She had a child. A baby!

No wonder Caitlin had felt so utterly bereft since she'd awoken in the hospital. She'd been aching for the child she couldn't remember!

"Caitlin, wait—"

She ignored her husband and ran up the stairs, following the sound of the baby's cries.

She found the infant in a crib in a nursery. Caitlin scooped up the small, wriggling bundle, and the crying stopped at once. The emptiness inside Caitlin was filled—everything *would* be all right. "Mommy's home now," she crooned.

"Caitlin." Dylan's voice was hoarse. "That is not our baby."

Dear Reader,

We've really got a treat in store for you this month, I promise. Many of you are already familiar with Rachel Lee's Conard County miniseries, which has been burning up the bestseller lists for Intimate Moments. Now she revisits Conard County—Shadows-style—in *Thunder Mountain,* a book that will have you on the edge of your seat (or hiding under it!) as you read. Remember the phrase "It's not nice to fool Mother Nature"? You'll never think of it the same way again after you climb the slopes of Thunder Mountain with Mercy Kendrick and Gray Cloud, keeper and protector of the mountain's secrets.

With only a few books behind her, Maggie Shayne has already made quite a reputation for herself with readers, and *Kiss of the Shadow Man* only proves what people already know: this lady is one top-notch talent. Heroine Caitlin Rossi's memory is gone. All she knows is that she's in danger—and it looks like the threat is coming from her husband, Dylan, a man she can't remember but knows she loves!

Turn on every light in the house, lock every door and window, then indulge yourself with a trip to the dark side of love, a trip that can be taken only one way— in the Shadows.

Yours,

Leslie J. Wainger
Senior Editor and Editorial Coordinator

Please address questions and book requests to:
Silhouette Reader Service
U.S.: 3010 Walden Ave., P.O. Box 1325, Buffalo, NY 14269
Canadian: P.O. Box 609, Fort Erie, Ont. L2A 5X3

MAGGIE SHAYNE

KISS OF THE SHADOW MAN

Published by Silhouette Books
America's Publisher of Contemporary Romance

 SILHOUETTE BOOKS

ISBN 0-373-27038-0

KISS OF THE SHADOW MAN

Copyright © 1994 by Margaret Benson

Books by Maggie Shayne

Silhouette Shadows

Twilight Phantasies #18
Twilight Memories #30
Kiss of the Shadow Man #38

*Wings In The Night

Silhouette Intimate Moments

Reckless Angel #522
Miranda's Viking #568

MAGGIE SHAYNE

lives in a rural community in Central New York with her husband and five daughters. She's currently serving as president of the Central New York chapter of the Romance Writers of America and has been invited to join the National League of American Pen Women. Maggie's first novel, *Reckless Angel*, appeared on the Waldenbooks bestseller list for series romance, and her second book, *Twilight Phantasies*, landed on the Waldenbooks mass-market romance bestseller list, also receiving an award and acclaim from critics. In her spare time, Maggie enjoys speaking about writing at local schools and conducting a romance-writing workshop at a local community college.

For my own Katie, a heroine as feisty and tough
as any I've ever written. And as smart and
beautiful, too. I love you.

CHAPTER ONE

Some there be that shadows kiss; Such have but a shadow's bliss.

—William Shakespeare

The pain lanced her head like a dull blade, sawing, cutting, ripping its way through. It was all-encompassing. At first, that was all she felt. Then, slowly, as if the lights were coming up in a darkened theater, she became aware of other sensations. The hard, irregular shape of her pillow. Her fists clenched around it, and the words "steering wheel" surfaced in her brain. She wasn't even certain what that meant. Then it came to her.

Next, the warm, steady trickle along her neck. She lifted her hand to touch the skin above the pulse point, only to find it soaked and sticky. Her fingers moved upward to trace the source, and located the gash at her temple. She pressed against it and a sharp pain made her wince. Still, she held the pressure there. It would stop the bleeding. She didn't know how she knew that, but she did.

Sounds filtered through the dense fog surrounding her mind. Sizzling…like bacon in a frying pan. No. Rain. It was rain. She lifted her head slowly, fighting the rush of dizziness the action brought, and peered through the darkness. Rainwater cascaded in sheets over the shattered windshield. She could see nothing beyond the spiderweb pattern of the broken glass, and the rain. Only darkness, filled with the howl of a vicious wind.

At first, she thought the wound to her head was what made her feel off center, out of balance. But when she tried to sit straight, she realized the car was at a strange angle, tilted with the driver's door pointing downward.

"I've been in an accident." She said it aloud, trying to take stock and finding it difficult. But the sound of her own voice made her gasp and jerk herself rigid. It wasn't her voice. It couldn't have been. It was the voice of a stranger, a voice she'd never heard before in her life. She blinked rapidly, looking around the car's interior, though she could see little detail in the darkness.

Then there was a flicker of light, a snapping sound, an acrid aroma.

Fire!

Her hand closed on the door handle, and she shoved desperately, again and again. It wouldn't budge. Panic giving her strength, she clambered up the sloping seat toward the opposite door. Her knee banged against something, a stick shift on the floor. Her skirt caught on it when she tried to move. She tore it free, and the sound of ripping fabric somehow added to the fear exploding inside her.

Her body shaking, she groped for the door. The latch gave when she wrenched at it. But the door wouldn't open. No. It would, it was just gravity making it difficult. The car was tipped on its side. The door, nearly horizontal above her. She pushed with all her might, bracing her feet against the hump in the center of the floor. The door lifted, and she growled deep in her throat and pushed harder. It wouldn't swing far enough to remain open on its own. She could only hold it up, her arms straining above her head, as she inched her way up and out. She braced one foot on the dashboard, the other on the seat's headrest and shoved herself upward, still holding the door. Another step. She pushed and shoved and hauled herself inch by inch through the opening, then out into the punishing rain and brutal wind.

Her legs gave way as soon as she hit the slick, muddy ground. She fell, curling into a small ball in the mud. Pain screamed through her brain. She could barely tell up from down, she was so dizzy. Her entire body throbbed with pains she couldn't isolate. She was cold, and afraid. So very afraid.

She only struggled to her feet again when the flames began to spread. Brilliant tongues of fire licked a path from the front of the vehicle toward the rear. The sharp scent of gasoline burned her nostrils. She pulled her mesmerized gaze from the hungry flames and bolted, only to skid to a halt in the mud. To her right, a sheer drop stretched endlessly into blackness and pouring rain. To her left, a steep, muddy embankment angled sharply upward.

Cold rain beating against her face, pummeling her body, frigid wind buffeting her every step of the way, she started up the bank. She clawed with her fingers and dug with her toes. She wore no shoes. She had no idea what had happened to them.

Countless times she slipped, losing more distance than she'd gained as the cold, wet soil scoured her palms, her knees, her chin. Each time, she grated her teeth and began once more. She'd be damned if she'd die here in this mud and misery. She gripped every protruding twig or outcropping of rock that she was fortunate enough to encounter. Slowly, agonizingly, with blood spilling over her neck and dampening her shoulder, she made her way to the top . . . to the twisting, narrow and utterly empty road.

An explosion rocked the ground beneath her, and she nearly fell from the force of its percussion. Bits of metal and glass rained around her and she shielded her face with her arms, frightened beyond rational thought. The car from which she'd escaped became a blinding ball of flame, and she had to turn her eyes away. The pounding in her head and the pressure against her temples grew stronger with every ragged breath she drew.

She heard the sirens then. In the road ahead of her, vehicles with flashing lights and flapping wipers screeched to a halt. Men emerged, and several hurried toward her, shouting.

Again she felt an inexplicable fear. She whirled from them and ran headlong in the other direction, bare feet slapping on cold wet pavement, raindrops ricocheting in front of her, lashing her face and legs. Headlights rounded a curve. The car swerved to miss her, skidding to a stop on the shoulder. She went rigid as the door opened.

She could only see his outline. He stepped around the car, the headlights at his back, rain pounding his body, and came toward her. He was no more than a powerful, menacing, black silhouette. A shadow.

Her heart hammered and she couldn't draw a breath. It was more than fear she felt. It was stark terror. He would hurt her, she was sure of it. He would kill her. He kept coming, closer, closer.

She screamed. It was a shriek of unbridled horror, and it froze the big, dark shadow-man in his tracks. Again, she turned to run blindly. The paramedics were in her path, hands held out as if to gentle a frightened pony, voices soft. "Easy now, just calm down. We're here to help you. Easy."

She shook her head, pressing her hands to the sides of it. One came away dripping crimson and her throat closed off. She backed away from them, turning again only to find the shadow-man there, so close she could smell the rain on his skin.

She screamed again when his arms closed around her like a steel trap. She fought, thrashing in his grip, kicking, pounding him with her fists.

"Dammit, Caitlin, that's enough!"

His voice was deep, loud, frightening. But it wasn't his voice that made her stop her struggling. She blinked, and shook her head, looking up into a face that was no more than a grouping of angles and planes in various shades of gray. A square, wide jaw. High, defined cheeks. Full lips. Prominent eyebrows.

Her voice a croak, she whispered, "What did you call me?"

His grip on her eased. She felt, rather than saw, the shock that rippled through him. "Caitlin." His arms freed her, but his large, hard hands gripped her shoulders. "Caitlin," he said again.

She was aware of the others closing in behind her. She shook her head, and dizziness swamped her like a small boat in a hurricane. "No...that's not my name." Her legs seemed to dissolve and her upper body sagged. She fought the sensation, leaned into the hands that supported her and managed to remain standing.

"Then what is?" It was nearly whispered, but there was a coarseness to the words that rubbed at all her nerve endings.

She closed her eyes, searched her mind. It was a simple enough question. What was her name? She squeezed her eyes tighter, trying to extract the information from her mind like juice from an orange. Nothing came. Her answer was an empty hole. A dark, empty hole in her mind where her identity should have been.

"I...I don't know."

"You don't know?" He seemed to be searching her face but she could barely see his. All crags and harsh lines, and beaded droplets of rain. Deep-set eyes. Wet hair that looked like a windstorm. No colors. Only shades of gray.

She felt the fear well up in her throat. She didn't know who she was. She didn't know where she was. But she did know that she was afraid, terribly, paralyzingly afraid. Of what, or whom, she had no clue. Right now, it was of everyone, everything. Most of all, this broad, hard-faced shadow man. She tried to pull free of him, but he wouldn't release her.

"Let me go!" She twisted her shoulders back and forth, heedless now of the icy rain pelting her, the streams of it running between her shoulder blades and soaking her clothes. "Let me go!" Again and again she screamed the words until the dizziness returned. The varying grays around her lost their form and blended into one cold, dark color. And then, even the pain in her head drowned in the gray sea.

Dylan Rossi stared through the double-paneled glass with the wire mesh between the panes into the room where they'd just wheeled his wife. He couldn't see her now. He only saw the backs of doctors and nurses in their pale green scrubs, with the white strings tied in neat little bows up their backs. He saw the dome of chromium steel above her, the blinding light it gave. And he saw the monitors. Their waving white lines coming erratically, the beeps without rhythm. The white sheets on the table that held her were spattered with crimson.

He couldn't see her. Not now. But he'd seen her less than an hour ago, when she'd struggled against his brutal grip in the pouring rain. In the glow of his headlights, he'd been able to see just fine. The gaping wound in her head, the blood pulsing from it, soaking her hair, her face, mingling with the rain on her neck.

And he remembered her eyes, the fear in them. It had been real. She'd been afraid...of him. And he couldn't say he blamed her. She had every reason in the world to be afraid of him.

Dylan paced away from the double doors marked Sterile Area, No Admittance. His wet shoes creaked over the polished tiles. The scent of the place turned his stomach.

No, no, it wasn't the damned scent that was making him sick. It was *him*. It was what he was thinking, what he was feeling right now that made him want to puke his insides out. But that didn't stop him from feeling it, and nothing could stop him from admitting it, at least to himself.

And he shouldn't hate himself for acknowledging what the rest of Eden, Connecticut, already knew. It would be best for everyone concerned if his coldhearted bitch of a wife never came out of that room.

Thirsty.

There had never been a desert dryer than her throat was right now. She forced her eyes open, but the room was blurry, dim. She licked her lips and tried to sit up. Her body responded with little more than a twitch of several muscle groups. And even that small effort left her limp with exhaustion. God, what was the matter with her?

"Caitlin?"

That voice sent a shiver up her spine. She tried to turn her head toward it, even as she felt herself instinctively cringe farther into the stiff sheets.

The form, dark as before, and blurred by her errant vision, rose from a chair to lean over the bed. "You're awake." His finger jammed repeatedly at a button on the side of her bed. "How do you feel?"

She twisted away from his touch, frightened to have him so near. Her back pressed against a cool metal rail at the far side of the bed. She turned fast, startled. Her head throbbed with pain.

"Take it easy. Caitlin, you're in a hospital. You're going to be fine."

She swung her head around to face him again, though the movement increased the pain abominably. "Who are you?"

He frowned. Her vision was steadily clearing, and while the room was only dimly lit, she could now see his features. His eyebrows were dense and dark. His hair a jumble of deep brown satin waves, mussed as though he'd run his hands through it.

In a flash, she saw him doing just that. Not here and now, but somewhere else . . . before. He was tall, solidly built and he looked as if he were trying to see through her eyes, into her mind as he stared at her.

The door was very wide and made of wood. She noticed that as it swung open and a miniature nurse came through, took one look at her and whirled to run out again.

The man never moved. He only continued staring at her, eyes like melted chocolate, glistening, probing. "You don't know who I am?"

She shook her head, then closed her eyes because the action hurt her.

"Do you know who you are?"

Tears stung her eyes, so she squeezed them tighter. She felt droplets work their way through to moisten her lashes and roll over her cheeks. He swore, low harsh words that made her spine stiffen.

She heard the door again, the shuffling of feet and a feminine voice, very low. "You'll have to wait outside, Mr. Rossi."

Rossi. The name meant something. Bells sounded in her mind, but there was no more. Nothing but the vague feeling that she ought to know the name.

"You told me there was no sign of brain damage." The deep, rumbling tenor voice, Rossi's voice, came to her as he was urged toward the door.

"I told you we couldn't be sure until she regained consciousness."

"She says she doesn't know who she is," he growled. He sounded as if he doubted it to be true. "So run your damned tests and tell me if this is legitimate, pronto."

"Please, try to be patient. I know you want your questions answered, but right now we need to examine your wife."

An electric shock zapped through her body at that word. "No!" The denial flew from her lips, riding her coarse voice to fill the sterile-smelling room. "No! I'm not his wife. I'm

not. I don't know that man. I don't know him, I swear it!
I—"

"Calm down, Mrs. Rossi." Cool hands on her shoulders, then her forehead.

"Don't call me that!" she shrieked. She sat up, flinging the covers from her. She had to get out of here. Everyone here was crazy. She swung her legs to the floor, only to feel her arm grabbed firmly and jabbed with something sharp. She caught her breath. By the time she drew another, her head was swimming, and someone was pushing her back onto the bed.

She looked toward the door. He still stood there, staring at her. She met his gaze and moved her lips, forcing words with an effort. "Keep him . . . away from me."

He shook his head, yanked the door open and left as quickly as possible.

Night again.

God, why was it dark whenever she opened her eyes? Was she to live in darkness from now on?

"You're sure she's not faking this?"

It was his voice. The man they'd said was her husband. And it was filled with contempt.

"Mr. Rossi, why on earth would she want to?" The feminine voice paused, awaiting an answer. There was none. "Amnesia is rare," she said at last. "But it does happen, and I'm convinced it has happened to her. She needs patience and understanding right now. Not suspicion and mistrust."

The shadow man's head turned toward her in the darkened room. Caitlin closed her eyes again, and lay utterly still, waiting.

"She's been through a terrible trauma, Mr. Rossi."

"All the more reason not to tell her. Not anything. If she's faking, I'll know soon enough. If not . . ." He let the sentence hang for a moment. "If not, then telling her would only do more harm." It wasn't, Caitlin thought, the ending he'd intended to tack on to the sentence.

"Quite frankly, I'm inclined to agree with you. She's better off not knowing too much. Yet. She'll have to be told, though."

"Yeah, well, I'm her husband, so I'm calling the shots. I decide when and how much."

"*I* am her doctor, Mr. Rossi. And as soon as she shows me that she is on stable mental ground, you'll no longer be in a position to decide anything about her care. If you haven't told her by that time, then I will. Make no mistake about that."

"Fine."

The door opened, closed again.

A sense of solitude slowly invaded the room. She was alone again. With no more answers than she'd had before. God, could she really have lost her memory so completely? Could that big, frightening shadow man really be her husband? And what was it they intended to keep from her?

Caitlin rolled over, very slowly so as not to aggravate the dull throbbing in her head. There was something else, something that was missing, something precious. She couldn't put her finger on what, exactly. She only knew a ball of loneliness rested in the pit of her stomach. She felt empty inside, aching for something she couldn't identify. Not her memory. Not the man who claimed to be her husband. Something else, something she missed so terribly that it was a gnawing pain in her heart.

A teardrop worked its way from between her lashes, and she closed her eyes tight before a flood of them could follow. She wrapped her arms around her pillow, hugged it tight to her chest. When the floodgates finally broke, the sounds of her sobs were muffled in the fabric.

* * *

"I've dimmed the lights, Caitlin. The brightness will aggravate the headache, and hurt your eyes. It's better this way."

She turned toward the woman's voice. The tall, blond doctor sat in a chair beside the bed. She wore a white coat, and the tag pinned to it read Dr. Judith Stone, M.D., Ph.D. She had a pretty face, but hid it behind oversize, black-rimmed glasses. Her hair was pinned to the back of her head.

"My name is Judith. Yours is Caitlin. Do you mind if I call you that?"

"How do you know?"

"Your name? Well, your husband told us, for one thing."

"He's not my husband. I don't know him."

Dr. Stone tilted her head to one side. "Caitlin, we're not just taking his word. He had photos of you. We checked your fingerprints, too. We'll bring your brother in to confirm it, if you like."

"I don't have a brother."

"Well, there is a man running around claiming to be your brother, with a birth certificate that has your parents' names on it. It's all a matter of public record." Dr. Stone paused for a moment, to let that sink in, she thought. Then she added, "Come to think of it, there is a marriage license that says you're married to Dylan Rossi. Also a matter of record."

Why did the name feel so...important? Unless it was true. He was her husband.

"If I have a brother, why hasn't he been in to see me by now?" No one had come to see her, she added in silence. Not her professed husband, or her parents, if she had any. No friends, no one at all.

"I thought it would be best not to allow visitors, Caitlin. Seeing a lot of strangers who claim they know you would only add to the stress."

She probably had a point. "Why can't I remember anything?"

Judith leaned forward in the chair, her eyes attentive. "How much *do* you remember, Caitlin?"

She shook her head slowly. The name still felt odd, like a pair of shoes broken in by someone else. It must be hers, though. The doctors were certain, had been insisting on it for days now. You couldn't argue with a birth certificate.

"Nothing. I woke up in a car, in the rain. Before that, there's just . . . nothing." She opened her eyes and faced Dr. Stone. "I've answered these questions before. Every doctor that comes in here asks me the same things. I'd like some of my questions answered now."

Dr. Stone blinked, but smiled gently and nodded. "All right."

All right. Just like that. She didn't know where to begin, there were so many things she wanted to know. Where she'd lived, what she'd done for a living, who her friends had been.

"Am I ever going to get better?"

Narrow fingers closed on the black-framed glasses and removed them. "Caitlin, you were in a serious accident. You saw firsthand the distance your car fell, and how much farther it could have gone. If you'd been unconscious another few minutes, you'd have died. If the car had landed differently, you could have been paralyzed, or worse. I want you to keep all of that in mind."

Caitlin—she was finally trying to think of herself by that name—braced herself. "As things stand," Judith Stone continued, "you escaped almost unscathed. The head injury was serious. You already know you spent a week in a state of coma before you woke up three days ago. Many times, patients who experience that never regain consciousness, or when they do, they're—"

"Please, stop preparing me and just say it. I'm not going to get my memory back, am I?"

She sighed. "I'm afraid I can't answer that. Not yet."

Caitlin sunk back against the pillows as tears threatened. She blinked against them.

"Only time will tell, Caitlin. There's just no medical way to predict whether you'll regain some or all of your memory. But in the meantime, you have to begin again. You have to start right now, today."

"Start what?"

Hands gripped hers and squeezed. "Learning who you are."

"I don't remember who I am." She wanted to wail the words, but she only whispered them.

"Not who you were, Caitlin. Who you are. Who you will be from this day on. That's the most important thing for you to accept. You aren't that woman anymore, and if you spend too much time trying to find her, to become her again, you'll drive yourself crazy. I want you to remember that." She tilted her head again, as if trying to read Caitlin's reactions on her face. "Anymore questions?"

She licked her lips. "My full name?"

"Caitlin Amanda O'Brien Rossi."

She turned that over in her mind. "So I'm Irish?"

"Sure sounds Irish to me."

Caitlin nodded. "It does, doesn't it. What about my family?"

"Parents are deceased. You have...no children. There's your brother, Thomas, and your husband, Dylan."

She nodded, glancing down at the rings on the third finger of her left hand. "How long have I been...married?" The word didn't come easily.

"Five years. You're thirty-three. Your brother is twenty-nine."

She met Judith's brilliant green gaze. "And Dylan?"

Pale brows rose. "I never asked him. Why don't you?"

"He hasn't been here since I woke up."

"No, that's not quite true. He's been a fixture around here. He only doesn't come into the room because you made it clear you didn't want to see him, and because I thought it would only upset you if he did."

"Oh."

"Do you want to see him now?"

She bit her lip. "I don't know."

"Caitlin, there's something else I need to let you know. Your stay in the hospital is no longer necessary. Physically, you're fine now. You need to start thinking about where you'll go when you leave here."

A cold finger of panic traced a path around her heart. Where could she go? "My b-brother?"

"He and his wife live with you and your husband."

The fear she'd felt right after the accident resurfaced, and she searched in vain for its source. "Doctor—"

"Judith," she gently insisted.

"Judith," Caitlin said. "What do you know about the accident? Where was I going? How did I end up going off the road?"

Judith licked her lips, and for the first time, she didn't meet Caitlin's eyes as she answered. "The police department would know more about that than I."

Caitlin sighed. The answer was no answer at all. She had a feeling the accident was important, somehow. Almost as important as that wellspring of sorrow she felt inside her. More pressing, though, was her situation now. It looked as if she would have no choice but to return to her former home, if Dylan Rossi would even have her.

And there was another thing bothering her. "Why are there no mirrors in here?"

Judith rose slowly. "I asked that they be removed. I wanted to be sure you were ready to see your reflection. It'll be kind of shocking at first. Like looking at someone else's face."

Caitlin drew a deep breath. She knew her hair was a deep, dark shade of auburn. She'd pulled a lock of it around her face to stare at it. It was very long, and she felt curly bangs on her forehead. "I'd like to have a mirror. I think I'm ready now."

"There's one in the room next door. Feel up to a walk?"

Caitlin nodded. Judith opened a closet and pulled a pretty, red satin dressing gown from it. "Here, put this on."

She got to her feet and let Judith help her slip the robe up over her arms. "Whose—"

"Yours. Your husband brought some things when you were still in the coma."

At the mention of her husband, Caitlin stiffened, and her nerves jumped. "When do I have to leave?"

Judith walked with her to the door, and held it open. "Tomorrow."

CHAPTER TWO

Dylan went rigid when she scuffed out of her hospital room, Dr. Stone at her side. He'd been at the desk only ten minutes, just getting the full report of how she'd passed the day and what progress had been made. He hadn't set foot in her room since she'd screamed that he be kept away from her. Seeing her now brought a sickening twist to his stomach and a jolt of memory to his mind. Again, he saw her caught in the beam of his headlights, frightened as a startled doe, as he moved toward her. Again, he saw her fear of him when he called her name, heard her scream, watched her turn and run away as if he were Satan himself.

Later, he'd wondered if she'd really had sense enough to think she might finally have pushed him too far, or if her fear had all been an act. One more scene in the never-ending play where she was always at center stage. One more bid to tear him apart a little more. He couldn't imagine what more damage she could hope to exact. But if there was anything, if she even imagined there was anything left that could hurt him, she would do her damnedest to use it. Cold, spoiled Caitlin. She would never change.

But she hadn't faked the injury, or the coma. And now this amnesia. Real, or a ploy? She had the doctors fooled, there was no doubt about that.

Dr. Stone opened the door to the room beside Caitlin's. "Do you want me to come with you?"

"No." Caitlin seemed to hesitate before answering, but when she did, her voice was firm. "No, I want to do this by myself."

"Okay. I'll be just down the hall if you need me. And I'll come back for you in five minutes."

Caitlin nodded and Judith Stone walked away. Dylan watched as Caitlin seemed to brace her shoulders, and stepped into the room, shoving the wide, brown door farther, and allowing it to swing slowly shut behind her. He was curious, and no one seemed to be paying much attention at the moment. He walked with deliberate casualness across the pale gray tiles of the hall, toward the door she'd entered. He pressed it open, just a little, and he peered inside.

She stood as if transfixed, staring into a full-length mirror on the inside of an open closet door. Dylan looked at her reflection, seeing everything she saw. The soft, ivory-toned skin, the high sculpted cheekbones that gave her a regal look. Her long, wavy hair, the color of an old penny. Her eyes, huge and round, wide-set and penetrating. They were wider right now than he thought he'd ever seen them, and greener. Like emeralds. Shocking, glittering green. Too green to belong to her.

Her hand rose slowly, and her fingers touched her cheek, then slipped slowly downward, over its hollow, tracing her jawline to her small, proud chin.

Her fingers were trembling.

Her gaze moved downward, over her slender frame, her endlessly long legs. When her eyes met those of her reflection again, there were tears brimming in both.

Dylan retreated in silence.

If she was acting, she was doing a hell of a job.

She was silent in the car, head turned away, eyes pretending to scan the roadside as they passed. Dylan kept a steady pressure on the accelerator as he negotiated the narrow, twisting strip of pavement that passed for a road.

She'd fastened her seat belt the second she'd slammed her door. It surprised him. Caitlin never used a seat belt. Oh, but he was forgetting Dr. Stone's lecture, wasn't he? This was not the same woman he remembered, not the woman he'd married, not the woman he'd known. This Caitlin was a new woman, a perfect stranger.

But that was the punch line, wasn't it? He and his wife had been strangers for a very long time now.

She certainly didn't look any different. At least, not now that she was dressed up in one of her chic, designer label skirts, with its brilliant yellow color. The matching jacket was cropped at the waist to show off its minuscule size, and flared at the hips to accentuate the way they would sway when she walked. The pumps were the precise shade of the suit. She did tug at the hem of the jacket once or twice, though. And she shifted in the seat as though uncomfortable with the amount of slender, long thigh exposed by the skirt. And she hadn't put her hair up. She hadn't gone out in public in more than a year without a classy French braid or a twisting chignon. Today, she just sat there with her coppery curls spilling all over the place.

So she'd forgotten how to braid her hair. So what? She hadn't changed in any way that mattered. It was still painfully obvious that she wished she were somewhere else, anywhere but with him. Not that the feeling wasn't one hundred percent mutual. So where was this big change he'd been told to expect?

He sighed and returned his attention to the pale gray ribbon that stretched ahead of him. In a way, it was good she'd continue being distant and cold. It would be easier to keep his secrets that way. There were some things she was far better off not remembering. He'd had a hell of a time convincing Dr. Stone of that, but in the end she'd agreed. If the amnesia was real—he glanced toward Caitlin, and felt a resurgence of doubt—she was better off.

She ran one hand over the supple leather seat. The car was an Infiniti Q-45. She knew, somewhere in the tangled jungle of her memory banks, that it was a luxury car. It seemed to have all the extras. The air conditioner silently cooled the interior, while the sun outside made heat waves dance above the pavement ahead. It smelled new, good. She tried to remember what the other car had looked like, the one she'd seen go up in a ball of white hot flame. She frowned, searching her mind, but nothing came.

"What is it?"

She jumped, startled by the suddenness and resonance of his deep voice. She was still afraid of him. Just being in the same car with him had her nerves standing on end, and seemed somehow to intensify that emptiness inside her. "I was trying to remember the car. The one that burned."

He slanted her a skeptical glance. "You don't remember your car?"

"Only that it was small, and there was a stick shift. I remember banging my knee on it when I was trying to climb out."

He shook his head. "It was a red Porsche." He released a low chuckle. "Figures that would be your first question. You thought more of that car than..." He shook his head, leaving the sentence unfinished. His face darkened, and his lips tightened.

His answer made her hesitate to ask any further questions. She sensed his disapproval. Still, there were things she needed to know. "What...what do I do?"

"What do you mean, what do you do?"

"For a living."

His eyebrows shot up and he stared at her for so long, he had to jerk the wheel when he finally glanced back at the road. He gave his head a quick shake. "For a living? You? Give me a break."

Caitlin felt a prickle of knowledge make its way into her brain. Dylan Rossi didn't like her. Not at all. In fact, she was feeling the touch of his intense dislike right across the space between them. She tried to find some patience for him. After all, he had lost a wife and gotten back a perfect stranger.

He had reason to be short-tempered. "Look, it would help if you could put a damper on the sarcasm and simply answer me. Do I have a job or not?"

He glanced at her from the corners of his eyes. "Not."

She nodded. "Can you tell me why not?"

He shrugged noncommittally, flipped down the visor, and pulled a pair of black sunglasses from it. When he slipped them on, his eyes were completely hidden.

She shook her head, exasperation growing with every minute. "I need to know. You were her husband—" She bit her lip. "I mean, my husband. If you don't know, then who does?"

"You don't work because you were born rich. You don't need to exert yourself any more than it takes to sign a check and you have all the money you could want. Happy?"

His words stung her. "No, I'm not."

"No," he repeated. "You never were."

He turned the car onto a long, winding driveway. She felt the crunch of the tires over gravel, but didn't hear it in the silent interior, as the car moved beneath a tunnel of overhanging trees. It was shadowy, and darker. He could easily have removed the sunglasses, she thought. He didn't.

They rounded a bend, and the house towered before her. Old red brick, everywhere, most of it covered with clinging, creeping vines that seemed to Caitlin as if they were trying to smother the place. The windows, narrow and arched at the tops, were surrounded with bricks in fan patterns. The entire place was a harsh combination of severe corners and dull colors. It frightened her, this house.

In an upper window, a curtain parted, and the shadow of a face peered out. Caitlin caught her breath, but before she could say anything, the curtain fell once more.

Dylan was already getting out of the car. He glanced in at her, as he replaced his sunglasses on the visor. He frowned when he saw she wasn't moving. "Something wrong?"

Yes. God, everything was wrong. Why would she feel such terror at the prospect of entering her own home? Why was there a gnawing sadness digging a pit into her soul? Why was she so uncomfortable with the man she'd married...perhaps even loved...once? She shook her head, and instead of asking any of the questions that truly troubled her, she asked a safe one. "Who else lives here, besides us?"

"Your brother and his wife, and..." He stopped, cleared his throat. His gaze moved away from hers for just a moment. A quick flicker of those dark eyes, and then he faced her again. "And my great-aunt, Ellen Rossi. Other than that, there are only Genevieve and Henri Dupres." He pronounced both names with a perfect French accent.

"Who are they?"

He sighed as if running low on patience. "The French siblings you insisted on hiring last year. Genevieve worked for your family once, but your old man let her go right after your parents' divorce. You always liked her."

As he spoke, he moved around the car to her side. His hand gripped her arm to urge her to her feet and draw her along beside him, an automatic gesture, she was sure. But the warmth of his touch, the pressure of each finger on her skin disturbed her. It sent her nerves skittering in a hundred directions, and a shiver over her nape.

"So when she showed up with her brother to answer your ad for hired help, you gave them the jobs. She's our maid and he's our cook."

Caitlin stopped walking, vaguely aware she'd missed most of what he'd said. Something tickled her consciousness, teased her senses, tugged at her. A scent. *His* scent, clean and pleasantly spicy... and familiar.

She frowned as an image flickered in her mind. His face, very close to hers. His eyes filled with dark fire, staring intensely into hers, as his strong hands held her to him. She felt his skin, hot and damp against hers, felt his warm breath on her face as his lips came nearer.

"Are you coming in or not?"

She gasped and blinked up at him. His brows drew close, and he reached out a hand. She instinctively took a step backward. Strong hands caught her shoulders, preventing her from going any farther.

"Caitlin, what in hell's the matter?"

She closed her eyes slowly, willing herself not to pull away from his touch. The image had shaken her, but she didn't want him to know. A heat spread up through her cheeks. Her skin seemed to burn where his hands rested, though that was all in her mind, of course.

"Nothing. I'm fine." She drew a steadying breath, and began walking at his side again, trying to act as if nothing had happened. Her feet sunk into the hot gravel. The humid, stifling air bathed her. Perspiration broke out on her forehead in the seconds it took to reach the steps. She felt her skin growing damp and her clothes sticking to her. And she smelled the Atlantic.

She frowned, tilting her head to listen to the sounds she hadn't noticed before. Waves crashing against rock in the distance, and the discordant harmony of sea gulls.

There seemed little lawn. Mostly the place was surrounded by shrubs and trees and plants of every size and variety. It was like a miniature jungle here, with the humid, heavy air to match. Not a single breeze stirred a single leaf. But she imagined that on the back side of the house, closer to the shore, there would always be a breeze. The idea was appealing at that moment.

"Caitlin?"

"Hmm?" She tore her mind away from the ocean and the gulls and the imaginary breeze, and glanced at him.

"Coming?"

She'd stopped again, at the base of the steps this time. She nodded, and made herself move. Already, the gravel she stood in was heating her feet right through the soles of her stylish, torturous pumps. Dylan walked beside her up the wide, stone stairs to the front door with the oval window of frosted glass through which one couldn't see. He opened it, held it and waited. Knees trembling for no reason she could name, Caitlin stepped inside.

The house had the chill of a meat cooler.

Her footsteps echoed over the deep blue, marble floor, floating up to the high, vaulted ceiling and vanishing there. A twisting stairway of darkly polished hardwood began at one end and writhed upward, out of sight. A tooled, gleaming banister supported by elegant spindles wound its way alongside the stairs. The place smelled of oil soap and old wood.

She absorbed it all, shuddering at the darkness of the decor, and at the cold. A woman descended the stairs, very slowly, one gnarled hand gripping the banister for support. Snow white hair was twisted into a smooth bun at the top of her head. She wore silver-rimmed glasses, Coke-bottle thick. And as she reached the bottom of the stairs and came nearer, Caitlin saw that her eyes were as brown as Dylan's.

Dylan rushed forward, extending a hand to help her. She waved him away. "Leave me be, boy. I'm not crippled."

Dylan's lips curved into a crooked smile, and he stepped back. Caitlin caught her breath. He was looking at the old woman with tenderness and a sort of indulgent smile. Real affection lit his eyes, and for some reason, it made her feel more alone than she could remember feeling.

"I've brought Caitlin home, Aunt Ellen." He walked beside his aunt, watchful, ready to reach out if she stumbled.

The old woman moved slowly, her feet scuffing the floor. "I can see that. I'm not blind, either." When she was standing six inches from Caitlin, she peered into her face. "So, you're back, are you?"

Caitlin smiled at the woman. "Yes. It feels good to be out of that hospital."

The woman sniffed. "Been better if you'd stayed there. For all of us."

"Ellen." Dylan's voice held a warning.

"What? She might as well know my feelings on the subject, or is that supposed to be a secret, too?" Caitlin shot Dylan a questioning glance. He averted his eyes. "You never liked me, girl. No more than I liked you. They tell me you've forgot all that, but I imagine it'll come back to you soon enough. Old habits die hard, you know."

Caitlin opened her mouth to deny it, then closed it again. How could she? She remembered nothing.

"Ellen, where is everyone?"

She faced her nephew, squinting. "How would I know? No one around here ever tells me anything."

Caitlin almost smiled. Despite Ellen's frosty attitude toward her, she was like a petulant child. And at least she was up-front with her feelings, not brooding and sending her veiled glances, the way Dylan had been doing.

Another woman entered the room then, coming through an arched doorway. She was tiny, with her jet hair cut in pixie style, and huge, dark, Liza Minelli eyes. She wore the regulation uniform of a maid, black dress with white collar and cuffs. Stiff white apron.

She came forward, smiling nervously when Caitlin's eyes met hers. "Madame Rossi, I am so glad to see you home. You look well." Her speech was laced with a silky French accent. She stretched both hands to clasp Caitlin's, and squeezed softly. A gesture that suggested familiarity, yet Caitlin felt none.

"I'm sorry. I don't—"

"I know," she said softly. "It is all right, you will be well soon, *non?* I am Genevieve—"

"Our maid," Caitlin filled in, more to solidify the information in her own mind than anything else.

Genevieve's hands fell away, and Caitlin noticed her nails. They were immaculate, not excessively long, but far from cropped. They were hot-pink at their bases, with a black diagonal line bisecting them. The top portions were white, with tiny black dots.

"More than your maid," Genevieve was saying. Her voice had dropped an octave, and was softer than before. "We are friends, as well."

Caitlin looked up, saw the expectancy in the woman's eyes, and offered her a smile that was far from genuine. "That's good to know, Genevieve. I could use a friend, right now."

Dylan cleared his throat, drawing both gazes toward him. Ellen had settled herself in a broad rocking chair that looked ancient, and was rocking back and forth rapidly.

"*Monsieur?*" Genevieve inquired. "Is there something I can get for you?"

"A cold drink would be terrific." Dylan all but ignored Caitlin, though the old woman's eyes never left her as she rocked.

"Ice tea?" the maid asked.

"Fine. It's pushing ninety again today. Air's so heavy you can barely breathe outside." He slanted a glance toward Caitlin. She felt his eyes on her face and knew it was beaded with perspiration, though not from the stifling heat he'd mentioned. The house was as cold as a tomb. "One for Mrs. Rossi, too. Ellen?"

"I'll get it myself. Haven't had any servants waiting on me in ninety-two years and damned if I need 'em now."

Dylan's mouth pulled upward at one corner, but he quickly remedied that twitch, and nodded toward Genevieve. She left, and Ellen stopped rocking all at once. "That gal's bucking for a raise, mark my words. Friends. Bah! I never did like her."

"You don't like anyone, Ellen," Dylan gently reminded her.

Caitlin shook her head, confused. "I don't understand. Am I friends with Genevieve, or not?"

Dylan shrugged. "Like I said before, you always liked her."

Ellen sniffed, pulled herself from the rocker and scuffed out through the arched doorway, taking the same path the maid had. Dylan was watchful of her every step until she moved through the doorway and out of sight.

"I guess your aunt and I didn't get along."

He faced her again, his eyes skeptical. He sighed, shook his head and walked to an elegant eggshell sofa, with scrolled wooden arms and clawed feet. He sat down, reaching for a newspaper on the matching end table. "She's my great aunt. And no, you never got along."

Caitlin remained standing, watching him as he shook the paper twice, then began scanning the headlines. "Why not?"

He lifted his head, his gaze meeting hers, still packing thinly veiled distrust. He opened his mouth, but snapped it shut again when Genevieve reappeared carrying a tray and two tall, dewy glasses. Caitlin moved forward and took one. "Thank you." Her throat was suddenly parched. She sipped the beverage gratefully.

Genevieve handed Dylan's glass to him, sent Caitlin an encouraging smile and vanished again. Dylan took a long drink. Caitlin's gaze affixed itself to him, the way his lips parted around the glass's rim, the rippling motions of his throat as he swallowed repeatedly.

A sound floated to her ears then, breaking the tense silence between her and her husband. A soft, demanding cry. It pierced Caitlin's nerves like a blade. She stiffened, and a second later heard the glass shattering at her feet. She didn't look down, only stepped past it, vaguely aware of the crunching beneath her shoes, and moved toward the staircase. Dylan jumped to his feet, then stood motionless, poised.

Again and again the tiny wail came. Caitlin felt her eyes moisten, and her heart twist. She turned to face Dylan. "My

God, no wonder I've felt so empty... Why didn't you tell me?"

"Caitlin, wait—"

She ignored him, whirling once more and racing up the stairs. She had a child. A baby! No wonder she'd felt so utterly bereft since she awoke in that hospital. It made perfect sense now. She'd been aching for her child.

She ran as fast as she could along the maze of corridors, following the sound of the baby's cries, paying no attention to the countless rooms she passed on the way. She didn't even pause when she came to the closed door of what had to be the nursery. She flung it open and hurried inside.

The infant lay on its back, eyes pinched tight, mouth round. Tiny arms and legs stretched out and trembled with every wail, then relaxed in between. Dark, thick hair swirled over a small head, and chubby fists clenched with frustration.

Without hesitation, Caitlin bent over the crib and scooped the small, wriggling bundle up into her arms. The child wore only a diaper and a tiny white T-shirt. Caitlin rescued the receiving blanket that had been kicked into a wad at one corner of the crib, and wrapped it around the baby, holding the child close to her chest, resting her cheek against the silken hair.

The crying stopped at once, and Caitlin looked down into huge eyes that were so blue the whites of them seemed tinted blue, and thick, long lashes and chubby cheeks. So soft, the skin on the pudgy arms and legs. And the baby smell that filled her senses was like pure heaven. Caitlin ran her hand over the baby's fuzzy dark hair, and bent to press her lips to a soft cheek. She closed her eyes as they filled with tears, and held the baby against her once more, rocking it slowly in her arms.

"God, I don't even know if you're a boy or a girl. But you're beautiful. You're beautiful, and Mommy is home now."

She heard his steps stop in the doorway, but she didn't turn. She just held that child to her breast and let the tears of joy and relief fall unchecked over her face. "Everything is all right now, little one." She felt as if her heart would explode, it was so full. That emptiness inside her was filled. She had the part of her that had been lacking. Everything *would* be all right.

"Caitlin." His voice was hoarse.

She turned slowly, smiling though her lips trembled. "You should have told me, Dylan. If I'd known we had a—"

"She's not ours."

Those three words spread a blanket of ice over her heart. She shook her head in denial and held the baby closer.

"Caitlin, that is not our child." He took a step closer, and she backed away.

"No."

His face was tight, his eyes glittering with something. Anger? "She's your brother's little girl, Caitlin. She's Thomas and Sandra's baby."

Again, she shook her head. "But...but—"

A young woman with a towel wrapped like a turban around her head joined them in the room then. She stopped when she saw them there, her wide blue eyes on the baby in Caitlin's arms. She wore a jade dressing gown, tied with a sash, but it gaped at the neck, giving a more than ample view of her swollen breasts.

"Cait." She shook her head, in self-deprecation, perhaps. "First day home an' here I've got you baby-sittin' already. Sorry," she said with a sexy southern drawl. She tipped her head back, fixing Dylan with a potent stare, her eyes huge and jewel-like. "I thought sure she'd sleep long enough for me to take a shower." She came forward, and took the baby from Caitlin's suddenly numb arms. "Come on, Lizzie, come to Mama."

Caitlin felt colder than ever all at once. She shivered, and tried to blink back a new rush of tears. This couldn't be true.

Holding the baby had felt so right, so natural. How could she not be her child?

"Caitlin, this is Sandra—" He broke off, his gaze leaving Caitlin's face when the narrow-faced woman sat down in a rocker near the crib, baring one plump breast as if she did so with an audience every day. Lizzie nuzzled, found her target and latched on with vigor.

Caitlin turned away, and pushed past Dylan into the hall.

Dylan braced one hand against the door frame, and watched her run away. She disappeared into one of the guest rooms, and he heard her lock the door after she'd slammed it.

"Gee, what's wrong with her?"

Dylan didn't answer. He couldn't, just then.

"What's wrong, little one? Not hungry?" She sighed. "I swear, she must have a tiny tummy. Eats just a little, and twenty times a day."

He heard the brush of fabric against skin as Sandra righted her robe, and then rose. "I'm taking Lizzie back to my room with me while I change. Then we're going out for a walk, aren't we, Lizzie?"

He ignored her artificially pitched voice as she murmured to her daughter all the way down the hall and out of sight. Dylan stepped back into the nursery and closed the door. He stared for a long time at the crib, and the litter of stuffed animals inside it. Mindlessly, he reached down, and stroked the silky fur of a teddy bear with a big red bow at its throat. When he'd walked in here, when he'd seen the way Caitlin held Lizzie in her arms, the ecstasy on her face, the relief, the tears of sheer joy...

It was like getting hit between the eyes with a two-by-four.

His hands clutched the brown fur until the bear was twisted into a grotesque blob, his chin fell to his chest and Dylan Rossi cried.

CHAPTER THREE

She had no idea how long she huddled on the bed in the obviously unused room. She cried, but she didn't know why. It was ridiculous to feel such devastation over a simple misunderstanding.

Then why was she devastated? Why did it hurt so much to have believed she was a mother for a few precious seconds, and then to learn that she wasn't? Why?

When the knock came, she sat up, and swiped at her tear-stained face with the backs of her hands. It would be Dylan, she had no doubt of that. She got to her feet, and pushed a nervous hand through her hair. She wanted it to be Dylan, she realized slowly. She wanted him to explain what she was feeling, and she wanted him to comfort her, perhaps even hold her, the way a husband would hold a wife. His arms were big, strong, his chest wide and firm. It would feel good to be cradled there, even if it was only a gesture. Even if it meant nothing at all.

She opened the door and frowned at Genevieve's curious, dark gaze.

"You are ill?" she inquired, scanning Caitlin's tear-stained face.

"No. I'm fine."

Genevieve shook her head slowly. "You do not look at all fine. Something troubles you, *non?*"

Caitlin only shook her head. "Really, it's just a headache. I'll be all right." Friend or not in the past, Genevieve was no more than a polite stranger in the present.

The maid looked Caitlin over with a narrow eye, and finally nodded sharply, just once. "Fine, then. Your husband asked me to show you to your rooms. You'll want to change for dinner." She shook her head in that way she had, that made it seem as if she were scolding herself. "I don't know why I did not think that you might not remember the way. My head is not, as you say, screwed straight, I think."

Caitlin smiled a little, looking down at the rumpled yellow suit she wore and nodding. Yes, she would like to change, into something that didn't look like an ad from some fashion magazine. But when the maid led her to her rooms, she began to wish she'd stayed where she was. She stood in the doorway for a moment, blinking. Crimson chintz draperies with blousoned valances adorned the tall windows like debs at a Southern ball. The bedspread was satin, as vividly red as the drapes. The wallpaper's soft ivory tone was splotched with huge scarlet roses.

For an instant, she saw that shattered windshield, splashed with blood. Her blood. She shivered.

"Is something wrong?" Genevieve's hand touched Caitlin's shoulder from behind. "It is beautiful, *non?*"

She turned slowly, tearing her eyes from the decor to stare at Genevieve. She blinked twice at the woman, who was glancing admiringly into the bedroom, then turned to look at it once more herself.

Beautiful? Maybe, to anyone but her. Maybe the colors seemed vibrant, and alive to the casual viewer. But all Caitlin could see was the red, and she could almost smell the blood, and beyond it, the sharp odor of gasoline, and the pungent smell of fire. The room might have seemed beautiful to her once, but, God, not anymore.

"I'll send Monsieur Rossi for you when dinner is served. If you have no memory, you won't find your way." She stepped back, and closed the door.

Caitlin drew a bracing breath and made herself walk through the bedroom. She peered into the adjoining bathroom and found it just as troublesome. Red curtains, even the shower curtain, with a frilly ruffle bordering it. The carpet was the same plush ivory tone as that in the bedroom, and that was a welcome relief. There were even red towels, huge and plush, hanging from the racks. She shook her head in disappointment. She hadn't needed one more bothersome thing to add to her list. She'd hoped for a haven, something familiar in her rooms, something that might jar her memory. The only memory this room jarred was that of the accident.

She returned to the bedroom and tugged open a closet. At least she could get rid of this expensive outfit now. But as she sorted through the items hung in neat rows, she found the clothes were all the same. Cropped and tight, in vibrant shades and noisy prints. All expensive, chic and sporting designer labels.

She sighed her disappointment—she'd been longing for something casual and comfortable—and turned to the bureau, already half-sure of what she'd find inside. One drawer spilled over with silken lingerie. Another was filled with spandex leotards, leggings and tops that looked as if they'd never been worn. Finally, buried in the bottom drawer, she uncovered a pair of designer jeans. She was so relieved, she could have cried as she pulled them on.

They were too tight to be comfortable, even though she'd lost weight. They must be old, she thought. Everything else was conspicuously loose on her, though obviously designed to fit like a second skin. She took a green silk, sleeveless blouse from one of the suits in the closet, buttoned it and tucked it in. She added a belt, from the fifty or so she found hanging on a special rack all their own, and knelt to search for footwear. The pumps that lined the closet floor were all alike, except in color. There seemed to be a pair to match every suit that hung above them. At last, she located a pair of running shoes, no doubt top of the line. It seemed the old Caitlin had never settled for anything less. They were as white as if they'd just come off the shelf, and she saw not a crumb of dirt in their tread.

She pulled them on, wondering if Caitlin had been the type who wanted to look great when she exercised, but rarely did so.

She was on the edge of the burgundy-cushioned Queen Anne chair, bending to tie the shoes, when she heard the door open. Dinner was served, then. And her hostile husband was here to fetch her. She felt again that emptiness inside her, and didn't turn to face him. She told herself not to be disappointed that her homecoming wasn't what she'd hoped for. What had she expected? For that hard-faced shadow man to take her in his strong arms and shower her with kisses? That he'd be so glad his wife was alive, he'd overlook the rest? Had she really expected this family to welcome a stranger into its midst?

Strong hands came to rest on her shoulders. She stilled utterly, shocked at the tenderness of that touch after his earlier coldness.

A second later, his head came downward, and lips nuzzled the crook of her neck. She closed her eyes.

They sprung open again when she felt the tickle of a moustache against her skin. She flew to her feet, whirling to face him at the same time. The man who stood there smiling at her was not Dylan. She'd never seen him before. He was shorter than Dylan, but just as powerfully built. His swarthy complexion and blue eyes were unfamiliar, as was the thick black mustache.

"Who are you!" She was breathing hard and fast in her anger.

The man looked stricken. "Surely, you have not forgotten me, *ma chérie?*" He studied her face for a long moment, then shook his head sadly. "Ah, but you have. It is I, Henri. Do you not remember the man who has begged at your feet for so long?"

Henri. Their cook, she recalled. My God, what on earth was going on in this house? She shook her head quickly and fought to find strength to put him straight. She stiffened her spine, and made herself meet his suggestive gaze head-on. "If you ever touch me again, Henri, I'll...I'll tell my husband, and he'll probably fire you on the spot. Is that understood?"

He smiled, one side of the moustache tilting upward. "Do you really believe he would care so much, *ma petite?*" He shook his head. "*Oui,* I dare much in saying so, but it is so clear to me, he does not know how to love a woman like you, he does not know what a treasure he holds. He is a fool—"

"That's enough!"

He stopped speaking, eyes downcast, lips tight. "My apologies. I forget myself in my joy to see you safe and sound once more. It is only that, I assure you, nothing more." His head came up, and his eyes, black and full of mystery, met hers. "Know that *someone,* at least, is happy to see you home again, and *alive* as well, *chérie.*"

His eyes were filled with meaning, and Caitlin felt a chill snake over her spine. "Maybe you'd better go, now." The words were spoken firmly, despite the tremor that shuddered through her body.

He nodded once. "Forgive me if I have upset you. It was not my intent." He turned and left the room.

Caitlin found herself slamming the door behind him, and throwing the lock. Stupid, senseless behavior, she told herself. He hadn't harmed her, or threatened to. And his affection would probably have been flattering, under any other circumstances. But, God, there was enough of a rift between her and Dylan without this added burden. Was Henri in the habit of flirting with Caitlin? Had she allowed such behavior in the past? Or was he truly only reacting to her close brush with death, as he'd implied?

She leaned her forehead against the cool, dark wood and closed her eyes. He'd implied that not everyone was glad to have her back, and the emphasis he'd placed on the word "alive" still rung in her ears. What had he meant by that? Was he giving her some cryptic warning? She'd felt sheer terror at her first sight of this house. Might there be a reason for that reaction?

She straightened and paced away from the door. They were keeping things from her. She already knew that. Part of her had agreed to come back here just to unravel the questions of her past, to learn what secrets Dylan was keeping from her and why. But another part, the part that had trembled at first sight of this house, and still trembled, in something other than fear, whenever she was close to her husband, wanted to leave. To go someplace where no one knew her and start fresh, and forget she'd ever had a past that had been erased from her mind.

She shook her head slowly, knowing even as the thought occurred to her that she wouldn't run away. She had to learn about her life before. Something inside was insisting on it. She might never be whole again, until she did.

Dinner was like a wake. A wake in a cold mausoleum filled with false smiles and stilted conversation. It was difficult for all of them, she realized dully. Sitting with a woman they'd once known well, a woman who was now a stranger. Knowing she didn't remember a thing about any of them.

The glasses were crystal, and the table shone with polished silver and the muted glow of the candelabra on the sideboard.

Caitlin wished she'd never come out of her room when the timid maid had found her there. But she had. She'd dried her eyes and tried to squelch the devastation she felt tearing her in two, and followed Genevieve to the formal dining room, achingly aware that Dylan hadn't wanted to come for her himself.

She picked at her food, eating little. She had no appetite tonight. The entire room was filled to the breaking point with tension, and she knew too well that she was the cause.

Dylan sat at the head of the glossy, dark wood table, eyes sharp and always moving. He paid close attention to every move she made, every bite she took. His features were tight, drawn as if he was in pain. He wasn't, though. She imagined he was just disgusted at having her in his house, in his elegant dining room with its dark-stained woodwork and its immaculate stucco ceiling. She certainly didn't feel she belonged here, beneath the muted glow of an antique brass chandelier.

"It would be a welcome relief if this weather would break," Dylan observed, spearing a bit of the succulent roast beef with his fork. "It isn't usually this bad here, Caitlin."

"I hardly notice the heat," she said. No, what she noticed was the lighted candles spilling their warm glow on his face, softening it in a way that was utterly false. "The house is so cool, and I haven't been outside at all."

"You used to..." Thomas stopped before he finished the sentence. He was just as tall and solidly built as Dylan, but his hair was brilliantly carrot-colored and wildly curly. Freckles spattered his face, and his eyes were troubled. "Sorry. You don't want to hear about what you used to do."

"Yes, I do," Caitlin told him. "What were you going to say?"

He met her gaze, a look of uncertainty in his. "You used to love to walk along the cliffs at night. Said you could hear the wind singing with the sea."

Caitlin closed her eyes, wishing she could recall that feeling.

"That was before. It wouldn't be a good idea to indulge in that habit now, Caitlin. You're not familiar with the cliffs, and there are some dangerous spots out there."

She frowned at Dylan, at the tone of command she heard in his forbidding voice. And then she stilled utterly, just staring into his dark eyes, glittering in the candlelight. She'd seen them glitter before…but in moonlight…and the strong emotion in their dark brown depths had been passion, not anger.

From somewhere far away, she heard an echoing whisper, a masculine voice, his voice. *Always, Caity. No matter what.*

"He's right, Cait." Thomas's voice intruded on her dream-state. "Better stay clear of the cliffs until… unless—until you're better." Her brother's lips thinned, and he broke eye contact with her to stare without much interest at his food.

Caitlin's stare was drawn back to Dylan. To the muscled column of his neck, the taut forearms revealed by his rolled-back sleeves. Her stomach twisted into a knot.

Across from Thomas, Sandra lifted her pale golden eyebrows. "It's not like she's crippled, you guys." She shook her head, and sent Caitlin a glance. "Don't let them start bossin' you around, or you'll never leave the house again. Believe me, I know 'em. Not just Tommy, but Dylan, too," she drawled sweetly. "Matter of fact, now that you lost your memory, I prob'ly know him better than anybody."

She glanced up at Dylan as she said it. He sat at her elbow, and returned her quick glance. His might have been slightly amused, but it was too short for Caitlin to be sure. She felt a sudden, swift jab of jealousy. It was ridiculous. After all, Thomas was only twenty-nine, and if Caitlin was any judge of ages, Sandra couldn't be more than twenty-two. She was practically a child, for God's sake.

Still, she was beautiful, her long, silvery blond hair hanging over one shoulder, her rounded breasts straining against the clingy fabric of her skintight black dress. It was short, exposing most of her shapely thighs to anyone who cared to look. Her voice, laced with that delicate Southern accent, made every sentence she spoke like a caress. Besides all that, she was the mother of the child Caitlin had thought was her own.

"We're in for a storm," Ellen remarked. "Been building up to it all week. I feel it in my joints."

"And your joints are usually right," Dylan returned, his gaze softening when it lit on Ellen's.

Caitlin picked at her food, and told herself not to feel animosity toward her sister-in-law. Sandra had done nothing to deserve it. She turned her attention to Thomas, who sat beside her. Her brother. How could her own brother seem like a perfect stranger to her? There was a strong resemblance between them, she noticed. His green eyes looked a lot like her own.

"Something wrong, Caitlin?"

He'd caught her staring at him. She shook her head. "No, I ... I was just trying to remember."

"To remember what?"

She shrugged. "Anything. What it was like growing up together. Whether you were a jock in high school, whether I..." She sighed and shook her head.

Thomas set his fork down with exaggerated care. "Our parents divorced while we were in high school. You stayed with Dad, I went with Mom."

She licked her lips. He seemed uncomfortable with the subject, but her curiosity was pestering her. "Why did they break up?"

"Because he was a bastard."

The sentence was clipped, and Thomas's eyes became hooded. "You never believed that, though."

"Is that why I stayed with him?"

He shook his head. "You were his princess, Caitlin. You blamed Mom for the breakup. No one really expected you to leave the lap of luxury and live the way we did."

Her eyes widened as he spoke, and she searched his reddening face, then glanced toward Dylan.

"That's enough, Thomas. What happened wasn't her fault."

"It's all right," Caitlin said quickly. "I want to know—"

"No, Cait." Thomas lowered his head, pushed one large hand through his curls and sighed hard. "Dylan's right. I'm sorry. It gets to me sometimes, that's all." He met her puzzled stare. "It was a mess. A big, ugly mess." He shoved his plate away from him, pushed his chair back and stalked out of the opulent dining room.

"Why'd you have to bring all that up? Dammit, Caitlin, he'll be ornery for the rest of the night, now."

Caitlin blinked rapidly at the woman who was her sister-in-law. "I'm sorry. I didn't mean—"

"Don't apologize, Caitlin." Dylan's gaze met hers for the first time that evening. "Your brother is still angry—"

"With good reason," Sandra cut in.

"Sandra O'Brien, it's time someone taught you some manners!" The declaration came loudly from Ellen, who sat across from Caitlin, and was accompanied by a wrinkled fist banging the table.

"Oh, hell, you're all treatin' her like she'll break in a strong wind!" She glanced at Caitlin. "If Thomas is still mad at you, it's no wonder, and I don't blame him!"

Dylan stood slowly, purposefully. "Go and see to your family, Sandra." His words were not shouted, but their tone carried the same impact as if they had been. And suddenly, the tall, powerful form of Caitlin's husband seemed terrifying. "Now."

Sandra rose, glaring at all of the them in turn. Dylan sat down slowly, saying nothing.

"Fine. That's just fine." She threw her linen napkin down on her plate, and hurried from the room.

Caitlin sighed, and leaned her head into her hands, elbows propped on the table. "I'm sorry. I didn't mean to spoil everyone's dinner."

A low, rasping chuckle brought her head up, and she met Ellen's glazed brown eyes, which were crinkled at the outer corners. "Didn't spoil mine, girl. I'd much rather eat without that kind of comp'ny."

Caitlin shook her head. She looked across the table to Dylan. "Why is my brother so angry with me?"

"He's not angry with you. Only at what happened. Your parents' divorce is ancient history now, Caitlin. He got over it a long time ago."

"But he was so—"

"It bothers him to talk about it, that's all. He was a kid, his family split up. It's understandable, isn't it?"

She bit her inner cheek, and finally nodded. "I suppose so."

"He doesn't resent you, Caitlin. When Sandra got pregnant, he didn't have two dimes to rub together. You're the one who offered to let them move in here—"

"And nagged Dylan until he gave the worthless bum a job," Ellen cut in.

"I did?" Caitlin shook her head. It was difficult to picture herself nagging Dylan. His very presence shook her to the marrow.

She looked up then, curious, scanning his handsome face with sudden interest. "What kind of job? God, do you realize, I don't even know what you do?"

He licked his lips, his eyes narrowing as if he wasn't sure she spoke the truth. "I'm an architect."

"Best architect in the state," Ellen added. "Owns his own firm, a whole office building's worth."

Caitlin nodded, looking around the richly furnished room. "That explains this place. You must make a lot of money."

His head came up, eyes alert. "You want to talk money now, Caitlin?"

She frowned, not understanding the sudden bitterness in his tone. Had she said something wrong?

"It's your house, not mine. I never wanted it. I still don't."

Caitlin was stunned. She sent a glance toward Ellen, who only nodded her affirmation. She shook her head. "I don't understand." She felt sick to her stomach. The more she learned about the past, the more confused she became. But she had to know, didn't she?

"Water under the bridge," Ellen declared all at once. "And here's dessert. You both better dig in, 'cause I hate to eat alone."

Genevieve crossed the room with a tray of dessert plates, laden with chocolate cake and whipped cream. She set one in front of Caitlin. Caitlin closed her eyes. "I don't think I can—"

"Sure you can. Barely touched your dinner, girl. You're already thin as a rake. Eat up."

Ellen lifted a forkful to her lips, and sighed as though she'd found ecstasy. Caitlin couldn't help but smile at the older woman. Ellen might dislike her, but Caitlin was beginning to wonder if she might have good reason. There had obviously been a lot of animosity in this marriage. Ellen pretty clearly adored her nephew.

"You really must try to eat," Genevieve put in. "I can see how much weight you have lost since the accident. You'll get well sooner if you eat."

She felt Dylan's eyes on her, and knew Genevieve was right. She had lost weight. The designer clothes hung looser than they should. Her curves didn't strain the seams the way

Sandra's did. She dipped her fork, and lifted it. She'd force herself.

The fork was slapped out of her hand with stunning force just before it reached her lips. It clattered to the floor, smearing cake and cream all over the marbled black tiles.

"Ellen, what the hell—"

"It's carob!" was her shouted answer to her nephew's unfinished question. "Did you eat any, girl?"

Ellen was shoving her own water glass into Caitlin's hands as she spoke. Dylan was on his feet, shouting at Genevieve. "What in God's name were you thinking?"

"I didn't know! I swear, Monsieur Rossi, I had no idea."

He brushed past the trembling maid and stood beside Caitlin. "Are you all right?"

She set the water glass down and stared up at him in shock. Was that concern or fury she heard in his tight voice? She nodded. "Yes, fine, but I don't understand. What in the world is carob?"

Dylan sighed hard and pushed a hand through his hair. "A bean from some Mediterranean evergreen. It's used as a chocolate substitute, among other things. You have violent reaction to carob, Caitlin. Rare, but potentially lethal. This damned dessert could have killed you."

His gaze met Ellen's, and there was some hidden knowledge that passed between them. "How did you know?"

Ellen shook her head. "I know real chocolate, boy. This stuff has a bitter aftertaste to it." She made a face.

Dylan glared at the maid, who was crying loudly. "Get Henri in here. I want to get to the bottom of this."

She nodded jerkily and hurried out of the room.

"You're sure you're all right?" Ellen asked. "You didn't eat any of it?"

"No, not a crumb." Caitlin felt the trembling in her hands, and she tried to force it to stop. First the accident, and then this, an inner voice whispered. Almost as if someone were deliberately out to get her. She gripped herself mentally, and shook. It was ridiculous. She was only being paranoid.

The dark look that passed between Ellen and Dylan just then made Caitlin's heart skip a beat.

She turned toward Dylan, certain there was something he wasn't telling her. She opened her mouth to demand an explanation, then closed it again. She was tired, upset. It was her first day home after a serious accident, a week in coma and a total loss of her own identity. Her judgment was far from what it should be. She was overreacting to what surely must have been an accident. Dylan disliked her enough without her shouting accusations of conspiracy at him over dinner. Her head throbbed. She rose slowly, closed her eyes at the increased pain in her skull.

"Caitlin?"

She opened her eyes and faced him. "I'm just going upstairs to lie down. It's . . . been a long day."

Genevieve reentered the dining room, with Henri at her side. His eyes met Caitlin's with a silent reminder of his earlier, veiled warning glowing from their onyx-black depths. Dylan moved toward Caitlin, one hand on her arm telling her to stay where she was.

"Henri, I want an explanation for this dessert. And it had better be a good one." Dylan's voice was dangerous, and its depth made her tremble. He shot her a brief, sidelong glance. He must have felt the vibrations shuddering through her arm, where his hand still rested. He took it away.

"Monsieur Rossi, I promise you, I had no idea the cake was made with carob. It was delivered this afternoon."

"*Oui,*" Genevieve added quickly. "I answered the door."

"Delivered from where?" Dylan demanded.

"The box said Alyce's Bakery. There…there was a card." Genevieve's voice trembled.

"Get it."

As she scurried out of the room once more, Caitlin looked up at the towering, angry form of her husband. "Dylan, I'm sure it was an honest mistake. Please don't—" She broke off at his quelling glance.

"The *madame* is right," Henri put in. "She must know *I* would never do anything to hurt her. This was simply a tragic error."

"I'll be the judge of that." Dylan snatched the small envelope from Genevieve's hand when she returned. He pulled out the card and read, "Wishing you a speedy recovery. It's signed, the Andersons."

"Who are they?"

He frowned down at the card, answering Caitlin's question without looking at her. "Our nearest neighbors. They live a mile farther down the road." He shook his head. "I'd better call them, just to be sure—"

"No chance of that, boy. They left for Europe yesterday. An extended vacation. Mahalia Anderson called to say goodbye just before they left." As she spoke, Ellen got up from the table.

Dylan sighed hard. "From now on, Henri, no food comes to this table unless it's prepared by you. This might have been a fluke, but it could happen again."

"Of course." Henri turned those knowing eyes on Caitlin. "I am terribly sorry, *madame*. I hope you believe that."

Caitlin only nodded. "Of course. It wasn't your fault." She glanced up at Dylan. "I really would like to go up and lie down now."

"Fine."

She licked her lips. "I'm not sure I remember the way. Genevieve brought me down and I wasn't paying much attention. This place is so big . . ."

His gaze slid past her to Genevieve and for an instant she thought he would abandon her to the maid's care. The Frenchwoman's eyes were wide, nervous, before she averted them. Poor thing. Caitlin knew *she'd* hate to be on the receiving end of Dylan's anger.

After a moment's hesitation, Dylan sighed, took her arm and turned her toward the doorway.

She felt three pairs of eyes on her all the way out, and she suppressed a shudder. Dylan led her up the stairs, through a number of tall, narrow corridors, all lined in that same gleaming, dark wood. The grim paintings all looked alike, abstract displays of dull colors that meant nothing. She was sure she'd never learn how to find her way around this mausoleum that was supposedly *her* house.

Finally, he paused and opened a door. Caitlin stepped inside and stopped, glancing around. The deep red decor stared back at her. Her feet sunk, but refused to move, in the plush carpet.

She shook her head and took a step backward into the hall. All that red. God, why couldn't she shut out the image of the blood-spattered windshield? She felt the sticky, warm flow on her neck again, and she closed her eyes tightly to block out the vision.

"You don't like it? Caitlin, you decorated it yourself."

She turned away from him, and drew several deep breaths. "It'll be fine."

He caught her shoulders and turned her to face him. "Look, Caitlin, if you don't want this room, say so. There are plenty of others." His hands stilled on her outer arms. He'd only need to bend his elbows to pull her against him. She almost wished he would. She almost longed for his hard chest as a pillow, his muscled arms as blankets, closing out the confusion, the pain.

She shook her head. And then she felt the phantom sensations like whispers on her body. Friction. Skin against skin. Hot, wet, frantic. Something skittered through her midsection. A tensing, a longing. Why didn't he pull her into his arms?

"I—um—" She fought to pull her thoughts into order. "I don't want to be difficult—"

"Since when?"

Her chin rose at the cynicism in his voice. It had hit her like a bucket of ice water, shocking her back to reality. She met his gaze and saw the censure in his eyes. Had she thought he might harbor a single spark of feeling for her? Was she insane?

"The room is fine. Thank you for bringing me up." She forced herself to step back inside, refusing to look at the stifling, dramatic red that surrounded her. She closed the door behind her.

CHAPTER FOUR

The disappointment was like some living force, draining the energy from her body. But then, what kind of homecoming had she expected? One where her loving family members would hug her hard, one by one, their eyes filled with genuine joy that she was alive and back with them, instead of suspicions and secrets?

And it wasn't only the anticlimactic first day home that was getting to her. It was compounded by the still unidentifiable sense of loss, the gnawing ache for something she couldn't identify, the feeling that she was on the brink of tears all the time. Not being able to remember the reason did nothing to dull the pain.

Then there was this other feeling, the invisible threat, the menace of this cold, echoing house. The way the circular knots in the wood's dark grain seemed like evil eyes, always watching, waiting.

God, waiting for what?

It was ridiculous to feel so vulnerable, so much at risk, and she knew it was more a result of the trauma she'd been through than any real danger. She was in *her* house, with *her* family. There was no reason for this insane feeling that she was being stalked, or that the carob-laced dessert had been a deliberate attempt to hurt her.

It had been a gift.

But Caitlin couldn't help but wonder if it was more than just a coincidence, as she recalled again the speaking glances Dylan had exchanged with his aunt, and Henri's earlier words, laden with meaning.

She hadn't lied when she'd said she was tired, but instead of resting, she paced like a condemned prisoner. Again and again she moved past the foot of the tall, four-poster bed, its wood nearly charcoal, gleaming, its posts rising as high as gallows.

Gallows? What made me think that?

Finally, when she knew she wouldn't close her eyes until she did so, she picked up the phone on her bedside stand, dialed information and got the number for Alyce's Bakery, in Eden. She dialed that number, and waited.

"'lyce's. What can I do for you?" The feminine voice was one that sounded as though it answered the phone in the same way many times each day, even dropping the "A" in "Alyce's."

Caitlin licked her lips. "My name is Caitlin Rossi. A cake was delivered to me today, but, uh, the card was missing. I wanted to thank whoever sent it to me, if I could."

"Just a minute." The answer was quick and brief. Not even a pause, as if Caitlin's story sounded fishy. "You said Rossi?"

"Yes."

"That cake was sent by Mr. and Mrs. Jacob Anderson."

"Oh."

"You have a nice—"

"Wait!" Caitlin drew a steadying breath. "Can I ask...how it was paid for? I mean, credit card, check or—"

"Sure, just a sec." Pages riffled in the background. "Cash, Mrs. Rossi. Was there a problem with the cake? Is someone looking for a refund, or—"

"No, nothing like that. There was just a question as to who sent it. The Andersons are in Europe, you see, so..."

"Hmm. Well, maybe they asked someone to take care of this for them. The order was waiting when we opened up this morning."

"Waiting?"

"Yup. Cash and instructions in an envelope, slipped through the mail slot in the door. We get those all the time, 'course they're not usually cash, but once in a while..."

"I see. And the instructions, did they specify carob instead of chocolate cake?"

"That's right."

No one actually saw the person who placed the order.

A tree branch scraped across the window glass, like fingernails on a chalkboard.

"Thank you for your help."

"Anytime, Mrs. Rossi."

And they paid in cash, so there's no way to trace the source.

Caitlin hung up the phone, an antique replica, gleaming black with brass trim and a bell-shaped mouthpiece. It was just coincidence. There was no reason to see diabolical plots around every corner. She could well imagine Mr. and Mrs. Anderson, whoever they were, hurrying to the airport to catch their flight early this morning before the shops opened, and remembering at the last minute that today was the day their critically injured neighbor was to come home from the hospital. So they'd improvised, stuffed some cash and some instructions in an envelope, and dropped it off at the bakery, barely breaking stride in their rush to catch their flight.

It was possible.

But not very likely.

She shook herself, vowing to put the entire incident out of her mind, and went into the adjoining bathroom. A long, hot soak might help her rest.

She'd only peeked in here briefly before. She was unprepared for a spigot in the shape of a lion's head. She shuddered, and adjusted the knobs until steamy water spewed from the gaping maw. The tub had clawed feet. She'd missed that before, too. She'd been too busy noticing the blood-red decor. She looked around a bit more now, while the tub filled. A spider wriggled its legs, in a high corner, while a fly struggled to free itself from the web. She bit her lip, trying not to liken herself to the fly. She was being ridiculous, melodramatic, overly afraid.

She forced grim thoughts aside and left the tub to fill while she searched for a comfortable nightgown. She had in mind an oversize football jersey or a dorm shirt. What she found, instead, were long and flowing, softly feminine nightgowns. Every fabric from cotton and soft white linen, to silk, and sheer gauze. Every color from one end of the spectrum to the other.

Apparently, the old Caitlin had a touch of a romantic inside her. Had she bought so many attractive nightgowns with her husband in mind? Or was it just that she'd been fond of pretty things?

Caitlin stilled, holding a white muslin gown held up by its spaghetti straps. One thing about this room was obvious. It was hers, and hers alone. There wasn't a single thing in it that suggested the presence of a man. Not a bit of masculine clothing anywhere. No men's colognes or shaving implements in the bathroom. Only one toothbrush, standing alone in a cup on the edge of the basin.

How long had they used separate bedrooms? she wondered. Had Dylan moved his things out since the accident, in an effort to make things easier on her? Or had it been this way far longer?

Another unanswered question to add to her growing list. Sighing, she took the nightgown with her into the bathroom, and twisted the knobs to stop the flow of steaming water. It brimmed near the overflow drain, and already the mirror and small window were coated in mist. Clouds of it rolled off the surface of the water, invitingly. Caitlin stripped off the designer jeans and silk blouse. She wasn't overly fond of either of them. They looked like the clothes of a rich, well-placed, confident woman.

Maybe that was why she felt so uncomfortable in them now. She didn't feel rich or well-placed, and she was anything but confident. She felt alone and afraid, unsure of herself and everyone around her. Putting on the expensive clothes was like putting on a disguise. They belonged to another woman. A woman she no longer knew.

The long, steaming bath she indulged in did little to settle her nerves, though she did her best not to look at the spigot, or the spider.

Her skin damp, she pulled on the nightgown, and slid beneath her satin sheets, but was unable to sleep for hours. Countless questions and myriad possible answers flooded her brain each time she closed her eyes. Finally, though, exhaustion took over, and she did sleep, only to be tormented by vivid, disturbing dreams.

She was standing in warm, wet sand. There was rain pelting her skin. Her wet hair clung to her neck and shoulders, until large, strong hands pushed it away, and moist lips moved over her skin where it had been.

There was a chilly wind. Goose bumps rose on her arms and naked thighs. Those hands moved down over the curve of her spine, long, graceful fingers kneaded her buttocks, pulled her close to hardness and heat, held her there.

She couldn't see, in the dream. Her head was tipped back and her eyes were closed. She could only *feel*, and what she felt made her breath come in short little gasps, and her heart beat faster.

A mouth covered hers, and she parted her lips in silent welcome. A tongue probed, thrust, suggesting things that heated her blood to boiling. She reveled in the feel of it and curled her arms around his neck, threaded her fingers in his hair, pressed her hips harder against his.

Then the mouth lifted just slightly, lips still brushing hers as they moved to form words. "I love you, Caity. I always will. No matter what."

"Dylan..."

She'd spoken his name aloud in her sleep, and the sound of her own voice roused her, broke the seductive spell the dream had wrapped around her, brought her back to cold, harsh, lonely reality.

She sat up in the bed, blinking in the darkness. Her fingers rose of their own volition to touch her lips, which seemed to burn with the memory of those phantom kisses, then brushed over her breasts to find their nipples taut and yearning. She shuddered. Had it been a dream, or a buried memory? Had Dylan ever held her, touched her like that? Had he ever whispered those words against her lips with such passion? Or had it all been a figment of her imagination?

She pressed a hot palm to her sweat-slick forehead and lay back down. Would she ever know? God, had she really had something that intense once, only to let it slip away?

It was 5:00 a.m. when the baby began crying. Caitlin was wide-awake, curled into a ball on her own bed, still shaken from her dream of making love with Dylan, still dreading its return . . . and longing for it. She lifted her head, listening, waiting for Lizzie's cries to be answered. But they went on and on. No one seemed to be in any hurry to check on the poor little thing.

Caitlin flung back her covers and got out of bed. She chewed her thumbnail and began to pace the room. Surely, someone would pick Lizzie up soon. They had to. She felt it wasn't her place to step in and care for the child herself. Sandra might resent the intrusion, and so might Thomas. She didn't want to do anything else to alienate her family.

"I'm being utterly ridiculous," she said firmly. "I'm her aunt, and no one else is bothering to take care of her."

Caitlin pulled her door open and strode out into the hall. Darkness greeted her. No light spilled through the drawn draperies, which stood between the night beyond the towering windows and the darker halls within. No lamp had been left aglow to show her the way. She glanced up and down, all the same, as a chill assaulted her body, and the hairs on her nape prickled with electricity. She narrowed her eyes, gazing into utter blackness as if by doing so she'd somehow sense if anyone was there, watching. There was only the scent of rich wood and oil polish, and the sound of Lizzie's cries. She told herself there was no reason to think anyone would be, but the shiver up her spine argued that point, so she looked, anyway. She felt nothing but emptiness. Utter isolation. She was alone, right to the soul of her.

The baby still cried and Caitlin turned in that direction, stepping softly, her bare feet making no sound on the plush carpet. She strained her ears to hear if anyone else was up, moving around, maybe answering the baby's demands already. She heard nothing. Or did she?

She halted, glancing over her shoulder, puckering her face in concentration as her heart was slowly filled with ice water. There was a sound. Not footsteps. No, something much more menacing than that.

Breathing, all but silent; slow inhales, deliberately quiet exhales came to her in steady rhythm. It seemed to grow louder as she listened. Or was it in her mind? Was the stalker coming nearer? Was that his heart she heard pounding, or her own?

She whirled and ran the rest of the way. The baby's cries still guided her, drawing her in as surely as a lighthouse guides a ship among the rocks and reefs, to shore.

She didn't slow down at the nursery door, only gripped it and flung it open, ducking inside and closing it behind her; turning the lock by sheer instinct.

She leaned back against the cool wood, fighting to catch her breath, and calm her rapid pulse as the baby kept crying in an odd sort of cadence that worked to ease her panic. She got her breathing under control. As jumpy as she was, it might well have been her own slow breaths she'd heard out there just now. Or even the rhythmic respirations of someone sleeping with the door open, in one of the bedrooms she'd passed.

It was neither of those and you know it.

She ignored the voice of her fears and moved toward the crib. There was a fluttering, then a clenching of Caitlin's abdominal muscles, a heavy sort of ache in her breasts.

She leaned over and scooped Lizzie up. "Hush, little one," she murmured, cuddling her close. "Ooh, you're wet, aren't you? No wonder you're so grouchy."

Her attention was only half-focused on Lizzie as she laid the child on the changing table, stripped her down and washed her pink bottom. The other half was busy glancing every few seconds at the locked door. Despite her silent rationalization, she almost expected to see the handle move as someone tried to get in. It didn't, and in a few more moments, Caitlin shook her head slowly, wondering if she were losing her mind.

Naked, Lizzie kicked her feet and waved her hands, cooing and chirping like a little bird on the first day of spring. As Caitlin taped a fresh diaper in place, Lizzie grinned broadly, dimples in her cheeks and her chin, toothless gums fully exposed.

Caitlin found herself smiling back. "Your auntie is a little bit paranoid, Lizzie. Must have been that bump on the head." She struggled to capture Lizzie's flying feet, one at a time, and fit them into the legs of a soft sleeper. Then her arms. "Anyone could have been out there in the hallway tonight. Right? You were crying loudly enough to wake the dead. Just because no one around here is overly fond of me, doesn't mean they spend their nights following me around this gloomy old place. Does it, Lizzie?" She fastened the snaps, and scooped the baby up once more, heading for the rocking chair near the window.

Her explanation wasn't very convincing. Sure, someone might have been on their way to see to the baby, but if so, why hadn't they spoken? Why try so hard to keep their presence behind her a secret? And even if she could make herself believe it was just a coincidence, it didn't erase the earlier incident. Somehow or other, a cake that was poison to her had wound up on her dessert plate tonight. She'd tried to explain it away as she lay in bed, but combined with the presence in the pitch-dark hallway just now, she wondered. The "accidents" and "coincidences" were beginning to pile high.

"I cannot find her, Monsieur Rossi."

Dylan frowned over the morning paper and his coffee cup at the maid. "What do you mean, you can't find her?"

"She is not in her room."

Dylan glanced at his watch, and shook his head. He had to be in the office today. He didn't have time to play Caitlin's games.

"Not thinkin' of going off to work without even seeing her, are you, boy?"

He tossed the newspaper down none too gently. "As a matter of fact, Ellen—"

A crooked finger was waggled near his nose. "Head injury like that, no tellin' what's become of her. Might have gone for a walk and taken a fall. Might be lost, maybe passed out somewhere. Can't just leave, Dylan Rossi, no matter how you feel about her. That explosive temper of yours makes you forget things. She's still your wife, your responsibility. I taught you better than that."

Dylan drew a deep breath, to keep his "explosive temper" from raining down on Ellen. "I'm not going anywhere until I know what she's up to."

"You're not worried?" Ellen demanded. "After the accident, and that close call last night?"

"Ellen, there was no proof that accident was anything but accidental."

"The brake line—"

"Was torn, not cut." He spoke slowly, carefully.

"You might try saying so without sounding so defensive, boy. And what about that cake last night?" Ellen squinted at him through her thick-lensed glasses.

"Are you sure she didn't send it herself, Ellen? Just another ploy, though God knows what she could hope to get out of it. Attention? Or maybe she's trying to set me up for attempted murder, so she can take the whole shebang."

Ellen looked stunned. She stopped eating and blinked down at the plate in front of her. "Well, I never heard of such a thing," she muttered.

"I'm not saying it's a fact, just that it's something to keep in mind. Don't get taken in by her acts. I don't intend to."

"Dylan!"

He looked up at Sandra's shout and saw her coming toward the table, wringing her hands. "What is it now, Sandra?"

"I can't get in the nursery. Door's locked from the inside, and I—" She broke off, glancing around the table. "Where is she?"

Dylan felt a small fist poke him in the gut. "Where is who?"

"Oh, Lord, she's in there with Lizzie, isn't she? That knock on the head was more serious than anyone thought. She's gone off the deep end and now she's holed up with my baby. Dylan, do somethin'!"

Dylan was on his feet before she finished her tirade, gripping Sandra's shoulders to calm her down. "Did you try knocking?"

"N-no. I didn't want to wake the baby. We can't just go up there and knock, Dylan, it might set 'er off." The more agitated Sandra became, the thicker her twang grew. "Git the key. Please, for God's sake, git the key."

"All right. All right, just calm down." She pressed herself to his chest, clinging to his shoulders as if she would fall down without his support. Dylan rolled his eyes. Sandra was nothing if not overly dramatic. "Caitlin would never do anything to hurt a baby, for God's sake."

"How do you know," she moaned. "She's different now. Like a stranger."

Dylan shook his head.

Ellen stood, slapping a hand to Sandra's shoulder from behind. "You want to blubber, girl, go find your own husband to hang all over and let Dylan get that door opened up."

She gave a rather ungentle tug and tore Sandra from Dylan's chest. Leave it to Aunt Ellen not to pull punches. Dylan knew damned well Thomas was still in bed, sleeping. Thomas had been up pacing the halls half the night. Dylan knew, because he'd been restless last night, too. After he'd called the bakery the cake had come from, only to be told his wife had already called, after he'd demanded they tell him, word for word, what they'd told her, he'd been too keyed up to sleep.

He turned toward the kitchen, and located the right key on the rack. Then he went back through the dining room, and on to the foyer and the stairway, with Sandra right on his heels. Thomas's young wife had one valid point. Caitlin was acting differently, strangely. Quiet, almost timid. Her usual assertiveness seemed to have disappeared along with her memory.

As he stopped outside the nursery door, a little ripple of apprehension went through him. Suppose Sandra wasn't overreacting? Suppose there *was* some lingering aftereffect of the accident that had left Caitlin less than sane, and suppose that baby in there was just the shove it took to push her over the edge? Maybe his problems would be solved in a way he hadn't even considered. If she were dangerous, maybe Caitlin would have to be institutionalized. Hadn't he wondered about her mental state all along? It was why he hadn't told her the secret he was keeping. She might know, though. She might have remembered. She might have some kernel of subconscious awareness buried in her mind, and it might be just a little more than her injured brain could take.

He turned the key in the lock, twisted the doorknob, and pushed it silently open.

Caitlin sat in the rocker, with her head leaning to one side, eyes closed, her long lashes just touching her sculpted cheekbones. Her hair was a wild tangle of auburn curls and there wasn't a trace of makeup anywhere to be seen. She wore a thin white nightgown, and her arms, thinner than he remembered, and bare to the shoulders, pale from being hidden from the sun for too long, were wrapped protectively around Lizzie. The baby was cradled to her chest, sleeping just as soundly as Caitlin. The relaxed little cherub-face was nestled in the crook of Caitlin's neck.

A searing hot blade sliced cleanly through Dylan's heart, and he grated his teeth against the flood of pain that would have liked to cripple him. He blinked twice, cleared his throat and made himself move forward as Sandra stood in the doorway, sighing in relief.

He leaned over, lifted a hand toward his wife's face, then lowered it. "Caitlin," he said.

Her eyes flew wide, and she stiffened.

"It's all right, it's only me." He searched her emerald eyes for any sign of insanity and found none. She calmed at once, drawing a breath, shaking her head self-deprecatingly. She lowered her gaze to the baby in her arms, and the most tender smile he'd ever seen whispered across her lips. She slowly got up, walked to the crib and lowered the baby into it, careful not to wake her, then tucked a tiny blanket over Lizzie and turned.

A finger to her lips for silence, she tiptoed into the hallway, past Sandra. Dylan followed, and pulled the door closed behind him.

Sandra turned on Caitlin the second the door was closed. "Do you mind tellin' me just what the hell you think you're doin'?"

"Ssh, you'll wake her." Caitlin frowned at the door, then at Sandra.

"She's my baby, Caitlin. I'll wake her if I want to."

Caitlin shook her head. "I know whose baby she is." She frowned until her auburn brows touched. "What I don't know is why you're so upset. Last night she cried for a half hour before I got up and went to her. She was soaking wet and probably hoarse from all that yelling. You didn't get up so I did. What's the problem?"

Sandra closed her eyes slowly. "Oh, God, it must have been the antihistamine I took last night. I never heard her." She opened her eyes again, and in an instant the anger and worry that had clouded them was replaced by regret. A second after that, her blue eyes narrowed again, searching Caitlin's face. "But that doesn't explain why you locked yourself in the nursery with Lizzie. I was scared half to death when I couldn't git that door open."

Dylan put a hand on Caitlin's shoulder, firm, not comforting. "Caitlin, why did you lock the door?"

She whirled to face him, blinking twice before she seemed to understand. "Oh... so that's what..." She lowered her head and pressed one palm to it. When she looked up again, it was to face Sandra. "God, no wonder you're ready to strangle me. I'm sorry I worried you, Sandra, really, I didn't mean to." She lifted her hands, palms up, and shook her head. "I did it without thinking. I was scared half to death, and I—"

"Scared of what?" Dylan caught her arm and turned her to face him again.

She licked her lips, and met his gaze only briefly, before looking away. "I don't know. It was probably nothing but a case of nerves."

Dylan frowned. "Tell me what happened." His hand still clasped her upper arm.

"Really, Caitlin. If somethin' scared you that bad—"

Caitlin shook her head slowly. "I didn't sleep well."

He nodded. He'd already noted the puffy eyes, the beginnings of dark circles forming beneath them. She was pale, too, and on edge. "Bad dreams?" he asked.

Her green eyes pierced his like arrows, and for just a second, he glimpsed a raw longing in their depths; a longing that shook him right to his frozen core. "Dreams. Not bad ones, though." Her cheeks flushed with color, and she turned away, facing Sandra instead of him. "I woke when I heard Lizzie, about 5:00 a.m. The halls were pitch-black, and I don't really know this place well enough to find light switches in the dark. I just followed the cries."

Her lips thinned, and Dylan saw her throat move as she swallowed. He jerked his gaze upward again. "Go on, Caitlin."

She shook her head. "I thought I heard something... behind me. Someone... breathing. It seemed to get louder, as if they were coming closer, and when I moved, it kept pace." She sighed. "I panicked, and ran the rest of the way. When I got to the nursery, it was a reflex to slam the door and throw the lock. I didn't even think about it, just did it." She lifted her gaze to Sandra's. "I'm really sorry I scared you, Sandra."

Sandra drew a deep breath, then let it out as she nodded. "It's okay." She shifted from one foot to the other. "Look, next time, why don't you just wake me up, all right? I'd really rather see to her myself."

Caitlin nodded. "If that's what you want." She couldn't keep the hurt from her voice, or hide it from her eyes.

Sandra nodded and turned to leave them. Dylan took Caitlin's arm and began walking. She tugged it free.

"We need to talk, Caitlin, and we can't do it here. Come on." He resumed walking, not touching her this time, and she followed. He stopped at her bedroom, opened the door and held it as she preceded him in.

She moved slowly toward the bed, then turned to face him. "What is it we need to talk about?"

"What happened last night? Did you see anyone?"

She looked down at the floor, closed her eyes slowly, shook her head from one side to the other. "This is like walking blind through a maze."

"*What?*"

She bit her lip, met his gaze again. "What kind of a marriage did we have, anyway?"

He opened his mouth to answer, but she hurried on. "I feel like I've just stepped into another woman's life, without a clue how she lived it. I've been handed this part to play, but the roles aren't what they're supposed to be, and the lines keep changing, and..." She turned, strode to the walk-in closet and whipped open the door. "Look at these things."

Dylan frowned. "Your clothes? What's wrong with your clothes?"

"Not *my* clothes, not anymore. There's nothing wrong with them, they're just wrong for me. Wrong for the *me* I am now, not the *her* that I was then." She reached in and began yanking tailored suits, narrow skirts, cropped jackets off hangers, and tossing them onto the bed. "They're bright, and expensive, and chic, and they're just not me."

He caught her shoulders, stopping her from emptying the closet entirely. He stood behind her, and her shoulders slumped forward, her chin touched her chest. "Didn't she even own a pair of jeans without a designer label? A sweatshirt?"

Dylan couldn't allow himself to fall for the act. This vulnerability, this confusion, was just a mask she'd put on. "Not in a long time," he said softly.

She turned toward him, searching his face. "You hated her and now you hate me."

"I never said I hated you, Caitlin—"

"Were the separate bedrooms your idea?"

He shook his head.

"No, I didn't think so." She closed her eyes, and the tensing of her throat muscles made him think she was fighting tears. Or at least, that was what she *wanted* it to make him think. "How long...how long since we made love?"

He licked his lips. "Eight months. Except..."

"Except?"

"There was one time."

Her face pinched tighter as he spoke the words. "One time. Why in God's name did you stay with her?"

He shook his head, fighting the image she was trying to project, angry that her apparent pain was so convincing. "You, Caitlin. Not *her*. You. Why did I stay with *you*." He said it as much to remind him as her.

Her brows lifted, green eyes meeting his, clear and direct. "Well?"

"I didn't have a choice."

She shook her head. "I don't know what that means."

He shrugged. "Doesn't matter. We've veered way off the subject here. You said someone was in the hall last night, following you."

She waited a long moment, and he thought she might insist on an explanation from him. It wouldn't matter if she did. He damned well wasn't going to say anymore. He wasn't even sure who she was anymore.

She stared at him for a long moment, searching his soul, it seemed. Finally, she sighed, long and low. "I've told you everything I can. I didn't hear anything except breathing. I saw nothing. No one touched me or said a word. I have no idea who it was, or even if I imagined the whole thing, and I wouldn't even have mentioned it, except to explain why I locked the nursery door. Okay?"

He examined her face with skepticism he didn't bother disguising. "Okay."

"I didn't mean to send Sandra into hysterics." She looked at the floor for a long moment, then shook her head slowly. "Maybe I just ought to leave."

Dylan was stunned. "Leave?"

She nodded and glanced again toward the closet. "I don't even need to pack. There's not a damned thing here I want."

"Caity, you love this place. You'd never leave—"

"What did you call me?" Her head had come up all at once, those sharp eyes probing again.

He shook his head, still confused by his own reaction to her suggestion. He'd known the end was at hand. He'd been eager to get it the hell over with. "Sorry. I know you hate it. It just slipped out."

"Caity," she said once, then again. A rush of air came through her lips even as they pulled upward at the corners. "God, all this time everyone's been calling me Caitlin, and I've felt like it was someone else's name. Not mine. But Caity..." She smiled fully. "That's who I am." She hugged herself and laughed softly as her eyes fell closed. "Oh, God, that's who I am."

Dylan saw a single tear work its way from beneath her lashes, and travel a slow path down her face. His gut twisted into a hard knot, and he had to clench his hands into fists to keep from reaching out. Whether to wring her slender neck for blatant deception, or to brush that tear away, he couldn't have said.

CHAPTER FIVE

Caitlin dashed the tear from her face with the back of her hand, nearly limp with relief at having found a shred of her identity to cling to.

Dylan shifted his stance. "Why don't you get dressed, come downstairs and get something to eat. You'll feel better."

She shook her head. She didn't want to put on the other woman's clothes, or eat at her table. She wasn't even sure she liked her. "No. I really think I need to get out of here."

"And go where?"

"I don't know. Anywhere. A hotel, a—"

His loud sigh stopped her from completing the sentence. "You're *not going* to any hotel. I've told you, this is your house."

"*Her* house. *I* don't want it."

Dylan turned from her, pushing one hand through his hair and pacing slowly away. "Look, you're two days out of the hospital. This is no time for you to be on your own."

"I don't care."

"Well, I do." He blinked fast after he said it.

"The hell you do," she said very softly.

He lurched forward, gripping her upper arms hard. "You're still my wife."

"Your wife is dead."

He stared hard into her eyes, and she felt his searching, probing, and doubting. She kept her gaze level with his, staring right back. She noticed for the first time how dark his eyes were, like melted chocolate. She felt the contained strength in the hands that held her, and glanced downward, at the corded muscles of his forearms extending from rolled up sleeves. Again, she felt herself wishing he'd fold her into those strong arms. That instead of digging his fingers into her flesh and despising her, he'd rock her against him and tell her that everything would be all right. She closed her eyes at the image, and battled back new tears.

His hands fell away, but when he spoke, his voice had not gentled. "Get dressed. You want out, I'll take you out. You can buy some clothes that meet your latest set of standards."

"I—I don't have any money."

His eyebrows rose slightly. "Caitlin, you're *rich*. When your daddy died, he left you every dime he had."

She shook her head. "Don't you understand? That isn't my money. It was hers. I'm not her, Dylan." She stepped nearer to him, and in her desperation to make someone understand, she caught his face between her palms and tipped it downward. "Look at me. She is gone. I'm not her. I'm not sure I even want to be."

For a long moment, he said nothing. Then slowly, one hand came up to stroke a slow, crooked path over her hair. For a fleeting moment, she saw his eyes lose their glittering harshness. "God, I wish I could believe that." Then his face hardened into the stone sculpture that was becoming familiar. "You'd like me to believe that, wouldn't you?"

Her hands fell to her sides, and she bit her lip. "But you don't, do you?"

"I can't."

"Why?"

He took a step away from her and shook his head slowly as she lifted her gaze to his face once more. "Sheer self-preservation, Caitlin. Go on and get dressed. If you feel you can't spend your own money, then consider it a loan."

She swallowed the lump that tried to choke her. She frowned, then, recalling what he'd just told her. "You said

I inherited everything from my father. What about Thomas?''

Dylan's face went still. "Thomas was excluded from the will. He and your father never got along, and when he took your mother's side in the divorce, the old man disinherited him.''

Caitlin blinked rapidly. "No wonder Thomas resents me.''

"He doesn't resent you. Let's not rehash all this now. I haven't got the time or the inclination. I'll meet you out front in an hour.''

She looked up briefly. "I'll only need twenty minutes.''

Aside from a brief frown, he said nothing. Then he was gone.

She saw that frown again and again that morning. Dylan drove in silence to the bank and helped her through the process of claiming the replacement bank credit cards they'd been holding for her. Hers had all burned with her car. He was quick, efficient and seemingly emotionless. She felt oddly guilty accepting a new card from the teller, but she took it, silently vowing she'd find a way to replace every dime she had to spend. She'd repay the woman she considered dead, the woman Dylan Rossi distrusted so openly.

Back in the front seat of his plush car, he turned to her. "I'll drop you at Eden Mists.''

"What's that?''

"Your favorite boutique. Very chic.''

She grimaced and shook her head quickly. Then her stomach rumbled loudly enough to be heard.

"Maybe we ought to start with breakfast. I forgot you hadn't eaten this morning. We'll swing by Milford's?''

"Another chic spot?''

"Four-star cuisine." His tone was deep, level, unfriendly.

"Don't we get enough of that at home? What about that?" She pointed to the golden arches in the distance.

"You're kidding, right?"

She shook her head and opened the car door, leaping to her feet. The gloom of the drafty house and its hostile atmosphere were wearing off fast. Even Dylan's grim face couldn't keep her mood from soaring, with the brilliant sun spilling all over the neat little city. There was so much to do, so much she must have done once, but couldn't remember. The small city of Eden was bustling, even this early in the morning. Cars buzzed up and down the broad lanes, people walked in groups of two and three, in and out of shops and businesses.

Dylan caught up with her, and they walked side by side to the fast-food restaurant, and through the double doors. Caitlin inhaled the delicious aromas, but hesitated at the crowd standing in front of the counter. She was suddenly uncertain of what to do. She didn't like the large number of strangers around her. She pressed closer to Dylan, not even fully aware she was doing it until he frowned down at her, and his arm came around her shoulders. It was like an automatic act. His face said he regretted it, but when she felt his arm begin to move away, she scrunched closer, and he let it remain.

"You want to leave?"

She gazed up at him, feeling the warmth of that arm around her, seeing the real concern in his black-fringed eyes. His strength seemed to flow into her. She wanted to turn into his embrace, feel his arms surround her...the way they had in her dream.

"No. I'll be fine." *As long as you hold me.*

Dylan's hand rested nervously on her shoulder, and he propelled her along beside him. "What'll you have," he asked, leaning closer as he spoke above the noise. His warm breath fanned her ear.

She shrugged, glancing at the menu high on the facing wall, then at the pastries under a clear cover on the counter. "Those look good."

"Cheese Danish?" He stared down at her for a moment, an odd look in his eyes, then he blinked it away and strode to the vacant spot near a cash register. "Two cheese Danish and two coffees."

A moment later, his arm was no longer around her, because he was carrying their meal on a cardboard tray as he made his way to an empty table. Caitlin sat across from him, unwrapped her pastry and took a bite, then closed her eyes in ecstasy. "Oh, this is terrific."

He only watched her and shook his head.

"What is it? Have I done something wrong, or—"

"We used to come here a lot," he said slowly, carefully, as if he was afraid something would slip through his lips against his will if he didn't watch every word. "You always ordered those."

She set the Danish down and studied his face. It seemed taut, as if he were in physical pain. "When?"

He averted his eyes. "A long time ago, Caitlin."

"Caity," she said quickly. "Can you please call me Caity?"

He lifted his Danish and met her gaze briefly over it. "I don't think so."

She was doing a hell of a number on him, and the worst part was, he felt himself starting to fall for it. First the fast food, then choosing K mart over all the stylish dress shops in the city, and now—

Dylan had to blink down his gut-wrenching memories when she came out of the fitting room in a pair of five-pocket Levi's jeans and a T-shirt. She had the T-shirt tucked in, and the jeans hugged her slender hips and buttocks just the way they had all those years ago, when she'd blown him away every time he looked at her. So long ago, before her mother's suicide, before she'd inherited all that money from her old man. Before she'd started to change, to close herself off from him, to change into the unfeeling woman she'd become.

They'd been something then. Like a live flame and gasoline. When they were together... He closed his eyes, remembering the way Caitlin used to make love to him. She'd put everything into it, heart, soul and body. But he'd soon begun to sense her slipping farther and farther from him, disappearing inside herself, drawing away. He'd responded by drawing back a little, himself. He'd poured even more time and attention into the business, stung by her coolness. And that had only seemed to make her build more walls. And eventually, what they'd had had died. He'd lost her. He'd finally accepted the facts, and resigned himself to ending his farce of a marriage.

And now, she was coming off like the girl she'd been before all that. She acted innocent, trusting and naive, and so damned vulnerable. Afraid, nervous. Pretending to enjoy his company. It was all an act. It was impossible for her to have changed so completely, virtually overnight. Impossible.

She picked out three more pairs of jeans, a half-dozen tops and a couple of simple sundresses, then added a pair of flat summer shoes to her collection. When they left the store, she balled up the bag that held the designer suit she'd arrived in, and stuffed it into a trash can.

She faced him smiling, her eyes glittering with pleasure, the wind whipping her long auburn tresses into mass chaos. "What next?"

Ah, damn, she looked like a teenager.

"We'd better call it a day. I need to go into the office so—"

"I'd love to see where you work!" She slung the shopping bag over her shoulder and started for the car.

He stood where he was, stunned into motionlessness. When she glanced back over her shoulder and saw him there, she stopped beside the car and turned. "What did I do now?"

Dylan shook his head. "You've never given a damn about the business." He made his legs carry him to the car, and slid in behind the wheel. "You sure you want to do this?"

She got in beside him, carelessly tossing her purchases onto the back seat, before studiously fastening her safety belt. "Of course I am." She looked up at him and her smile died. "Unless . . . you'd rather I didn't. I really didn't mean to monopolize your entire morning like this. I wasn't thinking—"

"It's all right, Caitlin."

She sighed and sat back in her seat. "You can take me back to the house if you want to."

He started the car, and backed out of the parking space. What the hell was she up to? She wasn't genuinely interested in the business all of the sudden. She couldn't be. She'd always seen it as a bother, a drain on his time and attention. She'd had enough money for them both, so why waste time on such a difficult project? She was just pretending, because she was up to something. He hadn't figured out what yet, but she was definitely up to something.

Or was she?

Doubts about his sanity pestered him, but he drove toward the office just the same. He'd give her enough rope to hang herself, and then he'd know for sure.

Caitlin stood just outside the glass-paneled office building, blinking. In gold letters across the front door were the words, Rossi Architectural Firm. Then his hand was on her arm again, and he marched her through the doors, into an elevator that whisked them up to the fifth floor.

The place even smelled successful, like new carpet and leather. He led her down a corridor, nodding to people who passed. They all greeted him with deference, "Hello, Mr. Rossi." "Good afternoon, Mr. Rossi." "Good to see you, Mr. Rossi." None smiled, though. They all looked rather pious when they looked at Dylan.

He took her through a door marked Dylan Rossi, CEO, into an office that would have suited the president of IBM. His desk was huge, his carpet, plush silvery gray. A drafting table stood near the windows with a stool in front of it. A computer terminal held court on the desk, with notepads and pencils and books piled around it.

"This is incredible."

He glanced at her once, and once only. He took the thronelike chair behind the desk, and began rummaging through file folders.

It didn't bother Caitlin. She moved around the office, impressed beyond comment at the place. And it was his. She wandered to the drafting table, and looked at the drawing there. The lines and angles, numbers and codes jotted all over the thing meant little to her.

She paid scant attention to Dylan as he spoke on the phone, and made notes in several files. When he finally took her on the promised tour, she felt a little guilty. He obviously had a lot more pressing things to do. Still, it was pleasant, and he seemed to swell a bit with pride as he showed her the various offices and storage rooms in the building, and introduced her to several young architects who worked with him. All the while, he was watching her, studying her reactions. What was he waiting for?

He showed her the small office her brother occupied, but Thomas seemed elbow-deep in something pressing, and only muttered a greeting.

Hours later, as Dylan led her back through the lobby and to the car, she looked back once more and shook her head.

"What?"

She glanced at him, seeing more of him than she had before. He was talented, successful, determined, capable. The people who worked for him respected him, and when he spoke to them, it wasn't with the same coolness in his eyes that always seemed directed at her. "Caitlin must have been proud to be your wife," she said, and her voice was strangely hoarse and soft.

He shook his head. "Not exactly."

Caitlin frowned hard. She couldn't believe the woman she'd once been had been indifferent to her husband's abilities. "She must have been. Maybe she just…never said so."

He looked at her for a long moment. "No, she never did."

"Then she was a fool." She swallowed hard, cleared her throat and made herself continue. She had to begin somewhere. She had to try to right some of the wrongs her old self had wrought. But first she had to find out what they were. She'd alienated her husband, somehow. She touched his arm as he leaned over to open the car door for her. He straightened. "She must have been a fool, Dylan, but for what it's worth, I'm not."

He searched her eyes so deeply, she felt his burn into her soul. Then he broke eye contact, leaving her feeling cold and alone. He jerked the car door open. "Get in, Caitlin. It's going to pour any minute."

Caitlin glanced up at the darkening sky. The sun was rapidly setting, and ominous black clouds roiled in masses overhead. She got in without another word, and they drove in silence.

By the time they approached the looming house, rain poured over the windshield in sheets. The headlights did little to pierce the wall of water, and Dylan drove slowly, braking with care as the drive came into view.

Caitlin sighed, drawing his attention.

"Something wrong?"

She shook her head. "I was just thinking…wishing…" She bit her lip and looked at him. "Wouldn't it be wonderful to just keep on going?"

He frowned, pulling to a stop at the end of the drive. "What?"

"Just keep driving," she rushed on. "Right past this house and on to...I don't know, someplace cozy and warm, and...and kind."

He looked at her strangely, then pulled the car into the long, curving drive and up to the house. A chill raced up the back of her neck when the house came into view. So grim, towering there with it's dark red bricks and masses of clinging vines. It seemed even more spectral in the middle of the night, with the rain pouring down. She fought to suppress it, but felt herself shiver, all the same.

"Running away wouldn't solve anything, Caitlin."

"Wouldn't it?" She faced him in the darkness of the car.

"You can't just walk away from your life, you know. It's not that simple."

She shook her head. "I know I can't. Not yet, anyway." She hurried on before he could ask what she meant by that. "I don't want to go inside yet. You know, all I've seen of this place is the front...all I can remember, anyway."

"Cait, it's raining."

She sighed long and low. "Feels good, doesn't it? It's been so hot." She opened the car door and got out. For a moment, she just stood still and let the rain pour over her. She tipped her face up and let the downpour bathe it.

She didn't hear him come toward her, only the sounds of the wind and the rain battering the ground, pinging and ricocheting on the car roof. His arm came around her shoulders and he urged her toward the house.

She pulled free. "No. I want to walk out back, by the ocean."

"The cliffs are dangerous at night, Caitlin, especially when it's raining. You could slip—"

"I'll be careful." They stood facing each other. His hair was already drenched, plastered to his head. His jaw was set and rigid.

"Cait, this is crazy." He pitched his voice loudly to fight the storm, and again it carried that tone of command that made her tremble.

"I'll be fine. Go on to the house, Dylan."

"That's exactly what I'm doing." In a second, he'd scooped her up into his arms and was striding toward the front door. He flung it wide, carried her through and kicked it closed behind him. The light in the foyer was too bright after the murky darkness outside. A shiver moved through her and his arms seemed to tighten just a little. He looked down, into her eyes. She stared back into his. Her arms had linked themselves around his neck, and their faces were close. She could feel the heat of his body through her wet clothes. And all at once, she wanted to kiss him. She wanted to know if it could be the way she imagined it . . . or had she remembered it?

Her fingers slid upward, into the dripping sable waves, and she brought her face closer to his. Her heart pounded harder. She closed her eyes, and eliminated the last inch of space between their mouths. She pressed her parted lips to his, felt them move in response, felt her mouth captured by his gentle suction. Then everything changed. His arms clutched her tighter, so tight she could barely breath. His mouth took hers in a frantic, desperate assault. His tongue plunged and dove, as if he couldn't taste enough of her. She kissed him back just as eagerly. Her body strained against his, her tongue twined with his in a sensual dance . . .

. . . that stopped all too soon.

He pulled away and abruptly set her on her feet. He looked at her once, his gaze narrow, almost wary. Then he shook his head and strode away.

CHAPTER SIX

She got turned around in the labyrinth of corridors on her way down to dinner. She knew she was on the ground floor, but she'd somehow taken a wrong turn from the foyer, and wound up in a part of the house she hadn't seen. The towering ceilings and darkly stained wood, the parquet floors and tall, arched windows, were the same as the rest of the place. The house was gloomy, unwelcoming, even with all the lights blazing. The rain slashing against the windows and the wind howling through the trees outside, only made it seem worse.

She walked over cold, hard ceramic tiles of the strange hallway, peering through one darkly stained door after another to try to get her bearings. She found a cluttered office, with wall-to-wall file cabinets, a desk full of computer equipment, and a fax machine. Maybe Dylan worked at home sometimes, she mused. She drew back, closed the door and moved along the hall to the next. She was just reaching for it when she heard soft voices farther down. She hurried toward them. Then stopped at the low, throaty laughter.

"Of course, I love you, *mon cher,* but I cannot wait forever." The voice was Genevieve's.

The one she heard whisper a reply startled her. It belonged to her brother. "It'll all be yours, baby. You just have to be patient."

"I run out of patience, playing servant to these people. And your wife, she treats me like a dog. How much longer, Thomas?"

"I need a little more time. I promise you, we'll be on top...and Dylan Rossi will be sorry he ever underestimated me. I'll show him. It'll be a lesson he won't forget."

Caitlin drew a sudden gasp and her brother's words stopped. A second later, he appeared in front of her, stepping out of the room—a cozy, private parlor, from what she could glimpse—where he'd been having his little chat with her maid.

"What are you doing here?" The words had the ring of an accusation, but the expression on his face was one of pure guilt—and something tugged at her mind.

"I, uh, got lost on my way to dinner." She fought to keep what she'd heard, and what she was feeling, from showing on her face. "I'm glad I ran into you. I was afraid I'd never get back on track."

Thomas's hooded green eyes tried to hide his offense, but at the same time he stole quick glances at her face to see if she knew. He took her arm and started off in the direction from which she'd come.

The image came to her then. The pudgy red-haired boy, in a grimy Little League uniform, looking up at her just the way he was right now, as he tried to wipe the white foam from his shirt.

She squinted, trying to fine-tune the memory, then clapped a hand to her mouth to stifle the burst of laughter when it all came clear. "Tommy, *you* were the one who shaved Mrs. Petrie's poodle!"

He stopped walking, faced her, blinking. "Mrs. Pe—" He grabbed her shoulders, smiling broadly. "You *remember* that?"

She grinned back, nodding hard, mentally hugging the memory to her, wanting never to let it go. "I covered for you. Helped you ditch the razor and cleaned the foam off you before anyone saw."

"Damned dog had it coming." He shook his head, and laughed. "Stole my lunch at practice. I thought I'd starve before I got home."

"I think you went overboard in your retaliation," she teased.

"I only shaved the puff from the top of the mutt's head." He turned, and began walking again. After a few moments, he said, "So, um, how long were you standing out there?"

She frowned up at him. She wanted very much to get close to her brother again, especially now, having regained such a cherished memory of him as a child. But she'd just heard him threaten her husband, unless she'd completely misunderstood. She couldn't trust him. Not yet. "Not standing, walking. I was just wandering aimlessly and you stepped right into my path."

"Oh." He looked relieved.

He guided her through the maze of corridors until things began to seem familiar to her. It seemed to take a long time, though. She realized why when she finally entered the dining room to find Genevieve had managed to get there before them. She was already setting covered platters on the formally set table. Dylan rose when Caitlin came in.

"There you are. I was getting ready to send out a search party." His voice was level, controlled, but there was tension in his eyes.

Caitlin sat down just as Ellen entered the room behind her, and did likewise. "Enjoy your day out, Caitlin?"

Caitlin glanced up at the older woman and nodded. "Very much."

"I see you got some new clothes." Ellen looked down at Caitlin's jeans and shook her head. "Not your usual style."

"It is now."

Platters were passed, and Caitlin frowned across the long table at her husband. "Shouldn't we wait for Sandra?"

Dylan shrugged. "You've always insisted on promptness at dinner. She knows that it's one of your favorite rules."

"It's a stupid rule."

Genevieve stopped halfway across the room with a bowl in her hand. Dylan paused in filling his plate. Thomas stared at her.

Ellen chuckled. "I always said so. Still, I think we may as well get on with it. Baby was fussing. Sandra probably won't be down for a while."

"Is Lizzie sick?" She directed the question toward her brother.

"I don't know. Just cranky, I think."

"Don't worry about it, Caitlin," Ellen said. "Tell me about your trip. What did you do?"

Caitlin was worried, and vowed to check on the baby after dinner. In the meantime, though, Ellen seemed genuinely interested, and Caitlin wanted to build some bridges with the woman.

"Dylan took me on a tour of his offices."

Ellen frowned, her silvery brows bunching behind those thick glasses.

"I had no idea how successful he was until I saw for my-'self. I was very impressed."

"Did he tell you he started in one room, and not a big room, either. Built everything from the ground up. Designed that building himself."

"No, he didn't."

Ellen nodded. "That's his, girl. I won't stand still to watch anybody try to take it from him, and that includes you." Her bony finger poked into Caitlin's shoulder as she spoke.

Caitlin only shook her head. "Why would you think I—"

"I know what you're up to. You just remember that."

"That's enough, Ellen."

Ellen shot her nephew an impatient glare, and returned her attention to her plate. Caitlin let her chin fall to her chest. She'd honestly believed she might be making some progress with the woman.

Sandra's hasty entrance brought her head back up, and then she shot to her feet. Sandra held little Lizzie in her arms. The child's eyes were heavy-lidded and dull. She lay limply, as if exhausted, her head resting against her mother's shoulder.

"She's burnin' up!" Sandra drawled thickly. "I cain't get the fever down."

Caitlin raced forward, instinctively placing her palm across Lizzie's forehead, feeling the unnatural heat and the clamminess of the baby's skin. Sandra's eyes were pleading as they met hers.

Thomas stood, but didn't make a move to approach his daughter. Ellen rose with effort, moving slowly forward.

"Landsakes, you're shaking like a leaf, girl. Give her here, before you drop her."

Sandra surrendered the child to Ellen, who, in turn, placed Lizzie in Dylan's arms, obviously unaware, or unconcerned that Dylan would prefer the child were anywhere other than in his grasp. He held her stiffly. The veins in his neck bulged.

"Take her upstairs," Ellen ordered. "Sandra, call the doctor if you think you can talk straight. I imagine by the time you get done on the phone, the fever will be down, but call anyway."

Dylan left the room with the baby clutched awkwardly to his chest. Ellen hobbled behind him. Sandra went to the living room and picked up the phone. Thomas, to Caitlin's amazement, sat back down to his dinner, but he didn't really eat any of it.

"Aren't you going to go up there?"

He shook his head. "It's not that I'm not worried. I am, I just...she's so tiny. I feel like a giant when I hold her. I'm...not comfortable, you know?"

Caitlin frowned at him and shook her head. "No, I really don't." She followed Ellen up the stairs, knowing she wasn't wanted or needed, but too afraid for Lizzie to stay behind. In the nursery, Ellen gave calm instructions.

"Dylan, just sit and hold her. Caitlin, make yourself useful and run some water in here." She handed Caitlin a small plastic tub. "Make it cool. Not cold, but cool to the touch. Go on, hurry it up."

Caitlin nodded and took the tub into the adjoining bathroom to fill it. She carried it back into the nursery, and placed it atop the changing table.

Dylan had the baby in his lap. He was peeling the little sleeper off the child, then removing the diaper. His lips were drawn into a thin line, brows furrowed.

As she watched, Caitlin felt her eyes fill. Ellen dipped a gnarled hand into the tub. "Just right. Set her in here, Dylan, but keep hold of her." Dylan rose. "Better get those sleeves rolled up first."

He looked down at his white shirt, then glanced at Caitlin. She hurried to him without a minute's hesitation, unbuttoned his sleeves and rolled them to his elbows. Her fingers moved over the curling hairs on his forearms and she felt a pain twist inside her.

Dylan stepped away from her, and haltingly lowered Lizzie into the tiny tub. The water just covered her chubby legs. "There now, Lizzie," he said softly, falteringly, clutching the infant under the arms as if afraid she'd dissolve in the water. "You like baths, don't you? Sure you do. There we go."

"Now cup your hand, Dylan, and just pour the water over her chest. That's it."

Dylan followed Ellen's instructions, bathing the hot little body in cool water as Lizzie stared trustingly up at him, looking sleepy. After a few minutes, Dylan leaned Lizzie forward, over his arm, and bathed her back in the same manner. He even managed to wet her head and neck, all without upsetting the baby at all, though his hands shook visibly.

Sandra burst into the room then. "What's happenin'? Is she all right?"

"What did the doctor say?" Caitlin asked.

Sandra glanced at Caitlin, then frowned. "You shouldn't be here, Caitlin. You can go now. *I'm* her mama."

God, was Sandra threatened by Caitlin's presence, her fondness for Lizzie? Was she jealous?

"Answer the question, Sandra, 'fore I cuff you upside the head for ignorance," Ellen scolded.

Sandra shot Ellen a nearly blank glance, before she answered. "He said to put her in a cool bath and keep her there until the Children's Tylenol has a chance to work."

"When did you give her the medicine?" Ellen asked.

"I—I couldn't get it down her. She was fussin' so much, and then she got so hot, I just—"

"Well, she isn't fussing now. Get that medicine in here."

Sandra went into the bathroom and returned with the little bottle, and a baby-size medicine spoon. She poured the dose and handed the spoon to Dylan.

"Uh…hey, Lizzie, look what Uncle Dylan has for you." He spoke as if he were talking to an adult. He slipped the spoon between Lizzie's lips and she took the medicine without a fight. Then he returned to his messy, nervous bathing of her heated body. His shirt was soaked, as were the fronts of his trousers and a good deal of the floor.

Sandra paced, Ellen sat in the rocker and Caitlin just stood and watched Dylan with the baby, a lump in her throat making it difficult to breathe. After twenty minutes, Ellen ordered the baby removed from the bath. Dylan scooped her out and wrapped her in a towel. As he patted her dry, she fell asleep in his arms. Dylan stared down at her, some secret turmoil in his eyes. He blinked it away at once.

"She feels cooler now." He placed her in the crib.

Ellen got up and touched the sleeping child's forehead. "Put a diaper on her, Sandra. Nothing else. Get that medicine down her every four hours. If you can't, or if that fever shoots up again, you come and get me."

"Yeah, okay. And I'll take her to the doctor in the mornin'. He said he'd see her first thing."

Ellen nodded and left the room. Caitlin turned to go, as well, but stopped cold when Sandra slipped her arms around Dylan's neck and pressed herself close to him. "I was so scared," she whispered. "Thank God you were here."

Caitlin saw Dylan's arms creep around Sandra's waist. Dylan's back was to Caitlin. But not Sandra's, and that blond head lifted from Dylan's shoulder just long enough to send Caitlin a look of unmistakable meaning.

Biting her lower lip to fight the tide of burning jealousy, pure and bitter, that rinsed through her heart, she turned and fled the room. It was obvious that Thomas's young wife had designs on Caitlin's husband. And from the looks of things, Dylan wasn't putting up too much of a fight. Not that Caitlin could blame him. After all, he hadn't slept in her bed in months and months. What had the old Caitlin expected him to do?

She raced past her bedroom, tears threatening. She felt more an outsider than she thought possible. Seeing Sandra in Dylan's arms, seeing the truth at last, in the other woman's eyes. God, she needed to get out of here!

She took the stairs at top speed, and went right out the front door into the rain-filled night. And then she stopped, and stood, tilting her head up into the black rains, razor winds and the night's bracing, icy hands.

It was almost as if the rain could wash away the person she'd been before, leaving her clean and free to begin again. She closed her eyes and let the drops roll over her heated lids, drenching her lashes, rinsing the hot tears from them, cooling the burn.

Almost without thinking, she began placing one foot ahead of the other, as her clothes slowly soaked through and began clinging to her skin. She followed a worn path in the grass that took her around to the rear of the house, down a mild slope, and through a small wood.

The sounds of waves hurling themselves against jagged rock were like a siren's call, luring her onward, until she stood at the very lip of a cliff. The wind blew in off the sea, razing her face with the stinging, chilled droplets it carried. It smelled of the ocean, and of the rain. Freshness and freedom. It sent her wet hair snapping behind her, and she closed her eyes and just felt its touch. She forced everything else from her mind, and lived only for the moment, for this experience.

God, it felt good.

She opened her eyes, but ahead there was only darkness, roiling clouds and curtains of rain. She edged closer to the granite lip, and let her gaze fall downward. White foam seethed from the surface around glittering fingers of rock, far below. More white exploded from each black wave that battered the shore.

She was as wet as if she'd been swimming, fully clothed, but she didn't care. She needed to think, and here was the best place to do it. She couldn't keep a clear head in that house.

The woman she'd been had left behind as much devastation as a hurricane. All of it, it seemed, was now hers to clean up. She had to begin somewhere.

But how?

She obviously couldn't mend any fences with Sandra. The woman was after her husband, there was no way around that. Sandra had declared her intentions in no uncertain terms.

The question was, what did Caitlin intend to do about it?

Would she surrender? Give up without a fight? Stand quietly by while the sleek little blonde seduced Dylan?

That the first option rubbed her wrong told her something about her personality. Whether it was the old Caitlin or the new one, she wasn't sure. But she knew that having something that belonged to her stolen while she watched was not a plausible answer. She couldn't do it.

And the only other option was to keep him for herself. And of course, she had no idea if she wanted that, either... or even if he'd have her.

She turned and walked along the edge for a time, letting the wind buffet her right side. When she came to an oblong boulder, she sat down upon its slick surface, and turned to face the sea again, her feet dangling over the rain-filled space between her and the shore.

"You should have died in the accident, Caitlin."

The voice rasped near her ear, just as she felt the gloved hands settle around her throat. She tried to turn around, but one fist closed in her hair, and she couldn't move her head. The voice went on, throaty and gruff, neither masculine nor feminine, unidentifiable.

"But you're about to have another one."

Even as the hands at her neck loosened, she felt the impact of a foot at the small of her back. Her body arched forward, pain slicing her spine. Her hands grappled for something, but only slid from the wet rock.

She was going over the edge. There was nothing to stop her. The cry she released was one of pure fear, and it split the night, pierced the walls of rain and drowned out the wind as she tumbled and twisted and grabbed for salvation.

Somehow, her fist closed on a jagged outcropping. Razor-edged stone cut into her palm, but she clung tighter, even as her body twisted and slammed into the sheer stone face. Frantically, she moved her toes and her other hand, in search of more support. One foot found a niche in the rock, and dug into it.

She was panting, breathless with fear. The rain battered her back and the sounds of the waves crashing to shore below were louder, echoing through her consciousness. She lifted her head, to look above at her assailant, but saw nothing. Only the jagged edge from which she'd fallen, and the inky sky above. She hadn't fallen far. Surely she could climb back up.

But what if he's still there, waiting? What if he pushes me again? She closed her eyes and prayed for courage, and strength to hold on. She dared not try to scale the wet, sheer wall. If she let go, she would fall, there was no question in her mind, but she couldn't remain where she was, either.

"Caitlin..."

The howling wind seemed to cry her name, then again, louder this time. It wasn't the wind. Someone was there, looking for her. The call came again, and she recognized Dylan's voice. She parted her lips to answer, then bit the cry off before it left her throat. What if Dylan was the one who had pushed her? What if he were only calling out now to ascertain whether his mission had been a success?

Seconds ticked by. Then other voices joined the first, calling her name. Thomas's, Henri's, even Sandra's.

"This way," Dylan's voice shouted into the wind. "I heard a scream."

"*Mon Dieu,* do you think she has fallen—" Henri began.

"Here," Caitlin cried out with every ounce of strength left in her. Whoever had pushed her, they wouldn't try again, not with all of them there to bear witness. "Down here. Help me!"

There were footsteps, then lights above her, glaring down into her eyes. She averted her face. "Hold on, Cait. Don't move, just hold on!" The light moved away, and she heard Dylan's voice once again, gruff and unsteady. "I can reach her, hold my legs, Thomas." There was shuffling, movements of bodies on the wet stone. She looked up again to see

Dylan's dark shape. He lay facedown above her, and bent at the waist until his upper body hung over the edge. His arms stretched down for her, his strong hands closed like vises around her wrists.

"Let go of the rock, Cait. Hold onto my arms."

She didn't. She couldn't. What if he just let her go?

"Let go," he said again. She tilted her head up, and looked at him. "Trust me for once, dammit! I won't let you fall."

She had no choice. She couldn't hang on much longer, anyway. Trusting Dylan with her life right now was her only option. She released her precarious hold on the stone, and gripped his wrists just as he was gripping hers.

"I have her," he shouted. "Pull me up."

Slowly, she was dragged up the wet, cold, washboard face of stone, and onto the blessedly level ground again. She lay facedown on the uneven stone, head buried in her arms. Dylan's hands on her shoulders urged her to her feet. His eyes scanned her face, her body, as the fear enveloped her all over again. With a strangled cry, she threw herself against him, and his arms closed around her. He held her against him with all the strength she'd known his arms would possess, and as she shook violently, she noticed that he was trembling, too.

His hands stroked her wet hair, her back and shoulders. "It's all right, Cait. It's over. You're safe now. It's all right."

She couldn't make the tears stop flowing. She couldn't let go of him. So she was glad when he scooped her up into his arms as if she weighed nothing at all, and turned to begin back toward the house. She kept her arms tight around his neck, her face pressed to the warm, wet skin of it. She knew the others walked with them. She felt their curious eyes on her, but she didn't care. She'd experienced raw terror in the last few minutes. She was clinging to her sanity by clinging to her husband. It didn't matter what they thought.

She knew he'd mounted the front steps. She heard the door open and felt the rain stop lashing her as he carried her inside. Then he was lowering her onto the sofa, leaning her head back against the armrest, sitting right beside her.

Caitlin couldn't take her eyes from his face, as he looked her up and down. His hands moved anxiously over her arms, then her legs. "Are you all right? Were you hurt?"

She shook her head as someone handed him a blanket, and he tucked it around her. Then he stared at her face, and shook his head, and the hardness crept over his features, little by little, until the ice sculpture was complete. "Dammit, Caitlin, I told you not to go out there tonight. I told you how dangerous it was, that you could fall—"

"I didn't fall." She blurted the words quickly, and everyone in the room stilled, looking toward her.

Dylan's face contorted then. He shook his head slowly as if in disbelief. "You didn't...my God, are you saying you..."

"Can't say it, Dylan?" Thomas's voice was laced with bitterness. "She jumped. Tried to take the same cowardly way out our mother did." Caitlin caught her breath, but Thomas went right on. "We all could've been killed trying to pull you up, big sister. Next time, try something a little smarter."

Dylan whirled on Thomas, fists clenched. Caitlin threw back the blanket and leapt to her feet, only to sway on weak knees. She gripped Dylan's arm, both to keep from falling at his feet, and to keep him from hitting her brother. "Stop it! For God's sake—"

"Caitlin, don't do this." Thomas's voice cracked and changed pitch. The next sentence was an octave higher, a plea. "I'll never forgive you if you do what she did—"

Caitlin released Dylan's arm, only to grip both of Thomas's. "My mother...are you saying...suicide?"

"It was cruel, Caitlin, and I hate her for it! Damn you, for trying—"

"I didn't!" she shrieked. Thomas went silent, and she saw actual tears swimming in his eyes as he searched her face. More calmly, she went on. "I didn't jump off that cliff. I was pushed."

"Pushed?" Dylan gripped her shoulders from behind, turned her to face him. He'd paled, and his eyes were wider than she'd seen them yet. "Who—"

"Did you say 'pushed'?" Caitlin turned her head to see Ellen, scuffing into the room, followed by Genevieve.

"Oh, *mon Dieu!* Are you all right?"

Caitlin's eyes met Dylan's, and she nodded. "For now I am." Silently, she heard her heart begging him, *Please don't be the one.*

CHAPTER SEVEN

The room went utterly silent. Dylan only stared at Caitlin, and said nothing.

"*I* think Caitlin ought to pay another visit to that shrink of hers."

She glanced toward Sandra's doubting eyes and shivered. Was the woman that desperate to latch on to Caitlin's husband? Desperate enough to kill?

Caitlin shivered. Dylan's gaze narrowed on her. "You need to get into some dry clothes before you get sick."

She turned toward him. "Is that all you have to say? Dylan, someone tried to kill me tonight!"

He searched her face, and she saw the skepticism in his eyes. "You don't believe me."

"I didn't say that."

"You didn't have to." She pulled free of the tempting warmth she could feel emanating from his body, turned and walked calmly toward the staircase and up it. She focused on the cool, smooth feel of the banister as her hand glided over it, on the number of steps her feet climbed, on the pattern of the wood grain on them. Anything but the feeling of their eyes on her back, and the fear that still made her heart thunder.

No one followed, only the grim specter of fear that seemed to grow larger with every minute she spent here. She closed the bedroom door, and flicked on the lights. Her nerves tingling, she moved slowly through the room. The closet loomed ahead of her like a dare, and she answered, stepping forward, flinging it wide and scanning the dim interior.

Nothing inside except the mounds of clothing she detested, and the few things she'd chosen for herself. But a chill raced up her spine, and she whirled. The bathroom door was closed. Hadn't she left it ajar?

She stood for an eternity, barely breathing as she listened. She heard only the howl of the wind and the hands of the rain slapping her windows. She moved forward, slowly, mindlessly closing her fingers around something cold and hard and heavy as she passed the nightstand. She gripped the doorknob, turned it and holding her breath, flung it wide.

When she saw only the dark shapes of the fixtures, she stiffened her spine, reached in for the light switch and snapped it on. Oh, God, the shower curtain was pulled tight.

She swallowed hard, snagged the curtain in one hand and lifted her makeshift weapon in the other. She tore it open. The porcelain tub stood gleaming, empty.

"Caitlin."

She spun at the sound of his voice, again lifting the weapon instinctively. Dylan stood near the bedroom door. It was closed behind him, and Caitlin's darting gaze quickly noted that it was locked, as well.

"What do you want?"

He frowned, his eyes focused on the object in her hand. "You won't need that, Cait. Put it down." As he spoke, he moved forward.

Caitlin blinked as her hand lowered. She studied her weapon, a shiny onyx-colored vase with a scarlet rose painted on the front. A thin rim of gold encircled the lip. It would be about as useful against a would-be killer as the pillow on her bed. She closed her eyes and stepped into the bedroom, replacing the vase on the stand.

She heard his sigh as he stepped closer. "You're still shaking."

She rubbed her arms and shrugged.

"Tell me you didn't try to jump, Cait."

She lifted her head, met his eyes. He stood very close to her now. "I didn't jump. I told you, I was pushed."

"By whom?"

She tipped her head up and studied the planes and angles of his face. It was a strong face, with deep brown eyes filled with emotions she couldn't begin to fathom. "I didn't see. He came up behind me."

"He? It was a man, then?"

She shrugged. "It could've been. I'm not sure, the voice was deliberately disguised."

"He spoke to you?"

She nodded. Dylan's hands came to her shoulders and her heart beat a little faster. It was a stupid reaction. For all she knew, it could've been him.

"Cait, what did he say to you?"

She swallowed hard. "That I should've died in the accident. That I'd die tonight, instead."

"And you still didn't get a look—"

"His hands were on my throat. I couldn't turn my head."

Brows bunching together, Dylan's glance dipped to her neck. His warm hands touched her skin there, and tilted her chin upward. His head lowered. An onlooker would have thought he was about to kiss her, she thought, and a shudder rippled through her at the vision. His long fingers touched her throat and she wished they'd explore lower. She knew those fingers had teased her breasts, had taunted her center to throbbing readiness.

How can I want a man who may have just tried to kill me?

"He left marks. There'll be bruises tomorrow."

"So now you have to believe me."

Dylan's hands fell away. "I believed you in the first place."

"Then why—"

"I thought it would be best if we discussed this alone."

Her eyes darted once again toward the locked door. She shivered.

"You're still soaking wet." He reached to the bedpost, where her red satin robe hung, and picked it up. "Here, get into this."

Cait took it from him and stepped into the bathroom, closing the door. She quickly shimmied out of her clothes, and wiped her skin dry with a towel. She scanned the room for something besides the robe to put on, but saw nothing. Not even underwear. Sighing in resignation, she pulled the robe on, and tied the sash tight.

When she stepped back into the bedroom, Dylan was pacing. He faced her and stopped, his eyes narrowing as his gaze moved briefly down her body. He snapped it upward again.

Caitlin felt the touch of his eyes as if they were hands, and she fought the wave of heat that rose to engulf her, even as goose bumps dotted her arms.

"So, what do you want me to do?"

She saw his eyes widen slightly. "What?"

"About tonight," she clarified. "Shouldn't I call the police?"

"I'll talk to them in the morning," he said.

Caitlin's heart skipped once, just once. "Why?"

"Because I'd like to keep this quiet if I can." He took a step toward her. "Cait, we have to handle this carefully." At his second step in her direction, she took one backward.

He froze where he was, his eyes narrowing. "What is it?"

She shook her head. "Nothing. Nothing, this is all just a lot to deal with. I just want to go to bed, and—"

"You're afraid of me, aren't you." It was a simple statement of fact. "You think it was me."

She licked her lips and forced herself to meet his gaze. "I don't know what to think."

He shook his head in disbelief. "You put down the vase."

"Maybe I ought to pick it back up."

"You think it would do any good?" He took another step forward, his hands closing on the outsides of her arms.

"I think you're trying to scare me."

"Am I succeeding?"

She felt her lips begin to tremble. "Yes," she whispered.

His eyes moved over her face in rapid, searching patterns. "Good. I hope you're scared enough to use some sense from here on in. Walking into that storm, going out to the cliffs on a night like this was insane, Caitlin. What on earth were you thinking?"

He still held her arms, and the angry sparks in his eyes were real. "I was upset. I just had to get out of this house."

"Why?"

She closed her eyes, shook her head quickly. "You don't know when to quit, do you?"

"I don't know the word 'quit,' lady. Tell me why you took off like that."

"Because I saw the way you were holding Sandra, all right?"

"The way I—"

"She was pressed so close, I couldn't have fit a matchstick between you."

Understanding seemed to dawn on his face. "In the nursery—"

"And you didn't seem to mind it at all, Dylan. And forgive me for being human, but seeing that hurt."

He shook his head slowly. "Hurt?" He repeated her own word as if trying to remember its meaning.

"She wants you, you know." She turned and paced away from him, relieved that she'd released the tension burning inside her. "And she intends to have you."

"How do you know?"

"She told me. No, not in words. Women can communicate without parting their lips sometimes, and she made her intentions perfectly clear to me. She wants you." Her back was still to him.

He came to stand close behind her. "And what do *you* want?"

A sob tried to escape, and she choked on it. "I don't know. I only know I want to believe you aren't trying to kill me. I want to believe it very much."

His hands crept up to her shoulders. "But you don't, do you?"

She sniffed, and shook her head. "No."

"What's my motive, Cait? You think I want your money? I've never given a tinker's damn about money. I could've let you fall out there if I'd wanted to get rid of you so badly. Have you thought of that?"

She laughed, though it came out as a short release of air. "What do you think?"

He turned her to face him, brows furrowed. "My God, you were thinking it at the cliff, weren't you? You were hanging over the side, clinging to nothing but my hands, half convinced I was going to let you go."

She nodded. There was no sense in being dishonest about it, no sense lying.

He shook his head hard and blew an angry sigh. "Believe what you want, Caitlin. Go to the police yourself if you don't trust me. Do whatever you have to do."

He turned toward the door, but her next words stopped him. "Have you slept with her, Dylan?"

He shook his head without turning to face her. He stood poised, his hand on the doorknob. "Do me a favor and stop worrying about my relationship with Sandra. It's none of your business ... unless you'd care to make me a better offer."

He stormed out and slammed the door behind him.

She took a long, hot bath to soak the chill from her bones, but it did little to soothe her frayed nerves. There was just too much she didn't know. Had her car accident been another attempt on her life? It seemed more than likely, given the assailant's words at the cliff. And the carob-laced dessert now looked like yet another. Someone wanted her dead, and badly.

But who? She knew so little about her life, it was difficult to judge who had a motive to want it to end. Did she have enough money to give Dylan a motive? Why wouldn't he simply divorce her if he wanted out of the marriage? And what about Thomas? She already knew he'd been disinherited. And she'd gotten everything. He'd sided with their mother in the divorce, and she'd apparently taken her father's side. What she hadn't known before tonight, was the manner in which her mother had died.

Suicide.

Had Caitlin been to blame for that? Had her decision to remain with her father added to her mother's depression in any way? And how could it not have? Maybe Thomas was resentful of the part she'd played in their mother's death, and maybe he was striking out against her, as a result.

Could she make amends with him now? And should she? She could offer him half of what she'd inherited from their father. It was only fair. He should have gotten it to begin with.

Snippets of the conversation she'd overheard between Thomas and Genevieve floated through her memory and she bit her lip. Thomas had said he would teach Dylan a lesson he'd never forget. Whatever he was planning, she couldn't very well help him along by giving him what he needed to carry it out. No, nor could she tell Dylan about what she'd overheard. She felt an instinctive urge to protect her brother, and sensed it was just the way she'd felt when they were growing up together. If she'd misunderstood, she might cost Thomas his job, and his wife and child their home, all without cause. That would only make him hate her.

God, she had so little to go on! If she had any sense at all, she'd probably pack her things and get out of here while there was still time. But something kept her from making that decision right now. Tomorrow, she decided. Tomorrow she would do some digging into her past, and decide how best to proceed. Tomorrow.

She dried her hair, and tried to get some sleep, but every time she began to drift off, she would hear footsteps outside her bedroom door, or the wind moaning at the window, and her eyes would fly wide once more.

She drifted off to sleep eventually, but the entire time, she tossed and turned in the throes of a nightmare she couldn't later recall.

A soft wail stroked at the edges of her consciousness, tugging her out of the dream. In the nick of time, it seemed, she emerged into the soft folds of her covers. The baby was crying.

Caitlin wiped the sweat from her forehead, and tried to settle her breathing into a normal pattern. It was just a dream. Nothing more. She was safe.

It was then she felt the presence in her room. She froze and held her breath, listening. There was no sound or movement. Just a feeling that she wasn't alone.

She tried to shake it. It was silly, she told herself. Of course no one was in her room. She was shaken, from the dream and from her close call on the cliffs, tonight.

The baby cried again, and Caitlin felt answering tears well up in her own eyes. She wished, with everything in her, that Lizzie was her own. During those few, brief times when she'd held the baby, she'd felt as if everything would be fine. It had seemed so perfect. She'd had an identity. She'd found something to cling to in this sea of unanswered questions. It hurt too much to hear that child cry, and then stop as someone, probably Sandra, picked her up. Why the hell did it hurt so much?

She rolled to her stomach and buried her face in the pillow, clutching it tightly. It absorbed her stinging tears, but gave no comfort.

Then she heard the audible click of the door closing, and sat bolt upright in the bed. Someone had just exited the room, she was sure of it. She shot to her feet, switching on the lamp. Its glaring light made her blink, and showed her nothing. The room was exactly as it had been before.

Caitlin went to the door and yanked it open, her eyes scanning the dim length of the hallway in both directions. There was no one in sight, but she heard, just for an instant, the soft padding of feet on the carpet.

Terror gripped her, and she backed into her room, closed the door and turned the lock. Someone had been in here, standing over her while she tossed in the throes of her nightmare. Someone had stood, silently, just watching her.

Why?

What would have happened if she hadn't awoke?

She sat on the bed, with her back to the headboard, and her knees drawn up to her chest. She didn't close her eyes again.

In fear and desperation, she finally got up, determined to find the guest room where she'd taken refuge that first day back. She would sleep there tonight. Not only would she feel better, but it would make finding her more difficult for the killer, if he decided to try again.

Dylan poured another shot and tossed it back in a single swallow. It did nothing to erase from his memory the feel of his wife in his arms. When he'd pulled her up from the cliff face and she'd thrown herself against him, he'd experienced a longing that was like an addict's craving for his drug of choice. He'd wanted her.

Wet. She'd been soaking wet, and shivering with cold, and her nipples had pressed against his chest so hard, he could feel them right through his shirt. And her face was damp, and her throat, and he'd wanted to lick the rainwater from her skin. God, how could he want any woman as badly as he wanted her, let alone one who'd caused him so much pain?

But she was different now. No longer the haughty princess of the manor, but unsure of herself, and softer-spoken, and—

Damn straight she's soft-spoken. She's scared to death I'm going to kill her and if I had half a brain I'd probably oblige her. Hell, I should have dropped her out there at the cliff.

His hand closed around the neck of the bottle and he splashed more scotch into the shot glass. Damn her for coming back when he'd thought he'd finally been rid of her for good. Damn her for changing everything just when he'd finally broken the grip she'd had for so long. Damn her for pretending she'd changed when he knew it was impossible. He'd waited five years for Caitlin to change. It hadn't happened. Why would a bump on the head do what all his arguing and pleading with her hadn't?

He poured the searing liquor down his throat and closed his eyes as it hit his stomach. He couldn't let her go now. He needed to watch her night and day until he settled this thing. And knowing that made him angry. And the anger made him reach for the bottle again. It was a night for anesthesia. Because as much as he'd vowed to set himself free of her, Caitlin was slowly drawing him in again.

And she wanted him to call her Caity.

For just a second, he let the image of her when she'd been Caity to him, rinse through his mind like a spring breeze. Then, she'd been as happy in tattered cutoffs as she was in a designer dress. She'd turned her nose up at her father's fancy meals to sneak out for pizza with him. God, if he could have that girl back again . . .

Ah, but that was idiocy! She didn't even remember those times. That Caity was dead and buried. So, she'd like him to believe, was the cold and distant woman she'd become.

But he wasn't so sure.

He drank and he paced, until his pacing became an unsteady weave and his head floated far above his shoulders. And then he mounted the stairs, thinking he ought to be drunk enough to sleep. As he climbed, clutching the banister for guidance, he recalled the conversation they'd had in her bedroom. She'd admitted that seeing him holding Sandra had hurt her. The old Cait never would have done that. And she'd looked at him like...like she wanted him. But he might have been seeing things that weren't there. And then he'd challenged her to make him a better offer. Like she would. And pigs would fly, too.

He forced himself farther along the hall, groped for the door handle and leaned heavily on it as it swung open. He stepped through, swaying slightly, but catching himself. He closed the door behind him and stood in complete darkness. He knew he was drunk. He didn't mind admitting it. The way he saw it, he had reason to get good and drunk tonight. Besides, he doubted he'd have been able to close his eyes sober. There was too much going on in his mind. Too many painful memories churning to life from the enforced death he'd imposed on them. Not memories of Caitlin. Memories of Caity.

He fumbled with his buttons, his fingers feeling too big. He dropped the shirt to the floor.

Hot, eager Caity. Her skin warm and coated in sweat, her body shuddering at his every touch, her soft whimpers as he played her. He knew how. He knew her every secret, knew her scent and her taste...

He groaned, and lurched forward, dragging the belt out of his pants and clumsily peeling them off. He kicked free of the rest of his clothes, amazed he managed to do so without falling on his butt.

Naked, he stood still a minute. The nearly frigid chill from the blasting central air unit felt good on his tormented flesh. It shot a little sanity back into his fevered mind. He pulled back the covers and crawled beneath them.

Warm, soft flesh was there to greet him. Long, silken tresses brushed against his unclothed chest. A curvy, bare backside rubbed over his groin, and he knew it was his wife. Naked, warm and waiting for him.

He released an anguished sigh and let his eyes fall closed. Finally, he thought in relief so great it was painful. Finally, the estrangement was at an end. She wanted him again.

His throat oddly tight, he rolled her onto her back, slipped his arms around her slender waist, and pressed his chest to hers as his mouth sought her lips. He found them and kissed her, and as long-denied passion hit him full force, his body grew fervent with need. He felt her slack, willing mouth tighten as she came fully awake, but he chose to ignore it. He forced his tongue inside, and he jammed his knee between her thighs to press them open. Already, he was hard and ready. He nudged against her opening, and felt it moisten in readiness. Oh, God, it had been so damned long.

He felt her hands pushing at his chest, and he was afraid she was changing her mind. Aided in his decision by the scotch, he gripped them both in one of his and pinned them above her head to the mattress. Her frantic twisting beneath him only served to heighten his lust. He kissed a hot trail from her lips to her jaw, and she immediately let out the beginning of a piercing shriek. His free hand clamped over her mouth.

"Baby, don't tell me to stop now," he said, panting with longing. "Please, don't tell me to stop. You don't know what I've gone through, night after night, always knowing you were just down the hall, always wanting you. God, how much I've wanted you."

He moved his mouth lower, captured one impudent breast between his teeth and worried it roughly, biting and tugging the hard little nipple until he felt it pulsate against his tongue. Muffled whimpering sounds escaped from beneath his palm, inflaming him beyond rational thought. Her nipple stood stiffer, hardened to a throbbing nub and he licked and sucked it before turning to the other one, and giving it equal attention.

Her opening wept for him, her juices coating his head where he pressed it against her. She was ready. So was he. He pulled back slightly. This first sheathing of him inside her would be to the hilt. It would be sheer ecstasy.

Her teeth closed on his hand so hard, he was certain she drew blood, and when he relaxed his hold on her in response to the pain, she yanked one hand free, and slammed it across his face.

"Get off me, you drunken lunatic! Get off me now or I swear I will scream until the windows rattle. I'll call a cop. Get off, get the hell off!"

He rolled to one side, swearing a blue streak and trying to figure out what the hell had happened. His arousal throbbed with need. His brain, with frustration. He felt her leave the bed on one side. He quickly left on the other, and unerringly found the light switch. As soon as the room was flooded with brilliance, he saw her. She'd been looking for something to put on, and apparently hadn't found it. She stood there, facing him, not a stitch covering her. Her lower lip was bleeding slightly. There were teeth marks on her dampened breasts, tiny little ridges around the nipples. Angry, red rings encircled her wrists.

But her nipples still stood in quivering hardness, gleaming with the moisture put there by his mouth, and he knew she'd been as aroused as he had been.

"Stop looking at me," she cried, snatching the comforter from the bed and tugging it up to her chin.

"If you didn't want me looking at you, why the hell were you naked, and waiting in my bed?"

"You're drunk," she cried. "This isn't your bed!" She gulped, blinked at tears that might have been manufactured, and shook her head.

Dylan frowned, and glanced around the room, now flooded with light. It was a guest room, the one right next door to his own. The furniture was situated in an almost identical pattern, and he had come in during utter darkness, not to mention falling-down drunk.

"You...said I could find another room if I didn't like the one I had. I—this was the only one I felt comfortable in."

He moved toward her, around the foot of the bed. She backed away until she was touching the wall. "And you didn't notice that it was right next door to my room? That didn't have anything to do with your choice?"

"As a matter of fact, it did. Someone was in my room tonight, watching me. I was terrified, and for some idiotic reason, I wanted to be closer to you." Her face fell, contorted with pain. "God, I'm a fool!"

Her words made their way through the scotch-induced haze of his brain, and he felt like groaning aloud. He looked at her again, at her dilated pupils, her tear-stained cheeks, her goose bump-dotted flesh. Then he glimpsed the corner of a dressing gown sticking out from under the bed. He reached for it and she jumped. Very slowly, he pulled it out and held it up to her.

She snatched it from his hands, held the blanket in her teeth and slipped the robe on. When she dropped the comforter at last, she lunged past him for the door.

He caught her arm. "This wasn't my fault, Caitlin. Not entirely. I stumbled into the wrong room by accident. What the hell was I supposed to think when I found you in what I mistook for my own bed, like this?"

She faced him, hair tousled, eyes blazing. "You damned near raped me, Dylan."

"If I were the kind of man to take a woman by force, you'd still be on your back under me, lady."

"If that—" she pointed an accusing finger at the rumpled sheets "—was an example of your technique, I'm not surprised your wife requested separate bedrooms."

His gaze lowered, and he ran the backs of his fingers over her still-distended nipple, where it poked through the material of the robe. "Oh, yeah. I can see how turned off *my wife* is."

"You're right," she shouted. "That's the worst part, Dylan. I thought I wanted you. I've stayed awake nights, wishing... Oh, God, I'm going to be sick!" Her face crumpled. She pushed her way blindly past him, and stumbled down the hall toward her own bedroom.

CHAPTER EIGHT

It was morning, but not yet dawn. And despite her night-long expenditure of energy, she was still thinking about him. Dylan.

Tears blurred her vision, and she sank onto the bed's edge, amid the piles of clothes, drained of all ambition. She'd wanted so badly to trust him, to believe he was the one person in this house she could turn to in the midst of this chaos. He was her husband. She should be able to trust him.

Then why didn't she?

Though she'd been determined not to, she recalled the events of last night with brutal clarity. His hands, holding her wrists to the bed. His mouth claiming hers with punishing force, his hardened groin digging into her. She'd felt the anger inside him, all of it, seemingly focused on her. She'd felt his contempt in his touch.

And his desire.

His throaty declaration haunted her, even now, ringing in her ears until she pressed her hands to them to stop it. But still she heard his gruff voice, the pain and frustration palpable in its timbre. "...night after night, always knowing you were just down the hall, always wanting you. God, how much I've wanted you..."

She closed her eyes as the tears spilled over her face. So many emotions assailed her, it was difficult to know what she was feeling.

So she told herself to stop analyzing and reliving it, and she stood up, and got back to work. She tightened the sash of her red satin robe, recalling as she did the coldness in

Dylan's eyes as he'd held it toward her in one outstretched hand. She shuddered. She'd have to add it to the pile of clothes to be discarded, just as soon as she returned to her room with some boxes.

Sleep, of course, had not been an option last night. She'd left the guest room devastated, and angry, and confused, and too full of emotions to rest. She tried to count the nights since she'd actually slept decently, and realized there'd been none. Not since she'd come back here.

She picked her way through the mounds of clothes, all separated into piles on the floor, and on the bed, and left the bedroom, stepping silently into the hall, flicking on every light switch she came to along the way. She'd memorized their locations since her last scare out here.

The house was cold, as always, and quiet as a tomb, which was fitting, she thought bitterly, since someone was trying so hard to make it hers. She wouldn't run into Dylan. No chance of that. As drunk as he'd been, he'd probably passed out right after she'd left him. He might not even remember... She almost hoped he didn't.

She padded softly down the stairs, barefoot, and made her way to the kitchen without interruption. She hoped to find Genevieve and ask for a box to pack the clothes in, or maybe just find the boxes herself.

But the kitchen was empty, spotless and dark. She didn't know where the light switch was in here. She stood for a moment, in the doorway, her eyes moving slowly over the shapes of gleaming pots and pans hanging from racks, the cabinets, the range. With a sigh of resignation, she slipped farther inside. She pressed her palm to the wall and walked sideways, feeling for the light switch. As soon as she let it go, the door swung closed, and Caitlin found herself surrounded by utter blackness.

Panic welled up in her throat until she almost choked on it. She walked faster, both hands racing over the wall now, in search of the switch. She'd been stupid to come down here. What was she thinking of, groping her way through a darkened room where a killer might very well be waiting?

Her fingers touched a switch. Limp with relief, her pulse thundering in her temples, she moved it, and the room filled with brilliant light.

A hand dropped to her shoulder. Caitlin whirled, a scream of terror catching in her throat.

"Do not be afraid, *chérie.*"

She took a step away from Henri, but her back touched the wall. "I . . . I was looking for Genevieve." Caitlin tried not to squirm at the notion of being alone with him, and standing so close. He hadn't lifted a finger to so much as touch her. And just because his eyes were so intense, it didn't really mean anything. So, he found her attractive. So what?

With her back to the wall, and him standing so close, she couldn't really move without shoving him aside, and looking like a total idiot. "Tell me what it is you need, what it is you want. I will take care of it."

Was it only admiration she was seeing in those dark eyes? Or was there more? A suggestion . . . a meaning she didn't get because she didn't remember. My God, had there ever been something going on between her and Henri? The thought shocked and shook her. Had the old Caitlin cheated on her husband? Was that why Dylan was so hostile toward her now?

She looked up, into the now-smiling face, and shook her head. No. If Dylan thought that, Henri certainly wouldn't still be employed here. Dylan wasn't the kind of man who'd take something like that lightly.

"*Chérie?*"

He was awaiting an answer. "Boxes. I, um, I need to pack some clothes I don't want, and I need boxes."

"Ah." He stepped back just slightly, pinching his chin. Then he snapped his fingers. "*Oui,* I have it. There are some in the storage room. Wait here."

And just like that, he was briskly walking across the kitchen, and out another door, beyond it. Caitlin slowly released all the air from her lungs. She knew she was simply overreacting to everything everyone said or did, because she knew that someone in this house hated her enough to kill her. She forced herself to calm down, and recalled that Henri tended to call every woman in the house *chérie*, even Ellen, on occasion. She shouldn't start reading a history of illicit liaisons into his friendliness.

He was back in seconds, with three boxes, each one fitted neatly inside another. She took them. "Thank you, Henri."

"It is nothing."

The sun never really rose. It was there, but you couldn't see it beyond the black clouds and pouring rain. Caitlin showered, hanging a washcloth over the ugly, lion-faced spigot, then slipped into jeans and a sweatshirt. She dried her hair and pulled it into a ponytail to keep it out of her face. When she stepped out of her bathroom, she folded the red robe over her forearm and dropped it into one of the boxes she'd filled with clothes.

And then she reached for the delicate antique-look phone. She'd come to only one conclusion all night long—that she needed to talk with Dr. Judith Stone. And then the police. She'd be damned if she'd sit here and wait for the next attempt on her life without taking some kind of action. The thought of just walking away from all of this pirouetted through her mind, but vanished just as quickly. She couldn't leave until she'd made some kind of sense of her life, found some shred of her identity. It wasn't even an option. This was her home; these people, her family. She'd never know peace until she solved this thing.

She brought the receiver from its elevated cradle to her ear. She was surprised to hear voices on the line.

"Just do it. Withdraw the bid."

The voice was low, resolute, and Dylan's. Caitlin was about to replace the receiver, but the answer came, and it caught her attention.

"Dylan, we need this contract. We're going to be in the red if we don't land it. Dammit, there are only two competitors, and one of the company's CEO is involved in that child molestation case. The state won't award a guy with so much scandal attached to him any kind of contract, so we—"

"We withdraw the bid."

Caitlin frowned, recognizing the young male voice on the other end as one of the architects she'd met at the office yesterday.

"We're about to have some scandals of our own come to light, Patrick. I'm on my way to the police right now, and you know how things leak from one government agency to another. Just pull out and maybe we can salvage our reputation."

"What scandal?"

"Not on the phone."

"It's a private line, Dylan. What scandal?"

Dylan sighed loudly into the mouthpiece. "Within the next hour, I will probably become the chief suspect in the attempted murder of my wife. Scandalous enough for you?"

There was a moment of stunned silence, then, "I don't need to ask if you did it."

"No?"

"No." There was a long sigh. "I'll pull the bid, Dylan. Call if you need anything."

"Right."

Two clicks sounded in Caitlin's ear, and she blinked down her shock. A second later, she placed her own call.

His idiotic boozing last night and the hangover it left him with had not in any way dulled his memory. Dylan almost wished it had. For the briefest of moments, he'd thought...hell, it didn't matter what he'd thought. He lifted his fist and pounded on her bedroom door harder than he needed to.

"Who's there?"

He closed his eyes and willed the throbbing that encompassed his skull to lessen. It didn't. She sounded scared and he imagined she was. Her fear wouldn't lessen when she knew he stood on this side of the door, either. Perhaps it would increase. He was madder than hell right now and rationalization didn't help. He hadn't hurt her last night. If anything, she'd been just as aroused as he was, but she'd never admit it. She'd hold his cavemanlike behavior over his head and make him squirm with guilt. Hell, she already had. The hurt in her eyes last night haunted him, even now. He felt like a bastard, and he was good and angry at her for that, even though it was his own fault. Not only that, but she was afraid of him. And that angered him still further.

"It's me," he said belatedly, in answer to her question.

He expected her to stand on her side of the door and speak through it. He was surprised when the handle turned and the door opened widely. Even more surprised at her murmured, "Come in."

He entered, and she closed the door behind him. She didn't meet his gaze as he looked her over. There were dark circles under her eyes that told of the sleepless night she'd spent. He might have been prone to insomnia last night, as well, if he hadn't been too drunk to stay conscious. Not too drunk to dream, though. And looking at her now, in the snug-fitting jeans, her face free of makeup, her eyes wide and wary, brought those dreams back to him full force. Dreams in which she hadn't stopped him, where he'd finished what he'd so clumsily begun last night.

He was aware of the stirring in his groin, and it only added to the discomfort he already felt. And that added to his irrational anger at her.

"You look like hell," she said, when she finally made her eyes move over his face.

"Good. I'd hate to feel this bad and not have it show."

"Hangover?"

"Mother of them all," he answered.

She nodded.

"You don't look too good yourself." He noticed the boxes of clothes stacked around the room, and the open, nearly empty closet.

She shrugged. "Couldn't sleep."

Here it came, he thought. The guilt trip. "Stay awake all night waiting for an apology?"

Her head came up and her gaze narrowed. "I was afraid if I closed my eyes, someone might sneak in and slit my throat."

"Me?"

"Maybe."

He sighed, and broke eye contact, turning to pace away from her. "I'm not going to apologize, Cait."

"I didn't ask you to."

"There's only so much deprivation a man can take."

"Then you *haven't* been sleeping with my brother's wife?"

He spun around to face her. "Show up naked in my bed again, Cait, and you're liable to get the same reaction."

"It wasn't your bed," she reminded him. "Or do you intend to get so falling-down drunk, you can't tell the difference often?"

She was so damned calm, so detached. He wanted to wring her neck. God, he couldn't get the image of her unclothed body out of his mind, or the feel of her moistened opening against his throbbing need, or the taste of her mouth, her skin, her tongue, her nipples.

"It won't matter if I'm drunk or sober."

Her fine auburn brows arched. "Thanks for the warning. I can't say much for your brand of lovemaking, so I'll avoid it from now on."

"That wasn't lovemaking. Just plain lust. And you can argue all you want, but it was mutual."

Finally, a hint of something flickered beneath the cool green waters of her eyes. She lowered them, and cleared her throat. "Was there some point to this visit, or did you just come here to harass me?"

"There's a point. I'm on my way to the police station, to report the unfortunate attempt on your life last night."

She released a short burst of air that might have been intended as a laugh. "What do you consider unfortunate, Dylan? That someone tried to kill me, or that he failed?"

He glared at her. "I came to ask if you want to come along. You're so convinced I might be the guilty party, I know you'll want to share that suspicion with the police."

She turned her back on him, walked toward the bed and sunk onto it as if too exhausted to stand up any longer. She closed her eyes.

Dylan carefully kept any hint of concern out of his voice. "Are you sick?"

She shook her head slowly. "Just tired. Mostly of you and your hostility. You're a real bastard, you know that?"

"And you're Sweet Mary Sunlight, babe. Are you coming with me, or not?"

"Yeah."

She didn't move, or look at him. She was pale this morning, he noted. Her cheeks hollow. She'd lost weight while she was in the coma, not that she'd had any to spare. And she didn't look as if she were putting any of it back on since coming home.

"Get something to eat. I'll wait in the foyer."

She shook her head, and rose slowly, like an old woman with aching joints. "No, let's just go."

She ought to eat. He ought to insist on it. Then again, she was a grown woman with a mind of her own. She didn't need a keeper.

"There's no hurry. We have time—"

"If I eat this morning, I'll probably puke in your fancy car. Let's just go, okay? And will you send Genevieve up for these clothes? I don't want them."

"What do you want her to do with them?"

"I don't care. Wear them, give them away, burn them, for all I care."

He was glumly silent on the short ride into Eden, and Caitlin felt nauseated, even though she hadn't eaten. It was fear gnawing at her gut, fear and confusion. As angry and afraid of him as she'd been last night, she now harbored a slight doubt he'd tried to hurt her. The phone call she'd overheard was strong evidence of that. He wouldn't risk his business by reporting this to the police unless he was innocent. He'd have tried to talk her out of going to the authorities.

Or was this his way of covering his tracks? Did he simply know she would report the incident either way, and want to be there when she did? She almost asked him to forget about it, or delay the visit, but she was too afraid he'd agree readily. She was also afraid the killer would try again, and the police were the only people she was sure would try to help her stay alive.

And there was something else…something she'd not been fully aware of in her fury over his rough treatment of her last night. Something that had only begun to dawn on her in the cold light of day, with his childish refusal to apologize, and his obvious guilt about his actions.

When she'd left him last night, there had been pain in his eyes. Stark, black agony. Loneliness as acute as her own. He had wanted her, had thought she was there waiting. And the truth had been like salt in an old wound. She'd hurt him.

Again. She'd obviously done the same in the past. Enough to make him hate her? she wondered. Enough to make him want her dead? He wanted her. She could feel it. Passion ricocheted between them in waves so thick, they were all but visible. But murder was a crime of passion. Wasn't it?

Police Detective Jack Barnes was a big man, with a voice to match. He sat behind his cluttered desk in a brilliant, touristy button-down shirt, leaned back in his chair and removed his rectangular bifocals, staring at Caitlin in the same distracted manner he'd had when she'd first walked into the beehive of activity.

"I'll have to come to the house, interview everyone who was there last night." His voice was deep, booming, as if it echoed back and forth in some cavern behind his barrel chest before floating out to her ears. "We'll send a forensics team to the scene, but with all this rain, I doubt there's any evidence left. Probably not even a footprint." He eyed Dylan for a long moment. "Might have been last night, if we'd been called right away."

"I don't think so, Detective. The cliffs are solid rock, not a very good receptacle for footprints."

Barnes nodded slowly. "So, you went to your wife's room, to check on her, found she wasn't there and got worried?"

Dylan nodded.

"Any particular reason you would worry so quick, Rossi?"

"Hell, Barnes, you're the detective. You figure it out. I've already told you about her condition. It was late at night, not to mention pouring rain."

Barnes's gaze narrowed, then softened just as quickly when he looked at Caitlin. "Why'd you go outside, Mrs. Ros—"

"Caity, please." She instinctively liked Detective Barnes, except for his gruff, suspicious manner with Dylan. Then again, she couldn't blame him for that. She was suspicious of Dylan, herself. "I was told I used to love to walk along the cliffs at night. I wanted to try it . . . see if I could remember." There was no sense telling him about how upset she'd been, or about the way Sandra had thrown herself into Dylan's arms. It was irrelevant.

"And who told you that?"

She frowned. "My . . . brother. Thomas." *Who happens to resent me for inheriting when he didn't, and who's having an affair with my maid, and who I overheard plotting against my husband.*

Thomas? Is he the one?

Barnes made a note. "Okay." He looked at Dylan again. "So, you found she wasn't in her room. Then what?"

Dylan glanced at her, and she thought he was uncomfortable having her hear him retell the story. "I searched the house, and then I realized she must have gone out to the cliffs. She'd mentioned earlier that she wanted to—"

"And Dylan warned me not to go out there alone," she put in quickly, then wondered why she'd defended him.

Dylan sent her a strange look, before returning his attention to Barnes. "Then I went out to look for her."

"Alone?"

Dylan shook his head. "I took Thomas, his wife, Sandra, and our chef, Henri, out with me. Genevieve and Ellen stayed in the house to look after the baby."

Barnes pulled a tissue from a box on his desk, and casually wiped the lenses of his glasses. He looked as if his full attention was focused on the rectangular specs. "You all left the house together?"

"Yes. We walked out to the cliffs, and then we split up."

"Who was closest to her when you heard her scream, Rossi?"

Dylan shook his head. "It's impossible to say. We all sort of ran in that direction from where we were."

Barnes replaced his glasses on his nose. "You have a will, Caity?"

She blinked. "I, um, I don't know." She looked at Dylan.

"Yes, she has a will. Last I knew, I was in it. So was her brother."

Barnes licked his lips. "Who's your lawyer, hon?"

She shook her head, not a bit put out by the endearment. He was at least fifteen years older than she, and he seemed to have some genuine concern for her. "I don't know."

Barnes shook his head, and glared at Dylan. "Done a good job of keeping her in the dark, haven't you, Rossi?"

"She's barely been home three days, Barnes. It hasn't come up in casual conversation." Dylan took his wallet from his pocket, pawed through it for a minute and extracted a business card. He snapped it down on the desk, and pushed it toward Detective Barnes. "Here's his card."

Barnes examined it, and nodded, slipping it into his shirt pocket. "You have any plans to leave Eden in the next few days, Rossi?"

Dylan opened his mouth, but Caitlin cut him off. "My husband makes a poor suspect, Detective Barnes."

The man's smile was obviously forced. "It's Jack, and I wish you'd let me decide who the suspects are."

She licked her lips and swallowed, refusing to glance Dylan's way as she spoke. "When this comes out, his business is going to suffer. He's already had to withdraw a bid on a government contract because of it. This whole thing is costing him money." She bit her lip, only now realizing how vehement she'd sounded. But she'd only spoken the truth, and Jack Barnes ought to have all the facts before he came to any conclusions.

Barnes pursed his lips and rose from his seat. He moved to the file cabinet across the room with measured strides, while Caitlin remained in her hard little chair beside Dylan. She felt her husband's eyes on her. She didn't look back.

Barnes returned, and slapped a file folder onto his desk. "This is the report on the accident you had, Mrs. Rossi. We were suspicious then, but there wasn't enough evidence to warrant an investigation. The brake line was torn, not cut. But I can tell you, it wouldn't be too difficult for someone to have done it deliberately. I suspected it then." He tapped the folder with his glasses for emphasis. "Now I'm certain of it." He slanted a glance at Dylan as he spoke. "You and your husband had a loud argument just before that accident, Caity. You left the house, driving like a bat out of hell, from what witnesses say. He went after you a few minutes later."

Caitlin wasn't aware of slowly shaking her head from side to side, or of rising to her feet. Her gaze turned inward, and when she spoke, she was addressing herself more than she was Jack Barnes. "But he pulled me up the side of that cliff last night. I wasn't holding on to anything but him, and if he'd wanted to drop me, he could have done it right then. No one would have believed it wasn't an accident. Not when he was hanging half over the side himself just to reach me."

Barnes sighed and got to his feet. "That doesn't prove anything," he said gently. "Caity, you're a nice girl. I don't want to see your name cross this desk in a homicide report. Take my advice. Move out for a while. Go stay with a relative—"

"I don't have any, except the ones who live with us."

"Then a hotel. You're somebody's target. You ought to get out of the line of fire."

She sighed hard, shaking her head. "I'll give it some thought." She already had given it thought, though. She just couldn't bring herself to leave. Not yet.

"I think there's another side to that argument, Barnes," Dylan said. She looked at him as he spoke, tried to read his motives in his fathomless, dark eyes. "In the house, there's one person who wants her dead—maybe—and four who don't. In a hotel, she'd be alone, and the killer wouldn't have much trouble tracking her down."

Did Dylan want her to stay, then? Why? To keep her from being killed . . . or to keep her within his reach?

The detective shook his head, ignoring Dylan. He addressed Caitlin. "Don't trust any of them. I'll be checking up on you."

She nodded. "Thank you."

"Stay in touch. Let me know if you decide to leave." His gaze sharpened when he turned it on Dylan. "Don't let anything happen to her, Rossi." His tone held a warning that couldn't be missed.

Dylan took her arm and walked her out to the car. Once he'd pulled out of the lot, he spoke without looking at her. "Since when are you my staunch defender?"

She shook her head at the sarcasm in his voice. "I was going to make a call this morning. I heard your conversation with Patrick Callen."

"So?"

"So it doesn't make sense that you would risk the business just to get rid of me. It would be simpler just to file for divorce."

"Oh, yeah. That would be a real simple solution, wouldn't it?"

She slammed her fists on the dashboard, and his head swung toward her. "Damn you!" She grated her teeth, squeezed her eyes tight, but the tears came, anyway. "You won't even deny it was you, will you? You can't even give me that much! Did it ever occur to you that I *need* to trust someone? That I need someone on my side right now? I can't . . ." She bit her lips to stop the endless flow of words that wanted to tumble through them.

"And you want that someone to be me, is that it? You want me to come to you on my knees and swear I'm innocent, beg you to believe me, vow to protect my loving little wife, no matter what?"

"Go to hell, Dylan."

"I'm already there. Don't expect me to come to you, swearing my innocence. If you can't trust me now, you have no one to blame but yourself."

"I don't even have that, Dylan. Because I wasn't around when some woman I don't remember was making you hate her. I was dropped into the middle of her life, not even knowing her name."

"Maybe *you* don't remember her, Caitlin. But *I do*." He braked to a stop at an intersection and waited for the light to change. "So are you going home, or to a hotel?"

She shook her head. "I don't have a home."

"How about a straight answer for once?"

She nodded, and swallowed the lump in her throat. "Take me to Dr. Stone's office. I have an appointment."

The light changed and he pressed the accelerator. "And then?"

"And then leave. When I decide where I'm going, I'll call a cab."

CHAPTER NINE

"I have to agree with Detective Barnes, Caity. It seems to me, you'd be safer somewhere else."

Caitlin continued pacing the length of Judith Stone's office. The knotty-pine walls and gas jet fireplace were supposed to be cozy, comforting, she supposed. But there was nothing comfortable about the way she felt.

"You're probably right."

"But?"

"I'm not sure I can leave yet. There are still too many things I don't understand about...about her."

"Caitlin Rossi?"

Caitlin nodded.

"You told me you considered her a stranger, one who's dead and buried. Someone you didn't know."

"I *don't* know her. But I feel I *have to*. I feel as if I'll never understand myself unless I come to grips with who I was."

Judith shifted in her chair, reaching for the cup of tea on her desk. "Is there one specific thing you want to know about, or just her life in general?"

Caitlin stopped, and faced the psychiatrist. "I need to know how she could have been so cold to her husband. How she managed to alienate him so completely, and why."

Judith calmly sipped her tea. She held up the mug. "Are you sure you won't have some? It's chamomile."

Caitlin only shook her head.

"Caity, are you developing feelings for Dylan?"

"I don't know. He acts like he can't stand to be near me most of the time."

"And the rest of the time?"

Caitlin walked to the huge window and looked down at the street. "When he took me shopping, there were moments when he let me glimpse the man behind the mask. But every time I started to feel some sort of closeness starting to develop between us, he pulled back."

"And you didn't want him to."

"No. I guess I didn't."

Judith lifted the tea bag from the mug with the spoon, wrapped the string around the spoon three times and gave the bag a dainty squeeze. "What do you want from him?"

Caitlin drew a slow breath and held it. She closed her eyes. "When he pulled me up from the cliff . . ."

Judith leaned forward in her chair. "Go on."

Caitlin swallowed hard. "He held me so tightly I could barely breathe." She closed her eyes and replayed the incident in her mind. Not the terror, but the crushing strength of his arms around her. The way his heart had thundered beneath her head, and the way his body had been shaking almost as much as hers. "For those few minutes, I didn't feel so alone. He told me everything was all right, and I believed him. He held me like he'd never let me go."

"You felt close to him then?"

Caitlin sighed. "Yes, I guess that's what I want. I want to be able to turn to him when I'm afraid, when I feel so alone I want to die. I want all that strength to be with me, not against me. I want to have someone I can depend on, trust in, and I want so much for it to be him."

"But it isn't?"

Caitlin faced Judith levelly. "How can it be? He won't even deny that he's the one who wants me dead."

"If he *were* the one, he'd probably deny it loudly. Sounds to me like his pride's been wounded."

"If it has, then it's because of the woman I was. I just don't know how to fix the damage she did." Caitlin began her pacing again. "He wants me."

"Physically?"

Caitlin nodded. "I went looking for another room last night, and chose the one nearest his. He came in later, drunk, and—"

"And what?" Judith rose from her seat.

"Things got a bit rough. He thought I was there waiting for him."

"Caity, are you telling me this man raped you?"

"No. It didn't go that far. But it was close."

Judith shook her head. "And how did you feel about that?"

"I don't know. I was afraid. There was so much anger in him, and it scared me. But I can't deny that there was a part of me that responded to him."

"You wanted to make love with him?"

"I did. I do." She turned in a small circle, pushing one hand through her hair. "I keep getting these flashes of us together, and it's... it's incredible."

"The sex?"

Caitlin nodded. "It's so frustrating. I don't know if they're memories or fantasies. I only know I want him. Madly. But not like that. God, how can I be attracted to a man who seems to despise me? Am I that sick?" She walked to a chair and slammed herself into it. "I disgust myself."

She closed her eyes, bit her lip. "But then, I look him in the eye, and I think he isn't being honest. I think he might not hate me as much as he pretends to. Dammit, if I could just go back and find out what went wrong, I might stand a chance of making amends." She lowered her head, then lifted it again as an idea occurred to her. "What about hypnosis? Could you put me under and make me remember my past?"

Judith crossed the room and knelt in front of Caitlin's chair. "It could work, Caitlin. But there is a very high risk factor involved in your case. The trauma of remembering might be more than your mind could take. You could end up worse off than you are now."

"It might be worth the risk."

Judith straightened, looked down at Caitlin and sighed. "That will be your decision. But I want you to give it careful thought. And I want you to try to work things out in the present, before you go delving into the past. If these flashes you've described *are* memories, hypnosis might not be necessary at all. Let's save it for a last resort, all right?

Caitlin nodded.

"In the meantime, Caity, why don't you try to get him into an honest, open conversation. He might be as confused about your feelings as you are about his."

"How's Lizzie?"

Sandra looked up from the book she was engrossed in, when Dylan crossed the room toward her. "She's gonna be just fine. The doctor put her on antibiotics. She's got a slight chest cold, is all." Her gaze swept the room behind him. "So where's the lady Caitlin?"

Dylan shrugged and said nothing. He had no idea where Cait was right now, and he told himself he didn't give a damn. The police had been roaming the place all afternoon. Detective Barnes in his loud shirt and khaki trousers, with his suspicion in his eyes every time he glanced Dylan's way had been almost too much. They'd questioned everyone, even Ellen. And their forensics crew had only just packed up and driven off, having found nothing on the cliffs.

Sandra rose and stood near him. Her hands rested lightly on his shoulders. "I don't know what I'd have done without you last night."

"I care about Lizzie." The glint in her eyes made him uncomfortable.

"More than her own daddy does."

"That's not true, Sandra. Thomas just—"

"Just what?" She shook her head. "He don't want her. Or me, either. You treat us better than he ever has."

"He needs time to adjust to the idea of being a father." Dylan went to step backward, but her hands slid around to the base of his neck.

"Lizzie's three months old. How much time you s'pose it's gonna take?" She sighed and a slight smile touched her full lips. "It doesn't matter. I don't want him either." Her grip tightened, pulling her body closer, until it pressed tight to his. "You know who I want."

"Sandra, for—"

Footsteps behind him made his spine stiffen. He knew without turning that Caitlin had come in. He caught the smug glance Sandra threw over his shoulder, before she lowered her head to it.

Dylan caught her hands, unwound them from his neck, pressing them to her sides, and stepped away from her. He turned, but only in time to see Caitlin's rigid back as she marched up the stairs. He swung his gaze back to Sandra. She was smiling.

"Dammit, Sandra! Do you know what she's probably thinking?

She shrugged. "I really don't care *what* she thinks."

"It was deliberate, wasn't it?" Dylan's voice was far louder than necessary, but he did nothing about it. He had enough trouble right now, without Sandra adding to it with her theatrics.

"She might as well know where things stand," Sandra yelled back. "You don't want her. I'd be so much better for you than she's ever been, can't you see that?" She lunged toward him again, throwing her arms around him.

Dylan shoved her roughly away. She staggered backward, tripped on the book she'd dropped and fell to the floor.

"What the hell is going on in here?" Thomas strode into the room, with Genevieve at his side. When Dylan glanced up, he saw Caitlin standing halfway up the stairs, staring downward. All of them had seen him shove Sandra. Cait must have heard the entire exchange.

Thomas crossed the room and reached down to take his wife's hand and pull her to her feet. "What are you two arguing about? We could hear you yelling all the way in the kitchen."

Sandra glared at Dylan. He pushed a hand through his hair and moved past them all, not saying a word. Let Sandra explain the fight. He had no doubt she could come up with a lie right on cue.

Dylan went to the library and reached for the bottle of scotch in the cabinet. Then he stopped himself. It had been stupid getting drunk last night. He needed a clear head, not anesthetic.

Caitlin's voice coming from behind him brought him around, still holding the bottle by its neck.

"I wish you wouldn't."

He glanced at the bottle, then at her. "Why not?"

"I want to talk to you. I'd prefer you sober."

He shrugged, and replaced the bottle. "So talk."

She came the rest of the way into the room, and turned to close the double doors behind her. Then she crossed the carpet to the sofa, and sat down. She pinned him to the spot with her eyes glittering like polished emeralds. "How do you feel about me, Dylan?"

He said nothing, but moved to the sofa, and sat on its opposite end.

"Do you hate me as much as you seem to?"

He shook his head. "I don't hate you."

"Dislike, then?"

He closed his eyes. "Why don't you just ask the question you came to ask. You want to know if I'm planning your murder, don't you?"

She shook her head. "No." She sighed, and averted her eyes. "You turned Sandra down. Thank you for that."

"I didn't do it for you. Contrary to what you might think, I'm not the kind of man who gets his kicks by sleeping with his sister-in-law."

"I know. More and more I'm seeing just what kind of man you are." She cleared her throat, licked her lips. She was nervous. "I want you to tell me...tell me about us. Our past. I want to know what went wrong. I need you to give me this one chance..."

"Chance to do what?"

She brought one knee up onto the sofa and leaned toward him. "To show you who I am. I'm not the woman who hurt you, Dylan. You can't keep hating me for the things *she* did. You don't even know me. I'm a stranger that looks like your wife, that's all."

"No, that's not true. You're a lot like her. The way she was when..." He stopped, blinking fast, averting his eyes. God, she was getting to him. He hated his weakness.

Caitlin frowned. "When what?" She slid nearer, placed her hands on his shoulders. "Please, tell me. Turn on a light so I can find my way through this maze. Give me a candle."

Dylan felt the heat of her hands through his shirt. He fought with the ridiculous arousal her touch brought, and he fought with the equally ludicrous hope that kept leaping up when she was like this. But he lost the battle. Her voice was almost a plea, and in her eyes he saw nothing but confusion.

"Fine. Fine, you want to hear a bedtime story, I'll give you one. But I warn you, the ending isn't happily-ever-after."

She sighed and gave him a soft smile that he couldn't keep looking at. He glanced away, toward the massive bookcase opposite the sofa. "We met in college. You were nineteen. We started dating the day we met, and stayed together right through your graduation. By then, I'd already started the business."

"What was I like then?"

He looked at her. He couldn't help himself. She was the image of the girl he'd known then, right now, and the pain of seeing her and knowing she wasn't *his* Caity was almost paralyzing.

"You were different." He fought to keep the emotions from his voice, his face, as he spoke. "You lived in a mansion, had more money than you could count, but never wore anything but jeans. And your hair was consistently in one of two styles. Either long and loose, or up in a ponytail. You hated what you called snobs. You treated your father's household staff like guests instead of employees. Genevieve was one of your favorites. And you never gave a damn if I couldn't afford to take you to the best restaurants or the hot concerts in town. You were just as happy to go for a walk, or a fast-food joint."

She turned to lean back on the cushions, and the act brought her side right up to his. She tipped her head backward and closed her eyes. "And what about you?"

Dylan wanted to recite the facts without getting caught up in the memories, but it was difficult. Her pale arching neck was right under his nose, and he had the ridiculous urge to run his lips and tongue over that satin skin.

He cleared his throat, and his mind. "I was struggling to get a new business going. I spent most of my time working. All I wanted was to be a success, so I could give you what your father could. You said it didn't matter. Maybe I knew, even then, that it really did."

"What kind of grades did I get?"

"Strictly Bs. You could have done better. You had this philosophy that spending too much time studying was unhealthy and a waste of your youth. You liked cutting classes now and then, dragging me away from my shabby little office to the beach." He licked his lips, remembering. "We used to strip down to our skin and swim. Then we'd get out of the water and make love in the sand." Even now, after all this time, Dylan could recall the feel of her warm, wet skin beneath his hands, the grate of the sand coating her damp body, taste her hungry mouth beneath his.

Her head tilted sideways until it rested on his shoulder. Part of him wanted to pull away, but most of him didn't. Against his better judgment, he kept on talking. "I remember once, a couple of the guys who worked for me followed us and stole our clothes. We drove back to my little apartment in nothing but our towels." He caught himself smiling at the memory. "I ran a red light and got pulled over. I'll never forget the expression on that cop's face."

She laughed aloud and the sound was like a knife in his heart, like a ghost from the past sneaking up on him to implant the blade. His smile died.

"When did we get married?"

The blade twisted.

"After you graduated. Your father insisted on throwing us a huge wedding, and you insisted we let him. I didn't like that he was footing the bill, but I wanted to make you happy, so I went along. By then, your parents had been divorced for years."

She turned her head, and when she spoke her breath fanned his neck. "What happened to them?"

"I don't know. It was one of those things you refused to talk about. Your mother and brother moved away, and you stayed with your father. I think that was when you started to change."

"In what way?"

Dylan shook his head. How many times had he cursed himself for missing the warning signs? "You kept things from me. You used to go and visit your mother, but you would never let me come along, even after we were married. You'd come home depressed and short-tempered, but you wouldn't tell me why. I do know that your mother took nothing when she left your dad. So I imagine she had it pretty rough."

She frowned, but in a moment went on with her questions. "Where did we live?"

"With Aunt Ellen. She had a big old house that was practically falling down around her. She wouldn't let us pay rent, but I chipped in what I could toward repairs. It wasn't much. Those first years were lean. And then your mother died."

She nodded, her hair brushing his neck with the action. "She killed herself."

Dylan nodded. "I was working that night, so I wasn't there when you got the news. You wouldn't talk about it at all, just said you wanted to forget. And the next thing I knew, you'd decided to buy a house. I wanted to wait until I could afford to do it, but you were adamant, almost obsessed with the idea. You picked this place, and just dipped into your trust fund to pay for it. It's all in your name. One big investment. You hired decorators and went crazy with remodeling it, and then we moved in. The one concession you made was to let Aunt Ellen move in, as well. I refused to leave her alone."

She gasped, and straightened to stare into his eyes. "I didn't want her?"

"She raised me. My parents were killed in a car crash when I was ten, and she was there for me. I wanted to return the favor. You didn't argue about it. You never really voiced an opinion at all. I have no idea how you felt."

She closed her eyes and gave her head a quick shake. "I don't know why I would have disagreed with you."

"It nearly killed her to leave her old house, but she couldn't afford to keep it up on her own. And I knew she shouldn't be by herself at her age."

"You were right."

He shrugged. "I couldn't seem to talk to you about anything then, Cait. You were so closed off from me. After a while, I stopped trying. I just poured everything I had into the business, while you worried about investments and stock options and whether our property value was increasing. You became so involved in making sure your money was gaining top interest, there was no room for me anymore. Things just went downhill from there."

"And then Thomas and Sandra moved in."

"Yeah. Your brother thought he'd be all set when your father died, but he was cut completely out of the will. I was surprised when you didn't offer to split your inheritance with him. But I guess I shouldn't have been. That money meant everything to you. By then, the business was on solid ground, so you pressured me into hiring him. About the same time, you hired Henri and Genevieve. We ended up with the life you'd always scoffed at. Our house was as big as your father's."

She shook her head slowly. "Dylan, why did you stay with me?"

He searched her face. It was as innocent and vulnerable as he'd ever seen it. Her sparkling green eyes wide and trusting. He couldn't tell her the rest. He couldn't cause her that kind of pain, not again, no matter what had happened between them. He wasn't looking at the woman he'd known a few months ago. He was looking at the image of the girl he'd fallen in love with. Even if she was no longer that girl on the inside.

"I can't answer that."

"Can you at least tell me why... why we slept apart?"

"You were afraid you'd get pregnant." That, at least, was true.

"But there are so many—"

"You didn't trust birth control, Cait. There's always a slight chance of failure and you just couldn't stand the idea of it. That's why you were so upset the night of the accident. We'd both had a few drinks that night. And we wound up in your bed, together." He shook his head, remembering how he'd thought then that maybe things were going to turn around. "When you woke later, found yourself naked, in my arms, you freaked. Accused me of taking advantage of you when you were drunk, said you'd never have allowed it sober. We had a hell of a row, and you threw on some clothes and stormed out, terrified I'd gotten you pregnant."

"And you came after me."

"I knew you shouldn't be driving."

She licked her lips. "I wish we did have a baby."

The blade ran right through him, and turned hot. Searing. Dylan had to close his eyes to hide the pain those words brought. "So do I." Suddenly, he felt her fingertips brush gently over his damp eyes, and he opened them. Hers were wet, too.

"Last night, in your room, I—"

He shook his head, and silenced her with a finger to her lips. "That's not the way it was with us, Caitlin. I was drunk and I was frustrated—"

"I know." She smiled, but it was shaky, watery. "How was it, before things went wrong? What was it like when we made love?"

He shook his head. He wouldn't feel anything. He *wouldn't*. "Explosive. Mindless." He closed his eyes, and thought of the nights they'd had together, despite his vow that he wouldn't. She knew him so well, knew how to touch him and make him tremble. And he was keenly aware of every sensitive spot on her body. He could reduce her to a trembling, whimpering mass of longing in minutes. Seconds.

She touched his face, her palm drifting over his cheek, until her fingertips traced his jaw, and his chin. He looked at her. "I want to start new, Dylan. I want to get to know you, to find out if it can be like that for us again."

He shook his head. She wanted him to trust her again, to let himself care again. And just when he was out of his mind in love with her, she'd get her memory back. She'd become the old Caitlin. She'd shut him out. "Not on your life, lady. I wouldn't go through that hell again for anything." It would kill him this time.

"It won't happen, I swear it." She looked at him intently as she spoke. "Dylan, I need you so much. I can't face all of this alone, please..."

"Ah, Caity..." He couldn't resist the plea in her eyes, the little cry in her voice. He wrapped his arms around her, cradling her head in one hand, and pulling her face close. He caught her mouth with his and her lips parted instantly. He licked her mouth inside and out, and her tongue responded. Her fingers curled in his hair and he kissed her, tasted her, held her close and wished she were closer.

He was in danger. He knew it, and only a supreme act of will made him draw away. Panting with need, he searched her face. Her breathing was just as ragged, her eyes glazed and damp.

"I want you, Cait. I want you so much it hurts, but that's all. I'll try to be your friend. I'll even be your lover, but I'm not going to love you again. Don't hope for that. Don't even consider it a possibility. It isn't going to happen."

She stiffened her spine and met his gaze. The light in her eyes faded slowly and her breaths, by sheer force, it seemed, grew more regular.

"My friend?"

He nodded. "I'll try not to hold the past against you, at least until it starts repeating itself."

"It will never repeat itself."

"I can't be sure of that. It's all I have to offer, Cait. Take it or leave it."

She nodded, but didn't look him in the eye. "Friends, then. I suppose it's better than enemies." She stood and turned toward the doors. "Thank you, Dylan." She moved forward, opened the doors and walked out, leaving him alone and painfully aroused. Apparently, friends was okay. Lovers was not.

CHAPTER TEN

She couldn't sleep. She wasn't surprised. She'd probably never have a good night's sleep in this house. But tonight, her reasons were different.

It was Dylan's kiss that kept her awake. The way he'd plundered her mouth, and the way she'd responded to the invasion. It hadn't been anger she'd felt emanating from him in waves this time. It had been desire. A desperate, long-denied desire that wouldn't be put off much longer. An answering need had flooded her body from the first touch of his lips on hers.

She wanted him. God, how she wanted him. And she still wasn't completely sure that was wise. She wanted to believe he could never hurt her. But the sight of him shoving Sandra to the floor haunted her. He was like two men in one body. He had a streak of brutality in him. She'd seen it when he'd pushed Sandra, felt it when he'd assaulted her in his bedroom so recently.

His passion was fierce, frightening. Especially where she was concerned. She'd felt its intensity when he'd pulled her from that cliff, been alternately touched by its warmth and burned by its heat. Then, last night, in the library, she'd seen the injured side of him as he'd told her things that obviously hurt him to talk about.

He'd said he could never love her again. Why, then, was there some fool inside her saying that he could? That he might?

She wondered which was the real Dylan Rossi. Which one would make love to her if she were to go to him, right now?

Would she feel the violent side of his passion? Or the side that wanted her as badly as she wanted him? Or would she encounter the wounded, wary man who was afraid she'd hurt him again?

"Hell, it doesn't matter, because I'm not going to him." She kicked her covers aside and rose, marching across the room and back again in her silky-soft green nightgown, her arms and shoulders bare. "He made it clear he doesn't want to try again to make our marriage work. Why on earth would I even consider sleeping with him under those conditions? Am I insane?"

He said he'd be my lover. All I have to do is go to his room.

She could have kicked herself for thinking about it. Even up and out of the bed, she kept envisioning erotic images of her and Dylan, their bodies wet and coated in warm sand, making frantic love on a deserted beach. She closed her eyes and willed the image away, but instead, it only intensified. She could feel his hot lips on her throat. She could feel the heat of the sun on his back as her hands moved urgently over it, and the cool spray of the surf as it showered them. She could taste the drying salt the sea had left on his skin.

Her eyes flew wide, and she gasped. She remembered! The images were too vivid, too real to have been imagined. Her breathing quickened and she fought for more. She scanned her mind in search of some other tidbit, something of her past to cling to. She saw the beach for just an instant, in her mind's eye. A horseshoe-shaped patch of sand, surrounded by craggy boulders. He was there, on her, inside her, thrusting, possessing. His lips whispered across hers, the words as soft as his breath. "I love you, Caity. I always will. No matter what."

And on one of the ragged stone faces that stood like protectors around them, someone had scratched a heart, with their initials inside. D.D.R. loves C.A.O.

She bit her lip as tears blurred her vision. In another brief flash, she saw Dylan, wearing cutoff denim shorts, barefoot, his hair longer, damp and tangled, painstakingly chiseling the stone with a pocket knife.

She searched for more, but there was nothing.

Oh, but it wasn't nothing, was it? She remembered. And in that one precious moment of remembering, she'd felt more than the physical sensations his touch evoked. She'd felt the warmth of his love surrounding her like invisible armor, and the strength of her own love pounding back to him.

How could she have had something so sweet, and let it slip away? Why? God, if she could only go back to that place, have that kind of love again, she'd cling to it with everything in her. She'd never let it die.

She brushed the tears away with a swipe of her hand. It was too late to try to change the past. The most she could hope for was to alter the present. Dylan had told her he'd never love her again. But that might change. Maybe with time, he'd see that she wasn't going to revert to the woman who'd hurt him so much. Maybe he'd believe in her, someday.

Exhaustion swamped her as she paced the room, wishing for memories, finding none. God, fate was cruel, giving her just that snippet and nothing more. Just enough to realize what she'd lost. Just enough to make her want it back.

Maybe she should go to Dylan right now, and tell him. She gripped the bedroom door, pulled it open and stepped into the hall before she stopped herself.

Tell him what? That she had a tidbit of their past and that it was killing her? That she wanted a time machine so she could go back there? That she wanted—now, more than ever—to believe he hadn't tried to kill her?

She shook her head sadly. Wanting things didn't make them true. Painful as it was to admit that, she had to force herself to accept it. She turned and stepped back into her room. Just before she closed the door, a strange sound caught her attention. A sort of rattling wheeze. Almost a choke. And it came from the foyer, or the stairway. She paused, one hand on the door, listening.

There was only silence, and the dull moan of the dying wind as the storm blew out to sea.

"Is someone there?"

No voice replied. The dark hallway loomed off in both directions, daring her to brave its blackness. She didn't want to take it up on that dare. But something was wrong. She felt it as surely as she felt the shiver of apprehension dance over her spine. She stepped into the hall, and turned toward the stairway.

The wall switch was at the top of the stairs. Just as soon as she reached it and filled the darkness with light, her fear, this *feeling*, would vanish right along with the shadows.

The house was utterly silent. The wind and rain of the past few days had finally died, the clouds were dispersing, and as she approached the stairway, she saw the full moon's glow filtering through its coat of clouds to streak the floor below.

She reached for the light switch, but her hand missed its mark, and fear tiptoed over her soul. A thrill of dread raced up her spine, and yet she felt some sense of urgency drawing her toward the stairs. She fought it, but took one step down, then another. A tingling sensation raced over her spine, and she stiffened. God, here she was wandering the darkened house alone, at night, knowing full well someone under this very roof wanted her dead. Should she go down, and try to locate the other light switch, or go back to her room?

She took a step backward, but couldn't seem to turn around. There was something tugging her gaze downward. Something down there wasn't right.

She took another step back, bringing her to the top of the stairs. The clouds shifted slowly. Moonlight streamed through the tall, tapering windows that lined the foyer below, and moved across the floor. Its soft glow spilled over the parquet, spreading like melted butter that coated everything in its path. Finally, it slowed to a crawl, having found its target. Like a spotlight, moonglow illuminated a mound of scarlet satin at the foot of the stairs.

Caitlin frowned. That looked like...

"My robe," she whispered. The light spread slower, as if it were congealing and could barely move, until it touched the pale skin of a still hand. And there it remained, motionless. Caitlin screamed at the top of her lungs.

She raced down the stairs, propelled by panic, her palm burning with friction as she clutched the banister too tightly. She fell to her knees at the bottom of the stairs, her hands gripping satin-clad shoulders, turning the woman onto her back.

The moon's light bathed the still face, and glinted on the crimson strand that trickled down one side from her ear, across her cheek. "Sandra!" Caitlin touched her face, and her voice was a shriek. "Sandra, wake up! For God's sake, wake up!"

There was no response and Caitlin's heart, once thudding wildly, seemed to skid to a painful stop in her breast. She was frantic, pressing her fingers into the warm skin of Sandra's throat in search of a pulse, when light flooded the room. She heard Henri's curse and Genevieve's sob, as both rushed in from the archway on the other side of the foyer. Caitlin felt no pulse beneath her fingers, and she rose slowly, moving toward them, dazed. "I think...I think she's dead."

Henri lurched forward, rushing to the body. Genevieve turned to lean against the wall, folding her arms to cradle her head. Caitlin kept walking, to the telephone on the other end of the room. She picked it up and dialed 911.

Vaguely, she heard steps in the hallway above, then Dylan's voice, hoarse and too loud. "Caity!" His steps pounded down the stairs, and she turned in time to see him stop short of the body on the floor, blink down at it and draw three openmouthed breaths that were ragged and deep. His gaze rose, and when he saw her, he closed his eyes. He looked down at Henri where the man knelt beside Sandra. Henri only shook his head.

"I need an ambulance, and the police." Caitlin's voice sounded dead as she spoke into the mouthpiece. "A woman's been killed." She muttered the address as Dylan crossed the floor toward her. He was barefoot, like her, and wore only a pair of briefs beneath a knee-length, terry robe that gaped open. His hair was wild, his eyes wide, and moving over her rapidly as she put the phone down.

For a long moment, he said nothing. Not a word. Then, very slowly, he lifted his arms, and she fell into them, clinging to his shoulders, shaking violently. He held her hard, his hands threading through her hair.

"Caity... I thought it was you."

She stiffened in his arms. *"What?"*

"The robe. It's yours. When I saw it from the top of the stairs, I thought..." He drew a deep breath and crushed her closer. "Doesn't matter. You're all right."

But the trembling that had begun in her from the moment she'd seen Sandra's body assaulted her anew, and fear made her dizzy. His words brought the truth to her with sickening clarity. "Someone else thought it was me, too," she whispered. "The person who killed her."

She heard an oath and looked up to see her brother on the floor beside his wife. His chalky face contorted, he pulled her upper body to his chest, and murmured her name. From above, she heard the baby crying, and tears filled her eyes. "Oh, God, Lizzie. Poor Lizzie."

Ellen appeared at the top of the stairs then and made her way slowly downward, stopping short of the bottom, clutching the banister until her knuckles whitened, sending a fear-filled glance toward Dylan and Caitlin on the other side of the foyer.

Dylan only held Caitlin tighter. She felt his heart hammering beneath her head, heard his ragged breaths. If he didn't care at all about her, he was certainly doing a good impression of someone who did. She closed her eyes, twined her arms around his neck and clung to him, her one anchor in a world gone crazy.

Dylan paced the library floor, feeling like a caged animal. He'd be arrested this time. There was no doubt in his mind of that as Thomas sat still as a stone, and told Detective Barnes about the argument he'd witnessed between Dylan and Sandra the day before.

"He was yelling at her. Loud enough to be heard in the kitchen."

"What was he saying?" Barnes wasn't bothering with his notepad this time. He had a tape recorder running. Henri was being questioned in another room. Genevieve had already given her statement, and was in the dining room, watching over Ellen, who was badly shaken. And Cait... Cait was upstairs with Lizzie. Thank God. Thank God it hadn't been her at the foot of those damned stairs.

But if he let himself get arrested, it might well be her next time. Damn, he felt helpless.

"I couldn't hear clearly," Thomas was saying. "I went to see what was going on, just as he pushed her."

"Pushed her," Barnes repeated. "Pushed her, how?" He walked right up to the overstuffed chair Thomas occupied. "Get up and show me."

Thomas rose as if his legs were too weak to hold him. He brought his hands upward to Barnes's shoulders and gave him a shove. "It was harder than that, though. She fell to the floor."

"It *wasn't* harder than that, and she only fell because she tripped over something."

Dylan stopped pacing to whirl around. Caitlin stood in the doorway. She hadn't bothered to change. She still wore the floor length, emerald green nightgown that shimmered like silk. Her auburn hair was as tousled as a lion's mane, and hanging down to the middle of her back. Her eyes were no longer frightened, or confused, though. They were glittering and angry.

Dylan crossed the room to stand beside her, ignoring the others. "How's the baby?"

"I managed to get her back to sleep. I didn't want to bring her down here with..." She didn't finish, only glanced in the general direction of the living room, where Dylan knew Sandra's body still rested. Barnes's faithful forensics team were as busy as ants in autumn. He could still hear the whir of the camera as the police photographer snapped pictures at the medical examiner's direction. He thought they'd have at least covered Sandra's face by now.

"Caity, if you don't mind...you witnessed this argument, too?"

"Yes."

"Then maybe you can tell me what it was about."

Her gaze shifted to Dylan. "Sandra had been doing her best to alienate me since I came back. I guess she didn't like me very much. I assumed Dylan was angry about that, but I'm not sure, since I came in at the tail end of the discussion. You ought to ask my husband if you want more details. Not that I think it's relevant. The killer obviously mistook Sandra for me in the dark."

Barnes looked skeptical, but turned to Dylan. "I suppose you're going to tell me you were alone in your room all night, and didn't hear a thing, right?"

"I—"

"Not quite alone, Detective," Caitlin said.

Dylan frowned at her.

"Before you go on, Caity, I ought to tell you I've already interviewed your employees. They said you and your husband haven't shared a bedroom in months."

"That was true, until last night."

"You telling me you two slept together last night?"

Her chin tilted upward. "I was afraid and alone. I needed someone with me last night, so I went to my husband. That isn't so farfetched, is it?"

"What time?"

"Early. Around nine, I guess."

Barnes cleared his throat, and he kept glancing at Dylan. Dylan fought to keep his surprise from showing on his face. He couldn't believe Caitlin was lying to a cop just to cover for him.

"But you slept sometime. He could have gotten up, and—"

"I didn't *sleep* at all." She sidled nearer Dylan and slipped her arm around his waist. "Dylan dozed off around midnight. I was still restless, so I got up to get a book from the library. That's when I found Sandra."

"Uh-huh." Barnes's gaze narrowed, and Dylan stiffened. If he caught on to Caitlin's lie, he'd be more suspicious than ever. "So what you're telling me is, that you and your husband have reconciled."

"Reconciled?"

"The divorce is off, right?"

Dylan felt the shock that jolted through Caitlin's body. He closed his eyes, and put his arm around her shoulders, squeezing her to his side. If she faltered now, he'd be behind bars before dawn. "Nothing's been decided, Barnes."

Caitlin pulled free of him, turned her back on Barnes and walked, on shaking legs, across the library. She reached into the liquor cabinet and pulled out a shot glass, and the same whiskey bottle Dylan had been holding earlier. Her back still to them, she unscrewed the cap, set it aside and poured a healthy splash into the glass.

"If that divorce is still on, Caity, your husband has a huge motive to try to kill you. I'm sure you're already aware of that, but I just want to remind you. The settlement you and your lawyers hammered out have you keeping everything you own, the house, too.''

She downed the shot, and sucked air through her teeth. She cleared her throat, but didn't turn. "Of course I'm aware of it.''

''Then you also know that your husband fought this settlement tooth and nail for months. Then, suddenly, agreed to everything without a hitch. Right before your accident.''

She said nothing. Instead, she only tipped the bottle again, then calmly replaced the cap and put it away.

''It wasn't the settlement I was fighting, Barnes. It was the divorce. I didn't want it.'' Dylan felt like wringing the bastard's neck for spilling everything that way. And he seemed to be enjoying it, too. He had to know Caitlin hadn't been aware of their pending divorce, just from her reactions. "I'd have nothing to gain by her death.''

''What you'd gain, Rossi, is half of everything she was planning to take in the settlement. What's hers is willed to her brother, and to you, in equal portions, more or less. Your share alone is a small fortune.''

Caitlin turned to face them, her face expressionless. She glanced toward Thomas, and downed half of the whiskey. ''I'm being rude. Would anyone else like a drink? I could make coffee.''

''No, thanks anyway.'' Barnes frowned at her. ''Will you reconsider what I said about getting out of here for a while?''

Dylan stiffened, waiting for her to say yes, and leave with the detective. If she walked out now, knowing what she knew, knowing he'd deliberately kept the truth about the divorce from her, she'd never come back. He was as sure of that as he was of his own name. He was equally sure he didn't want that to happen. Not like this. He hadn't realized it until he'd looked down those stairs at her satin robe, surrounding a dead woman's body, and thought for one heart-stopping second that it was her. But since then, he'd come to some damned painful conclusions.

She simply shook her head. "My niece needs me now, Detective Barnes. I can't leave her." She finished the drink and set the glass down. Her hands were shaking, but her face betrayed nothing.

"I'll need statements from each of you." He looked at Caitlin. "Caity, can you tell me why the victim was wearing your robe?"

She nodded. "I packed up some old clothes and asked Genevieve to get rid of them for me."

Thomas nodded. "Yeah, Genevieve brought them to our room, told Sandra to pick out anything she wanted, before the stuff went to charity."

"Did the maid go through the clothes herself?"

Caitlin shook her head. "I doubt she bothered. I'm so much taller than her, nothing would have fit."

Barnes nodded. "All right. You can go see to the kid, if you want. I'll get your statement later." She nodded, and started toward the door.

"You watch your back, Cait Rossi. This isn't over yet," Barnes added in a low voice.

She only nodded, and before she left the room, her gaze met Dylan's. There was a wounded look in her emerald eyes, a look of betrayal, and a shimmer of tears she refused to shed. She walked out with her back rigid, her shoulders so stiff, they shook with it. And all Dylan wanted to do was run after her.

CHAPTER ELEVEN

She felt his presence even before the bedroom door opened. It was like an energy, an awareness of him that preceded him into the room. She stayed where she was, lying on her side on the bed. She'd been wishing for sleep, even while knowing she'd find none.

Dylan stood in the doorway. She felt him there, and without looking up, she felt his gaze on her.

"I'm glad Lizzie's too young to know what's happening." Caitlin kept her voice very low. The entire house had the air of a funeral home, even though Sandra's body had finally been removed. "If I'd died in that accident, she might still have a mother."

"Caity—"

"When were you going to tell me about the divorce?" She blinked, and finally turned to face him.

His face was tight, and his eyes revealed nothing. "When I thought you could handle it."

Or maybe not at all. Maybe you weren't going to say anything, Dylan. Maybe you figured I'd be dead long before you had to.

"You think I did it, don't you?"

She stiffened a bit. Was her face so transparent? Or was he reading her mind? "I don't know what I think." She rolled over and sat up, with her legs dangling over the side of the bed.

"Last night, you believed I was innocent."

"Last night, I thought you didn't have a motive. But you did. And you kept it from me."

He stepped farther into the room and closed the door. He leaned back against the wall, his arms crossing over his chest. Her gaze followed his movements. He wore a snug-fitting black T-shirt that strained to contain his muscular shoulders. His forearms were hard, tight. His biceps, in this position, bulged. A soft stirring in her stomach troubled her. Was it because he was so attractive, because she still wanted him so badly? Or because she knew he could break her neck without working up a sweat?

"Why'd you lie to Barnes?"

His liquid brown eyes searched her face, but they were cold, without feeling. Or maybe he was deliberately hiding what he felt.

She got to her feet, walked to the window and gazed out. The sky was as brilliant as the meat of an orange. The sun's huge upper curve was just visible in the distance; neon fire. On impulse, she released the latch and pushed the windows open. Warm, sea-moistened wind bathed her face, blew through her hair. She tipped her head back and inhaled.

"It was like this that time on the beach," she said. "Early morning. Everything so fresh and new...like we were." She leaned out a little, wishing she could see the shore from here. She could hear it. Waves pounding stone. Foaming surf. Crying gulls. And she could smell the tang of saltwater in the air. She could even feel the sea. The breeze that caressed her face was wet with it. "That was the time you carved our initials into the rock."

She turned to gauge his reaction to that. He'd moved. He was standing nearer the bed now, stopped in the act of coming toward her. His gaze locked with hers over the bed.

"You remember."

She only nodded.

"When—"

"Last night. We were so happy together. What we had...it was so real, I wanted to believe it could be that way again, wanted to believe in us...in you." She sighed, and turned to the window once more. "That's why I lied to Barnes. I didn't want him locking you up when I was trying so hard to believe someone else was responsible."

She heard him coming toward her. She stiffened, but didn't turn. If he wanted to shove her out the window, here was his chance. She closed her eyes and bit her lip when his hands closed on her shoulders from behind. Then he turned her to face him, his eyes, for once, windows to the turmoil inside him. Emotion roiled in their melted-chocolate depths. But what kind of emotion? Regret? Longing? Anger? Hatred? God, how she wanted to believe in him! Would he tell her now that it wasn't him? That she'd been right to believe he could never hurt her? That he—

"How . . . much do you remember?"

Disappointment hit her with the force of a wrecking ball. She blinked as if she'd been slapped, and let her gaze fall to the floor. "Only that. Whatever other secrets you're keeping from me are still safe."

He frowned.

"There are others, aren't there, Dylan?"

"You can't expect me to tell you your life story within a few days, Cait. You'll know everything, in time."

"Unless I don't have time."

"You really *do* think it was me." He caught her face between two hands, tipping it up until his eyes could drill into hers. "So which theory are you buying? That I killed Sandra because she wanted to jump my bones, and I wasn't as hot for her? Or did I mistake her for you in the darkness?"

She felt her lips tighten, and tried not to let her features twist in misery. Despite her efforts, a tear slipped through, and trailed slowly down her face.

"Damn you, Caitlin." His palms on either side of her face holding her still, he brought his lips to hers. He kissed her hard, his lips moving against hers in an assault as his hands tilted and tipped her head to fit her mouth to his.

She hated it, and she loved it, and she'd craved it for what seemed like always. In spite of herself, her arms twined around his neck, tightening until they ached. Her body pressed itself to his, and her mouth moved rapidly. When his tongue thrust, she suckled it with a vicious hunger, then dipped her own into his mouth, until his joined hers in a desperate, urgent battle. His hands lowered, wrapped around her, held her tight. They pressed to the small of her back, and then her shoulders, and then her buttocks, and then her thighs. Her fingers clawed and twisted in his hair, and her breaths came in ragged, violent spasms.

His hands came between them, forced their way up to the neck of her gown, gripped and tugged and tore, and all the while he was feeding on her mouth, her tongue. But then his attention altered, and his lips dragged hotly down over her chin, across her throat. He took her breast like a madman, a starving man devouring his first crumb of food in days. He sucked hard, making her whimper with mindless need. Making her clutch at his hair as he bit and tugged just until she felt pain, then licked and sucked until she writhed with pleasure again. Small sounds escaped her throat, begging sounds, that only enraged him further.

Holding her to him, his hands at her back, his mouth at her breast, he began moving backward, dragging her with him. Then he was turning her, pushing her. Her back sunk into the mattress. His body pressed it deeper. His hands twisted and yanked at her panties, while his mouth moved back to hers. She moved her legs, lifted her hips, to help him, and the scrap of nylon slipped to the floor. She snagged the hem of the tight black T-shirt he wore, and tugged it upward, her hands skimming his muscled back, his shoulders, before pulling the shirt over his head.

His flesh was hot against hers. *She* was hot. Burning up with mindless, senseless need. His big arms encircled her waist, holding her tight to him, making her feel small and delicate as he ruthlessly plundered her mouth.

Then he tore himself away. All at once, she lay alone, completely exposed to him, and he stood beside the bed, yanking at the button of his jeans, his blazing eyes moving up and down over her body. She instinctively tried to pull the tattered edges of her nightgown together, but he lunged, gripping her wrists, stopping her.

"Don't."

She met his heated gaze, held it. He pushed the soft gown from her shoulders, pulling her up a little as he did. Then he let her lie back, and he tossed the garment to the floor. He knelt on the bed, and he pressed her thighs apart. His gaze burned her there, and then his fingers parted, and probed and pinched, all as he watched.

She moaned. It was too much. He still wore his jeans, though the fly gaped open, and she could see the curling, dark hairs there. She was fully exposed, more fully exposed than she could remember ever having been. He was kneeling over her, staring at her so intently, it burned as his fingers tormented her without mercy. He spread her folds, sunk his fingers into her. Against her will, her hips rose to meet them. His gaze seemed to darken, and he groaned deep and gruffly.

His fingers pulled back, but he still held her open, spread wide to his probing eyes. Then, suddenly, he bent over her, swooping down like a hawk diving on its prey. She gasped when his mouth touched her, his lips, his tongue. His mouth attacked her until she whimpered with passion, until her entire body trembled like a leaf in a strong wind, and until she'd have done anything he asked of her.

Then he stopped, leaving her completely insane. He stood only long enough to shed the jeans, and then he was back. He knelt, straddling her waist, staring down at her as she panted and twisted with agonizing need. His hands gripped her head, lifted her. His arousal stood before her, thick and hard. His hands were shaking as his fingers moved in her hair, urging her closer.

She opened her mouth and took him into it. He growled her name and his hips moved slightly. She sucked, and tugged him, and wanted to take in more than she possibly could. Then he withdrew, and pressed her back down to the bed.

His hard body lowered on top of hers. His arousal nested between her thighs, nudging her, testing her. She bent her knees and opened herself to him. Her hands glided down his back to grip his hard buttocks and pull him to her.

He answered her unspoken request with a single, powerful thrust. He sunk himself inside her so deep and so hard that she cried out. And then he drew back and stabbed into her again, and again, until her mind spun out of control. On and on he took her, until she clung to him, cried his name and exploded in sensation.

He thrust into her once more, and stiffened, holding himself there, pulsing inside her. She shuddered, and closed her eyes. Dylan slowly relaxed, the bunched muscles in his shoulders lost their tension, the air spilled from his lungs. He slipped off her, onto his side, and he searched her face.

Caitlin felt like crying. It hadn't been a fantasy. His touch held the same magic she'd felt in her mind. It was real, the passion that sizzled between them. She swallowed hard, closed her eyes and rolled away from him. She felt the morning sun slanting through her window, warming her face.

"You'd better go now," she said softly.

"Why?"

She said nothing, only bit her lip and prayed he'd leave before she cried in front of him.

"Are you having regrets, Caitlin? Are you going to pretend you didn't want this just as badly as I did?"

She shook her head. "I wanted it. The same way I wanted to walk along the cliffs the other night. The same way a drug addict craves his poison."

He was silent for a moment. Then she felt the bed move as he rolled over and sat up. "So, I'm your poison. Is that what you believe?"

"It doesn't matter what I believe, Dylan. I'm stupid where you're concerned, like a moth battering my wings against clear glass to get to the light on the other side. Only I'm going to beat myself to death, and the light is just an illusion."

"I still want you, Caitlin. That's no illusion."

"Physically." She sat up, too. Then stood, her back to him. "It's not enough." She reached for the bathroom door, unconsciously stiffening her spine. "I need to shower. I'm going out this morning."

She heard him turn toward her. "Out where?"

She lifted her chin, opened the door, stepped onto the threshold. "I want to have a talk...with my lawyer." She licked her lips. "I think it's about time, don't you?"

Before he could answer, she took another step, and closed the door behind her. She turned the lock, then twisted the knobs until rushing water drowned out the sounds of her sobs.

Sandra's body had been taken to the medical examiner's office. She had to be autopsied, it was required when someone was murdered.

Dylan would have liked to think she'd just fallen down the stairs. Barring that, he'd like to believe her killer had known who she was before he'd pushed her. But she'd been wearing Caitlin's unmistakable scarlet robe, and the halls at night were pitch-black.

Dylan wasn't blind. He knew there was something going on between Thomas and Genevieve. He also knew Henri had the hots for Caitlin, and he was equally certain, no matter what else Caitlin might have done in the past, that she'd never reciprocated the feeling.

Could Henri be acting out of anger over her rejection of him? Or was it Thomas? He could have had a motive to kill either Sandra or Cait. Sandra, to free himself so he could pursue Genevieve. Cait, to avail himself of the money in her will. And Genevieve . . . she was such a secretive little thing. Might she have pushed Sandra, knowing full well who the victim was, just to get Thomas all to herself?

Dylan pushed a hand through his hair. This was getting him nowhere. What he'd like to do, what he ought to do, was to take Caitlin the hell out of here. Get her somewhere safe until he could figure this out.

As if she'd go anywhere with him. She thought he was the one out to murder her. And right now, his wife was at her lawyer's office, putting the final touches on their pending divorce. And there wasn't a damned thing he could do about it. He'd already signed everything that needed signing.

But that was before, dammit!

He stalked into the living room, and found Ellen there, rocking Lizzie. He sent his aunt a smile that was forced and tight. "How's she doing?"

"Just fine, boy. No more signs of that fever. I've taken care of babies before, you know."

He nodded distractedly, and paced past her to gaze out the window, into the driveway. His car was there, as well as the old pickup he sometimes used for business, hauling lumber and supplies to smaller job sites. Cait must have taken a cab.

"She hadn't ought to be wandering around town on her own, Dylan."

He blinked and let the curtain fall over the glass.

"Somebody wants to hurt her." She shifted Lizzie from one knee to the other, and rocked a little faster as the baby started to fuss. "You're letting your emotions cloud your judgment, boy. Get on the ball."

He gave himself a mental shake, realizing she was right. Despite what his wife thought of him, and what that did to his insides, Cait was out there, alone and unprotected. A walking target.

He bent low to kiss his aunt's wrinkled cheek on his way out.

Cait sat in the cab, clutching the sheaf of papers in a white-knuckled grip. The visit to the lawyer had gone roughly. He'd been furious at what she wanted to do, considering all the time and effort he'd spent on her case. Caitlin had drawn herself up to her full height and stared down her nose at the man behind the desk. In a voice she thought the old Caitlin had probably used often, she'd reminded him that he worked for her, and would be paid the same fee, no matter what the results. He'd grumbled, but accepted her decision.

She glanced up at the back of the driver's head. "You know this area pretty well?"

"Born and raised. What do you need to know?"

She warmed to his smile and friendly eyes. "There's a little bit of beach, completely surrounded by craggy rocks in sort of a horseshoe pattern. Very private. You know it?"

Glancing over his shoulder, his smile grew wider. "Sure. It's only ten minutes away."

True to his promise, the cabby pulled off to the side of the road beside a steep drop, a short time later. He pointed. "Right down there. There's a path, see it?"

She looked where he was pointing, and spotted a worn track through the tall grass. "Yeah. Thanks." She fished in her pocket for a twenty, and handed it to him.

"Don't you want me to wait?"

She shook her head. "Eden's not far, and it's a perfect day for a walk, don't you think?" She'd call another cab when she was finished here. She wanted solitude, time to think.

"If you're sure." He took her money, and she got out of the car. She stood for just a second as he pulled away, then started down the path. At it's end, she found the little cove she'd remembered, just as she remembered it.

Waves lapped gently at the white sand. Caitlin toed off her shoes, peeled off her socks and tossed both aside. She dug her toes into the warm sand and closed her eyes. It felt good here.

She stripped off her jeans, feeling no embarrassment at doing so. Her T-shirt came to her thighs, so she was decently covered. She wanted to feel the sun on her legs. She wanted to feel warmth, to counteract the coldness she'd felt emanating in waves from that house. And the coldness that seemed now to have spread over her, through her, until her very soul was encrusted in ice.

She'd had what she'd been driving herself crazy longing for, so why was she still so frustrated? She'd had sex with Dylan. It had been hot, frantic, almost violently intense sex. But it hadn't been lovemaking. She'd wanted to make love with him. She'd wanted it slow, and languid, and emotional. The way it used to be between them. The way her snippets of memory told her it had always been.

Unable to resist the lure of the water, she moved toward it. She stepped into the cool, frothy sea and it lapped over her ankles. She walked out farther and the waves licked higher, embracing her shins, her knees, her thighs. She dove into the bracing cold, the shimmering blue, and swam beneath the surface, farther from shore. She broke the surface when she ran out of air, flipping her head backward so the sun blazed on her face. She stroked away, exerting herself full force, swimming hard, as if she were being chased by sharks, then turning and starting back again, just as fiercely.

Her lungs burned and her heart thundered in her chest. The muscles in her arms and legs burned with the effort after a while, but it felt good. Just pouring everything she had into physical exertion, forgetting everything else. Just for a tiny, safe space in time, losing herself in the burn, the effort.

But it couldn't last. She knew she had to get back to the house, back to the husband who didn't love her, and never would. Back to the elderly aunt who thought she'd ruined her nephew's life, and to the brother who resented her. Back to Lizzie. The poor little thing didn't have anyone now, except for Thomas, and he was awkward and uncomfortable with her.

And me. She has me.

Just thinking of the baby made her ache inside. How could she come to care so much for a child she'd only known a few days, a child that wasn't even hers?

She paused in her mindless stroking and tread water. It didn't matter how, it only mattered that she loved Lizzie. She knew she ought to leave that house, but she wasn't going to. She missed the baby, even after only a few hours of separation.

She stroked toward shore and emerged dripping, panting, her body heated despite the cold water dripping from it. Rivulets ran down her legs and she belatedly wished she'd brought a towel. But how could she have? This hadn't been planned. She'd come here on impulse to see . . .

The half circle of ragged stone rose up before her and she stopped. Then, slowly, she moved toward it. She didn't even have to look for the spot. She found it as if by sheer instinct. She walked right to the stone face and ran her fingers over its warm surface, feeling the deep ridges carved there. The heart. Her initials. Dylan's.

As she stood there, her fingers caressing the spot, she recalled the warmth; the protected, loved feeling that had flashed through her memory each time she'd envisioned their lovemaking. And the lack of it during their encounter this morning. A pain like nothing she'd dreamed of reached out to grab her and held her in its grip. She lowered her head. Tears burned her eyes, and her throat tightened until she could barely breathe.

Give in to it. You're alone here. No one to see you.

She nodded her agreement with the voice of her own reason. She *was* alone. God, she was so alone.

She sank slowly to the sand at the base of the rock, and drew her knees to her chest. The flood of emotion came the instant she'd locked her arms around her knees. Not silent tears. There was no dignity in the way she cried. No pride, no control. She sobbed out loud and moaned as the pain knifed through her. Her tears ran like endless fountains and her entire body trembled violently. Spasms ripped through her chest, as if they'd split her breastbone in half.

"Caity..."

She looked up fast at the hoarse voice. Dylan stood between her and the sea, between her and the path. She cleared her throat. "What are you—"

"I followed you."

Fear rippled over her spine, jelling the tears that remained in her eyes. She remained sitting there in the sand, looking up at him. "Why?"

Through her blurred eyes, she saw the brief flash of pain in his face, but it was just as quickly concealed. "Not to murder you, Cait. I got worried. I just wanted to make sure..." He sighed hard, shook his head. "I waited outside the law office and followed the cab."

So he'd been here the whole time, watching her?

She brushed her fingertips over her eyes and fought the lingering sobs that tore through her sporadically, against her will. "Why did you wait so long to come down here?"

"I wasn't going to come down at all." He moved forward, dropping to his knees in the sand. His hands reached out to cup her face, but she pulled free, and turned her head.

"Leave me alone."

"I can't. Not like this. Cait, I didn't tell you about the divorce because I didn't want to confuse you any more than you already were. I'm not the one who pushed Sandra down those stairs. I'm not the one who tried to kill you.''

She faced him then, searching his eyes with hers. ''Why now? You wouldn't deny anything before. Why are you bothering now?''

''It's important now.''

She shook her head. ''You're wrong. You have it all backward. It might have mattered before. It doesn't matter at all now.'' She stood and brushed the wet sand from her thighs and backside. She moved past him, to where she'd tossed her purse on the sand. She bent to pick it up, then pulled the folded papers from inside it. When she turned, he was behind her. She handed them to him. ''It's over, Dylan.''

He frowned down at the papers in his hand. She thought his lower lip trembled once, but she couldn't be sure. ''No matter what's written here, it's not over. Not until you understand—''

''You're the one who doesn't understand. Read them, Dylan. Sign them, and you're free.''

''I already signed—''

''Not this agreement. Look at it, will you?''

He nodded, unfolded the sheets and studied them for a long time. She stood and watched the emotions crossing his face, and tried to identify each one. Surprise? Shock? Sadness? Anger?

When he looked up again, his eyes were carefully blank. ''You don't want anything?''

She shook her head. ''Nothing. Not a dime. And I had the deed to the house transferred to you, too. I don't want it. I don't want anything that was hers—mine—before. I want to start over. And I hate that place.''

''The old agreement?''

She reached into her bag and pulled out the official-looking envelope with the original divorce papers inside. All contained Dylan's signature. ''I have both copies. Mine, and my lawyer's, right here. I knew you wouldn't trust me enough to take my word for it." She pushed the envelope into his hand. "Tear it up. Burn it. I don't care. It's up to you. I'm sure your lawyer will be happy to add his copies and yours to the bonfire."

Dylan shook his head. "Why?"

She shrugged and shook her head. The finality of handing those papers to him hit her and she felt tears threatening again.

"It was wrong. That first settlement was the act of another woman. Not me. It was just never my money. It was hers. It just felt...wrong."

"No." Dylan grabbed her purse and shoved both sets of documents inside, then tossed it to the sand. "You're taking away my motive. You're afraid I'm going to kill you, so you're taking away my motive." He stalked away from her, pushing a hand through his hair.

"I'm trying to make things right," she called after him. "I just want to cut my ties with the woman I was. I want to start over, try to build some kind of a life. Dammit, Dylan, I'm giving you what you wanted!"

He whirled to face her. "It was never what I wanted."

"Don't..." God, she couldn't stand for him to give her even a hint of false hope, not now. "Look, at least this way, if the killer succeeds, you won't be a suspect."

"Oh, thank you all to hell." He approached her, gripped her shoulders. "And what if the attempts just stop now, Caitlin? What are you going to believe then?"

"Does it really matter? Do you really care what I believe?"

He did. He knew it right then, and it hit him like a mallet between the eyes. He cared a lot what she believed; too much.

He saw the strain in her eyes when they met his, but she only bent to pick up her jeans and shoes, and her purse. She thumbed the strap of her bag over her shoulder, and carried her shoes dangling from one hand. The T-shirt she wore was soaked, clinging. It molded to her shape, and despite everything else he was feeling, he was aroused. He wanted her. He always had. It had been the one constant in their ever-changing relationship.

She walked in silence up the steep incline, over the path. He glanced back down the path, at the spot where they'd first made love, and wondered how much of it she recalled. Did she know how good it was, even then? How explosive? Did she realize yet, that she could bring him to his knees with a touch of her lips? Of her hands? That she'd driven him to the brink of insanity this morning? Had it been as good for her? He needed to know.

"Caity?"

She looked at him, eyes wide, searching.

"This morning—"

"I don't want to talk about this morning." She averted her eyes.

"You going to try to pretend it never happened?"

"It shouldn't have happened. It can't happen again. It won't." She closed her eyes, shook her head slowly.

He gripped her arm, pulled her around to face him. "It could. It could happen right now."

She opened her eyes. He saw moisture gathering there.

"It could," he insisted. He gripped her other arm, and drew her closer. She planted her feet, held herself away. "You want it, too, Cait. What are you so afraid of?"

"That you'll destroy me." She closed her eyes as the tears spilled over. "It wouldn't take much more, Dylan." The last sentence was a whisper, and a plea.

He let her go.

She was on her back, with the most horrible pains trying to crush her, like steel bands around her abdomen and back, tightening, crushing, squeezing. Her head swung back and forth on the pillows and someone ran a cool cloth over it.

She wanted to cry out, but couldn't catch her breath to do so. And the pain that took her breath away went on and on and on.

And then it was gone.

She sat up, gasping. Her face damp with sweat, her hair clinging to it, her eyes wide and unfocused as she scanned the blurry room. Dylan was there. Standing in the shadows, grim-faced. He held the baby in his arms, wrapped in a white receiving blanket. Caitlin lifted her arms toward him. And slowly, he moved forward.

He lowered the bundle into her arms. Caitlin cradled the child close, but frowned at its minuscule size. So small, so feather-light. And not moving. Not moving at all.

She parted the folds of the soft blanket, and looked down. The baby's skin was thin, translucent, and tinted a ghastly blue. Caitlin's hand touched the tiny cheek, and she recoiled at its feel. Unreal, unresponsive, dead.

Another pair of hands came—not Dylan's—to take the child from her arms. She clung, but they pried until her weak grasp gave way. "No," she begged, her voice choked, desperate. "No, please, don't take him away... No!"

But the stranger's hands, holding the lifeless infant, vanished into the mist. And Caitlin screamed aloud, her grief a living force in her soul.

She sat up in bed and reached for the lamp, knocking it over in her haste. It crashed to the floor, shattering, but she barely heard the sound. The panic ran like ice water in her veins as she staggered from the bed, lunged for the door. Glass razed her bare feet, but she was beyond caring.

She wrenched the door wide and ran through the hall to the nursery. She tore that door open and left it gaping as she reached for the crib, clutched it with trembling hands, leaned over it and willed the thundering in her heart to quiet.

Her hands shook, but she found Lizzie's rounded form beneath a light cover. She touched the warm, plump cheek with a forefinger, and Lizzie instinctively turned her head toward that touch, her lips smacking in her sleep.

Relief washed through her, transforming her muscles from tautly stretched wire to quivering, useless jelly. She sank in a heap to the floor at the side of the crib.

She heard the footsteps in the hall, her name being called. She saw the light spilling in from the nursery's open door. And then she was lifted in Dylan's strong arms, cradled close to his hard chest, held tight, her face pressed to the crook of his neck where his scent enfolded her.

"All right. It's all right, I have you. You're safe."

Her arms slipped around his neck, and she clung to him, crying harder, recalling the silent devastation she'd seen on his handsome face in the dream.

"What happened?"

She shook her head, but it moved very little. "Nothing." Her throat was painfully tight, too tight to speak more than a word or two at a time. "Bad dream."

But it wasn't a dream, was it? It hurts too bad to have been just a dream.

"You scared the hell out of me, Cait. The lamp in your room is smashed all to hell. There's blood in the hall all the way from your room to the nursery. Tell me what happened."

He was carrying her the wrong way, and she realized he was heading not to her bedroom, but to his. The light there was blazing, and he lowered her to the bed. He stood over her, wearing only his brief underwear that fit him like a second skin. "You sure you're okay?"

She closed her eyes. He looked so worried, as though he'd really been afraid for her. How could he look like that and not love her? How could he look like that and want her dead?

"I . . . cut my foot, I think. That's all."

"The lamp?"

She nodded as he bent to examine her foot. It was beginning to throb, and she could feel the blood that coated it now. She fought to control her breathing, to stop the sobs that sporadically rocked through her. She brushed her face dry with palms that were sweaty, and too warm. "I knocked it over."

He swore softly, left her there and walked into his bathroom, returning in a moment with his hands full of paraphernalia that he dumped on the foot of his bed. She saw tweezers, a roll of gauze and a tube of ointment, some tape. Without a word, Dylan sat on the bed's edge, and pulled her foot into his lap. Slowly, painfully, he began removing bits of the broken lamp from the sole of her foot.

When she winced, he stiffened. "Sorry. I think I got it all." He smeared ointment over her cuts, his fingers so gentle on her skin, they could have been caressing her instead of ministering to an injury. He wrapped her foot in gauze, taped the dressing in place and stood again, pushing a hand through his hair.

She sat up. "Thanks. I was clumsy—"

"You were terrified. Are you sure no one—"

"It was just a bad dream."

He nodded, searching her face with eyes so intense, she felt them cutting through her. "So you said. You want to tell me about it?"

She bit her lower lip. She couldn't tell him. Not now, not yet. Not until she was sure. She couldn't say the words out loud that would make that heartache real. God, but it already was real, wasn't it? It was tearing her apart inside, even now, with that one, devastating image. The baby, *her* baby. Her son, and Dylan's, lying lifeless in her arms.

She shook her head, stifling a new flood of tears. "I don't remember."

His eyes narrowed, but he nodded. She knew he didn't believe that, but he wasn't going to push. She started to get up, but Dylan's hands came to her shoulders. His touch wasn't firm, but tentative, light as a whispered promise, ready to lift away from her at a moment's notice. "Stay, Cait?"

The look in his dark, glittering eyes made her shudder inside. "Stay?"

CHAPTER TWELVE

"Yeah. Not so I can murder you in your sleep, and not so I can ravage you, either. I won't touch you unless ... unless you ask me to. I just want to know you're safe. Stay here tonight."

Here. In his bed. In his arms? She closed her eyes and nodded once. It did no good to question his motives. She wanted to be here with him, wanted it badly. Too badly to ignore, or even to deny.

She was grieving, suffering from a loss they must have shared, if her suspicion that it was more memory than dream was an accurate one. She needed to be held, to be comforted. As he pulled back the covers, peeled them from beneath her so she could slip under them, then slid in beside her, she knew she wanted this. Just to sleep in his arms, feel his heart beating close to hers. She wanted to lie close to him all night, with his scent filling her nostrils. She was stupid to put herself through it, stupid to let herself wallow in his presence. It only hurt her more deeply than ever. But she lay down beside him, anyway. She'd lie close to him tonight. Just that.

Not just that. More. Much more.

He reached for the lamp and snapped it off, plunging them into darkness. Then he lay still, on his back, not touching her. Drawing a breath, Cait rolled onto her side. She rested her head on his chest, and let her arm fall around him.

He stiffened. "Caity..."

"Hold me, Dylan." Her voice broke when she said his name.

His arms came around her, hard and fast. She felt his strength. His smooth, broad chest beneath her head, the taut heated skin touching her cool cheek. She turned her head slightly and pressed her lips to it, not caring that it might not be wise, only knowing that she wanted this man, even more than she had before. He wanted her, too.

He had the divorce papers. She'd given him his freedom, and she sensed it would only be a matter of time until he took it and ran with it. He'd be out of her life soon, leaving her with nothing but a single, vibrant memory of his passion, his touch. It wasn't enough.

She slid her leg over both of his, bending her knee, lifting it up over his body. She kissed his chest again, her lips brushing his nipple, and she heard him swear hoarsely. He gripped her shoulders and lifted her from his chest. "What the hell are you doing?"

There was anger in his voice, but desire in his eyes, glittering up at her even in the darkness. She felt its proof, pressing hard and insistent against her thigh. She moved her leg over him, gently. "Make it like it was, Dylan." She bit her lip when tears threatened. "Make it like it used to be."

His hands tightened on her shoulders. There was a moment of hesitation, a moment when she was terrified he was about to turn away from her. Then he drew her downward until his lips could reach hers. He kissed her long and slow, suckling her lips, tracing their shape with his tongue, nipping them. She opened her mouth to him and his tongue plunged inside her mouth to taste every part of it. Deepening the invasion with every second, he took from her, and he gave to her. His hands threaded in her hair, then danced down the column of her neck. His thumbs pressed little circles under her jaw, then his lips replaced them, so gently her throat tightened.

He moaned deep in his throat, and she moved over him more completely, until she straddled his powerful hips, bringing his hardness against her burning need. She rocked against him, and he trembled. She let her hands roam his body. She pressed her palms to the muscled wall of his chest, kneaded his shoulders, learned his shape all over again. She ran her hands up and down his arms, back and forth across his back. She kissed his face, his chin, his neck.

His hand left her back and she heard the snap of the bedside lamp. She opened her eyes to see the light falling on his face. She searched his burning yes.

"I want to see you, Caity. I love the way you look."

She nodded. She understood his need. She wanted to see him, too. To see the sensations pass over his face, through his eyes, to see the beautiful shape of him. To burn his image as she held him inside her one last time, into her heart, her soul, her memory. She'd never forget this night. Never.

She sat up, still straddling him, and the covers fell away behind her. He wanted to look at her.

She caught the hem of the nightshirt she wore, and lifted it, tugging it over her head, tossing it to the floor, keeping her gaze on his face all the while. His eyes darkened, slid slowly away from hers, downward, and fixed their attention on her breasts. His hands moved up over her back to her shoulders, and he drew her forward, lifting his head from the pillows at the same time. He captured one yearning peak in his mouth, and he sucked her hard, hungrily, using his teeth, worrying her flesh, nipping it until her head fell backward and her loins ached with wanting him. He released her only to move to the other breast, laving it with his tongue until it responded, then punishing it for the offense with his teeth and lips.

He caught her hips in his hands and lifted her from him. She braced her knees on the mattress as he shoved her panties down. One hand dove between her thighs, cupping the mound of curls. Then fingers parted, explored, pleasured her. He found the tiny nub that was the center of her desire, and ran the pad of his thumb over it. She shuddered and caught her breath. He pinched it between thumb and forefinger, squeezing, rolling, torturing her. She whimpered and all at once his free hand caught her chin, tipping her head down.

"Open your eyes, Caity. Look at me, let me watch you."

She did as he asked. She'd do anything he asked at that moment. And his deep, dark eyes stabbed into hers just as his fingers stabbed into her center. He slid them in deeper, then pulled them out again, watching the responses in her eyes.

She reached down between them, finding the waistband of his briefs, thrusting one hand beyond it. She held him, her grip tight, but trembling. He was like iron coated in silk. She squeezed and moved her hand up and down his turgid length, then up again until her fingers teased at his tip.

"Oh, yeah," he moaned.

She lowered her head to his chest, and worried his nipples just the way he'd done to hers. And then he was gripping her again, rolling her over, peeling her panties away and kicking free of his briefs all at once. He settled himself on top of her, nudging her thighs apart with his, positioning his need at her moist opening.

He entered her hard and fast and deep, groaning as he did. He gripped her buttocks in both hands, and drove himself to the very hilt, holding her hard against him, refusing to back down even when she stiffened, pressing harder, forcing her to take all of him.

He watched her face as she slowly relaxed, adjusting to her body's fullness, to the feel of him stretching her to his shape and size again. And as soon as she did, he knew, and he withdrew, slowly, until she was all but empty, before thrusting himself into her again. He set the pattern, and the pace continued. Deep, hard thrusts. Slow, mind-altering withdrawals. He kissed her hands, her fingers, one by one.

His lips traced a path over her forearms, making her tremble. Then his mouth dampened her shoulders, then her neck, and her ears. It was as though he wanted to taste every inch of her.

The force behind the thrusts grew stronger, harder, and faster with each stroke.

Her hips rose to meet his, her fingers dug into his shoulders. It was as if she were riding a hurricane, she thought vaguely. She felt possessed by him, filled with him and surrounded in him, all at once, and she moved without pause or forethought or planning. She moved according to her body's demands and the ones she could sense from his. And then he drove every thought from her mind as her entire body tightened until her muscles tried to tear from the bones.

Release pummeled her, exploding inside her. She clung to him as her body convulsed around his, and she cried out his name on a voice ragged and broken. He stiffened, plunging again, holding her hips to his. "Caity," he whispered, and then he collapsed atop her, panting, damp with sweat.

He lay there for a long time, his heart rumbling against her chest, his sweat dampening her body, mingling with her own, his breaths heating her skin as they slowed. He lifted his head after a long moment, when their lungs were functioning normally and their bodies began to cool. He searched her eyes, utter longing in his. He started to say something, then shook his head and rolled off her. He cradled her to his chest, held her in arms banded with steel, held her close, and warm and safe against him.

She cried softly, and silently, so he wouldn't know. This was what she'd wanted. She felt cherished, just as she had in her memory flashes. The sad part was, it wasn't real. But she could pretend. Just for tonight, she could pretend.

When she awoke, he was gone.
Dawn hadn't yet painted the horizon. But she was too

restless to lie in bed. There was so much to say. She needed to find Dylan, to beg him, if necessary, to give their marriage one more try. She wanted to tear up all of the divorce papers and start over. She wanted the cherished feeling he'd given her last night to live on and on. She wanted it to be real. She was determined to *make it* real.

She threw back the covers, got up and found her nightgown and panties on the floor. She pulled them on, then smiled as she spotted the roll of gauze and tube of ointment on the floor, recalling the tender way he'd cared for her wounded foot. She bent to pick them up, and reached for the tweezers, too. Then she carried the lot into the bathroom and opened the medicine cabinet to replace the items inside.

She set the gauze on a shelf, then froze as her gaze fell on a small, brown glass jar. She blinked at the words on the label, not willing to believe what she saw there.

"Pure ground carob."

"No." She stared at the bottle as though it might leap up and grab her, and backed away from the cabinet. "No, it can't be . . ."

God, the tenderness she'd felt in his touch last night, the sweet anguish in his eyes, the yearning . . . had it all been an act? One big performance to convince her once and for all that he was innocent? Could he have faked the passion, the affection, that she'd felt surrounding her all night long? She didn't want to believe it.

Maybe it's time you stopped believing what you want to believe, and start seeing what's staring you in the face.

Tears blurred her vision as she closed the cabinet and walked back into the bedroom. He hadn't returned. She stole in silence into the hallway, tiptoed along its dim length until she heard him, crooning a soft song, his voice deep, trembling, beautiful. "Good night, Sweetheart." She caught back a sob that leapt into her throat, and slipped nearer, peering through the open doorway into the nursery.

He walked slowly, barefoot, his calves naked beneath the hem of a terry robe. He cradled the tiny baby on his shoulder, patting her back with his huge hand. He sang very softly, and Lizzie, wide-eyed, seemed to be hanging on every note. He turned to pace the other way and Cait saw his face. His eyes were red, and there were marks on one cheek that looked like the tracks of hot tears.

She backed away slowly, bit her lips as her own eyes filled. How could she make sense of him? Of the tender man she saw holding Lizzie, of the man with the powder that was poison to her hidden in his medicine cabinet?

Blinded by tears, she made her way back to his bedroom. What other secrets was he hiding here? The keys to her past? His hidden motive for wanting her dead? She was tired of waiting to find the answers. She couldn't wait anymore.

He wouldn't come back any time soon. Lizzie was wide-awake, and it would take a while to get her back to sleep. Caitlin went to the dresser, opened the drawers, pawed their contents. She found nothing but clothes. She turned to the closet, and rummaged inside it. Nothing. Just more clothes, shoes, suits. A briefcase.

She drew it out, and lay it on the bed. She tried the snaps, half expecting it to be locked. It wasn't, and inside she found only papers pertaining to the business. Drawings. Blueprints. Invoices. Nothing to do with her.

She closed it and slipped it back into the closet. Then she spotted the fireproof security box on the top shelf. She reached for it, glancing over her shoulder toward the door as she did.

What if he returned, caught her snooping? What would he do then?

It didn't matter. She had to try. She drew the heavy box down, set it on the floor near enough the bed that she could shove it underneath if she heard him coming. She closed the closet.

The box was locked and she felt deflated. Then she saw his jeans from the day before hanging over the back of a chair. She went to them, searched the pockets and found a key ring. There were many keys on it, but it didn't take long to spot the small one that fit the lock. She sat on the floor, and opened the box.

There were photos. Dozens of them. Snapshots of her, in her youth. Pictures of the two of them together, mugging for the camera. She looked at all of them, blinking constantly to keep her eyes clear enough to see. They seemed so happy. So in love.

She found their marriage license. A large manila envelope held it, along with more photos, encased in a leather-bound album. Their wedding pictures. Her dress was off-the-shoulder, ivory-toned, spilling over with lace and pearls. She'd worn a sprig of baby's breath and yellow roses in her hair, carried a bouquet of the same in her hands.

She flipped through the album slowly, her heart aching for what they'd had, what they'd lost. There was a fat man in a dark suit, nearly bald, with hard, glassy blue eyes. He must have been her father, but she found no sense of recognition stirring inside her. Then she found the one of the woman. She looked just like Caitlin. Same auburn hair, only shorter, and permed in kinky curls to frame her petite face. Her green eyes held some secret pain, some deep sadness that belied the smile that curved her full lips. She didn't look old enough to be Caitlin's mother. But she knew that's who she was seeing right now. And her fingertips brushed over the troubled face.

God, she didn't remember her own mother! But she felt something, a pull, a heartache. A longing.

She closed her eyes, and then the album. There would be time to learn about her mother later. It was too late to mend the break she sensed in their relationship. Her mother was gone, dead and buried.

She set the album aside and continued pawing through the contents of the box. Her hand froze, her fingers tingling, when she picked up the envelope buried at the bottom, beneath titles to cars, and countless other documents.

Trembling for no reason, she opened it, and found inside the very item she'd most dreaded seeing. Across the top of the document, she read the words, Certificate of Fetal Death.

She caught her breath in her throat and tears stung her eyes. She swiped them away and forced herself to read all of it, the clinical, cold facts that told her she and Dylan had had a son. A tiny son, who'd weighed just over two pounds. Cause of death was listed as extreme prematurity. She blinked at the date. January 8th. Just over eight months ago. Her heart twisting, she scanned the page, and found the child's name. David Dylan Rossi.

So they'd named him. And if they had, then they'd probably buried him, as well. Where? Desperately, she reread the lines, but found no clue. Oh, God. She fought her shaking hands and replaced the paper in its envelope. But it wasn't empty. She shook out the folded card that was still inside. It read, In Memoriam. David Dylan Rossi. She found the name of the cemetery there, along with the date of his stillbirth and burial.

"My baby," she whispered, holding the card to her chest. And this was all she had of him. This, and the memory. It had been a memory, not a dream. A nightmare memory of the day she'd lost her child. And she knew, as surely as she knew anything, that losing the child had devastated her, that she'd been sure she could never survive going through it again. And that was why she'd been so afraid of getting pregnant. God, she'd been a fool.

She replaced everything else in the security box, but kept the card. She locked it, replaced it in the closet and returned the key ring to Dylan's pocket. Then she paused and took the keys back out. She needed to go there, she realized. She needed to see where her son rested. Yes, there were other things that must be done. She had to confront Dylan about this, and about the carob powder she'd found in his medicine cabinet. But first—before she could even think of anything else—she had to find her baby.

And she had to do it alone.

She found a pad and pen on the dresser and scrawled a note to Dylan. "I need to be by myself, to think. Please understand." She signed her name at the bottom, and left the note on the bed, then crept through the halls to her room, not making a sound, still clinging to the card that bore her son's name.

She set the card and the keys on the nightstand, avoiding the broken glass from the lamp while she dressed in jeans and a sweatshirt. She tugged a brush through her hair and snapped it into a rubber band.

She slipped on her shoes, quickly grabbed the keys and tiptoed out, locking the bedroom door from the inside and pulling it shut after her.

She paused at the top of the stairs, recalling the horror of seeing Sandra's broken body at the bottom. But she forced herself to move down them, through the foyer and then out the front door.

She got into Dylan's car, inserted the key, but didn't start the engine. She only turned the key enough to release the steering wheel, then shifted into neutral and coasted as far as she could down the drive. Only then did she start the car, and put it in gear. She flicked the headlights on when she reached the road.

She drove slowly, feeling her way. She hadn't driven a car since the accident, and it was terrifying to do so now. But she had to. She had to see . . .

She knew where the cemetery was. She'd passed it yesterday in the taxi. And she found it again with no trouble, despite the darkness. She pulled the car to the side of the road and shut off the engine. She left the keys in the switch, in her hurry to find her son.

The wrought-iron gate stood slightly crooked, like an aged sentry who put duty before comfort. It was closed, and a chain was wrapped around the bars with a padlock for a pendant. To prevent vandalism, she assumed. It had been open when she'd passed it by day. She moved through the damp, scraggly grass, along the short brick wall that surrounded the place, and easily climbed over it. It was really rather silly to have a padlocked gate when the wall was so easily scaled. She dropped to the ground on the other side, then just stood amid rows and rows of markers.

The night wind ruffled her hair. It smelled of fresh flowers, and old ones, and of the sea. Crickets chirped incessantly. The moon's whispered glow slanted into the place, making odd-shaped shadows around the stones. But the moon hung low in the sky, and soon it would disappear entirely. There were a few huge trees, looming like guardians of the dead.

She belatedly wished she'd brought along a flashlight. How would she ever find little David here?

But she began at the first row of markers, barely able to discern the names engraved in the stone in the pale moonlight. And she moved quickly, from stone to stone, searching, her heart breaking into millions of tiny bits. And when she finished with one row, she moved to the next.

It took the better part of an hour to find it. The marker was longer than it was high. The front was adorned with a tiny, sweet-faced angel, kneeling with hands folded in prayer. It read, Our Beloved Son, David Dylan Rossi. Fresh flowers covered the grave. Lilies, pale blue carnations, baby's breath for the baby who'd never drawn one. And yellow roses.

Caitlin ran her hand over the face of the cold stone, her fingers tracing the letters of his name. The pain was too much for anyone to bear and still live. Too much. She sank to her knees, pressing her face to the stone, giving way to the tears she'd cried too often lately. And then she sank lower, until her body was pressed to the fine, new grass that covered her child. She pushed her face into the moist, green blades, and sobbed as she never had before.

When the tears finally began to subside, she sat up again, shakily. She gathered the yellow roses to her breast and bent to inhale their scent. Who'd put them here? Dylan? God, was this as painful to him as it was to her? Why hadn't he told her? Why keep something so vital a secret?

Thinking of Dylan reminded her how long she'd been here. Though time had passed without her awareness, she knew she'd been gone a long while. The moon was gone now. Soon the sky would begin to lighten with the approaching dawn. She wanted to get back before anyone realized she'd gone.

She got to her feet, surprised at the weakness her crying had left in her. She shouldn't be surprised, she supposed. She hadn't been eating right, or getting much sleep at all. Her body needed some TLC, or she'd end up in worse shape than she'd been before.

She walked, dragging her feet, back to the short wall. Then stopped, turning abruptly. She'd heard something, some sound or movement behind her.

She scanned the darkness, senses alert, her pulse accelerating to a constant thrum in her ears. But every shadow could have concealed some waiting evil. There was nothing distinct. Fear shivered up her spine and she climbed over the wall, and hurried to the car. She got in, locked all the doors and reached for the switch, to turn the key.

Only the keys weren't there.

She frowned hard. *I know I left them in the switch. Didn't I?*

Maybe not. She'd been upset, not thinking clearly. She checked the pockets of her jeans and felt nothing. Oh, hell, could she have dropped them when she'd climbed the wall? Or when she'd lain prostrate on the ground, sobbing for her lost baby?

She glanced uneasily through the windshield, eyes straining. She saw no one. She was alone with her grief and her fears. She unlocked the door and got out, starting back for the cemetery. She stooped near the wall where she'd gone in and felt around in the grass, to no avail. Then she climbed over and repeated the vain process on the other side. Nothing. Sighing, she made her way back to the headstone. If she didn't find the keys there, she'd have to retrace her steps through the entire place as she'd searched for the grave. But as she approached her child's grave site, a slow, smooth motion caught her eye. She squinted in the darkness.

A length of rope dangled from a huge tree, a hangman's noose at its end. She froze, stark terror rinsing her in icy water. She screamed in horror and turned to run back the way she'd come.

Something came around her throat, something smooth and firm, and tight, growing tighter with every second, choking off her airway. She grasped at it with both hands, clawing her own skin, trying to get her fingers behind the leather. But the tightening only went on.

She couldn't breathe! She kicked backward with one foot, but connected with nothing. She was dying! God, someone was killing her and she was helpless to fight.

She was dizzy. Huge black spots danced in and out of her vision, followed by bright red ones that seemed like little explosions in her brain. And then utter blackness swallowed her up.

CHAPTER THIRTEEN

Dylan had tucked Lizzie in and returned to the bedroom to find Cait gone, and the note on his bed. That she wanted him to leave her alone was clear, but he was uncomfortable with the notion. He told himself it wasn't because he'd so looked forward to making love to her again, or because he'd dreamed for so long of holding her all night long and waking with her in his arms, snuggled against him. He told himself it was just that he was worried about her. She hadn't told him about her nightmare, but he didn't believe for a minute that she'd forgotten it. It was something she was keeping to herself. He tried to respect that, along with her need for privacy, but after an hour of tossing restlessly, he gave in to his greater need to know she was all right.

He pulled on jeans and a T-shirt, and went to her room, only to find the door locked from the inside. So he knocked, and waited.

No answer.

He knocked again, harder this time. "Caity. Come on, answer me. I'll go away if you want, I just want to know you're okay."

Still no answer, and panic began to spread through him. He pounded again. "Caity! Dammit, answer me! Caity!"

When he only heard silence, visions of her lying in a pool of blood on the floor assaulted him. He took two steps backward and kicked the door open.

She wasn't there. The room looked the same as it had earlier. The lamp shattered on the floor. The bloody footprints on the carpet. Then he spotted the little card on the nightstand and his heart flipped over. He picked it up, knowing already what it was.

He closed his eyes tightly. "Oh, God, she knows. But she wouldn't have gone there. Not at night, not alone..."

With dawning dread, he realized that his keys were no longer in his pocket, and when he raced down the stairs to the front door, he saw that his car wasn't out front, either.

But the battered pickup was. He ran to it, jumped in and found the extra key he kept in the ashtray, just in case. The engine roared to life, and Dylan shifted into gear and pressed the accelerator to the floor with his bare foot.

He was driving too fast. He knew he was, but he couldn't slow down. The feeling of impending doom assaulted him with killing force, and the pickup rocked up on two wheels as he rounded sharp curves without letting up. The headlights barely cut through the gloom enough to guide his way as he careered over the writhing roads toward Eden, toward the cemetery where he and Cait had buried their tiny child months ago... the cemetery where she'd fainted in his arms from sheer grief. He couldn't stand the thought of her there, alone, slowly regaining the memory of her most gut-wrenching experience. She couldn't handle it. Not yet, not alone. God, it still twisted *his* insides into knots to go there every week with fresh flowers.

He skidded to a stop when the pickup's headlights glinted off the metallic surface of his car, parked near the cemetery gates. He leapt out, and vaulted the wall.

He saw a flashlight moving through the darkness from the other side of the graveyard. Heard a gruff, male voice call, "What's goin' on out here? Who's there?"

He ran toward that voice, even as he heard the sound of running feet, retreating in another direction. He moved forward, tripping twice, falling down on hands and knees and lunging to his feet just as fast.

The third time he tripped, it was over a woman's still body.

"My God, Caity!" He gripped her shoulders, shook her gently. Then he saw the belt wrapped around her slender throat, and his heart tripped to a stop in his chest. He snatched the damned thing away and pulled her to him, holding her gently, rocking her, murmuring her name over and over. "Don't die, Caity, not now. Please, not now."

"Let go of that woman, mister."

He lifted his head, only to be blinded by the beam of a flashlight aimed directly at his face.

"She's my wife. Call an ambulance for God's sake, she's dying!"

"Already did that, when I heard the screams. Po-lice, too. So why don't you just stand up, nice and easy, and leave her be till they get here."

Dylan only shook his head and clutched her more tightly.

"Leave her be, mister. I got a twelve-gauge pointed at yer head, and I'd hate to have to use it."

Dylan stiffened, but he lowered her to the cool grass, and looked up, squinting in the beam of light. The light moved then, and caught a noose swaying slowly in the breeze, hanging from a tree right above him.

"Yer one sick son of a bitch, you know that?"

She was lying on a hard surface, in a small, enclosed place. Strangers hovered over her. A mask covered her face, bathing her nose and mouth in cold, sterile-smelling air. Her throat hurt. Her lungs burned. Her head throbbed.

"She's coming around."

"Mrs. Rossi. Mrs. Rossi, can you hear me?"

She nodded at the fresh-faced young man who leaned over her. He wore white, and beyond the open doors at her feet, she saw flashing lights, breaking the dawn with color. She tried to sit up, only to have the young man hold her shoulders in place. "Take it easy, now. You're going to be okay."

"Pulse is stronger. BP's gaining," another, older man said.

In the flashing light through the open doors, she saw Dylan looking rumpled, in jeans and a T-shirt. He was barefoot, and he stood nose to nose with Detective Barnes. It looked as if they were arguing.

Dimly, she recalled what had happened. The darkness, the noose, the grim certainty that she was going to die when her life was being choked out of her.

Dylan was here. What the hell was he doing here? Oh, God, it hadn't been him. It *couldn't have been* him.

The doors swung closed, and the vehicle lurched into motion.

Broad daylight filtered into her hospital room. She'd been examined, X-rayed, poked and prodded until the doctors were certain she was going to be all right.

Now she lay in the bed, sipping ice cola through a straw, letting it soothe her throat, and watching Detective Barnes pace the room.

"I need to get out of here."

He cocked one eyebrow at her, and stopped pacing. "I was told you'd have to stay overnight for observation."

"No."

He frowned at her, then shrugged. "Up to you, I guess. But not until you tell me everything. And don't leave anything out, Mrs. Rossi. Don't try to protect him anymore. We have him cold this time."

Her heart skipped a beat. "Have you arrested Dylan?"

His lips thinned. "He's being held for formal questioning. His answers at the scene didn't cut it."

"I want to be there."

"What?"

"When you question him. I want to be there. I want to hear the answers." She caught Barnes's gaze and held it. "I *need* to be there."

He was silent for a long time. Finally, he nodded. "Need to hear it for yourself, is that it? I can arrange it."

She sighed her relief, and leaned back on the pillows.

"So what happened last night?"

She closed her eyes. "I found out I'd had a child. He was stillborn, in January."

"Your husband hadn't told you about it?"

She shook her head.

"Then how did you find out?"

She licked her lips. "I found the fetal death certificate."

"Ah."

"I wanted to see the grave. I don't know why, I just felt this need to be there, close to him."

"Understandable." He paced again, nearer the bed, then sat in the chair beside it.

"But I wanted to be alone. I left Dylan a note, telling him not to bother me, and then took his car keys. I locked my bedroom from the inside. Then I took the car and drove to the cemetery."

"Anyone follow you?"

She shrugged. "I probably wouldn't have noticed if they had. I was pretty upset."

"I'll bet you were." He leaned forward in his chair. "So you found the place."

"Yes."

"See any other cars there? Anyone hanging around?"

"No."

"So?"

"I visited the grave for a while. I'm not sure how long. Then I went back to the car. Only the keys were gone. I thought I'd left them in the switch, but they weren't there." She sighed, pressing her hand to her pounding head. "I thought I might have dropped them, so I went back to the grave to look for them." She shuddered and closed her eyes tight. "There was a noose, hanging from a tree. I think I screamed, and I turned to run back to the car. But something came around my throat from behind.'' The horror of that feeling, of not being able to breathe, of certain death looming right in front of her, brought new tears to her eyes. She covered her face with both hands.

''It's all right.'' A heavy hand closed on her shoulder. ''It's all right, you're fine.''

She sniffed, lowered her hands and nodded. ''That's all I remember. I couldn't breathe. I passed out.''

He nodded. ''You didn't get a sense of who it was? Did he say anything? Maybe you caught a whiff of cologne, or—''

''No. Nothing.'' She met his concerned gaze, searched it. ''What stopped him from killing me? Why was that awful noose hanging there?''

Barnes shook his head. ''My best guess is that the killer planned to make it look like a suicide. Leave you...'' He didn't finish.

He didn't have to. ''Leave me hanging from the tree above my son's grave. Oh, God...'' A sob choked her.

''The caretaker lives right next door. He heard your screams. He had his wife call 911 while he grabbed his shotgun and headed out to see what was happening. I figure that your... that the killer stopped what he was doing when the old man called out.''

''Thank God,'' she whispered.

''Mrs. Rossi, when he got there, he found your husband crouching over you. He didn't see or hear anyone else.''

A cold feeling chilled her to the bone. ''What did Dylan say?''

Barnes frowned and shook his head. ''Let's go find out.''

The mirror was two-way, he had no doubt about it. But he didn't really give a damn. ''I want to know how she is.''

''You answer my questions, and then we'll discuss your wife, Rossi.''

Dylan clenched his fists on the surface of the table. "Is she alive?"

Barnes pursed his lips and Dylan felt like bloodying them for him. "Questions first. You want a lawyer present?"

"I don't need a freaking lawyer."

"Good. Sign here." He shoved a form across the table, then took a pen from his pocket and tossed it down. Dylan scratched his name across the bottom, and shoved it back.

Barnes took a long look at it, nodded and leaned back in the chair opposite Dylan's. "So tell me what happened last night."

"I told you at the cemetery."

"Take it from the top, Rossi. I have all day."

Dylan's glare did nothing to erase the smug expression Barnes wore. He'd get this over with so he could find out about Caity. The sooner the better. Dammit, if she'd died…he bit his lip at the thought. She couldn't have died. Not now.

"She had a bad dream. I found her crying in the nursery, took her to my room. I wanted her where I could be sure she was okay. Later, the baby was crying, so I got up to check on her. Cait was sound asleep when I left her."

"So far, so good. Keep going."

Dylan sighed hard and fought to keep a rein on his temper. "When I came back, she was gone. She left a note. I'm sure your guys have found that by now."

"Hell, yes. Found a few other goodies in your room, too." He took a plastic zipper bag from his huge manila envelope and dangled it like bait from a hook. "Ever seen this before?"

Dylan frowned and looked at the bottle encased in the plastic bag. "Carob powder?" He felt a chill pass over his spine.

"Have you seen it before?" Barnes repeated, his voice booming.

"No. Where did you—"

"Your medicine cabinet, Rossi."

Dylan nodded. "So, someone's trying to frame me. Isn't that pretty obvious, *Detective?*

Barnes only eyed him as though Dylan was something bad, as though he were a hunk of rotten meat on a platter. "So you found the note. Then what?"

"I lay in bed for a while. An hour or so. I couldn't sleep without knowing she was okay, so I went to check on her."

"Waited a whole hour, huh?"

"She made it clear she didn't want to be bothered." Dylan shook his head. "You aren't buying a word of this. It's bull, a waste of time. You've already decided I'm guilty."

"That's not my job, Rossi. You went to check on her…"

"The door was locked. She didn't answer. I got worried, kicked it in. Found the card on the dresser and guessed she'd gone to the grave. When I found the car gone, I was sure of it, so I took the pickup and went after her." He shook off the chill of precognition that had swept over him when he'd seen his car parked at the cemetery gate, and eyed Barnes. "How am I doing so far?"

"Word for word what you told me at the scene. Well rehearsed. You're smooth. I've seen smoother."

"Go to hell, Barnes."

"Been there for a long time now, Rossi. Finish the fairy tale, will you?"

Dylan shook his head. "I jumped the wall. Heard the old man call out, saw his light. I heard someone running away, and then I found her."

Barnes nodded. "You said that before, that you heard someone running away. Old man Crandall didn't hear a thing."

"He was running, too, toward me, ready to give me both barrels of that shotgun he was lugging. He might not have heard the other guy's steps over his own. But I did. Someone ran, toward the east side of the cemetery."

Barnes's eyes were still skeptical. He reached into the envelope again. A bigger plastic bag emerged this time, with a leather belt inside. "Reco'nize this?"

Dylan's neck prickled. He took the bag and examined the belt. There was no sense lying about it. His initials were engraved in the leather. "It's mine."

"Your fingerprints are on it, Rossi. And hers. No one else's."

"I took it off her neck, you bastard."

"How?"

The guy wasn't ruffled, not in the least. Dylan imagined he had lots of experience trying to make people sweat like this. "I don't know. I was scared. My wife was lying there as good as dead. I just yanked it off her, okay?"

"Your prints were here," Barnes pointed to one end of the belt. "And here," he added pointing to the other end. "Hers were only in the center, where she struggled to pull the thing away as she was being strangled." He stood and walked slowly away, then back again. "Your prints were where the killer would have been holding the belt, Rossi. Where you held it as you choked the life out of your wife."

Dylan felt a fist pummel his gut. "Are you saying...she's dead?"

Barnes only continued staring at him. Waiting for him to break?

Dylan came out of the chair like a shot, reached across the table and gripped Barnes by the front of his splashy print shirt. "Tell me, you bastard!"

The door burst open and two uniformed cops ran through, each gripping one of Dylan's arms and jerking him away from Barnes.

"Cuff him," Barnes ordered, straightening his shirt as if he hadn't a care in the world.

Then a soft cry from the still-open door drew Dylan's gaze. Caitlin stood there in the doorway. Her eyes huge, round, her pupils too dilated to be normal. She stood there, just staring at him, as handcuffs were snapped around his wrists, pulled behind his back.

"Caity..."

She blinked, but kept looking at him from those hollow, haunted eyes.

God, the relief that coursed through him almost made his legs give out. She was okay. He wanted to hold her, to run his hands through her wild hair, to kiss her. But his relief at seeing her on her feet, breathing, was short-lived. Her expressionless face, the hurt and fear he saw etched into it, were like daggers in his heart.

He saw the red marks at her throat, the purplish bruises that were already forming. There were garish scratches on her neck, and he shuddered as he envisioned her clawing at the belt, trying to pull it away. She was pale, too pale, and dark circles under her eyes made her look as if she'd been in a fight and lost.

The cops moved him forward until he stood right in front of her, at the doorway. He wanted to reach out, to pull her into his arms and hold her until that turmoil in her eyes calmed. But he couldn't with his hands cuffed behind him. He wished to hell she would say something. Anything. "Caity—"

"You'll have to step aside, Mrs. Rossi," Barnes ordered, tugging gently at her shoulders until she obeyed. But her eyes remained on Dylan, and his on her. "Dylan Rossi, I'm placing you under arrest for the attempted murder of your wife."

Caitlin's eyes fell closed, not softly or gently. They slammed shut like the doors of a prison, and squeezed themselves together hard. And then the two cops shoved him through the door.

"Don't go home, Caity!" Dylan shouted over his shoulder. "Don't go back there. It isn't safe!" He heard no answer as he was pushed through a hallway toward the back of the building.

Barnes opened a cell, and unceremoniously shoved him through. He closed the door. "Turn around and stick your hands through the bars so I can take the cuffs off."

Dylan did, putting his desperate hurt and paralyzing fear for his wife aside, converting it to anger, which he vented on the man who twisted a key in the manacles at his wrists. "You haven't Mirandaized me, Barnes. Slipping up in your old age?"

The cuffs fell free and Dylan turned to face the man. Barnes slipped a little card from his shirt pocket and stuck it through. "Read that."

Dylan took the card, glanced at it and read the first line. "You have the right to remain silent." He'd shot that one to hell already, hadn't he? And it had probably been a stupid mistake, but dammit, he'd had to know about Caity. He shook his head and slipped the card back to Barnes.

"Understand?"

Dylan looked at him, lifting his eyebrows. "What?"

"Your rights, do you understand them?"

"Oh, hell, yes, Barnes. You really have a knack for communication." Dylan won the stare-down. Barnes's gaze flicked away. Dylan's searched the man for a weak spot. "You don't have enough to indict me."

"I think I do." He shrugged. "Either way, you won't be offing your wife today. I'll sleep better knowing that."

"Don't sleep too soundly, Barnes. She still isn't safe. Dammit, it wasn't me, but someone sure as hell tried to kill her. She needs protection."

Barnes's gaze narrowed. "Nice try, Rossi."

"Dammit, I'm begging you. Give her some kind of protection. She's just stubborn enough to go back there today."

Barnes nodded. "Especially if she believes her attacker is safely behind bars. Looked to me like she was finally convinced, Rossi. How'd she look to you?"

"You're enjoying this, aren't you?"

Barnes shrugged again. "Can't help it. I honestly like the lady. She's got that innocent, trusting quality, makes a guy want to look out for her." He shook his head. "Makes a slug like you want to take her for everything she's got and throw her away. You're a fool, you know that?"

Dylan frowned, wondering at the softening in Barnes's voice, the slightly tormented look in his eyes. "You feel like protecting her, then go for it, Barnes. Look out for her, 'cause you've got me caged up and I can't. She still needs watching over. I swear it."

"You know, you almost have me convinced."

"Did she tell you about the divorce?" Dylan knew he was grasping at straws, but he had to try. "She canceled the old settlement. Had a new one drawn up. She doesn't get a damn thing, now. I have no motive to kill her."

"What, you think greed is the only motive that drives a man to murder his wife?"

"If she dies while I'm stuck here, Barnes, I'll make sure you pay."

"You don't scare me, Rossi."

"I'm the one that's scared here. Dammit, she's a walking target. Will you think about that? What if you're wrong, huh? What the hell is going to happen to her then?"

Barnes frowned through the bars. "You're damned convincing, I'll give you that." He turned to walk away from the cell, handcuffs dangling from his fingers.

"Assign a man to watch her, Barnes. If you have one decent cell in your body, protect her!" Dylan shouted after him as he got farther away. "Suppose you have the wrong man, Barnes! Suppose the real killer gets to her while I'm here. You gonna be able to live with that? Are you? Barnes!"

Barnes didn't answer, only kept strolling down the hall as though he were taking a walk through the park.

CHAPTER FOURTEEN

"Cait, God, I'm glad you're back." Thomas hugged her hard, but Caitlin remained stiff in his arms, feeling shell-shocked.

"Police have been here, snoopin' all over the place. That Barnes, he's a corker," Ellen snapped. "Said you were in the hospital, but wouldn't say why. Time we called, you'd checked out."

Caitlin freed herself from her brother's grip, and faced the older woman. How on earth was she going to tell her that Dylan had been arrested?

"You look ill, so pale and weak. You need to eat and rest, *non?*" Genevieve hovered with a worried expression. "I can get something for you—"

"No, Genevieve. I'll be fine, really." Her gaze moved around the living room, where they'd all gathered, but she didn't see Lizzie. Henri lurked in the arched doorway that led to the library, just watching, silent.

"What happened last night? There was another attempt on your life, wasn't there, Cait?"

She met her brother's concerned eyes, thinking his fear for her sounded genuine, and simply nodded. She hated suspecting he—or any of them—could be capable of murder. But if Dylan wasn't guilty, then someone else was. She'd only come back here to find out who... and for Lizzie.

His gaze narrowed, moving over her body as if in search of her injuries, then stopped on her vividly bruised throat, and widened. "Oh, my God."

"It isn't as bad as it looks."

"Where's Dylan?" Ellen demanded. "He took off outta here last night like his tail was afire, just a short while after that other car roared away. Made enough racket to wake the dead, that one did."

Caitlin closed her eyes tight. "They've arrested him."

Thomas froze, his eyes the only part of him that moved at all, and then, only to widen.

Caitlin dragged her feet as she made her way to the sofa, and sat down. "I went to the cemetery last night, to see my son. I guess Dylan came after me." She bit her lip hard, tasting blood on her tongue. "Someone tried to strangle me there, and then the caretaker came out to find Dylan bending over me."

"Did he do it, Cait?" Thomas sat beside her, gripped her hand in both of his.

"I was unconscious. I never saw—"

"But what do you *feel?*"

She shook her head slowly. "His fingerprints were on the belt that was twisted around my throat," she whispered, her voice straining painfully just to do that much. "The caretaker didn't see anyone else."

"But did he do it?"

She broke then. Sobs racked her frame, jerking her body with each assault, and she bent nearly double, covering her face with both hands. "I . . . I don't know."

"Damn fool girl!" Ellen's voice sounded close to Caitlin, and she felt her head jerked up by a cruel hand in her hair.

Thomas leapt to his feet, gripping Ellen's shoulders in a firm, but gentle hold. "Let her go! I know this is tough for you to take, Ellen, but—"

"The man's so in love with you, he doesn't know which way is up! And what does it get him? You're poison to him, Caitlin O'Brien. I always said you'd ruin him someday and now you've gone and done it!"

"Ellen, I—"

"And you're bound to stand by and watch him prosecuted for this. It's gonna kill him."

"Better him than my sister, Ellen."

"It wasn't Dylan who tried to wring your neck, girl, but it should'a been. He'd have left you long ago if it hadn't been for that baby. Him and his pipe dreams that it would change things, that you two could start over. He should have left then."

But he hadn't, Caitlin whispered to herself. He hadn't, and there were eight months between the stillbirth and the car accident. Why? She swallowed hard. No one could answer that question but Dylan.

"I won't see him tried for this, Caitlin," Ellen shouted, though she was standing so close, Caitlin could see the depth of each wrinkle in her face and the deep brown of her eyes. It was a little surprising to realize how very beautiful her eyes were, even now. So dark and deep. So like Dylan's. "I won't stand for it. I'll kill you myself first!"

The older woman turned to stalk out of the room, toward the stairs.

"Ellen, wait. You can't just condemn me like this when I—" Caitlin got to her feet and followed on Ellen's heels as the old woman kept on going. "Ellen, I'm the victim here. I'm the one who—oh, for God's sake. Where are you going?"

"Upstairs. Got some calls to make. A lawyer, and then my nephew, if they'll even let me talk to him. If not, I have a few things to say to that Barnes character." She struck off up the wide stairway, and disappeared into the hall.

Caitlin let her chin fall to her chest as all the air left her lungs. Thomas's hand on her shoulder gave little comfort. "You'll be okay, sis. I'll help you through this. I gotta say, I can't believe that Dylan..." His voice trailed off, and he shook his head. "I just can't believe it."

Caitlin was having trouble believing it herself. "Where's Lizzie?"

"The nursery. Having a nap, last time I checked."

Caitlin nodded, and gripped the banister in one hand. "I have to be with her for a little while. I need . . ."

"It's okay. I know."

She blinked fresh tears away as she stared up at her brother. "Don't ever forget how precious she is, Thomas." Then she turned and dragged one foot after the other, up the stairs. Part of her wanted to go to Ellen's room, to try to convince the woman that she wasn't out to destroy Dylan. But she knew it would be of little use.

She brought the baby into her room, and spread a blanket on the floor for her to lie on. Lizzie kicked her feet, and thrashed her arms, cooing and spitting and sticking out her tongue, as her wide eyes fixed first on one strange object, then another. Caitlin spread toys all around the baby, then got down on the blanket herself to play.

And as she did, shaking rattles to capture Lizzie's attention, letting the baby reach for them, seeing her huge blue eyes reflect joy and innocence and acceptance, Caitlin recalled the way Dylan had looked as he'd held Lizzie last night. Patiently, he'd paced the nursery's length, rubbing and patting her little back, snuggling her close to him. And singing.

"You wouldn't believe it, would you, Lizzie?" Cait lay on her side, her head close enough so Lizzie could catch handfuls of her aunt's hair and tug and twist it. "If you could talk, you'd swear your Uncle Dylan was the most gentle man on the planet. You'd never doubt him . . ."

A small hand smacked against Caitlin's cheek repeatedly as Lizzie made gurgling sounds.

". . . the way I have."

She sat up slowly, wrapping the baby up in her arms and holding her close. Lizzie chewed on Caitlin's chin. "It wasn't him, was it, Lizzie? It couldn't have been. And if it wasn't, then it had to be someone else. Someone else left this house last night after I did, followed me to the cemetery and..."

Her face fell, and she held Lizzie at arm's length, as the baby laughed out loud and kicked wildly. "Oh, but they couldn't have. Ellen was awake, and she said she only heard two vehicles leave, last night. First mine, and then—"

Cait blinked. "No. She *heard* two vehicles, but three drove out of here last night. She never heard me. Remember? I coasted the car all the way to the end of the driveway before I started it up, and then eased my way onto the road. No one could have heard me leave. There was someone else."

She lowered Lizzie to the blanket again. Lying beside her, with her head pillowed by a silky brown teddy bear. "Dylan is innocent," she whispered. "The question is, what can we do to prove it?"

Barnes led a team through the cemetery as soon as he'd closed the cell door on Rossi. There was something about this case that was bothering him. From day one, he'd been half-convinced Rossi was trying to kill his wife. But now that he'd locked the guy up, he wasn't so sure. He shook his head, and told himself not to lose his objectivity. It was tough, though. He wanted to protect Caitlin Rossi, and to catch the slug that was trying to hurt her more than he'd wanted anything in a long, long time.

He wanted Rossi to turn out to be innocent, because he could see how much Caitlin wanted it. The way she felt about the guy just about glared from those green eyes of hers. He knew she'd be devastated to find out her husband was capable of killing her. Now, he was probably letting that wishful thinking cloud his judgment, because there was no evidence that Rossi was anything *but* guilty.

Still, there'd been something in Rossi's eyes when he'd begged him to put a tail on his wife, to protect her. Fear.

Desperation. Sincerity. Frustration. All of it. Not a hint of cunning, or the whisper of deceit.

And that was why Barnes had dragged the forensics boys back here again. Rossi had said he heard someone running away, toward the east side of the boneyard. When Barnes thought about that, he realized that if another vehicle *had* been parked on that side, neither the victim, the suspect nor the witness would have been in a position to see it there. So he'd sent a car out to keep an eye on the Rossi house, and on Caitlin Rossi in particular. And he'd brought the crew to look for evidence of a fourth person here last night.

But after an hour of combing the place, they had little more to go on. The roadside was gravel, not a good receptacle for tire tracks. And the grass in the cemetery itself was too dense and close-cropped to pick up footprints.

Barnes was about to give up. He didn't want to believe Rossi was lying, but there was no evidence here to suggest he was telling the truth. Then one of his men yelled, and Barnes jogged toward him.

When Barnes reached him, Melbourne was picking the scrap of material from the brick wall with a pair of tweezers. He held it up for inspection, then dropped it into an evidence bag.

"What do you make of it?" Barnes asked.

Melbourne straightened his glasses, holding the bag in front of them and squinting at it as if he could read words written across the material inside. "It hasn't been here long. Two days at the most. A few hours at the least. The sun and rain would've faded some of this color if it had been out here longer. See? It's really vivid red."

"What'd it come from?"

Melbourne shrugged. "Could be just about anything. We'll run some tests on it, see if there's a hair, or a skin cell or a drop of blood, maybe sweat or saliva if we're lucky."

The square of cloth was uneven, and not more than three by four inches in size. Barnes wasn't hopeful. Then again,

Rossi hadn't been wearing anything red last night. Neither had his wife, nor Stanley Crandall, the caretaker.

She woke with a start, ashamed to have been sleeping so deeply when Dylan was sitting in a jail cell somewhere. Still, she supposed she'd be able to think more clearly now than she could have before. She'd been exhausted, and from the looks of the dim sky, she'd slept several hours.

Lizzie was still snoozing peacefully. The baby had a habit of sleeping the afternoon away. Storing up her energy to keep every adult in the house up all night, Caitlin theorized.

She got up, realized she was still wearing the jeans and sweatshirt from the night before, and thought longingly of a long bath and a hot meal. She conceded to the bath, and put a clean white muslin nightgown on. She intended to go down to the kitchen, fix herself a snack and plot her next move.

She tiptoed past Lizzie, stepped quietly into the hallway and then to the stairs. She was barefoot, and made little sound as she traversed the hall, and descended the stairs. The chill house was quiet, and the living room dim. Light spilled from the library door, though it was opened only a crack. She heard muted voices, padded footsteps, a clink of ice against glass. Caitlin stopped in her tracks. Her lack of sleep these past few nights, or the past few missed meals, must be dulling her senses. She'd come down here wondering how she could prove Dylan innocent. It followed then, that someone else was guilty of trying to kill her. Of murdering Sandra. Someone in this very house. That hadn't changed with Dylan's arrest.

A chill snaked up her spine. Part of her wanted to turn and run, but she refused to heed that part. She needed to know the truth.

Slowly, Caitlin moved toward the doorway.

She heard Genevieve softly whisper, "Thomas, why? I love you, you know that."

"I just can't live with the guilt anymore, Genevieve. This is wrong. It's always been wrong."

Genevieve, assuming he'd meant guilt about cheating on his wife, Caitlin surmised, sighed loudly. "How can it be wrong, when we love each other, Thomas? When is love wrong?"

"What I did to Sandra was wrong, dammit!"

Caitlin shivered violently.

"You never meant—"

"No, Genevieve. It's over. Don't make this any harder on me than it already is. Please. Just accept it. I have to focus on Lizzie now, try to be a good father to her, try to atone—"

"You are a fool to throw me away, Thomas O'Brien!"

Genevieve exited the room, slamming the door behind her, and came face-to-face with Caitlin. Caitlin swallowed her shock, and her fear. She felt a wave of pity for Genevieve. She was so quiet, so delicate-looking. It was awful that she'd been hurt. But God, she should have known better than to involve herself with a married man.

Caitlin put a hand on Genevieve's shoulder. "I'm sorry, Genevieve. If you want to take some time off, you know, think things through, I won't mind a bit."

Genevieve dipped her head, focusing on the little red cloak draped over her arm, rather than looking Caitlin in the eye, now that Caitlin obviously knew about the affair. "That is very kind of you, *madame*."

Genevieve sniffed. "I think I would like to lie down for a while, if you don't need me."

"Go ahead. Oh, and Genevieve, if you hear Lizzie crying, would you just give me a call? I hate to leave her alone in my room, but I need to talk to my brother."

Genevieve nodded, and smiled softly. "Do not worry. I will watch over little Lizzie for you."

Caitlin watched Genevieve ascend the stairs, then faced the library door again, biting her lip. Aside from Dylan, Thomas was the one person with the most to gain by Caitlin's death. He'd inherit half of her estate, which he probably felt he was entitled to, anyway. He'd also had a motive to kill his wife: his affair with Genevieve. Besides that, it seemed pretty clear that the guilty party not only wanted Caitlin dead, but Dylan convicted of the crime. And she'd heard with her own ears her brother's words about "showing" Dylan, teaching him a lesson.

But she'd never dreamed he'd meant anything like this. Her own brother! She'd just been beginning to feel some kind of bond with him. Could he really want her dead?

She looked up at the library door again, and suppressed a shiver. Was it wise to confront him now?

She licked her lips, stiffened her resolve. She couldn't let cowardice keep her from learning the truth. Henri and Genevieve were both within shouting distance. And there was the police cruiser, passing out front every few minutes like a shark circling its next meal.

Thomas was pouring whiskey into a shot glass when she entered, and she was painfully reminded of the night she'd walked in to see Dylan holding that same bottle. She missed him, she realized slowly. Missed him, hell, she ached for him.

But first things first. "Hello, Thomas."

He turned, startled, slopping a few drops from the shotglass onto the back of the hand that held it. "Caitlin."

She stayed a good distance away from him. She was still afraid, and not even her own mental reassurances that she was safe, dulled that fear. He wouldn't hurt her with witnesses so close, or with the police keeping such a close eye on the house.

"I think it's about time we had a talk. Don't you?" She tried to sound calm, but her voice trembled slightly.

He nodded, took a deep swig of whiskey and smacked his lips. "I'm not going to deny it. It's pretty obvious you overheard the whole thing. I've been a real bastard, Cait. I wanted so much..." He looked at the floor and shook his head.

"You wanted it all. With me dead, you'd inherit half of my money. With Dylan in jail for killing me, you'd probably end up with his share, as well."

She watched his face as she delivered her accusation. His head came up, his eyes widened and his skin paled. "You really believe all that?"

"What else am I supposed to believe?"

He frowned, shook his head. "Cait, I don't want to believe it was Dylan any more than you do, but for God's sake—"

"It wasn't him, Thomas. He wouldn't hurt me. He wouldn't hurt anybody."

"And you think *I would?*" He slugged back the rest of his drink, slammed the glass on a stand, and the sound reverberated through her nerve endings like an electric shock. "I'm your *brother!*"

"And you resent me for inheriting from our father when you didn't." She forced herself to go on, to carry this thing through and learn the truth. "You resent that I selfishly refused to share what I got from him, and to tell you the truth, I don't blame you for that." A lump leapt into her throat. "But it wasn't worth killing for, Thomas. My God, your own wife—"

"I didn't kill Sandra!"

"You thought she was me!"

"No!"

"Thomas, I just stood outside this door and heard you say you felt guilty for what you'd done to her."

He lifted his hands, palms up, and gaped, shaking his head in confusion. "I *do* feel guilty. For having an affair.

For being a lousy father to Lizzie and a worse husband. I feel guilty for what I've been planning..."

"To murder me and frame my husband and take everything we own? Is that what you've been planning, Thomas?"

His eyes turned accusatory and he lunged at her, gripping her wrists before she could back away. Her heart skidded to a stop and she prepared to cut loose with a scream that would bring someone running.

"I can't believe what I'm hearing! Dammit, Cait, all I was planning was to buy enough stock to force Dylan to make me his partner."

She blinked, and closed her gaping mouth. "Wh-what?"

Thomas eased his grip on her forearms and shook his head sadly. "Hell, I can't blame you for thinking the worst of me. I've been acting like an idiot. Blaming you for our father's rejection of me, hating you for having money when I didn't. Just like I blamed Sandra for making me marry her when she got pregnant. I felt trapped. I only wanted to get free. I didn't know how good I had it until she was gone." He lowered his eyes, turned and sunk onto the sofa as tears shimmered in them. "She deserved better than me, better than what I gave her."

Caitlin was shocked. She moved to the sofa, sat down beside her brother, touched his shoulder lightly, still uncertain. "Go on, Thomas. Explain this to me."

He sniffed, met her eyes. "Dylan only hired me because of you. He resented it, and for a long time, he never noticed I was actually doing a good job. I think he expected me to be a freeloader. I really do. I worked my butt off for him, Cait. I wanted more than I had and I was willing to pay for it."

He shook his head. "He promoted me a couple of times, sure. But never let me show him what I could really do. I thought if I bought enough stock to put me in a position of authority, he'd have to see. So I've been putting money aside, buying small chunks of stock whenever I can afford it. I knew he'd resent it at first, but I thought...hell, I don't know. I thought we'd end up working together, as equals, mutual respect and all that bull." He shook his head.

He stared into her eyes, and she felt him willing her to believe. "Cait, I was planning to divorce Sandra. I thought I wanted to be with Genevieve. I even told Genevieve about my buying the stock, and becoming Dylan's partner some day."

She didn't say a word, just sat there, wishing she could believe him.

"God, I can't believe you think I could actually try to kill you. Cait, we haven't been close in a long time. And I may have resented you and let myself become filled with bitterness and jealousy, but I never hated you. I swear it."

She wanted to believe him, but...

"If it wasn't you, Thomas...then who?"

He shook his head. "I don't know. I wish I did." ⸻

Caitlin didn't know what to believe, or whom. It was late. She wanted to be alone, to think through everything he'd told her, to come up with an alternative suspect, rather than believe one of the men she loved wanted to kill her. She just couldn't believe it of either of them. Beyond the library windows, night had fallen. Caitlin glanced out, then faced her brother. "I'm going to bed. I have a raging headache."

"For what it's worth, Cait, I don't think it was Dylan. Not really. At first, I was just too shocked to think about anything, but now—" He shook his head. "You're right. He wouldn't hurt you."

"Thanks for that, but it isn't exactly a relief. It means that the real killer is still free to try again."

She hugged her brother, felt his shoulders tremble beneath her light touch. Then she rose and walked on suddenly leaden legs out of the library. She wanted to get back upstairs to her room. She'd imposed on Genevieve long enough. The woman was heartbroken, she didn't need to watch a baby on top of all that.

But when she entered her bedroom, Lizzie wasn't there. Nor was Genevieve. Caitlin frowned for just a moment, then shrugged. Genevieve probably took her to the nursery for a fresh diaper or a clean outfit. She bent to pick up the little toys from the blanket on the floor. Then the pillows, and the blanket itself. She gathered her own discarded clothes from earlier last night, as well. Someone, probably Genevieve, had long since cleaned up the broken lamp. Other than that, though, the room was really in a clutter.

She frowned as she reached for the last item on the floor, and as she picked it up, she recognized Genevieve's hooded cloak. She smiled and still held it in her hands when she heard the shrill ring of the telephone on the stand beside her bed.

Thomas would get it, she thought, folding the cloak over one arm and heading for the door. But it shrilled again, and then again. Why wasn't her brother answering on the library extension?

Frowning, Caitlin picked up the receiver. "Hello?"

"Dammit, I knew you'd go back there. Why didn't you listen to me, Cait?"

"Dylan?" She was shocked, and glad to hear his voice. God, there was so much she wanted to say to him. She had to tell him that she believed in him, had to tell him that—

"Lock yourself in your room and wait for me. Don't let anyone else in. You hear me?"

"Dylan, what—"

"They found something, a scrap of red cloth at the cemetery, that proves someone else was there last night. They're releasing me. Look, it's complicated. I'll explain it all later, just do as I say. Are you in your bedroom now?"

"Yes, but—"

"Go right now and lock your door. Please, Caity."

"But Dylan, I don't under—"

"Will you try trusting me just this once, for God's sake? You want to hear it from Barnes? It wasn't me, Cait, and you have to—"

"I kn—"

"Go and lock yourself in. Now, Cait."

"All right." She set the receiver on the stand, and turned to go the door. Dylan was scaring her, and she wanted to know why. The urgency she heard in his voice had her hands trembling as she reached for the door, and she inadvertently let Genevieve's cloak slip to the floor. Shaking her head at her own nervousness, she bent to pick it up.

And then her blood slowed to a thick, jelled stop in her veins and her head swam. A tiny square with jagged edges gaped in the red material.

They found something, a scrap of red cloth . . .

"My God. She has Lizzie!"

CHAPTER FIFTEEN

She never returned to the phone. Dylan couldn't help but fear the worst as he and Jack Barnes sped through the night.

"That red scrap of cloth has three pieces of vital evidence on it, Rossi."

Dylan had demanded a detailed explanation of the evidence that had cleared him, even as Barnes's car roared through the night away from Eden, and toward Caitlin.

"One was a hair, and the boys in the lab have already determined that it came from your wife's head. That proves that the person who left the scrap of cloth there had contact with her. The second was a microscopic droplet of blood, and the type doesn't match yours, or old man Crandall's, or Caity's. That proves the person wasn't you. There was a fourth person in the cemetery last night, Rossi."

"You said three pieces of evidence," Dylan said softly, to fill the silence with something besides this gnawing fear for Cait. "What was the third?"

"A partial fingerprint. Slightly smudged, but we might still be able to use it."

"What about the blood? Can't you do DNA testing, or something, to identify the killer?"

"That would only work if we had a suspect to compare it to. DNA fingerprinting takes two weeks, Rossi. The ball's rolling, but I'm sure as hell hoping we have the bastard behind bars long before the results come in."

"And what do we do now?"

"We make sure Caity's okay. Then we work our tails off. I'm not planning to sleep until we get to the bottom of this."

Dylan's eyes narrowed. "Why?"

Barnes shrugged. "She's special. If you haven't figured that out yet, then you need some serious help."

Caitlin tore through the corridors to the nursery, knowing already that she wouldn't find Lizzie there. From there, she moved to Ellen's room, but no one was inside.

She raced down the stairs, shrieking for Thomas, running to the library and skidding to a stop in the doorway when she saw him, lying facedown on the floor, a gaping cut in the back of his head, thick, crimson blood coating his neck. She took a single step toward him when she heard Ellen's hoarse cry. "Damned if I'll let you— No!" And then a yelp like that of a wounded animal.

Caitlin forced herself to leave Thomas there, silently praying he'd be all right, and turned to race toward the front door where Ellen's cry had originated. She held the white nightgown up to her knees as she ran.

The door yawned wide. Ellen was pulling herself to her feet, staggering forward, and a car stood running, doors open, in the driveway.

Cait caught up to Ellen, saw the way she was limping. "Ellen, are you—"

"Stop 'em! Caitlin, they've got Lizzie!"

Caitlin gasped, and looked toward the car. Henri was just getting into the front seat. In the glowing panel lights, Caitlin saw Genevieve, with a wriggling bundle on her lap. She had no idea what was going on, but it didn't matter. She launched herself toward the car, bare feet bruising as each running step landed on loose stones. She gripped the open driver's door even as Henri began to pull away, reaching to shut it as he did. She was forced down into the gravel, but her hands gripped the handle tighter. Stones tore through the nightgown, clawed her flesh as she was dragged over the driveway.

And then, abruptly, the car stopped. She heard feet crunching gravel and looked up to see Henri standing over her, and in his hand, a black, evil-looking handgun. It was over, she realized. The smell of exhaust fumes, the sounds of the engine, and of the crickets chirping in chorus would be the last things she'd ever experience.

"Get up."

She blinked and struggled to her feet, shaking all over, her gaze darting past him into the car where Genevieve sat holding Lizzie in the passenger seat. The night wind cooled her sweat-dampened face, and made the muslin gown ripple. Her knees screamed in pain where the gravel had scraped them raw.

"Go on back inside, Caitlin."

She frowned. His French accent was gone. "Where— where are you taking the baby?"

"She's gonna be just fine, long as you and your husband pay what we'll ask for her. If not..." He shrugged, leaving the implication clear in her fevered mind.

"But why?"

"After all this work, you don't expect us to walk away empty-handed, now, do you?"

She didn't understand. She had no idea what he was talking about. She only knew she couldn't let them leave here with Lizzie. She wouldn't. "Dylan won't pay for someone else's child." She shook her head hard. "He won't, I swear it. This is all useless."

"You will, though."

She shook her head. "I won't. I can't. I lost my money, all of it. I signed a new divorce agreement, leaving Dylan everything, even the house. I was going to go away, start fresh." She sought Genevieve's gaze in the car's dimly lit interior. "You heard me say I didn't want the money, or anything that was hers...mine...before."

Henri, or whoever he really was, frowned, and shot a glance toward Genevieve.

"She might be telling the truth." Genevieve's cold glare raked her. "But I doubt it."

"It's true, I swear it. Look, take me, instead. Dylan would pay to get me back."

"Nice try," Henri said. "But why would he? He only wants to get rid of you."

"No, that's not true. He'd have to pay to get me back, it would ruin his reputation if he didn't. Besides, he doesn't hate me. He wouldn't want to see me dead." She saw that they were considering her words, and she rushed on. "It won't be easy to hide with a baby. She'll be so much trouble. She's been sick, remember? So fussy. Keeping everyone awake nights, crying every couple of hours. And there are diapers and feedings, and bottles to wash. If you take me, it'll be easier. Hell, I can wait on you. Think of the irony. The mistress serving the servants. Just leave her here. I'll come with you."

Right on cue, Lizzie began to squall. She twisted and writhed in Genevieve's lap, and made enough racket to wake the dead.

The car bounded over the driveway, headlights cutting through the darkness. They illuminated a hunched form, and the car skidded to a stop. Barnes jumped out, gun in his hand. Dylan ran forward as Ellen scooped the screaming baby up from the gravel. Ellen was crying, as well, when Dylan reached her.

"Ellen, are you—"

"Fine. And so's the little one." She shook her head. "Thomas needs an ambulance, though." Barnes was instantly reaching back into the car, gripping the mike mounted to the dashboard, barking orders.

"What about Caity?" Dylan felt himself tense as he awaited the answer.

Ellen chewed her lip. "They took her, boy. Henri and Genevieve. They were trying to take off with Lizzie, and

Caitlin...she stopped them.'' Ellen bounced the baby up and down in her arms to soothe her crying. ''I never saw anything like it. She grabbed on to the car door and they dragged her right down the driveway. Then they stopped and that Frenchman pointed a gun at her. But she got up and started arguin' and beggin' them to leave the baby. She told 'em to take her, instead. And that's what they did.''

Dylan swore, and Ellen looked at her nephew intently. ''I couldn't have stopped 'em. I was wrong about Caitlin, Dylan. She's got guts like a lion's got teeth. I'm sorry.''

The paramedics tended Thomas on the library floor, while Dylan paced. Thomas refused to be taken to the hospital, despite the fact that his head could use a dozen stitches. Someone had clobbered him from behind with a heavy brass lamp. He was lucky to be breathing. Barnes had set up roadblocks, but he'd grimly predicted they would do little good. He said he had a feeling these people were pros. Cold-blooded criminals who'd done this kind of thing before. Otherwise, they'd never have managed to avoid the squad car that had been patrolling the area. He had men working on that angle back at the station. Doing something he called ''profiling'' and comparing the facts in this case with others like it via the NCIC computer network. But finding a match would take time.

He'd also predicted the pair hadn't just taken Caitlin on a lark. They would want something, probably demand something, for her return. And he was right.

The call came at midnight. Dylan waited for Barnes's signal before picking up. He was to keep them on the line for the tracers. But they were one step ahead.

''We have her. We'll kill her. One million, Rossi. By this time tomorrow night, or she's dead.''

Barnes had told Dylan what to expect, but hearing the words was like a knife in his heart. He swore he felt his blood cool to a frigid chill. The man on the phone sounded nothing like Henri. "Let me talk to her."

"Just get the money."

"Not until I hear her voice," Dylan insisted. "How do I know she's not already dead?"

"Listen close, then."

Dylan closed his eyes as Caitlin's scream filled the phone line. They'd hurt her. His fear, his sick worry changed form and solidified into rage. The bastards were going to pay for this.

"Good enough?" The voice he barely recognized came back. He could still hear Caitlin sobbing in the background.

"Don't hurt her. I'll get the money."

"Good."

Barnes was making a stretching motion with his hands. He had to keep them on the line longer. He couldn't fail Caity now. "Uh, where should I bring it?"

"I'll call you tomorrow night. Same time. And tell the cops they're wasting their time. I know how long it takes to trace a call." The loud click in his ear told Dylan they'd hung up. He shot a glance to Barnes, who only shook his head.

"Damn!"

Henri turned off the cellular phone, glanced menacingly at the stubby black stun gun in his hand and then smiled at Caitlin. She couldn't move. She lay on the tilting, swaying floor, where she'd hit hard, every muscle limp, trembling. If he came at her again with that snapping, crackling menace, she wouldn't be able to get away.

But he didn't. He flicked a button and put the thing in his shirt pocket. Then he bent, gripped her shoulders and hauled her to her feet. "Sorry. But your hubby wanted to hear your voice. Think you yelled loud enough for him? Hmm? I do. He sounded damned frantic before I hung up.

Guess you were telling the truth about that much, anyway. He doesn't hate you."

She closed her eyes as he shoved her into a padded seat. She heard his footsteps retreating. He trotted up the shallow steps, through the open hatch and onto the deck. Then the hatch slammed down.

He wasn't Henri. It was as though a different being had come in and taken over Henri's body. Not only had his accent vanished, his entire manner was altered. The way he walked, moved, his facial expressions. He was no longer the devoted servant, or the hopeful admirer. He was mean, angry and ruthless.

But why? My God, why had he changed so drastically? And Genevieve. She seemed like a street thug now, instead of the sweet, timid woman Caitlin remembered. Why was she doing this? She'd worked for Caitlin's parents...

"I'm leaving, Scott. I know all about you and our maid..."

Her mother's voice, twisted with pain, came to her like a ghost from the past. Caitlin was eighteen, and had left for school, but had forgotten her American history textbook, and returned for it. Only to hear things she wasn't meant to hear. Learn things she'd never wanted to know.

"...and the other women, too. I know about all of them. I'm leaving today."

Caitlin burst into the den, where her parents were talking. Daddy stood, pacing the gray pile carpet, his face tormented. He turned abruptly at her sudden appearance. Mother remained sitting, stiff-backed, in the Queen Anne chair.

"It isn't true, Mom. Daddy would never—"

"Caity, what are you doing here? This wasn't meant for you to —"

"It's a lie!" Caitlin screamed the words at her mother. "You're making it up—or, or, someone else is telling you things that aren't true. It's a lie, isn't it, Daddy?"

She turned her tear-filled eyes toward her father whom she adored beyond reason. He moved toward her slowly, not easily, due to his rounded middle. "Of course it isn't true. Your mother is just upset, Cait. Go on to school now, and all this will be settled by the time you get home—"

"No, it won't." Sarah O'Brien rose with liquid grace. "You're practically an adult now, Caity. You're old enough to draw your own conclusions. I won't beg you to believe me. I'm leaving. I'll be gone when you get home today. If you want to come with me, you're welcome..." She paused there, huge brown eyes searching Caitlin's, with no trace of hope in them. "But I don't imagine you do."

"How can you do this? How can you break up our family this way?" Caitlin wailed and cried and threw a fit, but her mother only shook her head slowly.

"It wasn't my decision, it was his. I have no choice about it. I love you, Caity."

Caitlin blinked at the sudden onslaught of memory. It was like a riptide, dragging her out to sea. There was so much going on, so much she ought to be thinking about, doing, planning. But all she could do was remember that final confrontation between her parents, feel incredible remorse over her own choice to believe her lying father. God, she'd worshiped that man.

She turned her mother's accusations over in her mind now. She knew they'd been true. She wasn't certain how she knew it or when she'd learned it. It must have been later, because she'd certainly been in denial then.

I know about you and our maid.

Genevieve had worked for them then. But so had a half-dozen other women, most of them young and attractive. And even if Caitlin had believed her father had been sleeping with one of them, she would never have suspected Genevieve. Genevieve was her friend, even though she only remained with them for a few months. She'd moved to another job shortly after the divorce. Caitlin hadn't seen her again until years later, when she'd been looking for domestic help in her own household, and Genevieve had shown up at her door with her charismatic brother in tow.

"How do I know all this?" She shook herself, shook off the lingering effects of the paralyzing jolt of electricity that had so recently hammered through her body, and tried to analyze her newfound knowledge. She didn't remember the pertinent facts in a flashback or a visual image playing in her mind, the way she did that conversation between her father and her mother. No, she just *knew*. The information simply surfaced in her mind like a buoyant object released from underwater. Suddenly, it was just there.

And what else?

She searched her mind for more of the jigsaw pieces of her past. They were there. She could *feel* them there, just out of reach. Their familiar auras reaching out to her, teasing her, luring her, taunting her. God, she wanted her life to be whole again.

But first and foremost, she needed to be sure she would *have* a life. And that meant putting her past out of her mind, and concentrating on survival in the present. Regardless of what was motivating Genevieve and Henri, the dilemma was the same. She was their prisoner, their captive, and she had serious doubts they intended for her to leave their imprisonment alive.

Especially when Dylan refused to come across with the money. Because he wouldn't pay it. He couldn't. He didn't have that much money, and there was no way he could come up with it in time. The only way Dylan could get that much cash would be to put the business up as collateral.

And that was out of the question. He'd built that company from the ground up, and he wouldn't risk losing it to save the life of a woman he hated. Oh, he'd try to get her back. Caitlin had no doubt about that. He'd have every cop and private investigator he could get on her trail. He'd agree to pay the ransom, and he'd try to get her out alive. Because he was her husband, and he seemed to take that role seriously. He was a man of honor. He wouldn't let his worst enemy die if he could do something to prevent it.

The problem was, she didn't think he could prevent it. Not this time.

And she wouldn't want him to lose his business to save her. It was too great a price to pay for a woman who'd hurt him the way she had. She wouldn't allow it.

She wanted to get away on her own, just to be sure Dylan wouldn't do something foolish. She got to her feet. They hadn't tied her up. She was only locked into the cramped living quarters of a boat. It was a small space, lined on one side with a pair of wooden cupboards, above a two-burner propane cooking center, and a minuscule sink that could have been straight out of a child's playhouse. Below that, more cupboards. On the port side, a high bunk that was now folded to lie flat to the wall. Below was a table and two bench-type seats. Toward the bow, two more bunks, and in the stern, a tiny door that led to a bathroom smaller than a bread box.

She explored the entire area in a matter of minutes. In the bathroom, no hair spray or razors she might use to defend herself. Damn. She searched the galley and found the barest food supply in the cupboards and a little more in the twenty-four-square-inch refrigerator. She checked cupboards, then the two drawers that slid open after a bit of tugging. She found a small, sharp steak knife with a serrated edge. Her fist clenched around its plastic, fake woodgrain handle.

The hatch was flung open with a loud bang that seemed to rip through her nerves with an edge more jagged than the blade in her hand. She whirled, closing the drawer and slipping the knife into the folds of her nightgown, still holding it as inconspicuously as she could manage, just as Genevieve reached the lowest step and met her gaze with a curious, suspicious stare.

"What're you doing?"

Without the French accent, her voice wasn't sultry, it was coarse. She sounded rougher than sandpaper. "Nothing. I...I was hungry."

Genevieve's eyes narrowed, scanning the cupboards behind Caitlin. "Si'down. You eat when we do."

Caitlin nodded, and hurried back to her former chair. Genevieve passed her on her way to the cupboards, to whip them open and scan the contents. Caitlin stiffened when Genevieve opened the drawers. Would she miss the knife? God, what would she do if she knew Caitlin had taken it?

Genevieve closed the drawer at last, and turned toward Caitlin. The suspicion was gone from her eyes. She hadn't missed the knife.

"Your hubby is going to pay up. You won't be here long."

"How long?"

Genevieve shrugged. "Thirty-six hours at the outside."

"And if he doesn't get the cash?"

"He will. They always get the cash, honey. He's scared out of his mind right now. He'll come through, don't you worry."

Caitlin frowned. "You talk like you've done this before."

Rather than ashamed, she looked proud. Her chin rose a little. "That's 'cause I have."

"How many times?"

Her delicate brows rose. "You really wanna know? You talkin' kidnappings?" Caitlin nodded, feeling as if she were talking to a stranger, a street thug in tight black jeans and a skimpy purple bustier. Her accent sounded like Brooklyn. "You're the fourth."

"And all the others paid?"

"Every nickel. An' we got away clean every time. I tol' you, we're pros."

"And the other...hostages. You released them unharmed?"

Her lids lowered to half mast. "Yeah. Sure we did." She poked a hand into a high cupboard and retrieved a pack of cigarettes. She shook one loose, caught it from the pack in her lips and pulled it slowly out. She held the pack toward Caitlin, but Caitlin shook her head. Shrugging, Genevieve tossed the pack down, and twisted a knob on the stove. She turned, putting her back fully to Caitlin, and bending low to light the cigarette from the burner.

Now, Caitlin thought. Just get up, take the knife and jam it into her back. The thought made her stomach turn. She didn't move, and then Genevieve was facing her again, sucking on the filter, holding the slender white cylinder between two fingers tipped in elaborately decorated nails, and blowing the smoke slowly out.

"Why were you trying so hard to kill me?"

She wasn't aware she was going to ask the question. When it came out, it surprised her, and apparently, it surprised Genevieve, as well.

"You sure it was me? What makes you so certain it wasn't your lovin' man all along, hmm?"

"It wasn't Dylan."

Genevieve tilted her head, and shrugged. "Bigger payoff. You underground, him in jail and your brother wrapped around me like a clinging vine. We could have had it all."

"You and Henri?"

Genevieve threw back her head and laughed, a guttural, throaty sound. "It's Hank. And I'm Jen. I have about as much French in me as a two-dollar bottle of wine, Madame Rossi." She affected her old accent with the last two words, and laughed as if she hadn't had such a good joke in a long time.

Caitlin just shook her head. "That's quite a leap, from kidnapping to murder. And such a convoluted plan. What made you think it would work?"

Genevieve—Jen—narrowed her eyes and sent Caitlin a silent message.

"My God, you've done that before, too?"

She drew again on the cigarette, blew smoke rings and shrugged. "Didn't say that."

Caitlin frowned, the scope of their plotting hitting her hard. "How long have you been . . ." She didn't know what word to put at the end of the sentence. "Were you . . . even when you worked for my father?"

"Your parents' marriage was in trouble. It was all over the social grapevine."

"And those are the kinds of households you like to get into, where the marriage is in trouble?"

"You're putting words in my mouth, honey."

"And you were planning the same kind of thing with my parents?"

"I managed to get your old man in the sack when it looked like they might patch things up. It was easy to make sure she found out about it. The stupid bitch walked out without a fuss, though. Didn't demand even a nickel. That screwed things up big-time. I mean, your old man had no motive. Who'd believe he'd done it? And then the old bastard fired me before I could think of an alternate plan. He didn't want his little girl to ever know about our fun and games. God, you were blind to that sleaze-bag. Thought he made the world and everything in it just so you'd have a nice place to live, didn't you?"

Cait swallowed hard. "For a while."

"Yeah. The sweet little princess found out what a bastard her old man really was . . . and then she turned into a frog."

Caitlin frowned and searched the woman's face. "What do you mean by that?"

Jen shook her head, her short, slick hair not moving. "Nothin'. I wasn't around then. I'm just repeating what I heard. When I left your daddy's house, you were a nice kid. I even liked you, as much as I like anybody. When I met you later, in your own house, you were an arrogant bitch. I guess after your mother offed herself and your idol got knocked off his pedestal, you lost your innocence, hmm?''

Caitlin shook her head, eyes wide, searching inwardly to make sense of all this. "I don't know."

Jen glanced down at the glowing end of the stub she held, dropped it into the sink and rinsed it down the drain. "Yeah well, neither do I." She nodded toward the bunks in the stern. "You might as well get some sleep. Nothing's happening tonight."

Cait shook her head. "I'll never sleep."

And she didn't. She was sure they were going to kill her, anyway, when they got the ransom, no matter what they said. Jen wouldn't have admitted to so many other crimes if she planned to leave her alive to testify against them.

Jen went above and Caitlin laid on the hard little bunk, and tried not to listen to the sounds overhead, a short time later. Sounds that made her sure they were not brother and sister.

Dawn. All night they'd worked, staying in touch with the station by phone, and using the fax in Dylan's home office to send files back and forth. Dylan slugged back so much coffee he was practically floating in it. He drank it mindlessly, just to have something to do with his hands.

And then he heard Barnes say softly, "We have a hit."

Dylan spun to see Barnes scanning the sheets that had just come through the fax. "Tell me."

"Nine years ago, a couple name Hank and Jennifer Korbett were employed in the Garner household, in Bangor, Maine. They'd been working there for a little over a year, when Mrs. Garner was murdered. Hit and run. Her husband's car. They were in the middle of a divorce at the time. She'd been pushing for a big settlement, and that was his motive. He was tried and convicted in the death of his wife."

"But it wasn't him, was it, Barnes?"

Barnes shook his head. "Before his mother's body was cold, the surviving son, and heir to everything, Preston Garner, married Jenny Korbett, the family maid. A week later, his body was found in a ravine. All his accounts had been drained, and Jenny and Hank had disappeared. The partial print we found on that scrap of cloth belonged to Jenny Korbett, alias—"

"Genevieve Dupres," Dylan muttered.

"She's not even French. They're both from Brooklyn."

"So they've been planning to murder Cait, and pin it on me."

"Looks like," Barnes replied. "Then Jenny would marry Thomas, get him to put her name on his accounts, which by then ought to have included all of your wife's money. Then he probably would've suffered the same fate as the Garner kid."

"But it didn't work. Cait didn't die."

"Don't feel too relieved, there's no doubt in my mind that they have an alternate plan. They have a list of priors as long as my arm. Lots of cons, three kidnapping charges—Maine, Boston, Jersey. Their mugs have been on display in every post office in the Northeast. But they were both blond and from Brooklyn. No one was looking for a dark-haired pair of French siblings. They've never been brought to trial. They're wanted in eight states for various crimes. Three of them are murder charges."

"Which three?" Dylan knew just by the way Barnes's gaze fell. "The kidnappings, right? They killed their hostages, whether the ransom was paid or not, didn't they, Barnes?"

His lips tightening to a thin line, Barnes nodded once.

CHAPTER SIXTEEN

Dylan couldn't stay at home, restless, powerless. Guilt-ridden. The thought that he'd ever believed he could be better off without Caity in his life kept haunting him. Was some greater force trying to show him exactly what hell that would be, or was it one of those cases where you got what you wished for, and regretted it for the rest of your life? It didn't matter that she didn't love him, didn't trust him, didn't want to be with him. All that mattered was that she live. She deserved to live. If he had to lose her, if he'd already lost her, he'd find a way to deal with it. But not like this. He wouldn't lose her like this.

He huddled with Detective Barnes—Jack, now—in front of his desk at the station, and together they pored over the histories of Jenny and Hank Korbett, charge by charge, case by case, hour after hour, amid the strong aromas of coffee, and correction fluid and pencil shavings.

Dylan swilled his fourth cup of strong, mudlike coffee, and went over the list of assets Jenny had wound up with after Preston Garner's death. She'd managed to liquidate $1.5 million in stocks right after the heir's murder. An estimated $250,000 in cash, once she'd closed out all the accounts. A Mercedes and a Vette, both brand-new. A cabin cruiser, and a half-dozen pieces of art worth a cool 500 grand if she could hawk them.

"You suppose they sold all this stuff?"

"What?"

"Paintings, cars, boat. If they did, they should have been rolling in money. Why risk it all for more?"

Jack shrugged and sipped his cold coffee, grimacing. "Greed. The cars turned up in Jersey. A few of the paintings have been recovered, as well, but not all."

"And the boat?"

Jack shook his head. "Nope, not a sign of it."

Dylan's lips thinned. He closed the folder, and reached for another, hoping to find some clue that would help him get Caity out of the Korbetts' hands and back home, safe, with him.

Instead, he found only a grim trail of death behind the two, littering their path like bread crumbs. In all three kidnappings—the little girl in Cape May, New Jersey, the old man stricken with Alzheimer's they'd taken from his rich family in Bar Harbor, and the new young bride of a business tycoon in Boston—the hostages had been killed. All in the same horribly efficient manner, even though the ransom demanded had been paid. A single bullet, fired at close range, dead center of their foreheads. The thought of Caity, looking down the barrel of that gun, knowing she was about to die, gave him anger, fury that knew no bounds. He'd kill them if they hurt her. He'd kill them.

"Rossi?"

Dylan blinked and faced Barnes.

"You okay?"

He shook his head. "Far from it."

"Well, it's almost nine. You ought to get to the bank, see about raising the ransom."

Dylan nodded, but his eyes strayed back to the folder on the desk. "They killed the others. The families paid and they killed them, anyway. We both know that."

"I know, Rossi. But knowing that, maybe we can strike a better deal. Get them to bring her to us, and trade even up, instead of arranging a drop."

Dylan shook his head. "You don't believe that any more than I do."

The look in Jack's cornflower blue eyes was enough to

confirm it without words, but there was something else there, too. A determined stubbornness that wouldn't be banked by the fear. "We'll get her back alive."

"I wish I could be as sure of that as you are."

"I'm not sure, just damned determined. I like your wife, Rossi. She reminds me of someone…someone I knew once. I've been a cop a long time, but I've never wanted to protect a victim the way I want to protect her. And I've never wanted to collar any two-bit slug the way I want to collar these two. It's gonna happen. Count on it."

Dylan tried to believe in the light he saw in Jack Barnes's eyes, but found it difficult. He shook his head. "I don't know. It's like—" His throat closed off. "Dammit." He blinked and averted his face.

"I know what you're going through, Rossi."

"The hell you do."

A heavy hand fell on his shoulder. "My wife…I lost her two years ago. I *know*."

Dylan looked up slowly, saw the brittle, sad smile of encouragement. "Maybe you do." He sighed, a short, shallow rasp. "Dammit, Jack, for the past two years, all I've wanted was another chance with her. I prayed and fought and groped for the old Caity, the one I loved. The one I still love. Only I gave up too soon, and when the chance finally came, I was too freaking blind and bitter to see it. Now she's gone. I had her back and didn't even know it, and now she's gone."

His eyes burned. Oddly enough, he felt no shame at that. Jack slapped his shoulder hard. "Come on, I'll drive you to the bank. We'll talk this through, brainstorm, maybe come up with something. And on the way back, we'll stop for a good solid belt, hmm? I think we both could use one."

"It isn't a belt I need, Jack. It's a miracle."

"Get up." The hands that shook her shoulders were soft, small and brutal. "Get up, Caitlin. It's time for breakfast."

Caitlin blinked reality into focus. She'd been engrossed in a dream so vivid, it was hard to believe it hadn't been real. She'd been with Dylan, on that beach in the cove, with nothing between their heated bodies but gritty sand and saltwater. And he'd told her that he loved her. That he'd always love her, no matter what.

A tight fist squeezed her heart, and the tears wrung from that organ leaked into her eyes, filling them. She shook herself, and sat up. She was still wearing her torn, dirty nightgown. The knife tucked in the waistband of her panties had made for a restless night. But she'd have slept little, anyway. Barefoot, she got up, and moved toward the table.

"Not there," Jen said, her voice sharp and too loud. "The stove's on the other side. There are eggs and cheese in the fridge. Get to it. We're starved."

She glanced at the woman, saw the hardness in her eyes and understood. She recalled her own words about the mistress serving the maid. Genevieve must have liked the idea. Seen it as poetic justice. Well, okay. She could deal with that. "Can I use the bathroom first?"

"Make it quick."

Caitlin nodded and closed herself in the tiny cubicle. She quickly searched the inside of the minuscule medicine cabinet there, but found only aspirin tablets, sun block and an antiseptic ointment. No sleeping pills. Nothing that she might slip into their damned breakfast to render them harmless while she tried to escape. She emerged frowning, disappointed, grimly certain her time on this planet was nearing its end.

She couldn't remember the last time she'd told Dylan she loved him. She'd wanted to say it when they'd made love, when he'd held her so tenderly in his arms. But she hadn't. God, why hadn't she? She might never get the chance again.

She moved to the fridge and found the eggs and the cheese. She cracked the fragile shells one by one, and dropped their contents into a bowl. Her heart sinking lower with every stroke, she stirred.

"I'm willing to put the business up as collateral."

The banker, Frederick R. Pembroke, leaned back in his chair. "You don't own the entire company, Mr. Rossi."

"Fifty-one percent is well worth what I need."

Pembroke nodded, and fingered the few threads of oiled-down, dark hair that were combed to cover the bald spot in the middle of his head. "I'm aware of that. And I'm sure the loan can be approved, but to get you this amount of cash by the end of the day is nearly impossible."

Dylan shot to his feet. "Listen, you pompous little twit, my wife—"

Jack gripped Dylan's arms just as he would have reached across the desk to choke the man. Pembroke had jerked backward, slamming the chair and the back of his greasy head into the wall behind him.

"Mr. Pembroke, a woman's life is at stake here. I'm willing to personally guarantee this bank that the money will be repaid, if that's what it takes, but we need the cash today."

"Or they'll kill her," Dylan said. The words were low, soft and steady. "Make no mistake, Pembroke, they'll kill her."

"Surely that's an exaggeration."

"These people are wanted in connection with several other murders," Jack said calmly. "They have nothing to lose."

"And if she dies because you refuse the money, I'll come back here, Pembroke," Dylan told him, standing straighter, shaking Jack's restraining hands from his shoulders.

"Easy, Rossi." Jack glanced across the desk. "Can you do it or not? There are other banks in town, and we don't have all day."

Pembroke drew a series of short breaths, his eyes darting around the office, anywhere but on Dylan's face. "I'll try. We have two other branches in nearby towns. I ought to be able to get the cash between the three."

"How soon?" Dylan wanted to walk out of here with the money right now.

Pembroke glanced at his watch. "Before closing, certainly. I'll call you when you can pick it up."

Dylan nodded, yanked a business card from his wallet and tossed it onto the desk. It had his home and office numbers. "If I'm not there, you can reach me at the police station."

He turned and stalked out of the banker's plush office. He wanted to kick something, or slam the door so hard, the bastard's false teeth would rattle. But he didn't. He stalked all the way to Jack's car, and got in.

"How 'bout that drink?" Jack asked when he slid behind the wheel.

"How 'bout a couple?"

"You want to run home first. Change, shower? You look like hell."

"Screw it. I don't really give a damn how I look right now."

Jack sighed and pulled into traffic. Two blocks down, he turned again, into the parking lot of an apartment building. Dylan had expected a bar, but said nothing. He got out and followed Jack through a foyer, to an elevator. They got off at the sixth floor, and the detective opened a door and ushered him in.

"It's a shack compared to your place, but..."

Dylan walked in, barely noticing the decor, caring even less. He heard the ice chinking into the glasses, the gurgle of liquid. He smelled the whiskey. He saw none of it, though. He'd paused in front of a framed 8x10 color photo of a woman. A beautiful woman with shining emerald green eyes and long, wildly curling auburn hair. Her chin was pointy, rather than blunt like Caity's, and her nose was slightly larger. Her cheekbones were nowhere near as high, or regal, but there was no mistaking the similarities.

"She was tiny, too. Not short, but just...delicate, slender. I always loved that about her." Jack pressed a cool glass into Dylan's hand.

"Your wife?"

"Yeah. Holly. Perfect name, don't you think? Red and green?"

Dylan nodded. He tore his gaze away from the beautiful face and saw the stark agony in Barnes's gaze. "What happened?"

"Boating accident." He didn't elaborate.

"Here?"

Barnes shook his head. "We were visiting her family in Boston. Got plugged by a yacht full of drunken idiots driving on the wrong side, no lights. The bastards."

Dylan said nothing. Barnes tossed back a healthy slug of whiskey, licked his lips and went on. "I tried to find her. I knew she couldn't swim. Still, with the life jacket, I figured..." He closed his eyes. "It wasn't the water, though. She took a blow to the head on the way in. There wasn't a damn thing I could do for her."

"God." Dylan tilted his own glass to his lips, closing his eyes as the burn moved down his throat, spread heat in his belly. "I'm sorry, Jack." There was something tickling the fringes of his consciousness. Something Jack had said, setting little bells off in his mind, but he couldn't put his finger on it.

"Wish to hell we'd never gone to Boston that summer."

Boston.

"One of the kidnappings happened in Boston, didn't it?" Mentally, Dylan recounted the cases, the scams, the murders. "Boston, Bar Harbor. Where was the other one? Some cape or other. Dammit, Jack, do you see the pattern?"

The detective blinked and faced Dylan, his gaze no longer blank and stark, but sharp, piercing. "The northeast?"

"The coast. They were all on the Atlantic coast. Everything since the rich couple and their son were murdered has been on the coast. And you said Hank and Jen got a boat out of that one."

Jack whistled, and his nod was quick and decisive. "Ten to one that's where they're holding her. Off the coast on that boat. You ever think of goin' into police work, Rossi?"

Dylan shook his head. "Not on your life. What do we do now?"

The storm hit with a vengeance. The wind moaned and howled around the boat, and the waves tossed it with a violence Caitlin was certain would be the end of all of them. She clung to the bunk, facedown, and tried not to feel the nausea, the dizziness, the stark fear. But she felt it all the same.

"Don't look so damned terror-stricken. We've seen worse."

Hank's words didn't even put a dent in the haze surrounding her mind. She was sick. She was scared. God, she wanted Dylan. Needed him.

Waves slapped the boat, battered it until it shuddered with the force. Thunder rolled over the sea toward them, reverberating through the wood and into her soul.

"Look, maybe we oughta take it in. Tie up somewhere till it passes."

"For God's sake, Jen—"

"It's getting worse," she said in a firm, authoritative voice. "Let's just take it in."

"We weather it. We'll be fine. We get near shore, Jen, and we might be spotted. It isn't worth the risk."

"She's sick."

Hank's gaze moved to Caitlin, and she felt him staring in disdain. "So what?"

Caitlin lurched to her feet, groping for things to hold on to as she made her way to the toilet with the floor pitching beneath her feet. She pulled the door shut and fell to her knees, retching. God, what a time to be seasick. How could she plan or maneuver to keep herself alive when she felt this badly?

When she could stand again, she found a cloth and washed her face. She reached for the door.

"Whadda you care how sick she is? It isn't like she's gonna get better."

"She could."

"Dammit, Jen—"

"She *could!* We don't have to do it that way. Not this time, Hank."

"She knows us."

"So does everybody else in that family. They don't need her to tell 'em who did this. We don't have to do it this time, Hank."

"We do if I say we do. She knows about the boat. They'd be one step ahead of us next time."

"We don't need any next time. We have enough. God, can't we just quit this crap? Settle down somewhere? Rio, like we always planned."

"No. Just a couple more jobs, and then—"

"It's always just a couple more!" The words were shrieked at him, and Caitlin stiffened when she heard the ringing slap of a hand on skin, and Jen's startled cry. "You know what I think?" She was whispering now, harshly, loudly, but the words were punctuated by sobs. "I think you like the killing. I think you enjoy it and I think you only want her dead 'cause you couldn't get her into bed. That thing with the rope and the noose in the cemetery, when you know that's how her mother checked out—that was just to torture her. Just so you could get your kicks. You're sick, Hank, and gettin' worse all the time."

"Think what you want, bitch. I'm callin' the shots, and you better not forget it again. Or maybe I'll be flying to Rio alone." There was a short pause. "We stick out the storm, and then we kill her. Enough said."

Jen didn't answer.

"Another damned storm. I hate when it blows up like this."

Her mother's voice seemed to echo from the depths of her memory as Caitlin huddled on the bunk again later, feigning sleep amid the tossing waves and howling wind, waiting for Hank to place the call, praying he'd let her talk to Dylan before he killed her.

"But I won't see another one. Thank God for that at least. I'm through with storms."

Caitlin frowned as the memory solidified in her mind. She'd held the telephone receiver in her hand, felt the sweat of her palm making it slick. She'd slowly gone cold all over as it clicked and went silent. There'd been something in her mother's voice.

Caitlin had never believed her, never accepted that what her mother claimed had been true. Her adored father couldn't have, wouldn't have done the things she claimed. And if he was tightfisted after the divorce, it was only because he was hurt. Mom had ruined their family, torn them apart. Daddy was angry. That was all.

Still, visions of the squalor in which her mother lived had haunted her. And now the sound of despair in her voice. She was alone, in that little apartment. And Caitlin knew she had to go to her, make amends, try to mend the break in their mother/daughter bond.

And Dylan was at work, just like always. Aunt Ellen was already in bed, asleep. So she had to face it alone. She climbed into her modest car, a Mustang with one black door and one blue one, and rust spots everywhere, and drove through the deluge, wipers beating helplessly, to her mother.

Caitlin blinked as the memories rushed through her. Something told her she didn't want to know any more, some secret dread that lived in her soul. But she saw all of it, anyway. The dingy hallway, the peeling wallpaper, chipped plaster. She even smelled the mildew, the damp plaster, the rotting wood, as she climbed the dim stairs and knocked on the door of her mother's apartment.

But there was no answer, so she tried the knob. And it gave, and she went inside.

And there was a creaking sound, and she turned. Her mother's body swung very slowly from the end of a rope. Her head hung limp, chin to chest, auburn hair veiling her face. Plaster dust sprinkled from the ceiling into her hair. The light fixture she'd tied the rope to wasn't going to hold much longer.

Caitlin moved forward, slowly, as if in a trance. She reached up only slightly, and touched her mother's hand. It was cool. Not cold. Not yet. The two-hour drive had taken too long. Caitlin should've called the police. She should've called a neighbor. Anything. She could have prevented this.

She backed away, her chest heaving, wanting only to find Dylan, to feel his arms holding her tight, to feel his love surround and comfort her.

But there was something else, a small white envelope with her name scrawled across the front. She picked it up, opened it, and read with tear-blurred eyes.

It was all true, Caity. Oh, I don't blame you for not believing me. I know you love your father. I loved him, too. Don't blame yourself for this. You couldn't have known. It's him. He brought me to this. And I'm only writing to warn you, baby, because they're all the same. No matter how much they claim to love you at first, in the end it's always the same. I see the signs already, for you, my poor, trusting Caity. The late hours, the missed dinners, the nights he doesn't come home at all.

He'll take everything you have to give him, Caity, and then you'll end up just like me. Alone. And in too much pain for a human to bear. You'll see.

Prepare yourself, Caity. Don't depend on him for your happiness. Find a way to make your own. Don't give your entire soul to him the way I did to your father. He'll only throw it away. Please, don't let this happen to you.

Don't trust that man with your heart.

The letter hadn't been signed. But it had stamped itself on her heart. And in the morning, when Dylan had returned home after a long night at the office, she found she no longer craved the feel of the comfort his arms would offer. She never even told him about her midnight trip, or that she'd found her mother's body. Or about the note.

Because from that day on, it had become fairly obvious that her mother had been right. The late hours, the all-nighters. He was lying to her. She knew it, and she withdrew from him as much as she could manage. And the coldness she gave began to filter back to her, and the distance between them grew.

And then Daddy died, she thought in silence, and I had his money to cling to instead of my husband. Oh, God, how could I have been so stupid?

"Hank, it's twelve-thirty."

"I know what time it is. I want the bastard to squirm a little before I talk to him. You got a problem with that?"

Cait opened her eyes in time to see Jen shake her head quickly.

"You know, bitch, you're starting to be more trouble than you're worth."

CHAPTER SEVENTEEN

"They're late." Dylan slammed a fist into the wall beside the window. He'd been staring pensively into the storm-ravaged night, conjuring images of a splintered ship, of Caity's slender hands clinging to a jagged bit of wood until she couldn't hang on any longer. Of her face, pale and nearly lifeless, slipping away beneath the angry sea.

He forced the images away and whirled on Jack. "What the hell does it mean?"

"It means they want to make you crazy. Looks like it's working, isn't it, Rossi?"

"Damn straight it is."

Thomas paced. He'd been pacing for an hour now, and it didn't look as if he planned to stop anytime soon. His path was precise and repetitive and it was driving Dylan nuts.

"Calm down, Rossi. We have their coordinates. They're anchored less that ten minutes out. The Coast Guard's ready to move out the second this storm breaks, and when Hank calls, you're going to buy us enough time to last that long."

Ellen came in, carrying a pot of fresh coffee. She scuffed over the tiled floor looking weary, her housecoat floating just above her stretchy slippers. Jack held up his cup, and Ellen filled it. "Any word yet?"

"Nothing. This brew of yours sure puts mine to sha—" He broke off as the telephone bleated like a lost lamb calling for its mother.

Thomas jerked as if electrocuted, and finally stood in one spot. Dylan lurched for the phone, jerking it out of its cradle hard enough to hurt his arm.

"You have the money?"

"Yes. All of it."

"Very good. Now listen. Here's what I want you to do—"

"No, Hank. You listen. I know who you are, and I know what happened to your last three hostages. There's no way in hell I'm dropping this money anywhere, knowing you'll kill her, anyway."

"You don't have much choice, Rossi."

"I have one choice. I'll hang this phone up here and now. I'm not going to pay you to kill my wife."

There was a long moment of tense silence, and Dylan was terrified Hank would slam the phone down in his ear. Finally, his strange voice came back. "Talk."

Dylan's eyes met Jack's steady gaze. Jack shoved a scrap of paper at him. *Get them out of the water.*

"I want you to meet me...in the parking garage below my offices in Eden. And I want you to bring Caitlin. If I don't see her there, alive and well, then the deal's off. You hear me? We'll trade then. The money for Caity. You can take the cash and go, I won't try to stop you just as long as she's all right."

"Sounds like you have this all figured out."

Dylan licked his lips, swallowed the sand in his throat. "Unless you've already..." He couldn't say it. And he couldn't demand to talk to her, because he was afraid Hank would hurt her again. Make her scream in pain as he'd done last time.

"She's still alive." Hank muttered something, but had his hand over the mouthpiece, from the sound of it. When he came back, Dylan's hopes plummeted. "No deal. Forget it, Rossi. You can do this my way, or I'll off her as soon as I hang up the phone. What's it gonna be?"

"If you don't want to meet there, pick your own place. It doesn't matter where, as long as she's with you." Dylan felt desperation making his palms itch, his hands sweat.

"Bring the money to the cliffs, at dawn. I'll be watching you, so don't bring any cops with you. The first badge I see will be your wife's death warrant. Leave it in that little hollow the tide's made in the stone. You know where I mean?"

"Yes."

"Good. After I have it, after I've counted it, and I'm well out of reach, I'll call and tell you where to find your lady. All right?"

"No, it's not all right, you bastard. How do I know you won't kill her, anyway?"

"You don't. You only know that if the money isn't there, I will definitely kill her. Sweet dreams, Rossi."

He hung up. Dylan growled deep in his throat, tore the phone from the table and smashed it onto the floor. Pieces flew in a hundred directions.

"My God," Thomas muttered.

"They're gonna kill her. Dammit, Jack, they're gonna do it. We have to move now."

"Rossi, the storm—"

"They're out in it. They're still afloat. Dammit, Jack, we can't wait. You know it as well as I do. We have their location. It's time to move in. You can either come with me or I'll go by myself, but I'm going out there."

Hank slung the cellular phone across the table, and rubbed his hands together. "He'll do it. He'll pay. I could hear the fear in his voice. He's already figured it out, you know. He knows about the others. Practically begged me not to..." His voice trailed off, but he inclined his head toward Caitlin.

Jen looked at the floor. "Then don't. We don't have to—"

"We don't need her anymore. The money will be waiting in the morning, and we can take it and go. We don't need her for a damn thing."

"Hank—"

He pulled out his gun, and turned toward the bunk to waggle it at Caitlin. "Come on. We're going up on deck. Get some air."

"No...please, I—"

"Hank, stop it! I've had it with your sick games. I can't do it anymore."

He stood stock-still for a long moment. Caitlin clung to the knife hidden in the waistband of her panties, trembling inside because she knew the time had come and she was sure she wouldn't survive this.

Hank turned to face Jen. "So it's over, is it? You can't do it anymore?"

"I just...I hate the killing. I hate it, Hank. I can't—Hank?"

His arm lifted, and without a second's hesitation, he pulled the trigger. The blast was deafening in the closed-in area. Jen's head slammed backward as if she'd been punched, and then she was on the floor. Caitlin lunged from the bed, no longer thinking her actions through as terror took over. She would be next, she knew. She lifted the knife over her head, and brought it down in a deadly arc. The blade sunk into flesh, scraped against bone, and Hank twisted away from her with the steak knife embedded between his shoulder blades, as the gun clattered to the floor.

"You filthy little bitch!" He reached behind him in a feeble attempt to pull the knife free, but couldn't do it. "You're dead..."

Cait dodged his long reach, her gaze darting from the woman on the floor with the small round hole in her forehead and the unseeing stare in her slowly glazing eyes, and the widening pool of dark red spreading beneath her, to the closed hatch at the top of the steps. She ran toward it, flung it open and emerged into the darkness. Sheets of icy water lashed her body, tore at her face, carried by brutal winds. Waves slammed the boat, rocking it crazily.

There was nowhere to go. She glanced frantically behind her, to see Hank making his way up the steps, hunched over, his white T-shirt soaked in blood, the small woodlike handle protruding from his back. She reached for the hatch, and as she did, he brought up one hand. God, he had the gun again.

The shot echoed through her psyche as she slammed the hatch. Pain sliced into her midriff like a white-hot iron. Falling to the side, she grappled with the latches, hooking them to keep him where he was. Then she dragged herself away, toward the rail, her hand pressed to her side.

She felt the warmth of the blood, saw its dark stain spreading over the nightgown, felt it running down her body, coating one leg as it soaked through the muslin, dripping to the deck. She was going to die.

She clung to the rail, leaning out over the rioting sea as if in search of some trace of hope. Something. Someone.

Dylan.

A muffled crash brought her head around. Then another, and the hatch jumped from the force of it. Then another. He was battering the door with something. It wouldn't hold long. God, what could she do?

Again he hit the door, and again. The wood splintered. She cringed against the rail, moving backward farther from him, knowing there was no shelter, nowhere to hide.

One more crash and the hatch was swinging open. Panting, cursing, Hank emerged. He looked around as the vicious wind pummeled him. He couldn't see her. She crouched in the shadows near the bow, watching, water streaming over her, waves reaching for her as if to pull her into their frigid embrace.

Hank started forward, lifting the gun, his gaze narrow, searching, murderous. He'd find her sooner or later. And then he'd kill her.

Caitlin's hands clenched into fists, one against her bleeding side, the other on the watery deck. She bumped against something. A flotation device attached to the side. Her fingers fumbled to free it, careful not to make a sound. When she had the thing loose, she gripped it in shaking hands, whispered a prayer and threw it toward the starboard side.

The instant the ring landed, Hank fired a shot. She saw the flare of the gun in the inky, watery night. Silently, she crept backward, back against the rail, curving along the port side until she bumped another ring. She threw it, as well, drawing another shot.

"That's four," she whispered under cover of the wind. She'd had a good look at the gun. A better look than she'd ever wanted. A big revolver. And she assumed that meant it only held six bullets. "Two more. God, let me find two more." She scurried backward again, her side pulsing with pain, shivering from the cold wind and the brutal rain. He was coming toward her. She wasn't moving fast enough.

Turning, she gripped the rail and pulled herself upright. Clinging to it, she walked, but something hard tripped her and she fell facefirst onto the soaking deck. A shot rang out at the instant of impact, but she didn't think it had hit her. A swell smashed into the boat, lapping over onto the deck, dumping all over her body before fleeing back into the sea. She heard him coming closer, and dragged herself away. But she couldn't keep this up. The blood leaving her body so rapidly was weakening her, making her dizzy. Her movements slowed, and grew more clumsy and noisy with every inch of progress she made. And her killer was closing in.

"All right, hit the spotlight!"

The sudden illumination of the small boat just ahead

caught Dylan completely off guard. He hadn't even known it was there. The Coast Guard cutter's crew knew it, though.

Dylan stood in the bow, wearing a dark blue rain slicker with the hood thrown back, heedless of the water cascading over his face, running down his neck, soaking his hair. Thomas stood beside him. He squinted in concentration as the spotlight swept over the deck of the smaller boat. Then Dylan saw her, lying facedown on the deck, and he saw Hank, lifting a gun, pointing at the woman the light had just illuminated for him.

Dylan's agonized scream pierced the night, even above Thomas's coarse cry, and the bullhorn-enhanced voice that ordered Hank to drop the weapon or be shot. But Hank didn't, and as the cutter charged the boat as if to split it in half, a shot rang out. Dylan wasn't sure if it came from Hank's gun or one of the officers. He feared the worst, because Hank didn't falter, or collapse, or even drop his gun. He looked at it, then tucked it into his waistband and advanced on Caitlin.

Dylan's heart leapt when he saw her move. She gripped the rail and pulled herself to her feet. She staggered forward, and the spotlight danced on the blood-soaked nightgown, as Hank grabbed her.

"Shoot the bastard!" Dylan shouted, but no shots rang out. They couldn't risk hitting Caitlin. Hank held her from behind. He whirled her around in a slow-motion dance even as he was ordered to let her go.

Dylan gaped in horror as he watched Caitlin being wrenched off her feet, then cried out in stark agony as her body hurtled over the rail and into the angry sea. Hank pulled out the gun again, lifted it toward the cutter and then his body jerked like a marionette on a twitching string, as countless rounds hammered into him. Slowly, he sank to his knees.

Dylan didn't know if he sank any farther, because he was ripping off the slicker he wore, and diving through the space between the deck and the raging sea below.

He heard Jack shouting his name just before his body knifed into the angry waters. He stroked under the surface, propelling himself onward with every ounce of power he possessed. When he broke surface, saltwater streaming down his face, into his eyes, he was near the smaller boat. He looked around him, seeing only swelling whitecaps, pelting rain, darkness.

"Caity!" He tread water, scanning the sea in all directions. "Caity, where are you?"

The spotlight moved until he was caught in its glow, then swept slowly past him, searching the water for her. Dylan followed it, stroking swiftly, pausing at intervals to search. He had to find her. She couldn't die. He couldn't lose her. Not again. It would kill him.

He heard the difference in the sounds of sluicing water, and turned to see the lifeboat that was fighting its way toward him. As it drew nearer, he recognized the man in the bow.

Jack leaned out, over the water, pointing, shouting. "Near the stern, Rossi. Over your left shoulder!"

Dylan turned and swam in that direction, but he didn't see her. The swells blocked his view of anything, being down in the water. "She's going down!" Jack roared. "Get that light on her! Can't this thing move—dammit, Rossi . . ."

Dylan crested a huge swell just in time to see her limp hand let go of the rope it had been clutching, and disappear beneath the black water.

"No!" He drew a deep breath and dove under, angling toward her, and seconds later, his outstretched hands bumped something soft and limp, something that was sinking past them, and they gripped, clung, lifted. He pulled her to his chest as his feet propelled them upward. When he broke surface, dragging air into his burning lungs, it was with Caitlin crushed to his chest as he held her head out of reach of the angry waters.

He searched her face, pale, milky white in the harsh and erratic glow of the spotlights. Her eyes were closed, her lips, blue-tinted. Strands of her wet hair, dark with seawater, stuck to her face and neck, and she remained motionless, perfectly limp in his arms.

Frantically, he pushed his forefingers to her throat in search of a pulse. But he couldn't be certain the hammering in his fingertips came from the rush of her blood, or the current of his own. He brought her face to his with one hand, fighting to keep them both afloat with the other. He covered her lips with his open mouth, parting them with his tongue. He blew life into her again and again, praying desperately for a response, dying a little with each second that passed without one.

The shouts of men, Jack's louder than any other, grew louder in those nightmarish seconds, and then there were hands groping, and a pair of other bodies in the water. Caitlin was lifted by the three men in the water. Jack and Thomas pulled her gently into the lifeboat, and by the time Dylan hauled himself over the side, the cop was already kneeling beside her, pumping her heart with two hands, counting aloud, blowing air into her lungs. And crying. As he worked, twin rivers formed on Jack's face, and he didn't even try to swipe them away. Maybe he wasn't even aware of them.

He worked frantically, and when Thomas, rain-soaked and utterly silent, moved forward to assist him, Jack waved him away with a short bark of a command.

The lifeboat headed back toward the cutter, slicing the rolling sea. Dylan slumped down beside his still, pale wife. He clutched one of her hands in both of his as a puddle formed around him. "Don't die, Caity. Don't leave me like this."

Thomas sat near her, too, but only stared at her, as though he couldn't believe what he was seeing.

Jack sat back on his heels, his fingers pressing into the soft skin of her throat, his eyes intent. Then he looked across her body, and met Dylan's desperate gaze. "There's a pulse." The words were whispered so softly, Dylan wasn't sure he'd actually heard them. But then Jack cracked a wavering smile and said it again, louder. "There's a pulse!"

She drew a ragged, hoarse breath then, one loud enough for them both to hear. Dylan shook his head in silent wonder. Thomas bent until his head lay flat to Caitlin's chest, to hear her heart for himself. Jack blinked rapidly, seemingly aware all at once of his tear-stained face. He averted his gaze and barked at the men to get their butts into overdrive. Someone began packing the wound at her side, and the lifeboat picked up speed.

She was warm. Wet, but warm. And vaguely aware of motion, as if she were being carried at a high rate of speed by a vehicle that repeatedly *bumped*.

She opened her eyes. Dylan was pacing the little room. Thomas was sitting right at the bedside, and it took her a moment to connect the warm pressure on her hand with the fact that he was holding it in his.

He squeezed it suddenly tighter, looking at her face, and she winced.

"It's okay," he soothed. "We'll be at the hospital soon."

"Oh, God, not again."

Her voice seemed to have magically zapped Dylan from where she'd first glimpsed him, to her opposite side. She turned when he leaned over, gripping her shoulders so firmly, it hurt.

"You're awake. Caity, are you all right? How do you feel?" His dark eyes scanned hers with more fear than she'd ever seen in them.

"I'm hurting," she whispered.

His eyes fell closed and his lips thinned.

"Thomas is crushing my hand to sawdust, and your fingers are digging pits in my shoulders." Both grips immediately eased, and Dylan's eyes flew open. "You guys don't have to hold on so tight. I'm not going anywhere."

Dylan sat gingerly on the edge of the bed. His hands slid beneath her shoulders, and he lifted her gently, slowly, until her head was cradled on his chest, his fingers gently threading through her hair. "Damn straight, you're not going anywhere, baby."

She brought her arms around him, and held him as tightly as her pitiful amount of strength would allow. "I have so much to tell you."

"Maybe...maybe I ought to leave—"

"No, Thomas. You need to hear this, too." She released Dylan, though reluctantly, and slid herself higher on the bed, stopping in midmotion at the stabbing pain in her side. The gunshot wound. She'd forgotten. Dylan stacked pillows behind her and eased her upper body onto them. His touch was so tender, so careful, it nearly brought tears to her eyes.

Thomas touched her face. "You're pale."

"Lost a lot of blood," Dylan added.

"I'm fine. My side aches like hell, but—"

"You were shot," Thomas explained.

"I know I was shot. You think I'd forget something like that?" She made the words teasing. "What about Henri...I mean, Hank?"

"Dead."

She closed her eyes and shook her head. "Genevieve, too. He shot her. They've done this before, you know—"

"I know, honey. I know. Jack Barnes filled me in. But all of that is over now. It's over. All I'm worried about now is you."

She lifted a hand to his face. "Don't be. I'm going to be fine, I can feel it. And...and I remember now."

Dylan's brows rose. Thomas leaned forward. "Your memory is back? All of it?"

She smiled at her brother. "Most of it. There are less gaps, and I think they'll get smaller as time goes on. But even if they don't, it doesn't matter. I know what I need to know. I know why I became what I was, why I treated you—" she looked from Thomas to Dylan, "—both of you, the way I did."

Thomas nodded. "I already know. It was because of our father." His face tightened as he spoke. His eyes filled with pain, and anger. "You worshiped him, Cait. When you were finally forced to realize that everything Mom said about him was true, you were so disillusioned, you couldn't trust anyone again. Especially not men."

"That's a lot of it, but not all of it." She closed her eyes as the horrible memory threatened to engulf her as it had before. "That night, when our mother..." She shook her head. "She'd called me, and sounded so strange that I was worried, so I drove over there."

She opened her eyes to see Dylan's widen with concern. "It was storming, and you were at the office. I went alone. And when I got there, she was...it was already...done."

"*You* found your mother?"

"Hanging from the ceiling," she finished for him. "And right at her feet, there was a note with my name on it. A note telling me that all men were like my father, and that if I wasn't careful, I'd end up alone, just like her. She said that you'd start spending more and more time away from home, with work as your excuse..."

"And I'd already started doing just that," Dylan whispered. "But Caity, it *was* work. I swear it to you—"

"Shh. I know that...now. Then, I..." She grasped his hand. "We were so new, Dylan. I was still insecure, and you were so wrapped up in the business. I guess I started to believe her."

"And I knew you were keeping something from me. I sensed the walls you were putting between us, and I retreated even more."

She nodded, and turned toward her brother. "I wasn't right, Thomas. My mind just... *wasn't right*. Seeing Mom like that did something to me. It was like I started clinging to the money and the things it could buy, because it was the only thing I trusted, the only thing I dared to hold on to. Can you understand that?"

He nodded. "It's okay, sis. Honestly, I was an idiot to let the inheritance come between us—"

"I was the one who let it come between us. But that's over now. Everything I have, I want to share with you. It's only right, the way Daddy should have done it in the first place."

Thomas's face clouded. "He never really cared about me. I don't want anything that was his. I might have resented that he left it all to you, but I never wanted it. Can *you* understand *that?*"

She bit her lower lip, thinking. "Then it's Lizzie's. I'll put your share into a trust fund for her. Is that an acceptable solution?"

He smiled and nodded. "As long as you'll stay in her life... hers and mine. You're a lot more important to her... to both of us... than your money is."

She leaned forward and hugged him, tears blurring her vision. "My brother... I love you, Thomas."

"Me, too," he returned, hugging her back a little too hard. When he straightened, he brushed at his eyes with his knuckles. "*Now* I'll get out. You two need some time."

She met Dylan's gaze and held it as Thomas left them alone. "I'm sorry," she said softly.

"For what?" He seemed truly puzzled.

"Not loving you enough, not trusting you enough back then. If I'd come to you, told you what I was going through... God, all of this could've been so different."

"It doesn't matter."

She bit her lips, her eyes filling. "Yes, it does. Because you loved me once. I remember that, too, and I remember how wonderful it made me feel. But I ruined that love with my fears and distrust. I killed it, and now, you can't bring it back, even though I love you with everything in me."

"You do?"

She searched his face, misery gripping her heart. "I do. More, even, than I did then. It's not a little-girl love anymore, Dylan. It's real, and deep, and old, and ageless. And even if we have to be apart..." Her words stopped on a sob.

"Caity, I—"

"No, let me finish because this might be important, later. I hope... those precious times we had together... I hope there's a baby. And not because I want to replace the one I lost, or because I want to try to use it to cling to you. But because I want at least one part of you that I will always have near me. Your child, and I'd give it all the love I have for you inside... because it has to go somewhere. There's too much of it to hold back. And I—"

"Caity, let a guy get a word in, will you?"

She went quiet, sat utterly still while his fingers slipped into her hair, lifted it away from her head, sifted it. "I hope you have a baby, too."

"You do?"

He nodded. "But don't be too disappointed if you're not pregnant. Because if it didn't happen last time, it will next time, or the time after that, or..." He smiled down at her. "You get the idea. Because I'm not letting you go, Caity O'Brien Rossi. I love you. I never really stopped, that's why it hurt so much to think you didn't love me back."

She closed her eyes as all the air left her lungs and the weight of the world seemed suddenly to lift from her shoulders. "Say it again, Dylan."

"I love you, Caity. I always will. No matter what."

* * * * *

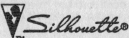

SILHOUETTE® Shadows™

Join award-winning author Rachel Lee as

CONARD COUNTY explores the dark side of love....

Rachel Lee will tingle your senses in August when she visits the dark side of love in her latest Conard County title, THUNDER MOUNTAIN, SS #37.

For years, Gray Cloud had guarded his beloved Thunder Mountain, protecting its secrets and mystical powers from human exploitation. Then came Mercy Kendrick.... But someone—or something—wanted her dead. Alone with the tempestuous forces of nature, Mercy turned to Gray Cloud, only to find a storm of a very different kind raging in his eyes. Look for their terrifying tale, only from Silhouette Shadows.

Dark secrets, dangerous desire...

Lovers
**DARK AND
DANGEROUS**

Three spine-tingling tales from the dark side
of love.

This October, enter the world of shadowy
romance as Silhouette presents the third in their
annual tradition of thrilling love stories and
chilling story lines. Written by three of
Silhouette's top names:

**LINDSAY McKENNA
LEE KARR
RACHEL LEE**

Haunting a store near you this October.

Only from

Silhouette®
...where passion lives.

MONTANA Mavericks

Stories that capture living and loving beneath the Big Sky, where legends live on...and the mystery is just beginning.

This September, look for

**THE WIDOW AND THE RODEO MAN
by Jackie Merritt**

And don't miss a minute of the loving as the mystery continues with:

SLEEPING WITH THE ENEMY
by Myrna Temte (October)
THE ONCE AND FUTURE WIFE
by Laurie Paige (November)
THE RANCHER TAKES A WIFE
by Jackie Merritt (December),
and many more!

Wait, there's more! Win a trip to a Montana mountain resort. For details, look for this month's MONTANA MAVERICKS title at your favorite retail outlet.

Only from **V** *Silhouette*® where passion lives.

The Loop™

Is the future what it's cracked up to be?

This August, find out how C. J. Clarke copes with
being on her own in

GETTING IT TOGETHER: CJ
by Wendy Corsi Staub

Her diet was a flop. Her "beautiful" apartment was
cramped. Her "glamour" job consisted of fetching
coffee. And her love life was less than zero. But
what C.J. didn't know was that things were about
to get better....

The ups and downs of modern life continue with

GETTING IT RIGHT: JESSICA
by Carla Cassidy in September

GETTING REAL: CHRISTOPHER
by Kathryn Jensen in October

Get smart. Get into "The Loop!"

MIRA ™

The brightest star in women's fiction!

This October, reach for the stars and watch all your dreams come true with **MIRA BOOKS**.

HEATHER GRAHAM POZZESSERE
Slow Burn in October
An enthralling tale of murder and passion set against the dark and glittering world of Miami.

SANDRA BROWN
The Devil's Own in October
She made a deal with the devil...but she didn't bargain on losing her heart.

BARBARA BRETTON
Tomorrow & Always in November
Unlikely lovers from very different worlds...they had to cross time to find one another.

PENNY JORDAN
For Better For Worse in December
Three couples, three dreams—can they rekindle the love and passion that first brought them together?

The sky has no limit with **MIRA BOOKS**

Paris Metro

*The stations Liège and Rennes are closed after 8pm and on Sundays and holidays.

Beyond the city limits, *Métro Urbain* tickets are not valid on the RER

13 Line Terminus
● Station
○ Transfer Station

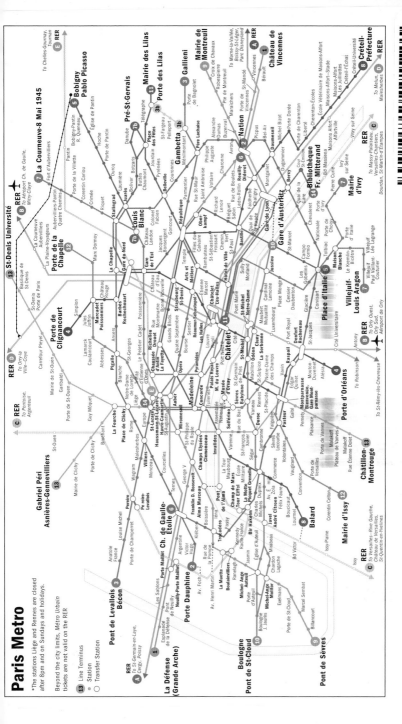

W9-DBZ-567

Paris: Overview and Arrondissements

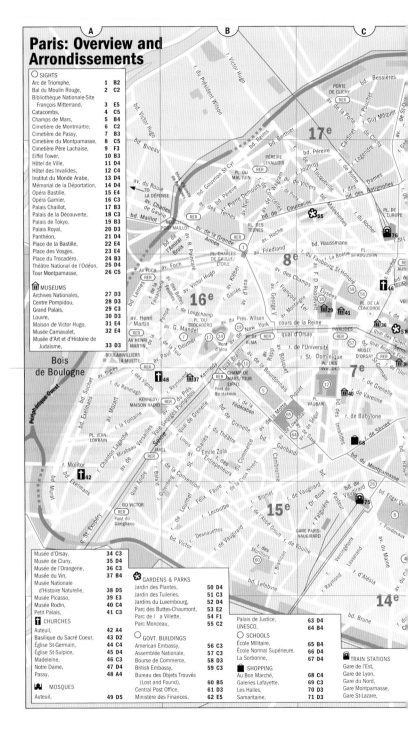

○ SIGHTS

Arc de Triomphe,	**1** B2
Bal du Moulin Rouge,	**2** C2
Bibliothèque Nationale-Site François Mitterrand,	**3** E5
Catacombs,	**4** C5
Champs de Mars,	**5** B4
Cimetière de Montmartre,	**6** C2
Cimetière de Passy,	**7** B3
Cimetière du Montparnasse,	**8** C5
Cimetière Père Lachaise,	**9** F3
Eiffel Tower,	**10** B3
Hôtel de Ville,	**11** D4
Hôtel des Invalides,	**12** C4
Institut du Monde Arabe,	**13** D4
Mémorial de la Déportation,	**14** D4
Opéra Bastille,	**15** E4
Opéra Garnier,	**16** C3
Palais Chaillot,	**17** B3
Palais de la Découverte,	**18** C3
Palais de Tokyo,	**19** B3
Palais Royal,	**20** D3
Panthéon,	**21** D4
Place de la Bastille,	**22** E4
Place des Vosges,	**23** E4
Place du Trocadéro,	**24** B3
Théâtre National de l'Odéon,	**25** D4
Tour Montparnasse,	**26** C5

🏛 MUSEUMS

Archives Nationales,	**27** D3
Centre Pompidou,	**28** D3
Grand Palais,	**29** C3
Louvre,	**30** D3
Maison de Victor Hugo,	**31** E4
Musée Carnavalet,	**32** E4
Musée d'Art et d'Histoire de Judaïsme,	**33** D3

Bois de Boulogne

Musée d'Orsay,	**34** C3
Musée de Cluny,	**35** D4
Musée de l'Orangerie,	**36** C3
Musée du Vin,	**37** B4
Musée Nationale d'Histoire Naturelle,	**38** D5
Musée Picasso,	**39** E3
Musée Rodin,	**40** C4
Petit Palais,	**41** C3

🛐 CHURCHES

Auteuil,	**42** A4
Basilique du Sacré Coeur,	**43** D2
Église St-Germain,	**44** C4
Église St-Sulpice,	**45** D4
Madeleine,	**46** C3
Notre Dame,	**47** D4
Passy,	**48** A4

☪ MOSQUES

Auteuil,	**49** D5

✿ GARDENS & PARKS

Jardin des Plantes,	**50** D4
Jardin des Tuileries,	**51** C3
Jardins du Luxembourg,	**52** D4
Parc des Buttes-Chaumont,	**53** E2
Parc de l a Villette,	**54** F1
Parc Monceau,	**55** C2

○ GOVT. BUILDINGS

American Embassy,	**56** C3
Assemblée Nationale,	**57** C3
Bourse de Commerce,	**58** D3
British Embassy,	**59** C3
Bureau des Objets Trouvés (Lost and Found),	**60** B5
Central Post Office,	**61** D3
Ministère des Finances,	**62** E5
Palais de Justice,	**63** D4
UNESCO,	**64** B4

○ SCHOOLS

École Militaire,	**65** B4
École Normal Supérieure,	**66** D4
La Sorbonne,	**67** D4

🛍 SHOPPING

Au Bon Marché,	**68** C4
Galeries Lafayette,	**69** C3
Les Halles,	**70** D3
Samaritaine,	**71** D3

🚉 TRAIN STATIONS

Gare de l'Est,
Gare de Lyon,
Gare du Nord,
Gare Montparnasse,
Gare St-Lazare,

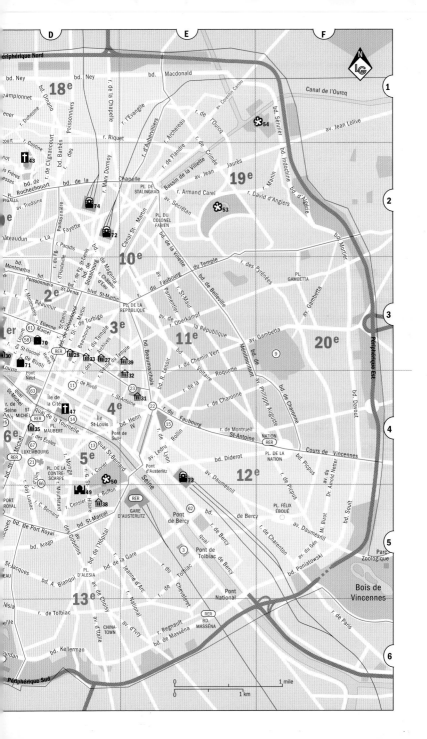

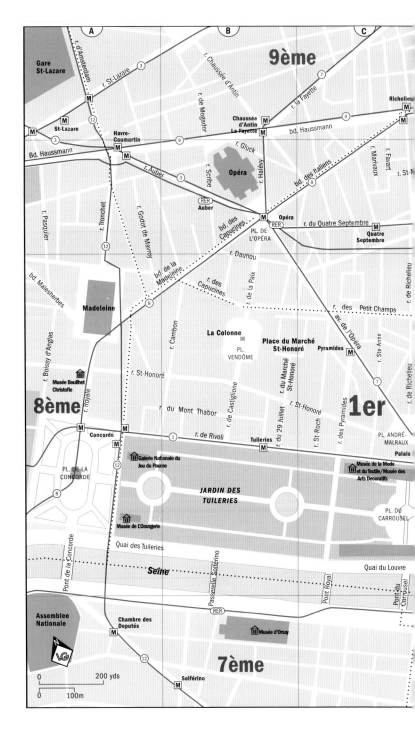

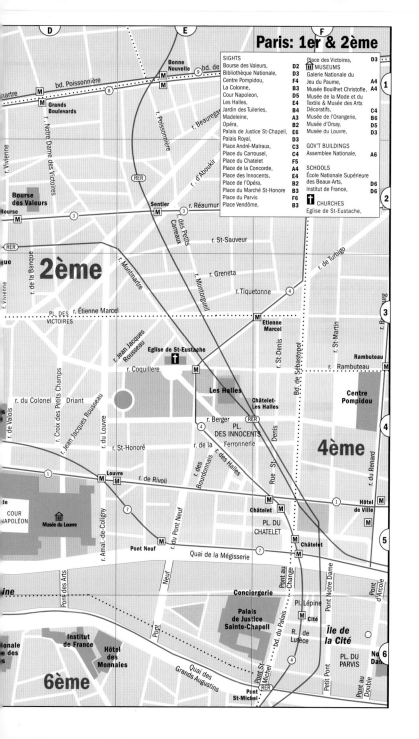

Paris: 1er & 2ème

SIGHTS	
Bourse des Valeurs,	D2
Bibliothèque Nationale,	D3
Centre Pompidou,	F4
La Colonne,	B3
Cour Napoleon,	D5
Les Halles,	E4
Jardin des Tuileries,	B4
Madeleine,	A3
Opéra,	B2
Palais de Justice St-Chapell,	E6
Palais Royal,	D3
Place André-Malraux,	C3
Place du Carrousel,	C4
Place du Chatelet,	F5
Place de la Concorde,	A4
Place des Innocents,	E4
Place de l'Opéra,	B2
Place du Marché St-Honore,	B3
Place du Parvis	F6
Place Vendôme,	B3

Place des Victoires,	D3
🏛 MUSEUMS	
Galerie Nationale du	
Jeu de Paume,	A4
Musée Bouilhet Christofle,	A4
Musée de la Mode et du	
Textile & Musée des Arts	
Décoratifs,	C4
Musée de l'Orangerie,	B6
Musée d'Orsay,	D5
Musée du Louvre,	D3
GOV'T BUILDINGS	
Assemblee Nationale,	A6
SCHOOLS	
École Nationale Supérieure	
des Beaux-Arts,	D6
Institut de France,	D6
🕆 CHURCHES	
Eglise de St-Eustache,	

Bonne Nouvelle

bd. de

bd. Poissonnière

Grands Boulevards

r. Notre Dame des Victoires

martre

r. Vivienne

r. Poissonnière

r. Beauregard

r. d'Aboukir

RER

Bourse des Valeurs

Bourse

M

Sentier

r. Réaumur

9

8

M

M

M

M

M

3

ue

r. de la Banque

r. Vivienne

2ème

r. des Petits Carreaux

r. Montmartre

r. St-Sauveur

r. Greneta

r. Tiquetonne

r. de Turbigo

RER

PL. DES VICTOIRES

r. Étienne Marcel

r. Montorgueil

r. Montmartre

4

3

r. Jean Jacques Rousseau

Eglise de St-Eustache

🕆

Etienne Marcel

r. St-Denis

r. St-Martin

Rambuteau

r. Rambuteau

M

r. Coquillere

M

r. du Colonel Driant

r. Croix des Petits Champs

r. Jean Jacques Rousseau

r. du Louvre

Les Halles

Bd. de Sébastopol

Centre Pompidou

r. de Valois

r. St-Honoré

Châtelet-Les Halles

r. Berger

RER

4

PL. DES INNOCENTS

Ferronnerie

r. de la

r. des Halles

Rue St-Denis

4ème

r. du Renard

r. des Bourdonnais

Louvre

M M

r. de Rivoli

M

Châtelet

M

1

Hôtel de Ville

M

M

de

COUR NAPOLÉON

🏛 Musée du Louvre

r. Amal.-de-Coligny

7

r. du Pont Neuf

PL. DU CHATELET

M

Châtelet

M

Pont Neuf

M

Quai de la Mégisserie

7

Châtelet

M

5

Pont des Arts

Pont Neuf

Pont au Change

Pont Notre Dame

Pont d'Arcole

ine

Conciergerie

PL. Lépine

Pont

Institut de France

Hôtel des Monnaies

Palais de Justice Sainte-Chapell

bd. du Palais

M **Cité**

R. de Lutèce

Île de la Cité

ionale e des

6ème

Quai des Grands Augustins

Pont St-Michel

4

Petit Pont

PL. DU PARVIS

No Da

Pont au Double

6

Pont St-Michel

RER

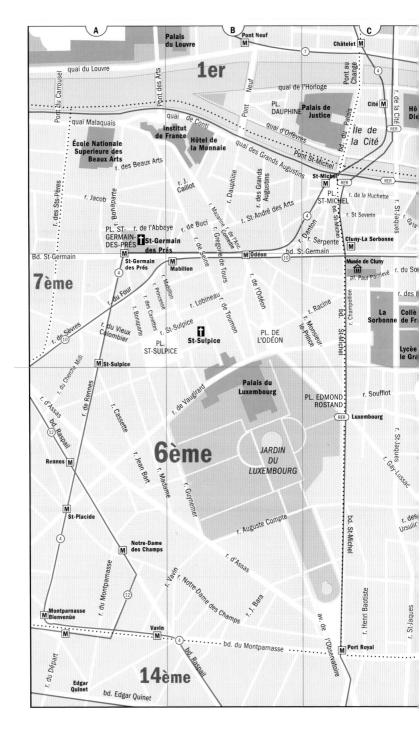

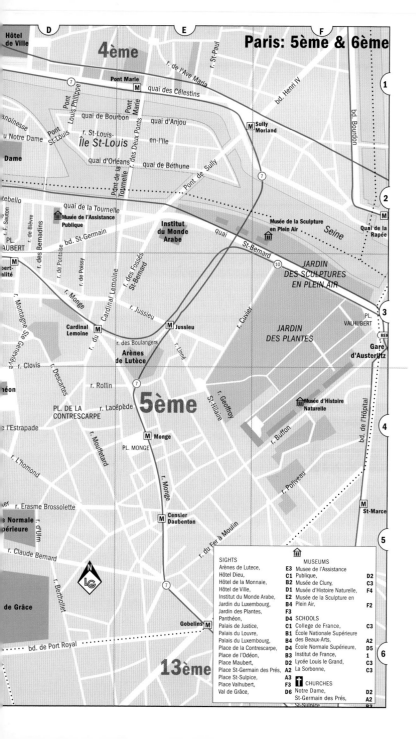

Paris: 5ème & 6ème

4ème

Hôtel de Ville

D · E · F

r. St-Paul
r. de l'Ave Maria

Pont Marie
M quai des Célestins

bd. Henri IV

bd. Bourdon

1

anoinesse
u Notre Dame

quai de Bourbon
Pont Louis Philippe
Pont St-Louis
r. St-Louis-en-l'Île

quai d'Anjou

M Sully Morland

Île St-Louis

Dame

quai d'Orléans
des Deux Ponts
Pont Marie

quai de Béthune

Pont de Sully

M

2

tebello

quai de la Tournelle
Pont de la Tournelle

III Musée de l'Assistance Publique

Institut du Monde Arabe

Musée de la Sculpture en Plein Air III

Quai de la Rapée

PL. AUBERT

r. F. Sauton
r. de Bièvre
r. des Bernadins

bd. St-Germain

r. de Pontoise
r. de Poissy

quai St-Bernard

Seine

M bert-alité

r. Monge

Cardinal Lemoine

r. des Fossés St-Bernard

r. Jussieu

10 **JARDIN DES SCULPTURES EN PLEIN AIR**

3

Cardinal Lemoine M

r. des Boulangers

M Jussieu

r. Linné

r. Cuvier

JARDIN DES PLANTES

PL. VALHUBERT

RER

Gare d'Austerlitz

néon

r. Montagne Ste Geneviève
r. Clovis
r. Descartes

Arènes de Lutèce

r. Rollin
7

r. Lacépède

5ème

r. Geoffroy St-Hilaire

Musée d'Histoire Naturelle III

bd. de l'Hôpital

4

PL. DE LA CONTRESCARPE

l'Estrapade

r. L'homond

r. Mouffetard

M Monge
PL. MONGE

r. Monge

r. Buffon

r. Poliveau

e Normale périeure
r. d'Ulm
r. Claude Bernard

M Censier Daubenton

r. du Fer à Moulin

M St-Marcel

5

LG

r. Berthollet

de Grâce

Gobelins M

bd. de Port Royal

13ème

7

III

SIGHTS

Arènes de Lutece,	E3
Hôtel Dieu,	C1
Hôtel de la Monnaie,	B2
Hôtel de Ville,	D1
Institut du Monde Arabe,	E2
Jardin du Luxembourg,	B4
Jardin des Plantes,	F3
Panthéon,	D4
Palais de Justice,	C1
Palais du Louvre,	B1
Palais du Luxembourg,	B4
Place de la Contrescarpe,	D4
Place de l'Odéon,	B3
Place Maubert,	D2
Place St-Germain des Prés,	A2
Place St-Sulpice,	A3
Place Valhubert,	F3
Val de Grâce,	D6

MUSEUMS

Musee de l'Assistance	
Publique,	D2
Musée de Cluny,	C3
Musée d'Histoire Naturelle,	F4
Musée de la Sculpture en	
Plein Air,	F2

SCHOOLS

College de France,	C3
École Nationale Supérieure	
des Beaux-Arts,	A2
École Normale Supérieure,	D5
Institut de France,	1
Lycée Louis le Grand,	C3
La Sorbonne,	C3

CHURCHES

Notre Dame,	D2
St-Germain des Prés,	A2
St-Sulpice	B2

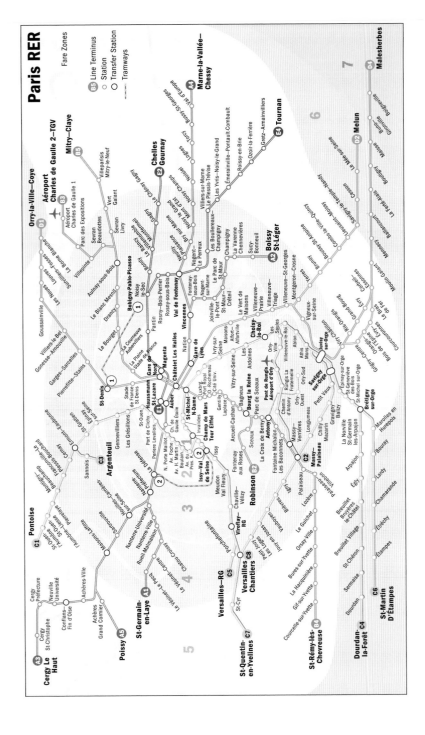

LET'S GO

PAGES PACKED WITH ESSENTIAL INFORMATION

"Value-packed, unbeatable, accurate, and comprehensive."

—*The Los Angeles Times*

"The guides are aimed not only at young budget travelers but at the independent traveler; a sort of streetwise cookbook for traveling alone."

—*The New York Times*

"Unbeatable; good sight-seeing advice; up-to-date info on restaurants, hotels, and inns; a commitment to money-saving travel; and a wry style that brightens nearly every page."

—*The Washington Post*

THE BEST TRAVEL BARGAINS IN YOUR BUDGET

"All the dirt, dirt cheap."

—*People*

"Let's Go follows the creed that you don't have to toss your life's savings to the wind to travel—unless you want to."

—*The Salt Lake Tribune*

REAL ADVICE FOR REAL EXPERIENCES

"The writers seem to have experienced every rooster-packed bus and lunar-surfaced mattress about which they write."

—*The New York Times*

"[Let's Go's] devoted updaters really walk the walk (and thumb the ride, and trek the trail). Learn how to fish, haggle, find work—anywhere."

—*Food & Wine*

"A world-wise traveling companion—always ready with friendly advice and helpful hints, all sprinkled with a bit of wit."

—*The Philadelphia Inquirer*

A GUIDE WITH A SPIRIT AND A SOCIAL CONSCIENCE

"Lighthearted and sophisticated, informative and fun to read. [Let's Go] helps the novice traveler navigate like a knowledgeable old hand."

—*Atlanta Journal-Constitution*

"The serious mission at the book's core reveals itself in exhortations to respect the culture and the environment—and, if possible, to visit as a volunteer, a student, or a teacher rather than a tourist."

—*San Francisco Chronicle*

LET'S GO PUBLICATIONS

TRAVEL GUIDES

Australia
Austria & Switzerland
Brazil
Britain
California
Central America
Chile
China
Costa Rica
Eastern Europe
Ecuador
Egypt
Europe
France
Germany
Greece
Hawaii
India & Nepal
Ireland
Israel
Italy
Japan
Mexico
New Zealand
Peru
Puerto Rico
Southeast Asia
Spain & Portugal
Thailand
USA
Vietnam
Western Europe

ROADTRIP GUIDE

Roadtripping USA

ADVENTURE GUIDES

Alaska
Pacific Northwest
Southwest USA

CITY GUIDES

Amsterdam
Barcelona
Boston
London
New York City
Paris
Rome
San Francisco
Washington, DC

POCKET CITY GUIDES

Amsterdam
Berlin
Boston
Chicago
London
New York City
Paris
San Francisco
Venice
Washington, DC

LET'S GO

PARIS

RESEARCHER-EDITORS
BRIANNA GOODALE
SARA O'ROURKE

R. DEREK WETZEL MAP EDITOR
SAMANTHA GELFAND MANAGING EDITOR

ST. MARTIN'S PRESS ✾ NEW YORK

HELPING LET'S GO. If you want to share your discoveries, suggestions, or corrections, please drop us a line. We appreciate every piece of correspondence, whether a postcard, a 10-page email, or a coconut. Visit Let's Go at **http://www.letsgo.com,** or send email to:

> feedback@letsgo.com
> Subject: "Let's Go: Paris"

Address mail to:

> Let's Go: Paris
> 67 Mount Auburn St.
> Cambridge, MA 02138
> USA

In addition to the invaluable travel advice our readers share with us, many are kind enough to offer their services as researchers or editors. Unfortunately, our charter enables us to employ only currently enrolled Harvard students.

HOW TO USE THIS BOOK

ORGANIZATION. Coverage is divided by the following neighborhoods: Île de la Cité, Île St-Louis, Châtelet-Les Halles (1*ème* and 2*ème*), The Marais (3*ème* and 4*ème*), Latin Quarter and St-Germain (5*ème* and 6*ème*), Invalides (7*ème*), Champs-Élysées (8*ème*), Opéra (9*ème*), Canal St-Martin and Surrounds (10*ème*), Bastille (11*ème* and 12*ème*), Butte-aux-Cailles and Chinatown (13*ème*), Montparnasse (14*ème* and 15*ème*), Passy and Auteuil (16*ème*), Batignolles (17*ème*), Monmartre (18*ème*), Buttes Chaumont (19*ème*), and Belleville and Père Lachaise (20*ème*). Within each neighborhood, sights are listed geographically and food and accommodations are listed by value. Maps for each neighborhood are in the Appendix at the end of the book.

PRICE DIVERSITY AND RANKINGS. Each listing in Accommodations and Food is followed by a price icon (❶-❺); see p. XI for a price range breakdown. Our favorite establishments are marked with the Let's Go thumbs-up (🖐).

TRANSPORTATION INFO. Let's Go lists the metro station nearest to each establishment. When there is no metro icon (Ⓜ) it means that no metro station is nearby. Check the Essentials chapter for more information on transportation and the Map Appendix for maps.

FEATURES AND SCHOLARLY ARTICLES. Throughout this book, you'll find sidebar features and longer articles—built-in reading material for waiting in line or hanging out in a cafe. You can read researchers' tales From the Road, learn what's been going on In Recent News, dive into the Insider's City with mini-walking tours, find explanations of items you'll see On the Menu, and much more. Don't miss the book's Scholarly Article, Haussmannia, on 19th-century urban planning in **Life and Times,** (p. 85).

COVERING THE BASICS. The first chapter, **Discover Paris,** contains highlights of the City of Light, complete with new Suggested Itinerary maps. **Essentials** has all the info you'll need to navigate Paris's airports, train stations, and metro system, while **Life and Times** should help you navigate even more complex constructs—Parisian history, culture, and customs. **Beyond Tourism** holds tons of options for travelers looking to volunteer and work in Paris, and our brand-new **Study Abroad** chapter, which was written entirely by students who studied abroad in Paris, could get any foreign student through the semester. **Practical Information** contains a list of local services, from dry cleaning to fitness clubs, while the **Appendix** has a phrasebook and maps for each neighborhood.

CONTENTS

DISCOVER PARIS 1
When to Go 1
Neighborhoods 2
ESSENTIALS 19
Planning Your Trip 19
Safety and Health 28
Getting to Paris 33
Getting Around France 41
Getting Around Paris 46
Keeping in Touch 50
Accommodations 54
Specific Concerns 56
Other Resources 59
LIFE AND TIMES 63
History 63
The Arts 78
Haussmannia 85
Sports and Recreation 91
Culture 92
Media 96
Festivals 97
National Holidays 101
BEYOND TOURISM 103
A Philosophy for Travelers 103
Volunteering 104
Studying 107
Working 111
STUDY ABROAD 117
Why Paris? 117
Honeymoon Period 118
Day to Day (Le Quotidien) 120
Bonne Santé (And Sanity Too) 124
Money in the Bank 125
Know Your Role: Go to École 126
Oh Yeah, And...Get a Life 133
PRACTICAL INFORMATION 135
Tourist and Financial Services 135
Local Services 138
Emergency and
  Communications 142
ACCOMMODATIONS 145
By Price 145
By Neighborhood 146
Île de la Cité 146
Châtelet-Les Halles 146
Latin Quarter and St-Germain 151

Invalides (7ème) 153
Champs-Élysées (8ème) 154
Opéra (9ème) 155
Canal St-Martin and Surrounds
  (10ème) 156
Bastille 156
Butte-aux-Cailles and
  Chinatown 158
Chinatown (13ème) 158
Montparnasse 159
Passy and Auteuil (16ème) 160
Batignolles (17ème) 161
Montmartre (18ème) 161
Buttes Chaumont (19ème) 162
Belleville and Père Lachaise
  (20ème) 162
FOOD 165
By Type 165
By Neighborhood 168
Île de la Cité 168
Île St-Louis 169
Châtelet-Les Halles 170
The Marais 172
Latin Quarter and St-Germain 178
Invalides (7ème) 184
Champs-Élysées (8ème) 186
Opéra (9ème) 187
Canal St-Martin and Surrounds
  (10ème) 189
Bastille 190
Butte-aux-Cailles and
  Chinatown (13ème) 193
Montparnasse 195
Passy and Auteuil (16ème) 198
Batignolles (17ème) 199
Montmartre (18ème) 201
Buttes Chaumont (19ème) 202
Belleville and Père Lachaise
  (20ème) 203
SIGHTS 205
Île de la Cité 205
Île St-Louis 209
Châtelet-Les Halles 210
The Marais 216
Latin Quarter and St-Germain 221
Invalides (7ème) 228
Champs-Élysées (8ème) 232

opéra (9ème) 236
Canal St-Martin and Surrounds
  (10ème) 238
Bastille 239
Buttes-aux-Cailles and Chinatown
  (13ème) 241
Montparnasse 243
Passy and Auteuil (16ème) 246
Batignolles (17ème) 248
Montmartre (18ème) 249
Buttes Chaumont (19ème) 252
Belleville and Père Lachaise
  (20ème) 253
Perimeter Sights 256

MUSEUMS 265
Île St-Louis 265
Châtelet-Les Halles 266
The Marais 270
Latin Quarter and St-Germain 275
Invalides (7ème) 279
Champs-Élysées (8ème) 284
Opéra (9ème) 286
Bastille 287
Butte-aux-Cailles and Chinatown
  (13ème) 288
Montparnasse 288
Passy and Auteuil (16ème) 289
Batignolles (17ème) 292
Montmartre (18ème) 292
Buttes Chaumont (19ème) 293
Belleville and Père Lachaise
  (20ème) 293

SHOPPING 297
A Brief History of Parisian
  Fashion 297
Île de la Cité 298
Île St-Louis 298
Châtelet-Les Halles (1er and
  2ème) 298
The Marais (3ème and 4ème) 300
Latin Quarter andSt-Germain (5ème
  and 6ème) 303
Invalides (7ème) 306

Champs-Élysées (8ème) 307
Opéra (9ème) 308
Bastille (11ème and 12ème) 308
Montmartre (18ème) 310

ENTERTAINMENT 313
Theater 313
Cabaret 314
Cinema 315
Music, Opera, and Dance 317
Guignol 319

NIGHTLIFE 321
Châtelet-Les Halles 321
The Marais 323
Latin Quarter and St-Germain 328
Invalides (7ème) 330
Champs-Élysées (8ème) 330
Canal St-Martin and Surrounds
  (10ème) 331
Bastille 332
Butte-aux-Cailles and Chinatown
  (13ème) 334
Montparnasse 335
Passy and Auteuil (16ème) 336
Batignolles (17ème) 336
Montmartre (18ème) 336
Buttes Chaumont (19ème) 337
Belleville and Père Lachaise
  (20ème) 337

DAYTRIPS 339
Versailles 339
Chartres 345
Fontainebleau 350
Chantilly 351
Giverny 354
Vaux-le-Vicomte 355
Auvers-Sur-Oise 357
Disneyland Resort Paris 359

APPENDIX 362
Climate 362
Measurements 362
Language 363
Map Index 365

INDEX 393

ACKNOWLEDGMENTS

BRI THANKS: Sara for laughter, sanity & dessert with *boules;* Sam for Foux Da Fa Fas & flexibility; Vinnie & Jenny for polishing Parisian prose; CUPA; Nicole, Michelle, Kate, Sara & Michael for table dancing; Muttie et Pepponne *pour une famille [et les fromages!];* my sisters for trans-Atlantic surprises; Mom, Dad & Cort for love always.

SARA THANKS: Bri, for delicious *dîners* and positive *pensées.* Sam, for getting it (the *fou* and *foux de fa fa*). Vinnie and his -isms. Derek, for coordination. The butcher, for *"C'est bon."* La Chaise and Le Fumoir, for *noisettes.* Sandrine, for becoming *chez moi.* Siblings and *famille,* for encouragement. Dad, for endless support and humor. Mom, *pour tout le reste.*

DEREK THANKS: Sammy, for her tireless dedication to a guide now truly improved. Bri and Sara for their amazing work abroad and at home; you two continued to shine when others would have stopped. Vinnie for helping out and always living STTW. Becca, Elissa, Gretchen, and Illiana for their help with the maps. And the rest of the office for keeping me sane!

VINNIE THANKS: 'O'Dork, Bri, and Sammy! Skeksis. RTGP and The Unstoppable Kovak. People who say, "Grill it!" And the company that makes Moxie.

SAM THANKS: Sara and Bri for a year of dedication. Jim for support. Derek for excellence and friendship. Alex and Lukas for wizardry and late nights. Colleen, Iya, Mary, Jenny, and Laura for help. Vinnie for tactility and the dog track. Lauren for sweet treats. Marissa for walks in the snow. Rach for the pie attempt. Bret for hugs. Family for genetic material. Mel for *crocodile.* Ben for being my bro/a bro. Grandma for shoes. Bertram for emails. And, my Chiefs, for 007, silly sticks, and that impeccable, life-changing, post-tubing pre-tubing communal nap. You know the one.

Researcher-Editors
Brianna Goodale, Sara O'Rourke
Contributing Editors
Vinnie Chiappini, Jenny Wong
Managing Editor
Samantha Gelfand
Map Editor
R. Derek Wetzel
Typesetter
C. Alexander Tremblay

LET'S GO

Publishing Director
Inés C. Pacheco
Editor-in-Chief
Samantha Gelfand
Production Manager
Jansen A. S. Thurmer
Cartography Manager
R. Derek Wetzel
Editorial Managers
Dwight Livingstone Curtis,
Vanessa J. Dube, Nathaniel Rakich
Financial Manager
Lauren Caruso
Publicity and Marketing Manager
Patrick McKiernan
Personnel Manager
Laura M. Gordon
Production Associate
C. Alexander Tremblay
Director of IT & E-Commerce
Lukáš Tóth
Website Manager
Ian Malott
Office Coordinators
Vinnie Chiappini, Jenny Wong
Director of Advertising Sales
Nicole J. Bass
Senior Advertising Associates
Kipyegon Kitur, Jeremy Siegfried,
John B. Ulrich
Junior Advertising Associate
Edward C. Robinson Jr.

President
Timothy J. J. Creamer
General Manager
Jim McKellar

RESEARCHER-EDITORS

Brianna Goodale   5ème, 6ème, 9ème, 10ème, 13ème, 14ème, 15ème, 17ème, 18ème, 19ème, 20ème

When Bri decided to live in a homestay during her semester abroad, she couldn't have dreamed she'd end up under the wing of a count and countess (who had everything from nightly four-course feasts to a family château outside of Paris). Though she got more than her fair share of lessons in formal French etiquette, this cross-country runner never hesitated to get down and dirty with her research. Between taking psychology classes at Nanterre and letting French beauty school students practice cutting and styling her hair (which now looks fabulous!), she even found time to explain to befuddled Parisians that yes, her name is Bri, but *non*, she is not *fromage*.

Sara O'Rourke   1er, 2ème, 3ème, 4ème, 7ème, 8ème, 11ème, 12ème, 16ème, Daytrips

Sara is a Let's Go All-Star and an expert in all things French. After working as an associate editor for *Let's Go France* in 2008, this Social Studies major decided she had done enough vicarious traveling and hit the road for a semester abroad in Paris. She settled into her cozy 4*ème* apartment, which she dubbed Sandrine, and soon made the Marais her own. Scoping out the best nightlife, cafes, and running paths, Sara even accomplished the impossible—making friends with Parisian waiters.

CONTRIBUTING WRITERS

Sarah Ashburn was a Researcher-Writer for *Let's Go: France* (2008).

Edward-Michael Dussom was a Researcher-Writer for *Let's Go: France* (2008).

Charlotte Houghteling has worked on Let's Go's *Middle East*, *Egypt*, and *Israel* titles. She wrote her senior thesis on the development of department stores during the Second Empire and then completed her M. Phil at Cambridge on the consumer society of Revolutionary Paris.

Sara Houghteling was a Researcher-Writer for *Let's Go: France* (1999) and has taught at the American School in Paris. She recently earned her MFA in creative writing from the University of Michigan.

PRICE RANGES
PARIS

We list establishments in order of value from best to worst; our favorites are denoted by the Let's Go thumbs-up (). Since the best value is not always the cheapest price, we have incorporated a system of price ranges for quick reference. Our price ranges are based on a rough expectation of what you will spend. For **accommodations,** we base our price range off the cheapest price for which a single traveler can stay for one night. For **restaurants** and other dining establishments, we estimate the average amount that you will spend in that restaurant. The table below tells you what you will *typically* find in Paris at the corresponding price range.

ACCOMMODATIONS	RANGE	WHAT YOU'RE *LIKELY* TO FIND
1	under €35	Mostly hostels; expect a basic dorm-style room and hall bathrooms. There may be lockout and/or curfew.
2	€35-54	Small hotels, sometimes far from major attractions. Expect basic, comfortable rooms and hall bathrooms.
3	€55-80	Small hotels in more central areas, and with more amenities or better decor than those in lower ranges. Some rooms have a shower, toilet, TV, and phone.
4	€81-100	Nicer hotels in convenient areas, with attention to decor and atmosphere. Rooms should have shower, toilet, TV, and phone.
5	over €100	Upscale hotels. If you're paying this much, your room should have all the amenities you want, and it should be exceptionally charming and comfortable.

FOOD	RANGE	WHAT YOU'RE *LIKELY* TO FIND
1	under €10	Mostly take-out food, like sandwiches, falafel, cafe fare, and crêpes.
2	€10-16	Small restaurants, cafes, and *brasseries;* you'll usually get a basic 1- or 2-course sit-down meal.
3	€17-25	Nicer restaurants or specialty cafes, usually featuring lunch or dinner *menus;* expect at least 2 courses (*plat* and *entrée* or dessert) and good service.
4	€26-35	Restaurants with great atmosphere, great service, and great food. You'll usually get a *menu* with 2 or 3 courses, wine, and coffee.
5	above €35	Classy, dressy restaurants with amazing food and flawless service: a memorable dining experience.

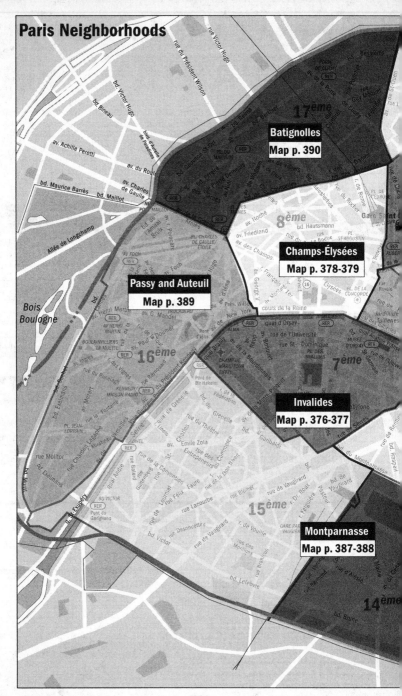

Paris Neighborhoods

17ème

Batignolles
Map p. 390

8ème

Champs-Élysées
Map p. 378-379

Passy and Auteuil
Map p. 389

Bois Boulogne

16ème

7ème

Invalides
Map p. 376-377

15ème

Montparnasse
Map p. 387-388

14ème

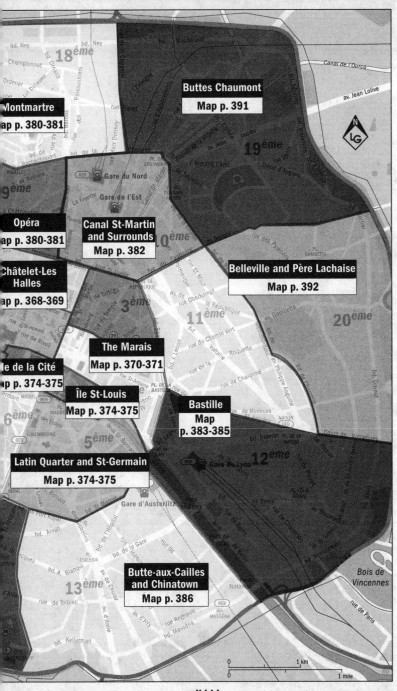

Montmartre
ap p. 380-381

Buttes Chaumont
Map p. 391

Opéra
ap p. 380-381

Canal St-Martin
and Surrounds
Map p. 382

Châtelet-Les
Halles
ap p. 368-369

Belleville and Père Lachaise
Map p. 392

le de la Cité
p p. 374-375

The Marais
Map p. 370-371

Île St-Louis
Map p. 374-375

Bastille
Map
p. 383-385

Latin Quarter and St-Germain
Map p. 374-375

Butte-aux-Cailles
and Chinatown
Map p. 386

Bois de
Vincennes

0 ____ 1 km
0 ____ 1 mile

XIII

DISCOVER PARIS

From students who obsess over Derrida's *Of Grammatology* to tourists who wonder why the French don't pronounce half the consonants in each word, everyone enjoys the city where, by decree of law, buildings don't exceed six stories, *pour que tout le monde ait du soleil* (so that all have sunshine). Though Parisians may English you (speak in English when you speak in French), and your feet may feel like numb petrified stubs *de bois* by the end of each day, this city pulls through for those who let themselves indulge in the sensory snapshots around every corner—the aroma of a *boulangerie*, the gleam of bronze balconies, the buzz of a *good* €2 bottle of red, the jolt of the new fave metro line 14. For all its hyped-up snobbery (and yes, the waiters *are* judging you), Paris is open to those willing to wander. The truth is, this city will charm and bitchslap you with equal gusto, but don't get too le tired—by your third or fourth sincere attempt at *s'il vous plaît*, even the waiters soften up. Stick around long enough, and you'll be able to tell the *foux* from the *foux de fa fa*, the Lavazza from the Illy, and the meta hipster bars from the wanna-be meta hipster bars. *Et puis*, we'll see who's judging whom.

FACTS AND FIGURES	
AGE: 2259 years old in 2009	**PERCENTAGE OF ANNUAL INCOME SPENT ON WINE:** 15
POPULATION: c. 2.2 million	
URBAN AREA: 2723 sq. km.	**KINGS NAMED LOUIS:** 18 (+ 1 Louis-Philippe)
LAND AREA: 86.928 sq. km.	
MOST VISITED SIGHT: Centre Pompidou (only because they keep count)	**ESTIMATED "ROMANTIC ENCOUNTERS" PER DAY:** 4,959,476
REVOLUTIONS: 4, to date	**NUMBER OF FILMS WITH THE EIFFEL TOWER AS A SIGNIFICANT FEATURE:** 65 and counting.
NUMBER OF STRIKES PER YEAR: 365, at least.	

WHEN TO GO

WEATHER. Spring weather in Paris is fickle, with rainy and sunny days in about equal numbers. Of the summer months, June is notoriously rainy, while high temperatures tend to hit in July and August. Occasional heat waves can be uncomfortable (and in extreme cases, devastating—a 2003 hot spell killed hundreds), and muggy weather aggravates Paris's pollution problem. By fall a fantastic array of auburn brightens up the foliage in the parks, and the weather is dry and temperate. Rain is more common than snow in the winter, which is typically mild and characterized by resplendent Christmas decorations.

CROWDS. Temperate weather lets everyone love Paris in the springtime, but in the summer, tourists move in and Parisians move out for vacation—smaller hotels, shops, and services usually close for the month of August. Many of Paris's best festivals are held during the summer (see Festivals, p. 97), and parts of the city can be quite peaceful. In the fall, the tourist madness begins to calm down—airfares and hotel rates drop, travel is less congested, and the museum lines are shorter. The winter is pretty low-key when it comes to crowds, but, as expected, many people love Paris in the springtime.

AVG TEMP (LO/HI), PRECIPITATION	JANUARY			APRIL			JULY			OCTOBER		
	°C	°F	mm	°C	°F	mm	°C	°F	mm	°C	°F	mm
Paris	1/6	34/43	56	6/16	43/61	42	15/25	59/77	59	8/16	46/61	50
Versailles	1/6	34/43	56	6/14	43/57	42	14/24	58/75	59	8/15	46/59	50
Reims	-1/4	30/40	46	4/16	40/60	48	13/24	56/76	66	6/14	43/58	66

NEIGHBORHOODS

The Seine River ("SEN") flows from east to west, splitting the city into two sections: Rive Gauche (Left Bank) to the south and Rive Droite (Right Bank) to the north. Two islands in the Seine, Île de la Cité and neighboring Île St-Louis, are situated in the geographical center of the city. Central Paris is divided into 20 *arrondissements* (districts) that spiral clockwise outward from the center of the city, like the shell of an *escargot*. Each *arrondissement* is referred to by its number (e.g. the third, the sixteenth). In French, "third" is said *troisième* (TRWAZ-yem) and abbreviated "3ème"; "sixteenth" is *seizième* (SEZ-yem) and abbreviated "16ème." The same goes for every *arrondissement* except the first, which is said premier (PREM-yay) and abbreviated 1er.

Although *arrondissements* are marked by official numerical divisions, Parisian neighborhoods often overlap more than one *arrondissement*. The Marais, for example, spans the *3ème* and *4ème arrondissements*. To ensure that our readers are *branchés* (literally, "plugged in," or in-the-know), we have divided our coverage by neighborhood, which we subdivide into *arrondissements* where necessary. This is the structure that we use throughout the book.

ÎLE DE LA CITÉ AND ÎLE ST-LOUIS

see map p. 374-375

Île de la Cité is situated in the very center of the Île de France, the geographical region surrounding Paris. From the 6th century, when Clovis crowned himself king of the Franks, until Charles V abandoned it in favor of the Louvre in the 14th century, the island was the seat of the monarchy. Construction of the **Notre Dame** (p. 205) began here in 1163, and the presence of the cathedral, as well as the **Ste-Chapelle** (p. 207) and the **Conciergerie** (p. 208), ensured that the island would remain a center of Parisian religious, political, and cultural life—and, now, a major center of tourism. All distances in France are measured from **kilomètre zéro**, a circular sundial in front of Notre Dame

Île St-Louis had less illustrious beginnings. Originally two small islands— the **Île aux Vâches** (Cow Island) and the **Île de Notre Dame**—the Île St-Louis was considered suitable for duels, cows, and little else throughout the Middle Ages. In 1267, the area was renamed for Louis IX after he departed for the Crusades. The two islands merged in the 17th century under the direction of architect **Louis Le Vau,** and Île St-Louis became a residential district. The island's *hôtels particuliers* (mansions, many of which were also designed by Le Vau) attracted an elite citizenry including Voltaire, Mme. de Châtelet, Daumier, Ingres, Baudelaire, Balzac, Courbet, Sand, Delacroix, and Cézanne. In the 1930s, the idiosyncratic inhabitants declared the island an independent republic. The island still retains a certain remoteness from the rest of Paris; older residents say "Je vais à Paris" (I'm going to Paris) when leaving by one of the four bridges linking Île St-Louis and the mainland. All in all, the island looks remarkably similar to its 17th-century self, retaining history and genteel tranquility. While tourists might clog the streets on weekends, St-Louis is nonetheless a haven of boutiques, specialty food shops, and art galleries that make for a pleasant wander.

CHÂTELET-LES HALLES (1ER, 2ÈME)

see map p. 368-369

Châtelet-Les Halles (chat-lay-lays-al) is home to much of Paris's royal history. Its most famous sight, the **Louvre,** (p. 266) was home to French kings for four centuries, but today, the bedchambers and dining rooms of the *ancien régime* palace house the world's finest art. The surrounding **Jardin des Tuileries** (p. 210) was redesigned in 1660 by Louis XIV's favored architect, André Le Nôtre, but the Sun King's prized grounds now play host both to strolling tourists and two other reputable art museums, the **Orangerie** (p. 269) and **Jeu de Paume** (p. 270).Meanwhile, a different kind of royalty dominates Châtelet-Les Halles: Chanel, Cartier, and the Ritz hold court here in the imposing **place Vendôme** (p. 211). Less glamorous souvenir shops crowd **rue du Rivoli** and **Les Halles,** (p. 298) while elegant boutiques line **rue St-Honoré,** also home to the **Comédie Française** (p. 313), where one of France's most talented *troupes* preserve the tradition of Molière. Farther west, jazz clubs (p. 322) rule the night on **rue des Lombards.**

 LET'S NOT GO. Although the 1er is one of the safest regions of Paris above ground, the area's metro stops (ⓂChâtelet and Les Halles) are dangerous and best avoided at night.

THE MARAIS (3ÈME, 4ÈME)

see map p. 370-371

The Marais is Paris's comeback kid. With a name that literally translates to "swamp," its origins are easy enough to discern—in short, it was all bog. Starting in the 13th century, the area began to find its bearings when monks drained the land to provide building space for the Right Bank. With Henri IV's construction of the glorious **Place des Vosges** at the beginning of the 17th century, the area became the city's center of fashionable living; *hôtels particuliers* built by leading architects and sculptors abounded, as did luxury and scandal. During the Revolution, former royal haunts gave way to slums and tenements, and the majority of the *hôtels* fell into ruin or disrepair. The **Jewish population,** a presence in the Marais since the 12th century, grew with influxes of immigrants from Russia and North Africa but suffered tragic losses during the Holocaust. In the 1960s the Marais was once again revived when it was declared a historic neighborhood. Since then, more than thirty years of gentrification, renovation, and fabulous-ization has restored the Marais to its pre-Revolutionary glory.

Once-palatial mansions have become exquisite museums, and the tiny twisting streets have been adopted by hip bars, avant-garde galleries, and some of the city's most unique boutiques. **Rue des Rosiers,** in the heart of the 4ème, is still the center of the city's Jewish population, though the steady influx of cutting-edge clothing stores threatens its existence. Superb kosher delicatessens neighbor Middle Eastern and Eastern European restaurants, and on Sundays, when much of the city is closed, the Marais remains lively. The Marais is also unquestionably the center of **gay Paris,** with its hub around the intersection of rue Ste-Croix de la Brettonerie and rue Vieille du Temple. Though recently heavy tourism has encroached upon the Marais's eclectic personality, the district retains its signature charm: an accessible, fun, and friendly mix of old and new, queer and straight, cheap and chic, classic and fresh, hip and historic.

RIVE GAUCHE (LEFT BANK). The *"gauche"* in Rive Gauche once signified a lower-class lifestyle, the kind flaunted by the impoverished students who lived there. Today, the Left Bank's appeal is ensured by its inexpensive cafes and bars, great shopping and sights, and timeless literary caché.

LATIN QUARTER AND ST-GERMAIN (5ÈME, 6ÈME)

see map p. 374-375

Named for the language used in the 5*ème*'s prestigious high schools and universities prior to 1798, the Latin Quarter *(le quartier latin)* is always buzzing with energy. The 5*ème* has been in the intellectual thick of things since the founding of the **Sorbonne** in 1263 (p. 222), and its hot-blooded student population has played a role in uprisings from the Revolution to the riots of May '68. In the 6*ème*, cafes on **boulevard St-Germain** were the stomping grounds of bigwigs like Hemingway, Sartre, Picasso, and Camus during the early 20th century.

Truth be told, the Latin Quarter has lost some of its rebellious vigor. While the reasons aren't easy to pin down—some cite the replacement of the old cobblestones, used by protesting students as projectiles in the old days—commodification of areas like **boulevard St-Michel** (now teeming with chain stores and hordes of camera-toting tourists) may have watered down the area's spirit. Nonetheless, the **bars** (p. 328) are some of the best in Paris, as are the **bookshops** (p. 304). The Latin Quarter is also the beating heart of that quintessential Parisian passion: **art house cinema.** The area's final claim to fame is its streetside past times; **place de la Contrescarpe** (p. 223) and **rue Mouffetard** (p. 223), both in the 5*ème*, are superb for people-watching, and the Mouff has one of the liveliest street markets in Paris. As for food, you'll probably have to drop some cash if you want more than a *crêpe*, and the area's accommodations (p. 151) aren't any more financially forgiving. However, if money is no object, there is terrific **boutique shopping** west and south of **Église St-Germain-des-prés** (p. 227).

INVALIDES (7ÈME)

see map p. 376-377

Between the grass of the **Champ de Mars** and the fashionable side streets surrounding **rue de Sèvres,** the 7*ème* offers the most touristy and the most intimate sights in Paris. The area became Paris's most elegant residential district in the 18th century, although many of its stunning residences have been converted to foreign embassies, especially near the **Musée Rodin** (p. 279). Though the 1889 completion of the **Eiffel Tower**

(p. 229) at the river's edge sparked outrage, it has secured Invalides's reputation as a Parisian landmark. Meanwhile, the **National Assembly** (p. 231) and the **Hôtel National des Invalides** (p. 231) add historical substance and traditional French character to this part of the Left Bank.

CHAMPS-ÉLYSÉES (8ÈME)

see map p. 378-379

The Champs-Élysées area is past its prime. Its boulevards are still lined with the vast mansions, expensive shops, and grandiose monuments that keep the tourists coming, but there's little sense of sophistication, progress, or style. The Champs-Élysées itself was synonymous with fashion in the 19th century, but now it houses charmless establishments ranging from cheap to exorbitant. Much of the neighborhood is occupied by office buildings and car dealerships; these areas are comatose after dark. Only the Champs itself throbs late into the night, thanks to flashy nightclubs, cinemas, and droves of tourists. A stroll along **avenue Montaigne, rue du Faubourg St-Honoré,** or around the **Madeleine** will give a taste of what life in Paris is like for those with money to burn. While low prices usually mean low quality here—particularly for accommodations—there are a few good restaurants (p. 186) and museums (p. 284). The northern part of the neighborhood, near the **Parc Monceau,** is a lovely, quiet area for walking.

OPÉRA (9ÈME)

see map p. 380-381

The 9ème is an example of Paris's cultural extremes. The lower 9ème gleams with the magnificent **Palais Garnier** (p. 237) and the haute couture in Paris' world-famous department stores, the **Galeries Lafayette** (p. 308) and **Au Printemps** (p. 308). The upper 9ème, near the northern border with the 18ème, offers a striking contrast: porn shops, X-rated cinemas, and prostitution define the neon-lit **Pigalle** neighborhood. Separating these two sectors is a residential neighborhood—the 9ème's geographical center. The area known as **Étienne-Marcel** has fabulously cheap clothing and great sales in more expensive stores. The Opéra Comique, now the **Théâtre Musicale** (p. 215), is between bd. des Italiens and rue de Richelieu.

CANAL ST-MARTIN AND SURROUNDS (10ÈME)

see map p. 382

Revolutionary fervor once gripped **place de la République,** but Haussmann doused their moxie with some clever urban planning (see Haussmannia, p. 83). Since then, the 10ème has quieted down. The area has striking juxtapositions—regal statues scrawled with graffiti line sunny, peaceful squares. Most travelers only visit the 10ème for the **Gare du Nord** and **Gare de l'Est,** but parts of it are well worth exploring. Good, cheap restaurants abound, and the blossoming area near Canal St-Martin makes for pleasant wandering.

 LET'S NOT GO. The 10ème is far from most tourist sights, and certain areas may be unsafe at night; be extra cautious around the bd. St-Martin and parts of rue du Faubourg St-Denis at any time of day. Use caution west of pl. de la République along rue du Château d'Eau.

BASTILLE (11ÈME, 12ÈME)

see maps p. 383-385

As its name attests, the Bastille (bah-steel) area is most famous for hosting the Revolution's kick-off at the Bastille prison on July 14, 1789. Hundreds of years later, the French still storm this neighborhood nightly in search of the latest cocktail, culinary innovation, and up-and-coming artist. Five Metro lines converge at Ⓜ République and three at Ⓜ Bastille, making the Bastille district a transport hub and mammoth center of action—the hangout of the young and fun (and frequently drunk). The 1989 opening of the glassy **Opéra Bastille** on the bicentennial of the Revolution was supposed to breathe new cultural life into the area, but the **party atmosphere** has yet to give way to galleries and string quartets. Today, with numerous bars along **rue de Lappe,** manifold original dining options on **rue de la Roquette** and **rue J.P. Timbaud,** and young designer boutiques, the Bastille is a great area for unwinding after a day at the museums.

North of the Bastille on **rue Oberkampf** and **rue Ménilmontant,** eclectic neighborhood bars (p. 332) provide the perfect end to a pub crawl. Budget accommodations (p. 156) also proliferate in the area. **Place de la Nation,** farther south, was the setting for Louis XIV's wedding in 1660 and the site of revolutionary fervor in 1830 and 1848. Today, this part of the Bastille district borrows youthful momentum from the neighboring 4*ème* and 11*ème arrondissements.* Its northwestern fringes are funky—the **Viaduc des Arts, rue de la Roquette,** and **rue du Faubourg St-Antoine** are lined with galleries and stores—and its core is working class, with a large immigrant population. Finally, for a taste of nature head to the 12*ème,* which borders the beautiful and expansive **Bois de Vincennes**—or, try the pretty **Yitzhak Rabin Garden** in the quirky **Parc Bercy.**

LET'S NOT GO. While the area is generally safe during the day, place de la République and bd. Voltaire are best avoided after sunset. Always be careful around Gare de Lyon, especially at night, and near the sleazy nightlife found at av. du Maine's northern end.

BUTTE-AUX-CAILLES
AND CHINATOWN (13ÈME)

see map p. 386

Until the 20th century, the 13*ème* remained one of Paris's poorest *arrondissements,* with conditions so terrible that Victor Hugo set **Les Misérables** there. Thankfully, the last two centuries have brought numerous changes to the 13*ème.* In 1910, the Bièvre was filled in, and environmentalists eventually won a campaign to close the neighborhood's tanneries and paper factories. Construction begun in 1996 on Mitterrand's ultra-modern **Bibliothèque de France,** (p. 242) ushering in a new wave of development aimed to transform the 13*ème*'s *quais* into Paris's largest cultural center. Associated with the **ZAC** (Zone d'Aménagement Concerté), recent projects include dormitories for over 20,000 University of Paris VII students and the **MK2 entertainment complex** (p. 242). Several immigrant communities make for a thriving **Chinatown.** Rising over the Seine, the Pont de Bercy connects the proletariat 13*ème* to the youthful 12*ème.*

DISCOVER

MONTPARNASSE (14ÈME, 15ÈME)

see maps p. 387-388

Named after the famous Greek mountain of lore (Mount Parnasse), Paris's 14*ème* revels in its **bohemian reputation.** During the 1920s, the *quartier* became a haven for the "Lost Generation," intellectuals and political exiles trying to process life after WWI. Famed Montparnasse residents F. Scott Fitzgerald, Ernest Hemingway, Man Ray, and Henry Miller conversed the night away in popular cafes like **Le Select** and **Le Dôme.** These legendary artists no longer roam the Montparnasse neighborhood (mostly because they're dead), but the area's affordability continues to attract artists (who are still alive) and students.

Unlike its neighbor to the east, the 15*ème* has never been a legendary area. The modern **Parc André Citroën** attracts families from all over Paris on weekends, but aside from the park, the 15*ème* has no tourist sights to speak of, and its atmosphere is often crowded, busy, and—around **Gare Montparnasse**—very industrial (a.k.a. ugly). As a result, the 15*ème* is one of Paris's least touristed areas, and streetwise travelers can benefit from low room rates and affordable restaurants. Locals have their pick among the many shops on rue du Commerce, the cafes at the corner of rue de la Convention and rue de Vaugirard, and the specialty shops along av. Émile Zola.

PASSY AND AUTEUIL (16ÈME)

see map p. 389

When Notre Dame was under construction in the 12th century, this now-elegant suburb was little more than some tiny woodland villages. With the architectural revolution of Haussmann, however, the area was transformed. The villages of Auteuil to the south, Passy in the east, and northernmost **Chaillot** banded together, joining the city to form what is now the 16*ème*. Today, the manicured, tree-lined streets of this elegant *quartier* provide a peaceful respite from the mobbed sidewalks of the nearby 8*ème*. The 16*ème* offers ideal views of the **Eiffel Tower,** framed by Art Nouveau and art deco architecture. The upper 16*ème* is populated with mansions and townhouses, while the lower half of the *arrondissement* is modest and commercial.

BATIGNOLLES (17ÈME)

see map p. 390

The 17*ème* is a diverse district where bourgeois turns working class and back again within a block. The *arrondissement's* eastern and southern parts share the bordering 8*ème* and 16*ème's* aristocratic bearing, while the *quartier's* western edge resembles the more tawdry 18*ème* and Pigalle. Removed from central Paris's suffocating crowds, the 17*ème* resonates with authentic French charm. Unlike the industrial briskness characterizing other *arrondissements*, a vibrant *joie de vivre* permeates its streets. Thanks in large part to its multicultural population, the 17*ème* offers a fabulous variety of restaurants spanning the price spectrum. Parents and young children stroll through the tree-lined **Village Batignolles,** while hip clientele frequent upscale bars at night.

> **LET'S NOT GO.** Especially at night, be careful at the border of the 17*ème* and the 18*ème* near pl. de Clichy, in the emptier northwestern corner of the 19*ème*, along rue David d'Angiers, bd. Indochine, av. Corentin Cariou, and by the *Portes* in the 19*ème*.

MONTMARTRE (18ÈME)

see map p. 380-381

Like Montparnasse and the Latin Quarter, Montmartre glows with the lustre of its bohemian past. Named "Mount of the Martyr" for St. Denis, who was beheaded there by the Romans in AD 260, the hill was for centuries a rural village covered with vineyards, wheat fields, windmills, and gypsum mines. In the late 19th and early 20th centuries, the city's rebellious artistic energies centered here. During the Belle Époque, its picturesque beauty and low rents attracted bohemians like painter Henri Toulouse-Lautrec and composer Erik Satie as well as performer and impresario Aristide Bruant. Toulouse-Lautrec, in particular, immortalized Montmartre by painting its disreputable nightspots like the infamous **Bal du Moulin Rouge.** Filled with *cabarets* like Le Chat Noir and proto-Dada artist groups like Les Incohérents and Les Hydropathes, the *butte* (ridge) became the Parisian center of free love, intoxicated fun, and liberated *fumisme:* the satirical jabbing of social and political norms. A generation later, just before WWI smashed its spotlights and destroyed its crops, the *butte* welcomed eccentric innovators Apollinaire, Modigliani, Picasso, and Utrillo.

Today, artsy Montmartre best embodies the stereotyped Parisian dream: nostalgic history on **rue Lepic,** pseudo-artistic schmaltz lingering in **place du Tertre,** and a dab of provocative sleaze from **boulevard de Clichy.** The *quartier* transcends its metropolis, however, with **functional vineyards,** an **official arboretum** in its cemetery, and a panorama of the city from the **Basilique du Sacré-Coeur.**

> **LET'S NOT GO.** Pl. Pigalle, bd. Barbès, and bd. de Rochechoart are notorious for prostitution and drugs, both of which become apparent at an early hour. The area is heavily policed, but travelers (particularly young women and those traveling alone) should still exercise caution. At night, Ⓜ Abesse is safer than Ⓜ Anvers, Ⓜ Pigalle, and Ⓜ Barbès-Rochechoart.

BUTTES CHAUMONT (19ÈME)

see map p. 391

The 19*ème* and the 20*ème*, both primarily working-class, have recently flourished as centers of Parisian bohemia. Between the romantic **Parc des Buttes Chaumont** and the famed **Cimetière du Père Lachaise,** a slew of performance spaces, artsy cafes, and provocative galleries have joined the neighborhood's ethnic eateries, markets, and shops. Historically lacking the artistic patronage that brought Montmartre fame, today the 19*ème* battles for cultural recognition; its modern **Cité de la Musique** (p. 253) and **Cité de la Science** (p. 252) encourage creative exploration through concerts and interactive museums. Home to Asian, Greek, Jewish, North African, and Russian communities, the 19*ème* and 20*ème* *arrondissements* include Paris's most dynamic neighborhoods.

LET'S NOT GO. Be careful at night in the more empty northwestern corner of the 19*ème arrondissement* and on rue David d'Angers, bd. Indochine, avenue Corentin Cariou, rue de Belleville, and by the "Portes" into the area.

BELLEVILLE AND PÈRE LACHAISE (20ÈME)

see map p. 392

The 20*ème*'s population swelled in the mid-19th century, when Hausmann's architectural reforms drove working-class Parisians from the central city. Thousands migrated east to **Belleville** (the northern part of the 20*ème*), **Charonne** (the southeastern), and **Ménilmontant** (the southern). By the late Second Republic, the 20*ème* had become a "red" *arrondissement*, characterized as proletarian and radical. Some of the heaviest fighting during the Commune suppression took place in its streets. Caught between the Versaillais troops to the west and the Prussian lines outside the city walls, the Commune fortified the **Parc des Buttes-Chaumont** (p. 253) and the **Cimetière du Père Lachaise** (p. 254) but soon ran out of ammunition. On May 28, 1871, the Communards abandoned their last barricade and surrendered (see **Life and Times,** p. 63). Following the government's retributive massacres, the surviving workers adopted the fairly isolated 20*ème* as their home. Today, the *arrondissement* is still working-class, with busy residential areas and markets catering to locals rather than visitors.

BANLIEUES

Parisian *banlieues* (suburbs) have gained attention as sites of poverty and racism, though in fact they run the socioeconomic gamut. The nearest suburbs, the *proche-banlieues*, are accessible by metro and bus and include the **Vallée de Chevreuse** towns to the south; **St-Cloud, Neuilly,** and **Boulogne** to the west; **St-Mandé** and **Vincennes** to the east; and **Pantin, Aubervilliers** and **La Courneuve** to the north. Farther afield and home to some striking sights (see **Daytrips,** p. 339), the *grandes banlieues* (**Chantilly, St-Germain-en-Laye,** and **Versailles**) can be reached by RER. The *banlieues* also host exciting cultural productions. Every summer brings the **Banlieue Jazz** and **Banlieue Blues** festivals (see **Festivals,** p. 97).

⬛LET'S GO PICKS

BEST PLACE TO MEDITATE: The Japanese garden at UNESCO (p. 230).

BEST PLACE TO MOURN YOUR POVERTY: Rue du faubourg St-Honoré in the 8*ème*, with the best clothes in Paris that you'll never afford.

BEST PLACE TO GET BUSY: La Défense, where business (and the occasional businessman) gets done (p. 261).

BEST POSTHUMOUS HANGOUT: Napoleon's tomb, Invalides (p. 231).

BEST WAY TO CATCH A DISEASE: Kiss Oscar Wilde's grave in the Cimitière du Père Lachaise (p. 254).

BEST BRIDGE BY NIGHT: The ornate Pont Alexandre III (p. 231), which connects the Esplanade des Invalides to the Grand and Petit Palais.

BEST PLACE TO SPEAK ENGLISH WITHOUT SHAME: Breakfast in America (p. 176). Also the best place for diner food.

BEST PLACE TO LEARN ABOUT SEX: The Musée de l'Erotisme (p. 292), conveniently open until 2am.

BEST NEW TAKE ON HANDBALL: The Jeu de Paume (p. 270), which hosts rotating contemporary art exhibits.

THE USUAL SUSPECTS

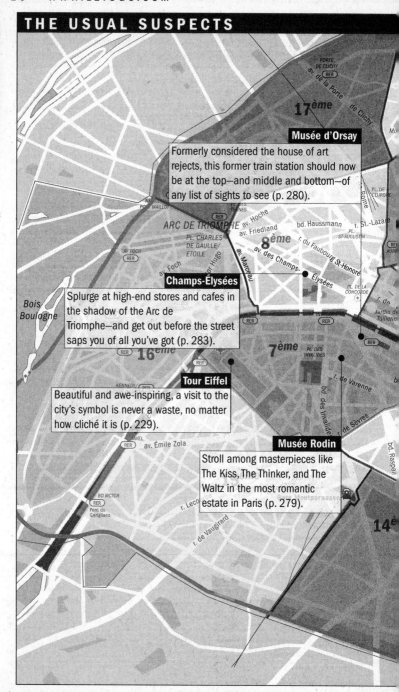

Musée d'Orsay

Formerly considered the house of art rejects, this former train station should now be at the top—and middle and bottom—of any list of sights to see (p. 280).

Champs-Élysées

Splurge at high-end stores and cafes in the shadow of the Arc de Triomphe—and get out before the street saps you of all you've got (p. 283).

Tour Eiffel

Beautiful and awe-inspiring, a visit to the city's symbol is never a waste, no matter how cliché it is (p. 229).

Musée Rodin

Stroll among masterpieces like The Kiss, The Thinker, and The Waltz in the most romantic estate in Paris (p. 279).

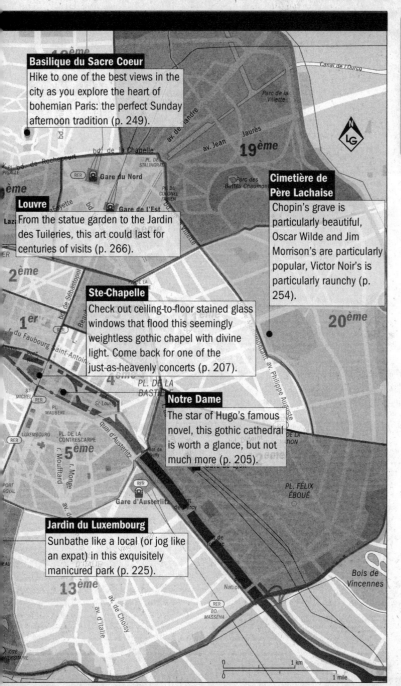

Basilique du Sacre Coeur
Hike to one of the best views in the city as you explore the heart of bohemian Paris: the perfect Sunday afternoon tradition (p. 249).

Louvre
From the statue garden to the Jardin des Tuileries, this art could last for centuries of visits (p. 266).

Cimetière de Père Lachaise
Chopin's grave is particularly beautiful, Oscar Wilde and Jim Morrison's are particularly popular, Victor Noir's is particularly raunchy (p. 254).

Ste-Chapelle
Check out ceiling-to-floor stained glass windows that flood this seemingly weightless gothic chapel with divine light. Come back for one of the just-as-heavenly concerts (p. 207).

Notre Dame
The star of Hugo's famous novel, this gothic cathedral is worth a glance, but not much more (p. 205).

Jardin du Luxembourg
Sunbathe like a local (or jog like an expat) in this exquisitely manicured park (p. 225).

LESSER-KNOWN WONDERS

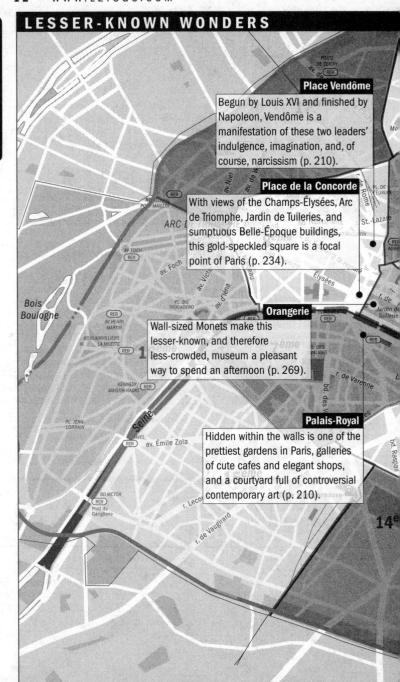

Place Vendôme

Begun by Louis XVI and finished by Napoleon, Vendôme is a manifestation of these two leaders' indulgence, imagination, and, of course, narcissism (p. 210).

Place de la Concorde

With views of the Champs-Élysées, Arc de Triomphe, Jardin de Tuileries, and sumptuous Belle-Époque buildings, this gold-speckled square is a focal point of Paris (p. 234).

Orangerie

Wall-sized Monets make this lesser-known, and therefore less-crowded, museum a pleasant way to spend an afternoon (p. 269).

Palais-Royal

Hidden within the walls is one of the prettiest gardens in Paris, galleries of cute cafes and elegant shops, and a courtyard full of controversial contemporary art (p. 210).

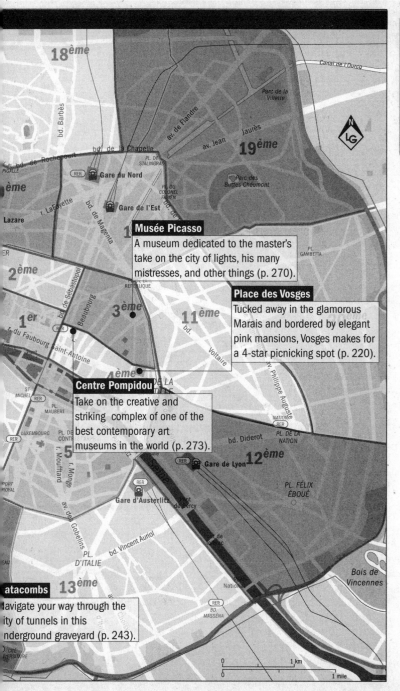

18ème

Canal de l'Ourcq

Parc de la Villette

bd. Barbès

av. de Flandre

av. Jean Jaurès

19ème

bd. de la Chapelle

PL. DE STALINGRAD

PIGALLE

RER Gare du Nord

r. LaFayette

bd. de Magenta

RER Gare de l'Est

Lazare

PL. DU COLONEL FABIEN

Parc des Buttes Chaumont

PL. GAMBETTA

2ème

bd. de Sébastopol

Beaubourg

PLACE DE LA RÉPUBLIQUE

3ème

11ème

bd. Voltaire

Musée Picasso
A museum dedicated to the master's take on the city of lights, his many mistresses, and other things (p. 270).

Place des Vosges
Tucked away in the glamorous Marais and bordered by elegant pink mansions, Vosges makes for a 4-star picnicking spot (p. 220).

1er

r. du Faubourg Saint-Antoine

RER

4ème

av. Philippe Auguste

ST-MICHEL RER

PL. MAUBERT

PL. DE LA

DE LA

RER NATION

PL. DE LA NATION

Centre Pompidou
Take on the creative and striking complex of one of the best contemporary art museums in the world (p. 273).

LUXEMBOURG RER

PL. DE CONTR

r. Mouffetard

5ème

r. Monge

bd. Diderot

RER Gare de Lyon

12ème

PORT ROYAL

av. des Gobelins

RER

Gare d'Austerlitz

Pont de Bercy

PL. FÉLIX ÉBOUÉ

bd. Vincent Auriol

PL. D'ITALIE

atacombs
lavigate your way through the ity of tunnels in this nderground graveyard (p. 243).

13ème

Nation

RER BD. MASSÉNA

CITE UNIVERSITE

Bois de Vincennes

0   1 km
0   1 mile

YOUR OWN MOVEABLE FEAST

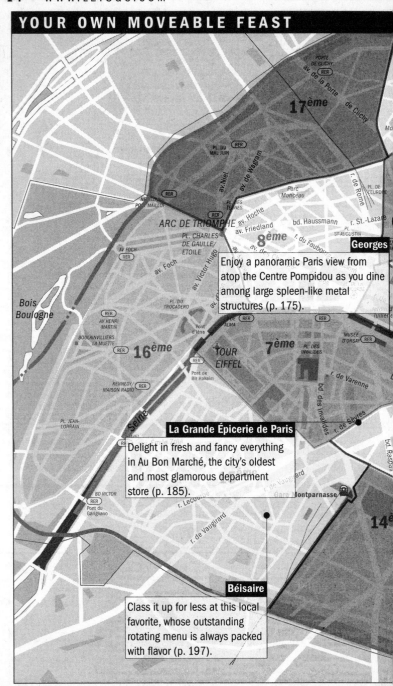

Georges

Enjoy a panoramic Paris view from atop the Centre Pompidou as you dine among large spleen-like metal structures (p. 175).

La Grande Épicerie de Paris

Delight in fresh and fancy everything in Au Bon Marché, the city's oldest and most glamorous department store (p. 185).

Béisaire

Class it up for less at this local favorite, whose outstanding rotating menu is always packed with flavor (p. 197).

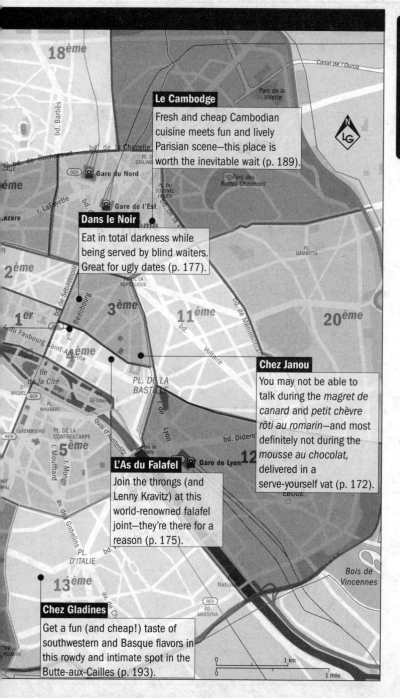

DISCOVER

Le Cambodge

Fresh and cheap Cambodian cuisine meets fun and lively Parisian scene—this place is worth the inevitable wait (p. 189).

Dans le Noir

Eat in total darkness while being served by blind waiters. Great for ugly dates (p. 177).

Chez Janou

You may not be able to talk during the *magret de canard* and *petit chèvre rôti au romarin*—and most definitely not during the *mousse au chocolat*, delivered in a serve-yourself vat (p. 172).

L'As du Falafel

Join the throngs (and Lenny Kravitz) at this world-renowned falafel joint—they're there for a reason (p. 175).

Chez Gladines

Get a fun (and cheap!) taste of southwestern and Basque flavors in this rowdy and intimate spot in the Butte-aux-Cailles (p. 193).

SOUVENIRS OF THE BELLE ÉPOQUE

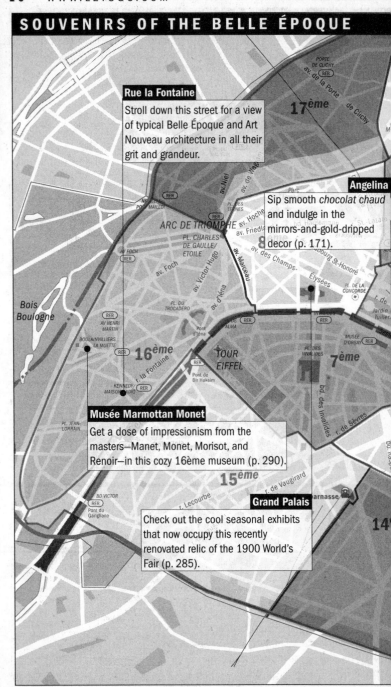

Rue la Fontaine

Stroll down this street for a view of typical Belle Époque and Art Nouveau architecture in all their grit and grandeur.

Angelina

Sip smooth *chocolat chaud* and indulge in the mirrors-and-gold-dripped decor (p. 171).

Musée Marmottan Monet

Get a dose of impressionism from the masters—Manet, Monet, Morisot, and Renoir—in this cozy 16ème museum (p. 290).

Grand Palais

Check out the cool seasonal exhibits that now occupy this recently renovated relic of the 1900 World's Fair (p. 285).

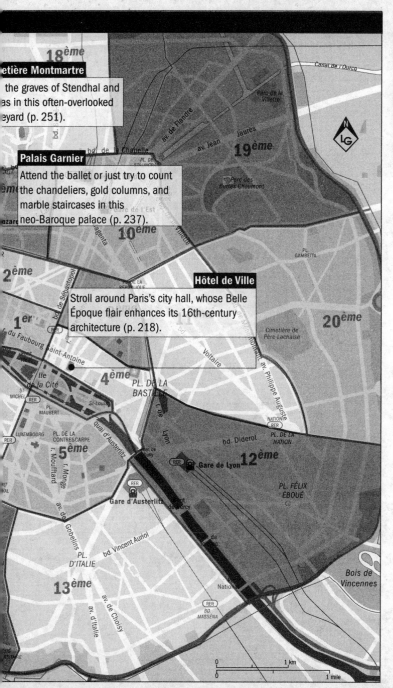

etière Montmartre

the graves of Stendhal and as in this often-overlooked eyard (p. 251).

Palais Garnier

Attend the ballet or just try to count the chandeliers, gold columns, and marble staircases in this neo-Baroque palace (p. 237).

Hôtel de Ville

Stroll around Paris's city hall, whose Belle Époque flair enhances its 16th-century architecture (p. 218).

ESSENTIALS

PLANNING YOUR TRIP

ENTRANCE REQUIREMENTS

Passport (p. 21). Required for non-EU citizens as well as citizens of the UK and Ireland.

Visa (p. 22). France does not require visas for EU citizens and residents of Australia, Canada, New Zealand, the US, and many more countries for visits of fewer than 90 days. To find out if you will need a visa, check with the French Ministry for Foreign Affairs (www.diplomatie.gouv.fr/en).

Study or Work Permit (p. 22). Required for all non-EU citizens planning to study or work in France.

EMBASSIES AND CONSULATES

FRENCH CONSULAR SERVICES ABROAD

All consulates will provide information on obtaining visas and travel to France in general. The hours listed below are for visa concerns unless otherwise stated. Most consulates will receive inquiries by appointment. The website **www.embassyworld.com** has a complete, up-to-date list of consulates.

Australia: Consulate General, Level 26, St-Martins Tower, 31 Market St., Sydney NSW 2000 (☎+64 02 9268 2400; www.ambafrance-au.org). Open M-F 9am-1pm.

Canada: Consulat Général de France à Montréal, 1501, McGill College, Bureau 1000, Montréal, QC H3A 3M8 (☎+1-514-878-4385; www.consulfrance-montreal.org). Open M-F 8:30am-noon. **Consulat Général de France à Québec,** 25 rue St-Louis, QC G1R 3Y8 (☎+1-418-266-2500; www.consulfrance-quebec.org). Open M-F 8:30am-noon without appointment; M-Th 2-5pm, F 2-4:15pm by appointment. **Consulat Général de France à Toronto,** 2 Bloor St. E., Ste. 2200, Toronto, ON M4W 1A8 (☎+1-416-847-1900; www.consulfrance-toronto.org). Open M-F 9am-12:30pm. By appointment only.

Ireland: French Embassy, 36 Ailesbury Rd., Ballsbridge, Dublin 4 (☎+353 1 277 5000; www.ambafrance.ie). Open M-F 9:30am-noon.

New Zealand: New Zealand Embassy and Consulate, 34-42 Manners St., 12th floor of Sovereign House, Wellington (☎+64 4 384 2555; www.ambafrance-nz.org). Open M-F 9:15am-1:15pm.

UK: Consulate General, 21 Cromwell Rd., London SW7 2EN (☎+44 20 7073 1200; www.consulfrance-londres.org). Open M-Th 8:45am-noon, F 8:45-11:30am. Visa service: P.O. Box 57, 6A Cromwell Pl., London SW7 2EW (☎+44 20 7073 1250).

US: Consulate General, 4101 Reservoir Rd. NW, Washington, D.C. 20007 (☎+1-202-944-6000; www.consulfrance-washington.org). Open M-F 8:45am-12:45pm; operator 8:45am-12:45pm and 2-5pm. Visa service ☎+1-202-944-6200. Open M-F 8:45am-

12:30pm. Consulates also in Atlanta, Boston, Chicago, Houston, Los Angeles, Miami, New Orleans, New York City, and San Francisco.

CONSULAR SERVICES IN FRANCE

Travelers visit these embassies only when they encounter trouble and need assistance. The most common concern is the loss of a passport or a question about potentially dangerous local conditions. If you encounter serious trouble, your home country's embassy or consulate can usually provide legal advice and may even be able to advance you money in emergency situations. But don't expect them to get you out of every scrape; you must always follow French law in France. In the case of arrest, your consulate can do little more than suggest a lawyer. **Dual citizens** of France cannot call on the consular services of their second nationality for assistance. Hours vary; call before visiting. Visa services tend to be available only in the morning.

Australia: 4 rue Jean Rey, 75724 Paris Cédex (☎01 40 59 33 00; www.france.embassy. gov.au). Open M-F 9am-5pm.

Canada: 35 av. Montaigne, 75008 Paris (☎01 44 43 29 00; www.international.gc.ca/ canada-europa/france). Open daily 9am-noon and 2-5pm.

Ireland: 12 av. Foch, 75116 Paris (☎01 44 17 67 00; www.embassyofirelandparis. com). Open M-F 9:30am-noon. Other offices in Antibes, Cherbourg, and Lyon.

New Zealand: 7ter rue Léonard de Vinci, 75116 Paris (☎01 45 01 43 43; www.nzembassy.com/france). Open July-Aug. M-Th 9am-1pm and 2-4:30pm, F 9am-2pm; Sept.-June M-Th 9am-1pm and 2-5:30pm, F 9am-1pm and 2-4pm.

UK: 18bis rue d'Anjou, 75008 Paris (☎01 44 51 31 02; www.amb-grandebretagne. fr). Open M-F 9:30am-12:30pm and 2:30- 4:30pm. Other offices in Bordeaux, Lille, Lyon, and Marseille.

US: 2 av. Gabriel, 75008 Paris Cédex 08 (☎01 43 12 22 22; http://france.usembassy. gov). 24hr. emergency assistance by phone. Open M-F 9am-noon. Tell the guard you want American citizen services. Other offices in Bordeaux, Lille, Lyon, Marseille, Nice, Rennes, Strasbourg, and Toulouse.

TOURIST OFFICES

The **French Government Tourist Office (FGTO),** also known as "Maison de la France," runs tourist offices in French cities and offers tourist services to travelers visiting France. The FGTO runs the useful website **www.franceguide.com.** *Let's Go* lists the tourist office in every town where one exists.

Australia and New Zealand: Level 13, 25 Bligh St., Sydney, NSW 2000 (☎+61 02 9231 5244; http://au.franceguide.com).

Canada: 1800 av. McGill College, Ste. 1010, Montréal, QC H3A 3J6 (☎+1-514-288-2026; http://ca-en.franceguide.com).

Ireland: See **UK** (http://ie.franceguide.com).

UK: Lincoln House, 300 High Holborn, London WC1V 7JH (☎+44 9068 244 123, 60p per min.; http://uk.franceguide.com).

US: 825 3rd Ave., New York City, NY 10022 (☎+1-514-288-1904; http://us.franceguide.com). Also at 9454 Wilshire Blvd., Ste. 210, Beverly Hills, CA 30212 (☎+1-310-271-6665).

DOCUMENTS AND FORMALITIES

PASSPORTS

REQUIREMENTS

Citizens of Australia, Canada, Ireland, New Zealand, the UK, and the US need valid passports to enter France and to re-enter their home countries. France does not allow entrance if the holder's passport expires in under six months; returning home with an expired passport is illegal and may result in a fine.

NEW PASSPORTS

Citizens of Australia, Canada, Ireland, New Zealand, the UK, and the US can apply for a passport at any passport office or at selected post offices and courts of law. Citizens of these countries may also download passport applications from the official website of their country's government or passport office. New passport and renewal applications must be filed well in advance of the departure date, though most passport offices offer rush services for a very steep fee. Note, however, that "rushed" passports still take up to two weeks to arrive.

ONE EUROPE. European unity has come a long way since 1958, when the European Economic Community (EEC) was created to promote European solidarity and cooperation. Since then, the EEC has become the European Union (EU), a mighty political, legal, and economic institution. On May 1, 2004, 10 South, Central, and Eastern European countries—Cyprus, the Czech Republic, Estonia, Hungary, Latvia, Lithuania, Malta, Poland, Slovakia, and Slovenia—were admitted into the EU, joining 15 other member states: Austria, Belgium, Denmark, Finland, France, Germany, Greece, Ireland, Italy, Luxembourg, the Netherlands, Portugal, Spain, Sweden, and the UK. On January 1, 2007, two others, Bulgaria and Romania, came into the fold, bringing the tally of member states to 27. What does this have to do with the average non-EU tourist? The EU's policy of **freedom of movement** means that most border controls have been abolished and visa policies harmonized. Under this treaty, formally known as the **Schengen Agreement,** you're still required to carry a passport (or government-issued ID card for EU citizens) when crossing an internal border, but, once you've been admitted into one country, you're free to travel to other participating states. Most EU states are already members of Schengen (minus Bulgaria, Cyprus, Ireland, Romania, and the UK), as are Iceland and Norway. In 2009, Cyprus, Liechtenstein, and Switzerland will bring the number of Schengen countries to 27. Britain and Ireland have also formed a **common travel area,** abolishing passport controls between the UK and the Republic of Ireland. For more important consequences of the EU for travelers, see **The Euro** (p. 24) and **Customs in the EU** (p. 23).

PASSPORT MAINTENANCE

Photocopy the page of your passport with your photo as well as your visas, traveler's check serial numbers, and other important documents. Carry one set of copies in a safe place, apart from the originals, and leave another set at home. Consulates recommend that you carry an expired passport or a copy of your birth certificate separate from other documents.

If you lose your passport, immediately notify the local police and your home country's nearest embassy or consulate. To expedite its replacement, you must show ID and proof of citizenship; it also helps to know all information previously recorded in the passport. In some cases, a replacement may take weeks to process, and it may be valid only for a limited time. Any visas stamped in your old passport will be lost forever. In an emergency, ask for immediate temporary traveling papers that will permit you to re-enter your home country.

VISAS AND PERMITS

VISAS

Citizens of Australia, Canada, Ireland, New Zealand, the UK, and the US do not need a visa for stays of up to 90 days for entrance into France, though this three-month period begins upon entry into any of the countries that belong to the EU's **freedom of movement** zone. For more information, see **One Europe** (previous page). Those staying longer than 90 days may purchase a *long séjour* (long-stay visa) at their local French consulate; all forms and fees must be presented in person. A visa costs US$155 and allows the holder to spend one year in France. All foreigners (including EU citizens) who plan to stay in France between 90 days and one year must apply for a *carte de séjour temporaire* at the prefecture in their town of residence within eight days of their arrival in France.

Double-check entrance requirements at the nearest embassy or consulate of France (listed under **French Consular Services Abroad**, p. 19) for up-to-date info before departure. US citizens can also consult http://travel.state.gov.

STUDY AND WORK PERMITS

Admission as a visitor does not include the right to work, which is authorized only by a work permit. Entering France to study requires a special student visa. Foreign visitors are not permitted to enter France as a tourist and then change their status to that of a worker or student; they may be required to return to their home country to apply for the appropriate visas and permits. For more information, see **Beyond Tourism**, p. 108.

IDENTIFICATION

French law requires that all people carry a form of official identification at all times—either a passport or an EU government-issued identity card. The police have the right to demand to see identification at any time. Minority travelers should be especially careful to carry proof that they are in France legally. Never carry all of your IDs together; split them up in case of theft or loss and keep photocopies of all of them in your luggage and at home.

STUDENT, TEACHER, AND YOUTH IDENTIFICATION

The **International Student Identity Card (ISIC)**, the most widely accepted form of student ID, provides discounts on some sights, accommodations, food, and transportation; access to a 24hr. emergency help line; and insurance benefits for US cardholders. In France, cardholders can receive discounts on plane and train tickets, on tours and excursions, or at museums. Applicants must be full-time secondary- or post-secondary-school students at least 12 years old. Because of the proliferation of fake ISICs, some services (particularly airlines) require additional proof of student identity.

For travelers who are under 26 years old but are not students, the **International Youth Travel Card (IYTC)** also offers many of the same benefits as the ISIC.

Each of these identity cards costs US$22. ISICs and IYTCs are valid for one year from the date of issue. To learn more about ISICs and IYTCs, try www.myisic.com. Many student travel agencies (p. 34) issue the cards; for a list of issuing agencies or more information, see the **International Student Travel Confederation (ISTC)** website (www.istc.org).

The **International Student Exchange Card (ISE Card)** is a similar identification card available to students, faculty, and children aged 12 to 26. The card provides discounts, medical benefits, access to a 24hr. emergency help line, and the ability to purchase student airfares. An ISE Card costs US$25; call ☎+1-800-255-8000 (in North America) or ☎+1-480-951-1177 (from all other continents) for more info or visit www.isecard.com.

CUSTOMS

Upon entering France, you must declare certain items from abroad and pay a duty on the value of those articles if they exceed the allowance established by France's customs service. Goods and gifts purchased at duty-free shops abroad are not exempt from duty or sales tax; "duty-free" means that you won't pay tax in the country of purchase. Upon returning home, you must likewise declare all articles acquired abroad and pay a duty on the value of articles in excess of your home country's allowance. In order to expedite your return, make a list of any valuables brought from home and register them with customs before traveling abroad. It's a good idea to **keep receipts for all goods acquired abroad.**

CUSTOMS IN THE EU. As well as freedom of movement of people (p. 21), travelers in the European Union can also take advantage of the freedom of movement of goods. This means that there are no customs controls at internal EU borders (i.e., you can take the blue customs channel at the airport), and travelers are free to transport whatever legal substances they like as long as it is for their own personal (non-commercial) use—up to 800 cigarettes, 10L of spirits, 90L of wine (including up to 60L of sparkling wine), and 110L of beer. Duty-free allowances were abolished on June 30, 1999, for travel between the original 15 EU member states; this now also applies to Cyprus and Malta. However, travelers between the EU and the rest of the world still get a duty-free allowance when passing through customs.

France requires a **value added tax (VAT)** of up to 19.8% (see **Taxes,** p. 27). Non-European Economic Community tourists bringing purchased goods home with them can usually be refunded this tax for purchases of over €175 (including VAT) per store. Ask for VAT forms at the time of purchase and present them at the *détaxe* booth at the airport. You must carry these goods with you at all times—at the airport and on the airplane. You must claim your refund within six months; it generally takes one month to process.

MONEY

CURRENCY AND EXCHANGE

The currency chart on the next page is based on August 2008 exchange rates between European Union euro (EUR€) and Australian dollars (AUS$), Canadian dollars (CDN$), New Zealand dollars (NZ$), British pounds (UK£), and US dollars (US$). Check the currency converter on websites like www.xe.com or www.bloomberg.com for the latest exchange rates.

EURO (€)		
AUS$ = €0.59	€1 = AUS$1.70
CDN$ = €0.62	€1 = CDN$1.62
NZ$ = €0.47	€1 = NZ$2.15
UK£ = €1.26	€1 = UK£0.79
US$ = €0.65	€1 = US$1.54

ESSENTIALS

As a general rule, it's cheaper to convert money in France than at home. While currency exchange will probably be available in your arrival airport, it's wise to bring enough foreign currency to last for at least 24-72hr.

When changing money abroad, try to go only to banks or *bureaux de change* that have at most a 5% margin between their buy and sell prices. Since you lose money with every transaction, it makes sense to convert large sums at one time (unless the currency is depreciating rapidly).

If you use traveler's checks or bills, carry small denominations (the equivalent of US$50 or fewer) for times when you are forced to exchange money at poor rates, but bring a range of denominations since charges may be applied per check cashed. Store your money in a variety of forms; at any given time you should carry some cash, some checks, and an ATM and/or credit card.

THE EURO. As of January 1, 2009, the official currency of 16 members of the European Union—Austria, Belgium, Cyprus, Finland, France, Germany, Greece, Ireland, Italy, Luxembourg, Malta, the Netherlands, Portugal, Slovenia, and Spain—will be the euro.

The currency has important—and positive—consequences for travelers hitting more than one euro-zone country. For one thing, money-changers across the euro-zone are obliged to exchange money at the official, fixed rate (below) and at no commission (though they may charge a small service fee). Second, euro-denominated traveler's checks allow you to pay for goods and services across the euro-zone, again at the official rate and commission-free. At the time of printing, €1 = US$1.54 = CDN$1.62 = NZ$2.15 etc. For more info, check a currency converter (such as www.xe.com) or www.europa.eu.int.

TRAVELER'S CHECKS

Traveler's checks are one of the safest and most convenient means of carrying funds. American Express and Visa are the best-recognized brands. Many banks and agencies sell them for a small commission. Check issuers provide refunds if the checks are lost or stolen, and many provide additional services, such as toll-free refund hotlines abroad, emergency message services, and assistance with lost and stolen credit cards or passports. Traveler's checks are readily accepted in regions of France with high tourist traffic, but credit and ATM cards are more typical. Ask about toll-free refund hotlines and the location of refund centers when purchasing checks and always carry emergency cash.

American Express: Checks available with commission at select banks, at all AmEx offices, and online (www.americanexpress.com; US residents only). AmEx cardholders can also purchase checks by phone (☎+1-800-528-4800). Checks available in Australian, British, Canadian, European, and Japanese currencies, among others. AmEx also offers the Travelers Cheque Card, a prepaid reloadable card. Cheques for Two can be signed by either of 2 people traveling together. For purchase locations or more information, contact AmEx's service centers: in Australia ☎+61 2 9271 8666, in New Zealand +64 9

367 4567, in the UK +44 1273 696 933, in the US and Canada +1-800-221-7282; elsewhere, call the US collect at +1-336-393-1111. In France, call ☎01 47 77 70 00.

Travelex: Visa TravelMoney prepaid cash card and Visa traveler's checks available. For information about Thomas Cook MasterCard in Canada and the US, call ☎+1-800-223-7373, in the UK +44 800 622 101; elsewhere, call the UK collect at +44 1733 318 950. For information about Interpayment Visa in the US and Canada, call ☎+1-800-732-1322, in the UK +44 800 515 884; elsewhere, call the UK collect at +44 1733 318 949. For more information, visit www.travelex.com.

Visa: Checks available (generally with commission) at banks worldwide. For the location of the nearest office, call the Visa Travelers Cheque Global Refund and Assistance Center: in the UK ☎+44 800 895 078, in the US +1-800-227-6811; elsewhere, call the UK collect at +44 2079 378 091. Checks available in American, British, Canadian, European, and Japanese currencies, among others. Visa also offers TravelMoney, a prepaid debit card that can be reloaded online or by phone. For more information on Visa travel services, see http://usa.visa.com/personal/using_visa/travel_with_visa.html.

CREDIT, DEBIT, AND ATM CARDS

Where they are accepted, credit cards often offer superior exchange rates—up to 5% better than the retail rate used by banks and other currency-exchange establishments. Credit cards may also offer services such as insurance or emergency help and are sometimes required to reserve hotel rooms or rental cars. **MasterCard** (a.k.a. **EuroCard** in Europe) and **Visa** (e.g., **Carte Bleue** in France) are the most frequently accepted; **American Express** cards work at some ATMs and at AmEx offices and major airports, but not at many establishments.

Credit cards are widely accepted in Paris, though usually only for purchases over €15. French credit cards are fitted with a microchip (such cards are known as *cartes à puce*) rather than a magnetic strip *(cartes à piste magnétique)*. Cashiers may attempt (and fail) to scan the card with a microchip reader. If this happens, explain: *"Ceci n'est pas une carte à puce, mais une carte à piste magnétique."* (This card doesn't have a chip, but a magnetic strip.)

PINS AND ATMS. To use a cash or credit card to withdraw money from a cash machine (ATM) in Europe, you must have a four-digit Personal Identification Number (PIN). If your PIN is longer than four digits, ask your bank whether you can just use the first four or whether you'll need a new one. Credit cards don't usually come with PINs, so, if you intend to hit up ATMs in Europe with a credit card to get cash advances, call your credit-card company before leaving to request one. Travelers with alphabetic, rather than numerical, PINs may also be thrown off by the lack of letters on European cash machines. The following are the corresponding numbers to use: 1 = QZ; 2 = ABC; 3 = DEF; 4 = GHI; 5 = JKL; 6 = MNO; 7 = PRS; 8 = TUV; and 9 = WXY. Note that if you mistakenly punch the wrong code into the machine three times, it will swallow your card for good.

Twenty-four hour cash machines are widespread in France. Depending on the system that your home bank uses, you can most likely access your personal bank account from abroad. ATMs get the same wholesale exchange rate as credit cards, but there is often a limit on the amount of money you can withdraw per day (usually around €500). Depending upon your domestic bank, there may be a surcharge of $1-5 per withdrawal.

The two major international money networks are **MasterCard/Maestro/Cirrus** (for ATM locations ☎+1-800-424-7787 or www.mastercard.com) and **Visa/PLUS** (for ATM locations ☎+1-800-847-2911 or www.visa.com). **American Express** cards are not as prevalent in France as elsewhere, but they may be accepted in more upscale restaurants or in heavily touristed areas.

> **BANKING ON IT.** Most ATMs charge a transaction fee (paid to the bank that owns the ATM), but Bank of America cardholders can withdraw euros at no extra charge from any BNP/Paribas ATM.

GETTING MONEY FROM HOME

If you run out of money while traveling, the easiest and cheapest solution is to have someone back home make a deposit to your bank account. Otherwise, consider one of the following options.

WIRING MONEY

It is possible to arrange a **bank money transfer** ("*virement*" in French), which means asking a bank back home to wire money to a bank in Paris. This is the cheapest way to transfer cash, but it's also the slowest, usually taking several days or more. Note that some banks may only release your funds in local currency, potentially sticking you with a poor exchange rate; inquire about this in advance. If your home bank has a relationship with a bank in France, make sure to use that bank, as the rate will be better. Money transfer services like **Western Union** are faster and more convenient than bank transfers—but also much pricier. Western Union has many locations worldwide, often at post offices. To find one, visit www.westernunion.com or call in Australia ☎1800 173 833, in Canada and the US 800-325-6000, in the UK 0800 833 833, or in France 08 00 90 32 75. To wire money using a credit card, call in Canada and the US ☎800-CALL-CASH, in the UK 0800 833 833. Money transfer services are also available to **American Express** cardholders and at selected **Thomas Cook** offices.

US STATE DEPARTMENT (US CITIZENS ONLY)

In serious emergencies only, the US State Department will forward money within hours to the nearest consular office, which will then disburse it according to instructions for a fee of US$30. If you wish to use this service, you must contact the Overseas Citizens Services division of the US State Department (☎+1-202-501-4444; from US ☎888-407-4747).

COSTS

The cost of your trip will vary considerably, depending on where you go, how you travel, and where you stay. The most significant expenses will probably be your round-trip (return) airfare to Paris (see **Getting to Paris: By Plane,** p. 33). Before you go, spend some time calculating a reasonable daily budget.

STAYING ON A BUDGET

To give you a general idea, a bare-bones day in Paris (camping or sleeping in hostels/guesthouses, buying food at supermarkets) would cost about US$37 (€50); a slightly more comfortable day (sleeping in hostels/guesthouses and the occasional budget hotel, eating one meal per day at a restaurant, going out at night) would cost US$70 (€100); and, for a luxurious day, the sky's the limit. Don't forget to factor in emergency reserve funds (at least US$200) when planning how much money you'll need.

TIPS FOR SAVING MONEY

Some simple ways include searching out opportunities for free entertainment, splitting accommodation and food costs with trustworthy fellow travelers, and shopping in supermarkets rather than eating out. Bring a **sleepsack** (see next page) to save on sheet charges in hostels and do **laundry** in the sink (unless you're prohibited from doing so). If you're eligible, consider getting an **ISIC** or an **IYTC** (p. 22); many sights and museums offer discounts to students and youths.

For getting around quickly, bikes are the most economical option, especially with Paris' new self-service bicycle transit system, **Vélib** (p. 135). Don't forget about walking, though; Paris is famous for catering to *flâneurs* (wanderers). In terms of saving money while taking advantage of Parisian nightlife, you may want to consider buying alcohol at a supermarket, pre-gaming, and avoiding absurdly priced drinks in bars and clubs. That said, don't go overboard. Though staying within your budget is important, don't do so at the expense of your health or a great travel experience.

 ART ON A BUDGET. Museums in Paris are often free the first Sunday of the month, and on special nights, usually Wednesdays or Thursdays.

BARGAINING AND TIPPING

You should inquire about discounts and less pricey options, but don't try to bargain at established places like hotels, hostels, restaurants, cafes, museums, and nightclubs. Bargaining is acceptable—and usually expected—at markets, and haggling is standard at flea markets like the **Puces St-Ouen** (p. 310). See **Life and Times**, p. 95, for a run-down of proper tipping practices in Paris.

TAXES

The **value added tax (VAT)** is a general tax on doing business in France; it applies to a range of services and goods (e.g., entertainment, food, and accommodations). The tax can be up to 19.8% of the price of the good, but the tax is 5.5% on food. Some of the VAT can be recovered (see **Customs**, p. 23).

PACKING

Pack lightly: lay out only what you absolutely need, then take half the clothes and twice the money. The **Travelite FAQ** (www.travelite.org) is a good resource for tips on traveling light. The online **Universal Packing List** (http://upl.codeq.info) will generate a customized list of suggested items based on your trip length, the expected climate, your planned activities, and other factors.

Luggage: If you plan to cover most of your trip on foot, a sturdy **internal frame backpack** is unbeatable. Unless you are staying in 1 place for a large chunk of time, a suitcase or trunk will be unwieldy. In addition to your main piece of luggage, a **daypack** (a small backpack or courier bag) is useful.

Clothing: No matter when you're traveling, it's a good idea to bring a warm jacket or wool sweater, a rain jacket (Gore-Tex® is both waterproof and breathable), sturdy shoes or hiking boots, and thick socks. Flip-flops or waterproof sandals are must-haves for grubby hostel showers, and extra socks are always a good idea. You may also want 1 outfit for going out and maybe a nicer pair of shoes. If you plan to visit religious or cultural sites, remember that you will need modest and respectful dress. See **Customs and Etiquette** (p. 95) for more info on fitting in. To get an idea of the climate, see the

ESSENTIALS

Appendix (p. 362); in general, France tends to be fairly temperate, but the August 2003 heat wave killed an estimated 14,802 people as it reached temperatures of up to 104°F, reminding all to come prepared for any weather.

Sleepsack: Some hostels require that you either provide your own linen or rent sheets from them. Save cash by making your own sleepsack: fold a full-size sheet in half the long way, then sew it closed along the long side and one of the short sides.

Converters and Adapters: In France, electricity is 230 volts AC, enough to fry any 120V North American appliance. 220/240V electrical appliances won't work with a 120V current, either. Americans and Canadians should buy an adapter (which changes the shape of the plug; US$5) and a converter (which changes the voltage; US$10-30). Don't make the mistake of using only an adapter (unless appliance instructions explicitly state otherwise). Australians, Brits, and New Zealanders (who use 230V at home) won't need a converter but will need a set of adapters to use anything electrical. For more on all things adaptable, check out http://kropla.com/electric.htm.

Toiletries: Condoms, deodorant, razors, tampons, and toothbrushes are often available, but it may be difficult to find your preferred brand; bring extras. Contact lenses are likely to be expensive and difficult to find, so bring enough extra pairs and solution for your entire trip. Also bring your glasses and a copy of your prescription in case you need emergency replacements.

First-Aid Kit: For a basic first-aid kit, pack bandages, a pain reliever, antibiotic cream, a thermometer, tweezers, moleskin, decongestant, motion-sickness remedy, diarrhea or upset-stomach medication (Pepto Bismol® or Imodium®), an antihistamine, sunscreen.

Other Useful Items: For safety purposes, you should bring a **money belt** and a small **padlock.** A needle and thread come in handy for small repairs, and electrical tape can patch tears. Other things you're liable to forget include a camera, sealable **plastic bags** (for damp clothes, soap, food, shampoo, and other spillables), an **alarm clock,** safety pins, rubber bands, a flashlight, earplugs, and garbage bags. A **cell phone** can be a lifesaver on the road; p. 52 for information on acquiring one that will work in France.

Important Documents: Don't forget your passport, traveler's checks, ATM and/or credit cards, adequate ID, and photocopies of all of the aforementioned in case these documents are lost or stolen (p. 22). Other helpful documents include: a hosteling membership card (p. 54); driver's license (p. 45); travel insurance forms (p. 31); ISIC (p. 22); and/or railpass (p. 42).

SAFETY AND HEALTH

GENERAL ADVICE

In any type of crisis, the most important thing to do is **stay calm.** Your country's embassy abroad (p. 20) is usually your best resource in an emergency; registering with that embassy upon arrival in the country is a good idea. The government offices listed in the **Travel Advisories** box (see opposite page) can provide info on the services they offer their citizens in case of emergencies abroad.

LOCAL LAWS AND POLICE

La police in France are generally very responsive to requests for help. The emergency call number is ☎**17.** The legal blood-alcohol level for driving is 0.05%, 0.03% less than in New Zealand, Ireland, the UK, and the US.

DRUGS AND ALCOHOL

Possession of illegal drugs (including marijuana) in France can result in a substantial jail sentence or fine. Police may arbitrarily stop and search anyone on the street. Prescription drugs—particularly insulin, syringes, or narcotics—should be left in their original, labeled containers and accompanied by their prescriptions and a doctor's statement. In case of arrest, your home country's consulate can suggest attorneys and inform your family and friends but can't get you out of jail. For more info, US citizens can contact the **Office of Overseas Citizens Services** (☎+1-202-501-4444; http://travel.state.gov).

The French love alcohol, but they drink carefully. Though there is no law prohibiting open containers, drinking on the street is considered uncouth. Restaurants may serve alcohol to anyone 16 or older. Though mention of France often conjures images of black-clad smokers in berets, **France no longer allows smoking in public as of 2008.** The government has no official policy on berets.

ESSENTIALS

SPECIFIC CONCERNS

DEMONSTRATIONS AND POLITICAL GATHERINGS

Demonstrations by students, labor groups, and other routine protesters have grown into more violent confrontations with the police. In 2006, opponents of a controversial labor deregulation bill sparked protests throughout France in February, March, and April. Millions of young protesters converged on France's urban centers to demonstrate their dissatisfaction. Although tensions have calmed somewhat, protests are a common threat in Paris. The most usual form of violence when demonstrations get out of hand is property damage, and though travelers typically are not targets, they are still advised to avoid demonstrations. In general, use common sense in conversation and, as in dealing with any sensitive issue, be respectful of other political and religious perspectives.

TERRORISM

Terrorism has not been as serious a problem in France as in other European countries, but after September 11, 2001, the French government heightened security in public places. Train stations no longer permit luggage storage. Still, Al Qaeda cells, as well as other terrorist groups, have been identified in France. In addition, France has had tense relationships with Algeria since its colonial period, a situation that has been a source of sporadic violent outbursts. Anti-Semites have firebombed several Jewish synagogues in the past few years. The box below lists resources with an updated list of your home country's government's advisories about travel.

TRAVEL ADVISORIES. The following government offices provide travel information and advisories by telephone, by fax, or via the web:
Australian Department of Foreign Affairs and Trade: ☎+61 2 6261 1111; www.dfat.gov.au.
Canadian Department of Foreign Affairs and International Trade (DFAIT): ☎+1-800-267-8376; www.dfait-maeci.gc.ca. Call for their free booklet, *Bon Voyage...But.*
New Zealand Ministry of Foreign Affairs: ☎+64 4 439 8000; www.mfat.govt.nz.
United Kingdom Foreign and Commonwealth Office: ☎+44 20 7008 1500; www.fco.gov.uk.
US Department of State: ☎+1-888-407-4747; http://travel.state.gov. Visit the website for the booklet, *A Safe Trip Abroad.*

PERSONAL SAFETY

EXPLORING AND TRAVELING

To avoid unwanted attention, try to blend in as much as possible. Respecting local customs (in many cases, dressing more conservatively than you would at home) may ward off would-be hecklers. Check maps in shops and restaurants rather than on the street. If you are traveling alone, be sure someone at home knows your itinerary. **Never tell a stranger that you're by yourself.** When walking at night, stick to busy streets. Violence in central Paris is very rare, but as in any city, it's safest to stay where other people are around.

There is no surefire way to avoid all the threatening situations that you might encounter while traveling, but a good **self-defense course** will give you concrete ways to react to unwanted advances. **Impact, Prepare,** and **Model Mugging** can refer you to local self-defense courses in Australia, Canada, Switzerland, and the US. Visit **www.modelmugging.org** for a list of nearby chapters.

POSSESSIONS AND VALUABLES

TRAVEL SAFETY 101. Never leave your belongings unattended; crime can occur in even the most safe-looking hostel or hotel. Bring your own padlock for hostel lockers and don't ever store valuables in a locker. Be particularly careful on overnight **buses** and **trains;** horror stories abound about determined thieves who wait for travelers to fall asleep. When traveling with others, sleep in alternate shifts. When alone, use good judgment in selecting a train compartment: use a lock to secure your pack to the luggage rack. Try to sleep on top bunks with your luggage stored above you (if not in bed with you) and keep important documents and other valuables on you at all times.

DON'T GET ROBBED. There are a few steps you can take to minimize the financial risk associated with traveling. First, **bring as little with you as possible.** Second, buy a few combination **padlocks** to secure your belongings either in your pack or in a hostel. Third, **carry as little cash as possible.** Keep your ATM/credit cards in a **money belt**—not a "fanny pack," which are as unsafe as they are uncool—along with your passport and ID cards. Fourth, **keep a small cash reserve separate from your primary stash.** This should be about €30 sewn into or stored in the depths of your pack, along with your traveler's check numbers, photocopies of your passport, your birth certificate, and other important documents.

COMMON CONS. In large cities like Paris, **con artists** often work in groups and may involve children. Beware of certain classics: sob stories that require money, rolls of bills "found" on the street, mustard spilled (or saliva spit) onto your shoulder to distract you while they snatch your bag. **Never let your passport and your bags out of your sight.** Beware of **pickpockets** in city crowds, especially on public transportation and around major monuments. Be alert in public telephone booths: say or type your calling-card number discretely.

HOMEOWNER'S INSURANCE. If you will be traveling with electronic devices, such as a laptop computer or a PDA, check whether your homeowner's insurance covers loss, theft, or damage when you travel. If not, you might consider purchasing a low-cost separate insurance policy. **Safeware** (☎ +1-800-800-1492; www.safeware.com) specializes in covering computers and charges US$90 for 90-day comprehensive international travel coverage up to US$4000.

INSURANCE

STA (p. 34) offers a range of plans that can supplement your basic coverage. Other private insurance providers in the US and Canada include: **Access America** (☎800-729-6021; www.acessamerica.com); **Berkely Group** (☎800-797-4514; www. berkely.com); **CSA Travel Protection** (☎800-873-9855; www.csatravelprotection. com); **Travel Assistance International** (☎800-821-2828; www.europ-assistance. com); and **Travel Guard** (☎800-826-4919; www.travelguard.com). **Columbus Direct** (☎0870 033 9988; www.columbusdirect.co.uk) operates in the UK.

PRE-DEPARTURE HEALTH

In your passport, write the names of any people you wish to be contacted in case of a **medical emergency** and list any **allergies** or **medical conditions.** Matching a prescription to a foreign equivalent is not always easy, safe, or possible, so, if you take **prescription drugs,** consider carrying up-to-date prescriptions or a statement from your doctor stating the medication's trade name, manufacturer, chemical name, and dosage. While traveling, be sure to keep all medication with you in your carry-on luggage. For tips on packing a **first-aid kit** and other health essentials, see p. 28.

French names for common drugs include *aspirine* (aspirin), *pénicilline* (penicillin), *antihistaminique* (antihistamines), and *ibuprofène* (ibuprofen).

IMMUNIZATIONS AND PRECAUTIONS

Travelers over two years old should make sure that the following vaccines are up to date: MMR (for measles, mumps, and rubella); DTaP or Td (for diphtheria, tetanus, and pertussis); IPV (for polio); Hib (for *haemophilus influenzae* B); and HepB (for Hepatitis B). For recommendations on immunizations and prophylaxis, consult the Centers for Disease Control and Prevention (CDC; below) in the US or the equivalent in your home country.

USEFUL ORGANIZATIONS AND PUBLICATIONS

The American **Centers for Disease Control and Prevention (CDC;** ☎+1-877-FYI-TRIP; www.cdc.gov/travel) maintains an international travelers' hotline and an informative website. Consult the appropriate government agency of your home country for consular information sheets on health, entry requirements, and other issues for various countries (see the listings in the box on **Travel Advisories,** p. 29). For quick information on health and other travel warnings, call the **Overseas Citizens Services** (M-F 8am-8pm from overseas ☎+1-202-501-4444, from US ☎888-407-4747; line open M-F 8am-8pm EST) or contact a passport agency, embassy, or consulate abroad. For information on medical evacuation services and travel insurance firms, see the US government's website at http://travel. state.gov/travel/abroad_health.html or the **British Foreign and Commonwealth Office** (www.fco.gov.uk). For general health information, contact the **American Red Cross** (☎+1-202-303-4498; www.redcross.org).

STAYING HEALTHY

Common sense is the simplest prescription for good health while you travel. Drink lots of fluids to prevent dehydration and constipation and wear sturdy, broken-in shoes and clean socks.

ESSENTIALS

ONCE IN PARIS

FOOD- AND WATER-BORNE DISEASES

Prevention is the best cure: be sure that your food is properly cooked. Many dishes in France include raw or partially cooked foods; eat at your own risk. Watch out for food from markets or street vendors that may have been cooked in unhygienic conditions. Other culprits are raw shellfish, unpasteurized milk, and sauces containing raw eggs.

Traveler's diarrhea: Results from drinking fecally contaminated water or eating uncooked and contaminated foods. Symptoms include nausea, bloating, and urgency. Try quick-energy, non-sugary foods with protein and carbohydrates to keep your strength up. Over-the-counter anti-diarrheals (e.g., Imodium®) may counteract the problem. The most dangerous side effect is dehydration; drink 8 oz. of water with ½ tsp. of sugar or honey and a pinch of salt, try uncaffeinated soft drinks, or eat salted crackers. If you develop a fever or your symptoms don't go away after 4-5 days, consult a doctor. Consult a doctor immediately for treatment of diarrhea in children.

OTHER INFECTIOUS DISEASES

The following diseases exist all over the world. Travelers should know how to recognize them and what to do if they suspect they have been infected.

AIDS and HIV: For detailed information on Acquired Immune Deficiency Syndrome (AIDS) in France, call the 24hr. National AIDS Hotline at ☎+1-800-342-2437.

Hepatitis B: A viral infection of the liver transmitted via blood or other bodily fluids. Symptoms may not surface until years after infection, and include jaundice, appetite loss, fever, and joint pain. It is transmitted through unprotected sex and unclean needles. A 3-shot vaccination sequence is recommended for sexually active travelers and those planning to seek medical treatment abroad; it must begin 6 months before traveling.

Hepatitis C: Like Hepatitis B, but the mode of transmission differs. IV drug users, those with occupational exposure to blood, hemodialysis patients, and recipients of blood transfusions are at highest risk, but the disease can also be spread through sexual contact or sharing items like razors and toothbrushes that may have traces of blood on them. No symptoms are usually exhibited. Untreated Hep C can lead to liver failure.

Sexually transmitted infections (STIs): Gonorrhea, chlamydia, genital warts, syphilis, herpes, HPV, and other STIs are easier to catch than HIV and can be just as serious. Though condoms may protect you from some STIs, oral or even tactile contact can lead to transmission. If you think you may have contracted an STI, see a doctor immediately.

OTHER HEALTH CONCERNS

MEDICAL CARE ON THE ROAD

France's socialized medical system provides care that is widely available and of high quality, but it may seem unfamiliar and intimidating to a foreigner, especially one who does not speak French fluently. The **American Hospital of Paris,** 63 bd. Victor Hugo (☎01 46 41 25 25) and **Hertford British Hospital,** 3, rue Barbes (☎01 46 39 22 22) are private hospitals staffed with English-speaking staff members. A visit to a doctor will cost around €50.

Pharmacies in Paris are ubiquitous and marked with a blinking green cross. Almost every drug (including allergy medications and fever reducers) **requires a prescription.** The shelves of pharmacies display only skin care products and other ephemera; for non-prescription medications you'll have to ask the pharmacist. See **Practical Information,** p. 143, for a list of pharmacies.

If you are concerned about obtaining medical assistance while traveling, you may wish to employ special support services. The **MedPass** from **Global-Care, Inc.**, 6875 Shiloh Rd. E., Alpharetta, GA 30005, USA (☎+1-800-860-1111; www.globalcare.net), provides 24hr. international medical assistance, support, and medical evacuation resources. The **International Association for Medical Assistance to Travelers** (**IAMAT**; US ☎+1-716-754-4883, Canada 519-836-0102; www.iamat.org) has free membership, lists English-speaking doctors worldwide, and offers detailed info on immunization requirements and sanitation. If your regular insurance policy does not cover travel abroad, you may wish to purchase additional coverage.

Those with medical conditions (such as diabetes, allergies to antibiotics, epilepsy, or heart conditions) may want to obtain a **MedicAlert** membership (US$40 per year), which includes, among other things, a stainless-steel ID tag and a 24hr. collect-call number. Contact the MedicAlert Foundation International, 2323 Colorado Ave., Turlock, CA 95382, USA (☎+1-888-633-4298, outside US 209-668-3333; www.medicalert.org).

WOMEN'S HEALTH

Women traveling in unsanitary conditions are vulnerable to **urinary tract (including bladder and kidney) infections.** Bring supplies from home if you are prone to infection, as they may be difficult to find on the road. **Tampons, pads,** and **contraceptive devices** are widely available, though your preferred brand may not be stocked—bring extras of anything you can't live without. **Abortions** are legal in France. Recent changes have relaxed restrictions on surgical and pharmaceutical abortions, permitting them up to 12 weeks into pregnancy. The *pillule du lendemain* (morning-after pill) is legal and available at pharmacies.

GETTING TO PARIS

BY PLANE

When it comes to airfare, a little effort can save you a bundle. Courier fares are the cheapest for those whose plans are flexible enough to deal with the restrictions. Tickets sold by consolidators and standby seating are also good deals, but last-minute specials, airfare wars, and charter flights often beat these fares. The key is to hunt around, be flexible, and ask about discounts. Students, seniors, and those under 26 should never pay full price for a ticket.

AIRFARE

Airfare to Paris peaks between June and September; holidays are also expensive. The cheapest times to travel are between November and April. Midweek (M-Th morning) round-trip flights run US$40-50 cheaper than weekend flights, but they are generally more crowded and less likely to permit frequent-flier upgrades. Not fixing a return date ("open return") or arriving in and departing from different cities ("open-jaw") can be pricier than round-trip flights. Patching one-way flights together is the most expensive way to travel.

If Paris is only one stop on a more extensive globe-hop, consider a round-the-world (RTW) ticket. Tickets usually include at least five stops and are valid for about a year; prices range US$1200-5000. Try **Northwest Airlines/KLM** (☎+1-800-225-2525; www.nwa.com) or **Star Alliance,** a consortium of 16 airlines including United Airlines (www.staralliance.com).

Fares for round-trip flights to Paris from the US or Canadian east coast cost US$600-2000, US$400-1000 in low season (Nov.-Mar.); from the US or Canadian west coast US$1100-2400/900-2200; from the UK, UK£100-200/50-150; from Australia AUS$2500-5000/1900-2500; from New Zealand NZ$3000-6000/2500-3500.

BUDGET AND STUDENT TRAVEL AGENCIES

While travel agents may seem to make your life easier, they may not spend the time to find you the lowest possible fare—they get paid on commission. Travelers holding ISICs and IYTCs (p. 22) qualify for big discounts from student travel agencies. Most flights from budget agencies are on major airlines, but in peak season some may sell seats on less reliable chartered aircraft.

The Adventure Travel Company, 124 MacDougal St., New York City, NY 10021, USA (☎+1-800-467-4595; www.theadventuretravelcompany.com.) Offices across Canada and the US including New York City, San Diego, San Francisco, and Seattle.

STA Travel, 5900 Wilshire Blvd., Ste. 900, Los Angeles, CA 90036, USA (24hr. reservations and info ☎+1-800-781-4040; www.statravel.com). A student and youth travel organization with over 150 offices worldwide (check their website for a listing of all their offices), including US offices in Boston, Chicago, New York City, Seattle, San Francisco, and Washington, DC. Ticket booking, travel insurance, railpasses, and more. Walk-in offices are located throughout Australia (☎+61 3 9207 5900), New Zealand (☎+64 9 309 9723), and the UK (☎+44 8701 630 026).

USIT, 19-21 Aston Quay, Dublin 2, Ireland (☎+353 1 602 1904; www.usit.ie). Ireland's leading student/budget travel agency has 20 offices throughout Northern Ireland and the Republic of Ireland. Offers programs to work, study, and volunteer worldwide.

 FLIGHT PLANNING ON THE INTERNET. The array of options on the internet can be overwhelming. Here's a run-down of the top sites:

STA (www.statravel.com) and **StudentUniverse** (www.studentuniverse. com) provide quotes on student tickets, while **Orbitz** (www.orbitz.com), **Expedia** (www.expedia.com), and **Travelocity** (www.travelocity.com) offer full travel services. **Priceline** (www.priceline.com) lets you specify a price and obligates you to buy any ticket that meets or beats it; **Hotwire** (www.hotwire. com) offers bargain fares but won't reveal the airline or flight times until you buy. Other sites that compile deals include www.bestfares.com, www.flights. com, www.lowestfare.com, www.onetravel.com, and www.travelzoo.com.

SideStep (www.sidestep.com) and **Booking Buddy** (www.bookingbuddy. com) are online tools that help sift through multiple offers; these two let you enter your trip information once and search multiple sites. French websites like **FranceGuide** (www.franceguide.com) and **All Travel France** (www.alltravelfrance.com) sometimes have better deals than American equivalents.

Air Traveler's Handbook (www.faqs.org/faqs/travel/air/handbook) is an indispensable resource on the Internet; it has a comprehensive listing of links to everything you need to know before you board a plane.

COMMERCIAL AIRLINES

The commercial airlines' lowest regular offer is the **APEX (Advance Purchase Excursion)** fare, which provides confirmed reservations and allows "open-jaw" tickets. Generally, reservations must be made seven to 21 days ahead of departure, with seven- to 14-day minimum-stay and up to 90-day maximum-stay restrictions. These fares carry hefty cancellation and change penalties (fees rise in summer). Book peak-season APEX fares early. Use **Expedia** (www.expedia.com) or **Travelocity** (www.travelocity.com) to get an idea of the lowest published fares, then use the resources outlined here to try to beat those fares. Low-season fares should be appreciably cheaper than the high-season (mid-June to Aug.) ones listed here.

Let's Go treats ☒**budget airlines** (see this page) separately from commercial airlines. For travelers who don't place a premium on convenience, we recommend these no-frills airlines for jetting around Europe. Even if you live outside the continent, you can save a lot of money by hopping the cheapest flight to Europe possible, then using budget airlines to reach your final destination.

TRAVELING FROM NORTH AMERICA

The most common ways to cross the pond are those you've probably heard of. Standard commercial carriers like **American** (☎+1-800-433-7300; www.aa.com), **United** (☎+1-800-538-2929; www.ual.com), and **Northwest** (☎+1-800-447-4747; www.nwa.com) will probably offer the most convenient flights, but they may not be the cheapest. Check **Lufthansa** (☎+1-800-399-5838; www.lufthansa.com), **British Airways** (☎+1-800-247-9297; www.britishairways.com), **Air France** (☎+1-800-237-2747; www.airfrance.us), and **Alitalia** (☎+1-800-223-5730; www.alitaliausa.com) for cheap tickets from destinations throughout the US. You might find an even better deal on one of the following airlines, if any of their limited departure points is convenient for you.

Icelandair: ☎+1-800-223-5500; www.icelandair.com. Stopovers in Iceland for no extra cost on most transatlantic flights. For last-minute offers, subscribe to Lucky Fares.

Finnair: ☎+1-800-950-5000; www.finnair.com. Cheap round-trips from San Francisco, New York City, and Toronto to Paris; connections throughout Europe.

TRAVELING FROM THE UK AND IRELAND

Cheapflights (www.cheapflights.co.uk) publishes bargains on airfare from the British Isles. Below is a list of a few commercial carriers with special deals, but there is really no reason for British and Irish globetrotters not to fly on budget airlines (see below).

Aer Lingus: Ireland ☎+353 818 365 000; www.aerlingus.ie. Return tickets from Dublin, Cork, Galway, Kerry, and Shannon to Paris (US$400-700).

KLM: UK ☎+44 8705 074 074; www.klmuk.com. Cheap return tickets from London and elsewhere to Paris.

TRAVELING FROM AUSTRALIA AND NEW ZEALAND

Qantas Air: Australia ☎+61 13 13 13, New Zealand +64 800 808 767; www.qantas.com.au. Flights from Australia and New Zealand to Paris for around AUS$2500.

Singapore Air: Australia ☎+61 13 10 11, New Zealand +64 800 808 909; www.singaporeair.com. Flies from Auckland, Christchurch, Melbourne, Perth, and Sydney.

Thai Airways: Australia ☎+61 1300 65 19 60, New Zealand +64 9 377 38 86; www.thaiair.com. Flights to international destinations including Paris.

BUDGET AIRLINES

Low-cost carriers are the latest big thing in Europe. With their help, travelers can often snag tickets for illogically low prices (i.e., less than the price of a meal in the airport food court), but you get what you pay for: namely, minimalist service and no frills. In addition, many budget airlines fly out of smaller regional airports several kilometers out of town, and may tack on extra charges. You'll have to buy shuttle tickets to reach the airports of many of these airlines, so add an hour or so to your travel time. Beauvais airport is 2 hours out of Paris (1-way; €14). After round-trip shuttle tickets and fees for services that might come standard on other airlines, that €1 fare can suddenly jump to €20-100. Prices vary dramatically; shop around, book months ahead, pack light, and stay flexible to nab the best fares. For a more detailed list of these airlines by country, check out www.whichbudget.com.

bmibaby: UK ☎0871 224 0224, elsewhere +44 870 126 6726; www.bmibaby.com. Departures from multiple cities in the UK to Paris Charles de Gaulle Airport.

easyJet: ☎+44 871 244 2366, 10p per min.; www.easyjet.com. London to Orly and Charles de Gaulle Airport.

Ryanair: Ireland ☎0818 30 30 30, UK 0871 246 0000; www.ryanair.com. From Dublin, Glasgow, Liverpool, London, and Shannon to Beauvais Airport.

SkyEurope: UK ☎0905 722 2747, elsewhere +421 2 3301 7301; www.skyeurope.com. 40 destinations in 19 countries around Europe. Flights to Orly Airport.

Sterling: Denmark ☎70 10 84 84, UK 0870 787 8038; www.sterling.dk. The 1st Scandinavian-based budget airline. Connects Denmark, Norway, and Sweden to 47 European destinations, including Paris Charles de Gaulle Airport.

Transavia: UK ☎020 7365 4997; www.transavia.com. Short hops from Cracow to Paris Orly Sud Airport from €49 one-way.

Wizz Air: UK ☎0904 475 9500, 65p per min.; www.wizzair.com. Paris Beauvais Airport from Budapest, Cracow, and Warsaw.

AIR COURIER FLIGHTS

Those who travel light should consider courier flights. Couriers help transport cargo on international flights by using their checked luggage space for freight. Generally, couriers are limited to carry-ons and must deal with complex flight restrictions. Most flights are round-trip only, with short fixed-length stays (usually 1 week) and a limit of one ticket per issue. Most of these flights also operate only out of major gateway cities, mostly in North America. Generally, you must be over 18 (in some cases 21). In summer, the most popular destinations (like Paris) usually require an advance reservation of about two weeks (you can usually book up to two months ahead). Super-discounted fares are common for "last-minute" flights (three to 14 days ahead).

FROM NORTH AMERICA

Round-trip courier fares from the US to Paris run about US$350. Most flights leave from Los Angeles, Miami, New York City, or San Francisco in the US; and from Montréal, Toronto, or Vancouver in Canada. The organizations below provide members with lists of opportunities and courier brokers for an annual fee. Prices quoted below are round-trip.

Courier Travel: (www.couriertravel.org). Searchable online database. Multiple departure points in the US to various European destinations, including Paris.

International Association of Air Travel Couriers: (IAATC; www.courier.org). From 7 North American cities to European cities, including Paris. 1-year membership US$45.

FROM THE UK, AUSTRALIA, AND NEW ZEALAND

The minimum age for couriers from the UK is usually 18. The **International Association of Air Travel Couriers** (www.courier.org; above) often offers courier flights from London to Tokyo, Sydney, and Bangkok and from Auckland to Frankfurt and London. **Courier Travel** (above) also offers flights from London and Sydney.

STANDBY FLIGHTS

Traveling standby requires considerable flexibility in arrival and departure dates. Companies dealing in standby flights sell vouchers rather than tickets, along with the promise to get you to your destination (or near your destination) within a certain window of time (typically 1-5 days). You call in before your specific window of time to hear your flight options and the probability that you will be able to board each flight. You can then decide which flights you want to try to catch, show up at the appropriate airport at the appropriate time, present your voucher, and board if space is available. Vouchers can usually be bought for both one-way and round-trip travel. You may receive a monetary refund only if every available flight within your date range is full; if you opt not to take an available (but perhaps less convenient) flight, you can only get credit toward future travel. To check on a company's service record in the US, contact the **Better Business Bureau** (☎+1-703-276-0100; www.bbb.org). It is difficult to receive refunds, and clients' vouchers will not be honored when an airline fails to receive payment in time.

TICKET CONSOLIDATORS

Ticket consolidators, or **"bucket shops,"** buy unsold tickets in bulk from commercial airlines and sell them at discounted rates. The best place to look is in the Sunday travel section of any major newspaper (such as *The New York Times*), where many bucket shops place tiny ads. Call quickly, as availability is extremely limited. Not all bucket shops are reliable, so insist on a receipt that gives full details of restrictions, refunds, and tickets and pay by credit card (in spite of the 2-5% fee) so you can stop payment if you never receive your tickets. For more info, see **www.travel-library.com/air-travel/consolidators.html.**

TRAVELING FROM CANADA AND THE US

Some consolidators worth trying are **Rebel** (☎+1-800-732-3588; www.rebel-tours.com), **Cheap Tickets** (www.cheaptickets.com), **Flights.com** (www.flights.com), and **TravelHUB** (www.travelhub.com). *Let's Go* does not endorse any of these agencies. As always, be cautious and research companies before you hand over your credit-card number.

CHARTER FLIGHTS

Tour operators contract charter flights with airlines in order to fly extra loads of passengers during peak season. These flights are far from hassle-free. They occur less frequently than major airlines, make refunds particularly difficult, and are almost always fully booked. Their scheduled times may change, and they may be canceled at the last moment (as late as 48hr. before the trip, and without a full refund). In addition, check-in, boarding, and baggage claim for them are often much slower. They can, however, be much cheaper.

Discount clubs and fare brokers offer members savings on last-minute charter and tour deals. Study contracts closely; you don't want to end up with an unwanted overnight layover. **Travelers Advantage** (☎+1-800-835-8747; www.travelersadvantage.com; US$90 annual fee includes discounts and cheap flight directories) specializes in European travel and tour packages.

AIRPORTS

Paris has three main airports: Roissy-Charles de Gaulle, Orly, and Beauvais.

ROISSY-CHARLES DE GAULLE (ROISSY-CDG)

Most transatlantic flights land at Aéroport Roissy-CDG, 23km northeast of Paris (www.adp.fr). The two cheapest and fastest ways to get into the city from Roissy-CDG are by RER and by bus.

RER

The RER train from Roissy-CDG to Paris leaves from the Roissy train station, which is in Terminal 2. To get to the station from Terminal 1, take the Red Line of the Navette, a free shuttle bus that leaves every 6-10 minutes. From there, the **RER B** (one of the Parisian commuter rail lines) will transport you to central Paris. To transfer to the metro, get off at **Gare du Nord, Châtelet-Les-Halles,** or **St-Michel,** all of which are RER and metro stops. You will need a ticket covering **five zones** to travel between Paris and Roissy-CDG. To get to the airport from central Paris, take the RER B3 to Aéroport Charles de Gaulle, which is the end of the line. Get on the free bus if you need to get to Terminal 1. The trip should take 35 minutes in either direction (RER every 15min. 5am-12:30am; €13).

BUS

Taking a shuttle bus the whole distance from the airport to Paris is simple, and it takes about the same amount of time as taking the RER. The ▨**Roissybus** (☎01 49 25 61 87) leaves from rue Scribe at **Place de l'Opéra** every 15min. during the day (5:45am-7pm) and every 20min. at night (7-11pm). You can catch the Roissybus from Terminals 1, 2, and 3 of the airport from 6am to 11pm (45min.; adults €9, children under 5 free). Roissybus is not wheelchair accessible.

The **Daily Air France Buses** (recorded info available in English ☎08 92 35 08 20) are faster and more expensive than the Roissybus and run to two areas of the city. Tickets can be purchased on the bus. Line 2 runs to and from the Arc de Triomphe (Ⓜ**Charles de Gaulle-Etoile**) at 1 av. Carnot (35min.; every 15min. 5:45am-11pm; one-way €10, round-trip €17, children one-way €5; 15% group discount), and to and from the pl. de la Porte de Maillot/Palais des Congrès (Ⓜ**Porte Maillot**) on bd. Gouvion St-Cyr, opposite the Hôtel Méridien (same schedule and prices). Line 4 runs to and from rue du Commandant Mouchette opposite the Hôtel Méridien (Ⓜ**Montparnasse-Bienvenue;** to Charles de Gaulle Airport every 30min. 7am-9pm; one-way €12, round-trip €20, children one-way €6; 15% group discount); and to and from **Gare de Lyon,** at 20bis, bd. Diderot (same schedule and prices). The shuttle stops are at or between Terminals 2A-D and F and at Terminal 1 on the departures level of the airport. The Air France buses are not wheelchair accessible.

DOOR-TO-DOOR SERVICE

While the RER B and buses are the cheapest means of transportation to and from the airport, it can be harrowing to navigate the train and metro stations when you're loaded down with luggage. As taxis are exorbitantly expensive (€40-50 to the center of Paris), **shuttle vans** are the best option for door-to-door service. Several companies run shuttles to and from both airports; prices range €15 to €30. See **Practical Information,** p. 137, for services and phone numbers.

TICKET VOCAB. Fares are either *aller simple* (one-way) or *aller-retour* (round-trip). "Period returns" require you to return within a specific number of days; "day return" means you must return on the same day. Unless stated otherwise, *Let's Go* always lists single one-way fares. Round-trip fares on trains and buses in France are usually double the one-way fare.

ORLY

Aéroport d'Orly (☎01 49 75 15 15 for info in English; 6am-11:45pm), 18km south of the city, is used by charters and many continental flights.

RER

From Orly Sud gate G or gate I, platform 1, or Orly Ouest level G, gate F, take the **Orly-Rail** shuttle bus (every 15min. 6am-11pm; €6, children €4) to the **Pont de Rungis/Aéroport d'Orly** train stop, where you can board the RER C2 for a number of destinations in Paris. (35min.; every 15min. 6am-11pm; adults €5.35, children €4.) The **Jetbus** (every 15min. 6:20am-10:50pm, €6) provides a quick connection between Orly Sud, gate H, platform 2, or Orly Ouest level 0, gate C and Ⓜ**Villejuif-Louis Aragon** on metro line 7.

BUS

Another option is the RATP Ⓜ**Orlybus** (☎08 36 68 77 14), which runs between metro and RER stop **Denfert-Rochereau** (lines 4 and 6) in the 14*ème* and Orly's south terminal. (25min.; every 15-20min. 6am-11:30pm from Orly to Denfert-Rochereau, 5:35am-11pm from Denfert-Rochereau to Orly; €7.) You can also board the Orlybus at **Dareau-St-Jacques, Glacière-Tolbiac,** and **Porte de Gentilly.**

　Air France Buses run between Orly and Gare Montparnasse, near the Hôtel Méridien, 6*ème* (Ⓜ**Montparnasse-Bienvenue**), and the **Invalides Air France** agency, pl. des Invalides (30min.; every 15min. 6am-11:30pm; one-way €14, round-trip €22). Buses stop at Orly Ouest and Orly Sud at the departure levels.

ORLYVAL

RATP also runs **Orlyval** (☎01 69 93 53 00)—a combination of metro, RER, and VAL rail shuttle—which is probably your fastest option. The VAL shuttle goes from **Antony** (RER line B) to Orly Ouest and Sud. You can either get a ticket just for the VAL (€8), or combination VAL-RER tickets (€10). Buy tickets at any RATP booth in the city, or from the Orlyval agencies at Orly Ouest, Orly Sud, and Antony. To Orly: Be careful; it splits into 2 lines right before the Antony stop. Get on the train that says **"St-Rémy-Les-Chevreuse"** or just look for the track that has a lit-up sign saying **"Antony-Orly."** (35min. from Châtelet; every 10min. M-Sa 6am-10:30pm, Su and holidays 7am-11pm.) From Orly: Trains arrive at Orly Ouest 2min. after reaching Orly Sud. (32min. to M: Châtelet, every 10min. M-Sa 6am-10:30pm, Su 7am-11pm.)

DOOR-TO-DOOR SERVICE

See **Practical Information: Transportation,** p. 137, for information on shuttle van service. Taxis from Orly to town cost around €25. Allow at least 30min.; traffic can make the trip much longer.

BEAUVAIS

Ryanair, easyJet, and other intercontinental airlines often fly into and depart from Aéroport de Paris Beauvais. Buses run between the airport and bd. Pershing in the 17*ème*, near the hotel Concorde Lafayette (Ⓜ**Porte Maillot**). Tickets are €13 and can be purchased in the arrivals lounge of the airport, at the kiosk just oustide the bus stop, or online. Call ☎03 44 11 46 86 or consult www.aeroport-beauvais.com for bus schedules.

ESSENTIALS

BY TRAIN

If you're traveling to Paris from another European city, trains can be a scenic and inexpensive option. Prices and number of trips per day vary according to destination, the day of the week, season, and other criteria. To find prices, schedules, and locations, check **www.raileurope.com** or **www.voyages-sncf.com.**

Gare du Nord: Trains to northern France, Britain, Belgium, the Netherlands, Scandinavia, Eastern Europe, and northern Germany (Cologne, Hamburg) all depart from this station. To: Amsterdam (4-5hr.); Brussels (1hr.); London (by the Eurostar Chunnel; 3hr.).

Gare de l'Est: To eastern France (Champagne, Alsace, Lorraine, Strasbourg), Luxembourg, parts of Switzerland (Basel, Zürich, Lucerne), southern Germany (Frankfurt, Munich), Austria, Hungary, and Prague. To: Luxembourg (4-5hr.); Munich (9hr.); Prague (15hr.); Strasbourg (1hr.); Vienna (15hr.); Zürich (7hr.).

Gare de Lyon: To southern and southeastern France (Lyon, Provence, Riviera), parts of Switzerland (Geneva, Lausanne, Berne), Italy, and Greece. To: Florence (13hr.); Geneva (4hr.); Lyon (2hr.); Marseille (3-4hr.); Nice (6hr.); Rome (15hr.).

Gare d'Austerlitz: To the Loire Valley, southwestern France (Bordeaux, Pyrénées), Spain, and Portugal. (TGV to southwestern France leaves from Gare Montparnasse.) To Barcelona (12hr.) and Madrid (12-13hr.).

Gare St-Lazare: To Normandy. To Caen (2hr.) and Rouen (1-2hr.).

Gare Montparnasse: To Brittany and southwestern France on the TGV. To Rennes (2hr.) and Nantes (2hr.).

CHUNNEL FROM THE UK

Traversing 31 miles under the sea, the Chunnel is undoubtedly the fastest, most convenient, and least scenic route from Britain to France.

Trains: Eurostar, Eurostar House, Waterloo Station, London SE1 8SE, UK (UK ☎08705 186 186, elsewhere +44 1233 617 575; www.eurostar.com). Frequent trains between London and the continent. Destinations include Paris, Disneyland Paris, Lille, Avignon, and Calais. Book online, at major rail stations in the UK, or at the office above.

Buses: Eurolines (www.eurolines.com) provides bus-ferry combinations to France. Service to major cities in France, including Paris, Lyon, and Marseille.

Cars: Eurotunnel, Ashford Rd., Folkestone, Kent CT18 8XX, UK (☎+44 8705 35 35 35; www.eurotunnel.co.uk). Shuttles cars and passengers between Kent and Nord-Pas-de-Calais. Return fares range UK£50-200 for a car, depending on length of stay. Travelers with cars can also look into sea crossings by ferry (below).

BY BUS

British travelers may find buses the cheapest (though slowest) way of getting to Paris, with round-trip fares starting around UK£50. The journey by bus entails either a ferry trip or a descent into the Channel Tunnel; these extra trips are typically included in the price of a ticket. **Eurolines** is Europe's largest operator of international coach services; their return fares between London and Paris start at €40. They have offices in London (☎+44 8705 80 80 80; www.eurolines.com) and Paris (☎+33 01 49 72 57 80; www.eurolines.fr).

GETTING AROUND FRANCE

If, for some unfathomable reason, you should choose to leave Paris and explore the rest of the country, you should carefully consider the following means of transport and choose the one which suits your budget and preferences.

BY PLANE

ESSENTIALS

COMMERCIAL AIRLINES

For small-scale travel on the continent, *Let's Go* suggests 🕮budget airlines (p. 35) for budget travelers, but more traditional carriers have made efforts to keep up with the revolution. The **Star Alliance Europe Airpass** offers economy-class fares as low as US$65 for travel within Europe to 216 destinations in 44 countries. The pass is available to non-European passengers on Star Alliance carriers, including **Air France** and **AirCorsica**. See www.staralliance.com for more information. In addition, a number of European airlines offer discount coupon packets. Most are only available as tack-ons for transatlantic passengers, but some are stand-alone offers. Most must be purchased before departure, so research in advance.

EuropeByAir: ☎+1-888-321-4737; www.europebyair.com. FlightPass allows you to hop between 500 cities in Europe and North Africa. Most flights US$99.

Iberia: ☎+1-800-772-4642; www.iberia.com. EuroPass allows Iberia passengers flying from the US to France to tack on a minimum of 2 additional destinations in Europe. US$125-155 each.

BUDGET AIRLINES

The recent emergence of no-frills airlines has made hopscotching around Europe by air increasingly affordable. Though these flights often feature inconvenient hours or serve less popular regional airports, with ticket prices often dipping into single digits, it's never been faster or easier to jet across the continent. See p. 35 for a list of budget airlines.

BY TRAIN

Trains in France are generally comfortable, convenient, and reasonably swift. Second-class compartments, which seat four to six, are great for meeting fellow travelers. Trains, however, are not always safe. For safety tips, see **Personal Safety,** p. 30. For long trips, make sure you are on the correct car, as trains sometimes split at crossroads. Towns listed in parentheses on European schedules require a switch at the town listed immediately before the parentheses.

You can either buy a **railpass,** which allows you unlimited travel within a particular region for a given period of time, or rely on buying individual **point-to-point** tickets as you go. Most countries give students or youths (usually defined as anyone under 26) discounts on regular domestic rail tickets, and many also sell a student or youth card that provides 20-50% off all fares for up to a year.

RESERVATIONS. While seat reservations are required only for selected trains (usually on major lines), you are not guaranteed a seat without one (usually €3-20). You should strongly consider reserving in advance during peak holiday and tourist seasons (at the very latest, a few hours ahead). You will also have to purchase a **supplement** (€5-15) or special fare for high-speed or high-quality trains, including certain French TGVs. InterRail holders must also purchase supplements (€2-10) for many TGVs, though they are often unnecessary for Eurail Pass and Europass holders.

OVERNIGHT TRAINS. On night trains, you won't waste valuable daylight hours traveling and you can avoid the hassle and expense of staying at a hotel. However, drawbacks include discomfort, sleepless nights, the lack of scenery, and, most importantly, safety concerns. **Sleeping accommodations** on trains differ from country to country, but typically you can either sleep upright in your seat (supplement about €4-6, if not free) or pay for a separate space. **Couchettes** (berths) typically have four to six seats per compartment (supplement about €10-20 per person); **sleepers** (beds) in private sleeping cars offer more privacy and comfort but are considerably more expensive (supplement €40-150). If you are using a railpass valid only for a restricted number of days, inspect train schedules to maximize the use of your pass: an overnight train or boat journey often uses up only one of your travel days if it departs after 7pm.

SHOULD YOU BUY A RAILPASS? Railpasses were conceived to allow you to jump on any train in Europe, go wherever you want whenever you want, and change your plans at will. In practice, it's not so simple. You still must stand in line to validate your pass, pay for supplements, and fork over cash for seat and couchette reservations. More importantly, railpasses don't always pay off. If you plan to spend extensive time on trains hopping between big cities, a railpass will probably be worth it. But in many cases, especially if you are under 26, point-to-point tickets may prove a cheaper option.

You may find it tough to make your railpass pay for itself in France, where train fares are reasonable and distances between destinations are relatively short. If, however, the total cost of your trips nears the price of the pass, the convenience of avoiding ticket lines may be worth the difference.

MULTINATIONAL RAILPASSES

EURAIL PASSES. Eurail is **valid in France,** as well as most of Western Europe, but **not valid in the UK. Eurail Global Passes,** valid for a consecutive given number of days, are best for those planning to spend extensive time on trains every few days. Global passes valid for any 10 or 15 (not necessarily consecutive) days within a two-month period are more cost-effective for those traveling longer distances less frequently. **Eurail Pass Saver** provides first-class travel for travelers in groups of two to five (prices are per person). **Eurail Pass Youth** provides parallel second-class perks for those under 26.

EURAIL GLOBAL PASSES	15 DAYS	21 DAYS	1 MONTH	2 MONTHS	3 MONTHS
Eurail Pass Adult	€503	€653	€810	€1145	€1413
Eurail Pass Saver	€426	€554	€688	€973	€1205
Eurail Pass Youth	€327	€423	€527	€745	€920

OTHER GLOBAL PASSES	10 DAYS IN 2 MONTHS	15 DAYS IN 2 MONTHS
Eurail Pass Adult	€594	€781
Eurail Pass Saver	€505	€665
Eurail Pass Youth	€387	€508

Passholders receive a timetable for major routes and a map with details on possible bike-rental, car-rental, hotel, and museum discounts. Passholders often also receive reduced fares or free passage on many boat, bus, and private railroad lines.

The **Eurail Select Pass** is a slimmed-down version of the Eurail Pass: it allows five, six, eight, 10, or 15 days of unlimited travel in any two-month period within three, four, or five bordering countries of 23 European nations. **Eurail Select Passes** (for individuals) and **Eurail Select Pass Saver** (for people traveling in groups of two to five) range from €319/270 per person (5 days, 3 countries) to €706/600 (15 days, 5 countries). The **Eurail Select Pass Youth** (2nd class) costs €207-459. You are entitled to the same freebies afforded by the Eurail Pass, but only when they are within or between countries that you have purchased.

SHOPPING AROUND FOR A EURAIL. Eurail Passes are designed by the EU itself and can be bought only by non-Europeans almost exclusively from non-European distributors. These passes must be sold at uniform prices determined by the EU. However, some travel agents tack on a handling fee, and others offer certain bonuses with purchase, so shop around. Also, keep in mind that pass prices usually go up each year, so, if you're planning to travel early in the year, you can save cash by purchasing before January 1 (you have 6 months from the purchase date to validate your pass in Europe).

It is best to buy your pass before leaving; only a few places in major European cities sell them, and at a marked-up price. You can get a replacement for a lost pass only if you have purchased insurance on it under the Pass Security Plan (€10). Eurail Passes are available through travel agents, student travel agencies like **STA (p. 34)**, and **Rail Europe** (Canada ☎800-361-7245, US 888-382-7245; www.raileurope.com) or **Flight Centre** (US ☎866-967-5351; www.flightcentre.com). It is also possible to buy directly from Eurail's website, www.eurail.com. Shipping is free to North America, Australia, and New Zealand.

EVERYONE NEEDS VALIDATION. In France, you must *composter* (validate) your ticket. Orange and yellow validation boxes can be found in every station, usually in front of the doors leading to the tracks, and you must have your ticket stamped with date and time by the machine before boarding the train.

OTHER MULTINATIONAL PASSES. If your travels will be limited to one area, regional passes are often good values. Eurail offers regional passes to France and Germany, France and Italy, France and Spain, and France and Switzerland. Rail Europe offers all of the above in addition to a France and Benelux pass.

For those who have lived for at least six months in one of the European countries where **InterRail Passes** are valid, they are an economical option. The InterRail Pass allows travel within 30 European countries (excluding the passholder's country of residence). The **Global Pass** is valid for a given number of days (not necessarily consecutive) within a 10-day to one-month period. (5 days within 10 days adult 1st class €329, adult 2nd class €249, youth 2nd class €159; 10 days within 22 days €489/359/239; 22 days continuous €629/469/309; 1 month continuous €809/599/399.) The **One Country Pass** limits travel within one European country. Passholders get free admission to many museums as well as **discounts** on accommodations, food, and some ferries. Passes are available at www.interrailnet.com and from travel agents, at major train stations throughout Europe, and through online vendors (such as www.railpassdirect.co.uk).

DOMESTIC RAILPASSES

Although Eurail and its brethren are great if you're spending some time out of France, a railpass on a smaller scale may be what you need for purely domestic travel. A national pass—valid on all rail lines of a country's rail company—is sometimes more cost-effective than a multinational pass. However, many national passes are limited and don't provide the free or discounted travel on private railways and ferries that Eurail does. Some of these passes can be bought only in Europe, some only outside of Europe; check with a railpass agent or with national tourist offices.

NATIONAL RAILPASSES. The domestic analogs of the Eurail Pass, national railpasses are valid either for a given number of consecutive days or for a specific number of days within a given time period. Usually, they must be purchased before you leave. The basic **France Railpass** (US$278-328) provides travelers with three days of unlimited train travel in one month. The **France Saverpass** (US$240-279) offers the same perks for people traveling with groups of two or more. Finally, the **France Day Railpass** (US$115-165) provides travelers with the opportunity to venture from Paris on daytrips to big cities like Lyon or Marseille. Senior and youth passes are also available. For more information on national railpasses, check out **www.raileurope.com/us/rail/passes/france_index.htm.**

BY BUS

European trains and railpasses are extremely popular, but in some cases buses prove to be the only option. Traveling by bus is generally inconvenient in France and typically only useful for short trips between destinations that are not served by train lines. However, **international bus passes** are often cheaper than railpasses and allow unlimited travel on a hop-on, hop-off basis between major European cities. The prices below are based on high-season travel.

Busabout, 258 Vauxhall Bridge Rd., London SW1V 1BS, UK (☎+44 20 7950 1661; www.busabout.com). Offers 3 interconnecting bus circuits covering 29 of Europe's best bus hubs. 1 circuit US$639; 2 circuits US$1069; 3 circuits US$1319.

Eurolines, 28 av. du Général de Gaulle, Paris (☎08 92 89 90 91; www.eurolines.com). The largest operator of Europe-wide coach services. Unlimited 15-day (high season €289, under 26 €238; mid-season €200/175; low season €178/150) and 30-day (high season €277/314; mid-season €276/226; low season €264/201) travel passes to 40 major European cities.

Ze Bus: ☎05 59 85 26 60; www.ze-bus.com. A hop-on, hop-off bus service that runs through western France. Stops include Paris, Cherbourg, Quiberon, La Rochelle, Biarritz, and smaller cities in between.

BY CAR

Cars offer speed, freedom, access to the countryside, and an escape from the town-to-town mentality of trains. Many places in France—especially the most popular tourist attractions, like the Loire châteaux or the D-Day beaches—are best reached by car. Other attractions can be reached in no other way. Although a single traveler won't save by renting a car, two to four usually will.

Before setting off, become acquainted with French driving laws (e.g., motorcycle drivers and passengers must wear helmets in France). For an informal primer on French and European road signs and conventions, check out www. travlang.com/signs. The **Association for Safe International Road Travel (ASIRT),** 11769 Gainsborough Rd., Potomac, MD 20854, USA (☎+1-301-983-5252; www.asirt. org), can provide more specific information about road conditions. ASIRT considers road travel (by car or bus) to be relatively safe in France. French drivers, along with other Western Europeans, use unleaded gas almost exclusively.

DRIVING PERMITS AND CAR INSURANCE

INTERNATIONAL DRIVING PERMIT (IDP)

If you plan to drive a car while in France, you must be over 18 and have a recognized driver's license. French law allows travelers to drive with a valid American or Canadian license for a year, but an **International Driving Permit (IDP)** is also sufficient. It is helpful to have an IDP in case you're in a situation (e.g., an accident or stranded in a small town) where the police do not speak English; information on the IDP is printed in 11 languages, including French. To apply, contact your home country's automobile association.

CAR INSURANCE

Most credit cards cover standard insurance. If you rent, lease, or borrow a car, you will need a **green card,** or **International Insurance Certificate,** to certify that you have liability insurance and that it applies abroad. Green cards can be obtained at car-rental agencies, car dealers (for those leasing cars), some travel agents, and some border crossings. Rental agencies may require you to purchase theft insurance in countries that they consider to have a high risk of auto theft.

If you are driving a conventional rental vehicle on an unpaved road in a rental car, you are almost never covered by insurance; ask about this before leaving the rental agency. Be aware that cars rented on an **American Express** or **Visa/MasterCard Gold** or **Platinum** credit card in France might not carry the automatic insurance that they would in some other countries; check with your credit-card company. Insurance plans from rental companies almost always come with an **excess** of around US$5-15 per day for conventional vehicles. This means that the insurance bought from the rental company only applies to damages over the excess; damages up to that amount must be covered by your existing insurance plan. Many rental companies in France require you to buy a **Collision Damage Waiver (CDW),** which will waive the excess in the case of a collision. **Loss Damage Waivers (LDWs)** do the same in the case of theft or vandalism.

RENTING A CAR

National chains often allow one-way rentals (picking up in one city and dropping off in another). There is usually a minimum hire period and sometimes an extra dropoff charge of several hundred dollars. Car rental in France is available through the following agencies:

Alamo (US ☎800-462-5266; www.alamo.com).

Auto Europe (☎+1-888-223-5555 or 207-842-2000; www.autoeurope.com).

Avis (France ☎08 20 05 05 05; www.avis.com).

Budget (US ☎800-472-3325, UK ☎0870 156 5656; www.budgetrentacar.com).

Europe by Car (☎+1-800-223-1516 or 212-581-3040; www.europebycar.com).

Europcar International, 3 av. du Centre, 78881 Saint Quentin en Yvelines Cedex (France ☎01 30 43 82 82, UK ☎0870 607 5000; US 877-940-6900; www.europcar.com).

Hertz (☎+1-800-654-3001; www.hertz.com).

Kemwel (☎+1-877-820-0668 or 800-678-0678; www.kemwel.com).

ON THE ROAD

DRIVING 101. Seat-belt use is mandatory in cars, and motorcycle drivers and passengers must wear helmets. Children under 10 years old are not permitted to sit in the front passenger seat. French police can fine anyone who does not comply with these laws. Always carry your driver's license, a vehicle registration document, and proof of auto insurance on the road.

RESOURCES. For directions, driving time estimates, and toll and gas costs, visit **www.iti.fr** or **www.prix-carburants.gouv.fr.** *L'essence* (gasoline) prices vary, but average about €1.60 per liter in cities and €1.40 per liter in outlying areas. *L'essence* tends to be cheaper than *l'essence sans plomb* (unleaded fuel). Ask at a French Government Tourist Office for *la carte de l'essence moins chère*—a map of supermarkets near highway exits, where gas is cheaper. For info on driving conditions in France, see the website of **Bison Futé** (www.bison-fute.equipement.gouv.fr.), an organization geared toward reducing road congestion.

CAR ASSISTANCE. Many car rentals include 24hr. roadside assistance. If you find yourself in trouble on the Autoroute without such service, go to a nearby orange SOS phone. Dial ☎15 for an ambulance and ☎17 for the police.

GETTING AROUND PARIS

BY PUBLIC TRANSPORTATION

The **RATP** (Régie Autonome des Transports Parisiens) coordinates a network of subways, buses, and commuter trains in and around Paris. For info, contact La Maison de la RATP, right across the street from Ⓜ**Gare de Lyon** (190 r. de Bercy) or the Bureau de Tourisme RATP, pl. de la Madeleine, 8ème (☎01 40 06 71 45; Ⓜ**Madeleine;** open daily 8:30am-6pm).

FARES

Individual tickets for the RATP cost €2 each, or €12 for a *carnet* of 10. Say, *"Un ticket, s'il vous plaît"* (UHN ti-KAY...), or *"Un carnet..."* (UHN car-NAY...), to the ticket vendor. Each metro ride takes one ticket. The bus takes at least one, sometimes more, depending on connections you make and the time of day. For directions on using the tickets, see Metro, p. 47.

🕭PASSES

If you're staying in Paris for several days or weeks, a **carte orange** can be economical. Bring an photo (machines take them in major stations) to the ticket counter and ask for a weekly *carte orange hebdomadaire* (€17) or the equally swank monthly *carte orange mensuelle* (€56). These cards have specific start and end dates (weekly pass runs M-Su; monthly starts at the beginning of the month). Prices quoted here are for passes in **Zones 1 and 2** (the metro and RER in Paris and suburbs), and **work on all metro, bus, and RER modes of transport.** If you plan to travel to the suburbs, you'll need RER passes for more zones (they go up to 5). If you're only in town for a day or two, a cheap option is the **carte mobilis** (€6 for a 1-day pass in Zones 1 and 2; available in metro stations; ☎08 91 36 20 20), which provides **unlimited metro, bus, and RER transportation** within Paris.

   🕭 **Paris Visite** tickets are valid for unlimited travel on bus, metro, and RER, as well as discounts on sightseeing trips, museum admission, and shopping at stores like Galeries Lafayette. These passes can be purchased at the airport or at metro and RER stations. The passes are available for one day (€8.50), two days (€14), three days (€19), or five days (€27.50). The discounts you receive do not necessarily outweigh the extra cost.

METRO

In general, the metro system is easy to navigate (pick up a colorful map at any station or use the one in the front of this book), and trains run swiftly and frequently. Metro stations, in themselves a distinctive part of the Paris landscape, are marked with an "M" or with the *"Métropolitain"* lettering designed by Art Nouveau legend Hector Guimard.

GETTING AROUND

The earliest trains of the day start running around 5:30am, and the last ones leave the end-of-the-line stations (the *portes de Paris*) for the center of the city at about 12:15am during the week, and at 2:15am on Friday and Saturday. For the exact departure times of the last trains, check the poster in the center of each station marked **Principes de Tarification** (fare guidelines), the white sign with the platform's number and direction, or the monitors above the platform. Transport maps are posted on platforms and near turnstiles; all have a *plan du quartier*(map of the neighborhood). Connections to other lines are indicated by orange *correspondance* signs, exits indicated by blue *sortie* signs. Transfers are free if made within a station, but it is not always possible to reverse direction on the same line without exiting the station.

USING TICKETS

To pass through the turnstiles, insert your ticket into the slot just to your right as you approach the turnstile. It disappears for a moment, then pops out about a foot farther along, and a little green or white circle lights up, reminding you to retrieve the ticket. If the turnstile makes a peevish whining sound and a little red circle lights up, your ticket is not valid; take it back and try another. When you have the right light, push through the gate and retrieve your ticket. **Hold onto your ticket until you exit the metro,** and pass the point marked *Limite de Validité des Billets;* a uniformed RATP *contrôleur* (inspector) may request to see it on any train. If caught without one, you must pay a hefty fine. Also, any *correspondances*(transfers) to the RER require you to put your validated (and uncrumpled) ticket into a turnstile in order to exit.

LATE AT NIGHT

Don't count on buying a metro ticket late at night. Some ticket windows close as early as 10pm, and many close before the last train arrives. Also, not all stations have automatic booths. It's a good idea to carry one more ticket than you need, although large stations have ticket machines that accept coins. Avoid the most dangerous stations **(Barbès-Rochechouart, Pigalle, Anvers, Châtelet-Les-Halles, Gare du Nord, Gare de l'Est)** after dark. Stay vigilant, as the stations are frequented by criminals looking to prey on tourists. When in doubt, take a bus or taxi.

RER

The RER *(Réseau Express Régional)* is the RATP's suburban train system, which passes through central Paris. The RER travels much faster than the metro. There are five RER lines, marked A-E, with different branches designated by a number: for example, the C5 line services Versailles-Rive Gauche. The newest line, the E, is called the Eole *(Est-Ouest Liaison Express)*, and links Gare Magenta to Gare St-Lazare. Within Paris, the RER works exactly the same way as the metro, requiring the same ticket. The principal stops within the city, which link the RER to the metro system, are Gare du Nord, Nation, Charles de Gaulle-Etoile, Gare de Lyon, and Châtelet-Les-Halles on the Right

ESSENTIALS

Bank and St-Michel and Denfert-Rochereau on the Left Bank. The electric sign-boards next to each track list all the possible stops for trains running on that track. Be sure that the little square next to your destination is lit up. Trips to the suburbs require special tickets. You'll need your ticket to exit RER stations. Insert your ticket just as you did to enter, and pass through. Like the metro, the RER runs 5:30am-12:30am, and until 2:30am on weekends.

TRAIN

Each of Paris's six train stations (p. 40) is a veritable community of its own, with resident street people and police, cafés, *tabacs*, banks, and shops. Locate the ticket counters *(guichets)*, the platforms *(quais)*, and the tracks *(voies)*, and you will be ready to roll. Each terminal has two divisions: the suburbs *(banlieue)* and the desti-nations outside the metropolitan area *(grandes lignes)*. Some cities can be accessed by both regular trains and *trains à grande vitesse* (TGV; high speed trains). TGVs are more expensive, much faster, more comfortable, and require reservations that cost a small fee. For train information or to make reservations, contact SNCF (☎08 90 36 10 10, €0.23 per min.; www.voyages-sncf.fr). Yellow ticket machines *(billet-teries)* at every train station sell tickets. You'll need to have a MasterCard or Visa card and know your PIN. SNCF offers many discounted round-trip tickets which go under the name *Tarifs Découvertes*—you should rarely have to pay full price.

> **SOYEZ PRUDENT.** Exercise caution in train stations at night; Gare du Nord and Gare d'Austerlitz, in particular, are home to after-hours drug traffic and prostitution. Also, buy tickets only at official counters; the SNCF doesn't have any outfits in refrigerator boxes, no matter what you're told.

BUS

Although slower and often costlier than the metro, a bus ride can be a cheap sightseeing tour and a helpful introductions to the city's layout.

TICKETS

Bus tickets are the same as those used in the metro, and they can be pur-chased either in metro stations or on the bus from the driver. Enter the bus through the front door and punch your ticket by pushing it into the machine by the driver's seat. If you have a *Navigo* or other transport pass, simply flash it at the driver. Inspectors may ask to see your ticket, so hold onto it until you get off. Should you wish to leave the earthly paradise that is the RATP autobus, just press the red button so the *arrêt demandé* (stop requested) sign lights up.

NIGHT BUSES

Most buses run daily 7am-8:30pm, although those marked **Autobus du nuit** con-tinue until 1:30am. Still others, named **Noctilien,** run all night. Night buses (€2) run from Châtelet to the *portes* of the city every hour on the half hour from 12:30-5:30am (1-6am from the *portes* into the city). Look for bus stops marked with a bug-eyed moon sign. Check out **www.noctilien.fr** or ask a major metro sta-tion or at Gare de l'Est for more information on Noctilien buses.

TOUR BUSES

The RATP's Balabus (☎01 44 68 43 35) stops at virtually every major sight in Paris (Bastille, St-Michel, Louvre, Musée d'Orsay, Concorde, Champs-Elysées,

Charles de Gaulle-Etoile; whole loop takes 1hr.). The circuit requires three standard bus tickets and starts at La Défense or the Gare de Lyon.

 THE BUS CODE. Buses with three-digit numbers travel to and from the suburbs, while buses with two-digit numbers travel exclusively within Paris.

ESSENTIALS

BY TAXI

For taxi companies, see **Practical Information**, p. 136. If you have a complaint, or have left personal belongings behind, contact the taxi company, or write to **Service des Taxis de la Préfecture de Police**, 36 rue des Morillons, 75015 (☎01 55 76 20 00; ⓂConvention). Ask for a receipt; if you want to file a complaint, record and include the driver's license number.

RATES

Tarif A, the basic rate, is in effect within the city limits 10am-5pm (€0.86 per km). Tarif B is in effect Monday through Saturday 7pm-7am, all day Sunday, and during the day from the airports and immediate suburbs (€1.12 per km). Tarif C, the highest, is in effect from the airports 7pm-7am (€1.35 per km). In addition, there is a *prix en charge* (base fee) of €2.20, and a minimum charge of €5.60. You should wait for taxis at the nearest **taxi stand**; taxis will not stop if you attempt to flag them down on the street. Lines at taxi stands can get long in the late afternoon during the week and on weekend nights. Should you call a taxi rather than hail one at a taxi stand, the base fee will increase according to how far away you are and how long it takes the driver to get there. For all cabs, stationary time (at traffic lights and in traffic jams) costs €27-31 per hour. Additional charges (€1) are added for luggage over 5kg. Taxis take three passengers; there is a €2.85 charge for a fourth. Some take credit cards (MC/V).

BY CAR

Traveling by car in Paris is only reasonable if your plans include significant travel outside the city. Parisian drivers are merciless. *Priorité à droite* gives the right of way to the car approaching from the right, regardless of the size of the streets, and Parisians exercise this right even in the face of grave danger. Technically, drivers are not allowed to honk within city limits unless they are about to hit a pedestrian, but this rule is broken more often than it is followed. The legal way to show discontent is to flash your headlights, and Parisian drivers are usually discontent (read: lots of flashing lights). A map of Paris marked with one-way streets is indispensable for drivers. Parking is expensive and hard to find. See **Practical Information**, p. 135 for info on **renting a car.**

BY TWO-WHEELER

BICYCLES

Thanks to frequent metro strikes, bike shops have come to the rescue of stranded citizens, and an emergent cycling community has approached its dream of an auto-free Paris. If you have never ridden a bike in heavy traffic, however, don't use central Paris as a testing ground. Bicycles can be transported on all RER lines anytime except rush hour (M-F 6:30-9am and 4:30-7pm) and on metro line 1 on Sunday before 4:30pm. Ask for a helmet (not legally required, but always a good idea) and inquire about insurance.

A new bike hire service, **Vélib,** has stationed over 20,000 bikes at over 1450 automated stations throughout Paris. With a subscription, bike rental is free for 30min. and very cheap for longer trips. For more info on Vélib and other bike rental companies, see **Practical Information,** p. 135.

SCOOTERS

Motorized two-wheelers, called *motos* or *mobylettes*, are everywhere in Paris. Everyone seems to own one, and just as many seem to have been injured on one. If you want to sacrifice safety for the speed and style that only a scooter can provide, you can rent one; no special license is required, though a helmet most definitely is. See **Practical Information,** p. 135.

KEEPING IN TOUCH

BY EMAIL AND INTERNET

Internet access is readily available in Paris. Many cafes offer free Wi-Fi, and most hostels offer a connection for a small (or not-so-small) fee.

Although in some places it's possible to forge a remote link with your home server, in most cases this is a much slower (and thus more expensive) option than using free **web-based email accounts** (e.g., www.gmail.com and www.hotmail. com). For a list of **Internet cafes** and free Internet terminals, see **Practical Information,** p. 139. For additional cybercafes in France, check out www.cybercaptive. com, www.netcafeguide.com, or www.world66.com/netcafeguide.

Increasingly, travelers find that taking their **laptop computers** on the road with them can be a convenient option for staying connected. Check out **Food,** p. 165, to find out which Parisian cafes offer free Wi-Fi.

WARY WI-FI. Wireless hot spots make Internet access possible in public and remote places. Unfortunately, they also pose **security risks.** Hot spots are public, open networks that use unencrypted, unsecured connections. They are susceptible to hacks and "packet sniffing"—ways of stealing passwords and other private information. To help prevent problems, disable ad hoc mode, turn off file sharing and network discovery, encrypt your email, turn on your firewall, beware of phony networks, and watch for over-the-shoulder creeps.

BY TELEPHONE

CALLING HOME FROM FRANCE

 SKIP THE FEES. If you buy an international phone card and are staying in a room with a telephone, call from your room rather than from a pay phone—*télécabines* charge large fees, which reduce your talk time by half.

Télécartes (prepaid phone cards) are a common and relatively inexpensive means of calling abroad. Each one comes with a Personal Identification Number (PIN) and a toll-free access number. You call the access number and then follow the directions for dialing your PIN. To purchase prepaid phone cards, check online for the best rates; **www.callingcards.com** is a good place to start. Online providers generally send your access number and PIN via email, with no actual "card" involved. You can also call home with prepaid phone cards purchased in France (see **Calling Within France,** below).

PLACING INTERNATIONAL CALLS. To call France from home or to call home from France, dial:
1. The **international dialing prefix.** To call from **Australia,** dial 0011; **Canada** or the **US,** 011; **Ireland, New Zealand,** the **UK,** or **France,** 00.
2. The **country code** of the country you want to call. To call **Australia,** dial 61; **Canada** or the **US,** 1; **Ireland,** 353; **New Zealand,** 64; the **UK,** 44; **France,** 33.
3. The **city/area code.** If the first digit is a zero (e.g., 01 for Paris), omit the zero when calling from abroad (e.g., dial 1 from Canada to reach Paris).
4. The **local number.**

Another option is to purchase a **calling card,** linked to a major national telecommunications service in your home country. Calls are billed collect or to your account. To call home with a calling card, contact the operator for your service provider in France by dialing the appropriate toll-free access number (listed below in the third column).

COMPANY	TO OBTAIN A CARD:	TO CALL ABROAD:
AT&T (US)	☎+1-800-364-9292 or www.att.com	☎0800 99 00 11
Canada Direct	☎+1-800-561-8868 or www.infocanadadirect.com	☎0800 99 00 16 or 0800 99 02 16
MCI (US)	☎+1-800-777-5000 or www.minutepass.com	☎0800 99 00 19
Telecom New Zealand Direct	www.telecom.co.nz	☎0800 99 00 64
Telstra Australia	☎+1-800 676 638 or www.telstra.com	☎0800 99 00 61

Placing a collect call through an international operator can be expensive but may be necessary in case of an emergency. You can frequently call collect without even possessing a company's calling card just by calling its access number and following the instructions.

CALLING WITHIN FRANCE

A simple way to make domestic or international calls is to use a card-operated pay phone. *Télécartes* carry a certain amount of phone time, and are usually the only way to pay at public phones, as coin-operated phones have largely been phased out. *Télécartes* are available in denominations of units; 120-unit cards cost about €24, and one minute of a local call uses about one unit. Emergency numbers, directory information (☎118 218), and *numéros verts* (toll-free numbers) beginning with ☎0800 can be dialed without a card. A bank card can often be used instead of a calling card at many public phones.

If the phone you use does not provide English commands, proceed with caution; French pay phones are notoriously unforgiving. *Décrochez* means pick up; *patientez* means wait. Do not dial until you hear *numérotez* or *composez*. *Raccrochez* means "hang up." To make another call, press the green button instead of hanging up. Phone rates tend to be highest in the morning, lower in the evening (after 3pm), and lowest on Sunday and late at night.

CABINE CALLBACK. Making international calls from France is easy— but getting the best deal on the dizzying array of phone cards offered at *tabacs* and post offices is anything but. While the spiffy *cabines* (public phone booths) that sit on most major streets have slots in which to insert a *télécarte* with a microchip, this is the most expensive way to call internationally. Savvy travelers ask for a **carte téléphonique internationale** at a *tabac*. These cards have a hidden trick that gets you **more minutes:** *cabine* callback. When using a non-*télécarte* phone card, don't dial the large, obvious four-digit number marked "free" on the instructions. Instead, when using a *cabine,* dial the smaller, less obvious 0800 number labelled "cabine callback" or just "callback." An automated voice will tell you, in French, to hang up. Do so, and in a minute or so the phone will ring. Pick up and dial your PIN and the number you're calling. It's a bit tedious, but this method will save you precious phone-card minutes otherwise wasted entering your PIN and dialing.

CELLULAR PHONES

If you plan to stay in Paris for several months, buying a French cell phone is worth the cost. Incoming calls to cell phones are often free (even from abroad), and making local calls is cheap. The cheapest phones are relatively inexpensive (from €60, but as low as €1 with certain plans), and French phones don't require long-term plans. **Orange** and **SFR** generally provide the best deals and reception. Cell-phone calls can be paid for without signing a contract with a **Mobicarte** prepaid card, available at Orage and SFR stores, as well as *tabacs.*

GSM PHONES. Just having a GSM phone doesn't mean you're necessarily good to go when you travel abroad. The majority of GSM phones sold in the US operate on a different frequency (1900) than international phones (900/1800) and will not work abroad. Tri-band phones work on all three frequencies (900/1800/1900) and will operate through most of the world. Additionally, some GSM phones are SIM-locked and will only accept SIM cards from a single carrier. You'll need a SIM-unlocked phone to use a SIM card from a local carrier when you travel.

The international standard for cell phones is **Global System for Mobile Communication** (GSM). To make and receive calls in France, you will need a GSM-compatible phone and a **SIM (Subscriber Identity Module) card,** a country-specific, thumbnail-size chip that gives you a local phone number and plugs you into the local network. Many SIM cards are prepaid, and incoming calls are frequently free. You can buy additional cards or vouchers (usually available at convenience stores) to "top up" your phone. For more information on GSM phones, check out www.telestial.com, www.orange.fr, www.roadpost.com, or www. planetomni.com. Companies like **Cellular Abroad** (www.cellularabroad.com) rent cell phones that work in a variety of destinations around the world.

Check with your service provider to see if your phone's band can be switched to 900/1800, which will register your phone with one of the three French servers: **Bouyges** (www.bouygtel.com), **Itineris** (www.ifrance.com/binto/itineris. htm), or **France Télécom** (www.agence.francetelecom.com).

TIME DIFFERENCES

Paris is usually 1hr. ahead of Greenwich Mean Time (GMT) and observes Daylight Saving Time (when it is 2hr. ahead) from March to October.

3AM	4AM	5AM	6AM	11AM	NOON	9PM*
Vancouver Seattle San Francisco Los Angeles	Denver	Chicago	Lima New York Toronto	London	**PARIS**	Sydney Canberra Melbourne

*Australia observes Daylight Saving Time from October to March, the opposite of the Northern Hemisphere. Therefore, it is 8hr. ahead of Paris from March to October and 10hr. ahead from october to March, for an average of 9hr.

BY MAIL

SENDING MAIL HOME FROM FRANCE

Airmail is the best way to send mail home from Paris. **Aerogrammes,** printed sheets that fold into envelopes and travel via airmail, are available at post offices. Write "airmail" or *"par avion"* on the front. Most post offices will charge exorbitant fees or simply refuse to send aerogrammes with enclosures. Surface mail is by far the cheapest and slowest way to send mail. It takes one to two months to cross the Atlantic and one to three to cross the Pacific—good for heavy items you won't need for a while, such as souvenirs that you've acquired along the way. Get insurance on anything you send internationally.

SENDING MAIL TO FRANCE

To ensure timely delivery, mark envelopes "airmail" or *"par avion."* In addition to the standard postage system, **Federal Express** (Australia ☎+61 13 26 10, Canada and the US +1-800-463-3339, Ireland +353 800 535 800, New Zealand +64 800 733 339, the UK +44 8456 070 809; www.fedex.com) handles express mail services from most countries to France. Sending a postcard within France costs €0.54, while sending letters (up to 20g) domestically requires €0.54.

 CODE OF CODES. Parisian *codes postales* (postal codes) end with the *arrondissement* number. That is, 75001 is the code for the 1*er arrondissement,* 75002 is the code for the 2*ème arrondissement,* and so on.

There are several ways to arrange pickup of letters sent to you while you are abroad. Mail can be sent via **Poste Restante** to post offices in Paris, but it is not very reliable. Address Poste Restante letters like so:

Jean Auguste Dominique INGRES
Poste Restante
75008, Paris
FRANCE

The mail will go to a special desk in the central post office, unless you specify a post office by street address or postal code. It's best to use the largest post office, since mail may be sent there regardless. It is usually safer and quicker, though more expensive, to send mail express or registered. Bring your passport (or other photo ID) for pickup; there may be a small fee. If the clerks insist that there is nothing for you, ask them to check under your first name as well. *Let's Go* lists post offices in the **Practical Information** section (p. 142).

American Express's travel offices throughout the world offer a free **Client Letter Service** (mail held up to 30 days and forwarded upon request) for cardholders who contact them in advance. Some offices provide these services to non-cardholders (especially AmEx Travelers Cheque holders), but call ahead to make sure. For a complete list of AmEx locations, call ☎+1-800-528-4800 or visit www.americanexpress.com/travel.

ACCOMMODATIONS

HOSTELS

Many hostels are laid out dorm-style, often with large single-sex rooms and bunk beds, although private rooms that sleep two to four are becoming more common. They sometimes have kitchens and utensils for your use, bike or moped rentals, storage areas, transportation to airports, breakfast and other meals, laundry facilities, and Internet. However, there can be drawbacks: some hostels close during certain daytime "lockout" hours, have a curfew, don't accept reservations, impose a maximum stay, or, less frequently, require that you do chores. In France, a dorm bed in a hostel will average around €10-25 and a private room around €20-80.

A HOSTELER'S BILL OF RIGHTS. There are certain standard features that we do not include in our hostel listings. Unless we state otherwise, you can expect that every hostel has no lockout, no curfew, free hot showers, some system of secure luggage storage, and no key deposit. See p. XI for a description of average Parisian accommodations and prices.

HOSTELLING INTERNATIONAL

Joining the youth hostel association in your own country (listed below) automatically grants you membership privileges in **Hostelling International (HI),** a federation of national hosteling associations. Non-HI members may be allowed to stay in some hostels, but they will have to pay extra to do so. HI hostels are scattered throughout France and are typically less expensive than private hostels. HI's umbrella organization's website (www.hihostels.com), which lists the web addresses and phone numbers of all national associations, can be a great place to begin researching hosteling in a specific region. Other comprehensive hosteling websites include www.hostels.com and www.hostelplanet.com.

Most HI hostels also honor **guest memberships**—you'll get a blank card with space for six validation stamps. Each night you'll pay a nonmember supplement (one-sixth the membership fee) and earn one guest stamp; six stamps make you a member. This system works well in most of France, but sometimes you may need to remind the hostel reception. A new membership benefit is the FreeNites program, which allows hostelers to gain points toward free rooms. Most student travel agencies (p. 34) sell HI cards, as do all of the national hosteling organizations listed below. All prices listed below are valid for one-year memberships unless otherwise noted.

Australian Youth Hostels Association (AYHA), 422 Kent St., Sydney, NSW 2000 (☎+61 2 9261 1111; www.yha.com.au). AUS$52, under 18 AUS$19.

Hostelling International-Canada (HI-C), 205 Catherine St., Ste. 400, Ottawa, ON K2P 1C3 (☎+1-613-237-7884; www.hihostels.ca). CDN$35, under 18 free.

Hostelling International Northern Ireland (HINI), 22-32 Donegall Rd., Belfast BT12 5JN (☎+44 28 9032 4733; www.hini.org.uk). UK£15, under 25 UK£10.

Youth Hostels Association of New Zealand Inc. (YHANZ), Level 1, 166 Moorhouse Ave., P.O. Box 436, Christchurch (☎+64 3 379 9970, in NZ 0800 278 299; www.yha.org.nz). NZ$40, under 18 free.

Youth Hostels Association (England and Wales), Trevelyan House, Dimple Rd., Matlock, Derbyshire DE4 3YH (☎+44 8707 708 868; www.yha.org.uk). UK£16, under 26 UK£10.

Hostelling International-USA, 8401 Colesville Rd., Ste. 600, Silver Spring, MD 20910 (☎+1-301-495-1240; www.hiayh.org). US$28, under 18 free.

HOTELS, GUESTHOUSES, AND PENSIONS

The cheapest hotel singles in Paris cost about €40 per night, doubles €50. All accredited hotels are ranked on a four-star system by the French government according to factors such as room size, facilities, and plumbing. You'll typically share a hall bathroom; a private bathroom or a shower with hot water may cost extra. If you want a double with two twin beds instead of one double, ask for *une chambre avec deux lits*. Some hotels offer *pension complet* (all meals) and *demi-pension* (no lunch). Smaller guesthouses and pensions are often cheaper than hotels. If you make **reservations** in writing, indicate your night of arrival and the number of nights you plan to stay. The hotel will send you a confirmation and may request payment for the first night. It is most often easiest to make reservations over the phone or online with a credit card.

OTHER TYPES OF ACCOMMODATIONS

UNIVERSITY DORMS

Many **colleges** and **universities** open their residence halls to travelers when school is not in session; some do so even during term time. Getting a room may take a couple of phone calls and require advanced planning, but rates tend to be low, and many offer free local calls and Internet access. For information on universities in France, consult the following source:

Centre National des Œuvres Universitaires et Scolaires (CNOUS), 69 *quai* d'Orsay, 75007 Paris (☎01 44 18 53 00; www.cnous.fr). A regional guide of universities and lodgings throughout France available on the website, under "La Vie Etudiante: Logement." Click on "Carte des Cités U" at the bottom.

HOME EXCHANGES AND HOSPITALITY CLUBS

Home exchange offers the traveler various types of homes (houses, apartments, condominiums, villas, even castles in some cases), plus the opportunity to live like a native and to cut down on accommodation fees. For more info, contact **HomeExchange.com Inc.,** P.O. Box 787, Hermosa Beach, CA 90254, USA (☎+1-310-798-3864 or toll-free 800-877-8723; www.homeexchange.com) or **Intervac International Home Exchange** (☎08 20 88 83 42; www.intervac.com).

Hospitality clubs link their members with individuals or families abroad who are willing to host travelers for free or for a small fee to promote cultural exchange and general good karma. In exchange, members usually must be willing to host travelers in their own homes; a small fee may also be required. **The Hospitality Club** (www.hospitalityclub.org) is a good place to start. **Servas** (www.servas.org) is an established, more formal, peace-based organization and requires a fee and an interview to join. An Internet search will find many similar organizations, some of which cater to special interests (e.g., women, GLBT travelers, or members of certain professions). As always, use common sense when planning to stay with or host someone you do not know.

LONG-TERM ACCOMMODATIONS

Travelers planning to stay in Paris for extended periods of time may find it most cost-effective to rent an **apartment.** A basic one-bedroom (or studio) apartment in Paris will range €500-1500 per month. Besides the rent itself, prospective tenants are usually required to front a security deposit (frequently 1 month's rent). Apartment hunters should be aware that landlords will often demand proof of income and a cosigner before agreeing to rent a space. For more information about renting an apartment, as well as helpful websites, see **Study Abroad: No Place Like Home,** p. 120.

SPECIFIC CONCERNS

TRAVELING ALONE

Traveling alone can be extremely formative, providing a sense of independence and a greater opportunity to connect with locals. On the other hand, solo travelers are more vulnerable targets of harassment and theft. If you are traveling alone, look confident, try not to stand out as a tourist, and be especially careful in deserted or very crowded areas. Stay away from areas that are not well lit. If questioned, never admit that you are traveling alone. Maintain regular contact with someone at home who knows your itinerary and always research your destination before traveling. For more tips, pick up *Traveling Solo* by Eleanor Berman (Globe Pequot Press, US$18), visit www.travelaloneandloveit.com, or subscribe to **Connecting: Solo Travel Network,** 689 Park Rd., Unit 6, Gibsons, BC V0N 1V7, Canada (☎+1-604-886-9099; www.cstn.org; membership US$30-48).

WOMEN TRAVELERS

Women exploring on their own inevitably face some additional safety concerns. Single women can consider staying in hostels that offer single rooms that lock from the inside or in religious organizations with single-sex rooms. It's a good idea to stick to centrally located accommodations and to avoid solitary late-night treks or Metro rides.

Always carry extra cash for a phone call, bus, or taxi. **Hitchhiking** is never safe for lone women, or even for two women traveling together. Look as if you know where you're going and approach older women or couples for directions if you're lost. Generally, the less you look like a tourist, the better off you'll be. Dress conservatively, especially in rural areas. Wearing a conspicuous **wedding band** sometimes helps to prevent unwanted advances.

Young women in France will frequently face verbal harassment; while most of it is harmless, it can be very uncomfortable. Your best answer to verbal harassment is no answer at all. The extremely persistent can sometimes be dissuaded by a firm, loud, and very public "Va-t-en!" ("VAH-TON"; "Go away!" in French). Don't hesitate to seek out a police officer or a passerby if you are being harassed. Memorize the emergency numbers in places you visit (police ☎17) and consider carrying a whistle on your keychain. A self-defense course will both prepare you for a potential attack and raise your level of awareness of your surroundings (see **Personal Safety,** p. 30). Also be sure you are aware of the **health concerns** that women face when traveling (p. 33).

GLBT TRAVELERS

Paris is fairly liberal toward gay, lesbian, bisexual, and transgendered travelers, and there are prominent gay and lesbian communities. However, overt displays of sexual identity can evoke an unfriendly response in more remote regions of France. Listed below are contact organizations, mail-order catalogs, and publishers that offer materials addressing some specific concerns. **Out and About** (www.planetout.com) offers a weekly newsletter addressing gay travel concerns. The online newspaper **365gay.com** also has a travel section (www.365gay.com/travel/travelchannel.htm).

Gay's the Word, 66 Marchmont St., London WC1N 1AB, UK (☎+44 20 7278 7654; http://freespace.virgin.net/gays.theword). The largest gay and lesbian bookshop in the UK, with both fiction and non-fiction titles. Mail-order service available.

Giovanni's Room, 345 S. 12th St., Philadelphia, PA 19107, USA (☎+1-215-923-2960; www.queerbooks.com). An international lesbian and gay bookstore with mail-order service (carries many of the publications listed below).

International Lesbian and Gay Association (ILGA), Avenue des Villas 34, 1060 Brussels, Belgium (☎+32 2 502 2471; www.ilga.org). Provides political information, such as homosexuality laws of individual countries.

ADDITIONAL RESOURCES: GLBT

Spartacus: International Gay Guide 2008. Bruno Gmunder Verlag (US$33).

Damron Men's Travel Guide, Damron Road Atlas, Damron Accommodations Guide, Damron City Guide, and *Damron Women's Traveller.* Damron Travel Guides (US$18-24). For info, call ☎+1-800-462-6654 or visit www.damron.com.

The Gay Vacation Guide: The Best Trips and How to Plan Them, by Mark Chesnut. Kensington Books (US$15).

Gayellow Pages USA/Canada, by Frances Green. Gayellow Pages (US$20). They also publish regional editions. Visit Gayellow pages online at http://gayellowpages.com.

TRAVELERS WITH DISABILITIES

The French Ministry of Tourism includes a branch called **Tourisme et Handicap,** 43 rue Marx Dormoy, 75018 Paris (☎01 44 11 10 41; www.tourisme-handicaps.com), which is devoted to providing information about access for disabled travelers at tourist sights and amenities in Paris and its suburbs. Disabled travelers can stay in Paris on a budget but may pay more than the average backpacker.

Those with disabilities should inform airlines and hotels of their disabilities when making reservations; some time may be needed to prepare special accommodations. Airports in France have published a guide for passengers with restricted mobility *(mobilité réduite)* that can be found at www.aeroportsdeparis.fr under the heading *"Départ."* Call ahead to restaurants, museums, and other facilities to find out if they are wheelchair-accessible *(accessible en chaise roulante)*. Guide-dog owners should inquire about quarantine policies of each destination country.

Rail is probably the most convenient form of transport for disabled travelers in Europe: many stations have ramps, and some trains have wheelchair lifts, special seating areas, and specially equipped toilets. The French national railroad offers wheelchair compartments on all TGV (high-speed) and Conrail trains. All Eurostar, some InterCity (IC), and some EuroCity (EC) trains are wheelchair-accessible, and CityNightLine trains, French TGV, and Conrail trains feature special compartments. For those who wish to rent cars, some major car-rental agencies (e.g., Hertz) offer hand-controlled vehicles.

USEFUL ORGANIZATIONS

Accessible Journeys, 35 W. Sellers Ave., Ridley Park, PA 19078, USA (☎+1-800-846-4537; www.disabilitytravel.com). Designs tours for wheelchair users and slow walkers. The site has tips and forums for all travelers.

Flying Wheels Travel, 143 W. Bridge St., Owatonna, MN 55060, USA (☎+1-507-451-5005; www.flyingwheelstravel.com). Specializes in escorted trips to Europe for people with physical disabilities; plans custom trips worldwide.

Mobility International USA (MIUSA), P.O. Box 10767, Eugene, OR 97440, USA (☎+1-541-343-1284; www.miusa.org). Provides a variety of books and other publications containing information for travelers with disabilities.

Society for Accessible Travel and Hospitality (SATH), 347 5th Ave., Ste. 610, New York City, NY 10016, USA (☎+1-212-447-7284; www.sath.org). An advocacy group that publishes free online travel information. Annual membership (US$49, students and seniors US$29) buys access to members-only section of website as well as discounts with companies facilitating travel with disabilities.

MINORITY TRAVELERS

Like much of Europe, France has experienced a wave of immigration from former colonies in the past few decades. The Maghreb—an ethnic group composed of North Africans and Arabs—make up the greatest percentage of the immigrants, at over a million, followed by West Africans and Vietnamese. Many immigrants are uneducated and face discrimination, which leads to poverty and crime in the predominantly immigrant *banlieues* (suburbs). In the fall of 2005, riots swept France in retaliation for the deaths of two Parisian immigrant teenagers following an altercation with the police. In turn, there has been a surge of support for the far-right National Front party and its cry, *"La France pour les français."* Anyone who might be taken for a North African or a Muslim may encounter verbal abuse and is likelier than other travelers to be stopped and questioned by the police. The following organizations can give you advice and help in the event of an encounter with racism.

SOS Racisme, 51 av. de Flandre, 75019 Paris (☎01 40 35 36 55; www.sos-racisme.org). Provides legal services and helps negotiate with police.

Mouvement Contre le Racisme et Pour l'Amitié Entre les Peuples (MRAP), 43 bd. Magenta, 75010 Paris (☎01 53 38 99 99; www.mrap.asso.fr). Handles immigration issues; monitors publications and propaganda for racism.

DIETARY CONCERNS

Paris has traditionally been unaccommodating to those with special dietary requirements, but the number of restaurants with vegetarian and began options is rapidly increasing. *Let's Go* lists many vegetarian- and vegan-friendly restaurants (see **Food,** p. 165. The travel section of **The Vegetarian Resource Group's** website, at www.vrg.org/travel, has a comprehensive list of organizations and websites that are geared toward helping vegetarians and vegans traveling abroad. They also publish *Vegetarian France,* which can be purchased at www.vegetarian-guides.co.uk. For more information, visit your local bookstore or health-food store and consult *The Vegetarian Traveler: Where to Stay if You're Vegetarian, Vegan, Environmentally Sensitive,* by Jed and Susan Civic (Larson Publications; US$16). Vegetarians will also find numerous resources on the web; try www.vegelist.online.fr, which lists vegetarian restaurants and *chambres d'hôtes* in France, www.vegdining.com, www.happycow.net, and www.vegetariansabroad.com, for starters.

  Lactose intolerance also does not have to be an obstacle to eating well in France. In restaurants, ask for items *sans lait* (milk), *fromage* (cheese), *beurre* (butter), or *crème* (cream). **Kosher** delis, restaurants, and bakeries abound in the 3*éme* and 4*éme*, particularly on rue des Rosiers and rue des Ecouffes. Contact the **Union Libéral Israélite de France Synagogue** (see **Religious Services** in **Practical Information,** p. 141) for more information on kosher restaurants. Travelers looking for **halal** restaurants may find www.zabihah.com a useful resource.

OTHER RESOURCES

USEFUL PUBLICATIONS

  Au Contraire! Figuring Out the French, by Gilles Asselin. Intercultural Press, 2001 (US$28). Provides a look into subtle cultural patterns.

  Culture Shock! France, by Sally Adamson Taylor. Marshall Cavendish, 2008 (US$16). Tips and warnings about France's cultural faux pas for travelers and expats.

WORLD WIDE WEB

Almost every aspect of budget travel is accessible via the web, but you can't trust every site you find. In 10min. at the keyboard, you can make a hostel reservation, get advice on travel hot spots from other travelers, or find out how much a train from Marseille to Paris costs. Listed here are sites to start off your surfing; other relevant websites are listed throughout the book.

  LET'S GO ONLINE. Plan your next trip on our newly redesigned website, www.letsgo.com. It features the latest travel info on your favorite destinations as well as tons of interactive features: make your own itinerary, read blogs from our trusty researcher-writers, browse our photo library, watch exclusive videos, check out our newsletter, find travel deals, and buy new guides. We're always updating and adding new features, so check back often!

THE ART OF TRAVEL

Backpacker's Ultimate Guide: www.bugeurope.com. Tips on packing, transportation, and where to go. Also tons of country-specific travel information.

How to See the World: www.artoftravel.com. A compendium of great travel tips, from cheap flights to self-defense to interacting with local culture.

Travel Intelligence: www.travelintelligence.net. A large collection of travel writing by distinguished travel writers.

Travel Library: www.travel-library.com. A fantastic set of links for general information and personal travelogues.

INFORMATION ON FRANCE

CIA World Factbook: www.odci.gov/cia/publications/factbook/index.html. Tons of vital statistics on France's geography, government, economy, and people.

Geographia: www.geographia.com. Highlights, culture, and people of France.

PlanetRider: www.planetrider.com. A subjective list of links to the "best" websites covering the culture and tourist attractions of France.

TravelPage: www.travelpage.com. Links to official tourist office sites in France.

World Travel Guide: www.travel-guides.com. Helpful practical info.

We'd rather be traveling.

LET'S GO
BUDGET TRAVEL GUIDES
www.letsgo.com

LIFE AND TIMES

HISTORY

ANCIENT PARIS

CAESAR STORMS GAUL. Paris was first settled around 300 BC by the Parisîi, a clan of Celtic Gauls who set up camp on the Île de la Cité. The Parisîi were successful fishermen and traders, and their settlement thrived until Julius Caesar's Roman troops arrived in 52 BC. According to Caesar's *Gallic Wars*, the Parisîi resisted alongside the ferocious Vercingétorix, but they eventually succumbed, initiating a two-millennia tradition of French military defeats. The Romans named the new colony **Lutetia Parisiorum** (Latin for "the Midwater-Dwelling of the Parisîi") and expanded the city, building new roads (including rue St-Jacques, in the 5ème), public baths (now the Musée de Cluny, p. 275), and gladiatorial arenas (like the Arènes de Lutèce, p. 224). A temple to Jupiter stood on the present-day site of the Cathédrale Notre Dame (p. 205), and Roman ruins are still on display in the cathedral's crypt. By AD 360, the Romans had fortified the Île de la Cité and shortened its name to "Paris." During this time, Paris was less powerful than other colonies in Gaul, including Lyons, Marseille, Vienne, and Arles.

CHRISTIANITY AND DYNASTIES. After three centuries of Roman prosperity, Paris was besieged by assaults from Vandals and Visigoths. Attila and the Huns tried to take the city in AD 451, but the prayers of **St. Genevieve**, henceforth the patron saint of Paris, turned them instead toward Orléans. (Orléans, by the way, had to wait until 1429 to be saved by their own patron Saint, Joan of Arc.) Meanwhile, the arrival of Christianity in the 3rd century threatened to erode Roman rule from within: when **St. Denis** appeared in Paris with orders from Pope Fabian to convert the population, he was beheaded by a mob of obdurate citizens (Basilique de St-Denis, p. 262). The overstretched Roman empire was losing its grasp on Paris. **King Clovis** of the Franks, who had converted to Christianity in 500, effectively founded France's first royal house, the **Merovingian Dynasty** (481-751), and named Paris its capital in 511. Clovis's descendants rules France with varying levels of actual power for almost 200 years and were succeeded by the more sophisticated **Carolingian Dynasty** (751-987).

CHARLES THE MAGNE. The second Carolingian king, Charlemagne took power in 768. Paris lost influence under big C, who took the title Holy Roman Emperor, expanded his territorial claims, and moved his capital to Aix-la-Chapelle (now Aachen, Germany). Charlamagne's patronage ignited the **Carolingian Renaissance**, a vigorous recovery of Europe's classical past that strengthened the imperial bureaucracy and enlivened all types of art and learning. When invading Normans (Vikings) and Saracens (Arav nomads) menaced Europe in the 9th and 10th centuries, Charlemagne's empire crumbled.

121 BC
Romans, doing as they do, colonize the south.

52 BC
Caesar conquers Vercingetorix's band of northern rebels and names present-day Paris "Lutetia Parisorum."

AD 486
Clovis I founds the Frankish Empire. Deciding to become one of the cool kids, he changes his name to "Louis."

AD 768
Charlemagne becomes king of the Franks and founds the Carolingian Dynasty.

AD 885-86
Vikings lay siege to Paris during the reign of Charles the Fat.

1146
Capetian king Louis VII and wife Eleanor of Aquitaine set out to join the Crusades together.

MIDDLE AGES TO THE RENAISSANCE

MEDIEVAL PARIS. By the end of the first millennium AD, France was a decentralized collection of **feudal kingdoms** with their own languages and traditions. In 987, **Hugh Capet,** the Count of Paris, was crowned King of France. Capet made Paris his capital, and under the 350-year rule of the Capetian Dynasty (987-1328), the city gradually consolidated power. The Capetians' most famous king, **Philippe-Auguste** (1179-1223), expanded the city and oversaw the construction of **Notre Dame** (p. 205) and **Les Halles** (p. 213). With the establishment of the University of Paris in 1215 and the Sorbonne in 1253, Paris was reorganized into two parts: the commercial **Rive Droite** (Right Bank) and the academic **Rive Gauche** (Left Bank).. By 1300, Paris was the largest city in western Christiandom and the center of learning.

UNICORNS AND BALLOONS (KIDDING, DEATH AND PLAGUE). The 14th century was a dark time for Europe. Three hundred years of rapid population growth had overcrowded cities and depleted food resources, and a mini **ice age** (1150-1450) had cooled and dampened the climate. These trends culminated in a widespread explosion of violence and disease: the **Black Death,** which ravaged Paris from 1348-49, killed more than a third of the city's population; hundreds more died in peasant uprisings.

FRANCE AND ENGLAND DUKE IT OUT. About ten years into **Philippe VI's** rule, England's **Edward III** decided to claim the throne of France for himself. In retaliation, the French **Philippe de Valois** (later King Phillip III) encroached upon English-owned Aquitaine, in what is now southwestern France. Edward III responded by landing his troops in Normandy, and the **Hundred Years' War** (1337-1453) began. The French took some serious battering over the course of the war. When the English crowned their own **Henry VI** king of France in 1418, legend has it that 17-year-old **Joan of Arc** was inspired by a choir of angels to lead the Valois troops in the **Battle of Orléans.** Despite her heroism, she was captured by the English and burned at the stake in 1431 for heresy.

THE RENAISSANCE. In the early 16th century, the imported ideals of the Italian Renaissance sparked interest in literature, art, and architecture in Paris. The **printing press** was introduced in the 1460s, and the universities on the Left Bank flourished. An unprecedented percentage of the population had access to literature, and writers like **Montaigne, Rabelais,** and **Ronsard** embodied the era's increasingly **secular humanism.** The 16th century also saw the strengthening of the monarchy as the French rallied around the Valois king **François I,** a popular patron of the arts and sciences. In 1527 François I had the Louvre rebuilt in the style of the Renaissance and moved the royal residence there. Under François's successor,

Henri II, the **Place Royale** (now called **Place des Vosges;** p. 220) became a masterpiece of French Renaissance architecture. When Henri died in a jousting accident, his wife, **Catherine de Médicis,** ordered it destroyed and began work on the **Tuileries Palace and Garden** and **Pont Neuf** (p. 209).

RELIGIOUS BLOODSHED. Paris's budding religious tension, sparked by the Protestant Reformation, played itself out brutally in the **Wars of Religion** (1562-98). The conflict unfolded in a series of military faceoffs and civilian clashes, fought between the **Huguenots** (French Protestants) and the **Catholics.** Catherine de Médicis, effective ruler of France after her husband's death, was particularly ruthless toward the Huguenots from the southwestern kingdom of Navarre. **Henri de Navarre** (who became Henry IV) agreed to marry Catherine's daughter, **Marguerite de Valois** (Queen Margot) as a peace-making gesture. Catherine played along, but when France's most prominent Protestants had assembled in Paris for the royal union, Catherine had 2000 of them slaughtered in the **St. Bartholomew's Day Massacre** (Apr. 24, 1572). Henri saved his life and his throne with a strategic conversion to Catholicism. In 1589, he ascended to the throne as Henri IV de Bourbon, uniting France and establishing the last of France's royal houses, the **Bourbons.** Upon his coronation, Henri IV made light of his sudden change of spiritual conviction with the remark, "Paris vaut bien une messe" (Paris is well worth a mass). His heart still lay with the Huguenots, though: in 1598, he issued the **Edict of Nantes,** which granted tolerance for French Protestants and quelled religious wars for almost a century.

THE 17TH CENTURY

LOUIS XIII AND RICHELIEU, BFF. The French monarchy reached its height of power, opulence, and egomania in the 17th century. **Henri IV** was assassinated in 1610 and succeeded by **Louis XIII.** Louis's ruthless minister, **Cardinal Richelieu,** consolidated political power in the hands of the monarch and created the centralized, bureaucratic administration characteristic of France to this day. He expanded Paris and built the **Palais du Luxembourg** (p. 211) for the Queen Mother, Marie de Médicis, and the Palais Cardinal (today the Palais-Royal; p. 211) for himself. Richelieu manipulated the nobility and tantalized the bourgeoisie with promises of social advancement, tightening the monarchy's hold over the state.

HERE COMES THE SUN KING. Proving their commitment to one another for eternity, Richelieu and Louis XIII died within months of each other in 1642 and were replaced by **Louis XIV** and his minister **Cardinal Mazarin.** Since Louis XIV was only five years old at the time, Mazarin took charge, but by 1661 the precocious 23-year-old was ready to rule alone. Louis adopted the title "Sun King" and took the motto, **"L'état, c'est moi"** (I am the state). He lent a personal touch to national affairs, moving the government to his new 14,000-room pal-

1337
The Hundred Years' War against England begins and continues for the next 116 years—but who's counting?

1348
The Paris leg of the Black Death world tour.

1431
Joan of Arc is burned at the stake by the English, who are not amused by her claims of divine conversation.

1562-98
The feud between Catholics and Protestants escalates into massacre during the Wars of Religion.

1642
Five-year-old Louis XIV inherits the throne.

1682
Louis XIV, lover of things bright and shiny, officially establishes his court at the Château de Versailles.

1744
The famous quote *"Qu'ils mangent de la brioche"* ("Let them eat cake") is attributed (perhaps inaccurately) to Marie Antoinette, making her the most hated woman in French history.

LIFE AND TIMES

1778
France comes to the rescue of rebellious colonists in the American Revolution.

ace, the extravagant **Château de Versailles** (p. 339). The court at Versailles was a spectacle of regal opulence and noble privilege, where the king himself was on display: favored subjects could observe him and his queen as they rose in the morning, groomed, and dined. The king kept the nobility under a close watch at Versailles to avoid challenges to his rule; the nobles, caught up in the elaborate choreography of the court, suffered a complete loss of political power.

June 1789
The French Revolution begins with the Tennis Court Oath and the storming of the Bastille.

QUITE AN EGO. Louis XIV reigned for 72 years by the principle of "un roi, une loi, une foi" (one king, one law, one faith). He revoked the Edict of Nantes in 1685 at the behest of his mistress and initiated the ruinous **War of the Spanish Succession** (1701-13). From Versailles, he commissioned the avenue des **Champs-Éysées** (p. 233) and the **Place Vendôme** (p. 211). His daughter, the Duchesse de Bourbon, commissioned the Palais Bourbon, today home to the **Assemblée Nationale** (p. 231).

August 1789
The National Assembly signs the Declaration of the Rights of Man.

THE BEGINNING OF THE END. Louis XIV finally died in 1715 and was succeeded by the two-year-old Louis XV. The light that had once radiated from the French throne could no longer eclipse the country's ruinous problems. The lavish expenditures of the Sun King left France in debt, and, after his death, the weakened nobility began to resent the monarchy.

THE FRENCH REVOLUTION

1792
Women of the Revolution sport figurines of the newly invented guillotine as earrings.

BOURBON ON THE ROCKS. When **Louis XVI** ascended to the throne in 1774, the country was in desperate financial straits. Civilians blamed the monarchy for their mounting debts, while aristocrats detested the king for his gestures toward reform. Queen Marie Antoinette's famous (if possibly fictional) "Let them eat cake" *("Qu'ils mangent brioche")* quip reflects the upper classes' ignorance about the peasants' suffering. In 1789, Louis XVI called a meeting of the **états généraux,** an assembly of delegates from three classes of society: aristocrats, clergy, and the Third Estate, the last of which included the vast majority of the population. On June 17, after weeks of wrangling over voting procedures, the Third Estate declared itself the independent **National Assembly** and was promptly expelled from the convention chamber. The National Assembly then reconvened on the Versailles tennis greens, and on June 20, they swore the **Oath of the Tennis Court,** promising not to disband until the king had recognized their constitution. As rumors of revolution multiplied, the initiative passed to the panicked Parisian masses, alarmed by astronomical bread prices and the tottering government.

1793
Louis XVI and Marie Antoinette are executed by guillotine.

1794
Maximilien Robespierre heads to the guillotine (pun unfortunately intended), officially ending the Reign of Terror.

STORMING OF THE BASTILLE. When a mob of almost 1000 citizens stormed the old fortress of the Bastille (p. 239) on July 14, peasants across France burned the records of their debts. *Le quatorze juillet* is now the Fête Nationale (p. 95), the equivalent of America's Independence Day. The Assembly joined the Revolution in August with the abolition of feudal law and the *Declaration of the Rights of Man*, which embodied the principles *liberté*, *égalité*, and *fraternité*. On October 5, a crowd of revolutionaries descended on Versailles, seized the king and queen, and brought them back to Paris.

REIGN OF TERROR. When the petrified Louis XVI tried to flee the country in 1791, he was caught and imprisoned. Meanwhile, a number of aristocrats and other counter-revolutionaries had fled the country to seek help from other European powers. Partly in response to the pleas of these émigrés, Austria and Prussia mobilized and prepared to stamp out the democratic disease. In 1793, the revolutionary armies miraculously defeated the invaders, and the radical Jacobin faction, led by **Maximilien Robespierre** and his **Committee of Public Safety,** took over the National Assembly. The period of suppression and mass execution under the Committee of Public Safety is known as the Reign of Terror. In January, the Jacobins guillotined Louis XVI and Queen Marie-Antoinette. By the end of the Reign of Terror, the ironically named **Place de la Concorde** (p. 234) had been the site of more than 1300 beheadings.

THE END OF THE FRENZY. With a republic declared, the *ancien régime* was history. The Revolution had taken a radical turn. The Church refused to submit to the National Assembly and so was replaced by the **Cult of Reason,** which renamed and renumbered the calendar and invented the **metric system.** As counter-revolutionary paranoia set in, power lay with Robespierre and his Committee of Public Safety. Even the slightest suspicion of royalist sympathy led to the block; Dr. Guillotine himself did not escape the vengeance of his invention. By 1794, Robespierre was physically exhausted and frustrated by divisions in the forces behind the Revolution. Like any egomaniacal autocrat, he faced heavy criticism from both the left and the right as his intimidation factor stagnated. Loyalists attacked Robespierre for his democratic ideals, while radicals criticized his leniency. On July 28, members of the National Assembly felt strongly enough in favor of a regime change that they beheaded Robespierre and all of his closest supporters. The terror was over, and power was entrusted to a five-man Directory.

NAPOLEON AND EMPIRE

THE RISE OF NAPOLEON. As wars raged on throughout Western Europe, an ambitious young Corsican general swept through northern Italy and into Austria. Riding a wave of public support, he deposed the Directory and declared himself First Consul of a triumvirate. In an 1802 fit of ego, Napoleon changed that title to Consul for Life, and ultimately to **Emperor** in 1804. In just one decade, Napoleon expanded France's empire, unified its people, and centralized its government. Portions of his **Napoleonic Code** still exist today, although it outlined an oppressively autocratic approach

1801
Jacques-Louis David reinvents history, depicting Napoleon crossing the Alps on a white stallion instead of his actual vehicle of choice—a mule.

1812
Napoleon's troops occupying Moscow freeze in the Russian winter, and the few who survive ignobly withdraw.

1814
Jean-Auguste Dominique Ingres paints *La Grande Odalisque,* igniting imaginations of men throughout France.

1816
Géricault paints *Le Radeau de la Méduse,* the masterpiece whose epic proportions (and politically charged content) prompted a hefty scandal.

1822
Louis Pasteur, darling of milk-drinkers worldwide, is born.

1829
Louis Braille brings dots into a whole new dimension.

LIFE AND TIMES

1830
Louis-Philippe, king of the French but not of France, forms a constitutional monarchy.

1853-70
Baron Haussmann reconstructs Paris, paving the way for its *haute couture* status.

1862
Victor Hugo publishes *Les Misérables* while exiled in Britain.

1867
Baudelaire extolls the importance of staying intoxicated in his prose poem, *Enivrez-Vous*

1888
Van Gogh goes half-deaf in Arles.

1898
The Dreyfus Affair exposes French anti-Semitism.

1903
Maurice Garin wins the first Tour de France.

LIFE AND TIMES

to life, re-establishing slavery and requiring wives to show unwavering obedience to their husbands.

NAPOLEON'S PARIS. Paris benefited from Napoleon's international booty. His interest in ancient civilizations brought sculptures from Alexandria and Rome into Paris, including the Louvre's Dying Gladiator and Discus Thrower. He ordered the constructions of two Roman arches, the **Arc de Triomphe** (p. 232) and the **Arc du Carrousel** (p. 210), topping the latter with a gladiatorial sculpture stolen from St. Mark's Cathedral in Venice. Napoleon's many new bridges, including the Pont d'Austerlitz, the Pont Iéna, and the Pont des Arts (p. 228) spanned the Seine in style. He ordered the construction of a neo-Greco-Roman temple, the Madeleine (p. 235), and he finished the Cour Carrée of the Louvre, originally ordered by Louis XIV. Meanwhile, when his wife Josephine failed to produce an heir, she and Napoleon amicably annulled their marriage. The Emperor was re-married to **Marie Louise d'Autriche,** and his armies pushed east to Moscow.

...AND HIS DOWNFALL. In the winter of 1812, after occupying a deserted Moscow, Napoleon was forced to withdraw. The freezing cold decimated the French ranks, and of the 700,000 men Napoleon had led into Russia, barely 200,000 returned. Having lost the support of a war-weary nation, Napoleon abdicated in 1814. He retired to the Mediterranean island of Elba, and the monarchy was reinstated under Louis XVIII, brother of the unfortunate Louis XVI. That's right, monarchy again, after all that revolution.

AN AMBIGUOUS HERO. But France had not seen the last of Napoleon. In a final spurt of delusional grandeur, he left Elba and landed near Cannes on March 26, 1815. As Napoleon marched north, Louis XVI fled to England. The adventures of the ensuing **Hundred Days' War** ended on the field of **Waterloo** in Flanders, Belgium, where the Duke of Wellington triumphed over Napoleon's army. The English banished him to the remote island of St. Helena in the south Atlantic, where he died in 1821. Oddly enough, Napoleon is popularly regarded as a hero in France; thousands still pay their respects at his tomb at **Les Invalides** (p. 231). After his death, the Restoration of the monarchy brought Louis XVIII to the helm, and the Bourbon dynasty went on...and on...and on...

RESTORATION AND MORE REVOLUTION

THE JULY REVOLUTION. Although initially forced to recognize the achievements of the Revolution, the reinstated monarchy soon reverted to its tyrannical ways (as monarchies are wont to do). But the precedent for rebellion had been set: when Charles X restricted the press and limited the electorate to the landed classes in 1830, the people launched the July Revolution, and Charles quickly abdicated. A constitutional monarchy was instated under **Louis-Philippe**, Duke of Orléans, whose more modest bourgeois lifestyle garnered him the name **"Citizen King."** The middle classes prospered under Louis-Philippe, but industrialization created a class of urban poor who were receptive to the ideas of socialism.

LIKE JULY, ONLY EFFECTIVE: THE FEBRUARY REVOLUTION. When the king's bourgeois government refused to oblige the demands of the working class, the people were well practiced: there followed the February Revolution of 1848, the declaration of the **Second Republic,** and France's first universal male suffrage. The late emperor's nephew, **Louis Napoleon,** was elected president. The constitution barred him from seeking a second term, but he ignored it and seized power in a coup in 1851, proving that megalomania must have some basis in genetics. Following a referendum in 1852, he declared himself **Emperor Napoleon III,** to popular acclaim. Napoleon III's reign saw the industrialization of Paris, the rise of urban pollution, and the abject poverty described in novels by Balzac and Victor Hugo. Still, France's prestige was restored during his reign: factories hummed, and Baron **Georges Haussmann** replaced Paris's medieval street plan (too conducive to social protests) with grand boulevards along which an army could be deployed (p. 85).

FRANCO-PRUSSIAN WAR. Napoleon III's downfall came in July 1870 with France's defeat in the Franco-Prussian War. The confident French didn't notice the storm clouds gathering across the Rhine, where **Otto von Bismarck** had almost completed the unification of Germany. The Iron Chancellor's troops swiftly overran France and captured the emperor. Paris held out for four months, with residents so desperate for food that they devoured most of the animals in the zoo, sparking the Parisian reputation for cutting-edge cuisine.

PARIS COMMUNE. When the government admitted defeat, placing a conservative regime led by **Adolphe Thiers** in power, the Parisian mob revolted again. In 1871, they declared the **Paris Commune,** which rejected the Thiers government, throwing up barricades and declaring the city a free Commune. When French troops were sent in to recapture the city, the *communards* burned the Hôtel de Ville, the Palais-Royal, and Catherine de Médicis's Tuileries Palace before retreating to their last stand, Père Lachaise Cemetery p. 254. The crushing of the Commune, like a good beheading, was quick and bloody. Many estimate that over 20,000 Parisians died, slaughtered by their compatriots; the last of the *communards* were shot against Père Lachaise's Mur des Fédérés (now a site of pilgrimage for radical leftists) on May 21, 1871.

BELLE ÉPOQUE

ART AND INDUSTRIALIZATION. After more than 80 years of violence and political instability, Paris finally took a hiatus

1914
The assassination of Archduke Franz Ferdinand sets off a chain reaction that marks the beginning of WWI.

1919
The Treaty of Versailles officially ends WWI, but France's excessive demands of Germany sow the seeds for WWII.

1940-44
The Nazi occupation of Paris leads to the establishment of a puppet regime in Vichy.

1940
Charles de Gaulle encourages the French Résistance in his June 18 radio address.

1943
Jacques Cousteau and Émile Gagnan invent the Aqualung, the first modern self-contained underwater breathing apparatus (scuba).

1944
De Gaulle declares the Fourth Republic after the liberation of Paris; French women attain the right to vote.

1954
The Algerian National Liberation Front (FLN) launches the colony's war of independence.

1957
Barthes sings the praises of *le bifstek* and *le vin* in *Mythologies*.

1968
Student protesters cripple France with massive strikes.

1974
Simone de Beauvoir becomes chair of the Women's Rights League.

1981
Socialist François Mitterand becomes President.

1995
Center-rightist Jacques Chirac succeeds Mitterand.

1996
Disney releases The Hunchback of Notre Dame; Hugo rolls over in his grave (in the Panthéon).

from chaos with a period of peace a aptly titled the **Belle Epoque** (Beautiful Time). The colors of the Impressionists (p. 84), the novels of **Marcel Proust** (p. 80), and the **Expositions Universelles** (World's Fairs) of 1889 and 1900 reflected the optimism and energy of the Belle Époque. The expositions gave Paris the **Eiffel Tower** (p. 229), the Grand and Petit Palais (see **Sights,** p. 233), and the first line of the **Métropolitain,** the Paris metro. At the same time, industrialization introduced many new problems to the Third Republic. While the government's reforms laid the foundation for the contemporary social welfare state, class-related tensions continued to grow.

DREYFUS AFFAIR. The **Third Republic** was further undermined by the Dreyfus Affair. Alfred Dreyfus was a Jewish army captain convicted and exiled in 1894 on dubious-at-best charges of treason. When the army refused to consider the case even after proof of Dreyfus's innocence was uncovered, France became polarized between the Dreyfusards—who argued for his release—and the reactionary, right-wing anti-Dreyfusards, to whom Dreyfus was an unpatriotic traitor, regardless of the evidence. These ethnic tensions foreshadowed the conflicts that France would later confront in its colonial territories.

WORLD WAR I

IN THE TRENCHES. After centuries of antagonism, the Entente Cordiale brought the British and the French into cooperation in 1904. Together with czarist Russia, this **Triple Entente** faced the **Triple Alliance** of Germany, Italy, and the Austro-Hungarian Empire. Tensions exploded in 1914, when a Serbian nationalist assassinated the heir to the Austrian throne, Archduke Franz-Ferdinand. Austria marched on Serbia, Russia responded, and suddenly almost all of Europe was at war. Paris itself survived the war unscathed, but close to 1,400,000 French soldiers had died by the time fighting stopped in November of 1918. This huge death roll reflected the clash of traditional war tactics with modern firearms, and the world was truly changed forever.

TREATY OF VERSAILLES. The Germans were forced to sign the **Treaty of Versailles** in the Hall of Mirrors, where Prussian King Wilhelm I had been crowned Kaiser of the German Reich in 1870 at the end of the Franco-Prussian War. The treaty contained a clause that blamed Germany for the war; the great resentment that would aid Hitler's rise to power was born in the Sun King's fabulous château.

ROARING 20S AND 30S DEPRESSION

LET THE GOOD TIMES ROLL. Parisians danced in the streets with British, Canadian, and American soldiers at the end of

WWI. The party continued into the Roaring 20s, when expatriate artists like Picasso, Chagall, and Man Ray and American writers like Gertrude Stein, Ernest Hemingway, Ezra Pound, and F. Scott Fitzgerald (p. 80) flooded Paris's cafes. Black American artists like Josephine Baker, faced with discrimination back home, found recognition in Paris. France's long-standing love affair with jazz began in this interwar period.

RISE OF FASCISM. The experimentative, artistic, and wild 20s eventually succumbed to the more practical and sober 30s. The era ended with the **Great Depression,** and Paris was rocked by a political crisis as well as an economic one: in the violent right-wing fascist demonstrations, thousands of Parisians marched on pl. de la Concorde and stormed the Assemblée Nationale. To combat the fascists, socialists and communists united under Léon Blum's left-wing **Front Populaire,** seeking better wages, unionization, and vacation benefits. The Popular Front split over the **Spanish Civil War,** when Blum decided not to aid the Republicans against the fascist General Franco. Internal political tensions made France ill-equipped to deal with Hitler's rapid rise to power and his impending mobilization on the opposite shores of the Rhine.

WORLD WAR II

NAZI OCCUPATION. After invading Austria, Czechoslovakia, Poland, Norway, and Denmark, Adolf Hitler's armies swept through the Ardennes in Luxembourg and blitzkrieged across Belgium before entering Paris on June 13, 1940, encountering almost no resistance. Curators at the Louvre, sensing the inevitable Nazi occupation, removed many works of art, including the Mona Lisa, and placed them in hiding. Stunned Parisians lined up along the Champs-Élysées to watch Nazi foot soldiers and SS troops goosestep through the Arc de Triomphe. The French signed a truce with the Germans, ceding the northern third of the country to the Nazis and designating the lower two-thirds to a collaborating government set up in **Vichy.** The puppet Vichy government under WWI hero **Maréchal Pétain** cooperated with Nazi policy, including the deportation of over 120,000 French and foreign Jews to Nazi concentration camps between 1942 and 1944.

DEPORTATION OF THE JEWS. Soldiers broke down doors in the largely Jewish neighborhoods of the Marais in the 3ème and 4ème *arrondissement*s and relocated Jewish families to the **Vélodrome d'Hiver,** an indoor winter cycling stadium. Here, Jews awaited transportation to concentration camps like Drancy, in the northeastern industrial suburb of Paris near St-Denis, or to camps in Poland and Germany (the **Mémorial de la Déportation** on the Île de la Cité honors those who perished in the Holocaust; p. 208). France was plagued by many profiteering and anti-Semitic collaborators *(collabos)* who aided the Gestapo. Recently, the French government has

1998
France wins the World Cup.

1999
The euro is introduced as the official currency. RIP, franc.

2004
France outlaws religious symbols in public schools.

May 2005
France rejects the European constitution.

Fall 2005
A storm of racial tension erupts as riots sweep France.

July 2006
Zinedine Zidane headbutts an Italian opponent during the World Cup Final, which France later loses in penalty kicks.

May 2007
Conservative Nicolas Sarkozy is elected president of France.

acknowledged some responsibility for the deportations and for their moral apathy, but the issue remains a controversial one.

THEY GRAY ZONE. Paris's theaters, cinemas, music halls, and cafes continued to operate for the Nazi soldiers and officers who flocked to Paris for recreation. Many of the establishments and individuals that the Nazis patronized for food and entertainment, including the Moulin Rouge, Maxim's, Yves Montand, Maurice Chevalier, and Edith Piaf, were maligned as traitors at the end of the war. Women who had taken German lovers had their heads shaved after the war and were forced to walk in the streets amid spitting and jeering.

LA RÉSISTANCE. Today, France commemorates the brave men and women of the Resistance who fought in secret against the Nazis throughout the occupation. In Paris, the Resistance fighters *(maquis)* set up headquarters in the sewers (p. 284) and catacombs (p. 243). In London **Général Charles de Gaulle** established the **Forces Françaises Libres** (Free French Forces), declared his Comité National Français the government-in-exile, and broadcast inspirational messages to his countrymen on the BBC (the first of which is now engraved above the Tomb of the Unknown Soldier under the Arc de Triomphe).

LIBERATION AND RECOVERY. On June 6, 1944, British, American, and Canadian troops launched the **D-Day invasion** on the Normandy coast. By August 25, after four years of occupation, Paris was free. Again, Parisian civilians and Resistance fighters danced and drank with the American, Canadian, and British soldiers. De Gaulle evaded sniper fire to attend mass at Notre Dame and give thanks for the liberation of Paris. His procession down the Champs-Elysées was met with the cheers of thousands of elated Parisians. After the war, as monuments to French bravery were established in the **Musée de l'Armée** (p. 282) and the **Musée de l'Ordre de la Libération** (p. 282), and as thousands of French Jewish survivors began to arrive at the main Repatriation Center in the Gare d'Orsay (p. 280), there was a move to initiate change and avoid returning to the stagnation of the prewar years. De Gaulle promised new elections once deportees and exiled citizens had been repatriated, and France drafted a new constitution. In 1946 French women finally gained the right to vote.

POSTCOLONIAL PARIS: 50S AND 60S

FOURTH REPUBLIC. The Fourth Republic was proclaimed in 1944, but de Gaulle, its provisional president, denounced the decentralizing agenda of the new constitution and resigned in 1946. The Fourth Republic lacked a strong replacement for de Gaulle, and in the following 14 years, France went through an astounding 25 different governments. Despite these problems, the Fourth Republic presided over an economically resurgent country.

COLONIAL INDEPENDENCE. The end of the war also signaled great change in France's residual 19th-century colonial empire. France's defeat in 1954 at the Vietnamese liberation of **Dien Bien Phu** inspired the colonized peoples of France's other protectorates and colonies, which all gained their independence in rapid succession: Morocco and Tunisia in 1956, Mali, Senegal, and the Ivory Coast in 1960. But in Algeria, France drew the line when Algerian nationalists, backed by the resistance efforts of the **Front Libération National** (FLN), moved for independence. With a population of over one million French *colons*, or *pieds-noirs* ("black feet" in French), who were either born in or had immigrated to Algeria, France was reluctant to give up a colony that it had come to regard as an extension of the French hexagone.

KNOW YOUR REPUBLICS. Everyone knows the French have seen a few governments in their day—so many, in fact, that it's tough to keep them straight. Here's a short tutorial so you can keep up with at least the most basic of political discussions:

Valois Dynasty (1329-1589): Rulers included the Fortunate, the Good, the Wise, the Well-Beloved (later the Mad), the Victorious or Well-Served, the Universal Spider, and the Affable as well as such bigwigs as François I and Catherine de Medici.

Bourbon Dynasty (1589-1792): Protestant Henry IV defeated the Medicis to launch this dynasty, converting to Catholicism in the process but making peace with Protestants in the Edict of Nantes. It took a revolution to finish these guys off—at least for the time being.

First Republic (1792-1804): This government had its own chaotic jumble of sub-governments, including the National Convention (during which France adopted universal male suffrage), the Directory (when five men shared power—a.k.a. four too many), and the Consulate (Napoleon's debut).

First Empire (1804-14): Napoleon became—or rather, named himself—emperor. The Napoleonic Code he established still dominates French law.

House of Bourbon (1814-30): France just couldn't shake those Bourbons.

House of Orléans (1830-48): Also known as the tumultuous July Monarchy—a constitutional monarchy in which the bourgeoisie held power.

Second Republic (1848-52): Began with a—comparatively—mini-revolution and ended with a—comparatively—mini-coup d'état.

Second Empire (1852-70): Another Napoleonic coup began this empire—this time, it was Napoleon III, Napoleon I's nephew.

Third Republic (1870-1940): Adolph Thiers said in 1870 that a republic was "the form of government that divides France least." At this point, unfortunately, it just wasn't enough. The French army clashes with protesters in the 1871 conflict of the Paris Commune.

Vichy France (1940-44): Named for the southern French town, this Nazi puppet government was led by Pétain and opposed by de Gaulle.

Provisional Government of the French Republic (GPRF, 1944-46): The Allies got their act together post-victory.

Fourth Republic (1946-58): Revival of the Third, meaning the same problems still existed. After the Algiers Crisis, de Gaulle took over—under the precondition that there would be a Fifth Republic.

Fifth Republic (1958-any day now): De Gaulle made the presidency stronger. A half-century later, it's still alive. At least for now.

ALGERIAN WAR. Fighting in Algeria lasted from 1954 to 1962. The Fourth Republic came to an end in the midst of this chaos overseas. De Gaulle was called out of retirement to deal with the crisis and voted into power by the National Assembly in 1958. Later that year, with a new constitution in hand, the nation declared itself the **Fifth Republic.** This, unsurprisingly, did nothing to resolve the Algerian conflict. Terrorist attacks in Paris by desperate members of the FLN led to **curfews** for African immigrants. At a peaceful demonstration against curfews in 1961, police opened fire on the largely North African crowd, killing hundreds. Amid the violence in Paris and the war in Algeria, a 1962 referendum granted **Algeria independence.** A century of French rule in Algeria came to an end, and the colonial empire crumbled in its wake. The repercussions of colonial exploitation continue to haunt Paris, where **racial tensions** exist today between the French and Arab North Africans, Black West Africans, and Caribbeans, many of whom are second- and third-generation citizens.

REVOLUTION OF MAY 1968. De Gaulle's foreign policy was a success, but his ideological conservatism spurred growing domestic problems. In May 1968, what started as a student protest against the university system rapidly grew into a full-scale revolt, as workers went on strike in support of social reform. Frustrated by racism, sexism, capitalism, an outdated curriculum, students seized the Sorbonne. Barricades were erected in the Latin Quarter, and an all-out riot began. Students dislodged cobblestones to hurl at riot police, and their slogan, **"Sous les pierres, la plage"** (Under the pavement, the beach), symbolized the freedom of shifting sand that lay beneath the rock-hard bureaucracy of French institutions. Police used tear gas and clubs to storm the barricades, while students fought back by throwing Molotov cocktails and lighting cars on fire. When 10 million state workers went on strike in support of the students, the government deployed commando units and tanks. Once the riot was quelled, the Parisian university system was almost immediately decentralized, with various campuses scattered throughout the city and the nation so that student power could never again come together so explosively. The aging General de Gaulle resigned following a referendum in 1969.

80S AND 90S

POLITICS. Four parties have dominated French politics since the era of de Gaulle. When de Gaulle's allies split in 1974, they formed two right-of-center camps: the **Union pour la Démocratie Française** (UDF), led by Valéry Giscard d'Estaing, and the **Rassemblement pour la République** (RPR), led by Jacques Chirac. In 2002, The RPR merged with the UDF to form the **Union pour un Mouvement Populaire** (UMP), which is now the dominant party in French government. On the left is the **Parti Socialiste** (PS)—which came to power throughout the 1980s under François Mitterrand—and the **Parti Communiste Français** (PCF), which currently holds few seats and little power in the modern government.

POMPIDOU AND D'ESTAING. After de Gaulle's resignation, many feared that the Fifth Republic would collapse. It has endured, but with substantial change. De Gaulle's prime minister, **Georges Pompidou,** was elected president in 1969. The years under Pompidou were fairly uneventful; he held a laissez-faire position toward business and a less assertive foreign policy than de Gaulle. He died suddenly in 1974 from Kahler's Disease and was succeeded by conservative **Valéry Giscard d'Estaing.** D'Estaing's term saw the construction of the Centre Pompidou (p. 273), famous for its architecture and excellent collection of modern art. D'Estaing carried on de Gaulle's legacy by concentrating on economic development and strengthening French presence in international affairs.

SOCIALISTS LEAVE THEIR MARK. Ending a lengthy period of conservative leadership, Socialist **François Mitterrand** took over the presidency in 1981, and the Socialists gained a majority in the National Assembly. Within weeks they had raised the minimum wage and added a fifth week to the French worker's annual vacation. Though workers' rights and social justice had begun to burgeon under Mitterrand's leadership, a widespread financial crisis soon after his election drove the political left to tatters, forcing Mitterrand to compromise with politicians on the right. Mitterrand began his term with widespread nationalization, but the international climate could not support a socialist economy.

In the wake of the 1983 recession, the Socialists met with serious losses in the 1986 parliamentary elections. The right gained control of parliament, and Mitterrand had to appoint the conservative Jacques Chirac as prime minister.

COHABITATION Meanwhile, in an unprecedented power-sharing relationship known as "cohabitation," Mitterrand withdrew from the domestic sphere to control only foreign affairs, allowing Chirac to assume power over all in-country business. To the right's delight, Chirac privatized many industries, but widespread terrorism and a large-scale transportation strike hurt conservatives, allowing Mitterrand to win a second term in 1988. He proceeded to preside over a series of unpopular Socialist governments, one led briefly by **Edith Cresson,** France's first female prime minister.

GRANDS PROJETS. Mitterrand's Grands Projets (p. 86) transformed the architectural landscape of Paris. Seeking immortality in stone, steel, and concrete, Mitterrand was responsible for the **Musée d'Orsay** (p. 280), the **Parc de la Villette** (p. 237) the **Institut du Monde Arabe** (p. 276), the **Louvre Pyramid** (p. 266), the **Opéra Bastille** (p. 240), the **Grande Arche de la Défense** (p. 261), and the new **Bibliothèque Nationale** (p. 215). Although expensive and at times as controversial as was the construction of the Eiffel Tower in 1889, Mitterrand's vision for a 21st-century Paris has produced some of the city's most breathtaking new architecture. Mitterrand's other great legacy was his Socialist project to decentralize financial and political power, shifting it away from Paris to local governments. Unfortunately, the people of France were more concerned with scandals involving Mitterrand's mistresses than his grand plans. Contributing to the level of intrigue, Mitterrand revealed two startling facts in the mid-90s—that he had worked with the Vichy government in WWII before joining the Resistance and that he had been seriously ill with cancer since the beginning of his presidency.

CHIRAC TAKES THE REINS. In 1995 Mitterrand chose not to run again because of his failing health, and Chirac was elected president. With unemployment at 12.2% at the time of the election, Chirac faced a difficult year. The crisis ended in a prolonged Winter Strike by students, bus drivers, subway operators, electricians, and postal workers, who protested against budget and benefit cuts proposed by Chirac and his unpopular prime minister, **Alain Juppé.** For weeks, Paris was paralyzed. Stores kept reduced hours, mail delivery came to a halt, and blackouts and traffic jams plagued the city. The following year proved to be an equally difficult one for Chirac and France. The nation mourned the loss of Mitterrand, who died in early January, and later that year, Chirac was denounced around the globe for conducting underground nuclear weapons tests in the South Pacific. The ascendancy of the right was short-lived; the 1997 elections reinstated a Socialist government. Chirac was forced to accept his one-time presidential rival, majority leader Lionel Jospin, as prime minister.

EUROPEAN UNION. One of the most important challenges for the Western world in the 80s and 90s was the question of **European integration.** Despite France's support of the creation of the **European Economic Community** (EEC) in 1957, the idea of a unified Europe has met considerable resistance among the French. Since the inception of the 1991 **Maastricht Treaty,** which significantly strengthened economic integration by expanding the 13-nation EEC to the European Union (EU), the French have manifested fear of a loss of French national character and autonomy. Hoping that a united Europe would strengthen cooperation between France and Germany, Mitterrand led the campaign for a "Oui" vote in France's 1992 referendum on the treaty. This position lost him prestige, and the referendum scraped past with a 51% approval rating. The **Schengen Agreement** (see p. 19) of 1995 created a six-nation zone without border controls. This zone extended to the entire EU and some other countries in 1999 (barring the UK, Ireland, and Denmark), as well as the birth of the euro, which in 2002 superceded the franc as France's official currency.

PARIS TODAY

2004 ELECTIONS. President Chirac's center-right suffered its worst defeat in years in the elections of March of 2004, with the Greens and Socialists gaining control of all but two regions of France. While Chirac's party, the UMP, has traditionally rallied around the president, its support has been waning. Most of the party was quite displeased with Chirac's reappointment of Prime Minister **Jean-Pierre Raffarin**. Meanwhile, **Alain Juppé**, an intimate ally of Chirac, resigned as head of the UMP in 2004 after being convicted for corrupt dealings. He was replaced by **Dominique de Villepin.**

IRAQ AND AMERICA. In early 2003, France joined with Germany and Russia to voice opposition to the US-led Iraq War, insisting on the use of political and diplomatic means to disarm Iraq. A breach in US-France relations opened as France criticized American unilateralism and defended a multi-polar world and a cohesive, unified Europe. After the June 2003 G-8 summit, Presidents Bush and Chirac made public displays of reconciliation, but tensions still existed. At the D-Day 60th anniversary ceremonies in June of 2004, President Bush attempted to draw a correlation between the WWII liberation of France and the Iraq takeover and was met with a stiff dismissal from the French president.

SARKO AND CHIRAC: A TUMULTOUS AFFAIR. The 2004 elections installed **Nicolas Sarkozy** as Finance Minister, and many looked to the energetic young politician for a solution to economic problems. In the fall of 2003, Sarkozy was one of the primary advocates of state investment in France's high-speed train company, **Alstom,** which found itself in dire financial straits. France was greatly criticized for the proposed bail-out, which was perceived as going against EU free-market principles. In May, France reached a compromise with the EU by which Alstom sell only a small portion of the company to private investors.

THE 2007 ELECTIONS. The 2007 presidential election was a dramatic moment in French history. After twelve years of Jacques Chirac, the French people were eager for change, and it showed in voter turnout. In the French system, all candidates stand for a first round of elections, and if none achieves a clear majority, the top two candidates face off against each other in a cage match to the death—or just a run-off election. In the first round of voting, Nicholas Sarkozy and **Ségolène Royal,** the Socialist candidate who would have been France's first female president. Missing the cut were **François Bayrou,** the centrist UDF candidate, and **Jean-Marie Le Pen,** the leader of the National Front who received 10.44% of the vote despite having advocated xenophobic positions, minimized the Holocaust, and remarked in 2006 that it was difficult to recognize the French World Cup team because of the number of players of color.

SARKO AND ROYAL. At least in terms of their promises and rhetoric, the differences between Sarkozy and Royal were clear. Sarkozy favored a more free market economy and drastic reforms, a **"rupture"** with the past quarter-century in France, which suffered from slow growth, high unemployment, high taxes, high public spending, a large and quickly rising national debt, and a culture that detested change. He wanted the French to work more hours and the government to in turn spend and tax less. On the other hand, Royal, while certainly wishing to break with Chirac and many of his policies, wanted to strengthen the socialist foundations of the French state. Preferring a "rupture," the French opted for Sarkozy by a significant margin.

SARKOZY'S HONEYMOONS. Nicolas Sarkozy entered office with a strong mandate from his own election and a parliamentary majority for his party. The country expected broad and bold reforms from the president who had made no secret of his affection for the American economic system while also espousing some traditionally French protectionist policies. He began with fair success abroad: he made progress with advancing the rejected EU constitution, brought France back in the NATO fold, and mended fences with the US by sending a combat battalion to Afghanistan with NATO and talking tough on Russia, China, and Iran. On the domestic front, he failed in many of his initiatives for deregulation, privatization, and changing the labor laws. At the end of his first year, he had the **lowest approval rating** of any Fifth Republic President at that point. Many blame the end of France's honeymoon with Sarkozy on his actual honeymoon. The French president's second wife left her lover to stand alongside Sarkozy during the campaign, but only five months after he was sworn in, they were divorced and she returned to her lover. Within two months, Sarkozy was seen floozing it up with **Carla Bruni,** an Italian-born ex-supermodel who is one of France's biggest pop stars. Two months after that, the beautiful Bruni, a woman who had reportedly dated Mick Jagger and Donald Trump, married Nicolas Sarkozy in Paris.

ONLY IN FRANCE. Sarkozy's presidency has had no shortage of non-marital distractions as well. He earned Youtube immortality when he looked quite *ivre* at a G8 press conference in June 2007. Then in February 2008, while shaking hands at the Paris Agricultural Show, Sarkozy responded to one man's "Don't touch me," with a phrase that could be roughly translated as, "Screw off, you worthless asshole." Of course, he did this without ever breaking his smile, but unfortunately for Sarko, the incident was caught on camera. Speaking of cameras, back in August 2007, Sarkozy also berated and almost broke one of the cameras of a group of US photographers who snapped some shots of him shirtless while he was vacationing at New Hampshire's Lake Winnipesaukee. As the hubbub of his marriage wanes, President Sarkozy has made signals that he wants to cut the Laguna-Beach-esque drama and get down to governing.

IN RECENT NEWS

DON'T GET TOO COZY, SARKOZY

In a recently released poll conducted by Paris Match magazine, 72% of French citizens voiced dissatisfaction with President Nicolas Sarkozy, the rightist UMP (Union pour un Mouvement Populaire) member who was elected just last year. Mr. Sarkozy, who championed reform of French economic and social policy in his campaign, can't seem to live up to his promises for change. Even worse, in a year that saw the French economy tumble almost as hard as Wall Street, nearly 60% of polled citizens cast doubt on his ability to affect change in the future. As of now, only 28% of those polled claimed satisfaction with him.

Faced with the same economic, social, and diplomatic problems as his predecessors, Sarkozy may soon look the fool if the French electorate leans back to the more familiar Socialist Party. The French may take comfort in the Socialists' approach to the problems of immigration, wages and labor, and foreign diplomacy—especially with the wisdom and know-how years of experience.

Conservatives have not held much sway in French politics in years, but with the addition of parliamentary seats on top of Sarkozy's decisive victory, *la droite* seemed to bear the people's mandate. However, it now seems that French conservatives have been dealt a public opinion blow from which they cannot recover.

ANTI-SEMITISM. Since early in the decade, anti-Semitic violence in France has been on the rise. France has the third largest Jewish population in Europe, including large numbers of Eastern European and North African Sephardic immigrants. There have been particularly harrowing conflicts between Jewish and Muslim North Africans in the Paris banlieu, but recent events have suggested that religious tensions penetrate all classes. There were 970 documented acts of anti-Semitic hatred in France in 2004, including cases of harassment and vandalism in synagogues and Jewish cemeteries. In July of 2004, Israeli Prime Minister Ariel Sharon urged French Jews to immigrate to Israel, citing France as unsafe because of its rampant anti-Semitism. President Chirac responded furiously to the accusation, defending his country's commitment to protecting its Jewish citizens, and while Sharon maintained that his comments had been misinterpreted, the incident brought France's racial and religious tensions into the international spotlight. In 2005, three reporters for Paris's Le Monde newspaper were found guilty of conscious anti-Semitism in their columns, and France still wrestles with its anti-Jewish reputation to this day.

GLBT RIGHTS. In 1999, France became the first traditionally Catholic country in the world to legally recognize same-sex unions. The **Pacte Civil de Solidarité,** known by its acronym PACS, was designed to extend to both same-sex and unmarried opposite-sex couples greater welfare, tax and inheritance rights. While PACS is now such a common term that it is used as both a verb *(pacser)* and an adjective (pacsé), it is has faced serious detractors. For many French people, official gay partnership is still an unwelcome concept; for others, PACS is an inadequate conciliatory gesture, designed to patch over the fact that gay marriage is still illegal. GLBT activists are currently struggling to attain the same parenting rights that heterosexual married couples enjoy.

THE ARTS

LITERATURE AND PHILOSOPHY

OLD SCHOOL HITS. Medieval France produced an extraordinary number of literary texts. Popular **chansons de geste** were epics in verse that recounted tales of eighth-century crusades and conquests. The most famous of these, the **Chanson de Roland** (1170), dramatizes the heroism of Roland, one of Charlemagne's chevaliers. While *chansons de geste* entertained 12th-century masses, the aristocracy enjoyed more refined tales of knightly honor and courtly love, such as the *Laïs* of **Marie de France,** the romances of **Chrétien de Troyes,** and Béroul's adaptation of the legend of Tristan et Iseult. During the 13th century, popular satirical stories called *fabliaux* celebrated the bawdy and the scatological.

RENAISSANCE INNOVATION. Renaissance literature in France challenged medieval notions of courtly love and Christian thought. Inspired by **Boccaccio's** *Decameron,* **Marguerite de Navarre's** *Héptaméron* used pilgrim stories to explore humanist ideas. Frenchman **John Calvin's** treatises criticized the Church and paved the way for the emergence of the **Protestant Reformation** in France. With **Jacques Cartier's** founding of Nouvelle France (Québec) in 1534, French writers began to expand their perspectives on themselves and the world. **Rabelais's** fantastical *Gargantua* and *Pantagruel* explored (and satirized) the world from a giant's point of view, and **Montaigne's** *Essais* pushed the boundaries of individual intellectual thought. While the poetry of **Ronsard** and **Du Bellay,** the memoirs of **Marguerite de Valois,** and the sonnets of **Louise Labé** contributed to the Renaissance's spirit of optimism and change, they also expressed anxiety over the atrocities of the 16th-century Wars of Religion.

RATIONALISM AND THE ENLIGHTENMENT. The **Académie Française** (p. 226) was founded in 1635 to regulate and codify French literature and language, and has since served as the guardian of French letters. There and elsewhere, French philosophers reacted to the musings of the Humanists with Rationalism, a school of thought that championed logic and order. In his *Discourse on Method*, **René Descartes** proved his own existence with the famous catchy deduction, "I think, therefore I am." **Blaise Pascal** misspent his youth inventing the mechanical calculator and the science of probabilities. He later became a devotee of Jansenism—an extremist sect of Catholicism that emphasized the need for grace—and retired from public life to write things like *"le coeur a ses raisons que la raison ne connait pas"* (the heart has reasons that reason cannot know) in his *Pensées* (1658). **Molière,** the era's comic relief, used his plays to satirize the social pretensions of the bourgeoisie. Molière founded the **Comédie Française**—the world's oldest national theater company—which still produces top-notch versions of French classics at its theater in Paris (p. 313).

In the 18th century the Enlightenment sought to promote reason and a definitive social code. **Denis Diderot** and **Jean D'Alembert's** *Encyclopédie* (1752-1780) was the ultimate compendium of Enlightenment thought, containing entries by philosophers **Jean-Jacques Rousseau** and **Voltaire.** Voltaire's famous satire *Candide* (1758) made jabs at any and all authorities, while Rousseau's *Confessions* (1766-1769) and novels like *Émile* (1762) suggested that society is not worth corrupting our souls. Playwright **Beaumarchais's** incendiary masterpieces *Le Barbier de Seville* (1775) and *Le Mariage de Figaro* (1784) were banned by Louis XVI for their criticisms of the aristocracy.

SEX AND REVOLUTION. The traumas of the era surrounding the French Revolution are perhaps best represented in literature by the works of the **Marquis de Sade.** In libertine novels like *Philosophy in the Bedroom* (1795) and *Justine* (1791), de Sade attacked hypocrisy and repression and dealt with what he perceived to be a mad world through the violently excessive representation of the sexual practice that now bears his name, Sadism.

ROMANTICISM AND REALISM. During the 19th century the expressive ideals of Romanticism, which first came to prominence in Britain and Germany, found their way to analytically minded France. **François-René de Châteaubriand** drew inspiration for his novel *Atala* from his experiences with Native Americans near Niagara Falls. **Henri Stendhal** *(Le Rouge et le Noir)* and **Honoré de Balzac** *(La Comédie Humaine)* helped to establish the novel as the new pre-eminent literary medium, but finally it was **Victor Hugo's** *The Hunchback of Notre Dame* (1831) that dominated the Romantic age. In the same period, the young Aurore Dupin left her husband and childhood home, took the *nom de plume* of **George Sand,** and published passionate novels condemning sexist social conventions. Sand was as famous for her scandalous lifestyle as for her prose, with a tendency to cross-dress and a string of high-profile relationships including a 10-year dalliance with **Frédéric Chopin.** The heroine of **Gustave Flaubert's** *Madame Bovary* (1856) spurned provincial life for romantic, adulterous daydreams in his famous realist novel. Flaubert was prosecuted for immorality in 1857 and was only narrowly acquitted. Poet **Charles Baudelaire** was not so lucky; the same tribunal fined him 50 francs. Although Baudelaire gained a reputation for obscenity during his own lifetime, today his *Fleurs du Mal* is considered the most influential piece of 19th-century French poetry.

SOCIALISM AND SCIENCE. Baudelaire participated in the 1848 revolution, and his radical political views closely resembled those of the anarcho-socialist innovator **Pierre-Joseph Proudhon.** Born into poverty and luckily brilliant, Proudhon received a scholarship to college at Besançon and then at Paris where, in 1840, he published the leaflet, *What is Property?* His inflammatory thesis stated that **"property is theft."** Put on trial in 1842, he escaped punishment only because the jury refused to condemn ideas it could not understand. A pivotal figure in the history of socialism, Proudhon inspired the *syndicaliste* trade-union movement of the 1890s. **Auguste Comte's** positivism provided a more optimistic philosophy, which anticipated that science would eventually give way to a fully rational explanation of nature.

NATURALISM AND SYMBOLISM. Like its artistic counterpart, Impressionism, literary Symbolism reacted against stale conventions and used new techniques to capture instants of perception. Led by **Stéphane Mallarmé** and **Paul Verlaine,** the movement was instrumental in the creation of modern poetry as we understand it, particularly through the work of the precocious **Arthur Rimbaud.** Naturalism, an outgrowth of Realism conceived around 1880, uses a scientific, analytic approach to dissect and reconstruct reality; the genre is represented by such famed writers like **Émile Zola** and **Guy de Maupassant.**

BELLE ÉPOQUE. Works that confronted the anti-Semitism of the Dreyfus Affair, like Zola's *J'Accuse,* laid the foundation for a whole new literature that would explore issues of individual identity—including sexuality, gender, and ethnicity—in 20th-century France. **Marcel Proust's** *À la Recherche du temps perdu* (1913-1927) inquired into the nature of time, memory, and love. Like most serious French authors of the time, Proust published in the influential **Nouvelle Revue Française.** Founded in Paris in 1909, the journal rose to prominence under **André Gide,** who won the Nobel Prize in 1947 for morally provocative novels like *The Counterfeiters* (1924). Throughout his career, Gide was engaged in a rivalry with Catholic revivalist **Paul Claudel.** Claudel struggled unsuccessfully to persuade Gide that divine grace would eventually overcome greed and lust, the basic theme behind plays such as *The Satin Slipper* (1924).

QUEER MODERNISM. Proust, Gide, and novelist/playwright **Colette** wrote frankly about homosexuality. Proust's portraits of Belle Époque Parisians in *Sodom and Gomorrah,* Gide's homoerotic novels like *l'Immoraliste,* and Colette's sensual descriptions of the opium dens of the 1920s and cabarets of the 1930s in *Le Pur et l'Impur* and *La Vagabonde* inspired later feminist and homoerotic writing. Authors who continued to explore these novel themes include **Jean Genet** in *Funeral Rites* (1949), **Monique Wittig** in *Les Guerillères* (1967), and **Hervé Guibert** in *Fou de Vincent* (Crazy about Vincent).

DADAISM AND SURREALISM. Like contemporary art, film, dance, and music, 20th-century French literature moved increasingly toward abstraction. Inspired by the nonsensical art movement called Dadaism, choreographer **Serge Diaghilev,** set-designer **Pablo Picasso,** composer **Erik Satie,** and writer **Jean Cocteau** laid the foundation for even further abstraction following the war. In France, Dadaism took a literary bent under the influence of Romanian-born **Tristan Tzara,** whose poems of nonsensically scrambled words attacked the structure of language. Tzara's colleagues **André Breton** and **Louis Aragon** soon became dissatisfied with Dadaism and set about developing a more organized protest, which exploded in 1924 with the publication of Breton's first *Surrealist Manifesto,* a proclamation of the artistic supremacy of the subconscious. But what is not created consciously is difficult to understand consciously—most Surrealist poetry defies analysis. Surrealism later influenced absurdist French theater, such as **Eugène**

Ionesco's *Rhinocéros*, expatriate **Samuel Beckett's** *Waiting for Godot*, and Jean-Paul Sartre's *Huis Clos*. Meanwhile, the rising threat of Nazi Germany spurred a literary call to arms, led by the indomitable **André Malraux,** who drew inspiration from the Chinese civil war for his masterpiece, *The Human Condition* (1933). Another adventurer, **Antoine de St-Exupéry,** used his experiences as an early aviation pioneer to create classics such as *The Little Prince* (1943).

EXISTENTIALISM. The period following the war was intellectually dominated by **Jean-Paul Sartre,** Existentialism's undisputed guru. His happy-go-lucky philosophy held that life as an independent entity is meaningless: only by choosing and then committing oneself to a cause can existence take on a purpose. Though **Albert Camus** is often grouped with Sartre, his brand of existentialism differs from Sartre's in its morality: Camus maintained that mere commitment was not enough to give life meaning if it was unfair to others. He achieved fame with his debut novel *L'Étranger* (1942), which tells the story of a dispassionate social misfit condemned to death for a cold-blooded murder.

FEMINISM. Acclaimed Existentialist feminist, Sartre's companion **Simone de Beauvoir** made waves with *The Second Sex* (1949), an essay attacking the idea of femininity. Its famous statement, "One is not born, but becomes a woman," planted the roots of the French second-wave feminism that would last through the 70s. With their exploration of gender identity, writers like **Marguerite Duras** *(L'Amant)*, **Nathalie Sarraute** *(Tropismes)*, **Hélène Cixous** *(Le Rire de la Méduse)*, and **Luce Irigaray** *(Ce Sexe Qui n'en est Pas Un)* carried the feminist torch worldwide. While American feminist literature emphasized practical action, French feminism tended to be more theoretical, influenced by Jacques Lacan's psychoanalytic writings and concerned with the structure of language. Specifically, French second-wave feminists advocated **femme écriture,** the philosophy of "writing the body" that inspired such sentiments as "deflating the phallus."

POSTCOLONIAL VOICES. In the 20th century, many voices emerged from France's former colonies and protectorates in the Antilles (Martinique and Guadeloupe), the Caribbean (Haiti), North America (Québec), North Africa (Algeria, Tunisia, and Morocco, known as the Maghreb), and West Africa (Senegal, Mali, Côte d'Ivoire, Congo, and Cameroon). Much of this literature speaks out against France's colonial exploitation and deals with the trauma of the decolonization process (p. 72). In Paris in the 1920s, intellectuals **Aimé Césaire** (Martinique) and **Léopold Sédar Senghor** (Senegal) founded the **Négritude** movement, which emphasized the shared history and identity of black Francophones. Their work and the subsequent founding of the press **Présence Africaine** on the Left Bank (p. 305) inspired generations of Francophone intellectuals on both sides of the Atlantic, the most celebrated of whom is Antillean writer **Frantz Fanon** *(Les Damnées de la Terre).*

Since the atrocities of the Algerian War in the 1960s (p. 73), much *maghrébin* literature has been characterized by a search for cultural identity, subjectivity, and the conflicts between colonial and postcolonial history. Some of the most prolific writers of the movement are **Assia Djébar** *(Les Femmes d'Alger Dans Leur Appartement)* from Algeria; **Driss Charibi** *(La Civilisation...Ma Mère!)* from Morocco; and **Albert Memmi** *(La Statue de Sel)* from Tunisia. Many second- and third-generation Maghrébin writers in France, such as **Mehdi Charef** *(Le Thé au Harem d'Archi Ahmed)*, have written about French-Arab culture and the difficulties of assimilation into French culture.

POSTMODERN -ISMS. From the 70s to the present day, postmodernism, a diverse confederation of ideas that reject the possibility of stable meaning and identity, has exerted a great influence over literary, political, and intellectual life worldwide. In *The Postmodern Condition: A Report on Knowledge* (1979), **Jean François Lyotard** turned a routine report commissioned by the Canadian government into a postmodernist manifesto. Among the most important postmodern thinkers are structuralist **Ferdinand de Saussure,** historical "archaeologist" **Michel Foucault,** psychoanalyst **Jacques Lacan,** poststructural feminist **Hélène Cixous,** and cultural critic **Jean Baudrillard.** Theory and literary criticism, both in France and in the United States, were transformed by deconstruction, a practice founded by **Jacques Derrida,** whereby a text's inherent oppositions are examined through careful analysis of language and form. Lyotard, Saussure, Lacan, Cixous, Baudrillard, and Derrida all spent most of their lives in Paris. The hugely popular public seminars given by Foucault, Lacan, and other thinkers are indicative of Paris's intellectual tenor: it seems that in Paris, literature and public life are more closely related than anywhere else in the world.

FINE ARTS AND ARCHITECTURE

ROMAN STONES. Paris's first achievements in architecture were the baths, arenas, and roads built by the Romans, which include the partially reconstructed **Arènes de Lutèce** (p. 224) and the baths preserved in the **Musée de Cluny** (p. 275). Though few of the ruins remain intact, this type classical architecture has been a model for many more recent constructions.

GOTHIC CATHEDRALS. Most Medieval art aimed to instruct 12th- and 13th-century churchgoers on religious themes. As most commoners were illiterate, stained glass and intricate stone facades, like those at **Chartres** (p. 345), **Ste-Chapelle** (p. 207), and **Notre Dame** (p. 205), served as large, pictorial reproductions of the Bible. The churches are stunning examples of Gothic architecture, characterized by flying buttresses and enormous stained glass windows.

THE RENAISSANCE. Inspired by the painting, sculpture, and architecture of the Italian Renaissance, 16th-century France imported much of its style from its boot-shaped neighbor to the east. **François I** had seen this art, which employed revolutionary techniques that transformed their subjects, during his Italian campaigns, and when he inherited France in 1515, he decided that the time had come to put his country, artistically, on the map. The king implored friends in Italy to send him works by **Titian** and **Bronzino.** He also imported the artists themselves to create **Fontainebleau** (p. 350), the most perfect example of French Renaissance architecture. **Leonardo da Vinci** appeared soon after, with the *Mona Lisa* in tow as a gift to the French monarch (p. 266). Some of the world's greatest Renaissance art can be seen at the **Louvre** (p. 266).

BAROQUE EXCESS. In the 17th century, the Baroque movement swept up from Italy to France, just in time for Louis XIV's to make everything gold and shiny. The architecture of **Versailles** (p. 339) benefited greatly from this Italian infusion. The Sun King drew inspiration from the château of **Vaux-le-Vicomte** (p. 355), the 1657 accomplishment of the architect-artist-landscaper triumvirate of **Louis Le Vau, Charles Le Brun,** and **André Le Nôtre.** But the Baroque period had room for realism, even as it indulged a monarch's penchant for gilt—the brothers **Le Nain** (who worked together on all their canvases) and **Georges de La Tour** (1593-1652) produced representations of everyday life.

ACADÉMIE ROYALE. Baroque exuberance was subdued by the more serious and classical works of painter **Nicolas Poussin** (1594-1665). Poussin believed that reason should be the guiding principle of art and was fortunate enough to promulgate these views with the endorsement of the Académie Royale. Under director Charles Le Brun (1619-90), the traditionalist Academy became the sole arbiter of taste in all matters artistic. It held **annual salons**—"official" art exhibitions held in vacant halls of the Louvre where the art can still be found—and it set strict, conservative guidelines for artistic technique and subject matter.

ROCOCO. The playful Rococo style emerged from the early 18th century. Its asymmetrical curves and profusion of ornamentation were far more conducive to Louis XV's interior design than to architecture itself. **Antoine Watteau** (1684-1721) captured the secret rendez-vous of the aristocracy in his paintings and **François Boucher** (1703-70) painted landscapes and scenes from courtly life.

NEOCLASSICISM AND REVOLUTIONARY ART. After the Revolution wreaked havoc on symbolic strongholds of the aristocracy like Versailles and Notre Dame, the reign of Napoleon I saw the emergence of **Neoclassicism,** exemplified architecturally by the **Église de la Madeleine** (p. 235)—a giant imitation of a Greco-Roman temple—and the imposing **Arc de Triomphe** (p. 232), both begun in 1806. In painting, **Jacques-Louis David** (1748-1825) exemplifies this aesthetic; his *Death of Marat* (1793) was a rallying point for revolutionaries and is considered by some critics to mark the onset of modernity. Later, he created giant canvases on classical themes like *Oath of the Horatii* (1784) which exploited the Greek and Roman iconography so admired by Napoleon (his employer). Following David, and encouraged by the deep pockets of Napoleon, painters created large, dramatic pictures, often of the emperor as Romantic hero and god, all rolled into one petit package. After Napoleon's fall, few artists painted nationalistic *tableaux.* One exception was **Théodore Géricault** (1791-1824), whose *Raft of the Medusa* (1819) hangs magnificently in the Louvre (p. 266).

ROMANTICISM AND ORIENTALISM. Nineteenth-century France was ready to settle into respectable, bourgeois ways after several turbulent years of transitioning from Republic to Empire. The paintings of **Eugène Delacroix** (1798-1863) were a shock to salons of the 1820s and 1830s. The *Massacre at Chios* (1824) and *The Death of Sardanapalus* (1827) both display an extraordinary sense of color and a penchant for melodrama. Delacroix went on to do a series of "Moroccan" paintings. He shared this Orientalist tendency with **Jean-Auguste-Dominique Ingres** (1780-1867), among others. Ingres's most famous representation of the sexual and racial otherness that so fascinated the Romantic imagination is the captivating reclining nude, *La grande odalisque.* The subject's exotic beauty is emphasized through exaggerated features; she would have had to have a few more verterbra than most humans for this stunning portrait to be true to life. Another influential Romantic, **Paul Delaroche** (1797-1859) created charged narratives on large canvases (*The Young Martyr,* 1855).

CLASSICISM AND THE INFLUENCE OF HAUSSMANN. Aside from a romantically inspired Gothic revival led by the so-called "great restorer" **Viollet-le-Duc,** Neoclassicism reigned in 19th-century architecture, supported by the strictly classical curriculum of the dominant École des Beaux-Arts. The ultimate expression of 19th-century classicism is **Charles Garnier's** Palais Garnier, built 1862-75 (p. 237). More influential to the face of today's Paris, however, was the direction of Baron **Georges Haussmann.** From 1852 to 1870, Haussmann transformed Paris from a medieval city to a modern metropolis. Commissioned by Napoleon III to modernize the city, Haussmann tore long, straight boulevards through the tangled clutter and narrow alleys of old Paris, displacing thousands of poor people and creating a unified network of *grands boulevards.*

REALISM. The late 19th and early 20th centuries saw the reinvention of painting in France: first, a shift of subject matter to everyday life, and then a radical change in technique. Impressionism found its beginnings in the mid-19th century with **Théodore Rousseau** (1812-67) and **Jean-François Millet** (1814-75), leaders of the **École de Barbizon**, a group of artists who painted nature for its own sake. Landscape paintings capturing a "slice of life" paved the way for Realism. The Realists were led by **Gustave Courbet** (1819-77), who focused on everyday subjects but portrayed them magnified many times on tremendous canvases.

MANET'S MODERNITY. **Edouard Manet** (1832-83) facilitated the transition from the Realism of Courbet to what we now consider **Impressionism;** in the 1860s, he began to shift the focus of his work to color and texture. Manet's *Déjeuner Sur l'Herbe* was refused by the **Salon of 1863** due to its less-than-kosher naked-lunch theme (two suited men and a naked woman are shown picnicking in the forest, in a formation taken from Raimondi's *Judgement of Paris*); it was later shown proudly at the **Salon des Refusés,** along with 7000 other rejected salon works. In the equally scandalous *Olympia* (1862), appropriating the form of Titian's *Venus of Urbino*, Manet boldly re-imagined the classically idealized female nude. He depicted a distinctly contemporary Parisian prostitute, wearing only a shoe and staring unapologetically at the viewer. This display of fleshy modernity disconcerted viewers, earned accusations of pornography, and inspired numerous caricatures, but eventually won him immortality. Both works can be seen at Paris's fantastic **Musée d'Orsay** (p. 280).

IMPRESSIONISM AND POST-IMPRESSIONISM. By the late 1860s Manet's new aesthetic had set the stage for **Claude Monet** (1840-1926), **Camille Pissarro** (1830-1903), and **Pierre-Auguste Renoir** (1841-1919), who began further to explore new techniques. They strove to attain a sense of immediacy; colors were used to capture scenes as they were (a very different agenda than classicism's emphasis on structure and stage-like set-ups) and light became subject matter in itself. In 1874 these revolutionary artists had their first collective exhibition, and one critic snidely labeled the group "Impressionists." The artists themselves found the label accurate, and their Impressionists' show became an annual event for the next seven years. In the late 1880s, the group inspired **Gustave Caillebotte** (1848-94), **Berthe Morisot** (1841-95), and **Henri Fantin-Latour** (1836-1904).

The **Post-Impressionists,** also called Neo-Impressionists, were for the most part loners. **Paul Cézanne** (1839-1906) painted landscapes using an early Cubist technique in Aix-en-Provence; **Paul Gauguin** (1848-1903) took up a solitary residence in Tahiti, where he painted in sensuous color; **Vincent van Gogh** (1853-90) projected his tortured emotions onto the countryside at **Auvers-sur-Oise** (p. 357). **Georges Seurat** (1859-91), something less of a social outcast, revealed his **Pointillist** technique at the **Salon des Indépendants** of 1884. Sculptor **Auguste Rodin** (1840-1917) focused on the energetic, muscular shaping of bronze (p. 279). Pieces by all of these artists can be found at the **Musée d'Orsay,** p. 279.

BOHEMIA AND ART NOUVEAU. As the 19th century drew to a close, Bohemia had moved its center to Montmartre, a refuge from the chaos of the modern city below. **Henri de Toulouse-Lautrec** (1864-1901) captured the spirit of the **Belle Époque** in vibrant silkscreen posters that covered Paris, as well as in his paintings of brothels, circuses, and can-can cabarets. The curves of **Art Nouveau** transformed architecture, furniture, lamps, jewelry, fashion, and even the entrances to the **Paris Métropolitain.** The **World's Fairs** of 1889 and 1900 led to the construction of the **Grand** and **Petit Palais** (p. 233) and the **Eiffel Tower** (p. 229), which, over a century after its controversial construction, remains France's most iconic landmark. Meanwhile, **Charles Frederick Worth** opened Paris's first house of haute couture, turning fashion into a sort of commodified art form (p. 297).

Haussmannia
How Paris Cleaned Up Its Act

Like a clock, 12 straight boulevards radiate outwards from the pl. Charles de Gaulle. A view through the arch at the foot of the Louvre aligns with the Obelisk in the pl. de la Concorde, the Arc de Triomphe, and the modern arch at La Défense. Cafe-lined streets and wide tree-lined boulevards seem as organic to Paris as the curving of the Seine. Yet none of this is an accident. The city's charm is calculated—and it wasn't always this beautiful.

Social commentator Maxime Du Camp observed in the mid-19th century: "Paris, as we find it in the period following the Revolution of 1848, was uninhabitable. Its population...was suffocating in the narrow, tangled, putrid alleyways in which it was forcibly confined." Sewers were not used until 1848, and waste and trash rotted in the Seine. Streets followed a maddening 12th-century design; in some *quartiers*, winding thoroughfares were no wider than 3.5m. Toadstool-like rocks lined the streets allowing pedestrians to jump to safety as carriages sped by. In the hands of the Seine prefect, Baron Georges-Eugène Haussmann, bureaucrat and social architect under Emperor Louis Napoleon, the city's medieval layout was demolished and replaced with a new urban vision.

Haussmann replaced the tangle of medieval streets with sewers, trains, and *grand boulevards*. Proclaiming the necessity of unifying Paris and promoting trade among the different *arrondissements*, Haussmann saw the old streets as antiquated impediments to modern commercial and political progress. His wide boulevards swept through whole neighborhoods of cramped row houses and little passageways; in doing so, he displaced 350,000 of Paris's poorest residents, many of whom were forced to live outside the city proper in the less crowded *balnieues*.

The widespread rage at Haussmann's plans reinforced the emperor's desire to use the city's layout to assert his authority. The old, narrow streets had been ideal for civilian insurrection in preceding revolutions; rebels built barricades across street entrances and blocked off whole areas of the city from the government's military. Haussmann believed that creating *grands boulevards* and carefully mapping the city could bring to an end the use of barricades, and more importantly, prevent future uprisings. He was dead wrong. During the 1871 revolt of the Paris Commune, which saw the deposition of Louis Napoleon and the rise of the Third Republic, the *grands boulevards* proved ideal for the construction of higher and stronger barricades.

Despite the underlying political agenda of Haussmannization, many of the prefect's changes were for the better. Haussmann transformed the open-air dump and grave at Montfauçon with the whimsical waterfalls, cliffs, and grottoes of the Parc

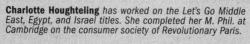

"Like a clock, 12 straight boulevards radiate outward from pl. de Gaulle."

des Buttes-Chaumont. Paris became eminently navigable, and to this day a glance down one of Paris's many grands boulevards will offer the *flâneur* (wanderer) an unexpected lesson in the layout of the city and the beauty of manipulation.

Charlotte Houghteling has worked on the Let's Go Middle East, Egypt, and Israel titles. She completed her M. Phil. at Cambridge on the consumer society of Revolutionary Paris.

Sara Houghteling was a Researcher-Writer for Let's Go: France 1999 and holds a Masters in Fine Arts from University of Michigan. Funded by a Fulbright Grant, Sara spent a year in Paris researcher for her novel.

CUBISM AND FAUVISM. Pablo Picasso, one of the most prolific artists of the 20th century, first arrived in Paris from Spain in 1900 and made a reputation for himself with collectors like writer **Gertrude Stein.** Together with fellow painter **Georges Braques** (1882-1963), Picasso patented Cubism, a radical movement de-emphasizing an object's form by showing all its sides at once. Many of Picasso's works can be found at the museum which bears his name (p. 270). The word "Cubism" was coined by **Henri Matisse** (1869-1964) as he described one of Braque's landscapes. Matisse, engaged in a lifelong rivalry with Picasso, chose to squeeze paint from the tube directly onto canvas. This aggressive style earned the name **Fauvism** (from *fauves*, or wild animals).

DADAISM. Marcel Duchamp (1887-1968) put Cubism in motion with his *Nude Descending a Staircase* (1912). The disillusionment that pervaded Europe after WWI kindled Duchamp's leadership of the Dada movement. Dadaists' production of "non-art" was a rejection of artistic conventions. This movement culminated in the exhibition of Duchamp's **La Fontaine** (The Fountain, 1917), a urinal that the guerilla artist turned upside-down and signed.

SURREALISM. Surrealism's goal was a union of dream and fantasy with the everyday to form "an absolute reality, a surreality," according to **André Breton,** leader of the movement. The bowler-hatted men of **René Magritte** (1898-1967), the dreamscapes of **Joan Miró** (1893-1983), the patterns of **Max Ernst** (1891-1976), and the melting timepieces of Salvador Dalí (1904-1989) all arose from time spent in Paris. Surrealist art can be found at the **Centre Pompidou** (p. 273).

1930S PHOTOGRAPHY AND ARCHITECTURE. During the 30s, photographers like **Georges Brassaï** (1889-1984), **André Kertész** (1894-1985), and **Henri Cartier-Bresson** began using small cameras to record the streets and *quartiers* of Paris in black and white. Meanwhile, architects began to incorporate new building materials in their designs. A Swiss citizen by the name of Charles-Edouard Jeanneret, known to Parisian citizens simply as **Le Corbusier,** pioneered the use of reinforced concrete in the city's modern architecture. A prominent member of the legendary International School, Le Corbusier dominated his field from the 1930s until his death in 1965. His **Villa La Roche** and **Villa Jeanneret,** today preserved by the **Fondation Le Corbusier** (p. 291).

NAZI DESTRUCTION AND THEFT. The arrival of WWII forced many artists working in Paris to move across the continent or the ocean, and, as the Nazis advanced, the Louvre's treasures were hidden in the basements of Paris. On May 27, 1943, hundreds of "degenerate" paintings by Picasso, Ernst, Klee, Léger, and Miró were destroyed in a bonfire in the garden of the Jeu de Paume. Tens of thousands of masterpieces belonging to Jewish collectors were appropriated by the Germans, most of which they held for several decades or destroyed.

GRANDS PROJETS. The 80s and 90s produced some of Paris's most controversial architectural masterpieces. Inspired by President Giscard d'Estaing's daring Centre Pompidou in the late 70s, **President Mitterrand** initiated his famous 15-billion-franc Grands Projets program to create modern monuments at the dawn of the 21st century (p. 75). New projects such as the **ZAC** (Zone d'Aménagement Concerté) in the 13ème, continue to transform the city.

CONTEMPORARY ART. Later 20th- and early 21st-century experiments in photography, installation art, video, and sculpture can be seen in the collections and temporary exhibitions of the Centre Pompidou (p. 273) and the **Fondation Cartier pour l'Art Contemporain** (p. 288), as well as in numerous galleries, evidence of the continuing vibrancy and creativity of the Parisian art scene.

MUSIC

EARLY MUSIC TO THE REVOLUTION. The early years of music in Paris date back to the **Gregorian chant** of 12th-century monks in Notre Dame. Early sacred music can still be heard in Paris's churches, including Notre Dame; check inside the churches and online for schedules. Other early highlights include the ballads of medieval troubadours, the Renaissance masses of **Josquin des Prez** (c. 1440-1521) and the Versailles court opera of **Jean-Baptise Lully** (1632-87). A century later, during the reign of Robespierre, Parisians rallied to the strains of revolutionary music, such as Rouget de Lisle's **War Song of the Army of the Rhine.** Composed in 1792, it was taken up with gusto by volunteers from Marseille; renamed **La Marseillaise,** it became the French national anthem in 1795.

GRAND AND COMIC OPERA. With the rise of the middle class in the early 19th century came grand opera, as well as the simpler *opéra comique.* These styles later merged and culminated in the Romantic **lyric opera,** a mix of soaring arias, exotic flavor, and tragedy; examples include **St-Saëns's** *Samson et Dalila* (1877), **Bizet's** *Carmen* (1875), and **Berlioz's** *Les Troyens* (1856-58).

ROMANTICISM TO THE BEGINNINGS OF MODERNISM. Paris served as a musical epicenter for foreign composers during the Romantic period, an 18th-century movement that influenced all types of art and shouldn't be confused with our modern use of "romantic": think of operas and orchestras, not candlelight and contraceptives. The half-French, half-Polish **Frédéric Chopin** (1810-49) started composing at the age of seven, and his mature works went on to transcend the Romantic style. In Paris, Chopin mingled with the Hungarian **Franz Liszt,** the Austrian **Félix Mendelssohn,** and the French **Hector Berlioz.**

Music at the turn of the 20th century began a new period of intense abstraction. Impressionist **Claude Débussy** (1862-1918) used tone color and nontraditional scales in his instrumental works, *Prélude à l'Après-midi d'un Faune* (1894) and *La Mer* (1905). Such technique also influenced his opera, *Pelléas et Mélisande* (1902). Meanwhile, **Maurice Ravel's** use of Spanish rhythm betrayed his Basque origins. When a listener screamed "but he is mad!" at the 1928 premiere of his Boléro, the composer retorted, "Aha! She has understood." Then along comes **Igor Stravinsky,** whose ballet, *The Rite of Spring,* caused a riot at its 1913 premiere at the **Théâtre des Champs-Elysées** (p. 318) was violently dissonant and rhythmic and effectively began the Modernist movement.

KLEIN AND NEOSERIALISM. Already famous for his monochromatic Blue paintings, **Yves Klein** presented to the world in 1960 **The Monotone Symphony:** three naked models painted a wall blue with their bodies while the artist conducted an orchestra on one note for 20 minutes. Composer **Pierre Boulez** (born 1925) was an adept student of the Neo-serialist school, which uses the 12-tone system developed in the 1920s by Austrian **Arnold Schönberg.** Always innovative, Boulez's work includes improvisational and partial compositions, but his greatest influence has been as director of the **IRCAM institute,** a research center in the **Centre Pompidou** (p. 273) dedicated to avant-garde music.

JAZZ AND CHANSONS. France recognized the artistic integrity of American jazz sooner than most Americans did. In the 1930s, French musicians copied the swing they heard on early Louis Armstrong records, but the 1934 **Club Hot** pair of violinist **Stéphane Grapelli** and stylish Belgian-Romany guitarist **Django Reinhardt** needed no help with their innovative style. After WWII, American musicians streamed into Paris. A jazz festival in 1949 brought the young **Miles Davis** across the pond for a dreamy April in the City of Love. Pianist **Bud Powell,**

drummer **Kenny Clarke,** and others stayed in Paris for the respect, dignity, and gigs that their race denied them in the United States. **Duke Ellington** and others played clubs like the Left Bank hot spot, **Le Caveau de la Huchette** (p. 329), and before long, the city's rain-slicked streets took on a saxophonic gloss.

While American standards are known and loved throughout France, the Parisian public has been happiest with the songs of crooner **Charles Aznavour** and the unforgettable **Edith Piaf,** whose *"La vie en rose"* is a cabaret classic. **Jacques Brel** and **Juliette Gréco's** popular *chansons* charmed smoky cabarets in the 1960s. Recent hit albums from **Francis Cabrel, Benjamin Biolay,** and **Isabelle Boulay** have resuscitated the genre, celebrated by the French as **Nouvelle Chanson Française.**

For those with a big travel budget (or a corporate credit card), Paris is a great place to see jazz. Nearly every type of jazz is represented here, from New Orleans to cool, acid to fusion. Brazilian samba and bossa nova are steadily growing in popularity together with music from the West Indies and Francophone Africa. Paris's jazz clubs charge either through inflated drink prices or a cover. Once you have paid your cover, you are not required to drink, though you should brace yourself for a disapproving look every time the server passes your table. You will probably not be disturbed if you choose to nurse one drink for the rest of the night. Frequent summer festivals sponsor free or nearly free jazz concerts. The **Fête du Marais** often features Big Band, while the **Villette Jazz Festival** has very big names and a few free shows (see **Festivals,** p. 97). In the fall, the **Jazz Festival of Paris** comes to town as venues open their doors to celebrity and up-and-coming artists. **Jazz Hot** (€7) and **Jazz Magazine** (€5) are great sources, as is the bimonthly LYLO (**Les Yeux, Les Oreilles;** free). *Pariscope* and *Figaroscope* (both available at any tabac) also have jazz listings.

THE ROCKSTARS. British and American rock 'n roll swept through France in the early 60s, inspiring the imitative *yéyé* craze. France's answer to Elvis was—and is to this day—**Johnny Hallyday.** France's legitimate pop icon, on the other hand, is the inimitable **Serge Gainsbourg,** a legend as famous for his public sex life and hard partying as for his commitment to musical innovation. As a musician, he bounced all over the spectrum, from rock to jazz to reggae, always astonishing fans with his newest inspiration. Gainsbourg also wrote songs for a wide range of artists, recorded his own albums, and penned more than 40 film soundtracks over the course of his career. He recorded his steamiest hit, "Je t'aime...moi non plus," with lover Brigitte Bardot in 1968, and again several months later with wife Jane Birkin. His daughter Charlotte Gainsbourg has become quite popular in recent years with a style similar to the unlikely new First Lady of the French state, Carla Bruni.

WORLD MUSIC. A vibrant music scene also emerged from the immigrant communities of the banlieue in the 80s and 90s, combining rap, hip hop, and the sounds of African, Arab, and French traditions. Cheb Khaled brought traditional Algerian raï to the mainstream dance floor with his 1996 hit, Aïcha, which remains popular over a decade later. The most well-loved French rapper throughout the 90s, MC Solaar, was born in Senegal. Some claim that the artistic output of the banlieue, including this music and its often caustic lyrics exploring the tensions of racism and ethnic identities, is where the most important and exciting possibilities for the future of French culture lie.

FILM

FRENCH CINEMA. Not long after he and his brother Louis presented the world's first paid screening in a Paris cafe in 1895, Auguste Lumière remarked,

"The cinema is a medium without a future." In defiance of this statement, the French have consistently sought to reveal the broadest possibilities of film and have always remained on the edge of celluloid innovation.

BEGINNINGS AND SURREALISM. The trick cinema of magician-turned-film-maker **Georges Méliès** astounded audiences with "disappearing" objects, but gave way by 1908 to an emphasis on narrative. At 14 minutes in length, Méliès's *Journey to the Moon* (1902) was the first motion picture to realize the story-telling possibilities of the medium. Paris was the Hollywood of the early days of cinema, dominating production worldwide. New movements in art engaged filmmakers and yielded the slapstick *Entr'acte* (1924) by **René Clair,** starring that grand-Dada of impertinence, **Marcel Duchamp.** Meanwhile, Spanish film-maker **Luis Buñuel's** *Un Chien Andalou* (1928) offered audiences a marvel of jarring associations featuring the work of **Salvador Dalí.**

THE 20S AND 30S. Although WWI allowed Hollywood to wrest celluloid domi-nance from a shattered Europe, in the 1920s and 1930s French cinema was the most critically acclaimed in the world under such great directors as **Jean Renoir,** son of the Impressionist painter. *La Grande Illusion*, which he directed in 1937, is a powerful anti-war statement, set in the POW camps of WWI. His *Les Règles du Jeu* (1939) reveals the erosion of the French bourgeoisie and his country's malaise at the doorstep of another world-altering war. The 1930s brought sound, crowned by **Jean Vigo's** *Zero for Conduct* (1933), which prefig-ured the growth of **Poetic Realism** under **Marcel Carné** and writer **Jacques Prévert** (*Daybreak*, 1939). Censorship during the Occupation led to a move from politi-cal films to nostalgia and escapist cinema. Carné and Prévert's epic *Children of Paradise* (1943-45) finds the indomitable spirit of the French in 1840s Paris.

NEW WAVE AUTHORS. **Jean Cocteau** carried the poetic into fantasy with *Beauty and the Beast* (1946) and *Orphée* (1950). The Surrealist *Beauty and the Beast* featured an early use of special effects. On the other end of the ideological spectrum, a group of young intellectuals gathered by critic **André Bazin** took issue with the "cinema of quality" that had dominated the French screen since WWII. Encouraged by government subsidies, they swapped the pen for the camera in 1959. **François Truffaut's** *The 400 Blows* and **Jean-Luc Godard's** *A Bout du Souffle* were joined the same year by **Alain Resnais's** *Hiroshima, Mon Amour* (written by Marguerite Duras) and together, the canon heralded the French New Wave *(Nouvelle Vague).* **Charles Aznavour** starred in Truffaut's *Shoot the Piano Player* (1960). Three years earlier, a star was born when **Jean Vadim** sent the incomparable **Brigitte Bardot** shimmying naked across the stage in *And God Created Woman.* Other directors of the New Wave are **Jean Rouch** (*Chronicle of a Summer*, 1961), **Louis Malle** (*The Lovers*, 1958), **Eric Rohmer** (*My Night with Maud*, 1969), **Agnès Varda** (*Cléo from 5 to 7*, 1961), and **Chris Marker** (*La Jetée*, 1962). These visionaries were unified by their interest in off-beat fiction and documentary, the fragmentation of linear time, and the thrill of youth. Their fascination with speed, cars, noise, and Hitchcock and Lang's films garnered them infinite popularity with teens and twentysomethings of the era.

NEW CLASSICS. The world impact of French cinema in the 60s led to wider recognition of French film stars in the 70s and 80s. The stunning **Catherine Deneuve, Gerard Depardieu,** and, more recently, **Juliette Binoche** and **Julie Delpy** have become faces almost as famous worldwide as they are in Paris. **Jean-Jacques Beineix's** *Betty Blue* (1985), **Louis Malle's** *Au Revoir les Enfants* (1987), **Marc Caro** and **Jean-Pierre Jeunet's** dystopic *Delicatessen* (1991), and Polish **Krzysztof Kieslowski's** three colors trilogy, *Blue* (1993), *White* (1994), and *Red* (1994) have all become classics of 20th-century French cinema. Explicitly artistic cinema now prospers under **Marcel Hanoun** (*Bruit d'Amour et de Guerre*, 1997) and **Jacques Doillon** (*Ponette*, 1997). A group of incendiary young directors like **Gaspar Noe** (*Irreversible*, 2003), **Catherine Breillat** (*Romance*, 1999), and **Claire Denis** (*Trouble Every Day*, 2002) have stirred controversy in their attempts to blur the boundaries between pornography and art while exploring heavy themes and proving that the French tradition of embracing content and technique far too provocative for Hollywood is alive and well. In 2001 **Jean-Pierre Feunet's** international hit *Le Fabuleux Destin d'Amélie Poulain* was the highest grossing film of the decade in France and a rare example of a French foreign film going mainstream in American markets.

SPORTS AND RECREATION

There are really only two sports of any importance in France: football and cycling. The others are just pleasant diversions.

FOOTBALL

The French take *le foot* very seriously. Their national team, **Les Bleus,** emerged in the late 90s from a half-century of mediocrity to perform spectacularly in recent years. They captured the 1998 World Cup, schooling perennial favorite Brazil 3-0 in the newly built Stade de France, outside Paris. The victory ignited celebrations from the Champs-Élysées to the Pyrénées. In the 2000 European Championship, Les Bleus took the trophy in an upset against Italy, and in the 2001 **Coupe des Confédérations,** France completed the Triple Crown of football. The charismatic star of the team, **Zinedine Zidane,** has attained a hero status second only to de Gaulle. The son of an Algerian immigrant, "Zizou" has helped unite a country divided by tension over immigration. Sadly, France failed to make it past the qualifying round of the 2002 Cup Mondiale, finishing even behind Uruguay. So shocking was the failure that President Chirac issued a message of condolence. This left the French eagerly awaiting their team's next shot at glory in the 2004 European Cup, but much to fans' disappointment they fell to Greece in the quarterfinals. In 2006, the team came close to winning the World Cup, but the season ultimately distinguished itself to fans everywhere for Zidane's excruciating **headbutt** to Italian player Marco Materazzi during their July 8th game. Zidane refused to apologize for his actions, citing a racist remark by Materazzi as his provocation. Despite the fiasco, he remains a French football hero. Most recently, the French had a disappointing showing at the 2008 European Cup, losing in the opening rounds of the tournament.

CYCLING

Cycling is another national obsession with an equally ardent following. France annually hosts the only cycling event anyone can name: the grueling three-week, 3500km **Tour de France,** which celebrated its 100-year anniversary in 2003. Unfortunately, competitors from the host country have not fared well in the competition lately, as American Lance Armstrong has triumphed over the rest of the field to capture the last seven championships.

OTHER ACTIVITIES

For those who prefer a bit less exertion, the game of **pétanque,** once dominated by old men, has been gaining popularity in younger age brackets. The basic premise of *pétanque*, also known as *boules* or bocce, is to throw a large metal ball as close as possible to a small metal ball. Old men playing pickup games of *pétanque* is a common sight in the parks around Paris.

Despite the objections of French traditionalists, sports from other continents are also gaining a foothold in France, particularly rugby, golf, basketball, and even the heresy that is American football.

CULTURE

America is like your mother—you go there for comfort, and for money. France is like your mistress—you go there for pleasure!
—Jean-Paul Jannot

FOOD AND DRINK

A BRIEF HISTORY. In the 16th century, Catherine de Médicis, disgusted with bland and dull French dishes, imported master chefs from her native Florence to spice things up. They taught the French to appreciate the finer aspects of sauces and seasonings, a culinary development elaborated upon by the great 19th-century chef **Antoine Carême,** acknowledged as the father of haute cuisine, the elegantly prepared foods now thought of as typically "French." He and others such as **George August Escoffier** made fine food an essential art of civilized life, and much of their wisdom on sauces and glazes is collected in the voluminous **Larousse Gastronomique,** a standard reference for French chefs today. The style made famous in the US by **Julia Child** is *cuisine bourgeoise,* quality home-cooking. A glance through her *Mastering the Art of French Cooking I & II* will give you ideas for dishes to try in France. Trendy and health-conscious nouvelle cuisine—tiny portions of delicately cooked, artfully arranged ingredients with light sauces—was made popular in the 1970s by the celebrated **Paul Bocuse.** Immigrant communities have shaken up the traditional French culinary scene: in addition to ubiquitous Greek gyros, there are outstanding Moroccan, Algerian, Tunisian, Senegalese, Ivorian, and Caribbean restaurants in Paris. Chinese, Thai, Vietnamese, Cambodian, Korean, Tibetan, Japanese, Indian, and Pakistani restaurants, especially in Chinatown in the 13*ème,* have brought vegetarian options to the traditionally meat-heavy Paris dining experience.

MEALTIMES. *Le petit déjeuner* (breakfast) is usually light, consisting of bread, croissants, or *brioches* (buttery breads) with jam and butter, plus an espresso with hot milk or cream (*café au lait* or the more trendy *café crème*) or a hot chocolate (*chocolat chaud,* often served in a bowl). *Le déjeuner* (lunch) is served between noon and 2:30pm, although some cafes and restaurants in tourist areas stay open throughout the day. Restaurants are most crowded from 1-3pm, when much of Paris takes a lengthy lunch break. During lunch, some shops, businesses, and government offices close; linger over a 2hr. lunch a few times and you'll be hooked too.

Le dîner (dinner) begins quite late. Most restaurants start at 7pm, but business really picks up around 8-9pm. Showing up at opening will make you feel like an awkward loser who punctually arrives before all other guests at a party held by an acquaintance and then must talk to the host with whom he has nothing in common. A complete French dinner includes an *apéritif,* an *entrée* (appetizer), a *plat* (main course), salad, cheese, dessert, fruit, *café,* and a *digestif* (after-dinner drink, typically a cognac or other brandy). However, the large majority of French diners content themselves with a three-course meal or less. Most Parisians drink wine with dinner.

HOW TO ORDER. Greet your server politely by looking him or her in the eye and saying, *"Bonjour."* In the evening, bring out your smoothest *"Bonsoir."* Starting your dining experience without a friendly greeting is considered impolite; the French are very polite to waiters, and visitors would do well to follow their lead. Without being obnoxious, try your best to speak French; the waiter will speak English—it's Paris—but he'll also appreciate the gesture. It is uncommon for French diners to split dishes or to take home any unfinished food. At the meal's end the bill will rarely come without your requesting it, so simply say *"L'addition, s'il vous plaît"* when you are ready to pay.

THE MENU. Most restaurants offer *un menu à prix fixe* (fixed-price meal) that is less expensive than ordering à la carte (when you pick individual items out). Lunch *menus* are often cheaper than dinner *menus*—if there is a pricier restaurant that you particularly want to try, consider going for lunch. A menu will usually include an appetizer *(entrée)*, a main course *(plat)*, cheese *(fromage)*, or dessert—or a choice of two or three of these options. Some also include wine or coffee. For lighter fare, try a *brasserie*, which has a fuller menu than a cafe but is more casual than a restaurant.

DRINKS. Sparkling water *(eau pétillante* or *eau gazeuse)* and flat mineral water *(eau plate)* are available in all restaurants, though you may have to ask for them. Ice cubes *(glaçons)* won't come with your drink; you'll have to ask for them if you can't live without them. To order a (usually free) jug of tap water for the table, ask for *"une carafe d'eau."* It is common to drink a sweet alcoholic *apéritif* before a nice meal; popular options include *kir,* a blend of white wine and cassis (black currant liqueur); *kir royale* (with champagne instead of wine); *pastis,* a licorice liqueur; *suze,* made from fermented *gentiane* (a sweet-smelling mountain flower that yields a wickedly bitter brew); *picon-bière,* beer mixed with a sweet liqueur; and the classic martini. During the meal, the only socially acceptable drinks are water and wine. Soda, beer, juice, and all other potable liquids that are not water or wine are forbidden under pentaly of shunning; if a restaurant offers these with your meal, it's a good sign that you're chowing down at a tourist trap. Finish the meal with an espresso *(un café),* which comes in lethal little cups with blocks of sugar. *Café au lait* and *café crème* are generally considered breakfast drinks, so if you prefer your afternoon coffee with milk, try a *noisette,* which is espresso with just a dash of milk. When *boisson compris* is written on the menu, you will receive a free drink (most often wine) with the meal.

WINE

In France wine is not a luxury; it is a necessity. The first French citizen to orbit the Earth brought along the indispensable beverage with him.

WINE-PRODUCING REGIONS. Wines from all over France can be purchased in supermarkets, specialty stores, and restaurants. The **Loire Valley** of France produces a number of whites, with the major vineyards at Angers, Chinon, Saumur, Anjou, Tours, and Sancerre. **Cognac,** farther south on the Atlantic coast, is famous for the double-distilled spirit of the same name. Centered on the Dordogne and Garonne Rivers, the classic **Bordeaux** region produces red and white Pomerol, Graves, and sweet Sauternes. The spirit armagnac, similar to cognac, comes from **Gascony,** while Jurançon wines come from vineyards higher up the slopes of the Pyrénées. Southern wines include those of **Langue-doc** and **Roussillon** on the coast and Limoux and Gaillac inland. The vineyards of **Provence** on the coast near Toulon are recognized for their rosés. The **Côtes du Rhône** from Valence to Lyon in the Rhône Valley are home to some of the most celebrated wines produced in France, including Beaujolais. **Burgundy** is especially renowned for its reds, from the wines of Chablis and the Côte d'Or in the north to the Mâconnais in the south. The white wines produced in **Alsace** tend to be much spicier and more pungent than others. Many areas of France produce sparkling wines, but the only one that can legally be called champagne is distilled in the **Champagne** region of the country, surrounding Reims.

SELECTING WINE. There are wines for every occasion and every type of meal, with pairings dictated by draconian rules. These rules, however, are not as hard and fast as they once were, so don't worry too much about them—go with your gut. White wines are lighter, drier, and fruitier. They go well with fish, chicken, and salads and many of the white dessert wines, like Barsac, Sauternes, or Coteaux du Layon, are great with fruit. Red wines tend to be heavier, more fragrant, and considerably older, but can overwhelm foods with gentler tastes. Red meat and red wine is a fine and common combination. Rosés are an excellent compromise between the two extremes and are becoming more popular, particularly during lunch. When confused about which wine to choose, just ask. Most waiters in restaurants and employees in wine shops will be more than happy to recommend their favorites to you. Or, fall back on the *vin de maison* (house wine), served in pitchers at reduced prices.

FOOD SHOPS AND MARKETS

WHERE TO BUY. A **charcuterie** is the French version of a delicatessen, and a **boucherie** has meat and poultry. A **crémerie** sells dairy products, and the corner **fromagerie** may stock over 100 kinds of cheese. **Boulangeries** will supply you with your daily bread—they're best visited in the early morning or right before mealtimes, when the baguettes are steaming hot. **Pâtisseries** sell pastries, and **confiseries** sell candy; both often have ice cream as well. You can buy your produce at a **primeur**, and prepared foods at a **traiteur**. **Épiceries** (grocery stores) have staples, wine, and produce. A *marché*, an open-air market, is the best place to buy fresh produce, fish, and meat. You can grab any simple food items, cigarettes, and lotto tickets at a corner **alimentation** (convenience store).

Supermarchés (supermarkets) are, of course, cheaper but lack the some of class, enjoyment, and selection of specialty shops. Do capitalize on the one-stop shopping at the **Monoprix** and **Prisunics** that litter the city. They carry men's and women's clothing and have photocopiers, telephone cards, and a supermarket. See **Study Abroad,** p. 117, and **Food,** p. 165 for more info.

MARKETS. In the 5th century, ancient Lutèce held the first market on Île de la Cité. More than a millennium and a half later, markets exude conviviality and neighborliness in every *arrondissement*, despite the ongoing growth of the *supermarché*. Most are open two to six days per week (always on Sunday). The freshest products are often sold by noon when many stalls start to close. Quality and price can vary significantly from one stall to the next, making it a good idea to stroll through the entire market before buying. See **Food,** p. 180.

SALONS DE THÉ. Parisian *salons de thé* (tea rooms) fall into three categories: stately salons that give off that tycoon-in-a-tux-with-a-mustache vibe, Seattle-style joints for pseudo-intellectuals, and cafes that simply want to signal that they also serve tea. For *salon de thé* culture at its best, enjoy delicate sandwiches and pastries at Sunday brunch—but be sure to reserve ahead, as lines often stretch out the door at the larger salons. See **Food,** p. 177.

ETIQUETTE

BLENDING IN. It's a good rule of thumb in Paris (and anywhere, really) to avoid fitting the stereotype of the tourist. The more of an effort that you make to blend in, the better your Parisian experience will be. For dress, what may look perfectly innocuous in your hometown might mark you out instantly in Paris. The French are known for their conservative stylishness: go for restrained sneakers or closed-toe shoes, solid-color pants or jeans, and plain T-shirts or button-down shirts, rather than Teva sandals, baggy pants, or cutoffs. Parisians rarely wear shorts, even in warm weather. Trying to blend in is also great excuse to shop for French clothes. If you're traveling in January or August, be sure to take advantage of massive sales *(les soldes)*—prices are often slashed as much as 75%. See Shopping, p. 297.

CHURCHES. "Cutoff," "tight," "short," "bare-shouldered," "sloppy," and "dirty" should not enter into your vocabulary for church-going clothes. Do not walk into the middle of a mass or other service unless you plan to give an impromptu homily. Do not take flash photographs or walk directly in front of the altar. Particularly at Notre Dame, which holds frequent services and is a common pilgrimage site, be considerate of those worshipping; like all churches, mosques, and synagogues, it is a house of prayer first and a tourist hotspot second.

ÉTAGES. In French, the ground floor is called the *rez-de-chaussée;* numbers begin with the first floor above the ground floor *(premier étage)*. In an elevator or call-box, the button labeled "R" (not "1") is typically the ground floor.

GREETINGS AND SALUTATIONS. Although customer service in Paris is more brusque than in the US and the UK, the French consider polite greetings to be essential. Say *"Bonjour, madame/monsieur"* when entering an establishment and *"bonne journée, au revoir"* when leaving. If you bump into someone on the street or the metro, it is polite to say *"pardon"*. The proper way to answer the telephone is *"âllo,"* but people greet each other that way in person.

HOURS. Most restaurants open at noon for lunch and then close for some portion of the afternoon before re-opening for dinner, while some bistros and most cafes remain open all afternoon. Small businesses, as well as banks and post offices, close for "lunch," which often lasts for two or three hours.

LANGUAGE. Even if your French is near-perfect, waiters and salespeople who detect the slightest accent will often respond in English (thereby Englishing you). This can be frustrating, especially if you came to Paris to practice your French, or if the Parisian in question speaks poor English. If your language skills are good, continue to speak in French. More often than not, they will both respect and appreciate your fortitude, and speak to you, in turn, in French.

POCKET CHANGE. Cashiers and tellers will often ask, "Avez-vous de la monnaie?" (Do you have change?) as they would rather not break your €20 note for a pack of gum. If you don't, say *"Non, désolée,"* and suffer the nasty look.

POLITESSE. Parisians are polite, especially to older people. In Paris, the difference between getting good and bad service is often the difference between a little *politesse* and disregard. Tone and facial expressions are important. Main-

LIFE AND TIMES

tain composure and act like you mean business; speak softly and politely (do employ the standard *"monsieur/madame"* and *"s'il vous plaît"*) to Parisians in official positions, especially if they are older than you.

PUBLIC RESTROOMS. The streetside public restrooms *(pissoirs)* in Paris are worth the €0.30 they require. These magic machines are self-cleaning after each use, so you're guaranteed a clean restroom. Toilets in train stations, major metro stops, and public gardens are tended to by *gardiens* and generally cost €0.40. Most cafes reserve restrooms for their clients only.

SERVICE. There is no assumption in Paris that "the customer is always right," and complaining to managers about poor service is rarely worth your while. Your best bet is to take your business elsewhere. When engaged in any official process (i.e., opening a bank account, purchasing insurance, etc.), don't fret if you get shuffled from one desk to another. Patiently explain your situation as many times as necessary, and you'll probably get the service you need.

SMOKING. The era of cafes foggy with tobacco smoke and smiled-at non-smoking sections in restaurants have passed. There was a time when after a night out a traveler would swear that the smoke had seeped through his pores, past his lungs, and into the very darkest depths of his soul. However on January 1, 2008, the ban on smoking in public passed in February of 2007 went into effect for places where people actually smoke, though the enforcement on New Year's was generously merciful. The ban is now enforced strictly, and fines for non-compliance are stiff. Suprisingly, the ban enjoys majority support, and while smokers have complained (in classic French fashion), many appreciate all the new opportunities to make friends as smokers huddle together on bar porches to smoke together in those chilly Parisian winters.

SUNDAY. Paris (non-Marais Paris, at least) appears to shut down entirely on Sundays. Minimarkets, supermarkets, shops, and restaurants will generally be closed, though some services may be available in the morning. Do as Parisians do and head for open-air markets to pack a picnic; or do as Parisians don't do and head to mass. Many establishments and most museums are closed on Mondays, and other hours vary: calling ahead is always a good idea.

TIPPING. Service is usually included in meal prices in restaurants and cafes, and in drink prices at bars; look for *service compris* on the menu, or just ask. If service is not included, tip 15-20%. If you're exceptionally pleased with the service at a cafe, bistro, restaurant, or bar, leave a *pourboire* of a euro or two. Tip your hairdresser well; do not tip taxis more than 15% of the metered charge.

MEDIA

TELEVISION AND RADIO

French television is notoriously bad. **TF1** is the most popular station in France. The public channel **ARTE** appeals to more intellectual tastes. **Cable TV** is also available; the pay channel **Canal Plus** shows recent films and live sporting events. TV guides are the most popular publications in France, with **Télé 7 jours** leading the pack. Second in line is **Télérama,** which provides commentary not only on TV but also on culture in general. French radio went commercial in 1984, although the success of large conglomerates means that few stations remain independent. National stations include **Fun Radio** for teens; **RTL2**, a pop rock station; **Skyrock,** a noisy and provocative rock station; and **Nostalgie,** an adult-oriented station with quiz shows and easy-listening music. **Radio FG,** once Paris's queer wavelength, has become the city's primary source for house, techno, dance, and R&B. Public stations include **France-Inter**—a quality general interest station—and **France Info,** an all-news station.

NEWSPAPERS AND OTHER PUBLICATIONS

NEWSPAPERS. The French are bombarded with views from many newspapers (and the various political factions that they represent). On the left are **Libéra-tion** (€1.20), a socialist newspaper that offers comprehensive news coverage of world events, and **L'Humanité** (€1.20), produced by the communist party. More to the middle (though sometimes with a socialist streak) is the widely read **Le Monde** (€1.30), which offers especially thorough political coverage. To the right are **Le Figaro** (€1.20) and **La Tribune,** the latter of which is France's version of the *Wall Street Journal*, providing international financial coverage.

MAGAZINES. Le Nouvel Observateur (€3) proffers an inquisitive take on French culture and society; **L'Express** (€2.30) is a weekly publication similar to *Time* magazine, with coverage of national and international news; **Marianne** (€2.50) resembles a French *Vanity Fair*, filled with gossip and world news; **Tetu** (€5) has the latest in queer politics and events; and **Technikart** (€4.90) is for the Parisian hipster. **Paris Match** (€2.40) dishes up the latest dirt on European royals and socialites as well as internationally known celebrities. For the best selection of English-language magazines, as well as copies of the Sunday edition of the *New York Times* (after noon on Mondays) try **W.H. Smith** (see **Shopping,** p. 300). Of course, if you are after cultural listings and reviews, you need only venture as far as the nearest *tabac*, as all carry the vital publications.

GOINGS-ON. Pariscope (€0.40) and **Officiel des Spectacles** (€0.35), both published Wednesdays, have the most comprehensive listings of movies, plays, exhibits, festivals, clubs, and bars. *Pariscope* may well be worth the extra €0.05; it has an English-language section called **Time Out Paris** and an easy-to-use (free) online counterpart at www.pariscope.fr. Also free is the tourist office monthly **Where: Paris,** which highlights exhibits, concerts, walking tours, and events, and the *Mairie de Paris*'s monthly **Paris le Journal,** which has articles about what's going on around the city. For other listings, check **Figaroscope,** a Wednesday supplement to Le Figaro, which lists happenings about Paris; **Free Voice,** a monthly English-language newspaper published by the American Church; and the bi-weekly **France-USA Contacts (FUSAC)** both of which provide job and housing listings, as well as general information for English speakers and are available for free from English-speaking bookstores, restaurants, and travel agencies throughout Paris.

FESTIVALS

For information on festivals, the **Paris Tourist Office** (see p. 135) has a home page (www.paris-touristoffice.com) and a pricey info line (☎08 92 68 30 00). You can also get a listing of festivals before you leave home by writing the French Government Tourist Office. We list our favorite festivals below. This isn't all of them—just the ones that promise to keep you fat, happy, or drunk (or all three). Be sure to check listings in Time Out and Pariscope (€0.40 at any news-stand) a week or more ahead of time for updates and details on all events.

SPRING

Foire du Trône, Apr.-May (☎01 46 27 52 29; www.foiredutrone.com). ⓜPorte Dorée. On Reuilly Lawn, Bois de Vincennes, 12ème. A 1063-year-old fair complete with carnival rides (€2-5), barbe à papa (cotton candy), and a freak show. Free navette (shuttle) from Nation to Pelouse de Reuilly. Open M-F and Su noon-midnight, Sa noon-1am.

Portes Ouvertes des Ateliers d'Artistes, May-June. Call tourist office or check Pariscope for details. For selected days during the year, each quartier's resident artists open their workshops to the public; the majority of expositions are in the 13ème.

SUMMER

▨ **Bastille Day (Fête Nationale),** July 14. France's independence day. Festivities begin the night before, with traditional street dances at the tip of Île St-Louis. The free *Bals des Pompiers* (Firemen's Balls) take place inside every Parisian fire station the night of July 13 and/or 14th from 9pm-4am, with DJs, bands, and cheap alcohol (€5). These balls are the best of Paris's Bastille Day celebrations. The fire stations on rue Blanche, bd. du Port-Royal, rue des Vieux-Colombiers, and the Gay Ball near quai de la Tournelle in the 5ème are probably your best bets. For information on the Bals, call the **Sapeurs Pompiers** (☎01 47 54 68 22) or visit them at 1 pl. Jules Renard in the 17ème. There is dancing at pl. de la Bastille with a concert, but be careful as young kids sometimes throw fireworks into the crowd. July 14 begins with the army parading down the Champs-Élysées at 10:30am (be prepared to get in place by 8 or 9am) and ends with fireworks at 10:30-11pm. The fireworks can be seen from any bridge on the Seine or from the Champs de Mars (get there as early as 3-4hr. beforehand to snag a decent spot). Be aware that for the parade and fireworks the metro stations along the Champs and at the Trocadéro are closed. Groups also gather in the 19ème and 20ème (especially in the Parc de Belleville) where the hilly topography allows a long-distance view to the Trocadéro. Unfortunately, the entire city also becomes a nightmarish combat zone with firecrackers underfoot; avoid the metro and deserted areas if possible. Vive la France!

▨ **Gay Pride,** last Sa in June (www.gaypride.fr). For additional information on dates and events, call the Centre Gai et Lesbien (☎01 43 57 21 47), Le Duplex bar (☎01 42 72 80 86), or Les Mots à la Bouche bookstore (☎01 42 78 88 30; www.motsbouche. com). Or check bars and cafes in the Marais for posters.

▨ **Fête de la Musique,** June 21 (☎01 40 03 94 70). Also called "Faites de la Musique" ("Make Music"), this summer solstice celebration gives everyone the chance to make as much racket as possible, as Paris's usual noise laws don't apply for the duration of the festival. The metro runs all night to transport tired revelers home.

▨ **Fête du Cinéma,** late June (www.feteducinema.com). Started in 1984, this festival aims to bring cheaper movies to all Parisians. Purchase 1 ticket at regular movie price (€6-8) and receive a passport for unlimited showings (during the 3-day festival) of participating films for €2 each. Arrive early for popular favorites, and expect long lines. Full listings of movies and events can be found online, at theaters, or in metro advertisements. Don't miss this opportunity to join the millions of movie-goers who relish the blockbusters, the indie flicks, the imports, and the ever-enduring classics that make the Parisian cinema scene one of the most diverse and enjoyable in the world.

■ **Paris Plages,** late July to late Aug. (☎08 20 00 75 75; www.paris.fr). For 4 weeks at the end of the summer, the banks of the Seine are decked out like St. Tropez, with white sand, deck chairs, cabanas, and swimming pools.

■ **Le Festival de Cinema en Plein Air,** early July to mid-Aug. (www.cinema.arbo.com). ⓂPorte de Pantin. At the Parc de la Villette. Families, couples, and large groups lounge on the grass and enjoy some of the greatest movies ever made. A limited number of lounge chairs are provided, so many people bring their own picnic blankets. Films start at nightfall—usually around 10:30pm—but arrive early to get a good spot on the grass.

Grandes Eaux Musicales de Versailles, early Apr. to early Oct. (info ☎01 30 83 78 88, tickets 01 30 83 78 89; www.chateauversailles-spectacles.fr). RER C7. Outdoor concerts of period music and fountain displays every Sa and Su at Parc du Château de Versailles. A magical event that displays Versailles's storied gardens in all their excess and glory. Tickets €7, concessions €5.50, under 10 free. For reservations through FNAC, call ☎08 92 68 36 22 or go to www.fnac.com.

Paris Jazz Festival, June-July (☎01 43 41 16 26; www.parcfloraldeparis.com). Excellent jazz artists from Europe and beyond play every Sa and Su afternoon in the Parc Floral. The park holds several other festivals throughout the summer, including children's theater events and classical concerts. All shows free with €3 park entrance, under 25 €1.50, under 7 free. Schedules at the tourist office and in Pariscope.

Festival Chopin, mid-June to mid-July (☎01 45 00 22 19; www.frederic-chopin.com). Route de la Reine Marguerite. From ⓂPorte Maillot, take bus #244 to Pré Catelan, stop #12. Concerts and recitals held at the Orangerie du Parc de Bagatelle in the Bois de Boulogne. Not all Chopin, but all piano, arranged each year around a different aspect of the master's oeuvre. Prices vary: €17-34, concessions only for afternoon concerts.

Feux de la St-Jean Baptiste (Fête Nationale du Québec), June 24 (☎01 45 08 55 61 or 01 45 08 55 25). Magnificent fireworks in the Jardin de Tino Rossi at quai St-Bernard, 5ème, honoring the Feast of St. John the Baptist. Sacré-Coeur offers a spectacular bird's-eye view. The festival also includes an elaborate display at the Canal de l'Ourcq in the Parc de la Villette. In addition, Québec's National Holiday is celebrated by Paris's Québecois community with dancing, *drapeaux fleurs-de-lys,* and music at various spots throughout Paris, including: the Délégation Générale du Québec, 66 rue Pergolèse, 16ème (☎01 40 67 85 00); the Association Paris-Québec, 5, r. de la Boule Rouge, 9ème; and the Centre Culturel Québécois, 5 rue de Constantine, 7ème (ⓂInvalides).

Fête des Tuileries, late June to late Aug. (☎01 20 00 75 75). ⓂTuileries. A large, spunky fair held on the terrace of the Jardin des Tuileries. The huge ferris wheel with views of nighttime Paris offers decisive proof that the carnival ethos is the same the world over. A mix of tame rides suitable for children and even some high-speed ones for thrill-seekers. The festival also manages to fit a water-*flume* ride in the Jardin des Tuileries. Open M-Th 11am-midnight, F-Sa 11am-1am. Free entrance; ferris wheel €5, under 10 €3.

POP GOES THE TOURIST. Commemorating the pivotal moment when enraged Parisians' stormed the king's armory, Bastille Day still ignites citizens's fierce pride and mob mentality. While the largest crowds celebrate benignly, firecrackers exploding underfoot turn the entire city into a mini-combat zone; avoid the Metro and deserted areas if possible.

Paris, Quartier d'Été, mid-July to mid-Aug. (☎01 44 94 98 00; www.quartierdete.com). This city-wide festival features dance, music from around the world, and a giant parade. Locations vary, but many events are held in the Jardin des Tuileries, Grand Palais, and Parc de la Villette. This is one of Paris's largest festivals and includes both world-class (i.e., international ballet companies and top-10 rock bands) and local artists, musicians, and performers. Prices vary, but much is free. Brochures at the tourist office.

Tour de France, enters Paris the 3rd or 4th Su in July (☎01 41 33 15 00; www.letour.fr). The Tour de France, the world's premier long-distance bicycling event, ends in Paris and thousands turn out at the finish line to see who will win the chemise d'or. Expect huge crowds at pl. de la Concorde as well as along the av. des Champs-Élysées.

Cinema au Clair de Lune, first 3 weeks in Aug. (☎01 44 76 63 00; www.clairdelune. forumdesimages.net). Classic French films projected on a giant screen that moves all over Paris, from the Hôtel de Ville to the Parc Choisy. Shows start around 9:30pm. Free.

FALL

☒ Jazz à la Villette, early Sept. (☎01 40 03 75 75 or 01 44 84 44 84; www.villette. com). Ⓜ Porte de Pantin. At Parc de la Villette. A week-long celebration of jazz from big bands to new international talents, as well as seminars, films, and sculptural exhibits. Past performers have included Herbie Hancock, Ravi Coltrane, Taj Mahal, and B.B. King. Marching bands parade every day, and an enormous picnic closes the festival. Concerts €18, under 26 €15. For reduced price tickets, you must call ahead.

Fête de l'Humanité, 2nd weekend of Sept. (☎01 49 22 73 86; www.humanite.fr). At the Parc de la Courneuve. Take the metro to Porte de la Villette and then bus #177 or one of the buses reserved especially for the festival. The annual fair of the French Communist Party. Charles Mingus, Marcel Marceau, the Bolshoi Ballet, and radical theater troupes have appeared. 3-day pass €15, under 12 free.

Festival d'Automne, Sept. 14-Dec. 19 (☎01 53 45 17 17; www.festival-automne. com). Notoriously highbrow and avant-garde drama, ballet, cinema, and music arranged around a different theme each year. Many events held at the Théâtre du Châtelet, 1er; the Théâtre de la Ville, 4ème; even some in the auditorium of the Louvre and in the Centre Pompidou. Ticket prices vary according to venue.

Journées du Patrimoine, 3rd weekend of Sept. (☎01 40 15 37 37; www.journeesdupatrimoine.culture.fr). The few days each year when certain ministries, monuments, and palaces are opened to the public. The Hôtel de Ville should be on your list, as well as the Palais de l'Élysée and the Palais Luxembourg. Offerings vary from year to year; check with the tourist office 2-3 days in advance. Free.

Fête des Vendanges de Montmartre, 2nd weekend in Oct. R. des Saules, 18ème (☎01 46 06 00 32; www.fetedesvendangesdemontmartre.com). Ⓜ Lamarck-Caulaincourt. A celebration of the harvest from Montmartre's vineyards. Folk songs, parades, and the picking and stomping of grapes. Much wine is consumed.

WINTER

Christmas (Noël), Dec. 24-25. At midnight on Christmas Eve, Notre Dame becomes what it only claims to be the rest of the year: the cathedral of the city of Paris. Midnight mass is celebrated with pomp and incense. Get there early to ensure yourself a seat. Christmas Eve is more important than Christmas Day in France. Families gather to exchange gifts and eat Christmas food, including *bûche de Noël* (Yule Log), a rich chocolate cake with heavy cream. During Advent, the city illuminates the major boulevards with holiday lights and decorations. A huge *crèche* (nativity scene) is displayed on pl. Hôtel-de-Ville. Restaurants offer Christmas specialties and special *menus*.

New Year's Eve and Day, Dec. 31-Jan. 1. Young punks and tons of tourists form throngs on the Champs-Élysées to set off fireworks, while restaurants host pricey evenings of foie gras and champagne galore. On New Year's Day, there is a parade with floats and dolled-up dames from pl. Pigalle to pl. Jules-Joffrin.

NATIONAL HOLIDAYS

When a holiday falls on Tuesday or Thursday, the French often take Monday or Friday off, which is known as *faire le pont* (to make a bridge). Banks and public offices close at noon on the nearest working day before a public holiday.

DATE	HOLIDAY (FRENCH)	HOLIDAY (ENGLISH)
January 1	Le Jour de l'An	New Year's Day
March 28	Le Lundi de Pâques	Easter Monday
May 1	La Fête du Travail	Labor Day
May 5	L'Ascension	Ascension Day
May 8	L'Anniversaire de la Libération	Anniversary of the Liberation of Europe
May 16	Le Lundi de Pentecôte	Whit Monday
July 14	La Fête Nationale	Bastille Day
August 15	L'Assomption	Feast of the Assumption
November 1	La Toussaint	All Saints' Day
November 11	L'Armistice 1918	Armistice Day
December 25	Le Noël	Christmas

LIFE AND TIMES

BEYOND TOURISM

A PHILOSOPHY FOR TRAVELERS

HIGHLIGHTS OF BEYOND TOURISM IN PARIS

TEACH French inmates how to dance, act, and paint (p. 106).

STUDY in the historic halls of the Sorbonne, France's oldest university (p. 110).

FLAMBÉ like the French and take cooking classes with a master chef (p. 111).

HELP needy families in Paris and beyond with the Action Contre la Faim (p. 105).

As a tourist, you are always a foreigner. Sure, hostel-hopping and sightseeing can be great fun, but connecting with a foreign country through studying, volunteering, or working can extend your travels beyond tourist traps. This is what's different about a *Let's Go* traveler—instead of feeling like a stranger in a strange land, you can understand Paris like a local. Instead of being that tourist asking for directions, you can be the one who gives them (and correctly!). All the while, you get the satisfaction of leaving Paris in better shape than you found it. It's not wishful thinking—it's Beyond Tourism.

As a **volunteer** in Paris, you can unleash your inner superhero, with projects that range from tutoring inmates to combating AIDS. This chapter is chock-full of ideas to get involved, whether you're looking to pitch in for a day or run away from home for a whole new life in French activism.

Whether through direct enrollment in a local university or an independent research project, **studying abroad** can be very fulfilling: it actually makes you feel sorry for those poor tourists who don't get to do any homework while they're here. Paris is home to some of the world's oldest universities—including *la Sorbonne*, founded in AD 1257—that are renowned for their programs in philosophy, literature, political science, and art history. If existentialism isn't your *tasse de thé*, France's distinguished array of culinary schools—including the world-famous *Cordon Bleu* in Paris—will refine your broiling abilities, and your palate. The study abroad opportunities in Paris are limitless, and the perfect way to indulge in French life.

Working abroad immerses you in a new culture and can bring some of the most meaningful relationships and experiences of your life. Yes, we know you're on vacation, but these aren't your normal desk jobs. (Plus, it doesn't hurt that it helps pay for more globetrotting.) Many travelers structure their trips around the work available to them along the way, and employment opportunities range from odd jobs on-the-go to full-time, long-term work. While such long-term work is tough to find for non-EU citizens without professional expertise, English and especially English-French bilingual skills are desirable and can facilitate the job search. Short-term work is more readily available and can range from working with children to busing tables at a street-side cafe. Both long-term and short-term jobs require a work permit, which is discussed in detail in the upcoming sections.

 SHARE YOUR EXPERIENCE. Have you had a particularly enjoyable volunteer, study, or work experience that you'd like to share with other travelers? Post it to our website, www.letsgo.com!

BEYOND TOURISM

VOLUNTEERING

Let's Go believes that travelers can have a positive influence on the natural and cultural environments they visit. Hostel-hopping and sightseeing can be great fun, but you may want to consider going Beyond Tourism. Volunteering can be a powerful and fulfilling experience, especially when combined with the thrill of traveling or living in a new place. Though Paris is considered wealthy by Western standards, there is no shortage of aid organizations that address the social issues France faces, and short-term volunteering positions are also abundant. Paris offers something to fit every volunteering preference, whether it is to work with the elderly, to advocate for the environment and work for wildlife conservation, or to aid needy families in the city.

Most people who volunteer in Paris do so on a short-term basis at organizations that make use of drop-in or once-a-week volunteers. The best way to find opportunities that match your interests and schedule may be to check with local or national volunteer centers listed below. The most common short-term volunteer activities include community groups that work with the disadvantaged, environmental protection efforts, and work camps that help restore Paris's historical monuments. As always, read up before heading out.

Those looking for longer, more intensive volunteer opportunities usually choose to go through a parent organization that takes care of logistical details and often provides a group environment and support system—for a fee. There are two main types of organizations—religious and secular—although there are rarely restrictions on participation for either. Websites like **www.volunteerabroad.com**, **www.servenet.org**, and **www.idealist.org** allow you to search for volunteer openings both in your country and abroad.

I HAVE TO PAY TO VOLUNTEER? Many volunteers are surprised to learn that some organizations require large fees or "donations," but don't go calling them scams just yet. While such fees may seem ridiculous at first, they often keep the organization afloat, covering airfare, room, board, and administrative expenses for the volunteers. (Other organizations must rely on private donations and government subsidies.) If you're concerned about how a program spends its fees, request an annual report or finance account. A reputable organization won't refuse to inform you of how volunteer money is spent. Pay-to-volunteer programs might be a good idea for young travelers who are looking for more support and structure (such as pre-arranged transportation and housing) or anyone who would rather not deal with the uncertainty of creating a volunteer experience from scratch.

GENERAL VOLUNTEER ORGANIZATIONS

Care France, CAP 19, 13 rue de Georges Auric, 75019 Paris (☎01 53 19 89 89; www.carefrance.org). An international organization providing volunteer opportunities that range from combating AIDS to promoting human rights to improving urban development. Over 130,000 supporting offices throughout France.

France Bénévolat (☎40 61 97 98; www.francebenevolat.org). With 180 offices nationwide, including one for each Parisian *arrondissement,* Bénévolat serves as a liaison between organizations and volunteers, matching individual skills and mutual interests.

International Volunteer Program, 678 13th St., Ste. 100, Oakland, CA 94612, USA (☎+1-866-614-3438; www.ivpsf.org). 4- to 12-week programs in arts and culture, humanitarian relief, environmental conservation, and community development. Fee of US$1450-3050, includes in-country transportation and room and board. Application fee US$100. Intermediate knowledge of French required. 18+.

International Volunteer Programs Association (IVPA), 1 Brattle Sq., Ste. 552, Cambridge, MA 02138, USA (☎+1-914-380-8322; www.volunteerinternational. org). International search site for volunteer and internship opportunities that includes general information about volunteering abroad.

Volunteers for Peace (VFP), 1034 Tiffany Rd., Belmont, VT 05730, USA (☎+1-802-259-2759; www.vfp.org). 2- to 3-week camps provide international volunteers the opportunity to live and work together in host communities while contributing to one of several projects, ranging from archaeological restoration to AIDS education. US$300 fee covers food, lodging, and supplies. Membership fee US$30.

YOUTH AND THE COMMUNITY

Community-based projects involve close work with disadvantaged populations in Paris, including at-risk youth and the poor, elderly, and disabled. A high unemployment rate has left many communities reliant on social programs, which range from elderly care to prison reform. These programs can be the most rewarding of all volunteer experiences, but due to their one-on-one nature, knowledge of French is often necessary.

Action Contre la Faim, 4 rue Niepce, 75014 (☎43 35 88 88; www.actioncontrelafaim.org). International organization combatting hunger seeks volunteers to help organize the nationwide Race Against Hunger, a fundraising running competition. Action Contre la Faim encourages high school and college youth in particular to become involved. Check their website for dates and times of tri-monthly info sessions.

L'Arche les Sapins, 9 rue Olivier de Serres, 75015 Paris (☎01 45 32 23 74; www.arche-france.org). Branch of an international Christian organization that places volunteers in a community home for the mentally challenged or learning disabled. 6-month commitment. Regular work hours, room, board, medical insurance, and monthly allowance provided. Ages 18-28.

GIVING BACK

HELPING THROUGH HUMOUR

At the age of 26, Michel Colucci adopted the name Coluche and—like so many before him with only one appellation—embarked on an entertainment career. Sure enough, the man with the razor-sharp political wit quickly became one of France's most beloved comedians. He ran for president in 1981—"I'll quit politics when politicians quit comedy"—but dropped out of the race when polls showed that he actually had a chance of winning. Before a motorcycle accident ended his life in 1986, Coluche founded the charity Restos du Cœur (Restaurants of the Heart), and in doing so left a permanent mark on France.

Restos du Cœur is a network of soup kitchens and other volunteer activities. Their emphasis on fostering personal relationships between those who volunteer and those who receive aid, along with their good humor—would a comedian have it any other way?—has set them apart as a uniquely positive force of goodwill. Volunteers can work the kitchens, provide face-to-face companionship, or help combat illiteracy, but they have to be able to do it for a few months. Coluche knew the importance of consistency and trust; it almost made him president.

Paris office: 4 cité d'Hauteville (☎53 32 23 23; www.restosducoeur.org). Meals distriubted daily in different regions of the city.

Fondation Claude Pompidou, 42 rue du Louvre, 75001 Paris (☎01 40 13 75 00; www.fondationclaudepompidou.asso.fr). Volunteers aid the sick, elderly, and disabled through home care and companionship.

Groupement Étudiant National d'Enseignement aux Personnes Incarcerées (GENEPI), 12 rue Charles Fourier, 75013 Paris (☎01 45 88 37 00; www.genepi.fr). Students work with inmates in French prisons to promote social rehabilitation. Offices throughout France. In operation for over 30 years.

Les Papillons Blancs de Paris—APEI, 44 rue Blance, 75009 (☎01 42 80 44 43; www.apei75.org). An NGO that aids the mentally handicapped and their families by providing transportation, assistance, homecare, and friendship.

Médecins Sans Frontières (Doctors without Borders), 8 rue St-Sabin, 75011 Paris(☎01 40 21 29 29; www.msf.fr). Non-governmental, non-religious organization that coordinates volunteers with at least 2 years of professional experience to provide health care to people affected by violence or neglect in developing countries worldwide. Interview required. Volunteers expected to make at least a 6-month commitment.

Ni Putes Ni Soumises, 70 rue des Rigoles, 75020 Paris (☎01 53 46 63 00; www.niputesnisoumises.com). The Ni Putes Ni Soumises (Neither Whores Nor Doormats) movement began in April, 2003 in response to violent acts against women in Parisian ghettos. NPNS campaigns against homophobia, racism, and sexism by organizing debates, marches, petitions, rallies, and seminars. The popular, highly publicized movement presents a great opportunity for social action.

Secours Catholique: Délégation de Paris, 13 rue St-Ambroise, 75011 Paris (☎01 48 07 58 21; www.quiaccueillequi.org). Catholic organization that works to support unemployed adults, children with social problems, immigrants, and other marginalized groups in Paris. Local branches throughout France.

Secours Populaire Français, 9-11 rue Froissart, 75140 Paris (☎01 44 78 21 00; www.secourspopulaire.asso.fr). National organization that provides food and clothing to poor children and families and arranges sporting and cultural activities. Aims to improve the quality of life of disadvantaged communities.

WICE, 20 bd. du Montparnasse, 75015 Paris (☎45 66 75 50, fax 40 65 96 53; www.wice-paris.org). Founded in 1978 as a part of the American College of Paris, WICE works to ease English-speakers transition into French life by providing expats with educational programs, a support network, library, social gatherings, and info on health care. Run almost entirely by volunteers, WICE's courses cover topics from art history to introductory French. Not satisfied with their program offerings? Plan and teach your own! Open M-F 10am-4:30pm. Closed during school vacations.

ENVIRONMENTAL CONSERVATION

After oil spills in France in 1999 and 2002 and similar disasters elsewhere in Europe, many EU nations enacted strict pollution controls to protect coastal areas. Yet France's natural resources still face challenges, and volunteers continue to supplement government efforts to preserve the environment.

Centres Permanents d'Initiatives pour l'Environnement (CPIE), 26 rue Beaubourg, 75003 Paris (☎01 44 61 75 35; www.cpie.fr). Organizes environmental volunteer programs and courses in mainland France, Corsica, and some Francophone countries.

Organisation Mondiale de Protection de l'Environnement,1 Carrefour de Longchamp, 75116 Paris (☎01 55 25 84 84; www.wwf.fr). Offers various opportunities for environmental activism regarding issues like climate change, endangered species, and sustainable living. Part of the World Wildlife Fund. Sites around France and the EU.

Worldwide Opportunities on Organic Farms (WWOOF), WWOOF France, 2 pl. Diderot, 94300 Vincennes (www.wwoof.fr). Provides volunteers the opportunity to learn first-hand organic farming techniques, such as biodynamic, permaculture, and micro-agri-culture. Volunteers receive room and board in exchange for work on organic farms. Must purchase book with a list of 300+ host farms (€25, €15 for electronic version).

HISTORICAL RESTORATION

The preservation and reconstruction of French landmarks is an ongoing concern. Volunteers looking for a more labor-intensive experience and an opportunity to learn about France's architectural history can assist in this process.

Association Chantiers Histoire et Architecture Médiévales (CHAM), 5-7 rue Guilleminot, 75014 Paris (☎43 35 15 51; www.cham.asso.fr). Organizes groups to restore medieval landmarks throughout France and select African nations. Office open M-F 9am-12:30pm and 1:30-5:30pm. Most projects restricted to volunteers older than 17. €30 membership fee; program costs from €12 per day.

Club du Vieux Manoir, Ancienne Abbaye du Moncel, 60700 Pontpoint (☎03 44 72 33 98; www.cvmclubduvieuxmanoir.free.fr). Projects of varying lengths to restore castles and churches. Membership and insurance fee €15 per year. Program fee €14 per day. Most programs ages 14 and up.

REMPART, 1 rue des Guillemites, 75004 Paris (☎01 42 71 96 55; www.rempart.com). Union of 170 nonprofit French organizations that offers 2- to 3- week work camps in monument restoration. Daily costs for room and board vary by camp. Registration fee covers accident insurance. Ages 18+.

BEYOND TOURISM

STUDYING

It's hard to dread the first day of school when Paris is your campus and exotic restaurants are your meal plan. A growing number of students report that studying abroad is the highlight of their learning careers. If you've never studied abroad, you don't know what you're missing—and if you have studied abroad, you do know what you're missing.

FOR STUDENTS BY STUDENTS. Check out **Study Abroad,** p. 117, written exclusively by college students who have studied abroad in Paris.

Study-abroad programs range from basic language and culture courses to university-level classes, often for college credit. In order to choose a program that best fits your needs, research as much as you can before making your decision—determine costs and duration, as well as what kind of students participate in the program and what sorts of accommodations are provided. Paris has a wide range of options that provide unique experiences, from direct enrollment in French universities to American programs with American professors using French resources. Back-to-school shopping was never this much fun.

In programs that have large groups of students who speak the same language, there is a trade-off. You may feel more comfortable in the community, but you will not have the same opportunity to practice a foreign language or to befriend other international students. For accommodations, dorm life provides a better opportunity to mingle with fellow students, but there is less of a chance to experience the local scene. If you live with a family, you could potentially build lifelong friendships with natives and experience day-to-day life in more depth, but you might also get stuck sharing a room with their pet iguana. Conditions can vary greatly from family to family, and apartment living is always an option. See **Study Abroad**, p. 117, for more info on how to choose accommodations during your study abroad experience.

VISA INFORMATION. Non-EU citizens hoping to study abroad in France must apply for a special student visa from the French consulate. There is a short-stay visa for stays up to 90 days, as well as two long-stay visas: one for three to six months, and one for six months to a year. Prospective students must fill out two to four—depending on the consulate—applications for the appropriate visa and provide a passport valid for at least three months after the student's last day in France, plus two extra passport photos. (When in doubt, bring extra copies of everything.) Additionally, students must give proof of enrollment or admission in a French learning institute, a letter from the home university or institution certifying current registration as a student, a financial guarantee with a monthly allowance of US$600 per month during the intended stay, and proof of medical insurance. Finally, there is a visa fee that can be paid during the time of application (€60 for short-stay visas, €99 for long-stay). When in France, students with long-stay visas for more than six months must obtain a *carte de séjour* (residency permit) from the local Préfecture de Police; students should file to obtain the card as soon as possible after arriving in France and will be required to provide much of the same information needed for a visa, and to undergo a medical check-up. EU citizens do not need a visa or, as of November 2003, a *carte de séjour*, provided they have alternate identification, including proof of address. See www.diplomatie.gouv.fr/en for more information.

UNIVERSITIES

See **Study Abroad**, p. 117, for an honest account of the French uni system.

AMERICAN PROGRAMS

American Institute for Foreign Study (AIFS), College Division, River Plaza, 9 W. Broad St., Stamford, CT 06902, USA (☎+1-866-906-2437; www.aifsabroad.com). Organizes programs for high-school and college study in universities in Cannes, Grenoble, and Paris. Program fees are around US$6000 for the summer, and US$16,000 per semester. Also holds offices in Paris, 19 r. de Babylone (☎+33 1 4439 0424).

Council on International Educational Exchange (CIEE), 300 Fore St., Portland, ME 04101, USA (☎+1-207-553-4000 or 800-40-STUDY/407-8839; www.ciee.org). One of the most comprehensive resources for work, academic, and internship programs around the world, including in Paris and Rennes. Summer course geared toward students with little or no background in French; semester-long programs require at least 2 years of college French. Program fees are US$3000 for the summer, US$11,600-14,250 per semester, and US$21,500-23,800 per academic year.

Cultural Experiences Abroad, France (CEA), 2005 W. 14th St., Ste. 113, Tempe, AZ 85281, USA (☎+1-800-266-4441; www.gowithcea.com). Programs in Aix-en-Provence, Grenoble, the Riviera, and Paris. Classes in English and French. US$5000 for the summer, US$10,000-17,000 per semester, and US$19,000-$29,000 per academic year.

European Institute for International Education, The Eur-Am Center, 32500 Telegraph Rd., Ste. 209, Bingham Farms, MI 48025, USA (☎+1-248-988-9341; www.euramcenter.com). Provides both educational and private-sector opportunities for people of all ages. Run by the University of Southern Mississippi. Tuition US$3800-4000 for the summer and US$9400 per semester.

International Association for the Exchange of Students for Technical Experience (IAESTE), 20 Av. Albert Einstein, Batiment 705, Villeurbanne Cedex, 69621, France (☎+33 472 438 391; www.iaeste.org). Chances are that your home country has a local office, too; contact it to apply for hands-on technical internships in France. Must be a college student studying science, technology, or engineering. "Cost of living allowance" covers most non-travel expenses. Most programs last 8-12 weeks.

The Center for University Programs Abroad (CUPA), P.O. Box 9611, North Amherst, MA 01059, USA (☎413 549 6960 or +33 01 42 2287 50; www.cupa-paris.org). Specializes in study abroad programs exclusively in Paris. Offers individualized courses of study; enrolls students in the University of Paris system and certain *Grandes Écoles*. Courses are conducted entirely in French.

The Experiment in International Living (☎+1-800-345-2929; www.usexperiment.org). Offers 3- to 5-week summer programs for high-school students. Programs include cross-cultural homestays, community service, ecological adventure, and language training in France (US$5300-6800).

FRENCH PROGRAMS

French universities are far cheaper than their American equivalents; however, it can be hard to receive academic credit at home for a non-approved program. Expect to pay at least €1200 in living expenses. EU citizens studying in France can take advantage of the three- to 12-month Socrates-Erasmus program (www.europe-education-formation.fr; in French only), which offers grants to support inter-European educational exchanges.

French universities are segmented into three degree levels: the first level involves a basic university degree, the second is the equivalent of a Master's degree, and the third is a Doctorat, or PhD. Programs at the first level—except the *Grandes Écoles*, described below—are two or three years long and generally focus on science, medicine, and the liberal arts. They must admit anyone holding a *baccalauréat* (French graduation certificate) or recognized equivalent to their first year of courses (British A levels or two years of college in the US). The more selective and demanding *Grandes Écoles* cover specializations from physics to veterinary medicine. These have notoriously difficult entrance examinations that require a year or more of preparatory schooling.

Foreign students can study throughout France at the many regional universities, although Paris is the hub of France's best-known universities and *Grandes Écoles*. Many French universities offer French language and cultural programs as well as general university classes, particularly during the summer.

Agence EduFrance, (www.edufrance.fr). A 1-stop resource for North Americans thinking about studying for a degree in France. Info on courses, costs, and grant opportunities. Housing options available in universities or with French families.

American University of Paris, 6 rue du Colonel Combes, 75007 Paris (☎+33 01 40 62 07 20; www.aup.fr). US admissions office: 950 S. Cherry St., Ste. 210, Denver, CO 80246 (☎+1-303-757-6333). Offers US-accredited degrees and summer programs in English on its Paris campus. Intensive French language courses offered. Tuition €12,587 per semester and €24,689 per year, not including living expenses.

Cité Universitaire, 17 bd. Jourdain, 14ème (☎44 16 64 00; www.cuip.fr). Ⓜ*Porte d'Orléans, RER: Cité Universitaire or Bus #88: Porte d'Arcueil.* 40 houses comprise a residential campus intended since its 1925 inauguration to promote cultural exchange. Close to 6000 students from 160 countries fill its *résidences,* organized by nationality. Each "dorm" has a unique personality typically inspired by its affiliated nation; for example, the Southeast Asia house resembles a Chinese palace. Candidates apply directly through their country-respective house with room costs varying by residency and type, averaging about €400-500 per month. At the Cité's center, the Maison Internationale houses the communal library, theater, and language center. The mini-campus also has a bank, frequent concerts, and a post office. Students can join in numerous activities from house government to club sports to musical ensembles. While never at a loss for Parisian eateries, residents may dine at any of the four on-site restaurants for less than €3. Interested students must apply before April 1st; summer housing also available. See p. 124 for more info.

Université Paris-Sorbonne, 1 rue Victor Cousin, 75005 Paris, Cédex 05 (☎01 43 18 41 00; www.paris-sorbonne.fr/en). In 1968, the Université de Paris split into 10 independent universities, each at a separate location offering a different program. The Sorbonne, or the Université de Paris IV, devotes itself to the humanities and, considering its 13th-century founding, has earned a reputation as the granddaddy of French universities. Offers 3- to 9-month-long programs for American students. Application online. See **Study Abroad,** p. 117, for info and tips on navigating the French school system.

LANGUAGE SCHOOLS

Enrolling at a language school has two major perks: a slightly less rigorous courseload and the ability to teach you to communicate effectively without looking like an obnoxious tourist. There can be great variety in language schools—independently run, affiliated with a larger university, local, international—but one thing is constant: they rarely offer college credit. Their programs are also good for high-school students who might not feel comfortable in a university program. Some worthwhile organizations include:

Alliance Française, École Internationale de Langue et de Civilisation Française, 101 bd. Raspail, 75270 Paris Cédex 06 (☎+33 01 42 84 90 00; www.alliancefr.org). Instruction at all levels, with courses in legal, medical, and business French. Courses last 1 to 12 weeks and cost approximately €50 per week for daily 2hr. sessions. Also offers private lessons starting at €60 per hour. Enrollment fee €55.

Cours de Civilisation Française de la Sorbonne, 47 rue des Écoles, 75005 Paris (☎01 44 10 77 00; www.ccfs-sorbonne.fr). French-language courses at all levels; also offers a comprehensive lecture program on French cultural studies taught by Sorbonne professors. Must be at least 18 and at baccalauréat level to enroll. Semester- and year-long courses €250-2750. 4-, 6-, 8-, and 11-week summer programs €250-2300.

Eurocentres, 56 Eccleston Sq., London SW1V 1PH, UK (☎+44 20 7963 8450; www. eurocentres.com). Language programs and homestays in Paris.

Institut de Langue Française (ILF), 3 av. Bertie-Albrecht, 75008 Paris (☎+33 01 45 63 24 00; www.ilf-paris.fr). Language, civilization, literature, and even au pair courses beginning at €75 for 4 weeks of instruction.

Institut Parisien de Langue et de Civilisation Française, 29 rue de Lisbonne, 75008 (☎01 40 56 09 53; www.institut-parisien.com). French language, fashion, culinary arts, and cinema courses. Also offers courses specifically for *au pairs.* Intensive language courses 10-25hr. per week, starting at €125 per week.

Language Immersion Institute, State University of New York at New Paltz, 1 Hawk Dr., New Paltz, NY 12561, USA (☎+1-845-257-3500; www.newpaltz.edu/lii). Short, intensive summer language courses and some overseas courses in French. Program fees are around US$1000 for a 2-week course, not including accommodations.

World Link Education: Study in France, Universitetsvägen 9, Box 50001, 104 05 Stockholm, Sweden (☎+46 55 803720; www.wle-france.com). US Office: 1904 3rd Ave., Ste. 633, Seattle, WA 98101 (☎800-621-3085 or 206-264-0941). French language and culture classes in Paris.

CULINARY SCHOOLS

Those truly devoted to food and its making should shell out the extra cash to enroll in a French culinary institute. The culinary capital of the world is the place for budding chefs to perfect their skills in semester- or year-long programs. For smaller, more intimate courses based in farms and homes—often with well-known chefs or food critics—amateur chefs should check out www.cookingschools.com, which lists private schools in France.

Cordon Bleu Paris Culinary Arts Institute, 8 rue Léon Delhomme, 75015 Paris (☎+33 01 53 68 22 50; www.cordonbleu.edu). The crème de la crème of French cooking schools, now with campuses in 15 different countries. In addition to its semester-long certificate programs, Cordon Bleu offers tourist-friendly desmonstrations and tastings (€42), hands-on culinary workshops (7hr. "Cooking for Friends," €160), and Parisian market tours (€125; includes lunch).

Françoise Meunier's Cours de Cuisine, 7 rue Paul-Lelong, 75002 Paris (☎01 40 26 14 00; www.fmeunier.com). €100 for a 3hr. class. Participants cook and share a 3-course meal. Typical class has 8-10 students; private lessons are available, as well as youth workshops for children ages 10-12. Classes taught in French, but *cuisinière* Meunier is also glad to speak English and limited Spanish. Also in conjunction with **Olivier Berté's Cours de Cuisine,** in the same building (www.coursdecuisineparis.com).

Promenades Gourmandes, 187 rue du Temple, 75003 Paris (☎01 48 56 84; www.promenadesgourmandes.com). Offers walking tours of culinary Paris and cooking classes in the intimate, top-of-the-line kitchen of Paule Caillat. Walking tours €110 per person. Cooking classes €250 per person for a half-day. English speakers welcome.

The International Kitchen, 330 N. Wabash, Ste. 2613, Chicago, IL 60611 (☎+1-800-945-8606 or +1-312-467-0560; www.theinternationalkitchen.com). Offers 2- to 8-night "cooking vacations" with famous chefs in Burgundy, Champagne, the Côte d'Azur, the Loire Valley, Paris, Provence, and the Southwest (US$695-3275). Also offers 1-day course in the Rhône-Alpes, Paris, Provence, and the Côte d'Azur (US$170-300), as well as wine- and chocolate-tastings (US$95-160).

WORKING

As with volunteering, work opportunities tend to fall into two categories. Some travelers want long-term jobs that allow them to integrate into a community, while others seek out short-term jobs to finance the next leg of their travels. With France's 7.2% unemployment rate, long-term jobs are hard to come by. Travelers without EU citizenship face a particular challenge when searching for a job in France: only employers who cannot find qualified workers in the EU may petition to bring in a long-term worker who is not an EU citizen. If you're undeterred by the less-than-welcoming attitude toward foreign workers, you may want to try a job that requires English-language skills, as bilingual candidates have a better chance of finding work. Working as an au pair or teaching English are both popular long-term employment options. If you're in the market for a short-term stint, be on the lookout for a service or agricultural job. **Transitions Abroad** (www.transitionsabroad.com) also offers updated online listings for work over any time span.

Many jobs in France are secured through alumni networks or personal contacts, but classified advertisements in newspapers and online are also great resources for job-hunters. **Agence Nationale pour l'Emploi** (www.anpe.fr) has listings for many skilled and unskilled jobs alike, while **Agence pour l'Emploi de Cadres** (www.apec.fr) catalogues professional job listings. **Michael Page** (www.michaelpage.fr) is another job recruiting agency with offices in major French cities as well as international locations. The **American Chamber of Commerce** (www.amchamfrance.org), located in Paris, fosters Franco-American business relations, and is currently generating an online job and internship directory. Note that working abroad often requires a special work visa.

MORE VISA INFORMATION. EU citizens have the right to work in France without a visa, and can easily obtain a *carte de séjour* (residency permit) by presenting a passport, proof of employment, and other identification documents. Visit www.infomobil.org for a complete list of requirements. Non-EU citizens hoping to work in France for less than 90 days must apply for an *Autorisation Provisoire de Travail* at a local branch of *Direction Départementale du Travail, de l'Emploi et de la Formation Professionnelle* (D.D.T.E.F.P.). A passport and proof of short-term employment are necessary to secure authorization; a short-term, or Schengen visa (US$62) is also sometimes required. Non-EU citizens wishing to work in France for more than 90 days must have an offer of employment authorized by the French Ministry of Labor (www.travail.gouv.fr/) before applying for a long-stay visa (US$131) through their local French consulate. Within 8 days of arrival in France, holders of long-stay visas must apply for a *carte de séjour.* International students hoping to secure a job must possess a *carte de séjour d'étudiant* (student residency card) and apply for an *Autorisation Provisoire de Travail* at a D.D.T.E.F.P. office. Students in France are permitted to work up to 19½hr. per week during the academic year, and full time during summer and holidays. Special rules apply for au pairs and teaching assistants; see www.consulfrance-washington.org for more info.

SHORT-TERM WORK

Many travelers try their hand at odd jobs for a few weeks at a time to help pay for another month or two of touring around. Seasonal work can be found in the hotel and restaurant businesses, in markets, and in agriculture. Another popular option is to work several hours a day at a hostel in exchange for free or discounted room and/or board. Most often, these short-term jobs are found by word of mouth or by expressing interest to the owner of a hostel or restaurant. Due to high turnover in the tourism industry, many places are eager for help, even if it is only temporary. Look in the "Positions Vacants" section of papers such as the "Guide du Job Trotter" for job listings, or visit www.jobs-ete.com for a summer job search engine.

Easy Expat (www.easyexpat.com/paris_en.htm). Provides a wealth of opportunities for those seeking summer, seasonal, or short-term jobs in Paris. The website lists positions in everything from teaching ski lessons to working at Disneyland Paris. Also has information about discount cards and student benefits.

Fédération Unie des Auberges de Jeunesse, 27 rue Pajol, 75018 Paris, France (☎01 44 89 87 27; www.fuaj.org). Offers short-term work in member youth hostels, from catering to reception. Submit application to individual hostel.

Transitions Abroad, (☎866-760-5340; www.transitionsabroad.com/listings/work). Provides accurate and up-to-date information about everything from au-pairing to farm jobs. Subscribe to the monthly magazine for how best to live (and make money) like a local while traveling, and to get some extensive resources for doing so. Website offers a comprehensive database of opportunities for short-term employment abroad, sorted by location and type of job desired.

LONG-TERM WORK

If you're planning on spending a substantial amount of time (more than 3 months) working in France, search for a job well in advance. International placement agencies are often the easiest way to find employment abroad, especially for those interested in teaching. Although they are often only available to college students, **internships** are a good way to ease into working abroad. Many say the interning experience is well worth it, despite low pay (if you're lucky enough to be paid at all). Be wary of advertisements for companies claiming to be able get you a job abroad for a fee—often the same listings are available online or in newspapers. Some reputable organizations include:

Council on International Educational Exchange (CIEE), 300 Fore St., Portland, ME 04101, USA (☎+1-207-553-4000 or 800-40-STUDY/407-8839; www.ciee.org). Tucked into their study-abroad listings is a resource for international internships.

Association for International Practical Training (AIPT), 10400 Little Patuxent Pkwy., Ste. 250, Columbia, MD 21044, USA (☎410-997-2200; www.aipt.org). Offers information on professional and academic exchange experiences.

American Chamber of Commerce in France, 156 Bd. Haussmann, 75008, Paris (☎01 56 43 45 67; www.amchamfrance.org). Supports Franco-American business relations.

Centre d'Information et de Documentation Jeunesse (CIDJ), 101 quai Branly, 75015 Paris (☎44 49 12 00; www.cidj.asso.fr). An invaluable state-run youth center providing info on careers, education, employment, and résumés. English spoken. Jobs posted on the bulletin boards outside. Open M-F 10am-noon and 1-6pm.

Fédération Familles de France, 28 place St-Georges, 75009 Paris (☎01 44 53 45 90; www.familles-de-france.org). Supports needy families by offering grants, conferences on parenting, and educational and vocational assistance. Branches in every French département, Guadeloupe, Guyane, Martinique, and Réunion.

French-American Chamber of Commerce (FACC), 122 E. 42nd St., New York, NY 10168, USA (☎+1-212-867-0123; www.faccnyc.org). Information on international career development programs.

TEACHING ENGLISH

While some elite private American schools offer competitive salaries, let's just say that teaching jobs abroad pay more in personal satisfaction and emotional fulfillment than in actual cash. Perhaps this is why volunteering as a teacher instead of getting paid is a popular option. Even then, teachers often receive some sort of a daily stipend to help with living expenses. In almost all cases, you must have at least a bachelor's degree to be a full-fledged teacher, although college undergraduates can often get summer positions teaching or tutoring. Because many bosses require that employees take English classes, demand for teachers is fairly high despite France's resilient pride in its language.

Many schools require teachers to have a **Teaching English as a Foreign Language (TEFL)** certificate. You may still be able to find a teaching job without one, but certified teachers often find higher-paying jobs. The French-impaired don't have to give up their dream of teaching, either. Private schools usually hire native English speakers for English-immersion classrooms where no French is spoken. (Teachers in public schools will more likely work in both English and French.) Placement agencies or university fellowship programs are the best resources for finding teaching jobs. The alternative is to contact schools directly or to try your luck once you arrive in France. In the latter case, the best time to look is several weeks before the start of the school year. The following organizations are extremely helpful in placing teachers in France.

International Schools Services (ISS), 15 Roszel Rd., P.O. Box 5910, Princeton, NJ 08543, USA (☎+1-609-452-0990; www.iss.edu). Hires teachers for more than 200 overseas schools. Candidates should have teaching experience and a bachelor's degree. 2-year commitment is the norm.

French Ministry of Education Teaching Assistantship in France, French Embassy, 4101 Reservoir Rd., Washington, D.C., 20007, USA (☎+1-202-944-6294; www.ambafrance-us.org). Program for US citizens sends up to 1700 grads and undergrads to teach English in France on a €900 monthly stipend.

AU PAIR WORK

Au pairs are typically women (although sometimes men) aged 18-27 who work as live-in nannies, caring for children and doing light housework in foreign countries in exchange for room, board, and a small stipend. One perk of the job is that it allows you to get to know France without the high expenses of traveling. Drawbacks, however, can include mediocre pay and long hours. In France, au pairs are paid between €50 and €75 per week. Much of the au pair experience depends on the family with which you are placed. The agencies below are a good starting point for looking for employment. There is also a database for au pair agencies at www.europa-pages.com/au_pair/france.html.

Accueil International Services, rue Ducastel, 78100 Saint Germain en Laye, France (☎01 39 73 04 98; www.accueil-international.com).

Agence Au Pair Fly, 16 rue Madeleine Fourcade, 69007 Lyon, France (☎03 34 37 65 70 83; www.aupairfly.com).

InterExchange, 161 6th Ave., New York City, NY 10013, USA (☎+1-212-924-0446 or 800-AU-PAIRS/287-2477; www.interexchange.org).

Childcare International, Trafalgar House, Grenville Pl., London NW7 3SA, UK (☎+44 20 8906 3116; www.childint.co.uk).

MEDICAL OUTREACH AND AIDS AWARENESS

Arcat-Sida, 94-102 rue de Buzenval, 75020 Paris (☎01 44 93 29 29; www.arcat-sida. org). Association of doctors, journalists, sociologists, and volunteers fighting to obtain easier access to treatment for HIV/AIDS patients. In addition to giving aid to victims, they also promote further research and publish an informational magazine.

AIDES, 119 rue des Pyrenées, 75020 Paris (☎01 53 27 63 00; www.aides.org). One of Europe's largest community-based organizations for people living with AIDS, providing education, support, and access to treatment. 360 staff members and 600 AIDES volunteers are active in over 70 French cities.

Sol En Si (Solidarité Enfants Sida), 9 bis rue Léon Giraud, 75019 (☎01 44 52 78 78; www.solensi.asso.fr). Sol En Si supports the children and families of HIV and AIDS victims, easing their suffering by offering help with day-to-day tasks. Seeks long-term volunteers to staff their daycare center and provide at-home childcare for ill parents.

FURTHER READING ON BEYOND TOURISM

Alternatives to the Peace Corps: A Guide of Global Volunteer Opportunities, edited by Paul Backhurst. Food First, 2005 (US$12).

The Back Door Guide to Short-Term Job Adventures: Internships, Summer Jobs, Seasonal Work, Volunteer Vacations, and Transitions Abroad, by Michael Landes. Ten Speed Press, 2005 (US$22).

Green Volunteers: The World Guide to Voluntary Work in Nature Conservation, by Fabio Ausenda. Universe, 2007 (US$15).

How to Get a Job in Europe, by Cheryl Matherly and Robert Sanborn. Planning Communications, 2003 (US$23).

How to Live Your Dream of Volunteering Overseas, by Joseph Collins, Stefano DeZerega, and Zahara Heckscher. Penguin Books, 2001 (US$20).

International Job Finder: Where the Jobs Are Worldwide, by Daniel Lauber and Kraig Rice. Planning Communications, 2002 (US$20).

Live and Work Abroad: A Guide for Modern Nomads, by Huw Francis and Michelyne Callan. Vacation Work Publications, 2001 (US$20).

Volunteer Vacations: Short-Term Adventures That Will Benefit You and Others, by Doug Cutchins, Anne Geissinger, and Bill McMillon. Chicago Review Press, 2006 (US$18).

Work Abroad: The Complete Guide to Finding a Job Overseas, edited by Clayton A. Hubbs. Transitions Abroad, 2002 (US$16).

Work Your Way Around the World, by Susan Griffith. Vacation Work Publications, 2007 (US$22).

BEYOND TOURISM

STUDY ABROAD

FOR STUDENTS BY STUDENTS. This year, Let's Go: *Paris 2009* was researched by us (Bri and Sara), two college students studying abroad in Paris over a six-month period. That means that, like all *Let's Go* researchers, we scoured the city for awesome restaurants (**Chez Janou;** p. 172) and clubs (**Favela Chic;** p. 332)—but we did so after 3hr. of poli sci at Paris 8 and 2hr. of psych at Nanterre. From late-night visits to the American Hospital, to Saturday morning appointments with the locksmith, from Disneyland Paris getaways with a countess host mom, to *maladroit* Americanisms at African dance classes, we have experienced our fair share of the best and worst that Paris—and more specifically, Parisians—have to offer. But we did it all with you in mind. Whether it was dropping our euros all over the floor at Monoprix while trying to pay *and* bag (a skill that is almost physically impossible), getting disapproving looks for not drying our hair, or attempting to outwit inappropriate waiters, we hope that our sacrifice and suffering, our enjoyment and experience, helps you live YOUR experience to the fullest.

LG Love,
Sara and Bri

WHY PARIS?

For us here at *Let's Go: Paris 2009*, this question is obvious at best and mildly offensive at worst, but we realize there exist people who might need convincing. Paris is inarguably one of the major "pulse" cities in the world. Abounding in culture, history, and everything aesthetically pleasing, Paris promises a dynamic and enriching environment that's hard to find elsewhere. At the same time, due to the wonderful French insistence on *joie de vivre*, Paris is more low-key and laid-back than other large cities you might encounter; the cafe culture, for example, continues to thrive. In addition, the French love their students, and because Paris is such a popular destination for study abroad, international students can get in on most student discounts and perks. From special museum nights, to special bar nights, to special train fares, study abroaders save money with almost every action—which is a definite plus in one of the most expensive cities in the world (an admitted disadvantage of Paris). Meanwhile, the French university system, though often reputed to be "slack" and even "a joke," is actually universally solid. While some students have noticeably easier educational experiences, the value of studying in a French environment—and getting to see its intricacies as well as its less subtle differences (such as the decided lack of campuses in Paris)—is priceless. Many Parisian universities are world renowned for their work in literature, philosophy, art history, and political science; there's a reason the Lost Generation came here for intellectual inspiration. Finally, and most importantly, it's *Paris*, and if that doesn't mean anything to you now, *veuillez patientez un semestre*—you'll learn soon enough the meaning of *Paris, je t'aime.*

OUNT ON A GOOD TIME

'No," I continued insisting in bro-
xen French, "I care about... the dirt.
.. the air..." I gestured a bit, "save
energy..." Raising an eyebrow, my
host mom repeated for the third
time, "I'll leave the hair dryer on
he counter," and walked out. My
irst Sunday abroad, I shrugged off
he conversation and proceeded à
table with wet hair.

The gourmet linner (lunch
and dinner) awaiting me hardly
seemed average; we started with
appetizers and champagne, dev-
led eggs for first course, duck
and potato gratin as the main
course, followed by salad, cheese,
and cinnamon and sugar apples
or dessert, all capped by coffee
and chocolate. To accent her royal
east, my host mom had perfectly
arranged the "daily" china set, fix-
ng knives so they lay on their knive
ests at a 35° angle. Impressed
by the decor, I remained oblivious
o the guests' shocked stares. As I
ound out in my study abroad program's Orientation one week too
ate, wet hair worn to dinner regis-
ers as a major offense in formal
French households.

Welcome to Chez D'Hautevilles,
a quintessential formal French
household. Modestly, my host
mom showed me her insignia
ing one afternoon, explaining her
husband's title as Count still car-
ied social weight despite having
ost aristocratic power centuries
ago. Life at their house followed
egal codes; no one walked bare-
oot in the house, we addressed
each other perpetually as "vous"

HONEYMOON PERIOD

Between the emotionally charged decision to study
abroad, the inevitable last-minute packing, and the
probably groggy and confused first steps in the
City of Light, the process of getting to Paris is overwhelming. The more you focus on organization the
better off you will be; we've come up with a list of
things to keep in mind, and some tips for staying
sane—for the most part, at least.

VISAS AND OTHER HELPFUL DOCUMENTS. Whether
you plan to study abroad for a semester or several
years, you will need a student visa, issued by your
local French consulate. (For a list of French consulates in your area, see **Essentials,** p. 19). Recently,
20 countries, including Canada and the US, have
switched to a solely online visa application process, which is regulated by **CampusFrance** (www.
campusfrance.org). You will need to set up a CampusFrance account before you apply for a visa and
bring proof of registration to the consulate. Other
documents you will need for your visa application
include: a **passport** valid for the entire length of
your visa, **proof of financial support** and existence of
a bank account from which funds will be drawn,
and a **letter of admission** from an educational institution. It's best to get started on this process as soon
as possible (and at latest, two months before your
departure date), as it will probably take at least a
couple of visits to the consulate before you actually have all the correct paper work, and then a
few weeks for the office to review your request and
send you your visa. For more detailed info on the
visa-application process, see **Beyond Tourism: Studying**, p. 107, and visit the CampusFrance website.

TIPS FOR TRANSITIONING. Most would agree that
Paris is one of the best study abroad destinations in
the world. However, the process of integrating into
a new environment—especially one as fast-paced
and close-knit as Paris—is always a challenge. You
have to deal with a new physical environment, living arrangement, and educational experience, all
in a new language and cultural context. Everyone's
process of integration is different, but after studying abroad in Paris, we have a few tips to share:

REMEMBER WHERE YOU CAME FROM. Having a
set plan of how to keep in touch with family and
friends back home is sometimes the best way to
remember you're in a different city as opposed to
a different universe. Many students find it comforting to bring or to have loved ones send care packages with reminders of home.

AMERICAN (OR CANADIAN OR BRIT OR...) IN PARIS. Many students expect to put on black skinny pants, don an accent, and fit right in. Try to remember that transitioning takes time and you will most likely feel like an idiot from time to time (or more consistently, which is nothing to be ashamed of). In the course of a semester, it is impossible to "become a local," but you can live your own version of Parisian life and make the city your own, in small ways *au moins.* Try to be realistic and forgiving of yourself (for example, skinny jeans are not for all—it's best to acknowledge and accept this fact as soon as possible).

JUST DO IT. In the first couple weeks—and possibly even throughout the semester—many students find themselves with more downtime than they are used to, and let's be honest—there is only so much cafe cruising you can do before you risk entering an espresso-induced coma. One tip that almost always come up is to just DO things—make a list of what you want to see and do in Paris and resolve to get it done. Another popular getting-to-know Paris activity is choosing a random metro stop, getting off, and exploring the area around it. Paris is one of the best walking cities in the world, so take advantage!

LOG (OR BLOG) IT. One of the best ways to keep track of your experience and to handle all the ups and downs is to write about it—for yourself, for your family, or for your friends. Not only does putting the pen to paper (or fingers to keyboard) help you get through the now, but it will also serve as a great souvenir of your experience. Besides, there's nothing more Parisian than going to a park or cafe and jotting down mysterious and potentially scandalous thoughts. (Bring your best brooding face.)

TREAT YOURSELF. Studying abroad can be taxing, and people tend to have high highs (I love Paris, I swear I was born French and my family abducted me, how can I think of ever living anywhere else again, etc.) and low lows (what am I doing here, this country is disfunctional, I miss parking lots, etc.). The best thing to do at times of low lows (besides eating your feelings in one of Paris's American diners; p. 165) is to do a reality check: bronze balconies, the serene Seine, delicious food—you're in a great place. And this is an amazing experience, one you'll look back on for the rest of your life, one that many people never get to enjoy. Take the time to indulge!

and ate 4-course dinners daily. The family had its own biographer and had been hosting students for over thirty years. During a photo-sharing session a month after my arrival, my host mom brought out several pictures of the family château, including a post card from the gift shop. My host mom, taught by her grandmother that pants "weren't feminine enough," had only ever worn skirts. At 64, persuaded by my insistence and the fear that Mickey Mouse might try to pick her up if not, she wore pants for the first time on our trip to EuroDisney. As she screamed while flying down Space Mountain, I really doubt she was thinking about not being feminine enough.

Noble in more than class, my host family shared their traditions and politesse; I brought my feminism and liberal ideals. Not all French *familles d'accueil* are the like. the d'Hautevilles, but most students who choose to stay in home stays do have memorable tales when they leave. Having returned home in time to celebrate the Fourth of July at home, I reveled in my *steak haché* slabbed between two buns and dripping ketchup. Despite eating (with my hands) at exactly the type of "cancer-causing BBQ" my host parents so feared, I would have done them proud, sporting a knee-length skirt, and, of course, freshly blow-dried hair.

—Brianna Goodale

DAY TO DAY (LE QUOTIDIEN)

One of the main differences between being a study abroader and a tourist is that as a student, you are actually setting up some semblance of a life in Paris. From discovering "your" *boulangerie* and cafe to creating Sunday afternoon traditions to paying the insurance, there are certain aspects to living and studying abroad that you might not have considered. When you are prepared for this process, it can be one of the most rewarding parts of your stay, but without careful thought, you can find yourself in some mad awk situations—from running out of Skype credit in the middle of a conversation with your girlfriend, to running out of toilet paper on a Sunday morning (and forgetting which Monoprix is open). We've tried to provide some damage control.

NO PLACE LIKE HOME

There are three main options for housing in Paris: living in a homestay, living with other students in a dorm, and living independently in an apartment. Many times your particular program will arrange your housing situation for you, but often they give you a choice. There are obviously pluses and minuses to each option, so its best to do extensive research before you decide.

HOMESTAYS

Generally organized by the college program you enroll in, homestays vary in accommodations and reciprocity. Not all families consider your arrival an "adoption"; some place very few restrictions on their students, granting them separate entrance and kitchen facilities. Others, however, expect hosted students to arrive home by curfew, call if they are going to miss dinner, and wear slippers or shoes at all times. You should consider the relationship you would like to cultivate with your host family before filling out the self-evaluation sheet most programs send to applicants. Your questionnaire will inquire about whether you play the piano—important for music majors, actually—and about your habits, and prospective host families fill out a similar form, indicating personality traits they would prefer a student to possess. **Honesty** in your responses is crucial to facilitate a good match. If you note you fear living in poverty because you secretly want your own bedroom and figure rich people are more likely to have spare rooms, be aware you could end up spending five months with a count and countess who still subscribe to strict social castes (see **Count on a Good Time,** p. 118). In particular, highlight vegetarian and **dietary concerns.** Your program may not notify host families about student food allergies; avoid the EpiPen fiasco by indicating problems on your form. Secondary concerns include proximity to Paris's center; if you like to stay out late, for example, you would do better with an accommodation close to the Bastille or Latin Quarter (see **Discover,** p. 1). Not only do *arrondissements* farther from the city center require longer commutes, having to switch several trains to arrive home could turn ugly should you miss the last train from the terminus. Think carefully about what you want from the experience.

FAMILLES D'ACCUEIL. Many students choose a homestay because they want to practice their French outside the classroom or—for better or worse—exchange cultural values. Forced to listen to the radio and watch the news in another language, you will become more proficient. Although no "typical" French family exists, a disproportionate number of old, divorced women host foreign students. Many may have grown-up children or grandchildren, and several families will have hosted previous students. Depending on the arrangement your program has provided, your families may have to provide breakfast and dinner several nights a week. Hating to waste food, French families expect you to arrive on time and eat what they serve you; on the plus side, you have someone who will cook exquisite food for you. If you get sick, an insider's advice can prove helpful when trying to navigate a foreign health-care system. Established French families may also own homes much bigger or grander than any apartment the typical college student—i.e. broke—could afford.

MAKE A GOOD IMPRESSION. Once assigned to a homestay, contacting them via email or phone before you leave may lessen your arrival's awkwardness. Yes, expect awkwardness; learning to laugh with your host family will soften linguistic stumbles and inevitably save your ego. Consider emailing your host family the time and date of your arrival; they may even offer to pick you up, saving you money and sweat. Everyone loves free stuff, even French people; as a thank-you offering, think about bringing your host family a typically American gift or an atypical local favorite. And, as the first few weeks roll by, remember that bonding takes time. Rome wasn't built in a day; you can't expect to destroy the French's close-minded reputation in a semester.

WHAT TO BRING YOUR HOST FAMILY. Despite scorning peanut butter and feeling generally unsure about maple sugar, most Parisian families will gladly gobble up noncommercial US honey and Girl Scout cookies.

LIVING INDEPENDENTLY

There are many reasons to consider living independently besides the potential that you'll meet a French hottie and want to bring them home. Living independently is a great opportunity to truly create your own Parisian experience—to determine your own schedule, social scene, and lifestyle. It's important to remember the operative word: independence. There are a couple of obvious perks that come with this: you are not tied to a host family's demands and plans, you can feel like a true Parisian resident as opposed to a "visitor" in someone else's house, and you can ensure that you won't end up in an house with a lonely cat lady or a dorm with a younger cat fan. (Or, you can be that cat man or lady without bothering anyone else about it.) However, living alone also brings with it great responsibility that you may not have otherwise dealt with as a student before, such as cleaning the apartment, paying bills on-time (insurance, electricity, etc.), cooking and shopping for yourself, dealing with nosy or otherwise odd neighbors, and most importantly, living by yourself. Coming back to an empty apartment can feel relaxing and liberating, but it can also be isolating, boring, and therefore lonely. For all of these reasons, it is probably best to have at least a solid handle on French before you decide to live independently—as you'll get fewer opportunities to speak the language (or will have to make a much greater effort to do so), and because dealing with the plumber is just less awkward when you can say more than *"Mon trou ne marche pas."* ("My hole doesn't work.")

CAMARADES DE CHAMBRE. In order to offset some of the disadvantages that come with living alone, many students decide to live with one or many roommates, either people from their home country or program, other international students, or even French students. Though this can make the experience less lonely and can relieve some of the burdens (someone else can take out the trash for once!), there are downsides as well—namely, the cat lady and the

RUNNING FROM PARIS

For study abroad students in Paris, there's always the question of "integrating" into the culture—how American can you be without feeling like an alien? There are some basic survival tricks that help tone down your stateside sheen—for women, skinny black jeans; for men, sunglasses and a man-purse. One of the main culture shocks, though, is in the area of exercise—for me, running functioned as a metaphor for overall socialization. Here is a chronicle of my path to Parisian-hood.

Step 1, Intolerance: At 10am, I exit my Marais apartment in long spandex pants, a tank top, and my iPod. As I hesitantly approach La Perle (the hippest place in the Marais at night), I see the owner perk up from behind the bar. In a flury of emotion, he rushes out into the street, stops me, points at me, and explodes in a loud "TSSSSSSKKKKK!" Think Salem Massachussetts, circa 1692.

Step 2, Humiliation: Two weeks later, I finally get up the courage to take on the city again. This time I wear more conservative cloths (i.e., long shirt), and attempt to hide my iPod. Two things happen: 1) a teenage boy decides to run along with me for about 500 yards, yelling "Cours, Forrest! Cours!" ("Run, Forrest, Run"—in case you couldn't piece that one together) and 2) an Old man turns to his wife and observes loudly: "Mais, il faut bronzer faire comme ça!" (Roughly, "One must

fact that it might deter you from branching out on your own (especially if you have English-speaking roommates.) While living with a roommate (*"co-location"* in French) used to be relatively rare, it is quickly becoming a popular trend, and there are now many websites dedicated to finding roommates, most of which also sponsor monthly meetings for roommate-seekers (a great way to meet people even if you're not looking for a roomie!). Some helpful sites include: **www.appartager.fr,** and **www.kel-koloc.fr, www.colocation.fr, www.easycoloc.com.** Another newer and therefore less user-friendly site is **www.recherche-colocation.com/paris.html.** Of course, once you find a roommate—or before you do—you'll need to find an actual place to stay, which is another story altogether.

HOW TO FIND AN APARTMENT. Finding the perfect apartment in Paris depends on a number of things: neighborhood or *arrondissement,* size and style of apartment, and price. Thankfully, many websites allow you to search by specifying these criteria (for a list of helpful websites, see **Essentials: Long-Term Accommodations,** p. 56). Due to Paris's natural dynamism, both long- and short-term apartments are always opening up. That being said, it is probably a good idea to begin the apartment search no less than one to two months before your planned arrival in Paris. Renting an apartment usually costs between €600 and €2000 per month; fortunately for you, the longer the stay, the lower the rate of pay (only more reason to prolong your Parisian experience as long as possible!). In addition to rent, you'll also most likely be asked to put down a security deposit (usually the amount of about two months rent) and to pay for extra utilities (such as Wi-Fi, heat, and electricity). When searching for an apartment through an online agency, you will also be charged an agency fee, which usually ranges from 30-75% one month's rent, depending on the length of stay. If you are lucky, your agency will also set you up with an insurer, but that doesn't mean you shouldn't do your own research to find the best rate (expect to pay about €125 per 6-month period).

ONLINE RESOURCES. Just remember: while searching online is much more convenient, it can also be less reliable: never send payment in advance without a solid guarantee (a contract) and always check to make sure the address actually exists (ideally, never settle on an apartment without seeing pictures). The French Yellow Pages *(Pages Jaunes)* sponsors a website called **Photos de Villes** (http://photos.pagesjaunes.fr), which allows you to see any pictures of any building in Paris just by typing in the address. Finally, make sure to keep track of all transactions and correspondences; while most contracts have to be signed in French, any reputable agency will allow you to see an English version as well. If you handle your rental with a private owner, it may be more of a hassle but you will avoid some of these fees. Some helpful websites include:

Craigslist Paris (http://paris.en.craigslist.org). Includes all the usual stuff you'd see on Craigslist, including housing, jobs, forums, services, and things for sale. In English.

▨ **Paris Attitude (www.parisattitude.com).** Allows you to search for short- or long-term furnished apartments using criteria of length of stay, type of apartment (studio, duplex, two-bedroom, etc.), and *arrondissement*. In English and French.

Paris CROUS (www.crous-paris.fr). A website that lists all student housing options in Paris. You'll need proof that you're a student; the university acceptance letter you used for your visa should work. The site also provides information about other aspects of student life. In French.

Lodgis.com (www.lodgis.com/en/paris). Allows you to search for furnished long- and short-term apartments by *arrondissement*, type of apartment, and length of stay. Each apartment is handled by a particular real-estate agency, who you will deal with when figuring out rent, contracts, etc. In 10 languages.

De Particulier à Particulier (www.pap.fr). Housing rentals and sales from private owners. Rents are on the expensive side. The paper version hits the newsstands every Thursday, and competition for apartments is fierce. You'll need to be the first in line to even have a chance at anything listed. Log on or purchase the paper early, then get on the phone ASAP. Have your paperwork ready to facilitate and speed up the process; most apartments are gone by noon. In French.

HOW TO CHOOSE AN APARTMENT. When deciding what type of apartment is right for you, there are a couple things you should consider. First off, what type of neighborhood do you want to live in? Do you want to live among the hip alternative crowd of the Bastille, the fabulously glamorous Marais, historical and intellectual St-Michel, or the more residential but adorable Butte-Aux-Cailles? As a general rule, the closer you get to the city center, the more you'll be paying. For a more in-depth take on the Paris neighborhoods, see **Discover**, p. 1. Another thing to consider is the location of the apartment *within* the *arrondissement*: how far is it from a metro or a park? Is it on a smaller, more quiet street or busy boulevard? Is it close to a gro-

surely go tanning before doing such a thing!")

Step 3, Slow Acceptance: Tired of Paris's attitude, I decided that the city would just have to "deal" with me. (Parisians are notorious for having a cold exterior until you push back; then they warm up.) Toward the end of one run, I approached the local butcher's shop while the daily meat was being loaded for delivery. The butcher was on his cell phone, but he ended the call to cross the street and stop me. I wait for another finger-pointing fiasco, but instead, the meat-man looks me up and down and concludes: *"C'est bon. C'est TRÈS bon!"* I sprinted happily home knowing at least one person in Paris appreciates my American ways.

Step 4, Enthusiatic Support (kinda): Now on my daily runs, I almost always receive thumbs-ups from policemen and taxi drivers, as well as comments like *"Je t'accompagnerai, mais je n'ai pas le courage!"* ("I would join you, but I don't have the courage!"). Waiters usually go in for a high-five, or at least clap as I pass. Is it mockery? Probably, but I like to take it as encouragement.

In conclusion, Paris loves to put its study abroaders and expats through intitiation before (quasi-)integration. Persistence is more than a virtue—it's a must.

—Sara O'Rourke

cery store, laundromat (if necessary), ATM, and *boulangerie?* Within the building, is the apartment on the first floor? Or is it a fifth-floor walk-up? (Literally a pain in the butt, but great for the quads and glutes!) Does it have a view of adorable Parisian roofs or a loud, growling, and potentially alive ventilator? The majority of apartments available for one person are studios, which consist of one "large" (usually around 20 sq. m) room with a bed (sometimes also the couch) and a kitchen "area" (this could just be a microwave and countertop), and smaller bathroom. While these can get a bit cramped, they are usually the perfect size for a student—and are oh-so-Parisian. Other options include lofts, duplexes, and standard one- and two-bedrooms, but these are usually more expensive and better suited for multiple residents. Finally, beware the eccentric (read: crazy) Parisian landlord; though he or she can at first seem endearing, the relationship can quickly escalate to a passive-aggressive Cold War.

DORMS AND FOYERS. Many students view dorm living as a happy medium between the homestay and apartment life, as well as a not-as-abrupt transition from university life in America. Dorms allow for more freedom in terms of schedule and lifestyle, but also provide the structure of community life. They are also a great way to meet other students. One tip is to apply as early as possible: student housing in Paris is a hot commodity, especially the weeks before the beginning of the semester or year. Also, you will want to take some of the same considerations as you would with apartment hunting (p. 56)—neighborhood, surroundings, amenities, etc. *Foyers* are located all over Paris and come in all shapes and sizes (from industrial and diverse to historical and unisex), so you should not feel limited by your decision to live in a dorm.

RESOURCES

Union nationale des maisons d'étudiants (www.unme-asso.com). Lists about 30 *foyers* in Paris and environs.

Association des résidences et des foyers de jeunes (www.arfj.asso.fr).

CROUS de Paris (www.crous-paris.fr). Find the housing section and click on "Foyers jeunes" on the menu; from there you can choose a location in Paris.

POPULAR DORMS

Cité Internationale Universitaire de Paris. (www.ciup.fr). "Cité U" is the most well-known of all Paris dorms, and therefore in the highest demand. It's incredibly hard to find reliable information about admission, mostly because their only advice is to apply and see what happens. So apply and see what happens. Submit online as early as possible. For more information, see **Sights: Montparnasse,** p. 245.

Foyer International des Étudiantes (☎01 43 54 49 63; www.fie.fr). Across from the Jardin du Luxembourg. All-female residency Oct.-June, coed hostel in summer. Term-time applicants must be women between 18- and 25-years-old and study at an University of Paris affiliated school. Applications available mid-April. See **Accommodations,** p. 152.

BONNE SANTÉ (AND SANITY TOO)

There are few things worse than being a sick stranger in a strange land, except when you're also trying to function in a strange language. Thankfully, health care in Paris is relatively accessible for internationals, and especially English speakers. However, health care can be more piecemeal than you might otherwise experience: you might visit a doctor at his or her residence, be sent to a

STUDY ABROAD

lab analysis center for tests and results, revisit the doctor for the actual analysis, and then pick up any prescriptions at a pharmacy. While this may be more of a hassle, it can also be a much more personal, and therefore more thorough (and comforting) experience. Depending on your insurance provider, you will be eligible for reimbursements for lab tests and results, doctors visits, and medications. Just make sure to keep receipts of all doctor's visits, tests, and medications; as well as any test results or written analyses. This will also be helpful if you should need to continue care upon return to your home country. For more detailed information on insurance, hospitals and doctors, and pharmacies, see **Essentials: Staying Healthy in Paris**, p. 31.

MONEY IN THE BANK

BANK ACCOUNTS. While it is sometimes possible to open an account from abroad, it's much easier to do so once in Paris. The process is usually pretty rough and French banks stick strictly to the French business mindset (more passive than efficient, more passive-aggressive than helpful), but having a French bank account is definitely helpful. Make sure the bank you choose is comfortable doing business in English, or the language in which you are fluent. The bank will want proof of reason for opening the account, proof of address in Paris, an ID (or multiple), and of course, money. Beyond that, demands vary from bank to bank—make sure you do not leave home without all the necessary banking records, and keep track of your account once in Paris. **Wiring money** from the US can result in unnecessary hassle and cost, and some businesses such as France Telecom insist on a *prélèvement* (direct debit automatic withdrawal). For more information on money in Paris, see **Essentials**, p. 23.

ACTIVE ACCOUNTS. Because you are most likely a non-resident, you will want to open up a *compte non-résident*, which is usually more restrictive than a resident account in terms of how much money you can withdraw per time period (but check with your bank to make sure). If you want to be able to access the money frequently, get a *compte courant*, a *compte à vue*, or a *compte de dépôt*, which are synonyms for "active account." This allows you (or your parents) to deposit money frequently and withdraw it almost immediately.

CARTE BLEU. The **Carte Bleu** contains a small chip instead of a magnetic strip. This may not seem like a huge discrepancy, but given the fact that most French credit-card accepting machines "live for the chip," as a strip holder you can often feel left out. When you've got 45min. before your TGV jets off for your rowdy weekend getaway to Amsterdam, and then the automatic *guichets* at Gare du Nord refuse your apparently unacceptable American Express, you'll be pining for that Carte Bleu. Especially for students staying in Paris for 5 months or more, it's a must—for shorter stays, it's still probably worth it.

GROCERY SHOPPING. Newcomers to Paris need to know the grocery shopping Golden Rule: **Stock Up Before Sunday,** and the Golden Rule's Amendment: Stock Up Before Sunday Or Know What Supermarkets Are Open On Sunday (for one, the Monop' at 69 ave. du Général Leclerc in the 14*ème*). Beyond the Saturday evening realization that you're out of your favorite brunch food (even more reason to explore Paris's rapidly increasing brunch options, p. 165), grocery shopping is otherwise a joy. French supermarkets have high quality food and are often much cheaper than in the US. While in the past, it was almost blasphemous to buy fresh produce and products such as meat and cheese at anything other than markets in Paris, supermarkets are starting to gain popularity, and they provide a larger range of goods. In particular, the grocery store chain **Picard (www.picard.fr),** stocked entirely with frozen foods and meals (sounds odd, is truly amazing), is the perfect quick-stop shop for dinner. For more information about supermarkets and grocery shopping, see **Life and Times,** p. 94.

CHEAP UNIVERSITY RESTAURANTS/CROUS. As a student in Paris, you will automatically have access to one of the delights of the French University system: university restaurants, run by the **Centre régional d'œuvres universitaires (CROUS).** While the cooks can't promise a four-star meal, they *can* offer a solid lunch or dinner for around €3. The CROUS offers 14 restaurants and 22 cafeterias around the city; to find a location near wherever you are or may be, check out **www.crous-paris.fr.** Just remember to bring your student card!

CELL PHONES. Most study-abroad students come to Paris with an International SIM card in the US, or they end up buying a pay-per-minute phone once they arrive. **PhoneHut** or **FNAC** (p. 307) sell several different phones from a variety of providers, allowing you to compare prices and service. **Bouygues, SFR,** and **Orange** also operate service centers in Paris. The cheapest "disposable" phones start at €20. You can purchase more minutes at most tabacs.

TIP **I'LL CALL YOU ... WAIT, YOU CALL ME.** Unlike American cell phones, French mobiles don't charge patrons for incoming calls. Most people rely on much cheaper text messaging to communicate.

STUDY ABROAD

KNOW YOUR ROLE: GO TO ÉCOLE

Qui a eu cette idée folle un jour d'inventer l'école?
—France Gall

When you tell most people that you're studying abroad in Paris, you'll probably get a the question, "Oh, the Sorbonne?" (In Anglo-speak, "The Sore Bun.") The historical cornerstone conjures up images of grand wood-outfitted lecture halls, elite professors, and Derrida. For some, a delight; for others, a bore. The truth is, Paris provides an overwhelming variety of study-abroad opportunities. Most are surprised to learn that the Sorbonne is not necessarily the most intensive educational institution—that would be the **Grandes Écoles.** Meanwhile, the Paris University system, numbered 1 through 11 based on subject area, includes a range academic environments, from the stuffy **Sorbonne** itself (No. 4), to the less-stuffy but ugly **Sorbonne Nouvelle** (No. 3), from the research power house **Paris 1—Panthéon,** to the radical, graffiti-covered concrete atmosphere of **Paris 8—St-Denis.** For almost all of these institutions, you can decide whether to direct enroll, or to enroll through a university or private program; there are pluses and minuses to both. Of course, in addition to French university courses, there are also cooking classes (**Cordon Bleu** is the *crème de la crème;* see **Beyond Tourism,** p. 111), language classes, and programs run by American universities that offer classes in English with Paris as a pretty backdrop. We can't tell you what to pick, but we hope the following info will help you decide.

UNIVERSITIES: A NUMBERS GAME

As mentioned above, Paris has a plethora of universities. While your choice will mostly be limited based on your area of study, be sure to consider other aspects of academic life: the physical surroundings, the atmosphere of the university (radical, liberal, conservative, indifferent), the types of professors (internationals, renowned researchers, lesser-knowns committed to teaching), the diversity (or lack thereof) of the student body, extracurriculars, and the intensity of academic experience. Here's a short profile of the Paris Us.

GRANDES ÉCOLES

The Grandes Écoles form a higher education system outside of the public university system. Instead of giving out degrees, these establishments groom France's next batch of high level men and women to serve *La République*. These schools are full of philosophers, scientists, statesmen, and clergy members. The application process requires years of preparation, but as a study abroad student, you can take advantage of these high-caliber classes without the pain that the average French student goes through. The **École Normal Supérieur** (a.k.a. Normal Sup, ENS, or Ulm, for its location on rue d'Ulm) is the best bet for a study abroader in Paris. The Harvard of French universities, Normal Sup specializes in science and the humanities and is located in the 5*ème*. Check out **www.ens.fr** for details.

GRANDS ÉTABLISSEMENTS

These are public universities under the ministerial charter. Consider them the second tier of universities in France, still putting out some of the best and brightest in a range of fields. Moreover, these institutions are also more research-oriented, so they also have some big name professors.

École Pratique des Hautes Études (www.ephe.sorbonne.fr), in the 7*ème*. A.k.a. **EPHE.** Offers master's degrees in biological sciences *(vie de la terre)* as well as philological, historical, and religious studies (so you can cover all your bases).

École des Hautes Études en Sciences Sociales (www.ehess.fr), in the 6*ème*. A.k.a. **EHESS.** Offers courses in social sciences, including international studies, immigration, race relations, etc. Many of their professors are at the cusp of major issues, such as affirmative action and immigration.

Institut d'Études Politiques de Paris (www. sciences-po.fr). A.k.a. **Sciences Po.** Courses in political science, economics, journalism, law, international relations, sustainable development, European studies, and history. One of the most welcoming to international students, as they have their own study-abroad requirement.

UNIVERSITÉ DE PARIS

The French public university system consists of 83 Académies spread throughout the country. These institutions practice free admissions, and any student who passed the *bac* (p. 132) has the right to attend. Don't think, though, that these institutions are therefore easy or slacker schools—a large number of students drop out each year due to the workload. That being said, the academic reins are certainly looser than the *Grandes* counterparts. The University of Paris consists of 13 universities distinguishable based on specialization (as well as environment); they are each assigned a number:

Paris 1: Panthéon-Sorbonne (www.univ-paris1.fr). Largest university in France, with humanities and social sciences. Spread all over central Paris, in prestigious buildings like the Sorbonne. Forefront of research and teaching in European studies, international relations, law, political science, management, and communications. Many professors are also major public figures. 40,000 students.

Paris 2: Panthéon-Assas. A.k.a. "Assas." Mostly law, but also business administration and social and political science. Centers on the Panthéon. Alumni include François Mitterand and several former prime ministers of France.

Paris 3: Sorbonne Nouvelle (www.univ-paris3.fr). The younger sibling of Paris's most ancient institution. Locations throughout the city; notoriously ugly. Specializes in arts and humanities—especially language and cultural studies. 20,000 students.

Paris 4: Sorbonne (www.paris-sorbonne.fr). The grandfather of them all—and just as set in its ways (read: conservative). Centered around the historical and stately Sorbonne building in the heart of St-Germaine, but also has locations in Malesherbes, Championnet, Clignancourt, and Michelet—and, actually, in Dubai. Specializes in literature, history, archaeology, art history, and philosophy. 14,000 students.

Paris Descartes (formerly **Paris 5**; www.univ-paris5.fr). Specializes in medical and social sciences, with a bit of law, math, and psychology. Located in Classical buildings off pl. Odéon in the 6ème. 32,000 students.

Paris 6: Pierre and Marie Curie (english.upmc.fr/UK/info/00). Largest medical and science complex in France; ranked #1 in the country. Over 180 labs. Once centered at Jussieu in the 5ème, the institutional, 70s-style buildings are currently under construction due to large amounts of asbestos found in the walls. Locations all over Paris. 22,000 masters students; 8000 med students.

Paris 7: Denis Diderot (www.univ-paris-diderot.fr). Humanities, science, and medicine. Once also located at Juisseu, it has moved to the 13ème. 26,000 students.

Paris 8: St-Denis (www.univ-Paris8.fr). The "liberal" (read: a bit radical) one. In the suburbs of Paris on the end of metro line 13. Concrete buildings and lots of anti-Sarko graffitti. Only public university with a Women's Studies Department (Cixous teaches here regularly.) Known for its radical Philosophy Department (begun by Foucault). Also specializes in communications, theater, and other arts classes. 24,000 students.

Paris Dauphine (formerly **Paris 9**; www.dauphine.fr). Founded as a university for economic and management studies in the former NATO headquarters in the 16ème. Changed status in 2004 to begin practicing competitive admissions, which means it's now technically a *grande établissement,* but that doesn't mean much to the study abroader, except that this place has a rep. Atmosphere is a bit "BCBG" (*"bon chic, bon genre"*—"good style, good class," or, more bluntly, *"beau cul, belle gueule"*—"nice ass, beautiful face"). 9000 students.

Paris 10: Nanterre (www.u-paris10.fr). Created according to the American campus model, with sports fields, dorms, cafeterias, Olympic-sized pool, and stadium. Along the same sort of radical lines as Paris 8; called *"Nanterre la Folle"* ("Nanterre the Crazy") or *"Nanterre la Rouge"* ("Nanterre the Red") during the 60s for its Commie leanings. Now a bit more bourgeois. Courses in social sciences, philosophy, literature, history, languages and linguistics, economics, law, political sciences, teacher training, acting, cinema, physiology and sports. About 1hr. from central Paris on the RER A. 35,000 students.

Paris 11: Paris Sud (http://old-www.u-psud.fr). Located in the southern suburb of Orsay. Known for its work in math and science (especially physics). Also has a quasi-campus that spans about 580 acres. Long tradition of international ties. 30,000 students.

Paris 12: Val-de-Marne (www.univ-paris12.fr). Largest multidisciplinary and professionalized university in Île-de-France. Located in the southeast suburb of Créteil and in the 14ème. 70s, institutional-esque architecture. Courses in law, arts and humanities, sciences and technology, economics and development, administration and exchange, educational science, and social sciences. 31,000 students.

Paris 13: Paris Nord (www.univ-paris13.fr). Campuses in the northern suburbs of St-Denis, Bobigny, and Villetaneuse. Research-focused courses in the areas of law, political science, literature, economics, communications, and technology. 23,000 students.

NON-"UNIVERSITÉ" UNIVERSITIES

Not technically allowed to be called "universities" because it's not a part of the "University system" (gotta love the French), the Institut Catholique de Paris is a university in the basic sense of the term.

Institut Catholique de Paris (www.icp.fr/icp/index.php). Courses in theology, but also secular studies such as letters, philosophy, education, social sciences, economics. Member of an international network of Catholic universities so has its eye on the global scene. 23,000 students; 3500 of which are study abroaders.

A-BROADEN YOUR HORIZONS

There is one major decision you need to make before or after choosing a university: to direct enroll or to enroll through a program? Like all decisions in life (sigh...), there are advantages and disadvantages on both sides.

DIRECT ENROLLMENT. The decision to direct enroll should be reserved mostly for those who are quasi-fluent in French and want an intensely independent experience. With direct enroll, you will probably have more freedom to decide which courses to take, where you will take them, and generally what your abroad experience will be like. Because you won't have a program scheduling activities for you, you'll also have more liberty in your free time—to travel on the weekends, to participate in extracurricular activities, etc. Socially, it may be more challenging to integrate at first, but it may also be more rewarding in the end: because you'll be surrounded mostly by French and international students, your experience will likely be more of an immersion. You can actually feel like a part of the university culture, as opposed to a perpetual outsider (which is a risk of being a "program kid" or "one of the Americans"). Of course, a lot is on you to be outgoing and to take initiative, which is especially challenging in a city that's known for its initially *froid* exterior.

STUDY-ABROAD PROGRAMS. There are almost as many study-abroad programs in Paris as there are *crêpe* stands—and that's not an exaggeration. From the university program with classes in English to the independent program that operates solely in French, the range of opportunities is vast. There are a number of things to keep in mind when choosing whether you want to do a program, and if so, which program best suits you:

1) What kind of **living situation** do you want? Many programs put you in dorms with other American students, which can be comforting but can isolate you from the "real Paris" world around you. Others put you in homestays or independent apartments, and still others let you choose where and how you'd like to live.

2) What kind of **study experience** do you want? Do you want to study in a French university in French? Would you rather be in a private program with other Americans? This will most likely depend on your language ability, but it also depends on how immersed you want to be in the Parisian academic experience.

3) How do you want to spend your **free time?** Many programs let you loose to cafe-, museum-, and monument-it-up; join university extracurriculars; or just hang in the Starbucks on the corner (blasphemy!), while others plan a couple "excursions" to plays, concerts, and even towns around Paris. Finally, some programs plan out your every

A NOTEWORTHY STUDENT

Flying fingers and clicking keys may have replaced spiral-bound notebooks in American classrooms, but French students have yet to embrace electronic note taking. Three-ring binders and graph paper remain à la mode, employed by serious studiers who highlight their petite, neat script in multiple colors. If your cramped hand and middle finger callus don't pain you enough, decoding French shorthand will leave you with a sizeable headache. Let's Go recognizes the difficulty in learning a new language abroad—and your social life's loss in productivity should someone else's notes remain indecipherable; hence, we've provided some common abbrevs employed by prof and peers alike that'll mos. def. prove helpful.

avt = avant
bcp = beaucoup
cad = c'est à dire
fê = femme
hô = homme
lg = long
mvt = mouvement
nv = nouveau
par ex. = par exemple
pcq = parce que
pq = pourquoi
pr = pour
q or qq = quelque(s)
qch or qqch = quelque chose
qd = quand
tt or ts = tout or tous
W = travail
^{o} = "ion" (e.g., frustrat^o)

minute. It's important to figure out how much time your program is planning to take over, so you're not tearing your hair out while sitting next to Overly-Spunky Susie-from-Sarasota, nor wandering the Paris streets with a blank, confused, and lost look on your face.

4) How much **hand-holding** do you want? Some programs just get you to Paris and say *bon voyage* from there. Others set you up with orientation programs to familiarize you with Paris life and times (not that you need it after reading **Life and Times,** p. 63). Others never let you out of their sight. Its important to know how the program handles the transition period and how much infrastructure they provide throughout the semester and year. Could you go to them for help with a paper or to find internships or activities in the area? Do they organize events? Is there an alumni network? Sometimes this "hand-holding" seems unnecessary, but it can often be quite helpful and supportive.

5) Finally, **How legit is it?** *Let's Go* suggests you make sure the program exists and that your "director" isn't about to go into hiding or something equally as unhelpful! Sounds like we're joking, but true story, my friends.

FRENCH SCHOOL 101

Getting to know the cultural and methodological intricacies (and eccentricities) of French academia can be one of the most adventurous experiences during your time abroad—for better or for worse.

PERFECT 10 ... OR 20. Instead of an A through F grading system, the French use a numbers scale up to 20. This might not seem like a culture-shockable difference until you receive an 11 on your first paper and wonder how all those hours in the Bibliothèque Nationale left you with just above a failing grade. Don't gorge yourself on Nutella *crêpes* in a hopeless self-pitying daze just yet—the numbers scale doesn't exactly correspond to a percentage-based sense of pass/fail. Below is a table of an approximate number-to-letter conversion.

LETTER GRADE	NUMBER EQUIVALENT
A+	17+
A	16
A-	15
B+	14
B	13
B-	12
C+	11
C	10
C-	9
F	8 and below

EXISTENTIALISM IS MORE THAN A PASTIME. One of the major differences between the American and French university experiences is the level of autonomy you are expected to exercise. American campuses are meant to provide a living environment—meaning they usually offer mental, emotional, and psychological support in the form of counselors, activities, tutors, etc. Professors (at least technically) are supposed to be approachable and available to student inquiries and concerns. There are usually actual assignments with actual due dates. In France, you're on your own, with initiative, discipline, and perseverance as your only friends. You'll often find that your class has no real syllabus, but rather an exhaustive list of books (anywhere from 5 to 60) that your professor thinks may be relevant to the topic at hand—or may just think are interesting in general. You may also have just one or two larger assignments as opposed to more frequent and less intense works; If you're prepared and organized, you can avoid the I'm-lost-in-a-world-of-nothingness feelings that have plagued Frenchies and study abroaders alike in the past.

IT'S NOT WHAT YOU SAY BUT HOW YOU SAY IT... The difference between your high-level French class at USA University and your history class at Normale Sup is not just that your papers are in French. The assignments themselves—and philosophy behind the assignments—are quite different. The French students you'll be studying with will have been instructed in French methodology since they were teething on wine corks, and you may be expected to be well-versed in the ways of French argumentation also. Moreover, like a lot of things in France—and Paris especially—presentation is often as or more important than content. Students have lost multiple points for forgetting to justify the margin (*always* justify!). We here at *Let's Go* can provide you with a brief overview, but for more information check out Guy Spielman's page at Georgetown (www9. georgetown.edu/faculty/spielmag/docs/index.htm), Site Magister (www.site-magister.com), www.lettres.net, and/or www.hisgeo.com.

La Dissertation: The difference between the essay and the dissertation basically boils down to this: in the US, your job is to assert; in France, your job is to reflect. While Americans are taught to form theses, summarize, analyze, and make conclusions about certain topics, French students are encouraged to discover the "questions behind the questions," reveal the many sides of the debate, and decide what there is to learn from the discussion (not the answer). Many think this is a metaphor for how Americans and Frenchies think in general, but *Let's Go* won't be so bold as to go that far.

Dossier de Synthèse: This is basically a summary of a major work—be it a novel or non-fiction. It's usually used in social science and humanities courses. Many study abroaders are confused by this type of assignment because it seems rather simple and mindless—you're just supposed to paraphrase what you've read in depth? Yes.

Fiche de Lecture: Usually assigned in political science or history classes, the *fiche de lecture* usually consists of reading a selection of texts, summarizing each, and explaining how they interact with one another—how the authors agree or disagree. The key to this is to be straightforward—they're looking not looking for creativity.

L'Exposé: The *exposé* can be one of the most harrowing aspects of a French education, especially at the grander universities. Often instead of lecturing each week, professors will assign a topic to each student, who has to research and then present his or her findings during class. Yes, study abroaders, too. And yes, it means that the same kid who gets Englished by waiters has to speak in French in front of potentially hundreds of people ... potentially for an hour or 2. Moreover, French professors seem to get a kick out of interrupting, questioning, and challenging students throughout the presentation—or better yet, they wait until the end before proceeding to re-do your *exposé* the way *they* would have given it. If all you get is a *"Pas mal,"* thank your lucky *étoiles*.

YOUR MASTER'S LICENCE? As you know, *Let's Go*'s got your back: we wouldn't let you set off on your abroad experience without knowing some of the major concepts and minor terminology so you can at least fake like you know what you're talking about (that's what we all do anyway, right?).

Le Baccalauréat: A.k.a *le bac*. The exam that all French teenagers take at the end of their version of *lycée*, or secondary school. You gotta pass to go to uni.

La Licence: Undergraduate studies in a specific discipline. Takes 3 years.

Le Master: Graduate studies with focus on research. Takes 2 years.

Le Doctorat: Like a PhD. Takes 3 years.

Le CM (cour magistral): Lecture, given by the main professor.

Le TD (travaux dirigés): A work session, or section as many people call them, usually with a second professor.

Devoir: Homework in general, but a paper more specifically.

Devoir sur table: In-class essay or test.

Partiel: Midterm.

UFR: "Unité de Formation et de Recherche". An academic department.

Inscription: Registration.

WHAT THE HÈQUE IS A BIBLIOTHÈQUE?

Cafes are great, and we would never claim otherwise, but sometimes you just need a more studious environment—that's where Paris's libraries come in. With large reading rooms, archives, and helpful staff, the *bibliothèques* in the City of Light will aid any search for enlightenment. Of course, Paris is also the City of Love, and therefore libraries are also prime locations for the *lycéen* dating scene, but the strict silence policies stop most trysts from getting too rowdy.

CITY LIBRARIES. Even if you find your workload significantly reduced while abroad, chances are you will have to check out a book or two to write that last-minute term paper or to beef-up for that obscure oral *exposé*. Most University of Paris campuses have their own—albeit severely limited—libraries. For serious research projects, you may find a trip to the *bibliothèque municipale* necessary. Most *arrondissements* have several branches; to find the location with the resources best suited for your particular project, search the Paris City Library's **online card catalogue** at http://dac-opac-pret.paris.fr/cyberpac/acceuil.asp. Alternatively, for a quiet place to study, you can locate **nearby libraries** at www.paris.fr/portail/Culture/Portal.lut?page_id=7973. In particular, eight branches offer more concentrated collections specializing in cinema, crime, feminism, graphic art, law, media, and Parisian history.

"INSCRIPTIONS," NOT SUBSCRIPTIONS. Borrowing books or magazines from any Paris City Library requires you to *s'inscrire*, or subscribe, to the entire municipal system. To sign-up for a free membership, just present your passport to the library clerk and answer a few questions about your birthday, current address, and occupation. Once enrolled, borrowers can keep up to five books, five cartoons, five magazines, and five reviews for three weeks and two new releases for one week. At any one time, however, a user cannot borrow more than 20 documents from any one library or 40 from the municipal system. The city libraries also offer annual subscription to their multimedia collection, charging €31 per year for CDs and €61 per year for CDs, DVDs, and VHS films.

Despite free *inscription*, the library charges €0.15 per day per document in late fees. Most but not all municipal libraries offer free Wi-Fi.

For more info, contact the **Bureau des Bibliothèques,** 31 rue des Francs-Bourgeois, 4è*me*. Library hours vary by branch and season; look online at www.bibliotheques.paris.fr or pick up a free library pocket map from a branch. Municipal libraries open just before or immediately after lunch and close by 7pm.

In addition to the *bibliothèque municipales* open to the public, free and specialized libraries may have useful resources for scholars. The two major specialty libraries are the BPI and the BNF:

La Bibliothèque Publique d'Information (**BPI;** www.bpi.fr). Located inside the Centre Pompidou (p. 217). With free Wi-Fi and late opening hours, this place is usually packed. The Sunday wait is rumored to be 2hr. at least. Free with student card. Open M and W-F noon-10pm, Sa-Su 11am-10pm.

Bibliothèque nationale de France (www.bnf.fr). In the 13è*me*. 4-buiilding complex is made to look like 4 open books facing each other. With a number of large and comfortable reading rooms, a sunken in garden, a huge selection of archives, and its own cafe, the BNF almost begs you to shack up inside it for days on end. Yearly student membership €18. Open Tu-Sa 10am-8pm, Su 1-7pm.

STYLIN' A STYLO

Besides the usual suspect (namely, **FNAC;** see p. 307), the following places can be useful for purchasing school supplies, grabbing a copy of Rousseau's *Confessions* that needs to be read within a week, and fixing that laptop that refuses to start. See also **Practical Information,** p. 135.

Gibert Jeune, 5 pl. St-Michel, 5è*me* (☎01 56 81 22 22; www.gibertjeune.fr). ⓂSt-Michel. Main location plus 7 specialized branches clustered around the Fontaine St-Michel; look for the tell-tale yellow canopies. With low-price books in many languages, Gibert Jeune draws a diverse group. Extensive stationary department downstairs. University text branch, 27 quai St-Michel, 5è*me* (☎01 56 81 22 22). Open M-Sa 9:30am-7:30pm. General books branch, 15bis bd. St-Denis, 2è*me* (☎01 55 34 75 75). Open M-Sa 10am-7pm. AmEx/MC/V.

ICLG, Apple Computer Service Center and Retail Store, 26 rue du Renard, 4è*me* (info ☎01 44 43 16 72, technical support 08 92 70 01 03; www.iclg.com). ⓂRambuteau. Fear not, oh frazzled *étudiant;* don't let a laptop on the fritz fluster your cafe cool. Licensed to sell Apple products, the ICLG also offers technical support for malfunctioning computers and iPods. Although damage reparation and part replacement could take several weeks, the local service will save you a pretty *centime* in shipping costs. Open M-F 9:30am-7pm, Sa 10am-1pm and 2-7pm. Also at 107 avenue Parmentier, 11è*me*, 35 avenue du Général Leclerc, 14è*me*, 15 avenue de la Grande Armée, 16è*me*.

OH YEAH, AND... GET A LIFE

Study abroad is a great opportunity to try things you never would think about doing at home.. From ballet, to yoga, to cooking classes, to volunteering, there are a million ways to get involved and meet people. You may find yourself getting out of class only to wonder: What now? Thankfully, that's what the rest of this book is for. From tips on staying fit, fine, and faithful (see **Practical Information,** p. 135) to ideas on how to get involved (see **Beyond Tourism,** p. 103), *Let's Go*'s got your back.

PRACTICAL INFORMATION

TOURIST AND FINANCIAL SERVICES

ACCOMMODATION AGENCIES
See also **Accommodations** (p. 145) and **Study Abroad** (p. 117).

Allô Logement Temporaire, 64 rue du Temple, 3ème (☎01 42 72 00 06; www.allo-logement-temporaire.asso.fr). ⓂHôtel-de-Ville. Open M-F noon-8pm.

Centre Régional des Oeuvres Universitaires et Scolaires de Paris (CROUS), 39 av. Georges Bernanos, 5ème (☎01 40 51 36 00, lodging 01 40 51 35 97; www.crous-paris.fr). RER: Port-Royal. With over 30 cafeterias and restaurants throughout Paris, CROUS offers students cheap alternatives to tourist-totting bistros. Choose from several fruit, grains, and veggie buffet options or pay with pocket change for the 3-course *repas complet* (€2.80). The CROUS also rents 3135 housing units to financially needy students in their third academic year. Restaurant Bullier at 39 avenue Georges Bernanos open daily 11:30am-2pm and 6:30-8pm; café open M-F 8:45am-4:30pm.

BIKE AND SCOOTER RENTAL

◼ **Vélib** (www.en.velib.paris.fr). Self-service bike rental. Over 1450 terminals and 20000 bikes throughout Paris. Buy a subscription (day €1, week €5, year €29) and rent bike from (and drop off at) any terminal in the city. All rentals under 30min. free. Day and week subscriptions give you access to an unlimited number of free rentals; year subscriptions involve extra charges for rentals longer than 30min. Available 24hr.

Paris à vélo, c'est sympa!, 22 rue Alphonse Baudin, 11ème (☎01 48 87 60 01; www.parisvelosympa.com). ⓂSt-Richard Lenoir. Rentals available with a €200 (or credit card) deposit. 24hr. rental €16; 9am-7pm €12.50; ½-day (9am-2pm or 2-7pm) €9.50. Open daily 9am-1pm and 2-6pm.

Roulez Champions, 5 rue Humblot, 15ème (☎40 58 12 22; www.roulezchampions.com). ⓂDupleix. Bikes €5 per 2hr., €10 per ½-day, €15 per day; in-line skates €9 per ½-day, €12 per day. Also repairs bikes, rollerblades, skateboards, and ice skates, Open Mar.-Oct. Tu-Sa 10:30am-1pm and 3:30-7:30pm, Su 10am-7pm; Nov.-Feb. Tu-Sa 10:30am-1pm and 3:30-7pm.

CAR RENTAL

Autorent, 98 rue de la Convention, 15ème (☎45 54 22 45, fax 45 54 39 69; www.autorent.fr). ⓂBoucicaut. Also, 36 rue Fabert, 7ème (☎45 55 12 54, fax 45 54 39 69) ⓂInvalides and 60 rue Gay-Lussac, 5ème (☎44 27 01 15, fax 45 54 39 69) RER B Luxembourg. Open M-F 8am-7pm, Sa 8:30am-noon. AmEx/MC/V.

Hertz, Carrousel de Louvre (☎01 47 03 49 12). ⓂLouvre. Open M-Th 8am-7pm, Sa 8am-1pm and 2-4pm, Su 8am-1pm. AmEx/MC/V.

Rent-a-Car, 79 rue de Bercy, 12 (☎01 43 45 98 99; www.rentacar.fr). Open M-Sa 8:30am-noon and 2-6:30pm. AmEx/MC/V.

TOP 10
METRO STATIONS

1. **Concorde** has mosaic-covered walls. Each tile displays a different letter. Take a stab at solving the world's largest word search (actually a series of long quotes). 1*er*.

2. **Cluny La Sorbonne** has signatures of the Sorbonne's luminaries all over the ceiling. 5*ème*.

3. **Arts et Metiers** is covered entirely in copper, reminiscent of Captain Nemo's submarine—or plumbing, depending on how you look at things. 3*ème*.

4. **Louvre** features replicas of the museum's artwork. 1*er*.

5. **Montparnasse-Bienvenüe** is a mega-station where you can choose your speed of moving sidewalk on the *trattoir roulant rapide* (fast-rolling sidewalk). 15*ème*.

6. **Bibliotheque Nationale Francois Mitterand** remains at the edge of innovation with the racy new automated line 14 and stairs covered in an array of foreign languages. 13*ème*.

7. **Varenne** displays replicas of Rodin sculptures. 7*ème*.

8. **Châtelet,** is a large, grimy, and disorienting station, but the musicians are sure to brighten your commute. 1*er*.

9. **Palais Royal** boasts a lavishly bejeweled entrance. 1*er*.

10. **Porte Dauphine** has a florid Art Nouveau entrance, designed by Hector Guimard. 16*ème*.

CURRENCY EXCHANGE

American Express, 11 rue Scribe, 9*ème* (☎01 53 30 99 00; parisscribe.france@kanoofes.com). ⓂOpéra or RER: Auber. Exchange counters open M-Sa 9am-6:30pm; member services open M-F 9am-5pm, Sa 9am-noon and 1-5pm.

Thomas Cook, 26 av. de l'Opéra, 1er (☎01 53 29 40 00, fax 01 47 03 32 13). ⓂGeorges V. Open M-Sa 9am-10:55pm, Su 8am-6pm.

TAXIS

Alpha Taxis, ☎01 45 85 85 85.

Taxis Bleus, ☎01 49 36 10 10.

Taxi Étoile, ☎01 41 27 27 27

Taxis G7, ☎01 47 39 47 39.

TOURIST OFFICES

Bureau Gare d'Austerlitz, 13*ème* (☎01 45 84 91 70). ⓂGare d'Austerlitz. Open M-Sa 8am-6pm.

Bureau Gare de Lyon, 12*ème* (☎01 43 43 33 24). ⓂGare de Lyon. Open M-Sa 8am-6pm.

Bureau Tour Eiffel, Champs de Mars, 7*ème* (☎08 92 68 31 12). ⓂChamps de Mars. Open daily May-Sept. 11am-6:40pm.

Montmartre Tourist Office, 21 place du Tertre, 18*ème* (☎01 42 62 21 21). ⓂAnvers. Open daily 10am-7pm.

TOURS

Bateaux-Mouches, ☎01 42 25 96 10, info 01 40 76 99 99; www.bateaux-mouches.fr. ⓂAlma-Marceau. 70min. tours in English. Departures every 30min. 10:15am-10:40pm (no boats 1-2pm) from the Right Bank pier near Pont d'Alma.

City Segway Tours, ☎01 56 58 10 54; www.citysegway-tours.com. See Paris from a Segway Human Transporter electric scooter. 4-5hr. tours leave at 10:30am and 6:30pm Mar.-Nov. from beneath the Eiffel Tower. €70 per person. Reserve by phone or Internet.

Canauxrama, 13 *quai* de la Loire, 19*ème* ☎01 42 39 15 00, fax 01 42 39 11 24; www.canauxrama.com. Reservations recommended. 2hr. boat tour of the St-Martin Canal. Departures either from Marina Arsenal (ⓂBastille) or Bassin de la Villette (ⓂJaurès) at 9:45am and 2:30p or 2:45pm. Ticket desk open 40min. before departure or buy online. €15, students except Sa-Su and holidays €11, under 12 €8, under 6 free; Sa-Su. Call ahead for departure point. Also offers 2 other boat cruises along the Seine and Marne Rivers; see website for more info.

Paris à vélo, c'est sympa!, 37, bd. Bourdon, 4ème (☎01 48 87 60 01). ⓂBastille. 3hr. tours 10am and 3pm. €30, under 26 €26. See Bike and Scooter Rental.

Paris-Story, 11bis, rue Scribe, 9ème (☎01 42 66 62 06; www.paris-story.com). ⓂOpéra. Features three separate attractions including a light-up model of the city and a 50min. film recounting Paris's history. Shows daily on the hr. 10am-6pm. €10, students and age 6-18 €6, under 6 free. AmEx/MC/V.

Vedette Pont Neuf Boats, ☎01 46 33 98 38. ⓂPont Neuf or Louvre. Many departures daily. Leave from the Pont Neuf. €9, under 12 €4.50, under 4 free.

Fat Tire Bike Tours, 24 rue Edgar Faure, 15ème (within France ☎56 58 10 54, toll-free from North America 1-866-614-6218; www.fattirebiketoursparis.com). Tours Apr.-Oct. 11am and 3pm; Nov.-Jan. 5 and Feb. 15-Mar. 11am. Ask about the tour of Monet's Garden. €24, students €22; includes bike rental.

TRANSPORTATION

For more on transportation, see **Essentials,** p. 19.

Aeroports de Paris, ☎01 48 62 22 80; www.adp.fr. One stop for all info related to Charles de Gaulle and Orly Airports—ground transportation, flight times, delays, etc. 24hr. English hotline.

Aéroport Beauvais, ☎08 92 68 20 66; www.aeroport-beuvais.com. 80km outside Paris. Caters to budget airlines including Ryanair and Wizzair. Flights to over 20 intercontinental destinations. Buses run between the airport and bd. Pershing in the 17ème, across from the Palais de Congrès (ⓂPorte Maillot). Tickets (€13) available online, in the arrivals lounge of the airport, or at the bus station. Passengers are asked to board the bus 3hr. before their flight. Call ☎08 9268 20 64 for bus schedules. Airport open daily 6am-11:30pm.

Aéroport d'Orly, info ☎08 92 68 15 15. Open 6am-11:45pm.

Air France Buses, ☎08 92 35 08 20; www.cars-air-france.com. Between Orly and Charles de Gualle and major metro stops in Paris. Daily 6am-11pm.

Airport Shuttle (to both airports), ☎01 30 11 11 90. Door-to-door service. €29, smaller additional fee for each person going to same destination.

Eurolines, ☎01 43 54 11 99. Intercity and international buses.

Paris Airports Service (to both airports), ☎01 55 98 10 80 or 01 55 98 10 89.

Paris Shuttle, ☎01 43 90 91 91. Serves both airports. Door-to-door service.

STREET SMARTS

Most French cities feature the same national heroes on its street signs. The usual suspects include:

1. Marquis de La Fayette: Short for Marie-Jean-Paul-Joseph Roche-Yves-Gilbert du Motier. Aristocrat who helped the Americans win their Revolution. Like it mattered, with a name like that.

2. Louis Pasteur: Enabled France's obsession with cream. Pioneered pasteurization.

3. Léon Gambetta: Had a vendetta. Statesman who opposed Napoleon III's imperialism.

4. Émile Zola: Promised to "live out loud"—and did. Novelist whose "J'Accuse" charged the government with anti-Semitism.

5. Jean Jaurès: These streets veer Left. WWI pacifist. Socialist defender of Dreyfus.

6. Joseph Joffre: a.k.a "Papa Joffre." WWI Commander in Chief. Used aggressive tactics and won.

7. Georges Clemenceau: WWI Premier and later Prime Minister. Wrote The Grandeur and Misery of a Victory, referring to his role in the Treaty of Versailles.

8. Ferdinand Foch: WWI Supreme Allied commander. Prophet. At Germany's surrender, he said: "This is not a peace. It is an armistice for 20 years."

9. Philippe Leclerc: WWII general who liberated Paris.

10. Charles de Gaulle: 1st President of the 5th Republic. Earned fame in WWII as leader of the Resistance. Baller.

Régie Autonome des Transports Parisiens (RATP), ☎08 92 68 77 14, €0.34 per min. Includes info on the Roissybus and Orlybus, RATP-run shuttles to both airports.

LOCAL SERVICES

CHUNNEL RESERVATIONS

Eurostar, reservation ☎01 49 70 01 75; www.eurostar.co.uk.

Eurotunnel, ☎03 21 00 61 00; www.eurotunnel.com.

DENTISTS AND DOCTORS

Centre Médicale Europe, 44 rue d'Amsterdam, 9ème (☎01 42 81 93 33). ⓂSt-Lazare. Open M-F 8am-7pm, Sa 8am-6pm.

SOS Dentaire, 87 bd. Port-Royal, 13ème (☎01 40 21 82 88). RER: Port-Royal. Open daily 9am-6pm and 8:30-11:45pm. No walk-ins.

SOS Médecins, ☎01 48 07 77 77. Makes house calls.

SOS Oeil, ☎01 40 92 93 94. Open daily 6am-11pm.

SOS Optique Lunettes, ☎01 48 07 22 00. Open 24hr.

Urgences Médicales de Paris, ☎01 53 94 94 94. Makes house calls.

DISABILITY RESOURCES

L'Association des Paralysées de France, Délégation de Paris, 17-19 bd. Auguste Blanqui, 13ème (☎01 40 78 69 00; www.apf.asso.fr). ⓂPlace d'Italie. In addition to promoting disabled individual's fundamental rights to state compensation, public transporation, and handicapped-conscious jobs, the association also organizes international and provencial vacations (10-16 days; €2500-4500). Open M-F 9am-6:30pm.

LAUNDROMATS

Multiservices, 75 rue de l'Ouest, 14ème (☎43 35 19 51). Wash €3.50, dry €2 per 20min. Open M-Sa 8:30am-8pm.

Laverie Net A Sec, 3 pl. Monge, 5ème. Wash €4 per 6kg., €4.50 per 7kg., €7.50 per 12kg., €9.50 per 16kg. Dry €1 per 9min. Soap €1. Open daily 7:30am-10pm.

DRY CLEANING

Arc en Ciel, 62 rue Arbre Sec, 1er (☎01 42 41 39 39). ⓂLouvre. Open M-F 8am-1:15pm and 2:30-7pm, Sa 8:30am-1:15pm.

Buci Pressing, 7 rue Ancienne Comédie, 6ème (☎01 43 29 49 92). ⓂOdéon. Open M-Sa 8am-7pm. MC over €13.

Pressing de Seine, 67 rue de Seine, 6ème (☎01 43 25 74 94). ⓂOdéon. Open M-Sa 8am-1:30pm and 2:30-7pm. Hours vary in Aug. MC/V.

Laverie Julice, 56 rue de Seine, 6ème (☎01 60 60 43 25). ⓂOdéon. Open daily from 7am-11pm. 6 kg, €3.50; dryers €1/10min. Also at 24 rue Monsieur le Prince, 6ème. ⓂOdéon. Open daily 7:30am-9:30pm. 6 kg, €3.50; 12 kg, €6.20. Cash only.

FITNESS CLUBS

Club Med Gym, (www.clubmedgym.com). With over 22 locations throughout Paris, Club Med offers classes for all interests and levels, including organized aqua aerobics, body sculpting, cycling, danse, qi kong, step, stretching, tai chi, and yoga instruction. Several facilities also have a pool, sauna, squash courts, and steam baths for individual use. The Carte Waou membership (€995) grants subscribers unlimited access for a year to personal trainers, pilates classes, and two spas. Carte Club annual membership €705; includes towel service and multi-risk insurance. Carte Base annual membership €650; access to 17 gyms only. Basic week-long pass €25. Month-long pass €185. 3-month pass €355. Most locations open daily 7am-11pm. MC/V.

Lady Fitness, (www.ladyfitness.fr). Accepting only women, Lady Fitness tailors their 30min. circuit program to the female figure. They promote six separate programs aiming to accommodate different slimming or toning goals, personalizing the standard routine for each client. " Tempo" membership €468 per year; grants gym access only M-F from 10am-noon and 2-5pm. "Club" membership €588 per year; unlimited access. Branches at: 20 rue de Sentier, 2ème (☎01 45 08 42 75), 47 rue des Vinaigriers, 10ème (☎01 40 36 01 32), 21 rue de la Voute, 12ème (☎01 43 40 10 45), and 131 rue de Cardinet, 17ème (☎01 43 18 00 12). Open M, W, and F 10am-8pm, Tu and Th 10am-9pm, Sa 10am-1pm. MC/V.

Club Quartier Latin, 19 rue de Pontoise, 5ème (☎01 55 42 77 88; www.clubquartier-latin.com). ⓂMaubert-Mutualité or Jussieu. Facilities include gym, jacuzzi, pool, sauna, squash courts, and weight room. Aquagym, salsa, squash, Tai Chi, and yoga classes available. Gym open M-F 9am-midnight, Sa-Su 9:30am-7pm. Pool open M and F 7-8:30am, 12:15am-1:30pm, and 4:30pm-8pm, Tu and Th 7-8:30am, 12:15am-1:30pm, and 4:30-7pm, W 7-8:30am and 11:30am-7:30pm, Sa 10am-7pm, Su 8am-7pm. Squash Courts open M-F 9am-11pm, Sa-Su 9:40am-6:20pm. Prices vary by activity and hour; see website for more info.

Club Energym, 6 rue Lalande, 14ème (☎43 22 12 02; www.club-energym.fr). ⓂDenfert-Rochereau. From the metro exit, walk along rue Froidevaux away from avenue du Général Leclerc; turn left on rue Lalande. The gym will be on your left. Lacking TVs and complex machines, the cramped Club Energym may disappoint enthusiastic body builders. Offers 8 different classes next door to a spa salon. €20 sign-up fee. Membership €665 per year, €495 per 6 months, €295 per 3 months; students €665/370/230. Open M-Tu and Th-F 9:30am-9pm, W noon-9pm, Sa 10am-5pm, Su 10am-2pm.

GLBT RESOURCES

ACT-UP Paris, 45 rue de Sedene, 11ème (☎01 48 06 13 89). ⓂBréguet-Sabin.

Boobs Bourg, 26 rue de Montmorency, 3ème (☎01 42 72 80 86). Sign up at this bar to join a Paris-wide lesbian email list with information on lectures and social events.

Centre Gai et Lesbien, 3 rue Keller, 11ème (☎01 43 57 21 47; fax 01 43 57 27 93). ⓂLedru-Rollin or Bastille. Open M-F 4-8pm.

Écoute Gaie, ☎01 44 93 01 02. Crisis hotline. Open M-Tu and F evenings; if no one answers, a message will give the hours for the next 2 weeks.

SOS Homophobie, 63 rue Beaubourg, 3ème. ☎01 48 06 42 41. Open M-F 8-10pm.

INTERNET ACCESS

Clickside, 14 rue Domat, 5ème (☎01 56 81 03 00). ⓂMaubert-Mutualité. €3 per hr. Open M-F noon-11pm, Sa-Su 2pm-11pm.

EasyInternetCafé, 6 rue de la Harpe, 5ème (☎01 55 42 55 42). ⓂSt-Michel. €3 per hr. Open M-Sa 7:30am-8pm, Su 9am-8pm.

Cyber Cube, 5 rue Mignon, 6ème (☎01 53 10 30 50). ⓂSt-Michel or Odéon. €0.15 per min., €30 for 5hr., €40 for 10hr. Open M-Sa 10am-10pm. MC/V.

Le Sputnik, 14-16 rue de la Butte-aux-Cailles, 13ème (☎01 45 65 19 82; www.sput-nik.fr). ⓂPlace d'Italie. From the metro, walk away from place d'Italie on rue Bobillot; turn right on rue de la Butte-aux-Cailles. Doubles as a hoppin' bar, ensuring real-world

NO WORK, ALL PLAY

GAY OLD TIME

Boasting a substantial GLBT population, Paris is a queer-friendly city bursting at the seams with entertainment and resources. Most notably, the City of Light participates in a campaign of marches across France to celebrate and raise awareness for queer communities. The highlight is the annual Gay Pride Festival, held on the last Saturday of June.

Nearly all of Paris's vibrant queer communities turn out for this infectiously exuberant parade. The festive din can be heard from several metro stops away; attendance is only partially optional if you're within the city limits, but that's for the best. A fabulous Carnaval scene greets visitors as they reach the festival. Drag queens in feathered costumes pose daintily next to scantily clad dancers shimmying, bumping, and grinding on floats.

This might be the only time the Communist Party, the Socialist Party, and the UMP root for the same cause. A sense of organized chaos ensues as the crowds and floats wiggle and bob from Montparnasse to the Bastille, dancing, chanting, and waving banners. While there is a hint of political consciousness, it hardly distracts from the parade's glittery, muscled, and celebratory mood.

Gay Pride Paris (p. 98), occurs every year the last weekend in June (www.gaypride.fr).

connections. Happy hour daily 6-8pm. Internet €0.90 per 15min., €25 per 10hr. Scanner use €2. Open M-Sa 2pm-2am, Su 4pm-midnight, holidays 4pm-2am.

Taxiphone, 6 rue Polonceau, 18ème (☎01 53 09 95 12). ⓂAnvers. €3 per hr. Open daily noon-10pm.

LIBRARIES
See also **Study Abroad,** p. 117.

The American Library, 10 rue Général Camou, 7ème (☎01 53 59 12 60; www.americanlibraryinparis.org). ⓂÉcole Militaire. Short-term and annual memberships available; see website. Open Tu-Sa 10am-7pm.

Bibliothèque Marguerite Duras, 79 rue Nationale, 13ème (☎01 45 70 80 30). ⓂNationale. Open Tu-Su 10am-7pm.

Bibliothèque Nationale de France, Mitterrand branch at 11 *quai* François-Mauriac, 13ème (☎01 53 79 59 59; www.bnf.fr). ⓂQuai de la Gare or Bibliothèque. Upper reading room open Tu-Sa 10am-8pm, Su 1-7pm; lower research library open M 2-8pm, Tu-Su 9am-8pm. Closed 2 weeks in Sept. For more info, see **Sights,** p. 242. Branches at 58 rue de Richelieu, 2ème (☎01 53 79 59 59), ⓂBourse; 2 rue de Louvois, 2ème (☎01 53 79 59 59), ⓂBourse; 1 rue Sully, 4ème (☎01 53 01 25 25), ⓂBastille; Bibliothèque de l'Opéra, 8 rue Scribe, 9ème (☎01 53 79 37 40), ⓂOpéra. Reader's card €3.30 per day, €35 per year, students €18.

Bibliothèque Publique, in the Centre Pompidou, 4ème (☎01 44 78 12 33). ⓂRambuteau. Open M and W-F 11am-9pm, Sa-Su 11am-10pm.

MINORITY RESOURCES

Association des Trois Mondes, 63bis rue du Cardinal Lemoine, 5ème (☎01 42 34 99 09; www.cine3mondes. fr). ⓂCardinal Lemoine. The Association des Trois Mondes helps researchers find audiovisual resources and potential interview candidates for projects inspired by African, Asian, and Latin American emigration.

Centre Culturel Algérien, 171 rue de la Croix-Nivert, 15ème (☎45 54 95 31; www.cca-paris.com). ⓂBoucicault. Library, art gallery, and theater all-in-one. Hosts occasional concerts and guest lecturers; check website for program details. Open M-F 9am-5pm.

Centre Culturel Egyptien, 111 bd. St Michel, 5ème (☎01 46 33 75 67; www.culture-egypte.com). ⓂLuxembourg. Opened in 1965 to welcome Egyptian students abroad, the Centre Culturel Egyptien has expanded its mission with weekly debates and a French-Arabic library. Check website for occasional concerts and film screenings. Open M-F 10am-7pm.

SOS Racisme, 51 avenue Flandre, 19ème (☎01 40 35 36 55). Open M-F 10:30am-6pm.

British and American Pharmacy, 1 rue Auber, Place de l'Opéra, 9ème (☎01 42 65 88 29). RER: Auber or Ⓜ Opéra. Hard-to-find Anglophone brands and French products. English-speaking. Open daily 8am-8:30pm.

RELIGIOUS SERVICES

American Cathedral (Anglican and Episcopalian), 23 av. George V, 8ème (☎01 53 23 84 00). Ⓜ George V. English services winter Su 9am, summer 9 and 11am. Open M-F 9am-5pm.

American Church in Paris, 65 quai d'Orsay, 7ème (☎01 40 62 05 00). Ⓜ Invalides or Alma-Marceau. Service in English Su 9 and 11am. Open M-Sa 9am-10:30pm.

Buddhist Temple, Centre de Kazyn Dzong, route de la ceinture du Lac Daumesnil, 12ème (☎01 40 04 98 06). Ⓜ Porte Dorée. Buddhist temple and meditation center. Meditations Tu-F 9:30am, 6, and 7:30pm; Sa-Su 10am-noon and 2:30-5:30pm.

Église Russe (Russian Eastern Orthodox), also known as Cathédrale Alexandre-Nevski, 12 rue Daru, 8ème (☎01 42 27 37 34). Ⓜ Ternes. Open Tu, F, Su 3-5pm. Services (in French and Russian) Su 10:30am.

Mosquée de Paris, Institut Musulman, 2bis pl. du puits de l'Ermite, 5ème (☎01 45 35 97 33; www.mosquee-de-paris.net). Ⓜ Place Monge. Open M-Th and Sa-Su 9am-noon and 2-6pm.

St. Joseph's Church (Catholic), 50 av. Hoche, 8ème (☎01 42 27 28 56). Ⓜ Charles de Gaulle-Étoile. English mass Su 11am and 6:30pm. Phone for other service times following renovations.

St. Michael's Church (Anglican and Episcopalian), 5 rue d'Aguesseau, 8ème (☎01 47 42 70 88). Ⓜ Concorde. Services in English Su 9:30, 11:15am, and 6:30pm. Open M-Tu and Th-F 10am-1pm and 2-5:30pm.

Union Libérale Israélite de France, 24 rue Copernic, 16ème (☎01 47 04 37 27). Ⓜ Victor Hugo. Services F 6-7pm, Sa 10:30am-noon, mostly in Hebrew with a little French. Services in the evenings and mornings of High Holy Days; call for info. Open M-F 9am-noon and 2-6pm, Sa 9am-5:30pm.

TICKET SERVICES

FNAC, 74 av. des Champs-Élysées, 8ème (☎01 53 53 64 64; www.fnac.fr). Ⓜ Franklin D. Roosevelt. Also at 1-7 rue Pierre Lescot, 1er; 30 av. d'Italie, 13ème; 136 rue de Rennes 6ème; Passage du Havre, 109 rue St-Lazare, 9ème; 26-30 av. des Ternes, 17ème.

Kiosque Info Jeune, 25 bd. Bourdon, 4ème (☎01 42 76 22 60). Ⓜ Bastille. Open M-F 10am-7pm.

THE LOCAL STORY

OF BATHS AND BIDETS

Befuddled American tourists have found an array of uses for the mysterious porcelain fixture lurking near the sink in their Paris hotel room: an ice-bucket for chilling champagne, a home for their globe-trotting goldfish. Good thing Goldie has no short-term memory, because he'd be pretty shocked to learn that his fishbowl was in fact a bidet, used for centuries to bathe Europeans' nether-regions.

The French are notorious for their lackadaisical attitude toward personal hygiene. While the stereotype is slightly outdated, it's true that they don't hold showers (douches, in French) as sacred as super-sanitized Americans do. Historically, France uses the smallest amount of soap per capita in Europe, and in some Paris apartments the stand-up, curtained-off shower is a rare amenity. In a culture that considers it normal to go a few days without bathing, the bidet is an economical way to clean where it counts.

The word bidet come from the French word for "pony." To saddle up, squat on the bidet with your front toward the fixture. Newer bidets have jets that squirt water upward, like a drinking fountain, but most use a simple faucet. Bidets should never be used as a toilet or—in Europe, anyway—in place of toilet paper. Today, however, as modern plumbing gains prominence, many Parisians use their bidets for washing feet, babies, and delicate laundry.

Virgin Megastore, 52 av. des Champs-Elysées, 8ème (☎01 49 53 50 00; www.virgin-mega.fr). ⓂFranklin D. Roosevelt. Open M-Sa 10am-midnight, Su noon-midnight.

WOMEN'S RESOURCES

Bibliothèque Marguerite Duras, 79 rue Nationale, 13ème (☎01 45 70 80 30). ⓂNationale. Open Tu-Sa 2-6pm.

Centre de Planification et d'Education Familiale, 27 rue Curnonsky, 17ème (☎01 48 88 07 28). ⓂPorte de Champerret. Offers information and services on AIDS, contraception, and STIs. Open M-F 9am-5pm.

EMERGENCY AND COMMUNICATIONS

EMERGENCY

Ambulance (SAMU), ☎15.

Fire, ☎18.

Poison, ☎01 40 05 48 48. In French, but some English assistance is available.

Police, ☎17. For emergencies only.

Rape: SOS Viol (☎08 00 05 95 95). Open M-F 10am-7pm.

SOS Help!, ☎01 46 21 46 46. An anonymous, confidential hotline for English speakers in crisis. Open daily (including holidays) 3-11pm.

HOSPITALS

American Hospital of Paris, 63 bd. Hugo, Neuilly (☎01 46 41 25 25). ⓂPort Maillot, then bus #82 to the end of the line.

Hôpital Bichat, 46 rue Henri Buchard, 18ème (☎01 40 25 80 80). ⓂPort St-Ouen. Emergency services.

Hertford British Hospital (Hôpital Franco-Britannique de Paris), 3 rue Barbès, in the Parisian suburb of Levallois-Perret (☎01 46 39 22 22). ⓂAnatole France.

HOTLINES AND SUPPORT CENTERS

AIDES, ☎0 800 84 08 00. Open 24hr.

Alcoholics Anonymous (AA), ☎01 43 25 75 00; www.aaparis.org. Holds both English and French meetings.

Free Anglo-American Counseling Treatment and Support (FACTS), HIV/AIDS information line ☎01 44 93 16 69. Open M-F 11am-2pm.

HIV, 43 rue de Valois, 1er (☎01 42 61 30 04). ⓂPalais-Royal or Bourse. Open M-W 9am-5pm. HIV testing at 218 rue de Belleville, 20ème (☎01 40 33 52 00). ⓂTélégraphe. Open M-F 1-6pm. 3-5, rue de Ridder, 14ème (☎01 58 14 30 30). ⓂPlaisance. Testing M-F noon-6:30pm, Sa 9:30am-noon.

International Counseling Service (ICS), ☎01 45 50 26 49. Open M-F 8am-8pm, Sa 8am-2pm.

SOS Crisis Help Line Friendship, ☎01 46 21 46 46. English spoken. Open M-F 3-11pm.

MAIL

There are several post offices in each *arrondissement*. Most open at 8am and close at 7pm on weekdays; on Saturday they are open from 8am-noon.

Federal Express, ☎0820 123 800. Call for pick up. Or, drop off at 63 bd. Haussmann, 8*ème*. Ⓜ Havre-Caumartin. Open M-F 9am-7:30pm, Sa 9am-5:30pm.

Poste du Louvre, 52 rue du Louvre, 1er (postal info ☎01 40 28 20 40). Ⓜ Louvre. Open 24hr.

PHARMACIES

Pharmacie des Halles, 10, bd. de Sébastopol, 1er (☎01 42 72 03 23). Ⓜ Châtelet-Les Halles. Open M-Sa 9am-midnight, Su 9am-10pm.

Pharmacie Beaubourg, 50 rue Rambuteau, 3è*me* (☎01 48 87 86 37). Ⓜ Rambuteau. Open M-Sa 8am-8pm, Su 10am-8pm. MC/V

Pharmacie Gacha, 361 rue des Pyrénées, 20è*me* (☎01 46 36 59 10). Ⓜ Pyrénées or Jourdain. Open M-F 9am-8pm, Sa 9am-7pm.

ACCOMMODATIONS

BY PRICE

UNDER €35 (❶)

Aloha Hostel (160)	15ème
Ass. Foyers de Jeunes: Tolbiac (159)	13ème
Aub. de Jeun. "Le D'Artagnan" (163)	20ème
Aub. de Jeun. "Jules Ferry" (157)	11ème
Ctr. Internt'l CISP "Kellermann" (159)	13ème
Ctr. Internt'l CISP "Ravel" (158)	12ème
Ctr. Internt'l (BVJ) Louvre (146)	1er
Ctr. Internt'l (BVJ) Quartier Latin (152)	5ème
Foyer de Chaillot (154)	8ème
Foyer Internt'l des Etudiantes (152)	5ème
Hotel Caulaincourt (162)	18ème
Hôtel Henri IV (146)	Île de la Cité
Hôtel des Jeunes (MIJE) (149)	4ème
Hôtel du Marais (148)	3ème
Hôtel de Milan (156)	10ème
Hôtel Palace (156)	10ème
Three Ducks Hostel (160)	15ème
Union Chrétienne de Jne. Filles (155)	8ème
Le Village Hostel (161)	18ème
Woodstock Hostel (155)	9ème
Young & Happy Hostel (151)	5ème

€35-55 (❷)

Cambrai Hôtel (156)	10ème
Delhy's Hôtel (153)	6ème
Eden Hôtel (162)	20ème
Hôtel des Argonauts (151)	5ème
Hôtel des Boulevards (147)	2ème
Hôtel Ermitage (163)	20ème
Hôtel de la Herse d'Or (150)	4ème
Hôtel Marignan (151)	5ème
Hôtel Montana La Fayette (156)	10ème
Hôtel Montebello (154)	7ème
Hôtel Notre-Dame (157)	11ème
Hôtel Picard (148)	3ème
Hôtel Printania (158)	12ème
Hôtel Rhetia (157)	11ème
Hôtel Riviera (161)	17ème
Hôtel du Séjour (148)	3ème
Hôtel Stella (152)	6ème
Hôtel Mistral (157)	12ème
Hôtel Tiquetonne (147)	2ème
Perfect Hôtel (155)	9ème
Plessis Hôtel (157)	11ème
Pratic Hotel (160)	15éme

€35-55 CON'T (❷)

Style Hôtel (162)	18ème
Super Hotel (163)	20ème

€56-80 (❸)

Crimée Hôtel (162)	19ème
FIAP Jean-Monnet (159)	14ème
Grand Hôtel Jeanne d'Arc (150)	4ème
Grand Hôtel Lévêque (154)	7ème
Hôtel Andréa Rivoli (150)	4ème
Hôtel de l'Aveyron (158)	12ème
Hôtel Beaumarchais (157)	11ème
Hôtel de Belfort (157)	11ème
Hôtel Bellevue et Chariot d'Or (148)	3ème
Hôtel de Blois (159)	14ème
Hôtel Boileau (160)	16ème
Hôtel Brésil (152)	5ème
Hôtel Camélia (160)	15ème
Hôtel Champerret Héliopolis (161)	17ème
Hôtel Chopin (155)	9ème
Hôtel de Nice (150)	4ème
Hôtel Esmeralda (151)	5ème
Hôtel Europe-Liège (154)	8ème
Hôtel Gay-Lussac (151)	5ème
Hôtel du Lion d'Or (146)	1er
Hôtel Montpensier (146)	1er
Hôtel de Nesle (152)	6ème
Hôtel du Parc (159)	14ème
Hôtel Paris France (149)	3ème
Hôtel Prince Albert Wagram (161)	17ème
Hôtel Roubaix (148)	3ème
Hôtel Stanislas (153)	6ème
Hôtel St-André des Arts (152)	6ème
Hôtel St-Honoré (147)	1er
Hôtel de Turenne (154)	7ème
Hôtel Vivienne (147)	2ème
Modern Hôtel (157)	11ème
Pacific Hôtel (160)	15ème
Paris Nord Hôtel (156)	10ème
La Perdrix Rouge (162)	19ème
Hotel Magendie (158)	13ème
Villa d'Auteuil (161)	16ème

€81-100 (❹)

Castex Hôtel (150)	4ème
Hôtel Bel Oranger (158)	12ème

€81-100 CON'T (④)		OVER €100 (⑤)	
Hôtel Amélie (154)	7ème	Hôtel Madeleine Haussmann (155)	8ème
▨ Hôtel Eiffel Rive Gauche (153)	7ème	Hôtel Prince Albert Lyon Bercy(158)	12ème
Hôtel de France (153)	7ème	Modial Hotel Européen (156)	9ème
Hôtel du Midi (160)	14ème	Timhotel Le Louvre (147)	1er
Hôtel Practic (150)	4ème		
▨ Hôtel St-Jacques (151)	5ème		

BY NEIGHBORHOOD

ÎLE DE LA CITÉ

▨ **Hôtel Henri IV,** 25 pl. Dauphine, Île de la Cité (☎01 43 54 44 53). Ⓜ Pont Neuf. Henri IV is one of Paris's best located and least expensive hotels. Named in honor of Henri IV's printing presses, which once occupied the 400-year-old building, this hotel has big windows and charming views of the tranquil pl. Dauphine. The spacious rooms have sturdy, mismatched furnishings and clean bathrooms. Breakfast included. Showers €2.50. Reserve one month in advance, earlier in the summer. Singles €29-34, with shower €48; doubles €38-48, with shower and toilet €58; triples €72. MC/V. ❶

CHÂTELET-LES HALLES

1ER ARRONDISSEMENT

Because the 1er is one of Paris's more heavily touristed areas, high-quality budget accommodations can be somewhat sparse. There is, however, a wide variety of mid-priced hotels and hostels whose locations can't be beat.

▨ **Hôtel Montpensier,** 12 rue de Richelieu, 1er (☎01 42 96 28 50; www.hotelmontpensierparis.com). Ⓜ Palais-Royal. Walk around the left side of the Palais-Royal to rue de Richelieu. Lofty ceilings, bright decor, plush carpets. Its good taste distinguishes it from most hotels in the area and price range. English-speaking staff. Great location near the Louvre and Palais-Royale. TVs in all rooms. Breakfast €8. Shower €4. Internet €10 for 2hr.; wireless €30 for 24hr. Reserve 1 month ahead in summer. Singles and doubles with sink €67-71; with sink and toilet €74; with sink, toilet, and shower €95; with sink, toilet, and bath €109. Triples and quadruples €129-149. AmEx/MC/V. ❸

▨ **Centre International de Paris (BVJ): Paris Louvre,** 20 rue Jean-Jacques Rousseau, 1er (☎01 53 00 90 90). Ⓜ Louvre or Palais-Royal. From Ⓜ Louvre, take rue du Louvre away from the river, turn left on rue St-Honoré and right on rue Jean-Jacques Rousseau. Unbeatable location near the Louvre and Seine. Large hostel (3 buildings in all) that draws an international crowd. Courtyard hung with brass lanterns and strewn with brasserie chairs. Bright, dorm-style rooms with 2-8 beds per room. Rooms single sex except for groups. English spoken. Breakfast and showers included. Lockers €2. Internet €1 per 10min. Laundromat down the street (24hr.). 3 nights max. per reservation, though you can extend the reservation once there. Reception 24hr. Weekend reservations up to 1 week in advance; reserve by phone only. Rooms held for only 5-10min. after your expected check-in time; call if you'll be late. Dorms €28, doubles €30. ❶

Hôtel du Lion d'Or, 5 rue de la Sourdière, 1er (☎01 42 60 79 04; www.hotelduliondor. com). Ⓜ Tuileries or Pyramides. From Ⓜ Tuileries, walk down rue du 29 Juillet away from the park and turn right on rue St-Honoré, then left on rue de la Sourdière. Carpeted, in a quiet area. Phone and TV in most rooms. English-speaking staff. Computer room; €4 per 30min., €6 per 1hr. Breakfast €8.50. Reserve 1 month ahead in summer. Singles and doubles with toilet and shower €75-85, with toilet and bath €95-115; executive suites €105-125. Impressive spacious studios with loft, kitchenette, and sitting area €125-165. 5% discount for stays of more than 3 nights. AmEx/MC/V. ❸

Hôtel St-Honoré, 85 rue St-Honoré, 1er (☎01 42 36 20 38 or 01 42 21 46 96; www.hotelsthonore.com). Ⓜ Louvre-Rivoli, Palais Royal, or Les Halles. From Ⓜ Louvre, cross rue de Rivoli on rue du Louvre and turn right on rue St-Honoré. Friendly, English-speaking staff. Standard, small rooms with bureau, desk, shower, toilet and TV. Refrigerator access. Breakfast €6. Internet €7 per hr. Reserve by phone or email 3 weeks ahead. Singles €70; doubles €89-95; triples and quads €95-120. AmEx/MC/V. ❸

Hôtel Louvre-Richelieu, 51 rue de Richelieu, 2ème (☎01 42 97 46 20; www.louvre-richelieu.com). Ⓜ Palais-Royal or Pyramides. See directions for Hôtel Montpensier. 14 simple but large, comfortable, clean rooms. English spoken. Breakfast €6. Internet access €2 per 15min., Wi-Fi €5 per day. Reserve 2 weeks ahead in summer. Singles €70, with shower €96; doubles €84/96-116; triples with shower and toilet €126. Extra bed €22. MC/V. ❸

Timhotel Le Louvre, 4 rue Croix des Petits-Champs, 1er (☎01 42 60 34 86; www.timhotel.com). Ⓜ Palais-Royal. Cross rue de Rivoli to rue St-Honoré and take a left onrue Croix des Petits-Champs. Although more expensive, this recently renovated 2-star Paris chain hotel has the only wheelchair-accessible rooms at reasonable prices in the 1er. Clean, modern rooms with bath, shower, and cable TV. Great location next to the Louvre. Small garden. Breakfast €10. Singles and doubles €109-190; 1 triple €190; 1 quad suite €210. Prices €20 higher in summer, discounts in low season; check online to verify. AmEx/MC/V. ❺

2ÈME ARRONDISSEMENT

The accommodations in the 2ème are as diverse and quirky as the arrondissement's attractions (indeed, often because of them).

▨ **Hôtel Vivienne,** 40 rue Vivienne, 2ème (☎01 42 33 13 26; www.hotel-vivienne.com). Ⓜ Bourse, Grands Boulevards, or Richelieu. From the lobby's hardwood floors to the flat-screen TVs and armoires of the luxurious rooms, Hôtel Vivienne adds a touch of refinement to budget digs. Well worth the extra money; most rooms are spacious, some with balcony. Rooms with toilet and shower by the courtyard are smaller. Breakfast €9; room service €10. Singles and doubles with shower €60-75, with shower and toilet €87-114, with bath and toilet €90-114. Extra bed 30% surcharge. AmEx/MC/V. ❸

▨ **Hôtel Tiquetonne,** 6 rue Tiquetonne, 2ème (☎01 42 36 94 58, fax 01 42 36 02 94). Ⓜ Étienne-Marcel. Walk against traffic on rue de Turbigo; turn left on rue Tiquetonne. Located near Marché Montorgueil and rue St-Denis's sex shops. Simple rooms generously sized (with high ceilings in case you want to practice your pogo stick moves)—especially considering the ritzy area and low price. Elevator. Breakfast €6. Hall showers €6. Closed Aug. and 1 week at Christmas. Reservations recommended at least 1 month in advance. Singles €35, with shower €45; doubles with shower €55. AmEx/MC/V. ❷

Hôtel des Boulevards, 10 rue av de la Ville Neuve, 2ème (☎01 42 36 02 29, fax 01 42 36 15 39). Ⓜ Bonne Nouvelle. Walk down bd. de Bonne Nouvelle and turn down rue de la Ville Neuve. In a cute and funky neighborhood between the busy boulevards of the northern 2ème. Quiet, simple and relatively spacious rooms with phone, wardrobe, and newer carpets. Friendly reception. Breakfast included. Reserve 2-4 weeks ahead. Singles and doubles €43, with shower and TV €54, with bath and TV €59. Extra bed €10. AmEx/MC/V. ❷

˙RENCH 101: A CRASH COURSE

˙raveling through France, you will ɹndoubtedly encounter many amiliar words on signs and on nenus. Though these cognates will seem to help in your struggle o comprehend *le monde franco-* ɔhone, beware! Some can also ead you astray. Here are some ˙aux amis (false cognates; literally, ˙false friends") to watch out for:

Blesser has nothing to do with spirituality (or sneezing). It means o hurt, not to bless.

Pain is anything but misery or the French: it's their word for ɔread.

Bras is not a supportive under-ɡarment, it's an arm.

Rage is not just regular anger, t's rabies.

Rabais, it follows, is not the ɟisease you can catch from a dog, ɔut a discount.

A **sale** is not an event with a lot ɔf *rabais;* it means dirty.

Draguer means to hit on, not o drag, unless you're doing it wrong.

Balancer is to swing, not to steady oneself.

A **peste** is slightly more serious han a bothersome creature. It is ȷ plague.

Puéril is not grave danger, just ɔhildhood.

Preservatif is not something ɔund in packaged food, but it can ɔe found in other packages, so to speak. This is the French word for ɔondom.

THE MARAIS

3ÈME ARRONDISSEMENT

This part of the Marais offers several quality accommodations, many of which are also friendly on the wallet and well located.

Hotel Picard, 26 rue de Picardie, 3ème (☎01 48 87 53 82; hotel.picard@wanadoo.fr). ⓂRépublique. Follow bd. du Temple and turn right on rue Charlot. Take the first right on rue de Franche Comte, which becomes rue de Picardie. A welcoming, family-run hotel with a superb location on a pleasant *place*. Bright and adorable rooms vary in size, but all have bathrooms, some of which are newly renovated. TVs in rooms with showers. Breakfast €5. Hall showers €3. Reserve 1 week ahead in summer and 2 weeks ahead the rest of the year. Singles with sink €44, with sink and shower €65, with full bath €75; doubles €53/83/94; triples €114. 5% discount if you flash your *Let's Go*. MC/V. ❷

Hôtel du Séjour, 36 rue du Grenier St-Lazare, 3ème (☎01 48 87 40 36). From ⓂÉtienne-Marcel, follow traffic on rue Étienne-Marcel, which becomes rue du Grenier St-Lazare. 1 block from Les Halles and the Centre Pompidou, this beloved hotel offers 20 bright, basic rooms and a warm welcome. Reception 7:30am-10:30pm. Reserve 2-3 weeks in advance. Singles €41-50; doubles €55, with shower and toilet €60-62. ❷

Hôtel de Roubaix, 6 rue Greneta, 3ème (☎01 42 72 89 91; www.hotel-de-roubaix.com). From ⓂRéaumur-Sébastopol, walk opposite traffic on bd. de Sébastopol; turn left on rue Greneta. Rooms are small and a bit outdated (check out the flowered wallpaper), but they are also clean, with high ceilings and soundproof windows. All rooms have small but clean bathrooms, phone, locker, and satellite TV. Some with balconies. Helpful staff. Elevator. Breakfast included. Reserve 1-2 weeks ahead. Singles €61-70; doubles €77-80; triples €87-95. MC/V. ❸

Hôtel Bellevue et du Chariot d'Or, 39 rue de Turbigo, 3ème (☎01 48 87 45 60; ww.hotelbellevue75.com). ⓂÉtienne-Marcel. A handsome Belle Époque lobby with bar and breakfast room. Clean, basic rooms with phone, cable TV, and spacious bathrooms. Some rooms with balcony. Quiet courtyard. Elevator. Breakfast €6. Reserve 3 weeks in advance. Singles €62; doubles €70-72; triples €85; quads €95. 5% discount if you flash your Let's Go. AmEx/MC/V. ❸

Hôtel du Marais, 16 rue de Beauce, 3ème (☎01 42 72 30 26; hotelmarais@voila.fr). ⓂTemple or Filles du Calvaire. From ⓂTemple, follow rue du Temple south; take a left on rue de Bretagne and a right on rue de Beauce. Dirt cheap without the dirt. This small hotel offers very simple but adequate rooms in a great location near an open-air market. Only for students and backpackers. Take the small stairs above the cafe owned by the same friendly man. Turkish style hallway toilets. 3rd fl. showers €3. Curfew 2am. Singles with sink €25; doubles €35-38. Cash only. ❶

Hôtel Paris France, 72 rue de Turbigo, 3*ème* (☎01 42 78 00 04; www.paris-france-hotel.com). ⓂRépublique or Temple. From ⓂRépublique, take rue de Turbigo. After extensive renovations, this hotel has gone from comfortable to downright luxurious. Rooms have plush carpets, flatscreen TVs, and sparkling modern bathrooms. 18th-century-style lobby with leather sofas, mosaic-tiled floors, chandeliers, and bar. Elevator. Wi-Fi €10 per stay. Breakfast €6. Reserve 2-4 weeks in advance. Singles €72-86; doubles €89-129; triples with bath €109-159; extra bed €25. AmEx/MC/V. ❸

4ÈME ARRONDISSEMENT

The trendy-yet-down-to-earth 4*ème* is home to some of the best deals and worthwhile splurges in the city. Take your pick from among numerous hotels, hostels, and *foyers* in the area.

🏠 **Hôtel des Jeunes (MIJE;** ☎01 42 74 23 45; www.mije. com). Books beds in Le Fourcy, Le Fauconnier, and Maubuisson (see below), 3 small hostels on cobblestone streets in beautiful old Marais *hôtels particuliers* (mansions) recognized as 17th-century historical monuments. Main welcome desk is at Le Fourcy. MIJE also arranges airport pick-up and drop-off and reservations for area attractions; call for details. No smoking. English spoken. The restaurant (located in an authentic vaulted cellar in Le Fourcy) offers a main course with drink (€9, lunch only) and 3-course "hosteler special" (€11). Breakfast, in-room shower, and sheets included (no towels). Public phones and free lockers (with a €1 deposit). Internet access €0.10 per min. with €0.50 initial connection fee. 7 day max. stay. Reception 7am-1am. Lockout noon-3pm. Curfew 1am; notify in advance if coming back after this time. Quiet hours after 10pm. Arrive before noon the first day of reservation (call in advance if you'll be late). Groups of 10 or more may reserve a year in advance. Individuals can reserve months ahead online and 2-3 weeks ahead by phone. MIJE membership required (€3). 4- to 9- bed dorms €29; singles €47; doubles €68; triples €90. Cash only. ❶

Maubuisson, 12 rue des Barres, 4*ème*. ⓂHôtel de Ville or Pont Marie. From ⓂPont Marie, walk opposite traffic on rue de l'Hôtel-de-Ville and turn right on rue des Barres. A former convent on a quiet street by the St. Gervais monastery. Accommodates individual travelers, rather than groups.

Crayon means pencil, not crayon, and **gomme** is not for chewing, unless you like the taste of rubber—it is an eraser.

An **extincteur** is not some sort of bazooka. It is a fire extinguisher.

Fesses is not a colloquial term for 'coming clean'; it means buttocks.

As is not another way to say *fesses* or even an insult. This is a French compliment, meaning ace or champion.

Ranger is neither a woodsman nor a mighty morpher. This means to tidy up.

A **smoking** has little to do with tobacco (or any other substance). It is a tuxedo or dinner suit.

Raisins are juicy grapes, not the dried-up snack food. Try *raisins-secs* instead.

Prunes are plums. *Pruneaux* are the dried fruit.

Tampons are stamps (for documents), not the feminine care item. If you are looking for those, ask for a *tampon hygiénique* or napkins. To wipe your mouth, you would do better with a *serviette*.

The **patron** is the boss, not the customer.

A **glacier** does translate literally, meaning glacier, but you are more likely to see it around town on signs for ice cream vendors; *glace* does not mean glass, but ice cream.

If the French language seems full of *deception*, think again. **Deception** in French actually means disappointment.

Le Fourcy, 6 rue de Fourcy, 4ème. ⓂSt-Paul or Pont Marie. From ⓂSt-Paul, walk opposite the traffic for a few meters down rue St-Antoine and turn left on rue de Fourcy. Hostel surrounds a large courtyard ideal for meeting travelers or for open-air picnicking.

Le Fauconnier, 11 rue du Fauconnier, 4ème. ⓂSt-Paul or Pont Marie. From ⓂSt-Paul, take rue du Prevôt, turn left on rue Charlemagne, and turn right on rue du Fauconnier. Ivy-covered, sun-drenched building steps away from the Seine and Île St-Louis. All rooms have shower and sink.

🏨 **Grand Hôtel Jeanne d'Arc,** 3 rue de Jarente, 4ème (☎01 48 87 62 11; www.hoteljeanne-darc.com). From ⓂSt-Paul, walk against traffic on rue de Rivoli; turn left on rue de Sévigné then right on rue de Jarente. This bright, clean hotel on a quiet side street features a country-style breakfast area with an extravagantly funky mosaic mirror. Feels more like a homestyle inn than a hotel. Small but comfortable and carpeted rooms with bath or shower, toilet, and cable TV. Wheelchair-accessible room on the ground floor. English spoken. Wi-Fi €1 per hr., €2 per day, €10 per week. Breakfast €6. Reserve 2-3 months in advance (longer for stays in Sept.-Oct.) by emailing or calling with credit card. Singles €60-84; doubles €84-97; triples €116; quads €146. MC/V. ❸

Hôtel de Nice, 42bis rue de Rivoli, 4ème (☎01 42 78 55 29; www.hoteldenice.com). ⓂHôtel de Ville. Walk opposite traffic on rue de Rivoli for about 4 blocks; the hotel is on the left. Quirky and extravagantly decorated (think shabby chic) hotel off the adorable place du Bourg-Tibourg. Prides itself on its "old-time Paris" appeal. Overly wallpapered and painted rooms featuring vintage prints, satellite TV, toilet, shower or bath, hair dryer, phone and A/C. A few have balconies with great views. Elevator. Breakfast €8; served in a beautiful salon. Reserve far ahead (2-4 weeks) by fax or phone with credit card. Singles €80; doubles €110; triples €135; quads €150. Extra bed €30. MC/V. ❸

Castex Hôtel, 5 rue Castex, 4ème (☎01 42 72 31 52; www.castexhotel.com). ⓂBastille or Sully-Morland. Exit ⓂBastille on bd. Henri IV and take the 3rd right on rue Castex. This luxurious hotel boasts large rooms decorated in the "style of Louis XIII"—think clean lines, dark mahogany furniture, and billowing curtains. All come with A/C, flatscreen cable TV, safe and full baths. Beautiful dining room in the vaulted, stone-walled cellar; tiled patio with colorful foliage. Pricier, but worth every penny. Breakfast €10. Reserve via fax, phone, or online with a credit card 2-4 weeks in advance. Singles €95-120; doubles €100-150; triples and quads €160-220. Discounts available for online reservation; see website for details. AmEx/MC/V. ❹

Hôtel Andréa Rivoli, 3 rue St-Bon, 4ème (☎01 42 78 43 93; fax 01 44 61 28 36). ⓂHôtel de Ville. Follow traffic down rue de Rivoli and then turn right on rue St-Bon. On a quiet street 2 blocks from Châtelet. A modern hotel with a family-run feel. Clean, carpeted rooms with phone, TV, A/C and bath. Some rooms have a sleek, black-and-white zebra motif. Top floor rooms have balconies. Elevator. Internet access €1 for 10min. Breakfast €9. Singles €66-74; doubles €80-120. MC/V. ❸

Hôtel Pratic, 9 rue d'Ormesson, 4ème (☎01 48 87 80 47; www.hotelpratic.com). ⓂSt-Paul. Walk opposite traffic on rue de Rivoli, turn left on rue de Sévigné and right on rue d'Ormesson. Timbered hotel on a cobblestone square in the Marais. Small rooms with busy decor. All have TVs, direct-dial phones, and hair dryers. English spoken. Breakfast included for long stays, €6 for stays under 5 days. Reserve online or by phone 2-3 weeks in advance. Book online for a discount. Doubles €89-95; triples €99-112. MC/V. ❹

Hôtel de la Herse d'Or, 20 rue St-Antoine, 4ème (☎01 48 87 84 09; www.hotel-herse-dor.com). ⓂBastille. Take rue St-Antoine from the metro; the hotel is about a block down on the right. Small, clean rooms with low ceilings. Cute timbered dining area; 2 courtyards. All rooms with hair dryer, phone, and TV. Breakfast €6. Wi-Fi in lobby. Singles with toilet €45, with full bath €70; doubles with sink €60, with full bath €76. MC/V. ❷

LATIN QUARTER AND ST-GERMAIN

5ÈME ARRONDISSEMENT

To stay in the 5*ème*, reserve well ahead, at least one week in winter and two months in summer. If foresight eludes you, don't despair: you may find same-day vacancies. In August, prices drop as tourist season wanes before students return in September, which increases rent at long-stay *foyers*.

Hôtel St-Jacques, 35 rue des Écoles, 5*ème* (☎01 44 07 45 45; www.paris-hotel-stjacques.com). ⓂMaubert-Mutualité. Turn left on rue des Carmes, then left on rue des Écoles, and cross the road. Audrey Hepburn and Cary Grant fans may recognize this chic hotel from the 1963 romantic murder mystery *Charade*. Spacious, elegant rooms with balcony, bath, and TV come at surprisingly reasonable rates. Chandeliers, Belle Époque frescoes, and walls decorated with *trompe-l'oeil* designs create a regal feel. English spoken. Breakfast €9.50-11. Free Wi-Fi. Singles €92; doubles €105-137; deluxe double €180; triples €168. AmEx/MC/V. Online discounts up to 25%. ❹

Hôtel Marignan, 13 rue du Sommerard, 5*ème* (☎01 43 54 63 81; www.hotel-marignan.com). ⓂMaubert-Mutualité. From the metro, turn left on rue des Carmes, then right on rue du Sommerard. Clean, freshly decorated rooms can sleep up to 5—a near impossible feat in Paris. Backpackers and families enjoy hostel friendliness without sacrificing hotel privacy. Fluent English-speaking owners post daily weather reports and will gladly suggest sight-seeing activities and tours. Rooms with TV by request. Kitchen available 12:45-9:30pm. Hall showers open until 10:45pm. Breakfast included. Free Wi-Fi. Free laundry open 8am-8pm. Check-out 11am. Reserve ahead. Singles €47-50, with toilet €55-60, with toilet and shower €75; doubles €60-68/69-80/82-90; triples €75-90/85-105/105-115; quads with toilet €100-125, with shower and toilet €120-140; quints with shower and toilet €105-155. Prices vary seasonally. AmEx/MC/V. ❷

Young and Happy (Y&H) Hostel, 80 rue Mouffetard, 5*ème* (☎01 47 07 47 07; www.youngandhappy.fr). ⓂMonge. Cross rue Gracieuse and take rue Ortolan to rue Mouffetard. A funky, lively hostel with 21 clean—if basic—rooms, some with showers and toilets. Staff speak English, some are less than friendly. Kitchen. Basic breakfast included. Sheets €2.50 with €5 deposit, towels €1. Internet €2 per 30min. Strict lockout 11am-4pm. Curfew 2am. 6-, 8-, or 10-person dorms €24; 3-, 4-, or 5-person dorms €26; doubles €28 per person. Jan.-Mar. €2 discount per night. MC/V. ❶

Hôtel Esmeralda, 4 rue St-Julien-le-Pauvre, 5*ème* (☎01 43 54 19 20; fax 01 40 51 00 68). ⓂSt-Michel. Walk along the Seine on *quai* St-Michel toward Notre Dame, then turn right at Parc Viviani. Antique wallpaper, ceiling beams, and red velvet create an ambience recalling a rustic Victorian epoch. Great location near a small park, within sight of the Seine and earshot of Notre Dame's bells. No breakfast. Reception 24hr. Singles €65, with shower and toilet €80; doubles €85-95; triples with shower and toilet €110; deluxe double with bath €120. AmEx/MC/V. ❸

Hôtel Les Argonauts, 12 rue de la Huchette, 5*ème* (☎01 43 54 09 82; www.hotel-les-argonautes.com). ⓂSt-Michel. With your back to the Seine, take the first left off bd. St-Michel on rue de la Huchette. Above a Greek restaurant sharing its name. Ideally located in a bustling, pedestrian quarter and a stone's throw from the Seine, this hotel's clean rooms flaunt a cheerful Mediterranean motif. Leopard-print chairs in the lobby boldly greet new customers. Breakfast €5. Free Internet and Wi-Fi. Reserve 2 weeks ahead. Singles with shower €50, singles with shower and toilet €70; doubles with bath €70-80; triples with shower €80. AmEx/MC/V. ❷

Hôtel Gay-Lussac, 29 rue Gay-Lussac, 5*ème* (☎01 43 54 23 96; www.paris-hotel-gay-lussac.com). RER: Luxembourg. Noisy neighborhood traffic detracts from the hotel's lodgings; lucky for respite-seeking patrons, peaceful shade pervades the nearby Luxembourg gardens. All rooms come with shower and toilet, some with non-functioning fireplace. Breakfast included. Free Wi-Fi. Reserve at least 2 weeks ahead. Singles €70; doubles €75; twins €80; triples €100; quads €120. Discounts in winter. MC/V. ❸

Hôtel Brésil, 10 rue Le Goff, 5ème (☎01 43 54 76 11; www.bresil-paris-hotel.com). RER: Luxembourg. With the Jardin du Luxembourg on your left, walk down bd. St-Michel from the RER station; turn right on rue Gay-Lussac, then left on rue Le Goff. While only a block away from the metro and Luxembourg Garden, Hôtel Brésil appears far removed from the 5ème's clamoring boulevards. If rooms with sound-proof windows, hair dryer, and cable TV fail to attract, sleeping in the same chamber as the hotel's famous past occupant, Sigmund Freud, may appeal to your subconscious. Breakfast €6. Free Wi-Fi. Sept.-July singles €78-82; doubles €84-89; twins €89-93, large twins €100-105; triples €110-120. Aug. singles €60; doubles €65; twin €70, large twins €80; triples €90. Up to €10 off 3-night weekend stays. AmEx/MC/V. ❸

Foyer International des Étudiantes, 93 bd. St-Michel, 5ème (☎01 43 54 49 63; www. fie.fr). RER: Luxembourg. Across from the Jardin du Luxembourg. This all-female student housing complex becomes a co-ed hostel July-Sept. Wood paneling and small balconies decorate the elegant rooms while each floor has its own kitchenette, showers, and toilets, Laundry facilities, library, marbled reception area, and TV lounge. Breakfast included. Free Internet and Wi-Fi. 3-night min. stay. Reserve in writing as early as Jan. for summer months. Apr.-June 2-person dorms €21; singles €30. July-Sept. 2-person dorms €25; singles €34. Oct.-Dec. 2-person dorms €32, singles €22. ❶

Centre International de Paris (BVJ): Paris Quartier Latin, 44 rue des Bernardins, 5ème (☎01 43 29 34 80; www.bvjhotel.com). Ⓜ Maubert-Mutualité. Walk with traffic on bd. St-Germain and turn right on rue des Bernardins. Faded jazz posters in the lobby try to spice up this generic, lackluster 100-bed hostel. In-room showers and a TV lounge comprise its basic amenities. English spoken. Breakfast, lockers, and sheets included. Internet €1 per 10min. Reception 24hr. Check-in 2:30pm. Check-out 10am. 3-night max. stay. Reserve at least 2-3 weeks ahead. 10-person dorms €28; 2- or 4-person dorms €32; singles €42; doubles €64. Cash only. ❶

6ÈME ARRONDISSEMENT

The 6ème is not exactly a budget paradise—there are cheaper places to stay within Parisian city limits. But for such proximity to the city center, the 6ème offers a balance of location and value in its smaller inns and hotels. Expect clean rooms and beds in doubles under €60, but not always your own *toilette*.

▨ **Hôtel de Nesle,** 7 rue du Nesle, 6ème (☎01 43 54 62 41; www.hoteldenesleparis. com). Ⓜ Odéon. Walk up rue de l'Ancienne Comédie, take a right on rue Dauphine and then take a left on rue du Nesle. Absolutely sparkling, the Nesle (pronounced "Nell") stands out in a sea of nondescript budget hotels. Every room is unique, representing a particular time period or locale. There is, for instance, a Molière room and an African room. The lobby's ceiling is made of bouquets of dried flowers. Garden with terrace and duck pond. Laundry room. Reserve by telephone; confirm 2 days in advance with arrival time. Singles €55-65; doubles €75-100, extra bed €12. AmEx/MC/V. ❸

▨ **Hôtel St-André des Arts,** 66 rue St-André-des-Arts, 6ème (☎01 43 26 96 16; hsaintand@wanadoo.fr). Ⓜ Odéon. Take rue de l'Ancienne Comédie, then turn right on rue St-André-des-Arts. Stone walls, high ceilings, and exposed beams create a country inn feeling, despite its location in the heart of St-Germain. Breakfast included. Reserve ahead. Singles €69; doubles €89-93; triples €113; quads €124. MC/V. ❸

▨ **Hôtel Stella,** 41 rue Monsieur-le-Prince, 6ème (☎01 40 51 00 25; http://site.voila. fr/hotel-stella). Ⓜ Odéon. Walk into the carrefour de l'Odéon then make a left on rue Monsieur-le-Prince. Takes the exposed-beam look to a whole new level with centuries-old woodwork. Rooms are huge, with high ceilings and an atmosphere that makes you glad to call this place home. Some rooms have pianos. Reserve at least 1 month ahead. Singles €45; doubles €55; triples €75; quads €85. Cash only. ❷

Hôtel du Lys, 23 rue Serpente, 6ème (☎01 43 26 97 57; www.hoteldulys.com). ⓂOdéon or St-Michel. From Odéon, turn left on rue Danton and then right on rue Serpente. If lodging and sights are equally important to you, this splurge is well worth it. Floral wall-prints, rustic beams, and antique tiles make this spotless hotel sublime. All rooms with bathtub or shower, TV, and phone. Breakfast and tax included. Reserve 1 month in advance in summer. Singles €100; doubles €105 for 1 bed, €120 for 2; triples €140. MC/V. ❹

Delhy's Hôtel, 22 rue de l'Hirondelle, 6ème (☎01 43 26 58 25; www.delhyshotel.com). ⓂSt-Michel. Just steps from pl. St-Michel and the Seine on a cobblestone way. Wood paneling, flower boxes, modern facilities, and quiet location. TV with satellite dish and phone in rooms. Breakfast included. Hall showers €4. Toilets in the hallways. Each night must be paid in advance. Reserve 10 days ahead. Singles €50-60, with shower €70-75; doubles €65-70 for 1 bed, €70-75 for 2; triples €114-128. Extra bed €15. MC/V. ❷

Hôtel Stanislas, 5 rue Montparnasse, 6ème (☎01 45 48 37 05; www.hotel-stanislas. com). This simple, well-kept inn is south of the Jardin du Luxembourg, well sheltered from the bustle of bd. St-Germain. All rooms with bath and TV. Reservations recommended 2 weeks in advance. Singles €63-66; doubles €65-69. MC/V. ❸

PAY FOR WHAT YOU GET. The city of Paris has a *taxe de séjour* of approximately €1.50 flat-rate per person per night. This does not have to be included in advertised or quoted prices but must be listed along with the room price on the price list posted on the back of the hotel room door. It is advisable to check for other add-on expenses such as direct telephone service (some hotels will even charge you for collect calls) before making your reservation. Also, always insist on seeing a room before you settle in, even if the proprietor is not amenable to the request.

INVALIDES (7ÈME)

The elegant environs and convenient location of the 7ème means there are few budget accommodations in the area. However, the *arrondissement* abounds with sophisticated, modern, and non-chain hotels that often have English-speaking staff. Plus, the view of Invalides' golden dome of is always pleasant.

▨ **Hôtel Eiffel Rive Gauche,** 6 rue du Gros Caillou, 7ème (☎01 45 51 24 56; www. hotel-eiffel.com). ⓂÉcole Militaire. Walk up av. de la Bourdonnais, turn right on rue de Grenelle, then left on rue du Gros Caillou. Located on a quiet street, this family-run hotel is a favorite of Anglophone travelers. With a bright, Spanish-style courtyard, a welcoming staff, and tastefully decorated rooms, Rive Gauche provides comfort, class, and calm. Rooms have flatscreen cable TV, phone, safe, and full bath; some have Eiffel Tower views. Wi-Fi access. Breakfast €12. Singles €95-155; doubles and twins €105-155; triples €115-175; quads €135-205. Extra bed €20. Prices vary seasonally. MC/V. ❹

Hôtel de France, 102 bd. de la Tour Maubourg, 7ème (☎01 47 05 40 49; www.hotelde-france.com). ⓂÉcole Militaire. On a corner directly across from the Hôtel des Invalides. Sparkling rooms with plush carpets, polished decor, and amazing views of the gold-domed Invalides, particularly from 5th fl. balconies. All rooms have phone, flatscreen cable TV, minibar, hair dryer, Internet jacks, and full bath. Staff gives advice on Paris in English, Spanish, German, and Italian. 2 wheelchair-accessible rooms (€95). Free Internet in lobby. Extensive buffet breakfast €9. Reserve 1 month in advance. Singles €88; doubles €110-140; triples €160; suites for families €220. AmEx/MC/V. ❹

Hôtel Montebello, 18 rue Pierre Leroux, 7ème (☎01 47 34 41 18; hmontebello@aol. com). ⓜVaneau. A bit far from the sights of the 7ème, and without the same sophistication of many other hotels in this upscale area, but with unbeatable rates and clean, cheery, colorful rooms, this hotel is great where it really counts. Breakfast €5. Reserve at least 2 weeks in advance. Singles and doubles with shower or bath €35-42; with shower or bath and toilet €44-55. Extra bed €17. ❷

Grand Hôtel Lévêque, 29 rue Cler, 7ème (☎01 47 05 49 15; www.hotel-leveque.com). ⓜÉcole Militaire. Take av. de la Motte-Picquet to cobbled rue Cler. Unbeatable location for those who like being in the action; rue Cler is the center of attention from morning until night. Modern, carpeted rooms with large beds and tall windows. Luggage storage. English spoken. Buffet breakfast in bistro-style dining room €8; room service €9. Showers for singles on the 5th fl. Satellite TV, safe deposit box (€5), Internet access, telephone, and A/C in all rooms. Reserve 2 months ahead, earlier for Sept.-Oct. Singles with sink €67; doubles with shower and toilet €90-102; 2-bed doubles with shower and toilet €90-122; triples with shower and toilet €130-137. AmEx/MC/V. ❸

Hôtel de Turenne, 20 av. de Tourville, 7ème (☎01 47 05 99 92, fax 01 45 56 06 04; hotel.turenne.paris7@wanadoo.fr). ⓜÉcole Militaire. Somewhat small, basic rooms with A/C, phone, safe and satellite TV. Spotless bathrooms and convenient location. Breakfast €9. Reserve 1-2 months ahead for Sept.-Oct., 2 weeks otherwise. Singles €66; doubles €70-86; triples €110. Extra bed €10. AmEx/MC/V. ❸

Hôtel Amélie, 5 rue Amélie, 7ème (☎01 45 51 74 75; www.hotelamelie-paris.com). ⓜLa Tour-Maubourg. Walk in the direction of traffic on bd. de la Tour Maubourg, make a left on rue de Grenelle, then a right on rue Amélie. Amélie is tiny but well-decorated. Mini-bar, TV, and full bath in all rooms. Breakfast €9. Prices higher Mar.-June and Sept.-Oct. Reserve 1 month ahead Apr. to mid-Jul., 1 week otherwise. Singles €90-105; doubles with shower €100-115, with bath €115-130; triples €115-130. AmEx/MC/V. ❹

CHAMPS-ÉLYSÉES (8ÈME)

As with everything in the posh 8ème, accommodations tend to be pricey—budget travelers might want to look elsewhere. For those set on the location, a few quality hostels present a more accessible option.

▨ Foyer de Chaillot, 28 av. George V, 8ème (☎01 53 67 87 27; www.foyer-galliera.com). ⓜGeorge V. Turn right on av. George V and walk about 3 blocks until you reach a high-rise silver office building called Eurosite George V. Take the elevator to the foyer on the 3rd fl. **For women only;** residents must be working or holding an internship and be between the ages of 18-25. Well-equipped rooms in an upscale dorm-like environment; Dinner included M-F. Full kitchen available for breakfast and weekend meals. Toilets and additional showers in each hall. Large common rooms equipped with stereo and TV. Full salle informatique with Internet. Fitness room. Laundry service. 3-month min. stay, 1-year max. stay. Guests permitted until 9pm. Bulletin boards advertise apartments for rent, theater outings, and other activities. €350 deposit required to reserve a room; applications on the website. Reserve 1-2 months ahead, especially for Sept.-Nov. €35 application/booking fee. Singles with sink €580-660 per month; doubles with sink and shower €500-590 per month per person. ❶

Hôtel Europe-Liège, 8 rue de Moscou, 8ème (☎01 42 94 01 51; fax 01 43 87 42 18). ⓜLiège. Turn left on rue de Moscou (on your left as you exit the metro); the hotel is on the right. Within the pricey 8ème this is the best bet. Cheerful, very clean rooms and a lovely interior courtyard. Many restaurants nearby. All rooms have TV, hair dryer, phone, and shower or bath. Breakfast €7. Wi-Fi available. Reservations recommended 3-4 weeks in advance, especially July-Aug. Singles €75; doubles €90. AmEx/MC/V. ❸

Hôtel Madeleine Haussmann, 10 rue Pasquier, 8*ème* (☎01 42 65 90 11; www.hotels-emeraude.com). ⓂMadeleine. Walk up bd. Malesherbes and turn right on rue Pasquier. Of the luxury hotels in the Paris's poshest neighborhood, Hôtel Madeleine Haussmann is the best value. Comfortable and professional, with a bathroom, hair dryer, TV, safe deposit box, and minibar in every room. Rooms are tiny, but the locale next to pl. de la Madeleine might make up for it. Wheelchair-accessible room on ground floor. Breakfast €12. Wi-Fi access. Reserve 1-2 months ahead Sept.-Nov., 2 weeks ahead otherwise. Singles and doubles €180-210; apartments €210-250. Discounts of 15-25% available with advance reservation outside of high season. AmEx/MC/V. ❺

Union Chrétienne de Jeunes Filles (UCJF/YWCA), 22 rue de Naples, 8*ème* (☎01 53 04 37 47; fax 01 53 04 37 54). ⓂEurope. Take rue de Constantinople and turn left on rue de Naples. Second location at 168 rue Blomet, 15*ème* (☎01 56 56 63 00; fax 01 56 56 63 12). ⓂConvention. For men and women in the 8*ème*. For women only in the 15*ème*; men should contact the YMCA Foyer Union Chrétienne de Jeunes Gens, 14 rue de Trévise, 9*ème* (☎01 47 70 90 94; fax 01 44 79 09 29). Spacious and quiet, if a bit worn. Rooms with hardwood floors, sinks, and desks. Large oak-paneled common room with fireplace, TV, VCR, books, theater space, and family-style dining room. Kitchen, laundry. Free Internet in the lobby. 1-month min. stay; 1-year max. stay. Reception M-F 8am-12:25am, Sa 8:30am-12:25pm, Su 9am-12:25pm and 1:30pm-12:30am. Guests permitted until 10pm; men not allowed in bedrooms. No curfew, but ask for key ahead of time. 1 month rent deposit required, which includes processing and membership fees. Singles, doubles and dorm-style triples €372-488 per month. ❶

OPÉRA (9ÈME)

Unless you reserve a more popular hotel along the southern border, the 9*ème* provides for a relatively quiet stay. Night owls and travelers returning late may wish to book rooms farther from the 18*ème*. Actual owls should look up aviaries in the phone book or consider public accommodations, like trees.

▨ **Hôtel Chopin,** 10 bd. Montmartre, 46 passage Jouffroy, 9*ème* (☎01 47 70 58 10; www.hotelchopin.fr). ⓂGrands Boulevards. Walk west on bd. Montmartre, away from the Hard Rock Cafe, and make a right into passage Jouffroy. At the end of a spectacular, covered passage lined with shops. Greeted by Chopin's masterpieces, guests can expect very clean, well-decorated rooms and a truly superb and personal staff. Hair dryer, phone, TV, and view of the Musée Grévin's wax studio (see **Museums,** p. 286) by request. Breakfast €7. Reception 24hr. Check-out noon. Reserve 2-3 months ahead. Singles €65, with shower or bath €73-81; doubles with shower or bath €88-102; triples €120. MC/V. ❸

▨ **Perfect Hôtel,** 39 rue Rodier, 9*ème* (☎01 42 81 18 86 or 01 42 81 26 19; www.paris-hostel.biz). ⓂAnvers. From the metro, walk against traffic on place Anvers, turn right on avenue Trudaine, and left on rue Rodier; across from the Woodstock. This hotel lives up to its name. Rooms with balcony available by request; upper floors offer a beautiful view. English-speaking staff takes care of guests' needs. Phones, communal refrigerator, well-stocked kitchen, free coffee, and a beer vending machine (€1.50). Be careful in neighborhood after dark. Breakfast included. Reception 24hr. Reserve at least 1 month ahead. Singles €44, with toilet €60; doubles €50/60. Extra bed €19. Cash only. ❷

Woodstock Hostel, 48 rue Rodier, 9*ème* (☎01 48 78 87 76; www.woodstock.fr). ⓂAnvers. From the metro, walk against traffic on place Anvers, turn right on avenue Trudaine, and left on rue Rodier. A Beatles-decorated VW Bug adorning its lobby wall hints at its fun, hippie vibe. A lovely terrace and relaxed air make the basic rooms worth your euros. Breakfast included. Sheets €2.50 plus €2.50 deposit; towels €1/1. Internet and Wi-Fi €2 per 30min. Communal kitchen, free safe deposit box, and hostel cat (not hostile). Max. stay 2 weeks. Lockout 11am-3pm. Curfew 2am. Reserve ahead. High-season 4- or 6-person dorms €22; doubles €50. Low-season €19/22. Cash only. ❶

Modial Hôtel Européen, 21 rue Notre Dame de Lorette, 9ème (☎01 48 78 60 47; www.hotelmodial.fr). ⓂSt-Georges. Across from the metro station, uphill. A charming hotel safely removed from the grimy debauchery of Pigalle. Spotless, comfortable rooms with direct telephone line, color TV, and full shower or bath. Reserve 2 weeks ahead. Twins €100; singles and doubles €150. Extra bed free. AmEx/MC/V. ❺

CANAL ST-MARTIN AND SURROUNDS (10ÈME)

The 10ème is full of budget accommodations. There is a glut of cheap hotels around the Gare du Nord and the Gare de l'Est. If the ones listed below are full, there is probably an adequate one nearby. However, the area immediately around the train stations can be a little intimidating at night, so make sure that whichever hotel you pick is accessible via a main road.

🏨 **Hôtel Palace,** 9 rue Bouchardon, 10ème (☎01 40 40 09 45). Ⓜ Strasbourg-St-Denis. Walk against traffic on bd. St-Denis until the small arch; follow rue René Boulanger on the left, then turn left on rue Bouchardon. A convenient (for the 10ème) hotel for hostel rates. Breakfast €4. Nearby laundromat and market. Reserve 2 weeks ahead. Singles €20-25, with shower €33; doubles €28-30/40; triples €55; quads €65-75. MC/V. ❶

Hôtel de Milan, 17 rue de St-Quentin, 10ème (☎01 40 37 88 50; www.HoteldeMilan.com). ⓂGare du Nord. Follow rue de St-Quentin from outside Gare du Nord; the hotel is on the right-hand corner of the 3rd block. This hotel's location is very well suited for access to the nearby gares, and the concierge is extremely friendly. Breakfast €5. Hall showers €4. Singles €34, with shower or bath €58; doubles €42/€61-63, 2-bed doubles €67; triples with shower €80. MC/V. ❶

Hôtel Montana La Fayette, 164 rue la Fayette, 10ème (☎01 40 35 80 80; fax 01 40 35 08 73). ⓂGare du Nord. Next to a bustling cafe-filled street near the Gare du Nord, yet still pleasantly quiet. Simple rooms with TV, and generous bathrooms, all with shower and toilet. Breakfast €5. Singles €46; doubles €68; triples €80. AmEx/MC/V. ❷

Cambrai Hôtel, 129bis bd. Magenta, 10ème (☎01 48 78 32 13; www.hotel-cambrai.com). ⓂGare du Nord. With your back to the Gare du Nord train station, turn right and follow rue de Dunkerque to pl. de Roubaix. The hotel is on the corner of bd. de Magenta. A family-owned hotel close to the Gare du Nord. Bright, 50s-style rooms with high ceilings and TVs. All rooms with shower. Breakfast €6. Singles €50, with toilet €54, with bath €60; doubles €54/60/65; 2-bed double €65, with full bath €75; triples €80/90. Quads €120. Extra bed €15. AmEx/MC/V. ❷

Paris Nord Hôtel, 4 rue de Dunkerque, 10ème (☎01 40 35 81 70; fax 01 40 35 09 30). ⓂGare du Nord. Facing the Gare du Nord, take rue Dunkerque to the right. Conveniently located between the 2 train stations. Clean rooms with hardwood floors and walls. All rooms have double beds and full bathrooms. Breakfast €5. Reserve 1 week in advance. €62 for 1 person, €65 for 2 people. AmEx/MC/V. ❸

BASTILLE

11ÈME ARRONDISSEMENT

The 11ème houses a wide range of accommodations, with ample options for budget travelers and big spenders alike.

⊠ **Auberge de Jeunesse "Jules Ferry" (HI)**, 8 bd. Jules Ferry, 11ème (☎01 43 57 55 60; paris.julesferry@fuaj.org). ⓜRépublique. Walk east on rue du Faubourg du Temple and turn right on bd. Jules Ferry. Great location next to a park, near pl. de la République. 99 beds. Modern, clean, and bright rooms with sinks, mirrors, and tiled floors. Doubles with big beds. Party atmosphere. Kitchen available. Breakfast, sheets, and showers included. Laundry €3, dry €2. Lockers €2. Internet access in lobby €1 per 10min. 1-week. max. stay. Reception and dining room 24hr. Lockout 10:30am-2pm. No reservations; arrive between 8am and 11am to secure a bed. If there are no vacancies, the staff will try to book you in a nearby hostel. 4- to 6-bed dorms and doubles €22. MC/V. ❶

⊠ **Hôtel Beaumarchais**, 3 rue Oberkampf, 11ème (☎01 53 36 86 86; www.hotelbeaumar-chais.com). ⓜOberkampf. Exit on rue de Malte and turn right on rue Oberkampf. This spacious hotel is worth the money. With funky, eye-popping colorful decor, the atmosphere is as fun and hip as the nearby nightlife. Rooms are comfortable and carpeted; all have safe, shower or bath, and toilet. Suites include TV room with desk and breakfast table. A/C. Buffet breakfast €10. Reserve 2 weeks in advance. Singles €75-90; doubles €110-130; 2-person suites €150-170; triples €170-190. AmEx/MC/V. ❸

Hôtel Notre-Dame, 51 rue de Malte, 11ème (☎01 47 00 78 76; www.hotel-notredame. com). ⓜRépublique. Walk down av. de la République and go right on rue de Malte. Nowhere near Notre Dame. Quality of rooms vary, but most are very clean and upbeat; those facing the street have large windows. Breakfast €6.50. Showers €3.50. Reserve 10 days ahead. Singles with sink €40, with shower €65, with shower and flatscreen TV €72, with bath and flatscreen TV €60; doubles with shower or bath and flatscreen TV €72-85; triples with bath and flatscreen TV €100-107. MC/V. ❷

Modern Hôtel, 121 rue du Chemin-Vert, 11ème (☎01 47 00 54 05; www.modern-hotel. fr). ⓜPère Lachaise. A few blocks from the Metro, on the right. Clean rooms with plush carpets and marble bathrooms. 6 floors; no elevator. All rooms have hair dryer, modem, and safe-deposit box. Breakfast included. Reserve 2-4 weeks ahead. Singles €65; doubles €75-78; triples €93; family room €135. Extra bed €15. AmEx/MC/V. ❸

Plessis Hôtel, 25 rue du Grand Prieuré, 11ème (☎01 47 00 13 38). ⓜOberkampf. Walk north on rue du Grand Prieuré. 6 floors of clean, bright rooms. Some rooms have great views of Parisian rooftops. Closed for renovation until March 2009. Lounge with TV and free Wi-Fi access. Breakfast €6.50. Singles or doubles with sink, €53, with shower €75-78, with bath €77. AmEx/MC/V. ❷

Hôtel de Belfort, 37 rue Servan, 11ème (☎01 47 00 67 33; hotelbelfortparis.com). ⓜPère-Lachaise, St-Maur, or Voltaire. From ⓜPère-Lachaise, take rue du Chemin-Vert and turn left on rue Servan. Dim corridors; clean, carpeted, functional rooms. All rooms with shower, toilet, TV, and phone. Breakfast €6. Reserve 1 week in advance, 1 month in advance Mar.-June and Sept.-Oct. Singles €60; doubles €75; triples €90. MC/V. ❸

Hôtel Rhetia, 3 rue du Général Blaise, 11ème (☎01 47 00 47 18; fax 01 48 06 01 73). ⓜVoltaire or St-Ambroise. From the Metro, take av. Parmentier, turn right on rue Rochebrune, and left on rue du Général Blaise. In a calm, quiet neighborhood, near a small park. Bright decor and basic, outdated furnishings in clean rooms. TV in all rooms. Breakfast €3. Reception 7:30am-9:30pm. Reserve at least 15 days in advance. Singles with shower €37, with shower and toilet €44; doubles €42/49-51; triples €61. ❷

12ÈME ARRONDISSEMENT

The 12ème offers relatively inexpensive and simple accommodations, with a good smattering of budget hotels around the Gare de Lyon. As usual, be sure to book considerably in advance in March, April, September, and October.

Hôtel Mistral, 3 rue Chaligny, 12ème (☎01 46 28 10 20; www.parishotelmistral.com). ⓜReuilly-Diderot. Walk west on bd. Diderot and turn left on rue Chaligny. Carpeted, endearingly old-fashioned rooms with new bathrooms. All rooms have shower, toilet, TV and phone. Cute and colorful dining room. Breakfast €6.50. 24hr. parking €10. Reserve 1 month in advance. Free storage. Singles €53; doubles €58; triples €66. MC/V. ❷

Hôtel Prince Albert Lyon Bercy, 108 rue Charendon, 12ème (☎01 43 45 09 00; http://hotelprincealbert.com). Ⓜ Gare de Lyon. Take bd. Diderot away from the tall buildings; the hotel is on the corner. A small chain hotel with modern, comfortable, and well-decorated rooms, all with full bath and cable TV. Breakfast €10. Reserve by phone 2 weeks ahead. Singles €105-110, doubles €115-125. Extra bed €18. AmEx/MC/V. ❺

Hôtel de l'Aveyron, 5 rue d'Austerlitz, 12ème (☎01 43 07 86 86; www.hotelaveyron.com). Ⓜ Gare de Lyon. Walk away from the train station on rue de Bercy and take a right on rue d'Austerlitz. On a quiet street, with clean, unostentatious rooms and oriental decor. Modern lounge with big-screen TV and leather chairs. Breakfast €5. Free Wi-Fi access. Wheelchair-accessible room. Reserve 2-3 months in advance for Sept.-Oct. and Mar.-Apr., 1 week ahead otherwise. Singles or doubles with toilet and shower €59-65; with bath €70; triples with bath €75; quads €100-110. MC/V. ❷

Hôtel Printania, 91 av. du Dr. A. Netter, 12ème (☎01 43 07 65 13; fax 01 43 43 56 54). Ⓜ Porte de Vincennes. Walk west on the cours de Vincennes and turn left on av. du Dr. A. Netter. Rooms with mini-fridge, large soundproof windows, and faux-marble floors. Breakfast €5. Reserve 1 month in advance for Sept.-Oct. and Mar.-Apr., otherwise 1-2 weeks. Doubles with shower €50, with shower and toilet €58, with shower, toilet, and TV €65-76. Extra bed €15. AmEx/MC/V. ❷

Hôtel Bel Oranger (Au Nouvel Hôtel Lyon), 9 rue d'Austerlitz, 12ème (☎01 43 42 15 79; fax 01 43 42 31 11). Ⓜ Gare de Lyon. Take rue de Bercy and then make a right on rue d'Austerlitz. Basic but clean rooms, all with bathroom and flatscreen TV. Breakfast €6. Wi-Fi access. Singles €90; doubles €100; triples €110. AmEx/MC/V. ❹

Centre International du Séjour de Paris: CISP "Maurice Ravel," 6 av. Maurice Ravel, 12ème (☎01 43 58 96 00; www.cisp.fr). Ⓜ Porte de Vincennes. Walk east on cours de Vincennes then take the 1st right on bd. Soult, left on rue Jules Lemaître, and right on av. Maurice Ravel. Large, clean rooms (most with fewer than 4 beds), art displays, auditorium, and outdoor public pool (€3-4). Offers guided tours of Paris. Attracts a diverse group of travelers, both individuals and groups. Cafeteria open daily 7:30-9:30am, noon-1:30pm, and 7-10:30pm (full meal €11). Restaurant open noon-3pm (lunch €17). Breakfast, sheets, and towels included. Free Internet. 24hr. reception; doors close at 1:30am, so arrange to have the night guard let you in after that. 1-week max. stay. Reserve at least 1-2 months ahead by phone or email. 8-bed dorm with shower and toilet in hall €20; 2-to 4-bed dorm €26. Singles with shower and toilet €39 per person; doubles with shower and toilet €28. AmEx/MC/V. ❶

BUTTE-AUX-CAILLES AND CHINATOWN (13ÈME)

Lacking tourists, the 13ème offers less expensive accommodations than neighboring quartiers, but it's a bit of a trek from central Paris. With strong legs or an unlimited metro pass, however, you could forget the mad throngs of the 5ème and 6ème and kick it like a local in the 13ème.

Hôtel Magendie, 2 rue Magendie, 13ème (☎01 43 36 13 61; magendie.magendie@belambra-vvf.fr). From Ⓜ Glacière, turn right off rue de la Glacière on rue des Cordeilières; turn left on rue Corvisart. Rue Magendie will be on your left. Offers a quiet stay in a bustling area. Basic, pristine rooms in a modern complex. 4 wheelchair-accessible rooms on the ground floor. Breakfast €7. Wi-Fi €3 per 30min., €5 per hr., €15 per 24hr. Parking €10 per day. Check-in noon. Check-out noon. Reserve at least 2 weeks ahead.

Singles €68; doubles €80; triples €100. Discounted 3-night weekend stay €60/72/90; includes breakfast. AmEx/MC/V. ❸

Centres Internationaux du Séjour de Paris: CISP "Kellermann," 17 bd. Kellermann, 13ème (☎01 44 16 37 38; www.cisp.fr). ⓂPorte d'Italie. Cross the street and turn right on bd. Kellermann. This 363-bed hostel resembles a retro spaceship on stilts. A cafeteria, laundry service, and TV lounge supplement its adequate rooms. Cafeteria open daily 7-9:30am, noon-1:30pm, and 6:30-8:30pm; buffet €11. Breakfast included. Free Wi-Fi and parking. Reception 24hr. Check-in noon. Check-out 9:30am. Reserve 1 month ahead. 8-bed dorms €20; 2- to 4-bed dorms €26; singles with shower and toilet €39; doubles with shower and toilet €28. MC/V. ❶

Association des Foyers de Jeunes: Foyer Tolbiac, 234 rue de Tolbiac, 13ème (☎01 44 16 22 22; www.foyer-tolbiac.com). ⓂGlacière. Walk east on bd. Auguste Blanqui, turn right on rue de Glacière, then left on rue de Tolbiac. Located in an unfortunate salmon-and-white building, the large, modern *foyer* provides housing for non-Parisian women age 18-25. Interns, professionals, and a few students share its 292 rooms. Kitchen and showers on each fl. Facilities include cafeteria, gym, laundry, library, and TV room. Organized activities held regularly. Free Wi-Fi. Sheets €6. Reserve at least 2-3 months ahead. Deposit €46 for stays over 2 nights, 1st month's rent for longer tenures. Mandatory annual €5 registration fee. Stays under 15 nights €20 per night; doubles €295 per month; singles €405 per month; large single with shower €465 per month. Financial aid available; see www.caf.fr for more info. MC/V. ❶

MONTPARNASSE

14ÈME ARRONDISSEMENT

▨ **Hôtel de Blois,** 5 rue des Plantes, 14ème (☎45 40 99 48, fax 45 40 45 62; www.hotel-deblois.com). ⓂMouton-Duvernet, Alésia, or Gaîté. Turn left on rue Mouton Duvernet, then left on rue des Plantes. Flowers adorn rooms with clean bathrooms, lush carpets, hair dryer, phone, and TV. The welcoming owner keeps thank-you notes from former guests in a proudly displayed scrapbook. 26 rooms on 5 floors; no elevator. Breakfast €6.50. Reception 7am-10:30pm. Check-in 3pm. Check-out 11am. Wi-Fi €5 per hr., €10 per 3hr., €26 per day. Reserve ahead. Singles and doubles with shower and toilet €55-70, with bath €75-85. AmEx/MC/V. ❸

▨ **FIAP Jean-Monnet,** 30 rue Cabanis, 14ème (☎43 13 17 00, reservations 43 13 17 17; www.fiap.asso.fr). ⓂGlacière. From the metro, walk straight down bd. Auguste Blanqui, turn left on rue de la Santé, then right on rue Cabanis. Resembling a standard college dorm, this 500-bed student center offers spotless rooms with bath and phone. The concrete complex has 2 restaurants, an outdoor terrace, and turns into a *discothèque* every W and F night. Wheelchair-accessible. Breakfast included; buffet €1.50 extra. Locker €3 per day. Internet €5 per hr., €10 per 2.5hr. 3-month max. stay. Reception 24hr. Check-in 2:30pm. Check-out 9am. Curfew 2am. Reserve 2-4 weeks ahead; the hostel often books up for the entire summer by the end of May. Be sure to specify if you want a dorm bed or risk paying more for a single. 3- to 4-bed rooms €32; 5- to 6-bed rooms €25; singles €55; doubles €70. MC/V. ❸

Hôtel du Parc, 6 rue Jolivet, 14ème (☎43 20 95 54, fax 42 79 82 62; www.hoteldu-parc-paris.com). ⓂEdgar Quinet. From the metro turn left on rue de la Gaîté, right on rue du Maine, then right on rue Jolivet. Well-lit rooms with A/C, big windows, hair dryer, phone, and TV. Breakfast €5.50. Internet €2 per 15min., €5 per hr.; free Wi-Fi. Book at least a month ahead in summer. Singles €70, with shower €90-110; doubles €110; 2-bed doubles €120. Extra bed €25. AmEx/MC/V. ❸

ACCOMMODATIONS

Hôtel du Midi, 4 av. Ren Coty, 14ème (☎43 27 23 25; http://midi-hotel-paris.com). ⓂDenfert-Rochereau. From the metro, take the av. du G. Leclerc côté du Nos Impairs exit; turn right at the corner on av. René Coty. Tight rooms in yellow and blue motifs have shower and toilet. Pricier rooms come with more space, a couch, and full bath. Breakfast €9, in-room €12. Parking €12. Dogs €4. Reserve at least a month ahead in summer. Single €80-108; doubles €98-138; triples €118-148; quads and suites €128-158. ❹

15ÈME ARRONDISSEMENT

Aloha Hostel, 1 rue Borromée, 15ème (☎42 73 03 03, fax 42 73 14 14; www.aloha.fr). ⓂVolontaires. Walk against traffic on bd. de Vaugirard then turn right on rue Borromée. Hosts a lively international crowd, with bright varnished doors and cheery checkered sheets. Free tour daily 10am. Breakfast included. Sheets €3, deposit €7; towels €3/6. Internet €2 per 30min.; free Wi-Fi. Key deposit €1. Reception 24hr. Check-in 5pm. Check-out 11am. Lockout 11am-5pm. Curfew 2am. Reserve at least 1 week ahead. No groups in Aug. Apr.-Oct. dorms €23, doubles €50; Nov. to Mar. €19/46. Cash only. ❶

Hôtel Camélia, 24 bd. Pasteur, 15ème (☎47 83 76 35, fax 40 65 94 98; www.hotel-cameliaparis15.com). ⓂPasteur. Walk away from rue de Vaugirard, down bd. Pasteur, to find the hotel on your right. Superbly situated next to the metro and on a shop-packed street. Small, comfortable doubles with shower, toilet, and TV. Its hopping location encourages trips into the nearby 14ème but bodes poorly for light sleepers. Breakfast €6. Free Wi-Fi in 1st- and 2nd-fl. rooms and lobby. Reception 24hr. Check-in 1:30pm. Check-out 11:30am. Reserve 1 month ahead. Doubles and twins €80. AmEx/MC/V. ❸

Pacific Hôtel, 11 rue Fondary, 15ème (☎45 75 20 49, fax 45 77 70 73; www.pacifichotelparis.com). ⓂDupleix or Emile Zola. A bit out of the way but among the 15ème's most elegant budget offerings. Spacious rooms have full bath, desk, hair dryer, and color TV. Breakfast €7. Internet €2 per 15min. Reception 24hr. Check-in 2pm. Check-out 11am. Reserve at least 2 weeks ahead. Singles €65; doubles and 2-bed doubles €75. €3-5 discount for online reservations. Reduced rates for stays 3 nights or longer. MC/V. ❸

Pratic Hôtel, 20 rue de l'Ingénieur Robert Keller, 15ème (☎45 77 70 58, fax 40 59 43 75; www.pratichotel.fr). ⓂCharles Michels. From pl. Charles Michels, walk up rue Linois, turn left on rue des Quatres-Frères Peignot, then right on rue de l'Ingénieur Keller. 38-room hotel in a location with few—how shall we say—distractions. Breakfast €7.70. Singles or doubles €52, with toilet €57, with shower or bath €77; twins with shower or bath €95; triples and quads €120-130. Extra child bed €14. AmEx/MC/V. ❷

Three Ducks Hostel, 6 place Étienne Pernet, 15ème (☎48 42 04 05, fax 48 42 99 99; www.3ducks.fr). ⓂFélix Faure. Head to the church from the Metro, walking against traffic; the hostel is on the left. With palm trees, beach-style shower sheds, airy rooms, and a fully equipped bar (open until 2am), this hostel guns for the seaside vagrant demographic. Small 4- to 12-bed dorm rooms and a modest small kitchen. Breakfast included. Sheets €3.50; towels €1. Internet €2 per 3hr. Reception 24hr. Lockout noon-4pm. Reserve online at least 1 week ahead, earlier for doubles. In summer 4- to 12-person dorms €19; 3-person dorms €21; 2 doubles €46. In winter €23/25/52. MC/V. ❶

PASSY AND AUTEUIL (16ÈME)

Affordable accommodations are difficult to find in the upper 16ème. The less posh but still genteel lower area has a smattering of inexpensive lodgings in a safe area, though you sacrifice quality and closeness to the city center.

Hôtel Boileau, 81 rue Boileau, 16ème (☎01 42 88 83 74; www.hotel-boileau.com). ⓂExelmans. Walk down bd. Exelmans away from its curving corner and turn right on rue Boileau. You'll be far away from most Parisian sights, and while the clean carpeted rooms come with flatscreen cable TVs, full baths (some of which are brand new), and a telephone, some also come with fading wallpaper. Breakfast €9-11.50. Internet access available. Reservations recommended 1 month in advance June-Sept. Singles €70-77; doubles €80-95, twins €92-98; triples €125-130. Extra bed €15. AmEx/MC/V. ❸

Villa d'Auteuil, 28 rue Poussin, 16ème (☎01 42 88 30 37; villaaut@aol.com). ⓂMichel-Ange Auteuil. Walk up rue Girodet and turn left on rue Poussin. At the edge of the Bois de Boulogne, this family-run hotel offers pastel rooms with high ceilings, wood-frame beds, shower, toilet, phone, and TV. Be prepared for chipped paint and fading furniture. Breakfast €6. Free Wi-Fi. Reserve 1 month ahead Feb. and July-Aug. Singles €66; doubles €68-72; triples €82. AmEx/MC/V. ❸

BATIGNOLLES (17ÈME)

Located far from the city center, the 17ème offers lodgings at budget prices.

▨ **Hôtel Champerret Héliopolis,** 13 rue d'Héliopolis, 17ème (☎01 47 64 92 56; www.champerret-heliopolis-paris-hotel.com). ⓂPorte de Champerret. With your back to the Periphery, walk away from the metro on venue de Villiers; turn right on rue d'Héliopolis. The hotel will be on your right. The superb, helpful staff maintain 22 brilliant blue-and-white rooms, all with hair dryer, phone, shower, and TV. Several rooms sport little wooden balconies opening onto a sunny, palm-lined terrace. Close to the metro, Hôtel Champerret Héliopolis remains one of Paris's best kept secrets. Wheelchair-accessible. Breakfast €9.50. Free Wi-Fi. Reception 24hr. Reserve 2 weeks ahead with credit card via email, fax, or phone. Singles €77; doubles €90, with bath €96; twins with bath €96; triples with bath €108. Check website for discounts of up to 15%. AmEx/MC/V. ❸

Hôtel Riviera, 55 rue des Acacias, 17ème (☎01 43 80 45 31; www.hotelriviera-paris.com). ⓂCharles de Gaulle-Étoile or Ternes. Walk north on avenue MacMahon, then turn left on rue des Acacias. Near the Arc de Triomphe, this well-situated hotel has modern, quiet rooms with hair dryer, phone, and TV. Decorated in soothing colors, several rooms also come with A/C. Elevator. Breakfast €7. Free Wi-Fi. Reserve 1 month ahead. Dogs €10. Singles with shower €53, with bath or shower and toilet €67-86; doubles with bath or shower and toilet €80-94; triples €105-115; quads €110-125. AmEx/MC/V. ❷

Hôtel Prince Albert Wagram, 28 passage Cardinet, 17ème (☎01 47 54 06 00; www.hotelprincealbert.com). ⓂMalesherbes. Follow rue Cardinet across bd. Malesherbes and rue de Tocqueville before turning left into passage Cardinet. In a quiet neighborhood, 10min. from the metro. Sleep off traveling's royal pains beneath the hotel's kitschy insignia-decorated headboard. Entirely renovated in a fresh mint-green, its clean, quiet rooms all come with shower, toilet, and TV. Dogs allowed with owner's assumption of responsibility. Breakfast €6. Internet and Wi-Fi €1.50 per 15min., €15 per 24hr. Reception 24hr. Check-in 2pm. Check-out noon. Reserve by email 2-3 months ahead. Singles €75; doubles €90. Extra bed €16. AmEx/MC/V. ❸

MONTMARTRE (18ÈME)

Staying in the bustling 18ème usually promises noisy quarters at rock-bottom prices. While it's easy to find a deal here, it's harder to spot a location where you'll actually be able to sleep.

▨ **Le Village Hostel,** 20 rue d'Orsel, 18ème (☎01 42 64 22 02; www.villagehostel.fr). ⓂAnvers. Go uphill on rue Steinkerque and turn right on rue d'Orsel. Despite daytime tourists swarming the Sacré-Coeur, Le Village Hostel offers a quiet repose removed from the 18ème's nighttime attractions. Several of its clean, cheap rooms face Montmartre's white majesty or open onto the communal patio. Breakfast included. Toilet and shower in every room. Kitchen, stereo, telephones, and TV in the lounge. English-speaking staff.

Internet and Wi-Fi €2 per 30min., €3.50 per hr. Reception 24hr. Check-in 4pm. Check-out 11am. Lockout 11am-4pm. 1-week max. stay. Reserve online at least 1 month ahead. 4-, 6-, or 8-bed dorms €24; doubles €60; triples €81. MC/V. ❶

☒ **Hôtel Caulaincourt,** 2 Square Caulaincourt, 18*ème* (☎01 46 06 46 06; www.caulaincourt.com). ⓜLamarck-Caulaincourt. Walk up the stairs above the metro and turn right, between no. 67 and 69 rue Caulaincourt. One of the best values around. Formerly artists' studios, the clean, simple rooms have wonderful views of Montmartre and the Paris skyline. Breakfast included. 30min. free Internet, €2 per hr. thereafter; free Wi-Fi. Check-in 4pm. Check-out 11am. Lockout 11am-4pm. Curfew 2am. Towels €1. Key deposit €1. Reserve online 1 month ahead. 4- to 6-bed dorms €25; singles with shower €50, with shower and toilet €60; doubles €63/73; 2-bed doubles €66/76; triples with shower and toilet €89. Extra bed €10. MC/V. ❶

Style Hôtel, 8 rue Ganneron, 18*ème* (☎01 45 22 37 59; fax 01 45 22 81 03). ⓜPlace de Clichy. Walk up avenue de Clichy and turn right on rue Ganneron. Close to the cemetery. No Internet. Breakfast €6. Reserve at least 3 weeks ahead. Singles with sink €35, with bath €45; doubles €35/50; triples €57; quads €67. Extra bed €6. MC/V. ❷

BUTTES CHAUMONT (19ÈME)

A quieter alternative than the neighboring 18*ème*, the 19*ème* offers similar deals with less hustle and bustle. If you choose to stay in this less-than-central location, plan for long transit times and multiple metro switches. Heavily seeped in its citizens' daily wind and grind, the "City of Love" becomes barely recognizable north of the Canal de l'Ourcq.

Crimée Hôtel, 188 rue de Crimée, 19*ème* (☎01 40 36 75 29; www.hotelcrimee.com). ⓜCrimée. Walk down avenue de Flandre and turn right on rue de Crimée. Its location in the northern, commercial 19*ème* adds to the hotel's business-conference feel. Though a bit sterile, the spotless rooms come with A/C, bath, and TV. Breakfast €7. Free Wi-Fi. Reception 24hr. Check-in and check-out noon. Reserve at least 2 weeks ahead. Singles €68-70; doubles €70-73; triple €15; quad €100. Extra bed €12. AmEx/MC/V. ❸

La Perdrix Rouge, 5 rue Lassus, 19*ème* (☎01 42 06 09 53; www.hotel-perdrixrouge-paris.com). ⓜJourdain. Facing a gorgeous church and steps from the metro, La Perdrix Rouge offers a peaceful repose away from the clamor of central Paris. Surrounded by a bank, grocery store, several bakeries, and restaurants, patrons will find the self-sufficient *quartier* surprisingly tourist-free. 30 clean, pleasant rooms come with bath or shower, hairdryer, toilet, telephone, and TV. Breakfast buffet €7.50. Free Internet. Singles €69; doubles €75, with bath €79, with twin beds €85; triples €97. Extra bed €12. €1-10 discount for online booking; €12-14 off minimum 3-night stays. MC/V. ❸

BELLEVILLE AND PÈRE LACHAISE (20ÈME)

Far from popular sights, the 20*ème* offers few budget accommodations to attract passing—or lost—tourists. Staying in this mostly-residential arondissement promises a glimpse into unembellished local life and metro rides too long for comfortable self-reflection. Agoraphobics will gleefully rejoice in the 20*ème*'s cheap, crowd-free lodgings.

Eden Hôtel, 7 rue Jean-Baptiste Dumay, 20*ème* (☎01 46 36 64 22, fax 01 46 36 01 11). ⓜPyrénées. Facing the church outside the metro, turn left down rue de Belleville; rue Jean-Baptiste Dumay is on the left. A good value for 2 stars, the Eden Hôtel's clean rooms, all with TV and WC, provide respite from hellish tourist mobs. Temptation may have you pining to stay longer. Breakfast €5. Hall showers €4. Free Internet and Wi-Fi. Dogs welcome. Reserve 1 week ahead. Singles €42-49, with bath €57; doubles with bath €60. Extra bed €10. MC/V. ❷

Auberge de Jeunesse "Le D'Artagnan" (HI), 80 rue Vitruve, 20ème (☎01 40 32 34 56; www.fuaj.org). ⓜPorte de Bagnolet. From the metro, walk downhill on bd. Davout and turn right on rue Vitruve. Claiming to be France's largest Youth Hostel, this 435-bed backpacker's colony signals a good time with flashing neon lights and a free in-house cinema. Breakfast included. Internet and Wi-Fi €2 per hr. Sheets included, towel €2.50. Lockers €2-4 per day. Laundry €3 per wash, €1 per dry. Restaurant (open noon-2pm and 6:30-9:30pm; plat €4.50), bar (open 8pm-2am; happy hour 9-10pm). 4-night max. stay. 24hr. Reception. Lockout noon-3pm. Reserve online. 3-, 4-, and 5-bed dorms €22; 9-bed dorms €20. Children under 10 half-price, under 5 free. International Youth Hostels Association membership required; on site €11-18. MC/V. ❶

Super Hotel, 208 rue des Pyrénées, place Gambetta, 20ème (☎01 46 36 97 48; http://superhotelparis.site.voila.fr). ⓜGambetta. From place Gambetta, hotel will be on your right off rue des Pyrénées. Less than a block from a bank, metro, pharmacy, and post office, Super Hotel saves the day with a bustling central location. Clean rooms with A/C, hairdryer, and TV vary greatly in size. Breakfast €8. Wi-Fi €10 per stay. Reception 24hr. Check-in 2pm. Strict check-out 11am. Single with sink €45, with shower €70, with bath €77; doubles with shower €77-95, with bath €85-120; triple with bath €95; quads €120. Extra bed €12. AmEx/MC/V. ❷

Hôtel Ermitage, 42bis rue de l'Ermitage, 20ème (☎01 46 36 23 44; http://hoteldelermitage.com). ⓜJourdain. Walk down rue Jourdain, turn left on rue des Pyrénées, and left on rue de l'Ermitage. This simple hotel provides 24 basic rooms with phone, safe, and TV for cheap. Wi-Fi €1 per 15min. Singles €35; doubles with shower €65. AmEx/MC/V. ❷

FOOD

French cooking is universally renowned and downright delicious. The preparation and consumption of food are integral to French daily life; while world-famous chefs and their three-star restaurants are a valued Parisian institution, you don't have to pay their prices for excellent cuisine, either classic or adventurous. Bistros provide a more informal, and often less expensive option. Even more casual are *brasseries*, often crowded and convivial, best for large groups and high spirits. The least expensive option is usually a *crêperie*, a restaurant specializing in thin Breton pancakes filled with meats, vegetables, cheeses, chocolates, or fruits, where you can often eat for less than you would pay at McDo. The offerings of specialty food shops, including *boulangeries* (bakeries), *pâtisseries* (pastry shops), and *traiteurs* (prepared food shops), make delicious, inexpensive picnic supplies and cheap meals on the go. A number of North African and Middle Eastern restaurants serve affordable dishes. At nouveaux bistros, French, Mediterranean, Asian, and Spanish flavors converge in a setting that is usually modern and artsy. Eating and drinking can easily be the most memorable part of any visit to Paris. *Bon appetit!*

BY TYPE

AFRICAN
404 (173) ❸
Babylone Bis (171) ❶
Chez Blondin (193) ❷
Chez Haynes (187) ❷
Djerba Cacher Chez Guichi (202) ❶
La Banane Ivoirienne (191) ❷
Saveurs & Coincïdences (188) ❷

AMERICAN
Breakfast in America (176) ❷
Central Perk (185) ❶
Charlie Birdy (196) ❷
McCoy Café (185) ❶

ASIAN
Au Coin des Gourmets (179) ❷
Chez Fung (197) ❷
Foyer Vietnam (179) ❶
Grannie (184) ❹
Guen-maï (181) ❶
Kintaro (172) ❷
Lao Siam (202) ❶
Le Cambodge (189) ❷
Le Dan Bau (201) ❷
Le Lotus Blanc (184) ❷
Le Pré Verre (179) ❸
Mood (186) ❸
Thabthim Siam (186) ❷
Tricotin (193) ❶
Wassana (201) ❷

BASQUE/SOUTHERN FRENCH
Chez Gladines (193) ❶
L'Aimant du Sud (194) ❷
Le Patio Provençal (199) ❷
Le Soleil Gourmand (201) ❷
Le Troquet (197) ❹

BISTRO
Au Pied du Fouet (184) ❷
Au Vieux Comptoir (170) ❸
Bistrot du Dome (176) ❷
Café des Musées (174) ❷
Chez Janou (172) ❸
Le Bistro d'Henri (181) ❷
Le Bistrot du Peintre (191) ❷
Le Comptoir du Relais (181) ❸
Le Dix Vins (197) ❸
Le Grenier de Notre-Dame (179) ❸
Le Grizzli (177) ❷
Les Fous de l'Île (169) ❸
Les Noces de Jeannette (171) ❹
Petit Bofinger (176) ❸

BRASSERIE
Brasserie de l'Île St-Louis (169) ❸

BRUNCH
3 Pièces Cuisine (200) ❷
Breakfast in America (176) ❷
Café Beaubourg (177) ❹
Café de l'Industrie (191) ❷

FOOD

Café des Lettres (184) ❸
Curieux Spaghetti Bar (176) ❷
La Boulangerie par V. Mauclerc (202) ❶
La Victoire Suprème du Coeur (175) ❷
Ladurée (187) ❸
L'Apparement Café (174) ❷
Le Fumoir (170) ❷
L'Endroit (200) ❸
Les Cocottes (184) ❷
Les Editeurs (182) ❸
Les Grandes Marchés (192) ❸
L'Oga (191) ❸
Mariages Frères (177) ❹
No Stress Cafe (188) ❷
The James Joyce Pub (199) ❷

CLASSIC CAFE
Au Bon Café (190) ❷
Au Roi du Café (198) ❶
Aux Artistes (198) ❷
Café de France (194) ❷
Café de la Paix (189) ❹
Café de l'Industrie (191) ❷
Café Delmas (180) ❷
Café du Commerce (195) ❷
Café Hortensias (200) ❷
Café Med (169) ❷
Café Vavin (183) ❷
Chartier (188) ❶
EXKi (172) ❶
Fouquet's (187) ❺
La Coupole (196) ❹
La Mer à Boire (203) ❶
La Maison Rose ❷
La Rotunde (198) ❷
L'Alfred (170) ❸
L'Apparement Café (174) ❷
Le Bar à Soupes (191) ❶
Le Café Marly (170) ❸
Le Fumoir (170) ❷
Le Kaskad' Café (202) ❷
Le Procope (183) ❷
Les Deux Magots (182) ❷
Les Editeurs (182) ❸
No Stress Café (188) ❷
Place Numéro Thé (168) ❷
Refuge Café (193) ❸
Royal Bar (174) ❶
Savannah Café (179) ❷

CRÊPERIE
Briezh Café (177) ❶
Café Delmas (180) ❷
Café Med (169) ❷
Crêperie Plougastel (195) ❶
Crêperie Saint Germain (181) ❶
Des Crêpes et des Cailles (194) ❶
La Bolée Belgrand (203) ❶
La Butte-aux-Cailles Crêperie (194) ❶
La Crêpe Rit du Clown (182) ❶

Page 35 (173) ❷
Ty Breiz (197) ❶
Ty Yann (186) ❶

FONDU
Pain, Vin, Fromage (176) ❷
Refuge des Fondus (201) ❷

FUSION/ECLECTIC
Au Trou Normand (190) ❸
Café Flèche d'Or (203) ❷
Café Rouge (174) ❷
Curieux Spaghetti Bar (176) ❷
Grannie (184) ❹
La Table d'Erica (181) ❷
Le Loup Blanc (171) ❷
Le Pré Verre (179) ❸
Mood (186) ❸

GREEK
Le Samson (194) ❷

ICE CREAM
Berthillon (169) ❶
Amorino (169) ❶
myberry (178) ❶

INDIAN
Anarkali Sarangui (188) ❷
L'Étoile du Kashmir (200) ❶
Pooja (190) ❷
Tandoori ❷

IRISH
The James Joyce Pub (199) ❷

ITALIAN
Curieux Spaghetti Bar (176) ❷
Fuxia (176) ❷
Piccolo Teatro (175) ❷
Villa des Ternes (199) ❷

JAZZ
Charlie Birdy (196) ❷
Les Broches à l'Ancienne (193) ❷
Les Grandes Marchés (192) ❸
Les Fous de L'Ile (169) ❸
The James Joyce Pub (199) ❷
Toi (186) ❸

KOSHER
New-Flash (190) ❸

MARKETS
Belleville Outdoor Market (203)
Marché Batignolles (199)
Marché Bastille (190)
Marché Beauvau St-Antoine (193)
Marché Berthier (200)
Marché Biologique (183)
Marché Monge (180)
Marché Mouffetard (180)

FOOD

Marché Popincourt (192)
Marché Port Royal (180)
Marché Président-Wilson (199)
St-Germain Covered Market (184)

MEXICAN
◾ Ay, Caramba! (202)   ❸
La Cucaracha (172)   ❷

MIDDLE EASTERN
Aquarius Café (196)   ❷
Babylone Bis (171)   ❶
Café de la Mosquée (180)   ❷
◾ Comptoir Méditerranée (178)   ❶
◾ Chez Hanna (175)   ❷
Chez Marianne (176)   ❷
◾ L'As du Falafel (175)   ❶
Samaya (197)   ❷

PÂTISSERIE
◾ La Fournée d'Augustine (199)   ❶

SALONS DE THÉ
◾ Angelina (171)   ❷
Le bien-être gourmand (186)   ❶
Le Petit Plateau (168)   ❷
◾ Mariage Frères (177)   ❹
Muscade (171)   ❶
Place Numéro Thé (168)   ❶

SCANDINAVIAN
◾ Café des Lettres (184)   ❸

SEAFOOD
Au Chien qui Fume (170)   ❹

SPANISH
Casa Tina (198)   ❹
Caves St-Gilles (173)   ❸
"Chez les filles" (194)   ❷
Chez Papa (196)   ❷
La Bodega (201)   ❶

SPECIALTY SHOPS
Au Coin du Pétrin (198)
Barthélémy (185)
◾ Bubbles (177)
Debauve et Gallais (185)
Izrael (178)
Fauchon (187)
Gérard Mulot (183)
Jadis et Gourmande (178)
Kusmi Tea (183)
◾ La Bague de Kenza (192)
La Boulangerie par Véronique Mauclerc (202)
◾ La Fournée d'Augustine (199)
La Maison du Chocolat (189)
◾ La Grande Épicerie de Paris (185)
L'entrée au dessert (186)
La Petite Scierie (169)
Le Gay Choc (178)

L'Empire des Thés (195)
myberry (178)
O&CO (170)
Pascal Beillevaire, Maître Fromager (196)
Poilâne (183)
◾ Tang Frères (195)

STEAK/MEAT
Les Broches à L'Ancienne (193)   ❷
Le "Relais de L'Entrecôte" (182)   ❸
Le Severo (195)   ❷

TRADITIONAL AND MODERN FRENCH
Au Général La Fayette (189)   ❷
◾ Au Petit Fer à Cheval (175)   ❷
Au Port Salut (180)   ❸
Au Rendez-Vous des Camionneurs (168)   ❸
Au Vieux Logis (199)   ❷
◾ Bélisaire (197)   ❹
Café du Marché (185)   ❶
◾ Chez Janou (172)   ❸
Chez Omar (174)   ❷
Chez Paul (190)   ❸
L'Alfred (170)   ❸
L'Amuse Bouche (196)   ❹
◾ L'Ébauchoir (192)   ❷
◾ Le Caveau du Palais (168)   ❹
Le Jardin des Pâtes (180)   ❷
◾ Le Perraudin (179)   ❸
Le Réconfort (174)   ❸
Le Scheffer (198)   ❸
Le Temps des Cerises (194)   ❷
L'Écurie (179)   ❷
Les Grandes Marchés (192)   ❸
◾ Les Noces de Jeannette (171)   ❹
Quai Quai (168)   ❸
◾ Robert & Louise (173)   ❷
Taxi Jaune (174)   ❷

TRENDY/INTELLIGENTSIA
3 Pièces Cuisine (200)   ❷
Bioboa (170)   ❷
Café Beaubourg (177)   ❹
Café Rouge (174)   ❷
◾ La Victoire Suprême du Coeur (175)   ❷
Le Petit Baigneur (196)   ❷
Le Troisième Bureau (191)   ❷
Les Editeurs (182)   ❸
L'Endroit (200)   ❸
L'Oga (191)   ❸
◾ Page 35 (173)   ❷
Pain, Vin, Fromage (176)   ❷
Pause Café (191)   ❷
Toi (186)   ❸

TURKISH
Le Cheval de Troie (192)   ❸
Restaurant Assoce (191)   ❷

FOOD

VEGETARIAN AND VEGAN / DETOX			
Aquarius Café (196)	❷	Chez Marianne (176)	❷
Au Grain de Folie (201)	❷	Guen-maï (181)	❶
Joy in Food (200)	❷	▨ La Victoire Suprême du Coeur (175)	❷
Savannah Café (179)	❷	Le Lotus Blanc (184)	❷
Bioboa (170)	❷	Le Loup Blanc (171)	❷
▨ Bubbles (177)		L'Heure Gourmand (183)	❶
▨ Chez Hanna (175)	❶	▨ Piccolo Teatro (175)	❷

BY NEIGHBORHOOD

VALUE. The following listings are in order of *value*; the top entry may not be the cheapest, but it will be the best value in its price range and area.

ÎLE DE LA CITÉ

The islands are crowded with tiny, traditional French restaurants with wood-paneled dining rooms and old-world charm, a vibe they pride themselves upon. Be warned, however, particularly on the Île St-Louis, that it's often an act. These restaurants cater largely to tourists, so expect to pay more than you would for an equivalent meal on the mainland—or just settle for some ice cream.

▨ **Le Caveau du Palais,** 17-19 pl. Dauphine, Île de la Cité (☎01 43 26 04 28). ⓜCité. Serves up hearty French fare like foie gras to *côte de boeuf*. An elegant dining room characterized by timbered ceilings and stone walls. Well-heeled locals crowd the terrace in the summer. The meat-heavy menu is pricey but worth the splurge. *Entrées* €9-20. *Plats* €18-50. Open M-F noon-2:30pm and 7-10:30pm. Reservations necessary for dinner and recommended for lunch. AmEx/MC/V. ❹

Quai Quai, 74 quai des Orfèvres, Île de la Cité (☎01 46 33 69 75). ⓜPont Neuf. The hip new-kid-on-the-Île opened by a popular group of *restauranteurs*. Modern and inventive decor, characterized by plush cushions, is well-suited to the creative-take-on-traditional cuisine. *Entrées* €9-14. Plats €15-26. Open Tu-Sa noon-2pm and 7-10pm. ❸

Au Rendez-Vous des Camionneurs, 72 quai d'Orfèvres, Île de la Cité (☎01 43 54 88 74). ⓜCité. Faces the Left Bank. Standard French fare, Italian decor, and a hearty sense of humor. €19 lunch *menu* (M-Sa) is a great deal. Meat and fish *plats* €19-20. Dinner *menu* €26. Open daily noon-11pm. AmEx/MC/V. ❸

CAFES

Place Numéro Thé, 20 pl. Dauphine, Île de la Cité (☎01 44 07 28 17). ⓜCité. A tiny, tastefully casual restaurant-*salon de thé* with a terrace looking out onto the calm, tree-lined pl. Dauphine. Light lunch fare and noteworthy desserts such as the *coulis* with *fromage blanc* (€5). Also has an array of exotic teas (€5). *Chocolat chaud à l'ancienne* €6. Open M-Tu and Th-F noon-5:30pm. MC/V. ❶

Le Petit Plateau, 1 quai aux Fleurs, Île de la Cité (☎01 44 07 61 86). ⓜCité. A cute, bright *salon de thé* overlooking Pont Marie. Not yet overrun by tourists. Fresh *tartes and salads.* Lunch *formules* €11-15. Tea-time *formule* €6 (includes pastry and coffee or tea). Open M-Sa 10am-7pm in summer, M-Sa 10am-6pm in winter. AmEx/MC/V. ❷

ÎLE ST-LOUIS

Île St-Louis is perhaps the best place in Paris to stop for a crêpe or some ice cream while strolling along the Seine. This isn't the spot for anything more formal (it's about place, not taste), but this is a snacker's heaven.

Berthillon, 31 rue St-Louis-en-l'Île, Île St-Louis (☎01 43 54 31 61). ⓂCité or Pont Marie. Reputed to have the best ice cream and sorbet in Paris. While Amorino is a worthy competitor, Berthillon has still been a family-run Île St-Louis institution since 1954. Choose from dozens of *parfums*, ranging from blood orange to gingerbread to the house specialty, *nougat miel* (honey nougat). Look for stores nearby that sell Berthillon treats; the wait is shorter, they usually offer a wider selection of flavors, and they're open in late July and Aug. when the main outfit is closed. Single scoop €2; double €3; triple €4. Open Sept. to mid-July W-Su 10am-8pm. Closed 2 weeks in Feb. and Apr. ❶

Amorino, 47 rue St-Louis-en-l'Île, Île St-Louis (☎01 44 07 48 08; www.amorino.fr/boutiques.htm). ⓂPont Marie. Cross the Pont Marie and turn right on rue St-Louis-en-l'Île. As a Paris chain, Amorinos are a dime a dozen, but even so, it's delicious. With a selection of over 20 *gelati* and *sorbetti* flavors (including nutella sensation *l'Inimitable*), Amorino serves amazingly creamy concoctions in more generous servings than its more famous neighbor, Berthillon. Your cup (€3-8) or cone (€3-5) will look like a work of art. Open daily noon-11pm. 22 other locations around the city. ❶

Brasserie de l'Île St-Louis, 55 quai de Bourbon, Île St-Louis (☎01 43 54 02 59). ⓂPont Marie. Cross the Pont Marie and turn right on rue St-Louis-en-l'Île; continue to the end of the island. This old-fashioned *brasserie* and island institution is known for its delectable Alsatian specialties, such as *choucroute garnie* (sausages and pork on a bed of sauerkraut; €18) as well as regional dishes like southern *cassoulet* (a casserole dish of meat and beans; €18). Also features an array of omelettes and typical cafe fare (€7-30). Outdoor *quai* seating with a view of the Panthéon through the Left Bank rooftops. Open daily noon-midnight. MC/V over €15. ❸

Les Fous de l'Île, 33 rue des Deux Ponts, Île St-Louis (☎01 43 25 76 67). ⓂPont Marie. A relaxed neighborhood bistro with a sense of humor; outfitted in everything from wine corks to Impressionist paintings to sculptures of Disney characters. Caters to the neighborhood crowd. Serves an array of dishes, from spaghetti with meatballs to *noix de St-Jacques* (scallops). Displays the work of local artists and has evening concerts (jazz, pop, piano, rock) every Th except in Aug. *Entrées* €9. *Plats* €14. Lunch *menus* €15-19; dinner *menus* €19-25. Open W noon-3pm and Th-Sa noon-11pm. ❸

Café Med, 79 rue St-Louis-en-l'Île, Île St-Louis (☎01 43 29 73 17). ⓂPont Marie. Cross the Pont Marie and turn right on rue St-Louis-en-l'Île; the restaurant is on the left. A small, red stucco restaurant that serves tasty *crêpes*, salads, and other French fare. For an island establishment, its prices and quality are hard to beat. Salads €9-10. Generous 3-course *menus* €10/11/13/20. Open daily noon-2pm and 6-9pm. MC/V. ❷

SPECIALTY SHOPS

L'Épicerie, 51 rue St-Louis-en-l'Île, Île St-Louis (☎01 43 25 20 14). Creative concoctions (everything from foie gras to mustard) and over 80 types of tea, line the walls of this tiny store. Perfumed sugars (€5), infused olive oils (€8), and variety of jams (€8) make perfect presents. Past patrons include Bill Clinton. Open daily 11am-9pm. MC/V.

La Petite Scierie, 60 rue St-Louis-en-l'Île, Île St-Louis (☎01 55 42 14 88). ⓂPont Marie. Foie gras, *rilettes*, quail eggs, and other house specialties and preserves are naturally prepared on a local farm. The owner has been selling her product on the Île for the last 25 years and is happy to offer tastings; a lunch deal of foie gras on a baguette with a glass of white wine is just €8. Open M and Th-Su 11am-7pm. AmEx/MC/V.

F O O D

O&CO, 81 rue St Louis en l'Île, Île St-Louis (☎01 40 46 89 37; www.oliviersandco. net). This Provençale company sells high-quality olive oils made in France. Olives are harvested from farms in Provence, Italy, Morocco, Portugal, Spain, and Tunisia. Gifts can be wrapped to make it safely home. Bottles range from €6-12. Also sells olive, fruit, and herb spreads, along with other gourmet food products and olive oil-related cooking accessories. 9 other branches around the city; most open M-Sa 10am-8pm.

CHÂTELET-LES HALLES

1ER ARRONDISSEMENT

The arcades overlooking the Louvre along rue de Rivoli are filled with chic and expensive spots, but visitors can enjoy the surroundings while sipping a tea or *chocolat chaud* at one of the many *salons de thé* without breaking the bank. Les Halles has louder, more crowded eateries, serving everything from fast food to four-course feasts. Diverse lunch and dinner options are also available along rue Jean-Jacques Rousseau. Those in search of a quieter meal should head to the many restaurants located off of rue St-Honoré or behind the Palais-Royal.

L'Alfred, 52 rue de Richelieu, 1er (☎01 42 97 54 40). ⓂLouvre. The celebrated (and upscale) new kid on the block, taking the place of the ancient Grillardin (a mainstay since 1827). In an excellent location (behind the Palais-Royal) for those needing rest after the Louvre. Menu changes daily and includes sophisticated takes on old favorites, like *magret de canard et poire à la vanille* (duck with vanilla pears). *Entrées* €9-12. *Plats* €20-24. Open M-F 12:30-2:30pm and 7:30-10:30pm. AmEx/MC/V. ❸

Au Chien qui Fume, 33 rue du Pont Neuf, 1er (☎01 42 36 07 42; www.au-chien-qui-fume.com). ⓂChâtelet or Les Halles. Even passersby who aren't hungry stop at this popular restaurant, just to see the cooks arrange beautiful plates of shellfish at its famous oyster bar. The Saint-Malo *menu* (€39), named after the fabled port, includes a tray of shellfish. Bazil's *menu* (€34) offers more of a selection, including steak and duck for those nonplussed by seafood. Sophisticated but light-hearted atmosphere, with pictures of dogs dancing, eating, and, of course, smoking on almost every wall, as well as statues of dogs on every counter top. Open daily noon-2am. ❹

Au Vieux Comptoir, 17 rue des Lavandières, 1er (☎01 45 08 53 08; www.au-vieux-comptoir.com). ⓂChâtelet. An extensive wine list accompanies delicious fish and meat *plats* (€16-33) in this wonderful little French bistro/wine bar, located on a corner perfect for people watching. Desserts €9. Seating inside amid wine barrel decor or outside under an awning. Tu-Sa noon-10:30pm; cold cuts and salads until 11:30pm. MC/V. ❸

CAFES

🖾 **Le Fumoir,** 6 rue de l'Amiral Coligny, 1er (☎01 42 92 00 24; www.lefumoir.com). ⓂLouvre-Rivoli. You may hear as much English as French while you sip a beverage in their leather sofas, but neighborhood favorite Le Fumoir is authentically Parisian in style. This part bar part tea house serves one of the best brunches in Paris (€22), Su noon-3pm. Leave-a-book-take-a-book library. Open daily 11am-2am. AmEx/MC/V. ❷

Le Café Marly, 93 rue de Rivoli, 1er (☎01 49 26 06 60). ⓂPalais-Royal. One of the classiest cafes in Paris; located in the Richelieu wing of the Louvre and well worth a visit. With one terrace facing the famed I.M. Pei pyramids and others overlooking the Louvre's Cour Napoléon, this is a prime spot for tourists (and **tourist-watching**). Enjoy a meal or sit back with a drink (coffee €3, beer €5). *Foie gras artisinal* (for two; €25). *Croque M.* or *Mme.* €12. *Plats* €21-31. Open daily 8-1am. AmEx/MC/V. ❹

Bioboa, 3 rue Danielle Casanova, 1er (☎01 42 61 17 67). ⓂPyramides. Take av. de l'Opéra toward Garnier and turn left on rue Danielle Casanova. A small "food spa," with fresh soups, salads, paninis, desserts, and pastries to eat-in or take away. 80% of ingredients are organic. Decor is simple and chic, like the menu. Smoothies (€5-8). Veggie or beef burger €10-11. *Menus* €11-13. Open M-Sa 11am-6pm. MC/V. ❶

> **TIP**
>
> **ENTRÉES AND PLATS.** In French, *entrée* means appetizer and *plat* means entree. Go figure. Check out **French 101: A Crash Course** (p. 148) for other false cognates.

SALONS DE THÉ

 Angelina, 226 rue de Rivoli, 1er (☎01 42 60 82 00). Ⓜ️Concorde or Tuileries. An old favorite of Audrey Hepburn and Coco Chanel. Little has changed here since its opening in 1903; the Belle Époque frescoes, mirrored walls, and marble tables are all original. It's touristy and a bit overdone, but that is more than compensated for by *Le chocolat à l'Ancienne dit 'l'africain'* (literally, "hot chocolate once called African"; €7), the heavenly house specialty. *Mont Blanc* (a mound of whipped cream, milk chocolate, hazelnut nougat) €7. Pastries €5-7. Tea €7. Open daily 9am-7pm. AmEx/MC/V. Also at 2 pl. de la Porte Maillot, 17ème (☎01 42 60 82 00). RER: Neuilly-Porte Maillot. ❶

Muscade, 36 rue de Montpensier / 67 Galerie de Montpensier, 1er (☎01 42 97 51 36). Ⓜ️Palais-Royal. In the Palais-Royal's northwest corner, within the courtyard. The hip, slightly rebellious sister of the ancient and traditional *salon de thés*. Magenta walls adorned with mirrors, paintings by John Cocteau, and arm-shaped candelabras. Checkered marble floors and bronze tables. *Le Chocolat a l'Ancienne* (€6.50) is a melted chocolate bar parading as liquid. An assortment of pastries (€7) and 23 kinds of tea (€5.50). *Café Muscade* (coffee and hot chocolate; €6.50). Reservations recommended, especially for terrace seating. Open May-mid-Sept. Tu-Su for tea 10-11:30am and 3-6pm, lunch 12:15-3pm, dinner 7:150-10:30pm; mid-Sept.-Apr. Tu-Su for tea 10-11:30am, lunch 12:15-3pm, tea and pre-theater dinner 3-8:30pm. AmEx/MC/V. ❶

2ÈME ARRONDISSEMENT

Châtelet-Les Halles has many inexpensive dining options. Rue Montorgueil is lined with bakeries, fruit stands, and cafe-bars, while side streets around Les Halles contain touristy cafes and hole-in-the-wall establishments. You'll find cheap food on passage des Panoramas and boulevard des Italiens.

 Les Noces de Jeannette, 14 rue Favart and 9 rue d'Amboise, 2ème (☎01 42 96 36 89). Ⓜ️Richelieu-Drouot. Exit on bd. des Italiens; turn left on rue Favart. Named after a 19th-century *opéra comique* playing across the street at the time of its opening, this elegant restaurant with a classic French feel will certainly impress a date. Menu du Jeanette (€28) includes *entrées* like the salad with goat cheese and pesto, *charcuterie Lyonnaise* (assorted dried meats), roasted fish and duck *plats*, and fabulous desserts. Kir included with meal. Menu Bistro is €3 more and includes a half-bottle of Bordeaux. Reservations recommended. Open daily noon-1:30pm and 7-9:30pm. ❹

Le Loup Blanc, 42 rue Tiquetonne, 2ème (☎01 40 13 08 35). Ⓜ️Étienne-Marcel. Walk against traffic on rue de Turbigo and go left on rue Tiquetonne. Relaxed, Mediterranean feel with wooden tables. Choose from a variety of "creative" meat, fish, and seafood dishes and add 2-4 sides, such as mashed potatoes, creamed corn, or tabbouleh (€16-19). Vegetarian option of 4-6 sides (€13-17). Open M-Th 7:30pm-midnight, F 7:30pm-12:30am, Sa 7:30pm-1am, Su 11am-4pm and 7:30pm-midnight. MC/V. ❷

Babylone Bis, 34 rue Tiquetonne, 2ème (☎01 42 33 48 35). Ⓜ️Étienne-Marcel. Walk against traffic on rue de Turbigo and turn left on rue Tiquetonne. With zebra skin on the walls, banana leaves on the ceiling, and loud *zouk* music blasting from speakers, this eatery fits right into its quirky neighborhood. Serves Antillean and African cuisine, including delicious *aloko* (fried bananas; €5.50) and stuffed crab (€9). It's also a late-night destination for celebrity musicians: pictures of Snoop Dogg, Stevie Wonder, and Marvin Gaye decorate the walls. Open daily 8pm-8am. MC/V. ❶

La Cucaracha, 31 rue Tiquetonne, 2*ème* (☎01 40 26 68 36). ⓂÉtienne-Marcel. Walk against traffic on rue de Turbigo and go left on rue Tiquetonne. Continuing the inexplicable trend of naming Mexican restaurants after the Spanish word for "cockroach," Cucaracha wins over a mostly French crowd with slightly kitschy Mexican decor and mole sauce (made with 39 spices). Dishes like *enchiladas verde* or fajitas run a reasonable €12-16. Open daily 7:30-11:30pm. MC/V. ❷

Kintaro, 24 rue St-Augustin (☎01 47 42 13 14). ⓂOpéra. Walk down av. de l'Opéra and turn left on rue St-Augustin. Delicious and popular Japanese restaurant with everything but sushi. Kintaro instead offers great noodle bowls (€8-10) and an array of menu combinations (€13-18). Sapporo €5. Open M-Sa 11:30am-10pm. MC/V over €23. ❷

CAFES

EXKi, 2 bd. des Italiens, 2*ème* (☎01 42 61 06 52; www.exki.fr). EXKi's philosophy of "fresh, natural, and ready-to-go" means delicious and often organic salads, sandwiches, and soups—to eat-in or takeout. A convenient rarity amongst a traditional cafe culture. Also serves breakfast and tea-time treats. Sandwiches €3-5, soups €5-7, salads €6-8. Open M-F 8am-10:30pm, Sa 9am-10:30pm. AmEx/MC/V. ❶

THE MARAIS

3ÈME ARRONDISSEMENT

The restaurants of the upper Marais serve an array of international and traditional French cuisine. Dozens of charming bistros line rue St.-Martin, and kosher food stands and restaurants are located around rue du Vertbois and rue Volta. Dinner in the Marais can be pricey, but lunchtime *menus* often offer good deals. Reservations are strongly recommended in the evening.

Chez Janou, 2 rue Roger Verlomme, 3*ème* (☎01 42 72 28 41). ⓂChemin-Vert. From the metro, take rue St-Gilles and turn left almost immediately on rue des Tournelles. Food so good it induces desert-island hypotheticals: if you were stranded on a desert island, would you bring an endless supply of Chez Janou's *magret de canard* and *chevre au romarin,* or the best lover you've ever had? We're just not sure. Tucked into a

DECODING DE CAFÉ

Paris's cafe culture is more than an institution, it's a way of life. A trip to the city wouldn't be complete without at least a few hours spent sitting, sipping, and soaking in the city life passing before you. Though commercialization has brought Starbucks and other chains to the City of Light, the French hold tight to their tradition of cafe dwelling, and buying a €2 still grants you the right to linger as long as you like.

However, there's more to this culture than initially meets the eye; indeed, throughout the years cafes have developed their own subcultures. While many cafes feature a melange of moods, it's helpful to peruse the crowd to see whether to bring out your Mac, Malthus, or Manolos.

It's usually pretty apparent from a glance at the patrons, but we've broken things down into a few general categories:

Student Spots: Free Wi-Fi is a pre-requisite for this atmosphere. At these cafes, it's ok to have your computer out and your table covered with papers. If you're lucky, it's also acceptable to bleed 5 hours out of a €2 espresso. Try Le Tresor or Les Chaises Au Plafond, both on rue Vieille du Temple.

Beauties and Businessmen: A mix of working lunchers and sophisticated daters make up this crowd—you can come with your laptop, but you better be striking a deal or tottering on heels. Le quiet corner of the 3ème, this Provençale bistro serves affordable ambrosia to a mixed crowd of enthusiasts. The chocolate mousse (€9) is brought in an enormous self-serve bowl, though Parisians count on self-control. Over 80 kinds of *pastis*. Reservations always recommended, as this local favorite is packed every night of the week. Open M-F noon-3pm and 7:45pm-midnight, Sa-Su noon-4pm and 7:45pm-midnight. ❸

🟦 **Page 35,** rue du Parc Royal, 3ème (☎01 44 54 35 35; www.restaurant-page35.com). You won't find a place like this outside the Marais: a hip, modern art gallery-restaurant-*crêperie* owned by a group of very accommodating gentlemen. Looks onto a quiet park. An extensive menu of light, fresh, and creative fare: beautifully presented buckwheat *crêpes* (€10-15) line up next to edgy versions French favorites (*confit de canard*, €15). Fantastic dessert *crêpes*, like the melt-in-your-mouth Crêpe au Salidou (made with salted butter caramel, €7). Open Sept.-July Tu-F 11:30am-3pm and 7-11pm, Sa-Su 11:30am-11pm; Aug. W-F 7-11pm, Sa-Su 11:30am-3pm and 7-11pm. AmEx/MC/V. ❷

🟦 **404,** 69 rue des Gravilliers, 3ème (☎01 42 74 57 81). Ⓜ Arts et Métiers. Walk down rue Beaubourg and take a right on rue des Gravilliers. A plain stone facade masks this sophisticated family-owned Maghreb restaurant. An intimate, rich decor of deep red curtains and dark carved wood. Seating in the airy, casual terrace in the back during lunchtime is a must. Features mouthwatering couscous (€14-24) and *tagines* (€14-18), with plenty of vegetarian options. Lunch *menu* €17, M-F only. Brunch *berbère* Sa-Su noon-4pm. Open M-F noon-2:30pm and 8pm-midnight, Sa-Su noon-4pm and 8pm-midnight. AmEx/MC/V. ❸

🟦 **Robert & Louise,** 64 rue Vieille du Temple, 3ème (☎01 42 78 55 89). Ⓜ St-Paul or Files du Calvaire. With red-checkered curtains, stone walls, and heavy wooden tables, Robert and Louise is exactly what it seems: a family-owned strictly-local fave serving up delicious French dishes. A lively crowd comes to feast on all the usual suspects—foie gras, *tête de veau*, *côte de boeuf*, *confit de canard*—made incredibly well in a wood fire-oven. Few vegetarian options. *Entrées* €6-8. *Plats* €11-20. Desserts €5-8. Reservations recommended. Open Tu-Su noon-2:30pm and 7:30-11pm. ❷

Caves St-Gilles, 4 rue St-Gilles, 3ème (☎01 48 87 22 62). Ⓜ Chemin Vert. A Spanish-style bistro outfitted with a mosaic tile floor, small wooden tables, and checkered tablecloths. Come here for *vino* and generous, filling portions of tapas (combination platters €16-19). The multilingual staff speaks French, Spanish, and English. Open daily noon-3pm and 7:30pm-midnight or whenever the lively crowd dies down. MC/V. ❸

Fumoir (in the 1er) perfects this aura, and don't they know it.

People-Watchers Paradises: Welcome to tourists, couples, and study-abroaders alike, all these cafes ask is that you face the street and keep the conversation light. Think off it as enforced joie de vivre. This culture dominates at any corner café.

Trendy Troughs: Usually seen in upscale neighborhoods and on grand plazas (ie Café Marché on rue Cler in the 7th or Café Beaubourg on the place in front of the Pompidou), these cafés are places to see and be scene. Models and playboys run the show here, with the occasional oblivious tourist. People-watching occurs, but its usually much more judgmental.

Alternative and Artsy: For the teenage crowd with raging hormones, this cafe culture can usually be found at dive bars during the day. Think cheap eats and a grundgy aesthetic. Like Saved by the Bell, but more angsty.

Philosopher Feel: To thrive in this culture, its best to have a cigarette in hand and an existential crisis in mind. Find this forum at the "classic" places, like the Bistro du Peintre in the 11ème.

Taxi Jaune, 13 rue Chapon, 3ème (☎01 42 76 00 40). ⓂArts et Métiers. Walk along rue Beaubourg and turn left on rue Chapon. A casual, intimate, and convivial atmosphere redolent of a 1930s French diner brings a devoted regular crowd who delight in the creative and original dishes. Menu changes regularly according to the seasonal produce—and the owner's whim. *Entrées* €7-13. *Plats* €16-25. Lunch *menu* €14. Open M-F 9am-midnight. Food served noon-3pm and 8-10:30pm. Closed 3 weeks in Aug. and winter holidays. Reservations strongly recommended. V. ❷

Le Réconfort, 37 rue de Poitou, 3ème (☎01 49 96 09 60). ⓂSt-Sébastien-Froissart. Walk along rue du Point-Aux-Choux to rue de Poitou. Plush red velvet French salon decor with an elegant vibe. Features a delightful melange of cuisines, from ratatouille with *chèvre* to coconut-lemon king prawns to pork filet mignon with balsamic sauce. Lunch menu €17-22. *Plats* €17-21. Reservations recommended for dinner. Open M-F noon-2pm and 8-11:30pm, Sa-Su 8-11:30pm. MC/V. ❸

Chez Omar, 47 rue de Bretagne, 3ème (☎01 42 72 36 26). ⓂArts et Métiers. Walk along rue Réamur, away from rue St-Martin. Rue Réamur turns into rue de Bretagne. One of the area's better Middle Eastern places, housed in an old-style French bistro with tall ceilings and a traditional bar. Come around 7:30pm for a relaxed ambience, later to see the local intelligentsia. Couscous with vegetables €12. The *steak au poivre* (€18) is served in a spectacular sauce. Other specialties like *brochettes* and ratatouille €18-24. Open M-Sa noon-2:30pm and 7-11:30pm, Su 7-11:30pm. Cash only. ❷

CAFES

🔲 **L'Apparrement Café,** 18 rue des Coutures St-Gervais, 3ème (☎01 48 87 12 22). ⓂSt-Paul. Behind the Picasso Museum, this cafe serves make-your-own gourmet salads (€12-16) and Su brunch (€16-21) to trendy young things in lounge chairs. Come to chat, play one of the many board games, or check out the art exhibit of the moment (see **Nightlife,** p. 324). Open M-Sa noon-2am, Su 12:30pm-midnight. Reservations recommended for brunch. MC/V. ❷

Royal Bar, 19 rue du Parc Royal, 3ème (☎01 42 72 33 03). ⓂChemin-Vert. An intimate and elegant cafe hidden behind a classic green facade. Perfect for a pre- or post-Picasso drink: the walls are covered with (tasteful) paintings of naked women (Picasso's favorite) and photos of the artist. Delicious, homemade pastries €6-7. Decadent *chocolat chaud* or *glacé* with a small pot of *chantilly* (whipped cream) €5-6. Wine €5. Hours vary—and the owner insists upon it; daily about 10am-7pm. Cash only. ❶

Café des Musées, 49 rue de Turenne, 3ème (☎01 42 72 96 17; fax 01 44 59 38 68). ⓂChemin Vert. Part bar, part cafe, part bistro—it may be undergoing something of an identity crisis, but it draws a diverse crowd as a result: businessmen finishing the workday, students with tattered backpacks, old couples enjoying morning coffee, and families out to dinner. Delicious *tartines,* salads, and sandwiches €4-9. *Plats* €12-19. Open daily 8am-midnight; food served noon-3pm and 9-11pm. MC/V. ❷

Café Rouge, 32 rue de la Picardie, 3ème (☎01 44 54 20 60). ⓂFilles du Calvaire or Temple. From ⓂFilles du Calvaire, walk along rue des Filles du Calvaire, turn right on rue de Bretagne and right on rue de Picardie. This trendy hidden cafe serves fashionable French fusion during the day and imaginative cocktails at night. A mix of young, old, professional, and artsy patrons try creations like curried lamb with *semoule* (€12) or hamburger with cantal, bacon, and sauteed onion (€14). Lunch *formule* €15. Salads €12. Open daily 9-2am; food served noon-3pm and 7:30-11pm. AmEx/MC/V. ❷

SPECIALTY SHOPS

🔲 **Palais des Thés,** 64 rue Vieille du Temple, 3ème (☎01 48 87 80 60; www.palaisdesthes. com). ⓂSt-Paul. Walk with traffic on rue de Rivoli and turn right on rue Vieille du Temple. Selling organic teas collected by the owners from 20 countries in Asia, Africa, and South

America, the Palais has become a worthy rival of long-standing fave, Mariage Frères. They may not have a *salon de thé*, but they do have over 200 teas (€8-135/100g), beautiful teapots (€40-165), and a welcoming staff eager to send you home with the perfect tea. Open M-Sa 10am-8pm. 4 other locations around the city. AmEx/MC/V.

4ÈME ARRONDISSEMENT

In the *4ème*, dining is less about the food and more about how you look eating it. But that doesn't mean you can't find a variety of restaurants, from authentic regional fare to new-age fusion. Dining in Marais isn't cheap, but living off salads and sandwiches from the many cafe/bar/restaurants or grabbing a falafel from rue des Rosiers won't break the bank. Sunday brunch is your chance to eat as much as you can at one of the many buffets. If you're in the mood for a bit of a splurge and a night in style, the Marais is your best bet.

- ▧ **Georges,** Centre Pompidou, 6th fl. (☎01 44 78 47 99). Enter via the center or, after hours, the elevator to the left of the Pompidou's main entrance. ⓂRambuteau or Hôtel de Ville. This cafe is almost more impressive than the museum—almost. With steel design aluminum spleen-shaped party rooms and pastel accents, the interior is an artistic experience. Then again, no artistic creation can compare with the Parisian skyline; the view from the rooftop terrace is unbeatable. Come for a glass of wine or champagne (€8-12) or a snack (*gateau au chocolat de costes* €12; fruit salad €11); splurge on a *plat* (king crab omelette €25, mandarin crispy duck €32); or just to take a peek at the menu, designed by Dior menswear creator Hedi Slimane. Dress to impress. Reservations suggested for dinner. Open M and W-Su noon-2am. AmEx/MC/V. ❹

- ▧ **L'As du Falafel,** 34 rue des Rosiers, 4ème (☎01 48 87 63 60). ⓂSt-Paul or Hôtel de Ville. Allegedly credited by Lenny Kravitz as having "the best falafel in the world," this kosher stand has become a landmark. Patrons line up outside for the famous "falafel special" (€5), perfect with the house lemonade (€4). Don't leave Paris without checking it out. Open M-Th and Su noon-midnight, F noon-7pm (5pm in winter). MC/V. ❶

- ▧ **Chez Hanna,** 54 rue des Rosiers, 4ème (☎01 42 74 74 99). ⓂSt-Paul or Hôtel de Ville. L'As du Falafel's resentful rival, Hanna is more of a local secret. Whether their falafel is better is a matter of taste, but it's definitely a more pleasant place to eat. Local families and couples come here for the people watching and the falafel special platter (€12). Open Tu-Su noon-midnight. MC/V over €15. ❶

- ▧ **La Victoire Suprême du Coeur,** 29-31 rue du Bourg Tibourg, 4ème (☎01 40 41 95 03; www.vscoeur.com). ⓂHôtel de Ville. Run by devotees of Sri Chinmoy, who have kept both body and soul in mind when creating the atmosphere and the cuisine. Try the *escalope de seitan à la sauce champignon* (seitan "steak" with mushroom sauce; €14) or the always creative *plat du jour* (€10.50). Meals marked "V" can be made vegan. 2-course *menu* (€13.50). Fresh-fruit smoothies and *lassis* (€4-5). Brunch de la Vie €21. Open M-Tu and Th-F noon-3pm and 6:30-10:30pm, Sa noon-11pm, Su 11am-5:30pm. ❷

- ▧ **Piccolo Teatro,** 6 rue des Écouffes, 4ème (☎01 42 72 17 79). ⓂSt-Paul. Walk with the traffic down rue de Rivoli and take a right on rue des Écouffes. A romantic vegetarian hideout draped in red velvet. Weekday lunch *menus* €9, €10.50, and €14.50. Appetizers €4-7.50. *Plats* €8-12. Open daily noon-3pm and 7-11pm. AmEx/MC/V. ❷

- ▧ **Au Petit Fer à Cheval,** 30 rue Vieille du Temple, 4ème (☎01 42 72 47 47; www.cafeine. com). ⓂHôtel de Ville or St-Paul. From ⓂSt-Paul, go with the traffic on rue de Rivoli and turn right; the restaurant will be on your right. An oasis of *chèvre*, kir, and Gauloises, graced by a low-key (but never boring) crowd of locals and expats. Hidden behind the bar are a few tables where you can order *filet mignon de veau* (€18) or the *Salade Au Petit Fer* (with *chèvre*, *magret de canard*, and ham €13; vegetarian version with avo-

FOOD

cado, *bleu d'auvergne*, and *chèvre* €11). The delicious *tarte tatin* is a house specialty (€8). Open daily 8-2am; food served noon-1am. MC/V. ❷

Breakfast in America, 4 rue Mahler, 4*ème* (☎01 42 72 40 21; breakfast-in-america. com). Ⓜ️St-Paul. BIA promises to be one thing: "An American diner in Paris." It passes with flying colors. From the shiny red booths to the toasters on the table; from the delicious fries and shakes to the bottomless mug o' Joe, it doesn't get more American than this. Delicious brunch (€15) includes an omelette or meat and eggs; a stack of pancakes, a muffin, a brownie, or a donut and yogurt; and an espresso or bottomless mug o' joe with OJ. Milkshakes €5. Burgers and sandwiches €9-12. Student *formule* of burger, fries, and drink €8. M-Sa breakfast served all day. Open daily 8:30am-11pm. Also at 17 rue des Écoles, 5*ème* (☎01 43 54 50 28). AmEx/MC/V. ❷

Pain, Vin, Fromage, 3 rue Geoffrey L'Angevin, 4*ème* (☎01 42 74 07 52). Ⓜ️Rambuteau or Hôtel de Ville. Tucked on a small side street right near the Centre Pompidou. A cozy and rustic Parisian classic with timbered ceilings. Combines France's 3 basic food groups for heartily comforting fare. Fondues (€14-16), *raclettes* (€13-19), and *croûtes compagnards* (grilled breads with toppings; €12) are accompanied by a winning wine list. Try the tasting platters of regional meats (€8-11) or cheese (€17). Open daily 7-11:30pm. Reservations recommended. AmEx/MC/V. ❷

Chez Marianne, 2 rue des Hospitalières St-Gervais, 4*ème* (☎01 42 72 18 86). Another rue des Rosiers attraction, Chez Marianne serves up unbeatable *mezzes* (called *assiettes composés*) with your choice of 4, 5, 6, or 10 dishes (€12, €14, €16, and €26 respectively). Choose from homemade hummus, falafel, kefta, tahini, tzatziki, pureed eggplant, tapenade, grape leaves, and more. Marianne is also known for her delicious desserts (baklava €5). Spacious terrace seating. Extensive wine list. Attached to the restaurant is a shop where you can buy the dishes and dessert to take home (*mezzes* €15-20/kg; desserts €2-3 each.) Open daily noon-midnight. AmEx/MC/V. ❷

Petit Bofinger, 6 rue de la Bastille, 4*ème* (☎01 42 72 05 23). Ⓜ️Bastille. The classic Parisian bistro experience: typically french cuisine in a relaxed yet refined atmosphere. Worth-the-splurge *prix fixe* (€21/29) includes wine and all the greatest hits of fine French cooking. Kids menu €9. Across the street, the original Bofinger attracts an older crowd dressed to the nines (dinner *menu* €32). *Entrées* €7-15. *Plats* €17-26. Desserts €7-11. Open daily noon-3pm and 7pm-midnight. AmEx/MC/V. ❸

Fuxia, 50 rue François Miron, 4*ème* (☎01 42 72 22 74; www.fuxia.fr). Ⓜ️ St-Paul. Rue F. Miron branches off the south side of rue de Rivoli and toward the river. This rustic-hip cafe-restaurant-caterer serves up Italian fare with the freshest of ingredients. Inventive pastas with veggies, fresh cheese, and meat or seafood €10-17; deliciously huge salads €10-12. Decadent Italian delicacies including *panna cotta,* tiramisu, and *crostata al cioccolata* (chocolate tarte) €7. Also sells imported olive oils, wines, and pastas. Open daily noon-3pm and 7-11pm. 6 other locations around Paris. AmEx/MC/V. ❷

Curieux Spaghetti Bar, 14 rue St.-Merri, 4*ème* (☎01 42 72 75 97; www.curieuxspag. com). Ⓜ️Rambuteau or Hôtel de Ville. A self-consciously hip restaurant-bar. The walls are decorated with pixelated, multicolored graphics, and patrons feast on generous helpings of pasta (€12-32) or risotto (€14-18) while listening to techno and hip hop. Lunch *formule* €14; lunch *menu* €17. Happy hour 4-8pm. Try a "CHUP!," a shot of perfumed vodka in fanciful flavors such as bubble gum and mojito. Buffet brunch Sa and Su noon-4pm (€26). Open M-W and Su noon-2am and Th-Sa noon-4am. MC/V. ❷

Bistrot du Dome, 2 rue de la Bastille, 4*ème* (☎01 48 04 88 44). Ⓜ️Bastille. Rue de la Bastille runs directly off pl. de la Bastille. This bright, refined restaurant serves up light, simple dishes of fresh fish like *thon à la planche* (€27) and *lotte au chutney* (€28). Also serves a variety of desserts, such as *tarte fine aux pommes* (€7-8). Open daily 12:15-2:15pm and 7:15-11pm. AmEx/MC/V. ❹

Le Grizzli, 7 rue St-Martin (☎01 48 87 77 56). ⓂChâtelet or Hôtel de VIlle. Take rue de Rivoli and turn on rue St-Martin. This cool bistro near the Pompidou serves meticulously prepared salads (€15) and other standard French fare (*plats* €12-20). Outdoor terrace seating overlooks a pleasant square. Look out for the bulldog. Su brunch €21. Open daily noon-2am. Food served noon-2:30pm and 7:30-11pm. AmEx/MC/V. ❷

CAFES

Briezh Café, 109 rue Vielle du Temple, 4*ème* (☎01 42 74 13 77; www.breizhcafe.com). ⓂFilles du Calvaire. A rare find in many ways, this relaxed Breton *crêperie* is full of surprises. In a city full of duds, Breizh makes inexpensive and inventive *crêpes* with the highest quality ingredients (organic veggies, raw milk and cheeses, normand sausage, etc.). In this extravagant and edgy *quartier,* Breizh offers a relaxed, welcoming, and understated atmosphere. Reservations recommended. Start or end your meal with the *"amuse-galettes"* or *"amuse-crêpes"* (€6). *Galettes* €3-11. *Crêpes* €4-8. Open W-Su noon-11pm. AmEx/MC/V. ❶

Café Beaubourg, 100 rue St-Merri, 4*ème* (☎01 48 87 63 96). ⓂRambuteau or Hôtel de Ville. Facing Centre Pompidou. Paris' take on a mix between NYC and LA, Beaubourg is a spot to see and be seen—especially from the front terrace. Clientele wear everything from the newest Lagerfeld to Dockers to nose piercings. 🍴**Charlotte au Toblerone** (Toblerone tarte) €9. Coffee €3. Mixed drinks €10. 3-course brunch €26. Open M-Tu and Su 8-1am, and W-Sa 8-2am. AmEx/MC/V. ❹

SALONS DE THÉ

🍴**Mariage Frères,** 30 & 35 rue du Bourg-Tibourg, 4*ème* (☎01 42 72 28 11). ⓂHôtel de Ville. Started by 2 brothers who found British tea shoddy, this salon offers 500 varieties of tea (€7-15 per 100g) and an in-house book detailing the history and uses of each. With white-suited waiters and sophisticated clientele, the *salon de thé* has become a French institution. Come for an elegant tea (*menu* includes sandwich, pastry, and tea; €30) or a Classic Brunch (eggs, brioche, smoked salmon, and pastries; €30). The tea shop sells a wide variety of books and tea kettles. Open daily 10:30am-7:30pm; lunch M-Sa noon-3pm; afternoon tea 3-6:30pm; Su brunch 12:30-6:30pm. Also at 13 rue des Grands-Augustins, 6*ème* (☎01 40 51 82 50); and at 260, rue du Faubourg St-Honoré, 8*ème* (☎01 46 22 18 54). AmEx/MC/V. ❹

SPECIALTY SHOPS

🍴**Bubbles,** 4 rue Mahler, 4*ème* (☎01 40 29 42 41; www. bubbles-dietbar.com). ⓂSt-Paul. This is technically a

ON THE MENU

A BITE IN THE DARK

It's no secret that Paris's cuisine is some of the world's best; what sets the restaurant Dans le noir apart is that you can't see your gourmet meal.

Founded in 2004 by Edouard de Broglie and Étienne Boisrond, the restaurant has charged itself with awakening senses other than sight—patrons dine in total darkness. After passing through a series of heavy curtains, diners are led to their table by the restaurant's staff. While you're free to order a la carte—the menu consists of inventive takes on traditional French cuisine—the more adventurous will opt for *le menu surprise.* You won't know what's on your plate until you taste it.

You may wonder how your servers are able to move through the dining room so easily. They're used to it—Dans le noir employs only blind waiters. In addition to its ambitions of sensory awakening, the restaurant has partnered with the Association Paul Guinot to help the blind find employment. Combining a disorienting, exciting experience with social change, Dans le noir is money well spent.

51 rue Quincampoix, 4ème. ⓂHôtel de ville. ☎01 42 77 98 04; www.danslenoir.com. Reservations 3-5 days ahead. 2-course menu €37, 3-course menu €43. Student discounts.

"diet bar" but it is best known for its deliciously thick smoothies (like banana, cocoa, and nutella; €5) and its creative fruit juice concoctions (try the orange, *carotte*, ginger; €5). Also has delicious dishes to-go (fresh salads and sandwiches €5-7; hot dishes like vegetable couscous €7-10). Open M-Sa 9:30am-8pm. MC/V.

Le Gay Choc, 45 Ste-Croix-de-la-Bretonnerie, 4*ème* (☎01 48 87 56 88). ⓜHôtel de Ville. A *boulangerie* with flare—and amazingly delicious breads and pastries. Creative concoctions like honey and almond or muesli loaf (€2-3), gooey *fondant au chocolat* (€2), and melt-in-your-mouth cookies (€1). The only Marais *boulangerie* open on Su. Go if only to see the ◼ **pain magique** (€2). Open M-Tu and Th-Su 8am-8pm. MC/V.

myberry, 25 Vieille du Temple, 4*ème* (☎01 42 74 54 48; http://myberry.fr). ⓜHôtel de Ville. Based on the non-fat frozen yogurt shop Pinkberry that has taken over New York and L.A., this lone Paris establishment is on its way to reaching the same level of popularity (it's already been written up by Elle). The yogurt is light, tangy, and delicious with one of the many toppings: mango, strawberry, kiwi, pineapple, granola, chocolate chips, almonds, coconut and more. The perfect afternoon snack. Free Wi-Fi. *Petit* €3; *moyen* €3.50, with 3 toppings €6; *grand* €2.50, with 3 toppings €7. Each topping €0.95. Special XXL €8, with 3 toppings €13. Smoothies €5-6. Fresh fruit juice €4-5. Open daily noon-midnight; closes earlier in winter. MC/V over €15.

Jadis et Gourmande, 39 rue des Archives, 4*ème* (☎01 48 04 08 03). ⓜRambuteau. Chocolate's equivalent to a flower shop. Violet perfumed chocolates and candy arrangements tucked into bamboo cases. Chocolate-shaped everything from Eiffel Towers to pencils. Custom-order chocolate messages. Smash-hit heart-shaped "Je t'aime" cookie €10-28. Open M-F 10am-7:30pm, Sa 10:30am-7:30pm, Su 2:30-7pm. AmEx/MC/V.

Izrael, 30 rue François Miron, 4*ème* (☎01 42 72 66 23). ⓜSt-Paul. Barrels and bins of orange lentils, brazil nuts, candied cherries, couscous, and other delicacies. Narrow shelves of Hershey's syrup and peanut butter jostle a large selection of curries and specialty alcohols. Best known for its pungent, aromatic spices from all over the world, sold from huge sacks. Open Tu-F 9:30am-1pm and 2:30-7pm, Sa 9am-7pm. MC/V.

TIP **TO INSURE PROPER SERVICE.** Leaving a tip in a restaurant or bar is a dead giveaway that you're foreign. Service is almost always included in meal and drink prices, so only tip if you don't see *"service compris"* on the check. For more info on etiquette in Paris, see **Life and Times, p. 95.**

LATIN QUARTER AND ST-GERMAIN

5ÈME ARRONDISSEMENT

A particularly diverse *arrondissement*, the 5*ème* hosts a score of inexpensive bistros as well as Middle Eastern, Tibetan, and Vietnamese eateries. All along rue Mouffetard, back-to-back restaurants serve high-quality food at surpassingly low prices; expect *menus* from €10-16. Sidewalk bistros crowd rue de la Montagne Ste-Geneviève in overwhelming quantities, continuing north of the Panthéon onto rue Descartes and place de la Contrescarpe. Greek and Middle Eastern stands on rue de la Huchette and rue Galande often offer cheap, delicious to-go crêpes and sandwiches.

◼ **Comptoir Méditerranée,** 42 rue du Cardinal Lemoine, 5*ème* (☎01 43 25 29 08; www. savannahcafe.fr). ⓜCardinal Lemoine. Savannah Café's little sister, run by the same welcoming owner. More deli than restaurant, Comptoir Méditerranée serves fresh, colorful Lebanese dishes easily ordered to-go. Select from 18 hot or cold dishes to make your own plate (€6.50-11.50). Sandwiches €4.20. Homemade lemonade €2.50. Espresso €1.70. Open M-Sa 11am-10pm. MC/V. ❶

🏶 **Le Perraudin,** 157 rue St-Jacques, 5ème (☎01 46 33 15 75; www.restaurant-perraudin. com). RER: Luxembourg. Walk down bd. St-Michel with the Luxembourg Garden on your left, turn right on rue Soufflot, then right on rue St-Jacques. Simple and elegant, Le Perraudin has a deep red exterior, an intimate garden, and red-and-white checkered tablecloths. Serves Parisian favorites like *tête de veau* and *boeuf bourguignon* to students and locals. *Plats* €16-29. 3-course *menu* (€30) includes house specialities like goat cheese *profiteroles* and *escargots.* Open M-F noon-2:30pm and 7-10:30pm. MC/V. ❸

🏶 **Le Pré Verre,** 8 rue Thenard, 5ème (☎01 43 54 59 47; www.lepreverre.com). ⓂMaubert-Mutualité. Walk against traffic on bd. St-Germain and turn left down rue Thenard. Always packed with locals, this French-Asian fusion restaurant displays the daily-changing menu on chalkboards at each table. The Delacourcelle brothers use only market-fresh ingredients to craft their unique dishes. *Entrées* and *plats* range from the experimental buckwheat grass soup to the more traditional suckling roast pig. Challenge your taste buds with a white chocolate mousse salad or *capu china au thé* for dessert. Lunch *formule* €14. 3-course *menu* €28. Open Tu-Sa noon-2pm and 7:30-10:30pm. ❸

Le Grenier de Notre-Dame, 18 rue de la Bûcherie, 5ème (☎01 43 29 98 29). ⓂSt-Michel. Walk along quai St-Michel to quai de Montebello; turn right on rue Lagrange and left on rue de la Bucherie. Sunflowers and organic plants decorate this upscale cafe's patio and interior. A haven for vegans, Le Grenier infuses macrobiotic and vegetarian specialties with an edgy French spin. Revolutionizing what it means to have "greens" as a main course, the Autumn salad (€16) combines chestnuts, endives, feta, ginger, hazelnuts, honey, olives, and oranges to create a tactile adventure for the mouth. 3-course lunch *formule* €16 or €18 for dinner; includes *entrée, plat,* and hot beverage. Open daily noon-11pm. MC/V. ❸

Savannah Café, 27 rue Descartes, 5ème (☎01 43 29 45 77; www.savannahcafe.fr). ⓂCardinal Lemoine. Follow rue du Cardinal Lemoine uphill, turn right on rue Clovis, and walk 1 block to rue Descartes. Decorated with eclectic knickknacks, this cheerful restaurant serves Lebanese food including *taboule* (€7). From its large pasta selection, try noodles stuffed with spinach and ricotta cheese in a basil cream sauce (€14), or, for the indecisive, the perfectly composed starter sampler for 2 (warm goat cheese, taboule, and baba ganoush; €16). *Plats* €14-16. Open M-Sa 7-11pm. MC/V. ❷

Au Coin des Gourmets, 5 rue Dante, 5ème (☎01 43 26 12 92). ⓂSt-Michel. Light Vietnamese and Cambodian cuisine along with classy, minimalist decor. Enjoy the *crêpe vietnamienne* or *rouleaux jardinières* ("garden" rolls packed with veggies) while lounging in a leather chair or outside on the small patio. Delicious lunch *menu* €12.50. Also at 38 rue du Mont Thabor, 1er (☎01 42 60 79 79). Open M 7-10:30pm, Tu-Su noon-2:30pm and 7-10:30pm. MC/V. ❷

Foyer Vietnam, 80 rue Monge, 5ème (☎01 45 35 32 54). ⓂPlace Monge. Meager decor foreshadows this local favorite's meager prices. Removed from crowded rue Mouffetard, Foyer Vietnam favors students with large portions and a 2-course lunch menu (€7). Try starting with the tasty *pho* before moving on to the *porc au caramel* or duck with bananas (€8.50). You'll have trouble finding another restaurant that offers lychees in syrup (€2.50) for dessert. Open M-Sa noon-2pm and 7-10pm. ❶

L'Écurie, 58 rue de la Montagne Ste-Geneviève, 5ème (☎01 46 33 68 49). ⓂCardinal Lemoine. Walk down rue du Cardinal Lemoine, turn right on rue Clovis, then right on rue de la Montagne Ste-Geneviève. On the corner with rue Laplace. Too weak-stomached for the French specialty horse? Eat like one instead at "The Stables." Metal hitches adorn the walls, and candles light the below-ground, 12th-century "dining rooms." The 3-course €17 dinner *menu* includes the house favorite, *bavette en trois sauces* (flank steak in three sauces). Same 3-course lunch *menu* €11.50. ½-pitcher house wine €5.20. Open M and W-Su noon-2:30pm and 7pm-midnight, Tu 7pm-midnight. Cash only. ❷

Le Jardin des Pâtes, 4 rue Lacépède, 5ème (☎01 43 31 50 71). ⓂJussieu. Walk up rue Linné and turn right on rue Lacépède. As calming and pleasant as the Jardin des Plantes around the corner. Bright white walls and tiled floors transport guests to a modern yogi's kitchen. Le Jardin's organic menu emphasizes fresh *pâtes* (pasta; €10-14) but its limited selection will disappoint dessert fanatics. Open daily noon-2:30pm and 7-11pm. AmEx/MC/V over €15. Also at 33 bd. Arago, 13ème (☎01 45 35 93 67). ❷

Au Port Salut, 163bis rue St-Jacques, 5ème (☎01 46 33 63 21). RER: Luxembourg. Down the road from Le Perraudin, on the corner with rue Fossés St-Jacques; walk down bd. St-Michel with the Luxembourg Garden on your left, turn right on rue Soufflot, then right on rue St-Jacques. Behind its iron portcullis, this old stone building once doubled as a cabaret with the same name; the remaining romanesque frescoes and bar-room piano recall its past heyday. Under new ownership, Au Port Salut now houses 3 floors of traditional French gastronomy. 3-course lunch *menu* €18, dinner *menu* €28. Gladly accommodates groups. Open Tu-Sa noon-3:30pm and 7:30-10pm. MC/V. ❸

STUDENTS EAT CHEAP. All students in Paris are free to eat at the university restaurants run by **Centre régional d'œuvres universitaires (CROUS)**. Solid meals go for about €3. For more info on student deals and how not to starve, see **Study Abroad,** p. 126.

CAFES

Café de la Mosquée, 39 rue Geoffrey St-Hilaire, 5ème (☎01 43 31 38 20). ⓂCensier-Daubenton. In the Mosquée de Paris. Adorned with blue tiled fountains and white marble floors, this cafe deserves a visit. Persian mint tea (€2) and *maghrebain* pastries (€2) make for a great late-afternoon snack, best savored on their shaded outdoor patio. For dessert, the *Coupe Orientale* (2 scoops of mint tea ice cream and 1 scoop of honey nougat; €6) is tasty. Couscous €13-25. Open daily 9am-11pm. MC/V. ❷

Café Delmas, 2-4, place de la Contre Escarpe, 5ème (☎01 43 26 51 26). ⓂCardinal Lemoine. Walk up rue du Cardinal Lemoine straight into place de la Contre Escarpe. Two-venues-in-one, Delmas is the place to while away the hours (stylishly) in this happening area. A modern *crêperie* along rue Descartes, it offers cheap, 3-crêpe *menus* (€12) until 6pm. In the salon and on the outdoor *terrace* overlooking the square, black-clad waiters serve trendy food like Chinese chicken salad (€13) and mixed drinks from a lengthy menu. Cafe €2.70. Mixed drinks €5.50. Happy hour 7-9pm. Open M-Th and Su 7:30-2am, F-Sa 7:30-5am. MC/V. ❷

MARKETS

▨ **Marché Monge,** 5ème. ⓂMonge. In pl. Monge at the metro exit. Busy but easy to navigate. Cheese, flowers, jewelry, shoes and much more. For the perfect picnic lunch, choose from among the very popular prepared foods and head to the Arènes de Lutèce (p. 224). Open W, F, and Su 8am-1pm.

Marché Port Royal, 5ème. ⓂLes Gobelins. Walk downhill to the major intersection, turn left on bd. de Port Royal, and look for the stalls just after the hospital entrance (about 10min.). Sells primarily cheese, fruit, meat, and fresh vegetables to mostly local patrons. Cheap clothes and houseware also available. Open Tu, Th, and Sa 7am-2:30pm.

Marché Mouffetard, 5ème. ⓂMonge. Walk through pl. Monge and follow rue Ortolan to rue Mouffetard. Shoppers wander the pedestrian block, picking up cheese, meat, and fish at the respective specialty stores or selecting fruits and veggies from the covered stalls outside St-Medard church. To quell your bread craving, seek out rue Mouffetard's highly-reputed *boulangeries*. Open Tu-Sa 8am-8pm, Su 8am-4pm.

6ÈME ARRONDISSEMENT

Restaurants with rock-bottom prices vie for space and customers in the streets enclosed by boulevard St-Germain, boulevard St-Michel, rue de Seine, and the river. Within the tangle, rue de Buci harbors bargain Greek restaurants and a rambling street market, while rue Grégoire de Tours has the highest density of cheap, greasy tourist joints. Rue St-Andre-des-Arts is lined with *crêperies* and panini purveyors. Around Odéon, the Carrefour d'Odéon has several traditional bistros, and rue Princesse, rue Guisarde, and rue des Canettes are jam-packed with cheap and pedestrian-friendly eateries. There is a **Marché Franprix** on 31, r. Mazarine (6*ème*. ⓂOdéon. Open M-Sa 8:30am-9pm. Closed Sunday. Many locations throughout Paris; check www.franprix.fr).

▨ **Le Comptoir du Relais,** 5 carrefour de l'Odéon, 6*ème* (☎01 44 27 07 97). ⓂOdéon. Though the focus is on pork and other meats at this truly outstanding bistro, there's no weak link in Le Comptoir's menu. Foie gras on toast (€11) is a good starter and makes a delightful dinner when coupled with another *entrée* (€17-20). The local-heavy, hyper-crowded atmosphere is the true highlight of this dining experience. Show up for a late lunch (after 3pm) or early dinner (before 8pm Sa-Su) to avoid a wait. Open M-F noon-6pm and for 8:30 dinner seating; Sa-Su noon-11pm. Reservations strongly recommended for weekday dinner, not accepted on weekends. MC/V. ❸

Le Bistro d'Henri, 16 rue Princesse, 6*ème* (☎01 46 33 51 12). ⓂMabillon. Walk down rue du Four and turn left on rue Princesse. This Left Bank bistro's food is prepared with the freshest ingredients, and its offerings are definitely representative of Parisian bistro fare (read: delicious, but heavy). Appetizers €6-7. *Plats* €12-18. Open daily noon-2:30pm and 7-11pm. MC/V. Around the corner is **Le Machon d'Henri,** 8 rue Guisarde , 6*ème* (☎01 43 29 08 70), with the same menu in a smaller, white-stone alcove. ❷

La Table d'Erica, 6 rue Mabillon, 6*ème* (☎01 43 54 87 61; www.tableerica.free.fr). ⓂMabillon. You'll hear only French in this Creole gem—it's the locals' shelter from the tourist-clogged main drag. Cuisine plays with Indian flavors while staying true to its Afro-Caribbean roots. The 3-course *menu* (€13) is the best deal, but the *Calou Creole*, a delicious stew of spinach, okra, chicken, and seafood (€16), is also a good option. Finish things off with the *gâteau chocolat* with orange *coulis* (€6). Open Tu-Sa noon-2:30pm and 6:30-11pm. AmEx/MC/V. ❷

Così, 54 rue de Seine, 6*ème* (☎01 46 33 35 36). ⓂMabillon. Walk down bd. St-Germain and make a left on rue de Seine. Enormous, tasty, reasonably-priced sandwiches on fresh, brick-oven bread. This is the original that inspired the now-popular American chain. Sandwiches €5-8. Desserts €3-4. Open daily noon-11pm. ❶

Guen-maï, 2bis rue de l'Abbaye, entrance at 6 rue Cardinale, 6*ème* (☎01 43 26 03 24). ⓂMabillon. Walk against traffic on bd. St-Germain and take a right on rue de la Petite Boucherie, then left on rue de l'Abbaye. This healthy-living oasis might have more appeal for vegetarians and vegans than for carnivores (though they do have fish); anyone who craves seitan and soy will find a little slice of macrobiotic heaven here. The all natural food products are made completely in-house. The lunch counter doubles as a *salon de thé* and bookstore, as well as a vitamin boutique. Choices include miso soup (€4.50), agar fruit salad (€5), *poisson crudités* (€10.50), lunch *formule* (either a *petite tart* or a *brochette*, €10.50), and daily specials (€11.50). Lunch served M-Sa 11:45am-3:30pm. Store open M-Sa 9am-8:30pm. MC/V. ❶

Crêperie Saint Germain, 33 rue St-André-des-Arts, 6*ème* (☎01 43 54 24 41). ⓂSt-Michel. Cross pl. St-Michel and walk down rue St-André-des-Arts. The low ceilings, stucco, and tiles give this otherwise typical *crêperie* a Grecian feel. Serves filling wheat-

F O O D

flour *galettes,* like the Chihuahua (chicken cooked with peppers, tomatoes, and onions; €9). Sweet dessert *crêpes,* like the Zanzibar (nougat ice cream, raspberries, chocolate sauce, and whipped cream; €7.50). €9 *menu* (M-F noon-3pm) includes 2 *crêpes* and a cider or soda. Open daily noon-1am. AmEx/MC/V. ❶

La Crêpe Rit du Clown, 6 rue des Canettes, 6è*me* (☎01 46 34 01 02). ⓂMabillon. Walk down rue du Four and turn left on rue des Canettes. Though the clown figure greeting patrons at the door is reminiscent of an unfortunate horror movie, the food is tasty and cheap. Compose a hefty salad from an array of fresh ingredients (€12). Lunchtime *formule* €10.50. Savory *crêpes* €7-9. Kir €4. Open M-Sa noon-11:30pm. MC/V. ❶

WHAT'S WHAT. The 6è*me* has a number of different types of eateries, with an array of prices to match. Supermarkets are obviously cheapest, but *traiteurs* have ready-made takeout that comes in handy for the busy traveler. Street cafes are a step up in price and quality, but they all serve more or less the same food. Highest on the list are, of course, restaurants and bistros—perfect for those with time and cash to spare.

CAFES

Forget fine dining; cafes are the heart—and stomach—of the 6è*me.* Ordering a *café express* will guarantee you a seat for as long as you like. While historic establishments like **Le Sélect** and **Café de Flore** still hold court along the boulevard Montparnasse and boulevard St-Germain-des-Prés, newer cafes cluster around Carrefour d'Odéon and north of bd. St-Germain near the galleries. This area contains many *brasseries* and is probably your best bet for eating cheap in Paris, though some establishments are better known for their famous clientele of old than any modern menu innovations.

Le "Relais de l'Entrecôte", 20 rue St-Benoit, 6è*me* (☎01 45 49 16 00). ⓂSt-Germain-des-Prés. The French bourgeois version of fast food; a far cry from your average McDonald's. One question takes the place of a menu: "How do you like your steak?"—the only main course at this wildly popular Parisian franchise. For €22, you can enjoy a salad with walnuts to start, followed by *steak frîtes* in their inimitable sauce (don't be fooled; any other chain's version is simply inferior). The scrambling waitstaff will eventually refill your plate, so don't fret if your portion seems small. Also offers dessert and an impressively lengthy selection of wine. Open daily noon-2pm and 7-10:30pm. MC/V. ❸

Les Editeurs, 4 carrefour de l'Odéon, 6è*me* (☎01 43 26 67 76). ⓂOdéon. Les Editeurs pays homage to St-Germain's literary pedigree with a small library of books on everything from Marilyn Monroe to Brassaï. Masterfully prepared food; the chicken tajine with purple artichokes is sumptuous, as is the classic salmon filet with green lentils (both €21.50). Coffee €3. Beer €4.50-5. Mixed drinks €9-9.50. Ice cream €8.50. Sa and Su brunch *menu* €25.50. Open daily 8am-2am. AmEx/MC/V. ❸

Café de Flore, 172 bd. St-Germain, 6è*me* (☎01 45 48 55 26). ⓂSt-Germain-des-Prés. Sartre composed *Being and Nothingness* here; Apollinaire, Camus, Artaud, Picasso, Breton, and Thurber all sipped brew here too. In the contemporary feud between Café de Flore and Les Deux Magots, Flore reportedly snags more intellectuals by offering a well-respected literary prize. While Brigitte Bardot preferred the terrace, the Art Deco seating upstairs is still the coolest (check out Sartre and de Beauvoir's booth on the left). Coffee €5.50. Pastries €5-10. *Salade flore* €14.50. Open daily 7:30-1:30am. AmEx/MC/V. ❷

Les Deux Magots, 6 pl. St-Germain-des-Prés, 6è*me* (☎01 45 48 55 25). ⓂSt-Germain-des-Prés. Just across the street from the Église St-Germain-des-Prés. The cloistered area behind the famous high hedges has been home to literati (from Mallarmé to Hemingway) since 1885, but is now favored mostly by Left Bank residents and tourists. The cafe is named for 2 Chinese porcelain figures (the originals are still inside), not for fly larvae. Sandwiches €7-14. Pastries from €8.70. Coffee €4.20. Hot chocolate €6.70. Breakfast *menu* €18. Open daily 7:30am-1am. AmEx/MC/V. ❷

Le Sélect, 99 bd. du Montparnasse, 6è*me* (☎01 45 48 38 24). ⓜVavin. Walk west on bd. du Montparnasse; across the street from La Coupole. An "American" bar of the Lost Generation once frequented by Trotsky, Satie, Breton, Cocteau, Picasso, and of course, Hemingway. Have the bartender mix you a mixed drink (€12), and enjoy it in the company of a surprisingly local crowd. Go at teatime and enjoy a *café au lait* (€4). Dinner *plats* start at €11, with a *formule* offered for €14. Simpler offerings like *croque monsieurs* start at €7. Open daily 7-3am. MC/V over €15. ❷

Le Procope, 13 rue de l'Ancienne Comédie, 6è*me* (☎01 40 46 79 00). ⓜOdéon. Walk against traffic on bd. St-Germain and go right on rue de l'Ancienne Comédie. Founded in 1686, making it the first cafe in the world. Voltaire drank 40 cups a day here while writing *Candide*; his table remains what the owners call "a testimony of permanence." Marat came here to plot the Revolution. Now a seafood restaurant—or history with a price. The *prix-fixe* menus are the most economical choice—the Procope (2 courses) is €26, and the Philosophe (3 courses) is €32. Open daily 10:30-1am. AmEx/MC/V. ❹

Café Vavin, 18 rue Vavin, 6è*me* (☎01 43 26 67 47). ⓜVavin. While the food isn't note-worthy, the students and nutty professors packing tiny tables make for a terrific atmo-sphere. *Entrecôte* and fries €13. Salads €9.50-12. Open 7-12:30am. MC/V. ❷

SALONS DE THÉ

L'Heure Gourmand, 22 passage Dauphine, 6è*me* (☎01 46 34 00 40). ⓜOdéon. Walk up rue de l'Ancienne Comédie and turn right on the passage Dauphine after the Carrefour Buci. A classy and quiet *salon de thé* with a terrace and romantic upstairs balcony over-looking a beautiful side street. Teas €5-6. Berthillon ice cream €3-4 per *boule* (scoop). Pastries and desserts €6-8. Open M-Sa 11:30am-7:30pm, Su noon-7pm. MC/V. ❶

SPECIALTY SHOPS AND MARKETS

Poilâne, 8 rue Cherche Midi, 6è*me* (☎01 45 48 42 59; www.poilane.fr). ⓜVaneau. Widely regarded as one of the best bread-makers in Paris, Poilâne has lines out the door every morning. Try the famous sourdough loaf (€3.80), which is very dense and infused with a smoky, rich flavor. For dessert, pick up a melt-in-your-mouth apple tart filled with great gobs of brown sugar (€2). Visitors can observe all baking processes done by hand behind the counter. Order online for international delivery, but beware of much higher prices. Open M-Sa 7:15am-8:15pm. MC/V over €20.

Gérard Mulot, 76 rue de Seine, 6è*me* (☎01 43 26 85 77). ⓜOdéon or St-Sulpice. Out-rageous selection of painstakingly crafted pastries, from flan to marzipan with virtually any kind of fruit. The *macarons* are heavenly (€3). Tarts around €3.50. Eclairs €2.50. *Délicieux* (and it is!) €3.10. Open M-Tu and Th-Su 6:45am-8pm.

Marché Biologique, on bd. Raspail between rue du Cherche-Midi and rue de Rennes, 6è*me*. ⓜRennes. French new-agers peddle everything from organic produce to 7-grain bread and tofu patties. Open Su 9am-2pm.

Kusmi Tea, 56 rue de Seine, 6è*me* (☎01 46 34 29 06; www.kusmitea.com). ⓜMabillon. Walk away from l'Église St-Germain-des-prés on bd. St-Germain; turn left on rue de Seine. Founded in 1867, Kusmi first made teas for Russia's tsars. The 1917 October Revolution put a dent in their consumer base, so they reopened in Paris. The sleek white decor and pretty trim tins might make you think you're only paying for packaging, but don't worry—the tea is outstanding. Try Prince Vladimir (black tea, citrus, and vanilla), their most popular blend. The full *salon de thé* upstairs offers a trendy alternative to Mariage Frères. 125g tins from €9.90. Open daily 11am-8pm. MC/V.

FOOD

St-Germain Covered Market, 6ème. ⓂMabillon. Exit the metro and walk down rue de Montfaucon. The market is inside the large building at the end of the street, at the back. While this market cannot keep up with its outdoor cousins in terms of size or ambience, it will appeal to travelers looking to get their food and go. Its selection—particularly of fresh seafood—is great. Open Tu-Sa 8am-1pm and 4-8pm, Su 8am-1pm.

INVALIDES (7ÈME)

The 7ème is not budget-friendly, but it has some of the best gourmet pâtisseries and boulangeries in Paris; try rue St-Dominique, rue Cler, or rue de Grenelle for great picnic fare. The restaurants below are worth the splurge.

🏶 **Les Cocottes,** 135 rue St-Dominique, 7ème (☎01 45 50 10 31). ⓂSolférino. The fourth restaurant of chef Christian Constant on this street alone, Les Cocottes is a simpler, less expensive version of his haute-cuisine establishments. A self-proclaimed "French version of an American diner," this sophisticated spot attracts a crowd of mostly young professionals. Food is fresh, beautifully presented, and comfortingly delicious. The specialty here are cocottes (€12-15), cast-iron skillets filled with ingredients such as pig's feet and pigeon or fresh vegetables. For dessert, don't miss La Fabuleuse Tarte au Chocolat de Christian Constant (€9). Open daily noon-2:30pm and 7:15-11pm. AmEx/MC/V. ❷

L'Auberge Bressane, 16 av. de la Motte Picquet, 7ème (☎01 47 05 98 37; www.auberge-bressane.com). ⓂÉcole Militaire or Tour Mauberg. This small, festive restaurant is bouncing with regular patrons enjoying dishes like butter-soft artichoke hearts in a light vinaigrette (€10) and their famous poulet à la crème et aux morilles (€28). Order one of the famous house soufflés (Grand Marnier or chocolate; €10) or omelettes Norvegienne (€10) at the start of your meal to ensure a fine finale. Menus €20 and €25; add €5 for a ½-bottle of wine. Reservations are a must. Open M-F and Su noon-2:30pm and 8-10:45pm, Sa 8-10:45pm. Closed in Aug. AmEx/MC/V. ❸

Le Lotus Blanc, 45 rue de Bourgogne, 7ème (☎01 45 55 18 89). ⓂVarenne. Walk on bd. des Invalides, toward the Invalides; turn left on rue de Varenne and then left again on rue de Bourgogne. Chef Pham-Nam Nghia has been perfecting Vietnamese dishes for over 25 years in this tiny, stone-walled restaurant. The specialties à la vapeur (€7-15) and the grillades are excellent. Lunch and all-day menus €10-33. Great vegetarian and vegan dishes (€4-15). Reservations encouraged. Open M-Sa noon-2:30pm and 7:30-11pm. Closed in Aug. AmEx/MC/V. ❷

Au Pied de Fouet, 45 rue de Babylone, 7ème (☎01 47 05 12 27). ⓂVaneau. Take rue Vaneau and turn left on rue de Babylone. Small, friendly, rough-and-tumble bistro with the typical checkered tablecloths and an added rustic feel. Attracts both cigarette-puffing locals and tourists; serves straightforward French home cooking at bargain prices. Entrées €3-5. Plats €8-11. Desserts (the crème de marron is awesome) €3-4. Open M-Sa noon-2:30pm and 7-11pm. Other locations at 3 rue St-Benoît, 6ème (☎01 42 96 59 10) and 96 rue Oberkampf, 11ème (☎01 48 06 46 98). ❷

Grannie, 27 rue Pierre Leroux, 7ème (☎01 43 34 94 14). ⓂVaneau. Walk west on rue de Sèvres and turn right on rue Pierre Leroux. French fare with a Japanese twist, served in country-style decor. Specializes in creative meat dishes like roast pigeon and magret de canard à la sauce teriyaki. Lunch menu €23; dinner menu €30. Open M-F noon-2:30pm and 7:30-10:30pm, Sa 7:30-10:30pm. Closed 2 weeks in Aug. MC/V. ❹

CAFES

🏶 **Café des Lettres,** 53 rue de Verneuil, 7ème (☎01 42 22 52 17). ⓂSolférino. Exit the metro on rue de Solférino, turn right on rue de l'Université, left on rue de Poitiers, and right on rue Verneuil. Hidden on a side street, this Scandinavian cafe serves fresh, healthy fare. Eat inside in large leather armchairs, or in the same sunny courtyard as the Maison des Écrivains, surrounded by statues. Enjoy platters of smoked salmon and *blinis* (€21) and other Danish seafood dishes (€14-25). Su Scandinavian-style brunch buffet (€29); reservations strongly recommended. Coffee €3. Beer €5. Open M-F noon-2:30pm and 8-10:30pm; also open Sa-Su in June noon-7pm. AmEx/MC/V. ❸

Café du Marché, 38 rue Cler, 7ème (☎01 47 05 51 27). ⓂÉcole Militaire. Walk up rue de la Motte Picquet and turn left on rue Cler. Frequented by the chic residents of this picturesque Anglophone corner (and American tourists); main draws are the crowd and the covered terrace perfect for people-watching. Surprisingly creative and generous salads, like the Indian-inspired tandoori chicken caesar salad or the "brick" of goat cheese (€9-10). Also serves hearty and traditional French standbys such as beef tartare (€11). Coffee €2. Open M-Sa 7am-midnight; food served 11am-11pm. MC/V. ❶

McCoy Café, 49 av. Bosquet, 7ème (☎01 45 56 00 00). ⓂÉcole Militaire. The best cure for homesickness. Indulge in all the American comfort food you grew up on: burgers (€5-7), hot dogs, bagels (€5-7), PB&J, and Philly cheese steak (€6). In the attached grocery store, you'll find the whole gang: Betty Crocker, French's, Newman's Own, Oreos, Swiss Miss, Orville Redenbacher's, Ritz, Pepperidge Farm, Pop Tarts, and even beef jerky. Oreo milkshake €7; marshmallow fluff €4. Open daily 8am-8pm. ❶

Central Perk, 47 rue Babylone, 7ème (☎01 47 05 56 24). ⓂSt-François-Xavier or Sèvres Babylone. This might not look like the *Friends* hangout, but it does have a sweeping selection of fresh and simple lunch fare—sandwiches, pizza, cookies, etc. Try the *Menu Friends* (€5-6), which comes with a sandwich or pizza, a cookie and a drink; add a dessert and coffee to make it a *Menu Central Perk* (€7-8). Open M-F 9am-5pm. ❶

SPECIALTY SHOPS

▨ **La Grande Épicerie de Paris,** 38 rue de Sèvres. The celebrated gourmet food annex of department store Au Bon Marché. Not cheap, but awesome in all other ways. You don't need to be hungry to enjoy La Grande Épicerie, which falls somewhere between supermarket and food museum. Featuring all things dried, canned, smoked, and freshly baked. Sa free tastings on every aisle. Open M-Sa 8:30am-9pm. AmEx/MC/V.

▨ **Stéphane Secco,** 20 rue Jean-Nicot, 7ème (☎01 43 17 35 20). ⓂLa Tour-Maubourg. Formerly the popular Poujaran, this *boulangerie-pâtisserie* has changed ownership but only gotten better. The perfect place to stop before a picnic on the Champs de Mars (p. 229); find creative salads, a range of quiches and *tartes* (€3 for a *petit*, €11 for a *grand*), intricately rich desserts (macaroons €1-2), and bread studded with everything from olives and herbs to figs and apricots (€1-3). Open Tu-Sa 7:30am-8:30pm. Another location at 25 bd. de Grenelle, 15ème (☎01 45 67 17 40).

Debauve et Gallais, 30 rue des Sts-Pères, 7ème (☎01 45 48 54 67; www.debauve-et-gallais.com). ⓂSt-Germain-des-Prés or Sèvres-Babylone. In 1800, a chocolate factory was founded near the Abbey St-Germain-des-Prés by the official pharmacist of Louis XVI. Since then, the dark, unsweetened chocolate has been the favorite of Marie Antoinette, Louis XVIII, Charles X, Louis-Philippe, as well as plebeians. Debauve et Gallais is still steeped in tradition: this flagship store is housed in a historic building designed by Napoleon's architects, and their chocolates continue to be produced without additives, dyes, or sweeteners. Customers pick and choose individual chocolates with flavors like peach and almond, nougat, and Earl Grey tea. Try the velvety bars of chocolate, also in a variety of flavors (€5). Golf-ball shaped pralines (300g, €34). Open M-Sa 9:30am-7pm. Also at 33 rue Vivienne, 2ème (☎01 40 39 05 50). AmEx/MC/V.

Barthélémy, 51 rue de Grenelle, 7ème (☎01 45 48 56 75). ⓂRue du Bac. A cluttered, old-fashioned storefront showcasing adorable livestock and poultry figurines; inside, the finest cheese in Paris. President Chirac has been known to stop in. Open Tu-F 8am-1pm and 4-7pm, Sa 8am-1:30pm and 3:30-7:15pm.

FOOD

L'entrée au dessert, 45 rue Babylone, 7ème (☎01 45 05 85 00; delentreeaudessert. com). ⓂSt-François-Xavier or Sèvres-Babylone. A cute, slightly cluttered shop filled with everything you might need for an elegant last-minute dinner party: freshly prepared salads, *plats*, and desserts; fresh cheeses and sausages; a sufficient selection of wine. Open M-F 8am-8pm and Sa 9am-pm. AmEx/MC/V.

CHAMPS-ÉLYSÉES (8ÈME)

The *8ème* has traditionally been Paris's center of glamorous dining and world-class cuisine. There are still plenty of extravagant establishments, particularly south of the Champs-Élysées, but lately the area has been losing importance as a culinary capital. The best affordable restaurants are on side streets around rue la Boétie, rue des Colisées, and place de Dublin.

▓ **Ty Yann,** 10 rue de Constantinople, 8ème (☎01 40 08 00 17). ⓂEurope. Turn right on rue de Rome and left on rue de Constantinople. The welcoming Breton chef and owner, M. Yann, cheerfully prepares outstanding and relatively inexpensive *galettes* (€8-10) and *crêpes* in this tiny restaurant, decorated with his mother's pastoral paintings. Try *La vaniteuse* (€8), sausage sauteed in cognac, Emmental cheese, and onions. Create your own crêpe (€6-7) for lunch. Takeout available for 15% less. Open M-F noon-3:30pm and 7:30-10:30pm, Sa 7:30-10:30pm. MC/V. ❶

Mood, 114 av. des Champs-Elysées and 1 rue Washington, 8ème (☎01 42 89 98 89; www.mood-paris.fr). ⓂGeorge V. A sensuous melange of Western decor and delicate Japanese accents reflects the fusion cuisine. Dine on the *prix-fixe* lunch (a great value at €20) in the calming upper dining room, or indulge your hedonistic side on the lower level's plush beds at night. A drink list with poetic and sultry mixed drinks (€12) such as *septembre en attendant* (waiting for September) and *Mademoiselle s'amuse* (Miss Fun). *Entrées* €8-13. *Plats* €14-27. Live music and DJ in the evenings. Reservations recommended for the restaurant, required for the lounge. Restaurant open M-Th and Su 10am-2am, F-Sa 10am-4am. Lounge open daily 10pm-4am. AmEx/MC/V. ❸

Thabthim Siam, 28 rue de Moscou, 8ème (☎01 43 87 62 56). ⓂRome. From the metro, take a right on rue de Moscou. A local favorite, with embroidered tapestries, silk-draped chairs, and bronze statues. An intimate restaurant with a romantic ambience, excellent curry dishes, and a rotating menu that allows patrons to experience all aspects of Thai cuisine. *Entrées* €8. *Plats* €13. The €16 lunch *menu* includes choice of *entrée, plat*, and drink. Open M-Sa noon-2pm and 7-10:30pm. AmEx/MC/V. ❷

Le bien-être gourmand, 17 rue de Constantinople, 8ème (☎01 44 70 00 72). ⓂEurope. Turn right on rue de Rome and left on rue de Constantinople. A cozy, organic hideaway in the northeast corner of the 8ème, this small, wood-bedecked restaurant-*salon de thé* offers delicious salads (€9), soups, and sweet and savory tarts (€5-6), all available for eat-in or takeout. Lunch *menus* (€11-13) are a deal. Also serves fresh fruit and vegetable juices. Open M-Sa 10am-6pm. MC/V. ❶

Toi, 27 rue Colisée (☎01 42 56 56 58). ⓂFranklin D. Roosevelt. Walk toward the arch on the Champs-Élysées and take the first street on the right. Deep red sofas; warm, dim lighting; and artfully black-clad waitstaff. A favorite hangout for the young and chic locals, who prefer the retro upper level, Toi is all about tantalizing and beautiful visual presentation in every aspect of the experience. Evenings feature themed *soirées* beginning 9pm. M Jazz Night, Tu Magic Night, Th Ladies' Night. The experimental cuisine menu rotates each season, with *entrées* €8-24, *plats* €14-31, and desserts €8-14. €17 lunch *menu* and €22 dinner *menu* (both M-F only). Reservations recommended for dinner. Open M-Sa noon-3pm and 6:30-2am. AmEx/V. ❸

CAFES

Fouquet's, 99 av. des Champs-Élysées, 8ème (☎01 47 23 50 00). ⓜGeorge V. Walk in and feel like a movie star. Decorated with sumptuous, red velvet upholstery and gilded fittings, Fouquet's is an experience of quintessential old-time Parisian glamour (see **Sights,** p. 233). Easy on the eyes but devastating for the bank account (starters run upwards of €30). Buy a coffee (€8) and soak in your surroundings. Open daily 8-2am. Food served all day in the cafe. Restaurant open daily 7:30-10am, noon-3pm, and 7pm-midnight in the restaurant. AmEx/MC/V. ❺

SALONS DE THÉ

⚑ Ladurée, 16 rue Royale, 8ème (☎01 42 60 21 79; www.laduree.com). ⓜConcorde. Ever wondered what it would be like to dine inside a Fabergé egg? The Rococo decor of this tea salon attracts a jarring mix of well-groomed shoppers and tourists. One of the first Parisian *salons de thé,* Ladurée shows its age but remains a must-see (and taste). Along with the infamous mini macaroons in the window (€2; in 16 different varieties), this spot offers little that hasn't been soaked in vanilla or caramel. Boxes of *"Chocolats Incomparable"* from €18. Ginger candies covered in dark chocolate €19. Specialty tea Ladurée *melange* €7.50. Su brunch €27. Open M-Sa 8:30am-7pm and Su 10-7pm. Lunch served until 3pm. AmEx/MC/V. Also at 75 av. des Champs-Elysées, 8ème (☎01 40 75 08 75); 21 rue Bonaparte, 6ème (☎01 44 07 64 87); and 62 boulevard Haussmann, 9ème (☎01 42 82 40 10). ❸

SPECIALTY SHOPS

Fauchon, 26-30, pl. de la Madeleine, 8ème (☎01 47 42 60 11; www.fauchon.com). ⓜMadeleine. Paris's favorite gourmet food shop comes complete with gourmet prices. Occupying two separate stores on pl. de la Madeleine alone, this *traiteur/pâtisserie/épicerie/charcuterie* has it all. Go home with a pretty tin of madeleines, check out the caviar bar, or browse their wine cellar—one of Paris's finest. Cute and creative box of chocolates €23 for 250g. *Épicerie/confiserie* (grocer/confectionary) open M-Sa 9:30am-8pm, *boulangerie* (bakery) 8am-6pm, *traiteur/pâtisserie* (caterer/pastry shop) 9am-9pm, tea room 9am-7pm. AmEx/MC/V.

OPÉRA (9ÈME)

Bordering the touristy 1er and 2ème, restaurants and eateries close to the Opéra cater to the posh after-theater and movie crowd; for cheaper meals, head farther north in the 9ème. Rue du Faubourg-Montmartre, only a short metro ride or brisk walk from Place de l'Opéra, brims with a seemingly limitless selection of inexpensive restaurants, including Chinese, Japanese, Mexican, and French options. Its cheap cafes, fast-food joints, *salons de thé,* and specialty shops vary in quality as well as cuisine.

⚑ Chez Haynes, 3 rue Clauzel, 9ème (☎01 48 78 40 63). ⓜSt-Georges. Head uphill on rue Notre Dame de Lorette and turn right on rue H. Monnier, then right again on rue Clauzel. Paris's first African-American owned restaurant, Chez Haynes opened in 1949. Louis Armstrong, James Baldwin, and Richard Wright all enjoyed Haynes's delicious New Orleans soul food and corn on the cob. Though a Portuguese/Brazilian couple now run the restaurant, its cuisine has remained relatively unchanged. There is no other place like this in Paris. Chez Haynes's very generous portions generally cost less than €16. Ma Sutton's fried honey chicken €14. Sister Lena's BBQ spare ribs €16. Chez Haynes's

GETTING THE SKINNY

Many theories have been put forward to explain the widely observed yet narrowly understood phenomenon of the slimness of the French, especially of French women. There seems to be no evidence of French cuisine's passion for cream and oil in the svelte hips of young Parisians. Just looking at clothing sizes in upscale boutiques, one can see that obesity is simply a rarity in Paris. But how can this be, in a country famous for its cheese and pâté?

A popular theory maintains that French women smoke constantly and drink copious amounts of coffee, thereby reducing their appetites and occupying their mouths in one unhealthy stroke. Smokers do indeed seem ever-present in Paris, but whether or not this prevents them getting hungry, many French can be seen in local cafes indulging in two- or three-course meals at lunchtime. A more convincing theory, and one that has been put forward on the basis of much research and many time-consuming studies, is that the French... wait for it... eat less than Americans and Brits. Genius.

Portion size is America's greatest weakness. Ever since McDonald's began offering to Super-Size your meal, it's been a slippery slope. The French, on the other hand, seem to have an ingrained Weight Watchers-style mentality of moderation. Although going to the gym is about as popular as the Atkins Diet in the country that invented the baguette, portion con-

soul food *menu* Tu-Sa, Brazilian food Su. Live music F-Sa nights; €5 cover. Open Tu-Su 7pm-midnight; hours vary. AmEx/MC/V. ❷

■ **Chartier,** 7 rue du Faubourg-Montmartre, 9*éme* (☎01 47 70 86 29; www.restaurant-chartier.com). ⓜGrands Boulevards. This Parisian fixture, tucked away down a covered passage, has been serving well-priced French cuisine since 1896; as tradition dictates, the waitstaff still adds up the bill on each table's paper tablecloth. While Chartier's classic Parisian character attracts patrons more than its diner-style food, French staples like *steak au poivre* (€8.50) and *langue de veau* (sheep's tongue; €9.80) are still sure to impress. Side dishes €2.50. Free Wi-Fi. Open daily 11:30am-10pm. AmEx/MC/V. ❶

No Stress Café, 24 rue Clauzel, 9*ème* (☎01 48 78 00 27). ⓜSt-Georges. Walk uphill on rue Notre Dame de Lorette and turn right on rue H. Monnier. A French crowd comes for American-sizes: enormous, flamboyant piles of vegetables and seasoned meats (€13-16). Fried onion rings with spicy sauce (€5). Vegetarian options. *Su brunch noon-3:30pm. Soirées Voyance* (psychic readings) F-Sa. Open Tu-Su 11am-2am. MC/V. ❷

Anarkali Sarangui, 4 pl. Gustave Toudouze, 9*éme* (☎01 48 78 39 84). ⓜSt-Georges. Walk uphill on rue Notre Dame de Lorette and turn right on rue H. Monnier. A rare North Indian restaurant with pleasant outdoor seating and a brightly-decorated interior. Tandoori and curries €7.50-12.50. Open Tu-Su 11am-2:30pm and 7-11pm. MC/V. ❷

Saveurs & Coincïdences, 6 rue de Trévise, 9*ème* (☎01 42 46 62 23; www.saveursetcoincidences.com). ⓜGrand Boulevards. The chefs here use only fresh, seasonal ingredients in creating their *cuisinal mélange,* which changes daily and draws inspiration from traditional French and North African dishes. €12-15 lunch *menu* includes vegetarian, salad, and white meat options. 3-course dinner *menu* €21; vegetarian entrees available by request. Open M-W noon-3pm, Th-F noon-3pm and 5-10:30pm. MC/V. ❸

Comme Par Hasard, 48 rue Notre Dame de Lorette, 9*ème* (☎01 06 28 25 51 23). ⓜSt-Georges. Although small, Comme Par Hasard offers outdoor seating and sandwiches more interesting than the standard *jambon beurre.* Try the €5.10 Pain "Pignon" sandwich with fig butter, smoked duck, and tomatoes or make your own salad (€3.50-7). Lunch menu €7.60-8.80; includes sandwich, dessert, and drink. Breakfast *formule* €5.80. Open M-F 7:30am-8:30pm. Cash only. ❶

CAFES

Au Général La Fayette, 52 rue la Fayette, 9ème (☎01 47 70 59 08). ⓜLe Peletier. With Art Nouveau lamps, mirrors, and decor from ceiling to floor, Au Général is one of the area's few classy cafe-bars. *Galettes* €10-11. Large salad selection €4.50-13.50. Bottled beer €5-6, on tap €2.30-3.50 at the bar. Open daily 10-4am. Kitchen open M-Sa noon-3am and Su noon-2am. AmEx/MC/V. ❷

Café de la Paix, 12 bd. des Capucines, pl. de l'Opéra, 9ème (☎01 40 07 36 36; www.cafedelapaix.fr). ⓜOpéra. Café de la Paix has drawn a classy crowd since its 1862 opening. Oscar Wilde frequented the restaurant regularly, while other international celebrities from Salvador Dalí to Buzz Aldrin (but not Neil Armstrong) have stopped by for a cup of expensive coffee (€4-6); tourists comprise the majority of today's clientele, however. Sandwiches €14-19. Desserts €11. Croissants €2. For cheaper prices, eat inside. Open daily 8am-11:30pm. AmEx/MC/V. ❹

SPECIALTY SHOPS

La Maison du Chocolat, 8 bd. de la Madeleine, 9ème (☎01 47 42 86 52; www.lamaisonduchocolat.com). ⓜMadeleine. From the rue de l'Église metro exit, turn left, walking away from the Madeleine; La Maison will be on your left. A chain with branches in Cannes, New York, London, and Tokyo, this Parisian emporium offers a range of exquisite milk and dark chocolates, along with a distilled chocolate essence drink (€4-6). Box of 2 chocolates €3. Mouth-watering chocolate eclairs €4. Also at Carrousel du Louvre, 99 rue de Rivoli, 1er (☎01 45 44 20 40); 19 rue de Sèvres, 6ème (☎01 45 44 20 40); 52 rue François, 8ème (☎01 47 23 38 25); and 225 rue du Faubourg Saint-Honoré, 8ème (☎01 42 27 39 44). Open M-Sa 10am-7:30pm. AmEx/MC/V.

CANAL ST-MARTIN AND SURROUNDS (10ÈME)

Many tourists never see more of the 10ème than their Gare du Nord layover allows. Those who venture out will find French, Indian, and African restaurants with reasonable prices, as well as cafes and brasseries on every corner.

🕮 **Le Cambodge,** 10 av. Richerand, 10ème (☎01 44 84 37 70). ⓜRépublique. It's no wonder that the youth of the 10ème flock to this small Cambodian restaurant. Main dishes cost a reasonable €7-10, and can be enjoyed from an outdoor terrace along a quiet side street. Expect to have to wait up to 90min. for a table,

trol seems to compensate entirely for the lack of exercise, speaking strictly in terms of slimness. If you do not consume so many calories, there's no need to sweat for an hour while reading Cosmo on the elliptical at your local gym.

Americans and other non-French who seek advice on how to achieve the svelte French figure have had their prayers answered by the book French Women Don't Get Fat. Author (and slim Frenchwoman) Mireille Guiliano has made a fortune from this book, which aims to enlighten the world as to how the French can stay so slim without cultivating a diet nation similar to that in the US (and England to a certain extent). Guiliano advocates savoring your food by turning off your television and focusing on what you are consuming. This way you can enjoy the taste and realize when you are full.

However, with the rise of McDonalds-style fast food and delivery pizza, who knows how long the French will stay ahead in the slimming game (only until 2020 according to BBC news)? So instead of trying to emulate the French, the United States et al could just sit tight and wait for them to catch up...and for the release of the next book, Whoops, French Women Got Fat.

as they don't take reservations. Thankfully, there are plenty of places nearby to get a *verre du vin* and anticipate the giant bowl of beef and noodles to come. Good vegetarian options also available. M-Sa noon-2:30pm and 8-11:30pm. MC/V. ❷

Au Bon Café, 2 bd. St-Martin, 10*ème* (☎01 42 02 14 57). Ⓜ République. Just off pl. de la République. A haven from the frenzy of the pl. de la République, and a nice alternative to the place's fast food chains. Patrons can grab one of its wooden tables and try a crisp salad with creative ingredients like *coquilles* (scallops), grapefruit, pear, avocado, and tomato. Salads €10-12. *Assiettes* €10-12, including specials that change daily. Karaoke and dance music on Friday and Saturday nights. Open daily 7-11pm. MC/V. ❷

Pooja, 91 passage Brady, 10*ème* (☎01 48 24 00 83; www.poojarestaurant. com). Ⓜ Strasbourg-St-Denis. Passage Brady is a small side street hidden away at no. 46 rue du Faubourg St-Denis. Pooja's Indian cuisine is best enjoyed at night, when the passage (which also houses many other Indian restaurants) is lit with hanging lanterns. The green astroturf that carpets the restaurant might turn you off, but a sip of the delicious green cocktail Pooja (€4) might just win you over. Lunch menu €12. Several vegetarian options. Open daily noon-3pm and 7-11pm. MC/V. ❷

New-Flash, 10 rue Lucien Sampaix, 10*ème* (☎01 42 45 03 30). Ⓜ Jacques Bonsergent. A rare find in Paris, this kosher restaurant is within walking distance from Place de la République. Serving standards like *côte de veau* (€18) at slightly elevated prices, this restaurant offers the primary attraction of kosher food regulated by the Beth-Din of Paris. Takeout sandwiches €8. Open M-F 11:30am-3:30pm. MC/V. ❸

SPECIALTY SHOPS

Marché St-Quentin, 85bis, bd. de Magenta, 10*ème*. Ⓜ Gare de l'Est or Gare du Nord. Outside: a massive construction of iron and glass, built in the 1880s, renovated in 1982, and covered by a glass ceiling. Inside: stalls of all varieties of produce, meat, cheese, seafood, and wine. A fun place to get inexpensive food basics and shop like a Parisian. Open Tu-Sa 8am-1pm and 3:30-7:30pm, Su 8am-1pm.

BASTILLE

11ÈME ARRONDISSEMENT

Although Bastille swells with fast-food joints, this increasingly diverse neighborhood offers Spanish, African, and Asian cuisines, among others. They are also a handful of nice restaurants for lower prices than the central *arrondissements*. The most popular haunts line the bustling rues de Charonne, Keller, de Lappe, and Oberkampf.

Chez Paul, 13 rue de Charonne, 11*ème* (☎01 47 00 34 57). Ⓜ Bastille. Go east on rue du Faubourg St-Antoine and turn left on rue de Charonne. Downstairs has a classic bistro feel; upstairs has a romantic atmosphere; both have fun, witty staff. The food? Not necessarily as fun and witty. Most come for farm-style favorites and traditional French dishes like *pot au feu* (a stew with meat and veggies; €17); the more daring go for St-Antoine's Temptation (pig ear, foot, tail, and groin; €18). Open daily noon-2:30pm and 7pm-2am. Kitchen closes 12:30am. Reservations required for dinner. AmEx/MC/V. ❸

Au Trou Normand, 9 rue J.P. Timbaud, 11*ème* (☎01 48 05 80 23; www.napacaro.com). Ⓜ République or Filles du Calvaire. Rue J.P. Timbaud intersects with bd. du Temple. A small, hidden-away, family-style restaurant. The welcoming staff serves up French, Italian, and Spanish-inspired meat and fish dishes; the menu changes every 3 months. Imported Italian olive oil in various flavors (like ginger and lemon) provides an accent for many dishes. Vegetarian options available. Entrées €6-12, *plats* €13-18, desserts

€7-8. Lunch *menus* €13-15; dinner *menu* €23-25. Open M-W and Su noon-3pm and 7:30-11:30pm, Th-Sa noon-3pm and 7:30pm-midnight. AmEx/MC/V. ❸

L'Oga, 82 rue Jean-Pierre Timbaud, 11*ème* (☎ 01 43 57 60 15; www.loga-resto.com). ⓂParmentier. A leather-and-lace style interior with red-and-black tables and delightfully mismatched antique chairs reflect this small restaurant's funky-elegant atmosphere. Salads (€7-14) with as much style and sophistication; from the Yacata, with guacamole and salsa, to the Lagon, with salmon, citrus, and mango. Le Brunch by L'Oga every Su, with 3 *assiettes* to choose from Anglaise, Asie, and Terroir (all €24-26). *Entrées* €7-14. *Plats* €15-24. Reservations recommended. Open M-Th noon-3pm and 8pm-midnight, F-Sa noon-3pm and 8pm-1am, Su brunch 11am-6pm. AmEx/MC/V. ❸

La Banane Ivoirienne, 10 rue de la Forge-Royale, 11*ème* (☎01 43 70 49 90). ⓂLedru-Rollin or Faidherbe-Chaligny. Rue de la Forge-Royale intersects with rue du Faubourg St-Antoine. Ivorian prints, palm trees, and African cuisine like shrimp *brochettes* (€16) and *foutou banane* (cooked plantains; for parties of 3 or more; €16 per person). Upbeat ambience. *Entrées* €5-8. *Plats* €10-16. Veggie *menu* €11. Dinner *menu* €29, includes wine. Live African music F 10pm; enjoy with Ivorian specialty drinks, €5-6. Reservations recommended. Open Tu-Sa 7pm-midnight. AmEx/MC/V over €15. ❷

Restaurant Assoce, 48bis rue St-Maur, 11*ème* (☎01 43 55 73 82). St-Maur. Serves excellent, inexpensive Turkish cuisine. Specializes in wood-fire-grilled meat platters (€10-12). Mediterranean desserts like *balli* yogurt and baklava (€5-7). Lunch *menu* is a steal at €10; dinner *menu* €16-20. *Plats* €9-11. Lots of veggie options. Open M-Sa noon-3pm and 7-11:30pm. MC/V. ❷

Le Bistrot du Peintre, 116 av. Ledru-Rollin, 11*ème* (☎01 47 00 34 39). ⓂLedru-Rollin. Le Bistrot du Peintre sticks to its Art Nouveau roots, sporting faded dark wood, curvy mirrors, ornate floral tiles, and an ivy-covered facade. An outdoor table here is just the place for the sociable clientele to watch the 11*ème* whirl, clang, and honk by. Impressive wine list. The traditional menu includes *charcuterie* (€5-12) and *confit de canard* (€14). *Plats* €13-15. Desserts €5-6. Open daily 7-2am. MC/V. ❷

CAFES

▩ **Le Bar à Soupes,** 33 rue Charonne, 11*ème* (☎01 43 57 53 79; www.lebarasoupes. com). ⓂBastille. Walk down rue Faubourg St-Antoine and turn left on rue Charonne. A small, bright cafe that features big bowls of delicious, freshly made soup (€5-6). 6 varieties change daily. The €9.50 lunch *menu* is an astonishing deal: it comes with soup; a crusty roll; wine or coffee; and salad, cheese plate, or dessert. The staff is very friendly. Try the gooey *gâteau chocolat* (€4) for dessert. Soups to go €4 per 1/4 liter, €6 per 1/2 liter. Open M-Sa noon-3pm and 6:30-11pm. MC/V. ❶

▩ **Café de l'Industrie,** 15-17 rue St-Sabin, 11*ème* (☎01 47 00 13 53). ⓂBreguet-Sabin. A happening cafe frequented by funky 20-somethings. Straddles a street. Both sides serve the same diverse menu: *tagliatelle* with pesto (€10) rubs elbows with marlin (€14). Coffee €3. *Vin chaud* €4.50. Salads €8.50-9. Popular brunch platter changes weekly (served Sa-Su; €12-15). Open daily 10-2am. MC/V. ❷

Pause Café, 41 rue de Charonne, 11*ème* (☎01 48 06 80 33). ⓂLedru-Rollin. Walk along av. Ledru-Rollin and turn left on rue de Charonne. Long the coffee and lunch spot of choice for a hip and lively crowd. All the cooler for having starred in the film *Chacun Cherche Son Chat*. Spacious, dressed-down interior and large outdoor seating area. The menu changes regularly—trust the fresh daily chalkboard specials. Creative salads €10-11. Beer €4-5. Mixed drinks €6-8. Open M-Sa 7:30-2am, food served noon-midnight; Su 9am-8pm, food served noon-5pm. MC/V. ❷

Le Troisième Bureau, 74 rue de la Folie-Méricourt, 11*ème* (☎01 43 55 87 65). ⓂOberkampf. Take rue de Crussol across bd. Richard Lenoir and turn left on rue de la Folie-Méricourt. A subdued cafe-bar-restaurant with a pared-down artistic aesthetic and

FOOD

a substantial wine list. Gets lively in the evenings to the sound of drum and bass and acid funk. Salads €10-14. Plats €16-22. *Formule* €12; *menu* €14. Open daily 10:30-2am. Lunch served noon-3pm; dinner served 7pm-midnight. MC/V. ❷

Babylone, 21 rue Daval, 11*ème* (☎01 47 00 55 02). Ⓜ️Bastille. In an area packed with cheap sandwich shops and crêpe stands, this shawarma and falafel spot stands out. A tiny, bar-like establishment with a 50s diner feel—but don't expect burgers. Order a falafel (€4-5), shawarma (€5-6), or falafel and shawarma (€5-6) sandwich. Beer €2.50. Open M noon-4pm, Tu-Sa noon-4pm and 7-11:30pm. Cash only. ❶

SPECIALTY SHOPS AND MARKETS

🏪 **La Bague de Kenza,** 106 rue St-Maur, 11*ème* (☎01 43 14 93 15). A famous Parisian treat. Piles of creatively sweet Algerian pastries—most of which are chock full of nuts, honey, and/or dried fruits €1.50-2.20. Beautiful fruit-shaped marzipan €2.20. Fluffy or dense Algerian bread €2.10-3.50. Open M-Th and Sa-Su 9am-10pm, F 2-10pm. AmEx/MC/V over €16. Also at 173 rue du Faubourg St-Antoine, 11*ème*.

Marché Bastille, on bd. Richard-Lenoir from pl. de la Bastille north to rue St-Sabin, 11*ème*. Ⓜ️Bastille. Produce, cheese, exotic mushrooms, bread, fish, meat, flowers, second-hand clothing, and housewares stretch all the way from Ⓜ️Richard Lenoir to Ⓜ️Bastille. A popular Su morning outing. Open Th 7am-2:30pm and Su 7am-2:30pm.

Marché Popincourt, on bd. Richard-Lenoir between rue Oberkampf and rue de Jean-Pierre Timbaud, 11*ème*. Ⓜ️Oberkampf. Fresh, well-priced fruits, vegetables, meat, and fish. A smattering of vendors selling essentials like socks, sunglasses, shoes, shirts and underwear. Open Tu and F 7am-2:30pm.

12ÈME ARRONDISSEMENT

In terms of food, the 12*ème* is a generally affordable *arrondissement,* where casual establishments serve a variety of cuisines, from North African to Middle Eastern to traditional French. Most of the better places are on side streets, scattered throughout the *arrondissement.* On rue du Faubourg St-Antoine you'll find some nice but overpriced restaurants and cheap fast food joints; meanwhile, the Viaduc des Arts hosts a couple of classy cafes.

🏪 **L'Ébauchoir,** 45 rue de Citeaux, 12*ème* (☎01 43 42 49 31; www.lebauchoir.com). Ⓜ️Faidherbe-Chaligny. Walk down rue du Faubourg St-Antoine, turn left on rue de Citeaux. A funky, lively, classy French restaurant. The menu (changes daily) features delicious concoctions of seafood and meat. Vegetarian dishes upon request. Impressive wine list. *Prix fixe* lunch *menu* €15. *Entrées* €8-15. *Plats* €17-25. Desserts €7. Open M 8-11pm and Tu-Sa noon-11pm. Food served noon-2:30pm and 8-11pm. MC/V. ❷

Le Cheval de Troie, 71 rue de Charenton, 12*ème* (☎01 43 44 24 44; www.chevaltroie. com). Ⓜ️Bastille. As you're facing the Opera, rue de Charenton is the street just to the left; the restaurant is on your left. Savory Turkish food in a traditionally festive setting populated with locals. Emphasis on kebabs and grilled meat platters, although vegetarian options are available. Light and refreshing desserts like *balli* yogurt (the house yogurt with honey and almonds; €4). Belly dancers Sa at 9:30pm. *Formules* €11-19. *Menu gourmand* €29, includes *aperitif* and *digestif.* Open M-Sa noon-2:30pm and 7-11:30pm. MC/V. 10% student discount. ❸

Les Grandes Marchés, 6 pl. de la Bastille, 12*ème* (☎01 43 42 90 32; www.lesgrands-marches.com). Ⓜ️Bastille. Adjacent to the opera. Sleek, air-conditioned, and expensive (but worth it), this is among the area's nicest restaurants. A popular place for power lunches and elegant dinners. Try one of the creative *entrées* like creamy mushroom soup with poached eggs (€9) before savoring one of the inspired meat or fish dishes

(€15-26). Outdoor seating overlooks the dynamic pl. de la Bastille. *Menus* €23 and €30. "Jazzy brunch" Su noon-4pm. Open daily noon-midnight. AmEx/MC/V. ❸

Les Broches à l'Ancienne, 21 rue St-Nicolas, 12ème (☎01 43 43 26 16). ⓂLedru-Rollin. Follow your nose: the meats here (from poultry to beef to boudin) are slow-cooked in a stone oven. Dark wood and crimson leather upholstery set the tone for serious, high-minded food at surprisingly low prices. Succulent shoulder of lamb with *frites* €19. *Entrées* €5-9. Photography displays in basement. Jazz F at 8pm; dinner and performance around €25. Reservations recommended. Open M-Tu and Th-Sa noon-2:30pm and 7-10:30pm, W noon-2:30pm. Closed middle two weeks of Aug. AmEx/MC/V. ❷

CAFÉS

▨ **Refuge Café,** 54 av. Daumesnil, 12ème (☎01 43 47 25 59). ⓂGare de Lyon. Marked by an old-fashioned metro sign, this whimsical, ivy-covered cafe and restaurant—with its magenta curtains and greenhouse-esque indoor patio—seems to be out of a fairy tale. Organizes art and photography exhibits every month. Salads €11-15. *Plats* €15-23. *Formules* €14-22. Open M-Sa 8am-midnight. ❸

SPECIALTY SHOPS

Marché Beauvau St-Antoine, on pl. d'Aligre between rue de Charenton and rue Crozatier, 12ème. ⓂLedru-Rollin. One of the largest and most diverse Parisian markets, lined with Muslim halal butcher shops, florists, and delis. Quality of produce varies between stands. Produce market open Tu-Sa 8am-1pm and 4-7:30pm, Su 8am-1pm.

BUTTE-AUX-CAILLES AND CHINATOWN (13ÈME)

A budget gourmand's dream, the 13ème turns dinner into a culinary foray. Locals fill the Butte-aux-Cailles's high-spirited restaurants and bars most nights of the week, and, believe it or not, scores of Asian restaurants fill Chinatown, south of place d'Italie on avenue de Choisy. North African eateries reign near ⓂSt-Marcel. Come with or without reservations; either way, with this many cheap venues, you are sure to find a restaurant that will keep you coming back.

▨ **Chez Gladines,** 30 rue des Cinq Diamants, 13ème (☎01 45 80 70 10). ⓂPlace d'Italie. Take bd. Auguste Blanqui and turn left on rue des Cinq Diamants; on the corner of rue Jonas. Intimate seating puts your right next to the locals at Chez Gladines, which serves southwestern French and Basque specialties (€7.30-11.60). Well-deserved city-wide acclaim has amped up Chez Gladine's Sa night popularity (read: it's delicious, cheap, and really crowded); gourmands seeking a leisurely repose should come before 7:30pm or after 11pm to avoid the crowds. Large salads (featuring lots of intestine and liver) €6.50-9. Beer €2. Espresso €1. Open M-Tu noon-3pm and 7pm-midnight; W-F noon-3pm and 7pm-1am; Sa-Su noon-4pm and 7pm-midnight. Cash only. ❶

Tricotin, 15 avenue de Choisy, 13ème (☎01 45 84 74 44). ⓂPorte de Choisy. Delicious food from Cambodia, Thailand, and Vietnam served in 2 large, cafeteria-style rooms. Start with the *Niems chaud* spring rolls (€4.90) before trying the sure-to-please *vapeur* (dim sum) dishes, such as the steamed shrimp ravioli (€3.80). Always busy, service always diligent. Picture menu available. Open daily 9am-11:15pm. MC/V. ❶

Chez Blondin, 33 bd. Arago, 13ème (☎01 45 35 93 67). ⓂLes Gobelins. Walk down avenue des Gobelins, then turn right on bd. Arago. Take rue Bobillot and turn right on rue de la Butte-aux-Cailles. Brightly colored walls and tables make this Senegalese restaurant pop. One fish and one meat dish per day, usually accompanied by a starch and veggies. Gained acclaim in Elle magazine. Exotic juice menu. West African speciality,

FOOD

bissop rouge (hibiscus extract; €3). Lunch *formule* €12, dinner €14; includes coffee, *plat,* and juice. Open M-Sa noon-2:30pm and 7-10:30pm. Cash only. ❷

Le Temps des Cerises, 18-20 rue de la Butte-aux-Cailles, 13ème (☎01 45 89 69 48; www.letempsdescerisesscop.com). ⓂPlace d'Italie. Take rue Bobillot and turn right on rue de la Butte-aux-Cailles. A local restaurant cooperative. All of Le Temps's workers, from cook to bartender, have shared ownership since 1976. Specializes in meat-heavy classic dishes like *andouillette* (€14); try the *assiette grècque,* piled high with cold cuts and veggies (€14) or the excellent *magret de canard* (€17). Lunch *menu* €10-13. Other *menus* €15-23. Open M-F 11:45am-2:10pm and 7:15-11:45pm, Sa 11:45am-2:10pm. Reservations recommended for dinner. AmEx/MC/V. ❷

Le Samson, 9 rue Jean-Marie Jego, 13ème (☎01 45 89 09 23). ⓂPlace d'Italie. Take rue Bobillot, turn right on rue de la Butte-aux-Cailles, and right again on rue Jean-Marie Jego; on the corner with rue Samson. This Greek-influenced restaurant offers cheap, extensive *menus* daily. Recline in its denim-covered booths while sampling moussaka (€12) or dessert profiteroles (€5). Lunch *menu* €11.50; M-F and Su 3-course dinner *menu* €14-25, Sa €17-25. Open daily noon-2:30pm and 7-11:30pm. MC/V. ❷

L'Aimant du Sud, 40 bd. Arago, 13ème (☎01 47 07 33 57). ⓂLes Gobelins. Walk down av. des Gobelins, then turn right on bd. Arago. This delightful restaurant serves Southern French favorites. Relax on their pleasant, leafy terrace while enjoying the *veau sauté à la mode Corse* (Corsican-style beef sauté) or *clafoutis aux pêches* (custard-like peach tart). Lunch menu €14-17, dinner menu €18-24. Wine €3-6. Open M noon-2:30pm, Tu-F noon-2:30pm and 7:30-10:30pm. MC/V. ❷

Des Crêpes et des Cailles, 13 rue de la Butte-aux-Cailles, 13ème (☎01 45 81 68 69). ⓂPlace d'Italie. Take rue Bobillot and turn right on rue de la Butte-aux-Cailles. Tiny, nautical-themed *crêperie* with brisk, efficient service and good food. *Galettes,* like *Le Rock and Roll* €3-8. *Crêpes* €2.50-7, takeout €2-5. Cider €3. Open M-F noon-2pm and 7:30-11:30pm, Sa-Su 12:30-2:30pm and 7:30-11:30pm. Cash only. ❶

La Butte-aux-Cailles Crêperie, 33 rue Bobillot, 13ème (☎01 45 80 07 07). ⓂPlace d'Italie. Take rue Bobillot away from the metro; restaurant will be on the left. Dine on traditional Breton cuisine at its quaint, wooden tables. 64 kinds of *crêpes.* Fresh seafood and cheese sauce fill the *galette St.-Malo* (€7.50), named for the seaside town in Brittany. Dinner *menu* €15.80; includes 2 *crêpes* and cider. Vegetarian options. Open M 7-10:15pm, Tu-Sa noon-2:15pm and 7-10:15pm. MC/V. ❶

"Chez les filles", 25 rue des Cinq Diamants, 13ème (☎01 45 80 53 20; www.restaurant-papagallo.com). ⓂPlace d'Italie. Take bd. Auguste Blanqui and turn left on rue des Cinq Diamants; across from Chez Gladines. With pictures of reggae artists hanging from its walls and a Spanish-inspired menu, this restaurant-bar has plenty of Latino flair. In addition to several set *formules* (€8.80-12.90), patrons can nibble on smaller tapas like guacamole or eggplant caviar (€5.50-7). Savvy locals come for the rum-infused mixed drinks (€6.10); why drink prune juice when you can have prune rum? Groups of up to 70 people welcome. Open M-F noon-2:30pm and 7pm-midnight, Su 7pm-midnight. Reserve ahead for dinner. MC/V. ❷

CAFES

Café de France, 12 place d'Italie, 13ème (☎01 43 31 19 86). ⓂPlace d'Italie. On the corner of avenue de la Soeur Rosalie. Almost lost among the other nondescript cafes on place d'Italie, Café de France emits a chill, hip vibe; recent French and American music videos play on several TV screens as locals commiserate over a glass of wine (€3) and *brasserie*-style food (€11.50-14.50). More for the ambience or company, however, you should come for their desserts; the 🔖**chocolate mousse** (€4.50) will have you shamelessly licking your spoon clean and contemplating seconds. *Entrées* €6.50-11.50. Espresso €2. Open daily 6:30-2am. MC/V. ❷

Café du Commerce, 39 rue des Cinq Diamants, 13*ème* (☎01 53 62 91 04). ⓂPlace d'Italie. Take bd. Auguste Blanqui and turn left on rue des Cinq Diamants; the restaurant will be on your left. This funky establishment serves up traditional food with a twist. Dinner (€12-22) and lunch (€12) *menus* both feature tantalizing options like *boudin antillais* (spiced bloodwurst; €10 à la carte). Happy hour 6-8pm; *menu* €12, beer €2-3.50. Free Wi-Fi. Open M-F noon-2:30pm and 6pm-1am, Sa-Su 11-1am. Reserve ahead for dinner and weekends. MC/V. ❷

SPECIALTY SHOPS

▨ **Tang Frères,** 48 av. d'Ivry, 13*ème* (☎01 45 70 80 00). ⓂPorte d'Ivry. Look for no. 44 and walk downstairs, or look for no. 48 and follow the sign through the parking lot; across from rue de la Pointe d'Ivry. A sensory-overload, this huge shopping center in the heart of Chinatown contains a bakery, *charcuterie*, fish counter, flower shop, and grocery store. Cheaper than competitors, Tang Frères stocks exotic fruits (durian €7.80 per kg), Asian beers (can of Kirin €0.85, 6-pack of Tsingtao €3.72), rice wines (€3.50 per 1/2 liter), and sake (€4.95-6.80). Noodles, rice, soups, spices, teas, and tofu in bulk. Also at 174 rue de Choisy. ⓂPlace d'Italie. Open Tu-Sa 10am-8:30pm. MC/V.

L'Empire des Thés, 101 av. d'Ivry, 13*ème* (☎01 45 85 66 33; www.empiredesthes. fr). ⓂPorte d'Ivry. From the metro, on your left along av. d'Ivry. Delicate flower and fruit blends from Asia in their tiny boutique. Perfect for couples but three may be a crowd. Patrons may "sample" each flavor before ordering by sniffing pots of crushed herbs. Porcelain tea sets and teas for sale in bulk. Pot of tea €3.30-7. Green tea *millefeuille* €4.50. Also at 69 rue du Montparnasse, 14*ème* (☎01 42 18 10 18) and 8 rue de la Chaussée d'Antin, 9*ème* (☎01 47 70 68 29). Tea salon open Tu-Su 11am-6pm. Boutique open Tu-Su 11am-7pm. V.

MONTPARNASSE

14ÈME ARRONDISSEMENT

On the busy boulevard du Montparnasse, which frames the top of the 14*ème*, travelers can chomp on everything from Tex-Mex to classic Parisian fare. Reasonably-priced Breton *crêperies* line rue du Montparnasse, which intersects the boulevard sharing its name. Rue Daguerre is like the United Nations of food; you can have Brazilian food for dinner, then hit up a Polynesian restaurant for dessert. Find inexpensive restaurants on rue Didot and rue Raymond Losserand, and cheap ethnic takeout and couscous joints line avenue du Maine.

▨ **Crêperie Plougastel,** 47 rue du Montparnasse, 14*ème* (42 79 90 63). ⓂMontparnasse-Bienvenue. Exiting the metro on bd. Montparnasse and facing the Centre Commercial Maine-Montparnasse, turn left. At the intersection of rue du Montparnasse, turn right. Friendly ambience and prompt staff set this cozy *crêperie* apart from its neighbors. *Formule* (generous mixed salad and choice from 2 *galettes* and 5 dessert *crêpes*, €14.50). Dessert *crêpes* feature the restaurant's home-made caramel. *Cidre* €2.90. Wine €2.70. Open daily noon-11:30pm. MC/V. ❶

Le Severo, 8 rue des Plantes, 14*ème* (☎45 40 40 91). ⓂMouton Duvernet. Exit the metro and walk down rue Brézin; cross av. du Maine and make a quick left on rue des Plantes. A prominent shout-out in the *New York Times* hasn't driven off Severo's local following. A former butcher, the owner prepares some of the city's best meat, and though the expensive dishes are worth the euros, inexpensive options are both available and delicious. House-recommended *pied de porc* (fried pig's feet) €8. *Plats* up to €26. Wine €3-6. Open M-F noon-2pm and 7:30-10pm, Sa noon-2pm. MC/V. ❷

Aquarius Café, 40 rue de Gergovie, 14ème (☎45 41 36 88). ⓂPernety. Walk against traffic on rue Raymond Losserand and turn right on rue de Gergovie. A celebrated local favorite, Aquarius Café offers a wide selection of protein-heavy vegetarian dishes, with moderately priced lunch (3 courses; €11) and dinner (2 courses; €15) *menus*. Although a bit difficult to find, Aquarius' original takes on Middle Eastern and Lebanese cuisine are worth the hunt. Open M-Sa noon-2:30pm and 7-10:30pm. MC/V. ❷

Chez Papa, 6 rue Gassendi, 14ème (☎43 22 41 19). ⓂDenfert-Rochereau. Walk down Froidevaux along the cemetery; the restaurant will be on the left at the intersection with rue Gassendi. Spanish influence pervades Chez Papa's dishes and decor. Specializing in southwestern cuisine, the restaurant offers a hearty lunch *formule* (M-F, 2 courses and coffee, €9.55). Supplement one of their numerous hot dishes (€13-27) or salads (€8-10) with the ◨ **pain sur la planche aux deux fromages** (toasted bread draped with *chèvre* and cheese from Auvergne; €8.60). Vegetarians beware: raw veggie appetizers are the only meatless options. Open daily 11-1am. AmEx/MC/V. ❷

L'Amuse Bouche, 186 rue du Château, 14ème (☎43 35 31 61). ⓂAlésia. Take av. du Maine to rue du Château. Classy but welcoming. Traditional French cuisine in a neighborhood removed from the main drag bustle. The 3-course dinner *menu* (€31.50) has options like duck filet with foie gras and St. Jacques scallops. Reserve ahead. Open Tu-Sa noon-2:15pm and 7:30-10pm. MC/V. ❹

Le Petit Baigneur, 10 rue de la Sablière, 14ème (☎45 45 47 12). ⓂMouton Duvernet. Exit the metro and walk down rue Brézin; cross av. du Maine and make a quick left on rue des Plantes. Numerous tables fill sizeable dining rooms, and metal signs and shelved bric-a-brac lend to its relaxed cafe vibe. Slightly less formal than other neighborhood eateries. 3-course dinner *menu* (€18.50), and delicate fruit and chocolate tartes tantalize customers. Beer €4. Wine €3.50-7. Mixed drinks €3-5. Open M-F noon-2:15pm and 7-10:15pm, Sa 7-10:15pm. MC/V. ❷

Charlie Birdy, 84 bd. du Montparnasse, 14ème (☎40 64 88 00; www.charliebirdy.com). ⓂMontparnasse-Bienvenüe. Take the rue d'Odessa exit and head straight down bd. du Montparnasse to the corner of rue du Montparnasse. Charlie Birdy remains a classy alternative to bd. Montparnasse's *crêpe* stands and high-priced cafes. Lounge on leather sofas surrounded by red-vased votives while enjoying the free concerts (see website for schedule). Burgers and salads (€11-17) might conjure up thoughts of Rocky and the ol' stars and stripes. Expensive mixed drinks (€12). Free Wi-Fi. DJ "Dancefloor Night" F-Sa. Live jazz Su noon-4pm. Open daily 10am-5am. ❷

CAFES

La Coupole, 102 bd. du Montparnasse, 14ème (☎43 20 14 20; www.lacoupoleparis.com). ⓂVavin. When exiting the metro, walk straight ahead on bd. du Montparnasse. A Montparnasse staple since 1927, La Coupole's Art Deco chambers have attracted celebrities like Albert Einstein, Ernest Hemingway, Edith Piaf, and Pablo Picasso. Though touristy and unabashedly overpriced, the trendy cafe merits a nostalgic splurge on coffee (€3.10), hot chocolate (€4.10), or a *croque monsieur* (€6). La Coupole also prides itself on its fresh seafood but sadly offers only 1 vegetarian dish. Open M-Th and Su 8-11am and 11:30-1am, F-Sa 8:30-11am and 11:30-1:30am. AmEx/MC/V. ❹

Pascal Beillevaire, Maître Fromager, 8 rue Delambre, 14ème (☎42 79 00 40). ⓂVavin. From the metro exit, take a right on bd. Montparnasse, followed by a quick right on rue Delambre; the *fromagerie* will be on your left. This small shop elevates a bread-and-cheese diet from student staple to fine dining. High-quality culinary classics like parmesan (€33.95 per kg.) are worth the cash, as are the cheaper alternatives, including *Barbeilleu au lait* (made from cow milk; €7.12 per unit). The store also sells fresh yogurt

(€1.40), cream desserts (€1.90), and various jams (€5-7). Open Tu-Sa 8:30am-1pm and 4-8pm, Su 9am-1pm. Cash only. ❶

15ÈME ARRONDISSEMENT

The 15ème offers a diverse range of restaurants, with traditional French cuisine alongside Middle Eastern and Asian specialties. Cheap eateries crowd rue du Commerce, rue de Vaugirard, boulevard de Grenelle, and Gare Montparnasse.

▨ **Bélisaire,** 2 rue Marmontel, 15ème. (☎01 48 28 62 24; m.garrel@free.fr). ⓂVaugirard. Turn left down rue de Vaugirard, then right on rue de l'Abbe Groult; the restaurant will be to your left, on the corner with rue Marmontel. Treat yourself to a splurge here. Fit for aristocratic celebrations, the sophisticated Bélisaire serves delicious French favorites at surprisingly reasonable prices. Options on the chalkboard menus rotate seasonally. Succulent salmon and lobster ravioli are to die for. Packed with locals daily, no matter what the hour; reservations are a must. 3-course lunch menu €22. 5-course dinner menu €40. Open daily noon-2pm and 8-10:30pm. MC/V. ❹

▨ **Le Dix Vins,** 57 rue Falguière, 15ème (43 20 91 77; http://ledixvins.free.fr). ⓂPasteur. Follow bd. Pasteur uphill and turn right on rue Falguière. This intimate bistro has an appropriate pun for a name—both the meals and the wines (fortunately numbering more than 10) indeed taste divin (divine). The menus, not quite cheap (€20-24), spice up regional Basque classics with tame nouvelle cuisine (a light, new taste). Open M-F noon-2:30pm and 8-11pm, Sa 8-11pm. MC/V. ❸

Ty Breiz, 52 bd. de Vaugirard, 15ème (☎43 20 83 72). ⓂPasteur. Walk out of the metro, up the hill, and turn left on bd. de Vaugirard. This classic crêperie claims a bit of Paris for Brittany. Wooden clogs and timbered walls evoke a feeling of chez Maman et Papa, a safe haven for enjoying a crêpe. For a filling dinner, try La savoyarde, a crêpe salée stuffed with bacon bits, onions, potatoes, and raclette cheese (€10.40). Crêpes sucrées €3.90-10. Open Tu-Sa 11:45am-2:45pm and 7-11pm. MC/V. ❶

Chez Fung, 32 rue Frémicourt, 15ème (☎45 67 36 99). ⓂCambronne. Walk across pl. Cambronne, then turn left on rue Frémicourt; the restaurant will be on the left. Authentic, and superb Malaysian cuisine, though the small portions may leave you hungry. Specialities include seafood cooked in banana leaves and unique combinations of sweet and salty, like the rojak Malaysian salad (shrimp, vegetables, and fresh fruit; €14). 3-course lunch menu M-F €15. Open M-Sa noon-2pm and 7:30-10pm. MC/V. ❷

Samaya, 31 bd. de Grenelle, 15ème (☎45 77 44 44; www.samaya.fr). ⓂBir-Hakeim. Head away from the river on bd. de Grenelle; Samaya will be to the left. Traditional Lebanese food with reasonable prices; great for a meal-to-go. Dinner menu €18. Lunch €13. Takeout sandwiches €4-4.50. Falafel €3.80. Open daily 11am-11:30pm. MC/V. ❷

Le Troquet, 21 rue François Bonvin, 15ème (☎45 66 89 00). ⓂSèvres-Lecourbe. Take rue Lecourbe and turn right on rue François Bonvin. A husband-and-wife team serve Basque-and-Parisian blended dishes. Although a daily-changing menu (3 plates €30) combats cuisinal apathy, hefty prices may discourage your frequent return. 6 plates for the table €40. Open Tu-Sa 12:30-2pm and 7:30-11pm. MC/V. ❹

Tandoori, 10 rue de l'Arivée, 15ème (☎45 48 46 72). ⓂMontparnasse-Bienvenüe. Take the bd. Montparnasse exit from the metro and cross the street, walking towards Tour Montparnasse along rue de l'Arivée; Tandoori will be on the left. Cheap, generous portions distinguish this Indian restaurant. M-F €10 lunch menu includes grilled chicken or lamb entree, with bread, cheese, veggies, basmati rice, and dessert. 3-course dinner menu €22. Musical Soirées W-F nights feature live, traditional Indian music; reserve ahead. Open M-Sa noon-2:30pm and 7-11pm. MC/V over €16. ❷

FOOD

CAFES

▩ **Aux Artistes,** 63 rue Falguière, 15ème (☎43 22 05 39). ⓜPasteur. Walk up the hill and turn right onto rue Falguière. This lively venue attracts a mix of students, professionals, and artists, including Amedeo Modigliani in his time. Despite surfboards and American license plates on the walls, the food adheres to traditional French cafe dictates. Lunch *menu* €11; choose from over 32 *entrées*, 16 *plats*, and 10 desserts. Dinner *menu* €14. Open M-F noon-2:30pm and 7:30pm-midnight, Sa 7:30pm-midnight. Cash only. ❷

Au Roi du Café, 59 rue Lecourbe, 15ème (☎47 34 48 50). ⓜSèvres-Lecourbe. A cheap cafe/bar frequented by both Parisians and expats. Simple cafe food served until 11pm. Enjoy a quiet drink at the bar or sit outside with friends on summer evenings. Undo your top button and start the night early with the €6 lunch *menu's* complimentary beer or wine. Happy hour 6-8pm; cocktails €4. Espresso €1.10-1.70. Beer €2-2.80. Open M-Sa 6:30am-midnight, Su 6:30am-5pm. ❶

SPECIALTY SHOPS

Au Coin du Pétrin, 96 rue des Entrepreneurs, 15ème (☎45 71 00 56). ⓜFelix Faure. Walk against traffic to the left of the church; turn left on rue des Entrepreneurs. Devotees gladly make the trek to this bakery, home to an award-winning *baguette traditionnelle* that lives up to the hype (€1.10). M-F lunch *formule* €6; includes sandwich, drink, and dessert. Open M-Sa 7:15am-8pm.

PASSY AND AUTEUIL (16ÈME)

There is high-quality fare to be had in the 16ème if you have deep pockets. For those with less to blow, budget-friendly ethnic restaurants crowd rue de Lauriston. Picnic fare can be purchased from *traiteurs* on rue Passy and avenue Mozart, and at the *marchés* on av. du Président Wilson, on rue St-Didier, along rue d'Auteuil, and at the intersection of rue Gros and rue la Fontaine.

Casa Tina, 18 rue Lauriston, 16ème (☎01 40 67 19 24; www.casa-tina.com). ⓜKléber. Walk down av. Victor Hugo toward the Arc de Triomphe, turn left on rue Presbourg and right on rue Lauriston going uphill. Spanish tiles cover the walls, tables are packed edge-to-edge, and dried peppers hang from the ceiling—it's all about intimacy here. The food and the sangria (€5) are both divine, but expect to sacrifice leg and elbow room. Tapas €4-16. Tapas *menu* €19; other *menus* starting at €35. Open daily noon-2:30pm and 7-11:30pm (last seating 11pm). Reservations recommended. MC/V. ❹

Le Scheffer, 22 rue Scheffer, 16ème (☎01 47 27 81 11). ⓜTrocadéro. Walk down av. Paul Doumer, then turn right on rue Scheffer. From the sound of clattering pans to the red-checkered tablecloths, Le Scheffer is a stronghold of traditional French cuisine. Slow service around lunchtime and suspicion of tourists add to the authenticity of this local favorite. *Plats* include *steak-frites* (€19) and *confit de canard maison garni de pommes sautées* (€15). Open M-Sa noon-2:30pm and 7:30-10:30pm. ❸

CAFES

La Rotonde, 12 Chaussée de la Muette, 16ème (☎01 45 24 45 45). ⓜLa Muette. 2min. from the metro down Chaussée de la Muette; head toward the Jardin de Ranelagh. Located in a beautiful *fin-de-siècle* building overlooking the tree-lined Chaussée de la Muette, this cafe draws a mostly local crowd. Indoors, the stylish red and yellow lamps, hip music, and plush burgundy seats take a sleek spin on the patio's classic feel, but the outdoor seating is the best. Grab a sandwich (€4-11), salad (€5.50-13.50), or the tart of the day (€6) before heading to the excellent Musée Marmottan (p. 289). Beer, mixed drinks, and wine available (€5-10). Open daily 7am-midnight. AmEx/MC/V. ❷

MARKETS

Marché Président-Wilson, av. du Président Wilson between rue Debrousse and pl. d'Iéna, 16ème. ⓜIéna or Alma-Marceau. The smart alternative to the 16ème's exorbitantly priced restaurants. Meat, fish, exotic breads, rich pastries and ready-to-eat Chinese and Middle Eastern fare. Flower stalls, clothing, table linens, and other household goods can all be found here. Uncovered market. Open W and Sa 7am-2:30 pm.

BATIGNOLLES (17ÈME)

Far from tourist attractions, the 17ème's restaurants depend on local support. Fortunately, the district's economic and ethnic diversity translates into delicious, gastronomical variety. For high-quality, cheap eats, wander around the Village Batignolles, around rue des Batignolles and north of rue des Dames.

🟦 **La Fournée d'Augustine,** 31 rue des Batignolles, 17ème (☎01 43 87 88 41). ⓜRome. With Gare St-Lazare to your right, walk down bd. des Batignolles, then turn left on rue des Batignolles. This closet-sized *pâtisserie* bakes an absolutely fantastic baguette (€1), and with lines out the door at lunchtime, it's hard to miss. Their fresh sandwiches (€3-4) range from light fare like goat cheese and cucumber to the more substantial grilled chicken and veggies. Grab a *pain au chocolat* (€1.05) or a delicately decorated brownie (€2.40) for later. Lunch *formule* €5.80-7; includes dessert, drink, and sandwich. Open M-Sa 7:30am-8pm. AmEx/MC/V over 10. ❶

🟦 **Le Patio Provençal,** 116 rue des Dames, 17ème (☎01 42 93 73 73). ⓜVilliers. Follow rue de Levis away from the intersection and turn right on rue des Dames. An airy, rustic restaurant, Le Patio Provençal serves southern French staples, such as *ravioles de Royans* (Dauphiné specialty, €8.50-12). Absinthe €4.60-6. 3-course *menu* €28. *Entrées* €7.50-8.50. *Plats* €12-20. Desserts €7.50. Often busy; service can be slow. Reservations recommended. Open M-Sa noon-2:30pm and 7-11pm. MC/V. ❷

🟦 **The James Joyce Pub,** 71 bd. Gouvion-St-Cyr, 17ème (☎01 44 09 70 32; www.kittyosheas.com). ⓜPorte Maillot. Take the Palais de Congrès exit from the metro; walk down bd. Gouvion St-Cyr past Palais de Congrès. On the corner of rue Belidor. Stained-glass windows dedicated to Joyce's novels and other Irish wordsmiths brighten the upstairs restaurant and downstairs bar. Good for a traditional Irish meal like stew with bacon and cabbage or ham with spuds and cheese (€10), the Joyce swells to capacity during televised rugby matches. Functions as an informal tourist office for middle-aged and young Anglophone expats. Beer €4.50-7. Mixed drinks €10. Sa-Su jazz brunch noon-3pm. F-Sa 10pm live DJ. Su 9:30pm open mic. Open daily noon-2am. Kitchen open M-F noon-3pm and 7-10:30pm, Sa-Su noon-3pm. AmEx/MC/V. ❷

Au Vieux Logis, 68 rue des Dames, 17ème (☎01 43 87 77 27). ⓜRome. Take rue Boursault to rue des Dames; the restaurant is on the corner. Despite heavy acclaim, this friendly provincial bar-restaurant has not lost local following. Its traditional but limited 3-course *menu* (€20) changes daily. *Plats* €12-16. "Summer Salads" made with fresh fruit and veggies €13. Open M-Sa noon-3pm and 7pm-midnight. AmEx/MC/V. ❷

Villa des Ternes, 35 rue Guersant, 17ème (☎01 45 74 23 86). ⓜPorte Maillot. Take bd. Gouvion-St-Cyr past the Palais de Congrès and turn right on rue Guersant. This quaint Italian *bistrot* specializes in simple pizzas (€10-14) crafted from basic ingredients like egg, fish, ham, and buffalo mozzarella. Pasta €9-11. Open M-Sa noon-2:30pm and 7:30-10:30pm. AmEx/MC/V. ❸

Joy in Food, 2 rue Truffant, 17ème (☎01 43 87 96 79). ⓂPlace de Clichy. Take bd. de Batignolles, turn right on rue Biot, then left on rue des Dames, then right on rue Truffaut. Vegetarian omelettes, *pâtés*, salads, tarts, and organic wine grace tables draped in blue and white gingham at this cozy, macrobiotic restaurant. Lunch *formule* €11, 3-course *menu* €14. Desserts like apple crumble €4. Open M-F noon-2:30pm. MC/V. ❷

L'Étoile du Kashmir, 1 rue des Batignolles, 17ème (☎01 45 22 44 70). ⓂRome. With Gare St-Lazare to your right, take bd. des Batignolles and turn left on rue des Batignolles. Serves Indian classics in a colorfully-lit interior. The 2-course lunch *formule* with vegetarian options (€7.50) appeals to the budget-conscious, while the adventurous spring for the two-person "chef's surprise" (€33). Open M-Sa noon-3pm and 6:30-11:30pm, Su 6:30-11:30pm. 15% off takeout. ❶

CAFES

3 Pièces Cuisine, 25 rue de Chéroy, 17ème (☎01 44 90 85 10). ⓂVilliers. From rue de Levis, turn right on rue des Dames. Walls blasted in bright colors and attractive bartenders courting locals create this cafe-bar's funky, hip vibe. The upbeat jazz music and cheap coffee (€1.50) provide the perfect pick-me-up. For a light dinner, try the Cléopatra or Marie-Antoinette salad (€8.80). Beer €2.70-3. Mixed drinks €7. Fries €2.30. Brunch €10, children €5. Open M-F 8:30am-2am, Sa-Su 9:30am-2am. Kitchen open daily noon-3pm and 8-10:30pm. MC/V. ❷

L'Endroit, 67 place du Dr. Félix Lobligeois, 17ème (☎01 42 29 50 00). ⓂRome. Follow rue Boursault to rue Legendre and turn right. Look for the blue exterior, the sprawling terrace, and the revolving tower of liquor. Too cool for school no matter what hour, L'Endroit is "the spot" to be seen day or night. 4-course weekend brunch (noon-4:15pm; €22) headlines a long menu packed with numerous big salads (€11-16) and toasted sandwiches (€13.70). Open daily 10am-2am. Kitchen open noon-11:45pm; lunch and dinner specials served noon-3pm and 7:30-11:15pm. AmEx/MC/V. ❸

Café Hortensias, 4 place du Maréchal de Juin, 17ème (☎01 47 63 43 39). ⓂPereire or RER C: Pereire Levallois. Just off bd. Pereire. A mostly local crowd enjoys simple, summery fare in an airy rotunda. Wine €6. Menu includes *croque monsieur* (€5.50), gazpacho (€8), and salads (€9.50). Most dishes €9-16. Dinner *menu* €20. Open M-F 9-1am, Sa-Su 8-1am. Food served 11am-11pm. AmEx/MC/V. ❷

SPECIALTY SHOPS AND MARKETS

Marché Berthier, on bd. de Reims between rue de Courcelles and rue du Marquis d'Arlandes, along place Ulmann, 17ème. ⓂPorte de Champerret. Turn left off bd. Berthier on rue de Courcelles, then right on bd. de Reims. Among the cheapest produce markets in Paris. Discover North African and Middle Eastern specialties like fresh mint, Turkish bread, and baklava in addition to the standard inexpensive clothes, perfumes, shoes, and seafood. Open W 7am-2:30pm, Sa 7am-3pm.

Batignolles Organic Produce Market, on the traffic divider along bd. des Batignolles, border of 8ème and 17ème. ⓂRome. Exit the metro and, with Gare St-Lazare on your right, walk down bd. des Batignolles. *Let's Go: Paris* meets *Let's Go: Green*—this market brings in the best organic produce around. Open Sa 9am-2pm.

Batignolles Covered Market, 96bis rue Lemercier, 17ème. ⓂBrochant. On the other side of rue des Batignolles, between rue Clairaut and rue des Moines. Provides faithful working-class and elderly locals with near daily fresh cheese, flowers, meat, and produce. Open Tu-Sa 8:30am-1pm and 4-7:30pm, Su 8am-1pm.

FOOD

MONTMARTRE (18ÈME)

Savvy Parisians have sought Montmartre's cheap eateries since the eighteenth century, when its duty-free food and wine drew them from the tax-torn capital. Many small bistros still serve modest meals between rue des Abbesses and rue Lepic, while touristy piano bars surround Place du Tetre and place St-Pierre.

> **DID YOU KNOW?** History of the word "bistro": When the Sixth Coalition defeated Napoleon in 1814, the Russian Cossacks quickly discovered Montmartre's hilly haven. Dissatisfied with the speed of service at restaurants, they would yell, *"Bystro!"* ("Faster!") at lingering waiters, and the name stuck.

 Refuge des Fondus, 17 rue des Trois Frères, 18*ème* (☎01 42 55 22 65; www.lerefugedesfondus.com). ⓂAbbesses. Walk down rue Yvonne le Tac and take a left on rue des Trois Frères. Only 2 main dishes: *fondue bourguignonne* (meat fondue) and *fondue savoyarde* (cheese fondue). The wine (2 choices: red or white) is served in baby bottles with rubber nipples. Leave your Freudian hang-ups at home, and join the family-style party at its 2 long tables. €17 *menu* includes wine, *amuse-gueule* (a light appetizer), fondue, and dessert. Open daily 5pm-2am. Kitchen open 7pm-2am. Cash only. ❷

Le Soleil Gourmand, 10 rue Ravignan, 18*ème* (☎01 42 51 00 50). ⓂAbbesses. Facing the church on pl. des Abbesses, head right down rue des Abbesses, and turn right (uphill) on rue Ravignan. Local favorite serves light *provençal* fare in a cheerful dining room decorated to match the restaurant's name. Try the bricks (grilled stuffed filo dough; €12), the 5-cheese *tartes* (€11), and the delicious homemade cakes (€5.80-6.80). Vegetarian options, like the *assiet sud* (a generous collection of grilled and marinated veggies; €13). Still suffering from Vitamin D deficiency? Brighten your Paris abode with any of the restaurant's radiant decorations, all for sale. Open daily 12:30-2:30pm and 7:30-11pm. Evening reservations recommended. Cash only. ❷

La Bodega, 54bis rue Ordener, 18*ème*. ⓂJules Joffrin. Facing the mairie, turn left on rue Ordener. Well removed from tourist central, this informal bar/restaurant specializes in Latin American cuisine with a Spanish twist. Low prices and great quality worth the trek. Patrons can order a fresh sandwich (€2.30-4.50) or an assiette of the day in one of 3 sizes (€5-9). Limited seating. Mixed drinks €5. Open Tu-Su noon-2am. Cash only. ❶

Wassana, 10 rue Ganneron, 18*ème* (☎01 44 70 08 54). ⓂPlace de Clichy. Walk up avenue de Clichy and turn right on rue Ganneron. Stylishly gold-decorated dining room and delicious Thai food 5min. from the Cimitière Montmartre. Lunch *menu* (€12) includes Thai chicken curry in coconut milk or beef in Thai herbs. Over ten vegetarian options available. *Entrées* €6.50-10. *Plats* €9-17.50. Open M-F noon-2:30pm and 7-11:30pm, Sa 7-11:30pm. AmEx/MC/V. ❷

Au Grain de Folie, 24 rue de la Vieuville, 18*ème* (☎01 42 58 15 57). ⓂAbbesses. From the metro exit, walk straight down rue Lavieuville. The restaurant will be on your right, near the intersection with rue des Trois Frères. This tiny vegetarian and vegan refuge serves four main menu plates each accompanied by mixed salad, lentils, grains, grilled veggies and a vegan apple crumble for dessert. Open Tu-Sa noon-2:30 and 7:30-10:30pm, Su 1-2:30pm. Cash Only. ❷

Le Dan Bau, 18 rue des Trois Frères, 18*ème* (☎01 42 62 45 59). ⓂAbbesses. Walk down rue Yvonne le Tac and take a left on rue des Trois Frères. The bamboo walls and clean-lined decor create a Zen-charged ambience rare in Pigalle. Well-crafted Vietnamese favorites like steamed shrimp in coconut juice (€12.80) contribute to Le Dan Bau's popularity. Incredible cheap 3-course lunch menu €9.50. Plats €7.50-22. Vegetarian options. Open M and F-Su noon-2pm and 7-11pm, Tu-Th 7-11pm. AmEx/MC/V. ❷

Djerba Cacher Chez Guichi, 76 rue Myrha, 18ème (☎01 42 23 77 99). ⓂBarbès-Rochechouart. Take bd. Barbès and turn right on rue Myrha. The area may make solitary travelers uncomfortable. Cheap, deli-style North African cuisine to local merchants. Parisians come from all over the city to sample Guichi's specialty, *brochette foie gras* (duck or goose liver kebabs; €14). Pizza €2. Sandwiches €5-6.50. *Plats* €7-11.50. Open M-Th and Su noon-4pm and 7-11pm, F noon-4pm. Cash only. ❶

La Maison Rose, 2 rue de l'Abreuvoir, 18ème (☎01 42 57 66 75). ⓂLamarck-Caulaincourt. Walk right on rue Lamarck, then turn right on rue des Saules. This small pink restaurant-cafe is something of a tourist trap, but a cute one. Once home to Maurice Utrillo, the ex-bachelor pad serves typical French fare with slightly jacked-up prices. €16.50 menu includes *entrée, plat,* and dessert. 12 escargots €13. Open M-Tu and Th-F 10:30am-2:30pm and 7pm-midnight, Sa-Su 10:30am-midnight. MC/V. ❷

BUTTES CHAUMONT (19ÈME)

Little Chinatown provides the finest budget dining in the ethnically diverse 19*ème*. Chinese, Malaysian, Thai, and Vietnamese restaurants cluster along rue de Belleville (ⓂBelleville). Greek sandwich shops and fast food joints line avenue Jean Jaurès and rue de Crimée. Hands down, Parc des Buttes-Chaumont is the winning spot for a picnic.

Ay, Caramba!, 59 rue de Mouzaïa, 19ème (☎01 42 41 23 80; http://restaurant-aycaramba.com). ⓂPré-St-Gervais. A bright, yellow establishment in a drab, residential neighborhood, this Tex-Mex restaurant transforms chic Parisan dining into a home-grown fiesta. Patrons salsa to live latino singers F-Sa nights. Mariachi and Mexican ballet performances. 3-course *menu* comes with coffee, wine, and additional beverage (€35). Pricey but generous fajitas and tacos (€18). Margaritas €7. *Nachos rancheros* €7. Open Su noon-3pm and 7:30pm-midnight, Tu-Th 7:30pm-midnight, F-Sa noon-3pm and 7:30pm-midnight. AmEx/MC/V. ❸

Lao Siam, 49 rue de Belleville, 19ème (☎01 40 40 09 68). ⓂBelleville. While nominally cheap, most dishes (€7-10) sneak a few more euros from your wallet by charging separately for rice (€2.20). The Thai-dried calamari salad (€6.30) makes for a light preamble to the *filet du poisson* with "hip-hop" sauce (€8.80) or *poulet aux pousses de bamboo au lait de coco* (chicken and bamboo in coconut curry sauce; €8.50). Open daily noon-3pm and 7-11pm. MC/V over €16. ❶

CAFES

La Kaskad' Café, 2 pl. Armand-Carrel, 19ème (☎01 40 40 08 10). ⓂLaumière. To the left of the *mairie,* La Kaskad' has a wonderful terrace, perfect for relaxing on after a morning strolling the Parc des Buttes-Chaumont. Varied, delicious cuisine includes iced coffees and tea (€6). Large salads €13.50-14.50. Dessert €7.50. Coffee €2.50. Open daily 7:30am-midnight. MC/V. ❷

SPECIALITY SHOPS AND MARKETS

La Boulangerie par Véronique Mauclerc, 83 rue de Crimée, 19ème (☎01 42 40 64 55). ⓂLaumière. Baking its divine bread in one of only four remaining wood-fired ovens in France, Mlle Mauclerc insists on using organic ingredients in her creations. This tiny *boulangerie* also serves Paris's cheapest Su brunch—for €11, gourmands can sample the numerous in-house breads, pastries and jam, washed down by fresh OJ and coffee or hot chocolate. Pastries like the highly recommended blueberry crumble, €3-4. Croissant €1.15. Baguette €1.25. Open M and Th-Su 8am-8pm. MC/V over €15.

Belleville Outdoor Market, 19ème & 20ème. ⓂBelleville. Not for the faint of heart, this Middle-Eastern influenced market provides an exhilarating experience. Belts, produce, sneakers, spices, and everything else you can imagine squeeze onto several blocks along bd. de Belleville. It's best to know what you're coming for; vendors behind the tables bellow at anyone who walks by, bewildering browsers. This is undeniably the place to find dates and figs, but beware of pickpockets. Open Tu and F 7am-2pm.

BELLEVILLE AND PÈRE LACHAISE (20ÈME)

A traditional meal amid Belleville's cobblestones will reinvigorate as well as refuel you after a day amid Paris's crowded center. To repose at one of the neighborhood's trendy bistros or cafes, head south to rue St-Blaise.

▨ **Café Flèche d'Or,** 102bis rue de Bagnolet, 20ème (☎01 44 64 01 02; www.flechedor. fr). ⓂAlexandre Dumas. Follow rue de Bagnolet until it crosses rue des Pyrénées; the cafe is on the right. Near Porte de la Réunion at Père Lachaise. In a defunct train station, this bar/cafe/performance space serves internationally inspired dishes. Let your taste buds wander from Holland (cheese, eggs, salad, and sausage tartine; €12) to New York (bagel with coleslaw, salad, and smoked salmon; €13.50). Almost nightly entertainment, including live bands and DJs (see **Nightlife,** p. 337). Entrées €12-14.50. Bar/ cafe open daily 10-2am. Kitchen open on performance nights 8pm-midnight. MC/V. ❷

La Bolée Belgrand, 19 rue Belgrand, 20ème (☎01 43 64 04 03). ⓂPorte de Bagnolet. Across the street from the Hôpital Tenon metro exit. A local crowd people watch through lace curtains and from outdoor tables while enjoying nationally-named crêpes. Served à la façon. "Hot Dog," the American (€9.50) features sausage and cheese with fries and salad on the side. Cidre €5. Lunch menu €10.50. Crêpes €3.10-7.50. Galettes €4.50-9.50. Open Tu-Sa noon-2:30pm and 7-10:30pm. MC/V over €15. 10% off takeout. ❶

CAFES

▨ **La Mer à Boire,** 1-3 rue des Envierges, 20ème (☎01 43 58 29 43; http://la.meraboire. com). ⓂPyrénées. Walk down the sloping rue de Belleville, turn left on rue Piat, and left on rue des Envierges. This multi-purpose cafe/bar across from Parc de Belleville offers spectacular views and simple, delicious food. Hosts art exhibits and occasional concerts. Brie and raisins or honey and goat cheese served on warm bread with corn, lentils, and tomato salad €10. Small tapas selection €5 each. Beer €2.50-5. Wine €2-7.50. Open M-Sa noon-1am. Kitchen open noon-2pm and 7:30-9pm. MC/V. ❶

SIGHTS

ÎLE DE LA CITÉ

If you're looking to be humbled by magnificent architecture and hundreds of years of impressive history, Île de la Cité is a wonderful place to start. Here lies the world-renowned Notre Dame Cathedral as well as a multitude of lesser-known but equally awe-inspiring locations like the Ste-Chapelle. Even without all this, the Île deserves a visit because it was the birthplace of Paris; a walk through the narrow streets offers a glimpse at the city's humble beginnings.

NOTRE DAME

Île de la Cité. ⓜCité. ☎ 01 42 34 56 10; crypt 01 55 42 50 10; towers 01 53 10 07 00. Cathedral open daily 7:45am-7pm. Towers open Jan.-Mar. and Oct.-Dec. 10am-5:30pm, Apr.-Sept. 10am-6:30pm, June-Aug. Sa-Su until 11pm. Last admission 45min. before closing. €8, ages 18-25 €5, under 18 free. Audioguides €5; includes visit of treasury. Tours begin at the booth to the right as you enter. In French M-F 2 and 3pm; call 01 44 54 19 30 for English, Russian, or Spanish, tours. Free. Mass M-F 8, 9am (except July-Aug.), noon, 6:15pm; Sa 6:30pm; Su 8:30am, 10am Mass with Gregorian chant, 11:30am international mass with music, 12:45, and 6:30pm. Free recital by one of the cathedral organists at 4:30pm. Vespers sung Sa-Su 5:45pm. Treasury open M-F 9:30am-6pm, Sa 9:30am-5pm, and Su 1-1:30pm and 6-6:30pm, last entry 15min. before closing. €3, ages 12-25 €2, ages 5-11 €1. Crypt open Tu-Su 10am-6pm, last entry 5:30pm. €4, over 60 €3, under 26 €2, under 12 free. MC/V over €15.

Once the site of a Roman temple to Jupiter, the ground upon which Notre Dame stands witnessed three previous churches before Maurice de Sully began construction of the cathedral in 1163. De Sully, the bishop of Paris under King Philip II, was anxious to avoid the poor interior design that characterized Notre Dame's dark and cramped predecessor. He aimed to create an edifice filled with air and light, in a style that would later be dubbed Gothic (see **Life and Times,** p. 63). De Sully died before his ambitious plan was completed, but the cathedral was reworked over several centuries into the composite masterpiece that stands today. The French royalty used Notre Dame for marriage ceremonies, most notably those of François II to Mary Queen of Scots in 1558 and of Henri of Navarre to Marguerite de Valois in 1572 (see **Life and Times**, p. 63). While royal burials were performed at the St-Denis cathedral, coronations took place at Reims (with the exception of Henri VI's, performed at Notre Dame in 1431), and relics went to Ste-Chapelle (p. 207), Notre Dame had an unrivaled hold on the public's attention from the beginning.

In addition to its royal functions, the cathedral was also the setting for notable events like Joan of Arc's trial for heresy in 1455. During the Revolution, secularists renamed the cathedral The Temple of Reason and encased its Gothic arches in Neoclassical plaster moldings. The church was reconsecrated after the Revolution and was the site of Napoleon's coronation in 1804. However, the building soon fell into disrepair, and for two decades, it was used to shelter livestock, until Victor Hugo's 1831 novel Notre-Dame de Paris (The Hunchback of Notre Dame) revived the cathedral's popularity and inspired Napoleon III and Haussmann to devote finances and attention to its restoration. Modifications by Eugène Viollet-le-Duc (including a new spire, gargoyles, and a statue of himself admiring his own work) reinvigorated the cathedral's image in the public consciousness, and Notre Dame once again became a valued symbol of civic unity. Indeed, in 1870 and again in 1940 thousands of Parisians attended masses in the church to pray for deliverance from the invading Germans. On August 26, 1944, Charles de Gaulle braved Nazi sniper fire to visit Notre Dame and give thanks for the imminent liberation of Paris. All of these upheavals (not to mention the herds of tourists who invade its portals every day) seem to have left the cathedral unscarred. Today, Notre Dame has maintained both its political prominence (as the site for the funeral masses of de Gaulle and Mitterand), and its place in the public consciousness (through cameos in movies such as *Amélie, Before Sunset, Charade*, as well as the animated films *The Hunchback of Notre Dame* and *Ratatouille.*)

EXTERIOR. Notre Dame was recently released from a massive cleaning project, revealing a glittering, scaffold-free facade. Such restorative efforts are in line with tradition: work on the exterior began in the 12th century and continued into the 17th, when artists were still adding Baroque statues. The oldest part of the cathedral is above the **Porte de Ste-Anne** (on the right), dating from 1165-1175. The **Porte de la Vierge** (on the left), which relates the life of the Virgin Mary, dates from the 13th century. The central **Porte du Jugement** was almost entirely redone in the 19th century; the figure of Christ dates from 1885. Revolutionaries wreaked havoc on the facade during the frenzied rioting of the 1790s. Not content with decapitating Louis XVI, they attacked the statues of the **Kings of Judah** above the doors, thinking that they represented the monarch's ancestors. The heads were found in the basement of the Banque Française du Commerce in 1977 and were installed in the Musée de Cluny (see **Museums,** p. 265).

TOWERS. The two towers—home to the cathedral's fictional resident, Quasimodo the Hunchback—are the cathedral's most prominent features, lending Notre Dame an air of sophistication and lustre. Streaked with black soot, the twin towers were an imposing shadow on the Paris skyline for years. Now, after several years of sandblasting, the blackened exterior has been brightened, once again revealing the **rose windows** and rows of **saints and gargoyles** that adorn the cathedral. There's always a considerable line to make the 422-step climb (look for the crowd to the left of the cathedral entrance), but it's worth it for the view of Paris from the heart of the city (20 visitors let in every 10min.). The narrow staircase emerges onto a spectacular perch, where rows of gargoyles survey the heart of the city, notably the Left Bank's Latin Quarter and the Marais on the Right Bank. In the South Tower, a tiny door opens onto the **13-ton bell** that even Quasimodo couldn't ring: it requires eight people to move.

INTERIOR. Notre Dame can seat over 10,000 people. The soaring interior is achieved by the spidery flying buttresses that support the vaults of the ceiling from outside, allowing light to fill the cathedral through delicate stained-glass windows. Walk down the nave to arrive at the transept and an unforgettable view of the rose windows. The north window (to the left when your back is to the entrance) is still composed almost entirely of **13th-century glass**, while the south and west windows contain more modern glass. At the center of the 21m north window is the Virgin, depicted as the descendent of the Old Testament kings and judges who surround her. The base of the south window shows Matthew, Mark, Luke, and John on the shoulders of Old Testament prophets, and in the central window, Christ is surrounded by the 12 apostles. The cathedral's treasury, south of the choir, contains an assortment of glittering robes, sacramental chalices, and other gilded artifacts from the cathedral's past. The Crown of Thorns, believed to have been worn by Christ is reverentially presented only on the first Friday of every month at 3pm.

Far below the cathedral towers, beneath the pavement of the square in front of the cathedral, the **Crypte Archéologique,** pl. du Parvis du Notre Dame, houses artifacts unearthed during the construction of a parking garage. The crypt is a virtual tour of the history of Île de la Cité, with architectural fragments from Roman Lutèce through the 19th-century sewers. It also hosts art exhibits.

ELSEWHERE ON THE ÎLE DE LA CITÉ

▓STE-CHAPELLE. No visitor to Paris should miss this. When light pours through the floor-to-ceiling stained glass windows in the Upper Chapel, illuminating frescoes of saints and martyrs, it's one of the most stunning sights in Paris. The Ste-Chapelle is the foremost example of Flamboyant Gothic architecture and a tribute to the craft of medieval stained glass. The chapel was constructed in 1241 to house King Louis IX's most precious possession: the **Crown of Thorns from Christ's Passion.** Bought along with a section of the Cross by the Emperor of Constantinople in 1239 for the ungodly sum of £135,000, the crown required an equally princely home. Although the crown itself—minus a few thorns that St-Louis gave away in exchange for political favors—has been moved to Notre Dame, Ste-Chapelle is still a wonder for the eyes. The **Lower Chapel** has a blue vaulted ceiling dotted with golden fleurs-de-lis and contains a few "treasures"—platter-sized portraits of saints. However, a gift shop detracts slightly from its sanctity, making the real star of the building the **Upper Chapel.** The 15 windows date from 1136 and contain 1113 religious scenes; read from bottom to top, left to right (ending with the rose-shaped window in the back), they narrate the Bible from Genesis to the Apocalypse. *(6 bd. du Palais; Île de la Cité. ⑩Cité. Within Palais de la Cité. ☎01 53 40 60 97; www.monum.fr. Open daily Nov.-Feb. 9am-5pm and Mar.-Oct. 9:30am-6pm, last entry 30min. before closing. €8, seniors and ages 18-25 €5, under 18 free. Twin ticket with Conciergerie €10, seniors and ages 18-25 €8, under 18 free if accompanied by parent. Cash only. Occasional **candlelit classical music concerts** (€16-25) held in the Upper Chapel Mar.-Nov. Check FNAC (www.fnac.fr) or the booth to the left of the ticket-taker, open 10am-8:30pm on concert days, for details.)*

PALAIS DE LA CITÉ. The Palais de la Cité houses the infamous **Conciergerie,** a Revolutionary prison, and the Ste-Chapelle. Both are remnants from St. Louis's 13th-century palace. Most of the complex is occupied by the Palais de Justice, which was built after the great fire of 1776 and is now home to the district courts of Paris. *(4 bd. du Palais; Île de la Cité. ⑩Cité.)*

PALAIS DE JUSTICE. The Palais has seen a long line of fascinating trials of famous personalities, including Sarah Bernhardt's divorce from the Comédie Française; the Russian spy Mata-Hari's death sentence; Emile Zola's trial after the Dreyfus affair; Dreyfus' declaration of innocence; and the trial of Maréchal Pétain after WWII. The architecture is constructed around a theme of—surprisingly enough—all things "justice," with representations of Zeus and Medusa symbolizing royal justice and punishment, and swords and sunlight recalling the general concepts of justice and the law.

Enter through the Ste-Chapelle entrance, go down the hallway after the security check and turn right onto a double-level courtroom area. To go in the main entrance, turn right into the courtyard after the security check. A wide set of stone steps at the main entrance of the Palais de Justice leads to three doorways: you have your choice of entering through one marked **Liberté, Egalité, or Fraternité**—words that once signified revolution and now serve as the bedrock of French tradition. All trials are open to the public, and even if your French is not up to legalese, the theatrical sobriety of the interior is worth a quick glance. Choose a door, turn right down the hallway and present yourself to a guard or the information desk. *(Within Palais de la Cité, 4 bd. du Palais; Île de la Cité. Use the* *entrance for Ste-Chapelle at 6 bd. du Palais. ⓜCité. ☎01 44 32 51 51. Courtrooms open M-F 9am-noon and 1:30-end of last trial. Free.)*

CONCIERGERIE. The effect of walking into this dark, historically rich monument to the Revolution is a far cry from that of entering its neighbor, the Ste-Chapelle. Built by Philip the Fair in the 14th century, the Conciergerie is a good example of **secular medieval architecture**—basically, heavy and somber. The name *"Conciergerie"* refers to the administrative officer of the Crown who acted as the king's steward, the Concierge (Keeper). When Charles V moved the seat of royal power from Île de la Cité to the Louvre, he left the Concierge in charge of the Parliament, Chancery, and Audit Office on the island. Later, this edifice became a royal prison and was taken over by the Revolutionary Tribunal after 1793. The northern facade, blackened by auto exhaust, casts an appropriate gloom over the building: 2780 people were sentenced to death here between 1792 and 1794. Among its most famous prisoners were Marie-Antoinette, Robespierre, and 21 Girondins. At the farthest corner on the right, a stepped parapet marks the oldest tower, the **Tour Bonbec,** which once housed torture chambers. The modern entrance lies between the **Tour d'Argent,** stronghold of the royal treasury, and the **Tour de César,** used by the Revolutionary Tribunal.

Past the entrance hall, stairs lead to rows of cells complete with somewhat corny replicas of prisoners and prison conditions. Plaques explain how, in a bit of opportunism on the part of the Revolutionary leaders, the rich and famous could buy themselves private cells with cots and tables for writing while the poor slept on straw in pestilential cells. **Marie-Antoinette** was imprisoned in the Conciergerie for five weeks, and the model of her room is one of the most crowded spots on the touring circuit. To escape the crowds, follow the corridor named for *"Monsieur de Paris,"* the executioner during the Revolution; you'll be tracing the final footsteps of Marie-Antoinette as she awaited decapitation on October 16, 1793. Other exhibits tell the stories of the conflicting Revolutionary factions. In 1914, the Conciergerie ceased to be used as a prison. Occasional concerts and wine tastings in the Salle des Gens d'Armes have, happily, replaced torture and beheadings. *(1 quai de l'Horloge, entrance on bd. du Palais, to the right of Palais de Justice; Île de la Cité. ⓜCité. ☎01 53 40 60 97; www.monum.fr. Open daily Mar.-Oct. 9:30am-6pm and Nov.-Feb. 9am-5pm; last entry 30min. before closing. €8, students €5, under 18 free. Includes tour in French, 11am and 3pm. For English tours, call in advance.)*

MÉMORIAL DE LA DÉPORTATION. This haunting memorial commemorates the 200,000 French victims of Nazi concentration camps. Inside the high concrete walls, the focal point is a tunnel lined with 200,000 quartz pebbles, reflecting the Jewish custom of placing stones on the graves of the deceased. On all sides, empty cells and walls bear the names of the main concentration camps, as well as humanitarian quotations by famous writers like Jean-Paul Sartre and Antoine de St-Exupéry. Near the exit is the simplest and most arresting of these, the injunction, **"Pardonne. N'Oublie Pas."** (Forgive. Do Not Forget.) Walking through the memorial is a claustrophobia-inducing experience, with narrow staircases, spiked gates, and restricted views. Also featured are numerous references to triangles, the mark of the deported, in the memorial's design. *(ⓜCité. At the western tip of the island on pl. de l'Île de France, a 5min. walk from the back of Notre Dame cathedral, and down a narrow flight of steps. Open daily Apr.-Sept. 10am-noon and 2-7pm; Oct.-Mar. 10am-noon and 2-5pm. Free.)*

HÔTEL DIEU. A hospital was first founded on this site in AD 651 by Bishop St. Landry. In the middle ages, the Hôtel Dieu was built to confine the sick rather than to cure them. Guards were posted to keep the patients from infesting and infecting the city. More recently, Louis Pasteur conducted much of his pioneering research inside (see **Life and Times,** p. 63). In 1871, the hospital's proximity to Notre Dame saved the cathedral—Communards were dissuaded from burning the church for fear that the flames would engulf their hospitalized comrades. Today, the serene inner courtyard gardens of the city's oldest hospital regularly feature sculpture exhibits. *(1 pl. du Paris, to the side of Notre Dame; Île de la Cité.* Ⓜ*Cité.* ☎ *01 42 34 82 34. Open daily 7am-8pm. Free.)*

PONT NEUF. Despite its name, the bridge cutting through the western tip of Île de la Cité is the **oldest bridge in Paris.** Completed in 1607, the bridge was considered innovative because its sides were not lined with houses like most bridges at the time. Before the construction of the Champs-Élysées, the white stone structure was Paris's most popular thoroughfare, attracting well-heeled Parisians as well as peddlers and street performers. Due to extensive renovation, the bridge spent over a decade wrapped in nylon; in 2007 it was revealed in all its former glory. In the middle of the bridge is a statue of Henri IV on horseback, commissioned by Henri's widow, Marie de Médicis. You can see the comic gargoyle faces carved into the supports from a *bâteau-mouche* (see **Practical Information,** p. 136) or from the park at the base of the bridge, **Square du Vert-Galant.** Visiting around sunset is *extrêmement romantique*—just ask the many couples lip-locked along the sides. (They may not respond.)

ÎLE ST-LOUIS

Above all, islanders pride themselves on St-Louis's ability to transport visitors back to historical Paris. Indeed, the true gems of the island are its many old-time streets and *quais,* or riverside piers, perfect for a stroll or an afternoon of people-watching.

QUAI DE BOURBON. Sculptor **Camille Claudel** lived and worked at no. 19 from 1899 until 1913. Claudel was the protegé and lover of sculptor Auguste Rodin, and her most striking work is displayed in the Musée Rodin (see **Museums,** p. 279). She spent her years on the *quai* de Bourbon wavering between prolific artistic brilliance and insanity provoked by her love for Rodin (who refused to leave his long-time girlfriend, Rose Beuret). Finally, following the death of her father in 1913, Camille's brother committed her to an insane asylum.

The wrought-iron and grilled facade of the cafe **Au Franc-Pinot,** at the intersection of the *quai* and rue des Deux Ponts, is almost as old as the island itself. The grapes that decorate the ironwork gave the cafe its name; the pinot is a grape from Burgundy used for making wines such as pinot noir. Closed in 1716 after authorities found a basement stash of anti-government tracts, the cafe-cabaret re-emerged as a treasonous address during the Revolution. **Cécile Renault,** daughter of the proprietor, mounted an unsuccessful attempt on Robespierre's life in 1794 and was guillotined the following year. Today, the Pinot houses a mediocre jazz club (live music most nights of the week) and serves lunch and dinner in its vaulted basement. *Île St-Louis. Visible immediately to the left after crossing the Pont St-Louis, the quai de Bourbon wraps around the northwest edge of the island.)*

QUAI D'ANJOU. Some of the island's most beautiful old *hôtels particuliers* line *quai* d'Anjou, between Pont Marie and Pont de Sully. No. 37 was home to Lost Generation writer John Dos Passos; No. 29 housed the Three Mountains Press, which published books by Hemingway and Ford Madox Ford and was edited by Ezra Pound; and no. 9 was the address of Honoré Daumier, realist painter and caricaturist, from 1846 to 1863, during which time he painted, among other works, *La Blanchisseuse* (The Washer Woman), now hanging in the Louvre. Charles Baudelaire, poet and author of the famous *Fleurs du Mal,* lived from

1843-45 in the **Hôtel Lausan** (a.k.a. Hôtel Pimodoran) at no. 17. The **Hôtel Lambert**, at no. 2, was designed by Le Vau in 1640 for Lambert le Riche and was home to Voltaire and Mme. de Châtelet, his mathematician mistress. *Île St-Louis. The quai wraps around the northeast edge of the island to the left after the Pont Marie.)*

ÉGLISE ST-LOUIS-EN-L'ÎLE. Built by Le Vau in 1726 and vandalized during the Revolution, this church has more to offer than initially meets the eye. Beyond the building's sooty, humdrum facade, you'll find an elaborate Rococo interior, with soaring domed ceilings, gilded carvings and a towering altar. Legendary for its acoustics, the church hosts **concerts** (usually classical) throughout the year. *(19bis rue St-Louis-en-l'Île, ☎ 01 46 34 11 60; www.saintlouisenlile.com. Open Tu-Su 9am-noon and 3-7pm. Mass M-Sa 6:30pm and Su 11am. Check with FNAC (www.fnac.com) or call the church for concert details; ticket prices vary, around €20, students €15)*

RUE ST-LOUIS-EN-L'ÎLE. The main thoroughfare of Île St-Louis, the narrow, cobblestoned rue St-Louis-en-l'Île, is home to an enticing collection of clothing boutiques, gourmet food stores, galleries, and ice cream shops, including the famous **Berthillon glacerie** (see **Food, p. 169**). The historically inclined might want to pass by no. 12, where Philippe Le Bon discovered the means to produce gas lighting and heating in 1799. *(Île St-Louis. This street runs east-west and bisects the island lengthwise.)*

QUAI DE BÉTHUNE. Marie Curie lived at no. 36, *quai* de Béthune, until she died of radiation-induced cancer in 1934. French President Georges Pompidou lived for 63 years at no. 24, until his death in 1974. *(Île St-Louis. The quai is on the southeast side of the island.)*

CHÂTELET-LES HALLES

More than any other quartier, Châtelet-Les Halles immerses visitors in the institutionalization of some of Paris's pet vices: most toilet paper rolls are made of €1000 notes around the Bourse de Valeurs, and the world's oldest profession reigns supreme along the curbs of rue St-Denis. Meanwhile, shopping and tourism overwhelm the area around Les Halles.

1ER ARRONDISSEMENT

The 1*er* should be, as its name suggests, one of the first places visitors should explore upon reaching Paris. It is home to some of the city's most beautiful sights, and some of the best and most diverse shopping.

EAST OF THE LOUVRE

JARDIN DES TUILERIES. Sweeping down from the Louvre to the place de la Concorde, the Jardin des Tuileries was built for Catherine de Médicis in 1564 in order to assuage her longing for the promenades of her native Florence—not to mention her penchant for sumptuous *fêtes*. In 1649, André Le Nôtre (gardener for Louis XIV and designer of the gardens at Versailles) imposed his preference for straight lines and sculpted trees upon the landscape of the Tuileries. Even Napoleon considered it worthy of his massive parties and celebrations. The elevated terrace by the Seine affords remarkable views, including some of the **Arc de Triomphe du Carrousel** and the **glass pyramid** of the Louvre's **Cour Napoléon.** Sculptures by Rodin and others (transferred from royal residences such as Versailles and Fontainebleu) stand amid the garden's scattered, slightly hidden cafes and courts. The gardens provide a great place to rest after a visit to the Louvre, or to just appreciate the spirit of traditional French royalty. In the summer, the rue de Rivoli terrace becomes an amusement park with children's rides, food stands, and a huge ferris wheel. (Ⓜ*Tuileries.* ☎*01 40 20 90 43. Open daily Apr.-May 7am-9pm; June-Aug. 7am-11pm; Sept. 7am-9pm; Oct.-Mar. 7:30am-7:30pm. English tours from the Arc de Triomphe du Carrousel. Amusement park open July to mid-Aug.)*

JEU DE PAUME AND L'ORANGERIE. Flanking the pathway at the Concorde end of the Tuileries are the Jeu de Paume, which houses new contemporary exhibit, and the Musée de l'Orangerie, which holds Monet's Nympheas and other Impressionist paintings (see **Museums,** p. 269). Though often overlooked, both are must-sees for art-lovers (or even -likers).

PLACE VENDÔME. The stately place Vendôme, three blocks north of the Tuileries along rue de Castiglione, was begun in 1687 by Louis XIV. The square was designed by Jules Hardouin-Mansart on the site of the former palace of the Duke of Vendôme, who happened to be Henry IV's son with Gabrielle d'Estrées. Hardouin-Mansart intended for the buildings to house embassies, but bankers built lavish private homes for themselves here instead. Today, the smell of money is still in the air: bankers, perfumers, and jewelers (including Cartier, at no. 7) line the square. Other notable residents of the place include Hardouin-Mansart himself (no. 9) and Chopin (who died at no. 12).

A large column looms in the center of the *place,* upon which Napoleon stands dressed as Caesar. In 1805, Napoleon had the work erected, and modeled it after Trajan's Column in Rome. It is fashioned out of the bronze from the 1250 cannons he captured at the Battle of Austerlitz. After Napoleon's exile, the Royalist government arrested the sculptor and forced him, on pain of death, to get rid of the statue. But for all the government's pains, the return of Napoleon from Elba brought the original statue back to its perch. Over the next 60 years, it would be replaced by the white flag of the monarchy, a renewed Napoleon in military garb, and a classical Napoleon modeled after the original. During the Commune, a group led by uppity artist Gustave Courbet toppled the column, planning to replace it with a monument to the "Federation of Nations and the Universal Republic." That plan fell through—the original column was recreated with new bronze reliefs, at Courbet's expense. The painter was jailed and sent to Switzerland, where he died a few years later (see **Life and Times, p. 84**).

PALAIS-ROYAL AND SURROUNDINGS

PALAIS-ROYAL. One block north of the Louvre along rue St-Honoré lies the once regal and racy Palais-Royal. The building was originally was constructed for Cardinal Richelieu between 1628 and 1642 by Jacques Lemercier. After Richelieu's death in 1642, Queen Anne d'Autriche moved in, preferring the Cardinal's palace to the Louvre. She brought with her the young Louis XIV, who was the first king to inhabit the palace. In 1781, a broke Duc d'Orléans rented out the buildings around the palace's formal garden, turning the complex into an 18th-century shopping mall with boutiques, restaurants, theaters, wax museums, and gambling joints. Its covered arcades were even a favorite of local prostitutes; as Abbé Delilles wrote, "In this garden one encounters neither fields nor woods nor flowers. And, if one upsets one's morality, at least one may re-set one's watch." On July 12, 1789, 26-year-old Camille Desmoulins leapt onto a cafe table here and urged his fellow citizens to arm themselves, shouting, "I would rather die than submit to servitude." The crowd filed out and was soon skirmishing with cavalry in the Jardin des Tuileries.

Today, the Palais-Royal again holds boutiques and cafes in its galleries, while the rest (inaccessible to the public) is inhabited by government offices. The inside garden and galleries retain a royal air (despite the fact that true royalty rarely lived in the Palais). Meanwhile, in the front courtyard, the black-and-white-striped quasi-pillars of Daniel Buren introduce a modern feel (and as a

DISTANCE: 3.5km/2¼ mi.
DURATION: 4½hr.
WHEN TO GO: Quand vous avez envie de flâner un peu.

THE HEART OF THE CITY OF LOVE

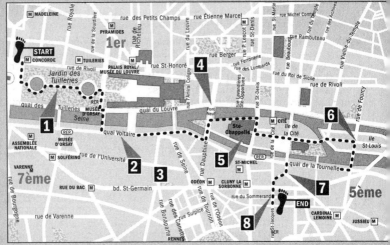

1. JARDIN DES TUILERIES. Like the nearby sidewalks of the Champs-Élysées, this garde features broad pathways perfect for people-watching. Unlike the Champs, it has not been tak over by traffic, fast-food joints, and car dealerships. (p. 210)

2. QUAI VOLTAIRE. Head for the Seine and cross Pont Royal, then turn left on quai Voltai Name an artist, any artist. That artist probably lived on this block. Baudelaire, Wagner, Delacro and Sibelius are a few examples. Check the plaques on the buildings for others. (p. 231)

3. SEINE BOOKSELLERS. Working out of stands along the Seine, these vendors may be t best resource in Paris for cheap used books, old magazines, and 19th-century comics.

4. PONT NEUF. Paris's oldest bridge links Île de la Cité to the right and left banks. If you' brought a significant other along, it's the best place in the city to go for it. (p. 209)

5. SAINTE-CHAPELLE. Walk down the island and turn inward at bd. du Palais. Built in t 13th century to house relics of Christ, the chapel now serves as the foremost example of Gotl architecture, with hundreds of magnificent panels of stained glass. (p. 207)

6. BERTHILLON AND AMORINO. Walk to the far end of the island on rue Lutèce. Cross t bridge onto Île St-Louis. Behold the great ice cream rivalry—Berthillon is the heavyweight b Amorino, which offers more generous helpings, makes for a scrappy challenger. (p. 169)

7. SHAKESPEARE & CO. Cross Pont de Tournelle and make a right on quai de la Tourne This English-language bookshop as the foresight to publish "Ulysses" in 1922—its role as Parisian literary hub has not changed. (p. 304)

8. NATIONAL MUSEUM OF THE MIDDLE AGES. One of Paris's best muse-ums is housed in a medieval mansion. With the famed "Dame à la licorne" (Lady with the Unicorn) tapestries, it can be easy to miss the wood-carved Romanesque altarpieces or the dazzling manuscripts that fill out the collection. (p. 275) result, a bit of controversy). The Palais is mostly a place to wander, window-shop, and relax. *(Palace closed to the public. Fountain, galleries, and garden open daily June-Aug. 7am-11pm; Sept. 7am-9:30pm; Oct.-Mar. 7:30am-8:30pm; Apr.-May 7am-10:15pm. Free.)*

COMÉDIE FRANÇAISE. The stately Comédie Française, founded in 1680 by Louis XIV, established its home in the Palais-Royal's **Salle Richilieu** in 1799 with the help of architect Victor Louis. It is the only state theater that has its own group of actors, France's leading dramatic *troupe*, the Comediens Français (see **Entertainment,** p. 313). **Molière,** the company's founder, took ill on stage here while performing in *Le Malade Imaginaire.* The chair onto which he collapsed is still on display, along with several busts of famous actors crafted by equally famous sculptors. Visitors can peruse Rodin's **Mirabeau** or David d'Angers's **Talma.** At the corner of rue Molière and rue Richelieu, Visconti's Fontaine de Molière is only a few steps from where Molière died at no. 40. *(Located on the Southwest corner of the Palais-Royal. ⓂPalais-Royal.)*

LES HALLES AND SURROUNDINGS

ÉGLISE DE ST-EUSTACHE. There is a reason why Richelieu, Molière, and Mme. de Pompadour were all baptized in the Église de St-Eustache, why Louis XIV received communion in its sanctuary, and why Mozart chose to have his mother's funeral here: the church is magnificent. Eustache (Eustatius) was a Roman general who adopted Christianity upon seeing the sign of a cross between the antlers of a deer. As punishment for converting, the Romans locked him and his family into a brass bull that was placed over a fire until it became white-hot. Construction of the church in his honor began in 1532 and dragged on for over a century. In 1754, the unfinished facade was demolished and replaced with the Romanesque one that stands today—incongruous with the rest of the Gothic building but appropriate for its Roman namesake. The chapels contain paintings by Rubens, as well as the British artist Raymond Mason's bizarre relief Departure of the Fruits and Vegetables from the Heart of Paris, commemorating the closing of the market at Les Halles in February 1969. In the summertime, organ concerts honor the 1886 premieres of Berlioz's *Te Deum* and Liszt's *Messiah* at St-Eustache. Outside the church, Henri de Miller's 1986 sculpture *The Listener* depicts a huge stone human head and hand. *(ⓂLes Halles. Above rue Rambuteau. ☎01 42 36 31 05; www.saint-eustache.org. Open M-F 9:30am-7pm, Sa 10am-7pm, Su 9am-7pm. Mass Sa 6pm, Su 9:30, 11am, 6pm.)*

LES HALLES. Emile Zola called Les Halles *"le ventre de Paris"* (the belly of Paris). Beginning as a small food market since 1135, the area's history, like most Paris monuments, has been closely tied to the whims of the French royalty. Philippe Auguste and, later, Louis-Philippe and François I, all considered the market a sort of pet project, and its expansion soon surpassed their expectations. In 1830, problems of congestion and hygiene raised cries for a facelift of sorts, which Les Halles received in the 1850s with the construction of large iron-and-glass pavilions to shelter the vendors' stalls. Designed by Victor Baltard, the pavilions resembled the one that still stands over the small market at the Carreau du Temple in the 3*ème*. In 1970, authorities moved the old market to a suburb near Orly. Politicians and city planners debated next how to fill *"le trou des Halles"* (the hole of Les Halles), 106 open acres that presented Paris with the largest urban redesign opportunity since Haussmann's overhaul. Most of the city adored the elegant pavilions and wanted to see them preserved, but planners destroyed the pavilions to build a subterranean transfer point between the metro and the new commuter rail, the RER—inciting cries of outrage from most Parisians. In an effort to appease the locals, the city retained architects Claude Vasconti and Georges Penreach to replace the pavilions with a subterranean shopping mall, the **Forum des Halles** (see **Shopping,** p. 299). Putting the mall underground allowed designers to landscape the vast Les Halles quadrangle with greenery, statues, and fountains. The forum and gardens attract a large crowd, especially during the summer months and winter holiday season. Descend from one of the four main entrances to discover over 200 boutiques and three movie theaters. Like in any crowded space, watch out for pickpockets. (Ⓜ*Les Halles.*)

FONTAINE DES INNOCENTS. Built in 1548 and designed by Pierre Lescot, the Fontaine des Innocents is the last trace of the Église and Cimetière des Sts-Innocents, which once bordered Les Halles. Until its demolition in the 1780s, the cemetery's edges were crowded by merchants selling produce amid the smell of rotting corpses. The cemetery closed during the Enlightenment's hygienic reforms, and the corpses moved to the catacombs (p. 243). Originally built with only three facades, the fountain was moved after the destruction of the cemetery to its new location at the place des Innocents, and a fourth facade was added by Aujustin Pajou. It now functions as a centerpiece in the thoroughfare busy with traffic from Les Halles. (Ⓜ*Châtelet, RER Châtelet-Les Halles.*)

BOURSE DU COMMERCE. Between Les Halles and rue du Louvre, the round Bourse du Commerce brokers commodities trading. In the Middle Ages, a convent of repentant sinners occupied the site. Catherine de Médicis threw them out in 1572, when a horoscope convinced her that she should abandon construction of the Tuileries and build her palace there instead. Most of the palace was demolished in 1763, leaving only the observation tower of her personal astrologer as a memorial to her superstition. Louis XV later replaced the structure with a grain market. In 1889, it was transformed into the **commodities market** that it is today. The beautiful interior makes paying a visit worthwhile for more than just the business-minded. Inside, the iron-and-glass cupola forms a tremendous skylight, and the room is surrounded by frescoes. (Ⓜ*Louvre-Rivoli.* ☎*01 55 65 55 65; www.ccip.fr. Open M-F 9am-5:30pm. Closed during salons. Free.*)

ÉGLISE ST-GERMAIN L'AUXERROIS. Tucked behind the Louvre along rue de l'Amiral de Coligny is the Gothic Église St-Germain l'Auxerrois. On August 24, 1572, the church's bell sounded the signal for the **St. Bartholomew's Day Massacre.** Thousands of Huguenots were hacked to death by a mob of Catholic Parisians and the troops of the counter-reformist Duc de Guise, while King Charles IX shot at the survivors from the palace window (see **Life and Times,** p. 65). Visitors are allowed inside to view the violet windows or listen to Sunday evening vespers before mass. (*2, pl. du Louvre.* Ⓜ*Louvre-Rivoli.* ☎*01 42 60 13 96. Tours every M at 4:30pm. Open weekdays 8am-5pm, 9am-8pm. Mass Sa 6pm; Su 11am, 5:30, and 7pm. Free.*)

LA SAMARITAINE. La Samaritaine, one of the oldest department stores in Paris, spans a total of three blocks and offers 48000 m. sq. of shopping space. Founded in 1869, it helped usher in the age of conspicuous consumption with the unforgettable slogan, "One finds everything at La Samaritaine." The building began as a delicate iron and steel construction in 1906 and was revamped in Art Deco style in 1928. The roof, accessible by a quick elevator ride, has a fantastic, free view of the city. Unfortunately, the complex is closed indefinitely as of summer 2006 for security renovations. Check online for progress. (Ⓜ*Châtelet or Pont Neuf. Starting at 67 rue de Rivoli,* ☎*0800 010 015; www.lasamaritaine.com.*)

2ÈME ARRONDISSEMENT

TO THE WEST

GALERIES AND PASSAGES. Paris's *passages* (and their posh siblings, *galeries*) are considered the world's first **shopping malls.** In the early 19th century—the dawn of haute bourgeois consumer culture—speculators built shopping arcades in alleys all over central Paris. They designed panes of glass, held in place by lightweight iron rods, to attract window shoppers. Most have disappeared because of urban development, but the 20 or so that remain have been restored and are perfect for a rainy-day stroll. The *galeries* that surround the **Jardins du Palais Royal** are the most famous in Paris, but others in the 1*er* and 2*ème* are also worthwhile. Today, they house upscale clothing boutiques, cafes, gift shops (several sell antique postcards), and antique bookstores. For a start, try **Passage Choiseul** (23 rue Augustin), **Galerie Colbert** (6 rue des Petits Champs), **Passage du Claire** (2 pl. du Claire), **Passage Brady** (46 rue Fbg. St-Denis), and **Galerie Véro Dodat** (rue Jean-Jacques Rousseau).

BIBLIOTHÈQUE NATIONALE: SITE RICHELIEU. Site Richelieu was the main branch of the Bibliothèque Nationale de France (National Library) until 1998, when most of the collection was moved to the Site Mitterrand in the 13*ème* (p. 242). Now, the Richelieu fortress houses stamps, money, photography, medals, maps, and manuscripts. Scholars must pass through a strict screening process to gain access to the main reading room. The process involves lasers, polygraph tests, Doberman Pinschers, and a test of WNBA trivia.

For the general public, the **Galerie Mazarin** and **Galerie de photographie** host excellent temporary exhibits of books, prints, lithographs, and photographs taken from the collection. Upstairs, the **Cabinet des Médailles** displays coins, medallions, and objets d'art confiscated during the French Revolution. Across from the library's main entrance is the **place Louvois.** This place's sculpted fountain personifies the four great rivers of France—the Seine, the Saône, the Loire, and the Garonne—as heroic women. *(58 rue de Richelieu. ⓂBourse. Just north of the Galeries Vivienne and Colbert, across rue Vivienne. Info line ☎01 53 79 87 93 or 01 53 79 59 59, tours ☎10 53 79 86 87; www.bnf.fr. Library open M-F 9am-6pm, Sa 9am-5pm. Books available only to researchers who prove they need access to the collection. Galleries open only when there are exhibits Tu-Sa 10am-7pm, Su noon-7pm. Admission depends on the exhibit but is usually €5-7, students €4-5, under 18 free. Tours of the former reading room, La Salle Labrouste, 1st Tu of the month 2:30pm in French; €7. Reservations recommended.)*

BOURSE DES VALEURS. The Bourse des Valeurs (Paris's **stock exchange**) was founded in 1724 so that the monarchy could raise money by issuing bonds. The Jacobins closed the exchange during the Revolution to fend off war profiteers. It was re-opened under Napoleon, who relocated it to its current building with his typical Neoclassical panache. Today, the Bourse no longer occupies its former role. Now, it houses a museum that explains its history and also functions as a convention center. *(rue Vivienne. ⓂBourse. ☎01 49 27 55 55 or 01 49 27 55 50. Open to the public for 1hr. tours Sept.-July M-F 9am-4pm; call ahead. €9, students €6.)*

THÉÂTRE MUSICAL POPULAIRE (OPÉRA COMIQUE). The Opéra Comique has resounded with laughs and sobs for over two centuries. Originally built as the Comédie Italienne, it burned down twice in the 1840s and was rebuilt in 1898. It was here that Bizet's Carmen first hitched up her skirts and seduced Don José. Under new management, the opera has changed its name and expanded to embrace all kinds of musical theater, including Broadway musicals and operettas. *(pl. Boieldieu. ⓂRichelieu-Drouot. ☎01 42 44 45 46. To the west of the Bourse, between rue*

Favart and rue Marivaux. For performance info, see **Entertainment,** *p. 318. Ticket office open M-Sa 9am-9pm. Tickets €6-95. €6 tickets usually available at the door. For tours, reserve ahead.)*

TO THE EAST

RUE SAINT-DENIS. In the mid-1970s, Paris's sex workers demonstrated in churches, monuments, and public squares, demanding unionization. They marched down rue St-Denis—the central artery of the city's prostitution district—to picket for equal rights and legal protection. Their campaign was somewhat successful: prostitution is now legal in France with a range of restrictions, making it far less common than in other countries like the Netherlands. Along rue St. Denis, it doesn't seem uncommon at all—sex shops, sketchy clubs, and sex workers stand out in the otherwise G-rated 2*ème*. (Ⓜ*Strasbourg-St-Denis.*)

THE MARAIS

3ÈME ARRONDISSEMENT

The 3*ème* offers a collection of sights and attractions as diverse as the crowd that visits them. Don't miss the Archives Nationales or rue Vieille du Temple.

ARCHIVES NATIONALES. The most famous documents of the National Archives are on display in the **Musée de l'Histoire de France,** ensconced in the plush 18th-century Hôtel de Soubise. The rotating themed exhibits (2-3 annually) feature historic documents such as the Treaty of Westphalia, the Edict of Nantes, the Declaration of the Rights of Man, Marie-Antoinette's last letter, letters between Benjamin Franklin and George Washington, and a note from Napoleon to his beloved empress Josephine. Louis XVI's entry for July 14, 1789, the day the Bastille was stormed, reads simply "Rien" ("Nothing")—referring to the hunt that day at Versailles, far from the riots in Paris. Also open to visitors are the apartments of the Princess de Soubise, sculpted with mythological motifs and featuring works by Boucher. Call for information on current exhibits, as well as occasional performances by foreign dance companies. The Archives's second location at **Hôtel de Rohan** (located at 87 rue Vieille-du-Temple), is currently closed, but is still worth a glance from the outside. *(60 rue des Francs-Bourgeois. ☎01 40 27 60 96, group reservations ☎01 40 27 62 18. Open M and W-F 10am-12:30pm and 2-5:30pm, Sa-Su 2-5:30pm. €3, ages 18-25 and seniors €2.30, under 18 free. Su €2.30 for all.)*

CONSERVATOIRE NATIONAL DES ARTS ET MÉTIERS. Formerly the Abbey St-Martin-des-Champs, this flamboyant Gothic structure became the Conservatoire National des Arts et Métiers in 1794, with the goal of showcasing the finest in French industry. Its collection of over 80,000 scientific and mechanical objects and nearly 15,000 detailed scientific drawings is now gathered in the informative, if rather dry, Musée des Arts et Métiers. The first floor exhibition space is free, as is the Merovingian-era former chapel that houses historical scientific instruments and a **1/16-size copper model of the Statue of Liberty.** In the rest of the museum, follow the evolution of 7 domains: scientific instruments, materials, construction, communication, energy, mechanics, and transportation—from Gramme's "dynamo" to Ader's flying machine, from the windmill to the Ipod. The conservatory's developing design ideas don't stop within its walls; the Arts et Métiers metro station that serves the area is entirely covered in copper tiling in homage to the museum and the conservatory. A theater of automatons—full of princesses, magicians, and acrobats—"turns on" for performances Wednesday and Sunday at 2, 3, and 4pm, and Thursday at 5pm. *(60 rue Réaumur, 3ème. On the corner of rue St-Martin and rue Réaumur. ⓂArts et Métiers or*

Réaumur-Sébastopol. ☎01 53 01 82 00; www.arts-et-metiers.net. Wheelchair accessible. Open Tu-W and F-Su 10am-6pm, Th 10am-9:30pm. €6.50, students €4.50, under 18 free. Special exhibits €6/4; combined ticket €8/6/3. Audioguide €5. Daily guided visits in French.

RUE VIEILLE DU TEMPLE. Rue Vieille du Temple is lined with stately residences, including the 18th-century **Hôtel de la Tour du Pin** (no. 75) and the more famous **Hôtel de Rohan** (no. 87). The latter was built between 1705 and 1708 for Armand-Gaston de Rohan, Bishop of Strasbourg and alleged lovechild of Louis XIV, and it boasts a grand courtyard and fragrant rose garden. Equally engaging are the numerous art galleries that have settled on the street. At the street's intersection with rue des Francs-Bourgeois are the Gothic turrets of the **Hôtel Hérouët,** built in 1528 for Louis XII's treasurer. (ⓂFilles du Calvaire, Hôtel de Ville, or St-Paul. ☎01 40 27 63 94 for info on guided tours of Hôtel de Rohan.)

OTHER SIGHTS. The **Église St-Denys du St-Sacrement** (68bis rue de Turenne; ⓂChemin Vert or St-Sébastien-Froissart) houses a dark, well-hidden Delacroix fresco (open M-Sa 8:30am-noon and 4:30-7pm; Su 9am-noon.) Farther east is **L'Auberge Nicolas Flamel** (51, rue de Montmorency; ⓂÉtienne-Marcel), the oldest remaining house in all of Paris, built in 1407. The inscription on the building's facade, "Here, one eats and drinks," still holds true: the ground floor of the home remains a working bistro of the same name, though the passage of time has added some weight to its prices (plats €17).

4ÈME ARRONDISSEMENT

The 4ème mixes modern and old; it is common to see Jewish rabbis walking just feet away from trendy fashionistas tottering on stilettos. Although the historical Marais sprawls over a considerable portion of the 4ème, bold and quirky architecture sprouts in the western part of the arrondissement in the form of the Centre Pompidou. Meanwhile, the east is crammed with old, adorable streets, a smattering churches and some of Paris's most beautiful mansions, or hôtels particuliers (particularly around the pl. des Vosges).

TO THE NORTH: BEAUBOURG

CENTRE POMPIDOU. Commissioned by President Pompidou in the early 70s as his presidential contribution to Paris culture, the Pompidou, according to the New York Times "turned the architecture world upside down." And not just the architecture world was affected: Parisians too were in shock. Erected in Beaubourg, a former slum quartier whose high rate of tuberculosis earned it classification as an îlot insalubre (unhealthy block) in the 1930s, the building is considered alternately an innovation and an eyesore. Pioneered by architects Richard Rogers, Gianfranco Franchini, and Renzo Piano, the design features color-coded electrical tubes (yellow), water pipes (green), and ventilation ducts (blue) along the exterior of the building. An ultra-modern exhibition, performance, and research space, the Pompidou also houses the **Musée National d'Art Moderne** (see **Museums,** p. 273). The **Salle Garance** hosts and adventurous film series, and the **Bibliothèque Publique d'Information** (entrance on rue de Renard) is a free, non-circulating library, which is almost always packed with students. Located in a separate building is the **Institut de la Recherche et de la Coordination Acoustique/Musique** (IRCAM), an institute and laboratory where scientists and musicians develop new technologies. The Pompidou was engineered to accommodate 5000 visitors a day, but the center now attracts over 20,000; more people visit the Pompidou every year than visit the Louvre. Don't miss the ■**spectacular view** from the top of the escalators, which can be reached only by purchasing a museum ticket or by dining at the rooftop restaurant, Georges (see **Food,** p. 175). The cobblestone square out front collects artists, musicians, punks, and passersby. As in all crowded spaces, keep an eye on your belongings. (ⓂRambuteau or Hôtel de Ville.)

IGOR STRAVINSKY FOUNTAIN. This novel installation features irreverent mobile sculptures by Niki de St. Phalle and Jean Tinguely. The whimsical elephants, lips, mermaid, and bowler hats are inspired by Stravinsky's works, and have been known to squirt water at unsuspecting bystanders. While the fountain's colorful quirkiness is in keeping with the Centre Pompidou, it stands in contrast to the nearby historic rue Brisemiche and Église de St-Merri. (In pl. Igor Stravinsky, adjacent to the Centre Pompidou on rue de Renard. ⓂHôtel de Ville.)

RUE DES ROSIERS. The heart of the Jewish community of the Marais, rue des Rosiers is packed with kosher shops, butchers, bakeries, and falafel counters (see **Food**, p. 175). Until the 13th century, Paris's Jewish population lived around Notre Dame, but when Philippe-Auguste expelled them from the city limits, many families moved to the Marais. During WWII, many who had fled to France to escape the pogroms of Eastern Europe were murdered by the Nazis. Assisted by French police, Nazi soldiers stormed the Marais and hauled Jewish families to the **Vélodrome d'Hiver,** an indoor cycling stadium. Here, French Jews awaited deportation to work camps like Drancy, in a northeastern suburb of Paris, or to camps farther east in Poland and Germany. The **Mémorial de la Déportation** commemorates these victims (p. 208). In the 1960s, new waves of North African Sephardim fleeing Algeria moved into the area. Today, the Marais's Jewish community thrives, with **two synagogues** (at 25 rue des Rosiers and 10 rue Pavée) designed by Art Nouveau architect Hector Guimard. The mix of Mediterranean and Eastern European Jewish cultures gives the area a unique flavor, with homemade *kugel* and the best falafel in Paris served side by side. (4 blocks east of Beaubourg, parallel to rue des Francs-Bourgeois. ⓂSt-Paul.)

RUE VIEILLE DU TEMPLE AND RUE STE-CROIX DE LA BRETTONERIE. Winter, spring, summer, fall—the intersection of rue Vieille du Temple and rue Ste-Croix de la Brettonerie is always hot. The epicenter of Paris's thriving GLBT community, these streets boast beautiful boys in tight pants and super-stylish girls walking hand-in-hand. The crowd here consists of variations of fabulous—dashing intellectuals frequent La Belle Hortense, a wine bar on the corner; loving couples share gelato at Amorino; trendy and aloof students hang out at the local bars; and women of all stripes come for some of the best **shopping** in the city. Especially on weekends, this is the place to see—and be seen in—an outift from one of the many surrounding boutiques. (ⓂSt-Paul or Hôtel de Ville. 1 block north of rue de Rivoli, runs the parallel rue du Roi de Sicile (which becomes rue de la Verrerie); rue Vieille du Temple meets it and, 1 block north, crosses rue Ste-Croix de la Brettonerie.)

HÔTEL DE VILLE AND SURROUNDINGS

HÔTEL DE VILLE. The Hôtel de Ville is the most extravagant non-palace building in Paris. The present structure is the second incarnation of the original edifice, which was built in medieval times and, during the 14th-15th centuries, served as a meeting hall for merchants who controlled traffic on the Seine. In 1533, King François I appointed Domenica da Cortona, known as Boccador, to expand and renovate the structure into a city hall worthy of Paris. The result was this building, in the Renaissance style of the Loire Valley châteaux.

On May 24, 1871, the Communards (see **Life and Times**, p. 69) doused the building with gasoline and set it on fire. Lasting a full eight days, the blaze spared nothing but the frame. The Third Republic built a virtually identical structure on the ruins, with a few significant changes. For one, the Republicans integrated statues of their own heroes into the facade: historian **Jules Michelet** graces the right side of the building while author **Eugène Sue** surveys the rue de Rivoli. They also installed crystal chandeliers, gilded every interior surface, and created a **Hall of Mirrors** in emulation of the original at Versailles. When Manet, Monet, Renoir, and Cézanne offered their services, they were all turned down in favor of the didactic artists whose work decorates the Salon des Lettres, the Salon des Arts, the Salon des Sciences, and the Salon Laurens. The information office holds exhibits on Paris in the lobby off the rue de Lobau.

Originally called pl. de Grève, the pl. Hôtel de Ville made a vital contribution to the French language. Poised on a marshy embankment (*grève*) of the Seine, the medieval square served as a meeting ground for angry workers, giving France the useful phrase *en grève* (on strike). In 1610, Henri IV's assassin was quartered alive here by four horses bolting in opposite directions. Today, place de Hôtel de Ville never sleeps: strikers continue to gather here, and less frequently, the square hosts concerts, special TV broadcasts, and light shows. Every major French sporting event—Rolland Garros, the Tour de France, and any game the Bleus ever play—is projected onto a jumbo screen in the *place*. *(Information office, 29 rue de Rivoli. ⓂHôtel de Ville. ☎01 42 76 43 43 or 01 42 76 50 49. Open M-F 9am-7pm when there is an exhibit; until 6pm otherwise. Group tours available with advance reservations, call for available dates. Special exhibit entry on rue de Lobau.)*

TOUR ST-JACQUES. Standing alone in its own park, this Flamboyant Gothic tower is the only remnant of the 16th-century Église St-Jacques-la-Boucherie. The 52m tower's meteorological station and the statue of Pascal at its base commemorate Pascal's experiments on the weight of air, performed here in 1648. The tower also marks Haussmann's *grande croisée* of rue de Rivoli and the bd. Sébastopol, the intersection of his east-west and north-south axes for the city. Currently, the tower is under renovation. *(39-41, rue de Rivoli. ⓂHôtel de Ville. 2 blocks west of the Hôtel de Ville.)*

SOUTH OF RUE ST-ANTOINE AND RUE DE RIVOLI

LA MAISON EUROPÉENNE DE LA PHOTOGRAPHIE. Located in the Hôtel Hénault de Cantobre, La Maison hosts both temporary exhibits featuring international contemporary photography and works from its permanent collection. The Hôtel also houses rotating galleries, an excellent library, and a *vidéothèque* with almost 600 films by photographers. *(5-7 rue de Fourcy. ⓂSt-Paul or Pont Marie. ☎01 44 78 75 00; www.mep-fr.org. Wheelchair accessible. Open W-Su 11am-7:45pm; last entry at 7:30pm. Admission €6, under 26 and seniors €3, under 8 free. W after 5pm free. Tours ☎01 44 78 75 30 or 01 44 78 75 24.)*

ÉGLISE ST-GERVAIS-ST-PROTAIS. St-Gervais-St-Protais was named after Gervase and Protase, two Romans martyred during Nero's reign. The Classical facade, Flamboyant Gothic vaulting, stained glass, and Baroque wooden Christ by Préault are part of a working convent. The exterior of the church dates to the 15th century, while the parish, going back to the 6th century, is thought to be the oldest on the Right Bank. *(Rue François-Miron. ⓂHôtel de Ville. Gregorian chant Tu-Sa 7am, Su 8am; vespers Tu-Sa 6pm, Su 6:30pm; mass Tu-Sa 6:30pm; high mass Su 11am.)*

HÔTEL DE BEAUVAIS. The Hôtel de Beauvais was built in 1654 for **Catherine Bellier**, wife of merchant Pierre de Beauvais and chambermaid/intimate of Anne d'Autriche. After the 40-year-old Mme. Bellier sexually "initiated" the Queen's son, the 16-year-old Louis XIV, her husband was promoted to royal advisor. In 1660, from the balcony of the *hôtel*, Anne d'Autriche and Cardinal Mazarin watched the entry of Louis XIV and his bride, the Spanish princess Marie-Thérèse, into Paris. A century later, Mozart played his first piano recital here as a guest of the Bavarian ambassador. Restored in 1967 and home to the Admin-

SIGHTS

istrative Court of Appeals since 1995, it is open to the public only through tours given by Paris Historique. *(Hôtel de Beauvais: 68, rue François-Miron.* Ⓜ*Hôtel de Ville. Paris Historique: 44-46, rue François Miron.* ☎*01 48 87 74 31. Open M-Sa 11am-6pm, Su 2-5pm.)*

HÔTEL DE SENS. One of the city's few surviving examples of medieval residential architecture and older than the Hotel de Cluny, the Hôtel de Sens was built in 1474 for Tristan de Salazar, the Archbishop of Sens. Its **military features** reflect the violence of the day: the turrets were designed to survey the streets outside, and the square tower served as a dungeon. An enormous Gothic arch entrance—complete with chutes for pouring boiling water on invaders—makes the mansion all the more intimidating. More importantly, as the former residence of Henri IV's first wife Marguerite de Valois, infamously known as Queen Margot, the Hôtel de Sens has witnessed some of Paris's most daring romantic escapades. In 1606, the 55-year-old queen drove up to the door of her home, in front of which her two current lovers were arguing. One opened the lady's carriage door, and the other shot him dead. Unfazed, the queen demanded the execution of the other, which she watched from a window the next day. The *hôtel* now houses the Bibliothèque Forney, a reference library for the fine arts open to the public, and a beautiful courtyard with an ornately designed garden. Special exhibits are held four times a year; call for schedule. *(1 rue du Figuier.* Ⓜ*Pont Marie.* ☎*01 42 78 14 60. Open Tu and F-Sa 1:30-7pm, W-Th 10am-7:30pm. Special exhibits €4, seniors and under 26 €2.)*

ÉGLISE ST-PAUL-ST-LOUIS. Dating from 1627 (when Louis XIII placed its first stone), the Église St-Paul dominates rue St-Antoine. Its large dome—a trademark of Jesuit architecture—is visible from afar but hidden by ornamentation on the facade. Paintings inside the dome depict four French kings: Clovis, Charlemagne, Robert the Pious, and St. Louis. The embalmed hearts of Louis XIII and Louis XIV were kept here in *vermeil* (ruby red) boxes before they were destroyed during the Revolution. The church's Baroque interior is graced with three 17th-century paintings of the life of St. Louis and Eugène Delacroix's dramatic Christ in the Garden of Olives (1826). The holy-water vessels were gifts from Victor Hugo. *(99 rue St-Antoine.* Ⓜ*St-Paul.* ☎*01 42 72 30 32. Open M-Sa 9am-10pm, Su 9am-8:30pm. Free tours in French at 3pm every 2nd Su of the month or upon request. Mass M 7pm; Tu-F 9am and 7pm; Sa 6pm; Su 9:30, 11am, 7pm.)*

17, RUE BEAUTREILLIS. **Jim Morrison** died here in his bathtub on the third floor, allegedly of a heart attack. There is no commemorative plaque, and today the building houses a massage parlor. In memoriam, visit his grave at the **Cimetière Père Lachaise** (p. 254). *(*Ⓜ*Bastille.)*

PLACE DES VOSGES AND SURROUNDINGS

◙**PLACE DES VOSGES.** At the end of rue des Francs-Bourgeois sits the magnificent pl. des Vosges, **Paris's oldest public square** and one of its best spots for a picnic or afternoon siesta. The central park **(sq. Louis XIII),** with manicured trees and four elegant fountains, is surrounded by Paris's most beautiful 17th-century Renaissance mansions. The Palais de Tournelles was built by Henri II, but his wife Catherine de Médicis had it destroyed after Henri died there in a jousting tournament in 1563. Henri IV later ordered the construction of a new public square as the first European project of royal city planning. During the Revolution, the statue of Louis XIII in the center of the park was destroyed (the current statue is a copy), and in 1800 the park was renamed pl. des Vosges, after the first department in France to pay its taxes. Today, the park is constantly full with frolicking families, cutesy couples, and snooty French teenagers.

All 36 buildings that line the square were constructed in the same design by Baptiste de Cerceau; each has arcades on the street level, two stories of pink brick, and a slate-covered roof. The largest townhouse, which forms the square's main entrance, was the **king's pavilion;** opposite is the smaller pavilion of the queen. Originally intended for merchants, the place Royale, as it was known, attracted nobility such as **Mme de Sevigné** (who was born at no. 1bis) and **Cardinal Richelieu** (who lived at no. 21). In the 18th century, **Molière, Racine,** and **Voltaire** filled the grand parlors with their *"bon mots,"* and **Mozart** played a concert here at the age of seven. Follow the arcades around the perimeter of pl. des Vosges for an elegant promenade, window shopping, and a glimpse at the plaques that mark the homes of famous residents. French poet **Théophile Gautier** and writer **Alphonse Daudet** lived at no. 8. **Victor Hugo** lived at no. 6, which is now a museum of his life and work (See **Museums**, p. 274). The corner door at the right of the south face of the *place* (between no. 5 and 7) leads into the garden of the **Hôtel de Sully.** (Ⓜ*Chemin Vert or St-Paul.*)

HÔTEL DE SULLY. Built in 1624, the Hôtel de Sully, was acquired by the Duc de Sully, minister to Henri IV. Often cuckolded by his young wife, Sully would say when giving her money, *"Voici tant pour la maison, tant pour vous, et tant pour vos amants"* (Here's some for the house, some for you, and some for your lovers). The classical composition of the building is adorned with elaborate, sculpted decoration representing the elements and the seasons. The inner courtyard accommodates fatigued tourists with benches, shade, and a formal garden. The building houses both an annex of the **Musée de Jeu de Paume** (see p. 274) and the **Centre d'Information des Monuments Nationaux,** which distributes free maps and brochures on Paris monuments and museums. The back garden contains an entrance into the pl. des Vosges. (*62 rue St-Antoine.* ⓂSt-Paul. Centre d'Information des Monuments Nationaux ☎01 44 61 20 00. Open M-Th 9am-12:45pm and 2-6pm, F 9am-12:45pm and 2-5pm.)

HÔTEL DE LAMOIGNON. Built in 1584 for Henri II's daughter, Diane de France, the Hôtel de Lamoignon is one of the finest *hôtels particuliers* in the Marais. The facade's Colossal style was copied later in the Louvre. Now the site of the Bibliothèque Historique de la Ville de Paris, a non-circulating library of Parisian history with 800,000 volumes, Lamoignon also hosts rotating art exhibits on Paris. The quiet courtyard on the rue des Francs-Bourgeois is great for picnicking or sunbathing. (*22 rue Malher.* ⓂSt-Paul. Exhibition hall ☎01 44 59 29 60. Open Tu-Su 11am-7pm. €4, students and seniors €2, under 8 free. Bibliothèque open M-Sa 9am-6pm.)

LATIN QUARTER AND ST-GERMAIN

5ÈME ARRONDISSEMENT

Paris's undisputed intellectual epicenter, the *5ème* brims with university campuses, musty bookstores, and cozy cafes. History buffs will adore the epic Panthéon, while those looking for a place to relax cannot miss the Mosquée de Paris's steam baths.

TO THE WEST: LATIN QUARTER

PLACE ST-MICHEL. The Latin Quarter meets the Seine at this monumental locale where the 1871 Paris Commune and the 1968 student uprising began. Although locals disdain from venturing here, tourists pose for photos in front of the square's centerpiece, a majestic 1860 **fountain** featuring St-Michel slaying a demon. Several branches of the **Gibert Joseph/Jeune** bookstore fan out along bd. St-Michel, while lesser known antiquarian booksellers and university presses surround the place, ready to indulge even the most arcane of literary appetites (see **Shopping,** p. 304). For those more interested in feeding their stomachs than their minds, an overwhelming number of crêpe stands and gyro counters pack rue St-Séverin and rue de la Huchette. Watch your belongings, as pickpockets like to operate in the busy place.

Modern stained glass and spiraling columns decorate the **Gothic Église St-Séverin.** *(1 rue des Prêtres-St-Séverin. ☎01 42 34 93 50. Follow rue de la Harpe away from the place and turn left on rue St-Séverin.)* One of Paris's oldest churches, the Église St-Julien-le-Pauvre, across bd. St-Jacques from St-Séverin, dates from 1120. *(1 rue St-Julien-le-Pauvre, ☎01 43 54 52 16.)* At the intersection of bd. St-Germain and bd. St-Michel, the **Musée de Cluny** houses an extraordinary collection of medieval art, famous tapestries, and illuminated manuscripts (see **Museums,** p. 275). Visitors can check out the traditional bistros on nearby rue Soufflot and rue des Fossés St-Jacques. *(Ⓜ St-Michel.)*

LA SORBONNE. Founded in 1257 by Robert de Sorbon as a dormitory for poor theology students, the Sorbonne has since diversified its curriculum and earned a place among the world's most esteemed universities. Soon after its founding, it became the administrative base for the University of Paris and the site of France's first printing house, opened in 1470. Growing in power and size, the Sorbonne often defied the French throne, even siding with England during the Hundred Years' War. Today, the French government controls the Sorbonne, integrating the college into its extensive public education system. Of the University of Paris's 13 campuses, "the Sorbonne" comprises four: **Paris I, Paris III, Paris IV,** and **Paris V.** Specifically, students studying at Paris IV take classes at the original 13th-century complex. Cardinal Richelieu commissioned the Sorbonne's main building, **Ste-Ursule de la Sorbonne,** in 1642. Befitting its elite status, the Sorbonne remains closed to the public through 2011, when the **Chapelle de la Sorbonne** will re-open after lengthy restoration. Bookstores, cafes, and students sprinkle the nearby place de la Sorbonne, making it a favorite people-watching destination. *(45-47 rue des Écoles, 5ème. Ⓜ Cluny-La Sorbonne or RER: Luxembourg. Walk away from the Seine on bd. St-Michel and turn left on rue des Écoles to see the main building.)*

COLLÈGE DE FRANCE. Created by François I in 1530 as an alternative to the Sorbonne, the Collège de France lies behind its more prestigious counterpart. The humanist motto **"Doce Omnia"** (Teach Everything) is emblazoned in mosaics in the interior courtyard. Originally the **"Collège Royal"** consisted of six lecturers including 1 math, 2 Greek, and 2 Hebrew professors. Courses at the Collège—given in the past by such luminaries as Henri Bergson, Pierre Boulez, Michel Foucault, and Paul Valéry—are free and open to all. Lecture schedules are posted around the courtyard. *(11 place Marcelin-Berthelot, 5ème. Ⓜ Maubert-Mutualité. Walk against traffic on bd. St-Germain, turn left on rue Thenard; the entrance to the Collège is at the end of the road, across rue des Écoles and up the steps. ☎01 44 27 11 47; www.college-de-france.fr. Courses Oct.-May. Reception open M-F 9am-6pm. Closed Aug.)*

PANTHÉON. Among Paris's most impressive buildings, the Panthéon displays geometric grandeur and a historical nod to the dead. Some of France's greatest citizens are buried in the Panthéon's crypt, including chemists Marie and Pierre Curie, politician Jean Jaurès, inventor Louis Braille, author Voltaire, philosopher Jean-Jacques Rousseau, writer Emile Zola, and playwright Victor Hugo. The crypt also contains the heart of Léon Gambetta in a big red urn. Fans of Le Petit Prince can pay homage to Antoine de St-Exupéry in the main rotunda. Alexandre Dumas became the crypt's most recent addition, following his November 2002 interment.

Intending to build his wife a basilica, King Clovis designed the original Panthéon in AD 507 to accommodate the royal couple's future tombs. In 512, **St. Geneviève,** believed to have saved Paris from the marauding Huns, was buried alongside the king and queen. Her tomb immediately became a pilgrimage site, with dedicated worshippers calling themselves Génovéfains. Ascribing his recovery from grave illness to the powers of Ste-Geneviève, Louis XV transformed the basilica into the awesome monument seen today. He entrusted the design to architect Jacques-Germain Soufflot but insisted on laying the first stone himself in 1764. On April 4, 1791, in the midst of the Revolution, the Panthéon was converted into a mausoleum for heroes. Compte de Mirabeau, a great orator during the Revolution, received the first nomination for a Panthéon burial. Although interred there, Mirabeau did not rest peacefully as the government expelled his ashes one year later when the public discovered his counter-revolutionary correspondence with Louis XVI. In 1806, Napoleon reserved the crypt for those who had given "great service to the State." An inscription in stone across the Panthéon's front declares, **"Aux Grands Hommes La Patrie Reconnaisante"** (To the great men, a grateful fatherland).

Beyond its crypt, the Panthéon's other main attraction is a famous science experiment: **Foucault's Pendulum.** The pendulum's plane of oscillation stays fixed as the Earth rotates around it, confirming the Earth's rotation. Louis Napoleon III was among those present at its February 1851 unveiling. *(place du Panthéon, 5ème. Ⓜ️Cardinal Lemoine or RER: Luxembourg. From rue Cardinal Lemoine, turn right on rue Clovis; enter on the other side. ☎01 44 32 18 04. Open daily Apr.-Sept. 10am-6:30pm, Oct.-Mar. 10am-6pm. Last entry 45min. before closing. Crypt open daily 10am-6pm. Dome visits Apr.-Oct. Dutch-, English-, French-, German-, Russian-, and Spanish-language tours. €7.50, ages 18-25 €4.80, under 18 and 1st Su of the month Oct.-Mar. free. MC/V. Conservative dress required.)*

ÉGLISE ST-ÉTIENNE DU MONT. Now outshadowed by its grander neighbor, the smaller Église St-Étienne once vied with the Panthéon for cryptic fame. The church has the French Revolution to blame for its disintegrated status; mathematician **Blaise Pascal** and dramatist **Jean Racine** were buried there until 1792. Its atypical facade blends Gothic windows, an ancient belfry, and a Renaissance dome. Inside, the church's central attraction still inspires awe. Sculpted from stone and flanked by spiral staircases, the **rood-screen** is among the last of its kind in Paris, after the other screens used to separate the priest from his congregation were removed to make way for an altar. To the right of the nave, check out a Herculean Samson holding up the wood-carved pulpit. *(30 rue Descartes, place de l'Abbé Basset, to the right of the Panthéon, 5ème. Ⓜ️Cardinal Lemoine. ☎01 43 54 11 79. Open M noon-7:30pm, Tu-F 8:45am-7:30pm, Sa-Su 8:45am-noon and 2-7:45pm. Mass Su-M 6:45pm, Tu-F 12:15pm and 6:45pm, Sa 9am, 11am, and 6:45pm.)*

ÉCOLE NORMALE SUPÉRIEURE. France's premier university, the École Normale Supérieure is located southeast of the Sorbonne and is part of the **Grands Écoles,** a consortium of prestigious French schools. Normale Sup'—as its students, the *normaliens,* call it—has programs in literature, philosophy, and the natural sciences. Its graduates include Michel Foucault, Louis Pasteur, and Jean-Paul Sartre. *(45 rue d'Ulm, 5ème. Ⓜ️Cluny-La Sorbonne or RER: Luxembourg. ☎01 44 32 30 00; www.ens.fr. Closed to the public.)*

TO THE EAST: PLACE DE LA CONTRESCARPE

RUE MOUFFETARD. The 5ème's rue Mouffetard, south of place de la Contrescarpe, hosts one of Paris's oldest and liveliest street markets (see **Food,** p. 180). The stretch up rue Mouffetard, past **place de la Contrescarpe,** and onto rue Descartes and rue de la Montagne Ste-Geneviève, is the quintessential Latin Quarter stroll, attracting a mix of Parisians and visitors. Hemingway lived on the Mouff at 74 rue du Cardinal Lemoine while poet Paul Verlaine died in the same neighborhood at 39 rue Descartes. *(5ème. ⓂCardinal Lemoine, Place Monge, or Censier Daubenton.)*

JARDIN DES PLANTES. In the *5ème*'s eastern corner, the Jardin des Plantes has 260,000 square meters of carefully-tended flowers and lush greenery. Opened in 1633 by Louis XIII's doctor, the gardens originally grew medicinal plants to promote His Majesty's health. Today, it seems like the soil is as good for nine-year-old French children as it is for flowers, and the constant hum of construction detracts from the peaceful atmosphere. The gardens also serve as a sanctuary for the natural sciences, surrounded on both sides by numerous state museums, research institutions, and scientific libraries. The gardens also include the fantastic **Musée d'Histoire Naturelle** (see **Museums, p. 276**) and the **Ménagerie Zoo.** Although no match for the Parc Zoologique in the Bois de Vincennes, the zoo houses 240 mammals, 500 birds, and 130 reptiles. During the 1871 siege of Paris, starving Parisians ate a few of the elephants; it wasn't cake but at least they got fed. An info hut adjacent to place Valhubert provides free maps and brochures. *(5ème. ⓂGare d'Austerlitz, Jussieu, or Censier-Daubenton. ☎01 40 79 37 94; www. mnhn.fr. Jardin des Plantes and Roserie open daily in summer 7:30am-7:45pm, in winter 7:30am-7:30pm. Free. Jardin Alpin open M-F 8am-5pm, Sa 1:30-6pm, Su and holidays 1:30-6:30pm. Free. Grandes Serres, 57 rue Cuvier. Due to re-open in 2009. Ménagerie Zoo, 3 quai St-Bernard and 57 rue Cuvier. Open Apr.-Sept. M-Sa 9am-6pm, Su and holidays 9am-6:30pm; Oct.-Mar. daily 10am-5pm. Last entry 30min. before closing. €7, students and ages 4-13 €5, under 3 free. Info desk open daily 10am-5pm. Mid-May to Oct. free guided tours; call ☎01 40 79 37 94 for more info.)*

MOSQUÉE DE PARIS. Built in 1920 to honor the role of North African countries in WWI, the **Institut Musulman** houses the elaborate *minaret* and shady porticoes of the Mosquée de Paris. The dense cedar doors lead to ascetic prayer rooms, visible from the courtyard but closed to the public. All visitors can relax in the exquisite hammam's **steam baths** or sip mint tea at the soothing cafe (see **Food,** p. 180). Dress appropriately: bare shoulders and legs are discouraged. *(2bis place du puits de l'Ermite, 5ème. Behind Jardin des Plantes at place du Puits de l'Ermite. ⓂCensier Daubenton. Walk down rue Daubenton and turn left at the end of the street onto rue Georges Desplas; the mosque is on the right. ☎01 45 35 97 33; www.mosquee-de-paris.net. Restaurant and steam baths ☎01 43 31 38 20; www.la-mosquee.com. Open Sa-Th 9am-noon and 2-6pm. Guided tour €3, students €2. Hammam open for men Tu 2-9pm, Su 10am-9pm; women M, W-Th, and Sa 10am-9pm, F 2-9pm; €15. 10min. massage €10, 30min. €30. Bikini wax €11. MC/V.)*

ARÈNES DE LUTÈCE. Once an outdoor theater, the Arènes de Lutèce now serves as a glorified sand-pit used for pick-up games of soccer or boules. Romans built the theater in the first century AD to accommodate 10,000 spectators but their arena suffered sever damage during 3rd-century invasions. Similar to the remains of oval amphitheaters in Rome and southern France, the ruins were unearthed in 1869 and restored in 1917; all the seats are reconstructions. *(At the intersection of rue de Navarre and rue des Arènes, 5ème. ⓂPlace Monge or Jussieu. Free Wi-Fi. Open in summer M-F 8am-9:30pm, Sa-Su and holidays 9am-9:30pm; in winter M-F 8am-5:30pm, Sa-Su and holidays 9am-5:30pm.)*

ALONG THE SEINE

SHAKESPEARE & CO. BOOKSTORE. Sylvia Beach's original Shakespeare and Co., at 8 rue Dupuytren (later at 12 rue de l'Odéon), is legendary among Parisian Anglophones. Expats gathered here in the 20s, and Hemingway described it memorably in *A Moveable Feast.* The shop is most famous for publishing **James Joyce's Ulysses** in 1922 when it was deemed too obscene to print in England and America. The original shop closed in 1941 when, as store legend recalls, the anglophone store clerk refused to sell books to a German. George Whitman—unrelated to Walt—opened the current rag-tag bookstore in 1951. Frequented by Allen Ginsberg and Lawrence Ferlinghetti, Shakespeare hosts **poetry readings,** free Sunday afternoon **tea parties** (4pm), a semi-annual **literary festival,** and other **funky events.** No traces of the Lost Generation remain, but there are plenty of lost boys and girls who call its burlap couches home. See **Shopping,** p. 304. *(37 rue de la Bûcherie, 5ème.* ⓂSt-Michel. 01 43 25 40 93; www.shakespeareco.org. Festival info at www.festivalandco.com. Open daily 10am-11pm.)

6ÈME ARRONDISSEMENT

The 6ème's grandest attraction is the big and beautiful **Jardin de Luxembourg** and the palace within it. The **Église de St-Sulpice,** also a significant site, has much increased in popularity thanks to Dan Brown's imagination and Tom Hanks's acting in *The Da Vinci Code.*

JARDIN DU LUXEMBOURG AND ODÉON

▨JARDIN DU LUXEMBOURG AND PALAIS DU LUXEMBOURG. "There is nothing more charming, which invites one more enticingly to idleness, reverie, and young love, than a soft spring morning or a beautiful summer dusk at the Jardin du Luxembourg," wrote Léon Daudet in an absolute **fit of sentimentality** in 1928. Parisians flock to these spectacular formal gardens—despite the truly violent winds—to sunbathe, stroll, and read by the rose gardens and central pool. The chairs conveniently placed along the paths and big, open views of the sky make it difficult to walk through without pausing to take a seat. Beware of **ostentatious PDAs,** though: kissing and touching in public is *à la mode* in Paris. The gardens themselves have been through many eras and uses; a residential area in Roman Paris, the site of a medieval monastery, and later the home of 17th-century French royalty, they were liberated during the Revolution and are now free to all. Children can sail toy boats in the fountain, ride ponies, and see the grand *guignol* (puppet show; see **Entertainment, p. 319**)while their granddads pitch *boules.* Visitors saunter through the park's sandy paths, passing sculptures of France's queens, poets, and heroes. The best and the brightest come to challenge the local cadre of aged chessmasters to a game under the shady chestnut trees, or sit and nap by the Renaissance facade of the Palais du Luxembourg. One of the loveliest spots in the Jardin is the **Fontaine des Médicis,** just east of the Palais, a vine-covered grotto complete with a murky fish pond and Baroque fountain sculptures. In 2005, a Swedish artist added a new touch to the ancient fountain: a **giant nose.** The sculpture is in complete contrast to the surroundings and well worth a visit. A mammoth task force of gardeners tends the grounds—each spring they plant or transplant 350,000 flowers and move 150 palm and orange trees out of winter storage. As in most public parks, you'll notice *"Pelouse Interdite"* signs forbidding you to sit on the grass; use the benches or find the grassy knolls where lounging is permitted. *(6ème.* ⓂOdéon or RER: Luxembourg. The main entrance is on bd. St-Michel. Open daily dawn-dusk. Guided tours in French Apr.-Oct. 1st W of every month at 9:30am and every W during June; depart from pl. André Honorat behind the observatory.)The **Palais du Luxembourg,** located within the park and built in 1615 for Marie de Medicis, is now home to the **French Senate** and thus closed to the public. Homesick for Florence, the Queen Marie tried to recreate her native architecture in her new Parisian home. During WWII, the palace was used by the Nazis as headquarters for the Luftwaffe. *(6ème. www.monum.fr.)*

MUSÉE DU LUXEMBOURG. The Musée du Luxembourg is housed in the historic Palais du Luxembourg and offers rotating art exhibitions featuring everything from classical to contemporary artists. With primary funding from the

Ministère de la Culture et la Communication, the Musée has recently exhibited the celebrated oeuvres of Maurice de Vlaminck and Giuseppe Arcimboldo. *(19, r. de Vaugirard. ⓂOdéon. Walk through the Carrefour de l'Odéon and down r. de Conde; turn right on r. Vaugirard; the museum entrance is on the left. €11, ages 10-25 €9. Open M, F, Sa 10:30am-10pm; Tu, W, Th 10:30am-7pm; Su 9am-7pm. Last entry 45min. before closing. Wheelchair accessible. Audioguides available for €3.50 in English, French, Spanish, German, Italian, and Dutch.)*

PALAIS DE L'INSTITUT DE FRANCE. The Palais de l'Institut de France broods over the Seine from beneath its famous black-and-gold dome. Designed by Le Vau to lodge a college established in Cardinal Mazarin's will, it has served as a school (1688-1793), a prison (1793-1805), and is now home to the **Académie Française,** devoted to the patronage of the arts, letters, and sciences. The *académicians,* who rather modestly call themselves "The Immortals," were symbolically militarized by Napoleon and thus wear snazzy green jackets and carry swords—very useful in their task of regulating the French language. The glorious building has housed the Académie since 1806 and also contains the Bibliothèque Mazarine, founded in 1643. The Palais is not open to the public, but peek inside the courtyard to the right—if the doors are open—to catch a glimpse of Mazarin's funeral sculpture. The grounds are frequently open for historical seminars and conferences. *(Pl. de l'Institut. ⓂPont Neuf. Walk west on quai du Louvre and cross the Seine on the Pont des Arts. 1 block to the east of the ENSB-A on quai Malaquai. Check Pariscope or Figaroscope for listings of frequent seminars, lectures, and openings. A schedule is also available from just inside the gates in the office on the left.)*

THÉÂTRE DE L'ODÉON. The Théâtre de l'Odéon is Paris's oldest and largest theater (see **Entertainment,** p. 314). Upon its completion in 1782, it was purchased by Louis XVI and Marie-Antoinette for the **Comédie Française,** Molière's celebrated theater troupe. Beaumarchais's *Marriage of Figaro,* which was nearly banned by Louis XVI for its attacks on the nobility, delighted aristocrats at its 1784 premiere. As the revolution approached, the *Comédie Française* splintered over political loyalties. Republican members moved to the Right Bank, settling into the company's current location near the Louvre. The actors who remained behind were jailed under the Reign of Terror and the theater closed. It later earned the name *théâtre maudit* (cursed theater) after two fires and a chain of flops left it nearly bankrupt. The Odéon's fortunes changed after WWII, when it became a venue for experimental theater. *(ⓂOdéon. Walk down the Carrefour and r. de l'Odéon to pl. de l'Odéon.)*

ÉGLISE ST-SULPICE. The Neoclassical facade of Église St-Sulpice dominates the large square of the same name, stomping ground for children and street vendors and home to a lovely fountain. Designed by Servadoni in 1733, the church is unfinished, and also in need of a restoration. Look for the set of Delacroix frescoes in the first chapel on the right (*Jacob Wrestling with the Angel* and *Heliodorus Driven from the Temple*), Jean-Baptiste Pigalle's *Virgin and Child* in a rear chapel, and a large organ used in frequent concerts. The stark, poorly-lit interior provides an unbecoming setting for these three gems. In the transept, an inlaid copper band runs along the floor from north to south, connecting a plaque in the south to an obelisk in the north. A ray of sunshine passes through a hole in the upper window of the south transept during the winter solstice, striking a marked point on the obelisk at midday. A beam of sunlight falls on the copper plaque during the summer solstice, and behind the communion table during the spring and autumn equinoxes. *(50, r. Vaugirard. ⓂSt-Sulpice or Mabillon. From ⓂMabillon, walk down r. du Four and make a left onto r. Mabillon, which intersects r. St-Sulpice at the entrance to the church.☎01 42 34 59 60; www.paroisse-saint-sulpice-paris.org. Open daily 7:30am-7:30pm. Guided tour in French Su 3pm.)*

ST-GERMAIN-DES-PRÉS

Known as the Village de St-Germain-des-Prés, the area around boulevard St-Germain between St-Sulpice and the Seine is packed with cafes, restaurants, galleries, cinemas, and expensive boutiques.

BOULEVARD ST-GERMAIN. Most famous as the former literati hangout of Existentialists (who frequented the **Café de Flore,** p. 182) and Surrealists (who preferred **Les Deux Magots, p. 182**), the bd. St-Germain is torn between nostalgia for its smoky, intellectual past and unabashed delight with all things fashionable and cutting-edge. It is home to scores of cafes, both new and old, where expensive coffee is *de rigueur.* The boulevard and the many sidestreets around rue de Rennes have become a serious shopping area (see **Shopping,** p. 303), filled with designer boutiques. (Ⓜ*St-Germain-des-Prés.*)

ÉGLISE ST-GERMAIN-DES-PRÉS. The Église St-Germain-des-Prés is the oldest church in Paris, and it shows: the only remaining decorations on the church's exterior are pink and white hollyhocks growing on one side. The last remnant of what was once one of the richest abbeys in the world, the church was the centerpiece of the **Abbey of St-Germain-des-Prés,** a center of Catholic intellectual life until it was disbanded during the Revolution. King Childebert I commissioned a church on this site to hold relics he had looted from the Holy Land. Completed in AD 558, it was consecrated by **Germain,** Bishop of Paris, on the day of King Childebert's death—the king was buried inside the church's walls. The rest of the church's history reads like an architectural Book of Job. Sacked by the Normans and rebuilt three times, the present-day church dates from the 11th century. On June 30, 1789, precocious revolutionaries seized the church two weeks before the storming of the Bastille. The church then had a brief stint as a saltpeter mill, and in 1794, 15 tons of gunpowder that had been stored in the abbey exploded. The ensuing fire devastated the church's artwork and treasures, including much of its monastic library. Haussmann destroyed the last remains of the deteriorating abbey walls and gates when he extended rue de Rennes to the front of the church and created pl. St-Germain-des-Prés. What remains of the abbey's exterior looks appropriately world-weary.

Completely redone in the 19th century, the magnificent interior is painted in shades of maroon, deep green, and gold—enough regal grandeur to counteract the building's modest exterior. Especially striking are the royal blue and gold-starred ceiling, frescoes (by a pupil of Ingres) depicting the life of Jesus, and decorative mosaics along the archways. In the second chapel—on the right after the apse—a stone marks the interred heart of 17th-century philosopher René Descartes, who died of pneumonia at the frigid court of Queen Christina of Sweden. Here, visitors can also find an altar dedicated to the victims of the September 1792 massacre, in which 186 refractory priests were slaughtered in the courtyard. The information window at the entrance has a schedule of the church's frequent concerts. *(3 pl. St-Germain-des-Prés.* Ⓜ*St-Germain-des-Prés. Walk through pl. St-Germain-des-Prés to enter from the front.* ☎*01 55 42 81 33. Open daily 8am-7:45pm. Info office open M 2:30-6:45pm, Tu-F 10:30am-noon and 2:30-6:45pm, Sa 3-6:45pm.)*

ÉCOLE NATIONALE SUPÉRIEURE DES BEAUX-ARTS. Napoleon founded France's most acclaimed art school in 1811 and it quickly became the stronghold of French academic painting and sculpture. Its current building, the **Palais des Études,** was finished in 1838 and represents a mix of architectural styles. Though the public is not normally permitted to tour the building, you may be able to prowl around its gated courtyard. The best shot at a glimpse of the life-blood of the École des Beaux-Arts, however, is the **Exhibition Hall** at no. 13, *quai* Malaquais, where you can get a look at the painting, photography, and installation work of an exciting new generation of Parisian *artistes*. *(14, r. Bonaparte, No. 13 at quai Malaquais.* Ⓜ*St-Germain-des-Prés.* ☎*01 47 03 50 00; www.ensba.fr. Tours by reservation; call ahead. Open Tu-Su 1-7pm. €4, students €2.50. 2 "open days" each year allow the public to peruse studios and teaching areas. Call for schedule and info.)*

ODÉON. Cour du Commerce St-André, branching off bd. St-Germain to the north, is one of the most picturesque walking areas in the 6*ème*, with cobblestone streets, age-old cafes (including **Le Procope**; see **Food**, p. 183), and outdoor seating. Beyond the arch at the north end of the Cour du Commerce stands the **Relais Odéon,** a Belle Époque bistro whose stylishly painted exterior, decked with floral mosaics and a hanging sign, is a fine example of Art Nouveau. The doorway of no. 7, rue Mazarine, several blocks north, is decorated in the same Belle Époque style. Farther down this passageway, on the top floor of the building on the left, is the site where a clandestine Revolutionary-era press published Jean-Paul Marat's *L'Ami du Peuple.* Marat was assassinated by Charlotte Corday in the bathtub of his home, which once stood at the spot where the *cour* meets rue de l'Ancienne Comédie. Just to the south of bd. St-Germain is the **Carrefour de l'Odéon,** a favorite Parisian hangout filled with sidewalk bistros and cafes that are a bit calmer than their counterparts on the bd. St-Germain, perhaps because their denizens are thinking and scribbling. *(*Ⓜ*St-Germain-des-Prés.)*

PONT DES ARTS. The footbridge across from the Institut de France, appropriately called the Pont des Arts, is one of the most beautiful bridges in Paris. Celebrated by poets and artists for its delicate ironwork, its unparalleled views of the Seine, and its spiritual locus at the heart of France's **Academy of Arts and Letters,** it was built as a toll bridge in 1803 and was the first bridge to be made of iron. On the day it opened, 65,000 Parisians paid to walk across it; today, it is less crowded, free, and perfect for a picnic dinner, a view of the sunset, and a little romance. The bridge is also occasional host to public art exhibits.

CAFÉ DE FLORE AND LES DEUX MAGOTS. These two literary landmarks—once the hangouts of Brigitte Bardot, Pablo Picasso, and Albert Camus—are now sadly filled with crowds of tourists and businessmen willing to pay for the history with exorbitantly priced coffee (€4-7). While neither merits a culinary stop, the cafes offer plenty of opportunities for intellectual idolatry. Sartre composed his seminal "*L'Être et le Néant*" ("Being and Nothingness") in Café de Flore, no doubt intertwined with lover Simone de Beauvoir in the upstairs Art Deco booth they shared. The Flore also distributes an annual literary prize for distinguished French language fiction, another vestigial tribute to its literary history. Not to be outdone, Les Deux Magots awards a much older annual award for 'best novel,' and boasts a cloistered area behind high hedges that was home to a legacy from Mallarmé to Hemingway. *(See Food, p. 182.)*

INVALIDES (7ÈME)

The 7*ème*'s undisputed focal point is the famous Eiffel Tower, but the *arrondissement* boasts plenty of other magnificent sights. The physical seat of the French national government and the home of a smattering of embassies, it is one of Paris' more serious and sophisticated areas. The neighborhood is extremely pleasing to the eye, as are many things that lack a soul.

TO THE WEST

▓ EIFFEL TOWER

Ⓜ️ *Bir-Hakeim or Trocadéro.* ☎ *01 44 11 23 23; www.tour-eiffel.fr. Open daily Jan. to mid-June and Sept.-Dec., elevator 9:30am-11:45pm (last access 11pm), stairs 9:30am-6:30pm (last access 6pm); mid-June to Aug., elevator 9am-12:45am (last access 11pm), stairs 9am-12:45am (last access midnight). Elevator to 1st fl. €5, under 12 €2.50, under 3 free; 2nd fl. €8/4.50/free; summit €12/7/free. Stairs to 1st and 2nd fl. €4, under 25 €3, under 3 free.*

Gustave Eiffel, who also engineered the Statue of Liberty, wrote of his tower: "France is the only country in the world with a 300m flagpole." The Eiffel Tower was designed in 1889 as the **tallest structure in the world**—a monument to engineering that would surpass the Egyptian pyramids in size and notoriety. Parisians were not impressed: before construction had even begun, shocks of dismay reverberated throughout the city. Critics dubbed it a "metal asparagus" and a Parisian Tower of Babel. After the tower's completion, writer Guy de Maupassant ate lunch every day at its ground-floor restaurant—the only place in Paris, he claimed, from which he couldn't see the offensive thing.

It wasn't until the tower was inaugurated in March 1889 as the centerpiece of the **World's Fair** that Parisians finally came around. Nearly two million people ascended it during the event. Of course, the tower was more than just an architectural controversy: in WWI it functioned as a radio-telegraphic center, which intercepted enemy messages, including the one that led to the arrest of Mata Hari, the Danish dancer accused of being a German spy. With the 1937 World's Fair, the Eiffel Tower again became a showpiece, Eiffel himself remarking: "I ought to be jealous of that tower; she is more famous than I am."

Since the expo, Parisians and tourists alike have reclaimed the monument in over 150 million visits. An icon of Paris represented on everything from postcards to neckties and umbrellas, Eiffel's wonder still takes heat from some who see it as Maupassant did: an "excruciating nightmare" overrun with tourists, trinkets, and false promises of clichéd romance. Don't believe the anti-hype, though. The tower is a wonder of design and engineering; no matter how much the aesthetic might turn you off, it's a sight to behold, especially up close. The top floor, with its unparalleled view, is especially deserving of a visit. And despite the 7000 tons of metal and 2.5 million rivets that hold together its 12,000 parts, the tower appears light and elegant. The distinctive bronze color is repainted every seven years and is graduated from a lighter tone at the summit to a darker one at the base to highlight the elegant line of perspective.

The cheapest way to ascend the tower is by walking up the first two floors. The third floor is only accessible by elevator. It's a good idea to wait until nightfall to make your ascent, as lines tend to be shorter after dark. At the top, captioned aerial photographs help you locate landmarks. On a clear day it is possible to see **Chartres** 88km away (see **Daytrips**, p. 345). From dusk until 2am (1am Sept.-May), the tower sparkles with light for 10min. on the hour.

NEAR THE TOWER

CHAMPS DE MARS. The tree-lined (and often lover-lined) expanse that stretches from the École Militaire to the Eiffel Tower is called the Champs de Mars (Field of Mars). Close to the *7ème*'s military monuments and museums, its history suggests a number of reasons why it should celebrate the Roman god of war. In the days of Napoleon's Empire, the field was used as a **drill ground** for the adjacent École Militaire, and in 1780, Charles Montgolfier launched the first **hydrogen balloon** from this site. During the Revolution, the park witnessed civilian massacres and political demonstrations. Nowadays, the series of bright green lawns are filled with hordes of tourists during the day and rambunctious French teenagers at night. In 2000, a glass monument to international peace was erected at the end of the Champs in quiet defiance of the École Militaire across the way. Named the **Mur pour la Paix** (Wall for Peace), the structure consists of two large glass walls covered from top to bottom with the word "peace" written in 32 languages.(Ⓜ*La Motte Picquet-Grenelle or École Militaire.*)

ÉCOLE MILITAIRE. In 1751, Louis XV founded the École Militaire at the urging of his mistress, Mme. de Pompadour, who hoped to make officers of "poor gentlemen." In 1784, 15-year-old Napoleon Bonaparte enrolled. A few weeks later, he presented administrators with a comprehensive plan for the school's reorganization, and by the time he graduated three years later, he was a lieutenant in the artillery. Teachers foretold he would "go far in favorable circumstances." Louis XVI made the building into a barracks for the Swiss Guard, but it was converted back into a military school in 1848. Today, the building houses the living quarters of the Chief of the National Army, the Minstry of Defense, and a variety of schools for advanced military studies, such as the Institute for Higher Studies of National Defense, the Center for Higher Studies of the Military, the Inter-Army College of Defense, and the School of Reserve Specialist Officers of the State. (*1 pl. Joffre.* Ⓜ*École Militaire.*)

UNESCO. The École Militaire's architectural and spiritual antithesis, UNESCO (United Nations Educational, Scientific, and Cultural Organization), occupies the Y-shaped, concrete-and-glass building across the road. Established in 1958 to foster science and culture throughout the world, the organization built this major international monument in Paris to represent its 188 member nations. The design itself is the work of three international architects: American Marcel Breuer, Italian Luigi Nervi, and Frenchman Bernard Zehrfuss. Don't be deterred by the institutional exterior: the organization welcomes visitors, and the exhibits and permanent pieces are worth the hassle of navigating the entrance.

In the outer courtyard, a huge sculpture by Henri Moore called **Figure in Repose** is joined by a **mobile** by the American Alexander Calder and a **walking man** by Swiss sculptor Alberto Giacometti. The large framework globe by Danish artist Erik Reitzel is eye-catching amongst the hedges. Two murals by Joán Miró and Josep Llorens Artigas, *The Wall of the Sun* and *The Wall of the Moon*, reside in the **Miró Halles.** Inside the foyer of Room I is Picasso's *Fall of Icarus*, and next door in the Salle des Actes is a tapestry by architect Le Corbusier. Behind Ségur Hall there is a lovely Japanese garden of peace by Japanese-American Isamu Noguchi. A serene oasis filled with goldfish and turtles, it lies to the side of metal sculptures by Vassilakis Takis and an angel from the facade of a Nagasaki church destroyed by the atomic bomb during WWII. (*7 pl. de Fontenoy.* Ⓜ*Ségur.* ☎ *01 45 68 05 16; www.unesco.org. Open M-F 9am-12:30pm and 2:30-6pm. Bookshop open M-F 9am-noon and 2:30-5:15pm; exhibits open M-F 9am-6pm. French or English tours M and W at 3pm upon reservation. Free; bring some form of identification. Pick up a map of the building at the information desk to your left, beyond the elevators after you enter.*)

AMERICAN CHURCH IN PARIS. The first American church founded on foreign soil has become an interdenominational meeting-place for expats and travelers. Besides being a good place for visitor information (such as job and apartment listings and language courses), the church hosts concerts—usually chamber music and solo classical performances—September through May on Sundays at 5pm. The brick and stone Gothic structure surrounds a charming courtyard. The church itself is only open during services. (*65, quai d'Orsay, at the corner of quai d'Orsay and rue A. Moissan.* Ⓜ*Invalides.* ☎ *01 40 62 05 00; www.acparis.org. Traditional services Su at 9, 11am; New Contemporary services Su 1:30pm.*)

TO THE EAST

INVALIDES. At the center of the 7ème, the gold-leaf dome of the Hôtel des Invalides glimmers conspicuously rain or shine, adding a touch of brilliance to the Parisian skyline. Most visitors assume that the building's history is just as scintillating, but Invalides has always led a life of seriousness and importance. Originally founded by Louis XVI in 1671 as a home for disabled soldiers, it is now the headquarters of the military governor of Paris and continues to serve, on a small scale, as a military hospital. Stretching from the building to the Pont Alexandre III is the tree-lined **Esplanade des Invalides** (not to be confused with the Champs de Mars). The Musée de l'Armée, Musée des Plans-Reliefs, Musée des Deux Guerres Mondiales, and Musée de l'Ordre de la Libération are housed within the Invalides museum complex (see **Museums, p. 281**)p. 281, as is Napoleon's tomb, in the Église St-Louis. To the left of the Tourville entrance, the **Jardin de l'Intendant** is strewn with benches and impeccably groomed trees and bushes, for those who have had their fill of guns and emperors. A ditch lined with foreign cannons runs around the Invalides area where a moat used to be, making it impossible to leave by any but the two official entrances. Be aware that certain areas are blocked to tourists in order to respect the privacy of the war veterans who still live in the hospital. *(127, rue de Grenelle, 7ème. ⓂInvalides. Enter from either pl. des Invalides or pl. Vauban and av. de Tourville.)*

ASSEMBLÉE NATIONALE. The Palais Bourbon serves as an architectural testament to the ever-changing nature of the French government. Built in 1722 for the Duchesse de Bourbon, the spunky daughter of the autocratic Louis XIV and his mistress, Mme de Montespan, the palace is now the home of the French parliament. Open only to French civil servants. *(33 quai d'Orsay. ⓂAssemblée Nationale. ☎01 40 63 50 00 or 01 40 63 77 77; www.assemblee-nat.fr.)*

QUAI VOLTAIRE. The *quai* Voltaire, known for its beautiful views of the monuments along the Seine, boasts an artistic heritage more distinguished than any other block in the city. Voltaire himself spent his last days at no. 27. No. 19 was home to Baudelaire while he wrote *Les Fleurs du Mal* (Flowers of Evil) from 1856 to 1858, to Richard Wagner as he composed *Die Meistersinger* between 1861 and 1862, and to Oscar Wilde while he was in exile. Eugène Delacroix and Jean Auguste Dominique Ingres had their studios at no. 9-11, followed by Jean-Baptiste-Camille Corot. The Russian ballet dancer Rudolf Nureyev lived at no. 23 from 1981 until his death in 1993. Finally, though more a patron than an artist himself, former President Chirac and his wife Bernadette lived briefly at no. 1 after leaving the Palais d'Élysée. *(Along the Seine between Pont Royal and Pont du Carrousel. Ⓜrue du Bac. Walk up rue du Bac to the river.)*

LA PAGODE. A Japanese pagoda built in 1895 by the Bon Marché department store magnate M. Morin as a gift to his wife, La Pagode endures as an artifact of the Orientalist craze that swept France in the 19th century. When Mme. Morin left her husband for his associate's son just prior to WWI, the building became the scene of Sino-Japanese soirées, despite the tension between the two countries. In 1931, La Pagode opened its doors to the public, becoming a cinema and swank cafe where the likes of silent screen-star Gloria Swanson were known to raise a glass. The theater closed during the Nazi occupation, re-opened in 1945, and closed again in 1998 due to a lack of funding, despite having been declared a historic monument by the Ministry of Culture in 1982. It was re-opened under private ownership in November 2000. The two-screen cinema continues to show smaller, independent films (see **Entertainment**, p. 316). *(57bis, rue de Babylone. ⓂSt-François-Xavier. ☎01 45 55 48 48. Cafe open daily between shows.)*

HÔTEL MATIGNON. Once owned by the royal family of Monaco and Talleyrand, Hôtel Matignon is now the official residence of the prime minister. It is considered one of the most stunning *hôtels particuliers* in Paris. Visitors are not permitted. Nearby, at 53, rue de Varenne, a plaque commemorates American novelist Edith Wharton, one of the first of the early 20th-century expats. She lived at this address from 1910 to 1920, what she describes as "happy years," "crowded years." *(57, rue de Varenne.* Ⓜ*Varenne.)*

ÉGLISE ST-THOMAS D'AQUIN. The 17th-century Église St-Thomas d'Aquin was originally dedicated to St. Dominique but was reconsecrated by revolutionaries as the Temple of Peace. While the church facade is an unassuming continuation of the city block, the interior is decorated with fantastic wall and ceiling murals, particularly behind the altar. The church holds organ concerts Sundays at 5pm. Information about group pilgrimages within Europe can be found on the bulletin boards inside the main entrance. *(On rue de Gribeauval, off rue du Bac.* Ⓜ*Rue du Bac.* ☎*01 42 22 59 74. Open in winter M-F and Su 9am-noon and 4-7pm, Sa 10am-noon and 4-7:30pm; in summer daily 9am-noon and 4-7pm.)*

ÉGLISE ST-FRANÇOIS-XAVIER. Built between 1861 and 1874, this beautiful church features bright blue-and-red stained-glass windows and provides respite from the noise of the serious 7*ème*. *(12, pl. du Président Mithouard, on bd. des Invalides.* Ⓜ*St-François-Xavier.* ☎*01 44 49 62 62; www.paroisse-sfx-paris.org. Open summer M-Tu and Th 7:45am-noon and 2:30-7:45pm, W 7:45am-12:45pm and 2:30-7:45pm, F 7:45am-12:45pm and 2:30-8pm; Sa 8:45am-12:30pm and 2:30-7:45pm, Su 8:45am-12:45pm and 3-7:45pm. Winter hours begin later and end earlier; check website for precise times and for mass schedules.)*

CHAMPS-ÉLYSÉES (8ÈME)

There's a reason that the 8*ème* remains Paris's most touristed *arrondissement* long after the Champs Élysées has ceased to be posh. With more architectural beauty, historical significance, and diverse shopping than many other areas in the city, it is a great—if hectic—place to spend a day.

ALONG THE CHAMPS-ÉLYSÉES

ARC DE TRIOMPHE. Situated at the top of a hill, the arch offers a stunning view down the Champs-Élysées to the Tuileries and Louvre. In 1758, architect Charles François Ribart envisioned the spot as a monument to France's military prowess—in the form of a giant, bejeweled elephant. Fortunately for France, construction of the monument was not undertaken until 1806 when Napoleon imagined a less kitschy tribute with which to welcome his troops home (modeled after the triumphal arches of victorious Roman emperors like Constantine and Titus). Napoleon was exiled before the arch was completed, and Louis XVIII took over construction in 1823. He dedicated the arch to the war in Spain and its commander, the Duc d'Angoulême, and placed its design in the hands of Jean-François-Thérèse Chalgrin. The Arc de Triomphe was consecrated in 1836. Yet the emperor wasn't forgotten: the names of Napoleon's generals and battles are engraved inside.

Since the days of Napoleon, the arch has been a magnet for various triumphant armies. After the Prussians marched through in 1871, the mortified Parisians purified the ground with fire. On July 14, 1919, the Arc provided the backdrop for an Allied victory parade headed by Maréchal Foch. During WWII, Frenchmen were reduced to tears as Nazis goose-stepped beneath the arch. After the demeaning years of German occupation, a sympathetic Allied army made sure that a French general would be the first to drive under the arch.

Today, this 165 ft. arch is dedicated to all French army soldiers and veterans. **The Tomb of the Unknown Soldier,** illuminated by an eternal flame, has lain under the arch since November 11, 1920. Its marker memorializes the 1,500,000 Frenchmen who died during WWI and bears this inscription: "Here lies a French soldier who died for his country, 1914-1918."

Visitors can climb up to the terrace observation deck for a brilliant view of the **"Historic Axis,"** from the Arc de Triomphe du Carrousel and the Louvre Pyramid at one end to the Grande Arche de la Défense at the other. There is also a permanent exhibit, **"Between Wars and Peace,"** which reads like the Arc's autobiography. (Ⓜ*Charles de Gaulle-Étoile. Expect lines even on weekdays, although you can escape the crowds if you go before noon. You will kill yourself (and face a hefty fine) trying to dodge the 10-lane merry-go-round of cars around the arch, so use the pedestrian underpass on the right side of the Champs-Élysées facing the arch. Buy your ticket in the pedestrian underpass before going up to the ground level. Open daily Apr.-Sept. 10am-11pm; Oct.-Mar. 10am-10:30pm. Last entry 30min. before closing. Wheelchair-accessible. €9, ages 18-25 €5.50, under 17 free. MC/V.)*

AVENUE DES CHAMPS-ÉLYSÉES. Radiating from the huge rotary surrounding the Arc de Triomphe, the Champs-Élysées seems to be a magnificent celebration of pomp and glory. Unfortunately, when you're walking along the avenue, you realize its role as the legendary epicenter of elegance is running away.

Born in 1616 when Marie de Médicis ploughed the Cours-la-Reine through the fields and marshland west of the Louvre, it remained an unkempt thoroughfare until the early 19th century, when the city built sidewalks and installed gas lighting. While it was the center of Parisian opulence in the early 20th century—with flashy mansions towering above exclusive cafes—the Champs has since undergone a bizarre kind of democratization, as commercialization has diluted its former glamor. Shops along the avenue now range from designer fashion to car dealerships to low-budget tchotchkes: the behemoth Louis Vuitton flagship store stands across from an even larger Monoprix, a low-budget all-purpose store. Overpriced cafes compete with fast-food outlets for the patronage of swarming tourists, while glitzy nightclubs and multiplex cinemas draw large crowds well into the evening.

Despite its slip in sophistication, the Champs continues to be known as the most beautiful street in the world. In 1860 Louis Vuitton spearheaded a committee to maintain the avenue's luxury, which it still strives to do so to this day, installing wider sidewalks and even preventing certain shops from moving in—H&M was refused a bid in 2007. With rents as high as €1.25 million a year for 1000 sq. m. of space, the Champs is the **second richest street in the world** after New York's 5th Avenue. The Champs continues to play host to most major French events: on **Bastille Day** the largest parade in Europe takes place on the avenue, as does the final stretch of the **Tour de France.** Meanwhile, many of the streets off of the Champs, like Avenue Montaigne, have picked up the slack and sweat class in their own right. (Ⓜ*Charles de Gaulle-Etoile. The Champs runs from pl. Charles de Gaulle-Etoile southeast to pl. de la Concorde.)*

FOUQUET'S. Fouquet's is a living monument to the Champs's glorious past. Once a favorite with French film stars, this outrageously expensive cafe/restaurant now has more celebrities in its picture frames than its seats. Open since 1899 and a designated historical monument, the somewhat over-the-top red-awninged eatery hosts the annual **César awards** (see **Food, p. 187**). *(99 av. des Champs-Élysées. Ⓜ*George V. ☎01 47 23 70 60.)*

GRAND AND PETIT PALAIS. At the foot of the Champs-Élysées, the Grand and Petit Palais face one another on av. Winston Churchill. Built for the 1900 World's Fair, they were lauded as a dazzling combination of "banking and dreaming" and exemplify Art Nouveau architecture; the Petit Palais's golden gate is especially dazzling. Today, the Petit Palais houses an eclectic mix of artwork, while the Grand Palais holds temporary exhibits on art, architecture, and French history. The Grand Palais also houses the **Palais de la Découverte,** a children's science museum; it is most beautiful at night when the statues are backlit and the glass dome glows from within. *(Ⓜ Champs-Élysées-Clemenceau.)*

PALAIS DE L'ÉLYSÉE. The guards pacing around the corner of av. de Marigny and rue du Faubourg St-Honoré are protecting the Palais de l'Elysée, the state residence for French presidents since 1870. The Palais was built in 1718 and later served as home to Louis XV's celebrated mistress Madame de Pompadour. Napoleon also lived here with Josephine. It wasn't until 1848, however, that the National Assembly officially declared Élysée the presidential residence. Napoleon III remodeled the Classical style a bit, with the help of architect Joseph-Eugène Delacroix. For the French, it remains a symbol of the Republic. Entrance requires a personal invitation, but since Sarkozy is always shopping for new wives, don't give up hope. *(Ⓜ Champs-Élysées-Clemenceau.)*

THÉÂTRE DES CHAMPS-ÉLYSÉES. Built by the Perret brothers in 1912 with bas-reliefs by Bourdelle, the Théâtre des Champs-Élysées is best known for staging the premiere of Stravinsky's ballet *Le Sacre du Printemps* (The Rite of Spring). The score, conducted by Pierre Monteux, was dissonant and arhythmic, and Vaslav Nijinsky's choreography had the dancers dressed in feathers and rags, hopping about pigeon-toed to evoke primitivism. The spectacle provoked the most famous riot in music history: the audience jeered and shouted so loudly that the dancers couldn't hear the orchestra. Today, the theater has three salles that host operatic, orchestral, and dance performances; it is also home to the **Orchestre National de France** and **Orchestre Lamoureux** (see **Entertainment,** p. 318). *(15 av. Montaigne. Ⓜ Alma-Marceau. ☎ 01 49 52 50 50, tours 01 44 54 19 30. €4.)*

PLACE DE LA CONCORDE AND SURROUNDINGS

PLACE DE LA CONCORDE. Paris's largest and most infamous public square is the eastern terminus of the Champs-Élysées. In the center of the *place*, 3300 years old and 72 feet tall, is the monumental **Obélisque de Luxor.** The spot was originally occupied by a statue of Louis XV (after whom the square was originally named) that was destroyed in 1748 by an angry mob. King Louis-Philippe, anxious to avoid revolutionary rancor, opted for a less contentious symbol: the 220-ton red granite, hieroglyphic-covered obelisk presented to Charles X from the Viceroy of Egypt in 1829. The obelisk, which dates back to the 13th century BC and recalls the royal accomplishments of Ramses II, wasn't erected until 1836. Gilded images on the sides of the obelisk recount its 2-year trip to Paris in a custom-built boat. Today, it forms the axis of what many Parisians call the **"royal perspective"**—from the Louvre, the straight-line view of Place de la Concorde, the Arc de Triomphe, and the Grande Arche de la Défense tells the history of Paris century by century, from the reign of Louis XIV to the Revolution to Napoleon's reign, and finally, all the way to the celebration of commerce.

Constructed between 1757 and 1777 by Louis XV to commemorate his monarchy, Concord quickly became ground zero for public grievances against the monarchy. During the Revolution and Reign of Terror, the *place* was called **place de la Révolution** when the **guillotine** severed 1343 aristocratic heads. In fact, Louis XVI met his end near the statue symbolizing Brest, while the obelisk marks the spot where Marie-Antoinette, Charlotte Corday (Marat's assassin), Lavoisier, Danton, and Robespierre all succumbed to the sharp reality of death.

With its monumental scale and heavy traffic, the *place* is not pedestrian-friendly. (Read: crossing the street here often feels like weaving through a zebra stampede.) On either side of Concord's intersection with the unusually wide Champs-Élysées are reproductions of Guillaume Coustou's **Cheveaux de Marly.** Also known as Africans Mastering the Numidian Horses, the original sculptures are now in the Louvre to protect them from pollution. Around the *place* stand eight large statues representing France's major cities: Brest, Bordeaux Lille, Lyon, Marseille, Nantes, Rouen, and Strasbourg.

At night, the ambience softens as the obelisk, fountains, and lamps light up. On Bastille Day, a military parade led by the President of the Republic marches through Concorde (usually around 10am) and down the Champs-Élysées to the Arc, and an impressive fireworks display lights up the sky over the *place* at night. At the end of July, the Tour de France finalists pull through Concorde and into the home stretch on the Champs-Élysées. (Ⓜ*Concorde.*)

MADELEINE. Mirrored by the Assemblée Nationale across the Seine, the Madeleine was begun in 1763 by Louis XV, who modeled it after a Greco-Roman temple. Construction of the church was halted during the Revolution, when the Cult of Reason proposed transforming the building into a bank, a theater, or a courthouse—anything but a church. When Napoleon came to power, he (unsurprisingly) wanted to dedicate it to his prestigious army, declaring it the "Temple of Glory of the Grand Army." Later, Louis XVIII would proclaim, "It shall be a church!" It wasn't until 1842 that construction was finally completed. Madeleine stands alone among Parisian churches, distinguished by her gigantic pediment, four ceiling domes, fifty-two 66 ft. exterior Corinthian columns, and a curious altarpiece adorned by an immense sculpture of the ascension of Mary Magdalene, the church's namesake. The reliefs on the impressive bronze doors depict the 10 Commandments. While the church is worth a visit because of its immensity, there isn't much else to see.

Today, clothing and food shops line the square surrounding Madeleine. Marcel Proust spent most of his childhood nearby at 9 bd. Malesherbes, which might explain his penchant for his aunt Léonie's madeleines with tea. You, too, can enjoy a sweet treat at the world-famous **Fauchon,** 24-30 pl. de la Madeleine, behind the church (see **Food, p. 187**). Meanwhile, the colorful flower market that thrives on east side of the church is always worth a stop. *(pl. de la Madeleine. Ⓜ Madeleine. ☎ 01 44 51 69 00; www.eglise-lamadeleine.com. Open daily 9am-7pm. Regular organ and chamber concerts; contact the church for a schedule and come to the church or call Virgin or FNAC for tickets (commission fee). Mass M 12:30, 6:30pm; Tu-F 7:45am, 12:30, and 6:30pm (crypt); Sa 12:30, 6pm; Su 9:30, 11am, and 7pm.)*

OTHER SIGHTS. On either side of the rue Royal, directly north of pl. de la Concorde, stand the **Hôtel de Crillon** (on the left) and the **Hôtel de la Marine** (on the right). Architect Jacques-Ange Gabriel built the impressive colonnaded facades between 1757 and 1770. The Crillon, which led former lives as a nobleman's home and a luxury hotel frequented by Marie Antoinette, now houses the world-famous Hôtel de Crillon (a reported fave of Madonna); it is especially beautiful at night, when it is the only building on the place that glows with light. The Marine served as furniture storage for the Louvre palace and is today the headquarters of the French national marines. On February 6, 1778, France became the first European country to recognize the independence of the United States of America, after the Treaty of Friendship and Trade was signed here by Louis XVI and American statesmen, including Benjamin Franklin. (A plaque on rue Royale commemorates the treaty.) World-renowned **Maxim's restaurant,** 3 rue Royale, once home to Cardinal Richelieu, stands nearby. A meal at this historic house may be beyond the budgets of most, but the souvenir shop and Cafe Minim's next door offer a more affordable slice of celebrity. (Ⓜ*Concorde.*)

TO THE NORTH

🔲**PARC MONCEAU.** The signs say *"Pelouse interdite"* (keep off the lawn), but on sunny days, everyone pretends to be illiterate. Lying behind gold-tipped, wrought-iron gates, the Parc Monceau is an expansive urban oasis especially popular with families. There's plenty of shade, courtesy of the **largest tree in Paris:** an oriental *platane* (or plane), 7m thick and two centuries old. The park was designed by painter Carmontelle for the Duc d'Orléans and completed by Haussmann in 1862. A number of architectural oddities—covered bridges, Dutch windmills, Roman ruins, and roller rinks—make this a kids' romping ground as well as a formal garden. As it is slightly out of the way, this local afternoon hangout has few tourists. (Ⓜ*Monceau or Courcelles. Open daily Apr.-Oct. 7am-10pm; Nov.-Mar. 7am-8pm. Last entry 15min. before closing.*)

CATHÉDRALE ALEXANDRE-NEVSKY. Known as the **Église Russe,** this shiny gold, 5-domed cathedral is Paris's primary Russian Orthodox church and Russian cultural center. The spectacular, recently restored interior, lavishly decorated in icons, was painted by artists from St-Petersburg in gold, reds, blues, and greens in the classic Byzantine style. An altar at the back of the church on the right dates from 1289 and is thought to have been taken during the Napoleonic Wars; it was given to the church by the Menier family (famous chocolatiers). The Virgin Mary icon to its right was a gift from a cavalier regiment of the Russian Imperial Guard. Dress appropriately; no shorts or uncovered shoulders are allowed inside. (*12 rue Daru.* Ⓜ*Ternes.* ☎ *01 42 27 37 34. Open Tu, F, Su 3-5pm. Services in French and Russian Sa 6-8pm, Su 10am-12:30pm; additional times on church calendar.*)

CHAPELLE EXPIATOIRE. Pl. Louis XVI is composed of the immense Chapelle Expiatoire, monuments to Marie-Antoinette and Louis XVI, and a lovely, quiet park excellent for picnicking. During the Revolution, when burial sites were in high demand, lime-filled trenches were dug here to accommodate heaps of hundreds of bodies. Louis XVIII had his brother's and sister-in-law's remains removed to St-Denis in 1815, and there are no graves remaining, despite rumors of Marat's assassin Charlotte Corday being buried here. Statues of the expiatory king and queen stand inside the Chapelle, symbolically guarding a tomb-shaped altar. Their touching final letters are engraved in French on the base of the sculptures. Otherwise, there is not much to see here. (*29 rue Pasquier, inside pl. Louis XVI, just below bd. Haussmann.* Ⓜ*Madeleine, Havre-Caumartin, or St.-Lazare.* ☎ *01 44 32 18 00. Open Th-Sa 1-5pm. €5, ages 18-25 €3.50, under 18 free. 45min. tours in French available 1:30 and 3:30pm. English-language pamphlets available at entrance.*)

OPÉRA (9ÈME)

The 9*ème* offers visitors a grand lesson in contrast: from the Opéra Garnier's serenely gorgeous frescoes to Pigalle's seedy side streets, this *arrondissement* exemplifies the distinctly Parisian cohabitation of vice and virtue.

OPÉRA AND SURROUNDINGS

The area around the southernmost border of the 9*ème* is known simply as l'Opéra after the area's incomparable landmark: the Opéra Garnier. Opéra and its surrounding *grands boulevards* are the 9*ème*'s busiest, most prosperous areas, touched by spill-over glamour from the ritzy 8*ème*. Those uninterested in the Opéra's world-class ballet can walk down the road to **L'Olympia** (see

Entertainment, p. 317), one of Paris's leading venues for American, Brazilian, and European jazz, rock, and pop rock concerts. North of the Opéra, the city's enormous department stores, **Galeries Lafayette** and **Au Printemps** (see **Shopping,** p. 308), offer some of Paris's best shopping. Look out for the sale seasons—crowded but fabulous—in January and July.

OPÉRA GARNIER. The exterior of the Opéra Garnier—with its restored multicolored marble facade, sculpted golden goddesses, and ornate columns and friezes—is one of Paris's most impressive sights. It's no wonder that Oscar Wilde once swore he saw an angel floating on the sidewalk while sitting next door at the Café de la Paix (see **Food, p. 189**).

Designed by Charles Garnier in the style of the Second Empire, the Opéra emphasizes both the era's ostentation and its lack of a definitive style. Asked whether his building was in the style of Louis XIV, Louis XV, or Louis XVI, Garnier responded that his creation belonged only to Napoleon III, the project's financier. Garnier was 35 and unknown when he won the Opéra commission in a contest among Paris's top architects; the building made him a superstar. After 15 years of construction, the Opéra opened its doors in 1875.

The Opéra's interior is decorated with Gobelin tapestries, gilded mosaics, and an eight-ton chandelier whose counterweight fell on an 1896 audience. The incident, along with rumors of a spooky lake beneath the building, inspired **Le Fantôme de l'Opera** (*The Phantom of the Opera*), Gaston Leroux's 1910 novel later incarnated in several films before bursting into song in 1986 with Andrew Lloyd Webber's megamusical. Be sure to pay a visit to the **Phantom's box,** no. 5. The Opéra's auditorium has 2200 red velvet seats and a ceiling painted by Marc Chagall in 1964. The five-tiered auditorium served several dramatic purposes; balconies were constructed so audience members could watch one another, as well as the show on stage. Since 1989, most operas have been performed at the **Opéra Bastille,** generally regarded as the Garnier's ugly stepsister who somehow resembles an airport (p. 318). Opéra Garnier has become mainly a ballet venue, where in 1992, Rudolf Nureyev danced for the last time.

The Opéra houses a library and museum that hosts temporary exhibits on theatrical personages like designer Christian Lacroix and dancer Vaslav Nijinsky. The museum's permanent collection includes sculptures by Degas and scale models of famous opera scenes. Paul Baudry's portrait of Charles Garnier hangs by the museum entrance. (Ⓜ*Opéra.* ☎ *08 92 89 90 90; www.operadeparis.fr. Concert hall and museum open daily 10am-5pm. Last entry 30min. before closing. Concert hall closed during rehearsals; call ahead. Admission €8, students and under 25 €4, under 10 free. 90min. English tours July-Aug. daily 11:30pm, 2:30pm; Sept.-June W and Sa-Su 11:30am, 2:30pm; €12, seniors €10, students €9, under 10 €6.*)

CAFE DE LA PAIX. Next to the Opéra Garnier, the Café de la Paix is the quintessential 19th-century cafe. Like its decadent neighbor, it was designed by Charles Garnier and sports frescoes, mirrored walls, and Neoclassical ceilings with winking "epicurean cherubs." Oscar Wilde frequented the cafe; today it caters to the after-theater crowd and other deep-pocketed patrons. (*12 bd. des Capucines, 9ème.* Ⓜ*Opéra. See also Food, p. 189.)*

NORTH OF OPÉRA

The upper 9*ème*, with its infamous red-light district, will please those in search of cheap thrills, while the less debaucherous visitor will probably choose to stay toward the south. A handful of kosher food stores line rue Notre Dame de Lorette and rue du Faubourg-Montmartre. Discount shops, pizza parlors, and car exhaust also fill this lively neighborhood.

ÉGLISE NOTRE DAME DE LORETTE. Built in 1836 to honor "the glory of the Virgin Mary," Église Notre Dame de Lorette exemplifies Neoclassical architecture. For almost two decades after its inauguration, Parisian journalists and citizens criticized the church for being too richly decorated. Frescoes inside its elevated chapel depict the four evangelists contemplating Mary and the four prophets hailing her while each portrait in the nave was painted in a color-scheme specifically designed to evoke religious symbolism. No longer angering Parisians on account of its good looks, the church has become slightly dilapidated; while the parish works to restore its interior, a lack of funding makes Église Notre Dame de Lorette's future uncertain. Noisy rue Notre Dame de Lorette is far less virtuous than the church after which it's named; the street was the debauched hangout of Emile Zola's *Nana* (whose name is now slang for "chick" or "babe"), while Lorette became a nickname for the quarter's young prostitutes in the 1960s. *(18bis. rue Choron, 9ème.* Ⓜ*Notre Dame de Lorette.* ☎*01 48 78 92 72; www.notredame-delorette.org. Exit the metro and the church will be in front of you on place Kossuth. Mass M 12:30, 6:45pm; Tu-F 8am, 12:30, 6:45pm; Sa 11am, 6:30pm; Su 9:30, 11am, 6:30pm.)*

PIGALLE. Bordering the 18*ème*, the generally naughty Pigalle area is a salacious, simmering stew of sleaze. Stretching along bd. de Clichy from place Pigalle to place Blanche, this neighborhood is home to **famous cabarets** (Folies Bergère, Moulin Rouge, Folies Pigalle) and overtly raunchy newcomers like Le Coq Hardy and Dirty Dick. Pigalle earned its reputation as Paris's un-chastity belt during WWII, when American servicemen stationed in the city nicknamed it "Pig Alley." Brothels, porn stores, sex shops, and leather and latex boutiques cram its alleys while prostitutes and drug dealers prowl its streets well before dark. Visitors traveling alone should exercise caution. *(9ème.* Ⓜ*Pigalle.)*

CANAL ST-MARTIN
AND SURROUNDS (10ÈME)

The 10ème is probably not anyone's first stop in Paris...or second...or third... but it can be a pleasant place to laze away an afternoon. While the Canal St-Martin might not offer the glamour or photo opportunities of the Seine, its bustling banks are a great place for a tourist to experience the real, lived-in Paris. This far from the Louvre, you'll probably be the only foreign passport around.

PORTES ST-DENIS AND ST-MARTIN. The grand Porte St-Denis looms triumphantly at the end of rue du Faubourg St-Denis. Built in 1672 to celebrate the victories of Louis XIV in Flanders and the Rhineland, the gate imitates the Arch of Titus in Rome. The site of the arch was once a medieval entrance to the city; today it serves as a traffic rotary and a gathering place for pigeons and loiterers alike. In the words of André Breton, "c'est *très belle et très inutile*" (it's very beautiful and very useless). On July 28, 1830, revolutionaries scrambled to the top and rained cobblestones on the monarchist troops below. The Porte St-Martin at the end of r. du Faubourg St-Martin, constructed in 1674, is a variation on a similar theme, with more subdued architecture on a smaller scale. On the bd. St-Martin side, a herculean Louis XIV dominates the facade, wearing nothing but a wig and a smile. *(*Ⓜ *Strasbourg-St-Denis.)*

PLACE DE LA RÉPUBLIQUE. Though Haussmann created it to separate some *beaux quartiers* from the revolutionary *arrondissements*, the pl. de la République is now an energized meeting point for the vastly different 3*ème*, 10*ème*, and 11*ème*. It also serves as the disorienting junction of av. de la République and bd. Magenta, Voltaire, Temple, Turbigo, and St-Martin. At the center of the place, Morice's sculpture of La République glorifies France's many revolutionary struggles, and the host of chain restaurants lining it feed the diverse crowds. The area buzzes with people during the day but can be a bit uncomfortable at night. (Ⓜ *République*.)

CANAL ST-MARTIN. The most pleasant area of the 10*ème* is unquestionably the tree-lined Canal St-Martin. Measuring 4.5km, the canal runs from r. du Faubourg du Temple to the Bassin de la Villette. It was built in 1825 as a shortcut for river traffic on the Seine, and it also served to remind the plebeians of their place in the city—that is to say, not in it. In recent years, the city has made efforts to improve water quality in the canal and clean up its banks; the result has been a sort of local renaissance. The residential area around the canal is being rediscovered by Parisians and tourists alike, and the tree-lined *quais* boast new, upscale boutiques and restaurants. Children line up along the banks to watch the several working locks lift barges and boats. Canauxrama runs boat tours on the canal (see **Practical Information,** p. 136). On Sundays, an antique market takes place along the *quai* de Valmy and the streets along the canal close to traffic, making room for bikes and rollerskates. (Ⓜ *République or Goncourt will take you to the most beautiful end of the canal.*)

BASTILLE

11ÈME ARRONDISSEMENT

There are few monumental sights (that still exist) in the 11*ème*, aside from the place de la Bastille. However, you might see some funny drunken antics during bar crawls on rue Oberkampf.

PLACE DE LA BASTILLE. Today, this busy intersection mainly ignores its past— except on Bastille Day, when the whole city parties in its honor. At the center of the square is a monument of winged Mercury holding a torch of freedom, symbolizing France's movement towards democracy. (*11ème.* Ⓜ*Bastille.*)

BASTILLE PRISON. This is the most visited sight in Paris that doesn't actually exist. On July 14, 1789, an angry Parisian mob stormed this symbol of royal tyranny, sparking the French Revolution. They only liberated a dozen or so prisoners, but nobody was counting. Two days later, the Assemblée Nationale ordered the prison demolished. Today, all that remains is the ground plan of the fortress, still visible as a line of paving-stones in the place de la Bastille.

The prison was originally commissioned by Charles V to safeguard the eastern entrance to Paris. Strapped for cash, Charles "recruited" a press-gang of passing civilians to lay the stones for the fortress. The Bastille towers rose 100 ft. above Paris by the end of the 14th century. Under Henri IV, they became the royal treasury, while Louis XIII made them a state prison. Internment there, generally reserved for heretics and political dissidents, was the king's business and, as a result, often arbitrary. But it was hardly the hell-hole that the Revolutionaries who tore it down imagined it to be—the Bastille's titled inmates were allowed to furnish their suites, use fresh linens, bring their own servants, and receive guests: the Cardinal de Rohan held a dinner party for 20 in his cell. Notable prisoners included the mysterious Man in the Iron Mask (made famous by writer Alexandre Dumas), the Comte de Mirabeau, Voltaire (twice), and the Marquis de Sade, who wrote his notorious novel Justine here.

On the day of the "storm," the Revolutionary militants, having ransacked the Invalides for weapons, turned to the Bastille for munitions. Supposedly an impenetrable fortress, the prison had actually been attacked during other periods of civil unrest. Surrounded by an armed rabble, too short on food to entertain the luxury of a siege, and unsure of the loyalty of the Swiss mercenaries who defended the prison, the Bastille's governor surrendered. His head was severed with a pocket knife and paraded through the streets on a pike. Yet despite the gruesome details, the storming of the Bastille has come to symbolize the triumph of liberty over tyranny. Its first anniversary was cause for great celebration in Revolutionary Paris. Since the late 19th century, July 14 has been the official state holiday of the French Republic. It is a time of glorious firework displays and copious amounts of alcohol, with festivities concentrated in the pl. de la Bastille (see **Life and Times**, p. 66). *(11ème.* Ⓜ*Bastille.)*

JULY COLUMN. At the center of the always-dynamic place Bastille lies this commemoration to a group of French freedom fighters—though not those that stormed the Bastille. Topped by the conspicuous gold cupid, the column was erected by King Louis-Philippe in 1831 to commemorate Republicans who died in the Trois Glorieuses, three-days of street fighting in July 1830. Victims of the Revolution of February 1848 were subsequently buried here, along with two mummified Egyptian pharaohs. The column is not open to the public. *(11ème.* Ⓜ*Bastille. In the center of pl. de la Bastille.)*

RUE DE LA ROQUETTE. Quieter than its neighbor, the buzzing rue de Lappe, the winding rue de la Roquette has some hidden gems. This 17th-century byway was home to poet Paul Verlaine, who lived at no. 17, and is now lined with offbeat cafes, bars, creative boutiques, an avant-garde church, and countless restaurants serving everything from Italian to Thai food. Above all, come here for the diverse and lively vibe. The charming sq. de la Roquette is an ideal endpoint to a stroll along this multi-faceted street. *(11ème.* Ⓜ*Bastille or Voltaire.)*

12ÈME ARRONDISSEMENT

The 12*ème* boasts giant monoliths of modern architecture, like the Opéra Bastille and the Palais Omnisports. Most of the construction is practical and commercial, as befits the working-class background of the area, but a bit of old-fashioned charm can be seen in the Viaduc des Arts near the Bastille.

AROUND PLACE DE LA BASTILLE

OPÉRA DE LA BASTILLE. President Mitterand made a bold move when he plunked the Opéra Bastille down in the working-class neighborhood around Place de la Bastille. The building was engineered by Carlos Ott, a Uruguayan architect, and it opened on July 14, 1989 (the bicentennial of the Revolution) to protests over its unattractive and dubious design. (In fact, the building is currently under renovated because the roof tiles have been tumbling off for years; work is to finish in 2009.) The "People's Opera" has been described as an airport, and as huge toilet because of its resemblance to the coin-operated *pissoirs* on the streets of Paris. Yet the opera has not struck a completely sour note, as it has helped renew local interest in the arts. The guided tour (expensive but extremely interesting) offers a behind-the-scenes view of the largest theater in the world. The immense granite and glass auditorium, which seats 2703, comprises only 5% of the building's surface area. The rest of the building houses exact replicas of the stage (for rehearsal purposes) and workshops for both the Bastille and Garnier operas. The Opéra employs almost 1000 people, from technies to actors to administrators to wig- and shoe-makers. *(130 rue de Lyon, 12ème.* Ⓜ*Bastille. Look for the words "Billeterie" on the building.* ☎*01 40 01 19 70; www. operadeparis.1hr. tour almost every day, usually at 1 or 5pm; call ahead for schedule. Tours are in French, but groups of 15 or more can arrange for English. €11, over 60 and students €9, under 18 €6. Open M-Sa 10:30am-6:30pm. For performance info, see* **Entertainment,** *p. 318.)*

VIADUC DES ARTS AND PROMENADE PLANTÉE. A surprisingly pleasant sight in the otherwise commercial 12ème, the *ateliers* (studios) in the Viaduc des Arts house artisans who make everything from haute couture fabric to hand-painted porcelain to space-age furniture. Restorators of all types fill the arches of the old railway viaduct; bring your oil painting, 12th-century book, grandmother's linen, or childhood dollhouse and they'll return it as good as new. Interspersed among the stores are gallery spaces, many of which are rented by new artists each month (see **Museums,** p. 287). High above the avenue, on the "roof" of the viaduct, runs the lovely Promenade Plantée, decorated with rose covered gazebos. Paris's skinniest park, it is ideal for a Sunday afternoon run or stroll. *(9-129 av. Daumesnil, 12ème. www.viaduc-des-arts.com.* Ⓜ*Bastille. The viaduct extends from rue de Lyon to rue de Charenton. Entrances to the Promenade are at Ledru Rollin, Hector Malot, and bd. Diderot. Park opens M-F 8am, Sa-Su 9am; closing hours vary, around 5:30pm in winter and 9:30pm in summer. Stores open M-Sa; hours vary, with many taking a 2hr. lunch break at noon.)*

ELSEWHERE IN THE 12ÈME

BERCY QUARTER. East of the Gare de Lyon, the Bercy quarter has seen rapid construction, beginning with Mitterrand's **Ministère des Finances** building, a modern monolith to match the similarly block-like **Bibliothèque** across the river. Any of the many new cafes and brasseries along the rue de Bercy offer a great locale from which to ogle the mammoth grass-and-glass **Palais Omnisports** concert and sports complex. Each of its sloping sides, which local youth and the occasional tourist try (unsuccessfully) to scale, is covered in green grass. The Parc de Bercy is not quite the calming getaway some visitors may seek, but it's still a popular hangout spot for locals. A lovelier (and less weird) site is the **Yitzhak Rabin Garden** at the eastern edges of the park, which offers rose arbors, grape vines, an herb garden, and a playground dedicated to the Nobel Prize-winning Prime Minister of Israel.

To top off this bizarre 21st-century construct, Frank Gehry added one of his psychedelic buildings at no. 51 rue de Bercy, which now houses the **Cinémathèque Française.** To one side of the park is what used to be Paris's wine depot; the rows of former wine storage buildings have now been converted into a Club Med (Ⓜ*Cour St-Emilion).* The club cafes lining **Cour St-Emilion** are cute in a contrived way; one even has hammocks outside instead of chairs. The Cour is jammed with tourists and locals in the summer. *(12ème.* Ⓜ*Bercy.)*

BUTTES-AUX-CAILLES AND CHINATOWN (13ÈME)

Unlike other more touristed *arrondissements*, the 13ème derives its character from its diversity, not from any one renowned landmark. A colorful Chinatown lies paces away from the working-class Butte-aux-Cailles and a Manufacture des Gobelins. A delightful, often overlooked melange of sights, the 13ème offers an ungilded glimpse into *la vie quotiedienne.*

QUARTIER DE LA BUTTE-AUX-CAILLES. Historically a working-class neighborhood, the Butte-aux-Cailles (Quail Knoll) district resembles a mini-village in the heart of a big city, with old-fashioned lampposts and cobblestone streets. The *quartier* sprawls out from Rue de la Butte-aux-Cailles and rue des Cinq Diamants, south-west of place d'Italie. One of the first areas to resist during the 1848 Revolution, the neighborhood became the unofficial headquarters of the *soixante-huitards*, the student and intellectual activists behind the 1968 Paris riots. Now fighting expensive, mundane eateries, la Butte-aux-Cailles sports funky new restaurants and drinking holes among its old standards, like the

SIGHTS

intellectual hang-out **La Folie en Tête** (see **Nightlife,** p. 334), and the cooperative restaurant **Le Temps des Cerises** (see **Food,** p. 194). The *arrondissement*'s nascent gentrification has attracted artists, intellectuals, and trendsetters, but, luckily for long-time residents, this process remains slow-moving. *(13ème. Ⓜ Corvisart. Exit onto bd. Blanqui and turn onto rue Barrault, which will intersect rue de la Butte-aux-Cailles.)*

QUARTIER CHINOIS (CHINATOWN). The core of Paris's Chinatown lies south of rue Tolbiac, in the blocks surrounding avenue de Choisy and avenue d'Ivry. Home to a large population of Cambodian, Chinese, Thai, and Vietnamese immigrants, this vibrant community offers the best—you guessed it—Asian food in Paris. The area's eateries focus on *entrées à la vapeur* (steamed). An afternoon spent window shopping can often turn up some unexpected finds among the legions of ceramic Buddhas. *(13ème. Ⓜ Porte d'Ivry, Porte de Choisy, Tolbiac, and Maison Blanche are near Chinatown.)*

BIBLIOTHÈQUE NATIONALE DE FRANCE: SITE FRANÇOIS MITTERRAND. The last, most expensive of Mitterrand's Grands Projets, this library opened in 1996 to accommodate the increasing number of books housed in the 2*ème*'s old Bibliothèque Nationale; since 1537, every book published in France has entered the national archives. Most of the Bibliothèque Nationale's 13 million volume collection, including **Gutenberg Bibles** and first editions from the Middle Ages, has been transferred to the Site Mitterrand. Dominique Perrault designed the library's four L-shaped towers to look like an open book from above. The pines emerging from the enormous sunken gardens at the center of the courtyard help to soften the buildings' stunning glassy planes and straight lines. Inside the imposing library you'll find large, **underground reading rooms,** and multiple galleries show temporary multi-media exhibits on various themes in French history. On sunny days, visitors linger on the stairs surrounding the library, watching the Seine drift by. *(Quai F. Mauriac, 13ème. Ⓜ Quai de la Gare or Bibliothèque François Mitterrand. From the Quai de la Gare metro, cross bd. Vincent Auriol and walk towards the Seine; turn right on Quai de la Gare to find steps leading up to the library on your right. ☎ 01 53 79 59 59; www.bnf.fr. Upper study library open Tu-Sa 10am-8pm, Su 1-7pm. Lower research library open M 2-8pm, Tu-Sa 9am-8pm, Su 1-7pm; closed 2 weeks in Sept. Ages 16+. €3.30. 15-day pass €20. Annual membership €35, students €18. MC/V.)*

MANUFACTURE DES GOBELINS. The Manufacture des Gobelins, a tapestry workshop over 400 years old, is all that remains of the 13*ème*'s manufacturing past. Established in 1601 by Henri IV for his imported Flemish tapestry artists, the Gobelins produced the priceless 17th-century tapestries now displayed in the **Musée de Cluny** (see **Museums,** p. 275). Still a state adjunct, the factory continues to receive commissions from French ministries and foreign embassies. The only way inside the Gobelin factory, tours (conducted in French) enable visitors to follow artisans as they meticulously craft their tapestries from start to finish. Following a 30-year renovation, the Galerie des Gobelins reopened in May 2007; dedicated to showcasing the state's Mobilier National collections, the gallerie hosts temporary exhibits on topics from Gobelin history to famous French furniture designers. *(42 avenue des Gobelins. 13ème. ☎ 01 44 08 53 49, group reservations 01 40 13 46 46; www.mobiliernational.culture.gouv.fr. Ⓜ Gobelins. 1hr. French-language tours W and F-Sa 1:15pm and 3pm. Tour €10, students and under 18 €7.50, under 13 free; includes temporary exhibits. Buy tickets at FNAC or online at http://fnac.com.)*

ÉGLISE STE-ANNE DE LA BUTTE-AUX-CAILLES. This Roman-Byzantine church owes its completion to the Lombard family who, in 1898, donated funds from their chocolate store to finish it. Locals nicknamed the front of the church *la façade chocolat* in their honor. *(189 rue de Tolbiac, 13ème. ☎ 01 45 89 34 73; www. paroissesainteanne.net. Ⓜ Tolbiac. From the metro, walk down rue Tolbiac, away from avenue d'Italie.*

Open daily 9am-7:30pm. Mass M 7pm, Tu and Th 9am and 7pm, W and F 9am and noon, Sa 9am and 6pm, Su 9, 10:30am, and 6:30pm. Reception open M-F 10am-noon and 4-6:45pm.)

JOSÉPHINE BAKER SWIMMING POOL. Paris's 37 thriving municipal swimming pools are a wonderful way to escape the heat—and the tourists. This particular pool does swimming as only Paris can, offering a relaxing dip in the middle of the Seine. Floating on the river itself, the pool also has an attached spa available for your post-swim indulgence. *(Quai François Mauriac. ⓂQuai de la Gare. Exit the Metro, walk to the Seine, and turn right. ☎01 56 61 96 50. Hours vary widely; call ahead. Entry €2.60, students and under 18 €1.50; 3-month pass €32.50/16.50. Spa €5.50.)*

MONTPARNASSE

14ÈME ARRONDISSEMENT

CIMETIÈRE MONTPARNASSE. The Tour Montparnasse (see p. 245) keeps the coffins cool on summer days at the beautiful Montparnasse Cemetery, which opened in 1824 and has served as the burial grounds for some of the city's most famous and fashionable former residents. Philosopher Jean-Paul Sartre, automobile giant André Citroën, Charles Baudelaire, and Simone de Beauvoir all hold permanent real estate here. The welcome center, just inside the bd. Edgar Quinet main entrance, provides free maps of the cemetery indicting celebrities' burial sites and their respective claims to fame. Fans of scandalous singer-songwriter Serge Gainsbourg have left beer bottle caps, cigarettes, flowers, and metro tickets on his modest concrete tomb. Samuel Beckett, Emile Durkheim, Alfred Dreyfus, Robert Desnos, Eugène Ionesco, Guy de Maupassant, and sculptors Constantin Brancusi and Frédéric Bartholdi, who designed both the Statue of Liberty and the imposing lion at nearby place Denfert-Rochereau, also lie here. Because Cimetière Montparnasse remains an active cemetery, please be respectful of other visitors. *(3 bd. Edgar Quinet. ☎44 10 86 50. ⓂEdgar Quinet. With your back to Café Odessa, walk to your left down bd. Quinet; the cemetery will be on your right, opposite sq. Delambre. Open 24hr. City-organized tours biannually; call for more info.)*

 KILLER LINES. Only 200 visitors are allowed below ground at one time, so the Catacombs often has long, slow-moving lines. Arrive as early in the morning as possible to avoid being bored to death while waiting.

CATACOMBS. Originally excavated to provide stone for building Paris, the Catacombs now attract tourists the world over. When much of the Left Bank was in danger of caving in during the 1770s, digging in the Catacombs stopped. The former quarry was converted into a mass grave in 1785 to solve the problem of the awful stench elicited by overcrowded cemeteries. Built twice as far underground as the Metro, Paris's "municipal ossuary" now comprises dozens of winding tunnels and hundreds of thousands of bones. They line the walls in gruesomely artful patterns, with skulls arranged into lines and crosses. After a dizzying descent down a spiral staircase, it's a .5km walk to the Catacombs themselves. While gates and signs rule out any possibility of getting lost, the dim lighting and sharp turns make for a surprisingly isolating experience. The catacombs are dark, chilly, and damp, and the morbid proverbs carved into its walls will hardly warm you up. The 45min. self-guided tour finishes with a long climb—another narrow spiral staircase of 83 steps—that spits you out two metro stops away from where you started. *(1 av. du Colonel Henri Roi-Tanguy, 14ème. ⓂDenfert-Rochereau. Take exit place Denfert-Rochereau, and cross avenue du Colonel Henri Roi-*

Tanguy with the lion on your left. You exit the Catacombs at 36 rue Rémy-Dumoncel. ⓂMouton Duvernet *is 2 blocks to the right at avenue du Général Leclerc.* ☎01 43 22 47 63. Open Tu-Su 10am-4pm. €7, over 60 €5.50, age 14-26 €3.50, under 14 free. AmEx/MC/V over €10.)

CITÉ UNIVERSITAIRE. Built in the 1920s to promote cultural exchange between international students, the Cité Universitaire now serves double duty as a residential campus and a tourist attraction. Near the complex's main entrance off bd. Jourdain, the Maison Internationale comprises the Cité's social and academic center. With topiary mazes and mansarde roofs modeled after the **Chateau de Fontainebleau** (p. 350), the building's old marble halls house the info desk and cafeteria, where visitors and residents alike can grab a quick bite. Reception distributes free brochures articulating the Cité's history and layout. Currently home to more than 5600 students from 160 countries, the Cité Universitaire organizes its dormitories by nationality. The houses *(résidences)* all have distinct personalities, most reflecting a cultural aspect of the country they represent. The Cité inaugurated its first *résidence*, the Fondation Deutsch de la Meurthe, in 1925. More modern and architecturally innovative houses like Le Corbusier's **Pavilion Suisse** (1933) and **Maison du Brésil** (1959) color the Cité's eastern end. The former reflects the architect's dream of a vertical city, and its roof garden housed anti-aircraft guns during WWII. At the park's other end lies the impressive Maison de l'Asie du Sud-Est, with its quintessentially Asian design. While the living quarters remain closed to the public and peeping toms in general, the grounds are free for exploration from 7am to 10pm daily. Behind the **Maison Internationale,** you'll find people picnicking, playing soccer and practicing Tai Chi on the *grande pelouse* (big lawn). Add a frisbee and some Birkenstocks, and you're back in the US. *(Main entrance 17 bd. Jourdain.* ⓂPorte d'Orléans. *Take on the place du 25 Août 1944 exits and walk down bd. Jourdain past the rue E. Faguet intersection. RER: Cité Universitaire. Bus #88: Porte d'Arcueil. With your back to rue E.D. de la Meurthe, walk down bd. Jourdain.* ☎44 16 64 00; www.ciup.fr. Reception open M-F 8am-1pm and 2-7:45pm, Sa 11am-2pm. Grounds open daily 7am-10pm. Free. Maison Heinrich Heine cafeteria open M-F 7am-2pm, Sa-Su 8am-2pm; coffee €1, formules from €3. Guided tours 1st Su of the month and start at the Collège Néerlandais; reserve ahead at ☎43 13 65 96; €8, students €3, Cité residents free.)*

BOULEVARD DU MONTPARNASSE. In the early 20th century, avant-garde artists like Chagall, Duchamp, Léger, and Modigliani moved to Montparnasse, many fleeing Montmartre's rising rents. Soviet exiles Lenin and Trotsky talked strategy over cognac in its cafes, including Le Dôme, Le Sélect, and La Coupole, presumably while wearing red suits and calling each other "comrade." Between the World Wars, Montparnasse attracted the "Lost Generation"— brooding, disillusioned American expatriates like Calder, Hemingway, and Henry Miller. Now, chain restaurants and tourists crowd the heavily commercialized boulevard. Although it is still possible to channel the quartier's artistic vibe, it comes at ever-increasing prices. Sip an espresso, read Apollinaire, and divine your destiny at Montparnasse's few remaining classical cafes. *(ⓂMontparnasse-Bienvenüe or Vavin. 14ème.).*

FONDATION CARTIER POUR L'ART CONTEMPORAIN. The Fondation Cartier's stunning modern glass facade surrounds natural plants and trees, giving the air of a forest from The Jetsons. The two-level gallery hosts rotating contemporary art exhibits, from Andy Warhol to African sculpture. The Fondation received a great deal of attention in 2004 for Pain Couture, a show featuring Jean-Paul Gaultier designs rendered in rolls and baguettes. On Thursday nights, during **Les Soirées Nomades,** enthusiasts can enjoy an eclectic set of dance, music, and performance art. *(261 bd. Raspail, 14ème.* ⓂRaspail *or Denfert-Rochereau.* ☎42 18 56 *50; http://fondation.cartier.com. Open Tu 11am-10pm, W-Su noon-8pm. Soirées Nomades Th 8:30pm; check website for performance details. Reserve ahead at* ☎42 18 56 72. €6.50, students and seniors €4.50, under 10 free.)

15ÈME ARRONDISSEMENT

Primarily a residential and business district, the 15ème has few well known attractions and consequently fewer tourists. A generally calm, safe area at night, it provides a glimpse into the authentic Parisian life.

▧PARC ANDRÉ CITROËN. Landscapers Alain Provost and Gilles Clément created the futuristic Parc André Citroën in the 1990s, following the Citroën automobile plant's closing. Located alongside the Seine, this Parisian jungle contains multi-level fountains, tall greenhouses, and a "wild" garden whose plants change annually. In the summer, sunbathers and picnickers recline on the grass. Those who need to find out whether that QT accepted their MySpace friend request can take advantage of the Parc's three free Wi-Fi zones. LOL! Hot-air balloon rides launch from the central garden and offer spectacular aerial views of Paris and the park. *(*ⓂJavel *or Balard. 15ème.* ☎44 26 20 00; www. aeroparis.com. No man-eating tigers in park; also, no tiger-eating men. Park open in summer M-F 8am-9:30pm, Sa-Su 9am-9:30pm; in winter M-F 8am-5:45pm, Sa-Su 9am-5:45pm. Guided tours leave from the Jardin Noir, between rue Balard and rue St-Charles; €3-6. Balloon rides daily in summer 9am-9pm; in winter 9am-5:15pm. Weekends and holidays 10min. balloon rides €12, ages 12-17 €10, ages 3-11 €6, under 3 free; weekdays €10/9/5/free.)*

INSTITUT PASTEUR. Founded by the French scientist Louis Pasteur in 1888, the Institut Pasteur is now a center for biochemical research, development, and treatment. A champion of 19th-century germ theory, Pasteur first developed the pasteurization technique for purifying milk products and beer. The institute has turned Pasteur's somber but magnificent home into a museum. Inside, the instruments Pasteur used in his discoveries of an anthrax vaccine and a cure for rabies will impress even those who don't know a mole from a groundhog. Meticulously preserved rooms and large portraits pained by a teenage Louis offer a closer look into the pionneer's life. While Pasteur's *tableaux* did not earn him eternal fame, his institute remains under the scientific spotlight as the lab where, in 1983, Dr. Luc Montaigner and Robert Gallo first isolated HIV. Visitors may also visit Pasteur's tomb, an awesome marble and mosaic construction, during the short (45min.) musuem tour. *(25 rue du Docteur Roux, 15ème.* ⓂPasteur. Walk uphill on bd. Pasteur; rue du Docteur Roux is the 1st right. ☎45 68 82 83; www.pasteur.fr. Open Sept.-July M-F 2-5:30pm. Box office located in a small building next to the museum, across from the institute. Tour times can be erratic. Admission €3, students €1.50; with English- or French-language tour and film €5/2.50.)*

TOUR MONTPARNASSE. The modern Montparnasse Tower dominates the 15ème's northeast corner. Standing 59 stories or 209m tall and completed in 1969, the building looks jarringly out of place amid Montparnasse's otherwise subdued 19th-century architecture. The structure, frequently maligned as an eyesore, spoils Baron Haussmann's carefully considered vistas. Shortly after the tower's creation, the city forbade the construction of similar monstrosities, designating the outer reaches of the La Défense district (p. 261) as the sole home for future *gratte-ciels* (skyscrapers). A monument to commercialism with offices filling 56 floors, the Tour Montparnasse boasts an incredible 360° of Paris from which you can see for 40km on a clear day. *(33 avenue du Maine, 15ème.* ⓂMontparnasse-Bienvenüe. Entrance on rue de l'Arrivée. ☎45 38 52 56. Open M-Th and

Su 9:30am-10:30pm, F-Sa 9:30am-11pm. Last entry 30min. before closing. Admission €9.50, student €6.80, handicapped €5.50, ages 7-15 €4; to 56th floor only €9/6.30/5/3.50.)

LA RUCHE. Although not open to visitors, La Ruche may still interest art aficionados. The building was originally constructed as a wine pavilion by Gustave Eiffel for the 1900 World's Fair. Sculptor Albert Boucher then bought and converted it into a studio and quasi-artists' colony. La Ruche ("The Beehive") received its name from its round shape, though its triangular cells prompted resident Ossip Zadkine to call it "a sinister wheel of brie." La Ruche has provided workspace for Chagall, Soutine, Léger, Zadkine, and other artists referred to by Boucher as *ses abeilles* (his bees). Today, La Ruche houses over 50 residents from 12 different countries who continue its mission to pursue creative endeavors. *(52 rue de Dantzig; on the passage de Dantzig, 15ème. ⓂConvention. Follow rue de la Convention toward place Charles Vallin; rue de Dantzig will be on the right.)*

PASSY AND AUTEUIL (16ÈME)

The 16*ème*, almost on the periphery, offers a break from the central Parisian pace. With residential avenues, peaceful parks and occasional architectural gems, this *arrondissement*, particularly in the prettier northern half, offers a glimpse into the life of the Parisian elite. Located southwest of Trocadéro, the exclusive ex-hamlets of Passy and Auteuil were once famous for their restorative waters (which attracted such visitors as Molière, Racine, and Proust) and later for their avant-garde architecture. Now, this pair is best known as the site where *Last Tango in Paris* was filmed and as a pricey shopping district. Streets named after the likes of Guy de Maupassant, Nicolas Poussin, Donizetti, among others, recall 18th-century salon culture. No. 59 rue d'Auteuil was the site of Mme. Helvetius's house, where the so-called "Notre Dame d'Auteuil" (a play on the church name, also meaning "Our Dame of Auteuil") hosted the Right Bank's well-read and best-dressed at her notorious salons for over five decades. Benjamin Franklin and Honoré de Balzac are other well-known ex-residents of these two posh Parisian boroughs.

RUE LA FONTAINE. Its name comes from the sulfurous thermal spring that brought the residents of Auteuil their water, but since the late 19th century, rue la Fontaine has been most famous for its Belle Époque architecture (though it often gives way to less-aesthetically-pleasing buildings). This street also boasts the first designs of Art Nouveau master Hector Guimard: Castel Béranger (1898), at no. 14, launched Guimard's career—look for the turquoise iron flourishes, carbuncular seahorses, and columns bulging with floral sea-growth. The red-paneled Bar Antoine at no. 17 (1911) has a painted-glass ceiling and is decorated with Art Nouveau tiles. Guimard designed the vine-entangled street signs of rue Agar, off rue la Fontaine, as well as the gnarled iron "branches" of the fence at no. 60 (1911), which now houses the Ministère de l'Education Nationale. Proust was born at no. 96 on July 10, 1871; look above the first-floor window for the information plaque. *(ⓂMichel-Ange Auteuil, Jasmin, or Église d'Auteuil, or RER: Kennedy. Rue la Fontaine extends from the intersection at ⓂMichel-Ange Auteuil to the Maison de Radio France, where it turns into rue Raynouard.)*

JARDIN DE RANELAGH. Surrounded by some of the most beautiful mansions in the 16*ème*, the lovely Jardin de Ranelagh has playgrounds, a carousel, puppets, and donkey rides. The people-watching is excellent: this is where the wealthy residents of the 16*ème* come out to play. *(ⓂLa Muette. Head away from the Eiffel Tower down Chaussée de la Muette, which becomes the pedestrian av. Ranelagh.)*

RUE BENJAMIN FRANKLIN. Rue Benjamin Franklin commemorates the statesman's one-time residence in Passy. Franklin lived at 66 rue Raynouard from 1777 to 1785 while negotiating a treaty between the newly formed US and Louis XVI. It was on this site that Franklin experimented with his electrifying lightning rod. (ⓂPassy. After exiting, take rue de l'Albinoni straight up and turn right onto rue Benjamin Franklin, past bd. Pelessert.)

STATUE OF LIBERTY. On a manmade islet in the middle of the Seine, the Allée des Cygnes, stands a very miniature version of the New York's Lady Liberty. Erected by French sculptor Frédéric Bartholdi, the little lady was donated by a group of American expats in 1885 and moved to this spot for the 1889 World's Fair. (ⓂPassy or Mirabeau. From Passy, walk down rue de l'Albinoni toward the Seine and cross av. du Président Kennedy onto the Pont Bir-Hakeim. From Mirabeau, walk on av. de Versailles toward the Eiffel Tower and turn right on the Pont de Grenelle.)

TROCADÉRO AND SURROUNDINGS

Although Trocadéro Place can be touristy due to the nearby Eiffel Tower, this part of the 16ème reveals an unexpected Paris.

PLACE D'IÉNA. The place d'Iéna positions you next to the rotunda of the Conseil Économique and opens onto the round Palladian facade of the Musée Guimet, which houses an exhaustive collection of Asian art. It is a 5min. walk west to the Trocadéro and 5min. east to the museums of the Palais de Tokyo, which houses cutting edge art expositions (see **Museums,** p. 289). (ⓂIéna.)

PALAIS DE TOKYO. Built for the 1937 World Expo, this austere, neoclassical, and arguably ugly Palais is home to the world-class ◨**Musée d'Art Moderne de la Ville de Paris** (see **Museums,** p. 289), which offers free admission to its permanent collection. The west wing of the Palais houses the excellent *site de création contemporaine,* which exhibits today's hottest and most controversial art. (11 av. du Président Wilson. ⓂIéna. ☎01 47 23 54 01; www.palaisdetokyo.com. Open Tu-Su noon-midnight. €6; seniors, under 25, and groups of 10 or more €4.50; artists and art students €1.)

PLACE DU TROCADÉRO. In the 1820s the Duc d'Angoulême built a memorial to his victory in Spain at Trocadéro. For the 1937 World's Fair, Jacques Carlu added two mirror-image white stone buildings called the **Palais de Chaillot,** block-like and situated in the shape of an arch, as well as an austere veranda between them. Guarded by Henri Bouchard's 7.5m bronze Apollo and eight other figures, the terrace attracts tourists, vendors, and roller bladers and offers the ◨**best view of the Eiffel Tower** and surrounding city, day or night. Beware pickpockets and traffic as you gaze upward. (ⓂTrocadéro.)

PALAIS DE CHAILLOT. The Palais de Chaillot houses the **Musée de l'Homme,** the **Musée de la Marine** (see **Museums,** p. 291), and the **Théâtre National de Chaillot** (see **Entertainment,** p. 314). It is the last of a series of buildings on the site: Catherine de Médicis had a château here, which was transformed into a convent by Queen Henrietta of England. Napoleon razed the convent and planned a palace for his son, but rotten luck at Waterloo brought construction to a halt. Architects Léon Azéma, Jacques Carlu and Louis-Hippolyte Boileau created the building as it now stands for the 1937 World's Fair. Their design, which beat out Le Corbusier's in a contest for the commission, is unusual for its lack of a central rotunda. Each side of each building is inscribed with an enigmatic quote by Paul Valery, like, "All men create without knowing how he breathes, but the artist feels to create. His act commits all of his being, his beloved pain fortifies him." (17 pl. de Trocadéro.)

JARDINS DU TROCADÉRO. Below the palace, the green swaths of the Jardins du Trocadéro stretch to the banks of the Seine. The gardens offer a stunning picnic spot and at night, an incredible view of the Eiffel Tower. Off to the right, there is a small park with towering trees, benches, and an equally impressive view of the tower. In the summer, children frolic in the wide, cool fountains. The unlit parts of the garden are best avoided after dark.

CIMETIÈRE DE PASSY. The hilly grotto that overhangs pl. du Trocadéro is a surprisingly pleasant place to wander, look out at the 16*ème* below, or mourn the legacies of some of Paris's most recognizable names. Art aficionados can pay homage to painters Edouard Manet and Berthe Morisot (off of Chemin Heugel) and composers Claude Débussy and Gabriel Fauré (in the back left of the cemetery, off of avenure Principeale). Fashionistas can see the entire Givenchy family site (off of chemin San Fernando, in the back left of the cemetery) or the founder of Samaritaine, Cognacq-Jay. Finally, French history buffs can visit the former President of the Republic, Alexander Millerand. The enormous wall on the cemetery's Trocadéro side was designed in the same Neoclassical style as the Palais de Chaillot. Find maps at the adjoining funeral home. *(2 rue du Commandant-Schloesing.* Ⓜ*Trocadéro.* ☎*01 47 27 51 42. Walk toward the far wing of the Palais de Chaillot, turn right on av. Paul Doumer, and veer right onto rue du Commandant-Schloesing. Open Mar. 16-Nov. 5 M-F 8am-6pm, Sa 8:30am-6pm, Su 9am-6pm; Nov. 6-Mar. 15 M-F 8am-5:30pm, Sa 8:30am-5:30pm, Su 9am-5:30pm. Last entry 15min. before closing. Conservation office open M-F 8:30am-12:30pm and 2-5pm.)*

BATIGNOLLES (17ÈME)

The western half of the 17*ème* is primarily residential, providing little entertainment for visitors. For a leisurely stroll, bargain shopping, or cemetery exploration, stick to the Village Batignolles area in the east.

VILLAGE BATIGNOLLES

The Village Batignolles, dynamic neighborhood in the eastern half of the 17*ème*, houses both working-class and bourgeois residents. It centers around **rue des Batignolles,** stretching from **boulevard des Batignolles** at the southern end to **place du Dr. Félix Lobligeois,** where several hip cafes overlook the tree-lined square.

CIMETIÈRE DES BATIGNOLLES. Stuck behind a noisy lycée and plagued by honking cars from the Périphérique, the cemetery hardly seems a place to rest in peace. Less glamorous than Père Lachaise (p. 254) or Montmartre (p. 251) graveyards, the Cimet ère des Batignolles nevertheless can claim verse poet Paul Verlaine and surrealist authors André Breton and Benjamin Peret among its interred. *(8 rue St-Just, 17ème.* ☎*01 53 06 38 68.* Ⓜ*Port de Clichy. Walk north along avenue Port de Clichy and turn right onto avenue du Cimetière des Batignolles. Open Mar. 16 to Nov. 5 M-F 8am-6pm, Sa 8:30am-6pm, Su and holidays 9am-6pm; Nov. 6 to Mar. 15 M-F 8am-5:30pm, Sa 8:30am-5:30pm, Su and holidays 9am-5:30pm. Conservation Bureau open M-F 8am-noon and 2-5:30pm; request free map inside. Last entry 15min. before closing. Free.)*

OTHER SIGHTS. Just north of the place du Dr. Félix Lobligeois, craggy waterfalls and duck ponds flush out **square des Batignolles;** this English-style park recalls its more famous southern neighbor, Parc Monceau (p. 236), but stands out for its historical merit. The meticulously landscaped oasis provided Monet with the western vantage point necessary to paint the train tracks stretching from Gare St-Lazare. From the park, Monet could walk to **Café Guerbois,** at 11 rue des Batignolles, where fellow Impressionists like Edgar Degas, Berthe Morisot, and Pierre-Auguste Renoir met regularly to share and critique their art. Today, an

organic produce market (see p. 200) occupies rue des Batignolles every Saturday. Tuesday through Sunday, local residents settle for regular cheese, meat, and produce at the **Marché Batignolles** (see p. 200). On the neighborhood's western edge, restaurants and cafes line rue des Dame, and shopping venues flourish on rue de Levis (Ⓜ Villiers). At the intersection with rue des Epinettes, **La Cité des Fleurs,** 59-61 rue de la Jonquière, is a row of exquisite private homes and gardens. Designed in 1847, this prototypical condominium complex required each owner to plant at least three flowering trees in his garden. (Ⓜ Villiers.)

MONTMARTRE (18ÈME)

No longer a local secret, Montmartre's captivating liveliness and bohemian spirit make it one of Paris's most touristed districts. Plan to spend at least a day and an evening here; the 18*ème* has enough nooks and crannies to keep you entertained for some time.

MOUNTING MONTMARTRE

No such thing as a simple stroll exists in Montmartre; rather, its stone staircase *"rues"* and sloping cobblestone hills provide for a physique-toning climb. The standard approach is from the south, via Ⓜ Anvers or Ⓜ Abbesses, although other directions provide interesting, less crowded uphill hikes. From Ⓜ Anvers, the short walk up rue Steinkerque to the ornate, switchbacked stairway attracts large numbers of tourists. The longer, more peaceful climb from Ⓜ Abbesses (fans may recognize this as Amélie's metro stop) passes by several worthwhile cafes and shops. Particularly feisty travelers up for a physical challenge should note that Ⓜ Abbesses, which lies 30m below ground, is also the metro stop with the most steps to its exit. Albeit less interesting than the graffiti scrawls plastering the metro walls a few years ago, the spiral staircase's mural-covered walls may suffice to distract you from the climb.

A glass-covered **funiculaire** ascends from the base of rue Tardieu to atop Montmartre (from Ⓜ Anvers, walk up rue Steinkerque and take a left on rue Tardieu). Operated by the RATP, the funicular functions similar to a ski lift and can be ridden with a normal metro ticket. *(Funicular runs cars every 10min. Open Su-F 7:35am-12:40am, Sa 7:35am-11:35pm. €1.50 or metro ticket.)* The **Syndicat d'Initiative de Montmartre,** located in place du Tetre, offers 2hr. **walking tours** of historic Montmartre for €10 per person. Call ahead to join a group tour or organize one of your own. Led in a multiple languages, the tours offer a unique perspective into some of the less touristed parts of the *butte.* (☎01 42 62 21 21).

▨**BASILIQUE DU SACRÉ-COEUR.** This ethereal basilica, with its signature white onion domes, was commissioned to atone for France's war crimes in the Franco-Prussian War. The chosen site, atop Montmartre ("mount of martyrs,") had religious as well as historical significance; home to Saint Denis, Paris's first bishop, it was where Saint Francois-Xavier and Saint Ignatius of Loyola founded the **Society of Jesus** (Jesuits) in 1534. A benedictine Abbey claimed the hill until the French Revoltution when, desiring a clean cut from their past, the revolutionaries beheaded its abbess and destroyed the nunnery. Construction on Sacré-Coeur began in 1876 and ended in 1914, and it was consecrated five years later. The basilica inspired even greater devotion in WWII when 13 bombs exploded in its vicinity, miraculously without injuring anyone.

Sacré-Coeur's architecture appears similarly divine. Its unusual rounded arches, onion domes, and white stone make it distinctive. Inside the basilica, the striking mosaics—especially Christ on the ceiling and the Passion mural behind the altar—attract large numbers of tourists, albeit fewer than its gothic cousin Notre Dame. Originally designed to accommodate the hordes of pilgrims who would otherwise interrupt praying parishioners, the covered ambulatory behind the high altar still succeeds at sweeping today's secular tourists away from the pews. Beneath the basilica, the crypt contains pieces of the heart of Alexandre Legentil, who was the first to vow to build a national chruch atop Montmartre. To the left of the crypt's entrance, a spiral staircase leads up to the top of Sacré-Coeur's dome. After a tiring, slightly claustrophobia-inducing climb, you can marvel at the 🗹view, which stretches 50km on clear days. The Eiffel Tower may trump the Sacré-Coeur in height, but the basilica reigns supreme with fewer tourists and a cheaper panorama. While the view makes climbing the grassy slopes worthwhile, beware foreigners who swamp the streets below. *(35 rue du Chevalier-de-la-Barre. 18ème.* Ⓜ*Anvers, Abbesses, or Château-Rouge.* ☎ *01 53 41 89 00; www.sacre-coeur-montmartre.fr. Basilica open daily 6am-11pm. Mass daily 10pm. Crypt open daily 9am-5:30pm. Dome open daily 9am-6pm; last entry 5:30pm. Wheelchair-accessible around the back. Basilica free. Dome €5; MC/V over €10.)*

AU LAPIN AGILE. A favorite of Guillaume Apollinaire, Max Jacob, Amedeo Modigliani, and Americans Charlie Chaplin and Ernest Hemingway, the establishment was known as the "Cabaret des Assassins" until André Gill decorated its facade with a painting of a lapin (rabbit) balancing a hat on its head and a bottle on its paw. The cabaret gained renown as the "Lapin à Gill" (Gill's rabbit). By the time Picasso began to frequent the establishment, walking over from his studio at no. 49 rue Gabrielle, the name had contracted to the "Lapin Agile." Today, the cabaret has become touristy, but you can still sip a *cerises maison* (€7) while taking in a mix of French *chanson* and comedy. *(22 rue des Saules, 18ème.* Ⓜ*Lamarck-Caulaincourt. Turn right on rue Lamarck, before walking right and up rue des Saules.* ☎ *01 46 06 85 87; www.au-lapin-agile.com. Call for reservations. Shows Tu-Su 9pm-2am. Tickets €24; Tu-F and Su excepting holidays students €17. Entry includes 1st drink; successive beverages €6-7. Knock on the door if arriving after 9pm. See* **Entertainment, p. 315***)*

LES VIGNES. A Montmartre staple since Gallo-Roman times, the vineyards were known in the 16th century for the diuretic wines they produced: a 17th-century saying even promises, "C'est du vin de Montmartre, qui en boit pinte en pisse quarte" (With Montmartre wine, he who drinks a pint pisses a quart). Now this lone surviving winery, perched on the hilly slope across from the Lapin Agile (see p. 315), is one of **Paris's last remaining vineyards.** It makes you feel like you're in Paris of the early 20th century. Montmartre's vignes have remained intact more for tradition than function, producing only a few dozen bottles of wine per year. Every October, the vineyard hosts the **Fête des Vendanges;** this boisterous weekend festival of wine-drinking, dancing, and folklore is the only time that the wine produced on the grounds is sold to the public (see **Life and Times,** p. 97). The area surrounding the vineyard, on the butte's northern slope, remains one of the loveliest in Montmartre. Still largely unspoiled by tourism, the streets around rue St-Vincent maintain their rural village charm with old stone walkways and shuttered farm houses. *(Rue des Saules, 18ème.* Ⓜ*Lamarck-Caulaincourt. Follow directions to the Lapin Agile; on the corner of rue des Saules and rue St-Vincent. Closed to the public, except during the Fête des Vendanges Oct. 10-12, 2008, Oct. 9-11, 2009, and Oct. 8-10, 2010; see www.fetedesvendangesdemontmartre.com for more info.)*

BATEAU-LAVOIR. There's not much to see here, but the history is interesting. Given its name by sardonic residents Max Jacob and André Salmon, who thought the building's winding corridors resembled the interior of a ship *(bateau)*, the Bateau-Lavoir has been home to several artists' *ateliers* (studios) since the early 20th century. Still serving as studio space for 25 contemporary painters and sculptors, the building celebrated its undisputed heyday in the early 1920s, when great artists and poets like Guillaume Apollonaire, Juan Gris, Amedeo Modigliani, and Pablo Picasso stayed there. In his studio here in 1907, Picasso finished his Cubist manifesto, the remarkable *Demoiselles d'Avignon*. The original building burned down in 1970, but a display to the left of the gate chronicles the site's history and residents. *(11bis place Emile Godeau, 18ème. ⓂAbbesses. Facing the church, head right up rue des Abbesses, and turn right, uphill, on rue Ravignan; follow the steps to place Emile Godeau. Closed to the public.)*

DOWNHILL

RUES ABBESSES, LEPIC, AND D'ORSEL. These days tasty restaurants, trendy cafes, and traditional *boulangeries* fill rue des Abbesses and rue Lepic, attempting to profit from a swell in tourism due to the international hit film *Amélie* (2002) which was filmed in the area. Predictably, longtime residents are complaining about the "Amélie Poulainization" of their neighborhood as devoted fans seek out the title character's home and haunts. Walking down rue Lepic will take you past the **Moulin Radet,** one of Montmartre's last remaining windmills. Farther down the street, you can visit the reconstructed **Moulin de la Galette,** now an expensive eatery but made famous during its prime in Auguste Renoir's 1876 painting *Bal au Moulin de la Galette.* One of Vincent van Gogh's former homes lies even further down rue Lepic at no. 54. Also noteworthy, beautiful 18th-century townhouses rest behind tall iron gates, architecturally true to their era. Shopaholics, disatisfied with the cheap **Puces St-Ouen** (see **Shopping,** p. 310), will find attractive boutiques along rue d'Orsel near ⓂAbbesses.

CIMETIÈRE MONTMARTRE. Though less star-studded than the legendary Père Lachaise (p. 254), the beautifully landscaped Cimetière Montmartre remains more secluded than its famous neighbor. Composers Hector Berlioz and Jacques Offenbach, dancers Marie Taglioni and Vaslav Nijinksy, filmmaker François Truffaut, painter Edgar Degas, physicians André Ampère and Léon Foucault, saxophone inventor Adolphe Sax, and writer Stendhal are buried here. People often leave ballet shoes on Taglioni's grave, as she was the first to dance an entire performance on point. The cemetery was also the site of mass graves after the 1871 suppression of the Commune. Emile Zola was originally interred here until a grateful French government transferred his remains to the Panthéon in 1908, with all the other *grands hommes*. The office to the left of the rue Rachel entrance distributes free maps. *(20 avenue Rachel, 18ème. ☎01 53 42 36 30. ⓂPlace de Clichy or Blanche. From either metro, walk down bd. de Clichy and turn down avenue Rachel. Open Nov. 6-Mar. 15 M-F 8am-5:30pm, Sa 8:30am-5:30pm, Su and holidays 9am-5:30pm; Mar. 16-Nov. 5 M-F 8am-6pm, Sa 8:30am-6pm, Su and holidays 9am-6pm.)*

BAL DU MOULIN ROUGE. Numerous Belle Époque cabarets and nightclubs line bd. de Clichy and bd. de Rochechouart to the north of the 18ème. None, however, have achieved the stardom—or notoriety—of the infamous Bal du Moulin Rouge, immortalized by Henri de Toulouse-Lautrec's paintings, Jacques Offenbach's music, and, most recently, Baz Luhrmann's Hollywood blockbuster. At the turn of the century, Paris's bourgeoisie came to the Moulin Rouge to play at being bohemian. Following WWI, the area around **place Pigalle** became an internationally renowned red-light district (p. 238). Today, despite the famous reconstructed windmill, there's not much to see from the street. If you're looking to splurge on one of the Moulin Rouge's splashy cabaret shows, see **Entertainment,** p. 314 *(82 bd. de Clichy, 18ème. ☎01 53 09 82 82; www.moulin-rouge.com. ⓂBlanche. Across from the Metro.)*

LA GOUTTE D'OR. Farther east, toward the railroad tracks, the 18ème becomes an immigrant ghetto attempting urban renewal. Still filled with crumbling buildings, the quartier takes its name, "drop of gold," from the prize-winning medieval vineyard that once stood here. Today, the area is one of the last few refuges for cheap housing in Paris. The large Virgin Megastore on bd. Barbès insinuates the neighborhood's desire for change, foreshadowing ambitious development plans that may soon raise the rents here, too. Discount clothing shops line bd. Barbès, and numerous African cloth, food, and gift shops can be found on rue Doudeauville and rue des Poissonniers. Be watchful of pickpockets in the neighborhood; those unfamiliar with the area might be uncomfortable at night. *(18ème. M:Barbès-Rochechouart, Château Rouge, or Marcadet-Poissonniers.)*

BUTTES CHAUMONT (19ÈME)

Modern, inventive, and extremely child-friendly, the sights of the 19*ème* are varied enough to keep any family on its toes for a day or more. La Villette showcases some of the Paris's significant architectural and social accomplishments of the past few decades, while the Parc des Buttes-Chaumont provides a wonderful picnic location.

LA VILLETTE

The realization of a successful urban renewal project, La Villette's 20-year metamorphosis proves you can't rush a good thing. Once a meat-packing district that provided Paris with much of its beef, the area became outmoded after the refrigerated truck's advent. In 1979, the slaughterhouses were replaced with an artistic park, and *voilà:* architect Bernard Tschumi's three-part vision took 461 teams from 41 difference countries to complete.

◧**PARC DE LA VILLETTE.** Cut in the middle by **Canal de l'Ourcq** and **Canal St-Denis,** Parc de la Villette separates the Cité des Sciences from the Cité de la Musique. Dominating the park, the steel-and-glass **Grande Halle** features concerts, films, and plays. The architecture fuses traditional Haussmann style and uber-modern glass facades. Twenty-six funny-shaped red buildings called *folies* dot the park at regular 120m intervals. Sharing a similar cube design, they serve numerous purposes from First Aid center to Le Quick hamburger stand. Before the Grande Halle, the **information Villette folie** distributes free maps and brochures.

During July and August, La Villette hosts a free open-air film festival with an international program. The **Zénith** concert hall welcomes rock and pop artists while the Trabendo jazz and modern music club—located in yet another *folie*—attracts new-wave and rock groups. Every September, an extremely popular, month-long jazz festival takes over La Villette (see **Life and Times, p. 97**).

Finally, the Promenade des Jardins links several thematic gardens, including the **Garden of Dunes and Wind,** reminiscent of a seashore; the **Garden of Childhood Fears,** which winds through a wooded grove resonant with spooky sounds; and the roller coaster **Dragon Garden.** If you can bypass the height requirement and pass yourself off as under 12, then you too can join the gaggle of kids leaping on trampolines, racing up hills, and zooming down slides. *(211 avenue Jean Jaurès, 19ème. ⓜPorte de Pantin. General info ☎01 40 03 75 75, Trabendo 01 42 01 12 12, Zénith 01 42 08 60 00; www.villette.com. Buy tickets online at www.fnac.com. Info office open M-Sa 9:30am-6:30pm. Promenade des Jardins open 24hr. Free.)*

◧**CITÉ DES SCIENCES ET DE L'INDUSTRIE.** The Cité des Sciences et de l'Industrie houses the fabulous **Explora Science Museum** (see **Museums,** p. 293), arguably the best destination for kids in Paris. The enormous **Géode** outside the Cité, a mirrored sphere mounted on a flower bed, looks like a gigantic disco ball thanks to the 6433 polished stainless steel triangles coating its exterior. Inside, **Omnimax movies** on deep sea creatures, glaciers, and other natural phenomena play on a 1000 sq. m hemispheric screen. To the right of the Géode, the **Argonaute submarine** details the history of submersibles from Jules Verne to present-day nuclear-powered subs. This 400-ton, 50m fighter submarine first served the French Navy in 1958, clocking more than 32,000hr. underwater during its 24-year tenure. Between the Canal St-Denis and the Cité, **Cinaxe** features innovative movies filmed from the first-person perspective; hydraulic pumps simulate every bump and curve as you explore the world in Formula One cars, low-flying planes, and Mars land rovers. Have lunch beforehand at your own risk. *(19ème. ⓂPorte de la Villette. ☎01 40 05 80 00; www.cite-sciences.fr. Géode: ☎01 40 05 12 12. Open M generally 10:30am-7:30pm, Tu-Su 10:30am-9:30pm; hours may vary. Shows hourly. Tickets €10.50, under 25 M-F except holidays €9, 2 films €15. Argonaute open Tu-Sa 10am-5:30pm, Su 10am-6:30pm. Admission €3; includes English- or French-languge audioguide. Cinaxe: ☎01 40 05 12 12. Open Tu-Su 11am-1pm and 2-5pm; shows every 15min. Admission €4.80.)*

CITÉ DE LA MUSIQUE. At the opposite end of La Villette from the Cité des Sciences, the Cité de la Musique opened in 1995. Christian de Pefrzamparc and Franck Hamoutène collaborated over this stunning complex's design, accentuating its glass ceilings and curving walls. For classical music lovers, the Musée de la Musique presents a rare treat. Visitors don headphones that tune in to musical excerpts and describe the pieces comprising the museum's vast collection of over 900 antique instruments, sculptures, and paintings. The Cité de la Musique's two performance spaces—the 900-seat **Salle des Concerts** and the 230-seat **Amphithéâtre**—host an eclectic range of concerts and shows year-round (see **Entertainment,** p. 317). The Cité de la Musique also houses the music info center and the **Médiathèque Pédagogique,** with 70,000 books, documents, music journals, and photographs. *(19ème. ⓂPorte de Pantin. ☎01 44 84 44 84, médiathèque 01 44 84 89 45; www.cite-musique.fr. Info center open Tu-Sa noon-6pm, Su 10-6pm. Musée de la Musique open Tu-Sa noon-6pm, Su 10am-6pm; last entry 5:15pm. Admission €6.50, under 18 €5.20. 1hr. French-language tour €10, under 18 €8. Extra charge for temporary exhibits. Médiathèque open Tu-Sa noon-6pm, Su 1-6pm. Free.)*

ELSEWHERE IN THE NINETEENTH

▨**PARC DES BUTTES-CHAUMONT.** Parc des Buttes-Chaumont, in the south of the 19ème, is a mix of manmade topography and transplanted vegetation, all created on a nostalgic whim. Napoleon III commissioned it in 1862 out of a longing for London's Hyde Park, where he spent much of his time in exile. Since the 13th century, the *quartier* had been host to a *gibbet* (an iron cage filled with the rotting corpses of criminals), a dumping ground for dead horses, a haven for worms, and a gypsum quarry (the source of "plaster of Paris"). Making a park out of the existing mess took four years and 1000 workers. Designer Adolphe Alphand had all the soil replaced and the quarried remains built up with new rock to create cliffs around a lake. Today's visitors walk the winding paths surrounded by lush greenery and hills, and enjoy a great view of the quartier from the Roman temple atop cave-filled cliffs. Watch out for the ominously named **Pont des Suicides,** or "Suicide Bridge." *(19ème. ⓂButtes-Chaumont or Botzaris. Open daily May-Sept. 7am-10:15pm; Oct.-Apr. 7am-8:15pm; some gates close early.)*

BELLEVILLE AND PÈRE LACHAISE (20ÈME)

Despite its largely residential reputation, the 20ème contains one massive, dominating attraction: the Père Lachaise Cemetery. Perusing the legendary graves at this historic location renders the long metro ride from the city

SIGHTS

center well worth it. For a more tranquil—and less morbid—place to relax, try the beautiful, layered Parc de Belleville.

PÈRE LACHAISE CEMETERY

16 rue du Repos, 20ème. ☎01 55 25 82 10. ⓂPère Lachaise. Open mid- Mar. to early Nov. M-F 8am-6pm, Sa 8:30am-6pm, Su and holidays 9am-6pm; Nov. to mid-Mar. M-F 8am-5:30pm, Sa 8:30am-5:30pm, Su and holidays 9am-5:30pm. Last entry 15min. before closing. Free. Free maps at the Bureau de Conservation near Porte du Repos; ask for directions at guard booths near the main entrances. Apr. to mid-Nov. free 2 1/2hr. guided tour Sa 2:30pm. For more info on "theme" tours, call ☎01 49 57 94 37.

With its winding paths and elaborate sarcophagi, the Cimetière du Père Lachaise has become the final resting place for many French and foreign legends. Balzac, Colette, Jacques Louis David, Eugène Delacroix, La Fontaine, Haussmann, Molière, and Proust are buried here, as are Modigliani, Jim Morrison, Stein, and Wilde.

"Streets" crisscross the 19th-century neighborhood-of-the-dead, bordered by marble and stone sarcophagi resembling little houses. Many of the tombs in this landscaped grove strive to remind visitors of the dead's worldly accomplishments: the tomb of French Romantic painter Théodore Géricault bears a reproduction of his Raft of the Medusa, the original painting now decorating the Louvre. On Frédéric Chopin's tomb sits his muse Calliope, sculpted beautifully in white marble, while larger-than-life Egyptian figures mark Oscar Wilde's grave. Although Wilde died destitute, an American admirer added the striking adornment in 1912. The sculpture was defaced in 1961, prompting false rumors that the cemetery director, finding a part of the sculpture's anatomy to be out of proportion, removed the offending jewels of the Nile and kept them as a paperweight. Despite an interdiction to kiss the tomb, dozens of lipstick marks from adoring fans cover Wilde's grave today.

Baron Haussmann, responsible for Paris's large boulevards, originally wanted to destroy Père Lachaise as part of his urban-renewal project; having relented, he now occupies one of the cemetery's mausoleums. The cemetery also commemorates modern dancer Isadora Duncan, Dada painter Max Ernst, and circus clown Achille Zavatta. The Doors's former lead singer, Jim Morrison remains popular even in death; the most visited, his grave attracts dozens of people bringing beer, flowers, joints, poetry, and Doors paraphernalia daily.

While over a million people are buried at Père Lachaise, only 100,000 tombs exist. This discrepancy arises from the old practice of burying the poor in mass graves. To make room for new generations of the dead, corpses are removed from these unmarked plots at regular intervals. Even with such purges, however, Père Lachaise's 44 hectares are filled to bursting; hence, the government digs up any grave unvisited in ten years and transports the remains to a different cemetery. To avoid being disenterred, some rich, solitary souls resort to hiring a professional "mourner" just before their death.

The monuments marking collective deaths remain the most emotionally moving sites in Père Lachaise. The **Mur des Fédérés** (Wall of the Federals) has become a pilgrimage site for left-wing sympathizers worldwide. In May 1871, a group of Communards, sensing their reign's imminent end, murdered the Archbishop of Paris, their hostage since the beginning of the Commune. They dragged his mutilated corpse to their stronghold in Père Lachaise and tossed it in a ditch. Four days later, the victorious Versaillais found the body. In retaliation, they lined up 147 Fédérés against the cemetary's eastern wall before shooting and burying them on the spot. Since 1871, the Mur des Fédérés has been a rallying point for the French Left, which recalls the massacre's anniversary every Pentecost. Near the wall, other monuments remember WWII

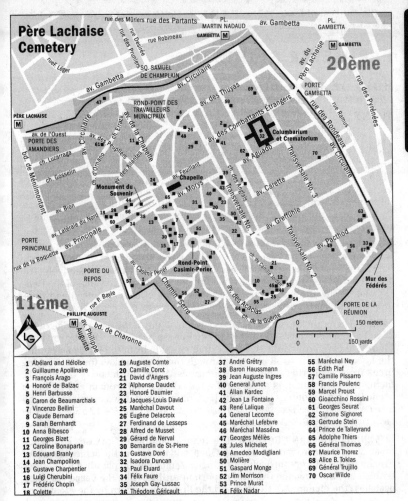

1 Abélard and Héloïse	19 Auguste Comte	37 André Grétry	55 Maréchal Ney
2 Guillaume Apollinaire	20 Camille Corot	38 Baron Haussmann	56 Edith Piaf
3 François Arago	21 David d'Angers	39 Jean Auguste Ingres	57 Camille Pissarro
4 Honoré de Balzac	22 Alphonse Daudet	40 General Junot	58 Francis Poulenc
5 Henri Barbusse	23 Honoré Daumier	41 Allan Kardec	59 Marcel Proust
6 Caron de Beaumarchais	24 Jacques-Louis David	42 Jean La Fontaine	60 Gioacchino Rossini
7 Vincenzo Bellini	25 Maréchal Davout	43 René Lalique	61 Georges Seurat
8 Claude Bernard	26 Eugène Delacroix	44 General Lecomte	62 Simone Signoret
9 Sarah Bernhardt	27 Ferdinand de Lesseps	45 Maréchal Lefebvre	63 Gertrude Stein
10 Anna Bibesco	28 Alfred de Musset	46 Maréchal Masséna	64 Prince de Talleyrand
11 Georges Bizet	29 Gérard de Nerval	47 Georges Méliès	65 Adolphe Thiers
12 Caroline Bonaparte	30 Bernardin de St-Pierre	48 Jules Michelet	66 Général Thomas
13 Edouard Branly	31 Gustave Doré	49 Amedeo Modigliani	67 Maurice Thorez
14 Jean Champollion	32 Isadora Duncan	50 Molière	68 Alice B. Toklas
15 Gustave Charpentier	33 Paul Eluard	51 Gaspard Monge	69 Général Trujillo
16 Luigi Cherubini	34 Félix Faure	52 Jim Morrison	70 Oscar Wilde
17 Frédéric Chopin	35 Joseph Gay-Lussac	53 Prince Murat	
18 Colette	36 Théodore Géricault	54 Félix Nadar	

Resistance fighters and Nazi concentration camp victims. The cemetery's northeast corner provokes greater solemnity than the well-manicured central plots' grand sarcophogi; sunbathers and picnickers had best frolic elsewhere.

OTHER SIGHTS IN THE 20ÈME

PARC DE BELLEVILLE. Built into the hillside, a series of terraces connected by stairs and footpaths comprise this well-landscaped park. From its high vantage points, the park offers spectacular views of Parisian landmarks, including the Centre Pomidou, the Eiffel Tower, and the Panthéon. Shrieking children clamor gleefully around the park's playground, located near the entrance, while parents rest weary legs on nearby benches. Dotted by flowers and napping couples in summer, the serene landscape floats above

SIGHTS

traffic-congested Paris. *(27 rue Piat, in front of La Maison de l'Air, 20ème. ⓂPyrénées. Walk downhill on rue de Belleville and turn left on rue Piat.)*

PERIMETER SIGHTS

BOIS DE BOULOGNE

ⓂPorte Maillot, Sablons, Les Sablons, Porte Dauphine, or Porte d'Auteuil. Open 24hr.

The Bois de Boulogne is an 846-hectare (over 2000 acres) green canopy at the western edge of Paris that hosts everything from the annual French Open tennis tournament to the regularly frolicking families to the occasional illicit sexual activity. Originally, the Bois was the vast **Forêt de Rouvray,** a royal hunting ground where deer and wild boar ran with wolves and bears. By 1852 it had become "a desert used for dueling and suicides," and was given to the city of Paris by Napoleon III. Acting on imperial instructions, Baron Haussmann dug lakes, created waterfalls, and cut winding paths through thickly wooded areas. By the turn of the century, the park was tame enough that aristocratic families rode there to spend a Sunday afternoon "in the country."

STADIUMS. The Bois de Boulogne contains several stadiums, including **Rolland Garros,** where the French Open is held; the **Hippodromes de Longchamp,** a flat race course; and the **Hippodromes d'Auteuil,** a steeplechase, respectively. The June **Grand Prix at Longchamp** was one of the premier annual events of the Belle Époque. Today, these stadiums host musical and athletic events. Meanwhile, the **Parc des Princes** hosts soccer, rugby, and concerts.

LAKES. There are two artificial lakes stretching down the eastern edge of the bois. The manicured islands of the **Lac Inférieur** can be reached only by rowboat. There is a path around the waterfalls that cascade from the **Lac Supérieur** into the Lac Inférieur; a stroll along it through the shade makes for a refreshing break from sweltering summer temperatures. At the north end of the islands, facing the boat rental, is a statue of a naked man and woman embracing, a scene that many couples around the park often re-enact, except clothed. Usually. *(ⓂPorte Dauphine. Boathouses open daily mid Mar. to early Nov. M-F 12-5:30pm, weather permitting. Rentals €10 per hr., €50 deposit.)*

■TENNISEUM ROLAND GARROS. The Tenniseum Roland Garros is a fantastic museum of the history of the French Open, and a salute to the achievements of French tennis players throughout the ages. A multimedia paradise for serious tennis fans, the museum displays important artifacts like the **Coupe des Mousquetaires** (the champion's trophy) and the first jacket, worn by the great René Lacoste, adorned with the now-famous crocodile logo. Visitors can also watch the archived matches of all the tennis greats of the Open era or test their tennis knowledge with quizzes on the computer terminals in the museum. *(ⓂPorte d'Auteuil or Michel-Ange Molitor. Enter at 2 av. Gordon-Bennett, off bd. d'Auteuil. ☎01 47 43 48 48; www.tenniseum.fr. Open Tu-Su 10am-6pm mid Feb. to Oct., W, F, Sa-Su Nov to mid Feb. Guided tour €10. €7.50, under 18 €4. Tours Tu-Sa, 3pm in English, 2 and 5pm in French.)*

JARDIN D'ACCLIMATATION. The Jardin d'Acclimatation offers a small zoo, some sports (mini-golf, riding, bowling), carnival rides, educational museums, picnic areas, and outdoor jazz concerts. Perfect for a day with the kids. Pick up a map from the ticket counter as you enter. Check website for theater performances, workshops, and other events. *(ⓂSablons. Cross the street, pass Monoprix, and walk 3 blocks. ☎01 40 67 90 82; www.jardindacclimatation.fr. Open daily May-Sept. 10am-7pm, Oct.-Apr. 10am-6pm. €3, seniors €1.50, under 3 free.)*

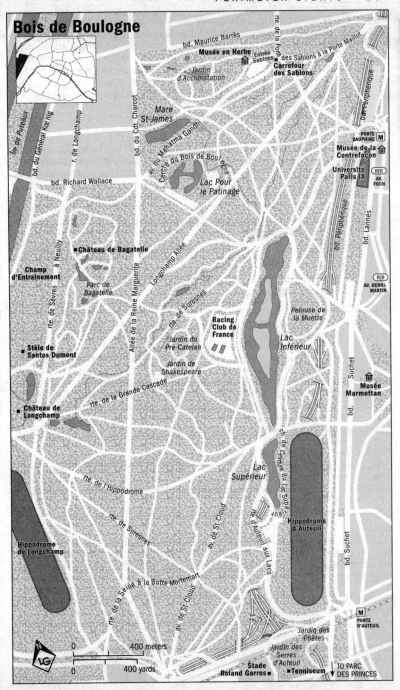

Bois de Boulogne

bd. Maurice Barrès

rte. de la Porte Maillot

Musée en Herbe

Entrée Sablons

Carrefour des Sablons

Jardin d'Acclimatation

rte. de Puteaux

bd. du Général Kœnig

r. de Longchamp

bd. du Cdt. Charcot

Mare St-James

PORTE DAUPHINE M

Musée de la Contrefaçon

av. du Mahatma Gandhi

Cercle du Bois de Boulogne

Université Paris IX

RER AV. FOCH

bd. Richard Wallace

Lac Pour le Patinage

bd. Lannes

Château de Bagatelle

Longchamp Allée

rte. de Sèvres à Neuilly

bd. Périphérique

Champ d'Entraînement

Parc de Bagatelle

Allée de la Reine Marguerite

RER AV. HENRI-MARTIN

rte. de Suresnes

Pelouse de la Muette

Stèle de Santos Dumont

Racing Club de France

Jardin du Pre-Catelan

Lac Inférieur

Suchet

Jardin de Shakespeare

Musée Marmottan

Château de Longchamp

rte. de la Grande Cascade

bd.

ch. de Ceinture du Supérieur

Lac Supérieur

rte. de l'Hippodrome

Hippodrome d'Auteuil

rte. de Suresnes

rte. d'Auteuil aux Lacs

Suchet

Hippodrome de Longchamp

av. de St-Cloud

av. de St-Cloud

M **PORTE D'AUTEUIL**

rte. de la Seine à la Butte Mortemart

Jardin des Poètes

0   400 meters

Jardin des Serres d'Auteuil

0   400 yards

Stade Roland Garros

Tenniseum

TO PARC DES PRINCES

MUSÉE EN HERBE. Celebrating the love story between art and the public, and created "with a little disrespect, a lot of humor and tenderness, and couple keys," the Musée en Herbe tells the history of European art. Designed for children ages 4-11, it showcases exhibits on all types of subjects, from farm animals to artists like Manet, Chagall, and Picasso. The museum also offers studio workshops on sculpture, pottery, papier-mâché, painting, and collage for children. A participatory theater company for children stages plays and puppet shows.*(In the Jardin d'Acclimatation. Directly on your left at the Entrée Sablons. ☎01 40 67 97 66; www.musee-en-herbe.com. Open daily 10am-6pm. €4, with temporary exhibit €8. Call to make reservations for special studio sessions. Also has a location at 21 rue Harold, 1er.)*

PRÉ CATELAN. The Pré Catelan is probably named after Théophile Catelan, master of the hunt under Louis XIV, but legend has it that this neatly manicured meadow was actually named after a murdered delivery boy, Arnault Catelan. Catelan was ordered to ride from Provence to Paris to deliver gifts to Philippe le Bel from Beatrice de Savoie, so he hired a group of men to protect him on his journey. The men killed him in the night, believing that Arnault carried gold, when in fact, the gifts were only perfumes from the South of France. Authorities later captured the marauders, who, doused in a rare Provençale scent, were easy to identify. Inside the Pré Catelan, there is an insanely overpriced restaurant (*entrées* start at €70), as well as the **Jardin de Shakespeare,** a popular open-air theater. *(From Ⓜ Porte Maillot, exit onto av. de Neuilly. Take bus #244 to Bagatuel-Pré-Catelan. Jardin de Shakespeare ☎01 40 19 95 33, tours of Pré Catelan 01 40 71 75 60. Jardin open daily 2-4pm. Pré Catelan open daily 9am-8pm. Guided tours €6, reduced €3).*

PARC DE BAGATELLE. Parc de Bagatelle was once a private estate and became a public park in 1905. In 1777, in an impetuous act that could not have helped his image in pre-revolutionary Paris, the future Charles X bet his sister-in-law, Marie-Antoinette, that he could build the Château de Bagatelle in three months. Marie-Antoinette was game, so Charles employed 1000 workers of all descriptions to complete the job. The Bagatelle Garden is now famous for its **rose exhibition** (3rd Th of June). The tulips are magnificent in April, irises bloom in May, and August is the month for the water lilies the gardener added in tribute to Monet. *(Same bus stop as Pré Catelan, above. ☎01 53 64 53 80; www.parcbagatelle.com. Open daily Mar.-June 9:30am-6:30pm; June-Sept. 9:30am-8pm; Oct.-Nov. 9:30am-6pm; Dec.-Feb. 9:30am-5pm. Ticket office closes 30min. earlier. €3, under age 26 €1.50).*

BOIS DE VINCENNES

Ⓜ Château de Vincennes or Porte Dorée. To best enjoy the park, rent a bike from the Lac des Minimes (☎01 30 59 68 38): open W and Sa 1:30-7:30 or 8pm, Su and holidays 9:30 or 10am-7pm (closed 6pm in winter), daily during school holidays; €5 for 1hr. ID deposit required. Lac Daumesnil (☎06 81 34 47 19): open W and Sa-Su 10am-7pm; daily during school holidays 9am-8pm (6pm in winter); €5 for 1hr. ID or €150 required.

Once a royal hunting forest, the Bois de Vincennes is now the largest expanse of greenery in Paris, encompassing nearly 1000 hectares. Until the 19th century, it lay beyond the reach of Parisian authorities, making it a favorite dueling venue. Alexandre Dumas challenged a literary collaborator to a duel in the Bois for claiming to have written *Le Tour de Nesle*. Although the duel was a debacle—Dumas's pistol misfired—the experience gave the author the inspiration for a scene in *Les Frères Corses*. Like the Bois de Boulogne, the Vincennes forest was given to Paris by Napoleon III, to be transformed into an English-style garden. Not surprisingly, Haussmann oversaw the planning of the lakes and pathways. Annexed to a much poorer section of Paris than the Bois de Boulogne, Vincennes was never as fashionable or as formal. Today, the Bois de Vincennes's bike paths, horse trails, zoo, and Buddhist temple offer an escape

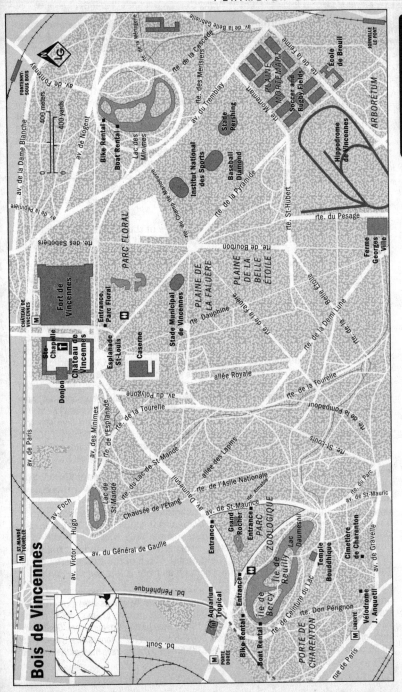

Bois de Vincennes

FONTENAY-SOUS-BOIS

av. de Fontenay

av. de la Dame Blanche

400 meters
400 yards

av. de la Pépinière

av. de Nogent

Bike Rental
Boat Rental

Lac des Minimes

rte. des Sabotiers

rte. de la Belle Gabrielle

av. de la Cascade

rte. des Merisiers

av. du Tremblay

Stade Pershing

rte. de la Pyramide

Institut National des Sports

Baseball Diamond

PLAINE MORTEMART

Soccer and Rugby Fields

rte. du Mortemart

rte. de la Ferme

JOINVILLE LE PONT

École de Breuil

ARBORÉTUM

Hippodrome de Vincennes

rte. St-Hubert

rte. du Pesage

Ferme Georges Ville

rte. de Bourbon

PLAINE DE LA BELLE ÉTOILE

Belle Étoile

rte. de la Demi Lune

rte. de la Faluère

PLAINE DE LA FALUÈRE

rte. Dauphine

PARC FLORAL

Entrance, Parc Floral

Stade Municipal de Vincennes

Esplanade St-Louis

Caserne

Fort de Vincennes

CHÂTEAU DE VINCENNES

Château de Vincennes

Ste Chapelle

Donjon

av. de Paris

av. des Minimes

av. de l'Esplanade

rte. de la Tourelle

av. du Polygone

allée Royale

rte. de la Tourelle

rte. de la Pompadour

rte. St-Louis

allée des Lapins

av. Daumesnil

rte. de l'Asile Nationale

rte. de St-Mandé

Lac de St-Mandé

rte. du Lac-de-St-Mandé

Chaussée de l'Étang

av. Foch

av. Victor Hugo

av. du Général de Gaulle

bd. Périphérique

bd. Soult

ST-MANDÉ TOURELLE

Aquarium Tropical

Bike Rental

Boat Rental

Île de Bercy

PORTE DORÉE

Entrance

Entrance

Grand Rocher

PARC ZOOLOGIQUE

rte. aimée

av. de St-Maurice

Île de Reuilly

Lac Daumesnil

Temple Bouddhique

rte. de Ceinture du Lac

rte. Don Pérignon

Cimetière de Charenton

av. de St-Maurice

av. du Parc

av. de Graville

Vélodrome J. Anquetil

LIBERTÉ

rue de Paris

PORTE DE CHARENTON

SIGHTS

from the city. The flat terrain is given definition by two irregularly shaped lakes and numerous thematic gardens. The park also houses the Vélodrome Jacques Anquetil, the Hippodrome de Vincennes, and other sports facilities.

PARC ZOOLOGIQUE DE PARIS. In a country not known for its zoos, the Parc Zoologique de Paris is considered the best of the bunch. The entrance is dominated by a manmade mountain especially designed for the zoo's population of alpine **goats**. A troupe of **Japanese macaques** pass the day sliding down rocks, swinging from trees, and chewing on hats that people throw into their habitat. The **phoques** (the French word for seal, pronounced just like you hope it is) are fed daily at 4pm (**pelicans** at 2:15pm, **penguins** at 2:30pm, and **otters** at 3pm). The zoo is undergoing comprehensive **renovation** until 2010, and the elephants, rhinos, and bears have decamped, but it is still open and fun to explore. *(53, av. de St-Maurice. ⑩Porte Dorée. ☎01 44 75 20 10. Open daily Jan. 9am-5pm; Feb.-Mar. 9am-5:30pm; Apr.-Sept. M-Sa 9am-6pm and Su and holidays 9am-6:30pm; Oct. 9am-6pm; Nov.-Dec. 9am-5pm. Ticket office closes 30min. before zoo. Admission €5, under 4 free. Train tour leaves from giraffe enclosure. €1.50, children €1.)*

CHÂTEAU DE VINCENNES. Called "the Versailles of the Middle Ages," the Château de Vincennes was the favored court residence of French kings as early as the 13th century. Although the Louvre was the principal royale abode, every French monarch from Charles V to Henri IV spent at least part of his time at Vincennes. Henri III took refuge here during the Wars of Religion, and Mazarin and the court found the château's defenses useful in the wake of the Fronde. In the 18th century, Vincennes became a country-club prison for well-known enemies of the state like the Comte de Mirabeau and the infamous Marquis de Sade. When Diderot was imprisoned in the château, Rousseau walked through the forest to visit him. In 1917, the infamous spy Mata Hari, convicted of espionage on behalf of the Germans, faced a firing squad within its walls. In 1940, the château was the headquarters of General Maurice Gamelin, Commander of the French Land Forces. Today, the 17th-century apartments house the archives of the French armed forces, and much of the château is only accessible by guided tour. *(⑩Château de Vincennes. On the northern edge of the park. Château doors open daily Apr.-Sept. 7:30am-7pm and Oct.-Mar. 9am-6:50pm. Information office (Accueil Charles V) located in second building to the right. ☎01 48 08 31 20. Open Sept.-Apr. 10am-noon and 1-5pm, May-Aug. 10am-noon and 1-6pm. Tour of Ste-Chapelle and château history (45min.) 11:45am, 1:30, and 5:15pm. €5, ages 18-25 €3.50, under 18 free. Tour of Ste-Chapelle, Etude du Roi, and Donjon (1hr.) 11am, 2:15, 3, 3:45, 4:30pm. €6.50/4.50. Tour information liable to change.)*

STE-CHAPELLE AND DONJON. Not to be confused with the better-known Ste-Chapelle on Île de la Cité, Ste-Chapelle is looking better than ever these days after restoration of its exterior. Built between 1336 and 1370, the 52m high donjon (big square tower) is a striking example of medieval architecture. It has been closed for restoration since 1995, and is expected to have a lavish re-opening in spring of 2007. Guided tours are the only way to get inside the church for a close-up look at the 16th-century stained-glass windows but most of the tour is devoted to historical background. Much of the structure's beauty can be appreciated from the outside as much as from inside the ramparts.

PARC FLORAL DE PARIS. The park has a butterfly garden, bonsai display, miniature golf, and assorted games for kids, and hosts festivals and concerts in summer. Check the park's website for details. *(Esplanade du Château. ⑩Château de Vincennes. ☎01 49 57 15 15, tours 01 40 71 75 60; www.parcfloraldeparis.com. Open daily Mar.-Apr. 9:30am-6pm; Apr.-Sept. 9:30am-8pm; Oct.-Feb. 9:30am-5pm. Admission €1, ages 7-25 €0.50, under 7 free; during events and concerts €3/1.50. €3-6 guided tours meet at the entrance of the park, and are themed by particular flowers.)*

LAC DAUMESNIL AND LAC DES MINIMES. Joggers, cyclists, horseback-riders, and people-watchers share the banks of the lovely Lac Daumesnil, while rowboats paddle around in it. The mysterious **caves** near the lake—topped off by a small temple—are not to be missed. The more remotely located Lac des Minimes is quiet and great for boating and picnicking. *(Lac Daumesnil boat rental (☎01 60 94 45 75) on av. Daumesnil. Open daily Mar.-Nov. 20 9:30am-6pm in winter and until 8pm in summer. 1-2 people €9.50 per hr., 3-4 people €10.50 per hr.; additional €10 deposit. Lac des Minimes boat rental (☎06 86 08 01 12) on av. de Nogent. Open Mar.-Nov. W and Sa-Su and holidays 1:30-7pm in winter. Open 1:30-8pm in summer daily 1:30-7pm; 1-2 people €9, 3-5 people €10; additional €15 deposit.*

LA DÉFENSE

Ⓜ/RER La Défense, or the #73 bus. The RER is slightly faster, but the metro is pretty quick and cheaper. If you take the RER, buy your ticket before going through the turnstile. A normal metro ticket may get you into the RER station in Paris, but won't get you out without a fine at La Défense. Consider either coming or going by the Esplanade de la Défense metro stop so you can savor the architecture, gardens, and outdoor sculpture around the arch. Grande Arche open daily 10am-7pm; last ascent 6:30pm. €7.50; under 18, students, and seniors €6. Beyond the small lawn, the Info Défense booth offers free maps, guides, and a free permanent exhibit on the architectural history and future of La Défense. ☎01 47 74 84 24. Open Oct.-Mar. M-F 9:30am-5:30pm, Apr.-Sept. 10am-6pm. Daily French Petit Train tours Apr.-Oct. every hr. 10am-5pm (6pm in Aug.), lasting 35min., from under the Grande Arche. €5, under 16 €3.

Just outside Paris's most exclusive suburbs lies a gleaming, teeming space crammed with eye-popping contemporary architecture, enormous office buildings, and one very geometric arch. Great efforts have been made since La Défense's initial development in 1958—especially by Mitterrand and his Grands Projets program—to inject social spaces, monuments, and art into La Défense's commercial landscape. Shops, galleries, gardens, and sculptures by Miró, Calder, and César cluster around the Grande Arche de la Défense, a 35-story building in the shape of a white hollow cube.

After the construction of the Tour Montparnasse was somehow permitted in 1973 (p. 245), Parisian authorities restricted further building of *gratte-ciels* (skyscrapers) within the 20 *arrondissements*, rightly fearing that new high-rises would mar the Paris skyline. As a result, new construction projects moved to La Défense. To maintain the symmetry of the Historic Axis (the line that stretches from the arch in front of the Louvre to La Défense, passing up the Champs-Élysées and through the Arc de Triomphe), I.M. Pei suggested a plan for a monument to anchor the La Défense end of the axis. Danish architect Otto von Spreckelsen's **Grande Arche** was chosen for the La Défense monument, and Pei was asked to design the eastern terminus in the courtyard of the Louvre. Spreckelsen backed out of the project midway, disheartened by red tape and by his own design, which he deemed a **"monument without a soul."** British engineer Peter Rice finished the work and designed the canvas tent "clouds" suspended to soften the arch's austere angles.

The arch was inaugurated on the French Republic's bicentennial, July 14, 1989. It took 300,000 tons of steel, 2800 marble and glass facade pieces, 2.6 billion francs and the efforts of 2000 workmen (2 of whom died in construction accidents) to complete the 87,000 sq. m building. The roof of this unconventional office space covers one hectare—Notre Dame could nestle in its hollow core. The arch's walls are covered with white marble and mirrors, which gleam in sunlight (bring your shades or you'll be squinting).

THE INSIDE SCOOP. The outdoor glass elevators on the Grande Arche de la Défense make for a unique ride, with fantastic views all the way up. The view from the top of the arch, however, is less than spectacular, given the number of tall buildings between it and the far-off center of Paris. It doesn't quite match the views from the Eiffel Tower, the Basilica of Sacré-Coeur, the Parc de Belleville, or the top of the Centre Pompidou.

OTHER SIGHTS AT LA DEFENSE. Other La Défense buildings include the **Bull Tower**; the tent-like **Palais Défense**; a space-age **IMAX dome**; and the **CNIT building**, a center for congresses, exhibitions, and conferences that, at age 39, is La Défense's oldest building. Underneath the Arche is the **Sources d'Europe European** information center, which houses a quiet cafe and holds exhibits on topics like the European Union. *(Open M-F 10am-6pm. Free.)* The arch is surrounded by eight **gardens** (maps available at Info Défense). The huge **Quatre Temps** shopping center, one of the largest shopping malls in Europe, contains cafes, supermarkets, a cinema, and 30 restaurants. But visitors may be disappointed by the stores themselves—serious shoppers have better luck in Paris proper. *(Enter from the Grande Arche metro or from behind the Miró sculpture. Shops open M-Sa 10am-8pm. Supermarkets open M-F 9am-10pm, Sa 8:30am-10pm. Cinema and restaurants open daily until 11pm.)*

SAINT-DENIS

North of the 18*ème* and easily accessible by metro, the town of St-Denis is most noted for its stunning 12th-century **basilica** that has served for centuries as the spiritual home and final resting place of French royalty. The basilica is an architectural marvel—especially in comparison to the rather grubby modern buildings beside it. The town itself has little else to offer in the way of tourist sights, and if you're looking for a bite to eat, you'll find plenty of fast-food outlets and cheap eats but not much in the way of fine dining. Its most recent claim to fame was as the venue for the **1998 World Cup**, which necessitated the construction of a new 75,000-seat stadium that today hosts rock concerts and sporting events. An **open-air market** is held three times a week (Tu, F, Su) in the square by the Hôtel-de-Ville (on the way from the metro stop to the basilica).

PRACTICAL INFORMATION. The most direct route to St-Denis is by metro (Ⓜ Basilique St-Denis, line 13); visitors headed to the stadium should take the RER (RER Stade de France, line B5 or RER St-Denis, line D1). The tourist office, 1, rue de la République, has English-speaking guides, info on the basilica and the town of St-Denis, maps, suggested walks, restaurant guides, and a ticket outlet for events in the Stade de France. From the metro, take exit 1; turn left down r. Jean Jaurès, following the signs to the tourist office; and turn right on r. de la République. (☎ 01 55 87 08 70; www.ville-saint-denis.fr. Open daily Apr.-Sept. 1am-1pm and 2-4pm; Oct.-Mar. 10am-2pm.)

BASILIQUE DE ST-DENIS. Surrounded by modern buildings, markets, and non-Christian communities, the Basilique de St-Denis stands as an anachronistic and archaic symbol of the French monarchy. Buried in the transept, crevet, and crypt are the remains of three royal families (the Capets, the Valois, and the Bourbons), 41 kings, 32 queens, 63 princes and princesses, 10 dignitaries, and the relics of three saints. During the height of the French monarchy, the basilica acted as the national church, housing political artifacts like the Oriflamme (the royal banner) and coronation paraphernalia.

St. Denis, Paris's first bishop, was martyred by the Romans in AD 260 for trying to Christianize the city. After being beheaded on Mt. Mercury, which was renamed Montmartre ("Mount of the Martyr;" p. 249) in his honor, he allegedly picked up his head and walked north with it to the church. His tragic tale is told in stained glass on the northern side of the nave. **King Pepin the Short** turned it into a larger basilica to accommodate the many pilgrimages to this site. Denis has been joined by the royal remains of Clovis, François I, Catherine de Medicis, Anne d'Autriche, Louis XIV, Louis XVI, and Marie-Antoinette.

The basilica's 12th-century ambulatory was the **first appearance of Gothic architecture in Europe** (the scornful term "Gothic" was coined by Italian critics to describe St-Denis's extravagant style). Nicknamed *"Lucerna"* (Latin for "lantern") for its luminosity, the basilica features enormous stained-glass windows, high vaults, and exceptionally wide, airy transepts. These and other innovations were ordered by St-Denis's great patron, **Abbot Suger** (1122-1151), an influential clergyman and politician. Dissatisfied with the dark interiors of Romanesque churches, Abbot Suger famously began rebuilding the basilica in 1136 to open it to the "uninterrupted light of the divine."

Suger's shocked contemporaries worked to outdo him in technical brilliance, building ever more intricate interiors, larger stained-glass windows, and loftier vaults. But few were able to rival the luminous eastern end of the church: Suger's celebrated, color-flooded crevet. Dubbed the "manifesto" of the new Gothic style, the crevet was built to displace the crowds of pilgrims, which became so immense that, as rumor has it, some would faint and even suffocate in the tiny, air-deprived vault. The crevet is still home to some of the finest stained glass in France, with wall-to-wall ripple effects and intricate patterns.

Suger died in 1151, well before the basilica was finished, but he had already established it as France's seat of theological power. Several queens were crowned here, and in 1593, underneath the nave, Henri IV converted to Catholicism (see **Life and Times**, p. 65). With such a royalist pedigree, St-Denis made a prime target for the wrath of the Revolution. Tombs were destroyed, windows were shattered, and the remains of the Bourbon royal family were thrown into a ditch. With the restoration of the monarchy in 1815, Louis XVIII ordered the re-establishment of the necropolis, and Louis XVI and Marie-Antoinette were buried here with great pomp in 1819. Louis XVIII also retrieved the Bourbons' remains, placing them in a small ossuary in the crypt, and replaced the original tombs and funerary monuments. *(1, rue de la Légion d'Honneur and 2, rue de Strasbourg. From the metro, head toward the town square on rue Jean Jaurès and turn left at the tourist office on rue de la République. ☎01 48 09 83 54. Open Apr.-Sept. M-Sa 10am-6:30pm, Su and holidays noon-6:30pm; Oct.-Mar. M-Sa 10am-4:30pm, Su noon-4:30pm. Last entry 30min. before closing. Admission to nave, side aisles and chapels free. Transept, ambulatory, and crypt €6.50, ages 18-25 €4.50, under 18 and first Su of month from Nov.-Mar. free. Open daily Apr.-Sept. 10am-5:45pm; Oct.-Mar. 10am-4:45pm. Enter through the right fence gate of the basilica and go to the ticket kiosk. Audioguide in various languages €4, 2 people €6. Tours in French M-Sa 11:15am, 3pm; Su 12:15, 3pm. Mass M-Sa 9am, Su 8:30, 10am, and 6pm.)*

MUSÉE D'ART ET D'HISTOIRE. Located in a former convent (the nuns' cells are still intact), the Musée d'Art et d'Histoire features exhibits on daily life in medieval St-Denis and on the convent's most famous resident, **Mme Louise**. The interesting array of religious paraphernalia, archaeological finds, and historical artifacts is especially notable for the impressive collection of documents from the Paris Commune of 1871. A small room on the second floor in the far corner has been made into a literary shrine to the famous early 20th-century poet **Paul Eluard**. *(22bis, r. Gabriel Péri. Walk down r. de la République away from the basilica and then take the first left onto r. Gabriel Péri. The road forks left; follow signs. ☎01 42 43 05 10; www.musee-saint-denis.fr. First floor wheelchair accessible. Open M, W, and F 10am-5:30pm, Th 10am-8pm, Sa-Su 2-6:30pm. €4; students, seniors, and Su €2; under 16 and first Su of month free.)*

MUSEUMS

If you're going to be doing the museum circuit while in Paris—and you definitely should—you may want to invest in a **Carte Musées et Monuments,** which offers admission to 65 museums in greater Paris. The card is cost-effective if you plan to visit more than three museums or sights every day and will enable you to sail past admission lines. It is available at major museums, tourist office kiosks, and many metro stations. Ask for a brochure listing participating museums and monuments. A pass for two days is €30, for four days €45, for six days €60. For more information, call **Association InterMusées,** 4 rue Brantôme, 3ème (☎01 44 61 96 60; www.intermusees.com). Most museums, including the Musée d'Orsay, are closed on Mondays, while the Louvre, Centre Pompidou, and Musée Rodin are closed on Tuesdays.

ÎLE ST-LOUIS

The **Bibliothèque Polonaise de Paris** hosts the only official "museums" on the island, but the elegant *hôtels particuliers* that abound can be considered museums in their own right. Many of them have small plaques explaining the historical significance of the building—a walk along any of the *quais* will reveal a number of historical monuments.

MUSÉE ADAM MICKIEWICZ. Adam Mickiewicz, one of the most best-known and celebrated Polish poets, was considered the greatest Polish Romantic poet of the 19th century. Born in Nowogródek, he emigrated to France during the 1830 war for independence, and became a major actor in the intellectual and cultural circles of Paris at the time. The museum, located in the Bibliothèque Polonaise de Paris and dedicated to the poet, also presents the social and historical context of Mickiewicz's life in Poland and elsewhere. Founded by the poet's son, the museum includes letters from Goethe and Hugo as well as a sketch by Delacroix on George Sand's letterhead. In the same building are the **Musée Boleslas Bregas,** featuring a collection of paintings, and the **Salon Chopin,** a small room displaying letters, music scores and the death mask of the celebrated composer. There are also free temporary exhibits on the Polish historical and literary legacy several times a year. *(6 quai d'Orléans, Île-St-Louis. ⓂPont Marie. ☎01 55 42 83 83. Ring buzzer marked "gardien," enter and present yourself at the information office to the right. Admission to Musée Adam Mickiewicz, Musée Boleslas Bregas, and Salon Chopin. €5, students, over 60 and under 18 €2; under 12 free. Temporary exhibits free. Open Th 2:15, 3, 3:45, 4:30, and 5:15pm; Sa 9, 10, 11am, and noon. You must arrive at one of these times to be admitted to the museum.)*

GALLERIES

Galerie Alizé, 45 rue St-Louis en l'Île, Île St-Louis (☎01 46 34 26 32). ⓂPont Marie. A quirky and fascinating collection of original porcelain, bronze, and wooden animal sculptures and decorative pieces, many from such far off places as Burkina Faso, Indonesia, and Zimbabwe. From figurines of frogs dancing, reading, and teaching, to gigantic and colorful roosters to sombre hippos and elephants. Open M and W-Su noon-8pm.

CHÂTELET-LES HALLES

1ER ARRONDISSEMENT

Museums in the first are, of course, dominated by the most renowned of all art showcases in the country (and perhaps the world): the Musée du Louvre. This *grand monument* is an essential part of any first-time visit to Paris, as much for the building and surroundings (notably, I.M. Pei's famed glass pyramid) as for the thousands of priceless works inside. However, the smaller museums of the 1er, although overshadowed by the Louvre in size as well as fame, are some of the best in Paris. The newly re-opened Musée de l'Orangerie, with its impressive Impressionist collection, is not to be missed, and it's much less overwhelming than the enormous Louvre.

⊠MUSÉE DU LOUVRE

Ⓜ*Palais-Royal-Musée du Louvre.* ☎01 40 20 53 17; www.louvre.fr. Open M, Th, and Sa 9am-6pm, W and F 9am-10pm. Last entry 45min. before closing; closure of rooms begins 30min. before closing. Admission €9, after 6pm (W and F only) €6. Free for the unemployed, under 18, under 26 F after 6pm, everyone on the first Su of every month. Prices include both permanent and temporary collections, except for those in the Cour Napoléon. Tickets also allow same-day access to the Musée Delacroix. 1½hr. tours in English, French, or Spanish daily 11am, 2, 3:45pm; sign up at the info desk. Check website for tours in French sign language and tours for the visually impaired.

The Louvre was built on the foundations of a medieval castle that housed French kings for four centuries and was restructured by a 20th-century Socialist politician and a Chinese-American architect. Filled with priceless objects from tombs of Egyptian pharaohs, halls of Roman emperors, studios of French painters, and walls of Italian churches, it is a monument and a museum that transcends national and temporal boundaries. Explore the endless exhibition halls; witness new generations of artists at work on easels in the galleries; catch a glimpse (if only a glimpse) of the Louvre's most famous residents: the Mona Lisa, the Venus de Milo, the Winged Victory of Samothrace, and the The Right Hand of the Victory of Samothrace; and then come back for more...

PRACTICAL INFORMATION

Entrance and Organization: Enter through I.M. Pei's glass pyramid in the center courtyard of the building itself; an escalator descends into the Cour Napoléon, the museum's lobby, where you'll find tickets, information, and updated maps. There are 3 wings that branch off the Cour Napoléon: **Sully, Richelieu,** and **Denon.** Each wing is divided according to the art's period, national origin, and medium. To find out which rooms will be open on your visit, check the website, ask the info desk, or call **museum info** (☎01 40 20 53). See **Straight to the Art** tip box for time- and sanity-saving strategy.

Collection: The collection is divided into 7 departments: Oriental Antiquities; Egyptian Antiquities; Greek, Etruscan, and Roman Antiquities; Painting; Sculpture; Decorative Arts; and Graphic Arts. Color-coding and room numbers on the Louvre's free maps correspond to the colors and numbers on the plaques at the entrances to every room. Getting lost is an inevitable part of the Louvre experience, but there are plenty of docents who can point you in the right direction.

Audioguides: Available at the Richelieu, Sully and Denon entrances or reserve them online before the visit. They describe over 350 of the museum's highlights. Rental €6,

MUSEUMS

under 18 €2; deposit of driver's license, passport, or credit card; available to reserve online. There are also thematic audioguides based on current events at the museum.

Tours: Plastic info cards *(feuillets)* found in gallery corners provide detailed commentary and historical context.

Wheelchair rental: The Louvre is wheelchair-accessible. Wheelchairs are available for free at the central info desk, however a passport deposit is required; call information for disabled visitors (☎01 40 20 59 90).

Workshops: Subjects range from hieroglyphics to painting in perspective for children ages 4-13 in English. See the info desk in the Cour Napoléon.

Concerts and Films: Concerts and films are held in the auditorium in the Cour Napoléon. Concerts €3-30; films, lectures, and colloquia €2-10. Call ☎01 40 20 53 17 for more information. There is a small theater in the hall with free 1hr. films in French relating to the museum (films every hr. 10am-6pm).

Student Discount: Visitors under 26 years old can benefit from the Carte Louvre Jeunes, which provides 1year unlimited entrance to the permanent collection and temporary exhibits, visits with a guest W and F nights 6-10pm, free tickets to concerts and movies F nights, and discounts on all books, tours, concerts, movies, and classes. Call ☎01 40 20 53 72 or inquire at main desk for more info.

STRAIGHT TO THE ART. The lines stretching across the courtyard at the Louvre can be disheartening. To sail past, try the following strategies:
- —Don't enter through the glass pyramid; instead, follow the signs from the metro to the Carrousel du Louvre. Or, enter through one of the wings off the main courtyard.
- —Carte Musée et Monuments (see p. 265) and the Carte Louvre Jeunes (p. 267) will let you skip ticket lines.
- —Use coins or a credit card in the automatic ticket machines in the Cour Napoléon, or buy tickets online (valid to the end of the calendar year).
- —Visit on a weekday afternoon or on Monday or Wednesday evening, when the museum is open until 9:45pm. You'll cut down on waiting time, and get up close and personal with Mona.

HISTORY

Construction of the Louvre began in 1190—and it still isn't finished. King Philippe-Auguste built the original structure as a fortress to defend Paris while he was away on a crusade. In the 14th century, Charles V converted the fortress into a residential château. The monarchs of the 15th century avoided the narrow, dank, and rat-infested building, but François I returned to the Louvre in 1528 in an attempt to flatter the Parisian bourgeoisie. François razed Charles's château and commissioned Pierre Lescot to build a new palace in the open style of the Renaissance. All that remains of the original Louvre are its foundations, unearthed in the early stages of Mitterrand's 1990s renovations and displayed in an underground exhibit called Medieval Louvre on the ground floor of the Sully wing (admission included in museum ticket).

François I was succeeded by Henri II, whose widow, Catherine de Médicis, had the **Tuileries Palace** built in the Italian-style **Jardin des Tuileries.** Henri IV embarked on what he called the Grand Design—linking the Louvre and the Tuileries with the two large wings you see today in a "royal city." He oversaw completion of only a fraction of the project before his death in 1610.

After fleeing the Palais-Royal in 1650, Louis XIV moved into the Louvre. The **Cour Carrée** owes its classicism to Sun King, who hired a trio of an architect, a painter and a physician—**Le Vau, Le Brun,** and **Perrault,** respectively—to transform the Louvre into the grandest palace in Europe. However, Louis XIV eventually abandoned the Louvre for Versailles, and construction did not get past the enormous Renaissance courtyard.

In 1725, after years of relative abandonment, the halls were converted into a space for annual salons held by the Academy of Painting to showcase its members' work. In 1793, the Revolutionaries made the exhibit permanent, thus establishing the **Musée du Louvre.** For over a century, French painting revolved around the Louvre salons. Napoleon filled the Louvre with plundered art from continental Europe and Egypt (much of which had to be returned after his defeat at Waterloo).

More enduring, however, was Napoleon's construction of the **Arc de Triomphe du Carrousel,** a copy of Rome's Arch of Septimus Severus, to commemorate his victories. His imperial successor, Napoleon III, continued Henri IV's Grand Design, extending the Louvre's two wings to the Tuileries Palace and remodeling the facades of the older buildings.

For most of the 20th century, the Louvre was a confusing maze of government offices and inaccessible galleries. In the early 1990s, Mitterrand's **Grands Projets** campaign (see Life and Times, p. 63) transformed the Louvre into a well-organized museum. American architect I.M. Pei came up with the idea of moving the museum's entrance to an underground level in the Cour Napoléon, surmounted by his magnificent but controversial glass pyramid. Some saw the construction—made of 666 panes of glass—as sacrilege, others as genius, but it is now a world-renowned monument of Paris (made even more famous by its guest appearance in the 2006 film *The Da Vinci Code*).

COLLECTIONS

MESOPOTAMIAN COLLECTION. The cradle of civilization, the fertile crescent, the land of epithets—Mesopotamia was also the birthplace of Western Art. The **Victory Stela of Naram Sim** (Room 2) is a highlight of the collection, depicting the Akkadian King ascending the heavens, trampling his enemies along the way and sporting the crown of a god. The **Winged Bulls of Sargon II** (Room 4) served as guardians of the king's Assyrian palace. While modern times have delegated that kind of job to highly trained armed guards, the bulls' massive size is still impressive. On a more historical note, **Hammurabi's Code** holds center stage in Room 3. The object itself is a modest stela inscribed with 282 laws for Hammurabi's Babylonian civilization. It's in the Louvre because it is a physical memento of the first public **codified law,** a democratic gesture of such importance that it's easy to overlook the fact that dismemberment was the sentence for minor crimes like petty theft. *(Richelieu; ground fl.)*

GREEKS, ROMANS, & CO. The **Venus de Milo** is the ultimate classical beauty, even if she is missing her arms. Located in Room 74 on the first floor, the size-14 lady is always surrounded by enthusiastic hordes of camera-waving admirers. Overlooking a nearby stairway, the **Winged Victory of Samothrace** proves that a head is not a prerequisite for Greek masterpieces; beware the crowds. Located on the lower ground floor of the Denon wing is a display devoted to Cycladic Art, which employed such a highly geometricized style that the sculptures and idols actually look modern. *(Denon and Sully; 1st fl., ground fl., and lower ground fl.)*

THE ITALIANS. Ok, fine. We know you didn't come for the Cycladic Idols. You came for Da Vinci's **Mona Lisa** (Room 6), the most famous image in the world. While the lady's mysterious smile is still charming, there is nothing mysterious or charming about the experience of looking at it in person. The crowds are fierce, the painting is hidden in a glass box that constantly reflects hundreds of camera flashes, and you won't be allowed within 15 ft. We don't want to be heretical, but if you're pressed for time, you might consider skipping the lady. In the adjacent hall, an astonishing group of Renaissance masterpieces awaits—everything from Da Vinci's **Virgin on the Rocks** to Raphael's **Grand Saint Michel** to Fra Angelico's **Calvary.** It's an impressive bunch that outlines the rise of Humanism in the West. This wing is best visited as soon as the museum opens, as it turns into a circus within 30min. *(Denon; 1st fl.)*

HOLLAND, FLANDERS, THE NETHERLANDS. A more civilized museum experience lies on the second floor. Vermeer's astonishing **Astronomer** and **Lacemaker** occupy Room 38. While this resident of Delft left behind no drawings or other clues to his preparatory methods, some scholars believe that he used a camera obscura in composing his works. Indeed, one can make out subtle effects of light that could not have appeared to Vermeer's naked eye without a little assistance. This section is also filled with works by **Rembrandt, Van Eyck,** and **Van der Weyden,** as well as a monumental 24-painting cycle by **Rubens.** *(Richelieu; 2nd fl.)*

FRANCE. It is only fitting that a French palace would be filled with French paintings. The 17th-, 18th-, and 19th-century works that occupy the second floor of the Sully wing can be as fluffy and sugary as a chocolate soufflé, but don't lose interest quite yet. Keep an eye out for Watteau's **Pilgrimage to Cytheria** (Room 36), a melancholy ode to the **impermanence of love.** La Tour's fascination with hidden sources of light produced the haunting works that occupy Room 28. Once you've had your fill of peace and quiet, head back to the first floor of Denon, where the French heavyweights keep a close eye on the Mona Lisa. In Rooms 75, 76, and 77, large-format works dominate the walls. Géricault's **Raft of the Medusa,** ripped straight from the headlines in 1819, depicts the Medusa's abandoned passengers struggling to survive as they catch the attention of a passing ship. A large "X" formed by the bodies on the raft lends the painting its compositional stability, and the horrifying depiction of hunger, cannibalism, and despair packs an emotional wallop. The second most famous painting in these galleries is Delacroix's **Liberty Leading the People,** in which Liberty, like almost everything in Western Art, is symbolized by a partially nude woman. David's enormous paintings **The Coronation of Napoleon, The Oath of the Horatii,** and **Sabine Women** all showcase the painter's Neoclassical style. Finally, check out Ingres's body-twisting **Grande Odalisque** (go ahead, try and put your legs like that) and Delacroix's **Death of Sardanopolous.** Both are examples of Orientalism, a product of France's imperial adventures in North Africa. Within France itself, the "Orient" was imagined as a paradise of indulgence, sexually generous women, and crazy drugs. *(Sully, 2nd fl.; Denon, 1st fl.)*

OTHER MUSEUMS IN CHÂTELET-LES HALLES

▨**MUSÉE DE L'ORANGERIE.** The Orangerie has come a long way from its original role as the greenhouse of the Jardin des Tuileries. Opened as a museum in 1927, the intimate building is home to a phenomenal set of works, collected by two men wholly unconnected to one another, except that they were both married to the same woman (at different times). The collection includes works by Renoir, Cézanne, Modigliani, Rousseau, Matisse, and Picasso. But the admitted highlight is Monet's enormous **Les Nymphéas** (Water Lilies), which cover the walls of two oval-shaped rooms that form the sign for infinity. Recently renovated and consequently crowded, the Orangerie's popularity should not deter visitors; the art is worth the wait. *(Southwest corner of the Jardin des Tuileries; 1er. ⓂConcorde. ☎01 44 77 80 07; www.musee-orangerie.fr. Open M, W-Su 12:30-7pm; open until 9pm on F. €7.50, under 26 €5.50; audioguides €5, under 26 €3. Wheelchair accessible.)*

MUSEUMS

JEU DE PAUME. Not be confused with the Jeu de Paume of the **Tennis Court Oath** at Versailles, this Jeu de Paume, in the Tuileries, was built in the 19th century and soon converted into an art gallery. In the 1930s, the museum showcased the masters of modern art; during WWII it was a warehouse for art confiscated from Jewish Parisians; and in 1958 it became home to a collection of Impressionist works. In 1986, the Impressionist works were moved to the new Musée d'Orsay (p. 280), and the Jeu de Paume closed for extensive renovations. In 1991, President Mitterand inaugurated the revived building, whose new role would be a gallery displaying contemporary art—from well-known to new-on-the-scene artists. Its latest incarnation, as of summer 2006, is a center for photography and video. *(1 pl. Concorde; northwest corner of the Jardin des Tuileries; 1er. ⓜConcorde. ☎01 47 03 12 50; www.jeudepaume.org. Open Tu noon-9pm, W-F noon-7pm, Sa-Su 10am-7pm. €6, seniors and under 25 €4, under 10 free.)*

MUSÉE DES ARTS DÉCORATIFS. Housed in the northwestern wing of the Louvre, the Musées des Arts Décoratifs displays much more creativity than its name suggests. Packed with decorative art from the middle ages to today, the museum showcases some more predictable things (extravagant gold plates, embroidered chairs) and many that may surprise you—like clothing designer Jeanne Lanvin's marble-outfitted bathroom, a bright red kiss-shaped couch, or an apparently useless gold encrusted boat, gift from Empress Eugenie to her husband Ferdinand. Regardless of what it is, you can expect it to be over-the-top. *(107 rue de Rivoli, Palais du Louvre; 1er. ⓜPalais-Royal. ☎01 44 55 57 50; www.lesartsdecoratifs.fr. Open Tu, W, F 11am-6pm, Th 11am-9pm, Sa-Su 10am-6pm. Admission €8, under 26 €6.50, under 18 free. MC/V. Wheelchair-accessible.)*

MUSÉE DE LA MODE ET DU TEXTILE. Housed in the Louvre with the **Musée des Arts Décoratifs,** the Musée de la Mode et du Textile is a huge collection of all that has been en vogue since the 18th century. Exhibits rotate annually and trace the history of costume from 17th-century brocade evening dresses to the runway fashions of Chanel and Dior. *(107 rue de Rivoli, Palais du Louvre; 1er. ⓜPalais-Royal. ☎01 44 55 57 50; www.lesartsdecoratifs.fr. Open Tu, W, F 11am-6pm, Th 11am-9pm, Sa-Su 10am-6pm. Admission €8, under 26 €6.50, under 18 free. MC/V. Wheelchair accessible.)*

THE MARAIS

3ÈME ARRONDISSEMENT

Even if you're not the traditional museum-going type, the 3ème will surprise you with its range of options, from beautiful and elaborate mansions to unconventional and well-maintained attractions. The Musée Picasso is an undisputed must-see, while underrated Musée Carnavalet is sure to please.

▧MUSÉE PICASSO. When Picasso died in 1973, his family paid the French inheritance tax in artwork. Twelve years later, the French government put the collection on display in the 17th-century **Hôtel Salé,** so named because its original owner made his fortune by raising the *gabelle*, a salt tax. The museum is the world's largest catalogue of the life and 70-year career of one of the most prolific artists of the 20th century. Arranged chronologically, it leads viewers through the evolution of Picasso's artistic and personal life. From his earliest work in Barcelona to his Cubist and Surrealist years in Paris to his Neoclassical work on the French Riviera, each room situates his art within the context of his life: his many mistresses, his reactions to the World Wars, his changing philosophies, etc. This chronological arrangement has provoked attention and a good deal of criticism. You can follow the *Sens de Visite* arrows around the building—or feel free to go your own way.

Though born in Málaga, Spain in 1881, Picasso loved Paris and moved to the studios of the **Bateau-Lavoir** in Montmartre in 1904 (see **Sights**, p. 249). There he painted one of his masterpieces, **Les Demoiselles d'Avignon** (1907), currently in the New York Museum of Modern Art, but represented here by various preliminary studies. In the late 1920s, Picasso moved to Montparnasse (see **Sights**, p. 243), where he frequented the Café Sélect and La Closerie des Lilas along with Jean Cocteau and Surrealist guru André Breton. Unable to return to Spain during the Franco regime, Picasso adopted France as his permanent home. Later, he moved to Cannes on the French Riviera, where he died in 1973.

Highlights of the collection include the haunting blue **Autoportrait, Le violon et la musique** (Violin with Sheet Music), the post-Cubist **Deux femmes courant sur la plage** (Two Women Running on the Beach), and sculptures from the 1930s that experiment with human morphology. Picasso's experiments with abstraction often went hand in hand with his love affairs: check out the many studies of **La Tête d'une Femme,** inspired by his lover Marie-Thérèse Walter; **La femme qui pleure** (Woman Crying), based on the Surrealist photographer Dora Maar; and **The Kiss,** painted later in his life while he was married to Jacqueline Roque. By the time of their wedding, Clouzot's film *Le Mystère Picasso* and retrospectives at the Petit Palais were already celebrating his life's work. The museum also houses paintings from Picasso's personal collection, including those by **Matisse, Renoir, Cezanne,** and **Corot.** *(5 rue de Thorigny, 3ème.* Ⓜ*Chemin Vert.* ☎*01 42 71 25 21; www.musee-picasso.fr. Open Apr.-Sept. M and W-Su 9:30am-6pm, Oct.-Mar. 9:30am-5:30pm; last entry 45min. before closing. Admission €6.50, ages 18-25 €4.50, under 18 free. First Su of every month free.)*

MUSÉE CARNAVALET. Housed in Mme. de Sévigné's 16th-century *hôtel particulier* and the neighboring **Hôtel Le Peletier de Saint-Fargeau,** this meticulously arranged museum traces Paris's history from its origins to the present. The chronologically themed rooms follows Paris's evolution as a city, from prehistory and the Roman conquest to medieval politics; 18th-century splendor to Revolution; 19th-century urban, literary, and artistic growth; and Mitterrand's *Grands Projets.* Highlights include Proust's fully reconstructed bedroom, a piece of the Bastille prison wall, and Sévigné's interior decor itself—check out the **Wendel Ballroom,** painted by Jose-Maria Sert, the Charles Le Brun ceilings in Rooms 19 and 20. Of course, Madame didn't neglect the outside; the courtyard gardens, with symmetrically designed bushes and bright pink flowers, are a lovely place to relax after perusing the collections. The museum also regularly hosts special exhibits featuring the work of cartoonists, sculptors, and photographers. *(23 rue de Sévigné, 3ème.* ☎*01 44 59 58 58; www.paris.fr/musees/ musee_carnavalet.* Ⓜ*Chemin Vert. Take rue St-Gilles, which turns into rue de Parc Royal, and turn left on rue de Sévigné. Open Tu-Su 10am-6pm; last entry 5pm. Admission free. Special exhibits €7, under 26 €4, seniors €6, under 14 free. MC/V over €15.)*

MUSÉE D'ART ET D'HISTOIRE DU JUDAÏSME. Housed in the grand **Hôtel de St-Aignan**—once a tenement for Jews fleeing Eastern Europe—this museum displays a history of Jews in Europe, France, and North Africa with a focus on communal traditions and rituals throughout the diaspora. Modern testimonials on the Jewish identity are interspersed among exquisite ancient relics. Highlights include an ornate 15th-century Italian ark and a small collection of Chagall and Modigliani paintings, Lissitzky lithographs, and art collections looted by the Nazis from Jewish homes. There is also a notable collection of letters and articles concerning Captain Alfred Dreyfus, a French Jew accused of treason and espionage in the greatest socio-political controversy of the late 19th century. *(71 rue de Temple, 3ème.* Ⓜ*Rambuteau.* ☎*01 53 01 86 60; www.mahj.org.*

MUSEUMS

Wheelchair accessible. Open M-F 11am-6pm, Su 10am-6pm; last entry at 5:30pm. Admission €7, ages 18-26 €4.50, under 18, art and art history students free; includes an excellent English audioguide. Special exhibits €5.50, ages 18-26 4, combined ticket €8.50/6. MC/V over €12.)

MUSÉE COGNACQ-JAY. Ernest Cognacq (a founder of the famous Samaritaine department store) and his energetic wife Louise Jay were prolific philanthropists and collectors. They bequeathed the bulk of their fortune to the city of Paris to form the Musée Cognacq-Jay. The 16th-century Hôtel Donon was built for a royal councilor, who was also the son-in-law of sculptor Girolamo della Robbia. It is notable for the austere purity of its lines, exemplified by its lack of external sculpted decoration. The museum's five floors house Enlightenment art and furniture, including minor works by Rembrandt, Rubens, Greuze, La Tour, and Fragonard. The sumptuous house features interior designs by Natoire, Van Loo, and Boucher, as well as a bucolic collection of German porcelain sculpture. *(8 rue Elzévir, 3ème. Walk up rue Pavée and take a left on rue des Francs-Bourgeois and a right on rue Elzévir. ⓂSt-Paul. ☎01 40 27 07 21. Open Tu-Su 10am-6pm; last entry 5:30pm. Access to garden mid-May to mid-Sept. 10am-12:45pm and 4-5:35pm. Admission to permanent collection and special exhibits free.)*

MUSÉE DE LA POUPÉE. This small museum, nestled in a cul-de-sac, is devoted to everything to do with dolls. The first rooms are devoted to a permanent collection of dolls from 1805 to the present, while the rest of the museum hosts exhibits such as **"The 1001 Lives of Barbie"** and **"The Arousal of the Senses."** The museum also hosts special events, including puppet shows (W 2:30pm; €7-11), appraisal of antique dolls (W 11am; €12), and "torch visits" in the dark (one Th per month; €10). A great place to bring the kids, though grown-ups may find it slightly creepy. The attached shop sells ancient dolls and performs restorations. *(Impasse Berthaud, 3ème. ⓂRambuteau. ☎01 42 72 73 11; www.museedelapoupeeparis.com. Open Tu-Su 10am-6pm; last entry 5:30pm. €7, under 26 and seniors €5, ages 3-17 €3.)*

GALLERIES

The swank galleries in the Marais, concentrated in the *3ème*, display some of Paris's most exciting and avant-garde art. Cutting-edge paintings, sculptures, and photographs peek out of store-front windows along rue de Perche, rue de Thorigny, rue Debellyme, rue Vieille du Temple, rue Quincampoix, rue des Coutures St-Gervais, rue de Poitou, and rue Beaubourg. Especially in summer, the *vernissages* (gallery openings) are some of the most exclusive events in town—look for the crowds of gorgeous model-like women. Most galleries are closed Sundays, Mondays, and the entire month of August.

GALERIE THUILLIER. Featuring over 1500 pieces of art each year at 21 annual expositions across two sizable shopfronts, this is among the city's most active galleries. It thrives commercially by displaying a variety of media and styles, as well as both temporary and permanent artists. *(13 rue de Thorigny. ⓂSt-Sébastien-Froissart, behind the Picasso Museum ☎01 42 77 33 24; www.galeriethuillier.com. Exhibition Tu evening starting at 6pm. Open M-Sa noon-7pm.)*

FAIT & CAUSE. Aiming at spreading humanist and humanitarian consciousness, mostly through documentary photography, the popular exhibits at this gallery draw large crowds. Past featured artists have included Jacob Riis, Jane Evelyn Atwood, and Robert Doisneau. *(58 rue Quincampoix. ⓂRambuteau or Étienne-Marcel. ☎01 42 74 26 36. Open Tu-Sa 1:30-6:30pm.)*

GALERIE EMMANUEL PERROTIN. A celebrated visionary in the art world, Perrotin first made waves with his "ambitious" Miami gallery. Situated in a courtyard building once occupied by the directors of the Bastille prison, the Paris counterpart displays everything from installation art to sculpture and features artists from around the world. *(76 rue Turenne and 10 impasse St-Claude.* Ⓜ*St-Sebastien Froissart.* ☎*01 42 16 79 79; www.galerieperrotin.com. Open Tu-Sa 11am-7pm.)*

GALERIE DANIEL TEMPLON. Tucked away from the chaos near the Centre Pompidou, this is one of Paris's most respected contemporary galleries, with a special focus on promoting French contemporary artists. It features 20th-century painting and sculpture and an impressive roster of artists, including Ross Bleckner, Arman, and Jim Dine. *(30 rue Beaubourg. Walk north on rue Beaubourg. Enter at no. 30; the gallery is at the back of the courtyard.* Ⓜ*Rambuteau.* ☎*01 42 72 14 10; www. danieltemplon.com. Open M-Sa 10am-7pm. Closed Aug.)*

GALERIE MICHÈLE CHOMETTE. This gallery features six to eight exhibitions per year of contemporary and historic photography. *(24 rue Beaubourg. Walk north on rue Beaubourg. Ring the buzzer at no. 24 and proceed upstairs.* Ⓜ*Rambuteau.* ☎*01 42 78 05 62; mc.galerie@free.fr Open W-Sa 2-8pm. Closed Aug.)*

GILLES PEYROULET & CIE. Showcases contemporary photographers like Waplington. Design exhibits, including highly conceptual clothing, are across the street in Espace #2. *(75 and 80 rue Quincampoix.* Ⓜ*Rambuteau.* ☎*01 42 78 85 11; www. galeriepeyroulet.com. Open Tu-Sa 2-7pm. Closed July 15-Sept. 1.)*

GALERIE ZÜRCHER. Focuses on young, emerging artists in France and abroad, featuring abstract painting, photography, and video. *(56 rue Chapon. Walk south on rue Beaubourg, turn right on rue Chapon, and enter at no. 56—gallery is at back of courtyard.* Ⓜ*Arts et Métiers.* ☎*01 42 72 82 20; www.galeriezurcher.com. Open T-Sa noon-7pm.)*

POLARIS. Showcases promising new artists with an edgy aesthetic, especially in photography and painting. *(8 rue St-Claude.* Ⓜ*St-Sébastien-Froissart.* ☎*01 42 72 21 27; www.galeriepolaris.com. Open Tu-F 1-7pm, Sa 11am-1pm and 2-7:30pm.)*

GALERIE DENISE RENÉ. Since the end of WWII, René has been committed to experimentation and the expression of absolute liberty and limitless possibility. Her gallery presents primarily abstract art, and she has had an exhibit at the Centre Pompidou. *(22 rue Charlot.* Ⓜ*St-Sébastien-Froissart.* ☎*01 48 87 73 94; www.deniserene.com. Open Tu-Sa 2-7pm. Closed in Aug. Second location at 196 bd. St.-Germain, 6ème.* ☎*01 42 22 77 57. Open Tu-Sa 10am-1pm and 2-7pm. Closed in Aug.)*

4ÈME ARRONDISSEMENT

The 4*ème*'s undeniable attraction is the Centre Pompidou, but those looking for a less touristed way to explore can enjoy the Musée de Jeu de Paume or take a tour of author Victor Hugo's stately residence.

▧CENTRE POMPIDOU. The Musée National d'Art Moderne is the Centre Pompidou's main attraction. While its collection spans the 20th century, the art from the last 50 years is particularly brilliant. It features everything from Philip Guston's uncomfortably adorable hooded figures to Eva Hesse's uncomfortably anthropomorphic sculptures. Those looking to escape the discomfort will want to see Cai Guo-Qang's *Bon Voyage*, an airplane made of wicker and vine hanging from the ceiling and studded with objects confiscated from passengers' carry-on luggage at the Tokyo airport. On the museum's second level, early 20th-century heavyweights like Duchamp and Picasso hold court. Most of the works were contributed by the artists themselves or by their estates; Joan Miró and Wassily Kandinsky's wife are among the museum's founders. For more on the Centre Pompidou, see **Sights**, p. 217 *(Pl. Georges-Pompidou, rue Beaubourg.* Ⓜ*Rambuteau or Hôtel de Ville. RER Châtelet-Les Halles.* ☎*01 44 78 12 33; www.centrepompidou.fr. Centre open M and W-Su 11am-10pm; museum open M, W, and F-Su 11am-9pm, Th 11am-11pm; last ticket sales 1 hr. before closing. Library*

MUSEUMS

open M and W-F noon-10pm, Sa-Su 11am-10pm. Library and Forum free. Museum admission to permanent collection and exhibits €12, under 26 €9, under 18 free. First Su of month free for all visitors. Visitors' guides available in bookshop.)

AN ANNUAL AFFAIR. The Centre Pompidou rotates its permanent collection regularly and therefore constantly offers a new experience. If you plan to be in Paris for a while (ahem, students), you may want to purchase an annual pass, *le laisser passer*, sold in the Centre under the left escalator. (€48, over 60 €37, under 26 €22).

MUSEUMS

MÉMORIAL DE LA SHOAH. Opened in 2005, the Mémorial de la Shoah literally translates to Museum of the Holocaust. Also functioning as a resource center and archives, the memorial's formal mission is to teach: to form a bridge between the generation that experienced the Holocaust and that which did not. Beautifully conceived and intensely moving, the museum accomplishes much more. Visitors enter into a small courtyard that features a series of monuments: the memorial to the **Unknown Jewish Martyr,** a large bronze cylinder bearing the names of the major concentration camps; and the **Wall of Names,** inscribed with the names of the 76,000 Jews, including 11,000 children, deported from France during the Nazi regime. Inside, there are an extensive series of exhibits recounting the deportation itself, as well as the somber but beautiful black marble crypt, shaped in the Star of David. In a dark room lit by a single flame, the crypt symbolizes the tomb of the six million Jews who died without a proper burial and contains the ashes of martyrs taken from the death camps and from the ruins of the Warsaw Ghetto. While an emotional experience, the Mémorial de la Shoah is a must-see. *(17 rue Geoffroy l'Asnier, 4ème. Ⓜ Pont Marie or St-Paul. From Ⓜ Pont Marie, walk along rue de l'Hôtel de Ville with the river on your left and turn right on rue G. l'Asnier; the museum will be on your left . ☎ 01 42 77 44 72; www.memorialdelashoah.org. Tours every Su 3pm or upon request. Wheelchair access. Open M-W and Su 10am-6pm, Th 10am-10pm. Free.)*

MUSÉE DE JEU DE PAUME. Located in the Hôtel de Sully (on the lower left-hand of the courtyard), this is an annex of the main Musée de Jeu de Paume at pl. de Concorde. It shows only temporary photo exhibitions, but they are usually well worth the visit. Check the website for current showings. *(62 rue St-Antoine. Ⓜ St. Paul. ☎ 01 42 74 47 75 and 01 47 03 12 52; www.jeudepaume.org. Wheelchair accessible. Open Tu-F noon-7pm and Sa-Su 10am-7pm. €5, seniors and under 25 €2.50. Admission to both Concorde and Sully €8/4. Call for tours.)*

MAISON DE VICTOR HUGO. Dedicated to the father of the French Romantics and housed in the building where he lived from 1832 to 1848, the museum displays Hugo memorabilia, including little-known paintings by his family and his writing desk. On the first floor, one room is devoted to paintings of scenes from *Les Misérables,* another to *Notre Dame de Paris,* and a third to other featured plays and works. Upstairs are Hugo's apartments, a recreation of the bedroom where Hugo died, and the *chambre chinoise,* which reveals Hugo's flamboyant interior decorating skills. *(6 pl. des Vosges. Ⓜ Chemin Vert or Bastille. ☎ 01 42 72 10 16; maisonsvictorhugo@paris.fr. Wheelchair accessible. Open Tu-Su 10am-6pm. Permanent collection free, special exhibits around €8, seniors €5, under 26 €4. MC/V over €15.)*

GALLERIES

It seems as though the Centre Pompidou area has become the queen bee to a bevy of galleries clustered around the giant landmark. You might also stumble upon several tucked away on side streets while strolling in the Marais.

◪ **GALERIE RACHLIN & LEMARIÉ BEAUBOURG.** This is the leading gallery of cutting-edge contemporary painting. *(23 rue de Renard. ⓜRambuteau or Châtelet. ☎01 44 59 27 27; www.galerieljbeaubourg.net. Open Tu-Sa 11am-7pm.)*

ATELIER CARDENAS BELLANGER. This gallery doesn't let its tiny size stand in its way. Recent exhibitions include Henry Taylor's wickedly funny paintings on race and a series of contemporary drawings. Devendra Banhart, a bearded freak-folk hero, has curated here. *(43 rue Quincampoix. ⓜRambuteau. ☎01 48 87 47 65; www.ateliercardenasbellanger.com. Open Jan. to mid-July and Sept.-Dec. Tu-Sa 11am-7pm.)*

GALERIE NATHALIE OBADIA. Gallery features new works by young artists who might just make it into the nearby Pompidou someday—come see the newest attempts to get the medium of painting back on the road to glory. *(3 rue Cloître St-Merri. ⓜHôtel de Ville. ☎01 42 74 67 68; www.galerie-obadia.com. Open M-Sa 11am-7pm.)*

GALERIE DU JOUR AGNÈS B. This small contemporary gallery features photography and multimedia art, and also sells books by the gallery and documents from past expositions. *(44 rue Quincampoix. ⓜRambuteau. ☎01 44 54 55 90, library ☎01 44 54 55 98; www.galeriedujour.com. Open Tu-Sa noon-7pm. Closed late July to mid-Sept.)*

GALERIE DE FRANCE. This well-established gallery is known for showing the work of artists like Richard Avedon, Pier Paolo Calzolari, and Patrick Faigenbaum. *(54 rue de la Verrerie. ⓜHôtel de Ville. ☎01 42 74 38 00. Open Tu-Sa 11am-7pm.)*

GALERIE NELSON. Features several installations a year, running from sculpture to painting to video to photography. Most are by young French artists, but other European countries are represented. *(59 rue Quincampoix. ⓜRambuteau. ☎01 42 71 74 56; www.galerie-nelson.com. Open Tu-Sa 11am-1pm and 2-7pm or by appointment.)*

LATIN QUARTER AND ST-GERMAIN

5ÈME ARRONDISSEMENT

Any visit to Paris would be incomplete without a stop at the resplendent **Musée de Cluny**. Its elegant, varied, and accessible exhibits thrill the artsy, the intellectual, and the young-at-heart. The **Institut du Monde Arabe** showcases Middle Eastern art, and is an essential and diverse cultural resource.

◪**MUSÉE DE CLUNY.** The Hôtel de Cluny houses the **Musée National du Moyen Âge**, one of the world's finest collections of medieval art, including jewelry, sculpture, and tapestries. It presents a variety of mediums for exploration, from cloth and shoes to sculptures and stonework. The museum has only two floors with 23 rooms, enabling visitors to pass through quickly or linger for hours over each artifact; either way, you should not miss this intriguing throwback to life without cars or Q-tips. The *hôtel* itself is a flamboyant 15th-century manor built atop 2nd-century Roman ruins. In the 13th-century, the site became home to the Cluny abbots. Jacques d'Amboise revived the Parisian monastic order in the 15th century. In 1843, the state converted the hôtel into the medieval museum; post-WWII excavations unearthed the baths.

The museum's collection, brilliantly curated so as to be impressive but not overwhelming, includes art from Paris's most important medieval structures: Ste-Chapelle, Nôtre Dame, and St-Denis. Panels of brilliant stained glass in ruby reds and royal blues from Ste-Chapelle line the ground floor. The brightly lit **Galerie des Rois** contains sculptures from Notre Dame—including a series of marble heads of the kings of Judah, severed during the Revolution. The museum's medieval jewelry collection includes royal crowns, brooches, and daggers. Wandering eyes will discover veteran chess pieces and ornate iron keys flushing out the Cluny's armour and sword displays. Perhaps the most impressive work of goldsmithing is the exquisite 14th-century **Gold Rose,** on the first floor. Tucked away among gilded reliquaries and illuminated manuscripts is the gruesome sculpture of the head of **St. John the Baptist on a platter.** But a series of allegorical tapestries, **La Dame à la Licorne** (The Lady at the Unicorn), outshines other pieces as the museum's coveted star. Claiming a room all their own, the woven masterpieces depict the five senses. If they look familiar to you, it may because you've seen them before—they deck the halls of the Gryffindor Common room in the Harry Potter films. George Sand made the tapestries famous after discovering them hanging in the **Château Broussac** in Chantelle, south of Paris. The complete cycle comprises the centerpiece of the museum's collection of 15th- and 16th-century Belgian weaving.

Outside, irises, mint, and primroses grow in the **Jardin Médiéval,** a 5000 sq. m replica of a medieval pleasure garden. The grounds are divided into several sections, including the **Forest of the Unicorn,** containing uncultivated wild plants, **Le Jardin Céleste** (The Heavenly Garden), dedicated to the Virgin Mary, **Le Jardin d'Amour** (The Garden of Love), used for medicinal and aromatic purposes, and **Le Tapis de Mille Fleurs** (Carpet of a Thousand Flowers), inspired by the *mille fleurs* tapestries. The museum also sponsors chamber music concerts during the summer. *(6 pl. Paul-Painlevé, 5ème. ⓂCluny-La Sorbonne. Info ☎01 53 73 78 00, reception 01 53 73 78 16. Open M and W-Su 9:15am-5:45pm; last entry at 5:15pm. Closed Jan. 1, May 1, and Dec. 25. Temporarily free; prices TBD. English-, French-, German-, Italian-, Japanese-, and Spanish-language audioguides €1. Garden open in winter M-F 9:30am-5pm, Sa-Su and holidays 9am-5pm; summer M-F 9:30am-9:30pm, Sa-Su and holidays 9am-9:30pm. Free. Call ☎01 53 73 78 16 for info on weekly concerts. €6.)*

INSTITUT DU MONDE ARABE. The Institut du Monde Arabe (IMA) is located in one of the city's most striking buildings. Facing the Seine, the IMA was built to look like a ship, recalling how Algerian, Moroccan, and Tunisian immigrants sailed to France. On its southern face, ▧**240 Arabesque portals** open and close, powered by light-sensitive cells designed to determine the amount of light necessary to illuminate the building's interior without damaging its art. Inside, the spacious museum exhibits 3rd- to 18th-century art from Arab regions of the Maghreb, the Middle East, and the Near East. Level Six displays artifacts of the Arab world's scientific achievements in astronomy, mathematics, and medicine, while Level Four is devoted to contemporary Arab art. The extensive public library houses over 85,000 documents and provides free Wi-Fi. In July, the IMA shows Arabic movies with English- and French-language subtitles outside. Their cultural outreach programs also sponsor music and theater productions, lecture series, and children's activities. Check out the IMA's website or pick up their monthly InfoMag brochure for more info. The ▧**rooftop terrace** has a fabulous— = free—view of Montmartre, Île de la Cité, Sacré Coeur, and the Seine. *(1 rue des Fossés St-Bernard, 5ème. ⓂJussieu. Walk down rue Jussieu away from the Jardin des Plantes, and make your first right onto rue des Fossés St-Bernard. ☎01 40 51 38 38; www.imarabe.org. Museum open Tu-Su 10am-6pm. Closed May 1. €4, under 26 €3, under 12 free. Library open Sept.-June Tu-Sa 1-8pm; July-Aug. Tu-Sa 1-6pm. Free. Cinema €4, under 26 €3.)*

MUSÉE D'HISTOIRE NATURELLE. Three science museums actually comprise the "Museum of Natural History," all beautifully situated within the Jardin des Plantes. The hyper-modern, four-floor **Grande Galérie d'Evolution** illustrates evolution with an ironically Genesis-like parade of naturalistic stuffed animals and numerous multimedia tools. A section of the permanent exhibit is dedicated to human interaction with the environment, with displays on farming and sustainable development, as well as a slightly alarming world population counter estimating future figures. Temporary exhibits dominate the basement level. Allow yourself at least 2hr. to take in the whole museum. Next door, the **Musée de Minéralogie** displays rubies, sapphires, and other minerals, but it's by no means a riveting exhibit. The **Galeries d'Anatomie Comparée et de Paléontologie** are at the garden's far end, with an exterior resembling a Victorian house of horrors. Inside, a ghastly cavalcade of femurs, rib-cages, and vertebrae form pre-historic animals. Despite some snazzy new placards, the place doesn't seem to have changed much since its 1898 opening; it's almost more notable as a museum of 19th-century grotesquerie than as a catalogue of anatomy. Check out the fossils, lined up in a grand procession of death, on the first floor. *(57 rue Cuvier, in the Jardin des Plantes. ⓂGare d'Austerlitz or Jussieu. ☎01 40 79 30 00; www.mnhn.fr. Grande Galerie de l'Evolution open M and W-Su 10am-6pm. €8, age 4-13 and students under 26 €6. Musée de Minéralogie open Nov.-Mar. M and W-Su 10am-5pm, Apr.-Oct. M and W-F 10am-5pm, Sa-Su 10am-6pm. €7, students under 26 €5. Galéries d'Anatomie Comparée et de Paléontologie open Nov.-Mar. M and W-Su 10am-5pm; Apr.-Oct. M and W-F 10am-5pm, Sa-Su 10am-6pm. Last entry 45min. before closing. €6, students €4, under 4 free. Weekend passes for the 3 museums and the ménagerie €20, reduced €15; valid for one entry at each museum Sa or Su. MC/V.)*

6ÈME ARRONDISSEMENT

The Latin Quarter's alternative to large-scale, conventional museums is its bounty of private galleries, which offer contemporary art displays with enough variety to suit every taste. Rue de Seine and the area north of bd. St-Germain are especially dominated by these little galleries, making for a delightful stroll.

MUSÉE ZADKINE. Installed in 1982 in the house and studio of Russian sculptor Ossip Zadkine (1890-1967), the pleasantly tourist-free Musée Zadkine houses a collection of his work, along with moving contemporary art exhibits. Zadkine, who immigrated to Paris in 1909, worked in styles from Primitivism to Neoclassicism to Cubism, and the museum's collection represents all 12 of his creative periods. The tiny sculpture garden is a wonderful place to recover from time spent in the busy northern part of the 6ème. *(100bis rue d'Assas, 6ème. ⓂVavin. Walk north along rue Vavin and take the third right on rue d'Assas. ☎01 55 42 77 20; www.paris.fr/musees/zadkine. Open Tu-Su 10am-6pm. €4, under 26 €2.)*

MUSÉE DELACROIX. The Musée Delacroix offers a surprisingly intimate and scholarly perspective on 18th century Romanticist Eugène Delacroix, the artistic master behind the famous *Liberty Leading the People* (1830). The museum is situated in the refurbished three-room apartment and atelier where Delacroix lived and worked for much of his life. Sketches, watercolors, engravings, and letters to Théophile Gautier and George Sand are part of the permanent holdings, while sporadic traveling exhibits showcase significant achievements in Delacroix scholarship. There is a lovely enclosed garden between the *atelier* —equipped with Delacroix's original palettes and studies—and the artist's private apartment. *(6 rue de Furstemberg, 6ème. ⓂSt-Germain-des-Prés. Behind the Église St-Germain, off rue de l'Abbaye. At the courtyard, follow the sign to the central atelier Delacroix. ☎01 44 41 86 50; www.musee-delacroix.fr. Open M and W-Su 9:30am-5pm; last entry 4:30pm. €5, under 18 free. Free same-day entry with a Louvre ticket. MC/V.)*

MUSÉE DE LA MONNAIE. Housed in the Hôtel des Monnaies, a mint until 1973, the Musée de la Monnaie (Currency Museum) is not just for coin collectors. Displays in this small museum document the history of French coinage from Roman times to the present, with everything from medieval coins the size of dinner plates to answers for any question you've ever had about the euro. There is also a stellar exhibition of international currencies. The museum occasionally hosts traveling exhibitions on non-pecuniary topics. *(11 quai de Conti, 6ème. ⓂPont Neuf. Cross the Pont Neuf and turn right on quai de Conti. ☎01 40 46 55 35; www.mon-*

naideparis.fr. Wheelchair-accessible. Open Tu-F 11am-5:30pm, Sa-Su noon-5:30pm. €5, under 16 free; includes audioguide available in English, French, Spanish, German, and Italian. MC/V.)

GALLERIES

North of bd. St-Germain, back-to-back galleries cluster on rue de Seine, rue Mazarine, rue Bonaparte, rue Jacques Callot, rue Dauphine, and rue des Beaux-Arts. Most are marked with colorful "Art of St-Germain des Pres" flags. Posted hours tend to be flexible; most galleries close at lunchtime (usually 1-2:30pm) and on Mondays. In addition, most galleries will offer neighborhood maps giving the locations and information for nearby exhibitions. While all galleries are worth a browse, these are our personal favorites.

GALERIE PATRICE TRIGANO. Down the street from the École des Beaux-Arts, Galerie Trigano finds inspiration in the artistic ideals of the 20th century. The works on display may have been created in the last few years, but the abstract and expressionist styles they embody have been around for decades. Don't forget to check out the basement and the small sculpture garden in the back. *(4bis rue des Beaux-Arts, 6ème. ☎01 46 34 15 01. Open Tu-Sa 10am-1pm and 2:30-6:30pm.)*

GALERIE LOEVENBRUCK. An outstanding gallery, specializing in politically engaged Dada- and Pop-inspired contemporary sculpture, video, photography, and painting—most of it with a sense of humor. Pick up free postcards advertising art events in Paris. *(2 rue de l'Echaudé. Enter off rue Jacob, 6ème. ☎01 53 10 85 68; www.loevenbruck.com. Open Tu-Sa 11am-7pm. Closed Aug.)*

KAMEL MENNOUR. A hip gallery with a young staff. It exhibits prized work by stars like Annie Leibovitz and Larry Clark, and some of the best photography, video, and painting that the 6ème's up-and-comers have to offer. *(60 rue Mazarine, 6ème. ☎01 56 24 03 63; www.galeriemennour.com. Open Tu-Sa 11am-7pm.)*

GALERIE SEINE 51. With one of the flashiest collections of contemporary art on the Left Bank and innovative curatorial projects—including occasional pink walls and astroturf—Seine 51 is an amusing foray into experimental art, with a mischievous feel. Exhibits range from Pop-inspired installations, photography, and furniture to works in standard mediums. *(51 rue de Seine, 6ème. ☎01 43 26 91 10; www.seine51.com. Open Tu-Sa 10:30am-1pm and 2:30-7pm.)*

GALERIE ALBERT LOEB. Modern art and classy black-and-white photography with a tendency toward social critique are the lifeblood of this stripped-down gallery space. *(12 rue des Beaux-Arts, 6ème. ☎ 01 46 33 06 87; www.galerieloeb.com. Open Tu-Sa 10am-1pm and 2-7pm. Closed Aug.)*

GALERIE LOFT. Galerie Loft features expressive and politically oriented Chinese avant-garde art, unlike anything else you'll find in St-Germain. *(3bis, rue des Beaux-Arts, 6ème. Enter the courtyard at no. 3 and climb the stairs. ☎01 46 33 18 90; www.galerieloft.com. Open Tu-Sa 10am-1pm and 2-7pm.)*

CLAUDE BERNARD. An expansive art space, Claude Bernard is perhaps one the most prestigious galleries of rue des Beaux-Arts. The space holds a mix of traditional photographs and off-the-wall collages and modern art. It has showcased such famous artists as Dubuffet, Balthus, David Levine, and Henri Cartier-Bresson. *(7-9, rue des Beaux-Arts, 6ème. ☎01 43 26 97 07; www.claude-bernard. com. Open Tu-Sa 9:30am-12:30pm and 2:30-6:30pm.)*

GALERIE DI MEO. This gallery specializes in multimedia painting and sculpture, and features a fabulous retinue of neo-Pop and Abstract-Expressionist contemporary artists. *(9 rue des Beaux-Arts, 6ème. ☎01 43 54 10 98; www.dimeo.fr. Open Tu-F 10am-1pm and 2:30-7pm, Sa 10am-7pm. Closed Aug.)*

GALERIE LELIA MORDOCH. Superior individual and group shows of Pop- and Minimalist-inspired sculpture, painting, photography, and installation displayed, all with a very clean aesthetic. *(50 rue Mazarine, 6ème. ☎ 01 53 10 88 52; www. galerieleliamordoch.com. Open Tu-Sa 1-7pm.)*

GALERIE PIECE UNIQUE. As the name suggests, this gallery offers a collection of eclectic pieces whose arresting subjects are bound to make for interesting conversation when your mother-in-law decides Thanksgiving should be at your house this year. *(4 rue Jacques Callot, 6ème. ☎ 01 43 26 54 58; www.galeriepieceunique.com. Open Tu-F 11am-1pm and 2:30-7pm, Sa 11am-1pm and 2:30-5pm.)*

INVALIDES (7ÈME)

The *7ème* is a museum lover's dream, with most of its best stretched along the *quais* lining the Seine. Visitors can indulge themselves in the best of Impressionism and satisfy their curiosity about sewers all in one day. The **Musée Rodin** and the **Musée d'Orsay** are the best and most-visited museums in Paris next to the Louvre, so be prepared for crowds during the summer and on weekends.

🖾 MUSÉE RODIN

79 rue de Varenne, 7ème. Ⓜ Varenne. ☎ 01 44 18 61 10; www.musee-rodin.fr. Open Tu-Su Apr.-Sept. 9:30am-5:45pm; Oct.-Mar. 9:30am-4:45pm; last entry 30min. before closing. Gardens open Tu-Su Apr.-Sept. 9:30am-6:45pm, Oct.-Mar. 9:30am-5pm. Café open Apr.-Sept. 9:30am- 5:30pm, Oct.-Mar. 9:30am-4:30pm. €6, seniors and ages 18-25 €4; special exhibits €7/5. Free first Su of the month and for under 18. Garden €1. Audioguides in 7 languages €4 each for permanent and temporary exhibits, combined ticket €6. Temporary exhibits housed in the chapel, to your right as you enter. Touch tours for the blind and educational tours available (☎ 01 44 18 61 24). Ground floor and gardens wheelchair accessible. MC/V.

The museum is located in the elegant 18th-century **Hôtel Biron,** where Auguste Rodin lived and worked at the end of his life, sharing it with the likes of Isadora Duncan, Cocteau, Matisse, and Rilke. During his lifetime (1840-1917), Rodin was among the country's most controversial artists, classified by many as the sculptor of Impressionism (Monet was a close friend and admirer). Today, he is universally acknowledged as the father of modern sculpture.

According to many Parisians, the Musée Rodin is one of the best museums in Paris, and they're right. Besides housing many of Rodin's better known sculptures, including Le Penseur, Le Baiser and L'Homme au Nez Cassé, the *hôtel* and its surrounding garden are aesthetically appealing in their own right.

The *hôtel's* garden displays Rodin's works amid rosebushes and fountains, including the piece nearly all visitors go to the museum to see: **Le Penseur** (The Thinker), situated on the right side of the garden as you enter. Originally entitled The Poet, the piece was meant to depict Dante pondering his great epic poem, **La Commedia Divina.** Across the garden a miniature of this contemplative man can be seen atop **La Porte de L'Enfer** (The Gate of Hell), which depicts the hellish cast of characters from *The Inferno*, the first third of *La Commedia Divina*. Viewing machines placed in front of the sculpture (which is six meters high, four meters wide and one meter deep) allow visitors to look more closely at the anguished faces of souls damned to purgatory. Originally commissioned as the entrance doors for the new École des Arts Décoratifs, the Gates were never finished. In response to his critics, the master of French sculpture asked, "Were the cathedrals ever finished?"

Near Le Penseur stands the sculpture of a haughty man in robes: **Balzac.** Commissioned in 1891 by the Société des Gens de Lettres., the sculpture took years for Rodin to design and complete, causing a cold war to erupt between the sculpture and Société. After years of battle, Rodin cancelled the commission and kept the statue himself. Later in his life, he noted, "Nothing that I made satisfied me as much, because nothing had cost me as much; nothing else sums up so profoundly that which I believe to be the secret law of my art."

After thoroughly exploring the gardens, enter the hotel for a concentrated dose of artistic mastery. Many of Rodin's sculptures were based on characters or scenes from *The Inferno*. ▧**Le Baiser,** for example, tells the story of **Francesca da Rimini,** who fell in love with her brother-in-law, **Paolo Malatesta.** Parallel to Dante's compassionate portrayal of Francesca in Canto V of *The Inferno*, Rodin's depiction shows the lovers in a moment of passion right before Rimini's husband discovered and killed them—and never has adultery looked so good. The lovers' urgency shows through in small details—Paolo's muscular right arm, which becomes tender and graceful at his caressing hand, and Francesca's clenching toes, which rest on Paolo's foot. Rodin truly mastered masculine and feminine sensuality in this piece, whose hypnotizing momentum and force resound with Francesca's words in Canto V: *Amor, che a nullo amato amar perdona mi prese del costui piacer sì forte che, come vedi, ancor non mi abbandona.* (Love, which pardons no loved one from loving, seized me with a pleasure so strong for him that, as you can see, still it does not leave me.) Romantics, prepare thyselves. It doesn't get better than this.

Other sculptures rest on antique furniture, and walls are casually adorned with works by artists like Renoir, Munch, van Gogh, Géricault, and Steichen. Rodin's sculptures decorate the staircase and doorways; **Les Bourgeois de Calais,** a study of six men walking toward certain death, takes up an entire room.

The museum also has several works by ▧**Camille Claudel,** Rodin's muse, collaborator, and lover. Claudel striking **L'Age Mûr** has been read as her response to Rodin's decision to leave her for another woman; the powerfully moving ensemble shows an angel of death dragging a man away from his pleading lover. Many, however, claim that it was Claudel who left Rodin, and it has recently been argued that she was also responsible for some of Rodin's most celebrated works. Either way, her talent for capturing the essence of romance is undeniable—if you liked Rodin's Le Baiser, spend some time (a few hours in front of Claudel's **La Valse,** a union of staggering complexity and beauty.

▧ MUSÉE D'ORSAY

62, rue de Lille, 7ème. Ⓜ Solférino, RER Musée d'Orsay. Access to visitors at entrance A of the square off 1 rue de la Légion d'Honneur. ☎01 40 49 48 14; www.musee-orsay. fr. Wheelchair-accessible; call ☎01 40 49 47 14 for more information. Open Tu-W and F-Sa 9:30am-6pm (last ticket sales 5pm), Th 10am-9:45pm (last ticket sales 9:15pm); June 20-Sept. 20 Su 9am-6pm. Admission (includes most exhibits) €7.50, ages 18-25 €5, under 18 free. Su and after 4:15pm (after 8pm on Th) €5.50. English tours 1hr. usually Tu-Sa 11:30am and 2:30pm; call ahead to confirm. €6.50/5. Bookstore open Tu-Su 9:30am-6:30pm, Th until 9:30pm. AmEx/MC/V. Tickets available online through FNAC.

If only the unimaginative *Académiciens* who turned the Impressionists away from the Louvre salon could see the Musée d'Orsay today. Now considered masterpieces of art, these "rejects" are well worth the pilgrimage to this mecca of 19th and 20th century modernity. The collection, installed in a former railway station, includes paintings, sculpture, decorative arts, and photography from 1848 until WWI. The museum is one of the most popular in Paris and has crowds to match. Visit on Sunday mornings or Thursday evenings to avoid the masses.

PRACTICAL INFORMATION

Entrance: A clearly marked escalator at the far end of the building ascends to the Impressionist level, and maps and English-language information are available at the entrance.

Guides and Maps: Guide to the Musée d'Orsay: (€15) by Caroline Mathieu, the museum's director, is worth the splurge. Practical Musée d'Orsay Pocket Guide €6. Handheld audioguides (2hr.; €5), available in English and other languages, provide anecdotal histories and analyses of 60 of the museum's masterpieces.

Tours: Every 1hr. from the group reception area

Cafes: Café des Hauteurs sits on the 5th fl. behind one of the huge iron clocks (open Tu-W and F-Su 10am-5pm, Th 10am-9pm). A self-serve food stand is located directly above the cafe (open Tu-Su 11am-5pm). The **Restaurant du Musée d'Orsay** on the middle floor is a museum piece all its own; designed by Gabriel Ferrier in Belle Époque style, it features magnificent chandeliers and a spectacular view of the Seine (open for lunch Tu-Su 11:30am-2:30pm; tea 3:30-5:30pm except Th; dinner Th 7-9:30pm).

HISTORY

Built for the 1900 World's Fair, the Gare d'Orsay's industrial function was carefully masked by architect Victor Laloux behind glass, stucco, and a 370-room luxury hotel, so as not to mar the elegance of the 7*ème*. For several decades, it was the main departure point for southwest-bound trains, but newer trains were too long for its platforms, and it closed in 1939. After WWII, the station served as the main French repatriation center, receiving thousands of concentration camp survivors. Orson Welles filmed *The Trial* here in 1962. Twenty-four years later, Musée d'Orsay opened here as one of Mitterrand's *Grands Projets*, gathering works from the Louvre, Jeu de Paume, Palais de Tokyo, Musée de Luxembourg, provincial museums, and private collections.

COLLECTION

The museum is curated in a chronological fashion from the ground floor to the top floor to the mezzanine. The ground floor, dedicated to Pre-Impressionist paintings and sculpture, contains the two scandalous works that started it all, both by Manet: *Olympia*, whose confrontational gaze and nudity caused a stir, and *Déjeuner sur l'Herbe*, which shockingly portrayed a naked woman accompanied by fully clothed men. At the back, the detailed section study of the **Opéra Garnier** is definitely worth a visit. The top floor includes all the big names in Impressionist and Post-Impressionist art: Monet, Manet, Seurat, Van Gogh, and Degas (his famed dancers and prostitutes are a highlight). In addition, the balconies offer supreme views of the Seine and a jungle of sculptures below. Among the decorative arts on the middle level, Rodin's imperious *Honoré de Balzac* and Pompon's adorably big-footed *Ours Blanc* are not to be missed. Besides the permanent collection, seven temporary exhibition spaces, called *dossiers*, are scattered throughout the building. Call or pick up a free copy of **Nouvelles du Musée d'Orsay** for current installations. The museum also hosts conferences, special tours (including children's tours), and concerts.

INVALIDES MUSEUMS

Esplanades des Invalides, 7ème. Ⓜ*Invalides or Saint François-Xavier.* ☎ *01 44 42 37 72; www. invalides.org. All open M and W-Su Apr.-Sept. 10am-6pm, Oct.-Mar. 10am-5pm; Tu 10am-9pm. Last ticket sales 30min. before close. Closed first M of the month. Buy tickets to all museums in the building's southeast corridor, to the left when facing dome from pl. Vauban. Admission to all museums €8, students under 26 €6, under 18 free. Tu after 5:30pm €6, under 26 free. Audioguide for Napoleon's Tomb included (€1 supplement for free ticket holders). MC/V.*

In 1670, Louis XIV decided to "construct a royal home, grand and spacious enough to receive all old or wounded officers and soldiers." Architect Libéral Bruand's building accepted its first *invalides* in 1674, and veterans still live on the grounds today. Of course, for all his beneficence toward the wounded soldiers, Louis XIV requested the Dome Church have two separate entrances so that he could attend mass without mingling with, well, the masses. Jules Hardouin-Mansart provided the final design for the imposing double chapel. The restoration monarch, Louis-Philippe, had Napoleon's remains returned to the French as a political move in 1840, but it wasn't until the reign of Napoleon's nephew, Louis-Napoleon, that the mosaic floor of the Église du Dôme was destroyed to build the huge, circular crypt for Napoleon I.

Completed in 1861, **Napoleon's tomb** consists of six concentric coffins, made of materials ranging from mahogany to lead. The tomb is viewed first from a round balcony above it, forcing everyone who visits to bow down to the emperor even in his death; this delighted Adolf Hitler on his visit to Paris in 1940. Names of significant battles are engraved in the marble floor surrounding the coffins; oddly enough, Waterloo isn't there. Bas-reliefs recall Napoleon's institutional reforms of law and education, portraying him as a Roman emperor in a toga and laurels. Upstairs, a display case holds the hat and grey coat that defined Napoleon's actual wardrobe. His only child (Napoleon divorced his beloved Josephine to marry Marie-Louise of Austria), titled King of Rome and Duke of Reichstadt, was buried near him after succumbing prematurely to tuberculosis. Six chapels dedicated to different saints lie off the main room and harbor the tombs of French Marshals and Napoleon's brothers. In 1989, the 107m high Église du Dôme was regilded, making the glorious Hôtel des Invalides the only monument in Paris to glint with real gold—12kg of gold, to be exact. The Athena project, undertaken over a decade ago and with no deadline in sight, aims to restore the entire building complex for public visitation.

MUSÉE DE L'ARMÉE. The Musée de l'Armée celebrates French military history. It lies in two wings on opposite sides of the Invalides's main cobblestone courtyard, the Cour d'Honneur. The West Wing (Aile Occident) is filled almost exclusively with French armor from medieval times onward (including that of some of France's more powerful kings), along with a variety of Asian metal and a 20th-century exhibit. The East Wing (Aile Orient) is more well-rounded, with uniforms, maps, royal ordinances, medals, and portraits in addition to armor, focusing on the 17th, 18th, and 19th centuries. Beautiful sets of Chinese and Japanese armor provide a fascinating contrast with the Western displays.

MUSÉE DES DEUX GUERRES MONDIALES. Opened in 2005, this museum in the West Wing features a chronological presentation on the World Wars. Focusing on the historical context, socio-political triggers, and technological developments, of the Wars, the collection includes uniforms, weapons, videos, interactive maps, and propaganda.

MUSÉE DES PLANS-RELIEFS. Housed in a dimly-lit attic-like room, the Musée des Plans-Reliefs is a collection of about 20 models of fortified cities from 1668 to 1870. Citadels, châteaux, and entire areas of the French countryside are intricately modeled and displayed beside aerial photographs of the land today to show interesting comparisons. Highlights include the surreal Mont-St-Michel and Fort Paté, which does in fact resemble its namesake.

MUSÉE DE L'ORDRE DE LA LIBÉRATION. Just beyond the West Wing of the Musée de l'Armée, this museum tells the story of those who fought for the liberation of France during WWII. A diverse collection of de Gaulle-related paraphernalia is complemented by tributes to the *Résistance* fighters of Free

France. Radio broadcasts, video footage, and newspaper clippings immerse the visitor in the era. On the top floor, sketches of concentration camp prisoners provide a moving glimpse into their lives and personalities.

OTHER MUSEUMS IN THE 7ÈME

■**MUSÉE DE MAILLOL.** In an *arrondissement* with some of the best art museums in Paris, the Musée de Maillol holds its own. Aristide Maillol was a sculptor, artist, and painter who, inspired by Paul Gauguin, focused most of his work on the human—especially female—form. When she was 15 years old, Dina Vierney met Maillol and became his muse, eventually finding her own passion as a collector of modern art. The museum's permanent collection combines the careers of these two art lovers (and possible lovers); it includes Maillol's work as well as pieces by Matisse, Kandinsky, Gauguin, Redon, Poliakoff, and Couturier, among others. Opened in 1995, the Musée has chosen to display its permanent collection in a series of temporary expositions that never fail to impress. *(61 rue de Grenelle, 7ème. ⓂRue du Bac. ☎01 42 22 59 58; www.museemaillol.com. Open M and W-Su 11am-6pm. Admission €8, students €6, under 16 free. AmEx/MC/V.)*

■**MUSÉE DE QUAI BRANLY.** In 2006, President Chirac jumped on the controversial presidentially-commissioned-architecture bandwagon by offering Paris this new cultural monolith of artifacts from Oceania, the Americas, Asia, and Africa. During its construction, the museum's architecture aroused as much speculation as its collections. Designed by Jean Nouvel, the massive and wildly inventive building is ensconced behind a looming glass shield (to deflect traffic noise) surrounded by a lush imitation jungle. Once inside, visitors are greeted by a stark white, winding ramp with video displays of nature projected onto the neutral ground—the beginning of the "fresh approach" Branly promises. Divided into four geographically themed sections, the museum's collection is exhaustive: 3500 of the overall 300,000 pieces fill the dimly lit display cases. But it is the pieces themselves that are truly impressive: towering totem poles stand next to ceremonial masks the size of a small car; enormous, intricately-carved ivory tusks are displayed above quirky and creative statuettes. The **Garden Gallery** (admission separate) hosts special exhibits that include rotating pieces from the permanent collection as well as loans from other museums. *Quai* Branly also hosts consortiums, workshops, and lectures in art history, philosophy, and anthropology, as well as concerts, dance performances, cinema, and theater, establishing itself as a diverse and rich source of cultural growth. Props to you, Chirac. *(27, 37, and 51 quai Branly, 7ème.ⓂAlma-Marceau. Cross the Pont de l'Alma and turn right onto quai Branly. ☎01 56 61 70 00; www.quaibranly.fr. Open Tu-W and Su 10am-6:30pm (last ticket sales 5:45pm); Th-Sa 10am-9pm (last ticket sales 8:15pm). Admission to permanent collection and mezzanine galleries €8.50, students €6, under 18 free; temporary exhibits in the Garden Gallery €8.50/6; combined ticket €13/9.50. Free first Su of the month. Audioguide €5/7. English tours available; call ☎01 56 61 71 72 for more information.)*

MUSÉE NATIONAL DE LA LÉGION D'HONNEUR ET DES ORDRES DE CHEVALERIE. Rewarded to individuals who have given outstanding service to the Republic, the National Order of the Legion of Honor is the highest honor in France. Famous recipients include Queen Elizabeth II, Winston Churchill, Chiang Kai-shek, and President Eisenhower. Recent recipients include Vladmir Putin and designer Valentino (2006), Clint Eastwood (2007), and Steven Spielberg and Celine Dion (2008). Housed in the 18th-century **Palais de la Légion d'Honneur,** this museum mostly displays medals of the French Legion of Honor, made of everything from enamel to precious stones. The carpet-sized embroidered ceremonial robes, as well as medals of honor from other countries around the world, are also worth a look.

MUSEUMS

Once the elegant **Hôtel de Salm,** the Palais de la Légion d'Honneur was built in 1786 by architect Pierre Rousseau for the Prince de Salm-Kyrburgh. The mansion came into Napoleon's hands in 1804. Though it burned down during the Commune of 1871, the members of the Légion rebuilt it soon after using the original plans. Both the Palais and the museum re-opened in November 2006 after extensive renovations. *(2 rue de la Légion-d'Honneur, 7ème. At the corner of rue de Lille and rue de Bellechasse.* Ⓜ*Solférino. Walk up rue Solférino and turn right onto rue de Lille; the short rue de la Légion d'Honneur will be on your left.* ☎*01 40 62 84 25; www.legiondhonneur.fr. Open W-Su 1-6pm. Free)*

MUSÉE DES ÉGOUTS DE PARIS (MUSEUM OF THE SEWERS OF PARIS). From 1892 to 1920, a brave and curious few observed the bowels of the city of Paris via subterranean boats. Luckily, today's tourists get to travel on foot through tunnels that are only slightly moist and smelly (don't worry: the friendly tour guides will warn you before you enter the more fragrant tunnels). The displays showing Paris's struggle for potable water and a clean Seine are arguably worth the slightly uncomfortable journey. *(Pont de l'Alma, 7ème. Across from 93 quai d'Orsay. Tickets are sold in a hut by the Mairie de Paris.* Ⓜ*Alma-Marceau.* ☎*01 53 68 27 81. Open M-W and Sa-Su May-Sept. 11am-5pm, Oct.-Apr. 11am-4pm. Closed 2 weeks in Jan. €5; students, over 60, and under 10 €4; under 5 free. English and French tours depending on volume of visitors.)*

CHAMPS-ÉLYSÉES (8ÈME)

You'll find a variety of museums, especially of *objets d'art* in the north of the *arrondissement,* while modern and diverse expositions take the stage on and around the Champs-Élysées. The former are often located in *hôtels particuliers,* once part of the private collections.

▉**MUSÉE JACQUEMART-ANDRÉ.** Nélie Jacquemart's passion for art and her husband Edouard André's wealth combined to create this extensive collection, housed in their gorgeous late-19th century home. During the couple's lifetime, Parisian high society admired their extravagant, double-corniced marble and iron staircase; however, only very special guests got a glimpse of their precious collection of English, Flemish, French, and Italian Renaissance artwork, which included a **Madonna and Child** by Botticelli, **St-George and the Dragon** by Ucello, and **Pilgrims at Emmaeus** by Rembrandt. Today, you can wander through the mansion (a sight in itself, with its wealth of gold embellishments, towering windows, and marble columns), which houses a collection worthy of the most prestigious museums. The couple imported the magnificent fresco on the upper level, set above a walled indoor garden, from Italy. Visitors can also enjoy a light lunch in the tea room (open 11:45am-5:30pm; *formule* €17), or admire the museum's facade while resting in the courtyard. *(158 bd. Haussmann, 8ème.* ☎*01 45 62 11 59.* Ⓜ*Miromesnil. Open daily 10am-6pm. Last entry 30min. before closing. €10, students and ages 7-17 €7.30, under 7 free. 1 free child ticket per 3 purchased tickets. English headsets free with admission. AmEx/MC/V.)*

PETIT PALAIS. Also called the **Musée des Beaux-Arts de la Ville de Paris,** the Petit Palais offers a mix-and-match batch of works, from 19th century sculpture to 17th century portraiture to Renaissance *objets d'arts* to ancient Greek relics—as well as the largest public collection of Christian Orthodox icons in France. Themed displays include 19th-century Impressionist works (think Monet and Cézanne) and decorative art as well as 17th-century Flemish and Dutch masterpieces (including Rubens and Rembrandt). Don't miss the beautiful exotic **garden,** which displays more of the Palais' grandiose architecture. *(av. Winston Churchill, 8ème.* ☎*01 53 43 40 00; www.petitpalais.paris.fr.* Ⓜ*Champs-Élysées-*

Clemenceau or Franklin D. Roosevelt. Follow av. Winston Churchill towards the river; the museum is on your left. Open Tu-Su 10am-6pm, Tu open until 8pm for special exhibits. Last entry 15min. before closing. Wheelchair-accessible. Admission to permanent collection free. Special exhibits €9, ages 14-27 €4.50, seniors €6, under 14 free. Audioguide €4. MC/V with €15 min. charge.)

MUSÉE NISSIM DE CAMONDO. This museum was dedicated by a wealthy Turkish banker to the Musée des Arts Décoratifs in memory of his son who died in WWI. The extensive collection of mostly 18th-century decorative arts includes Chinese vases, Savonnerie carpets, and magnificent sets of Sèvres porcelain. The museum also explains life in a grand mansion at the turn of the century: wandering through the sitting rooms, bedrooms, bathrooms, and kitchen, you may get the eerie sense that you and Doc Brown just landed the De Lorean on rue de Monceau. *(63 rue de Monceau, 8ème. From ⓂVilliers, walk down rue de Monceau; the museum is on the right. ☎01 53 89 06 50. Ground floor is wheelchair accessible. Open W-Su 10am-5:30pm. €6, ages 18-25 €4.50, under 18 free. Closed national holidays and Aug. 15. English-language audioguide free with admission. MC/V.)*

PALAIS DE LA DÉCOUVERTE. Kids tear around the Palais's interactive science exhibits, and it may be hard not to join them—nothing brings out your inner child like buttons that start comets on celestial trajectories, spinning seats that demonstrate angular motion, and displays of creepy-crawlies. What's more, adults and children alike are likely to learn a surprising amount about the physics, chemistry, astronomy, and geology, biology, and more. The temporary exhibits (4 per year) are also crowd-pleasers; the most recent, entitled "Volcanos, Earthquakes, and Tsunamis: Living with Risk," featured a volcano-simulation machine (more like a mini carnival ride). The exhibit is set to return to the museum in mid-October 2009. The planetarium has four shows (11:30am, 2, 3:15, 4:30pm) per day; arrive early during school vacation periods. *(In the Grand Palais, entrance on av. Franklin D. Roosevelt, 8ème. ⓂFranklin D. Roosevelt or Champs-Élysées-Clemenceau. ☎01 56 43 20 20; www.palais-decouverte.fr. Open Tu-Sa 9:30am-6pm, Su 10am-7pm. Wheelchair-accessible through a side entrance. €7; students, seniors, and under 18 €4.50; under 5 free. Families with at least 2 children €4.50 per adult. Planetarium €3.50. AmEx/MC/V.)*

MUSÉE CERNUSCHI. France's second-largest museum of Asian art lies just outside of the beautiful Parc Monceau. Between 1871 and 1873, during a trip around the world, Italian banker Henri Cernuschi gathered this assortment of ancient to 18th-century Asian art, including a three-ton Japanese buddha. The permanent collection is mostly from China and is organized in chronological order from the Wei-Sui dynasties to the Qing dynasty, including excellent Tang pottery pieces. Don't miss the Henri Cernuschi Memorial Room in the basement. *(7 av. Velasquez, outside the gates of Parc Monceau, 8ème. ⓂVilliers or Monceau. ☎01 53 96 21 50; www.cernuschi.paris.fr. Wheelchair-accessible. Open Tu-Su 10am-6pm. Admission to permanent collection free; special exhibits €7, seniors €5.50, under 26 €3.50. MC/V over €15.)*

GALERIES NATIONALES DU GRAND PALAIS. Designed for the 1900 World's Fair, most of the Grand Palais is occupied by the **Palais de la Découverte** (see p. 233); it also hosts 2 temporary exhibit spaces in the Galeries Nationales. The main exhibit space at 3 av. du Général Eisenhower boasts four special expositions a year. (In 2008, they ranged from "Marie Antoinette" to "Figuration Narrative.") In the other space, just around the corner, exhibits change seasonally; call ahead or check the website for more information. Make sure an exhibit is ongoing before you visit, as the Palais is closed if there are none. *(3 av. du Général Eisenhower, 8ème. ⓂChamps-Élysées-Clemenceau. Follow av. Winston Churchill towards the river; the museum is on your right. ☎01 44 13 17 17; www.rmn.fr. Open M, W, F-Su 10am-10pm, Th 10am-8pm. Last entry 45min. before closing. Wheelchair-accessible. €10, students €8. For special exhibits, admission varies; expect €7-15 and €5-8 for students, free for art students.)*

Reservations suggested; call FNAC (☎ 08 92 68 46 94) or go to www.rmn.fr or any FNAC, Virgin, or department store. Audioguide availability depends on exhibit, €5. AmEx/MC/V.)

GALLERIES

The upper 8*ème* is dotted with a variety of art galleries, hidden in sidestreets behind discrete facades. Given the opulence of the *arrondissement*, they tend to be quite high-brow. Most require ringing before entry, hours vary widely, and many close in August. If you're unable to make it to the galleries during regular hours, call ahead for a private viewing.

GALERIE LELONG. A popular gallery with a select display of 20th-century art, including works by Robert Ryman, Tàpies, and Richard Serra. It also has a good selection of contemporary art books, many edited by Daniel LeLong. There are two floors, so be sure to see both. *(13 rue de Téhéran, 8ème. Ⓜ Miromesnil. ☎ 01 45 63 38 62. Open M-F 10:30am-6pm, Sa 2-6:30pm. Closed Aug. and Dec. 24-Jan. 2.)*

GALERIE LOUIS CARRÉ & CIE. An expansive, novel array of contemporary painting, photo, and sculpture from the francophone world, this fresh and welcoming space with leather couches has about five to six exhibits per year. *(10 av. de Messine, 8ème. Ⓜ Miromesnil. ☎ 01 45 62 57 07. Open M-F 10am-12:30pm and 1:30-6pm; Sa during exhibits 10am-12:30pm, and 2-6:30pm.)*

OPÉRA (9ÈME)

MUSÉE GUSTAVE MOREAU. This monographic museum, housed in Gustave Moreau's home and *atelier* (studio), opened in 1896, two years before the artist's death. Symbolist master, Matisse and Roualt's instructor, and École des Beaux-Arts professor, Moreau left behind a fantastic body of work, much of which depicts mythological scenes. The museum overflows with more than 6000 drawings, models, sculptures, paintings, and watercolors. Climb the Victorian staircase to find Moreau's famous *L'Apparition*, an opium-inspired painting of Salomé dancing before John the Baptist's severed head. *(14 rue de La Rochefoucauld, 9ème. Ⓜ Trinité. Make a right on rue St-Lazare and then a left onto rue de La Rochefoucauld. ☎ 01 48 74 38 50; www.musee-moreau.fr. Open M and W-Su 10am-12:45pm and 2-5:15pm. Admission €5, under 26 and Su €3, under 18 and 1st Su of the month free. MC/V.)*

MUSÉE GRÉVIN. It's easy to lose your grip on reality in the garish, mirrored halls of Paris's wax museum, a treat but probably *un peu trop cher* for most budgets. Musée Grévin boasts models of everyone from Molière to Harrison Ford. Even in wax, the characters remain true to life: Charlie Chaplin is still silent and Michael Jackson is still creepy. Some gruesome scenarios involving Black Plague victims and a pre-execution Joan of Arc are also on display. The museum releases temporary exhibits every few months; past models have included a busty Madonna and a befuddled George Bush. *(10 bd. Montmartre, 9ème. Ⓜ Grands Boulevards. From the metro, walk west on bd. Montmartre, towards Opéra Garnier. ☎ 01 47 70 85 05; www.grevin.com. Open M-F 10am-6:30pm. Last entry 30min. before closing. Admission €18.50, seniors and students €16, ages 6-14 €11, under 6 free. AmEx/MC/V.)*

GALLERIES

🔲FONDATION TAYLOR. This gallery is run as a not-for-profit art space, and serving the Parisian and international art community with annual prizes in architecture, engraving, painting, and sculpture. *(1 rue la Bruyère, 9ème. ☎ 01 48 74 85 24; www.fondationtaylor.com. Ⓜ St-Georges. Take r. Notre Dame de Lorette away from Pl. St-Georges, turn left onto r. la Bruyère. Open Sept.-July Tu-Sa 1-7pm. Free.)*

BASTILLE

11ÈME ARRONDISSEMENT

GALLERIES

ESPACE D'ART YVONAMOR PALIX. Small gallery displays contemporary abstract painting with a special focus on Mexican contemporary art. White gravel covers the ground floor and exhibits change monthly. *(13 rue Keller, 11ème. Walk up av. Ledru-Rollin, turn left on r. de Charonne and right on r. Keller. Ⓜ Ledru-Rollin. ☎01 48 06 36 70; yapalix@aol.com. Open Tu-F 2-5pm and Sa 2-7pm.)*

GLASSBOX. Independently run by volunteers, this all-but-conventional gallery displays the work of young artists yet to get their big break—some of it installation art, some sculpture, some defying characterization. *(113bis rue Oberkampf, 11ème. Located below the post office; walk down the staircase in front of the post office entrance. Ⓜ Oberkampf. ☎01 43 38 02 82; glassbox.free.fr. Open Th-Sa 2-6pm.)*

12ÈME ARRONDISSEMENT

There are more hospitals than museums in the 12*ème*, which isn't necessarily a cultural hotspot. However, in October 2007 the *arrondissement* welcomed a new museum, the Cité Nationale de l'Histoire de l'Immigration, which is a must-see if only for its present relevance. It is housed in the Palais de la Porte Dorée along with the aquarium; if you make it there, hop on over to the nearby Bois de Vincennes (p. 256) for the impressive château and grounds.

CITÉ NATIONALE DE L'HISTOIRE DE L'IMMIGRATION. It is both appropriate and ironic that the newly opened (as in, October 2007) museum on immigration is housed in the **Palais de la Porte Dorée,** which was built during France's colonial expansion and thus features not-so-politically-correct friezes of "native culture" on its outside walls. The museum inside, however, is a much-needed and much-anticipated commemoration of the tumultuous history of immigration in France. Presented chronologically, the permanent collection traces the arrival and subsequent attempts at integration of immigrants in France, from 1830 to today. Videos, testimonials, photos and factual displays provide a surprisingly unbiased account of both France's experience and the experiences of the immigrants themselves. *(In the Palais de la Porte Dorée. 293 av. Daumesnil, 12ème. ⓂPorte Dorée. On the western edge of the Bois de Vincennes. ☎01 53 59 58 60; www.histoire-immigration.fr. Wheelchair-accessible. Open Tu-F 10am-5:30pm, Sa-Su 10am-7pm; last admission 45min. before museum closes. €3, ages 18-26 €2, under 18 and 1st Su of every mo free. Cité and Aquarium €6, during exhibits €7. AmEx/MC/V.)*

AQUARIUM TROPICAL. This tropical aquarium was originally conceived as part of the 1931 Colonial Exposition to display exotic fauna from the French colonies. Though it has mostly fish, it holds over 5000 creatures representing 300 species. The hands-down highlight is the perpetually dozing **crocodiles** of all sizes. *(293 av. Daumesnil, 12ème, ⓂPorte Dorée. On the western edge of the Bois de Vincennes. ☎01 44 74 84 80; www.aquarium-portedoree.fr. Wheelchair accessible. Open T-Su 10am-5:30pm; last entry 4:45pm. Admission €7.50, ages 18-26 €4.20, under 18 and first Su of every month free. Cité and Aquarium €6, during exhibits €7. AmEx/MC/V.)*

GALLERIES

The Viaduc des Arts, with its intimate artisan workshops and gallery spaces, runs through the 12*ème* (see **Sights,** p. 241; ⓂBastille), and the fabulous Jean-Paul Gaultier has a gallery at no. 30 rue du Faubourg St-Antoine. Establishments on avenue Daumesnil offer strollers a funky but swanky artisans' haven in the heart of the Bastille.

■**MALHIA KENT.** A behind-the-scenes look at fashion. Watch artisans weaving fabric that becomes haute couture for houses like Dior and Chanel. Also sells clothing and accessories. *(19 av. Daumesnil, 12ème. ☎01 53 44 76 76; www.malhia.fr.* Ⓜ*Gare de Lyon. Jackets and blazers €190-220. Open M-F 9am-6pm, Sa-Su 11am-7pm.)*

■**VERTICAL.** Twisted and mangled Amazonian wood turned into mesmerizing, zen-like art. *(63 av. Daumesnil, 12ème. ☎01 43 40 26 26; www.vertical.fr.* Ⓜ*Gare de Lyon. Open Tu-F 10am-1pm and 2:30-7:30pm, Sa 11am-1:30pm and 3-7:30pm.)*

55-57. These gallery spaces are rented out every month by a variety of artists and craftsmen—usually a good place for international contemporary art. *(55-57 av. Daumesnil, 12ème.* Ⓜ*Gare de Lyon.)*

GALERIE CLAUDE SAMUEL. This is the only fixed contemporary art gallery in the Viaduc; the artists in this sparse space change every six weeks. *(69 av. Daumesnil, 12ème.. ☎01 53 17 01 11; www.claude-samuel.com.* Ⓜ*Gare de Lyon. Open Tu-F 10am-1pm and 2:30-7pm, Sa 11am-7pm.)*

BUTTE-AUX-CAILLES AND CHINATOWN (13ÈME)

GALLERIES

The 13*ème* has a coterie of new galleries along rue Louise-Weisse (Ⓜ Chevarelet) and the perpendicular rue Duchefdelaville. Expect glossy, colorful photos, loopy (and looping) videos, and gleefully bold installations. Any one of the show spaces can provide you with the Louise pamphlet, which gives descriptions of each gallery and plots them on a mini-map.

MONTPARNASSE

14ÈME ARRONDISSEMENT

■**FONDATION CARTIER POUR L'ART CONTEMPORAIN.** The Fondation Cartier looks like an avant-garde indoor forest, with a stunning modern glass facade surrounding the natural wildlife and local flora of the grounds. Inside the main building, the gallery hosts exhibits of contemporary art, from Andy Warhol to African sculpture. The gallery received a great deal of attention in 2004 for Pain Couture, a show of Jean-Paul Gaultier designs rendered in rolls and baguettes. On Thursdays, art hounds can scope out an eclectic set of dance, music, and performance art at the Soirées Nomades. *261 bd. Raspail, 14ème.* Ⓜ *Raspail or Denfert-Rochereau. ☎01 42 18 56 50; www.fondation.cartier.com. Open Tu-Su noon-8pm. €6, students and seniors €4.50, under 10 free. Soirées Nomades Th 8:30pm; check website for performance details. Reserve ahead ☎01 42 18 56 72.*

15ÈME ARRONDISSEMENT

MÉMORIAL DE LA LIBÉRATION DE PARIS. Opened in 1994 to commemorate the 50th anniversary of the French Liberation, the **Mémorial du Maréchal Leclerc de Hauteclocque** and the **Musée Jean Moulin** honor two beloved French WWII heroes. Leclerc led the Free French in North Africa and was at the head of the first Allied division to liberate Paris from German occupation in August

1944. As the National Council of Resistance's founder, president, and martyr, Moulin collaborated with Charles de Gaulle to overthrow the German occupation. Secretly parachuting back into France from British exile in 1942, Jean "Max" Moulin fell captive to the *Gestapo* barely a year later, betrayed by his own side. The museums, both of which are filled with official documents and letters relating to the Liberation, present a comprehensive timeline of WWII France. Furthermore, situated in the fantastic Jardin Atlantique, on the roof over the tracks of Gare Montparnasse, the museum provides a serene picnic ground. *(23 allée de la 2ème D.B., Jardin Atlantique, 15ème. ⓜMontparnasse-Bienvenüe. On the roof above the tracks of the Gare Montparnasse. Follow signs to the Jardin Atlantique from the train station, place du Pont des Cinq Martyrs du Lycée Buffon, or rue Commandant René Mouchotte. ☎ 40 64 39 44. Open Tu-Su 10am-6pm. Wheelchair accessible. Admission to permanent collection free; exhibitions €4, students and seniors €3, ages 14-26 €2.)*

MUSÉE BOURDELLE. Rodin's pupil and Matisse's mentor, Emile-Antoine Bourdelle (1861-1929) sculpted the reliefs that adorn the Théâtre des Champs-Élysées and the Marseilles Opera House. Housed in the expressionist sculptor's studio and home, the museum displays over 500 works in bronze, marble, and plaster, including Bourdelle's masterpiece, **Heracles the Archer** (1909). While Greek-inspired sculptures dominate the museum, two Beethoven busts hint at the artist's virtuosity; Bourdelle celebrated the German composer in 28 other sculptures and over 20 paintings. Wander the spacious gardens to admire the sculptor's more sizable works not displayed in the "Great Hall." The museum's smaller inner rooms provide insight into Bourdelle's creative methodology, featuring his studies and casts in addition to his finished pieces. *(16 rue Antoine Bourdelle,15ème. ⓜMontparnasse-Bienvenüe. From place Bienvenüe, take avenue du Maine, turn left onto rue Antoine Bourdelle. ☎49 54 73 73; www.paris.org/Musees/Bourdelle. Open Tu-Su 10am-6pm. Last entry 15min. before closing. Admission €4-7, ages 14-16 €3.50. MC/V.)*

PASSY AND AUTEUIL (16ÈME)

▧**MUSÉE D'ART MODERNE DE LA VILLE DE PARIS.** The magnificent Palais de Tokyo (see **Sights**, p. 247) is home to one of the world's foremost museums of modern art. Though the collection is smaller than that of the Centre Pompidou, it is free and less touristed. One room is dedicated to Matisse's enormous *La Danse Inachêvée*, which was executed with the help of a brush attached to a long bamboo pole. Other rooms are organized around significant movements—New Realism, Fauvism, and Abstraction, to name a few-and showcase works from the likes of Modigliani, Vuillard, Braque, Klein, and Picasso. The museum has fantastic special exhibits of both contemporary art and retrospective displays. There is also a cafe, which opens onto a terrace in the summer. *(Palais de Tokyo, 11 av. du Président Wilson, 16ème. ⓜIéna. Follow av. du Président Wilson with the Seine on your right. ☎01 53 67 40 00; www.mam.paris.fr. Open Tu-Su 10am-6pm, last entrance 5:45pm; W night open until 10pm for special exhibits, last entrance 9:45pm. Wheelchair-accessible. Admission to permanent exhibitions free; special exhibits admission varies, expect approximately €4.50-7 for contemporary art and €6-9 for retrospective exhibits, large families, seniors, under 27 €3-6; under 13 free. For guided tours, call ☎01 53 67 40 80.)*

▧**MUSÉE MARMOTTAN MONET.** Housed in the former hunting villa of the Duc de Valmy (later the private home of Jules and Paul Marmottan), this hidden museum holds Impressionist treasures, started from the personal collection of Dr. Georges de Bellio, former physician to Manet, Monet, Pissarro, Sisley and Renoir. All of the patients have works showcased here, as do Morisot, Gauguin, Daumer and Caillebotte. But it's called the Marmottan Monet for a reason: the basement has the collection's centerpiece: wall-sized paintings of the Impressionist's waterlilies, weeping willows, and wisterias. Meanwhile, the mansion, with its intricate furnishings and elaborate decor, is a sight in itself. *(2 rue Louis-Boilly, 16ème. ⓜMuette Follow directions to the Jardin Ranelagh, and walk through the Jardin; the museum will be visible on the right side of rue Louis-Boilly. ☎01 44 96 50 31; www.marmottan. com. Open Tu-Su 10am-5:30pm; last admission 1hr. before closing. €8, seniors and students under 25 €4.50, under 8 free; including temporary exhibit €9/5.50. Audioguide €3.)*

▧**MAISON DE BALZAC.** Honoré de Balzac hid from bill collectors (under the pseudonym of M. de Breugnol) in this three-story hillside *maison*, his home from 1840-47. In this tranquil retreat, he completed a substantial part of *La Comédie Humaine*, and wrote many other famous works, such as *A Dark Affair*. Visitors can see the desk and beautifully embroidered chair where Balzac supposedly wrote and edited for 17 hours a day. (He is quoted as saying, "To work is to wake at midnight, write until 8am, lunch for a quarter of an hour, work until 5pm, have dinner, go to bed, and start again the next day.") In the fantastic **Manuscript Room,** you can observe his excruciating editing process. View over 400 printing block portraits of his characters, organized into genealogical sequences, in one of the last rooms. Information *plaques* are in both English and Japanese. *(47 rue Raynouard, 16ème. ⓜPassy. Walk up the hill and turn left onto rue Raynouard. ☎01 55 74 41 80; www.paris.fr/musees/balzac. Open Tu-Su 10am-6pm. Last entry 5:30pm before closing. Permanent collection free. Guided tours and temporary exhibits €4, families and seniors €3, students under 26 €2, under 12 free. Call for schedule.)*

MUSÉE NATIONAL DES ARTS ASIATIQUES (MUSÉE GUIMET). The clean grey and white lines of this architectural marvel display a beautiful collection of Asian art from 17 different countries and spanning over 5 millennia. Over 45,000 works in stone, metal, paper, and canvas serenely occupy a five-floor maze of rooms organized by country and era, from China's Wei Dynasty to India's Gupta Era, from 12th century Vietnam to 14th century Tibet. The Riboud Gallery, a dazzling display of decorative objects and jewelry from Mogul India, is a highlight. Don't miss the lovely rotunda on the second floor and the lacquer screen room on the top floor. To get the full experience, rent a free audioguide, which provides explanations of the historical and religious significance of selected pieces. Just around the corner, the annexed Panthéon Bouddhique, 19 av. d'Iéna packs in more art from Japan and China and has a tranquil garden out back. *(6 pl. d'Iéna, 16ème. ⓜIéna. ☎01 56 52 53 00; www.museeguimet.fr. Open M and W-Su 10am-6pm; last entrance 5:45pm. Wheelchair-accessible. Admission to permanent collection €6.50, ages 18-25 and all visitors on Su €4.50, under 18, disabled persons and all visitors on the first Su of the month free. Temporary exhibits €7, ages 18-25 €5; combined tickets €8.50/ 6. Free audioguide in 8 languages.)*

MUSÉE DE LA MODE ET DU COSTUME (MUSEUM OF FASHION AND CLOTHING). The elegant **Italian Palais Galleria,** in which the museum is housed, was originally conceived in 1892 as a repository for the Duchess of Galliera's sizable collection of Italian Baroque art, which was sent to Genoa instead. Now the Palais holds an even larger collection of the quintessential Parisian art form: clothing. With 30,000 outfits, 70,000 accessories, and a relatively small space in which to display them, the museum rotates exhibits to showcase various fashions of the past three centuries. This is the place to go for the history of Parisian chic, written in beads, brocade, and *bouclée*. *(In the Palais Galliera, 10 av. Pierre, 1er de Serbie, in the pl. de Tokyo, 16ème. ⓜIéna. Walk down either av. du Président Wilson or av. Pierre 1er de Serbie with the Eiffel Tower to your right. The museum entrance is in the center of the Palais and can be reached from the pl. de Rochambeau side. ☎01 56 52 86 00. Open Tu-Su 10am-6pm; last entrance 5:30pm. Admission depends on exhibit: €7, students and seniors €5.50,* *ages 14-26 €3.50, under 14 free. Availability of audioguide depends on exhibit. For guided visits, call ☎01 56 52 86 20. MC/V over €15.)*

MUSÉE DE LA MARINE (MUSEUM OF NAVAL HISTORY). Contructed to commemorate the evolution of France's relationship with the seas, this museum is more interesting than you might think, though it is only a must-see for serious sailors. Large model ships of astounding detail, exhaustive exhibits on the French Navy in the two World Wars, and impressive maritime equipment from the days of Napolean and Louis XIV make for a diverse experience. A few real boats from the 17-19th centuries are anchored here, including a lavishly-embellished golden "dinghy" built for Napoleon in 1810, which takes up an entire room. Oil paintings of stormy sea battles and French ports round out the collection. *(17 pl. du Trocadéro, 16ème. ⓂTrocadéro. In the Palais de Chaillot, immediately to the right of the entrance. ☎01 53 65 69 69; www.musee-marine.fr. Open M and W-Su 10am-6pm; last entry 5:15pm. Admission to permanent collection €6.50, students, academia, large families €4.50, under 18 free. Joint admission to permanent and temporary exhibits €8, students €6, ages 6-18 €4, ages 3-6 €3. AmEx/MC/V over €15.)*

FONDATION LE CORBUSIER. The foundation is located in **Villa La Roche** and **Villa Jeanneret,** both designed and furnished by the Swiss architectural master Le Corbusier (1887-1965); it might not blow you away unless you are an architectural guru. Villa Jeanneret houses the foundation's scholarly library, but the real attraction is the reduced geometry, understated curvature, and creative spaciousness of Villa La Roche's interiors, which reflect the architect's maxim that "a house is a machine you live in!" *(Villa La Roche 8-10, sq. du Docteur Blanche, 16ème. ⓂJasmin. Walk up rue de l'Yvette and turn left on rue du Docteur-Blanche and left again at no. 55 into sq. du Docteur-Blanche; go down to the cul-de-sac and ring the bell inside the gate at your right. ☎01 42 88 41 53; www.fondationlecorbusier.asso.fr. Open M 1:30-6pm, Tu-Th 10am-12:30pm and 1:30-6pm, F 10am-12:30pm and 1:30-5pm, Sa 10am-5pm, last entry 15min. before closing. Admission €4, students €2. Groups of 10-15 €2, under 14 free. Groups must reserve ahead. Library in Villa Jeanneret (on your right before end of cul-de-sac open by appointment only, specify the Villa when calling. Book consultation free, archive access €3/1.50.*

MUSÉE GEORGES CLEMENCEAU. The museum, oddly hidden through a courtyard behind an unassuming residential facade, thoroughly documents the life of revered and vilified journalist and statesman Georges Clemenceau (1841-1929). Publisher of Emile Zola's *J'accuse, Prime Minister of France,* and the much-criticized negotiator of the Treaty of Versailles, Clemenceau lived here from 1895 until his death in 1929. The museum contains personal mementos (letters to his wife, clothes, etc.) as well as official documents (newspaper articles, war propaganda, books, etc.). Those who are not French history lovers need not make it a point to visit. Ring a doorbell for access to the museum. *(8 rue Benjamin Franklin, 16ème. ⓂPassy. ☎01 45 20 53 41. Open Tu-Sa 2-5:30pm; closed Aug. Last entry 30min. before closing. Admission €6, ages 12-25 €3, under 12 free. Free audioguide.)*

MUSÉE DU VIN. Located in the cool, subterranean corridors of the renovated 15th-century Passy Monastery, which once produced one of Louis XIII's favorite wines, the Musée du Vin is appealing more for its symbolic role than anything else. With whimsical (and occasionally creepy) wax models, the museum meticulously recreates the life cycle of wine from vine to *verre,* highlighting each French wine, from Champagne to Bordeaux to Grand Marnier. The content of the museum is dry but exhaustive; the hundreds of objects on display date to the 18th century, including wine bottles, corkscrews of all shapes, and agricultural implements. After the tour, you may have to remind the receptionist to give you a free tasting. If that whets your appetite, a wine-heavy lunch is available in the adjacent restaurant. *(Rue des Eaux, or 5-7 pl. Charles Dickens, 16ème.*

Ⓜ*Passy. Go down the stairs, turn right on pl. Alboni, and then right on rue des Eaux; the museum is at the end of the street. ☎45 25 63 26; www.museeduvinparis.com. Open Tu-Su 10am-6pm. Admission including 1 glass of wine €9, seniors €7.50, students €7, under 15 free. MC/V.)*

MUSÉE DE L'HOMME. This anthropology museum has been considerably reduced: its entire ethnology collection was moved in 2005 to Musée du Quai Branly. However, there are still a handful of exhibits on the human life cycle, centered on everything from birth control to physical differences among peoples. With most exhibits directed at children, this museum might only be worth the price of admission for the typically intriguing temporary exhibits, conferences, and films. *(17 pl. du Trocadéro, 16ème.* Ⓜ*Trocadéro. In the Palais de Chaillot, on the right-hand side if you're facing the Eiffel Tower. ☎01 44 05 72 72; www.mnhn.fr. Open M and W-F 10am-5pm, Sa-Su 10am-6pm, last entry 1hr. before closing. Wheelchair-accessible. €7, under 26 €5; under 4 free. Films in the afternoon Tu, Sa, Su. MC/V.)*

BATIGNOLLES (17ÈME)

MUSÉE JEAN-JACQUES HENNER. Three full floors display works by Alsatian artist Jean-Jacques Henner (1829-1905). The exhibits feature landscapes, nymphs, and soft-focus subjects. Closed for renovations through early 2009; call for more info including opening hours and ticket prices. *(43 avenue de Villiers, 17ème. ☎01 47 63 42 73.* Ⓜ*Malesherbes. Across from the metro.)*

MONTMARTRE (18ÈME)

The 18*ème*'s museums are as varied as the *arrondissement* itself. At the northern end past the Basilique du Sacré-Coeur (p. 249) is the historic Musée de Montmartre, which stands in stark contrast to the fantastically explicit Musée de l'Erotisme bordering the 9*ème*.

▉MUSÉE DE L'EROTISME. Bronze statues in the missionary position, Japanimation sex cartoons, vagina-shaped puppets—seven floors of steamy creations await visitors at Paris's shrine to sex. The museum celebrates multicultural erotic art across all media, from painting to sculpture to video—and even includes King Alfonso XIII of Spain's pornos. Organized to provide a more edifying experience than expected, the 2000-item collection places the museum high on the City of Love's "to-do" list. Temporary exhibits on the top three floors insuring novel excitement at each visit. Despite the scholarly nature of the museum's contents, it is not advised to bring children here. *(72 bd. de Clichy, 18ème.* Ⓜ*Blanche. ☎01 42 58 28 73; www.musee-erotisme.com. Open daily 10am-2am. €8, groups of 4 or more €6, seniors and students €5.)*

HALLE SAINT-PIERRE. Within a former 19th-century marketplace, this gallery and cultural center holds temporary exhibits of contemporary drawing, painting and sculpture. It features mostly folk and naive artists from around the world, including France, Haiti, and North America. The Halle Saint-Pierre also hosts a bookstore, community auditorium, and various art workshops for children. A quiet, ground-floor cafe enables pleasant reflection on the gallery's collections, relatively removed from the hoards of tourists outside. Halle Saint-Pierre is also home to the **Musée d'Art Naïf Max Fourny,** a one-room permanent collection of international folk art. *(2 rue Ronsard, 18ème.* Ⓜ*Anvers. Walk up rue Steinkerque, turn right at place St-Pierre, and left on rue Ronsard. ☎01 42 58 72 89; www.hallesaintpierre. org. Open Sept.-July daily 10am-6pm, Aug. M-F noon-6pm. Last entry at 5:30pm. Workshops for children over 6 W 2:30-6pm; reserve ahead. Wheelchair accessible. Temporary exhibits €7.50, students under 26 €6, under 4 free. Children's workshops €8.)*

MUSÉE DE MONTMARTRE. Located in the quartier's oldest house, the Musée de Montmartre guides visitors through the neighborhood's history, embellishing local stories with drawings, letters, and relics. The house was built for an actor in Molière's company, Roze de Rosimond, who, like Molière bizarrely enough, died onstage during a performance of *Le Malade Imaginaire.* Painters Raoul Dufy, Auguste Renoir, Maurice Utrillo, and conductor Gustave Charpentier also called the place home; the museum hosts their original work and personal relics in an upper room. On other floors, cabaret posters, journal entries, and mediocre paintings by celebrated Montmartre residents line the walls. On the topmost floor, a maquette (miniature model) displays the relatively-unchanged neighborhood as it stood in 1956. Finally, the view of the *butte* from the garden is not to be missed. (*12 rue Cortot, 18ème.* Ⓜ*Lamarck-Caulaincourt. Turn right on rue Lamarck, right again up steep rue des Saules, then left on rue Cortot.* ☎*01 49 25 89 37; www. museedemontmartre.fr. Open Tu-Su 11am-6pm. Last entry 5pm. €7, students, seniors, and under 26 €5.50; includes English- or French-language audioguide. MC/V.*)

BUTTES CHAUMONT (19ÈME)

▨**EXPLORA SCIENCE MUSEUM.** Dedicated to making science youth-friendly, the Explora Science Museum is La Villette's star attraction, located in the complex's **Cité des Sciences et de l'Industrie** (see **Sights**, p. 252). The museum's intriguing exhibits rock just as much as the buildings' futuristic architecture. Kids will love them, and even adult visitors may find themselves unexpectedly enthralled. The museum hosts 11 permanent and 4 temporary exhibits, ranging from astronomy and mathematics to computer science and sound. Explora also features a **planetarium** (level 2), the **Cinéma Louis Lumière** (level 0) with 3D movies, a modest **aquarium** (level -2), and **Médiathèque,** a multimedia scientific and technical library with over 3500 films. The museum's **Cité des Enfants** offers one set of programs for kids ages 2-7 and another for ages 5-12. Most programs are in French, but the interactive exhibits are just as fun for English-speaking explorers. The *vestiaire* on the ground floor lends strollers and wheelchairs for free with purchase of a museum ticket. (*30 av. Corentin-Cariou, 19ème.* Ⓜ*Porte de la Villette.* ☎*01 40 05 80 00; www.cite-sciences.fr. Museum open Tu-Sa 10am-6pm, Su 10am-7pm. Last entry 30min. before closing. €8, under 25 or families of 5 or more €6, under 7 free. Planetarium supplement €3, under 7 free. Médiathèque open Tu-Su noon-6:45pm. Free. Aquarium entry free. 1½hr. Cité des Enfants programs Tu-Su 10:30am, 12:30, 2:30, and 4:30pm. €6.*)

MUSÉE DE LA MUSIQUE. Spanning three-centuries of music, this museum enables you to hear history in action. Its over 900-piece collection includes antique instruments, sculptures, and paintings from around the world. Completely renovated in 2007, the stimulating audio complex comprises only part of the **Cité de la Musique** (see **Sights**, p. 253). Don headsets tuning into classical excerpts and forget the surrounding honking grind of working-class Paris. (*221 avenue Jean-Jaurès, 19ème.* Ⓜ*Porte de la Villette.* ☎*01 40 05 80 00; www.cite-musique.fr. Open Tu-Sa 10am-6pm, Su 10am-7pm. Permanent collections €7, under 18 free.*)

BELLEVILLE AND PÈRE LACHAISE (20ÈME)

While not really worth a separate trip, the 20*ème*'s sole museum, La Maison de l'Air, makes for an interesting addendum to a leisurely afternoon spent lounging in the Parc de Belleville (p. 255).

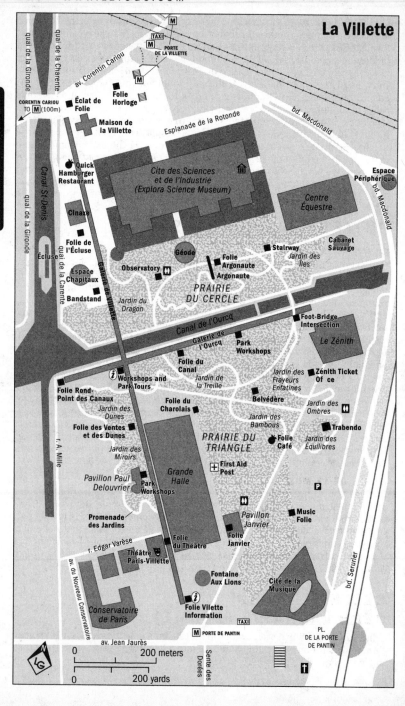

La Villette

MUSEUMS

quai de la Gironde
quai de la Charente
av. Corentin Cariou
M
TAXI
M
PORTE DE LA VILLETTE
M

CORENTIN CARIOU TO M (100m)

Éclat de Folie
Folie Horloge

Maison de la Villette

Esplanade de la Rotonde

bd. Macdonald

Quick Hamburger Restaurant

Canal St-Denis

Cinaxe

Cité des Sciences et de l'Industrie (Explora Science Museum)

Espace Périphérique

bd. Macdonald

Centre Équestre

Folie de l'Écluse

Écluse

Espace Chapitaux

Bandstand

Galerie de la Villette

quai de la Carente

Géode

Observatory

Folie Argonaute
Argonaute

Stairway
Jardin des Îles

Cabaret Sauvage

PRAIRIE DU CERCLE

Jardin du Dragon

Canal de l'Ourcq

Foot-Bridge Intersection

Le Zénith

Galerie de l'Ourcq

Park Workshops

Workshops and Park Tours

Folie du Canal

Jardin de la Treille

Jardin des Frayeurs Enfatines

Zénith Ticket Office

Folie Rond-Point des Canaux

Jardin des Dunes

Folie du Charolais

Belvédère

Jardin des Ombres

Folie des Ventes et des Dunes

Jardin des Bambous

Trabendo

Jardin des Miroirs

PRAIRIE DU TRIANGLE

Folie Café

Jardin des Équilibres

Pavillon Paul Delouvrier

Grande Halle

Park Workshops

First Aid Post

P

Promenade des Jardins

Pavillon Janvier

Music Folie

r. Edgar Varèse

Folie du Théâtre

Folie Janvier

av. du Nouveau Conservatoire

Théâtre Paris-Villette

Fontaine Aux Lions

Cité de la Musique

bd. Sérurier

Conservatoire de Paris

Folie Vilette Information

TAXI

M PORTE DE PANTIN

PL. DE LA PORTE DE PANTIN

av. Jean Jaurès

Sente des Dorées

0   200 meters

0   200 yards

LA MAISON DE L'AIR. Aimed at children age 8-11 years old, this one-floor museum helps you hear, smell, and touch your way into a broader understanding of the air around you. Interactive exhibits investigate the atmosphere, meteorology, and pollution—a major problem in Paris. Occasional themed weekends encourage further hands-on investigation, and the surrounding Parc de Belleville provides amazing views. (*27 rue Piat, 20ème.* ☎ *01 43 28 47 63.* Ⓜ*Pyrénées. Walk down the sloping rue de Belleville and turn left on rue Piat. Open Apr.-Sept. Tu-F 1:30-5:30pm, Su 1:30-6:30pm; Oct. and Mar. Tu-Su 1:30-5:30pm; Nov.-Feb. Tu-Su 1:30-5pm. Free.*)

MUSEUMS

SHOPPING

Fashion is born by small facts, trends, or even politics, never by trying to make little pleats and furbelows, by trinkets, by clothes easy to copy, or by the shortening or lengthening of a skirt.
—Elsa Schiaparelli

In a city where Hermès scarves function as slings for broken arms and department store history stretches back to the mid-19th century, shopping is nothing less than an art form. Be prepared to expend every ounce of your energy out in the boutique battlefield, but rest assured that your efforts will pay off. Almost everything in this city, from the world's most expensive dresses to kitchen appliances, is astoundingly stylish. The brave and experimental, willing to splurge on the independent designs of off-the-beaten path boutiques in the 18ème or the Marais, will be especially rewarded with one-of-a-kind pieces—wearable evidence of your exploits in the fashion capital of the world.

A BRIEF HISTORY OF PARISIAN FASHION

Paris has been at the vanguard of fashion since the Romans got tunic-making tips from the Gauls. Things really took off during the 17th century, when the costumes of royals and aristocrats inspired the envy of both the wealthy and the lowly, who eventually got so fed up with those 5ft. high powdered wigs and 10ft. wide bejeweled skirts that they started a Revolution. Post-Revolutionary **Empire style,** perhaps aware of the decadent fastidiousness of the previous century, was all about a "simple" Neoclassical ideal. Fashion as we know it today came into being in the 1800s, when the first **department stores** were built (p. 306). The bourgeoisie became consummate consumers; artists like **Edouard Manet** and writers like **Charles Baudelaire** began to represent fashion as a harbinger of modernity—a unique expression of "the moral and aesthetic feeling" of the era. Soon thereafter, the **couturier** (designer; see Couture Culture) was born.

The first modern *couturier* was **Charles Frederick Worth,** whose House of Worth opened in Paris in 1858. Worth invented the fashion show, the designer-as-celebrity (clothing-makers had previously been considered lowly artisans), and the fashion label as a status symbol. In the early 20th century, designers like **Madeliene Vionnet** and **Paul Poiret,** influenced by Art Nouveau and Orientalist trends, "liberated" women from corsets and heavy petticoats, designing whimsical shapes and flowing bias-cut dresses. In the 1920s, the iconic **Coco Chanel** revolutionized women's dress with her boyish elegance, insistence on comfort, legendary suits, and invention of the "little black dress." Meanwhile, the designs of innovators like **Elsa Schiaparelli** echoed radical art movements like Surrealism and Cubism (**Salvador Dalí** designed the fabric for some of her dresses). During WWII, strict regulations were enforced on fabric and design, and patriotic self-denial came into fashion. But in 1947, **Christian Dior** aroused shock, anger, and delight with the cinched waists and outlandishly full skirts of his **New Look,** re-establishing Paris as the center of the fashion world and, once again, reinventing the way the female form was idealized. In the 1960s,

André **Courrèges** and **Paco Rabanne** moved fashion in fantastically futuristic directions, employing bold shapes and radical new materials. **Yves Saint Laurent** dominated Parisian fashion throughout the second half of the 20th century with his embrace of androgynous style and Left Bank beatnik chic.

Today, designers like **Jean-Paul Gaultier** and **Christian Lacroix** display their creations in extravagant bi-annual spectacles, the Paris fashion shows. Fashion continues to exist at the crossroads of art and consumerism; to reinvent the past and imagine the future; and to shape—and be shaped by—the way we perceive our desires, bodies, and eras. And Paris is where it all goes down.

ÎLE DE LA CITÉ

Le Marché aux Fleurs, pl. Louis-Lépine, Île de la Cité. ⓜCité. The market is to your left as you exit the Metro. An open secret to Parisians for many years, this covered flower marketplace is open year-round, rain or shine. Dangling wicker baskets, quaint garden knicknacks, and spiral-shaped bushes are just some of the attractions. This leafy oasis turns into the **Marché aux Oiseaux** (bird market) on Su, attracting delighted children who poke at cuddly furballs and chirpy birds nestled in cages. Open daily 8am-7pm.

ÎLE ST-LOUIS

Shopping on Île St-Louis is not for the faint of heart: one could easily spend a fortune on antiques, rare books, or overpriced tourist trappings. However, the island also contains some small, unusual (and reasonable) boutiques, where you just might find that one-of-a-kind hat (or toaster) you've been looking for. Most worthwhile stores can be found on rue St-Louis-en-l'Île.

CLOTHING AND ACCESSORIES

Pylônes, 57 rue St-Louis-en-l'Île (☎01 46 34 05 02). ⓜPont Marie. Sells all the items that you'll never really need (but will certainly want). Exuberantly youthful, artful, and adorable concept. Bright, spunky housewares such as gnome-shaped piggy banks (€36), dog-shaped spatulas (€18), and the slightly sinister "voodoo knife holder" (€90). Open daily 10:30am-7:30pm. 5 other locations throughout the city. AmEx/MC/V.

Sobral, 79 rue St-Louis-en-l'Île (☎01 43 25 80 10; www.rsobral.com.br). ⓜPont Marie. This boutique features funky accessories influenced by pop art with a dash of retro Italian flavor. Colorful earrings, necklaces, and bracelets (€10-40). Key chains (€12-21). For those with deep pockets, the stools, mirrors, and coffee tables covered with sea flora and fauna are artsy and fun (€150-330). Open daily 11am-7:30pm. AmEx/MC/V.

Le Grain de Sable, 79 rue St-Louis-en-l'Île (☎01 46 33 67 27; www.legraindesable.fr). ⓜPont Marie. Hats of every outrageous-but-sophistiated color, shape, and size imaginable (approx. €15-150). Women bring in dresses to match hat colors, and staff are more than willing to spend hours with each customer. Also stocks brightly colored espadrilles, dressy knits, and costume jewelry. Open daily 11am-7pm. MC/V.

CHÂTELET-LES HALLES (1ER AND 2ÈME)

Sugar and spice, and all things naughty. In the tourist-packed 1*er* and 2*ème arrondissements*, the fabrics are a little cheaper and the style is younger, especially around rue Tiquetonne. A stroll down rue Étienne-Marcel will delight shoe fetishists. The popular Forum Les Halles and the streets that surround it offer everything you'll need for a full urban-warrior aesthetic.

Zadig & Voltaire, 15 rue du Jour, 1er (☎01 42 21 88 70; www.zadig-et-voltaire.com). ⓂÉtienne-Marcel. 6 other locations in the city. Funky, sleek, and expensive women's designs by Paul & Jack, Holly, etc. Their own label does soft, feminine, bohemian-rocker-chic. A big selection of handbags. Opening hours vary by branch. Main branch open M 1-7:30pm, Tu-Sa 10:30am-7:30pm. AmEx/MC/V.

Samaritaine, 67 rue de Rivoli, on the quai du Louvre, 1er (☎01 40 41 20 20; www.lasa-maritaine.com). ⓂPont Neuf, Châtelet-Les Halles, or Louvre-Rivoli. 4 large, historic Art Deco buildings between rue de Rivoli and the Seine, connected by tunnels and bridges (see **Sights,** p. 205). Not as chic as Galeries Lafayette or Bon Marché, as it dares to sell souvenirs (gasp!) and merchandise at down-to-earth prices (the horror!), but still a presence in the Parisian shopping scene, and not just due to tradition. The rooftop observation deck provides one of the best views of the city; take the elevator to the 9th floor and climb the short, spiral staircase. Some hotels offer 10% discount coupons for use in the store. Closed indefinitely for construction; usually open M-W and F-Sa 9:30am-7pm, Th 9:30am-10pm. AmEx/MC/V.

Forum des Halles, ⓂLes Halles or RER: Châtelet-Les Halles, 2ème (☎01 44 76 96 56). Why anyone thought Paris needed an American-style shopping mall is a puzzling ques-tion. The 4 main entrances lead down to over 200 stores, including FNAC, the cosmetics wonderland Sephora, boutiques featuring independent designers, and a 4-story H&M. It can get confusing, so pick up a map from the welcome desks. Open M-Sa 10am-7:30pm (later during the *soldes*).

Celio, 65 rue de Rivoli, 1er (☎01 42 21 18 04). ⓂPalais-Royal. An French clothing line (the first store was opened on rue St-Lazare) that prides itself on its international appeal. Exhaustive collection of pretty-preppy shirts, jeans, pants, and sweaters. The Celio Sport section of the store carries basic athletic wear. More than reasonably priced. Other locations throughout the city; most open M-Sa 11am-7pm. AmEx/MC/V.

Kookaï, pl. Carrée, Nouveau Forum des Halles, 1er (☎01 40 26 59 11). Quintessential French fashion chain for fun-loving *jeune filles.* Beware the small sizing. Open M-Sa 10:30am-7pm. Also at 155 rue de Rennes, 6ème (☎01 45 48 26 36); 66, bd. de Montparnasse, 15ème (☎01 45 38 74 30); and 16 other locations in the city. MC/V.

Esprit, Carrousel du Louvre, 99 rue de Rivoli, 1er (☎01 42 60 41 51). ⓂChâtelet. Other locations throughout the city. Modern, sporty basics for the whole family. Done with a trendy twist. AmEx/MC/V.

SHOES AND ACCESSORIES

▨ **Gabrielle Geppert,** 31-34 Galerie Montpensier, 1er (☎01 42 61 53 52; www.gabriel-legeppert.com). ⓂPalais-Royale. A true gem. A tiny store tucked away in the back of the Palais-Royale; a favorite of Sharon Stone. Gold leather and snakeskin bags, rhine-stud-ded sunglasses in all colors, fur purses, enormous necklaces and earrings—all by vin-tage designers: Chanel, Louis Vuitton, Prada, and Gucci. The exuberant, smartly-dressed owner, Gabrielle, handpicks all pieces herself. Open M-Sa 10am-7:30pm.

Longchamp, 404 rue St-Honoré, 1er (☎01 43 16 00 16; www.longchamp.com). ⓂConcorde. This flagship store inspired an endless trend of classic leather-strapped canvas totes that fold up flat when need be. (A whole wall is devoted to them.) Original bags start at €48. Also sells more conventional totes, as well as lots of leather acces-sories like wallets, belts, key chains, and even pencil cases. Open M-Sa 10am-7pm. AmEx/MC/V. Also at 21 rue du Vieux-Colombier, 6ème (☎01 42 22 74 75).

Colette, 213 rue St-Honoré, 1er (☎01 55 35 33 90; www.colette.fr). ⓂTuileries. Unthink-ably cool lifestyle store whose bare display tables feature an eclectic selection of art books, make-up, clothes, shoes, jewelry, music, magazines, and food. Find the likes of Marc Jacob, Doc Marten, and Burberry Prorsum here. A lifeline for those with a lot of money and maybe less taste. The fabulously outfitted mannequins on the 2nd fl. are worth a visit. Downstairs cafe has free Wi-Fi. Open M-Sa 11am-7pm. AmEx/MC/V.

La Droguerie, 9-11 rue du Jour, 1er (☎01 45 08 93 27). ⓜÉtienne Marcel. Every sewing, knitting, or beading supply you could possibly need, whether you're patching a hole in your backpack or making a ballgown. Beads, wool, yarn, and ribbon of all shapes, sizes, colors and materials. Open M 2-6:45pm, Tu-Sa 10:30am-6:45pm.

BOOKS AND MUSIC

WHSmith, 248 rue de Rivoli, 1er (☎01 44 77 88 99; www.whsmith.fr). ⓜConcorde or Tuileries. Large general selection includes many scholarly works in English. A solid array of international magazines and tourist guidebooks. Occasional events and book signings. A legitimate parent to the smaller branches that populate most US airports. *The New York Times* available daily. Open M-Sa 9am-7:30pm, Su 1-7:30pm. AmEx/MC/V.

Monster Melodies, 9 rue des Déchargeurs, 1er (☎01 40 28 09 39). ⓜLes Halles. Downstairs supplies used CDs while upstairs overflows with records. Mostly American pop and rock, but some techno and indie rock. Open M-Sa noon-7pm.

THE MARAIS (3ÈME AND 4ÈME)

Shopping in the Marais is a complete aesthetic experience: boutiques of all colors and flavors pop out along medieval streets and among chic, tree-shaded cafes. (ⓜSt-Paul or Hôtel-de-Ville.) What the Marais does best are independent designer shops selling truly unique creations and vintage stores lining rue Vieille du Temple, rue de Sévigné, rue du Roi de Sicile, and rue des Rosiers. The best selection of affordable-chic menswear in Paris can be found here, especially along rue Ste-Croix de la Bretonnerie; stores outfit a largely GLBT clientele, but anyone up for some metrosexual Euro-style should check them out. Womenswear runs the gamut from downtown deconstructed to all-out glamo—often in the same edgy boutique. Rue des Francs-Bourgeois, the center of the Marais shopping scene, features high-end but smaller and uniquely-French labels, like Les Petites and Zadig & Voltaire. Most stores are open Sundays.

MEN AND WOMEN'S CLOTHING

Loft Design By, 12 rue de Sévigné, 4ème (☎01 48 87 13 07; www.loftdesignby.com). ⓜSt-Paul. A men and women's clothing store that takes itself seriously. Well-tailored shirts, fine-gauge casual sweaters (from €60) and pants (around €85), all in a spectrum of blacks, whites, and grays. Loft's selling points are refinement and style rather than innovation, but it has a strong local following. Open M-Sa 10:30am-7pm, Su noon-7pm. 4 other locations around the city. AmEx/MC/V.

BHV, 52-64, rue de Rivoli, 4ème (☎01 42 74 90 00). ⓜHôtel-de-Ville. Dior, Lacoste, and John Deere? An immense, all-encompassing, and completely unpretentious department store spanning more than a block. Clothes, accessories, books, home furnishings, and the best hardware store in central Paris. Wheelchair-accessible. Sporadic access to roof, but if it's available, ascend for a stellar view of Paris. A classy and inexpensive cafe is located in the flower shop on 11 rue des Archives (*menu* €11-15). Open M-Tu and Th-Sa 9:30am-7:30pm, W 9:30am-9pm. AmEx/MC/V.

TIP POLITESSE. When you enter and leave store in Paris, it is polite to greet the salespeople, even if you're just browsing. A simple *"bonjour"* when you come in and *"bonne journée"* when you leave will do the trick.

WOMEN'S CLOTHING

⬛ **Culotte,** 7 rue Malher, 4ème (☎01 42 71 58 89; www.poidsnetparis.com). Ⓜ︎St-Paul. The deconstructed is de *rigeur* at this tiny, eclectic vintage boutique. Designs range from ripped, printed tees to 40s-style dresses, all handmade and reasonably priced. Bold and funky vintage jewelry, especially of the mod and 80s variety. Most items under €100. Open Tu-Sa 12:30-7pm, Su 2-7pm. AmEx/MC/V.

⬛ **Abou d'abi Bazar,** 10 rue des Francs-Bourgeois, 3ème (☎01 42 77 96 98). Ⓜ︎St-Paul. Flirty, feminine French fashion in simple and chic styles and a variety of bright and neutral colors. Most items €50-200. Features lots of Paul & Joe as well as some Chloé, Tara Jarmon, Étoile by Isabel Marant, and smaller French labels. Often features new designers. Open M and Su 2-7:15pm, Tu-Sa 10:30am-7:15pm. Also at 125, rue Vieille-du-Temple (☎01 42 87 36 64). Closed Su. AmEx/MC/V.

⬛ **I Heart Ethel,** 47 rue de Turenne, 3ème (☎01 40 29 97 32). "I heart Ethel" and so will you. One of many girly, boutiques with designer-like digs for much less. Flowy *chemises*, girly dresses, and going-out tops in pretty prints and cute cuts. Most items €40-110. Open daily 10:30am-7:30pm. AmEx/MC/V.

Bel'Air, 2 rue des Rosiers, 4ème (☎01 48 04 82 16). Ⓜ︎St-Paul. At the intersection with rue Malher. Beads, sequins, and appliqué flowers abound. Casual, flowing cotton-based frocks and smocks with a whimsical edge (€50-100). Open M-Sa 10:30am-7:30pm, Su 2-7:30pm. Several other locations throughout Paris. MC/V.

Sucrées..., 10 rue Roi de Sicile, 4ème (☎09 54 11 78 97). Carries all things feminine. Specializes in cutesy dresses (€35) and skirts (€30) but also sells belts (€30), scarves (€15), and bags (€60). Open Tu-Sa 10:30am-7:30pm, Su 1:30-7:30pm. MC/V.

MEN'S CLOTHING

Boy'z Bazaar, 5 rue Ste-Croix de la Bretonnerie, 4ème (☎01 42 71 94 00 or 01 42 71 67 00). Ⓜ︎Hôtel de Ville. They "make boys look better." A large selection of all that's "sharp" and trendy in casual menswear, including Energie, Paul Smith, and Sonia Rykiel. Caters to a largely GLBT clientele, though anyone who wants to soak up the Euro-metro vibe is welcome. Piles of Replay denim from €100. D&G tees from €100. Open M-Th noon-8pm, F-Sa noon-10pm, Su 1-8:30pm. Also an annex at 5 rue des Guillemites, 4ème (☎01 42 71 63 86). AmEx/MC/V.

Factory's Paris, 3 rue Ste-Croix de la Bretonnerie, 4ème (☎01 48 87 29 10; factorys@noos.fr). Ⓜ︎Hôtel de Ville. Factory's professes to be "an urban men's clothing and accessories store," which basically translates to collared shirts, cargo shorts, messenger bags, and other pieces of the hipster-faux vintage-prep variety. Main brands include Fred Perry, Deeluxe, Scotch and Soda, and Ben Sherman. Open M-Sa noon-8pm, Su 2-8pm. AmEx/MC/V.

IEM, 16 rue Ste-Croix de la Bretonnerie, 4ème (☎01 42 74 01 61; www.iem.fr). Ⓜ︎Hôtel de Ville. This sex-y boutique flies the rainbow flag—as well as rainbow keyrings, belts, and other paraphernalia. Popular with a mixed crowd looking for a kinky kind of chic. Leather handcuffs (€70) and dog collars (€50-225). Museum-like display of leather masks and sex paraphernalia in the basement. Extensive collection of queer porn in back. "Sexy Boy" t-shirt €33. Open M-Th 1-8pm, F-Sa 1-10pm, Su 2-9pm. AmEx/MC/V.

Fabien Nobile, 7 rue Ferdinand Duval, 4ème (☎01 42 78 52 48; www.fabien-nobile.com or www.fabiennobile.com). Ⓜ︎St-Paul. In a recent attempt to streamline his own line, the designer no longer carries other brands and now caters only to men. Emphasis on simple, artfully cut shapes in solid colors. From casual to professional. Pants and tops €100-200. Open M-Sa noon-7pm. AmEx/MC/V.

SHOPPING

VINTAGE AND CONSIGNMENT CLOTHING

Free 'P' Star, 8 rue Ste-Croix de la Bretonnerie, 4*ème* (☎01 42 76 03 72). ⓜHôtel de Ville. Enter as Plain Jane and leave as a star—from the 80s or 90s, that is. Wide selection of vintage dresses (€20), velvet blazers (€40), boots (€30) and a €10 jean pile. Worn military-style blazers €5. Open M-Sa noon-11pm, Su 2-11pm. Also at 61 rue de la Verrerie, 4*ème* (☎01 42 78 0 76). MC/V over €20.

Vertiges, 85, rue St-Martin, 3*ème* (☎01 48 87 36 64). ⓜRambuteau. A bit musty, but a consignment shopper's heaven—well-organized racks of shirts (from Nike to Lacoste) and skirts (€5), dresses and pants (€10), fabulous leather jackets, and velvet blazers (€40-100). Small selection of Burberry trenches at €120. Converse All-Star €25. Open M-Sa 10am-8pm and Su 11:30-8pm. Cash only.

SHOES AND ACCESSORIES

Brontibay, 4 rue de Sevigné, 4*ème* (☎01 42 76 90 80; www.brontibay.com). ⓜSt-Paul. Vibrant and artistic bags come in all shapes and sizes; materials range from canvas to leather to delicate silk. Most bags €100-200, printed silk clutches €35, leather and silk wallets in delicious shades €80. Open M-Sa 11am-8pm and Su 1:30-7:30pm. Also at 13 rue Lafayette, 9*ème*. AmEx/MC/V.

Monic, 5 rue des Francs-Bourgeois, 4*ème* (☎01 42 72 39 15). ⓜChemin Vert or St-Paul. A fantastic, transgenerational boutique selling all types of jewelry. Silver, gold, precious, and semi-precious stones; from handmade Bohemian antique pieces to up-to-date Nina Ricci (€1-300; most under €50). Large selection of charms from €9. Open M-Sa 10am-7pm and Su 2:30-7pm. Also at 14 rue de l'Ancienne-Comedie, 6*ème* (☎01 43 25 36 61). ⓜOdéon. AmEx/MC/V.

BOOKS

Les Mots à la Bouche, 6 rue Ste-Croix de la Bretonnerie, 4*ème* (☎01 42 78 88 30; www.motsbouche.com). ⓜHôtel de Vile. A 2-level bookstore offering mostly queer literature, photography, magazines, and art. Don't miss the international DVD collection (with titles somewhere between art and porn) in the corner of the bottom level (€10-28). Also a small English section. Open M-Sa 11am-11pm, Su 1-9pm. AmEx/MC/V.

ETC.

Fleux, 39 rue Ste-Croix de la Bretonnerie, 4*ème* (☎01 42 78 27 20; www.fleux.com). With all things trendy, cutesy, and downright edgy, this is the go-to place to fab-out your pad. Fluorescent globe-like feather chandeliers €150-360. Life-size Lego pieces to build your own couch €15-35 each. "Smoochee" mirror €57. NYC skyline cushions €55. Open M-Sa 1130am-8pm, Su 1:30-8pm. AmEx/MC/V.

SHOPPING FOR POCKET CHANGE. Twice a year, Parisians and tourists alike hit the pavement for the shopping version of the Tour de France, Paris's semi-annual sales. The two great *soldes* (sales) of the year start right after New Year's and at the very end of June. If you don't mind slimmer pickings, the best prices are at the beginning of February and the end of July. And if at any time of the word *braderie* (clearance sale) appears in a store window, that is your signal to enter said store without hesitation.

LATIN QUARTER AND
ST-GERMAIN (5ÈME AND 6ÈME)

While you'll find plenty of chain clothing and shoe stores around boulevard St-Michel and numerous little boutiques selling scarves and jewelry, the bookstores are the truly characteristic shopping attraction of the *5ème*. Wealthy St-Germain-des-Prés, meanwhile, is saturated with high-budget names, particularly in the triangle bordered by boulevard St-Germain, rue St-Sulpice, and rue des St-Pères. Rue du Four has fun, wallet-friendly designers.

CHILDREN'S CLOTHING

▧ **Petit Bateau,** 26 rue Vavin, 6ème (☎01 55 42 02 53). ⓂVavin or Notre-Dame-des-Champs. Locations throughout the city. A children's store, but fashionistas flock here for the soft cotton t-shirts and tanks. A kid's size 16 is about an American 6; sizes go up to 18. Tees start around ^9.50. Open M-Sa 10am-7pm. AmEx/MC/V.

MEN AND WOMEN'S CLOTHING

Vanessa Bruno, 25 rue St-Sulpice, 6ème (☎01 43 54 41 04). ⓂSt-Sulpice. Chic, trendy, simple, exotic, wild—all could describe Vanessa Bruno's beautiful, well-cut clothing. Color schemes and fabrics that will fit any wardrobe—even if the prices won't fit any budget. Blazers and skirts around €150. Open M-Sa 10:30am-7:30pm. AmEx/MC/V.

Moloko, 53 rue du Cherche-Midi, 6ème (☎01 45 48 46 79). ⓂSèvres-Babylone, St-Sulpice, or Rennes. Simple, Asian-inspired women's clothing with surprising colors, shapes, and closures. Buy a piece here and wear it for life—the compliments will keep coming. Dresses from €120. Branches in the 4ème and Forum des Halles. Open Tu-Sa 11am-2pm and 3-7pm. Closed Aug. MC/V.

Tara Jarmon, 18 rue du Four, 6ème (☎01 46 33 26 60). ⓂSt-Germain-des-Prés or Mabillon. Classic, feminine styles in lovely fabrics. Silk-chaffon dresses starting at €170, tops €120. Open M-Sa 10:30am-7:30pm. MC/V. Also at 73, av. des Champs-Élysées, 8ème (☎01 45 63 45 41) and 51, rue de Passy, 16ème (☎01 45 24 65 20).

agnès b., 6 and 12 rue du Vieux-Colombier, 6ème (☎01 44 39 02 60). ⓂSt-Suplice. Men's apparel at 12, women's at 6, plus several other locations throughout the city. Legendary knitwear and other separates in classic cuts and colors. Selling timeless pieces rather than the latest fashions, this Parisian staple represents understated elegance at its best. Open daily 10am-7pm. AmEx/MC/V.

Naf Naf, 25 bd. St- Michel, 5ème (☎01 44 27 06 02). Just another link in the growing population of French chain stores, Naf Naf sells consistently affordable, generally fashionable clothes to a teenage crowd. Open M-Sa noon-7pm. MC/V. Also at 33 rue Étienne Marcel (☎01 42 36 15 28), 52 av. des Champs-Élysées, 8ème (☎01 45 62 03 08), and other locations throughout the city.

Mango, 3, pl. du 18 Juin, 6ème (☎01 45 48 04 96). This Spanish retailer sells festive, fashionable European styles for both sexes at reasonable prices. Sizable range of basics. Open M-Sa 10am-8pm. AmEx/MC/V. Also at 82 rue de Rivoli, 8ème (☎01 44 59 80 37) and 6 bd. des Capucines, 9ème (☎01 53 30 82 70).

Cacharel, 64 rue Bonaparte, 6ème (☎01 40 46 00 45). ⓂSt-Germain-des-Prés. The house of Cacharel has lately gone upscale and more mature. Emphasis is on retro-inspired patterns and bright colors. Dresses €180-400. Open M-F 10am-7pm, Sa 10am-7:30pm. AmEx/MC/V.

SHOES AND ACCESSORIES

Muji, 27 and 30 rue St-Sulpice, 6ème (☎01 46 34 01 10 and 01 44 07 37 30). ⓂOdéon. Affordable, modern, and minimalist bric-a-brac made in Japan. Everything from candles to magazine racks to bathrobes. Lots under €15. Open M-F 10am-7:30pm, Sa 10am-8pm. AmEx/MC/V.

No Name, 8 rue des Canettes, 6ème (☎01 44 41 66 46). ⓂSt-Sulpice. Stylish sneakers in every color, fabric, and shade of glitter. Sandals €53-61, sneakers €60-90. Open M and Th 10am-1pm and 2-7pm; Tu-W, F 10am-7pm, Sa 10am-7:30pm. AmEx/MC/V.

Free Lance, 30 rue du Four, 6ème (☎01 45 48 14 78). ⓂSt-Germain-des-Prés or Mabillon. Some great and stylish shoes alongside a few less posh picks. *Très cher* rainbow stilettos and patterned knee-high leather boots call to the stylistically outrageous. Some more basic merchandise falls just below the €200 mark. Come for the *soldes*, when prices become infinitely more reasonable. Open M-Sa 10am-7pm. AmEx/MC/V.

Om Kashi, 7 rue de la Montagne Ste-Geneviève, 5ème (☎01 46 33 46 07). ⓂMaubert-Mutualité. Its name translating to "The City of Lights," this welcoming shop sells imported boxes of henna, more than 80 kinds of incense, and shelves of clothing and jewelry. Its owners individually select each product from India and Asia, from the 18th-century furniture to the Himalayan singing bowls. Carries unusual scarves and fabrics with which Parisians love to accessorize. Open M 2-7pm, Tu-Sa 10am-1pm and 2-7pm. 15% discount if you bring your *Let's Go: Paris*.

BOOKS AND MUSIC

▧ **Abbey Bookshop,** 29 rue de la Parcheminerie, 5ème (☎01 46 33 16 24; www.abbey-bookshop.net). ⓂSt-Michel or Cluny. Located on a road steeped in literary history, this laid-back shop overflows with new and used English-language titles, as well as Canadian pride furnished by its friendly expat owner Brian. A good selection of travel books including titles like How to Survive at the North Pole. Impressive basement collection of anthropology, sociology, history, music, motherhood, and literary criticism titles. Also carries English-language fiction and French-Canadian work. Brian occasionally offers free coffee to browsers, complete with a dollop of maple syrup for Canadian flair. Ask about the Canadian club's author events and Su hikes, or add your name to their email list. Happy to take special orders. Open M-Sa 10am-7pm, sometimes later.

▧ **Shakespeare & Co.,** 37 rue de la Bûcherie, 5ème. (☎01 43 25 40 93; www.shake-speareco.org). ⓂSt-Michel. Across the Seine from Notre-Dame. A terrific English-language bookshop and miniature socialist utopia, where the books on the 2nd fl. are just for reading, not for buying. Scenes from the film *Before Sunset* were shot here. The owners allow passing "tumbleweeds" to sleep for free, provided they volunteer in the shop and read a book a day. An adjacent storefront holds an impressive collection of first editions, with emphasis on the Beat Generation. Bargain bins outside include French classics translated into English. Open daily 10am-11pm. MC/V. See **Sights,** p. 224.

▧ **Gibert Jeune,** 5 place St-Michel, 5ème (☎01 56 81 22 22; www.gibertjeune.fr). ⓂSt-Michel. Main location plus 7 specialized branches clustered around the Fontaine St-Michel; look for the telltale yellow canopies. With books in any language and low prices, Gibert Jeune draws young and old alike. Extensive stationary department downstairs. University text branch, 27 quai St-Michel, 5ème (☎01 56 81 22 22). Open M-Sa 9:30am-7:30pm. General books branch, 15bis bd. St-Denis, 2ème (☎01 55 34 75 75). Open M-Sa 10am-7pm. AmEx/MC/V.

▧ **L'Harmattan,** 16 and 21bis rue des Ecoles, 5ème (☎01 40 46 79 10; www.editions-harmattan.fr). ⓂCluny-La Sorbonne. Walk with traffic down bd. St-Germain, make a right on rue St-Jacques, and a left on rue des Ecoles. Over 50,000 titles of Francophone literature from Africa, the Antilles, Asia, the Indian Ocean, Latin America, and the Middle East. So packed with books that it's hard to navigate. General catalogue available online. Open M-Sa 10am-12:30pm and 1:30-7pm. AmEx/MC/V.

The Village Voice, 6 rue Princesse, 6ème (☎01 46 33 36 47; www.villagevoicebookshop. com). ⓂMabillon. Named for the Parisian neighborhood, not the Manhattan paper. An excellent Anglophone bookstore and the center of the city's English literary life, featuring readings, lectures, and discussions Sept. to early July. A good selection of English-language travel books. Open M 2-7:30pm, Tu-Sa 10am-7:30pm, Su 1-6pm. AmEx/MC/V.

San Francisco Book Co., 17 rue Monsieur le Prince, 6ème (☎01 43 29 15 70; www. sanfranciscobooksofparis.com). ⓂOdéon. This old bookshop's towering shelves hold scads of secondhand English-language books, both literary and pulp—including some rare and out-of-print titles. A great place to trade in used paperbacks. Open M-Sa 11am-9pm, Su 2-7:30pm. MC/V.

Tea and Tattered Pages, 24 rue Mayet, 6ème (☎01 40 65 94 35; www.teaandtattered-pages.com). ⓂDuroc. This place's funky collection of secondhand English-language books is a lot of fun for browsing. Books €3-11. If they don't have what you want, sign the wish list and you'll be called if it comes in. Tea room serves root beer floats, brownies, and American coffee with free refills. Occasional poetry readings, and lots of info for English speakers in Paris. Open M-Sa 11am-7pm, Su noon-6pm. MC/V over €20.

Gibert Joseph, 26-34, bd. St-Michel, 6ème (☎01 44 41 88 88). ⓂOdéon or Cluny-La Sorbonne. A gigantic *librairie* and music store with new and used selections. Frequent sidewalk sales with books from €2. Good selection of used dictionaries and guidebooks. There are several branches along bd. St-Michel. Open M-Sa 10am-7:30pm. MC/V.

La Chaumière à Musique, 5 rue de Vaugirard, 6ème (☎01 43 54 07 25; www.chaumi-ereonline.com). ⓂOdéon. The sophisticated patrons at this store move quietly and speak softly, as if they're attending a classical concert rather than browsing classical music. Knowledgeable staff. Bargain bin CDs start at €4. Will buy back and trade used CDs. Open M-F 10am-7:30pm, Sa 10am-8pm, Su and holidays 2-8pm. MC/V

Présence Africaine, 25bis rue des Écoles, 5ème (☎01 43 54 15 88; www.presenceaf-ricaine.com). ⓂCluny-La Sorbonne. Also a publishing company, this was Paris's first bookstore to specialize in African history, literature, and social science. The well-organized shelves display everything from contemporary political analysis to Francophone children's stories. Open M-F 10am-7pm, Sa 10am-1pm and 2-7pm. MC/V.

Crocodisc, 40-42 rue des Écoles, 5ème (☎01 43 54 47 95 or 01 43 54 33 22). ⓂMaubert-Mutualité. Music from the enormous speakers entertains patrons browsing 2 rooms of used CDs, records, and tapes. Mainly stocks classical, funk, pop, reggae, rock, and techno, reggae, funk. Buys CDs for €8-15. Nearby **Crocojazz,** 64 rue de la Montagne-Ste-Geneviève (☎01 46 34 78 38) stocks jazz and blues. Both stores open mid-Aug. to July Tu-Sa 11am-7pm. MC/V over €10.

ETC.

Au Vieux Camper, around 48 rue des Écoles, 5ème (☎01 53 10 48 48; www.au-vieux-campeur.fr). A crunchy backpacker's dream, Au Vieux Camper has 26 different locations throughout the 5ème, each specializing in a different outdoor activity. While passing seasons dictate the selection, stores cater to avid skiers, chilled-out surfers, and everyone in between. One branch sells only shoes while another just backpacks. Also stocks books, running gear, canoes, diving equipment, hiking clothes, kayaks, sailing supplies, and tents. Check online for specific store locations. Open M-W and F 11am-7:30pm, Th 11am-9pm, Sa 10am-9:30pm.

INVALIDES (7ÈME)

Affordable luxury goods are not to be found in the 7*ème*, but that shouldn't stop you from looking. Specialty shops abound, and it's easy to spend an entire day window-shopping. Begin your trek along rue du Bac (entire guidebooks have been written about the shops on this street), taking in everything from fountain pens to baby clothes, until you arrive at Au Bon Marché on rue de Sèvres.

CLOTHING AND ACCESSORIES

La Femme Écarlaté, 42 av. Bosquet (☎01 45 51 08 44). ⓜÉcole Militaire. Forgot to pack your €3000 evening gown? Friendly and attentive sales ladies will help you select a Lacroix, Azzaro, Balmain, or other designer gown to rent. Almost every color, texture, and style. Also rents bridal gowns, €300-600 per day. 1-night rentals €150-300. Open Tu-Sa 11am-7pm. Cash only.

Misia Rêve, 87 rue du Bac (☎01 42 34 20 52). ⓜRue du Bac. Accessories for grown-up girls, all designed by the very quirky but tasteful Misia. Whimsical coin purses featuring cherries, polka dots, and cutesy French phrases (€15); leather bags with colorful appliqués and whimsical patterns (from €50); as well as t-shirts, scarves and other accessories. Open Tu-Sa 11am-7:15pm. AmEx/MC/V.

Au Bon Marché, 24 rue de Sèvres, 7*ème* (☎01 44 39 80 00). ⓜSèvres-Babylone. Paris's oldest department store, Au Bon Marché has it all, from scarves to smoking accessories, *haute couture* to home furnishings. Don't be beguiled by the name (*bon marché* means cheap)—this is the most exclusive and expensive department store in Paris. Across the street, **La Grande Epicerie de Paris** (38 rue de Sèvres), Bon Marché's celebrated gourmet food annex, features all things dried, canned, smoked, and freshly baked. Store open M-W and F 9:30am-7pm, Th 10am-9pm, Sa 9:30am-8pm. La Grande Epicerie open M-Sa 8:30am-9pm. AmEx/MC/V.

BOOKS, ETC.

Ciné-Images, 68 rue de Babylone (☎01 47 05 60 25; www.cine-images.com). ⓜSt-François Xavier. A cinephile's paradise, this boutique has endless catalogues of stock: original movie posters from the beginning of film history to the late 1970s. Prices range from €30 (*Le Vampire Sexuel*) to as high as €20,000 (the original German poster for Fritz Lang's *M* ̀), but it's worth a browse even if you can't afford a thing. The enthusiastic English-speaking owner also does amazing restorations and mounting work *(entoilage)* for around €120. Open Tu-F 10am-1pm and 2-7pm, Sa 2-7pm. MC/V.

Florent Monestier, 47bis av. Bosquet (☎01 45 55 03 01). ⓜÉcole Militaire. All manner of nostalgic bric-a-brac to perfect that cluttered, shabby-chic look. Nautical baubles nestle against Chinese vintage-inspired porcelain. A mix of classic toiletry items and retro household goods, this is a treasure trove of quintessential Parisian gifts for anyone fed up with tacky souvenirs. Open M-Sa 10am-7pm. MC/V.

Librairie Gallimard, 15 bd. Raspail (☎01 45 48 24 84; www.librairie-gallimard.com). ⓜRue du Bac. The main store of this famed publisher of French classics features a huge selection of pricey Gallimard books. Basement filled with folio paperbacks. Only French language books here. Open M-Sa 10am-7pm. AmEx/MC/V.

PROTECT YOUR POCHE. In Paris, pickpocketing is common at department stores, particularly on the escalators. Pickpockets and con artists often work in groups, and children are among the most effective extortionists.

CHAMPS-ÉLYSÉES (8ÈME)

The 8*ème* is not wallet-friendly, but it's perfect for a day of **window shopping.** Take a break from the exhausting Champs-Élysées and walk along **avenue Montaigne** to admire the great couture houses. Their collections change every season, and they're always innovative, gorgeous, and jaw-droppingly expensive. Check out Chanel at no. 42, Christian Dior at no. 30, Emanuel Ungaro at no. 2, and Valentino at no. 17-19. **Rue du Faubourg Saint-Honoré** hosts Gucci (no. 2), Lanvin (no. 22), Hermès (no. 24), Jean-Paul Gaultier (no. 30), Yves Saint Laurent (no. 32-38), Chloé (no. 54-6) and Versace (no. 62). Around the Madeleine, you'll find Burberry and some big American names. Keep in mind that many of these shops have an unspoken dress code. You'll find it difficult to browse their collections if you don't look like you can afford them. A more accessible way to peruse couture collections is department stores (p. 306).

Back on the Champs-Élysées, you can purchase everything from CDs at the Virgin Megastore (open until midnight) to perfumes and chocolates. Stores in this area usually stay open until a much later hour than in the rest of Paris. Some BMOCs ("big men on Champs") include:

FNAC (Fédération Nationale des Achats et Cadres), 74 av. des Champs-Élysées, 8*ème* (☎01 53 53 64 64; www.fnac.com). The big kahuna of Parisian music/technology chains—selling DVDs, CDs, cell phones, video games, stereo equipment, even books—and has 9 locations throughout the city. This branch and the ones in Bastille (4 pl. de la Bastille; ☎01 43 42 04 04) and around Étoile (26-30 av. des Ternes; ☎01 44 09 18 00) are the largest. Use scanners to listen to any CD in the store. Tickets to nearly any concert and many theater shows can be purchased at the FNAC ticket desk located on the ground level of the store. For detailed and helpful information (in French), visit the website at www.fnac.com. All branches open at 10am and most close at 7:30 or 8pm. The Champs-Élysées branch closes at midnight. MC/V.

Sephora, 70-72 av. des Champs-Élysées, 8*ème* (☎01 53 93 22 50). ⓜCharles de Gaulle-Étoile. The fairest cosmetics store of them all offers an enormous array of beauty products to color your world pretty. The enormous and chaotic corridor is lined with almost every eau-de-toilette on the market for both men and women. Frequent makeover promotions by prestigious cosmetics companies. With products from Dior to Diesel to Disney, prices run the gamut from reasonable to absurd. Open M-Th and Su 10am-midnight, F-Sa 10am-1am. 16 other locations around the city. AmEx/MC/V.

 SHOPPING FOR POCKET CHANGE. A *stock* is the French version of an outlet store, selling big name clothing for less—often because it has small imperfections or dates from last season. Many *stocks* are on rue d'Alésia in the 14*ème* (ⓜAlésia), including **Cacharel Stock,** no. 114 (☎01 45 42 53 04; open M-Sa 10am-7pm; AmEx/MC/V); **S.R. Store** (Sonia Rykiel) at no. 112 and no. 64 (☎01 43 95 06 13; open Tu 11am-7pm, W-Sa 10am-7pm; MC/V); **Stock Patrick Gerard,** no. 113 (☎01 40 44 07 40). A large **Stock Kookaï** bustles at 82 rue Réamur, 2*ème* (☎01 45 08 17 91; open M 11:30am-7:30pm, Tu-Sa 10:30am-7pm); **Apara Stock** sits at 16 rue Étienne Marcel (☎01 40 26 70 04); and **Stock Opéra,** with names like Diesel, Versache, and Dolce & Gabbana, has three locations: 9 rue Scribe, 9*ème* (☎01 40 07 10 20; open M-Sa 10am-7pm; M:Opéra); 66 rue de la Chaussée d'Antin, 9*ème* (☎01 40 16 06 00; open M-Sa 10am-7pm; ⓜChaussée d'Antin); and 7-9 passage Choiseul, 2*ème* (☎01 49 26 94 10; open M-Sa 10am-7pm; ⓜQuatre Septembre).

SHOPPING

OPÉRA (9ÈME)

Galeries Lafayette, 40 bd. Haussmann, 9*ème* (☎01 42 82 34 56; www.galerieslafayette.com). ⓂChaussée d'Antin-Lafayette or Havre-Caumartin. Chaotic (the equivalent of Paris's entire population visits here each month), but the *Galeries* carries it all, including Kookaï, agnès b., and Cacharel. It can be difficult to find a middle ground between high-end labels and ultra-edgy "streetwear." The astounding food annex on the 1st fl., **Lafayette Gourmet,** has everything from a sushi counter to a mini-boulangerie, not to mention a great view. Open M-W and F-Sa 9:30am-7:30pm, Th 9:30am-9pm. AmEx/V.

Au Printemps, 64 bd. Haussmann, 9*ème* (☎01 42 82 57 87). ⓂChaussée d'Antin-Lafayette or Havre-Caumartin. One of the two biggies on the Parisian department store scene along with Galeries Lafayette. Visitors to this mega-complex can escape into air-conditioned bliss with hundreds of other Parisians and tourists, but should be prepared to be pushy or be pushed. Bringing your credit card is advisable if you want to hit the 2nd fl. Open M-W and F-Sa 9:35am-7pm, Th 9:35am-10pm. AmEx/MC/V.

Passage Jouffroy, 10 bd. Montmartre, 9*ème*. ⓂGrands Boulevards. Walk west on bd. Montmartre, away from the Hard Rock Cafe; the passage will be on your right. Leading naturally into Passage Verdeau, a second covered walk, Passage Jouffroy provides numerous unique shops perfect for perusing on a day that has better weather for ducks than people. Collectors and gourmands alike will revel at the mall's eclectic collection of antique dealers, bookshops, *épiceries*, oriental fabric stores, and tea salons. Built in 1847, Passage Jouffroy was the first passage built completely from metal and glass and the first to employ floor-heating. Today's visitors can peer into the **Musée Grévin,** Paris's wax musuem, from a side window (see **Museums,** p. 286). Open daily 7am-9:30pm.

BASTILLE (11ÈME AND 12ÈME)

The 11*ème* and 12*ème* collectively form one of the best shopping areas in Paris. Emerging designer labels and alternative music stores cling to the edgy rue Keller, while nearby rue de Charonne hosts a variety of eclectic, feminine boutiques. Rue de la Roquette is a one-stop shop for young, funky fashion (occasionally veers toward Eurotrash but makes for cute clubbing gear). Find everything from Gap to Lacoste to cheaper stores on rue du Faubourg St-Antoine.

WOMEN'S CLOTHING

Des Petits Hauts, 5 rue Keller, 11*ème* (☎01 43 38 14 39; www.despetitshauts.com). ⓂLedru-Rollin. Take av. Ledru-Rollin, turn left on rue de Charonne, and turn right on rue Keller. Feminine and flirty clothes; fun and flashy shoes and bags. Featured in Elle Paris. Open M 1:30-7:30pm, Tu-F 11:30am-7:30pm, Su 11am-7:30pm. AmEx/MC/V.

Doria Salambo, 38 rue de la Roquette, 11*ème* (☎01 47 00 06 30). ⓂBastille. Cotton and linen sundresses and skirts in bohemian, tie-dye, and African patterns (€80-100) with a smattering of jackets. Open M 3:30-8pm, Tu-Sa 11am-8pm. MC/V.

Incognito, 41 rue de la Roquette, 11*ème* (☎01 40 21 86 55). ⓂBastille. Tiny boutique stocked with trendy dresses (€140), tops (€60-80), and fur-trimmed leather jackets (€300). Menswear also available. Open Tu-Sa 11am-8pm. MC/V.

Planisphere, 19 rue de la Roquette, 11*ème* (☎01 43 57 69 90). ⓂBastille. Miss Sixty rules the roost in this store, with a smattering of Diesel, D&G, and We Are Replay. Jeans €120-280. Tops €50-120. Open M-Sa 11am-8pm and Su 2-8pm. AmEx/MC/V. Additional location at 19 rue des Rosiers (☎01 48 04 01 05). Men's location at 78 rue de la Roquette (☎01 48 05 10 55) and 32 rue des Rosiers (☎01 40 27 07 31).

Atelier 33, 33 rue du Faubourg Ste-Antoine, 11ème (☎01 43 40 61 63). ⓂBastille. If you can flash the cash: choose from over 200 designs, wait one month, and take home a glamorous gown (€300-3000) in any fabric imaginable. Evening gown showroom accessible by appointment only. All clothes can be tailored, including the ready-made jackets (€35-200), pants (€80-100), and flirty frocks. The floral prints, liberal sequencing, and wild colors resemble the most outlandish Versace styles. Prices negotiable. Open M-Sa 10:30am-7:30pm. AmEx/MC/V.

MEN'S CLOTHING

Stone Company, 6 rue Bréguet, 12ème (☎01 47 00 56 81). ⓂBastille. Swiss owned and operated but specializing in all things Italian. Shoes (€180), shirts (€60), and leather jackets (up to €2500) by Alkis, Portland, and others. No wardrobe is complete without a cheetah-print belt (€78). Open M 1-8pm, Tu-Su 10am-noon and 1-8pm. MC/V.

ACCESSORIES

Total Eclipse, 40 rue de la Roquette, 11ème (☎01 48 07 88 04). ⓂBastille. It's time to accessorize. Purchase you-can't-find-me-anywhere-else jewelry with chunky stones in bright colors. One-of-a-kind necklaces (from €30). Where-did-you-get-that bracelets (€30-50). Also a wide range of men and women's watches from Diesel, Fossil, and Opex (from €30). Open M-F 11am-7:30pm and Sa 10:30am-8pm. AmEx/MC/V.

La Baleine, 11 rue Boulle, 11ème (☎01 43 14 94 94). ⓂBastille. Classic toys and accessories by Hello Kitty and Groovy Girls, animal- and food-shaped lamps (penguin, rabbit, *champignon*) €39-70. Porcelain figurines €4. Check out the remote-controlled mobiles €30-69. Open M-Sa noon-8pm. MC/V.

Automates & Poupées, 97 av. Daumesnil, 12ème (☎01 43 42 22 33). ⓂGare de Lyon. Dolls, dolls, and more dolls; delicate music boxes; and a variety of other ancient toys. Restorations and a moderate selection of new and used dolls for purchase. Petit Prince knick-knack box €30-60. Some dolls exceed €1000. Open Tu-Sa 10:30am-6:30pm.

St-Charles de Rose, 16 rue Keller, 11ème (☎01 48 05 47 37; fax 01 40 21 85 12). ⓂLedru-Rollin. Take av. Ledru-Rollin, turn left on rue de Charonne, right on rue Keller. Everything you need to throw an adorable tea party—from colorful curtains and tablecloths (€45-56), to trays and plates, to dresses and cover-ups (€58-60). Small *salon de thé* inside (coffee €2, tea €4, hot chocolate €3). Open M-Sa 11:30am-7:30pm.

BOOKS AND MUSIC

Les Soeurs Lumière, 18 rue St-Nicolas, 12ème (☎01 43 43 13 15; www.soeurslumiere.fr). ⓂLedru Rollin. With the motto *"Un livre, un film,"* this cinema-centered bookstore sells DVDs and the books that they are based on. The selection includes classics like *The Importance of Being Earnest* and more recent works like *Harry Potter,* with an emphasis on English-language titles. Open M-Sa 11am-7pm. MC/V.

L'Arbre à Lettres, 62 rue du Faubourg St-Antoine, 12ème (☎01 53 33 83 23). ⓂBastille. A small bookstore with a sizeable selection of French and other European literature, poetry, and nonfiction. Intellectual atmosphere. Regular readings and lectures. Consult store for details, and pick up their gazette at the desk. Open M-Sa 10am-8pm, Su 2-7pm. Closed Su July-Aug. MC/V.

La Manoeuvre, 58 rue de la Roquette, 11ème (☎01 47 00 79 70). ⓂBastille. A tiny French-language bookstore with a vast selection of international literature, from Anglo-Saxon, to Italian, to Maghrebin. Smaller selection of non-fiction works. Open Tu-Sa 10:30am-8pm, Su 3-8pm. AmEx/MC/V.

SHOPPING

Born Bad Record Shop, 17 rue Keller, 11ème (☎01 43 38 41 78). ⓂBastille. Walk along rue de la Rocquette and turn left on rue Keller. Vintage records from a variety of genres, including soul, funk, garage, punk, ska, and more (most €10-20). Also sells music miscellany (stickers, badges, zines), comic books, and t-shirts (16-20). Open M-Sa noon-8pm. MC/V.

Downtown Records, 57 rue du Faubourg St-Antoine, 11ème (☎01 44 74 64 18). ⓂBastille. House, garage, techno, disco, hip-hop (the entire upper floor is devoted to it), jazz, and R&B on tape, CD, and vinyl. Learn to spin records with instructional videos or DVDs (€20-30) or just go ahead and buy your turntables (€800). Open M noon-8pm, Tu-Sa 11:30am-8pm. AmEx/MC/V.

Wave, 36 rue Keller, 11ème (☎01 40 21 86 98). ⓂBastille. This tiny store packs a great selection of techno, house, electronic, and jungle music. Record and CD players for those who want to listen before buying. Also has a board with posters and flyers listing upcoming shows and other events. Open M-F 1-7:30pm and Sa noon-7:30pm. MC/V.

MONTMARTRE (18ÈME)

The 18ème is just south of the granddaddy of all flea markets, the **Puces de St-Ouen**—an overwhelming, eclectic mix of clothes, furniture, and records. Opening early and nominally closing late, the market will take serious hunters the better part of a day to navigate. Over 270 stalls sell everything from lighting systems to porcelain pottery. In general, merchandise is either dirt-cheap and shoddy or expensive and antique, but if you're willing to slog through the sneaker stands and smoking paraphernalia, you may find a great deal. In 1908, the Paris metro opened its first station at the *"Foire aux Puces"* (Flea Fair), referring to the reduced hygiene standards of the area's original inhabitants. After the Franco-Prussian war in 1870, the French government attempted to purge the capital's streets by forcing the Paris's *chiffonniers* (vagabonds) outside city limits. Resettling north of the 18ème, the poverty-stricken families established their own self-sufficient community, complete with vegetable gardens and open-air dance halls. An influx of antique and second-hand furniture dealers post-WWII earned the Puces de St-Ouen greater social recognition. In 2001, the Puces became classified as a national heritage zone. True to its origins, today's market lacks the haut couture typifying French fashion but offers diverse style and pieces at prices unmatched anywhere else in Paris. For more info and an official map, visit the **Saint-Ouen Office de Tourisme,** located within the market at 7 impasse Simon (☎01 58 61 22 90).

PUCES DE ST-OUEN

Official Market, 18ème. (www.parispuces.com). ⓂPorte-de-Clignancourt or Garibaldi. From the Porte-de-Clignancourt stop, walk 10min. down av. de la Porte de Clignancourt, past the Renegade Market, under the highway bridge, and left on rue Jean Henri Fabre. Spanning rue des Rosiers and rue Jules Vallès, the regular market is officially divided into 15 sub-markets, each theoretically specializing in a certain type of item. Don't try to follow a set path or worry about hitting every *marché*, as the same eclectic collection of antiques pervades them all. Most of the official markets have posted individual maps, extremely helpful in navigating the labyrinth of stalls inside. Open Sa 9am-6pm, Su 10am-6pm, M 11am-5pm; most vendors close well before 5pm.

Renegade Market, 18ème. ⓂPorte-de-Clignancourt. On avenue de la Porte de Clignancourt, before the bridge. From the moment you exit the metro, you will be surrounded—and hassled—by sellers. Jammed together, the tiny stalls sell flimsy new clothes, cheap woven scarves, fake designer get-ups, and cheap, colorful jewelry. If the renegade bazaar turns you off, continue on to the official market, where you'll be able to browse more leisurely in a slightly less crowded setting. Although many of the official stalls close early, some renegade vendors open at 5am and don't pack up until 9pm.

COMMENT DIT-ON "RIP-OFF"? Some tips for first-time flea market visitors: **There are no €1 diamond rings here;** if you find the Hope Diamond in a pile of schlock jewelry, well, you haven't. **Be prepared to bargain;** sellers at flea markets don't expect to get their starting prices. **Pickpockets love crowded areas;** "three Card Monte" con artists proliferate. Don't be pulled into the game by seeing someone win lots of money; he's part of the con, planted to attract suckers. **This is the place to find rare records.** Record peddlers generally know what they have, but if you look long enough, you might just find a priceless LP for next to nothing.

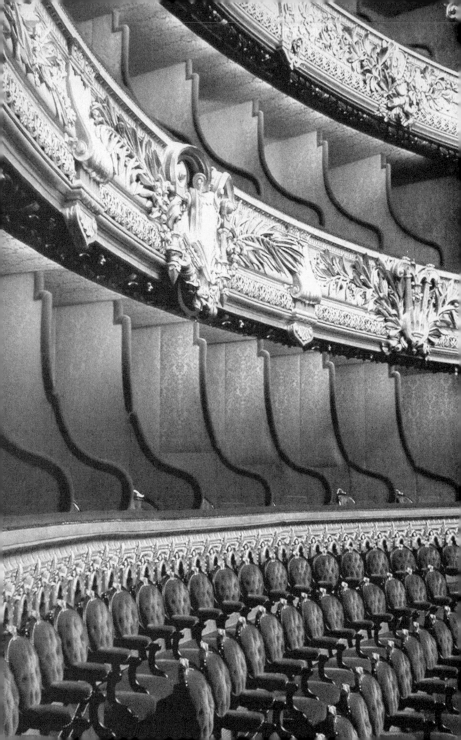

ENTERTAINMENT

When it comes to entertainment, Paris satisfies all tastes. The best resources are the weekly bulletins *Pariscope* (€0.40) and *Figaroscope* (€1), both on sale at newsstands. Even if you don't understand French, you should be able to decipher the listings of times and locations. You can also contact Info-Loisirs, a recording in English and French that keeps tabs on what's on in Paris (☎08 92 68 31 12; €0.40 per min.).

You don't need to speak fluent French to enjoy the theater scene. Paris's theaters present productions whose music, physical comedy, and experimental abstraction lend themselves to any audience. The comedy-oriented *café-théâtres* and the music-oriented *cabarets* recall the ambience of 1930s Paris. Paris's ballet and modern dance companies often host performances by visiting companies, including the Kirov Ballet, the Alvin Ailey Dance Company, and the Dance Theater of Harlem. Paris's new Stade de France and other athletic venues offer spectator and participatory sports galore.

Among Paris's many treasures, music and film top the list. West-African music, Caribbean calypso and reggae, Latin-American salsa, North-African raï, and European house, techno, and rap are fused by the hippest of DJs in the coolest of Paris's clubs (see **Nightlife**, p. 321). Classical concerts are staged in both expensive concert halls and churches, particularly during the summer. Parisians are inveterate filmgoers, greedy for movies from all over the world. Frequent English-language film series and festivals make Parisian cinema accessible, inventive, challenging, and entertaining.

 A VIEW TO KILL FOR. At almost every theater or concert venue in Paris, there are a couple seats—usually in prime seating areas—that are sold just to students at extremely discounted prices (usually €5-12). Look online or visit a FNAC or department store to reserve.

THEATER

Fortunately for the non-fluent, much of Parisian theater is highly accessible, thanks in part to its dependence on the classics and in part to its love of a grand spectacle (read: physical humor). Four of France's five national theaters are located in Paris (the fifth is in Strasbourg). Unless you're banking on last-minute rush tickets (which are sometimes available), make reservations 14 days in advance. Paris's private theaters, though less celebrated than their state-run counterparts, often stage outstanding productions. Most theaters have shows every day except Monday and are closed for July and August. *Pariscope* (€0.40) and *Figaroscope* (€1), at any newsstand, provide listings of current shows, as well as information on one of the best ways to see theater in Paris: half-price previews. Many theaters offer student tickets at discounted prices. For ticket services, see **Practical Information**, p. 141.

▩ **La Comédie Française,** pl. Collette, 1*er* (☎ 08 25 10 16 80 or 01 44 58 14 00; www. comedie-francaise.fr). ⓜPalais-Royal. Founded by Molière, this is now the granddaddy of all French theaters (see **Sights**, p. 213). Expect anything from the likes of *Le Misanthrope* to wildly gesticulated slapstick farce; you generally don't need to speak French to understand the jokes. Performances take place in the 862-seat Salle Richelieu. Box office open daily 11am-6pm and 1hr. before shows. Tickets €11-35. Rush tickets available 1hr. before show. Disabled patrons are asked to make reservations in advance. If you plan to stay in Paris for a long time, invest in the Passeport Comédie-Française, which allows you to make reservations at reduced prices. Check the website (in French) for details. The *comédiens français* perform the same sort of plays in the 300-seat **Théâtre du Vieux Colombier,** 21 rue des Vieux Colombiers, 6ème (☎01 44 39 87 00 or 01 44 39 87 01). ⓂSt-Sulpice or Sèvres-Babylone. AmEx/MC/V.

Bouffes du Nord, 37bis, bd. de la Chapelle, 10ème (☎01 46 07 34 50; www.bouffes-dunord.com). ⓂLa Chapelle. Bouffes du Nord is an experimental theater (headed by Micheline Rozan and famous British director Peter Brook) that produces cutting-edge performances and concerts. Offers occasional productions in English. Wheelchair-accessible, but you must call in advance. Closed July and Aug. Box office open M-Sa 11am-6pm. Concerts €26, under 26 and over 60 €11. Plays €10-26, under 26 €10-20.

Comédie Italienne, 17 rue de la Gaîté, 14ème (☎43 21 22 22; www.comedie-italienne.fr). ⓂEdgar Quinet. Exit the metro; rue de la Gaîté will be to your left. French-language adaptations of classic and contemporary Italian comedies in a 100-seat venue decorated with exquisite costumes, masks, and *trompe l'œil* murals. Most shows Tu-Sa 8:30pm, Su 3:30pm. Box office open M-Sa noon-7:30pm, Su noon-3pm. Tickets Tu-Th €15, F-Su and Christmas €21. Cash only.

Odéon Théâtre de l'Europe, 1 pl. Odéon, 6ème (☎01 44 85 40 40 for tickets and information; www.theatre-odeon.eu). ⓂOdéon. Programs in this elegant Neoclassical building range from classics to avant-garde, but the Odéon specializes in foreign plays in their original language. The 2009 season will include production of *Les Européens, Faust,* and *Le Soulier de Satin.* 1042 seats. Wheelchair-accessible. Box office open M-Sa 11am-6pm and 2hr. before the show. Tickets €7.50-30 for most shows; fewer than 30 rush tickets (€3-5) available 1hr. before performance. MC/V.

Théâtre de la Huchette, 23 rue de la Huchette, 5ème (☎01 43 26 38 99; www.theatre-huchette.com). ⓂSt-Michel. 100-seat theater where Eugene Ionesco's *La cantatrice chauve (The Bald Soprano)* and *La leçon (The Lesson)* premiered in 1957 and have played continually since. Actors change regularly, promoting a bastion of Left Bank intellectualism; high-school French will suffice. Wheelchair-accessible. Shows Tu-Sa. *La cantatrice chauve* starts at 7pm, *La leçon* at 8pm. No one admitted after curtain. Box office open M-Sa 5-9pm. Tickets €20, students under 25 M-F and Su €15; both shows on the same night €30/22. Only 30 student tickets available M-F. MC/V over €15.

Théâtre National de Chaillot, 1 pl. du Trocadéro, 16ème (reservations ☎01 53 65 30 00, 24hr information ☎01 53 65 30 04; www.theatre-chaillot.fr). ⓂTrocadéro. In the Palais de Chaillot. Innovative plays, music, and dance concerts in 2 rooms, one with 1250 seats and the other with 420. Each season's shows are listed on the website and in a brochure available at the box office, which is open M-F 11am-6pm and Sa 11am-7pm. Ticket prices vary with show but average €27-33, groups of 10 or more and seniors €21-27, students under 26 €12-17. Disabled and hearing impaired individuals should call ☎01 53 65 30 74 in advance to request special seating and headsets.

CABARET

Bal du Moulin Rouge, 82 bd. de Clichy, 9ème (☎01 53 09 82 82; www.moulin-rouge.com). ⓂBlanche. Directly across from the Metro. This world-famous cabaret has hosted such international stars as Ella Fitzgerald and Johnny Rey. The crowd consists of tourists out for an evening of sequins, tassels, and skin. The reviews remain risqué, but the price of admission is prohibitively expensive. While the late show may be cheaper, be prepared to stand if it's a busy night. Elegant attire required; no shorts, sneakers, or sportswear permitted. Shows nightly 9, 11pm. Ticket for 9pm show €99, 11pm show €89;

includes ½-bottle of champagne. 7pm dinner and 9pm show €145-175. Occasional lunch shows €95-125; call for more info. MC/V.

Au Lapin Agile, 22 rue des Saules, 18ème (☎01 46 06 85 87; www.au-lapin-agile.com). ⓂLamarck-Coulaincourt. Turn right on rue Lamarck, then right up steep rue des Saules. Apollinaire, Picasso, Renoir, and Verlaine hung out here in Montmartre's heyday; now, a touristy audience crowds in for comical poems and songs. The *chansonnier* inspired Steve Martin's 1996 hit play *Picasso at the Lapin Agile.* Shows Tu-Su 9pm-2am. Admission and 1st drink €24, M-F and Su students €17. Drinks €6-7. MC/V.

Caveau de la République, 1 bd. St-Martin, 3ème (☎01 42 78 44 45; www.caveau.fr). ⓂRépublique. A Parisian crowd fills the 482 seats of this 100-year-old venue for political satire. The *tour de champs* (tour of the field) consists of 6 separate comedy and song acts. Solid French skills and knowledge of French politics are a must to get the gags. Tickets sold up to 6 days in advance, M noon-6pm, Tu-Sa noon-7pm, Su noon-4pm. Shows Jan.-June and from mid-Aug. to Dec. Tu-Sa 8:30pm, Su 3:30pm. Admission Tu-Th €31, F-Su €37; students €16/20. MC/V.

CINEMA

Every night, swarms of Parisians populate the city's cafes after a night at the movies, continuing Paris's century-long love affair with the cinema (see **Life and Times,** p. 89). You'll find scores of cinemas throughout the city, particularly in the Latin Quarter and on the Champs-Élysées. You may not notice them at first, but take a wander around pl. St-Michel and La Sorbonne, especially the side streets, and you'll see theaters playing everything from the latest from Iran to Lars von Trier retrospectives. The two big theater chains—Gaumont and UGC—offer *cartes privilèges* discounts for five visits or more. In late June, the wonderful three-day **Fête du Cinéma** offers great discounts and great films (see **Life and Times,** p. 98).

Check the publications *Pariscope* or *Figaroscope* (€0.40 and €1, respectively; available at any newsstand) for weekly film schedules, prices, and reviews. Cinemas are conveniently listed by *arrondissement.* The notation "VO" (*version originale*) after a non-French movie listing means that the film is being shown in its original language with French subtitles; watching an English-language film with French subtitles is a great way to pick up new vocabulary. "VF" (*version française*) means that the film has been dubbed—an increasingly rare

THE LOCAL STORY

LOST IN TRANSLATION

Hollywood movies and American television may have captivated an enthusiastic market in France, but little rhyme or reason regulates the translation of their titles:

Lolita in Spite of Myself (Mean Girls): Nabokov and Lindsay Lohan: the perfect pop culture union.

The Counter Attack of the Blondes (Legally Blond): Perhaps a little aggressive for a movie about Reese Witherspoon and handbags.

The Little Champions (Mighty Ducks): From the Flying V to the quack chant, the canard is the heart and soul of this film.

Rambo (Rambo): Some words just transcend linguistic and cultural barriers.

The Man who would Murmur at the Ears of Horses (The Horse Whisperer): Just in case there was any ambiguity in the original title.

A Day with No End (Groundhog Day): If you don't get the Groundhog Day reference, this is going to be a long movie.

La Grande Evasion (The Great Escape): If they didn't translate this literally, Steve McQueen probably would've just taken everyone down.

The Big Lebowski (The Big Lebowski): The French recognize that The Dude does not appreciate name changes.

Lost in Translation (Lost in Translation): Apparently this one wasn't.

MAKE SOME NOISE

When France was inhabited by the ancient Gauls, the summer solstice was celebrated with feasting, dancing, and human sacrifice, as any reader of the French comic book Astérix knows. These days, thanks to former Culture Minister Jack Lang, the country enjoys a raucous music festival instead.

The Fête de la Musique takes place every June 21. In Paris, official concerts in major squares combine with impromptu jam sessions to make sweet sounds all over the city. While you can catch a few acts as early as noon, things don't get humming until about 8pm. A gigantic show on the Champ de Mars features big international musicians.

There's no real center of festivities—the fête extends all over the city. Cafes and bars stay open through the night, pumping music into the street. Everything is free—including entry into normally pricey venues—and vendors blanket the city with cheap beer and merguez. Some subway lines stay open late, and night buses run regularly. For €2.50 you can buy an unlimited metro pass good from the evening of June 21 through the next morning, but you'll have a tough time getting home between midnight and 6am. Do what the Parisians do—stay out until the sun comes up. See p. 98 for details.

phenomenon. Like most European and American cinemas, Paris's cinemas offer student, senior, and family discounts, although these discounts are usually restricted to matinee screenings. On Monday and Wednesday, all prices drop by about €1.50.

Accattone, 20 rue Cujas, 5ème (☎01 46 33 86 86). RER: Luxembourg. Carefully selected classics from art-house maestros ranging from Salvador Dalí to Peter Greenaway. All VO. €6.50, students €5.50.

Action Christine, 4 rue Christine, 6ème (☎01 43 25 85 78). ⓂOdéon. Off rue Dauphine. International selection of art and classic films from the 40s and 50s. Many golden-era Hollywood pics and classic French hits. Always VO *(version originale)*, without subtitles. €8; early show (usually 6 or 7pm), M, and students €6. 1-year pass for 10 movies €45. Cash only.

L'Arlequin, 76 rue de Rennes, 6ème (☎01 45 44 28 80). ⓂSt-Sulpice. A revival cinema with occasional visits from European directors and first-run previews. Some films VO, others dubbed. Buy tickets in advance. €9, students M-F and all tickets W €6.80, matinee €6. 6-month pass for 10 movies €57. MC/V.

Cinémathèque Française, 51 rue de Bercy, 12ème (☎01 71 19 32 00; www.cinemathequefrancaise. com). ⓂBercy. Formerly located in the 16ème. Moved to its current location in 2005. A must for film buffs. 4-5 classics, near-classics, or soon-to-be classics per day. Non-film exhibits include costumes (over 1000), objects, and apparatuses from the past and present world of film. Foreign films usually VO. Buy tickets 20min. early. Temporary and permanent "collections" open M and W-F noon-7pm, Th noon-10pm, Sa-Su 10am-8pm. €6, under 26 and seniors €5. Discounted packages available; check website for more.

Musée du Louvre Auditorium, 1er (☎01 40 20 53 17; www.louvre.fr). ⓂLouvre. Concerts and artsy films. Open Sept.-June. Prices vary.

La Pagode, 57bis, rue de Babylone, 7ème (☎01 45 55 48 48). ⓂSt-François-Xavier. A pseudo-Japanese pagoda built in 1895 and re-opened as a cinema in 2000, La Pagode screens independent and classic French films, as well as the occasional American new release (see **Sights,** p. 231). Stop in at the cafe in between shows. €8; over 60, under 21, students, and M and W €6.50. MC/V.

Saint André des Arts, 30 rue de St-André des Arts. 6ème (☎01 43 26 48 18). ⓂSt-Michel. A revival theatre with the typical French fondness for Woody Allen. Screenings are based on a weekly theme. All movies VO. €8, students €6.50. Cash only.

Les Trois Luxembourg, 67 rue Monsieur-le-Prince, 6ème (☎08 92 68 93 25; www.lestroisluxembourg.

com). Ⓜ️Luxembourg. Turn left on bd. St-Michel, right on rue Racine, and left on rue M-le-Prince. Independent, classic, American and foreign films, all with French subtitles. €7. Reduced ticket price M-Tu. Cash only.

MUSIC, OPERA, AND DANCE

Acclaimed foreign and provincial dance companies visit Paris frequently; watch for posters and check the listings in **Pariscope.** Connoisseurs will find the thick, indexed *Programme des Festivals* (free at tourist offices) an indispensable guide to seasonal music and dance series. Be wary of rock-bottom ticket prices, as seats are often obstructed (like at Opéra Garnier). For seasonal events, consult **Festivals,** p. 97. For listings of public concerts, check the magazine *Paris Selection,* available at tourist offices throughout the city. Free concerts are often held in churches and parks, especially during summer festivals; these are extremely popular, so plan to arrive at the host venue early. **The American Church in Paris,** 65, quai d'Orsay, 7*ème*, sponsors free concerts (Sept.-May Su 6pm; ☎01 40 62 05 00; Ⓜ️Invalides or Alma Marceau). **Église St-Germain-des-Prés** (see **Sights,** p. 227) and **Église St-Merri** (78 rue St-Martin, 4*ème*) also hold concerts; check the information booth just inside the door for times. Concerts take place W-Su in the **Jardin du Luxembourg's band shell,** 6*ème* (☎01 42 34 20 23); show up early if you don't want to stand. Occasional free concerts are held in the **Musée d'Orsay,** 1 rue Bellechasse, 7*ème* (☎01 40 49 49 66; Ⓜ️Solférino).

VENUES AND COMPANIES

Le Bataclan, 50 bd. Voltaire, 11*ème* (☎01 43 14 00 30; www.bataclan.fr). Ⓜ️Oberkampf. A 1500-person concert space and cafe-bar that hosts the likes of Metallica, Oasis, Blur, and Prince, as well as indie rock bands. Tickets start at €15 and vary with each show. Call or look online for schedules and reservations. Open Sept.-July. MC/V.

La Cigale, 120 bd. Rochechouart, 18*ème* (☎01 49 25 89 99; www.lacigale.fr). Ⓜ️Pigalle. One of Pigalle's 2 large rock clubs. Seats over 950 for international hardcore, indie, pop, and punk bands. Also stages modern dance shows. Concerts begin 7-8:30pm. Most shows €25-60; buy tickets online or at FNAC (see **Shopping,** p. 307). MC/V.

Cité de la Musique, La Villette, 221 avenue Jean-Jaurès, 19*ème* (☎01 44 84 45 00; www.cite-musique.fr). Ⓜ️Porte de Pantin. Opened in 1995 as one of Mitterrand's Grands Projets (see **Sights,** p. 253, and **Life and Times,** p. 75), this modern venue hosts everything from lute concerts to American gospel in its enormous *salle des concerts* and smaller *amphithéâtre*. Shows at 8pm; box office open Tu-Sa noon-6pm, Su 10am-6pm; open until 8pm on performance nights. Tickets generally €10-40. AmEx/MC/V.

Élysée Montmartre, 72 bd. Rochechouart, 18*ème* (☎01 44 92 45 36; www.elysee-montmartre.com). Ⓜ️Anvers. The most famous rap, reggae, and rock venue in Paris. Montmartre opens its stage to well-known American and British groups as well as young, homegrown talent. Large dance floor for disco, salsa, and techno nights. Drinks €5-8. Shows €15-40; buy tickets online. AmEx/MC/V.

L'Étoile du Nord, 16 rue Georgette Agutte, 18*ème* (☎01 42 26 47 47; www.etoiledunord-theatre.com). Ⓜ️Guy Môquet. A small, 200-seat independent dance space showcasing impressive modern choreographers. Box office open M-F 2-6pm. Tickets €19; students, seniors, groups of 10 or more €14; under 26 €10; children €8. MC/V.

L'Olympia, 28 bd. des Capucines, 9*ème* (☎08 92 68 33 68; www.olympiahall.com). Ⓜ️Opéra or Madeleine. Paris's oldest music hall, having hosted The Beatles and Sinatra. L'Olympia still draws big-name acts like James Taylor and French favorites MC Solaar and Yves Simon. Box office open daily 11am-7pm. Tickets €25-130. AmEx/MC/V.

Opéra de la Bastille, pl. de la Bastille, 12ème (☎08 92 89 90 90; www.operadeparis. fr). ⓂBastille. Opera and ballet with a modern spin. Subtitles in French. Check website for the season's events. The '08-'09 season will include operas *Macbeth* and *Tristan and Isolde* and will feature ballets by the New York City Ballet Company and the National Ballet of China. Tickets can be purchased by Internet, mail, phone (M-Th 9am-6pm, Sa 9am-1pm), or in person (M-Sa 10:30am-6:30pm). Rush tickets 15min. before show for students under 25 and seniors. For wheelchair-access, call 2 weeks ahead (☎01 40 01 18 50). Tickets for '08-'09 season €7-196. AmEx/MC/V.

Opéra Comique, 5 rue Favart, 2ème (☎01 42 44 45 46 or 08 25 01 01 23; www.opera-comique.com). ⓂRichelieu-Drouot. Operas on a lighter scale. Founded in 1714 to give theatergoers an alternative to the dominant Italian opera, the company has produced operas composed by Berlioz and Bizet, as well as the premiere of Debussy's only opera. Box office open M-Sa 9am-9pm. Tickets €6-95. Cheapest tickets (limited visibility) usually available until the show starts. MC/V.

Opéra Garnier, pl. de l'Opéra, 9ème (☎08 92 89 90 90; www.operadeparis.fr). ⓂOpéra. Hosts mostly ballet, chamber music, and symphonies. Tickets usually available 2 weeks before the show. Box office open M-Sa 10:30am-6:30pm. Last-minute discount tickets go on sale 1hr. before show-time. For wheelchair access call 2 weeks ahead. Ticket prices vary; operas €7-160, ballets €6-80. AmEx/MC/V.

Orchestre de Paris, 252 rue du Faubourg St-Honoré, 8ème (☎01 42 56 13 13; www. orchestredeparis.com). ⓂTernes. This internationally renowned orchestra, one of the largest with 119 permanent musicians, celebrated its 40th year during the 2007-08 season. Season runs mid Sept. to mid-June. Call, check the website, or stop by for concert calendar. Box office open M-Sa 11am-7pm, 8pm on concert nights. Shows at 8pm. Tickets €10-130; €10 tickets for students, seniors, and 30min. before show. MC/V.

Palais Omnisports de Paris-Bercy, 8 bd. de Bercy, 12ème (☎08 92 39 01 00; www. bercy.fr). ⓂBercy. Only the biggest names in popular music play here—after all, it's tough to fill a stadium. In 2008 alone, Bercy hosted Celine Dion, Elton John, Jack Johnson, Alicia Keys, Kiss, Queen, and Radiohead, among others. Box office open M-Sa 11am-6pm. You can also call M-F 2-6pm or reserve online. Call ahead for wheelchair-access (☎08 92 39 04 90). Tickets €22-90. MC/V.

Théâtre des Champs-Élysées, 15 av. Montaigne, 8ème (☎01 49 52 50 50; www. theatrechampselysees.fr). ⓂAlma-Marceau. Top international dance companies and orchestras, from world music to chamber music, as well as opera. Season runs early Sept. to early June. Buy tickets 2-3 months in advance. Reserve by phone M-F 10am-noon and 2-6pm (€2 charge per ticket); box office open M-Sa 1-7pm. Call ahead for wheelchair-access. Tickets €5-130. AmEx/MC/V over €15.

Théâtre du Châtelet, 2 rue Edouard Colonne, 1er (☎01 40 28 28 40; www.chatelet-theatre.com). ⓂChâtelet. Superb 2300-seat theater hosts world-class orchestras, ballet companies, and operas. Magnificent acoustics. Call ahead for wheelchair access. Season runs Oct.-June. Tickets €10-120. Last-minute discount tickets available 15min. before show. Box office open daily 11am-7pm. AmEx/MC/V.

Théâtre de la Ville, 2 pl. du Châtelet, 4ème (☎01 42 74 22 77; www.theatredelaville-paris.com). ⓂChâtelet. Primarily known for its innovative (and often daring) dance productions, this venue also offers a selection of classical and world music concerts. Season runs Sept.-June. Call for program and discounts. Tickets sold by phone M-Sa 11am-7pm; box office open M 11am-7pm, Tu-Sa 11am-8pm. Call ahead for wheelchair access. Tickets €12-24. AmEx/MC/V.

Zénith, 211, av. Jean-Jaurès, Parc de la Villette, 19ème (☎01 42 08 60 00; www.le-zenith.com). ⓂPorte de Pantin. This loud, large venue on the edge of the city hosts major pop and rock artists. Tickets start at €16. Most around €45. MC/V.

GUIGNOL

Grand-Guignol Theater features the *guignol*, the classic stock character of the traditional Parisian **marionette show.** Although the puppets speak French, they're very urbane, and you'll have no trouble understanding the slapstick, child-geared humor. Nearly all parks have *guignols;* check *Pariscope* for more info. During the months of July and August, all *guignols* switch to a daily schedule to accommodate the French school vacations.

Marionnettes du Luxembourg, in the Jardin du Luxembourg (see **Sights,** p. 225), 6*ème* (☎01 43 26 46 47, groups 01 43 29 50 97). ⓂVavin. The best *guignol* in Paris. This theater has played the same classics since its opening in 1933, including *Le Petit Chaperon Rouge* (Little Red Riding Hood), *Pinocchio*, and others. Running time approx. 40min. Arrive 30min. early for good seats. Performances during the summer months at 4pm daily with a matinée performance Sa-Su 11am. €4.40. Cash only.

ENTERTAINMENT

NIGHTLIFE

Il faut être toujours ivre. Tout est là, c'est l'unique question.
  —Charles Baudelaire

The City of Light is no less bright at night. Bars in Paris are either chic night-time cafes bursting with people-watching potential, house-party-esque joints that are all about rock music and teenage angst, or laid-back neighborhood spots that often double as Anglo havens. In the 5*ème* and 6*ème*, bars draw French and foreign students, while the Bastille and Marais teem with Paris's young and hip, queer and straight. The Châtelet-Les Halles area draws a slightly older set, while the outer *arrondissements* cater to the full range of locals in tobacco-stained bungalows and yuppie drinking holes. Paris also harbors a ton of quality **jazz bars,** the best of which are listed in this chapter. For more on jazz bar culture and etiquette, see **Life and Times,** p. 95.

Clubbing in Paris is less about hip DJs and cutting-edge beats than it is about dressing up, getting in, and being seen. Drinks are expensive, and Parisians drink little beyond the first round, included in most cover charges. Many clubs accept reservations, which means that on busy nights there is no available seating. It's best to dress well and be confident but not aggressive about getting in. Come early and bring or be in a group of girls if you can. Once inside, the dance scene depends on the club—sometimes it's hopping, sometimes its an excuse to sway next to the one you *kiffe*. Clubs are usually busiest 2-4am. Tune in to **Radio FG** (98.2 FM) or **Radio Nova** (101.5 FM) to find out about upcoming events.

One of Europe's most queer-friendly cities, Paris boasts a plethora of GLBT nightlife hotspots, both calm and cruisy. The Marais is the center of GLBT life in Paris. Most queer bars and clubs cluster around rue du Temple, rue Ste-Croix de la Bretonnerie, rue des Archives, and rue Vieille du Temple, in the 4*ème* (p. 325). A number of more-subdued lesbian bars can be found in the 3*ème* (p. 323). For the most comprehensive listing of GLBT restaurants, clubs, hotels, organizations, and services, consult *Illico* (free at queer bars and restaurants), Gai Pied's annually updated book *Guide Gai* (€15 at kiosks and bookstores), or Zurban magazine's annual *Paris Gay and Lesbian Guide* (€6 at any kiosk). **Les Mots à la Bouche,** Paris's largest queer bookstore, is an unofficial information center for GLBT life; they can tell you what's hot now (see **Shopping,** p. 302).

CHÂTELET-LES HALLES

1ER ARRONDISSEMENT

Nightlife in the 1*er* is dominated by the many jazz bars in the area. Rue des Lombards is home to three of the best, as well as other bars, cafes, and crêpe stands. The 1*er* is a great area to go out at night, as it's mostly safe and the bars are usually fun and full. Getting home can be a chore, however, as on busy nights cabs are difficult to find. If France wins a football game by day, tired clubbers might find themselves walking home by night.

▓ **Le 18 Club,** 18 rue Beaujolais, 1*er* (☎42 97 52 13; www.club18.fr). ⓂPyramides. Walk toward the Opera on av de l'Opéra, turn right on rue des Petits Champs, and take another right at rue Vivienne; rue Vivienne dead-ends into rue Beaujolais. The oldest gay club in Paris, Le 18 is still going strong. A mostly male crowd dances to lighthearted pop music. Intimate bar and dance floor. Mixed drinks €6-9. Cover €10; includes 1 drink. Open W and F-Sa midnight-6am.

☒ **Banana Café,** 13 rue de la Ferronerie, 1er (☎01 42 33 35 31; www.bananacafeparis. com). ⓂChâtelet. Take rue Pierre Lescot to rue de la Ferronerie. This *très branché* (way cool) evening arena is the most popular GLBT bar in the 1er, and it draws an extremely mixed group. Patrons can enjoy the loud dance music and tropical decor while watching scantily clad males pole dance. Head downstairs for a lively piano bar and more dancing space. Legendary theme nights. "Go-Go Boys" Th-Sa midnight-dawn. 2 for 1 drinks during happy hour 6-9pm; mixed drinks excluded. Beer €5.50. Mixed drinks €8. F-Sa €10 cover with a drink. Open daily 5:30pm-6am. AmEx/MC/V.

Café Oz, 18 rue St-Denis, 1er (☎01 40 39 00 18; www.cafe-oz.com). ⓂChâtelet. Take the rue de Rivoli exit, walk down rue de Rivoli, and make a left on rue St-Denis. Huge, friendly Australian bar with pine benches, long wooden tables, and obliging bartenders. Popular with study-abroaders looking to dance or hook up. Pints €7. Mixed drinks €8. Happy hour daily 5-8pm; pint €6, mixed drinks €5. Soirées featuring Reggae, Hip Hop, R&B, or Funk W at 10pm. Open M-Th and Su 5pm-3am, F 5pm-6am, Sa 1pm-6am. Sa €10 cover; includes drink and coat check. Also at 1 rue de Bruxelles (☎01 40 16 11 16) and 8 bd. Montmartre (☎01 47 70 18 52), both 9ème. MC/V.

Le Slow Club, 130 rue de Rivoli, 1er (☎01 42 33 84 30). ⓂChâtelet. This cellar used to be a banana-ripening warehouse; now it looks like a cave with plush seating. A DJ plays music from the 60s to today, to 25+ French crowd that actually likes to dance. No cover but dress well. Some nights host private functions. Open W-Sa midnight-6am

Le Fumoir, 6 rue de l'Amiral Coligny, 1er (☎01 42 92 00 24; www.lefumoir.com). ⓂLouvre. As cool and ritzy by night as it is by day. 30-something crowd. Extra dry martini €11-12. Champagne-infused mixed drinks €11.40. Happy hour 6-8pm; €6 mixed drinks. See full listing in **Food,** p. 170.

JAZZ CLUBS

☒ **Au Duc des Lombards,** 42 rue des Lombards, 1er (☎01 42 33 22 88; www. ducdeslombards.com). ⓂChâtelet. From rue de Rivoli exit, take rue des Lavandières St-Opportune. Cross the street to follow rue St-Opportune, turn right on rue des Lombards. Murals of Ellington and Coltrane cover the exterior of this premier jazz joint. Still the best in French jazz, with occasional American soloists and hot items in world music. 3 sets each night—lower cover and concessions if you reserve in advance by phone. Cover €19-25, student €12 if you call in advance. Couples €30 in advance. Beer €3.50-5. Mixed drinks €8; prices vary depending on show. Music 10pm-1:30am. Open M-Sa 5pm-2am. MC/V.

☒ **Le Baiser Salé,** 58 rue des Lombards, 1er (☎01 42 33 37 71; www.lebaisersale. com). ⓂChâtelet. A few doors down from Au Duc des Lombards. Cuban, African, and Antillean music featured together with modern jazz and funk in a welcoming, mellow space. Month-long African music festival in July. Jazz concerts start at 10pm, music until 2:30am (typically 3 sets); mainly new talent. Cover around €20. Free M jam sessions at 10pm with 1-drink min. Beer €6.50-11.50. Mixed drinks €9.50; prices vary depending on show. Happy hour 5:30-8pm. Open daily 5pm-6am. AmEx/MC/V.

Le Sunside, Le Sunset, 60, rue des Lombards, 1er (☎01 40 26 21 25 or 01 40 26 46 60; www.sunset-sunside.com). ⓂChâtelet. Next door to the Baiser Salé, down the street from Au Duc des Lombards. An easy-going double club with an old and widespread reputation (especially with Anglophones), Le Sunside and Le Sunset are in fact 2 separate jazz venues; Le Sunside is above Le Sunset and opens 1hr. earlier. Sometimes both have concerts, sometimes only one; check online. Concerts M-Sa 8pm-1am. Happy hour 6-8:30pm; beers €3-5, mixed drinks €5. Beer €5-6. Mixed drinks €9-10. Cover €20-25, occasional student discount. Open daily 6pm-2am. MC/V.

WINE BARS

Willi's Wine Bar, 13 rue des Petits Champs. 1er (☎01 42 61 05 09; www.williswinebar. com). ⓂPalais-Royal. Behind the Palais. Popular since its opening in 1980, this place is fancier than its name suggests. Exposed wood beams, chic decor, and huge windows looking out onto the Palais and apartment of author Colette. Friendly staff and international clientele. Huge selection of French wines €13.50-17 per glass, though by the bottle is customary. Open M-Sa noon-midnight. MC/V.

Wine and Bubbles, 3 rue Française, 1er (☎01 44 76 99 84). ⓂÉtienne Marcel. Tastetest bubbly without breaking the bank. A classy but casual place for a late 20s to early 30s crowd of professionals—perfect for finding a spouse. Also doubles as a *marchand de vin,* so if you like what you try you can buy it. From €4 per glass and €16 per bottle. *Assiettes* of cheese and charcuterie €5-16. Bar open M-Tu 6pm-midnight, W-Sa 6pm-2am; shop open M-Tu 4-9pm, W-Sa 11am-9pm. AmEx/MC/V.

2ÈME ARRONDISSEMENT

When it comes to throwing a great party, few *arrondissements* can top the 2ème. A welcoming destination for English-speaking expats from around the globe, the neighborhood is home to several Anglophone pubs (ⓂÉtienne Marcel and Opéra) and some of the best dancing in Paris (around bd. Poissonière). It's also the most GLBT-friendly nightspot outside of the Marais.

Le Champmeslé, 4 rue Chabanais, 2ème (☎01 42 96 85 20; www.lachampmesle.com). ⓂPyramides. Take av. de l'Opéra and make a right on rue des Petits Champs and a left on rue Chabanais. This welcoming lesbian bar is Paris's oldest and most famous. Both men and women enjoy the popular cabaret shows (Sa 10pm) and monthly art exhibits. Beer €5 before 10pm, €7 after. Mixed drinks €8/10. No cover. Open M-Sa 3pm-dawn.

Frog and Rosbif, 116 rue St-Denis, 2ème (☎01 42 36 34 73; www.frogpubs.com). ⓂÉtienne-Marcel. At the corner of rue St-Denis and rue Tiquetonne. One of several Anglo-French "Frog and..." pubs in Paris. The Frog and Rosbif shows live rugby and football broadcasts, which can get pretty intense when England plays. Frog pubs also brew their own lagers and bitters. Happy hour 5:30-8pm; pints €5, mixed drinks €5. Thirsty Thursdays; students €4.50 beer and mixed drinks, €2 shots. Quiz nights Su 8pm. Beer €6. Mixed drinks €7. Also serves decent pub food (M-F lunch menu €13; English breakfast Su). Free but cranky wireless Internet. Open daily noon-2am. MC/V.

Rex Club, 5 bd. Poissonière, 2ème (☎01 42 36 10 96; www.rexclub.com). ⓂBonne-Nouvelle. A non-selective club that presents the most selective of DJ line-ups. Young clubbers crowd this casual venue to hear cutting-edge techno, jungle, and house fusion from international DJs on one of the best sound systems in Paris. Large dance floor and surrounded by colorful leather booths. Beer €6-8. Mixed drinks €9-11. Cover €10-15 (some nights free). Open (roughly) W-Th 11:30pm-6am, F-Sa midnight-6am.

THE MARAIS

3ÈME ARRONDISSEMENT

Nightlife in the 3ème is more subdued than the scene found in the neighboring 4ème—for the most part, women (and men, too) can leave their stiletto heels at home. There are a number of GLBT bars in the area on and around rue aux

Ours, rue St-Martin, and rue Michel Le Comte but the area's focus is on casual bar-cafes with live music--especially around the Pompidou.

Andy Wahloo, 69 rue des Gravilliers, 3ème (☎01 42 71 20 38). ⑩Arts et Métiers. Walk down rue Beaubourg and turn left on rue des Gravilliers. The happening and hip lounge bar of the moment, this Moroccan themed bar is an offshoot of the popular **404** restaurant next door. The environment is funky and eclectic, featuring ingenious paint-bucket seats and a cushioned corner poised on plastic crates. The tiny bar stirs after 11pm, but come early to claim a seat on the casual terrace, where patrons smoke hookah to the beat of DJs spinning tunes. Beer €5-6. Mixed drinks €9-10. Happy hour 5-8pm; beer and mixed drinks €5. Open M-Sa 5pm-2am, Su 11am-5pm. AmEx/MC/V.

L'Apparement Café, 18 rue des Coutures St-Gervais, 3ème (☎01 48 87 12 22). ⑩Chemin Vert. Beautiful wood and red lounge with games and a chill, young crowd. Display of local artists' paintings that you can buy if you so desire. Late-night meals €12-15, served until 11:30pm. Mixed drinks €9 (see **Food**, p. 174).

Le Duplex, 25 rue Michel Le Comte, 3ème (☎01 42 72 80 86) ⑩Rambuteau. Small and intimate atmosphere features a computer where the 30-something patrons can snap photos to remember their evening. Local artists display photographs and paintings in rotating exhibits on the walls. Not an exclusively male bar—anyone is welcome—but few women hang out here. The bar becomes lively after 11pm and plays lots of jazz and electronic music. Beer €2.50 until 10pm, €3.50 after. Mixed drinks €7.50. Open M-Th and Su 8am-2am and F-Sa 8am-4am. MC with €15 min. charge.

Le Connétable, 55 rue des Archives, 3ème (☎01 42 77 41 40). ⑩Arts et Métiers. Walk down rue Beaubourg and turn left on rue Michel Le Comte; restaurant is at the corner of rue des Archives and rue des Haudriettes. Housed in a former *hôtel particulier*, this 3-level bar-restaurant-theatre is a cross between a tavern and a classic parlor. The atmosphere follows: an unpretentious but cultured young crowd comes for nightly concerts in the basement, starting at 8:30 and 10pm; come early to secure a good seat in the tiny concert room. Beer and wine €4-7. Mixed drinks €8. Dinner menu €21. Main dishes €15-2. Open M-F noon-3pm and 7pm-4am, Sa-Su 7pm-4am. Food served noon-3pm and 7-11pm. AmEx/MC/V.

La Perle, 78 rue Vieille du Temple, 3ème (☎01 42 72 69 93). ⑩ St-Paul. Walk with traffic along rue de Rivoli and turn right on rue Vieille du Temple. Day or night, hot or cold, crowds of fashionably cool 20-somethings spill outside of this corner bar for no apparent reason—except that everyone else is doing it. Sandwiches €3-5; wine and beer €3-6. Open daily 6am-midnight or whenever the party dies down.

Le Tango, 11 rue au Maire, 3ème (☎01 48 87 25 71; www.tangoparis.com). ⑩Arts et Métiers. This 70-year-old establishment is the last vestige of the traditional musette (accordion) club. The columns and bar and the casual, down-to-earth ambience have changed little since the club's inception. Managed by the GLBT organization "La Boite à Frissons" (The Thrill Box), this is not your typical sweaty, over-sexed queer club. Partners' dancing to tango and chacha between 10:30pm and 12:30am; disco and world music (with lots of Madonna) thereafter F and Sa. Sunday parties are organized by various GLBT organizations; check website for details. Regular theme nights, usually F. Popular singles ball every 2 mo. Heterosexuals—both men and women—welcome. Cover €8, with membership €5.50. Drinks €4-7.50. Open F-Sa 10:30pm-5am, Su 6-11pm. Cash only.

L'Enchanteur, 15 rue Michel Le Comte, 3ème (☎06 17 11 90 13). ⑩Rambuteau. Laid-back bar works its magic with purple fittings, psychedelic lighting, and techno/dance tunes. Club downstairs Sa; festivities begin at 9pm. Older men are the predominant species, but women welcome. Karaoke W-Sa. Happy Hour 6-8pm; same prices, bigger sizes. Beer €2.50. Mixed drinks €7. Open M-Th and Su 4pm-2am, F-Sa 4pm-4am. V.

DANCE CLUBS

Le Dépôt, 10 rue aux Ours, 3ème (☎01 44 54 96 96; www.ledepot.com). ⓂÉtienne-Marcel. Take rue Étienne-Marcel east; it becomes rue aux Ours. The queen of Paris's gay club scene, Le Dépôt inspires dancing with everything from disco to house to techno. Find a boy toy in the designated "cruising" area while watching porn on mounted TVs. Once you do, don't waste time on small talk—check out the rooms in the downstairs labyrinth. Women not welcome (exceptions include Pride Week, when a few lesbians can enter). The 5pm post-Su brunch Gay Tea Dance is especially popular. Cover (includes 1st drink) M-Th €8.50, Su before 11pm and F €10, Sa €12. Open daily 2pm-8am. V.

WINE BARS

🕮 **L'Estaminet,** 39 rue de Bretagne, Marché des Enfants Rouges, 3ème (☎01 42 72 34 85).ⓂTemple. Walk down rue du Temple and turn left on rue de Bretagne. Enter the Marché des Enfants Rouges; the bar is on the upper right corner, marked by an arching grapevine. This tiny, clean-scrubbed, and airy wine bar is a place for relaxation, not partying. It features a delightful selection of inexpensive wines by the glass (€3-3.50) or bottle (€5-25). Accompaniments available, or better yet, traipse through the market and pick up something to munch on. In summer, the yellow-checkered picnic tables are a great way to meet friendly locals. MC/V.

> **DRINKING AND FRENCHING.** French is full of nasal sounds, but practice makes perfect. You know you're good when you can order *un bon vin blanc* without making the waiter or bartender cringe. Too easy? Try having some *bon vin blanc* and *then* saying it, ten times fast.

4ÈME ARRONDISSEMENT

No matter where you are in the 4ème, a bar or club is close by. Spots with outdoor seating are piled on top of one another on rue Vieille du Temple, from rue des Francs-Bourgeois to rue de Rivoli. Unarguably the center of Paris's GLBT nightlife scene, fun and fashionable men's and women's bars and clubs crowd rue Ste Croix de la Bretonnerie (though most are more concerned with how you're dressed than whom you're dressing for). The places on rue des Lombards have a more rough and convivial—though often touristy—atmosphere.

🕮 **Le Yono,** 37 rue Vieille-du-Temple, 4ème (☎01 42 74 31 65). Ⓜ St-Paul or Hôtel de Ville. In a cool courtyard, this bar channels Casablanca with its stone interior, hidden balcony, slowly spinning ceiling fan, and shadow-casting palm leaves. The bar recently underwent a name and attitude change, adding a nightly DJ to liven things up. Now, Le Yono has it all with a mellow, table-filled area upstairs and dancing below. Happy hour 6-8pm; mixed drinks €8.50, beer €4. Open daily 6pm-2am. MC/V.

🕮 **Amnésia Café,** 42 rue Vieille-du-Temple, 4ème (☎01 42 72 16 94). Ⓜ St-Paul or *Hôtel de Ville*. A largely queer crowd comes to lounge on plush sofas in Amnésia's classy wood-paneled interior. 1st fl. cafe, 2nd fl. lounge and basement club with music beginning 9pm. This is one of the top see-and-be-seen spots in the Marais, especially on Sa nights. Don't forget to close your tab. Espresso €2. Kir €4. Mixed drinks €7.50-10. Open Tu-Th and Su 11am-2am, M and F-Sa 11am-2am. V.

🕮 **Raidd Bar,** 23 rue du Temple, 4ème. ⓂHotel de Ville. Take the ⓂHotel de Ville exit and walk up rue du Temple. The most hip and happening GLBT club in the Marais and probably in Paris. Spinning disco globes cast undulating shadow and light in the intimate space, illuminating the muscular, topless torsos of the sexy bartenders. After 11pm, performers strip down in glass shower cubicles built into the wall showcase (yes, they take it all off every hour on the hour starting at 11:30pm). Happy hour 5pm-9pm for all drinks, 5-11pm for beer; size doubles. Tu disco night, W 80s and house, Th "DJ VIP," F-Sa club, Su 90s. Beer €4. Mixed drinks €8. Notoriously strict door policy—women are not allowed unless with a greater ratio of (gorgeous) men. Open daily 5pm-5am.

Open Café, 17 rue des Archives, 4ème (☎01 42 72 26 18). Ⓜ Hôtel de Ville. A very popular Marais GLBT-friendly bar, Open Café draws a large crowd of loyal customers to its corner. Always crowded, this is one of the hottest bars in Paris with outdoor terrace seating and sleek metal decor. Most patrons are men, but women are welcome. Happy hour 6-10pm; half-price beer only. Beer €3.50-6.50, mixed drinks €7.50. Open M-Th and Su 11am-2am, F-Sa 11am-4am. MC/V.

Stolly's, 16 rue Cloche-Perce, 4ème (☎01 42 76 06 76). ⓂSt-Paul. On a dead-end street off rue du Roi de Sicile. This small Anglophone hangout, run by the same folks who own Lizard Lounge, does dive-bar cool. The €14 pitchers of cheap blonde ensure that the bar lives up to its motto, "hangovers installed and serviced here." Life-size papier-mâché animals and a decidedly non-trendy crowd. When there's an open mic night at the LL, come here to hang with the band beforehand. Occasional live music. Happy hour 5-8pm; mixed drinks and beer €5. Open M-F 4:30pm-2am, Sa-Su 3pm-2am. Terrace closes at midnight. MC/V.

Le Pick-clops, 16 rue Vieille du Temple, 4ème (☎01 40 29 02 18). The new kid on an already over-popular block, the diner-esque Pick-Clops draws trendy 20-somethings day and night with its choice corner locale (perfect for people-watching and -judging), rock and alternative music, and good food and drink. Doesn't take itself too seriously because it doesn't need to. *Punch maison* €5; mixed drinks €7-8. Delicious salads €9-13. Open daily 7am-2am. MC/V.

Café Klein Holland, 36 rue du Roi de Sicile, 4ème (☎01 42 71 43 13). ⓂSt-Paul. From St-Paul, take rue de Pavée and turn left on rue du Roi de Sicile. A Dutch bar with a friendly, lively atmosphere. Goes out of its way to cater to students: drinks are cheap (esp. for the *quartier*), happy hours begin at noon, and you can rent out the place (including dancefloor) for free. M quiz night 9-11pm. Happy hour noon-10pm; pints €4-5; special mixed drinks such as the "multiple orgasm" €5. After 10pm beer €5, mixed drinks €7. Open daily noon-2am. MC/V.

Les Étages, 35 rue Vieille du Temple, 4ème (☎01 42 78 72 00). Ⓜ St-Paul or Hôtel de Ville. 18th-century hotel-turned-bar. 4 *étages* populated by dressed-down, relaxed 20-somethings. Limited selection of €4.50 mixed drinks during happy hour (5-9:30pm) with side of nuts and olives. Open daily 3:30pm-2am. MC/V with €15 min. charge.

Lizard Lounge, 18 rue du Bourg-Tibourg, 4ème (☎01 42 72 81 34; www.cheapblonde. com). ⓂHôtel de Ville. A happening split-level space for rowdy American college kids. Underground cellar has DJs every night from 10pm. Happy hour on ground floor 5-8pm, underground 8-10pm. Select pints and mixed drinks €5. Open daily noon-2am. Good, if somewhat pricey American grub served M-F noon-3pm and 7-10:30pm, Sa-Su noon-4pm, 7:30-10:30pm. Su brunch €12-18, no *menu* available on Sundays, just a sparse buffet. MC/V with €15 min. charge.

Le Carré, 18 rue du Temple, 4ème (☎01 44 59 38 57). ⓂHôtel de Ville. Take the Hôtel de Ville exit and walk up rue du Temple. Le Carré is working hard to stay chic; stained glass decor, a red back-lit bar, and smoky taupe velvet chairs characterize this happening bar of the moment. A favorite drinking hole for chic and well-dressed 20-somethings, thanks to the cheap happy hour beers and tapas. Beer €3.40-4. Mixed drinks €8-10. Happy hour 6-9:10pm, half off beers on tap. Lunch menu €13.50-14.50. Brunch €18 every Su 11am-5pm. Open daily 10pm-4am. AmEx/MC/V.

Okawa, 40 rue Vieille du Temple, 4ème (☎01 48 04 30 69). Ⓜ St-Paul. Walk up rue de Pavée, turn left on rue des Rosiers and left on rue Vieille du Temple. This friendly, casual Franco-Québécois bar-cafe is run by a Canadian expat. Plop down on one of the leather tufted stools and ogle passersby, or check out a cabaret-concert in the basement (W 8:30pm, €40 for dinner and show), which features chunky stone wells from the reign of Philippe-Auguste. The €7 speed-dating nights on M (includes 1 drink) are popular with singletons; sign up beforehand. Happy hour 7-9pm; beer €3.50-3.70. Coffee €2.50. Mixed drinks €8.50. Open M-Th and Su 11:30pm-2am, F-Sa 11:30pm-4am. MC/V.

3W Kafé, 8 rue des Ecouffes, 4ème (☎01 48 87 39 26, www.3w-kafé.com). ⓂSt-Paul. Walk with traffic along rue de Rivoli and turn right on rue des Ecouffes. Formerly "Les Scandaleuses," the Marais's hippest lesbian bar got a face-lift and a new name—3W stands for "women with women." Sleek interior, great angry indie music. Men welcome if accompanied by women. Downstairs club with DJ F-Sa from 10pm. Beer €4-5. Mixed drinks €8-9. House punch €5. Free GLBT maps of Paris. Open daily 6pm-2am. MC/V.

Au Petit Fer à Cheval, 30 rue Vieille du Temple, 4ème (☎01 42 72 47 47). ⓂHôtel de Ville. A Marais institution with a horseshoe bar, sidewalk terrace, and small restaurant in the rear. Best mojito in Paris (€8-9), especially the 3rd one. Beer €2.50-10. Mixed drinks €7.50-8.50. Drinks cheaper if served at bar. See also **Food,** p. 175. Open daily 10-2am. MC/V.

Le Quetzal, 10 rue de la Verrerie, 4ème (☎01 48 87 99 07). Ⓜ Hôtel de Ville. Nicknamed *l'Incontournable,* this black-lit men's bar plays everything from rap to techno and runs the gamut from stylish to shady. Opposite the rue des Mauvais Garçons (Bad Boys). Women welcome by management, not necessarily by patrons. Happy hour 5-11pm, beer half-price. Beer €3.80-5. Mixed drinks €7.50-10. Open daily 5pm-5am. MC/V.

Cox, 15 rue des Archives, 4ème (☎01 42 72 08 00). Ⓜ Hôtel de Ville. As the name suggests, this is a buns-to-the-wall men's bar that caters to an older clientele. So crowded that the guys waiting to get in often block traffic on the street. Cruisy and hypersexualized, with a slightly seedy tang; not the place for a quiet weekend cocktail. Happy hour 6-9pm; draft beer half-price. Beer €3.50-4.50. Open daily 12:30pm-2am. Cash only.

WINE BARS

La Belle Hortense, 31 rue Vieille du Temple, 4ème (☎01 48 04 71 60; www.cafeine.com). ⓂHôtel de Ville. Walk against traffic along rue de Rivoli and turn left on rue Vieille du Temple. A literary bar/gallery/cafe, the intimate Hortense draws an oxymoronic crowd of down-to-earth intellectuals. Walls and walls of books (literature, art, philosophy, children's) and mellow

THE LOCAL STORY

SOIRÉES ON THE SEINE

It might seem cliché, but there are few places in Paris more popular than the Seine at night. More than a lovers' hangout, the *quais* have bred a culture of their own. From nightfall until sunrise, the river's edges feature a variety of activity, from lip-locking to fist-fighting. While sometimes intimidating, if approached with a sense of humor the Seine can be a great (and cheap) nightime hangout. Here are some of the usual suspects you're bound to see:

Parisian Punks: crowds of Parisian teens come here to accumulate street cred. The louder and more obnoxious they are, the more respect they accrue: expect everything from drums to dreds.

Didactic Drunkard: usually enraged and occasionally homeless, there is at least one man whose self-appointed job includes pacing up and down the *quais* asking for substances—tobacco, alcohol, or weed.

Showy Study Abroaders: just as loud as the Parisian Punks, this crowd also travels in groups and totes cheap bottle sof wine.

Lustful Lovebirds: you'd think the rowdy surroundings would get to them, but they're usually too busy making out to notice.

Inquisitive Oddball: a tourist or older couple who wanders along the *quais* until, bewildered, they realize it's not their scene.

music to go with your merlot. Frequent exhibits, readings, lectures, signatures, and discussions in the small leather-couch-filled back room; advertised on the front window. Free Wi-Fi. Varied wine selection from €4 per glass, €8 per bottle. Wine of the month €8. Open daily 5pm-2am. MC/V.

LATIN QUARTER AND ST-GERMAIN

5ÈME ARRONDISSEMENT

A decidedly student-dominated scene, the 5ème offers an astoundingly diverse array of nightlife, much of it with a retro pastiche. Down rowdy pint at the L'Academie de la Bière or groove to the jazz at Le Petit Journal.

▓ **L'Académie de la Bière,** 88bis bd. de Port Royal, 5ème (☎01 43 54 66 65; www. academie-biere.com). ⓜVavin. Take the bd. Raspail exit and walk against traffic on bd. du Montparnasse, which becomes bd. de Port Royal. With 12 kinds of beer on tap and more than 300 more in bottles, this bar doesn't mess around. Fortunately, it doesn't matter what you pick—there's not a weak link on the menu. According the Academy, "Hunger has no hour, nor does thirst," so service is continuous. Extensive menu featuring salads and *tartines* (€8-9), *assiettes* of cheese and *charcuterie* (€13-17), mussels (€7-9), and hot *plats* (€8-13). The outdoor tent seating is a plus. Beer €6-9. Happy hour 3:30-7:30pm. Open M-Th and Su 10am-2am, F-Sa 10am-3am.

▓ **Le Caveau des Oubliettes,** 52 rue Galande, 5ème (☎01 46 34 23 09). ⓜSt-Michel. Head away from pl. St-Michel on *quai* de Montebello and turn right on rue Petit Pont, then left on rue Galande. 2 scenes in 1, both with a mellow, funky vibe. The upstairs bar (La Guillotine) has sod carpeting, ferns, and a real guillotine. The downstairs cellar is an outstanding jazz club. This cellar's previous incarnation was an actual *caveau des oubliettes* (literally "cave of the forgotten ones"), where criminals were locked up and forgotten. Free *soirée boeuf* (jam session) M-Th and Su 10pm-1:30am: M Pop Rock, Tu Swing, W groove, Th Funk, Su Blues; F-Sa free concerts. Drinks from €5-9. Happy hour daily 5-9pm. Open daily 5pm-2am, later on weekends.

▓ **Le Piano Vache,** 8, rue Laplace, 5ème (☎01 46 33 75 03; www.lepianovache.com). ⓜCardinal Lemoine or Maubert-Mutualité. From Maubert, walk up rue de la Montagne Ste-Geneviève and make a right on rue Laplace. This place has character: once a butcher shop, now a dim, poster-plastered bar with cow paraphernalia. A local favorite and film site for music videos, Piano Vache always promises an interesting time; the crowd ranges from alternative-trendy students to 30-something brains to Johnny Depp, who has been known to stop by. Beer €3.50, before 9pm €2.50. Mixed drinks €7/6. M live Jazz concerts. Theme nights 9pm-2am: W Gothic, Th 80s. F "Soirée Chewing-Gum des Oreilles" (don't ask us) rock night. Sa rock and punk. Japanese rock night every second Tu of the month. Open M-F noon-2am, Sa-Su 9pm-2am.

Le Who's Bar, 13 rue Petit Pont, 5ème (☎01 43 54 80 71). ⓜSt-Michel. Walk away from pl. St-Michel on *quai* Montebello and make a right on rue Petit Pont. This hopping bar stays open super late for Paris and is right in the swing of things—close to the Seine and the center of the Latin Quarter's bar scene. Live pop and rock music every night at 10:30pm; some of its not too bad (think Placebo covers). Disco in the basement W-Su 10:30pm-midnight. Beer €6-7. Mixed drinks €10-12. Shots €5. Happy hour daily 4-10pm, all drinks half-price. Open M-Th and Su 5pm-5am, F-Sa 6pm-6am.

Finnegan's Wake, 9 rue des Boulangers, 5ème (☎01 46 34 23 65). ⓜJussieu. An Irish pub set in a renovated ancient wine cellar with low, black-beamed ceilings. Have a pint (€6) with the boisterous but down-to-earth crowd of students and professionals. Occasional live concerts of traditional Irish music in the downstairs *cave* from 5pm. Happy hour daily 6-9pm; pints €4.50. Open M-Th 6am-2am, F-Sa 6pm-4am.

JAZZ CLUBS

Le Petit Journal St-Michel, 71 bd. St-Michel, 5ème (☎01 43 26 28 59; www.petit-journalsaintmichel.com). ⓜCluny-La Sorbonne; RER Luxembourg. Follow bd. St-Michel away from the Seine. Le Petit is another of the early jazz strongholds that draws a mostly middle-aged crowd. Low ceilings and tables right next to the band create memorable atmosphere. First-class New Orleans and Big Band acts frequently perform here. The *menu* is excellent but pricey. Concerts start at 9:15pm. Obligatory 1st drink €17-20, students €11-15; subsequent drinks €7-9. Open M-Sa 9pm-1:15am. Closed Aug.

Le Caveau de la Huchette, 5 rue de la Huchette, 5ème (☎01 43 26 65 05; www.cave-audelahuchette.fr). ⓜSt-Michel. From bd. St-Michel, turn down rue de la Huchette. In the past, the Caveau was a meeting place for secret societies and directors of the Convention; downstairs you can still see the prison cells and execution chambers filled by the victims of Danton and Robespierre. Now a diverse crowd comes prepared to listen, watch, and participate in jitterbug, swing, and jive in this extremely popular (if touristy) club. Bebop dance lessons Sept.-June; call for times. Live music 10pm-2am. Wine €5-6. Beer €6-7. Mixed drinks €10. Cover M-Th and Su, F-Sa €13; students €9; no cover after 2am. Open M-W and Su 9:30pm-2:30am, Th-Sa 9:30pm-dawn. AmEx/MC/V.

Aux Trois Mailletz, 56, rue Galande, 5ème (☎01 43 54 00 79 or 01 43 54 42 94; before 5pm 01 43 25 96 86). ⓜSt-Michel. Walk along the Seine on *quai* St-Michel, make a right on rue du Petit Pont and a left on rue Galande. What you'd expect a cool jazz club to look like. The crowded basement *cave* features world music and jazz vocals (from around 11pm) and welcomes a crowd of all ages. The upper floor is packed with a well-dressed mix of students and 40-somethings there for cabaret or subdued piano concerts (starting around 10pm). Weekend cover for club around €20; no bar cover. Beer and wine €7-10. Mixed drinks €13. Bar open daily 5pm-dawn; *cave* 10pm-dawn.

6ÈME ARRONDISSEMENT

The 6*ème*'s great nightlife is oriented toward bars and pubs, not clubs. There are lots of great little bar-cafes around Carrefour Buci and Carrefour de l'Odéon, and also some *crêpe* stalls for the journey home at the end of the night.

▨ **Le 10 Bar,** 10 rue de l'Odéon, 6*ème* (☎01 43 26 66 83). ⓜOdéon. Walk against traffic on bd. St-Germain and make a left on rue de l'Odéon. Le 10 Bar is a classic student hangout where Parisian youth indulge in philosophical and political discussion. Either that or they're getting drunk and making inside jokes. After several glasses of their famous spiced sangria (€3.50), you might feel inspired to join in. Jukebox plays everything from Edith Piaf to Aretha Franklin. Open daily 6pm-2am.

▨ **Chez Georges,** 11 rue des Cannettes, 6*ème* (☎01 43 26 79 15). ⓜMabillon. Walk down rue du Four and turn left on rue des Cannettes. Upstairs is a wine bar with a crowd spanning the ages: chain-smoking college students, 30-somethings, and quiet types playing chess against themselves are equally at home here—maybe it's the cheap wine. Downstairs is a smoky, candlelit cellar where students drink and dance. Beer €3.50-4. Wine €1.50-4. Upstairs open Tu-Sa noon-2am; cellar 10pm-2am. Closed Aug.

Bob Cool, 15 rue des Grands Augustins, 6*ème* (☎01 46 33 33 77). ⓜOdéon. Walk up rue de l'Ancienne Comédie, turn right on rue St-André-des-Arts and left on the small rue des Grands Augustins. One of the city's best expat hangouts, Bob Cool has a laid-back clientele, colorful paintings and photographs, and a friendly vibe (*baba cool* means "hippie"). The music is at the discretion of the bartender and ranges from salsa to The Corrs to Buddy Holly. Beer by the pint €5.50. Mixed drinks €5-6. Open daily 5pm-2am.

Fu Bar, 5 rue St-Sulpice, 6*ème* (☎01 40 51 82 00). ⓜOdéon. Take Carrefour d'Odéon to rue de Condé, then turn right on rue St-Sulpice. A multilevel haven for a boister-ous Anglophone crowd, this hip bar serves an astounding array of tantalizing martinis

NIGHTLIFE

(€7.50) along with the regular bar fare. Name is misleading—this place is far from FUBAR. Tu is student night, when martinis are €2 off and those under 25 pack the place almost to bursting. Happy Hour daily 5-9pm. Open daily 5pm-2am.

The Moose, 16 rue des Quatre Vents, 6ème (☎01 46 33 77 00; www.mooseheadparis. com). ⓂOdéon. Head toward rue d'Odeon and go right on rue des Quatre Vents. Decorated in typical Canadian fashion—that is to say, with hockey sweaters and bilingual beer posters—The Moose is the place to rub elbows with friendly Canadian expats. Restaurant serves North American bar fare—nachos, burgers, and wings—until midnight. Those yearning for Canadian beer can treat themselves to an ice-cold bottle of Moosehead (€5.50). Happy hour 4-8:30pm. Tu happy hour all night; mixed drinks €5.50, Moose head €3.50. Bar open M-Sa 4pm-2am, Su 11:30pm-2am. MC/V over €15.

INVALIDES (7ÈME)

The 7ème may be the poshest address in town, but its respectable citizens retreat early, and quality nightlife spots are thus sparse. A few wannabe-cool corner cafe-bars at École Militaire are expensive and touristy, but the rue St-Dominique has a couple of cafes and bars staked out by locals. In the hotter months, teenagers and couples hang on the Champs de Mar until the wee hours, absorbing the magic of the Tour Eiffel—which increases with every drink.

Le Club des Poètes, 30 rue de Bourgogne, 7ème (☎01 47 05 06 03; www.poesie.net). ⓂVarenne. Walk up bd. des Invalides with the Invalides behind you and to your left; go right on rue de Grenelle and left on rue de Bourgogne. Since 1961, Jean-Pierre Rosnay has been making "poetry contagious and inevitable." A restaurant by day, the old-style, timbered Poètes is transformed into a poetry club 9-10pm each night. A troupe of readers and comedians, including some of Rosnay's family, bewitch the audience with poetry from Villon, Baudelaire, Rimbaud, and others. If you arrive after 10pm, wait to enter until you hear clapping or a break in the performance. Lunch menu €15. Wine about €4-8. Open Tu-Sa noon-3pm and 8pm-1am. Food served until 10pm. Closed Aug. MC/V.

O'Brien's, 77 rue St-Dominique, 7ème (☎01 45 51 75 87). ⓂLa Tour-Maubourg. Follow traffic along bd. de La Tour Maubourg. A sophisticated Irish pub (apparently not an oxymoron) with a horseshoe-shaped bar. Attracts a largely Anglophone crowds who come to watch the sports event of the moment (everything from darts to football). Happy hour M-F 5-8pm; pints €6. Pub quiz nights Su 9pm. Beer 25cl €5, 50cl €7. Mixed drinks €8. Open M-Th and Su 5pm-1am, F-Sa 5pm-2am. MC/V over €15.

CHAMPS-ÉLYSÉES (8ÈME)

Glam is the word at the trendy, expensive bars and clubs of the 8ème. Whether you're going for a mystical evening at buddha-bar or a surprisingly more accessible evening at Le Queen, make sure to bring your wallet, dashing good looks, and if possible, a super-important and/or famous friend.

buddha-bar, 8 rue Boissy d'Anglas, 8ème (☎01 53 05 90 00; www.buddha-bar.com). ⓂMadeleine or Concorde. Too cool for capital letters. Perhaps the most glamorous drinking hole in the city (Madonna drops by when she's in town). If you're sufficiently attractive, wealthy, or well connected, you'll be quickly led to 1 of the restaurant-bar's 2 dim, candlelit levels, where your internal organs will gently vibrate to hypnotic "global" rhythms. A two-story Buddha watches over the chic ground-floor restaurant, while the luxurious upstairs lounge caters to those looking to unwind in style with one of the creative mixed drinks (€16-17). buddha may break the bank, but the experience is totally enlightening, and possible worth it. Beer €8-9. Sake €8. Wine €8-11. Open M-F noon-3pm and 6pm-2am, Sa-Su 6pm-2am.

Charlie Birdy, 124 rue la Boétie, 8è*me* (☎01 42 25 18 06; www.charliebirdy.com). ⓂFranklin D. Roosevelt. Walk toward the arch on the Champs; rue la Boétie will be the second street on your right. A friendly and spacious restaurant-bar with an Anglo design concept (as they claim, "between the New York loft and English lounge"). Serves up affordable drinks (mixed drinks €8, special drinks €11) and fusion food (burgers €12-15, salads €11-13) in a chill and casual atmosphere. Perfect post-work atmosphere. Flat-screen TVs show the soccer or rugby game of the moment. Free Wi-Fi. Weekly soirées; check website for details. Happy hour M-F 4-8pm, drinks half-price. Wine €3-6. Beer €4-7. Open daily 10am-5am. AmEx/MC/V.

World Place, 34-36 rue Marboeuf, 8è*me* (☎01 56 88 36 36). Hyper-trendy bar-restaurant formerly known as Mandala Ray. Owned by Johnny Depp, John Malkovich, and Sean Penn. To get in, look like a celebrity or bring one. Busy bar on the upper level (beer €10, mixed drinks €15-20) with live jazz, salsa, soul, and latin music. Restaurant in the lower level accented with a purple glow and white armchairs (entrées €10-25; plats €21-40). On weekends, DJs spin tunes for the beautiful crowd after 11pm (€20 cover). Open daily 6:30pm-2:30am. Restaurant open 8pm-midnight. AmEx/MC/V.

DANCE CLUBS

Le Queen, 102 av. des Champs-Élysées, 8è*me* (☎01 53 89 08 90; www.queen.fr). ⓂGeorge V. A renowned Paris institution where drag queens, superstars, tourists, and go-go boys get down to the mainstream rhythms of a 10,000-gigawatt sound system. Her Majesty is one of the cheapest and most accessible GLBT clubs in town and has kept its spot on the Champs for a reason. Women have better luck with the bouncer if accompanied by at least one male. All drinks €10. M disco, W Ladies' Night, Th-Sa house, Su 80s. Cover Tu-Th and Su €15, M and F-Sa €20; includes 1 drink. Bring ID and come in small groups. Open daily midnight-dawn. AmEx/MC/V.

CANAL ST-MARTIN AND SURROUNDS (10ÈME)

While it's relatively safe during the day, the 10è*me* becomes a haven of pick-pocketing and prostitution after sundown, so *Let's Go* recommends avoiding the area if at all possible. For intrepid travelers who feel particularly inclined to hear some jazz, New Morning is the best option for nightlife in the area.

JAZZ CLUBS

New Morning Jazz Club, 7-9 rue des Petites-Ecuries, 10è*me* (☎01 45 23 51 41; www.newmorning.com). ⓂChâteau d'Eau. The club's entrance—a small, nondescript metal door—is easy to miss, so be on the look out. Dark and crowded, New Morning is everything a jazz club should be. This 400-seat former printing plant now plays host to some of the biggest American headliners in the city. All the greatest names in jazz have played here—from Chet Baker to Stan Getz and Miles Davis. These days it continues to attracts big names like Wynton Marsalis, Betty Carter, and John Scofield. The venue's best acoustics are in the lower front section or near the wings of the stage. Tickets can be purchased from the box office, any branch of FNAC, or the Virgin Megastore; they average €16-20. Check performance schedule and reserve tickets online (four days in advance). Drinks €6-10. Open daily Sept.-July 8pm on. Most concerts begin at 9pm. MC/V.

NIGHTLIFE

BASTILLE

11ÈME ARRONDISSEMENT

Nightlife in the 11ème is a tale of two scenes. With a few exceptions, rue de Lappe and its neighbors offer a big, raucous night on the town dominated by Anglophiles, while rue Oberkampf, rue Amelot, and rue Thaillandiers are more eclectic, low-key, and local. Both streets are definitely worth your time, even if you have only one night in the area. Rue Faubourg St-Antoine is a world of its own, dominated by enormous nightclubs expecting a well-dressed crowd.

■ **Le Pop In,** 105 rue Amelot, 11ème (☎48 05 56 11). ⓜSt-Sébastien Froissart. Living a double life as a neighborhood bar and rock club, but with the air of a 90s house party, this broken-in, crowded spot is a favorite hangout for Paris's young, carefully bedraggled cool kids. Pop, rock, folk, and indie folk concerts Tu, W, and Su at 9pm in the tiny basement. Beer €3-5.50, cheaper before 9pm. Open Tu-Su 6:30pm-1:30am.

■ **La Mécanique (Ondulatoire),** 8 passage Thière, 11ème. ⓜBastille. Walk along rue de la Roquette away from pl. Bastille and take a right on passage Thière. A local hang out with a lighthearted sense of humor, rough-and-tumble aesthetic (note the skis, gas pump, and scooter as decor), and an obsession with rock music. Has a 50s/60s meets 90s feel. Live concerts every night at 9pm. Dancefloor downstairs, lively bar and sitting room upstairs. Specializes in quality drinks, with over 90 kinds of whiskey and 30-40 types of rum. Beer €5-6. Wine €3-4. Mixed drinks €6-9. Open M-Sa 6pm-2am.

■ **Le Bar Sans Nom,** 49 rue de Lappe, 11ème (☎01 48 05 59 36). ⓜBastille. Take rue de la Roquette and make a right on rue de Lappe. The No-Name Bar is a laid-back oasis amid the clamor of rue de Lappe, catering to an older crowd than most other bars. Dim, seductive lounge with tall ceilings and huge, Bohemian wall hangings. Famous for its creative mixed drinks (€9-10), posted on oversized wooden menus; don't leave Paris without trying their mojito. Their free tarot-card reading (Tu 7-9pm, come early to grab a seat) has become something of an institution. Beer €5-6.50. Shots €6.50. Open Tu-Th 6pm-2am and F-Sa 6pm-4am. MC/V over €12.

■ **Favela Chic,** 18 rue du Faubourg du Temple, 11ème (☎01 40 21 38 14; www.favelachic. com). ⓜ République. Walk down rue du Faubourg du Temple, turn right into the arch at no. 18; the club is to your left. Self-proclaimed Franco-Brazilian joint in the middle of working class République. Little Franco and lots of brassy Brazilian. Wildly popular with locals, this restaurant-bar-club has eclectic decor and equally colorful clients. Dinner in the restaurant segues into unbridled and energetic table-dancing to salsa-latino-brazilian rhythms. Exceedingly crowded with gyrating bodies during the weekend and a long line snaking out the door. Mixed drinks €9, made strong enough to justify the cost; cover F-Sa €10, includes a drink. Open Tu-Th 7:30pm-2am, F-Sa 7:30pm-4am. MC/V.

Café Charbon, 109 rue Oberkampf, 11ème (☎01 43 57 55 13). ⓜParmentier or Ménilmontant. The beautiful, soaring ceiling and burnished mirrors are proud traces of this place's fin-de-siècle dance-hall days. These days, the cafe maintains a casual, modern atmosphere. The crowd varies with the act playing at the attached Nouveau Casino (p. 333), but usually consists of laid-back 20- to 30-somethings. Happy hour daily 5-8pm; beer €3. Mixed drinks €8. Salads €8. Tapas €6 each. Open M-W and Su 9am-2am and Tu-Sa 9am-4am. Food served noon-3pm and 8pm-midnight. MC/V.

Le Bar à Nénette, 26bis rue de Lappe. 11ème (☎01 48 07 08 18; www.lebaranenette. com). ⓜBastille. Walk down rue de la Roquette and make a right on rue de Lappe; look for the sparkling lights. Saloon-style bar with wooden facade, wall-sized mirrors, and a cool, casual vibe. Popular with a local young-professional crowd. Friendly owner and pretty bartenders complement the welcoming atmosphere. Happy hour 5-10pm; mixed drinks €5, beer €4, shots and apéritifs €3). Open daily 5pm-2am. AmEx/MC/V.

Le Lèche-Vin, 13 rue Daval, 11ème (☎01 43 55 98 91). ⓜBastille. This irreverent bar greets visitors with a large statue of a nun and other religious paraphernalia. The holy kitsch doesn't prevent the artsy crowd from enjoying their beers (€6). Happy hour 6-10pm; beer and mixed drinks €4. Open Tu-Sa 6pm-2am. MC/V over €15.

Le Kitch, 10 rue Oberkampf, 11ème (☎01 40 21 94 14). ⓜOberkampf or Filles-du-Calvaire. A crazy, dream-like of a cafe-bar with painted clouds scudding across the ceiling, marble-mosaics, and rainbow brooms flying across the wall. Eclectic, welcoming crowd. M DJ. Happy hour 5:30-9pm; mixed drinks and beer €5. Open daily 5:30pm-2am.

DANCE CLUBS

🏵 **Wax,** 15 rue Daval, 11ème (☎01 40 21 16 18). ⓜBastille. Take bd. Richard Lenoir, then make a right on rue Daval. A rare Parisian miracles: a place that is always free and fun. Set up in a concrete bunker with retro orange, red, yellow and white couches, this mod bar/club is packed with a mix of locals and tourists. W and Su disco/funk, Th R&B, Sa-Su house. Beer €5-7. Mixed drinks €10. Open daily 9pm-dawn. MC/V over €15.

Nouveau Casino, 109 rue Oberkampf, 11ème (☎01 43 57 57 40; www.nouveaucasino. net). ⓜParmentier or Ménilmontant. This hot spot draws in the Bastille crowd with concerts and clubbing. Music ranges from electropop to hip-hop to pop to rock. Occasional art exhibits and video shows; check the website or call for a weekly schedule. Cover €5-10. Tickets available through FNAC. Open midnight-dawn when there are events.

Sanz Sans, 49 rue du Faubourg St-Antoine, 11ème (☎01 44 75 78 78). ⓜBastille. Popular, upbeat bar/club/restaurant with moderate bouncer control (during peak hours, there must be a female in your group) but no cover. It's not classy, but fun on weekend nights when the dancefloor gets crowded. For the voyeur in each of us: a large, baroque-framed screen projects scenes from the bar like a black-and-white movie. M funk/groove, Tu R&B, W mix, Th hip hop and reggae, F-Sa house. Outdoor seating; indoor A/C. Beer €5. Mixed drinks €10. Open M-W 9am-3am, Th 9am-4am, F-Sa 9am-5am. MC/V.

WINE BARS

🏵 **Jacques Mélac,** 42, rue Léon Frot, 11ème (☎01 43 70 59 27; www.melac.fr). ⓜCharonne. Walk down rue Charonne, and turn left on rue Léon Frot. A cozy, family-owned wine bar and bistro with strong local following since 1938. The menu features 35 wines, at least 2 of which are made in M. Mélac's vineyards. Mid-Sept., Mélac lets children harvest, tread upon, and extract wine from grapes growing in the bar's storefront. Wine €3 per glass, bottles €15-38. Salads €8-12. Cheese and *charcuterie* platters €13-15. Open Tu-Sa 9am-3:30pm and 8-10:30pm. Closed Aug. MC/V.

Le Clown Bar, 114 rue Amelot, 11ème (☎01 43 55 87 35; www.clown-bar.fr). ⓜFilles du Calvaire. Cross bd. du Filles du Calvaire to rue Amelot. Located next to the circus, Le Clown Bar is a neighborhood hangout that has attracted considerable buzz for its reasonable prices, friendly service, and delicious sampler menu. Perfect for students who want to drink and *discuter,* not rage. As for the aesthetic, its written in the name: clown paintings, posters, and sculptures adorn every surface. Wine by the glass from €3.50. Dinner *menu* €25. Open M-Sa noon-3pm and 7pm-1am, Su 7pm-1am. Cash only.

La Muse Vin, 101, rue de Charonne, 11ème (☎01 40 09 93 05). ⓜCharonne. A bit more modern and trendy than your average wine bar; pulls in a mix of young and not-so-young couples and professionals. Wine by the glass from €4; bottles from €10. *Plats* €18. Open M-Sa 5pm-midnight. MC/V.

12ÈME ARRONDISSEMENT

Rue du Faubourg St-Antoine is the dividing line between the lively 11ème and its tamer 12ème sister. Buzzing nightlife spills out from both sides of the road, and you can hop from one club-lounge to another all night—but it won't be cheap in the 12ème. Be prepared to make it rain.

Barrio Latino, 46-48 rue du Faubourg St-Antoine 12ème (☎01 55 78 84 75; www.buddhabar.com). ⓂBastille. The Latin, less famous counterpart to buddha-bar (p. 330)—it's basically the same place minus the 3-story Buddha. 4 dim floors of lounge chairs, low tables, couples, and groups ready to eat, drink, and above all, dance. The giant dancefloor heats up around 11pm and doesn't stop until closing. Shove the flip-flops in the closet; the bouncers are picky with footwear. Su brunch is an institution among stylish locals (noon-4pm, €29) and includes a free salsa lesson (2:30pm). DJ arrives at 10pm. Cover €20. Mixed drinks €10-15. Open daily noon-2am. AmEx/MC/V.

China Club, 50 rue de Charenton, 12ème (☎01 43 46 08 09; chinaclub.cc). ⓂLedru-Rollin or Bastille. 2 levels of sophisticated socializing, one level of high-class clubbing. The first and second floors feature a restaurant/piano bar/smoke lounge atmosphere, with high ceilings, marble floors, oriental carpets, and luxurious lounge chairs; downstairs in Club Chin Chin, things get more intimate with red velvet and dimmed lights. A bit pricey but the drink list features creative concoctions like "Roasted Almond." Mixed drinks €10-15. 3-course dinner menu €40-45. Dinner reservations recommended. Restaurant open daily 8pm-2am. Club open daily Th-Sa 10pm-5am. AmEx/MC/V.

WINE BARS

Le Baron Rouge, 1 rue Théophile-Roussel 12ème (☎01 43 43 14 32). ⓂLedru-Rollin. Follow the rue du Faubourg St-Antoine away from the opera and take a right on rue Charles Baudelaire. Théophile-Roussel is your first left. A laid-back but cool crowd mingles around enormous wine barrels that serve at tables. The boisterous bartender will suggest one of the dozens of wines on the menu (a steal at €1-3 a glass). Assiettes of cheese, charcuterie, or fruits de mer €5-14. Open Tu-Th 10am-3pm and 5-10pm, Sa 10am-2pm, Su 10am-4pm. MC/V.

BUTTE-AUX-CAILLES AND CHINATOWN (13ÈME)

The thirteenth is mostly filled with businesses and residences, but there are pockets of excitement. The area around Place d'Italie, especially rue de la Butte-aux-Cailles, has a few local bars perfect for kicking back. If you'd rather kick up your heels, head for the new boat bars along the Quai de la Gare.

La Dame Canton, Porte de la Gare, 13ème (☎01 53 61 08 49 or 01 44 06 96 45; www.damedecanton.com). Starting in the early afternoon, couples and groups populate the picnic tables and beach chairs on the terrace. The pirate ship behind the bar hosts concerts at 8pm and "DJ parties" on weekends. Tickets available at FNAC. Also a restaurant; menu starts at €24. Cover €5. Open Tu-Th 7pm-2am, F-Sa 7pm-5am.

La Folie en Tête, 33, rue de la Butte-aux-Cailles, 13ème (☎01 45 80 65 99). ⓂPlace d'Italie. Take rue Bobillot south; rue de la Butte-aux-Cailles branches right. The artsy axis mundi of the 13ème. Exotic instruments line the walls of this beaten-up wood-fronted hole in the wall, but it keeps a laid-back vibe. Beer €3. Ti punch €6. Happy hour 6-8pm; mixed drinks €5, kir €3. Open M-Sa 6pm-2am, Su 5pm-midnight. MC/V over €15.

Bateau El Alamein, Port de la Gare, 13ème (☎01 45 86 41 60; elalamein.free.fr). ⓂQuai-de-la-Gare or Bercy. A mix between an abandoned pirate ship, a garden party, and an exotic island. The stage downstairs features local performers nightly at 9pm. Entrance €8. Delicious drinks €8-10; try the mojito or the TGV (tequila, gin, vodka). Open daily 8:30pm-2am, earlier on performance nights.

DANCE CLUBS

▥ **Batofar,** facing 11 *quai* François-Mauriac, 13è*me* (☎01 53 60 17 30; www.batofar. fr). ⓜQuai de la Gare or Bibliothèque Nationale de France. Look for red lights. This 45m long, 520-ton barge/bar/club has made it big with a variety of music—mainly electronic, techno, hip hop, reggae, and house—but attracts a friendly, rather than obnoxious, crowd. Live artists daily; check website for more info. In summer, the terrace restaurant features a happy hour from 7-11pm. Cover €8-15; usually includes 1 drink. Open M-Th 11pm-6am, F-Sa later; hours change for special film and DJ events. MC/V.

MONTPARNASSE

14ÈME ARRONDISSEMENT

▥ **L'Entrepôt,** 7 rue Francis de Pressensé, 14è*me* (☎45 40 07 50, restaurant reservations 45 40 60 70; www.lentrepot.fr). ⓜPernety. Proving that nerds can throw down, L'entrepôt offers a quadruple combo: a 3-screen independent cinema, a restaurant with a garden patio, a modern art gallery, and a trendy bar featuring live Th night jazz, and F-Sa world music (9:30pm; cover €7-10). Young clientele enjoys free weekly debates and lectures on topics ranging from literature to Olympic families. Ciné-Philo, a screening, lecture, and discussion cafe, is held every other Su 2:20pm (€8); check the monthly schedule in the main foyer. Free improv theater (with audience participation) fills alternating Su 6:30pm. Movie tickets €7, students €5.60, under 12 €4. Check website for other special events, including jam and slam sessions. Su buffet brunch noon-3pm (€25). Complex open daily 9am-midnight; art gallery open daily 10am-7pm; bar open M-W and Su noon-3pm and 7:30-10:30pm, Th-Sa noon-3pm and 7:30pm-1am. Kitchen open M-W and Su noon-3pm and 7:30-10:30pm, Th-Sa noon-3pm and 7:30-11pm. AmEx/MC/V.

Café Tournesol, 9, rue de la Gaîté, 14è*me* (☎43 27 65 72). ⓜEdgar Quinet. From the metro, turn left on rue de la Gaîté; the bar is on the left, at the corner of impasse de la Gaîté. With fake sunflowers hanging above the bar and lyrical techno music, industrial chic meets country cool at this ultra-mod cafe-bar. Wine €2.50-3. Beer €2.70-3.50. Open M-F 8:30am-1:30am, Su 9am-1:30am. AmEx/MC/V.

15ÈME ARRONDISSEMENT

The 15è*me* is largely residential and doesn't have much to offer in terms of nightlife. There are a few good cafe-bars, popular with businessmen during the week, but the weekends are generally quiet.

Au Roi du Café, 59 rue Lecourbe, 15è*me* (☎01 47 34 48 50). ⓜSèvres-Lecourbe. This is a great little cafe/bar frequented by both Parisians and expats. Super friendly staff gives it a great atmosphere, and the drinks are generous. Simple but delicious cafe food served until 10:45pm. You can enjoy a quiet drink at the bar or come with friends and sit at an outside table on summer evenings. Happy hour 6-9pm; mixed drinks €4. Beer €2-3. Mixed drinks €7. Open M-Sa 7am-midnight, Su 7am-5pm.

Mix Club, 24 rue de l'Arrivée, 15è*me* (www.mixclub.fr). ⓜMontparnasse-Bienvenüe. The entrance to this underground club is right next to the Tour Montparnasse. Though horribly cheesy and a bit generic, Mix can be amusing for the open-minded, drunk, or cynical. Expect red, orange, and purple fluorescent lights; disco-like effects; and an eclectic mix of house, rock, German ska, Greek tunes, oldies and hip-hop. Popular with studyabroaders on Th "Erasmus nights" (students get in free). €15 for entrance, a drink, and a healthy lung full of the ambient, machine-generated smoke. Huge neon signs flash "party," just in case you forget. Mixed drinks from €8.

PASSY AND AUTEUIL (16ÈME)

The 16*ème* is a residential district, and most of its nightlife lies on the edge of the upper half bordering the more lively 8*ème* and the Champs-Élysées.

Duplex, 2bis av. Foch, 16*ème* (☎01 45 00 45 00; www.leduplex.com). Ⓜ️Charles de Gaulle-Étoile. Take the av. Foch exit; the entrance is marked by a red awning leading to the underground nightclub. During the week a young, mostly-French crowd lets loose, while the weekends bring businessmen and their arm candy. 2 or 3 separate rooms play music ranging from techno to R&B to hip-hop to house. Also contains the expensive Le Living restaurant (open Tu-Sa 8:30-11:30pm; DJ Sa 9pm-midnight), which contrasts with the rest of the club. Themed nights; check website for details. Cover and first drink Tu-Th and Su €15, F-Sa €20; Sa women free before midnight. All drinks Tu-W and Su €10, Th €9, F-Sa €11. Open Tu-Su 11pm-dawn. Closed July 30-Aug. 25.

Sir Winston, 5 rue de Presbourg, 16*ème* (☎01 40 67 17 37). Ⓜ️Kléber. Walk toward the Arc de Triomphe, take a right, and take the first right again. This hip bar/restaurant/lounge/club is a watering hole for young Parisian bobos (bohemian bourgeois, the French version of American yuppies). Indian shrines, romantically dim lighting, wrought-iron lanterns and superb ceiling frescos. Downstairs is a dance space with a DJ spinning lounge and jazzy tunes. Wine €4-9. Beer €4.50-7. Mixed drinks €9-12. "Live Gospel Brunch" Su noon-4pm €24. Open M-Tu and Su 9am-3am, Th-Sa 9am-4am. MC/V.

BATIGNOLLES (17ÈME)

The 17*ème* doesn't have much to offer in night-time revelry. The cafes near the pl. du Dr. Félix Lobligeois are always filled with crowds of young things sipping cocktails and chatting away, but that's about as wild as it gets.

▨ **L'Endroit,** 67 pl. du Dr. Félix Lobligeois, 17*ème* (☎01 42 29 50 00). Ⓜ️Rome. Follow rue Boursault to rue Legendre and turn right. Hip, young 17*ème*-ers come for the snazzy diner-esque bar and idyllic spot on a tree-lined place. Popular choices include the mojito and the apple martini. The alcohol is kept on a giant rotating shelf. Wine €4-5. Beer €3-5. Mixed drinks €8-10. Open daily 10am-2am, often later F-Sa. MC/V.

MONTMARTRE (18ÈME)

Much of the 18*ème*'s nightlife lies in the sleazy southern end of the *butte*, in the red light district around Place Pigalle and bd. Rochechouart. The streets are lined with peep-show hawkers and the odd drug dealer; stay in well-lit, busy areas if you want to avoid hassles. Don't get us wrong, it can still be a blast—the area is packed with bars of all shapes and sizes, and dance clubs range from classy to crude. Tourists traveling alone, especially women, should avoid Ⓜ️Pigalle, Ⓜ️Anvers and Ⓜ️Barbès-Rochechouart at night. For live music in Montmartre, see **Entertainment,** p. 313.

La Fourmi, 74 rue des Martyrs, 18*ème* (☎01 42 64 70 35). Ⓜ️Pigalle. Head east on bd. Clichy; La Fourmi is on the corner of rue des Martyrs. An artsy atmosphere with a large zinc bar and industrial-trendy decor, complete with burnt orange walls, a mosaic-tiled floor, and a chandelier made of green chianti bottles. A hyper-hip, energetic, and scrappy young crowd takes refuge here from the otherwise sleazy Pigalle. Also hosts rotating art exhibits. Beer €3-7. Wine €5-7. Mixed drinks €7-9. Open M-Th 8am-2am, F-Sa 8am-3:30am, Su 10am-1:30am. MC/V.

Chez Camille, 8 rue Ravignan, 18*ème* (☎01 42 59 21 02). Ⓜ️Abbesses. Facing the church in pl. des Abbesses, head right down rue des Abbesses and go right (uphill) on rue Ravignan. Small, bright yellow bar on the upper slopes of Montmartre with a small terrace looking down the *butte* to the Invalides dome (especially dramatic at night). Come for the view, not the aging and lethargic crowd. Cheap coffee (€2) and tea (€2.50). Beer €2-4. Wine €4. Mixed drinks €5.50. Open Tu-Su 3pm-2am.

DANCE CLUBS

Folies Pigalle, 11 pl. Pigalle, 18*ème* (☎01 48 78 55 25; www.folies-pigalle.com). ⓂPigalle. The largest, wildest club in the sleazy Pigalle *quartier*—not for the faint of heart. A former strip joint, the Folies is popular with both gay and straight clubbers and is perhaps the most trans-friendly club in the city. Mostly house and techno, usually crowded. Soirées Transsexuelles Th, all types welcome. Drinks €10-15. Cover €20, includes 1st drink. Open M-Th and Su midnight-8am, F-Sa midnight-11am. AmEx/MC/V.

Bus Palladium, 6 rue Fontaine, 18*ème* (☎01 42 23 18 62; www.lebuspalladium.com). From ⓂPigalle, walk down rue Jean-Baptiste Pigalle (left of Folies Pigalle), turn right on rue Fontaine, and look for the bright blue facade. Getting past the bouncers can be tough; most F and Sa are open to the public. Cover is usually €15-20. AmEx/V.

BUTTES CHAUMONT (19ÈME)

The 19th is dominated by large boulevards and office buildings, but there are a couple of popular cafes and bars lining bd. de la Villette that have great people watching, especially in the summer.

Café Chéri(e), 44 bd. de la Villette, 19*ème* (☎01 42 02 02 05). ⓂBelleville. With cheap drinks, nightly DJ sets, and outdoor seating, this is quickly becoming one of the hottest spots in the 19*ème*. Beer starts at €5 and comes with free chips. Indie atmosphere. Nightly DJ sets (pop and electronic) start around 7pm. No cover. Open daily 8am-2am.

BELLEVILLE AND PÈRE LACHAISE (20ÈME)

A laid-back place to enjoy a drink and possibly a little bit of live music, the 20*ème* provides visitors with nightlife that is mellow yet still hip. Come here on a Friday night to wind down like the locals do.

▨ Café Flèche d'Or, 102bis rue Bagnolet (☎01 44 64 01 02; www.flechedor.fr). ⓂPorte de Bagnolet. A live indie rock (and more) concert venue that draws crowds upon crowds. Cool, intense, and a little rough around the edges. Music ranges from reggae to hip-hop to electro pop to Celtic rock; Girl Talk brought down the house in early '08. Art videos, dance classes, and crazy theater on the tracks below the terrace. DJ set Th-Sa midnight-6am. Free entry for concerts 8pm-2am. Beer €4-6. Mixed drinks €8-20. Open W-Sa 10am-3am, Th-Sa open until 6am. MC/V. Also a restaurant; see also **Food, p. 203**.

Lou Pascalou, 14 rue des Panoyaux, 20*ème* (☎01 46 36 78 10; www.loupascalou.com). ⓂMénilmontant. Follow bd. de Belleville and make a left on ruedes Panayaux. A local hangout a little bit out of the way, with open-air seating on a shady terrace. Occasional concerts (about every Su), slam poetry (2nd Tu of the month), and improvisational theater and art displays. Beer €3-5. Wine €2-3. Open daily 9:30am-2am. MC/V.

NIGHTLIFE

DAYTRIPS

TRIP	TRAVEL TIME
Versailles	40-60min.
Chartres	65-75min.
Fontainebleau	55-65min.
Chantilly	45-75min.
Giverny	1-1hr.
Vaux-le-Vicomte	1-2hr.
Auvers-sur-Oise	1-1hr.
Disneyland Resort Paris	45-50min.

VERSAILLES

By sheer force of ego, the Sun King converted a hunting lodge into the world's most famous palace. The sprawling château and gardens testify to Louis XIV's absolute power, and absolute ego. What started off as extravagance became absurdity during the reign of Louis XVI and Marie-Antoinette; it takes only one visit to this royal playground to understand why the (starving) rest of the country got their *culottes* all up in a bunch and staged a revolution (see **Life and Times,** p. 63). Versailles still glitters with the sheen of excess luxury, but at least now nobody gets beheaded for enjoying it.

🛈 PRACTICAL INFORMATION

Transportation: RER trains beginning with "V" run from Ⓜ️Invalides or any stop on RER Line C5 to the Versailles Rive Gauche station (30-40min., departs approx. every 15min., €5.60 round-trip). Buy your RER ticket before going through the turnstile to the platform; when purchasing from a machine, look for the Île-de-France ticket option. While a metro ticket will get you through these turnstiles, it will not get you through RER turnstiles at Versailles and could ultimately result in a significant fine. From the RER Versailles station, turn right down av. de Général de Gaulle, walk 200m, and turn left at the first big intersection on avenue de Paris; the entrance to the château is straight ahead. Like pornography, you'll know it when you see it.

Tourist Office: Office de Tourisme de Versailles, 2bis avenue de Paris (☎01 39 24 88 88; www.versailles-tourisme.com). From the RER Versailles train station, follow directions to the château; the office will be on your left before the château courtyard. A great place to plan your Versailles exploration before succumbing to the palace's tourist mayhem. The office has info on local accommodations, events, restaurants, and sightseeing buses. Also sells tickets for historical, guided tours of the town. Open Oct.-Mar. M 11am-5pm, Tu-Su 9am-6pm; Apr.-Sept. Tu-Su 9am-6pm.

Food: While numerous tourist-focused eateries—including a MacDo—exist along the walk from the train station to the palace, packed picnics present the most enjoyable and affordable warm-weather solution; munch on a cheap baguette or light quiche snagged from a Parisian *boulangerie* while you sprawl out near the Swiss Lake. On the weekends, many French locals do the same, still profiting from Louis XIV's greediness. Moderately priced snack bars occupy various hidden niches off the main pathway leading up to the castle, and food at over-priced restaurants is available just outside the garden gates.

LET THEM STEAL FURNITURE

October 5, 1789 was a good day for the French Revolution and a very bad one for the Château de Versailles. Taking a cue from the crowd that stormed the Bastille prison, another, even larger group made their way to Versailles, hijacked the king and queen, and brought them back to Paris.

After those shenanigans, the revolutionaries auctioned off several of the chests, chairs, and tables that filled the Versailles palace. All of the artwork was transported to the Louvre for safekeeping. Many of the rooms and buildings at Versailles were later restored to their pre-Revolutionary glory, with reproductions put in place of the original furnishings; however, of the roughly 17,000 items sold off at public auction, a majority have been lost forever.

Gerald van Kemp, a French curator who died in January 2002, made it his life's work to track down missing pieces and return them to their rightful place. Nicknamed "The Man Who Gave Us Back Versailles," he retrieved some Riesener commodes made for Marie Antoinette and a Savonnerie carpet, for which the Versailles estate paid millions of dollars. Versailles's most prized former possession is Leonardo da Vinci's Mona Lisa, but let's hope she doesn't leave the Louvre anytime soon—the lines at Versailles are long enough already.

👁 SIGHTS

PALACE HISTORY. When Louis XIV was just 10 years old, a mob invaded his bedroom in Paris during the Fronde (a civil war among nobles). Traumatized by the malodorous commoners, he decided to move his government away from the politically unreliable capital to the safety of Versailles. In 1661, the Sun King renovated the small hunting lodge in Versailles and enlisted the help of architect **Louis Le Vau,** painter **Charles Le Brun,** and landscape architect **André Le Nôtre** (all of Vaux-le-Vicomte fame) just months after their previous patron, Nicolas Fouquet, had been sentenced to lifetime imprisonment (see Vaux-le-Vicomte, p. 355). Indeed, Versailles's Vaux-esque fountains and grandiloquent scale provided a not-so-subtle reminder of the monarchy's power. The Versailles court soon became the nucleus of noble life, where France's aristocrats vied for the king's favor and navigated a highly structured social hierarchy.

No one knows just how much it cost to build Versailles; Louis XIV burned the accounts. Though every aspect of life was a minutely choreographed public spectacle, things there were less luxurious than one might imagine: courtiers wore rented swords and urinated behind statues in the parlors, wine froze in the drafty dining rooms, and dressmakers invented the color *puce* (literally, "flea") to camouflage the bugs crawling on the noblewomen. The king also lacked the necessary funds to keep all his fountains flowing at once; instead he had his gardeners turn the water on and off to correspond to his guest's pre-chosen walking path, giving the illusion that all the fountains functioned continuously. Louis XIV died on September 1, 1715; his great-grandson Louis XV succeeded him. Louis XV commissioned the **North Wing Opera** for the marriage of Austrian Marie-Antoinette to his grandson, the crowned prince or *dauphin*. The newlyweds inherited the throne and Versailles when Louis XV died in 1774. The new king Louis XVI and Marie-Antoinette barely changed the château's exterior, but they did create Marie-Antoinette's personal pretend playland, the **hameau.** The Queen would spend hours in her hamlet village, pretending to live simply like a peasant. On October 5, 1789, 15,000 National Guardsmen and angry Parisian stormed Versailles and brought the royal family back to Paris, where Louis and his wife would eventually be victims of the Revolution.

During the 19th century, King Louis-Philippe established a museum to preserve the château,

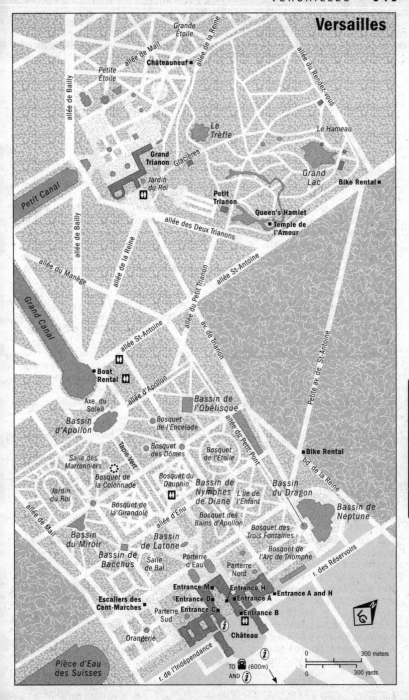

Versailles

Grande
Étoile

Petite
Étoile

allée de Mail

Châteauneuf

allée de la Reine

allée du Rendez-vous

allée de Bailly

Le
Trèfle

Le Hameau

Grand
Trianon

Glacières

Jardin
du Roi

Grand
Lac

Bike Rental

Petit Canal

allée de Bailly

allée de la Reine

allée des Deux Trianons

Petit
Trianon

Queen's Hamlet

Temple de
l'Amour

allée du Manège

allée St-Antoine

allée du Petit Trianon

av. de Trianon

Grand Canal

allée St-Antoine

Petite av. de St-Antoine

Boat
Rental

allée d'Apollon

Axe du
Soleil

Bassin
d'Apollon

Bassin de
l'Obélisque

Bosquet
de l'Encelade

Bosquet
des Dômes

Bassin de
l'Étoile

allée du Petit Pont

Bike Rental

bd. de la Reine

Salle des
Marronniers

Tapis Vert

Bosquet de
la Colonnade

Bosquet du
Dauphin

Jardin
du Roi

Bosquet de
la Girandole

allée d'Enu

Bassin de
Nymphes
de Diane

L'Île de
l'Enfant

Bassin
du Dragon

Bassin de
Neptune

allée de Mail

Bosquet des
Bains d'Apollon

Bosquet des
Trois Fontaines

Bassin
du Miroir

Bassin
de Latone

Salle
de Bal

Parterre
d'Eau

Bosquet de
l'Arc de Triomphe

r. des Réservoirs

Bassin de
Bacchus

Parterre
Nord

Escaliers des
Cent-Marches

Parterre
Sud

Entrance M

Entrance D

Entrance C

Entrance H

Entrance A

Entrance B

Entrance A and H

Orangerie

Château

Pièce d'Eau
des Suisses

r. de l'Indépendance

TO   (600m)
AND

0   300 meters

0   300 yards

against the wishes of many Frenchmen; Louis Philippe's opponents wanted Versailles demolished, preferring it to share the Bastille's fate (see **Sights,** p. 205). In 1871, the château regained historical importance when King Wilhelm of Prussia became Kaiser Wilhelm I of Germany in the Hall of Mirrors. That same year, as headquarters of the conservative Thiers regime, Versailles sent an army against the Paris Commune. The Versaillais pierced the city walls and crushed the Communards. On June 28, 1919, the Hall of Mirrors was again the setting for a momentous occasion, this time the signing of the Treaty of Versailles, a document ending WWI and instituting a flawed peace.

GUIDED TOURS. By arriving early in the morning, you can avoid the heavy crowds who swarm the château on Sundays from May to September and especially in late June. Figuring out how to get into the château is the hardest part, as there are half a dozen entrances. Most visitors enter at Entrance A, located on the right-hand side in the north wing, or Entrance C, located in the archway to the left. Both locations rent audio guides for €6-10. Entrance B is reserved for groups, Entrance D is where guided tours begin, and Entrance H is for visitors in wheelchairs. General admission grants entry to the following notable rooms: the **Grands Appartements,** the **War and Peace Drawing Rooms,** the **Galerie des Glaces** (Hall of Mirrors), and Marie-Antoinette's public apartment, the **hameau.** From Entrance D, at the left-hand corner as you approach the palace, you can choose between seventeen different English- or French-language guided tours each exploring a different area or theme. After the tour, you'll be able to explore the rest of Versailles on your own, without waiting in the general admission line. To avoid a long wait for guided tours, arrive before 11am. (☎ *01 30 83 78 89; www.chateauversailles.fr. Château open Tu-Su Apr.-Oct. 9am-6:30pm, Nov.-Mar. 9am-5:30pm. Last entry 30min. before closing. Admission to palace and self-guided tour through Entrance A €8, after 3:30pm €6, under 18 free. Supplement with 1hr. audio tour €6. 1-day pass is self-guided but includes entrance to the private apartments, temporary exhibitions, and the Grand and Petit Trianons, as well as the usual Grands Apartments, Mesdames Apartments, and the Hall of Mirrors on weekends; pass also includes audio guides for both the Grands and private apartments. 1-day pass Sa-Su in summer over 18 €25; in winter €16. Guided tours €22, under 18 €5.50. For group discounts and reservations call ☎ 08 10 81 16 14.)*

SELF-GUIDED TOURS. With a general admission ticket or day pass, you can begin at Entrance A and start your visit in the **Musée de l'Histoire de France,** created in 1837 by Louis-Philippe to celebrate his country's glory. The 21 rooms, arranged in chronological order, lay out a historical context for the château. The museum occasionally closes with no fixed schedule, so be sure to call.

Up the main staircase to the right, the king heard mass in the dual-level royal chapel. Architect **Hardouin-Mansat** constructed the chapel from 1699-1710. Back toward and to the left of the staircase, a series of gilded drawing rooms in the State Apartments are dedicated to Roman gods like Hercules, Mars, and the ever-present Apollo (the Sun King identified with the sun god, naturally). The ornate **Salon d'Apollo** was Louis XIV's throne room. The French citizens demonstrated great respect for the king's prestige, bowing or curtseying when passing the throne, even when it was empty. The **War and Peace Drawing Rooms** frame the recently-renovated **Hall of Mirrors,** originally a terrace until Mansart added a series of mirrored panels and windows to double the light in the room and reflect the gardens outside. These mirrors were the largest that 17th-century technology could produce and therefore an unthinkable extravagance. Le Brun's ceiling paintings (1679-1686) tell the history of Louis XIV's heroism, culminating with The King Governs Alone.

The Queen's Bedchamber, where royal births were made public in order to prove the legitimacy of the heirs, appears exactly as the Queen last left it on

October 6, 1789. A version of **Le Sacre de Napoleon** (1808) by David depicting Napoleon's self-coronation dominates the **Salle du Sacré** (also known as the Coronation Room). **The Hall of Battles,** installed by Louis-Philippe, is a monument to 14 centuries of France's military.

GARDENS. Numerous artists, including Coysevox, Le Brun, and Mansart created statues and fountains for Versailles's gardens, but master gardener André Le Nôtre provided the overall plan. Louis XIV wrote the first guide to the gardens, entitled the Manner of Presenting the Gardens at Versailles. Today the grounds remain a spectacular example of obsessive landscaping with neatly trimmed rectangular hedges lining the geometric *bosquets* (groves). The Sun King added further visual intricacies to his design; by making the cross-shaped canal wider on its western most end, he created a perspective-defying illusion evident when viewed from the terrace.

Though the château offers several different 1.5hr. tours of the gardens, the best way to visit the park is during the spectacular summer festival, **Les Grandes Eaux Musicales.** Weekends and holidays from Apr.-Sept., almost all the fountains are turned on at the same time and chamber music groups perform among the groves (see **Festivals,** p. 97). Any self-guided tour of the gardens must begin, as the Sun King commanded, on the terrace. To the left of the terrace, the **Parterre Sud** graces the area in front of Mansart's **Orangerie,** once home to 2000 orange trees; the temperature inside still never drops below 6°C (43°F). In the center of the terrace lie the fountains of the **Parterre d'Eau,** while down the steps, the **Bassin de Latone** features Latona, the mother of Diana and Apollo, shielding her children as Jupiter turns villains into frogs. For a truly spectacular fountain finale, make your way to the **Bassin of Neptune** at 5:20pm, to the right of the castle and behind the Bassin du Dragon.

Past the Bassin de Latone and to the left is one of the Versailles gardens' undisputed gems: the fragrant, flower-lined sanctuary of the **Jardin du Roi,** accessible only from the easternmost side facing the **Bassin du Miroir.** Near the grove's south gate lies the magnificent **Bassin de Bacchus,** one of four seasonal fountains depicting the Greek god of wine crowned in vine branches reclining on a bunch of grapes. Behind the Bassin de Bacchus, the **Bosquet de la Salle de Bal** features a semi-circle of cascading waterfalls and torch holders enabling royal revelers to host late-night balls; a large clearing in the middle provided ample space for dancing and merrymaking. Working your way north toward the center of the garden brings you to the exquisite **Bosquet de la Colonnade,** where the king used to take light meals amid 32 violet and blue marble columns, sculptures, and white marble basins. The north gate to the Colonnade exits onto the 330m long **Tapis Vert** (Green Carpet), the central mall linking the château to the garden's conspicuously central fountain, the **Bassin d'Apollon,** whose charioted Apollo rises out of the water to enlighten the world.

On the garden's north side, you'll find the incredible Bosquet de l'Encelade. When the fountains on, a 25m high jet bursts from Titan's enormous mouth, which is plated with shimmering gold and half buried under rocks. Flora reclines on a bed of flowers in the **Bassin de Flore,** while a gilded Ceres luxuriates in wheat sheaves in the **Bassin de Cérès.** The **Parterre Nord,** full of flowers, lawns, and trees, overlooks some of the garden's most spectacular fountains. The **Allée d'Eau,** a fountain-lined walkway, provides the best view of the **Bassin des Nymphes de Diane.** The path slopes toward the sculpted **Bassin du Dragon,** where a beast slain by Apollo spurts water 27m into the air. Next to the Bassin du Dragon, 99 jets of water issue from sea horns encircling Neptune in the **Bassin de Neptune,** the gardens' largest fountain.

Beyond Le Nôtre's classical gardens stretch wilder farmland, meadows, and woods perfect for a picnic away from the Versailles's manicured perfection. Stroll along the **Grand Canal**, a rectangular pond beyond the Bassin d'Apollon that measures an impressive 1535m long. To explore destinations farther afield around Versailles, rent a bike or a boat, or go for a horse-drawn carriage ride. (*Gardens open daily Apr.-Oct. 8am-8:30pm; Nov.-Mar. 8am-6pm. Free. Grandes Eaux Musicales Apr.-Sept. Sa-Su, and holidays €8, students and under 18 €6, under 6 free.*

The most convenient place to rent **bikes** *is across from the base of the canal.* ☎ *01 39 66 97 66. Open Feb.-Nov. daily 10am-7pm. 30min. €4, 1hr. €6. There are 2 other bike rental locations: one to the north of the Parterre Nord by the Grille de la Reine, another by the Trianons at Porte St-Antoine. Rent a 4-person electric car next to entrance C2 on the terrace.* ☎ *01 39 66 97 66. 1hr. €28; driver must be over 18. Rent boats for 4 at the boathouse to the right of the canal.* ☎ *01 39 66 97 66. Open daily 10am-6:30pm. 30min. €10, 1hr. €14; refundable deposit €10. Horse-drawn carriages depart Tu-Su from right of the main terrace.* ☎ *01 30 97 04 40.*)

TRIANONS AND MARIE-ANTOINETTE'S HAMEAU. Marie-Antoinette's *hameau* provides interesting insight into how French royalty escaped social stresses. Marie-Antoinette's solution was of course to build palaces, have trysts with lovers, and play at peasantry. We all know how that turned out.

On the right down the wooded path from the château, the **Petit Trianon** was built between 1762 and 1768 for Louis XV and his mistress Mme. de Pompadour. Marie-Antoinette took over the Petit Trianon in 1774, and it soon earned the nickname **Little Vienna.** Napoleon's sister (Empress Marie-Louise) later inhabited The Petit Trianon. In 1867, the Empress Eugénie, one of Marie-Antoinette's few admirers, turned the house into a museum devoted to the hapless queen.

Exit the Petit Trianon and follow the path to the left to arrive at the libidinous **Temple of Love,** a domed rotunda with 12 white marble columns and swans. Marie-Antoinette held many intimate nighttime parties in the small space, illuminated by torchlight. The queen was perhaps at her happiest and most ludicrous when spending time at the *hameau*, her own pseudo-peasant "hamlet" down the path from the Temple of Love. Inspired by Jean-Jacques Rousseau's theories on the goodness of nature and the *hameau* at Chantilly (p. 351) the queen aspired to a so-called "simple" life. She commissioned Richard Mique to build a 12-building compound comprised of a dairy farm, gardener's house, and mill, all surrounding a quaint artificial lake. Marie-Antoinette could play at a country life, imagining the starving Third Estate must not really suffer all that much. Any naïve illusions of rough living disappear upon entering the **Queen's Cottage** at the hamlet's center. Ornate furniture, marble fireplaces, and walk-in closets where Marie-Antoinette kept her monogrammed linens fill its rooms.

The single-story, stone-and-pink-marble **Grand Trianon** was intended as a château-away-from-château for Louis XIV. When life was getting him down—you know, his nobles were bickering or his mistresses were having bad hair days—the King got in a boat and rowed (well, was rowed) to this spot of refuge. Erected in 1687 and designed by Mansart, the palace consists of two wings joined by a large central porch. Lovely, simple formal gardens located behind the colonnaded porch are a relief from the rest of Versailles's showy *bosquets*. Stripped of its furniture during the Revolution, the mini-château was later restored and inhabited by Napoleon and his second wife. In the last century, President Charles de Gaulle installed presidential apartments and rooms for visiting heads of state at the Grand Trianon while the Maastricht Treaty's constitutional amendment was also written here. (*Shuttle trams from the palace to the Trianons and the hameau leave from the North Terrace. www.train-versailles.com. 50min. ride, 1-4 trains per hr. Round-trip €6, age 11-18 and handicapped visitors €4.50, under 11 free. Audio guides for the garden ride €1.20. The walk takes 25min. Both Trianons open daily Apr.-Oct. noon-*

6:30pm; Nov.-Mar. noon-5:30pm. Last entry 30min. before closing. Trianons admission Apr.-Oct. €9, 2hr. before closing €5, under 18 free; Nov.-Mar. €5, under 18 free.)

CHARTRES

Nothing compares to Chartres. It is the thinking of the Middle Ages itself made visible.
   —*Émile Male*

Were it not for a scrap of fabric, the cathedral and town of Chartres might still be a sleepy hamlet. But the cloth that the Virgin Mary supposedly wore when she gave birth to Jesus made Chartres a major medieval pilgrimage center. The spectacular cathedral that towers over the city isn't the only reason to visit: the *vieille ville* (old city) is also a masterpiece of medieval architecture, which almost lets you forget the zooming highways that have encroached upon it.

   Founded as the Roman city Autricum, Chartres is an ancient hilltop village at heart. Its oldest streets, still named for the trades once practiced there, cluster around the cathedral and gaze over the tranquil Eure River. These winding paths offer some of the best views of the cathedral and are navigable using the well-marked tourist office circuit (map available at tourist office). Chartres's medieval tangle of streets can be confusing, but getting lost here is enjoyable.

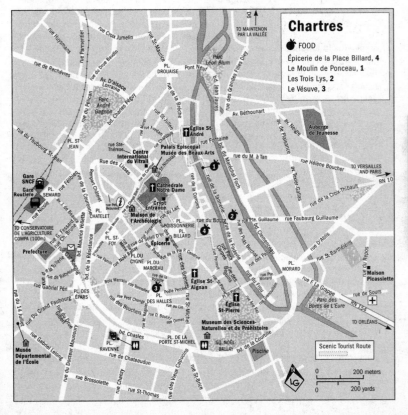

Chartres

🍴 FOOD

Épicerie de la Place Billard, **4**
Le Moulin de Ponceau, **1**
Les Trois Lys, **2**
Le Vésuve, **3**

DAYTRIPS

Timing is important if you want to fully enjoy your visit to Chartres, as everything closes during lunch time, casual visits to the cathedral are not permitted during mass, and English tours are only given twice a day. For an ideal daytrip, arrive around 10 or 10:30am, pick up the invaluable walking-tour map of the *vieille ville* from the tourist office, and head straight for the Musée des Beaux-Arts to catch it before it closes at noon (those particularly interested in stained glass can walk through the smaller Centre International du Vitrail afterward; it closes at 12:30pm). You can start your walking tour in the northward direction after visiting the museum and stop en route for lunch at the beautiful Moulin de Ponceau on the bank of the river. A stop at the Maison Picassiette makes for an enjoyable detour. Finish with a trip to some of the still-spectacular smaller churches, and make it back to the cathedral in time for Malcolm Miller's English tour (p. 347). Visitors can rest at one of the cafes surrounding the cathedral and finish the day with brief visits to any of the small museums.

☑ PRACTICAL INFORMATION

Transportation: Chartres is accessible by frequent trains from **Gare Montparnasse,** Grandes Lignes, on the Nogent-le-Rotrou line. About 1 train per hr. runs during the summer; best to pick up a schedule ahead of time in both summer and winter, as times are irregular. (50-75min.; round-trip €25, under 25 and seniors €19.40, under 12 €12.50. Discount of 20-40% available if bought up to 2 weeks ahead of time.) To reach the cathedral from the train station, walk straight along av. Jehan de Beauce to pl. de Châtelet and turn left into the place, right on rue Ste-Même, and left on rue Jean Moulin (head toward the massive spires).

Tourist Office: Located in front of the cathedral's main entrance at pl. de la Cathédrale (☎02 37 18 26 26; www.chartres-tourisme.com). Helps find accommodations (€2 surcharge) and supplies visitors with a free and helpful map that includes a walking tour and a list of restaurants, hotels, and sights. For those with difficulty walking or who want a relaxed tour of the town, *le petit train* Chart'train runs late Mar. to early Nov. with 35min. narrated tours (in French and English) of the old city. (☎02 37 25 88 50). Tours begin in front of the tourist office every hr. starting at 10:30am and running until 6pm. €6, under 12 €3. English-language walking tours (1hr.) depart from the tourist office every Sa from July-Aug. at 4:15pm (€5, under 14 €3.50, young children free). Audio guide of the *vieille ville* (1hr.) available for €5.50, and €3 for the second. Tourist office open Apr.-Sept. M-Sa 9am-7pm, Su and holidays 9:30am-5:30pm; Oct.-Mar. M-Sa 9am-6pm, Su and holidays 9:30am-5pm. Closed Jan. 1 and Dec. 25.

◖ FOOD

▨ **Le Moulin de Ponceau,** 21/23 rue de la Tannerie (☎02 37 35 30 05; www.lemoulinde-ponceau.fr). Located on one of the lower medieval stone landings along the stream, this classic French restaurant is worth every penny. *Menu dégustation* €51, 3-course *menus* at €38. Single entrée €13, plat €20. Make reservations before visiting Chartres—you'll regret it if you don't. Open daily 12:15-2pm and 7:30-9:30pm. Closed Su evenings in the summer. Oct. 1-Mar. 31, closed W and Sa lunch and Su dinner. AmEx/MC/V. ❸

Épicerie de la Place Billard, 19 rue des Changes (☎02 37 21 00 25). A friendly, inexpensive grocery store that sells basics alongside bottles of perfumed *limonade* (a fizzy drink) and flavored *sirops* (€6). Choose from over 40 flavors of *limonade* (€5), ranging from cotton candy to violet. Open M-Sa from 6:30am-7:30pm and Su 6am-6pm. ❶

Les Trois Lys, 3 rue Porte Guillaume (☎02 37 28 42 02). This casual *crêperie,* right by the river and just off the walking tour, serves a formidable assortment of *crêpes* (€2-6.50) and galettes for a delicious price (€5.50-8.50). Try the salade Sud-Ouest (smoked duck, *foie gras*, apples, and greens; €10). Open Tu-Sa noon-2pm and 7-10pm. Reservations suggested F-Sa evenings. MC/V. ❶

Le Vesuve, 30 pl. des Halles (☎02 37 21 56 35). Good food at reasonable prices. A variety of pizzas baked on bread so good it must be French (€9-12). Salads piled high with cheese and veggies (€9-14). Wine €2-8. Beer €2-4. Open M-Th and Su 10:30am-11pm and F-Sa 10:30am-11:30pm. MC/V. ❷

👁 SIGHTS

THE CATHEDRAL

☎02 37 21 75 02; www.cathedrale-chartres.com. Call the tourist office for info on concerts in the cathedral, the annual student pilgrimage in late May, Chartres in Lights in mid-summer, and other events throughout the year. English-language audio guides available at the gift shop (€3.50, €4.50, €6.50, depending on tour) require a piece of identification as a deposit. English tours of the cathedral by Malcolm Miller (see below) begin outside the gift shop in the cathedral. 1hr. Easter to early Nov. M-Sa noon and 2:45pm; call ☎02 37 28 15 58 for tour availability during winter months. €10, students and children €5.

The Cathédrale de Chartres is the best-preserved medieval church in Europe, having miraculously escaped major damage during the French Revolution and WWII. A patchwork masterpiece of Romanesque and Gothic design, the cathedral was constructed by generations of masons, architects, and artisans. Its sheer size dominates the town—with spires visible from most locations—and its place in French history is equally as prominent. It was here, for example, that Henri IV was crowned in 1594 (see **Life and Times,** p. 63). Approaching from the pl. de la Cathédrale, you can see the discrepancy between the two towers: the one on the left, finished in 1513, is Late Gothic (or Flamboyant); the one on the right, built just before the 1194 fire, is Romanesque and octagonal (the tallest of its kind still standing). The statues of the **Portale Royale** present an assembly of Old Testament figures. The 13th-century **Porche du Nord** depicts the life of Mary, while the **Porche du Sud** depicts the life of Christ.

The only English-language tours of the cathedral are given by ◆**Malcolm Miller,** an authority on Gothic architecture who has been leading visitors through the church for over 40 years. His presentations on the cathedral's history and symbolism are intelligent, witty, and enjoyable for visitors of all ages. If you can, take both his morning and afternoon tour—no two are alike.

FROM THE ROAD

FLYING WHAT?

"Those," he crooned, "are the flying buttresses." As Malcolm Miller gazed lovingly up at Chartres Cathedral, I envied the tenderness in his voice as he spoke to the tour group.

Call me ignorant, but up until this fateful tour of Chartres I could not have named even one architectural property belonging to a cathedral. And call me juvenile, but the term "buttress" is funny. No matter what it is referencing. Further investigation revealed that a flying buttress is actually not something to be taken lightly—figurative or literally.

Used since the Romans, a flying buttress is an arc connecting a load-bearing wall with a wall outside the building, removing stress from the building. Before the heyday of flying buttresses, the heavy stone that made up church walls required a great deal of support and it was difficult to create windows. Churchgoers were therefore left in the dark. In the 12th century, architects began to realize the decorative appeal of the flying buttress and incorporated it into churches across Europe. We therefore have the buttresses to thank for the beautiful stained glass we can still in Chartres today.

I still laugh when I hear the term buttress. Buttress. I can't help it. But also have a newfound respect, and I feel grateful to M Miller—and the you-know-whats—for shedding some light.

—Sara Ashburn

SANCTA CAMISIA. The year after he became emperor in AD 875, Charlemagne's grandson—unfortunately named Charles the Bald—donated to Chartres the **Sancta Camisia,** the cloth believed to have been worn by the Virgin Mary when she gave birth to Christ. Although a church dedicated to Mary had existed on the site as early as the mid-700s, the emperor's bequest required a new cathedral to accommodate the growing number of pilgrims. Thousands journeyed to the church to kneel before the sacred relic in hope that it would heal them and answer their prayers. The sick were nursed in the crypt below the sanctuary. The powers of the relic were confirmed in AD 911 when the cloth supposedly saved the city from invading Goths and Vikings; the Viking leader Rollon converted to Christianity and became the first Duke of Normandy. Today, the relic is on display in the back of the church on the left-hand side.

STAINED GLASS. At a time when books were rare and the vast majority of people illiterate, the cathedral served as a multimedia teaching tool. Most of the 172 stained-glass windows date from the 13th century and were preserved through both World Wars by heroic town authorities, who dismantled over 2000 sq. m of glass and stored the windows pane by pane in Dordogne. The famous *Blue Virgin, Tree of Jesse,* and *Passion and Resurrection of Christ* windows are among the surviving originals. The medieval merchants who paid for the windows are represented in the lower panels, which provide a record of daily life in the 13th century. The windows are characterized by a stunning color known as "Chartres blue," which has not been reproduced in modern times. The center window depicts the story of Christ from the Annunciation to the ride into Jerusalem. Stories read from bottom to top, left to right.

LABYRINTH. The windows of Chartres often distract visitors from the treasure below their feet: a winding labyrinth pattern that is carved into the floor in the rear of the nave. Designed in the 13th century, the labyrinth was laid out for pilgrims as a substitute for a journey to the Holy Land. By following this symbolic journey on their hands and knees, the devout would enact a symbolic voyage to Jerusalem. Now the labyrinth is uncovered on Fridays.

TOUR JEHAN-DE-BEAUCE. The adventurous, the athletic, and the non-claustrophobic can climb the narrow staircase to the cathedral's north tower, Tour Jehan-de-Beauce (named after its architect), for a stellar view of the cathedral roof, the flying buttresses, and the city below. If you don't make it all the way to the top, the first viewing platform offers a slightly obstructed but nonetheless impressive sight. (☎02 37 21 75 02. Open May-Aug. M-Sa 9:30am-12pm and 2-5:30pm, Su 2-6pm; Sept.-Apr. M-Sa 9:30am-12:30pm and 2-5pm, Su 2-5pm; last entrance 30min. before closing. Access to roof structure May-Aug. starting at 4pm, Sept.-Apr., Sa-Su and school holidays starting at 3pm. Tours of the upper stained-glass windows available upon request. Closed Jan. 1 and 5 and Dec. 25. €6.50, ages 18-25 €4.50, under 18 free.)

CRYPT. Visitors may enter the 110m long subterranean crypt only as part of a guided tour. Parts of the crypt, including a well down which Vikings tossed the bodies of their victims during raids, date back to the 9th century. Information sheets in English are available at the La Crypte store. ☎02 37 21 56 33. Tours (in French) leave from La Crypte store, opposite the cathedral's south entrance at 18, Cloître Notre Dame. English leaflets available. (☎02 37 21 56 33. French-language tours 30min. Apr.-Oct. M-Sa 11am (except bank holidays), 2:15pm, 3:30pm, 4:30pm; Nov.-Mar. M-Sa 11am and 4:15pm (except bank holidays); additional 5:15pm tour June 22-Sept. 21. €2.70, students €2.10, under 7 free. Groups should call ahead ☎02 37 21 75 02.)

ELSEWHERE IN THE CATHEDRAL. Inside the church, the intricate Renaissance choir screen, begun by Jehan de Beauce in 1514, depicts the life of the Virgin Mary. The lovely, candlelit shrine to "Notre Dame de Pilier" is near the Sancta Camista. Both are worth a visit.

OTHER SIGHTS

MUSÉE DES BEAUX-ARTS. The Musée des Beaux-Arts is housed in the former Bishop's Palace, which is itself an impressive sight. Built in the 17th and 18th centuries (on a site occupied by bishops since the 11th century), the palace houses an eclectic collection of painting, sculpture, and furniture, including works by Vlaminck, Navarre, and Soutine. A harpsichord collection dating back to the 17th century and a collection of Oceanic art are also on display. The multi-terraced park is perfect for a picnic. It includes a miniature labyrinth and plenty of shady spots overlooking the town. *(29, Cloître Notre-Dame. Behind the cathedral. ☎ 02 37 36 41 39. Open May-Oct. M and W-Sa 10am-noon and 2-6pm, Su 2-6pm; Nov.-Apr. M and W-Sa 10am-noon and 2-5pm, Su 2-5pm, last entry 30min. before closing. Closed Jan. 1, May 1 and 8, Nov. 1 and 11, and Dec. 25. €2.50, students and seniors €1.50, under 12 free.)*

OTHER MUSEUMS. Chartres has a number of small museums that cater to specific interests. The small **Centre International du Vitrail,** 5 rue du Cardinal Pie, housed in a small 13th-century barn once used by the clergy, hosts two temporary exhibitions on stained glass each year. *(☎ 02 37 21 65 72; www.centre-vitrail.org. Open M-F 9:30am-12:30pm and 1:30-6pm, Sa 10am-12:30pm and 2:30-6pm, Su 2:30-6pm. €4, students €3, under 14 free. English-language tours available upon reservation (€6.50-17.50).* The **Maison Picassiette,** 22 rue du Repos, is an extraordinary house covered entirely in mosaic tiles, inside and out. *(☎ 02 37 34 10 78. Open Apr.-Oct. M and W-Sa 10am-noon and 2-6pm, Su 2-6pm. €4.50, students €2.50; combination ticket with the Musée des Beaux-Arts €6, students €3.)* There is also a substantial natural history museum, the **Muséum des Sciences Naturelles et de Préhistoire,** 5bis bd. de la Courtille. *(☎ 02 37 88 43 86. Open July to mid-Sept. and school holidays M-Sa 2-6pm; mid-Sept. to June W and Su 2-5pm. Free.)* The **Maison de l'Archéologie,** 1 rue de l'Étroit Degré, has a fascinating collection of archaeological finds relating to the history of the town. *(☎ 02 37 30 99 38. Open Oct.-June W and Su 2-5pm and by appointment; July-Sept. M and W-Su 2-6pm. Closed Dec. 19-Jan. 8 and May 1, July 14 and Aug. 15. €1.50; under 18, students, disabled persons free.)* The **Conservatoire de l'Agriculture COMPA,** Pont de Mainvilliers, the largest agricultural museum in France, displays a huge array of tractors and other farm machinery, as well as one temporary exhibit at a time, on subjects like horses and farm life. *(☎ 02 37 84 15 00; www.lecompa.com. Open Tu-F 9am-12:30pm and 1:30-6pm, Sa-Su and holidays 10am-12:30pm and 1:30-7pm. €4, students €3, ages 6-18 €1.50, under 6 free. French-language guided tours holidays, Sa and Su 11am, 3pm, 5pm.)*

CHURCHES. All three churches are on the tourist office's walking tour. All hours listed are tentative. Rebuilt in the 16th century, the feudal **Église St-Aignan,** on rue des Greniers, hosts summer concerts and has magnificent ceiling frescoes, a true rarity. *(Open M-F 10-noon and 2-5:30pm, Sa 2-5pm. Mass Su 10:30am, Tu-F 7am, M and Sa 9am.)* The 12th-century Romanesque **Église St-André** sits on rue St-André on the banks of the Eure River. *(Open daily 10am-noon and 2-6pm.)* Once part of a Benedictine monastery, the **Église St-Pierre** on pl. St-Pierre, is a 12th-century Gothic masterpiece. *(Open daily 10am-noon and 2-6pm, mass at 10:30am.)*

MONUMENT TO JEAN MOULIN. This monument to WWII hero Jean Moulin consists of a giant stone hand gripping the hilt of a broken sword. Moulin, who was Prefect of Chartres before the war, attempted suicide to avoid signing a Nazi document accusing French troops of atrocities. Tortured and killed by the Gestapo in 1943, he was eventually buried in the Panthéon. The monument is included on tourist office's walking tour. *(On rue Jean Moulin off bd. de la Résistance.)*

DAYTRIPS

FONTAINEBLEAU

More digestible and less crowded than Versailles, the Château de Fontaine-bleau achieves nearly the same grandeur while preserving a distinct charm among the great royal châteaux. With lush gardens and luxurious apartments, the estate ranks among the best daytrips from Paris. French kings hunted on these grounds since the 12th century, when the exiled Thomas Becket con-secrated Louis VII's manor chapel. In 1528, François I rebuilt the castle to be closer to the game he loved to hunt, and introduced Renaissance art to France with masterfully rendered galleries and frescoes he commissioned for his gal-lery. A great patron of the arts, François sought out Italian artists to design his Fontainebleau, among them Leonardo Da Vinci. Since then, Fontainebleau has hosted a number of epic events: Louis XIII was born here in 1601, Louis XIV revoked the Edict of Nantes here in 1685, and Louis XV was married here in 1725. In 1814, Napoleon signed his abdication and bid goodbye to the Empire from the central courtyard, now called the Cour des Adieux in his honor.

🛈 PRACTICAL INFORMATION

Transportation: Hourly trains from Gare de Lyon on the banlieue sud-est line (45min., €16 round-trip; keep your ticket to be punched on the train). At Gare de Lyon, follow signs to the Grandes Lignes, and buy your ticket from the **"Billets Île de France"** coun-ter. From the station, Veolia (☎01 64 22 23 88) runs buses (€1.50) after each train arrival from Paris; take **bus "A"** in direction "Château-Lilas" and get off at the château stop in front of the tourist office. Otherwise, the château is a 25min. walk away (follow the signs from the station), through the tiny towns of Avon and Fontainebleau.

Tourist Office: 4 rue Royal (☎01 60 74 99 99; www.fontainebleau-tourisme.com). Turn right from château entrance and left up rue Royal. Finds accommodations, organizes tours of the village, sells audio tours of the château's exterior, and distributes maps of Fontainebleau and Barbizon. Open May-Oct. M-Sa 10am-6pm, Su 10am-1pm and 2-5:30pm; Nov.-Apr. M-Sa 10am-6pm, Su 10am-1pm.

🍴 FOOD

The bistros immediately surrounding the château are not the only dining options when visiting Fontainebleau. Walk a couple of minutes into town, fol-lowing rue de Ferrare, and you'll find several quality establishments serving up traditional French cuisine. There are also many *patisseries*, *boulangeries*, and pizza and crêpe places along rue Grande and rue de France.

Le Caveau des Ducs, 24 rue de Ferrare (☎01 64 22 05 05; www.lecaveaudesducs.com). A medieval-style bistro serving up traditional fare; expect foie gras, *terrine,* salmon, and *magret de canard.* Menus €24-41. Classic desserts €7-8. Giant salads €10-20. Open daily noon-2pm and 7-10:30pm. AmEx/MC/V. ❸

La Petite Alsace, 26 rue de Ferrare (☎01 64 23 45 45). As the name implies, this tra-ditional restaurant serves up hearty Alsacian specialties like *choucroute, Flammenkuch,* and of course, beer. Lunch *formule* €12.50. *Entrées* €6-7. *Plats* €14-21. Open daily M-F noon-2pm and 7-10:30pm, Su noon-2:30pm and 7-10:30pm. AmEx/MC/V. ❸

🗺 SIGHTS

CHÂTEAU DE FONTAINEBLEAU

☎01 60 71 50 60 or 01 60 71 50 70; www.musee-chateau-fontainebleau.fr. *Château open Apr.-Sept. M and W-Su 9:30am-6pm; Oct.-Mar. 9:30am-5pm. Gardens and courtyard open Nov.-Feb. 9am-5pm; May-Sept. 9am-7pm; Oct. 9am-6pm. Last entry 45min. before closing. Wheelchair accessible. Free. Audioguide €8, ages 18-25 €6, under 18 €1. Admission including audioguide and 1hr. guided tour of petits appartements €12.50, ages 18-25 €11, under 18 €5. Call ahead for tour schedule. Admission to Musée Chinois de l'Impératrice Eugénie is included, but sometimes closed due to low staffing, so call ahead. AmEx/MC/V.*

GRANDS AND PETITS APPARTEMENTS. Throughout the eight centuries that French kings lived here, Fontainebleau experienced a number of epic historical events and impressive architectural innovations, both of which have been documented in the decor of the **Grands Appartements.** The **Celebration Gallery** and **Gallery of Plates** both commemorate Fontainebleau's noteworthy history: the former, commissioned by Napoleon III, through large frescoes and paintings; the latter, designed by Dubreuil, through 128 porcelain plates fitted into the woodwork. The castle's most famous room, the **Galerie de François I** both glorifies the king's royal egotism and serves as a testament to his patronage of the arts. Peppered with "F"s, the royal *fleurs de lis,* and François's personal salamander emblem, the *galerie* boasts vivid mythological frescoes glorifying François's line and French royalty. Meanwhile, Henri II's legacy pervades throughout his ballroom; note the "H"s for Henri, and the entwined "C"s for his wife Catherine de Medici—which could also be "D"s for Diane de Poitiers, his mistress. It was here that Richelieu was knighted and the Duc d'Orleans (Louis-Philippe's son) was wed in 1837. The **Gallery of Diana** holds 16,000 volumes from Napoleon's original library, while every queen and empress of France since Marie de Médici has slept in the gold-and-green **Empress's Bed Chamber;** the gilded wood bed was built for Marie-Antoinette. Napoleon, in all his humility, outfitted the **Throne Room** with maroon and gold; today it is the only existing throne room in France that is still furnished. He also had two bedrooms, though he rarely slept: the first, a monument to both his narcissism and eroticism, is sandwiched between two mirrors, while the second is more austere, containing a narrow military bed. In the Emperor's private room, known today as the **Abdication Chamber,** Napoleon signed off his empire in 1814 before bidding farewell to his troops in the château's entry courtyard. The tour ends with the impressive 16th-century **Trinity Chapel,** with soaring vaulted ceilings and more Italian frescoes illustrating the *Redemption of Man.* The **Petits Appartements** feature the private rooms of Napoleon and the Empress Josephine, as well as the impressive **Map Room** and **Galerie des Cerfs;** they can be seen only by guided tour.

MUSÉE NAPOLÉON. The Musée Napoléon features an extensive collection of the Emperor's personal effects, including his toothbrush, tiny shoes, field tent, and gifts from European monarchs. (☎*01 60 71 50 60. Only open to guided 1hr. tours; average of 8 per day, but call ahead for exact tour schedule; in French.)*

⬛GARDENS. Fontainebleau's serene **Jardin Anglais** and **Jardin de Diane** shelter quiet grottoes guarded by statues of the huntress Diana. The **Étang des Carpes,** a carp-filled pond, can be explored by rowboat. (☎*01 64 22 92 61 or 01 81 50 09 20. Boat rental available on an irregular basis. Coach driving in the park, €4, children €3.)* The lake was a swamp, which François I altered into an ornamental body of water. On the outskirts of the garden is a 1200m canal perfect for picnicking. The **Forêt de Fontainebleau** is a wooded 20,000-hectare preserve with hiking trails, bike paths, and rock-climbing. Find maps at the tourist office or in the château.

CHANTILLY

The French don't call whipped cream "Chantilly" for nothing—this 14th- to 19th-century château is as whimsical and fluffy as the delicious dessert supposedly invented on its grounds. An amalgam of Gothic extravagance, Renaissance geometry, and flashy Victorian ornamentalism, the triangular-shaped château is surrounded by a moat, lakes, canals, and the elegantly simple Le Nôtre gardens. Between the architecturally masterful **Grandes Écuries** (stables) and the world-class **Musée Condé**, it's a wonder that Chantilly has stayed a hidden treasure for so long. The whole package makes for a delightful foray into the French countryside; just 30min. from the city, visitors can stroll through the dense woodland surrounding the castle and hear nothing but the melodious singing of the **tilleul**, the bird from which the town derives its name.

A Roman citizen named Cantilius originally built his villa here, and a succession of medieval lords added elaborate fortifications. In the 17th century, Louis XIV's cousin, the Grand Condé, commissioned a château and asked André Le Nôtre to create the gardens. It was while the Prince played at peasantry in these magnificent grounds that the now-famed *crème chantilly* was invented. Though the original castle was razed during the revolution, the Duc d'Aumale (King Louis-Philippe's fifth son) rebuilt it in the 1870s, complete with the eclectic facade, modern wrought-iron grillwork, copies of Michelangelo marbles, lush greenery, and extravagant entrance hall you see today.

PRACTICAL INFORMATION

Transportation: Take the train from the Gare du Nord RATP (Grand Lignes) to Chantilly Gouvieux (up to 35min., approximately every hr. 6am-10pm, round-trip €14, under 25 €11). Schedule varies with season. The château is a scenic 25min. walk from the train station—go straight up rue des Otages about 50m, and the well-marked path (1.5km) runs directly through the woodland opposite. Alternatively, by road (2km), turn left on av. du Maréchal Joffre, and then right on rue de Connetable, the town's main street. There is also a free but irregular *navette* (shuttle) service; catch one just to the left as you exit the train station. Approximately every hr. M-Sa until 6pm.

Tourist Office: 60 av. du Maréchal Joffre (☎03 44 67 37 37; www.chantilly-tourisme. com). From the train station, walk straight up rue des Otages about 50m. Offers brochures and maps. The tourist office can also call you a taxi (€6; ☎03 44 57 10 03) or rent you a bike to explore the town and caste grounds (€10 per 1/2-day, €15 per day). Open May-Sept. M-Sa 9:30am-12:30pm and 1:30-5:30pm, Su 10am-1:30pm. Oct.-Apr. M-Sa 9:30am-12:30pm and 1:30-5:30pm.

FOOD

Rue de Connetable runs through the middle of the town of Chantilly to the Grandes Écuries, offering a number of reasonable dining options—cafes, *crêperies*, and *boulangeries*. Near the entrance to the château grounds, you'll find ice cream and sandwich stands, while the château itself has a pricey restaurant. In the gardens, you'll find fresh farm-style fare at **Le Hameau** (☎03 44 57 46 21 or 03 44 56 28 23). From the château, bear left and go down the stairs toward the fountains; turn right and walk along canal des Morfondus. Cross the canal by one of the two wood-planked bridges and you'll see the restaurant on your right once you clear the woods. The menu offers fresh cheese, salads, *gesiers*, *magret de canard*, *paté*, *terrines* and foie gras—the **assiette gourmande** (€22) is a nice sampler. For dessert (starting at €5), it's chantilly with fruit, chantilly with ice cream, chantilly with pie, or just chantilly. (Beer €5. Plenty of outdoor seating. Reservations suggested in the summer. Open mid-Mar. to mid-Nov. daily noon-6pm; no lunch after 3pm. MC/V.)

🜰 SIGHTS

CHÂTEAU, GARDENS, AND MUSÉE CONDÉ. Maps of the gardens suggest a walking tour of the grounds, but wandering is just as effective. A bike can help you explore the château's 115 hectares of parks and grounds. Directly in front of the château, the gardens' central expanse is designed in the French formal style, with neat rows of carefully pruned trees, statues, and geometric pools. To the left, hidden within a forest, the Romantic English garden attempts to re-create untamed nature. Here, paths meander around pools where lone swans glide across the surface. Windows carved into the foliage allow you to see fountains in the formal garden as you stroll. To the right, the gardens hide an idyllic play-village *hameau* (hamlet), the inspiration for Marie-Antoinette's hamlet at Versailles. Farther in, a statue of Cupid reigns over the "Island of Love." Recent additions include the kangaroo enclosure—the 15 or so wallabies gathered in the far right corner of the formal gardens—and a labyrinth, near the hamlet; both represent a move back toward the former royal flare.

Chantilly's biggest attraction lies inside the château: the spectacular **Musée Condé** houses the Duc d'Aumale's private collection of pre-modern paintings and is one of only two museums in France to boast three Raphaels (the other is the Louvre). The sky-lit picture galleries contain 800 paintings; 3000 drawings; and hundreds of engravings, sculptures, and tapestries, among them works by Titian, Corot, Botticelli, Delacroix, Reynolds, Watteau, and Ingres. Marble busts and drawings of royals and nobles attest to the château's illustrious litany of owners: the powerful noble Montmorency family, and the royal Bourbon and Condé princes. Following the Duke's will, the paintings and furniture are arranged as they were over a century ago, in the distinctively 19th-century frame-to-frame (academic) style. But the Musée's absolute gem is the tiny velvet-walled **sanctuary;** this hidden gallery contains what the Duke himself considered the finest works in his collection: illuminated manuscripts by Jean Fouquet, a painting by Fra Filippo Lippi, and two Raphaels. Alas, the museum's two most valuable pieces, a **Gutenberg Bible** and the illuminated manuscripts of the **Très Riches Heures** (1410), are too fragile to be kept in public view—but a near-perfect digitized facsimile of the latter can be seen in the illustrious library, second only to the Bibliothèque Nationale in prestige. The rest of the château's *appartements* can be visited only by taking a guided tour in French. (☎03 44 62 62 62; www.domainedechantilly.com. *Château open Apr.-Nov. M and W-Su 10am-6pm, gardens until 8pm; Nov.-Mar. M and W-F 10:30am-12:45pm and 2-5pm, Sa-Su and holidays 10:30am-5pm, gardens until 6pm. Gardens €5, large families, seniors, disabled persons, students €4, ages 4-12 €3; to gardens and château (the Musée Condé) €10/8/4. Passe Domaine (château, gardens, Musée Vivant du Cheval) €17, students €14, ages 4-17 €7. Petit trains with 30min. tour of gardens and grounds in French and English €5/3. Audio guides €2 in English and French. Guided visit to private apartments 2-3 times per day, reserve ahead; €5. Program of daily children's activities available at ticket office. AmEx/MC/V.*)

GRANDES ÉCURIES. Another great (if slightly less sweet-smelling) draw to the château is the Grandes Écuries (stables), whose immense marble corridors, courtyards, and facades are masterpieces of 18th-century French architecture. Commissioned by Louis-Henri Bourbon, who hoped to live here when he was reborn as a horse, the Écuries boast extravagant fountains, domed rotundas, and sculptured patios that are enough to make even the most cynical believe in reincarnation. From 1719 to the Revolution, the stables housed 240 horses and hundreds of hunting dogs, and now are home to the **Musée Vivant du Cheval,** an extensive collection (supposedly the largest in the world) of all things equine. In addition to the stables's 30 live horses, donkeys, and ponies, the museum displays saddles, merry-go-rounds, and a horse statue featured in a James Bond film. The museum also hosts equestrian shows (1st Su of month at 4pm) and daily dressage demonstrations. The **Hippodrome** on the premises is a major racetrack: two of France's premier horse races are held here in June. *(On rue Connetable; entrance is through the Jeu de Paume gate, to the right. ☎03 44 57 13 13; www.museevivantducheval.fr. Open Apr. and Sept.-Oct. M and W-F 10:30am-5:30pm, Sa-Su 10:30am-6pm; Nov. and Jan.-Mar. M and W-F 2-5pm, Sa-Su 10:30am-5:30pm; Dec. M, W-F Sa-Su 10:30am-5pm; May-June M-F 10:30am-5:30pm, Sa-Su 10:30am-6pm; July-Aug. M and W-F 10:30am-5:30pm, Sa-Su 10:30am-6pm. Museum €8.50, students €7.50, children €6.50. Educational demonstration equestrian shows Apr.-Oct. daily 11:30am, 3, 4:30pm; Nov.-Mar. M-F 3pm, Sa-Su 11:30am, 3, 4:30pm. Hippodrome matches €3, schedule upon request at the tourist office.)*

LE POTAGER DES PRINCES. The Prince's Kitchen Garden is a cultivated 2-hectare expanse of greenery modeled on the château's original 17th-century working garden. First designed by Le Nôtre as a pheasantry for the Grand Duke Condé in 1682, it was later converted into a "Roman pavilion" of terraced gardens. Abandoned during the Revolution's pruning of excess, the gardens were restored in 2002 to their former verdant glory, this time as a public attraction. Catering mostly to children, the garden is arranged in themed areas, including a fantasy region replete with bridges and grottoes, a romantic and aromatic rose garden, and a *ménagerie* that features goats, squabbling chickens, and over 100 varieties of pheasant. It also hosts occasional concerts and plays by the likes of Shakespeare and Marivaux in the summer months; check website for details. *(☎03 44 57 40 40; www.potagerdesprinces.com. 300m from the stables down rue Connetable toward the town, turn on rue des Potagers; garden is at end of road. Wheelchair-accessible. Open mid-Mar. to mid-Oct. M and W-Su 2-7pm; last entry M and W-F 5:30pm, Sa-Su 6pm. Gardener talks in French for children M and W-F 2:30pm; free with entry. €8, ages 13-17 €7, ages 4-12 €6.)*

GIVERNY

Drawn to the verdant hills, woodsy haystacks, and lily-strewn Epte River, painter Claude Monet and his eight children settled in Giverny in 1883. By 1887, John Singer Sargent, Paul Cézanne, and Mary Cassatt had placed their easels beside Monet's and turned the village into an artists' colony. The cobblestone street that was the setting for Monet's *Wedding March* is instantly recognizable. At the **Fondation Claude Monet,** visitors admire Monet's cheerful home and stroll across his Japanese footbridge over a lily pad-strewn pond. In spite of tourists retracing the steps of the now-famous Impressionists (see **Life and Times,** p. 84), Giverny retains its rustic tranquility.

▐ PRACTICAL INFORMATION

Transportation: From Paris to Vernon: The SNCF runs trains regularly from Paris's Gare St-Lazare to Vernon, the station nearest Giverny. To get to the Gare St-Lazare, take the metro to St-Lazare and follow the signs to the Grandes Lignes. From there, proceed to any ticket line marked "France," or use an SNCF machine to avoid the lines (French credit cards only). To schedule a trip ahead of time, call the SNCF (☎08 36 35 35 35). Round trip around €24, ages 18-25 €18. **From Vernon to Giverny:** The fastest way to Giverny is by bus (☎08 25 07 60 27; 10min.; Tu-Su.) Buses leave every day for Giverny just a few minutes after the train arrives in Vernon, so hurry over. 4 buses per day go from Giverny to Vernon; look for the schedule inside the information office in the train station; €4 return (as many times as you want in a day). You can rent a **bike** (☎02 32 21 16 01) from many of the restaurants opposite the Vernon station for €10 per day, plus deposit. The 6km pedestrian and cyclist path from the Vernon station to Giverny is unmarked. It begins at the dirt road that intersects rue de la Ravine above the highway (free map at most bike rental locations). **Taxis** run from the train station for a flat rate: M-F €10 for up to 3 people; €11 for 4 people; sometimes more on Sa-Su and holidays.

FOOD

Ancien Hôtel Baudy, 81 rue Claude Monet (☎ 02 32 21 10 03, www.giverny.fr). From the Fondation, walk 500m up rue Claude Monet (when facing the Fondation, walk right). In addition to its delicious Normandy-style cuisine, this renovated hotel (once frequented by Monet, Cézanne, and Cassatt) has an exquisite terrace garden. Also on the premises is a reconstructed ivy-covered artist's *atelier*. Menus €22.30. Salads €7.50-13.50. Open Apr.-Oct.Tu-Su 10am-9:30pm. MC/V. ❸

Les Nymphéas, rue Claude Monet (☎02 32 21 20 31). Adjacent to the parking lot opposite the Fondation. After a day of roses and honeybees, visitors can decompress at Les Nymphéas, named after Monet's famous water lilies. The building was originally part of the artist's farm. Cuisine nouvelle-Normandie is served in an indoor terrace decorated with Toulouse-Lautrec posters. *Menu* €20.50, wine €3-4.50. The salade Monet (€11.50) is a masterpiece: mixed greens with mushrooms, smoked salmon, crab, tomatoes, green beans, asparagus, and avocado. Open Apr.-Oct. Tu-Su 9am-5pm. MC/V over €20.

SIGHTS

FONDATION CLAUDE MONET. From 1883 to 1926, Claude Monet, a leader of the Impressionist movement, resided in Giverny. His home, with its thatched roof and pink, crushed brick facade, was surrounded by ponds and immense gardens, two features central to his art. Today, Monet's house and gardens are maintained by the Fondation Claude Monet. From April to July, the gardens overflow with wild roses, hollyhocks, poppies, and fragrant honeysuckle. The **Orientalist Water Gardens** contain the water lilies, weeping willows, and Japanese bridge recognizable from Monet's paintings. To avoid the rush, go early in the morning and, if possible, during the low season. Inside the house, with its big windows and pastel hues, the original decorations have been restored or recreated. Highlights include the artist's cheerful, brimming kitchen and his collection of 18th- and 19th-century Japanese prints. The house also boasts a great view of the gardens from Monet's bedroom window. (*84, r. Claude Monet.* ☎*02 32 51 28 21; www.fondation-monet.com. Open Apr.-Oct. Tu-Su 9:30am-6pm, last entry 5:30pm. €5.50, students and ages 12-18 €4, ages 7-12 €3. Gardens €4.*)

MUSÉE D'ART AMÉRICAIN. The modern Musée d'Art Américain, near the Fondation Monet, is the sister institution of the Museum of American Art in Chicago. It houses a small number of works by American expats like Theodore Butler and John Leslie Breck, who came to Giverny to study Impressionist style. Outside the museum, a garden designed by landscape architect Mark Rudkin features an array of flowers separated by large, rectangular hedges. While not as impressive as Monet's garden, this smaller labyrinth is worth the free visit. It affords a scenic view of **Giverny Hill,** the inspiration for many Impressionist *œuvres*. (*99, r. Claude Monet.* ☎*02 32 51 94 65; www.maag.org. Open Apr.-Oct. Tu-Su and M holidays, 10am-6pm. €5.50; students, seniors, and teachers €4; ages 12-18 years €3; under 12 free. Free the first Su of each month. Audio guides available for €1.50.*)

VAUX-LE-VICOMTE

Nicolas Fouquet, Louis XIV's Minister of Finance, assembled the triumvirate of Le Vau, Le Brun, and Le Nôtre (architect, artist, and landscaper) to build

Vaux-le-Vicomte in 1641. On August 17, 1661, upon the completion of what was then France's most ornate château, Fouquet threw an extravagant party in honor of the Sun King. Louis and his mother Anne of Austria were among the 6000 guests at the event, which premiered poetry by Jean de la Fontaine and a comedy-ballet, *Les Fâcheux*, by Molière. After novelties like elephants wearing crystal jewelry and whales in the canal, the evening concluded with an exhibition of fireworks that featured the King and Queen's coat of arms and pyrotechnic squirrels (Fouquet's family symbol). But the housewarming bash was the beginning of the end for Fouquet. Since his appointment to the office in 1653, the ambitious young Minister of Finance had fully replenished the failing Royal treasury. His own lavish lifestyle, however, sparked rumors of embezzlement that were nourished by jealous underlings like Private Secretary Jean-Baptiste Colbert, Fouquet's eventual successor as master of Vaux-le-Vicomte. The August 17 revelry gave 22-year-old Louis XIV an opportunity to publicly question the Minister's source of income, and shortly after the fête he ordered Fouquet's arrest. In the words of Voltaire, "At six o'clock in the evening, Fouquet was king of France; at two the next morning, he was nothing." In a trial that lasted three years, Fouquet was found guilty of embezzlement and banished from France (just barely escaping a death sentence). Louis XIV, however, overturned the sentence in favor of life imprisonment—the only time in French history that the head of state overruled the court's decision in favor of a more severe punishment. Fouquet was to remain imprisoned at Pignerol, in the French Alps, until his death in 1680. The Fouquet intrigue has been repeatedly dramatized by the popular and literary imagination: Alexandre Dumas, for example, retells the story in *Le Vicomte de Bragelonne.* Some have postulated that Fouquet was the legendary "man in the iron mask," and while evidence refutes the claim, Hollywood's 1999 film *The Man in The Iron Mask* starring Leonardo diCaprio was filmed in part at Vaux-le-Vicomte.

🔊 PRACTICAL INFORMATION

Vaux is one of the most exquisite French châteaux, and it's much less crowded than Versailles, whose construction was based in large part on Vaux. Getting there during the week can be an ordeal, as there is no shuttle service from the train station in Melun to the château 7km away.

Transportation: Take the RER (D line) to Melun from Châtelet-Les Halles, Gare de Lyon, or Gare du Nord (30min.-1hr.; round-trip €14). Then catch a shuttle to the château (€6-8 round-trip, weekends only) or take a taxi (around €15). The château staff will call you a cab for the return trip. By car, take Autoroute A4 and exit at Troyes-Nancy by N104. Head toward Meaux on N36 and follow the signs. The château is about 50km from Paris.

Tourist Office: Service Jeunesse et Citoyenneté, 2 av. Gallieni (☎01 60 56 55 10; www. ville-melun.fr). By the train station in Melun. Information on accommodations and sightseeing, plus free maps. Open Tu-Sa 10am-noon and 2-6pm.

Tour Groups: Several tour companies run trips from Paris to the château with varying frequencies and prices; call ahead to book a trip. **ParisVision** (☎01 42 60 30 01; www. parisvision.com) offers regularly scheduled trips (€25-154). Dinner and visit to candlelight shows Sa at 6pm May-Oct. (€154).

👁 SIGHTS

CHÂTEAU. While Vaux doesn't appear ostentatious when viewed from the front, it is quite Baroque in the back. The garden-side facade is covered with ornate "F"s, squirrels (Fouquet's symbol), and the family motto, *"Quo non ascendet"* (What heights might they not reach). The castle's interior is even more opulent. **Madame Fouquet's**

DAYTRIPS

Closet, once lined with tiny mirrors, was the decorative precedent for Versailles's Hall of Mirrors, while the **Room of the Muses** is one of Le Brun's most famous decorative and detailed displays. The artist had planned to crown the cavernous, Neoclassical **Oval Room** (or **Grand Salon**) with a fresco entitled **The Palace of the Sun,** but Fouquet's arrest halted all decorating activity, and only a single eagle and a patch of sky were painted in to fill the space. Fouquet's successor and great enemy, Colbert, removed even more of his predecessor's mark, seizing the tapestries that once bore Fouquet's menacing squirrels and replacing them with his own adders. Meanwhile, the **King's Bedchamber** boasts a marble-and-gold ceiling featuring an orgy of cherubs and lions circling the centerpiece, Le Brun's *Time Bearing Truth Heavenward.* (☎01 64 14 41 90; www.vaux-le-vicomte.com. Not wheelchair-accessible. Open Mar. 15-Nov. 9 M-F 10am-1pm and 2pm-5:30pm, Sa-Su 10am-5:30pm; Dec. 23-Jan. 7 daily 10am-5:30pm. Admission to château, gardens, and carriage museum €13; students, seniors, and ages 6-16 €10; under 6 free. Candlelight visits (visites aux chandelles) Sa evenings (8-11pm) May to mid-Oct., and F in July and Aug. €16; students, seniors and ages 6-16 €14. Fountains open Apr.-Oct., 2nd and last Sa of each month 3-6pm. Château audio tour with good historical presentation in English; €2.50. Golf carts for rent to the right of the garden from the entrance; €15 per 45min., €18 per hr. AmEx/MC/V.)

GARDENS. The classical French garden was invented at Vaux-le-Vicomte by Le Nôtre, the Sun King's gardener, who became famous for forcing nature to conform to strict geometric patterns. Vaux's multilevel terraces, fountained walkways, and fantastical *parterres* (literally "on the ground;" these are low-cut hedges and crushed stone arranged in arabesque patterns) are still the most exquisite example of 17th-century French gardens. The collaboration of Le Nôtre with Le Vau and Le Brun ensured that the same patterns and motifs were repeated with astonishing harmony in the gardens, the château, and the tapestries inside. But not all is visibly seamless: Vaux owes its most impressive *trompe l'oeil* effect to Le Nôtre's adroit use of the laws of perspective. From the back steps of the château, it looks as if you can see the entire landscape at a glance, but as you walk toward the far end of the garden, the grottoes at the back seem to recede, revealing a sunken canal known as **La Poêle** (the Frying Pan), which is invisible from the château. The **Round Pool** and its surrounding 17th-century statues mark an important intersection: to the left, down the east walkway, are the **Water Gates,** the backdrop for Molière's performance of *Les Fâcheux.* Closer to the château along the central walkway is the **Water Mirror,** which was designed to reflect the building perfectly. A climb to the **Farnese Hercules** earns the best vista of the grounds. The tremendous Hercules sculpture at the top was at the center of Fouquet's trial; in an age when kings enjoyed divine rights to their royalty, the beleaguered Fouquet likened himself to Hercules, the only mortal to become a god. If you don't want to venture that far, a visit to the castle's dome is worth the bird's eye view of the garden as well as the castle's complex (€2). The old stables, **Les Equipages,** also house a surprisingly extensive carriage museum. But by far the best way to see Vaux's gardens is during the ◪**visites aux chandelles,** when the château and grounds are lit up by thousands of candles, and classical music plays through the gardens in imitation of Fouquet's legendary party; arrive around dusk to see the grounds in all their glory.

AUVERS-SUR-OISE

> I am entirely absorbed by these plains of wheat on a vast expanse of hills—like an ocean of tender yellow, pale green, and soft mauve.
> —Vincent van Gogh, 1890

This once-sleepy little hamlet has transformed into a self-proclaimed "Cradle of Impressionism," proud of having hosted famed artists such as Daubigny,

Corot, Daumier, Cézanne, and a certain van Gogh. The 70 canvases van Gogh produced during his 10-week stay in Auvers bear testimony to what he called the "medicinal effect" of this bit of countryside, only 30km northwest of Paris. Fleeing Provence, where he had been diagnosed with depression and possible epilepsy, van Gogh arrived in May 1890 at Auvers-sur-Oise, where he would be treated by a Dr. Gachet. But neither the doctor nor the countryside were enough to lift his depression. On the afternoon of July 27, he set off with his paints to the fields above the village, crawling back into his room that evening with a bullet lodged deep in his chest. Gachet, van Gogh's brother Théo, and even the police had a chance to demand an explanation from the painter as he lay smoking his pipe and bleeding for two days. "Sadness goes on forever," he told his brother, and died. Visitors to this tranquil town will find a number of vistas remarkably unchanged from those portrayed in van Gogh's work. Various festivals and fairs are held here throughout the year; check www.auver-scama.com for more information.

PRACTICAL INFORMATION

Transportation: Take the RER C from Gare d'Austerlitz (☎01 30 36 70 61) toward Pontoise. Disembark at St-Ouens L'Aumone (approx. 1hr.). Switch to the Persan Beaumont Creil line (walk downstairs and change to opposite platform; consult screen for departures) and get off at Gare d'Auvers-sur-Oise (approx. 15min.). €10 round-trip.

Tourist Office: Manoir des Colombières, rue de la Sansonne (☎01 30 36 10 06; www.tourisme.fr/office-de-tourisme/auvers-sur-oise.htm or www.auvers-sur-oise.com). Helpful free walking maps and event brochures. Open Tu-Su Apr.-Oct. 9:30am-12:30pm and 2-6pm, Nov.-Mar. 9:30am-12:30pm and 2-5pm. 1hr. guided tours in French Apr.-Oct. Su 3pm; €6. Free audiovisual guide (15min.) in the office.

SIGHTS

The walk below takes about 2hr. Turn left directly from the train station.

To begin, on the right you'll see the small **Parc van Gogh**, which includes a Zadkine statue of the artist, and offers a shady rest and a great picnicking spot. Farther down on the right is the **Auberge Ravoux** where van Gogh stayed while in Auvers-sur-Oise and where he ultimately killed himself. The **Maison de van Gogh,** 8 rue de la Sansonne, is just around the corner. Though it has little to offer beyond a glimpse of van Gogh's bare room and a pretty (and pretty uninformative) slide show, the cost of admission includes a souvenir "passport" to Auvers-sur-Oise that details the history of the *auberge* and van Gogh's sojourn here. The Maison also gives out information on other museums, walking tours in the region, and discounts to four of the museums. (☎01 30 36 60 60; www.maisondevangogh.fr. Open Mar.-Oct. W-Su 10am-6pm; last entry 5:30pm. Van Gogh's room/Auberge Ravoux €5, ages 12-18 years €3, under 12 free.)

A visit to the **Cimetière d'Auvers**, where van Gogh and his brother Théo are buried, is worth the 15min. walk from the Maison de van Gogh. To get to the cemetery, take the uphill path past the tourist office, following the signs labeled *"Les tombes de Théo et Vincent"*. After the path becomes rue Daubigny, you will reach a narrow staircase on your left. Follow the steps to the elegant **Notre Dame d'Auvers** (open daily 9:30am-6pm), which served as the 12th-century subject of van Gogh's 1890 Église d'Auvers, which currently hangs in the Musée d'Orsay (see **Museums**, p. 265). The entrance to the church is on the left side.

From the right side of the church, take the steep road curving uphill, which levels with a wheat field. The cemetery is on your right, and the tombs are located against the far left wall, covered by an unimpressive ivy bush. Outside

DAYTRIPS

the cemetery, facing the field, take the dirt path to your right labeled *"Château par la Sente du Montier"* to the wheat field where van Gogh painted his *Champs de Blé aux Corbeaux* (Wheatfields with Crows). Turn left at the end of the road and you will see on your right the **Atelier de Daubigny,** 61 rue Daubigny, once the home and studio of pre-Impressionist painter Charles-François Daubigny. (☎01 34 48 03 03; www.atelier-daubigny.com. Open Easter-Nov. Th-Sa 2-6:30pm, Su 11am-6:30pm; closed mid-July to mid-Aug. €5.) Turn right on rue de Léry, and on a side street to the left you'll find the **Musée de l'Absinthe,** 44 rue Alphonse Callé, a tribute to the ⬛potent green liqueur immortalized in various paintings by Degas and Manet. Samples of a legal but much less toxic (read: less fun) version of the supposedly psychedelic drink that van Gogh liked so much are on sale at the museum's small gift shop. (☎01 30 36 83 26. Open Mar. to mid-Sept. W-F 1:30-6pm and Sa-Su 11am-6pm; mid-Sept. to mid-Dec. Sa-Su 11am-6pm. €5, students €4, under 14 free.) From the museum, follow rue de Léry up to the **Château d'Auvers,** which houses a tranquil *orangerie* and a modest collection of engaging Impressionist paintings. (☎01 34 48 48 45; www.chateau-auvers.fr. Open Apr.-Sept. M-F 10:30am-6pm and Sa-Su 10:30am-6:30pm; Oct.-Mar. M-F 10:30am-4:30pm and Sa-Su 10:30am-5:30pm. Closed mid-Dec. to mid-Jan. €12, students and ages 6-18 €8.)

⬛ FOOD

Inexpensive cafes and *crêperies* can be found throughout the town, but visitors willing to splurge should experience the **Auberge Ravoux 4,** 52, rue de Général-de-Gaulle (☎01 30 36 60 60), in all its historical glory. The ultimate van Gogh experience, the restaurant is located in the house where the painter lived and died over 100 years ago. Elaborate glasswork, lace curtains, and old-fashioned wooden benches complement €29 two-course or €37 three-course *menus* of classic French dishes such as 7hr. leg of lamb, beef Bourgignon, and homemade foie gras. (Open W-F noon-3pm for lunch and 3-5pm; Sa-Su first lunch service noon, second lunch service 2:15pm, *salon de thé* 3:20-5pm. Serves dinner only to groups of 30-45; reservations required. Closed Nov.-Feb. AmEx/MC/V.)

DISNEYLAND RESORT PARIS

It's a small, small world, and Disney is hell-bent on making it even smaller. When EuroDisney opened on April 12, 1992, Mickey Mouse, Cinderella, and Snow White were met by the jeers of French intellectuals and the popular press, who called the Disney theme park a "cultural Chernobyl." Resistance has subsided since Walt & Co. renamed it Disneyland Resort Paris and started serving wine. Pre-construction press touted the complex as a vast entertainment and resort center covering an area one-fifth the size of Paris. In truth, the theme park doesn't even measure the size of an *arrondissement*, though Disney owns (and may eventually develop) 600 hectares. Technologically advanced, the special effects on some rides will blow you away. If you have bottomless pockets, indulging in one of the park's seven world-class hotels, like the palatial Disneyland Hotel, may be worth the luxury. For the more frugal—and those with a low tolerance for toddlers—a daytrip will more than suffice.

⬛ PRACTICAL INFORMATION

Catering to both English and French speaking tourists, the park provides detailed bilingual maps at its entrance. The **Guests' Special Services Guide** has info on wheelchair accessibility. For more info on Disneyland Paris, call ☎08 448 008 111, or visit their website at www.disneylandparis.com.

Transportation: Take RER A4 from either Ⓜ Gare de Lyon, Opéra (RER: Auber) or Châtelet-Les Halles (dir. Marne-la-Vallée/Chessy) to the last stop, Ⓜ Marne-la-Vallée-Chessy. Before boarding the train, check the boards hanging above the platform to make sure there's a light next to the Marne-la-Vallée stop and not the Boissy-Saint-Leger stop (40min., departs every 30min., round-trip from Opéra-Auber €12.50). The last train to Paris leaves Disney at 12:20am, but the metro closes just before 1am M-Th and Su, so you'll have to catch an earlier train if your route involves taking a second line home. **TGV** service from de Gaulle reaches the park in a under 10min., making Disneyland Paris easily accessible for travelers with Eurail passes and international visitors (www.tgv.fr. 18 trains per day, €23-30). **Eurostar** trains now run directly between Waterloo Station in London and Disneyland. (☎ 00 44 1233 617 575 from outside the UK, from within the UK 08705 186 186; www.eurostar.co.uk. 1 train per day to and from Disney, 23/4hr., from €250.) By car, take the A4 highway from Paris and get off at Exit 14, marked "Parcs Disney/Bailly-Romainvilliers". Parking €8 per day; 11,000 spaces.

Tickets: Instead of selling tickets, Disneyland Paris issues *passports*, valid for 1 day and available online and at the entrance. *Passports* are also sold at Paris tourist office kiosks (see **Practical Information,** p. 135), FNAC, Virgin Megastores, any Disney Store, many hotels in Paris, and at any of the major stations on RER line A, such as Châtelet-Les Halles, Gare de Lyon, or Charles de Gaulle-Étoile. Any of these options beats buying tickets at the park where unwieldy, long lines dominate. Buy online in advance for the best deals at www.disneylandparis.com.

Admission: A 1-day ticket allows entry to either Disneyland Park or Walt Disney Studios. For an extra €10, you can visit both theme parks. Apr.-Nov. €49, children €31. 2- and 3-day *passports* also available (€110-135, child €92-114); days do not need to be consecutive. Year-long season tickets €89-179; entitles holder to entrance to the 2 parks 300-365 days of the year plus additional reductions on hotel, parking, and shops. Free ▧ **Fastpasses** allow guests to make reservations on attractions, enabling them to cut the standard line at their designated ride time. Print your Fastpass from the Fastpass counters outside each attraction; patrons may only reserve one ride at a time.

Hours: Disneyland Park open Jan. M-F 10am-6pm, Sa 10am-9pm; Su 10am-8pm; Feb. M-F 10am-7pm, Sa 10am-9pm; Su 10am-8pm; Mar., May, and Sept. M-F 10am-7pm, Sa 10am-10pm, Su 10am-9pm; Apr. M-F 10am-8pm, Sa 10am-9pm, Su 10am-8pm; June M-F 10am-8pm, Sa 10am-10pm, Su 10am-9pm; July-Aug. daily 10am-11pm; Oct.-Nov. M-Th 10am-6pm, F 10am-7pm, Sa 10am-10pm, Su 10am-9pm; Dec. M-F 10am-7pm, Sa-Su 10am-10pm. Walt Disney Studios open Feb.-Aug. daily 10am-7pm; Sept.-Jan. M-F 10am-6pm, Sa-Su 10am-7pm.

🜨 SIGHTS

DISNEYLAND PARK. Divided into five areas, each filled to bursting with families, Disneyland Park showcases American cultural imperialism. **Main Street, Frontierland, Adventureland, Fantasyland,** and **Discoveryland** circle around the park's central plaza—a flowery garden in front of **Sleeping Beauty Castle.** Employing old-fashioned streetcars and bubble gum facades, **"Main St., U.S.A."** attempts to recreate the 20th-century charm of small-town America. Giant floats and dancing Disney characters stream down Main Street and pass before Sleeping Beauty Castle weekdays at 4pm and weekends at 5pm during the **Once Upon A Dream Parade.** Carefully choreographed, the parade will delight the young at heart. During the summer, Disney caps off the magical night with fireworks.

The park's main draws, of course, are its 45 rides and attractions. Smaller than its American counterparts, Disneyland Paris feels less overwhelming; the whole park can easily be conquered in a day. Perennial favorites, the slow-moving **Pinocchio's Fantastic Journey** and **Snow White and the Seven Dwarves** recount

Disney classics; colorful and amusing, they are perfect for small children or die-hard fans. For iron-stomached guests seeking more action, **Indiana Jones and the Temple of Peril** and **Space Mountain** are sure to thrill. Passengers ride on a turbulent "rocket-powered" spaceship that climbs, drops, loops, and twists through complete darkness. For a swash-buckling good time, stow away on the **Pirates of the Caribbean** attraction that inspired the 2003 American movie of the same name. **It's A Small World** presents a more peaceful boat ride through a Disney-fied Earth; all smiles and waves, and of course, the miniature inhabitants share the same utopian melody.

WALT DISNEY STUDIOS. More technical than Disneyland Park, Walt Disney Studios features several motor stunt shows daily, an Armageddon special effects exhibit, and an entire building dedicated to the art of Disney animation. Coaster-enthusiasts fret not: the **Rock 'N' Roller Coaster with Aerosmith** is a thrilling indoor coaster with loud music, strobe lights, and dizzying loops. Lines in Walt Disney studios are usually much shorter than those in its sister park, but with good reason: the thrills in this park are few and far between. Children may enjoy an **Animagique** show with Mickey, Donald, and the rest of the gang (daily at 11:30am, 12:25, 1:20, 2:15, 4:30, and 5:25pm).

DAYTRIPS

APPENDIX

CLIMATE

While spring and autumn in Paris have been known to deliver unpredictable precipitation, temperatures throughout the year remain palatably moderate. Summer highs rarely rise above 80°F; winters, while often wet, hardly ever see temperatures colder than 30°F. From October through April, it may be a good-idea to pack outerwear. In all seasons, remember comfortable rain gear.

	AVG. HIGH TEMP.		AVG. LOW TEMP.		AVG. RAINFALL		AVG. NUMBER OF WET DAYS
January	6°C	43°F	1°C	30°F	56mm	2.2 in.	17
February	7°C	45°F	1°C	30°F	46mm	1.8 in.	14
March	12°C	54°F	4°C	40°F	35mm	1.4 in.	12
April	16°C	61°F	6°C	43°F	42mm	1.7 in.	13
May	20°C	68°F	10°C	50°F	57mm	2.2 in.	12
June	23°C	73°F	13°C	55°F	54mm	2.4 in.	12
July	25°C	77°F	15°C	59°F	59mm	2.1 in.	12
August	24°C	75°F	14°C	57°F	64mm	2.5 in.	13
September	21°C	70°F	12°C	54°F	55mm	2.2 in.	13
October	16°C	61°F	8°C	46°F	50mm	2.0 in.	13
November	10°C	50°F	5°C	41°F	51mm	2.0 in.	15
December	7°C	45°F	2°C	36°F	50mm	2.0 in.	16

To convert from degrees Fahrenheit to degrees Celsius, subtract 32 and multiply by 5/9. To convert from Celsius to Fahrenheit, multiply by 9/5 and add 32.

°CELSIUS	-5	0	5	10	15	20	25	30	35	40
°FAHRENHEIT	23	32	41	50	59	68	77	86	95	104

MEASUREMENTS

Like the rest of the rational world, Paris (and the rest of France) uses the metric system. The basic unit of length is the meter (m), which is divided into 100 centimeters (cm) or 1000 millimeters (mm). One thousand meters make up one kilometer (km). Fluids are measured in liters (L), each divided into 1000 milliliters (mL). A liter of pure water weighs one kilogram (kg), the unit of mass that is divided into 1000 grams (g). One metric ton is 1000kg.

MEASUREMENT CONVERSIONS	
1 inch (in.) = 25.4mm	1 millimeter (mm) = 0.039 in.
1 foot (ft.) = 0.305m	1 meter (m) = 3.28 ft.
1 yard (yd.) = 0.914m	1 meter (m) = 1.094 yd.
1 mile (mi.) = 1.609km	1 kilometer (km) = 0.621 mi.
1 ounce (oz.) = 28.35g	1 gram (g) = 0.035 oz.
1 pound (lb.) = 0.454kg	1 kilogram (kg) = 2.205 lb.
1 fluid ounce (fl. oz.) = 29.57mL	1 milliliter (mL) = 0.034 fl. oz.
1 gallon (gal.) = 3.785L	1 liter (L) = 0.264 gal.

LANGUAGE

French is the official language of France, and the French have always been beyond proud of it. *Par example*, Cardinal Richelieu started *L'Académie française* (The French Academy) in 1635, and the establishment's efforts to preserve language's integrity continue to this day. Nevertheless, choice words like *cool* (cool) and *téléphone* (telephone) have crept in, and most people in larger cities—especially the student population—speak at least some English. Knowing elementary French can't hurt, particularly in smaller towns, but don't be surprised if a native interrupts halfway through your butchered *"Comment ça va?"* to ask if you wouldn't prefer conversing in your own tongue.

PHRASEBOOK

THE BASICS		
Hello/Good day	Bonjour	bohn-jhoor
Good evening	Bon soir	bohn-swah
Hi	Salut	sah-lu
Goodbye	Au revoir	oh ruh-vwah
Have a good day/evening	Bonne journée/soirée	buhn jhoor-nay/swah-ray
Yes/No/Maybe	Oui/Non/Peut-être	wee/nohn/p'tet-ruh
Please	S'il vous plaît	see voo play
Thank you	Merci	mehr-see
You're welcome/My pleasure	De rien/Je vous en prie	duh rhee-ehn/jh'voo-zohn-pree
Pardon me	Excusez-moi/Pardon	ex-ku-zay-mwah/pahr-dohn
Go away	Allez-vous en	ah-lay vooz on!
What time do you open/close	Vous ouvrez/fermez à quelle heure	vooz oo-vray/ferh-may ah kel-uhr
Help!	Au secours!	oh suk-oor!
I'm lost	Je suis perdu(e)	jh'swee pehr-du
I'm sorry	Je suis désolé(e)	jh'swee day-zoh-lay
Do you speak English?	Parlez-vous anglais?	par-lay-voo ahn-glay?
I don't understand.	Je ne comprends pas.	jh'ne kohm-prahn pas
JUST BEYOND THE BASICS		
Who/What/When/Where	Qui/Quoi/Quand/Où	kee/kwah/kahn/oo
How/Why	Comment/Pourquoi	ko-mahn/pour-kwah
Speak slowly.	Parlez moins vite.	par-lay mwehn veet
I would like...	Je voudrais...	jh'voo-dray
How much does this cost?	Ça coûte combien?	sa coot comb-yen
Leave me alone.	Laissez-moi tranquille	less-say-mwah trahn-keel
I need help.	J'ai besoin d'assistance.	jhay bezz-wehn dah-see-stahnss
I am (20) years old.	J'ai (vingt) ans.	jhay vehn-tahn.
I don't speak French.	Je ne parle pas français.	jh'ne parl pah frahn-SAY.
My name is ( ). What's your name?	Je m'appelle ( ). Comment vous appelez-vous?	Jh'ma-pell ( ). kuh-mahn voo-za-pell-ay-voo?
What is it?	Qu'est-ce que c'est?	kess-kuh-say?
This one/That one	Ceci/Cela	suh-see/suh-lah
Stop!	Arrêtez!	ahr-eh-tay
Please repeat.	Répétez, s'il vous plaît.	reh-peh-TAY, see voo play.
How do you say ( ) in French?	Comment dit-on ( ) en français?	kuh-mahn deet-ohn ( ) ohn frahn-SAY?
Do you understand?	Comprenez-vous?	kohm-prehn-ay-voo?
I am a student.	Je suis étudiant(e).	jh'sweez eh-too-dee-ahn(t)
Hell is other people.	L'enfer, c'est les autres.	l'ahn-fehr, say lay zoh-truh
EMERGENCY		
Where is the nearest hospital?	Où est l'hôpital le plus proche?	oo ay l'oh-pee-tal luh ploo prohsh

Where is the nearest emergency pharmacy?	Où est la pharmacie de garde la plus proche?	oo ay lah farm-ah-see duh gard lah ploo prohsh
Where is the police station?	Où est la station de police?	oo ay lah stah-si-ohn duh poh-leess
I am ill/hurt.	Je suis malade/blessé(e).	jh'swee mah-lahd/bleh-say
I was attacked.	J'ai été attaqué(e).	jhay ay-tay ah-tah-kay
I was raped.	J'ai été violé(e).	jhay ay-tay vee-oh-lay
I think I broke my arm/my leg/ something.	Je pense que je me suis cassé(e) le bras/le jambe/quelque chose.	jh'pohnss kuh jh'me swee kah-sau luh bra/luh jhahmb/kel-kuh showz
I need a doctor.	J'ai besoin d'un médecin.	jhay buh-zwahn duhn med-sahn
Help me!	Aidez-moi!	eh-day-mwah
Someone stole...	Quelqu'un m'a volé...	kel-kahn mah voh-lay
... my camera.	... mon appareil photo.	mohn a-par-ray foh-toh
... my purse.	... mon sac.	mohn sahk
... my wallet.	... ma portefeuille.	mah port-foy
... my passport.	... mon passport.	mohn pass-pore

GLOSSARY

BOISSONS (DRINKS)			
bière	beer	chocolat chaud	hot chocolate
bouteille de champagne	bottle of champagne	eau platte/gazeuse	flat/sparkling water
café (crème/au lait)	coffee (with cream/milk)	thé	tea
carafe d'eau (du robinet)	pitcher of water (from the tap)	vin rouge/blanc	red/white wine

VIANDE (MEAT)			
agneau	lamb	foie gras d'oie/de canard	goose/duck liver pâté
andouillette	tripe sausage	jambon	ham
bavette	flank (cut of meat)	lapin	rabbit
bœuf	beef	poulet	chicken
brochette	kebab	rillettes	potted meat
canard	duck	saucisson	cooked sausage (like salami)
coq au vin	rooster stewed in wine	saucisse	uncooked sausage
côte	chop (cut of meat)	steak	steak
cuisses de grenouilles	frog legs	steak tartare	raw steak mixed with raw eggs
dinde	turkey	veau	veal
entrecôte	side (cut of meat)	à point	medium
escalope	thin slice of meat	bien cuit	well done
faux-filet	sirloin steak	saignant	rare
coquilles st-jacques	a scallop dish	huîtres	oysters
crevettes	shrimp	moules	mussels
escargots	snail	poisson	fish
homard	lobster	thon	tuna

FRUITS ET LÉGUMES (FRUITS AND VEGETABLES)			
ananas	pineapple	fraise	strawberry
asperge	asparagus	framboise	raspberry
aubergine	eggplant	haricots verts	green beans
champignons	mushrooms	petits poids	peas
chou-fleur	cauliflower	poire	pear
compote de fruits	stewed fruit	poireaux	leeks
cornichon	pickle	pomme	apple
épinards	spinach	pomme de terre	potato
figue	fig	raisins	grapes

MAP INDEX

Bastille (11ème) 384-385
Bastille (12ème) 383
Batignolles (17ème) 390
Belleville and Père Lachaise (20ème) 392
Bois de Boulogne 257
Bois de Vincennes 259
Buttes Chaumont (19ème) 391
Buttes-aux-Cailles and Chinatown (13ème) 386
Canal St. Martin and Surrounds (10ème) 382
Champs-Élysées (8ème) 378-379
Chartes 345
Châtelet-Les Halles (1er & 2ème) 368-369
Invalides (7ème) 376-377
La Villette 294
Latin Quarter and St-Germain (5ème & 6ème), Île de la Cité, and Île St-Louis 374-375
Montparnasse (14ème and 15ème) 388
Montparnasse (14ème) 387
Opéra and Montmartre (9ème & 18ème) 380-381
Paris Neighborhoods XII-XIII
Paris Overview and Arrondissements 366-367
Passy and Auteuil (16ème) 389
Père Lachaise Cemetery 255
Suggested Itinerary: Lesser-Known Wonders 12-13
Suggested Itinerary: Souvenirs of the Belle Époque 16-17
Suggested Itinerary: The Usual Suspects 10-11
Suggested Itinerary: Your Own Moveable Feast 14-15
The Marais (3ème & 4ème) 370-371
Versailles 341

MAP LEGEND

✚ Hospital	✈ Airport	🕌 Mosque
Police	🚌 Bus Station	🏰 Castle
✉ Post Office	🚆 Train Station	🏛 Museum
ⓘ Tourist Office	Ⓜ METRO Station	🏛 Arch
$ Bank	METRO Line	🏠 Hotel/Hostel
Embassy/Consulate	RER RER Station	🍎 Food & Drink
▪ Sight or Point of Interest	🚻 Public Restroom	🛍 Shopping
☎ Telephone Office	✝ Church	★ Nightlife
Theater	✡ Synagogue	💻 Internet Café

Pedestrian Zone
Steps

Park

Water

Forest

The Let's Go compass always points NORTH.

Paris: Overview and Arrondissements

○ SIGHTS

Arc de Triomphe,	1	B2
Bal du Moulin Rouge,	2	C2
Bibliothèque Nationale-Site François Mitterrand,	3	E5
Catacombs,	4	C5
Champs de Mars,	5	B4
Cimetière de Montmartre,	6	C2
Cimetière de Passy,	7	B3
Cimetière du Montparnasse,	8	C5
Cimetière du Père Lachaise,	9	F3
Eiffel Tower,	10	B3
Hôtel de Ville,	11	D4
Hôtel des Invalides,	12	C4
Institut du Monde Arabe,	13	D4
Mémorial de la Déportation,	14	D4
Opéra Bastille,	15	E4
Opéra Garnier,	16	C3
Palais Chaillot,	17	B3
Palais de la Découverte,	18	C3
Palais de Tokyo,	19	B3
Palais Royal,	20	D3
Panthéon,	21	D4
Place de la Bastille,	22	E4
Place des Vosges,	23	E4
Place du Trocadéro,	24	B3
Théâtre National de l'Odéon,	25	D4
Tour Montparnasse,	26	C5

🏛 MUSEUMS

Archives Nationales,	27	D3
Centre Pompidou,	28	D3
Grand Palais,	29	C3
Louvre,	30	D3
Maison de Victor Hugo,	31	E4
Musée Camavalet,	32	E4
Musée d'Art et d'Histoire de Judaïsme,	33	D3

Musée d'Orsay,	34	C3
Musée de Cluny,	35	D4
Musée de l'Orangerie,	36	C3
Musée du Vin,	37	B4
Musée Picasso,	38	E3
Museum Nationale d'Histoire Naturelle,	39	D5
Petit Palais,	40	C3

🛐 CHURCHES

Auteuil,	41	A4
Basilique du Sacré Coeur,	42	D2
Église St-Sulpice,	43	D4
Madeleine,	44	C3
Notre Dame,	45	D4
Passy,	46	A4

☪ MOSQUES

La Mosquée,	47	D5

❀ GARDENS & PARKS

Jardin des Plantes,	48	D4
Jardin des Tuileries,	49	C3
Jardins du Luxembourg,	50	D4
Parc des Buttes Chaumont,	51	E2
Parc La Villette,	52	F1
Parc Monceau,	53	C2

○ GOVT. BUILDINGS

American Embassy,	54	C3
Assemblée Nationale,	55	C3
Bourse de Commerce,	56	D3
British Embassy,	57	C3
Bureau des Objets Trouvés (Lost and Found),	58	B5
Central Post Office,	59	D3
Ministère des Finances,	60	E5

Palais de Justice,	61	D4
UNESCO,	62	B4

○ SCHOOLS

École Militaire,	63	B4
École Normal Supérieure,	64	D4
La Sorbonne,	65	D4

🛍 SHOPPING

Galeries Lafayette,	66	C3
Les Halles,	67	D3

🚉 TRAIN STATIONS

Gare de l'Est,
Gare de Lyon,
Gare du Nord,
Gare Montparnasse,
Gare St-Lazare,

APPENDIX

17ème
16ème
15ème
14ème
8ème
7ème

Bois de Boulogne

PORTE DE CLICHY

Périphérique Nord

bd. Ney
bd. Ney
bd. Macdonald

18ème

Championnet
Ordener
rue Duhesme
rue de la Chapelle
rue de l'Evangile
rue de l'Ourcq
rue de l'Ourcq
av. Corentin Cariou

Canal de l'Ourcq

av. Jean Lolive

bd. Sérurier

52

rue Archereau

rue de Flandre

Junot
42
bd. de Clignancourt
rue des Poissonniers
rue Marx Dormoy
rue Riquet
rue d'Aubervilliers

bd. d'Indochine
bd. d'Algérie

Trois Frères
Abbesses
bd. de Rochechouart
PIGALLE
av. Trudaine
Chapelle
PL. DE STALINGRAD

Bassin de la Villette
rue de Crimée
av. Jean Jaurès

19ème

bd. Mortier

9ème
Châteaudun
rue La Fayette
Poissonnière
70

rue Armand Carel
av. Secrétan

rue David d'Angiers

58

Canal St-Martin
PL. DU COLONEL FABIEN

Montmartre
Poissonnière
bd. de Strasbourg
rue du Château d'eau
rue de Magenta

10ème

bd. de la Villette

rue des Pyrénées

PL. GAMBETTA

2ème
Réaumur
rue Etienne Marcel
rue St-Denis
rue du Temple

du Temple
bd. de Belleville
rue St-Maur

av. Gambetta

1er
rue du Louvre
56
59
St-Honoré
rue de Rivoli
67

PL. DE LA RÉPUBLIQUE

3ème
28
33
27
38

av. du Faubourg
rue St-Martin
blvd. St-Martin

av. de la République
rue du Faubourg
av. Parmentier

11ème

rue de Oberkampf

av. Gambetta

20ème

30
Louvre
Pont Neuf
61
Île de la Cité

32
31
23

rue de Rivoli
rue du Temple
bd. Beaumarchais
rue du Chemin Vert

rue du Voltaire
rue de la Roquette

bd. de Ménilmontant

Périphérique Est

11
45
14
4ème
St-Louis

22
15

rue du Faubourg
St-Antoine
bd. Henri IV

rue de Charonne

av. Philippe Auguste

bd. de Charonne

bd. Davout

ST-MICHEL
35
MAUBERT
25
Seine
St-Germain

13
65
LUXEMBOURG
21
64
rue Cuvier

5ème
48
47
39

Pont de Sully
Pont d'Austerlitz

av. Ledru Rollin

rue de Montreuil
St-Antoine
NATION

Cours de Vincennes

PL. DE LA NATION

bd. Diderot
bd. Picpus

PORT ROYAL
bd. de Port Royal
bd. Arago

rue Buffon
Hilaire
rue Censier
rue C. Bernard
rue Monge

GARE D'AUSTERLITZ

69

av. Daumesnil

12ème

PL. FÉLIX ÉBOUÉ

av. Daumesnil

rue de Picpus
av. du Dr Arnold Netter

Parc Zoologique

St-Jacques
REAU
bd. A. Blanqui
D'ALESIA
av. des Gobelins
bd. St-Marcel
rue de l'Hôpital
rue Jeanne d'Arc
bd. de la Gare

60
Pont de Bercy
rue de Bercy
quai
de Bercy

rue de Charenton

av. du Gén

bd. Poniatowski

Alésia
rue de Tolbiac
av. d'Italie

3
rue du Tolbiac
Pont de Tolbiac
Pont de Bercy

Bois de Vincennes

Reille
Jourdan

13ème

rue de Chevaleret
bd. National
CHINA-TOWN
av. de Choisy
rue Regnault
av. d'Ivry

Pont National

rue de Paris

bd. Kellerman

bd. de Masséna
BD. MASSÉNA

Périphérique Sud

0   1 mile
0   1 km

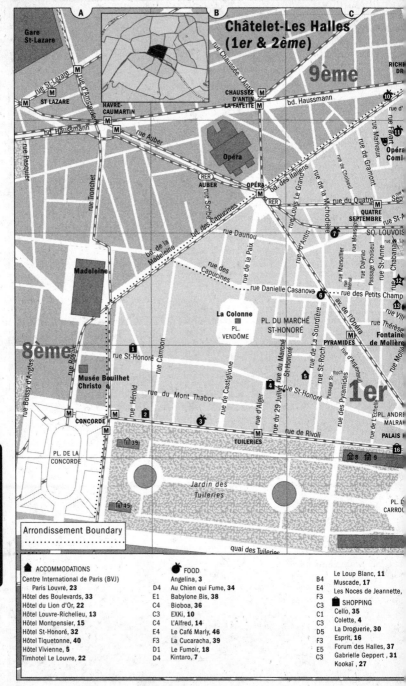

Châtelet-Les Halles
(1er & 2ème)

APPENDIX

Arrondissement Boundary

🔺 ACCOMMODATIONS		
Centre International de Paris (BVJ) Paris Louvre, **23**	D4	
Hôtel des Boulevards, **33**	E1	
Hôtel du Lion d'Or, **22**	C4	
Hôtel Louvre-Richelieu, **13**	C3	
Hôtel Montpensier, **15**	C4	
Hôtel St-Honoré, **32**	E4	
Hôtel Tiquetonne, **40**	F3	
Hôtel Vivienne, **5**	D1	
Timhotel Le Louvre, **22**	D4	

🍎 FOOD		
Angelina, **3**		
Au Chien qui Fume, **34**		
Babylone Bis, **38**		
Bioboa, **36**		
EXKi, **10**		
L'Alfred, **14**		
Le Café Marly, **46**		
La Cucaracha, **39**		
Le Fumoir, **18**		
Kintaro, **7**		

Le Loup Blanc, **11**	B4
Muscade, **17**	E4
Les Noces de Jeannette,	F3
🛍️ SHOPPING	
Cello, **35**	C3
Colette, **4**	C1
La Droguerie, **30**	C3
Esprit, **16**	D5
Forum des Halles, **37**	F3
Gabrielle Geppert , **31**	E5
Kookaï , **27**	C3

	Longchamp, **1**	A4	Frog & Rosbif, **45**	F3
F3	Monster Melodies, **38**	F5	Le Fumoir, **25**	E5
D4	Samaritaine, **28**	E5	Rex Club, **26**	E1
C2	W. H. Smith, **2**	A4	Le Slow Club, **49**	E5
	Zadig & Voltaire, **29**	E3	Le Sunside, Le Sunset, **47**	F4
E5			Willi's Wine Bar, **21**	D3
B4	★ NIGHTLIFE		Wine and Bubbles, **41**	F3
E3	Le 18 Club, **20**			
C4	Le Baiser Salé, **44**	D3	🏛 MUSEUMS	
F4	Banana Café, **42**	F4	Galerie Nationale du Jeu de Paume, **39**	A4
D4	Café Oz, **48**	F4	Musée des Arts Décoratifs, **9**	C4
E5	Le Champmeslé, **12**	F5	Musée du Louvre, **24**	D5
	Au Duc des Lombards, **43**	C3	Musée de la Mode et du Textile, **8**	C4
		F4	Musée de l'Orangerie, **45**	A5

The Marais (3ème & 4ème)

see key p. 372

Arrondissement Boundary

200 meters

200 yards

0

0

10ème

11ème

3ème

St-Ambrose

bd. Richard Leno

BRÉGUET

bd. Richard Lenoir

rue du Chemin Vert

CHEMIN
VERT

PARMENTIER

OBERKAMPF

FILLES DU
CALVAIRE

RICHARD
LENOIR

RÉPUBLIQUE

PL. DE
LA RÉPUBLIQUE

RÉPUBLIQUE

TEMPLE

ARTS ET
MÉTIERS

RÉAUMUR-
SÉBASTOPOL

RAMBUTEAU

ST-SÉBASTIEN
FROISSART

bd. Beaumarchais

rue Amelot

rue St-Sébastien

rue St-Gilles

rue des Arquebusiers

rue St-Claude

rue des
du Calvaire

bd. des Filles

Froissart

rue des Filles du Calvaire

rue de Poitou

rue du Pont aux Choux

rue de Bretagne

rue de Normandie

rue de Saintonge

rue Charlot

rue de Picardie

rue Debelleyme

rue de Turenne

rue Ste-
Anastase

Église
St-Denis
du St-Sacrement

rue de Saintonge

Hôtel Salé

rue Vieille du Temple

rue des Coutures

rue de la Perle

Hôtel
Libéral
-Bruant

rue de Thorigny

rue du
Roi Doré

rue Commines

rue de Bretagne

rue de France Comté

rue Béranger

av. de la République

bd. Voltaire

bd. du Temple

rue du Temple

rue de Turbigo

rue des Fontaines

rue Dupetit Thouars

rue G. Dupetit Thouars

rue Dubois

rue Perrée

SQ.
DU TEMPLE

rue Portefoin

rue de Picardie

rue de Beauce

rue Caffarelli

rue du Vertbois

rue Meslay

bd. St-Martin

rue Notre Dame de Nazareth

rue Volta

rue Réaumur

rue Réaumur

rue des Vertus

rue des Gravilliers

rue Chapon

rue Michel Le Comte

rue du Grenier St-Lazare

rue Beaubourg

rue du Temple

rue des Archives

rue Pastourelle

Archives
Nationales

Hôtel
de Rohan

Hôtel de la

rue des Haudriettes

rue des-4-Fils

rue de Brac

Passage Ste-Avoie

rue de Montmorency

rue de Braintome

rue St-Martin

rue Quincampoix

rue aux Ours

rue du
Bourg l'Abbé

rue Molière

bd. de Sébastopol

bd. de Sébastopol

SQ. ÉMILE
CHAUTEMPS

Conservatoire
Nationale
des Arts
et Métiers

rue St-Martin

rue Réamur

rue Greneta

rue au Maire

rue Vaucanson

rue Mongolfier

rue des Vertbois

rue Borda

rue Bonté

rue de Turbigo

rue Imp.
Berthaud

LG

The Marais (3ème & 4ème)
see map p. 370-371

🏠 **ACCOMMODATIONS**

Castex Hôtel, **106**	F5
Le Fauconnier, **94**	D5
Le Fourcy, **93**	D5
Grand Hôtel Jeanne d'Arc, **101**	E4
Hôtel Andréa Rivoli, **13**	A4
Hôtel Bellevue et du Chariot d'Or, **1**	A2
Hôtel de la Herse d'Or, **105**	F4
Hôtel du Marais, **39**	C2
Hôtel de Nice, **54**	C4
Hôtel Paris France, **20**	B2
Hôtel Picard, **68**	D2
Hôtel Pratic, **91**	D4
Hôtel du Séjour, **17**	B3
Maubuisson, **66**	C5

🍎 **FOOD**

404, **3**	A2
L'Apparement Café, **70**	D3
L'As du Falafel, **60**	D4
Au Petit Fer à Cheval, **57**	C4
Bistrot du Dome, **104**	F4
Breakfast in America, **87**	D4
Briezh Café, **75**	D3
Bubbles, **89**	D4
Café Beaubourg, **14**	A4
Café des Musées, **79**	D3
Café Rouge, **67**	D2
Caves St-Gilles, **29**	E3
Chez Hanna, **41**	C4
Chez Janou, **38**	E4
Chez Marianne, **42**	C4
Chez Omar, **98**	C2
Curieux Spaghetti Bar, **27**	B4
Fuxia, **51**	C5
Le Gay Choc, **30**	B4
Georges, **15**	A4
Le Grizzli, **12**	A4
Izrael, **91**	C5
Jadis et Gourmande, **26**	B3
Mariage Frères, **48**	C4
myberry, **51**	C4
Page 35, **78**	D3
Pain, Vin, Fromage, **96**	B3
Petit Bofinger, **64**	F4
Piccolo Teatro, **62**	C4
Le Réconfort, **69**	D3
Robert & Louise, **80**	D3
Royal Bar, **77**	D3
Taxi Jaune, **19**	B3

⭐ **NIGHTLIFE**

3W Kafé, **61**	C4
Amnésia Café, **55**	C4
Andy Wahloo, **2**	A2
L'Apparement Café, **73**	D3
Au Petit Fer à Cheval, **58**	C4
La Belle Hortense, **52**	C4
Café Klein Holland, **59**	C4
Le Carrée, **29**	B4
Le Connétable, **40**	C3
Cox, **32**	B4

Le Dépôt, **5**	A3
Le Duplex, **18**	B3
L'Enchanteur, **19**	B3
Les Etages, **46**	C4
Le Quetzal, **34**	B4
Lizard Lounge, **50**	C4
Okawa, **56**	C4
Open Café, **33**	B4
La Perle, **84**	D3
Le Pick-clops, **53**	C4
Raidd Bar, **31**	B4
Stolly's, **63**	C4
Le Tango, **18**	B2

🛍️ **SHOPPING**

Abou d'abi Bazar, **99**	E4
Bel' Air, **86**	D4
BHV, **100**	B4
Boy'z Bazaar, **47**	C4
Brontibay, **92**	D4
Culotte, **88**	D4
Fabien Nobile, **83**	D4
Factory's Paris, **49**	C4
Fleux, **28**	B4
Free 'P' Star, **44**	C4
IEM, **45**	C4
I Heart Ethel, **97**	E3
Loft Design By, **90**	D4
Monic, **37**	E4
Les Mots à la Bouche, **43**	C4
Palais des Thés, **g**	C4
Sucrées..., **85**	D4
Vertiges, **11**	A4

🎨 **GALLERIES**

Atelier Cardenas Bellanger, **10**	A4
Galerie Daniel Templon, **22**	B3
Galerie Denise René, **95**	F3
Galerie Emmanuel Perrotin, **72**	D3
Fait & Cause, **8**	A4
Galerie de France, **36**	B4
Gilles Peyroulet & CIE, **6**	A3
Galerie du Jour Agnès B, **9**	A4
Galerie Michèle Chomette, **23**	B3
Galerie Nathalie Obadier, **#**	A4
Galerie Nelson, **7**	A3
Galerie R&L Beauborg, **35**	B4
Galerie Thuillier, **71**	D3
Galerie Zürcher, **4**	A2

🏛️ **MUSEUMS**

Centre Pompidou, **16**	A4
Maison de Victor Hugo, **103**	E4
Mémorial de la Shoah, **p**	C5
Musée d'Art et d'Histoire du Judaïsme, **21**	B3
Musée Carnavalet, **82**	D4
Musée Cognacq-Jay, **81**	D4
Musée de Jeu de Paume, **102**	E4
Musée Picasso, **74**	D3
Musée de la Poupée, **24**	B3

Latin Quarter and St-Germain (5ème & 6ème), Île de la Cité, and Île St-Louis

(see map p. 374-375)

🏠 ACCOMMODATIONS

Centre International de Paris (BVJ) Paris Quartier Latin, **73**	D3
Delhy's Hôtel, **23**	C2
Foyer International des Étudiantes, **92**	C5
Hôtel des Argonauts, **25**	C2
Hôtel Brésil, **76**	C4
Hôtel Esmeralda, **27**	C2
Hôtel Gay-Lussac, **90**	C5
Hôtel du Lys, **38**	C3
Hôtel Marignan, **67**	C3
Hôtel de Nesle, **20**	B2
Hôtel St-André des Arts, **36**	B2
Hôtel St-Jacques, **69**	D3
Hôtel Stanislas, **98**	A5
Hôtel Stella, **63**	B3
Young and Happy (Y&H) Hostel, **91**	D5

🍎 FOOD

Au Port Salut, **86**	C4
Au Coin des Gourmets, **19**	C2
Le Bistro d'Henri, **51**	A3
Café Delmas, **84**	D4
Café de Flore, **40**	A3
Café de la Mosquée, **89**	E4
Café Vavin, **95**	A6
Comptoir Méditerranée, **77**	D3
Le Comptoir du Relais, **93**	B3
Così, **35**	A2
La Crêpe Rit du Clown, **50**	A3
Crêperie Saint Germain, **22**	B2
Les Deux Magots, **41**	A3
L'Écurie, **54**	D3
Les Editeurs, **55**	B3
Foyer Vietnam, **72**	E4
Gérard Mulot, **44**	B3
Le Grenier de Notre-Dame, **30**	D2
Guen-Maï, **34**	A2
L'Heure Gourmande, **42**	B2
Le Jardin des Pâtes, **85**	E4
Kusmi Tea, **45**	B2
Poilâne, **65**	A4
Le Perraudin, **82**	C4
Le Pré Verre, **88**	C3
Le Procope, **37**	B2
Le "Relais de L'Entrecôte," **32**	A2
Savannah Café, **83**	D4
Le Sélect, **97**	A6
La Table d'Erica, **59**	A3

⭐ NIGHTLIFE

Le 10 Bar, **62**	B3
L'Académie de la Bière, **16**	C6
Bob Cool, **21**	B2
Le Caveau de la Huchette, **98**	C2
Le Caveau des Oubliettes, **29**	C2
Chez Georges, **48**	A3
Finnegan's Wake, **78**	E3
Fu Bar, **61**	B3
The Moose, **60**	B3
Le Piano Vache, **75**	D3
Le Petit Journal St-Michel, **81**	C4
Aux Trois Mailletz, **99**	C2
Le Who's Bar, **28**	C2

🛍 SHOPPING

Abbey Bookshop, **39**	C2
agnès b., **52**	A3
Cacharel, **53**	A3
La Chaumière à Musique, **102**	B3
Crocodisc, **68**	C3
Free Lance, **46**	A3
Gibert Jeune, **24**	C2
Gibert Joseph, **64**	C3
L'Harmattan, **74**	D3
Mango, **101**	A4
Moloko, **79**	A4
Muji, **57**	B3
Naf Naf, **100**	C3
No Name, **47**	A3
Om Kashi, **71**	D3
Petit Bateau, **94**	A6
Présence Africaine, **70**	D3
San Francisco Book Co., **56**	B3
Shakespeare and Co., **26**	C2
Tara Jarmon, **43**	A3
Tea and Tattered Pages, **80**	A4
Vanessa Bruno, **58**	B3
Au Vieux Camper, **103**	C3
The Village Voice, **49**	A3

🏛 MUSEUMS

Institut du Monde Arabe, **31**	E2
Musée de Cluny, **66**	C3
Musée Delacroix, **33**	A2
Musée d'Histoire Naturelle, **87**	F4
Musée de la Monnaie, **18**	B2
Musée Zadkine, **96**	B6

Île de la Cité and Île St-Louis

🏠 ACCOMMODATIONS

Hôtel Henri IV, **2**	B1

🍎 FOOD

Amorino, **13**	D3
Au Rendez-Vous des Camionneurs, **1**	B1
Berthillon, **15**	E2
Brasserie de l'Île St-Louis, **4**	B1
Café Med, **9**	D2
Le Caveau du Palais, **6**	D1
L'Épicerie, **11**	D2
Les Fous de l'Île, **14**	E1
O&CO, **104**	D1
Le Petit Plateau, **18**	D1
La Petite Scierie, **12**	D1
Place Numéro Thé, **3**	B1
Quai Quai, **19**	B1

🛍 SHOPPING

Le Grain de Sable, **8**	D2
Le Marché aux Fleurs, **5**	C1
Pylônes, **10**	D2
Sobral, **7**	D2

🏛 MUSEUMS

Musée Adam Mickiewicz, **17**	E2

1er

quai du Louvre
Palais du Louvre
PONT NEUF
CHÂTELET

Pont du Carrousel
Pont des Arts

Pont au Change
Pont Notre Dame

quai Malaquais
quai de Conti
SQ. DU VERT GALANT
PL. DAUPHINE
Conciergerie
Palais de Justice
Ste-Chapelle
CITÉ
Hôtel Dieu

École Nationale Superieure des Beaux Arts
Institut de France
quai d'Orfèvres
Palais de Justice
Île de la Cité

Hôtel de Monnaies
quai des Grands Augustins
ST-MICHEL

rue des Beaux Arts
rue Visconti
rue de Furstemberg
rue J. Caillot
rue du Nesle
passage Dauphin
rue Christine
rue de l'Hirondelle
PL. ST-MICHEL
rue de la Huchette
rue du Petit Pont
rue St Severin
Église St-Jul le-Pa

rue des Sts-Pères
rue Jacob
rue Bonaparte
PL. de l'Abbaye
ST-GERMAIN-DES-PRÉS
St-Germain Des Prés
rue de Buci
rue St-André des Arts
Église St-Séverin

bd. St-Germain
ODÉON
bd. St-Germain
CLUNY-LA SORBONNE
Hôtel Cluny

ST-GERMAIN DES PRÉS
MABILLON
rue de l'École de Médecine
p. Paul Painlevé
rue du Som

rue du Dragon
rue du Four
rue Princesse
rue Guisarde
rue de Seine
rue Lobineau
rue Monsieur-le-Prince
rue Racine
rue de Delavigne
La Sorbonne
Collège de Franc

rue de Sèvres
rue des Canettes
rue St-Sulpice
rue de Condé
PL. DE L'ODÉON
PL. DE LA SORBONNE
Lycée Lou le Grand

rue du Vieux Colombier
PL. ST-SULPICE
St-Sulpice
rue Garancière
Odéon Théâtre de l'Europe
rue Cujas

ST-SULPICE
rue du Cherche Midi
rue de Tournon
rue de Médicis
rue Soufflot

TO 65 (50m), 79 (350m), 80 (700m)
rue de Vaugirard
rue Férou
Palais du Luxembourg
PL. EDMOND ROSTAND
LUXEMBOURG

rue d'Assas
rue de Rennes
Musée du Luxembourg
rue Royer Collard
rue St-Jacques

RENNES
6ème
Fontaine des Médicis
rue P. et M.

ST-PLACIDE
Marionettes de Luxembourg
Jardin du Luxembourg
LUXEMBOURG
rue Gay Lussac

NOTRE-DAME DES CHAMPS
rue Auguste Compte
rue des Ursulines

rue du Montparnasse
rue Vavin
rue Notre-Dame des Champs
bd. St-Michel
rue des Fe

VAVIN
MONTPARNASSE BIENVENÜE
14ème
bd. du Montparnasse
PORT ROYAL
rue Henri Baptiste
rue Pierre Nicole
av. de l'Observatoire

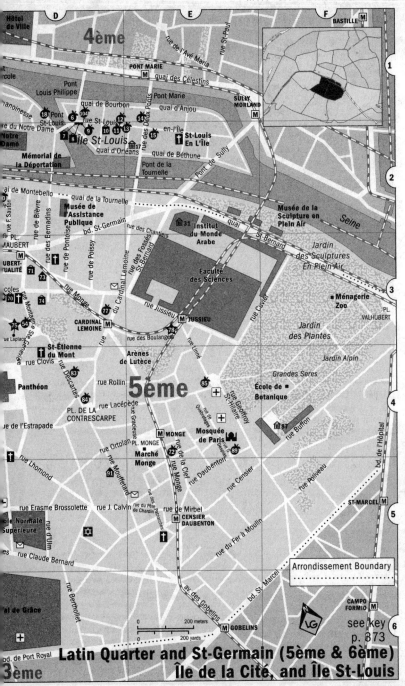

Latin Quarter and St-Germain (5ème & 6ème)
Île de la Cité, and Île St-Louis

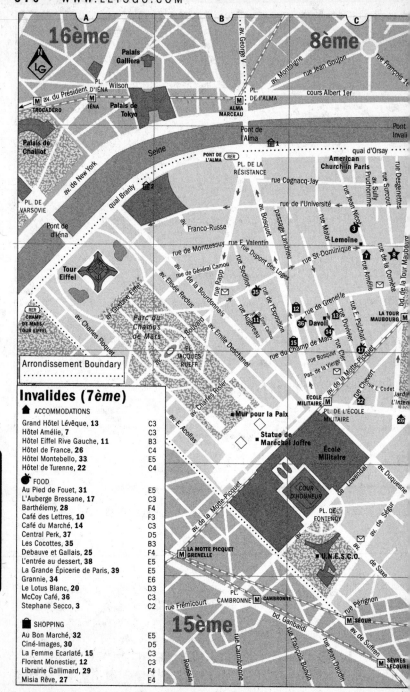

16ème

8ème

Palais
Galliera

av. George V

av. Montaigne

rue Jean Goujon

rue François 1e

PL.
Wilson

av. du Président D'IÉNA

PL.
DE L'ALMA

cours Albert 1er

Pont
Invali

M TROCADÉRO

M IÉNA

Palais de
Tokyo

M ALMA
MARCEAU

Palais de
Chaillot

Pont de
l'Alma

quai d'Orsay

American
Church in Paris

rue Desgenettes

Seine

PONT DE
L'ALMA **RER**

PL. DE LA
RÉSISTANCE

av. Sully Prudhomme

rue Surcout

PL. DE
VARSOVIE

av. de New York

quai Branly

rue Cognacq-Jay

rue de l'Université

rue Jean Nicot

Pont de
d'Iéna

av. Franco-Russe

av. Bosquet

passage Landrieu

rue Malar

3

Lemoîne

rue de Monttessuy

rue F. Valentin

rue Dupont des Loges

rue St-Dominique

7   **9**

Tour
Eiffel

av. de Général Camou

av. Elisée Reclus

rue Rapp

rue du Sédillot

rue de l'Exposition

rue St-Dominique

rue Amélie

RER
CHAMP
DE MARS/
TOUR EIFFEL

av. Gustave Eiffel

Parc du
Champs
de Mars

av. Charles Floquet

av. de la Bourdonnais

av. Augereau

rue Cler

35

12

rue de Grenelle

13

rue Duvivier

LA TOUR
MAUBOURG **M**

11

36 Davoli

14

rue E. Psichari

J. Bouvard
av. Emile Deschanel

PL.
JACQUES
RUEFF

15

rue du Champ de Mars

rue Bosquet

Pas. de la Vierge

av. de la Motte-Picquet

rue Chevue L Codet

17

Arrondissement Boundary

av. Charles Risler

av. E. Acollas

Mur pour la Paix

ECOLE
MILITAIRE

PL. DE L'ECOLE
MILITAIRE

22

Jardi
L'Inter

26

Invalides (7ème)

🏠 **ACCOMMODATIONS**

Grand Hôtel Lévêque, **13**	C3
Hôtel Amélie, **7**	C3
Hôtel Eiffel Rive Gauche, **11**	B3
Hôtel de France, **26**	C4
Hôtel Montebello, **33**	E5
Hôtel de Turenne, **22**	C4

🍎 **FOOD**

Au Pied de Fouet, **31**	E5
L'Auberge Bressane, **17**	C3
Barthélemy, **28**	F4
Café des Lettres, **10**	F3
Café du Marché, **14**	C3
Central Perk, **37**	D5
Les Cocottes, **35**	B3
Debauve et Gallais, **25**	F4
L'entrée au dessert, **38**	E5
La Grande Épicerie de Paris, **39**	E5
Grannie, **34**	E6
Le Lotus Blanc, **20**	D3
McCoy Café, **36**	C3
Stephane Secco, **3**	C2

🛍 **SHOPPING**

Au Bon Marché, **32**	E5
Ciné-Images, **30**	D5
La Femme Ecarlaté, **15**	C3
Florent Monestier, **12**	C3
Librairie Gallimard, **29**	F4
Misia Rêve, **27**	E4

Statue de
Maréchal Joffre

École
Militaire

av. de Lowendal

av. Duquesne

COUR
D'HONNEUR

PL. DE
FONTENOY

av. de Ségur

av. de Saxe

av. de la Motte-Picquet

M LA MOTTE PICQUET
GRENELLE

U.N.E.S.C.O.

M SÉGUR

15ème

PL.
CAMBRONNE **M** CAMBRONNE

rue Frémicourt

bd. Garibaldi

rue Pérignon

M SÉVRES
LECOURB

rue Cambronne

rue François Bonvin

rue Jean Daudin

av. de Suffren

Roussin

APPENDIX

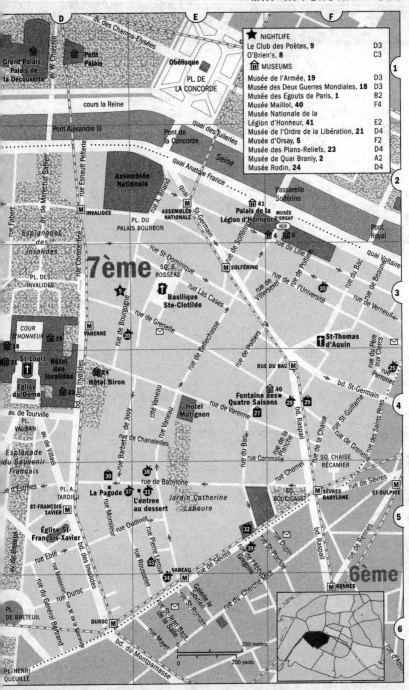

★ NIGHTLIFE
Le Club des Poètes, 9 — D3
O'Brien's, 8 — C3

🏛 MUSEUMS
Musée de l'Armée, 19 — D3
Musée des Deux Guerres Mondiales, 18 — D3
Musée des Egouts de Paris, 1 — B2
Musée Maillol, 40 — F4
Musée Nationale de la
Légion d'Honneur, 41 — E2
Musée de l'Ordre de la Libération, 21 — D4
Musée d'Orsay, 5 — F2
Musée des Plans-Reliefs, 23 — D4
Musée de Quai Branly, 2 — A2
Musée Rodin, 24 — D4

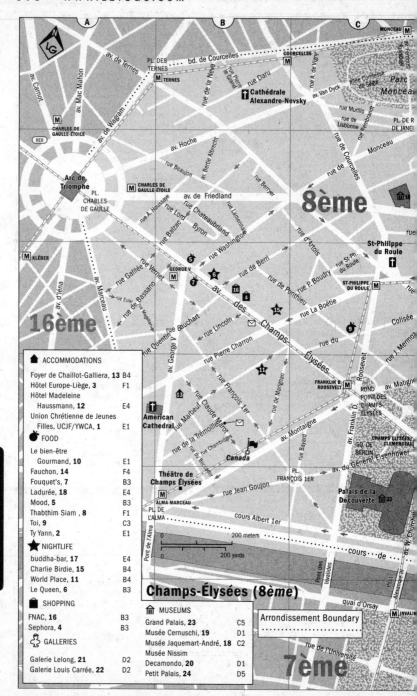

Champs-Élysées (8ème)

Arrondissement Boundary
· ·

APPENDIX

ACCOMMODATIONS

Foyer de Chaillot-Galliera, **13**	B4
Hôtel Europe-Liège, **3**	F1
Hôtel Madeleine Haussmann, **12**	E4
Union Chrétienne de Jeunes Filles, UCJF/YWCA, **1**	E1

FOOD

Le bien-être Gourmand, **10**	E1
Fauchon, **14**	F4
Fouquet's, **7**	B3
Ladurée, **18**	E4
Mood, **5**	B3
Thabthim Siam , **8**	F1
Toi, **9**	C3
Ty Yann, **2**	E1

NIGHTLIFE

buddha-bar, **17**	E4
Charlie Birdie, **15**	B4
World Place, **11**	B4
Le Queen, **6**	B3

SHOPPING

FNAC, **16**	B3
Sephora, **4**	B3

GALLERIES

Galerie Lelong, **21**	D2
Galerie Louis Carrée, **22**	D2

MUSEUMS

Grand Palais, **23**	C5
Musée Cernuschi, **19**	D1
Musée Jaquemart-André, **18**	C2
Musée Nissim Decamondo, **20**	D1
Petit Palais, **24**	D5

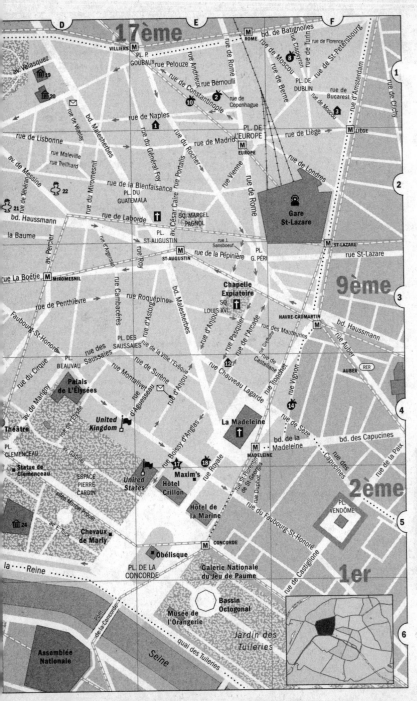

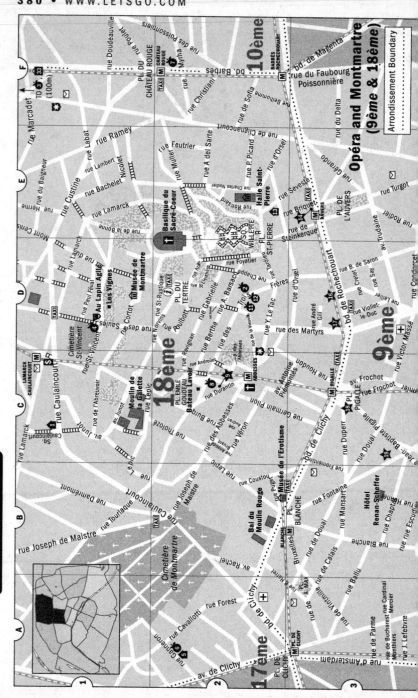

Opéra and Montmartre
(9ème & 18ème)

Arrondissement Boundary

ACCOMMODATIONS	
Hôtel Caulaincourt, 1	C1
Hôtel Chopin, 30	D6
Modial Hôtel Européen, 26	C4
Perfect Hôtel, 23	D4
Style Hôtel, 5	A2
Le Village Hostel, 13	E2
Woodstock Hostel, 24	E4
FOOD	
Anarkali Sarangui, 21	C4
Au Général La Fayette, 27	D5
Au Grain de Folie, 11	D2
La Bodega, 3	F1
Café de la Paix, 32	B6
Chartier, 31	D6
Chez Haynes, 25	D4
Comme Par Hasard, 20	C4
Le Dan Bau, 2	C4
Djerba Cacher Chez Guichi, 7	D2
La Maison du Chocolat, 31	F2
La Maison Rose, 4	A6
No Stress Café, 22	D1
L'Olympia, 15	C4
Refuge des Fondues, 12	A6
Le Soleil Gourmand, 8	D2
Saveurs & Coincidences, 32	C2
Wassana, 6	E5
★ **NIGHTLIFE AND ENTERTAINMENT**	A2
Bus Palladium, 19	C3
La Cigale, 9	C2
Elysée Montmartre, 14	D3
Folies Pigalle, 18	E3
La Fourmi, 17	C3
■ **SHOPPING**	D3
Au Printemps, 28	A5
Galeries Lafayette, 29	B5
Passage Jouffroy, 10	D6
Puces de St-Owen, 33	F1

8ème

2ème

rue de Rochechouart
rue de Belleford
SQ. DE MONTHOLON
rue de Maubeuge
rue La Fayette
Folies Bergère
rue de Trévise
rue de la Tour d'Auvergne
rue Rodier
imp. Boviare
rue Mayran
CADET
rue Saulnier
rue Ste-Cécile
rue Milton
rue de l'Agent Bailly
rue Lamartine
rue de Montholon
rue Cadet
rue de la Boule Rouge
rue Manuel
rue Choron
rue Buffault
rue du Faubourg Montmartre
rue Richer
rue G. Marie
rue Hippolyte Lebas
rue de Châteaudun
rue de Provence
rue de la Grange Batelière
rue Montyon
rue Bergère
Cité Bergère
rue des Martyrs
rue de Navarin
rue Clauzel
St-Georges
PL. ST-GEORGES
rue Notre Dame de Lorette
Notre-Dame-de-Lorette
NOTRE DAME DE LORETTE
rue St-Georges
rue Drouot
RICHELIEU DROUOT
Musée Grévin
GRANDS BOULEVARDS
bd. Montmartre
rue de Richelieu
Fondation Taylor
SQ. ALEX BISCARRE
rue Laferrière
LE PELETIER
rue Le Peletier
rue de la Victoire
rue Lafayette
rue Chauchat
bd. Montmartre
rue d'Aumale
Musée Gustave Moreau
rue de la Tour des Dames
rue de Châteaudun
rue de Provence
rue La Fayette
rue Taitbout
bd. Haussmann
rue Pinel Will
rue de la Bruyère
rue La Bruyère
rue Taitbout
rue Le Peletier
bd. des Italiens
4 SEPTEMBRE
rue St-Lazare
rue de la Chaussée d'Antin
Galeries Lafayette
rue du Helder
CHAUSSÉE D'ANTIN LA FAYETTE
rue Meyerbeer
Capucines
rue de Clichy
Ste-Trinité
Théâtre Mogador
SQ. PL. D'ESTIENNE D'ORVES
TAXI
TRINITÉ
rue Mogador
PL. DIAGHILEV
rue Gluck
Opéra Garnier
PL. DE L'OPÉRA
av. de l'Opéra
OPÉRA
rue de Liège
rue de Milan
rue d'Athènes
rue de Londres
Cité de Londres
rue St-Lazare
av. du Coq
rue Joubert
rue de Caumartin
rue Auber
AUBER
rue Scribe
bd. des Capucines
LIÈGE
rue Blanche
Gare St-Lazare
PL. DU HAVRE
ST-LAZARE HAVRE
rue de Bydapest
rue du Havre
HAVRE CAUMARTIN
PL. EDOUARD VIII
rue Godot de Mauroy
rue Boudreau
PL. DES MATHURINS
bd. de la Madeleine
rue Tronchet
rue de Sèze

0   100 meters
0   100 yards

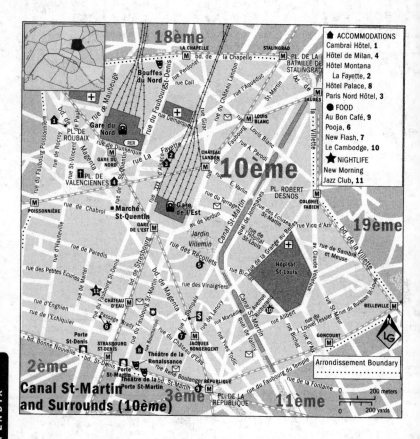

ACCOMMODATIONS
Cambrai Hôtel, **1**
Hôtel de Milan, **4**
Hôtel Montana
  La Fayette, **2**
Hôtel Palace, **8**
Paris Nord Hôtel, **3**
● **FOOD**
Au Bon Café, **9**
Pooja, **6**
New Flash, **7**
Le Cambodge, **10**
★ **NIGHTLIFE**
New Morning
Jazz Club, **11**

Canal St-Martin
and Surrounds (10ème)

Arrondissement Boundary

0   200 meters
0   200 yards

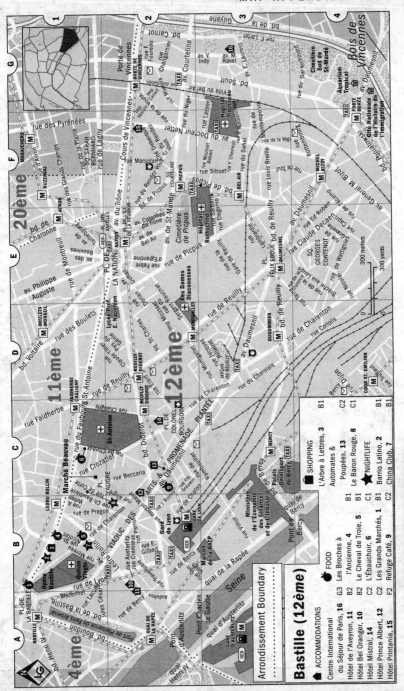

Bastille (12ème)

···· Arrondissement Boundary

ACCOMMODATIONS

Centre International	
du Séjour de Paris, **16**	G3
Hôtel de l'Aveyron, **11**	B2
Hôtel Bel Oranger, **10**	B2
Hôtel Mistral, **14**	C2
Hôtel Prince Albert, **12**	C2
Hôtel Printania, **15**	F2

FOOD

Les Broches à	
l'Ancienne, **4**	B1
Le Cheval de Troie, **5**	C1
L'Ébauchoir, **6**	C1
Les Grands Marchés, **1**	B1
Refuge Café, **9**	C2

SHOPPING

L'Arbre à Lettres, **3**	B1
Automates &	
Poupées, **13**	C2

NIGHTLIFE

Le Baron Rouge, **8**	C1
Barrio Latino, **2**	B1
China Club, **7**	C2

Bastille (11ème)

▲ ACCOMMODATIONS

Auberge de Jeunesse "Jules Ferry", 2	C1
Hôtel Beaumarchais, 8	C2
Hôtel de Belfort, 17	E3
Hôtel Notre-Dame, 3	C1
Hôtel Rhetia, 15	D3
Modern Hôtel, 16	E3
Plessis Hôtel, 4	C1

● FOOD

Au Trou Normand, 31	C2
Babylone, 21	B4
La Bague de Kenza, 23	E2
La Banane Ivoirienne, 13	C5
Le Bar à Soupes, 36	C4
Le Bistrot du Peintre, 35	C4
Café de l'Industrie, 19	B4
Chez Paul, 32	C4
L'Oga, 6	E2
Pause Café, 34	C4
Restaurant Assoce, 14	E3
Le Troisième Bureau, 5	D2

★ NIGHTLIFE

Le Bar à Nénette, 29	B4
Le Bar Sans Nom, 33	C4
Café Charbon, 10	E2
Le Clown Bar, 7	C2
Favela Chic, 1	C1
Jacques Mélac, 39	E4
Le Kitch, 9	C2
Le Lèche-Vin, 18	B4
La Mécanique Onudlatoire, 27	C4
La Muse Vin, 38	D4
Nouveau Casino, 11	E2
Le Pop In, 12	C2
Sanz Sans, 30	B4
Wax, 20	B4

Cimetière Père Lachaise

bd. de Charonne

M AVRON

M ALEXANDRE DUMAS

M PHILIPPE AUGUSTE

rue de la Roquette

rue de Nice

rue Alexandre Dumas

rue Nueve des Boulets

rue des Immeubles Industriels

rue de Montreuil

av. Philippe Auguste

rue de Tunis

imp. Mortel

PL. DE LA NATION

M NATION

M BOULETS MONTREUIL

rue des Boulets

rue Chevreul

ROQUETTE

rue Léonrt Frot

rue Mercœur

rue A. Laurent

PL. LÉON BLUM

bd. Voltaire

M VOLTAIRE

rue Vrue de Belfort

M CHARONNE

rue Titon

rue de Charonne

bd. Diderot

rue J. Macé

rue Chanzy

rue Godefroy Cavaignac

rue Richard Lenoir

rue Faidherbe

M REUILLY DIDEROT

rue de Reuilly

rue Basfroi

av. Ledru Rollin

rue Charles Delescluze

rue de Charonne

rue Trousseau

St. Bernard

Foire Roland

rue du Faubourg St-Antoine

M FAIDHERBE CHALIGNY

rue de Cîteaux

rue Chaligny

12ème

rue Keller

rue de la Roquette

rue des Taillandiers

pas. Thiéré

M LEDRU ROLLIN

rue Crozatier

25

28 22 36 34

26 35

27

rue Charenton

rue de Lappe

21 29 32

30

rue Daval

M BASTILLE

Opéra Bastille

M GARE DE LYON

av. Daumesnil

rue Villiot

M QUAI DE LA RAPÉE

M Gare de Lyon

RER

rue de Charenton

rue Traversière

rue de Lyon

bd. de la Bastille

av. Ledru Rollin

bd. Diderot

rue de Bercy

quai de la Rapée

Seine

SHOPPING	
Born Bad Record Shop, **28**	C4
Doria Salambo, **24**	B4
Des Petits Hauts, **22**	C4
La Manoeuvre, **26**	C4
St. Charles de Rose , **25**	C4

Arrondissement Boundary — — —

4

5

6

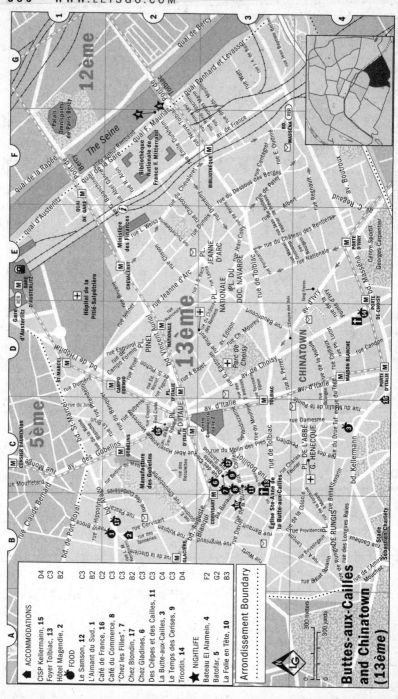

Buttes-aux-Cailles and Chinatown (13ème)

▲ ACCOMMODATIONS	
CISP Kellermann, 15	D4
Foyer Tolbiac, 13	C3
Hôtel Magendie, 2	B2
● FOOD	
Le Samson, 12	C3
L'Aimant du Sud, 1	B2
Café de France, 16	C2
Café du Commerce, 8	C3
"Chez les Filles", 7	C3
Chez Blondin, 17	B2
Chez Gladines, 6	C3
Des Crêpes et des Cailles, 11	C3
La Butte-aux-Cailles, 3	C4
Le Temps des Cerises, 9	C3
Tricotin, 14	D4
★ NIGHTLIFE	
Bateau El Alamein, 4	F2
Batofar, 5	G2
La Folie en Tête, 10	B3

Arrondissement Boundary

APPENDIX

Montparnasse (14ème)

see key p. 388

14ème

Tour Montparnasse
MONTPARNASSE BIENVENÜE
PL. DU 18 JUIN 1940
rue de l'Arrivée
rue du Départ
rue d'Odessa
rue Delambre
rue Delambre
rue Huyghens
PL. PABLO PICASSO
NAVIN
rue de la Gaîté
bd. Edgar Quinet
EDGAR QUINET
Passage d'Enfer
rue Campagne Première
rue Boissonade
PORT ROYAL
Maternité Port Royal Clinique Baudelocque
Hôpital St-Vincent de-Paul
rue Cassini
Hôpital Cochin
RASPAIL

Gare Montparnasse
rue du Maine
Impasse de la Gaîté
Comédie Italienne
GAÎTÉ
Cimetière du Montparnasse
rue Froidevaux
rue Émile Richard
rue Schoelcher
bd. Raspail
Fondation Cartier pour l'Art Contemporain
TAXI
Observatoire de Paris
rue du Faubourg St-Jacques
PL. ST-JACQUES
ST-JACQUES

MONTPARNASSE BIENVENÜE
rue du Cdt. René Mouchotte
rue Vercingétorix
rue Jean Zay
rue Lebouis
rue J. Guesde
rue de Texelloi
rue du Château
TAXI
rue Cels
rue Fermat
rue Deparcieux
rue Roger
rue Daguerre
rue Lalande
rue Victor Considérant
PL. DENFERT ROCHEREAU
TAXI
av. Denfert Rochereau
SQ. GEORGES LAMARQUE
SQ. CLAUDE NICOLAS LEDOUX
DENFERT ROCHEREAU
The Catacombs
SQ. DE L'ABBÉ MIGNE
RER
rue de la Tombe Issoire

PL. DE CATALOGNE
SQ. CAL WYSZYNSKI
Église Nôtre Dame du Travail
rue Niepce
rue Raymond Losserand
rue du Château
Maison Dieu
av. du Maine
rue Asselineau
rue Liancourt
rue Charles Divry
rue E. Cresson
Mairie
SQ. F. BRUNOT
PL. F. BRUNOT G. PERROY
rue Boulard
Duvernet
MOUTON DUVERNET
rue Sophie Germain
av. du Général Leclerc
Hôpital La Rochefoucauld
rue Hallé
av. René Coty
TO (100 m)

rue Des Prez
PERNETY
rue de l'Ouest
rue Francis de Pressensé
rue de Gergovie
av. Villemain
PLAISANCE
rue d'Alésia
rue des Suisses
PL. DE LA GARENNE
rue Pernety
rue de Plaisance
rue Boyer Barret
rue du Moulin des Lapins
rue Maurice Ripoche
rue de l'Eure
rue Bénard
rue Hippo
rue du Didot
rue du Moulin Vert
rue Léonidas
rue O. Noyer
Melendon
rue Sévero
rue de la Sablière
rue Brézin
St-Pierre de Montrouge
ALÉSIA
PL. VICTOR BASCH
rue du Couëdic
rue Rémy-Dumoncel
rue du Commandeur
rue d'Alés
TO (90 m)
rue Montebrun
rue du Loing
rue de Lunaire
rue Marie-Rose
rue Bezout

rue Décrès
rue de Gergovie
rue Jonquoy
rue Pauilly
rue Pierre Larousse
Hôpital St-Joseph
Hôpital Broussais
rue des Mariniers
rue Furtado-Theine
rue Delbert
rue Lecuirot
rue Jacquier
rue L. Morard
rue de l'Abbé Carton
rue Collet
v. Brune
sq. Alice
al. G. Bachelard
rue d'Alésia
Villa d'Alésia
rue de Châtillon
rue Antoine Chantin
passage Assas
villa Mallebay
rue Boulitte
villa Duthy
rue Deshayes
rue Ledion
Hôpital Notre-Dame-de-Bon-Secours
TAXI
rue des Plantes
rue G. Bruno
av. Jean Moulin
rue Friant
rue Alphonse Focillon
rue Alphonse Daudet
av. du Général Leclerc
rue Sarrette
rue de Coulmiers
rue Poirier de Narcay
Clinique St-Geneviève
bd. Brune
rue Morère
Chapelle St-Paul
PORTE D'ORLÉANS
PORTE D'ORLÉANS
PL. DE LA PORTE DE CHÂTILLON
PL. DU 25 AOÛT 1944
TAXI
rue Lacaze
rue H. Regnault
rue Beaunier
rue Paul Faure
TO (75 m)
bd. Jourdan
av. Paul Appell

bd. Brune
rue du Gal Humbert
av. Georges Lafenestre
rue du Gal Mistre
rue H. de Bournazel
av. Maurice d'Ocagne
av. Ernest Reyer
rue G. Lefort
rue A. Sorbier
rue A. Luchaire
av. de la Pte de Montrouge
SQ. DU SERMENT DE KOUFRA
rue de la Légion Étrangère
Porte d'Orléans
Porto-Riche
Cimetière de Montrouge
Porte de Châtillon
av. de la Porte de Châtillon
Périphérique
av. de la Porte d'Orléans

Arrondissement Boundary

0   500 meters
0   500 yards

15ème

 **ACCOMMODATIONS**

Aloha Hostel, **11**
Hôtel Camélia, **3**
Pacific Hôtel, **7**
Pratic Hôtel, **12**
Three Ducks Hostel, **15**

FOOD

Au Coin du Pétrin, **14**
Aux Artistes, **6**
Bélisaire, **8**
Chez Fung, **9**
Le Dix Vins, **5**
Samaya, **1**
Le Troquet, **10**
Tandoori, **13**
Ty Breiz, **4**

Montparnasse (14ème)
see map p. 387

ACCOMMODATIONS

FIAP Jean-Monnet, **7**	D3
Hôtel de Blois, **9**	C4
Hôtel du Midi, **6**	D3
Hôtel du Parc, **5**	B1

FOOD

Aquarius Café, **12**	A4
Pascal Beillevaire, **13**	B1
Chez Papa, **5**	C2
La Coupole, **1**	B1
Charlie Birdy, **14**	B4
Crêperie Plougastel, **8**	A1
Le Severo, **2**	C3
Le Petit Baigneur, **3**	B4

NIGHTLIFE

Au Roi du Café, **16**	
Mix Club, **2**	

NIGHTLIFE

Café Tournesol, **4**	A2
L'Entrepôt, **10**	A4

APPENDIX

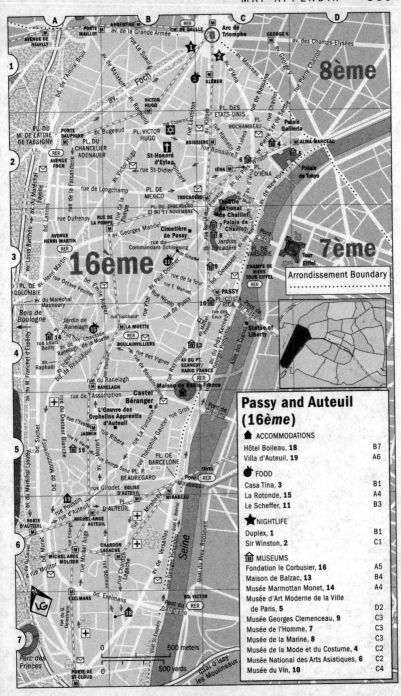

Passy and Auteuil (16ème)

🛏 ACCOMMODATIONS

Hôtel Boileau, **18**	B7
Villa d'Auteuil, **19**	A6

🍴 FOOD

Casa Tina, **3**	B1
La Rotonde, **15**	A4
Le Scheffer, **11**	B3

⭐ NIGHTLIFE

Duplex, **1**	B1
Sir Winston, **2**	C1

🏛 MUSEUMS

Fondation le Corbusier, **16**	A5
Maison de Balzac, **13**	B4
Musée Marmottan Monet, **14**	A4
Musée d'Art Moderne de la Ville de Paris, **5**	D2
Musée Georges Clemenceau, **9**	C3
Musée de l'Homme, **7**	C3
Musée de la Marine, **8**	C3
Musée de la Mode et du Costume, **4**	C2
Musée National des Arts Asiatiques, **6**	C2
Musée du Vin, **10**	C4

APPENDIX

Batignolles (17ème)

♦ **ACCOMMODATIONS**

Hôtel Champerret Héliopolis, 1	C2
Hôtel Prince Albert Wagram, 3	E2
Hôtel Riviera, 13	C4

🍴 **FOOD**

Au Vieux Logis, 8	F3
L'Endroit, 4	F2
Café Hortensias, 2	D2
The James Joyce Pub, 11	B3
L'Étoile du Kashmir, 17	G3
Le Patio Provençal, 6	B3
Villa des Ternes, 10	G2
La Fournée d'Augustine, 14	G2
Joy in Food, 15	F3
3 Pièces Cuisine, 16	

★ **NIGHTLIFE**

L'Endroit, 5	F2

Arrondissement Boundary

500 meters

500 yards

LEVALLOIS-PERRET

PEREIRE-LEVALLOIS

17ème

8ème

16ème

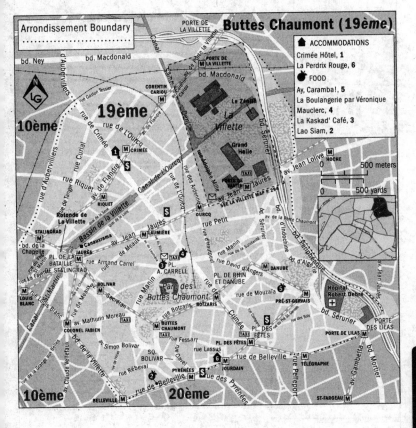

Arrondissement Boundary

Buttes Chaumont (19ème)

ACCOMMODATIONS
Crimée Hôtel, **1**
La Perdrix Rouge, **6**

🍎 FOOD
Ay, Caramba!, **5**
La Boulangerie par Véronique
Mauclerc, **4**
La Kaskad' Café, **3**
Lao Siam, **2**

APPENDIX

rue de Belleville
PYRÉNÉES
rue J. Prat
rue Julien Lacroix
Rouvé
La Maison de l'Air
Parc de Belleville
rue des Couronnes
COURONNES
rue du Transvaal
rue des Envierges
rue de la Mare
rue des Cascades
l'Ermitage
rue des Pyrénées
rue de la Duée
rue de Ménilmontant
PL. DE MÉNILMONTANT
MÉNILMONTANT
rue des Panoyaux
rue des Cendriers
rue Boyer
bd. de Belleville
av. de la République
rue de Chemin Vert
rue de — Tlemcen
rue des Partants
rue Gaspier
rue des rue de la Bidassoa
PÈRE LACHAISE
av. Gambetta
bd. de Ménilmontant
rue de la Roquette
rue de la Folie-Regnault
rue Léon Frot
Cimetière du Père Lachaise
PHILIPPE AUGUSTE
20ème
SEE PÈRE LACHAISE MAP P. 255
ALEXANDRE DUMAS
rue de Charonne
CHARONNE
rue Neuve des Boulets
rue Alexandre Dumas
PHILIPPE AUGUSTE
bd. de Charonne
bd. Voltaire
BOULETS MONTREUIL

JOURDAIN
rue de Belleville
TÉLÉGRAPHE
rue du Télégraphe
PORTE DES LILAS
rue des Tournelles
rue Pixérécourt
rue Pelleport
rue du Borego
rue Haxo
rue Olivier Métra
rue Levert
rue de la Chine
rue Pelleport
rue St-Fargeau
ST-FARGEAU
rue de Surmelin
rue E. Marey
bd. Mortier
PELLEPORT
av. Gambetta
rue Villiers de l'Isle Adam
rue Orfila
GAMBETTA
Hôpital Tenon
PLACE GAMBETTA
rue Belgrand
rue de la Cour des Noues
PORTE DE BAGNOLET
rue de la Py
rue des Prairies
rue Stendhal
rue des Rondeaux
rue de Bagnolet
bd. Davout
rue Virtuve
SQ. VIRTUVE
PL. ST-BLAISE
rue de la Réunion
rue des Orteaux
PL. DE LA RÉUNION
rue des Vignoles
rue des Halles
rue des Pyrénées
rue St-Blaise
rue Florian
rue des Balkans
rue Louis Lumière

11ème

Arrondissement Boundary

♠ ACCOMMODATIONS
Auberge Jeunesse
Le D'Artagnan, **9**
Eden Hôtel, **1**
Hôtel Ermitage, **4**
Super Hotel, **2**

🍴 FOOD
La Bolée Belgrand, **6**
Café Flèche d'Or, **8**
La Mer à Boire, **3**

★ NIGHTLIFE
Café Flèche d'Or, **7**
Lou Pascalou, **5**

AVRON
MARAÎCHERS
rue d'Avron
rue du Volga
Jardin de la Gare de Charonne
PORTE DE MONTREUIL
PL. DE PORTE DE MONTREUIL
rue des Grand Champs
PL. DU GÉNÉRAL TESSIER
rue de la Plaine
rue Philidor
rue de Lagny
bd. Davout
cours de Vincennes
rue Reynaldo Hahn
rue Maryse Hilsz
rue Christino Garcia
PL. DE LA NATION
NATION
av. Dorian
av. de Bel-Air
av. de Ste-Mandé
av. de Picpus
PL. PICPUS
COURTELINE
rue de Picpus
bd. de Picpus
av. Docteur Netter
rue des Maraîchers
rue des Pyrénées

300 meters
300 yards

Belleville and Père Lachaise (20ème)

INDEX

Symbols

3 Pièces Cuisine 200
3W Kafé 327
10 Bar, Le 329
18 Club, Le 321
55-57 288
404 173

A

Académie de la Bière, L' 328
Académie Française 79
Accommodations 145
  accommodation agencies 135
  Batignolles (17ème) 161
  Butte-Aux-Cailles and Chinatown
    (13ème) 158
  Buttes Chaumont (19ème) 162
  By Price 145
  Canal St-Martin and Surrounds
    (10ème) 156
  Châtelet-Les Halles (1er and
    2ème) 146
  dorms and foyers 55, 124
  home exchanges and hospitality
    clubs 55
  Île de la Cité 146
  Invalides (7ème) 153
  Latin Quarter and St-Germain
    (5ème and 6ème) 151
  long-term accommodations 56
  Montmartre (18ème) 161
  Montparnasse (14ème and
    15ème) 159
  Opéra (9ème) 155
  Passy and Auteuil (16ème) 160
  The Marais (3ème and 4ème)
    148
Accueil International Services
  114
Action Contre la Faim 105
Agence Au Pair Fly 114
Agence EduFrance 109
Agence Nationale pour
  l'Emploi 112
Agence pour l'Emploi de
  Cadres 112
AIDES 114
Aimant du Sud, L' 194
Alfred, L' 170
Algerian War 73
Alliance Française 110

Aloha Hostel 160
ambulance 142
American Chamber of Com-
  merce 112
American Chamber of Com-
  merce in France 113
American Church in Paris 230
American Express 24
American Hospital of Paris
  142
American Institute for Foreign
  Study (AIFS) 108
American Programs 108
American University of Paris
  109
Amnésia Café 325
Amorino 169
Amuse Bouche, L' 196
Anarkali Sarangui 188
Andy Wahloo 324
Angelina 171
anti-semitism 78
apartments 122
Apparement Café, L' 174,
  324
Apple Store 133
Aquarium Tropical 287
Aquarius Café 196
Arcat-Sida 114
Arc de Triomphe 232
Arche les Sapins, L' 105
architecture 82
Archives Nationales 216
Arènes de Lutèce 224
Art Nouveau 84
As du Falafel, L' 175
Assemblée Nationale 231
Association des Foyers de
  Jeunes: Foyer Tolbiac 159
Association for International
  Practical Training (AIPT) 113
Atelier Cardenas Bellanger
  275
ATM cards 25
Auberge Bressane, L' 184
Auberge de Jeunesse "Jules
  Ferry" (HI) 157

Auberge de Jeunesse "Le
  D'Artagnan" (HI) 163
Auberge Nicolas Flamel,
  L' 217
Au Bon Café 190
Au Chien qui Fume 170
Au Coin des Gourmets 179
Au Coin du Pétrin 198
Au Duc des Lombards 322
Au Général La Fayette 189
Au Grain de Folie 201
Au Lapin Agile 250, 315
au pair work 114
Au Petit Fer à Cheval 175, 327
Au Pied de Fouet 184
Au Port Salut 180
Au Roi du Café 198, 335
Au Trou Normand 190
Au Vieux Comptoir 170
Au Vieux Logis 199
Aux Artistes 198
Aux Trois Mailletz 329
Ay, Caramba! 202

B

Babylone 192
Babylone Bis 171
Bague de Kenza, La 192
Baiser Salé, Le 322
Banana Café 322
Banane Ivoirienne, La 191
bank accounts 125
Banlieues (overview) 9
Bar à Nénette, Le 332
Bar à Soupes, Le 191
Baron Rouge, Le 334
Barrio Latino 334
Bar Sans Nom, Le 332
Barthélémy 185
Basilique de St-Denis 262
Basilique du Sacré-Coeur 249
Bastille Day (Fête Nation-
  ale) 98
Bastille (overview) 6
Bastille Prison 239

Bataclan, Le 317
Bateau El Alamein 334
Bateau-Lavoir 250
Batignolles Covered Market 200
Batignolles Organic Produce Market 200
Batignolles (overview) 7
Batofar 335
Beauvais 39
Bélisaire 197
Belle Hortense, La 327
Belleville and Père Lachaise (overview) 9
Belleville Outdoor Market 203
Bercy Quarter 241
Berthillon 169
Beyond Tourism 103
  Studying 107
  Volunteering 104
  Working 111
Bibliothèque Nationale de France: Site François Mitterrand 242
Bibliothèque Nationale: Site Richelieu 215
Bien-Être Gourmand, Le 186
bikes 49, 135
Bioboa 170
Bistro d'Henri, Le 181
Bistrot du Dome 176
Bistrot du Peintre, Le 191
Bob Cool 329
Bodega, La 201
Bohemia and Art Nouveau 84
Bois de Boulogne 256
Bois de Vincennes 258
Bolée Belgrand, La 203
Bouffes du Nord 314
Boulangerie par Véronique Mauclerc, La 202
Boulevard du Montparnasse 244
Boulevard St-Germain 227
Bourse des Valeurs 215
Bourse Du Commerce 214
Brasserie de l'Île St-Louis 169
Briezh Café 177
Broches à l'Ancienne, Les 193
Bubbles 177
buddha-bar 330

budget airlines 34, 35, 39
budget tips 27
buses 40, 44
Bus Palladium 337
Butte-Aux-Cailles and Chinatown (overview) 6
Butte-aux-Cailles Crêperie, La 194
Buttes Chaumont (overview) 8

C
cabaret 314
Café Beaubourg 177
Café Charbon 332
Café Chéri(e) 337
Café de Flore 182, 228
Café de France 194
Café de la Mosquée 180
Café de la Paix 189, 237
Café de l'Industrie 191
Café Delmas 180
Café des Lettres 184
Café des Musées 174
Café du Commerce 195
Café du Marché 185
Café Flèche d'Or 203, 337
Café Hortensias 200
Café Klein Holland 326
Café Marly, Le 170
Café Med 169
Café Oz 322
Café Rouge 174
Café Tournesol 335
Café Vavin 183
calling cards 51
Cambodge, Le 189
Cambrai Hôtel 156
CampusFrance 118
Canal St. Martin and Surrounds (overview) 5
Care France 104
Carré, Le 326
cars 44, 45, 49, 135
Carte Bleu 25, 125
Casa Tina 198
Castex Hôtel 150
Catacombs 243
Cathédrale Alexandre-Nevsky 236

Caveau de la Huchette, Le 329
Caveau de la République 315
Caveau des Oubliettes, Le 328
Caveau du Palais, Le 168
Caves St-Gilles 173
cell phones 52, 126
Center for University Programs Abroad (CUPA) 109
Centers for Disease Control and Prevention (CDC) 31
Central Perk 185
Centre d'Information et de Documentation Jeunesse (CIDJ) 113
Centre International de Paris (BVJ): Paris Louvre 146
Centre International de Paris (BVJ): Paris Quartier Latin 152
Centre International du Séjour de Paris: CISP "Maurice Ravel," 158
Centre Pompidou 217, 273
Centre régional d'œuvres universitaires (CROUS) 123
Centres Internationaux du Séjour de Paris: CISP "Kellermann" 159
Centres Permanents d'Initiatives pour l'Environnement (CPIE) 106
CHAM 107
Champmeslé, Le 323
Champs de Mars 229
Champs-Élysées 233
Champs-Élysées (overview) 5
Chantilly 351
Chapelle Expiatoire 236
Charlie Birdy 196, 331
Chartier 188
Chartres 345
Château de Versailles 339
Château de Vincennes 260
Châtelet-Les Halles (overview) 3
Cheval de Troie, Le 192
Chez Blondin 193
Chez Camille 336
Chez Fung 197
Chez Georges 329
Chez Gladines 193
Chez Hanna 175

Chez Haynes 187
Chez Janou 172
"Chez les Filles" 194
Chez Marianne 176
Chez Omar 174
Chez Papa 196
Chez Paul 190
Childcare International 114
China Club 334
Chinatown 242
chunnel 40, 138
Cigale, La 317
Cimetière de Passy 248
Cimetière des Batignolles 248
Cimetière Montmartre 251
Cimetière Montparnasse 243
cinema 315
Cinema au Clair de Lune 100
Cité de la Musique 253, 317
Cité des Sciences et de
l'Industrie 252
Cité Nationale de l'Histoire de
l'Immigration 287
Cité Universitaire 109, 244
Classicism 83
Clown Bar, Le 333
Club des Poètes, Le 330
Club du Vieux Manoir 107
clubs 325, 331, 333, 335,
337
Cocottes, Les 184
Collège de France 222
Comédie Française 213
Comédie Italienne 314
Comme Par Hasard 188
Comptoir du Relais, Le 181
Comptoir Méditerranée 178
Conciergerie 208
Connétable, Le 324
Conservatoire National des
Arts et Métiers 216
consulates 19
converters and adapters 28
Cordon Bleu 111
Così 181
Council on International
Educational Exchange (CIEE)
108, 113
Coupole, La 196
Cours de Civilisation Fran-

çaise de la Sorbonne 110
Cox, 15 327
Craig's List Paris 123
credit cards 25
Crêperie Plougastel 195
Crêperie Saint Germain 181
Crêpe Rit du Clown, La 182
Crimée Hôtel 162
CROUS 180
Cubism 86
Cucaracha, La 172
culinary schools 111
Cultural Experiences Abroad
(CEA) 108
culture 92
Curieux Spaghetti Bar 176
currency exchange 23, 136
customs 23
cycling 91

D

Dadaism 80, 86
Dame Canton, La 334
Dan Bau, Le 201
Daytrips 339
　Chantilly 351
　Chartres 345
　Disneyland Resort Paris 359
　Fontainebleau 350
　Giverny 354
　Versailles 339
Debauve et Gallais 185
debit cards 25
Delhy's Hôtel 153
dentists 138
De Particulier à Particulier 123
Dépôt, Le 325
Des Crêpes et des Cailles 194
Deux Magots, Les 182, 228
dietary concerns 59
disabled 57, 138
Discover Paris 1
Disneyland Resort Paris 359
Dix Vins, Le 197
Djerba Cacher Chez Guichi 202
doctors 138
Doctors Without Borders (Mé-
decins Sans Frontières) 106
dorms 55, 124
Dreyfus Affair 70

driving permits 45
drugs and alcohol 29
dry cleaning 138
Duplex 336
Duplex, Le 324

E

Easy Expat 112
easyJet 39
Ebauchoir, L' 192
École des Hautes Etudes en
Sciences Sociales 127
École Militaire 230
École Nationale Supérieure
des Beaux-Arts 227
École Normale Supérieure 223
École Pratique des Hautes
Études 127
Écurie, L' 179
Eden Hôtel 162
Edict of Nantes 65
Editeurs, Les 182
Église de St-Eustache 213
Église Notre Dame de Lorette
238
Église St-Denys du St-
Sacrement 217
Église Ste-Anne de la Butte-
Aux-Cailles 242
Église St-Étienne du Mont 223
Église St-François-Xavier 232
Église St-Germain-des-Prés
227
Église St-Germain
l'Auxerrois 214
Église St-Gervais-St-Protais
219
Église St-Louis-en-l'Île 210
Église St-Paul-St-Louis 220
Église St-Sulpice 226
Église St-Thomas D'Aquin 232
Eiffel Tower 229
Élysée Montmartre 317
embassies 19
Empire des Thés, L' 195
Enchanteur, L' 324
Endroit, L' 200, 336
Entertainment 313
Entrance Requirements 19
Entrée au Dessert, L' 186

Entrepôt, L' 335

environmental conservation 106

Épicerie, L' 169

Espace d'Art Yvonamor Palix 287

Essentials 19
Accommodations 54
Documents and Formalities 21
Embassies and Consulates 19
Getting Around France 41
Getting Around Paris 46
Keeping in Touch 50
Money 23
Other Resources 59
Packing 27
Safety and Health 28
Specific Concerns 56

Estaminet, L' 325

Étages, Les 326

etiquette 95

Étoile du Kashmir, L' 200

Étoile du Nord, L' 317

EU 21

Eurail passes 42

Eur-Am Center 109

Eurocentres 110

European Economic Community (EEC) 21, 75

Existentialism 81

EXKi 172

Experiment in International Living 109

Explora Science Museum 293

F

Fait & Cause 272

familles d'accueil 120

fashion 297

Fauchon 187

Fauconnier, Le 150

Fauvism 86

Favela Chic 332

Federal Express 143

Fédération Familles de France 113

Fédération Unie des Auberges de Jeunesse, 113

Feminism 81

festivals 97

FIAP Jean-Monnet 159

film 89

fine arts 82

Finnegan's Wake 328

fitness clubs 138

flights 33, 41

Foire du Trône 98

Folie en Tête, La 334

Folies Pigalle 337

Fondation Cartier pour l'Art Contemporain 244, 288

Fondation Claude Pompidou 106

Fondation le Corbusier 291

Fondation Taylor 286

Fontainebleau 350

Fontaine des Innocents 214

Food 165
Bastille (10ème and 11ème) 190
Batignolles (17ème) 199
Belleville and Père Lachaise (20ème) 203
Butte-aux-Cailles and Chinatown (13ème) 193
Canal St-Martin and Surrounds (10ème) 189
Champs-Élysées (8ème) 186
Châtelet-Les Halles (1er and 2ème) 170
Île de la Cité 168
Invalides (7ème) 184
Latin Quarter and St-Germain (5ème and 6ème) 178
Montmartre (18ème) 201
Opéra (9ème) 187
Passy and Auteuil (16ème) 198
The Marais (3ème and 4ème) 172

food shops and markets 94

football 91

Foucault's Pendulum 223

Fouquet's 187, 233

Fourcy, Le 150

Fourmi, La 336

Fournée d'Augustine, La 199

Fous de l'Île, Les 169

Foyer de Chaillot-Galliera 154

Foyer International des Étudiantes 152

Foyer Vietnam 179

France Bénévolat 104

Françoise Meunier's Cours de Cuisine 111

French-American Chamber of Commerce (FACC) 113

French Government Tourist Office (FGTO) 20

French Ministry of Education

Teaching Assistantship in France 114

French Programs 109

French Revolution 66

Frog and Rosbif 323

Fu Bar 329

Fumoir, Le 170, 322

Fuxia 176

G

Galerie Alizé 265

Galerie Claude Samuel 288

Galerie Daniel Templon 273

Galerie de France 275

Galerie Denise René 273

Galerie du Jour Agnès B 275

Galerie Emmanuel Perrotin 272

Galerie Lelong 286

Galerie Loevenbruck 278

Galerie Louis Carré & Cie 286

Galerie Michèle Chomette 273

Galerie Nathalie Obadia 275

Galerie Patrice Trigano 278

Galerie Rachlin & Lemarie Beaubourg 275

Galeries and Passages 215

Galerie Seine 51 278

Galeries National du Grand Palais 285

Galerie Thuillier 272

Galerie Zurcher 273

Gay Choc, Le 178

Gay Pride Festival 98

GENEPI 106

Georges 175

Gérard Mulot 183

Gilles Peyroulet & CIE 273

Giverny 354

Glassbox 287

GLBT resources 57, 139

GLBT rights 78

Goutte d'Or 251

grading system 130

Grande Épicerie de Paris, La 185

Grandes Eaux Musicales de Versailles 99

Grandes Écoles 127
Grandes Marchés, Les 192
Grand Hôtel Jeanne d'Arc 150
Grand Hôtel Lévêque 154
Grand Palais 233
Grands Établissements 127
Grands Projets 75, 86, 268
Grannie 184
Grenier de Notre-Dame, Le 179
grocery shopping 125
GSM phones 52
Guen-maï 181
guesthouses 55
guignols 319

H

halle Saint-Pierre 292
Halles, Les 213
Haussmann 83
Hertford British Hospital (Hôpital Franco-Britannique de Paris) 142
Heure Gourmand, L' 183
historical restoration 107
history of Paris 63
homestays 55
Hôpital Bichat 142
hospitals 142
Hostelling International 54
Hôtel Amélie 154
Hôtel Andréa Rivoli 150
Hôtel Beaumarchais 157
Hôtel Bellevue et du Chariot d'Or 148
Hôtel Bel Oranger (Au Nouvel Hôtel Lyon) 158
Hôtel Boileau 160
Hôtel Brésil 152
Hôtel Camélia 160
Hôtel Caulaincourt 162
Hôtel Champerret Héliopolis 161
Hôtel Chopin 155
Hôtel de Beauvais 219
Hôtel de Belfort 157
Hôtel de Blois 159
Hôtel de France 153
Hôtel de la Herse d'Or 150

Hôtel de Lamoignon 221
Hôtel de l'Aveyron 158
Hôtel de Milan 156
Hôtel de Nesle 152
Hôtel de Nice 150
Hôtel de Roubaix 148
Hôtel des Boulevards 147
Hôtel de Sens 220
Hôtel des Jeunes (MIJE) 149
Hôtel de Sully 221
Hôtel de Turenne 154
Hôtel de Ville 218
Hôtel Dieu 208
Hôtel du Lion d'Or 146
Hôtel du Lys 153
Hôtel du Marais 148
Hôtel du Midi 160
Hôtel du Parc 159
Hôtel du Séjour 148
Hôtel Eiffel Rive Gauche 153
Hôtel Ermitage 163
Hôtel Esmeralda 151
Hôtel Europe-Liège 154
Hôtel Gay-Lussac 151
Hôtel Les Argonauts 151
Hôtel Louvre-Richelieu 147
Hôtel Madeleine Haussmann 155
Hôtel Magendie 158
Hôtel Matignon 232
Hôtel Mistral 157
Hôtel Montana La Fayette 156
Hotel Montebello 154
Hôtel Montpensier 146
Hôtel Notre-Dame 157
Hôtel Palace 156
Hôtel Paris France 149
Hotel Picard 148
Hôtel Pratic 150
Hôtel Prince Albert Lyon Bercy 158
Hôtel Prince Albert Wagram 161
Hôtel Printania 158
Hôtel Rhetia 157
Hôtel Riviera 161
hotels 55
Hôtel St-André des Arts 152
Hôtel Stanislas 153

Hôtel Stella 152
Hôtel St-Honoré 147
Hôtel St-Jacques 151
Hôtel Vivienne 147
Hundred Days' War 68
Hundred Years' War 64

I

Île de la Cité (overview) 2
Île St-Louis (overview) 2
immunizations 31
Impressionism 84
Institut Catholique de Paris 129
Institut de Langue Française (ILF) 110
Institut d'Études Politiques de Paris 127
Institut du Monde Arabe 276
Institut Parisien de Langue et de Civilisation Française 110
Institut Pasteur 245
insurance 31
InterExchange 114
International Association for the Exchange of Students for Technical Experience (IAESTE) 109
International Schools Services (ISS) 114
International Volunteer Programs Association (IVPA) 105
Internet Access 139
Invalides Museum 281
Invalides (overview) 4
Izrael 178

J

Jacques Mélac 333
Jadis et Gourmande 178
Jardin d'Acclimatation 256
Jardin de Ranelagh 246
Jardin des Pâtes, Le 180
Jardin Des Plantes 224
Jardin des Tuileries 210
Jardin du Luxembourg 225
Jardins du Trocadéro 248
jazz 88
Jazz à la Villette 100

jazz clubs 322, 329, 331
Jeu de Paume 270
Jeu de Paume and l'Orangerie 211
Joséphine Baker Swimming Pool 243
Journées du Patrimoine 100
Joy in Food 200
July Column 240

K

Kamel Mennour 278
Kaskad' Café, La 202
Kintaro 172
Kitch, Le 333
Kusmi Tea 183

L

Lac Daumesnil And Lac Des Minimes 261
Ladurée 187
Language Immersion Institute 110
language schools 110
Lao Siam 202
Latin Quarter and St-Germain (overview) 4
laundromats 138
Lèche-Vin, Le 333
Le Grizzli 177
Les Bleus 91
libraries 132, 140
Life and Times
  Culture 92
  Festivals 97
  History 63
  Media 96
  National Holidays 101
  Sports and Recreation 91
  The Arts 78
literature 78
Lizard Lounge 326
Lodgis.com 123
Lotus Blanc, Le 184
Lou Pascalou 337
Loup Blanc, Le 171
Louvre 266

M

Maastricht Treaty 75

Madeleine 235
magazines 97
mail 53, 142
Maison de Balzac 290
Maison de la France 20
Maison de l'Air, La 295
Maison de Victor Hugo 274
Maison du Chocolat, La 189
Maison Européenne de la Photographie, La 219
Maison Rose, La 202
Malhia Kent 288
Manufacture des Gobelins 242
Marais (overview) 3
Marché Beauvau St-Antoine 193
Marché Berthier 200
Marché Biologique 183
Marché Monge 180
Marché Mouffetard 180
Marché Popincourt 192
Marché Port Royal 180
Marché Président-Wilson 199
Marché St-Quentin 190
Mariage Frères 177
Marionnettes du Luxembourg 319
Maubuisson 149
McCoy Café 185
Mécanique (Ondulatoire), La 332
Médecins Sans Frontières (Doctors Without Borders) 106
media 96
medical outreach and aids awareness 114
Mémorial de la Déportation 208
Mémorial de la Libération de Paris 288
Mémorial de la Shoah 274
Mer à Boire, La 203
metro 47
minorities 58
minority resources 140
Mix Club 335
Modern Hôtel 157
Modernism 80, 88
Modial Hôtel Européen 156
Montmartre (overview) 8

Montparnasse (overview) 7
Mood 186
Moose, The 330
Mosquée de Paris 224
Moulin Rouge 251, 314
Muscade 171
Musée Adam Mickiewicz 265
Musée Bourdelle 289
Musée Carnavalet 271
Musée Cernuschi 285
Musée Cognaco-Jay 272
Musée d'Art et d'Histoire 263
Musée d'Art et d'Histoire du Judaïsme 271
Musée d'Art Moderne de la Ville de Paris 289
Musée de Cluny 275
Musée de Jeu de Paume 274
Musée Delacroix 277
Musée de la Marine 291
Musée de la Mode et du Costume 290
Musée de la Mode et du Textile 270
Musée de la Monnaie 277
Musée de la Musique 293
Musée de la Poupée 272
Musée de l'Armée 282
Musée de l'Erotisme 292
Musée de l'Homme 292
Musée de l'Orangerie 269
Musée de l'Ordre de la Libération 282
Musée de Maillol 283
Musée de Montmartre 293
Musée de Quai Branly 283
Musée des Arts Décoratifs 270
Musée des Deux Guerres Mondiales 282
Musée des Égouts de Paris 284
Musée des Plans-Reliefs 282
Musée d'Histoire Naturelle 276
Musée d'Orsay 280
Musée du Louvre 266
Musée du Luxembourg 225
Musée du Vin 291
Musée en Herbe 258
Musée Georges Clemenceau

291
Musée Grévin 286
Musée Gustave Moreau 286
Musée Jacquemart-André 284
Musée Jean-Jacques Henner 292
Musée Marmottan Monet 289
Musée National de la Légion d'Honneur et des Ordres de Chevalerie 283
Musée National des Arts Asiatiques 290
Musée Nissim de Camondo 285
Musée Picasso 270
Musée Zadkine 277
Museums 265
  Bastille (11ème and 12ème) 287
  Batignolles (17èmes) 292
  Belleville and Père Lachaise (20ème) 293
  Buttes Chaumont (19ème) 293
  Champs-Élysées (8ème) 284
  Châtelet-Les Halles (1er and 2ème) 266
  Île St-Louis 265
  Invalides (7ème) 279
  Montmartre (18ème) 292
  Montparnasse (14ème and 15ème) 288
  Opéra (9ème) 286
  Passy and Auteuil (16ème) 289
  The Marais (3ème and 4ème) 270
Muse Vin, La 333
music 88
myberry 178

N
national holidays 101
Naturalism 80
Nazis 86
neighborhood overview 2
Neoclassicism 83
Neoserialism 88
New Morning Jazz Club 331
newspapers 97
New Wave 90
Nicolas Sarkozy 77
Nightlife 321
  Batignolles (17ème) 336
  Belleville and Père Lachaise (20ème) 337
  Butte-aux-Cailles and Chinatown (13ème) 334
  Buttes Chaumont (19ème) 337
  Champs-Élysées (8ème) 330

  Châtelet-Les Halles (1er and 2ème) 321
  Invalides (7ème) 330
  Latin Quarter and St-Germain 328
  Montmartre (18ème) 336
  Montparnasse (14ème and 15ème) 335
  Passy and Auteuil (16ème) 336
  The Marais (3ème and 4ème) 323
Ni Putes Ni Soumises 106
Noces de Jeannette, Les 171
No Stress Café 188
Notre Dame 205
Nouveau Casino 333
Nouvelle Revue Française. 80

O
Oath of the Tennis Court 66
O'Brien's 330
O&CO 170
Odéon 228
Odéon Théâtre de l'Europe 314
Okawa 326
Olympia, L' 317
Open Café 326
Opéra Comique 318
Opéra de la Bastille 240, 318
Opéra Garnier 237, 318
Opéra (overview) 5
Orangerie 269
Orchestre de Paris 318
Organisation Mondiale de Protection de l'Environnement 106
Orientalism 83
Orly 39
Orlyval 39
Overnight Trains 42

P
Pacific Hôtel 160
packing 27
Page 35 173
Pagode, La 231
Pain, Vin, Fromage 176
Palais de Chaillot 247
Palais de Justice 207
Palais de la Cité 207
Palais de la Découverte 285
Palais de l'Élysée 234

Palais de L'Institut de France 226
Palais des Thés 174
PalAis de Tokyo 247
Palais du Luxembourg 225
Palais Omnisports de Paris-Bercy 318
Palais-Royal 211
Panthéon 222
Papillons Blancs de Paris (APEI), Les 106
Parc André Citroën 245
Parc de Bagatelle 258
Parc de Belleville 255
Parc de la Villette 252
Parc des Buttes-Chaumont 253
Parc Floral de Paris 260
Parc Monceau 236
Parc Zoologique de Paris 260
Paris Attitude 123
Paris Jazz Festival 99
Paris Nord Hôtel 156
Paris Plages 99
Paris Visite Tickets 46
Parti Communiste Français (PCF) 74
Parti Socialiste (PS) 74
Pascal Beillevaire, Maître Fromager 196
passports 21
Passy and Auteuil (overview) 7
Patio Provençal, Le 199
Pause Café 191
Perdrix Rouge, La 162
Père Lachaise Cemetery 254
Perfect Hôtel 155
Perle, La 324
Perraudin, Le 179
pétanque 91
Petit Baigneur, Le 196
Petit Bofinger 176
Petite Scierie, La 169
Petit Journal St-Michel, Le 329
Petit Palais 233, 284
Petit Plateau, Le 168
pharmacies 143
philosophy 78
Piano Vache, Le 328

Piccolo Teatro 175
Pick-clops, Le 326
Pigalle 238
Place de la Bastille 239
Place de la Concorde 234
Place de la République 238
Place d'Iéna 247
Place du Trocadéro 247
Place Numéro Thé 168
Places des Vosges 220
Place St-Michel 221
Place Vendôme 211
Plessis Hôtel 157
Poilâne 183
Polaris 273
politics 74
Pont des Arts 228
Pont Neuf 209
Pooja 190
Pop In, Le 332
Portes Ouvertes des Ateliers d'Artistes 98
Portes St-Denis and St-Martin 238
Poste, La 53
Post-Impressionism 84
Postmodernism 81
post offices 142
Practical Information 135
   Emergency and Communications 142
   Local Services 138
   Tourist and Financial Services 135
Pratic Hôtel 160
Pré Catelan 258
Pré Verre, Le 179
Procope, Le 183
Promenades Gourmandes 111
Protestant Reformation 78
public transportation 46
Puces de St-Ouen 310

Q

Quai d'Anjou 209
Quai de Béthune 210
Quai de Bourbon 209
Quai Quai 168
Quai Voltaire 231
Queen, Le 331
Quetzal, Le 327

R

Raidd Bar 325
railpasses 42, 43
Rassemblement pour la République 74
Realism 83
Réconfort, Le 174
Refuge Café 193
Refuge des Fondus 201
"Relais de l'Entrecôte," Le 182
religious services 141
REMPART 107
Renaissance 64, 78
renting a car 45
RER 39, 47
Restaurant Assoce 191
Rex Club 323
Robert et Louise 173
rockstars 89
Roissy-Charles de Gaulle (Roissy-CDG) 38
Roland Garros 256
Romanticism 83, 88
Rotonde, La 198
Royal Bar 174
Ruche, La 246
Rue Benjamin Franklin 247
Rue de la Roquette 240
Rue des Rosiers 218
Rue La Fontaine 246
Rue Mouffetard 223
Rues Abbesses, Lepic, and d'Orsel 251
Rue Saint-Denis 216
Rue St-Louis-en-l'Île 210
Rue Vieille du Temple 217
Rue Vieille du Temple and Rue Ste-Croix de la Bretonerie 218
Ryanair 39

S

Saint-Denis 262
Samaritaine, La 214
Samaya 197
Samson, Le 194
Sanz Sans 333
Savannah Café 179

Saveurs & Coincïdences 188
Scheffer, Le 198
Schengen Agreement 21, 75
scooters 50, 135
Secours Catholique: Délégation de Paris 106
Secours Populaire Français 106
Sélect, Le 183
Severo, Le 195
Shakespeare & Co. Bookstore 224
Shopping 297
   Bastille (11ème and 12ème) 308
   Champs-Élysées (8ème) 307
   Châtelet-Les Halles (1er and 2ème) 298
   Île de la Cité 298
   Île St-Louis 298
   Invalides (7ème) 306
   Latin Quarter and St-Germain 303
   Montmartre (18ème) 310
   Opéra (9ème) 308
   The Marais 300
Sights 205
   Batignolles (17ème) 248
   Belleville and Père Lachaise (20ème) 253
   Bois de Boulogne 256
   Bois de Vincennes 258
   Buttes-Aux-Cailles and Chinatown (13ème) 241
   Buttes Chaumont (19ème) 252
   Canal St-Martin and Surrounds (10ème) 238, 331
   Champs-Élysées (8ème) 232
   Châtelet-Les Halles (1er and 2ème) 210
   Île de la Cité 205
   Île St-Louis 209
   Latin Quarter and St-Germain (5ème and 6ème) 221
   Montmartre 249
   Montmartre (18ème) 249
   Montparnasse (14ème and 15ème) 243
   Opéra (9ème) 236
   Passy and Auteuil (16ème) 246
   The Marais (3ème and 4ème) 216
Sir Winston 336
Slow Club, Le 322
Soleil Gourmand, Le 201
Sol En Si (Solidarité Enfants Sida) 115
Sorbonne, La 110, 222
SOS Help! 142
standby flights 37
Statue of Liberty 247
St. Bartholomew's Day Massacre 65

Ste-Chapelle 207
Stéphane Secco 185
St-Germain Covered Market 184
St-Germain-des-Prés 227
Stolly's 326
Stravinsky Fountain 218
Study Abroad 107, 117, 129
  Health 124
  Homestays 120
  Honey-Moon Period 118
  Living Independently 121
  Money 125
  University Overview 126
  Why Paris? 117
study permits 22, 112
Style Hôtel 162
Sunside, Le Sunset, Le 322
Super Hotel 163
support centers 142
Surrealism 80, 86, 90
Symbolism 80

T

Table d'Erica, La 181
Tandoori 197
Tang Frères 195
Tango, Le 324
tax 27
taxe de séjour 153
Taxi Jaune 174
taxis 49, 136
teaching English 113
temperature chart 2
Temps des Cerises, Le 194
terrorism 29
Thabthim Siam 186
Theater 313
Théâtre de la Huchette 314
Théâtre de la Ville 318
Théâtre de l'Odéon 226
Théâtre des Champs-Élysées 234, 318
Théâtre du Châtelet 318
Théâtre Musical Populaire 215
Théâtre National de Chaillot 314

The International Kitchen 111
The James Joyce Pub 199
Three Ducks Hostel 160
ticket consolidators 37
ticket services 141
time differences 53
Timhotel Le Louvre 147
Toi 186
Tour de France 100
tourist offices 20, 136
Tour Montparnasse 245
tours 136
Tour St-Jacques 219
trains 41
Transitions Abroad 113
transportation 137
travel advisories 29
traveler's checks 24
Travelex 25
Travelite FAQ 27
Treaty of Versailles 70
Tricotin 193
Troisième Bureau, Le 191
Troquet, Le 197
Ty Breiz 197
Ty Yann 186

U

UNESCO 230
Union Chrétienne de Jeunes Filles (UCJF/YWCA) 155
Union pour la Démocratie Française (UDF) 74
Union pour un Mouvement Populaire (UMP) 74
Université de Paris 127
US State Department 26

V

value added tax (VAT) 23
Vélib 135
Vertical 288
Viaduc des Arts and Promenade Plantée 241

Victoire Suprême du Coeur, La 175
Villa d'Auteuil 161
Villa des Ternes 199
Village Hostel, Le 161
Visa 25
visas 22, 108, 112, 118
Volunteers for Peace (VFP) 105

W

War of the Spanish Succession 66
Wars of Religion 65
Wassana 201
Wax 333
Who's Bar, Le 328
WICE 106
Wi-Fi 50
Willi's Wine Bar 323
wine 93
Wine and Bubbles 323
wine bars 323, 325, 327, 333, 334
wiring money 26
women's health 33
women's resources 142
Woodstock Hostel 155
work permits 22, 112
World Link Education 111
World Place 331
World War I 70
World War II 71
Worldwide Opportunities on Organic Farms (WWOOF) 107

Y

Yono, Le 325
Young and Happy (Y&H) Hostel 151

Z

Zénith 318

SMART TRAVELERS KNOW:
GET YOUR CARD BEFORE YOU GO

An HI USA membership card gives you access to friendly and affordable accommodations at over 4,000 hostels in more than 85 countries around the world.

HI USA Members receive complementary travel insurance, airline discounts, free stay vouchers, long distance calling card bonus, so its a good idea to get your membership while you're still planning your trip.